ST. ANDREW'S ROAD

Scarlet Well

No. 17

FORT STREET

MOAT ST.

BATHROW

STREET

SCARLETWELL STREET

SPRING LANE

Spring Lane Terrace

MONKSPOND STREET

CRANE STREET

Spring Lane
School

LOWER CROSS ST.

R CROSS ST.

CRISPIN STREET

COMPTON STREET

LOWER HARDING STREET

Claremont Court
(from 1962)

GRAFTON SQUARE

Beaumont Court
(from 1962)

HERBERT STREET

LTHORP STREET

COOPER STREET

BELL BARN STREET

St. Andrew's
church

GRAFTON STREET

ST. ANDREW'S STREET

AD STREET

Timber
yard

NARROW LANE

REGENT STREET

CROMWELL STREET

FITZROY TERRACE

REGENT SQUARE

St. Sepulchre's
church

M P T O N

¼ Mile

500

100

Feet 0

JOHN COULTHART • MMXVI

JERUSALEM

Also by Alan Moore

Voice of the Fire

Alan Moore

JERUSALEM

A Novel

Liveright Publishing Corporation
A Division of W. W. Norton & Company
Independent Publishers Since 1923
New York   London

Publisher's Note: Some of the people named or depicted in this book are loosely inspired by real people, but this is a work of fiction and the usual rules apply.

Excerpt from *An Einstein Encyclopedia* by Alice Calaprice, Daniel Kennefick, and Robert Schulmann, copyright © 2015 by Princeton University Press. Reprinted by permission.

For information about permission to reproduce selections from this book, write to Permissions, Liveright Publishing Corporation, a division of W. W. Norton & Company, Inc., 500 Fifth Avenue, New York, NY 10110

For information about special discounts for bulk purchases, please contact W. W. Norton Special Sales at specialsales@wwnorton.com or 800-233-4830

Manufacturing by RR Donnelley, Harrisonburg, VA
Book design by Daniel Lagin
Production manager: Anna Oler

Library of Congress Cataloging-in-Publication Data

Names: Moore, Alan, 1953– author.
Title: Jerusalem : a novel / Alan Moore.
Description: First edition. | New York : Liveright Publishing Corporation, [2016]
Identifiers: LCCN 2016014957| ISBN 9781631491344 (hardcover) | ISBN 9781631492433 (paperback)
Classification: LCC PR6063.O593 J47 2016 | DDC 823/.914—dc23 LC record available at https://lccn.loc.gov/2016014957

Liveright Publishing Corporation
500 Fifth Avenue, New York, N.Y. 10110
www.wwnorton.com

W. W. Norton & Company Ltd.
15 Carlisle Street, London W1D 3BS

2 3 4 5 6 7 8 9 0

For my family, for the people of the Boroughs, and for Audrey Vernon, the best piano-accordionist our cracked lanes ever knew.

CONTENTS

BOOK THREE–VERNALL'S INQUEST

AFTERLUDE

Based on a "true story."

JERUSALEM

PRELUDE

WORK IN PROGRESS

Alma Warren, five years old, thought that they'd probably been shopping, her, her brother Michael in his pushchair and their mum, Doreen. Perhaps they'd been to Woolworth's. Not the one in Gold Street, bottom Woolworth's, but top Woolworth's, halfway along Abington Street's shop-lit incline, with its spearmint green tiled milk-bar, with the giant dial of its weighing machine trimmed a reassuring magnet red where it stood by the wooden staircase at the building's rear.

The stocky little girl, so solid she seemed almost die-cast, had no memory of holding back the smeary brass and glass weight of the shop's swing doors so that Doreen could steer the pram into the velvet bustle of the main street glistening outside. She struggled to recall a landmark that she'd noticed somewhere along the much-trodden route, perhaps the lit-up sign that jutted out from Kendall's rainwear shop on Fish Street corner, where the marching *K* leaned boldly forward against driving wind, cartoon umbrella open and held somehow by the letter's handless, out-flung arm, but nothing came to mind. In fact, now that she thought about it, Alma couldn't honestly remember anything at all about the expedition. Everything before the lamp-lit stretch of paving along which she now found herself walking, with the squeak of Michael's pram and rhythmic clacking of their mother's heels, everything prior to this was a mysterious fuzz.

With chin tucked in her mackintosh's buttoned collar against dusk's pervasive chill, Alma surveyed the twinkling slabs that steadily unwound beneath the mesmerising back and forth of her blunt, buckled shoes. It seemed to her that the most likely explanation for the blank gap in her recollection was plain absent-mindedness. Most probably she'd daydreamed through the whole dull outing, and had seen all of the usual things but paid them no attention, caught up in the lazy stream of her own thoughts, the private drift of make-believe and muddle going on between her dangling plaits, beneath her butterfly-slides, faded pink and brittle like carbolic soap. Practically every day she'd wake up from a trance, emerge from her cocoon of plans and memories to find herself a terrace or two further on than the last place she'd noticed, so the lack of any memorable details from this current shopping trip was no cause for concern.

Abington Street, she thought, was the best bet for where they'd been, and would explain why they were now making their way along the bottom edge of a deserted Market Square towards the alley next to Osborn's, where they'd next slog up the Drapery, pushing Michael past the seaside-flavoured brick slab of the Fish Market with its high, dust-veiled windows, then down Silver Street, across the Mayorhold and into the Boroughs, home amongst the tilt and tangle of its narrow passages.

As comforting as Alma found this notion, she still had the nagging feeling there was something not quite right about her explanation. If they'd just left Woolworth's then it couldn't be much after five o'clock, with all of the town centre shops still open, so why weren't there any lights on in the Market? No pale greenish glow crept from the gated mouth of the Emporium Arcade up on the slanted square's top side, while on the western border Lipton's window was blacked out, without its usual cheese-rind coloured warmth. Shouldn't the market traders, for that matter, still be packing up their wares, closing their stalls down for the day, cheerfully shouting to each other as they kicked through the spoiled fruit and tissue paper, folding trestle tables up to load with hoof-beat clang and clatter into bulky, spluttering vans the shape of ambulances, tin frames echoing like gongs with each fresh armful?

But the wide expanse was vacant and its draughty incline swept away uphill to empty darkness. Rising from the gooseflesh of wet cobbles there were only listing posts dividing up the absent stalls, drenched timbers chewed like pencils at one end and jutting from square, rust-rimmed holes between the hunchback stones. One tattered awning had been left behind, too miserable for anyone to steal, the sodden flap of its sole wing slapping at intervals above the low, half-waking murmur of the wind, the sound snapped back by the high buildings framing the enclosure. Looming from its centre, black on sooty grey, the market's iron monument poked up into the dirty wash-water of night, ornate Victorian stem rising to blossom in a scalloped capital crowned by a copper globe, much like some prehistoric monster flower, alone and petrified. Around its stepped plinth, Alma knew, were small unnoticed bursts of emerald grass, doggedly bristling from the cracks and crevices, perhaps the only living things beside her mother, brother and herself to be about the square that evening, even if she couldn't see them.

Where were all the other mothers dragging children through the shining and inviting pools outside shop windows, home for tea? Where were the tired, unhappy-looking men slouching along their solitary paths back from the factories, with one hand in a sorry pocket of their navy trousers and the frayed strap of a shouldered kitbag in the other? Over the slate roofs that edged the square there was no pearly aura shading up into black sky, no white electric rays spilled from the Gaumont's streamlined front, as if Northampton had been suddenly switched off, as if it were the middle of the night. But then, what were they doing in town centre when it was so late, with all the shops shut and the oblong glass eyes of their bolted doors become unfriendly, distant, staring blankly like they didn't know you, didn't want you there?

Trotting beside her mum, one hot hand clenched on the cool tubing of the pushchair's handle, dragging slightly so that Doreen had to tow her, she began to worry. If things were no longer going on the way they should be, didn't that mean anything could happen? Glancing up towards her mother's scarf-wrapped profile, Alma could find no sign of concern in the soft, sensible blue eyes fixed on the pavement up ahead, or in the uncomplaining line that sealed the small rose mouth. If there were any reason to be frightened, if they were in danger, surely Mum would know? But what if there was something horrible, a ghost or bear or murderer, and their mother wasn't told? What if it got them? Chewing on her lower lip, she made another effort to remember where the three of them had been before this haunted cobblestone enclosure.

In the shadows puddled at the market's bottom flank not far in front, the heavyset child noticed with relief that there was at least one light burning in the otherwise apparently deserted murk, a rectangle of ivory brightness falling from the big front window of the paper-shop on Drum Lane's corner, angling across the boot-worn yellowed flags outside. As if she had been listening in upon her daughter's mounting apprehension, Alma's mother looked down at her now and smiled, nodding towards the shop-front that was barely more than three pram-lengths before them. "The'yar. Ayr's wun blessid place as ent shut up, ay?"

Alma nodded, pleased and reassured, while in his creaking pushchair Michael kicked against the footboard in approval, with his curly golden head that looked like Bubbles in the painting bouncing up and down. As they drew level with the newsagent's the little girl peered through its tall clean panes into the dazzle of a stripped interior where it appeared that work was going on, carpenters labouring through the hours of darkness at their renovations, no doubt so as not to intrude on the normal trading times of the establishment. Four or five men were busy over sawhorses there on the bare, new-looking floorboards, hammering and planing under an unshaded light-bulb, and she noticed that their feet were naked in the dust and shavings piled like curls of butter. Wouldn't they get splinters? All of them were wearing plain white gowns that reached their ankles. All of them had close-trimmed nails, had smooth skin that was radiantly clean as if they'd just come from a proper sit-down bath, still had lavender talcum crusting on damp shoulders into shapes like continents. They all looked serious and strong but not unkind, and most of them had hair that hung down to the collars of their freshly laundered robes, heads bent above robust and rasping toil.

One man amongst the labour detail stood aside from his four colleagues, watching as they worked. Alma supposed he was in charge. She noticed that, unlike those of the other men, his gown rose to a cowl so that none of his face was really visible above the nose. His hair was covered, but she somehow felt sure it was dark and shorter than that of his workmates, the neck shorn to suede below the folds of his dove-coloured hood. He was clean-shaven, like the rest of them, ruggedly handsome from those features she could see beneath the inky cowl-cast shade that filled his sockets and concealed his eyes behind a phantom burglar mask. Seeming to feel the child's attention through the glass, the man in question turned to smile in her direction, lifting one hand casually in greeting, and with an astounded, disbelieving lurch somewhere inside her Alma understood who he must be.

The measured pram-squeak and the ringing cap-gun detonations of her mother's heels slowed to a stop as Doreen also paused to stare through the illuminated window, in at the nocturnal labourers and their hooded foreman.

"Well, I'll goo ter ayr ace. Look 'ere, you two, it's the Frit Burr un 'iz angles."

Alma thought that 'angles' was most likely an expression from the Boroughs meaning carpenters or joiners, but the other term was foreign to her and she frowned up questioningly into Doreen's gently mocking gaze, as if her mum thought Alma was just being dense and should have known at her age what a 'Frit Burr' was.

Doreen gave a mild tut. "Ooh, yer a sample, you are. 'E's the Frith Borh. The Third Burrer. All the times you've 'eard me gooin' on abayt 'im, un yuh look ut me gone ayt."

Alma had heard of the Third Borough, or at least it seemed she had. The words were teasingly familiar, and she knew this was a way the person that she'd understood the hooded man to be the moment that he'd waved was known, something that people called him when they wanted to avoid his other name. 'Third Borough', if she'd got it right, meant something like a rent-man or policeman, only much more friendly and respected, more magnificent than even the Red Earl, Earl Spencer, swinging on a pub sign she'd once seen. She looked back from her mother to the tableau of the partly reconstructed paper-shop, the figures at their earnest graft there in a flood of brilliance, the newsagent's with its glass front like a fish tank where the men worked under water that was warm and luminous. The cowled man, the Third Borough, was still smiling out at Doreen and her children, but he wasn't so much waving now as beckoning, inviting them to come inside.

Mum scraped the pushchair round in a tight quarter-circle on the pavement bordering the hushed, abandoned market, steering Michael and his pram into the shop's glass entranceway, set back with grubby beige and turquoise chips in a mosaic ramp between the doorframe and the slippery street. With one plump hand still clenched upon the carriage handle and pulled in her mother's wake, Alma hung back uncertainly, dragging her feet. She'd heard somewhere, or somehow gathered the impression that you only got an audience like this if you were dead, dead being an idea she hadn't really taken in as yet but knew she wouldn't like. One of the men with flowing locks, this one with hair so fair that it was white, was setting down his handsaw now and crossing to the door to hold it open for them, genial creases forming at the corners of his eyes. Sensing the girl's reluctance, Alma's mother turned and spoke to her encouragingly.

"Gor, you are a soppy date, ayr Alma. 'E ent gunner urcha, un 'e dun't see people very orften. Goo on in un say 'ello or else 'e'll think we're rude."

With head tipped forward and her brown roller-provided curls concealed beneath the headscarf's charcoal check, her winter coat's line falling from the full bust in a prow-like swoop, Doreen had something in her manner that made Alma think of pigeons and their careless calm, their paint-box mottled necks, the ruffling music of their voices. She remembered having had a dream once in which she'd been sitting with her mother in their living room down Andrew's Road, on the west boundary of the Boroughs. In the dream Doreen was ironing while her daughter knelt there in the armchair, sucking absently upon the threadbare padding of its rear and gazing through the back-yard window out into the twilight. Over next door's wall there loomed the disused stable with black holes like crossed-out bits in documents, where slates were missing from its roof. Through these the flickering shapes of pigeons lifted and descended, barely visible, pale twists of smoke against the darkness of the school hill rising up beyond. Mum turned to Alma from her ironing board and solemnly explained about the roosting birds.

"They're where dead people goo."

The child had woken before she could ask whether this meant that pigeons were all human ghosts, forms that dead people had gone into and become, or whether they somehow existed simultaneously in Heaven, where dead people go, and up amongst the rafters of the derelict barn in the neighbour's yard at the same time. She had no idea why the dream should come to mind now as she followed Michael and her mother through the door, still patiently held open by the silver-haired and gown-draped carpenter, out of the night into the light-soaked store.

Having one entrance on the market and another round the corner in Drum Lane, the shop's inside seemed bigger than she'd thought it would be, although Alma realised this was partly due to there not being any paper racks, cash registers or counters; any customers. Filling the room was the perfume of fresh-shaved wood, somewhere between the scents of tinned peach and tobacco, and beneath her feet the new-laid floorboards were as satisfyingly resilient as longbows, sawdust heaping in the unswept corners. Woman, girl and baby having stepped within, the white-haired workman who'd been holding back the door went to his partially cut plank, grinning at Alma and her brother with a gruff wink that included them in some unspoken and yet wonderful conspiracy, before returning to his interrupted task.

Unsure of what to make her face do in response to this, Alma attempted a half-hearted grimace that came out as neither one thing nor the other, then looked round at Michael. He was sitting up enthusiastically out of the pushchair, tugging forward on the chewed straps of his harness – the same one Alma had worn just a few years ago – made of red leather, with the flaking and much picked-at gold leaf outline of a horse's head gradually disappearing on its front. Michael was chortling in delight, arms raised with fingers opening and closing, trying to grab onto the milky light, the air, the tingling Christmas atmosphere of that peculiar moment at the corner of the eerie midnight square, as if he wanted to take hold of it all, cram it in his mouth and eat it. His large head tipped back upon the jiggling infant body with a profile like the Fairy Soap child, blinking up at everything and gurgling with such enjoyment that his sister privately suspected he was rather shallow for a two-year-old, far too concerned with having fun to take life seriously. Behind him, out through the shop's window there was only blackness, with the market gone and nothing but their lantern-slide reflections hanging in the dark, as if the news and magazine store was alone and falling through the emptiness of space. Above her, in the adult chatter closer to the paper shop's high plaster ceiling, Doreen and the hooded man were talking as her mum thanked him for asking them inside and introduced him to her children.

"This wun in the pram's ayr Michael, un that's Alma. She's ut school now, ent yer, up Spring Lane? You come un say 'ello t' the Third Burrer."

Alma looked up bashfully at the Third Borough, managing a weak "Hello". Seen from close up he was a little older than her mother, and perhaps might have been thirty. Unlike all the other workers who were white as chapel marble, his complexion was much darker, brown from hard work in the sunshine. Or perhaps he was from somewhere hot and far away like Palestine, one of the lands she'd heard the older children sing about in the big school-hall where they went for prayers, up three stone steps from Alma's first-year infant's cloakroom, pegs identified by locomotives, kites and cats rather than boys' and girls' names. "Quinquereme of Nineveh and distant Ophir ..." went the song, places and words that sounded lovely, sad, and gone now.

The Third Borough crouched to Alma's level, still with the same kindly smile, and she could smell his skin, a bit like toast and nutmeg. She could see the cowboy hero dimple in his chin, as if someone had hit it with a dart, but she still couldn't see his eyes beneath that band of shadow falling from the cowl's peaked brim. When he addressed her, she could not remember later if his lips had moved, or what his voice had been like. She was sure it was a man's voice, deep and honest, that it hadn't sounded posh, yet neither had it sounded like the pokey fireside-corner accents of the Boroughs. It was more a wireless intonation, and she didn't seem to hear it with her ears so much as feel it in her stomach, warm and welcome as a Sunday dinner. *Hello, little Alma. Do you know who I am?*

Alma shivered, thoughts all of a sudden filled with thunder, stars and people weeping with no clothes on. Far too shy to speak his name aloud but wanting him to know she recognised him, she tried singing the first verse of 'All things bright and beautiful', which always made her think of daisies, hoping that he'd get her awkward, timid little joke and not be cross. His smile grew very slightly wider and, relieved, she knew he'd understood. Still crouching, the robed figure turned his covered head to study Michael for a moment before reaching out one sun-browned hand to run its fingers through the golden bedsprings of the toddler's hair. Her brother clapped and laughed, a pleased budgerigar squawk, and the Third Borough straightened from his stoop, resuming his full stature to continue talking with their mum.

Alma half-listened to the adult dialogue going on above her head as she gazed idly round the shop at the four labourers, still busy with their hammers, lathes and saws. Despite identical white gowns and similarly-cut fair hair the men were not alike ... one had a large mole in the centre of his forehead, while another one was crew-cut, dark and a bit foreign-looking ... yet they looked as though they came from the same family, were brothers or close cousins at the least. She wondered what their robes were made from. The material was plain and strong as cotton but looked soft, with ice-blue shadows hanging in its folds, so probably it cost more. These must be the aprons worn by senior carpenters or 'angles', Alma reasoned, and she had the muddy recollection of a word or brand name that she'd heard once which described the fabric. Was it 'Might', or 'Mighty'? Something like that, anyway.

Doreen was making polite conversation with the hooded eminence and venturing at intervals the reassuring coos that Alma recognised from those times when she'd tried explaining one of her more complicated drawings to her mother, sounds which meant that Mum had no real understanding of whatever she was being told but didn't want to give offence or seem disinterested. She must have casually enquired of the Third Borough how the work was coming on, Alma decided, and was now compelled to stand and cluck with hopefully appropriate surprise, appreciation or concern while he replied. As with much of the talk between her elders, Alma only caught the slender gist of it and wasn't really sure most of the time if she'd caught even that. Odd phrases and occasional expressions would lodge somewhere in her mind, provide a coat-rack of precarious hooks from which she could drape tentative connecting strings, threads of conjecture and wild guesswork linking up one notion with another until Alma either had a sketchy comprehension of whatever she had eavesdropped, or had burdened herself with a convoluted and ridiculous misunderstanding that she would continue to believe for years thereafter.

In this instance, standing listening to her mother's varyingly pitched and wordless interjections into the Third Borough's monologue, she picked her way between the stumbling blocks of grown-up language and tried hard to make a picture of what the discussion was about, one of her crayon dioramas but inside her head, a scene that had its different bits all in one almost-sensible arrangement. She supposed her mother had asked what the men were building, and from the reply it sounded as though they were making ready something called the Porthimoth di Norhan, which were words that Alma knew she'd never heard before and yet which sounded right, as if she'd known them all her life. It was a court of some kind, wasn't it, the Porthimoth di Norhan, where disputes would all be aired and everyone would get what they were due? Although in this case, Alma thought it sounded more like the Third Borough meant the term another way, relating to his carpentry, with 'Porthimoth di Norhan' as the name for an ingeniously complicated type of joint. Some words were said about it being where the rising lines converged, which Alma thought meant something similar to 'come together', so she could imagine that it was perhaps an octopus-armed junction such as she supposed you might get up inside a wooden church dome, bringing all the curving, varnished beams into a clever-cornered knot there at the middle. She imagined for some reason that there'd be a rough stone cross inlaid, set back into the polished rosewood at the heart of the arrangement.

Seeming to confirm the child's interpretation, the Third Borough was now saying it was just as well there were so many oaks here at the centre to support the weight and tension. As he said this, he placed one bronzed hand on Doreen's shoulder, which to Alma made the comment seem two-sided. Was he talking about all the oak trees studding the town's grasslands, or paying Doreen a form of compliment, saying their mother was an oak, a timber pillar that would take the strain without complaint? Her mum seemed pleased by the remark, however, pursing her lips diffidently, tutting to deride the thought that she was worthy of such praise.

The hooded man removed his hand from Doreen's sleeve, continuing his explanation of the labour he was overseeing which required completion by a certain time, demanding that his men work day and night to finish up their contract. There was something contradictory in this, it seemed to Alma. She was sure that the Third Borough's business must be one of the town's longest standing, older than the firms who had their premises in Bearward Street, with splintering gateways over which the peeling signs of former owners were still partly visible, leading to queerly-shaped mysterious yards. Some of the pubs, her dad once told her, had been here since Jacobean times, and she sensed that the building of this Porthimoth di Norhan had been going on for just as long, would still be going on a hundred years from now with the Third Borough still checking each detail of its craftsmanship to make sure that they'd got it right. Why did it sound so urgent, then, she asked herself? If there were centuries to go before the job was done, why all this talk of pressing deadlines to be met? Alma expected that the cowl-draped man just had to plan ahead more than most people did, perhaps because of his more serious long-term responsibilities.

She stood there on the tight new boards of the shop's floor that made her think of a ship's deck, one from the same song that she'd heard the juniors singing in their hall, a stately Spanish galleon sailing from an isthmus or the like. One hand still clasped around the push-bar of her brother's pram, she watched the four industrious carpenters hard at their grating, thumping work and thought they seemed a bit like sailors even if their long white aprons made her think of bakers. She was barely listening to their foreman's conversation with her mother anymore, having belatedly and with a start realised that all the workers' saw-blades, hammer-heads and drill-bits looked like they were made from actual gold, with diamonds twinkling in their handles where the screw heads ought to be. Bemused as to why she'd not noticed this before, Alma became aware of the Third Borough and her mother only when a name she knew arose from the low mumble of their discourse.

They were talking about something they referred to as a Vernall's Inquest, which she gathered was a kind of hearing to decide the gutters, corners, walls and edges of the world, where they all were and who they all belonged to. From what Doreen and the hooded governor were saying, it seemed this inquiry was the sole event that the assize under construction there, the Porthimoth di Norhan, was intended to contain – the only reason it was being built at all – but it was more the inquest's title than its import that had seized the girl's attention. Vernall was a family name, from Alma's dad's side. As she thought it over, Alma realised that she'd picked up quite a bit about her clan's immediate history from overheard grownup discussions, things she knew but hadn't previously known she knew. For instance May, Dad's mum, Alma and Michael's ironclad and ferocious nan, had been a Vernall before marrying Tom Warren, Alma's grandfather who'd been already dead some years when she was born. Her other granddad had been dead as well, now that she thought about it, Doreen's dad Joe Swan, a cheerful, barrel-chested fellow with a walrus-style moustache, dead of TB from working on the barges and known only from a bleaching oval photograph hung in the living room down Andrew's Road, up in the gloom beneath the picture rail. She'd never known her grandfathers and so their influence was absent from her life and was unmissed. The same could not be said about her grandmothers, not their gran Clara, Doreen's mother who they lived with, and not May, their nan, in her house at the bottom of the green behind St. Peter's Church, upon the Boroughs' weed-bound southwest fringe.

May Warren, formerly May Vernall, was a stout and freckled dreadnaught of a woman, rolling keg-shaped down the tiled lanes of the covered Fish Market most Saturdays, leaving a cleared path in her wake and gathering momentum with each heavy pace like an accumulating snowball of cheery malevolence, the speckled jowls in which her chin lay sunken shuddering at every step, the darting currants of the eyes pressed deep into the heaped blood-pudding of her face glittering with anticipation of whatever awful treat she'd visited the market to procure. It might be tripe, or whelks like muscle-bound and orange slugs, or chopped-up eels in lard. Alma believed her nan would probably eat anything, might be the sort of person who'd eat other people if it came to it, but then May was the deathmonger for Green Street and that general stretch. The deathmongers were women who brought people in and laid them out when they were done, so you could bet they'd seen some things all right. May had been born, so legend went, on Lambeth Walk itself, amidst the spit and sweepings of its gutters. Now she lived alone on Green Street's corner in a gas-lit, mildewed house with doors halfway up crooked stairs that nobody could fathom, there where Tommy, who was Alma's dad, and half her aunts and uncles had been raised. Family opinion had it that May had grown mean and ogress-like with age after a disappointed life, but family opinion also had it that there was a streak of madness in the Vernalls.

May's dad Snowy Vernall, Alma's great-grandfather, had gone what the family called 'cornery' and by the end was eating flowers, which sounded succulent and colourful to Alma, but not really wrong. Snowy had red hair as a baby, people said, but this lost all its hue during his later childhood, at around the same time Snowy's father Ernest, Alma's great-great-grandfather, had lost his mind and had his hair go white while he was working on St. Paul's Cathedral as a painter and restorer down in London in the nineteenth century. Ernest had passed his madness on to Snowy and to Snowy's sister, Thursa Vernall. Thursa was reputedly a great success on the accordion despite her lunacy, as was Alma's dad's pretty cousin Audrey Vernall, daughter of Snowy's son Johnny. Audrey had been in a dance band managed by her father at the finish of the war, and was now locked up in the madhouse round the turn at Berry Wood.

The turn, the bend, the twist, the corner: there were quite a few in Alma's family who'd gone round it. She imagined it must be a sudden angle in your thinking that you couldn't see approaching in the way that you could see a corner of the street in front of you. It was invisible, or nearly so, possibly see-through like a greenhouse or a ghost. This corner's lines ran a completely different way to all the others, so instead of going forward, down or sideways they went somewhere else, in a direction that you couldn't draw or even think about, and once you'd turned this hidden corner you were lost forever. You were in a maze you couldn't see and didn't even know was there, and everybody would feel sorry for you when they saw you blundering about, but probably they wouldn't want to still be friends with you the way they were before.

For saying just how many people had gone round this bend, Alma remained convinced that whatever existed past the unseen corner must be lonely, empty, and there'd always be nobody there but you. It wouldn't be your fault, but it would still be something shameful, something her gran Clara wouldn't like, a family embarrassment. That's why nobody talked about the Vernalls, and that's why Alma was almost startled now to hear her mum and the Third Borough speaking in such reverential tones about this Vernall's Inquest he had planned, the boundary-hearing all this work was being done for. Was this branch of Alma's relatives secretly special in some way, or was the inquest's name just a coincidence? And if it wasn't Alma's family that the words referred to, then what was a Vernall?

She thought it might once have been the term for some old-fashioned trade that people used to have, which could across the years become a family's surname. For example, Alma's father Tommy Warren, who worked for the brewery, had once told her that a cooper, years ago, was what you called a person who made barrels, so her best friend Janet Cooper's ancestors were very likely barrel-makers. This still didn't tell her what a Vernall was, of course, or what the job of being one entailed. Perhaps the name had been connected to an inquest about edges because tending borderlines and corners was a Vernall's duty? Alma wondered if amongst the corners they looked after was the bend that Ernest, Snowy, Thursa and poor Audrey Vernall had all gone around, but couldn't work out where that thought was leading and so let it fizzle out.

For no good reason that she could determine, the name Vernall also made her think of grass and how the scruffy little meadow over Andrew's Road near Spencer Bridge smelled when it had been mowed, of green blades pushing from the darkness underground into the sunlit world above, although how this had anything to do with boundaries and corners was beyond her. In her thoughts she saw her nan's house at the ragged end of Green Street, weeds and even poppies growing from between bricks, rooted in the railway soot that was the Boroughs' outdoor wallpaper, black curds that hung in drooping pleats from the burnt orange brickwork like a veil over the widowed neighbourhood. Across the street and a low dry-stone wall the green rose to the back of Peter's Church, beside the rear gate of the Black Lion's yard. This was the grassy slope she pictured Jesus walking on when people sang the hymn about the pleasant land, in his long dress with lights all round his head and nothing on his feet, strolling downhill from the pub gate towards the bottom of Narrow Toe Lane and Gotch's sweetshop, on the other end of Green Street from her nan's house. Finding herself trying to guess if Jesus had a favourite sweet she realised that her thoughts were wandering away with her and forced her restless cloud of concentration back to what her mum and the man in the white hood were discussing.

The Third Borough was concluding his account to Doreen of how things were going, reassuring Alma's mother that working with wood had been his family's business since time immemorial. He was telling her that though the job was long and would break many backs before its finish, all went well and would be done on time. Alma could not explain why this pronouncement filled her with such joy. It was as if nobody had to worry anymore about how things turned out because it would be all right in the end, like when your parents reassured you that the hero wasn't going to die and would get well before the story finished.

All around her in the glimmer of the shop the carpenters bent conscientiously to their unceasing toil, shouldering planes upslope against the grain, but Alma caught them looking to see if she'd understood what welcome news this was for everyone and smiling with a quiet satisfaction when they saw she had, proud of themselves yet blushing with embarrassment at their own pride. The Porthimoth di Norhan would be built, was in a sense already good as done. She looked around at Michael sitting up alertly in his pram. Even he seemed aware that there was something special going on and eagerly locked gazes with his sister, highlights dancing in his huge blue eyes as he communicated his delight along their private wordless channel, rattling his reins excitedly. Alma could tell that even if her brother wasn't old enough to give things names yet, he still knew in some way who the hooded foreman really was. You couldn't meet with him and not know, even if you were a baby. Michael was by nature a contented child but at that moment looked about to burst from all the wonderment inflating him, as if he understood exactly what this grand completion meant to everybody. It occurred to her from nowhere that one day when she and Michael were both old they'd probably sit on a wall together somewhere and have a good laugh about all this.

Doreen was thanking the Third Borough now for having asked them in while at the same time she made ready to depart, checking that Michael was strapped back securely and instructing Alma to do up her mackintosh's belt. Either the lights inside the shop were getting brighter, Alma thought, or else the darkness of the empty square outside had turned an unknown colour that was worse than black. She wasn't looking forward to the walk home, not to the vague, muffled dread she sometimes felt in Bath Street nor the night jaws

of the entrance to the alleyway, the jitty, where it ran along behind their row
of terraced houses down between Spring Lane and Scarletwell Street, but she
felt that it would seem ungrateful if she said so. Even if it meant a chilly trudge
Alma would not have missed this for the world, although she still wished she
could jump through the next twenty windswept minutes of her life to find
herself already tucked in bed.

The lights inside the shop were definitely getting brighter, she decided, as
she struggled to do up her mac's all-of-a-sudden awkward belt. In front of her,
or possibly above her, there were shiny rectangles of greater whiteness hanging
from the air, which Alma realised must be the reflections of the windowpanes
behind her as she stood beside the pushchair trying to do up her coat. Except
that wasn't right. You sometimes got a lit-up room reflected in a window, but
not windowpanes reflected in the empty spaces of a room, suspended there in
nothing, getting whiter and more blinding by the moment. Somewhere near,
Doreen was telling her to hurry up with fastening her belt so they could leave
the gentlemen to get on with their work. Alma had let go of the buckle-end
and lost it down a complicated tuck she hadn't known was there. The more she
tried to extricate the belt the more she found that extra swathes of gabardine
unfolded from recesses in her coat that only outfitters would understand and
tangled Alma in their shoelace-coloured creases. There above or possibly in
front of her the levitating panes of light blazed fiercer. Nearby mum was telling her to get a move on but the situation with her mackintosh was getting
worse. Alma was wrestling on her back against endless, engulfing fabric when
she noticed that the glowing oblongs floating there before her had a pair of
curtains pulled across them. Patterned with grey roses, they were very like the
ones in Alma's bedroom.

That in substance was the dream that Alma Warren, who grew up to be a moderately famous artist, had one February night in 1959 when she was five years
old. Within a year her brother Michael choked to death and yet somehow
got better and was back from hospital unharmed, at home with them down
Andrew's Road inside a day or two, which neither he nor Alma really mentioned afterwards although it scared them at the time.

Their father Tommy Warren died in 1990, Doreen following a short while
later in the sweltering summer heat of 1995. A little under ten years after
that Mick Warren had an accident at work, where he was reconditioning steel
drums. Rendered unconscious in a slapstick way and only woken by cold jets
of water that workmates were using to sluice caustic dust out of his eyes, Mick
was returned to life this second time with a variety of troubling thoughts
inside his head, strange memories churned up to the surface while he'd been
knocked out. Some of the things he thought that he remembered were so odd

they couldn't possibly have happened, and Mick started to become concerned that he was taking on the feared and thus unmentioned trait that simmered in the family blood, that he was going cornery.

When he'd at last worked up the nerve to tell his wife Cath of his fears she'd straight away suggested that he talk to Alma. Cathy's family, like Mick's, had been evicted from the grime-fields of the Boroughs, the square mile of dirt down by the railway station, when the council had the final remnants of the area cleared away during the early 1970s. Solid and sensible and yet proud of her eccentricities, Cath had those qualities that Mick recalled the Boroughs women having: the decisiveness and unshakeable faith in intuition, in their own ability to know what it was best to do in any given circumstance, no matter how peculiar.

Cathy and Alma got on like a house on fire despite or possibly because of their vast differences, with Cathy openly regarding Alma as a mad witch who lived in a rubbish tip and Alma scathing in return about her sister-in-law's fondness for Mick Hucknall out of Simply Red. Nevertheless, the women harboured nothing but respect towards each other in their separate fields of expertise, and when Cath recommended that her husband have a word with Alma if he thought that he was going Radio Rental, Mick knew that this was because his wife believed his older sister to be an authority on having not just lost the plot but having wilfully flushed the entire script down the shitter. Furthermore, he knew that she was more than likely right. He made a date to meet with Alma for a drink the following Saturday and for no reason that he could articulate arranged to see her in the Golden Lion on Castle Street, one of the few surviving pubs out of the dozens that the Boroughs had in its day boasted, and coincidentally where he'd met Cath when she was working there, before he'd lived the dream by marrying the barmaid.

Even on a Saturday these days, he found out when he rendezvoused with Alma, the once packed establishment was all but empty. Evidently the flat-dwelling residents remaining in the gutted neighbourhood who weren't confined to their front bedrooms by an ASBO usually preferred to head up to the sick- and spunk- and stabbing-friendly zoo of the town centre rather than endure the mortuary still of premises closer to home. His sister sat there at a corner table in her uniformly black ensemble: jeans, vest, boots and leather jacket. Black, Alma had recently explained to Mick, was the new iPod. She was nursing fizzy mineral water whilst trying to balance a round Strongbow beer-mat on its edge, watched with what looked to Mick like clinical depression by the man behind the bar. The only customer that he'd had in all night and it was a teetotal ugly bird.

Other than to her face, Mick would admit that Alma was what you'd call striking more than ugly, even at this late stage in the game. What was she,

fifty-one now? Fifty? Striking, definitely, if by that you meant actually frightening. She was five-eleven, one inch shorter than her brother, but in heels was
six feet two, her long uncut brown hair that greyed to dusty copper here and
there hanging like safety curtains to each side of her high cheek-boned face
in a style Mick had heard her once describe as 'bombsite creeper'. Then of
course there were her eyes, spooky and massive when they weren't myopically
screwed shut, with warm slate irises against which an extraterrestrial citrus
yellow flared around the pupil like a full eclipse, thick lashes creaking from
the weight of her mascara.

She'd had, across the years, at least her fair share of admirers but the truth
was that the great majority of men found Alma to be "generally alarming"
in the words of one acquaintance, or "a fucking menopausal nightmare" in
the blunter phrasing of another, although even this was said in what seemed
almost an admiring tone. Mick sometimes thought his sister was just the
wrong side of beautiful, but it was funnier if he insisted that she looked like
Lou Reed on the cover of *Transformer*, or "a solarized glam Frankenstein" as
Alma had with glee reworked it, saying that she'd use it in the catalogue biography next time she had an exhibition of her paintings. Revelling in the receipt
or dishing out of insults with an equal verve, Alma could more than hold her
own, maintaining with deadpan sincerity that her angelically good-looking
young brother had been simpering and effeminate since birth, had actually
been born a girl, was even chosen as Miss Pears at one point, but then under-
went a sex-change operation since their mum and dad had wanted one of
each. She'd first tried this painfully earnest routine out on Mick himself when
he was six and she was nine, reducing him to mortified, bewildered tears.
Once when he'd told her, not entirely without accuracy, that she came across
to people as a homosexual man trapped in a rough approximation of a woman's body, she'd said "Yeah, but so do you", then laughed until she coughed and
ultimately retched, inordinately pleased as usual by her own *bon mot*.

Stopping off at the bar to wrap a fist around the pleasing icicle of his first
pint he made his way over a threadbare floral-patterned carpet like a diagram of suicide towards his sister's chosen table, unsurprisingly located in
the empty lounge's furthest angle from its door, the misanthrope's retreat of
choice. Alma looked up as he scraped back a chair to sit opposite her across
the wet veneer with its sparse archipelago of beer mats. She rolled out her
usual smile of greeting which he thought was probably intended to give the
impression that her face lit up to see him, but since Alma's tendency to overdo
things was extended to her Grand Guignol theatre of expressions the effect
was more one of religiously-themed murderess or pyromaniac, that burst of
yellow arson in the centre of each eye.

"Well, if it isn't Warry Warren. How in God's name are you, Warry?"

Alma's voice was smoke-cured to an ominous bass organ chord reverberating in a Gothic church, at times even a little deeper than Mick's own. He grinned despite his current mental health concerns and felt sincerely glad to see his sister, re-establishing all their arcane connections, being with somebody comfortingly further gone than he was. Mick took out his cigarettes and lighter, placing them beside his beaded glass in preparation for the evening as he answered her.

"Just about had it, Warry, if you want the truth."

Each of the pair had called the other 'Warry' since a moment during 1966 of which neither had any clear, reliable memory. Alma, thirteen, may have begun it all by using Warry as a ridiculing term when speaking to her younger brother, and he may have hurled it back at her because, as she had always privately suspected, he was far too frivolous in his essential attitude towards existence to make up an insult of his own, even a stupid one like 'Warry'. Once the pair had taken up referring to each other in this way it would have all become an idiotic war of wills that neither could remember why they were involved in, but where neither felt that they could be the first to call the other by their given name without conceding an unthinkable defeat. This nominative tennis match had carried on, pathetically, for the remainder of their lives, long after they'd begun to find the cognomen affectionate and had forgotten utterly its half-baked origins. If asked why they both called each other Warry, Mick would usually reply that coming as they did from an insolvent background in the Boroughs, Mum and Dad had been unable to afford a nickname for each child, so that they'd had to make do with just one between them. "Not like posh kids", as he'd sometimes add with an authentic tone of bitterness. If Alma were around she'd look up at their audience with an accusing veal-calf stare and solemnly instruct them not to laugh. "That name was all we got for Christmas one year."

Now his sister planted the grazed leather of her elbows in the film of liquid covering their table, cupped her chin between long fingers and leaned forward through the weak-tea atmosphere inquiringly, head to one side so that the longer locks of hair dragged through the table's wet meniscus, tips becoming sharp as sable brushes.

"Truth? Why would I want the truth? I was just making conversation, Warry. I weren't asking for the *Iliad*."

They both admired her callousness, and then Mick told her how he'd had the accident at work, had been knocked out and had his face burned, had been blinded for an hour or two and had been worried ever since that he was going mad. Alma looked at him pityingly then shook her disproportionately massive head and sighed.

"Oh, Warry. Everything's about you, isn't it? I've been dog rough, half blind and barking mad for years but you don't catch me going on about it. Whereas you, you catch one face-full of corrosive chemicals for cleaning battleships, you fall to bits."

Mick put his fag out in the ashtray's sea-blue porthole and then lit another.

"It's not funny, Warry. I've been having weird thoughts since I woke up in the yard with everybody trying to hose me down. It's not so much the stuff that I'd got in me eyes or having banged me head, it's when I come round. For a minute it was like I'd got no memory of being forty-nine or working down the reconditioning yard. I'd got no memory of Cathy or the lads or anything."

He paused and sipped his lager. Alma sat across the sopping table, gazing flatly at him, paying genuine attention now she knew that he was serious. Mick carried on.

"The thing is, when I first come round I'd got it in me head that I was three and waking up in hospital, that time I had the cough-sweet when me throat swelled up."

Alma's defiantly unplucked brows tightened to a puzzled frown.

"That time you choked, and Doug next door drove you up Grafton Street, over the Mounts to hospital, sat in his vegetable lorry? We all thought that's probably where you contracted brain damage, or at least I did."

"I didn't get brain damage."

"Oh, come on. You must have done. Three minutes without oxygen and that's your lot. They all said you weren't breathing, right from Andrew's Road to Cheyne Walk, and that has to be ten minutes in a rusty truck like Doug's. Ten minutes without breathing and you're talking brain death, mate."

Mick laughed into his pint and flecked his nose with foam.

"And you're supposed to be an intellectual, Warry? Try ten minutes without breathing sometime and I think you'll find that it's all-over death."

That silenced both of them and made them think for a few moments without reaching any practical conclusions. At last, Mick resumed his narrative.

"So what I'm saying is, when I woke up in hospital when I was three, I'd no idea of how I'd got there. I'd no memory of choking or of being in Doug's truck although he said me eyes were open all the way. This time when I woke, it was different. Like I say, just for a minute I thought I was three again and coming round in hospital, but this time I remembered where I'd been."

"What, in the back yard with the cough-sweet, or Doug's truck?"

"Nothing like that. No, I remembered I'd been in the ceiling. I'd been up there for about a fortnight, eating fairies. I suppose it was a sort of dream I had while I was out, although it wasn't like a dream. It was more real, but it was more bizarre as well and it was all about the Boroughs."

Alma was by this point trying to interrupt and asking him if he knew he'd just said that he remembered being in the ceiling eating fairies for a fortnight, or did he assume he'd only thought it? Mick ignored her, and went on to tell her his entire adventure, the recaptured memory of which had so disturbed him. By its end, Alma sat slack jawed and unspeaking, staring in amazement at her brother with those medicated panda eyes. At last she ventured her first serious comment of the night.

"That's not a dream, mate. That's a vision."

Earnestly for once the pair resumed their talk, there in the gloom of the bereft pub lounge, replenishing their drinks at intervals with Alma sticking to the mineral water, her preferred drug being the half-dozen Bounty Bar-sized slabs of hashish strewn around her monstrous flat up on East Park Parade. About them as they sat the Golden Lion was steeping in the opposite of hub-bub, anti-clamour dominated by the wall-clock's mortal thud. The brightness of the bar-shine fluctuated subtly at times, as if the absences of all the missing customers were milling through the room, brown and translucent like old celluloid, occasionally overlapping with enough of their fly-specked non-bodies to occlude the light, if only imperceptibly. For hours Mick and his sister spoke about the Boroughs and about their dreams, with Alma telling Mick the one she'd had about the lit-up shop in the deserted market, where the carpenters were hammering through the night. She even told him how within the dream she'd thought about another dream she'd previously had, the one where Doreen had said pigeons were where people went when they were dead, although Alma admitted that upon awakening she'd not been sure if this were something that she'd really dreamed, or only dreamed she'd dreamed.

Eventually, when some while later they stepped out into the gusty shock of Castle Street, Alma was thrumming with excited energy and Mick was luminously pissed. Things were much better after talking to his sister and enduring her enthusiastic ranting. As they walked down Castle Street to Fitz-roy Street through the ghost-neighbourhood, Alma was talking about how she planned to do a whole new run of paintings based on Mick's near-death experience (which she'd by now convinced herself that his recovered memory really was) and her own dreams. She mocked her brother's fears for his own sanity as just one more example of his girlishness, his terror-stricken unfa-miliarity with anything resembling creative thought. "Your problem, Warry, is you have an idea and you think it's a cerebral haemorrhage." Listening to her spooling out impractical and transcendental picture-concepts like a hyper-ventilating tickertape he felt the weight lift from him, floating in a sweet and putrid lager fart to dissipate beneath the starry, vast obsidian pudding bowl of closing time, inverted and set down upon the Boroughs as though keeping flies away.

Down from the Golden Lion's front doorway and its carious sage-green tiles they stumbled, with – across the vehicle-forsaken street upon their right – the fading 1930s Chinese puzzle of scab-textured brick that was the rear of Bath Street flats, Saint Peter's house, breaks in the waist-high border wall allowing access to triangular stone stairways shaped like ziggurats, steps dropping from the apex to the base at either side. Past that there were the flats themselves with chiselled slots of Bauhaus shadow, double doors recessed beneath their porticos; gauze-cataracted windows, most of them unlit. Police car sirens skirled like radiophonic workshop banshees from the floodplains of St. James's End, west of the river, and Mick thought about his recent revelation, realising that despite the uplift of his sister's fervid, near fanatical response there was still a hard kernel of unease residing in the pit of him, albeit sunk beneath a lake of numbing amber slosh. Seeming to catch his shift of mood, Alma broke off her rapturous description of exquisite landscapes she had yet to capture and looked past him in the same direction he was looking, at the backside of the silent and benighted flats.

"Yeah. That's the problem, isn't it? Not 'What if Warry's going round the corner?' but 'What if he's not?' If what you saw means what I think it does, then that thing over there is what we've really got to deal with." Alma nodded to the dark flats and by implication Bath Street, running unseen down their furthest side.

"The business that you saw when you were with the gang of dead kids, the Destructor and all that. That's what we're up against. That's why I'd better make these paintings great, to change the world before it's all completely fucked."

Mick glanced at Alma dubiously.

"It's too late, sis, don't you think? Look at all this."

He gestured drunkenly around them as they reached the bottom of the rough trapezium of hunched-up ground called Castle Hill, where it joined what was left of Fitzroy Street. This last was now a broadened driveway leading down into the shoebox stack of 'Sixties housing where the feudal corridors of Moat Street, Fort Street and the rest once stood. It terminated in a claustrophobic dead-end car park, block accommodation closing in on two sides while the black untidy hedges, representing a last desperate stand of Boroughs wilderness, spilled over on a third.

When this meagre estate had first gone up in Mick and Alma's early teenage years the cul-de-sac had been a bruising mockery of a children's playground with a scaled-down maze of blue brick in its centre, built apparently for feeble-minded leprechauns, and the autistic cubist's notion of a concrete horse that grazed eternally nearby, too hard-edged and uncomfortable for any child to straddle, with its eyes an empty hole bored through its temples. Even that, more like the abstract statue of a playground than an actual place, had been less awful than this date-rape opportunity and likely dogging hotspot, with its hasty skim of tarmac spread like cheap, stale caviar across the pink pedestrian tiles beneath, the bumpy lanes and flagstone closes under that. Only the gutter margins where the strata peeled back into sunburn tatters gave away the layers of human time compressed below, ring markings on the long-felled cement tree-stump of the Boroughs. From downhill beyond the car park and the no-frills tombstones of its sheltering apartment blocks there came the mournful shunt and grumble of a goods train with its yelp and mutter rolling up the valley's sides from the criss-cross self-harm scars of the rail tracks at its bottom.

Alma looked towards the vista Mick had indicated, tightening her thick-caked lashes into a contemptuous spaghetti western squint so that her eyes were jumping-spiders tensing for the fatal pounce.

"Of course it's not too late, you girl. There's no point sending you a vision if there's nothing to be done about it, is there? And, look, I'm a genius. They said so in the *NME*. I'll do these paintings and we'll get this sorted. Trust me."

And he did, implicitly. While it was obvious to a blind man that Mick's sister was both self-infatuated and delusional, in his experience Alma also often turned out to be right. If she said that she could repair a cataclysm with some tubes of paint, Mick was inclined to put the money on his sister rather than the meteor strike or whatever it was had happened to the Boroughs. All her life she'd made perverse decisions that had worked out for her against all the odds and nobody could say their Alma hadn't done well for a Boroughs kid. Mick had got faith in her, though not the wide-eyed faith of her devoted audience, many of whom appeared to think of her as having origins within the region of the supernatural or else the field of clandestine genetic research, a god-sent mutation who could talk to stones and raise the unborn, let alone the dead.

"I can't believe you're Alma Warren's brother", he'd had more than one fan of his sister's paintings tell him, mostly female workmates of his wife's whom Alma was convinced only responded to her as "a badly misjudged lesbian icon" rather than an artist. Sometimes, if they knew Mick's background, they'd sit looking thoughtful before asking him how anyone like Alma Warren could have possibly emerged from a notorious urban soul-trap like the Boroughs. He considered this a stupid question, as if there were any other place she could have come from, Hell or Narnia or somewhere. How long was it since there'd been even a trace of the authentic working class, if its conspicuous products were today unrecognisable as dodos? What had happened to that culture? Other than those parts of it which had been tempted up into the low boughs of the middle classes or drained off into the cardboard jungle, how had it all vanished so that these days if they saw it, no one had a clue what they were looking at? Where had it gone? Why hadn't somebody complained?

They'd turned left and were walking down the lowest edge of Castle Hill, towards the wall of Doddridge Church, heading for Chalk Lane, Marefair and the cab rank of the station at the bottom, on the end of their beloved Andrew's Road. Alma was back to conjuring another as yet non-existent masterpiece, eyes staring fixedly into the ink-wash empty space before her as if she already saw it framed and hanging there.

"I had this idea, right, when we were talking. I could do my dream, the one about the carpenters down at the corner of the market in the middle of the night. I could do something really big, a bit like Stanley Spencer with enormous figures bent over their lathes, facing away from us. I'll do some bits in loving detail but I'll leave the rest unfinished with, like, dangling pencil lines. I'll call it 'Work in Progress' ..."

Alma trailed off, stopping in her tracks to gaze up at the eighteenth-century Nonconformist church that they were passing. Set into the toffee-coloured stonework of its upper storey was a closed pitch-painted doorway that led into empty air, clearly a loading bay of some sort, except why would anybody need one halfway up a church? It looked as if it was intended to lead to an unseen upper floor of the impoverished district, one long since demolished without trace, or possibly a planned extension yet to be constructed. She looked from the senseless angel-door to Mick and when she spoke her train-wreck voice was small and marvelling, more like that of a little girl than when she'd been one.

"That's one of the places, Warry, isn't it? From in your seizure or whatever?"

Alma's brother nodded and then indicated the turfed-over wasteland up beyond another car park, on Chalk Lane approaching to their right as they resumed their walk.

"Yeah. That's another, but that's like an earthworks. It's much bigger though, and older, and the puddles have unfolded, sort of, into a lagoon."

His sister nodded slowly, taking it all in as she surveyed the tuft of land rising behind the car-crèche, its surveillance camera babysitter monitoring her charges from a litter-pocket corner. One forked tree or maybe a close-planted pair stretched up out of the mound in silhouette against the sodium lamp bleed above the nearby station. Trees were the enduring features of a landscape, its true face beneath the pantomime dame crust of leisure centre and dual carriageway, cosmetic affectations wiped away at intervals. The oak and elm defined the view across great tracks of time, were vital structural elements, constant as clouds and like the clouds mostly unnoticed.

As they reached the top of Chalk Lane, to the east past Doddridge Church on its grass hillock were the flats and houses of St. Mary's Street where the great fire was started, and past that the traffic rush of Horsemarket, running

uphill to void into the dead monoxide junction where the Mayorhold used to
be. Ahead of them the crack of Chalk Lane dipped through darkness, south and
down to Marefair's headlight ribbon with the devil-decorated eaves of Peter's
Church across the way, an ibis hotel and attendant entertainment complex
up towards town on the left. A neon tumour styled by Fabergé, this had been
raised upon the site of the demolished Barclaycard headquarters, previously
an endearing tangle of small businesses and hairline alleyways, Pike Lane,
Quart Pot Lane, Doddridge Street and long before that a royal residence that
governed Mercia and with it most of grunting Saxon England. There weren't
ghosts here; there were fossil seams of ghosts, one stacked upon another and
compressing down to an emotive coal or oil, black and combustible.

Alma tried to imagine the whole listing quarter right from Peter's Way to
Regent Square, from Andrew's Road to Sheep Street and Saint Sepulchre's, a
petrifying side of boar still with the jutting tower-block arrows that impaled
and brought it down, still with its street lamp bristles and its alehouse crackling; tried imagining it all in context of Mick's vision as if the distressed
topography and broken skyline still plugged into something humming and
impalpable, some legendary machinery long disappeared but still perhaps in
working order. It was awesome and it made her need a joint. Campaigners said
it wasn't possible to get addicted to old-fashioned hashish, but to Alma's way
of thinking they just couldn't have been trying.

They stepped out of Chalk Lane onto Black Lion Hill, a million years of
gradient presided over by four hundred years of public house at the arse-end
of Marefair. By the alley-mouth there'd been another paper-shop where Alma
from the age of seven had bought comics for their pictures, garish flotsam
shipped here from America as ballast with skyscraper-scented pages and
electrifying banners: *Journey into Mystery*, *Forbidden Worlds* and *My Greatest Adventure*. Over the resurfaced lane had stood a melancholy guesthouse
hanging back behind a screen of elders, with existing photos from a date still
earlier showing a mill-like structure dominated by a lantern cupola that previously ruled the corner. There was a short row of faceless 1960s houses perched
there now, behind the high wall overlooking the main road, with tenants
hanging on until the area was one day gentrified, part of a 'Cultural Mile' that
council wonks had blue-skied and attempted to talk up, before they sold high
and bailed out for somewhere less accusing, somewhere without all the bad
dreams trapped like astral rising damp in the foundations. Alma had from
somewhere the impression that a local councillor had occupied one of the
buildings once, but whether he still lived there she had no idea. Rounding the
corner to their right, they walked down to the lights and crossed St. Andrew's
Road, continuing to the approach of Castle Station.

This was where the sex-commuters pulled in at the weekends, prostitute away-teams hot from Milton Keynes or Rugby riding in upon a Silverlink express to the well-publicised red-light zone of the Boroughs, the rich pickings of the all night truck-stop on its northwest corner, where the hump of Spencer Bridge met Crane Hill at the foot of Grafton Street, the area's northern boundary. Walking AIDS vectors and their managers routinely filtered through the station forecourt, through the former medieval castle where Shakespeare's *King John* commences, where reputedly they held the world's first parliament during the thirteenth century and raised the poll tax that sparked off Wat Tyler's uprising of 1381, where various Crusades were planned, where Becket was condemned, here at the end of the soot-blasted road where Mick and Alma had grown up, their derelict arcadia. As they descended to the hackney cabs unwinding round the station's yard from its front entrance, Alma was reflecting on the grave enormity of what she'd promised she'd see through. She wasn't going to have to simply do these pictures. She was going to have to do the fuck out of them.

———

And she did. Fourteen months later on a cold Spring Saturday in 2006 Mick had lunch with his wife and boys up at their house in Whitehills, then walked down through Kingsthorpe to the Barrack Road, coming upon the Boroughs from its northeast corner and the crater that had formerly been Regent Square. He'd passed his driving test but still preferred to go by foot, sharing his family's antipathy to motor vehicles. Neither his sister and their parents nor all save one of their various aunts and uncles had ever possessed a car, and Mick still felt uneasy on the rare occasions that his designated driver Cathy was away, obliging him to climb behind the wheel.

Alma had called him weeks ago to say she'd finished with the paintings she'd commenced after their meeting at the Golden Lion the year before. She planned to kick the exhibition off with a small viewing that she'd set up at the playgroup where Pitt-Draffen's dance school used to be, up on one sawn-off corner edge of Castle Hill. His sister had invited him to see the images his vision had inspired, including 'Work in Progress' with its midnight carpenters, a piece that she particularly wanted him to see called 'Chain of Office', and another work that Alma said was 'three dimensional' and which might only be available for viewing at this opening event.

In slacks and loafers and a plain tan sports shirt underneath a jacket he still wasn't sure if he was going to need he strolled facing the breeze down Grafton Street, a fit and handsome forty-nine-year-old who still maintained a gleam of infant animation in his pale blue eyes, which were at least one normal colour and weren't something out of *Village of the Damned* like Alma's. She of course would counter that she'd kept her hair while his had made the dignified retreat into a cloud of golden fuzz high on his suntanned brow, not wholly different from the burnished, lonely ringlets of his babyhood. If he was feeling rash or lucky he might point out in riposte that he'd kept all his teeth, a literal sore point with the munchie-prone and periodontinitis-stricken Alma who would probably then glare at him, go dangerously quiet and that would be the end of that. He realised that rehearsing these encounters with his sister and stage-managing their banter that might never happen was a mark of insecurity, but in Mick's previous experience with Alma it was always best to be prepared.

The plunge of Grafton Street gushed with a growling steel and rubber torrent, vehicle flow swollen by a rain of lunchtime drinkers, weekend shopping trips and booming penis publicizers, threatening to overspill its banks. An anaconda laminate of molten tyre that snaked across the pavement just ahead of Mick bore testament that such a breach had happened only recently, most probably during the Friday night just gone. White-water driving by some Netto Fabulous crash-dummy who bled Burberry, shooting the traffic island rapids in his hotwired kayak, home to Jimmy's End across the river in the west, head full of *Grand Theft Auto San Andreas* and horse tranquilliser, pinprick pupils, squinting in the spindrift of oncoming headlights.

Ambling down the draughty slope beneath a panoramic sky, Mick passed the Sunlight building that was on the road's far side, a Chinese laundry once that breathed out lonely bachelor steam, become an oily car-repair shop still, with the incongruous solar trademark of the previous establishment raised in relief from its white Art Deco façade. A little further down on the same side there stood the dismal shell of the old Labour Exchange where both Mick and Alma and the great majority of their associates had at one point or other stood amongst the shuffling and obscurely guilty abattoir processions, lining up to be inspected by a merciless nineteen-year-old with bolt-gun phrasing. Mick was grimly satisfied to note that the dour arbiter of worker's fortunes was itself these days redundant, the indifferent prison-warder gaze its windows used to have replaced now by the look of tremulous, disoriented dread that comes with growing old in a declining neighbourhood. They never like it when it's them, Mick thought, as he passed by St. Andrew's Street there on his left and carried on downhill into the wind.

St. Andrew's Street, receding now behind him, had once led to the raised bump where stood St. Andrew's Church, long since torn down, itself built on the site of the St. Andrew's Priory that had been there hundreds of years before and which accounted for the great preponderance of phantom Cluniac monks amongst the district's roster of reported ghosts. At one time, Mick remembered, almost all the half-a-square-mile's multitude of pubs – what was it, eighty-something? – were alleged to have a chanting apparition seeking absolution in the snug, or drawing painstaking illuminated pricks with gilded scrollwork on the lavvy wall. Mick wondered where the spectres had all gone in 1970 or so, when the last fag ends of the area were swept away. The Boroughs' mortal residents were siphoned off to flats in King's Heath like the one that his nan May had died in, or to the genetic sumps of Abington like Norman Road, where his and Alma's gran upon their mum's side, Clara, had dropped off the twig, both grandmas passing within weeks of their uprooting from the Boroughs where they'd buried husbands, where they'd buried kids. What struck Mick was that clearly it had never been a big priority to suitably relocate Boroughs dregs like him and Alma and their family, who, although possibly dishevelled, were at least alive. How much less effort had gone into the rehousing of the region's wraiths, who'd all been dead, gruesomely so, for years? Did spooks from pulled-down pubs now shiver and clutch tight their glowing bed-sheets under the shop doorways of Northampton's centre, like its other dispossessed? Did they have shelters for the bodiless as well as for the homeless; magazine street-vendor schemes for revenants, like *The Dead Issue*, maybe?

It had been along St. Andrew's Street that he and Alma had once known a barber, forty years ago, with the unlikely name Bill Badger. They'd pretended, just between themselves, that he was one of Rupert Bear's accomplices grown up, shaved by his own hand to appear more human, forced by circumstance to get a proper job. His shop had been an odditorium, its crowding walls filled to the ceiling with unfathomable, strangely charismatic products like Bay Rum and styptic pencils that would seal up cuts and which, during his childhood, Mick had thought might be a handy thing to carry round with you so that there was at least a chance that you could stick your head back on if you'd been guillotined. Of course, the shop was gone now, both it and the church replaced by the same blocks of flats with which the district had been steadily and surely tiled since 1921 or thereabouts. Last year there'd been a young, mentally ill Somali under armed police siege up St. Andrew's Street, threatening to kill himself, while still more recently a cousin of Mick's lovely and formidable wife Cathy, herself a benignant outgrowth of the town's notorious and hydra-headed Devlin clan, had put St. Andrew's Street into the news again by strangling his spouse. She'd been "doing his head in", so he claimed.

The place was cursed. Only that lunchtime Mick had seen a hoarding for the local *Chronicle & Echo* that reported yet another hooker raped and beaten in the small hours of the night before and left for dead down at the base of Scarletwell Street, only saved by intervention from a resident, such incidents reported every month although occurring every week. Nothing good happened in the Boroughs anymore but once, down Grafton Street towards Crane Hill there lived a woman that Miss Starmer who had run the post office would speak of, who'd been standing on her step one morning when a passing stranger thrust a newborn child into her arms and ran away; was never seen again. The child was taken in and raised, brought up as though the woman's own, and fought in World War One. "You can tell what a lovely family they were to bring him up", Miss Starmer used to say, "but they were in the Boroughs. That's the kind of families that we had in the Boroughs then." And it was true. Even confronted by the stark reality of how the neighbourhood had ended up, as an environmental head-butt where the woman's stunning act of altruism was today unthinkable, Mick knew that it was true. There'd been a different sort of people then that seemed another race, had different ways, a different language, and were now improbable as centaurs.

He turned left from Grafton Street and into Lower Harding Street, a long straight track that would deliver him to Alma's exhibition on the Boroughs' far side by the most direct route. This was where his sister's lefty activist mate Roman Thompson lived, another bloody-minded kamikaze from the 'Sixties just like Alma was. 'Thompson the Leveller' she called him fondly, probably one of her know-all references, and he lived with his slinky, stroppy boyfriend here in Lower Harding Street. Roman had been a firebrand since the UCS ship-workers' strike four decades earlier, had broken through police lines to punch out one of the leaders in a National Front march through Brick Lane and had once wreaked terrible revenge upon a unit of drunk squaddies who'd made the mistake of thinking that this wizened terrier posed less of an immediate threat alone than they, en masse and army-trained, could muster. Rome was in his early sixties now, some ten years older than Mick's sister, but still closed his jaws upon the arse of an oppressor with undimmed ferocity. At present he was on the militant arm of the local Boroughs action group, campaigning to prevent the sale and demolition of the area's few remaining council dwellings. Alma had consulted with her old friend once or twice while she was working on this current run of paintings, she had told her brother, who would not have been surprised if Thompson and his chap should turn up at the exhibition Mick was making for.

Over a narrow road the yard of a car salesroom had replaced the wasteland on which he and Alma had amused themselves as children, scrabbling urgently across 'The Bricks' as they had called their improvised apocalyptic theme-park, clambering oblivious through spaces where once men and women had their rows and sex and children. Further on were business premises formerly owned by Cleaver's Glass, the national interest where their great-grandfather, barmy Snowy Vernall, had refused a co-director's job back at the company's inception, spurning millionaire life for no reason anyone could fathom and returning to his family's slum accommodation at the end of Green Street, where some decades later he would end his days hallucinating, sat between parallel mirrors in an endless alley of reflections, eating flowers.

Beyond the factory's southern boundary Spring Lane went trickling down to Andrew's Road past the rear side of Spring Lane School and its unmodified caretaker's house, on past the factory yard down near the bottom where a baffling and precarious spike of brick rose up that had a single office shed just slightly larger than the tower itself balanced on top, the overhang held up by bulky wooden struts. This made Mick think about his unearthed memories from the year before and of the pointless loft halfway up Doddridge Church, subjects that had a feathered whisper of uncertainty about them, so that he directed his attention to the hillside school itself, its fenced top edge now passing slowly on his right.

It was a sorry sight, but didn't have the morbid overtones stirred by that inexplicable brick spar. Alma and he had both been pupils here, when all was said and done, as had their mum Doreen before them. They'd all loved the huddled red brick building that had somehow shouldered the responsibility for educating several generations in that surely unrewarding province, had all been upset when the original establishment was finally dismantled and replaced by a prefabricated substitute. The school was still a good one, though, still with some of those qualities that Mick remembered from his boyhood. Both of Mick and Cathy's children, Jack and Joseph, had attended Spring Lane Primary and had enjoyed it, but Mick missed the steep slate roofs, the bull's-eye windows keeping watch from underneath a sharply angled ridge, the smooth gunmetal crossing-barriers outside stone-posted gates.

Down at the bottom of the hill, beyond the schoolhouse and its playing fields there stretched the strip of grass on Andrew's Road where Mick and Alma's house had been, a startlingly narrow patch, barely a verge, where by one estimate upwards of one hundred and thirty people had existed, there between Spring Lane and Scarletwell Street. There was only turf now underneath which the brick stump of someone's garden wall could still be found, and a few trees that stood in the approximate location of their former home. The size and sturdiness of these always surprised Mick, but then, when you thought about it, they'd been growing there for over thirty years now.

Puzzlingly, towards the plot of ill-kept ground's south end, two houses from the Warren's block still stood unharmed, knocked into one and facing onto Scarletwell Street, all alone with everything about them levelled, taken back eight hundred years to featureless green Priory pasture. Mick thought that the dwellings might have been built after all the others in the row, possibly where the filled-in space of an old yard had been, owned by some other landlord who'd resisted when all the surrounding properties had been sold out from under their inhabitants and then knocked down. He'd heard that the anomalous surviving home had at one time been used as sheltered housing, possibly by those in care of the community, but didn't know if this was true. The solitary structure that still hulked from the grassed-over reach where he'd been born had always struck Mick as in some way indefinably uncanny, but since his experience that nebulous unease had gained a new dimension. Now, he found, the place reminded him of Doddridge Church's pointless aerial door or else the unbelievable brick growth protruding from the factory in Spring Lane; things from the interred past that poked up inconveniently into the present, halfway houses with their portals that went nowhere, that led only into a suggestive nothing.

Lower Harding Street had turned to Crispin Street just past its juncture with Spring Lane. Up on the left ahead two hulking monoliths rose up, the tall Kray-brother forms of Beaumont Court and Claremont Court, bird-soiled and lime-streaked headstones slowly decomposing over the community that had been cleared to raise them. Easily impressed, the soon to be dispersed folk of the Boroughs had all oohed and ahhed about what they mistook for the space-age pizzazz of the twelve-storey heaps, failing to understand the high-rise blocks for what they were: two upended and piss-perfumed sarcophagi that would replace the tenant's back-wall badinage and summer doorstep idylls with more vertical arrangements, thin-air isolation and the tension rising with each number lit up in the climbing after-curfew lift, a suicide's-eye view of what had been done to the territory around them that was inescapable.

In what might have been taken for a moment of lucidity two or three years ago, the town belatedly deplored the squalid stack-a-prole insensitivity of the constructions and proposed to bring them down, which had made Mick's heart soar, if only briefly, at the thought that he and Alma might outlive the monster breeze blocks that were used to smash their home ground into crack dens, knocking shops and a despairing dust that settled everywhere on people's heartstrings. His unreasonable optimism proved short lived, and elements within the council had instead decided on the option of offloading the dual eyesores to a private housing firm for sums that Mick had heard amounted to a penny each. His sister's activist mate Roman Thompson had made dark insinuations about backroom deals and former members of the council now ensconced upon the housing company's board, but Mick had heard no more about this for a while and guessed that it had come to nothing. Bedford Housing had refurbished the two cheaply-purchased buildings and they now stood waiting for a promised influx of key workers, cops and nurses and the like, to be imported to the town and take up occupancy. If you had a population that were miserable and restless because they had nowhere bearable to live, then the preferred solution seemed not to be spending money on improving their condition but on hiring more police in case things should turn ugly, housing these new myrmidons in properties from which the itchy and disgruntled man-herds were already serendipitously purged.

Off from behind the reappointed and Viagra-fuelled atrocities of the two rearing giants, from the more humanly-proportioned residences spread between them and the constant rumble of the Mayorhold at their rear, Mick caught what sounded like a garbled shriek immediately followed by a door-slam, the report slurred by the distance and the dead acoustic of the concrete flat-fronts. Running or more properly careening over the bleached lawn extending round the high rise edifices came a gangling, panic-stricken figure, looking to Mick's slightly narrowed eye to be a teenager around nineteen, brown-haired and pale-complexioned, just a few years older than Mick's eldest son. The flailing boy was barefoot, clad in jeans that seemed intent on merging crotch and ankles, and a FCUK top that looked too large and likely borrowed, fitting the distraught young man like an Edwardian nightshirt. He was gurgling and gasping, making a repeated sound of horrified denial that came out as 'nnung' and taking frantic looks behind him as he ran.

Whether this clump of gibbering tumbleweed had spotted Mick and veered towards him or whether their separate trajectories had simply happened to converge he couldn't later say. The youth's flight from whatever frights pursued him ended in a wheezing halt some feet in front of Mick, compelling him in turn to stop dead in his tracks and take stock of this sudden and as yet inscrutable arrival. The scared boy stood doubled over with hands planted on his knees, staring with red eyes at the earth beneath his feet while trying to draw breath and whimper simultaneously with neither effort an unqualified success. Mick felt obliged to say something.

"Are you all right, mate?"

Gazing startled up at Mick as if he hadn't realised there was anybody there until he heard a voice, the lad's face was a bag lady of physiognomy, trying to wear all its expressions at the same time. Pasty white skin at the corners of the eyes and lips twitched and convulsed through a succession of attempts at an emotional display, embarrassment, amazement, blanked-out disassociation, each without conviction, each immediately abandoned as the trembling individual sorted frantically among his clearly ransacked wardrobe of responses. Drugs of some sort, Mick decided, and most likely something synthesized last Tuesday rather than the limited array of substances that he himself was very distantly familiar with, mostly through Alma who had tripped for England in her schoolgirl years. This wasn't acid, though, where people burned all their evaporating sweat away into an incandescent peacock shine, nor was this like the knowing grin of magic mushrooms. This was something different. Random winds stroked the half-hearted grass, funnelled by tower-block baffles until they were lost, bewildered, disappearing in frustrated eddies, turning on themselves. The kid's voice, when he found it, was a piping yelp that Mick seemed to recall from somewhere, just as he had similarly started to detect a nagging shadow of familiarity in the teenager's dough-toned features with that shake of cinnamon across the nose.

"Yes. No. Fuck me. Oh, fuck me, I was up the pub. The pub's still up there. I was in it. It's still up there, and they're all still there. Me mate's still there. That's where I've been all night, up in the pub. They wouldn't let us go. Fuck me. Fuck me, mate, help us out. It was a pub. It was a pub, still up there. I was up the pub."

All this was said with wild-eyed urgency, apparently unconscious of its tics or its obsessive repetitions, its conspicuous lack of any point. Mick found himself with nothing he could read in the by now disturbingly familiar young- ster's fractured body language or his babbling conversation. On the street's far side a gnome-like woman in a headscarf walked along beside the Upper Cross Street maisonettes with circulation-dodging fingers hooked about the handles of her plastic shopping bag. She stared at Mick and his unasked-for company, a glowering disapproval that went without saying, so that he wished there were some convenient semaphore by which he could convey that he had simply been accosted by this raving stranger in the street. Other than point- ing to his temple and then to the auburn-haired kid he could think of nothing, so he switched his gaze from the old lady back to his incomprehensible assail- ant with the pleading eyes. Mick tried to tease a thread of sense out from the tumbling rubble of the young man's opening speech.

"Hang on, you've lost me, mate. Was this a lock-in, then, this pub they kept you at all night? Which was it, anyway? Up where?"

The boy, no more than eighteen, Mick decided, stared imploringly from out behind the glass of his own failure to communicate. He waved one skinny forearm and its baggy, flapping sleeve in the direction of the Mayorhold, up behind them. There'd been no pubs on the Mayorhold for some decades now.

"Up there. Up in the roof. I mean the pub. The roof's a pub. The pub's still up there, in the roof. They're all still there. Me mate's still there. That's where I was all night. They wouldn't let us go. Oh fuck me, I've been up the pub, the pub up in the roof. Oh, fuck, what's happened? Something's happened."

Mick was startled and could feel his scalp crawl at the nape, but made an effort not to let it show. No point in getting jumpy when you're trying to talk somebody back into their skin, although that bit about the roof had gotten to him. It was too much like the way that he'd described his recalled memories to Alma as adventures in the ceiling. Obviously, it had to be just happenstance, a space-case turn of phrase that by some fluke chimed ominously with his own childhood experience, but combined with the still-gnawing sense that he'd met with this lad before somewhere, it bothered him. Of course, it also loaned him an at least imaginary commonality with the young man, a way he could respond compassionately to the poor kid's helpless gibberish.

"Up in the roof? Yeah, I've had that. Like when there's people in the corners trying to pull you up?"

The youth looked dumbstruck, with his pink-rimmed eyes wide and his mouth hung open. All the panic and confusion fell away from him, replaced by something that was almost disbelieving awe as he stared, suddenly transfixed, at Mick.

"Yeah. Up the corners. They were reaching down."

Mick nodded, fumbling in his jacket for the brand new pack of fags he'd picked up half an hour back on the way down Barrack Road. He peeled the cuticle of cellophane that held the packet's plastic wrap in place down to its quick, shucked off the wrapper's top and tugged the foil away that hid the tight-pressed and cork-Busbied ranks beneath, the crinkled see-through wrapping and unwanted silver paper crushed to an amalgam and shoved carelessly into Mick's trouser pocket. Taking one himself he aimed the flip-top package at the grateful teenager in offer and lit up for both of them using his punch-drunk Zippo with the stutter in its flame. As they both blew writhing, translucent Gila monsters made of blue-brown vapour up into the Boroughs air the boy relaxed a little, letting Mick resume his pep-talk.

"You don't want to let it get you down, mate. I've been up where you've been, so I know how it can be. You can't believe it's happened and you think you're going mental, but you're not, mate. You're all right. It's just when you come back from one of them it takes a while before this all feels real and solid like it did. Don't worry. It comes back. Just take it easy, have a think about it all, and gradually the bits all fall back into place. It might take you a month or two, but this will all get better. Here."

Mick pulled a clump of cigarettes out from the pack, approximately half a dozen thick, and gave them to the barefoot psychotropic casualty.

"If I were you, mate, I'd go off and find yourself a quiet place to sit down where you can sort your head out, somewhere out of doors without the ceilings and the corners and all that. I'll tell you what, down at the other end of Scarletwell Street over there, there's a nice bit of grass with trees for shade. They'll be in blossom around now. Go on, mate. It'll do you good."

Incredulous with gratitude, the youngster stared adoringly at Mike, as if at something mythical he'd never seen before, a sphinx or Pegasus.

"Thanks, mate. Thanks. Thanks. You're a good bloke. You're a good bloke. I'll do that, what you said. I'll do it. You're a good bloke. Thanks."

He turned away and stumbled barefoot off across the grit and shattered headlight glass of Scarletwell Street corner, where it joined with Crispin Street and Upper Cross Street, as the former had by that point technically become. Mick watched him go, tenderly picking his way over the rough paving by the chain-link fence of Spring Lane School like a concussed flamingo, stuffing the donated cigarettes into a misplaced pocket of his low-slung pants. As he began to head off down the hill towards Mick's recommended quiet spot, he stopped by the school gates and glanced back. Mick was surprised to see that there appeared to be tears streaming down the youngster's cheeks. He looked towards Mick gratefully and with some difficulty worked his face into a kind of smile. He gave a helpless shrug.

"I was just up the pub."

Resignedly, he carried on away from Mick and was soon out of sight. Mick shook his head. Fuck knew what that was all about. As he resumed his own walk along Upper Cross Street, taking tight drags on his cigarette at intervals, it struck him that he felt in some way oddly lifted by the lunatic encounter. Not just by the dubious warm glow of having lent a modest hand to somebody in need, but by the hard-to-explain reassurance that the mad boy offered. An authentic Boroughs nutcase, just like he'd run into when he was a child, when the insane were that much easier to spot and someone walking down an empty street towards you yelling angrily into the air was certain to have paranoid psychosis rather than a Bluetooth earpiece. Mick just wished he could remember where he'd met the lad before.

The stuff about him being in the roof had knocked Mick back a bit, but that had got to be coincidence, or 'synchronicity' as Alma had attempted to explain it to him back when she was in her twenties and still had a crush on Arthur Koestler, before finding out he'd been a wife-beating bipolar rapist, which had rather shut her up. As far as Mick could understand the concept, it defined coincidences as events that had some similarity or seemed to be connected, but which weren't linked up in any rational way, with one causing the other for example. But the people who'd come up with the word 'synchronicity' still thought that there might be some kind of bond between these intriguing occurrences, something we couldn't see or understand from our perspective and yet obvious and logical in its own terms. Mick had an image in his mind of koi carp gazing upward from the bottom of their pool to see a bunch of waggling human fingers dipping through the ceiling of their universe. The fish would think that it was several separate and unusually meaty bait-worms, could have no idea these unconnected wrigglers were all part of the same unimaginable entity. He didn't know how this related to his meeting with the barefoot boy, or to coincidence in general, but it seemed in some way muddily appropriate. Taking a last pull on his cigarette he flicked the smouldering butt-end to the ground ahead of him, its arc like space junk burning up upon re-entry, then extinguished the crash-landed ember underneath his shoe-sole without breaking step. Still thinking foggily about coincidence and carp he looked up with a start to find he was in Bath Street.

He'd been wrong. He'd been quite wrong to think that he was over his unsettling dream, his sojourn in the ceiling. He'd been wrong to tell the freaked-out teenager that it would all get better, because actually it didn't. It just faded to a deep held chord, a pedal-organ drone behind the normal noise of life, a thing that you forgot about and thought you'd put away forever, but it was still there. It was still here.

He looked across the street at Bath Street flats, their front and not the rear he'd seen by dark a year ago with Alma. Since he'd had no call to venture through the Boroughs since that night, he realised that this must be the first time he'd been confronted by the bad side of his vision since he blinded himself, knocked himself out and recalled it, all those months ago. The sickening punch he felt, a bunch of fives impacting in his gut and driving all the air out of him was much worse than he'd expected. Leadenly, as if toward a scaffold, Michael Warren walked across the road.

Of course, he didn't have to cut across the flats, up the wide central avenue with lawns to either edge, concluding in the broad brick-sided stairs that would deliver Mick practically to the doorstep of his sister's exhibition. He could turn right and walk down to Little Cross Street, which would take him by the lowest edge of the shunned living units into Castle Street, thus circumventing the whole business, except that would prove Alma's contention that she'd always been more of a man than he was, and he wouldn't suffer that. Besides, this was all rubbish and Mick didn't even know for sure if all that stuff that he'd remembered really was what happened when he'd choked that time, or whether it was all a dream he'd dreamed he dreamed, a spastic rush of images that had come to him only when he lay there flat out on the tarmac of the reconditioning yard with fireballs in his eyes. Even Mick's youngest, Joseph, had long since ceased to let bad dreams colour waking life, had learned that the two realms were separate, that night-things couldn't get you in clear daylight when your eyes weren't shut, and Joe had just turned twelve. Attempting an indifferent air, Mick sauntered through the central gap in the low bounding fence and up the spacious walkway, heading for the steps just sixty or so feet ahead, just twenty paces off. What was it, anyway? For fuck's sake, it was just a block of flats, in many ways more pleasant than the others that he'd passed that day.

He'd gone a step or two before the dreadful stench of burning garbage made him flinch and snap his head back, scanning the surrounding terra cotta chimneys for a source and finding none. Alma had told him once that to smell burning was a symptom schizophrenics suffered from, adding "but then they probably set fire to things quite often, so it's bound to be a tricky judgement call." Strangely enough, he found himself preferring the idea of schizophrenia and its olfactory hallucinations to the worse alternative that had occurred to him. As he remembered Alma pointing out during their meeting of the previous year, it wasn't that he might have gone insane that was the prime cause for concern, but rather the alarming possibility that he might not have done. Clenching his nostrils against the pervasive charnel reek he carried on towards the stairs that, as he neared them, turned out to have been replaced during the last few years by a more wheelchair-friendly ramp.

A clot of blackness on the gravel path ahead of him fragmented into whirring charcoal specks like the precursor to a migraine, with a looping ochre turd briefly revealed, a footprint breaking its mid-section into ridge and trough, before the cloud of blowflies regrouped and resettled. Coming this way had been a mistake. The verdant swathes to either side of him were bounded at their far rims by long walls that ran along in parallel beside the central footpath and its bordering tracks of grass. The walls, built in the same dark red brick mottle as the rest of the accommodation, were alleviated by faux-Bauhaus half-moon windows that allowed an interrupted view of the wide, empty stretches of split-level concrete, the flats' gardens, sulking bird-less there beyond. When he'd first heard of Limbo he had visualised these courtyards, somewhere dismal where the dead might spend eternity, sat on a flight of granite steps below a featureless white sky. The semi-circles had been recently adorned by fans of iron spokes that made them look like cartoon eyes, the black rails forming radii across a negative-space iris. Seen in pairs they looked like the top halves of Easter Island faces buried to their ears in soil but still alive with begging, suffocating gazes. Young trees on the verges, more contemporary additions, threw their gloss-black shadows on the stifling masks, liquid and spider-like, ink droplets blown to form runny mascara patterns by an infant's straw.

Despite the speed with which the wave of smothering depression was upon him, Mick was not aware of its arrival, and was instantly convinced that what was now roiling like toxic fumes inside his mind had always been his point of view, his usual optimism nothing but a fraud, a flimsy tissue behind which he hid from what he knew was the inevitable truth. There was no point. There was no point and there had never been a point to all this grief and graft and grovelling, to being alive. When the heart failed or the brain died, he'd always really known inside, we just stopped thinking. Everyone knew that within their sinking, secret heart, whatever they might say. We all stopped being who we were, we just shut down and there was nowhere that we got beamed up to after that, no Heaven, Hell or reincarnation as a better person. There was only nothing after death, and nothing else but nothing, and for everyone the universe would all be gone the moment they exhaled their final breath, just as though they and it were never there. He didn't really sometimes feel the warmth and presence of his parents still around him, he just kidded himself now and then that this was what he felt. Tom and Doreen were gone, dad from a heart attack and mum from cancer of the bowel that must have hurt so much. He wasn't ever going to see them anymore.

Mick had by this point reached the bottom of the ramp, and the incinerator odour was now everywhere. He tried to raise a flutter of resistance to the irrefutable awareness that pressed down upon him, tried to summon all the arguments that he was sure that he'd once had against this hopeless blackness. Love. His love for Cathy and the kids. That had been one of his protective mantras, he was certain, except love just made things crueller, gave you so much more to lose. One partner dies first and the other spends their final years alone and crushed. You love your kids and watch them grow to something wonderful and then you have to leave them and not meet with them again. And all so short, seventy years or so, with him near fifty now. That's twenty years, assuming that you're lucky, less than half of what had already slipped by, and Mick felt certain that these final decades would flash past with grim rapidity.

Everyone went away. Everything vanished. People, places, turned to painful shadows of their former selves and then were put to sleep, just like the Boroughs had been. It was always a half-witted district anyway, even its name. The Boroughs. One place with a plural word describing it. What was that all about? Nobody even knew why it was called that, some suggesting that the name should be spelled 'Burrows' for its nest of streets seen from the air, for its inhabitants who bred like rabbits. What a load of bollocks. People like his grandparents may have had six or seven kids but that was only so that they had some who reached adulthood. It was always a bad sign when better-off types drew comparisons between unsightly ghetto populations and some animal or other, most especially those species that we had, reluctantly, to poison periodically. Why didn't people keep their lame excuses to themselves?

Mick realised that he was no longer thinking about death at the same moment that he realised he had reached the ramp's top and was stepping onto Castle Street. He stopped, astounded by the sudden on/off light-switch change within him, and gazed back at Bath Street, looking down the sunlit path between the two halves of the flats that he'd just walked along. The lawns were luscious and inviting and the saplings hissed and whispered in the lulling breeze. Mick stood dumbfounded, staring at it.

Fucking hell.

Blinking his eyes exaggeratedly as if to banish sleep, Mick turned his back upon the flats and made his way down Castle Street towards the base of Castle Hill, the rectangle of turf there on its corner, much reduced since Mick's day, where that man and woman had once tried to drag his sister into their black car when she was seven, only letting her go when she screamed. He hoped her paintings would be good enough to do whatever she intended, because what just happened to him was a demonstration of the force that threatened to eat everything they cared about, and other than his sister and her doubtful counter-strategy Mick couldn't think of anyone who had a plan.

Rounding the bend of Castle Hill to Fitzroy Street he saw that the small exhibition was already in full swing. His sister, in a big turquoise angora sweater leaned upon the wood frame of the open nursery door, anxiously looking out to see if he was really going to show, beaming and waving like a pastel-coloured children's TV muppet when she spotted him. Standing with Alma was a grizzled stickman that Mick recognised as Roman Thompson, and beside him lounged a lavishly disreputable-looking feline thirty-something with a cream vest and an opened beer can, evidently Roman's boyfriend, Dean. Sat on the step next to Mick's sister was Benedict Perrit, the itinerant poet with the sozzled grin and tragic eyes who'd been in the same class as Alma at Spring Lane, two years above Mick's own. There were some others there he knew, as well. He thought that the good-looking black guy with the greying hair was probably Alma's old friend Dave Daniels, with whom she had shared her longstanding enthusiasm for science-fiction, and he saw his sister's tough and sunburnt former 1960s co-conspirator Bert Reagan standing near an elderly yet strong-looking old woman that Mick thought might be Bert's mother, or perhaps an aunt. There were two other women of about the same age, although these were genuine old gargoyles, hanging back on the group's fringes, more than likely friends of the old dear stood by Bert Reagan there. He raised a hand to all of them and smiled, returning Alma's greeting as he walked towards the exhibition's entrance. Oh, our sis, Mick thought. Oh, Warry.

This had better be much more than good.

Book One

THE BOROUGHS

He [Ludwig Wittgenstein] once greeted me with the question: "Why do people say that it was natural to think that the sun went round the earth rather than that the earth turned on its axis?" I replied: "I suppose, because it looked as if the sun went round the earth." "Well," he asked, "what would it have looked like if it had *looked* as if the earth turned on its axis?"

—Elizabeth Anscombe,
An Introduction to Wittgenstein's Tractatus

A HOST OF ANGLES

It was the morning of October 7th, 1865. The rain and its accompanying light were foul against the squinty attic window as Ern Vernall woke to his last day of sanity.

Downstairs the latest baby wailed and he heard his wife Anne already up and shouting at their John, the two-year-old. The blankets and the bolster, both inherited from Anne's dead parents, were a rank entanglement with Ernest's foot snagged in a hole through the top sheet. The bedding smelled of sweat, infrequent spendings, farts, of him and of his life there in the shacks of Lambeth, and its odour rose about him like resigned and dismal music as he knuckled gum from barely-open eyes and roused himself, already bracing to receive the boulder of the world.

Feeling a pang beneath his left breast that he hoped was his digestion, he sat up and, after extricating one from the torn bedclothes, placed both naked feet upon the homemade rug beside his cot. For just a moment Ern luxuriated in the tufted scraps of knitting wool between his toes then stood up, with a groan of protest from the bedstead. Blearily he turned himself about to face the mess of charcoal army blanket and slipped counterpane below which he had until recently been snoring, and then kneeled upon the variegated bedside mat as if to say his prayers, the way he'd last done as a seven-year-old child a quarter-century ago.

He reached both hands into the darkness underneath the bed and carefully slid out a slopping jerry over the bare floorboards, setting it before him like a pauper's font. He fumbled for his old man in the itchy vent of the grey flannel long johns, staring dully into the sienna and blood-orange pool already stewing in its chip-toothed china pot, and made an effort to recall if he'd had any dreams. As he unleashed a stair-rod rigid jet of piss at the half-full receptacle he thought that he remembered something about working as an actor, lurking backstage at a melodrama or a ghost-tale of some kind. The drama, as it now came back to him, had been about a haunted chapel, and the rogue that he was playing had to hide behind one of those portraits with the eyes cut out, such as you often found in that sort of affair. He wasn't spying, though, but rather talking through the picture in a jokey frightening voice, to scare the fellow on the other side that he was looking at, and make him think it was a magic painting. This chap that he'd played the trick on in the dream had been so rattled that Ern found himself still chuckling at it in mid-stream as he knelt by the bed.

Now he'd thought more on it, he wasn't sure if it was a theatrical performance that he'd dreamed about or a real prank played on a real man. He had the sense, still, that he'd been behind the scenery of a pantomime, delivering lines as the employee of a repertory company of sorts, but didn't think now that the victim of the gag had also been an actor. A white-haired old pensioner but still young-looking in his face, he'd seemed so truly terrified by the enchanted daubing that Ern had felt sorry for him and had whispered an aside from there behind the canvas, telling the poor beggar that he sympathised, and that Ern knew this would be very hard for him. Ern had then gone on to recite the lines out of the play that he apparently had learned by heart, blood-curdling stuff he hadn't really understood and was unable now to bring to mind, except that part of it, he thought, was about lightning, and there was another bit concerning sums and masonry. He'd either woken at this point, or else could not now recollect the story's end. It wasn't like he placed a lot of stock in dreams as others did, as his dad John had done, but more that they were often smashing entertainment that cost nothing and there wasn't much you could say that about.

Shaking the last few drops from off the end he looked down in surprise at the great head of steam that brimmed above the po, belatedly apprised of just how icy the October garret was.

Pushing the now-warmed vessel back under the bed-boards he rose to his feet and made his creaking way across the attic to an heirloom washstand by the far wall opposite the window. Bending to accommodate the sharp decline in headroom at the loft-room's edges, Ern poured some cold water from his mam's jug with the picture of a milkmaid on into the rusty-rimmed enamel washbowl, splashing it with cupped hands on his face, ruffling his lips and blowing like a horse at the astringent bite of it. The brisk rinse turned his mutton-chops from arid, fiery scrub to freshly-watered ringlet fronds, dripping below his jutting ears. He rubbed his face dry with a linen towel, then for a while looked on its faint reflection that gazed from the shallow puddle in the bowl. Craggy and lean with straggling wisps of pepper at the brow, he could see in its early comic lines the doleful cracks and seams of how Ern thought he might appear in later life, a scrawny tabby in a thunderstorm.

He dressed, the fraying clothes chilled so that they felt damp when first he put them on, and then climbed from the attic to the lower reaches of his mother's house, clambering backward down pinched steps that were so steep that they required one's hands to mount or to descend, as with a ladder or a quarry face. He tried to creep across the landing past the doorway of his mum's room and downstairs before she heard him, but his luck was out. A cowering, curtain-twitching tenant when the rent-man called, his luck was always out.

"Ernest?"

His mum's voice, like a grand industrial engine that had fallen into disrepair stopped Ern dead with one hand on the round knob of the top banister. He turned to face his mother through the open door that led into her bedroom with its smell of shit and rosewater more sickly than the smell of shit alone. Still in a nightgown with her thinning hair in pins, Mum stooped beside her nightstand emptying her own room's chamber pot in a zinc bucket, after which she would go on to make the rounds of both the nippers' room and his and Annie's quarters, emptying theirs as well and then later depositing the whole lot in the privy at the bottom of their yard. Ernest John Vernall was a man of thirty-two, a wiry man with a fierce temper whom you wouldn't seek as an opponent in a fight, with wife and children, with a trade where he was quietly respected, but he scuffed his boots against the varnished skirting like a boy beneath his mother's scornful, disappointed frown.

"Are you in work today, 'cause I shall 'ave to be along the pawn shop if you're not. That little girl won't feed 'erself and your Anne's like a sleeve-board. She can't feed 'em, baby Thursa or your John."

Ern bobbed his head and glanced away, down to the worn, flypaper-coloured carpet covering the landing from its stair-head to his attic door.

"I've got work all this week up at St. Paul's but shan't be paid 'til Friday. If there's anything you've hocked I'll get it back then, when I've 'ad me earnings."

She looked to one side and shook her head dismissively, then went back to decanting the stale golden liquid noisily into her bucket. Feeling scolded, Ern hunched down the stairs into the peeling umber of the passageway, then left and through a door into the cramped fug of the living room, where Annie had a fire lit in the grate. Crouching beside the baby's chair and trying to get her to take warmed-up cow's milk from a bottle meant for ginger ale that they'd adapted, Annie barely raised her head as Ern entered the room behind her. Only their lad John looked up from where he sat making a pig's ear of his porridge by the hearth, acknowledging his father's presence without smiling.

"There's some fried bread doing in the kitchen you can 'ave for breakfast, but I don't know what there'll be when you get 'ome. Come on, just take a spot o' milk to please your mam."

This last remark Anne had directed at their daughter, Thursa, who was still red-faced and roaring, turning with determination from the weathered rubber teat as Ern's wife tried to steer it in between the baby's yowling lips. It was a little after seven in the morning, so that the dark-papered cuddle of the room was mostly still in shadow, with the burnished bronze glow from its fire-place turning young John's hair to smelted metal, gleaming on the baby's tear-tracked cheek and painting half his wife's drawn face with light like dripping.

Ern went through and down two steps into the narrow-shouldered kitchen, its uneven whitewashed walls crowding and spectral in the daybreak gloom, a memory of onions and boiled handkerchiefs still hanging in the bluish air, cloudy as though with soap scum. The wood-burning stove was going, with two end-cuts of a loaf frying upon its hob. Clarified fat was sizzling in a pan black as a meteor that fell out of the stars, and spat on Ernie's fingers as he carefully retrieved the noggins with a fork. In the next room his baby daughter wearily allowed her furious weeping to trail off into accusing hiccup-breaths at sulking intervals. Finding a crack-glazed saucer that had lost its cup to acci-dent he used it as a plate, then perched upon a stool beside the knife-scarred kitchen table while he ate, chewing upon his mouth's right side to spare the bad teeth on its left. The taste of singed grease flooded from the sponge-pores of a brittle crust as he bit down, scalding and savoury across his tongue, bring-ing the phantom flavours of their last week's fry-ups in its wake: the bubble 'n' squeak's cabbage tang, the pig cheek's subtle sweetness, a crisped epitaph for Tuesday's memorable beef sausage. When he'd swallowed the last morsel Ern was pleased to find his spittle thickened to a salty aspic where the resurrected zest of each meal still enjoyed its culinary afterlife.

Re-crossing the now subdued living room he said goodbye to everyone and told Anne he'd be back by eight that night. He knew that some blokes kissed their wives goodbye when they went off to work, but like the great majority he thought that kind of thing was soppy and so did his Anne. Fastidiously scraping a last smear of porridge from the bowl their two-year-old son John, their little carrot-top, watched stoically as Ern ducked from the fire-lit room into the dingy passageway beyond, to fish his hat and jacket down from off the wooden coat-hooks and then be about his business in the city, somewhere John had dimly heard of but had thus far never been. There was the sound of Ernie's shouted farewell to his mum, still on her night-soil rounds upstairs, followed by the expectant pause that was his mother's failure to reply. A short while after that Anne and the children heard the front door close, its judder-ing resistance when shoved into its ill-fitting jamb, and that turned out to be the last time that his family could honestly say they'd seen Ginger Vernall.

Ern walked out through Lambeth to the north, the sky above a stygian forest canopy swaying upon the million tar-black sapling stems of fume that sprang from every chimney, with the sooty blackness of the heavens only starting to dilute there at its eastern edge, above the dives of Walworth. Exit-ing his mother's house in East Street he turned right down at the terrace end and into Lambeth Walk, onto the Lambeth Road and up towards St. George's

Circus. On his left he passed Hercules Road where he had heard the poet Blake lived once, a funny sort by all accounts, though obviously Ern had never read his work or for that matter anybody else's, having failed to really get the trick of books. The rain was hammering in the buckled gutters of the street outside an uncharacteristically quiet Bedlam, where the fairy-painter Mr. Dadd had been until a year or so before, and where they'd been afraid Ern's father John would have to go, although the old man died before it had been necessary. That was getting on ten years ago, when he'd yet to meet Anne and wasn't long back from Crimea. Dad had gradually stopped talking, saying that their conversations were all being overheard by "them up in the eaves". Ern had enquired if Dad meant all the pigeons, or did he still think there might be Russian spies, but John had snorted and asked Ern just where he thought that the expression 'eavesdropping' had come from, after which he'd say no more.

Ern passed by the rainswept asylum on the far side of the street, and speculated distantly if there might be some antic spirit bred in Bedlam, squatted over Lambeth with eyes rolling, that infused the district's atmosphere with its own crackpot vapours and sent people mad, like Ernest's dad or Mr. Blake, though he supposed that there was not, and that in general people's lives would be sufficient to explain them going silly. Down St. George's Road heading for Elephant and Castle swarmed, already, a great number of horse buses, pushcarts, coal wagons and baked potato sellers dragging stoves like hot tin chests-of-drawers piled on their trolleys, a vast multitude of figures in black hats and coats like Ern, marching with downcast eyes beneath a murderous sky. Turning his collar up he joined the shuffling throng of madhouse-fodder and went on towards St. George's Circus where he would begin his long hike up the Blackfriars Road. He'd heard that they had train-lines running underground now, out from Paddington, and idly speculated that a thing like that might get him to St. Paul's much quicker, but he hadn't got the money and besides, the thought gave him the willies. Being underground like that, how would it ever be a thing that you got used to? Ern was well-known as a steeplejack who'd work on rooftops without thinking twice, sure-footed and quite unconcerned, but being underneath the ground, that was a different matter. That was only natural for the dead, and anyway, what if something should happen down there, like a fire or something? Ernest didn't like to think about it and decided that he'd stop the way he was, as a pedestrian.

People and vehicles eddied there at the convergence of a half-a-dozen streets like suds about a drain. Making his way around the circus clockwise, dodging in between the rumbling wheels and glistening horseflesh as he crossed Waterloo Road, Ern gave a wide berth to a broadsheet vendor and the gawping, whispering gaggle he'd attracted. From the burrs of chat that Ern picked up passing this pipe-smoke shrouded mob on its periphery he gathered it was old news from America about the blackies having been set free, and all about how the American Prime Minister had been shot dead, just like they'd done to poor old Spencer Perceval, back when Ern's dad had been a boy. As Ern recalled it, Perceval was from the little boot and shoe town of Northampton, sixty miles from London to the north, where Ern had family upon his father's side still living, cousins and the like. His cousin Robert Vernall had passed through last June on his way down to Kent for picking hops, and had told Ernest that much of the cobbling work that he'd relied on in the Midlands had dried up because the greycoats in America, for whom Northampton had supplied the army boots, had lost their civil war. Ernest could see it was a shame for Bob, but as he understood things, it was all the greycoats as what kept the slaves, the blackies, which Ern didn't hold with. That was wrong. They were poor people just like anybody else. He walked across the awkward corner with its little spike of waste-ground where the angle was too sharp to fit another house, then turned left and up Blackfriars Road, making across the smouldering rows of Southwark for the river and the bridge.

It took Ern some three-quarters of an hour, bowling along at a fair pace, before he came on Ludgate Street over the Thames' far side and the approach to the West Front of the cathedral. In this time he'd thought about all sorts of things, about the slaves set free out in America, some of them branded by their masters as though cattle, he'd been told, and of black men and poor people in general. Marx the socialist and his First International had been about more than a year already, but the workers still weren't any better off as far as anyone could tell. Perhaps things would be better now that Palmerston was dying, as it was Lord Palmerston who'd held back the reforms, but to be frank Ern wasn't holding out much hope on that one. For a while he'd cheered himself with thoughts of Anne and how she'd let him have her on the blade-grooved kitchen table while his mam was out, sat on its edge without her drawers on and her feet around his back, so that the memory put him on the bone under his trousers and his flannels, hurrying through the downpour over Blackfriars Bridge. He'd thought about Crimea and his luck at coming home without a scratch, and then of Mother Seacole who he'd heard about when he was out there, which returned him to the matter of the blacks.

It was the children that concerned him, born as slaves on a plantation and not brought there as grown men or women, some of them being set free just now across the sea, young lads of ten or twelve who'd never known another life and would be flummoxed as for what to do. Did they brand kids as well, Ern wondered, and at what age if they did? Wishing he hadn't thought of this and banishing the awful and unwanted picture of young John or Thursa brought beneath the glowing iron he mounted Ludgate Street with the majestic hymn-made-solid of St. Paul's inflating as he neared it, swelling up beyond the slope's low brow.

As often as he'd seen it, Ern had never ceased to be amazed that such a beautiful and perfect thing could ever come to be amongst the sprawl of dirty closes, inns and tapering corridors, amongst the prostitutes and the pornographers. Across the puddle-silvered slabs it rose with its two towers like hands flung up in a Hosanna to the churning heavens, grimmer than when Ern had left for work despite the way the day had lightened naturally as it wore on since then. The broad cathedral steps with raindrops dancing on them swept down in two flights calling to mind the tucks around a trailing surplice hem, where over that the six pairs of white Doric columns holding up the portico dropped down in billowed folds, unlaundered in the city's bonfire pall. The spires that flanked the wide façade to either side, two hundred feet or more in height, had what seemed all of London's pigeons crowded on their ledges under dripping overhangs of stonework, sheltering against the weather.

Huddling amongst the birds as if they had themselves just flown down from unfriendly skies to roost in the cathedral eaves were stone apostles, with St. Paul himself perched on the portico's high ridge and gathering his sculpted robes up round him to prevent them trailing in the grime and wet. At the far right of the most southern tower sat a disciple, Ern had no idea which one, who had his head tipped back and seemed to watch the tower's clock intently, waiting for his shift to finish so that he could flap off home down Cheapside through the drizzle, back to Aldgate and the East. Climbing the soaked and slippery steps with fresh spots drumming on his hat-brim, Ernest had to chuckle at the irreligious notion of the statues intermittently producing liquid marble stools, Saints'-droppings that embittered parish workers would be paid to scrape away. Taking a last peer at the boiling mass of bruised cloud overhead before he slipped between the leftmost pillars and towards the north aisle entrance, he concluded that the rain was getting worse if anything, and that today he would undoubtedly be better off indoors. Stamping his boots and shaking off his sodden jacket as he crossed the threshold into the cathedral he heard the first muffled drum-roll of approaching thunder off at the horizon's rim, confirming his suspicion.

In comparison to the October torrent pouring down outside, St. Paul's was warm and Ern felt briefly guilty at the thought of Anne and their two children drawn up shivering to the deficient fire back home in East Street. Ernest walked along the North Aisle under the suspicious frowns of passing clergy towards the construction and activity at its far end, only remembering to snatch his sopping bonnet off at the last minute and to carry it before him humbly in both hands. With every ringing step he felt the vistas and the hidden volumes of the stupefying edifice unfolding up above him and upon all sides, as he veered from the north aisle's curved recesses on his left and passed between the building's great supporting columns to the nave.

Framed by St. Paul's huge piers there in the central transept space beneath the dome milled labourers like Ern himself, their scruffy coats and britches a dull autumn palette of dust greys and browns, shabby against the richness of the paintings hung around them, the composure of the monuments and statues. Some of them were lads Ern knew of old, which was the way he'd come by this appreciated stint of paid work in the first place, with a word put in to them as were contracted for the cleaning and restoring. Men were scrubbing with soft cloths at lavishly-carved choir-stalls bossed with grapes and roses at the far end of the quire, while in the spandrels between arches underneath the railed hoop of the Whispering Gallery above were other fellows, giving the mosaic prophets and four Gospel-makers something of a wash and brush-up. Most of the endeavour though, it seemed to Ern, was centred on the mechanism overshadowing the nearly hundred-foot-wide area immediately below the yawning dome. It was perhaps the most ingenious thing that Ern had ever seen.

Hanging from the top centre of the dome, fixed to the crowning lantern's underside at what Ern guessed must be the strongest point of the vast structure, itself with a tonnage in the tens of thousands, was a plumb-straight central spindle more then twenty storeys high that had on one side an assemblage nearly as tall made of poles and planks, while on the other side what had to have been London's largest sandbag hung from a gigantic crossbeam as a counterweight. The sack sagged from a hawser on the left, while to Ern's right the heavy rope-hung framework that it balanced out was shaped like an enormous pie-slice with its narrow end towards the centre where it joined securely with the upright central axis. This impressive scaffolding contained a roughly quarter-circle wedge of flooring that could be winched up and down by pulleys at its corners, so as to reach surfaces that needed work at any level of the dome. The mast-like central pivot was hung almost to the decorative solar compass in the middle of the transept floor, with what looked like a smaller version of a horizontal mill-wheel at its bottom by which means the whole creaking arrangement could be manually rotated to attend each vaulted quadrant in its turn. The pulley-hoisted platform in the midst of its supporting struts and girders was where Ern would be employed for the remainder of the day, all being well.

A fat pearl cylinder of failing daylight coloured by the worsening storm outside dropped from the windows of the Whispering Gallery to the cathedral's flooring down below, dust lifted by the bustling industry caught up as a suspension in its filmy shaft. The soft illumination filtering from overhead rendered the workmen with a Conté crayon warmth and grain as they bent diligently to their various enterprises. Ern stood almost mesmerised admiring this effect when to the right ahead of him, out of the south aisle and its stairs from the triforium gallery above there came a striding, rotund figure that he recognised, who called to him by name.

"Oi, Ginger. Ginger Vernall. Over here, you silly beggar."

It was Billy Mabbutt, who Ern knew from different pubs in Kennington and Lambeth and who'd landed him this opportunity to earn a bit of money, like a good 'un. His complexion florid to the point of looking lately cooked, Bill Mabbutt was a heartening sight with his remaining sandy hair a half-mast curtain draped behind his ears around the rear of that bald cherry pate, the braces of his trousers stretched across a button-collared shirt with sleeves rolled boldly back to show his ham-hock forearms. These were pumping energetically beside him like the pistons of a locomotive as he barrelled towards Ern, weaving between the other labourers who drifted back and forth through rustling, echoing acoustics on their disparate errands. Smiling at the pleasure that he always felt on meeting Billy mingled with relief that this much-needed job had not turned out to be a false alarm, Ernest began to walk in the direction of his old acquaintance, meeting him halfway. The high lilt of Bill's voice always surprised Ern, coming as it did from those boiled bacon features, lined with sixty years and two campaigns – in Burma and Crimea – with this last being the place the two had met. The older man, who'd been a quartermaster, had adopted what appeared to be the shot-and-shell repellent Ernie as his red-haired lucky charm.

"Gor, blow me, Ginger, you're a sight for sore eyes. I was upstairs in the Whispering Gallery just now, looking at all the work there is to do and getting in a right commotion 'cause I swore blind as you'd not show up, but now you've come and made me out a liar."

"Hello, Bill. I've not got 'ere too late, then?"

Mabbutt shook his head and gestured in between the hulking piers to where a gang of men were struggling as they adjusted the immense contraption there at the cathedral's heart, dependent from its dome.

"No, you're all right, boy. It's the mobile gantry what's been messing us about. All over everywhere, she was, so if you'd got 'ere sooner you'd have only been sat on your 'ands. I reckon as we've got 'er settled now, though, by the looks of things, so if you want to come across we'll get you started."

One fat and the other thin, one with a pale complexion and red hair, the other with its opposite, the two men sauntered down the nave, over the resonant and gleaming tiles, and passed between its final columns to where all the work was going on. As they drew nearer to the dangling monster that Bill had referred to as the mobile gantry, Ern revised with each fresh pace his estimate regarding the thing's size. Close to, that twenty floors of scaffolding was more like thirty, from which he inferred that he'd be at his job two or three hundred feet above the ground, a disconcerting prospect even given Ernest's celebrated head for heights.

Two labourers, one of whom Ernest knew was brawling Albert Pickles from up Centaur Street, were stripped down to their singlets as they pushed the cog-like mill wheel in the middle round a final notch or two, rotating the whole feat of engineering on its axis while they trudged their orbit-path round the mosaic sun at the dead centre of the transept, its rays flaring to the cardinal directions. With their efforts, the men brought about the groaning framework on the spindle's right until it was aligned exactly with one of the eight great orange-segment sections into which the overarching bowl had been divided up. As the huge scaffold moved, so too did its enormous sandbag counterweight off to the left side of the axial pole, suspended from the crossbeam far above. Four or five navvies stood about it, walking round beside the hanging sackcloth boulder, steadying it as it wobbled with a foot or two of clearance over the church floor.

Ern noticed that the bag had sprung a leak, a small hole in the fabric of its underside with an apprentice of fourteen or so scuffing about there on his knees beside the sack, sweating and swearing as he tried to darn the rend with thread and needle. The boy was disfigured by what people called a strawberry mark staining his skin across one eye from cheek to forehead in a mongrel puppy patch, whether from birth or from a scald Ern couldn't say. The milky, stormcloud-filtered radiance dropped down upon the youth from overhead like in Greek dramas as he grovelled at his mending, with the hourglass grains spilling across his darting fingers, falling in a thin stream on the lustrous slabs below. As Ern gazed idly on this scene, thinking inevitably of the sands of time, the picture's lighting jumped and lurched, followed not several seconds later by a cannon fusillade of thunder. The squall's eye was evidently drawing nearer.

Billy Mabbutt led Ern past where men were fastening the gantry's trailing guy-ropes down to anchor it now it had been positioned properly, over to a trestle that had been set up between the statues of Lord Nelson and the late Viceroy of Ireland Lord Cornwallis, who'd surrendered in the Yankee independence war to General Washington if Ern remembered all his history right. Lord knows why they should want to give him such a grand memorial. The kit that Ern would need to make his restorations was set out upon the makeshift table where another young apprentice, this one slightly older, was already separating eggs by pouring them from one cracked china teacup to another. Workmen stood about the trestle waiting to begin their tasks and Billy loudly introduced Ern as the pair rolled up to join the crew.

"It's all right, chaps, the decorator's come. This 'ere is me old 'oppo Ginger Vernall. A right Rembrandt on the quiet, is Ginger."

Ern shook hands with all the men and hoped they didn't grudge the fact that he was the skilled labour on this job and would be getting more than they did. Probably they understood that he might not have any work like this again for months, while brawny labourers were always needed, and at any rate the money was so poor that neither party had a cause for envy. Him and Billy Mabbutt conferred briefly on the ins and outs of what he was to do, and then Ern went about transferring his required materials and tools from off the tabletop onto the quarter-cheese shaped wooden flooring slung inside the framework of the moveable arrangement.

He selected an array of squirrel brushes from the tin-full that the St. Paul's clergy had provided and, as well, the cardboard lid off an old shoebox serving as a tray for all the cleaned-out varnish tubs containing the cathedral's range of powder-paints. Of these, the purple and the emerald green had caught the damp and clotted into crumbly gems, but Ern didn't expect that he would need these colours and the other pigments seemed to have been kept in a much better state. The surly youngster who'd been put in charge of separating out the eggs was finishing the last of half a dozen when Ern asked if he could have his yolks. These were unbroken in one basin while another pot held the unwanted whites, a viscous slop that looked obscenely like collected drool which would no doubt be put to other use and not go wasted. Carefully transporting his receptacle with the six yellow globs sliding around each other at its bottom, Ern set it upon the pulley-mounted platform with the brushes and the colours then fetched mixing bowls, a two-pound sack of gypsum and half-gallon cider flagon washed and filled with water. Adding glass paper and three or four clean cloths, Ern climbed onto the swaying wedge of deck beside the trappings of his craft and with a tight grip on one of its corner-ropes, he gave the signal for Bill Mabbutt's men to winch him up.

The first jolt of his footing when it lifted had another momentary splash of silver from outside for its accompaniment, the subsequent protracted boom coming just instants later as the storm-head neared. One of the burly fellows hauling down upon his rope with a bell-ringer's grip made some crack about God moving his furniture around upstairs at which another of the gang protested, saying the remark was disrespectful in that great Mother of Churches, although Ern had heard the saying since his boyhood and saw nothing wrong with it. There was a practicality behind the phrase that tickled him, for while within his heart of hearts Ern wasn't altogether sure if he believed in God, he liked the notion of the Lord as someone down-to-earth who might occasionally, as did we all, have call to rearrange things so that they were better suited to His purposes. The pulleys shrieked as Ern made his ascent in measured stages, eighteen inches at a time, and when the lightning flashed again to out-line everything in sudden chalk the deafening explosion in its wake was near immediate.

The broad curve of his platform's outmost edge eclipsed more of the ground below with every squealing half-yard that it gained in height. The greater part of Ernest's gang of workmates was already gone from sight beneath the sway-ing raft of planks he stood upon, with Billy Mabbutt at the group's rear lifting up one ruddy palm in a farewell before he too was out of view. Now Ern took stock of the wood floor beneath his feet he realised that it was much larger than he'd first supposed, almost as big as a theatre stage with his small heap of jugs and pots and brushes looking lonely and inadequate there at its centre. Fully raised, he thought, and a full quadrant of the transept would be made invisible to Ern, and he to it. The heads of first Cornwallis then Lord Nel-son vanished, swallowed by the elevating podium's perimeter, and Ernest was alone. Tilting his head he gazed at Sir James Thornhill's eight vast frescoes on the dome's interior as he rose by instalments up into their company.

Back when he'd been a small boy in the early 1840s Ern had learned to draw a bit when he'd risked piles by sitting on a cold stone step and watch-ing Jackie Thimbles recreate in chalk the death of Nelson at Trafalgar on the flagstones by the corner of the Kennington and Lambeth Roads, day after fas-cinated day. Jackie was in his sixties then, a veteran of the Napoleonic Wars who'd lost two fingertips on his left hand to gangrene and concealed the stumps beneath a pair of silver thimbles. Making now a threadbare living as a pavement artist, the old man had seemed quite glad of young Ern's daily com-pany, and was a mine of information about painting. He'd regale the boy with long accounts, shot through with yearning, of the marvellous new oil paints that were then available to them as had the money, bright laburnum yellows and rich mauves or violets like a copse at dusk. Jackie had taught Ern how to mix a realistic flesh tone from a range of hues you'd never think were in pink skin, and how the fingers could be useful when it came to blending, smoothly smudging a white highlight cast by burning warships down the dying admi-ral's cheek or on the polished timbers of the *Victory*. Ernest had thought his mentor the most talented of men, but looking up at Thornhill's masterpieces now he understood them to be from a realm as far above the blood and fire washed decks of Jackie Thimbles as the halls of Heaven surely were above the streets of Lambeth.

Episodes from Saint Paul's life surrounded Ern as he rode his ramshackle elevator up amongst them, from the Damascene conversion to a vividly depicted shipwreck, with the various disciples under-lighted as though by a forge or opened treasure chest while ray-pierced cloudscapes roiled behind. The fresco that Ern planned to clean up and retouch today, over upon the echoing concavity's southwestern side, was one that he was not familiar with from sermons. In its background was a place of warm, rough stones that might have been a gaol, with stood before this a wide-eyed and wretched man whose awe seemed to be at the very brink of terror, gazing at the haloed saints or angels who looked back with lowered eyes and small, secretive smiles.

Ern's wooden dais climbed now past the Whispering Gallery where one could fancy that the walls still crept with century-old prayers and where the windows allowed Ern his final glimpse out over a drenched London to Southwark Cathedral's tower in the south-east before he was moved higher, up into the dome itself. Around the lowest rim of this, on the encircling tambour just above the gallery, he was dismayed to note that a whole swathe of border detail at the bottom of each fresco had been covered over in stone-coloured paint, no doubt to easily and inexpensively mask water-damage that had been discovered during earlier renovations. Ern was muttering beneath his breath about the shameful lack of pride in one's endeavours showing in this shoddy workmanship when blinding brilliance and tumultuous din so close they were a single thing exploded all about him and his platform dropped a sickening inch or two as startled bruisers far below lost then regained their grips upon the pulley-ropes. Ern's heart was thudding while his suddenly precarious stand resumed its screeching progress upwards and he cautiously approached its right rear crook thinking he'd risk a peek down just to see if all was well.

As he wrapped one tight round the rope, Ern found his hands were wringing wet with perspiration, so that he supposed he must be frightened of heights after all, despite what everyone had always said. He peered down past the planking's rough-cut ends and, though he could not see his fellow workers, was astounded to find how far up he was. The St. Paul's clergy looked like earwigs inching over the white, distant floor and Ernest watched with some amusement as two of the clerics waddled unaware towards each other along the adjacent sides of a giant pier, colliding at the corner in a flurry of black skirts. It wasn't the mere sight of a downed clergyman that made Ern chuckle, but his realisation that he'd known the two priests would bump into one another before they themselves did, just by virtue of his lofty vantage point. To an extent he had been able to perceive the destinies of land-bound people moving back and forth on their flat plane from the superior perspective of a third dimension up above theirs that they seldom thought about or paid attention to. Ernest imagined this was why the Romans had got on so well, seizing the tallest peaks as lookout posts and watchtowers in their conquests, their perceptions and their strategies both wonderfully advantaged by the higher ground.

His perch had by now reached the level he'd agreed with Billy Mabbutt, where it came to rest and was tied off, securely Ernest hoped, more than two hundred feet below. He was around the upper reaches of his first appointed fresco with the cloudburst's flickering, percussive heart an almost constant presence right above him now. Once his expanse of floor space had stopped moving, Ern decided to begin his restorations with a halo-sporting figure in the picture's upper left, angel or saint he couldn't tell, the face of which had been somewhat discoloured by decades of censer-fume and candle smoke. He started gently with his cloths, stood there upon the platform's brim wiping the smuts and layered dust from a visage he was surprised to find measured at least four feet from crown to chin when seen from right up next to it, the almost girlish features turned halfway towards the right and looking down demurely with the small lips pursed in that same smugly knowing smile. An angel, Ern decided, on the basis that those saints he could remember all had beards.

Ern was all on his own in what seemed the bare-boarded attic of the world, much more elaborately decorated and more spacious than the one at his mum's house in East Street. Once he'd cleaned off as much superficial grime as he could manage from a quarter-profile near as long as he was, Ernest settled to the serious affair of mixing up a shade that would exactly match the holy being's weathered peach complexion. Using the least mucky-looking handle of a brush that he could find he whipped the six yolks in their basin, then allowed a miserly amount of the resulting copper cream to pour into one of his mixing bowls. Another brush-handle served as a slender spoon with which Ern measured minute servings of what he believed to be the necessary colours from their varnish-tubs, wiping the brush-stem after every measure with a rag and stirring different quantities of lurid powder in his mixing bowl amongst the beaten egg.

He started with an earthy, rich Burnt Ochre, adding Naples Yellow for its touch of summer afternoon then followed this with a restrained pinch of Rose Madder. Next the bloody and translucent drizzle of rich crimson was mixed vigorously with the combination, tiny beads of yolk frosted with colour crushed into each other by the stirring squirrel hairs. He supplemented the already-satisfying mixture with his secret touch, the trick he'd learned from Jackie Thimbles, which was to employ a sprinkling of Cobalt Blue, this simulating the depleted veinal blood that circulated just below the human epidermis. If the blue and reds should prove too much Ern would offset them with a drop of white, but for the moment he was pleased with how the blending had turned out and set about preparing his light skim of gesso, shaking the blanched gypsum from its bag into a little water and then pouring his flesh tempera to colour the thin plaster once it had been mixed. Taking a useful range of brushes in his trouser pocket Ernest walked across the aerial theatre's boards, holding his bowl containing the painstakingly assembled medium between both hands, back to the platform's southwest point where he commenced to work on the gigantic countenance, his head tipped back as he reached upward slightly to the image on the concave wall directly over him.

Applying first a shallow coating of the fleshy-coloured gesso down the long sweep of the angel's side-lit jaw line, Ernest waited until it was dry before he rubbed it down to a fine finish with his glass paper and then got ready to lay on a second coat. He'd barely started slapping this with hurried, practiced motions on the yard-wide face before he noticed to his consternation that the tints upon its far side, which he hadn't touched yet, had begun to run. The storm outside had mounted to its zenith with a staggering barrage of thunders as Ern squinted up, bewildered and alarmed through an incessant lantern-Morse of lightning, at the dribbling colours moving on the angel's flat and slightly in-bowed head and shoulders.

Squirming droplets, each a different shade, were running up and down and sideways on the inner surface of the dome round the angelic face, with their trajectories in shocking contravention of all reason's laws. Moreover, the fast-swarming rivulets did not appear to Ern to have the glisten that they would if they'd been wet. It was instead as if dry streams of grains, infinitesimal and rushing, poured across the brushwork features following their inward curve like bright-dyed filings swimming over a weak magnet. This was an impossibility and, worse, would almost certainly be stopped out of his wages. He took an involuntary, faltering step back, and as he did so widened his appreciation if not comprehension of the frantic, trickling activity and motion going on before him.

Neutral greys and umbers from the shadows on the far right of the giant face where it was turned away were crawling on a steep diagonal towards its upper left, where they pooled to a blot of shading such as you might get to one side of a nose if whomever it might belong to looked straight at you. Radiant Chrome Yellow and Lead White bled from the halo, forming an irregular bright patch with contours roughly like the angel's rightmost cheek if it were slightly moved so that it was illuminated. With a bleak, numb horror moving up his spine Ern realised that without its modelling disturbing the almost-flat plane on which it was described or breaking from the confines of its two-dimensional domain, the angel's massive face was turning slowly, still within the surface of the fresco, to regard him with a gaze that was head-on. New creases of Payne's Grey coagulated at the corners of its eyes as loaf-sized lids, formerly downcast shyly, fluttered open with small flakes of paint falling from fresh-created wrinkles into Ernest's mouth as he stood there beneath the spectacle with jaw hung wide. His circumstances were so wholly unbelievable he didn't even have the wits to scream but took another step back with one hand clapped tight across his gaping maw. At the far edges of the figure's epic mouth, also migrated up and to the left now, dimpled cracks of mingled Ivory

58   Alan Moore

Black and crimson crinkled into being as the pale, foot-long lips parted and the painted angel spoke.

"Theis whille beye veery haerdt foure yew" it said, sounding concerned.

The 'is' or the essential being of this coming while as, from your viewpoint, it apparently goes by will be a sudden and extreme veer in the pathway of your heart with things that you have heard concerning a fourth angle of existence causing difficulties to arise within your mortal life, that is concluded in a graveyard where the yew trees flourish, and this will be very hard for you. Ern understood this complicated message, understood that it was somehow all squeezed down into just seven mostly unfamiliar words that had unfolded and unpacked themselves inside his thoughts, like the unwrapping of a children's paper puzzle or a Chinese poem. Even as he struggled to absorb the content bound in this exploded sentence, the mere noise of it unravelled him. It had a fullness and dimension to its sound, compared to a whole orchestra performing in a concert hall, such as the latter might have in comparison with a tin whistle blown inside an insulated cupboard. Every note of it seemed to be spiralling away in countless fainter and more distant repetitions, the same tones at an increasingly diminished scale until these split into a myriad still smaller echoes, eddying minuscule whirlwinds made of sound that spun off into the persistent background thunderclaps and disappeared.

Now that it had completed that first startling quarter turn the table-sized face seemed almost to settle down into its new configuration. Only at its edges and around the mobile mouth and eyes were particles still creeping, dots of pigment skittering in little sand-slides round the fresco's curvature and making small adjustments to accommodate the slight and natural movements of the figure's head, the shift of gleam and shadow on its opening and closing lips.

In the few moments that had actually elapsed since the commencement of the episode Ernest had clutched at and as soon discarded several desperate rationalizations of his situation. It was all a dream, he thought, but then knew instantly that it was not, that he was wide awake, that those teeth on the left side of his mouth still ached, with those upon the right retaining fragments of fried bread from breakfast. He decided that it was a prank, perhaps accomplished with a Magic Lantern, but was instantly reminded that the pictures cast by such devices do not move. A Pepper's Ghost, then, like they had at Highbury Barn so that the shade of Hamlet's father seemed to walk upon the stage, but no, no, the effect required a sheet of angled glass and there was nothing in Ern's working-space save Ern himself and his materials.

As each fresh explanation turned to shreds of flimsy tissue in his hands he felt the panic terror welling in him until he could take no more of it. His tightening throat choked out a sob that sounded womanly in his own ears and turning from the apparition he began to run, but as the footing shuddered under his first step the dreadful fact of where he was, alone and at great altitude, returned to him with overwhelming force. Above, the thunderstorm had clambered to its flashing, crashing peak and even if Ern could have overcome the clenched paralysis that gripped his vocal cords for long enough to scream, nobody down below would ever hear him.

He'd just jump, then, get the whole thing over with and better that, the flailing fall, the pulverising impact, better that than this, this thing, but he had hesitated far too long already, knew he couldn't really do it, knew he was and always had been in the last analysis a coward when it came to death and pain. He shuffled back around to face the angel, hoping against hope that when he did the trick of light or hearing would have been corrected, but the mammoth physiognomy was looking straight towards him, its peripheral lines still squirming faintly and the highlights on its lids slithering quickly to change places with the eye-whites as it blinked, then blinked again. The roseate tones in which its lips had been depicted swirled and curdled as it tried what seemed intended as a reassuring smile. At this, Ern started quietly weeping in the way he'd wept when he had been a boy and there was simply nothing else save crying to be done. He sat down on the planks and sank his face into his hands as that transfixing voice again began to speak, with its unwinding depths and curlicued reverberations scurrying away to shimmering nothing.

"Justiiyes abdoveer thier straeelthe."

Just I, yes, I, just my affirming presence and my just eyes watching from above, around a veer or corner in the heavens where the doves and pigeons fly, among the hierarchies and the hierophants of this higher Hierusalem, over the straight and honest straitened trails which are the aether of the poor that I have made my great tribunal whereby do I now announce that Justice be above the Street.

Ern had his stinging eyes closed and his palms pressed to his face, but found he could still see the angel anyway, not through his finger-cracks or eyelids as with a bright light but more as if the rays had swerved around these obstacles by some route Ern could not determine. His attempts to block the sight out proving useless he next clasped his hands across his ears instead, but had no more success. Rather than being muffled by the intervening pads of gristle, bone and fat, the entity's cascading voice seemed to be circumventing these impediments to sound with crystal clarity, almost as if its source were inside Ernest's skull. Remembering his father's madness, Ern was coming rapidly to the conclusion that in fact this might well be the case. The talking fresco was just a delusion and Ern had gone round the bend like his old man. Or, on the other hand, he was still sane and this uncanny intervention was a real event, was genuinely taking place there in the dangling loft above St. Paul's, there in Ern's world, there in his life. Neither of these alternatives was bearable.

The sparkling music of each angel-word, its shivering harmonic fronds and its disintegrating arabesques, was crafted so the sounds were subdivided endlessly in ever-smaller copies of themselves, just as each branch is like its tree in miniature, each individual twig a scaled-down reproduction of its branch. A river that fragmented into streams and at last rivulets upon its delta, every syllable would trickle through a thousand fissures and capillaries into Ern's core, into the very fabric of him, all its meaning saturating him in such a way that its least nuance could not be misheard, misunderstood or missed.

"Justice above the Street", the vast, flat face had said, or that at least had been a part of it, and in his thoughts he found a strong and sudden visual image to accompany the phrase. In his mind's eye he saw what was, in short, a set of scales hung up above a winding band of road, but the stark crudeness of the imagery bewildered Ern, who'd always thought he had a fair imagination for such things. These were no gleaming balances suspended in the glorious streaming sky above a rustic lane as in some Bible illustration, but the rough marks of a child or imbecile. The hanging pans and their supporting chains were no more than uneven triangles, joined near and not exactly at their apex by an oblong drawn in an unpracticed hand. Below this was a wavering and elongated rectangle that may have been a street or may as well have been a strip of curling ribbon.

With as few lines to its making as the angel's utterance had words, the simple sketch unloaded all its diverse implications into Ern by much the same means that the being's voice had utilised, implanting modest parcels of awareness that unwrapped themselves into a thing much bigger and more complicated. Studying the slipshod mental picture, Ernest comprehended that it was related in a mystifying way to every idle thought he'd had while on his walk to work that day, as though those notions had been foggy and inverted memories of this immediate revelation, memories that in some puzzling fashion one might have before their subject had occurred. The image in his head, he understood, had a connection to his earlier musings on the difficulties of the poor, to his consideration of the shoe-trade in Northampton and seemed even relevant to the rude, loving thoughts he'd had about his wife. It also called to mind his ponderings upon his offspring, John and little Thursa, and what would become of them, as well as his brief conjuring of Heaven as located at great height above the streets of Lambeth. Chiefly, though, Ern was reminded of the black men that he'd thought of in America, the freed slaves and his horrid visualisation of the branded children. He still wept, sat helpless there upon the filthy floorboards, but his tears were not now wholly for himself.

Having succeeded in attracting Ern's attention, the big painting of a face proceeded to impart its lesson, there amidst the crackling wrath and rage that seemed locked in a course which circled the cathedral's spire. From the continual and subtle shifts of its demeanour, it seemed anxious to convey instruction of profound importance on a staggering range of topics, many of them seeming to be matters of mathematics and geometry for which Ern, though illiterate, had always had a flair. The knowledge, anyway, decanted into him so that he had no choice as to whether he took it in or not.

The vision first explained, using its mangled and compacted bouillon-words, that the surrounding storm was a result of something, in this instance the angel itself, moving from one world to another. In with this Ern heard an inference that storms themselves had a geometry that was to human senses unperceivable, that bolts of lightning that might strike in different places and on different days were yet the selfsame discharge, though refracted, with reflections even scattering through time, into the past and future. The phrase by which it expressed this wisdom was "Foure lerlaytoernings maarcke iyuour entreanxsists ..." *For lightnings mark our transits ...*

Ernest lifted up his shining flash-lit cheeks to stare despairingly at the quartet of archangels picked out in blue and gold upon the skullcap of the dome above the frescoes. Tranquil and expressionless they offered no assistance, were no consolation, but at least weren't moving. As he let his gaze sink back to the expanse of slowly writhing specks that was the face of his interlocutor, Ern distantly realised that this was the only area of the fresco, or of any of the frescoes, which was thus afflicted. In a sense, this made things worse because if he were mad then wouldn't he be seeing visions bubbling everywhere and not just in one place? He wished he could pass out or even have his heart pack in and die, so this insufferable horror would be over, done with, but instead it just went on and on and on. Looking towards him patiently across the boards that cut it off at chest-height, the huge head appeared to shrug its robe-draped shoulders sympathetically, an energetic ripple of displaced mauves and burnt umbers moving through the garment's folds and then resettling as the glimmering impossibility resumed Ern Vernall's education, much of it related to the field of architecture.

" ... aeond thier cfhourvnegres orfflidt Heerturnowstry awre haopended."

And there at the higher convergence of the aeons that is fourfold on the dim benighted verges of our Heaven, at the 'or' of things, the golden-lighted hinge of possibility that in this hour when are black people freed hove off the lid of an eternal here and now of history that is already happened, has turned out, has ended happily with hope and awe or is in your awareness unresolved and open-ended, yet rejoice that Justice be above the Street, for lightnings mark our transit and the corners of Eternity are opened.

This continued for two and three-quarter hours.

The lecture was expansive, introducing Ern to points of view he'd never really thought about before. He was invited to consider time with every moment of its passing in the terms of plane geometry, and had it pointed out that human beings' grasp of space was incomplete. An emphasis was placed on corners having unseen structural significance, being located at the same points on an object whether realised in plan or elevation, constant though they be expressed in two or three or more dimensions. Next there was a discourse on topography, albeit one in which that subject was projected to a metaphysical extreme. It was made clear to him that Lambeth was adjacent to far-off Northampton if both were upon a map that should be folded in a certain way, that the locations although distant could be in a sense conceived as being in the same place.

Still on matters topographic, Ern was introduced to a new understanding of the torus, or 'the life-belt shape' as he inwardly called it, an inflated round pierced by a hole. It was remarked upon that both the human body with its alimentary canal and humble chimney with its central bore were variations on this basic form, and that a person might be seen as an inverted smoke-stack, shovelling fuel into its top end with brown clouds of solid smoke erupting from the other to disperse in either earth or sea, in anything save sky. It was this point, despite the tears still coursing down his cheeks, despite the fact that he felt he was drowning, at which Ern began to laugh. The idea of a man or woman as a chimneypot turned upside down was just so comical he couldn't help it, with the picture that it called up of long streaming turds unfurling over London from the city's foundry towers.

Ern laughed, and as he did so did the angel, and its every scintillating intonation was brim-full with Joy, with Joy, with Joy, with Joy, with Joy.

Bill Mabbutt noticed that the storm had finished when the nearby churches chimed for noon and he first realised that he could hear them. Setting down his mortarboard with the last scrapes of grout that he'd been using to fill in between some problematic tiles, he turned and clapped his raw-beef hands so that the men would heed him. His light tenor voice reverberated in the galleries, careening in the aisles like a lost gull as he announced a stoppage for some tea and bread.

"All right, lads, that's your lot for 'alf an 'our. Let's 'ave our bit o' bup and get the kettle on."

Remembering the decorator, Mabbutt nodded his pink, glistening head towards the scaffolding.

"We'd better wind old Ginger down, and all. I've seen 'im lose his rag and you can trust me that it's not a pretty sight."

Big Albert Pickles, lumbering across the polished checkers with his filmy, incomplete reflection swimming in the sheen beneath his boots, looked up at Bill and grinned as he took his position by one of the cage's corner winches.

"Aye. 'E's ginger and 'e's barmy and 'is dad's still in the army."

Several of the other fellows smirked at this old ragamuffin taunt as they prepared to man the scaffolding's remaining ropes, but Bill was having none of it. A tubby bloke who had a piping voice he may have been, but Bill had won a medal fighting the Burmese and all the men, including Albert Pickles, knew they'd best not go upsetting him.

"'Is dad's passed on, Bert, so we'll 'ave no more of that, eh? 'E's a decent chap who's 'ad 'ard luck and just got a new baby. Now, let's 'aul 'im down, then all of you can 'ave your break."

The men accepted the reproof good-naturedly, then took the strain upon their cables as Bill ventured a shout up into the glorious well above them, telling Ginger to be ready so he shouldn't spill his pots or knock them over when the platform started to descend. There was no answer, but with the suspended planking up at such an altitude Mabbutt had not really expected his announcement to be heard. He bobbed his ruddy chin in the direction of the labourers, whence they began to let sink the broad arc of wood down from the murmuring, gilded firmament of the cathedral to the brawny back-or-forth and subdued hubbub of its thronging floor.

The pulleys overhead struck up their measured, intermittent squealing like a horde of women lowering themselves by inches into the cold waters of a public bath. Pulling a hanky from his trouser pocket, Billy Mabbutt mopped the liquid glaze of perspiration from his rosy crown and thought of Ginger Vernall as he'd been out in Crimea, battering one of his fellow squadders bloody in their barracks when this other chap made some remark about the sort of background Ginger came from. Bill felt sorry for the man, that was the truth of it, to see how proud he'd been back in the war and see him now brought low by everything. No sooner was he back from fighting Russians when old John, his dad, went potty and then died not many years thereafter. Still shook up from all of that, Bill shouldn't wonder, Ginger had took up with his young girl then married her, and right away she'd had first one kid then another. Billy never had a lot of truck with women, being more at ease with other men, but he'd seen such a lot of fellows get through muck and musket balls only to have their legs cut out from under them by wife and family. Ginger was stuck with hungry mouths to feed and no place of his own where they could live, still at his mam's out Lambeth and a miserable old biddy she was too, from Mabbutt's one encounter with her.

Ninety or a hundred feet above, the underside of Ginger's podium came closer to a rhythmical accompaniment of groaning hawsers, grunting workers and shrill pulley-wheels. Stuffing the handkerchief back where it came from Bill turned round to face the trestle table where he'd put his mortarboard so he could give it a wipe down before he had a cup of tea. The clergy of St. Paul's had been persuaded after an unseemly bout of haggling to boil up a big tub of water over the cathedral's stove so that the two capacious teapots made of earthenware and brought along by the contracted labour could be filled. These steamed there at the table's far end now, alongside a collection of the dirtiest tin mugs that Bill had ever seen, another loan from the begrudging clerics. Dented and dilapidated, these had blotchier complexions than poor Strawberry Sam, Bill's young apprentice at St. Paul's. Shit-coloured rust was crusted at their rims, and one was gnawed through by a bum-wipe of corrosion so you could see daylight. Rubbing the last scabs of grout from off his board, Bill made a mental note to see as neither him nor Ginger got the cup that had a hole, unless they wanted hot tea pissing in their laps.

He was made gradually aware of a commencing ruction somewhere to his rear and so looked back towards the scaffold just in time to see the platform winched down below head-height, now a yard or two at most above the ground. Old Danny Riley with his beard like Mr. Darwin's and that same gent's monkey mouth was saying "Who's that? Blessed Mary, now, who's that?" over and over like the village fool, so that Bill glanced about to see if some Archbishop or important man like that had stepped out from behind a post and come amongst them. Finding no one he looked back towards the wedge of boards that skimmed now only inches from the tiling and which with another scream from its four pulleys would be landed.

Coming from the figure squatting there at the construction's centre was a stammering "hoo-hoo-hoo" noise, only audible once all the winches were at rest, and even then you couldn't tell if it were laughter or the sound of weeping you were hearing. Tears rolled, certainly, across the figure's grubby cheeks, but ran into the crevices of what might have appeared a blissful smile were not the eyes filled with confusion and with pain. Upon the boards in front of it, writ by a fingertip dipped in Venetian Yellow and with wobbling characters such as a young child might attempt was the word TORUS, that Bill knew to be a term come from astrology by virtue of the fact that he himself was born in May. What Mabbutt couldn't fathom, though, was how the word came to be written on the planks at all, when he knew full well as the man that he'd sent up there to retouch the frescoes couldn't write his name, perhaps might copy out a letter's shape if he were so instructed, although obviously that had not been the case alone there in the upper dome.

Billy walked leadenly as in those nightmares of pursuit towards the heaping cage of scaffolding, pushing aside the navvies stood stock still and gawping in his way. Amidst the susurrus of gasps surrounding him he heard Bert Pickles saying, "Fuck me! Fuck my arse!" and heard the clattering footfalls of the priests come running to see what the noise was all about. Someone beside the figure shipwrecked there upon his raft had started crying. From the sound, Bill thought it was young Sam.

Looking up from the scattered pots and brushes that he sat amongst and from the inexplicable bright scrawl, the person who'd come down from the high gantry's pinnacle stared back at Mabbutt and his other workmates, and then giggled in a sobbing sort of fashion. It was not as though there was no recognition there in his expression, but more as if he had been away so long that he had come to think his former occupation and companions all a dream, and was surprised to find they were still there. Billy could feel hot tears well in his own eyes now, returning that destroyed, uncomprehending gaze. His voice twisted an octave higher than it's normal pitch when Billy tried to speak. He couldn't help it.

"Oh, you poor lad. Oh, my poor old mate, whatever 'as become of you?"

One thing was sure. For the remainder of his life no one would ever, when they spoke of Ernest Vernall, call him Ginger.

Billy walked his broken friend home over Blackfriars Bridge and stayed a while with Ernie's wailing family once they'd recognised the stranger brought home early from his work. Even Ern's mam was weeping, which Bill was surprised by, having never thought she had an ounce of pity in her, though her son's condition would have made a stone cry. Not so much the way Ern looked now as the things he talked about – trees, pigeons, lightning, corners, chimneypots – a tumult of plain, ordinary things that he would mention in the same hushed tones with which one might discuss a mermaid. The one person not in tears amongst the household was the two-year-old, young John, who sat there staring at his trans-formed father with those big dark eyes whilst mother, grandmother and baby sister wept, and all that time he never made a sound.

Ernest refused to speak about what had occurred up in the storm clouds over London, save to John and Thursa some years later, when his son was ten years old and Thursa only eight. For their part, Ernest's children never would reveal what they'd been told, not even to their mother or to John's own off-spring when he married and had kids a decade later, at the tail end of the 1880s.

On the morning after and in fact on every day that week Ern Vernall, hav-ing by that point regained at least some of his senses, made a brave attempt to take up his employment in St. Paul's again, insisting there was nothing wrong with him. Each morning he would reach the foot of Ludgate Street and stand there for a time, unable to go any further, before turning round in his despondent tracks and making back for Lambeth. He had some work for a while, just on and off, though not in churches anymore and not at any height. Anne had two further children by him, first a girl named Appelina, then a boy that Ernest was insistent should be christened Messenger. In 1868 Ern's wife and mother for the first time in their lives agreed on something and allowed him to be placed in Bedlam, where Thursa and John and sometimes the two younger kids would make first monthly and then yearly visits until the July of 1882 when, in his sleep and aged just forty-nine, Ern perished from a heart attack. Except his eldest children, no one ever found out what he'd meant by the word TORUS.

ASBOS OF DESIRE

What Marla thought was, it had all gone wrong when the royal family had killed Diana. All of it was bad things what had happened after that. You knew they'd killed her, 'cause there was that letter what she wrote, how she'd thought, like, they'd do it with a car crash. That was proof. Diana was expecting it, what happened to her. Marla wondered if she'd had a whatsit, premonition, a prediction thing that night it happened. That bit what you always see with her and Dodie and the driver coming out the Ritz where it's like on the hotel cameras and they go through the revolving doors. She must have known in some way, Marla thought, but it was like Diana's destiny what couldn't be avoided. Marla thought she must have known when she was walking towards the car.

She'd been, what, ten? Ten when they'd had the car crash. She remembered it, just being on the settee with a blanket all that Sunday crying, in her fucking mum's house up on Maidencastle. She remembered it, but then she'd thought she could remember watching telly when she was a baby, when Prince Charles and Princess Di got married in St. Paul's. She could remember it as clear as anything and she'd go on about it to her mates but then, like, Gemma Clark had said how that was 1981 and Marla was nineteen now, what meant she'd been born in 1987 or whatever, so she can't have done and must have seen it on a video. Or it was, like, Edward and Sophie and she'd got mixed up, but Marla wasn't having it. They could do all this stuff now, where they faked things? Like September the Eleventh or the Moon landing and that, or like – who was it? – Kennedy. Who was to say they'd not got married after 1987, but it was all covered up and all the pictures changed with CSI effects? Nobody didn't know nothing for sure, and they were fucking liars if they said they did.

What made her think of Di was she'd just popped back in her flat from where she'd been up Sheep Street, that way, just popped back 'cause she'd remembered where she thought she might have left some, and when she was looking down beside the sofa she'd found all her scrapbooks with Diana in instead. There was her Jack the Ripper books and all her Di stuff, where she thought she'd lost it or she'd lent it out to somebody. Other than that, what she'd been looking for weren't down there, but she'd jumped on what turned out to be a bit of cellophane from off a fag-pack thinking it was something else, how everybody must have done one time or other, when you see that glint down in the carpet and you think you might have dropped some, or somebody might. But there was nothing in the flat except for Jack the Ripper and Diana. If she wanted it that bad she'd have to earn it, wouldn't she?

She had a king-size Snickers, then she made herself boil up a kettle for Pot Noodle so as she could say she'd had a healthy meal, although who would she say it to, now Keith and them had cut her out? Oh, fucking hell. She only had to think about it and it made her stomach do that sort of drop thing and she'd go right into one, start thinking about everything there was might happen and what would she do and all of that, all of the usual, and it really made her need a smoke. She sat there in her armchair with its straps all busted under the foam cushion, spooning worms and gristle in hot dishwater into her mouth and staring at the wallpaper where it was starting to peel back up in the corner, looking like a book was opening. Whatever else she did, she wasn't going out tonight, not on the Beat, not down the Boroughs. She'd go out and get the homeward traffic later on this afternoon, but not tonight. She promised herself that. She'd sooner go without it altogether than risk that.

To give her brain something to gnaw on until she could sort things out, she thought back to when she'd last had some and it had been good. Not just this Thursday, yesterday, which was the actual last time, obviously, 'cause that was shit. Not any time before that in the last five months, when she'd been getting fuck all out of it, no matter how much she was doing, but the last time it was good. That had been January, just after Christmas when her mate Samantha, who'd worked further up the Andrew's Road in Semilong, had come to put her hair in rows. She was still in with Keith then – both of them were in with Keith – and things were still all right.

After they'd seen to Marla's hair, which had took ages but looked great, they done a pipe and give each other half-and-half. She weren't a les and neither was Samantha but it gave a boost to it, it was well known. It pushed it up another level, you'd be sucking on the pipe while they kneeled down and sucked you off, then you'd change round. Down on the fucking old Jamaican flag rug what her mum had given her when she moved out, still there six inches from her toe where she was sitting now, eating her noodles. It was January, so they'd had both bars on of the fire and had their knickers off, in just their T-shirts. Marla let Samantha have first go because she'd come and done her hair, so she could hear the whistling noise like blowing down an empty biro when Samantha sucked the smoke in and when Marla got down on the floor and licked her out. It tasted like the lemon from a gin and tonic, and Franz Ferdinand were on the radio, cassette, whatever, doing 'Walk Away'. When it was her turn next, Samantha was well off her face and gobbled at her like a dog with chips while Marla stood and took it back and it was fucking perfect, not quite how it was the first time but still magic.

What it was, when it was good, it felt like that was you, that was how you were meant to feel, that was the life that you deserved and not all this, this walking round like you're asleep and feeling like you're dead. Up there it was so good you thought you were on fire and could do anything, even in just a T-shirt by a two-bar fire with red spots on your legs and someone's pubes gone down your throat. You felt like fucking Halle Berry, somebody like that. You felt like fucking God.

This wasn't helping anything, it was just making Marla want some even worse. Putting the empty plastic pot down on the coffee table that she'd covered with some gift-wrap paper under glass after she'd seen it done on a make-over show, she picked up her Diana book instead, from where she'd placed it on the sofa with her Ripper paperbacks. A great big thing with coloured sugar-paper pages, Marla had begun collecting articles to put in it when she was ten and when Diana died. The cover had a picture that she'd done stuck over it with Pritt Stick so there were all bumps and creases in it. It was an old photo Marla had cut from a Sunday magazine, showing a place in Africa at sunset with the clouds all lit up gold, but what Marla had done was cut a face of Princess Di out from another page and glued it over where the sun was, so it looked like Di was up in Heaven lighting everything. It was so beautiful she hardly could believe, now, that she'd done it, specially not when she'd been ten, and she'd not seen anywhere else since then where anyone had come up with a picture that was half as clever an idea as hers. She'd probably been like a genius or something back then, before everybody started going on at her.

She had another look beside the sofa, just in case, and underneath as well, then sat back in the armchair, sighing, running one hand back over her head, over the rows where they were coming all to frizzy bits. That was because Samantha wasn't round there anymore. Marla had heard she'd gone back to her parents up in Birmingham when she'd come out of hospital, so there'd been nobody to see to Marla's rows. It wasn't like she had the money to have them done properly, so she was letting them unravel until some time when she could afford to have them seen to. Marla knew they made her look a state and they were bad for business, but what could she do? She'd had a tooth fall out three weeks ago from all the sweets and that weren't helping neither, but at least with that she could still practice smiling with her mouth shut.

That was bad, what happened to Samantha. She'd got in the wrong car, or been dragged in. Marla hadn't seen her since to ask her. These two blokes had took her over Spencer Bridge to do it, round the back of Vicky Park, and left her half dead in the bushes, pair of fucking cunts. There was a girl got done like that it must be every week, but it weren't one in four of them that got reported. Not unless it was a big event, like that last August when there was the rape gang in the BMW took women off from Doddridge Street and

Horsemarket, and that girl what got dragged from near the poolroom down in Horseshoe Street then took up Marefair round the green behind St. Peter's Church. Five rapes in ten days that had been, got on the television news and everything, everybody saying something would get done about it. That had been a good six months before what happened to Samantha. Marla sat there in her busted armchair thinking about how Samantha had got up from off the floor wiping her chin when Marla finished coming, then they'd had a little kiss, still rushing, tasting all the smoke and love-juice in each other's mouths. Later that night they'd had another go because it was just after Christmas, but it wasn't such a hit and neither of them had got off that second time, they'd just kept at it 'til their jaws hurt and they'd got fed up.

Thinking about it – and it was one of the only things that didn't frighten her to think about – Marla would bet there wasn't a room anywhere inside these flats what hadn't had somebody fucking in it. Not a kitchen or a lavatory or anything where someone hadn't stood there with their pants off doing something or else having something done to them. She could still sort of see her and Samantha gobbling each other down on the Jamaican flag, and if she thought about it she could picture other people too, in the same room as she was but perhaps from long ago like 1950 or whenever. What if there'd been someone like her mum, some slag who's in her forties and when the old man's out, bang, she's got some tramp in off the streets and giving her one up against the wall? Marla could see them, with the woman old and fat and wobbling standing with her hands up on the wall just over Marla's mantelpiece above the two-bar fire, her great big bum out and her skirt up, while this comical old tramp with an old trilby covering his bald patch gives it to her from the back, still with his hat on. Marla laughed and was dead tickled at how she'd imagined it in such a lot of detail when she never normally called pictures to her mind like that, or even managed any dreams. What little sleep she got was empty darkness like a big black fag burn that you fell in and climbed out of later not remembering a single thing. She was still looking at the fat lass and the tramp that she imagined, doing it against the wall above the fireplace, when the doorbell rang and made her jump.

She crept along the passageway to the front door, past where the bathroom and her messy bedroom both led off, and wondered who it was. She thought it might be Keith come back to say he'd take her on again, but then she thought it might be Keith come back to say she owed him still and smack her round the room. She was relieved and disappointed both at once when she opened the door up on its chain and it was only that bloke Thompson from up Andrew's Street, the ferrety old queer bloke who banged on about the politics and that. He was all right, and always sounded kind when he was talking to you, never talking down at you like most of the political ones did, the black ones and the whites. He'd called round once or twice in the past year or eighteen months, just going round from door to door and getting signatures for some petition or else telling people about meetings there were going to be, to stop the high-ups selling off the council houses and all that, and Marla always said she'd go along but never did, 'cause she'd be either working or else smoking.

This time he was going on about some painting exhibition that this artist woman what he knew was doing, in the little nursery up on Castle Hill five minutes' walk away. She wasn't really listening much while he explained, but it was all to do with how this artist was supporting one of his political campaigns that he was doing in the Boroughs, and how she'd come from that area herself, like that meant anything. The Boroughs was a shit-heap that was full of rotten cunts like them next door who'd had the ASBO put on her, and if it weren't that it was where they'd given her a flat and where she worked, for all she cared they could tear the whole fucking place down and then bury it. The Thompson bloke was telling her this exhibition thing was in the afternoon on the next day, the Saturday, and Marla said she'd definitely go though they both knew she wouldn't, just so she could shut the door without offending him. Tomorrow afternoon, Marla would either be all right, in which case she'd be round here in her flat and getting out of it, or else she wouldn't be all right, and either way she wasn't going to want to look at paintings. They were all a fucking con and people just said they could see all deep things in them when they wanted to look clever.

Shutting her front door on the old guy, Marla was hoping that come the next afternoon she'd definitely be all right, rather than not all right, whatever that might mean. Probably nothing worse that slogging round by Grafton Street and Sheep Street like she had today, in hope of lunchtime trade. That was as bad off as she'd be, she told herself. She knew she definitely wasn't going out down Scarletwell tonight, no matter how bad it might get, no way, so that was one alternative she didn't have to worry over.

After she'd got rid of Thompson or he'd gone on to the next house or whatever, she went back into the living room and sat back down where she'd been sitting, but she found she couldn't now imagine the two people fucking by the fireplace like she had before. They'd gone. She checked again beside the sofa and beneath it, then sat down again and thought about how it was all her fucking mum, Rose, was to blame for this. A little skinny white slag always chasing after niggers with her hair in dreadlocks, doing all the talk like Ali G and fucking giving it Bob Marley this, Bob Marley that. She'd even named her brown kid fucking Marla with Roberta as a middle name. Marla Roberta Stiles, and Stiles was just what Marla's mum's last name was, and not Marla's dad's. He'd been long gone and Marla didn't blame him, not one fucking bit. No fucking woman, no cry.

All the time while Marla had been growing up, her mum had been there making fucking curry with her headphones on and bellowing to lively up yourself or one of them. Or she was sitting by the telly spliffing up from little deals of ropey weed and saying it was fucking ganja. Then there was her boyfriends, every one some fucking nigger who'd be gone in six weeks or six minutes when they found out that she'd got a kid. When Marla was fifteen she'd fucked one of them, one of Rose's boyfriends, Carlton with the funny eye, just to get back at Rose for all the … just for everything. Just all of it. Marla still didn't know whether her mum had ever found out about her and Carlton, but he'd been kicked out the Maidencastle house within the month and there was such an atmosphere that Marla hadn't stuck it for much longer and fucked off herself soon as she turned sixteen. It was around then that she'd met Samantha and all Gemma Clark and them, and Keith.

Her mum had only been round once since Marla had got fixed up with the flat. She'd sat on the settee there with a skinny little spliff, Marla could see her now, and told her daughter what, in Rose's own opinion, she was doing wrong, how she was messing up her life. "It's all these drugs. It's not just like a lickle bit of 'erb. You'll end up like a slave to it." Yeah, like you're not a slave to cider and black cock, you fucking hypocrite. But Rose would have just said something like "At least I'm not out and selling it down Grafton Street." You couldn't, mum. You couldn't fucking sell it and you couldn't fucking give it away free, you just, you fucking couldn't. "There's no love in what you do." Oh, fucking hell. You stupid fucking … what, you think there's any in what you do? In what anybody does? It's all just FUCKING SONGS and FUCKING BIRTHDAY CARDS, you cunt, you old cunt. DON'T YOU FUCKING TELL ME, RIGHT, don't you fucking tell me because YOU, you've got NO fucking right, no fucking right. You sit there with your fucking SPLIFF, your fucking GAN-JAH, fucking smiling 'cause you're monged and saying to chill out. YOU WHAT? You fucking WHAT? I'll fucking chill YOU out, you old cunt. Fucking leave YOU with your face in stitches and your ribs all kicked in, see how YOU like it, you fucking, FUCKING …

There was no one there. She was all on her own. I tell you, man, you've seriously got to watch that. Seriously. She'd been shouting, not just in her head but out loud. It was getting a bit regular with Marla, that was, shouting. Shouting at Miss Pierce, her form teacher from Lings. Shouting at Sharon Mawsley when they were in first year, shouting at her mum, shouting at Keith. Yeah, right. As if. At least it was all people what were real and what she knew, or at least mostly. At least so far. There'd been only once, no, twice, when Marla had been shouting at the Devil, and a lot of people got that all the time. Samantha used to get that. She'd said that for her he was a red cartoon one with a pitchfork, but that's not the way that Marla saw him.

It had been the middle of the night about three months back, after what had happened to Samantha. She'd not had a proper smoke, 'cause there'd been none about but somebody – who was it? – somebody had given her some pills, fuck knows what, just to get her through. She'd been here in the flat, the same place where she always was, sat up in bed there in the dark having a fag just so that she'd be smoking something. She was staring at her fag end, like you do, and in the dark there it looked like a little face, a little old man's face with pink cheeks and pink mouth and two black flecks for eyes. The bits of grey and white ash were his hair and eyebrows and his beard. There were two glowing sparks up at the top, bright red so that they looked like horns, a little devil man there on her fag end and it looked like he was grinning. Where the hot coal at the end was burning through the paper from the other side to make his mouth it sort of went up at one side, and Marla had been all, like, Yeah? What are you laughing at, you ugly cunt? And he was like, Who do you think I'm laughing at? I'm laughing at you, ain't I? Because when you die you're going to go to hell if you're not careful.

That had been when Marla laughed at him instead, or snorted at him anyway. Well, what the fuck is hell supposed to be, you ash-faced twat? I'll tell you, hell for me would just be being stuck in Bath Street here forever, and he'd said, Precisely, and that really fucking freaked her out. Where had she got a word like that? When she was talking to her people in her head they talked like she did, and she'd never said "Precisely" in her life. She'd stubbed him out, she'd squashed his little burning brains out in the ashtray by the bed and then she lay there until morning with it running round her head, the thing he'd said. She didn't understand it and she didn't understand why she was letting it get to her like it had. For fuck's sake, what did he know? He was just a fucking fag end.

When Marla saw him the other time, that had been just a week or two ago, when Keith had told her he was having nothing more to do with her. She'd been here afterwards, been in the bathroom sorting out her mouth, which had looked much worse than it really was. She'd felt that low, though, that she'd thought about the fag-faced little devil and the things he'd said, fucking "Precisely", all that, and she'd thought about it so much he was in her head like a real person, like Miss Pierce or Sharon Mawsley, and like all her people in her head he had a go at her. It was like he was sitting on the edge there of her little bathtub while she stood above the basin to one side of him and swabbed her chin with Dettol. He weren't like the little red end off a fag though, this time, even if he sort of had the same face. He was a whole person like her mum or like the shagging tramp she'd thought about. He was all sort of dressed in what was like a monk's robes or it might have been old rags, and it was either red, or green, or both. He had the curly hair and horns and beard and eyebrows like he'd had when he was made of ashes and, as Marla saw him in her

head, he was still grinning at her, laughing when the Dettol stung and made
her cry again when she'd only just stopped, only just got herself together.

He was pissing himself, this old Devil, and she'd lost it. She'd completely
fucking lost it and she shouted Why don't you leave me alone? He'd just looked
back at her and done a face, taking the piss like, and he'd said it back to her, the
same words, in a nasty whiny voice she knew was meant to sound like hers.
He'd just said Why don't *you* leave *me* alone, and then she'd just been crying
after that and when she'd stopped he'd gone. She hadn't seen him since, and
didn't want to see him but the other people who'd had demons said they got
more regular, not less. He was her nasty fag-end devil prophet and she'd even
got a name for him. Ash Moses, that was what she called him. Sometimes
when she got that burning smell she often had when she was in the flat, the
smell she thought was just her nerves all frying up, she'd laugh and say Ash
Moses was about. But that was when she'd got some and was in a good mood
and it all seemed funnier.

Marla was searching down beside the couch again when she looked at the
carriage-clock there on the mantel and saw that she'd been here for more than
an hour and half when she'd just meant to pop in on the off chance of some
little lick she might have lost. Fuck. If she didn't get a move on she'd have no
chance of the knocking-off time trade, the blokes home for the weekend from
the places that they worked in Milton Keynes or London or wherever. It had
better be a bigger turn out than she'd seen at dinner time up Regent Square
and Sheep Street and round there, 'cause if she didn't get some money soon
she'd, well, she'd stay in. Stay in, read her Di book and her Ripper books and
just put up with it, that's what she'd do. She definitely, definitely wasn't going
out tonight, no way. No way.

She sorted out her make-up best she could but there weren't much that
she could do about her hair. She put the scrapbook and the murder paperbacks inside the bedroom chest of drawers in the clean clothes space, so that
she'd remember where they were, then went out through her little kitchen
and her back door, into the big concrete gardens of the flats. It wasn't a bad
day, but just the sight of all the gravel paths and shrubs and steps stretching
away towards the backs of all the flats there on the far side, or towards the big
brick arches near the middle avenue, it always got her down and almost always
kicked off the Ash Moses smell, though not today. This was a fucking awful
place. She bet there hadn't ever been a time when everything what happened
here weren't horrible.

One of the girls round there was thirteen and for this last month she'd
been the rage with the Somalis, the poor lucky little fucker. Still, that wouldn't
last. She wouldn't last. Then there was that old spastic bloke what used to live
across the middle path on the next block somewhere, mentally handicapped

whatever, what had been put out in the community. Next thing, he's met some geezer in the pub, right, bloke asks himself back, says what a nice place that the mental feller's got and how he'll bring some mates of his round, it'll be a bit of company, yeah? Next thing there's all these fuckers moving in and taking over, telling this poor cunt they'll kill him if they're fucked about and he's too mental to know any different and besides they might do. Doing gear and putting girls out round there and the handicapped bloke, he's out living on the street. This was a place, these Bath Street flats, where any rubbish, anybody that the council wanted rid of, nutters, Kosovans, Albanians all that, they could put all the shit here and just wait for it to disappear, go up in smoke like everybody round here seemed to, like Samantha and the other girls, Sue Bennett and Sue Packer and the one what had a gap between her teeth, banjo string cleaner what they called her. Kerry? Kelly? Her what had been found up round Monk's Pond Street anyway, the blonde one with the teeth. There weren't nobody killed yet, but some of them had been fucking close. Samantha had been close by all accounts. There weren't no way what she was going out tonight.

There was her ASBO. That was one good reason what she had for staying home, even without the other stuff, Samantha and all that. The fucking Robertses next door, that's who she had to blame for that. It was like, three, four months ago when Keith was seeing to it that she got more work. There'd been, what, two or three nights, five nights at the very most when she'd brought punters round the flat. Not even late, only like two o'clock or that, and fucking Wayne and Linda Roberts on their fucking doorstep every fucking time and banging on at her about the noise, giving it this about their fucking baby, all this with her punters looking on and listening while she got called every cunt under the sun and is it any wonder she'd had a go back? Five fucking times. Six times at most, and then they'd had them put the ASBO on her.

Fucking ASBOs. What that was, it was so they could keep control of places like the Boroughs without wasting any cash on extra coppers. Just stick every fucker under ASBOs and then let the fucking cameras keep an eye on things. The cameras, that was what you call it, zero fucking tolerance. If anyone shows up on film what's breaking their conditions, then that's it, you can just lock them up. Don't matter if what they've done is a proper criminal offence or not. Marla had heard about some woman got an ASBO for sunbathing, right, in her own back yard. What the fuck was that about? Some fucking neighbour cunt, some old cunt who can't stand to see somebody having a good time, see someone with her baps out, so they fucking, what they do, they fucking get a fucking ASBO took out on you and then they ...

Fat Kenny. That was who she'd had the pills off that night when she'd seen Ash Moses the first time, the big bald kid who lived in the flats up on the Mayorhold at the back of Claremont, Beaumont Court there, what they called

the Twin Towers. She'd gone round his flat and wanked him off and he'd give
her the pills. It was a funny thing, how when there was some little detail what
you wanted to remember, if you just stopped trying and forgot about it, it
would come to you. She walked across the courtyard to the gateway at one
end of the brick arches where she could see it was open and she wouldn't need
a key, because she'd lost hers or she'd put it somewhere and forgotten where.
Wearing her little sexy mac what she'd not took off all the while when she was
in the house, she walked up by the middle path towards the ramp and told the
dog halfway along to fuck off what was laying a big cable.

Stepping off the top end of the ramp and out the little half-walled exit into
Castle Street she got a sort of lift from nowhere when the sun come out just
for a minute, from behind a cloud. She felt more sort of positive whatever, and
she thought that was a good sign, that was like a lucky whatsit. Not charm, but
the same thing. It would be all right. She'd find somebody down Horsemarket
or in Marefair and then after that, who knows, perhaps things might start
looking up in general. If she could get sorted out a bit then Keith might say she
could come back with him or, fuck him, there might be somebody else, one of
the Kosovans or that, she didn't care. It was about half four when she walked
out from the no-entry at the end of Castle Street and onto Horsemarket. Right
then. Let's see who was about.

There was a lot of traffic, but all going fast and in a hurry to get home,
nobody idling along at twenty with an eye out on the curb. Across the busy
road she could see the arse-end of Katherine's Gardens, what the wrinklies
round there called 'Gardens of Rest', around the back of College Street and
that dark-looking church. There were some old girls lived in Bath Street flats,
ones who'd been on the batter in the old times and were all, like, in their
sixties and that. Marla couldn't even think what it would be like to be in her
thirties. These old dears said as St. Katherine's Gardens and the top of College
Street was where all of the trade got done back in the 1950s and the 1960s,
back then during wartime or whenever. Up where College Street met King
Street there'd been this one pub called the Criterion and just across the road
another called the Mitre. That was where the girls all used to knock about,
back then. They'd either do the business in the bushes round in Katherine's
Gardens, or they had this taxi company next to the Mitre what would run
them and the punters back down Bath Street, wait outside the flat five minutes
for the bloke to finish and then run them both back up the pub. It sounded
really nice to Marla, sort of cosy and all friendly. There'd be people round to
keep an eye on you.

Of course, in them days the Old Bill were different. What their plan was
then, it was to keep all of the different sorts of trouble to a different pub. So all
the hippies and the druggies were all off in one pub, all the bikers in another,

queers and lezzers up the Wellingborough Road somewhere and all the girls down here, up the top end of College Street. By all accounts it worked quite well, then you got all new coppers coming in with new ideas who probably just wanted to be seen as doing something, and to look good in the papers. They went in and busted all these pubs and scattered everybody everywhere, so now you'd got all of the different sorts of trouble spread through nearly every pub in town. Marla supposed it was a bit like with Afghanistan, when all the terrorists whatever were all in one place until they sent the soldiers in and now they're fucking everywhere. Fucking result. Marla thought how it must have been when Elsie Boxer and the other old girls from her flats were on the game, back in the 1960s when it was all whatsit, all Dickensian and that. It must have been like really nice.

Elsie had said there used to be a statue just along from the Criterion on the edge of Katherine's Gardens, that was like this woman with bare tits, holding a fish, but people all the time were fucking with it, putting paint all on its tits and that, then someone broke its head off. After that they probably thought like the people round here shouldn't have a statue so they moved it off down Delapre, Delapre Abbey where it was all posh and old, over the back of Beckett's Park what Elsie said they used to call Cow Meadow. Marla thought that was a shame, about the statue. It was fucking typical. Something that's sexy, yeah? Some woman, or like statue, with the tits and that, there's always going to be some cunt, some bloke who wants to smash it up. Anything lovely, like Princess Diana or Samantha. Fucking kill it. Fucking knock its head off. That was just the way things were, and it had always been like that. Some fucking people, they'd got no respect for fucking anything.

She stood there for a minute, sizing up her prospects. Looking uphill to her left there was the Mayorhold, somewhere else that Elsie said had used to be all right, a sort of village square thing, where there was just like this junction now. That could be a good patch for trade, or had been in the past at any rate, but only after it got dark and not around this time of day. Her best bet was downhill towards the traffic lights down at the bottom, on the corner there where Gold Street and Horsemarket joined with Horseshoe Street and Marefair. She'd get any trade coming up Marefair from the station, then there was whatever business might be passing by the other way, down Horsemarket and Horseshoe Street to Peter's Way and out of town. Plus, right, there was the ibis, where they pulled the Barclaycard place down in Marefair. People off from home in a hotel, you never knew. Shoving her hands into the pockets of her little PVC mac, she walked down the hill.

Down at the bottom Marla went over Horsemarket to the Gold Street side there where the pizza place is, then crossed Gold Street to the corner where it joined with Horseshoe Street, then stood there while she lit a fag. That was the only good thing with all these no smoking laws. You got so many women worked in offices whatever who got made to go outside for fag breaks that if you were standing smoking on a corner these days, looking dodgy, no one automatically assumed that you was on the game or none of that. She watched the crowd, the people filing to and fro over the zebra crossings, coming back from work or home to make their kids' teas. Marla wondered what was in their heads and bet it was like really fucking boring stuff like fucking football fucking telly shit, not like all what she thought about, all fucking wonderful and all imagination and all that, like anybody else would think of gluing Princess Di down on the sun. Watching her crowd for any possibles she let herself go off onto a daydream, thinking about who she'd like to have come up to her if she could have like anybody, any man.

He wouldn't be a big bloke, and he wouldn't be all blokey. Not a gay, but pretty. A bit girly, how he looked not how he acted. Nice eyes. Nice eyelashes and all that and really fucking fit, wiry and like he'd be dead good at dancing and dead good in bed. Black curly hair and he's like got this little beard … no, no, this little moustache … and he'd be GSOH like in the adverts, a good sense of humour what could make her laugh a bit 'cause she'd not had a laugh in fucking months. He'd be GSOH but not N/S. And he'd be white. No special reason, he just would be. He'd be standing here, right on this corner with her and he'd chat her up, he'd flirt a bit, he wouldn't just ask how much for a blow-job. He'd be fluttering his eyes and making little jokes and looking at her like they both knew where all this was going, looking really dirty in a real way, not like on a DVD. Oh, fucking hell. Marla was giving herself fizzy knickers. She pulled harder on her fag and stared down at the ground. This bloke, this bloke so fucking fit you wouldn't even charge him, right? You'd fucking pay for it. This bloke, she'd take him up her flat and on the way there he'd be kissing her, he'd kiss her on the neck and maybe he'd feel round her bum and she'd say not to but he'd just look up at her, right? He'd look up from under his eyelashes like a little boy and he'd say something really fucking funny and she'd let him just do anything, man. Anything. When they got round the flats he'd probably steer her up against her flat's door, right there in the hallway, and he'd have his hand down on her pubes and they'd be kissing, she'd be saying no, oh fucking hell, just let me open the front door.

And then the Robertses would have her put in prison.

She heard All Saints' clock up at the top of Gold Street strike for the three-quarter hour, quarter to five, and ground her fag out underneath her shoe. She gave the passing crowd another once-over, but there was fuck all there. Some really pretty white girl with red hair who had this fucking gorgeous baby in one of them slings goes round the front. Yeah, nice one, darling. Nice tits. Fucking good for you, yeah? Probably you don't even deserve that baby, probably you'll fuck her up and she'll grow up wishing you'd never had her, that she'd died when she was little and still happy, 'cause that's what you feel like. That's what fucking happens. That's what fucking happens all the time.

There was a nice old black guy on a bike, white-haired with a white beard, clocked off and going home, stopped on his bike there with one leg down, waiting for the lights, and some fifteen-year-olds with skateboards underneath their arms, but nothing what had any prospects. Marla glanced down Horseshoe Street there on her left and wondered if it might be worth a visit to the pool hall that was halfway down towards the pub, the Jolly Wanker or whatever it was called, what Elsie Boxer said had been the biker pub, the Harborough something. Harbour Lights. That was a nice name, cosy sounding, better than the fucking Jolly Wanker. There might be the odd bloke in the pool hall, maybe won a bit of money, feeling lucky.

On the other hand, she didn't like the pool hall much. Not because it was dark or sleazy, but ... oh, look, this was completely fucking mental, right, but the one time she'd been in there it was like in the afternoon? And there was hardly anybody there, and it was dark with the big lamps above the tables shining down these big blocks of just light, white light and Marla had got creeped out so she'd just, like, left. She couldn't even say 'til later what it was had got to her, the spooky feeling what she knew she'd had before and then she realised it was like when she'd been little and had gone inside a church. She'd told Keith that, one night in bed, and he'd said she was fucking mad, said it was rocks. "It's rocks, gal. All them rocks inside your head." She hated churches. God and all that, all that thinking about dying, or how you were living, all that bollocks, it was fucking morbid. If she wanted the religious thing she'd think of Princess Di. Any trade waiting down the holy pool hall could fuck off, Marla decided, and she stuck her hands down in her pockets, tucked her chin in and then waited for the lights to go back green so she could cross the top of Horseshoe Street to Marefair. She'd have better luck down at the station.

Marla took it easy as she made her way down Marefair, on the far side of the street from the hotel and all the leisure place whatever. No point being in a hurry, that was all off-putting, looking like you'd mind somebody stopping you to have a word. She walked by all the fed-up looking little restaurants and all that, and when she got along towards that bit what runs down off from Marefair, Freeschool Street, she passed this couple looked like they were married, in their forties, and the fucking faces they had on them. Miserable as sin, like the whole world had fallen in, heading up Marefair out of Freeschool Street, uphill towards town centre. They weren't holding hands or talking, looking at each other, nothing. Marla didn't even know why she thought they were married but they had that look, walking along both staring into space

like something fucking horrible just happened. She was wondering what it
was, thinking about them, when she almost walked into the bloke stood in the
road there at the top of Freeschool Street, just staring down it like he'd lost
something, his dog or something.

He was quite a tall bloke, white bloke, getting on but in good shape with
curly black hair what hadn't gone grey yet, but that was as close to Marla's
dream-bloke as he got. No pretty lashes and no little moustache but a great
big nose instead, with sad eyes where the eyebrows went up in the middle and
looked stuck like that, and with a big sad smile across his face. He was dressed
funny too, with this all sort of orange yellow red whatever waistcoat on over a
real old-looking shirt with rolled up sleeves and one of them things, not cra-
vat, not tie, like coloured handkerchief thing round his neck like farmers had
in books. With the big nose and curly hair he had a sort of pikey look, standing and staring off down Freeschool Street after his dog or his old woman or
whatever else it was he'd lost. He was no fucking painting and was older than
what Marla liked, but she'd done older and she knew full well as she'd done
uglier. As she stepped back from nearly running into him she looked at him
and smiled and then remembered where the tooth was gone so sort of turned
it to a pout, a little kiss thing with her lips pushed forward when she spoke.

"Ooh, sorry, mate. Not looking where I'm going."

He looked round at her, with his sad eyes and brave-face-on-it smile. She
realised that he'd had a drink or two, but then so much the better. When
he answered he'd got this high funny voice what had a sort of twang to it. It
wasn't even high all of the time, but sometimes went down in a kind of Farmer
Giles 'Arrrr', same as with the scarf what he had round his neck, all countri-
fied or something, Marla didn't know, but then it would go up in this weird
laugh, this giggle, sort of nervous laugh thing. He was definitely pissed.

"Aa, that's all right, love. You're all right. Ah ha ha ha."

Oh fucking hell. It was all she could do to keep from cracking up, like
when she'd be getting a lecture from some teacher back up Lings and trying
not to laugh, that noise you make up in your nose and cover up with coughing.
This bloke was a fucking one-off. There was something really mental to him,
not like dangerous or like the wombles what they put out into the community,
but just like he weren't on the same world everybody else was on, or like he
might be the next Doctor Who. Whatever it was up with him he wasn't biting,
so she went for the direct approach.

"Fancy a bit of business?"

How he acted, she'd never seen anything quite like it. It weren't like he was
all shocked by what she'd said, but more like he was acting shocked and being
all exaggerated, making it into a sort of funny turn. He jerked his head back
on his neck and made his eyes go wide like he was startled, so his big black

eyebrows lifted up. It was like he was being someone in a film what she'd not seen, or more old fashioned, like somebody from a pantomime or what you call it, music hall whatever. No. No, that weren't it, what he was doing. It was more like films before they had the words in, when it was just music and all black and white and that. The way they made all their expressions right over the top so you'd know what they meant when they weren't saying anything. He started wobbling his head a bit while he was doing this surprised face, just to make it look more shocked. It was like they were acting out a play at school together, or at least he thought they were, with all the different things you had to say writ out and learned beforehand. How he acted, though, it was like there were telly cameras on them, doing some new comedy. He acted as though she were in on it as well. He broke off the surprised look and his eyes went sad and kind again, all sort of sympathetic, then he turned his head away round to one side like he was looking at this audience or these cameras what she couldn't see, and did his laugh again like this was just about the funniest fucking thing what ever happened. In a weird way, probably because it had been so long since she'd had some, Marla thought he might be right. This was all pretty fucking funny when you had it pointed out.

"Ah ha ha ha. No, no, no, you're all right, love, thanks. No, bless your heart, you're all right. I'm all right. Ah ha ha ha."

The giggle at the end went really high. It sounded like it might just be he was embarrassed, but he was so fucking freaky that she couldn't tell. She was out of her depth here. This was just, like, whoosh. She tried again, in case she'd read him wrong or something.

"Are you sure?"

He tipped his head back, showing this great whopping Adam's apple, and then twisted it about from side to side, doing his giggle. She'd heard all the "he threw back his head and laughed" and that, but just in books. She'd not seen anybody try and do it. It looked really fucking loony.

"Ah ha ha ha. No, love, I'm all right, ta. You're all right. I'll have you know that I'm a published poet. Ah ha ha."

And he was like, that said it all. That was, like, everything explained, right there. She sort of nodded at him with this fixed grin that was, Yeah, all right, mate, nice one, see you, and then Marla carried on along the Peter's Church side, past them places made from all brown stones with criss-cross windows, Hazel-fucking-whatsit house and all of them. She looked back once and he was still there on the corner, staring down the little side-street waiting for his dog to come back up the hill, or whatever it was had run away from him. He looked up, saw her looking and he did the head thing. Even from this far away she could see that he'd done the giggle too. She turned away and walked on past St. Peter's Church towards the station, where you could already see the people coming home, crowds of them pushing up towards town on Marefair's far side, none of them looking at each other, or at Marla.

On her left, past its black railings and the grass all round it, Peter's Church looked really fucking old, yeah? Really fucking Tudor or Edwardian or one of them. She looked to see if there was anybody sleeping underneath the cover of its doorway, but there wasn't anybody there. Marla supposed the time was getting on now, five o'clock or round there, and they didn't let you sleep in doorways over night, just in the day. At night they moved you on which, actually, was fucking stupid. She'd been by St. Peter's yesterday round lunchtime and there'd been two fellers sleeping underneath the front bit then. Oh, no, hang on, there hadn't been two, had there? There'd been one. That had been sort of funny, now she thought.

She'd seen two people lying in the doorway, or at least she'd seen the bottoms of their feet, where they stuck out from under all the sleeping bag and stuff. Their toes pointed together, inwards, so she'd thought that they were lying facing one another and thought no more of it. Then she'd looked again when she drew level with the gate, and there was only one pair of soles showing she could see. The other one had disappeared. She'd done a great big complicated working out inside her head, trying to figure out, like, where the other feet had gone. Perhaps, like, what it was, when she'd first seen them there'd been one pair of bare feet and this bloke had just took his shoes off, with them down beside his feet there, toe to toe. Then in between the first and second time she's looked, he'd put them on, so she could only see one pair of feet the second time and thought someone had disappeared or was a ghost, whatever. Not that Marla thought that there was ghosts, but if there was then Peter's Church would be like the big hangout, innit? Somewhere from their own times, all the Tudors and the Edwards, all of that lot.

Walking past its gate now, Marla couldn't help but have a little peep in, just to see, but the space underneath the arch outside the closed black door was empty, except where they had the posters up for some other religion that was renting out the place, Greek Cypriots or Pakis, one of them. She went on, past the front of the Black Lion, where she stopped and looked towards the great big spread-out crossroads with the rush hour traffic, down there near the station. There were tons of people pouring out still, heading off up Black Lion Hill and Marefair into town, and there were all the black cabs in all different colours coming out the station entrance on this side of the West Bridge to wait there at the lights with all the vans and lorries. This was, like, well pointless. What the fuck was she down here for? She could no more walk down in that station forecourt just across the road than she could fly there.

It was Friday night. The girls would all be coming in from Bletchley, Leighton Buzzard, fucking London for all Marla knew, them and their fucking daddies, looking better than what she did 'cause they were looked after and like, looking at her, knowing what she was, how she was one of them but not even as good. That fucking look, yeah? And then there was Keith. Keith might be down there, scouting out new talent. He'd done that on Fridays sometimes and she knew she couldn't handle that, not having Keith see she was desperate. For fuck's sake, nobody did their business in the station anyway, not with the cameras. What the fuck had she been thinking? I mean, like, hello? Earth calling Marla. She weren't going down there, but then she'd have nothing for tonight, but, like, she didn't care, she still weren't going down there. But then she'd have nothing for tonight. Oh fuck.

What she could do, she'd see Fat Kenny. He'd have nothing proper, but he just liked drugs so he'd have something. He could sort her out, then she could get through 'til tomorrow, even if she sat up all night talking to herself again. There's worse ways she could spend the night than that. She waited for the lights to change so they were in her favour, then she tottered in between the waiting traffic and across Black Lion Hill to Marefair's other side, where there was Chalk Lane running up to Castle Street and where she lived in Bath Street flats.

Chalk Lane always made Marla think of Jack the Ripper, at least since she'd read a bit some years back in the *Chronicle & Echo*, where some local bloke said how he thought the Ripper might have come from round there. Mallard, this bloke's name was, both the one who'd writ the thing about it and the bloke he thought had done the killings. He'd been looking up his family tree and found this other family called Mallard what were the same name but not related and who lived down Doddridge Church, Chalk Lane, round that way. They'd had madness in the family, the dad had topped himself and one son had gone down to London, working as a slaughterer in the East End the time the murders happened. Marla had read all the theories and she didn't reckon there was much in that one. It was just a laugh, that there was her all mad on Jack the Ripper and somebody thought he'd come from down her street.

Some of the other girls were all, like, what d'you want to read all that for, specially with the line you're in, but Marla was, like ... well, she didn't know what she was like. She didn't know why she was into Jack the Ripper nearly the same way that she was into Princess Di. Perhaps it was because it had all happened back in history, like with *Lord of the Rings* and that. Perhaps it didn't feel like it had much to do with 2006 and what it was like being on the batter now. It was like an escape thing, the Victorian times, *Tipping the Velvet* and all them. It wasn't real. That's why she liked it. And the ins and outs of it were really, really interesting once you knew it all, how the Royal Family had ordered all them women murdered which was just the same as with Diana. Not like cutting her all up, but the same thing.

Now that she thought about it, there'd been other suspect Rippers passing through Northampton, not just this bloke Mallard from the local paper. Duke of Clarence, he'd come here and opened the old church, St. Matthews up in Kinsgley. Then there was the bent bloke, the bent poet bloke what hated women. J.K. something. J.K. Stephen. He'd died in the nuthouse up the Billing Road, the posh one where they said like Dusty Springfield, Michael Jackson and all them had been. This Stephen bloke, he was the one who wrote the poems dissing women. Had he written the Kaphoozelum one? It went, like, all hail Kaphoozelum, the harlot of Jerusalem. It had stuck with her 'cause the name was funny. Fuck, she'd rather she was called Kaphoozelum than Marla.

She walked up the entry of Chalk Lane from Black Lion Hill and thought for, like, two seconds about going round the front doors of the houses off the Chalk Lane entry to her left. Sometimes the girls she'd knew, they'd had to do that, if there weren't no trade about or if the truckers down the Super Sausage car park showed no interest. They'd go round, like, door to door, houses they knew had single blokes in, widowers whatever, or they'd take pot luck, just knock on any door and ask if anybody wants a bit of business, just like pikeys selling pegs. Samantha once, right, she'd said how she'd knocked round Black Lion Hill, nowhere she knew, just on the off-chance, and it was that Cockie bloke, the councillor whose wife's a councillor too. The wife was in, and everybody was all fucking outraged, saying as they'd have Samantha and all them looked into, so she'd took her shoes off and she'd legged it.

No, Marla was fucked if she'd go round Black Lion Hill. She'd wank Fat Kenny off. Perhaps he'd have an E to spare or something.

She was passing by the car park on her left there when she heard a noise, a voice or voices over its far side, what made her look up and take notice. Over the far corner, where there was a way up to that bit of grass around the back of the high wall on Andrew's Road, what they said was where the old castle was, there were some kids just climbing up out of the car park to the grassy bit. She couldn't see how many, 'cause the last one was just climbing up when Marla looked across, but she'd done business on the grass up there and felt a bit bad that it was where kids were playing. They were only fucking eight or something, younger than you'd think their mums and dads would let them play out in the street how things are now with fucking perverts everywhere. It would be dark inside another hour, and when she'd been in Marefair she'd thought it already looked sunsetty, up behind the station.

The last kid to climb up to the grass, the one what Marla saw, she was this little girl who'd got a dirty face but really pretty, like a little fucking elf whatever with the messy fringe and clever little eyes where she was looking back over her shoulder and across the car park straight at Marla. It was more than likely 'cause she was so far away and because Marla only saw her for a minute and had been mistaken like with the two pairs of feet in Peter's doorway, but it looked like she was wearing a fur coat. Not coat, just that bit round the collar like a mink stole. Stole. The little kid looked like she'd got a stole on, something furry round her little shoulders, but Marla just saw her for a second and then she was gone and Marla carried on, to up by Doddridge Church. It must have been a fluffy top, Marla concluded.

Doddridge Church was all right, not so fucking miserable as all the other churches 'cause it hadn't got a steeple, it was just this decent-looking building. Mind you, there was that door halfway up the wall what did her head in. What was that about? She'd seen doors halfway up old factories so they could make deliveries, but what would anybody need delivered in a church? Hymn books and that you could just take in through the door.

She went up Castle Street and round the top by the no-entry, how she'd gone out to Horsemarket earlier, but this time though she went the other way, up to the Mayorhold past the subway entrances and then along there by the Kingdom Life Church place, round to the flats behind the Twin Towers where Fat Kenny lived. He was at home, and had a plate of beans on toast in one hand when at last he come to see who it was at the door. He'd got his brand name sweatshirt on over his great fat belly, where it looked at least a size too small. So did his little face, a size too small for his shaved head, his big ears with the rings in one of them. He went, Oh, hello ... and then sort of trailed off so she knew he'd got no idea what her name was and hardly remembered her, well thanks a fucking lot. Spend twenty minutes getting cramp over his little prick and that was all the thanks you got. But still, she smiled and sort of flirted with him, butting in when he trailed off, just to remind him who she was and what she'd done for him that time.

She asked him if he'd anything would take the edge off things, but he just shook his big bald head and said he'd only got this legal high stuff, stuff what you could order out the back of like *Bizarre* and them, and other stuff he'd grew himself. He'd got a mate of his round later. They were going to try these legal high things out. Marla said she was really desperate and if he'd give her a bit of whatever it was to see her through, then she'd see him all right, better than last time. She'd meant giving him a nosh, but he like thought about it for a minute then said that he might if it was anal and she'd said to fuck off, fuck right off and die you fat cunt. Have your fucking mate round and bum him instead, she'd sooner fucking go without. He'd done a shrug and gone back in his house to eat his beans on toast and she'd turned round and marched round by the front of the Twin Towers, up Upper Cross Street and along to Bath Street.

Fuck. She went in by the entrance in the half-fence, up the middle walkway in between the bits of grass. Fuck. Fuck, what was she going to fucking do? All fucking night with nothing, not even Ash Moses in her fag end she could talk to. Fuck. The black iron gate what she'd come out by was still open under the brick archway. She went through and down three steps into the courtyard and she got the smell, Ash Moses smell like someone burning shit, like someone burning shitty nappies, probably it was the FUCKING ROBERTSES. Fuck. Past the shrubs all fucking grey and up some steps under the little sheltered bit where the back doors ran off from. Marla saw the back of Linda cunt-face Roberts's head when she was passing by their kitchen window, but got through her own back door and in the flat before the fucking bitch turned round and saw her too. Fuck. This was fucking shit. All fucking night. All fucking night and even the next morning, who said she was going to get some then?

The way it worked, when you were starting out with it, was that first time it felt like you were taken up, inside your body and your head, up somewhere you were meant to be where you could feel how you were meant to feel, a fucking angel or whatever, what they feel like. After that it wasn't quite as good again, and it got worse 'til by the end, the way you'd felt before you took it that first time, well, that's the level that you dream of getting back to now. Not feeling like a fucking angel all on fire, forget that, that's not going to happen for you anymore, no, no, just feeling like a fucking person like you was again for just ten fucking minutes, that's your fucking big ambition these days. Heaven, where you went the first time, that's all shut. The ordinary world you used to be in, that's shut too, most of the time, and you're stuck somewhere else, somewhere that's under all of that, like being under fucking ground.

Marla supposed that it was hell, like what she'd said when she was talking to Ash Moses. Being stuck here doing this in Bath Street, but forever.

The smell inside her flat, the smell of her all bottled up inside there, it was fucking minging coming back indoors to it like that. She knew she didn't wash much, this last while, and always thought her clothes would do another day, but it was fucking bad in there. It was like she could hardly tell the smell of her from the Ash Moses smell, the burning shit smell. It was her and she was it. What was she going to do in here all night? Because this was where she was going to fucking be, that much was fucking certain. She was not YOU ARE NOT going out, you FUCKING TWAT. She would be staying in. All night. With fucking nothing.

She'd do like she said. She'd read her Ripper books, read her Diana book … she'd had an idea. The Diana book, the picture what she'd done there on its front, best fucking picture what she'd ever seen. That was, like, fucking art. People give money all the time for art and some of it was fucking shit, just pickled things and beds what they'd not made. Marla's Diana picture had to be at least as good as that, had to be worth at least as much as that was. Just 'cause she was living down in Bath Street didn't mean she couldn't be an artist.

That bloke Thompson who'd been round, the bender with the politics, he'd said that artist he knew, her was going to be on Castle Hill having her exhibition the next day, he'd said she was a woman had come from the Boroughs, fucking just like Marla. That was fucking destiny whatever, like coincidences, with him coming round putting the idea in her head like that. This was all going to happen. Fucking hell, you sometimes heard where people had give fucking thousands for some picture. Fucking millions.

Think what you could buy if you had that. She'd never have to go out anymore, never go begging round Fat Kenny's, Keith could just fuck off. Yeah, you. You heard. Just fuck off. What are you to me, you little cunt, now I've got all this money? All the fucking bling-bling. I could have you fucking killed, mate. Just like that, a fucking hit man, bang and then I'll go out on the piss with Lisa Mafia. She'll be all like "You're Marla, yeah, the fucking artist done that picture of Diana on the sun and all that? Fucking wicked. Fucking sorted, yeah? You fucking go, girl." This was going to be so fucking good. She went to get the scrapbook with the picture on from where she'd left it on the coffee table and that's when she realised she'd been fucking burgled.

What the fuck? Someone had been in, though there weren't like nothing broken. Had she locked the back door, had she locked it when she went out? Had she needed to unlock it when she come back in? For fuck's sake. Someone had been in while she was out. They'd been in and they'd taken not the telly, not the beatbox thing, not even took the carriage clock. No, now she looked around they hadn't taken nothing except Marla's scrapbook. And her Ripper books. She'd left them there as well, there on the coffee table so that she'd know where they were. Oh, fuck. Someone had been in, had her scrapbook with her picture of Diana on and the worst of it was that she'd been right. Been right about the picture. Why would someone nick it if it wasn't valuable? Oh fucking hell, the millions that she could have got for that. Now look. Now look at her, she's fucking crying. Fucking crying. Keith thinks she's a cunt and Lisa Mafia thinks she's a cunt as well. Princess Diana thinks that she's a cunt.

Cry all you want. Cry all you want you stupid, stupid fucking cunt. Cry all you want 'cause you're not going out.

It was a new moon like when they're all sharp and pointed, over Scarletwell what run downhill to Andrew's Road. That was the only place, where there were customers but where there were no cameras what could see you, although they kept saying they were going to put some there. On Marla's left across the road there were the maisonettes what had their front round Upper Cross Street. Most of them were dark where you could see over the balconies but some with lights on, shining through all coloured curtains. On her right across the criss-cross wires that made the fence she had the grass bit at the top of Spring Lane

School. Marla thought schools always looked haunted when it was at night and there weren't kids there. She supposed it was because a school had such a lot of noise and kids all running round during the day, it made you notice more when it was dark and quiet and there weren't nothing moving.

She went down past the school gates and carried on down by the bottom playing fields. Over the road now there were other flats, Greyfriars flats had she heard them called? They looked sort of the same as Marla's flats, about as old, perhaps in better nick, you couldn't really tell at night. Some of the balconies down here had rounded corners, though, and that looked sort of better than round hers. She carried on, down past where Greyfriars ended on the road's far side and Bath Street's bottom end curved round to join with Scarletwell. She went on past the empty playing fields, where they were fenced off at their bottom on her right and other than the traffic in the distance over Spencer Bridge all she could hear were her own footsteps on the bumpy path what had all weeds come up between its stones.

There was that little house all on its own there, little red-brick house at one end of this strip of grass by Andrew's Road, just where it met with Scarletwell Street. It weren't big, but looked as if it might have been two really little houses once what had been knocked together. It shit Marla up, shit her up every time she saw it and she'd no idea why. Perhaps it was because she couldn't work it out, why it was standing there when what looked like the terrace it had been on had been pulled down years ago. It had a light on through thick curtains, so there must be someone living there. She pulled the collar of her mac tight and went clacking past the funny house and round the corner to its right, along the pavement by St. Andrew's Road, between the road and that long strip of grass that ran towards Spring Lane, the bit where all the other houses must have used to be. Up in the sky, just here and there between the brown bits from the street lights, she could see all stars.

She knew. She knew exactly what was going to happen, in her guts she knew. There'd be a car along now, any minute. That would be the one. There wasn't anything what she could do to stop it, nothing she could do so she was somewhere else. It was as if it had already happened, was already in the script of that bloke with the waistcoat's comedy and there weren't nothing she could do except just go along with it, go through the moves that she was meant to make, take one step then another up along beside the grass towards Spring Lane, then at the end turn back and walk along the other way, to Scarletwell Street, with the house all dark there on the corner and no windows lit from this side.

Walking back to Scarletwell, there were the noises from the station yards, behind the wall across St. Andrew's Road, just shunting noises, but she could hear kids as well, kids' voices giggling. They were coming from the big dark row of bushes on the far side of the strip of grass, that ran along the bottom there of the school playing fields to Marla's left. It must be them what she'd seen earlier, the little girl with the fur stole from up Chalk Lane. What were they doing, all still out this late? She listened but the voices didn't come again from up behind the hedge. She'd probably imagined them.

The little house was black against the grey sky up the hill behind it, up towards the railway station and up Peter's Way. The car was coming down St. Andrew's Road from up the station end towards her, moving slow, its headlights getting slowly nearer. She knew what would happen but it was like it would happen anyway. It was all set, the minute that she'd left the flat, all set in stone like with a church or something where it was already built and nobody could change it. The car stopped, pulled in across the road and stopped there at the corner on the other side of Scarletwell, across from where the house was. Marla couldn't hear the kids now. There was nobody about.

She walked towards the car.

ROUGH SLEEPERS

It had been in one sense forty years since Freddy Allen left the life. One day he might go back to it, there was always that possibility. That door was always open, as it had turned out, but for the moment he was comfortable the way he was. Not happy, but amongst familiar faces and familiar circumstances in a place that he was used to. Comfortable. Somewhere that you could always get a bite to eat if you knew where to look, where you could sort of have a drink and sort of have some of the other, now and then, although the now and then of it could be a pain. But there was always billiards, up the billiard hall, and there was nothing Freddy loved more than he loved to watch a cracking game of billiards.

He could remember how he'd got out of the life, the business, the proverbial 'Twenty-five Thousand Nights', as he'd heard it referred to. Far as Freddy was concerned, it might have happened yesterday. He'd been under the arches down Foot Meadow, sleeping out the way he did back then, when he'd been woke up sudden. It was like he'd heard a bang that woke him up, or like he'd just remembered there was something that was happening that morning that he'd better be alert for. He'd just come awake with such a start that he'd got to his feet and he was walking out from underneath the railway arches and across the grass towards the riverside before he knew what he was doing. Halfway to the river it was like he'd woken properly enough to think, hang on, what am I jumping up like this for? He'd stopped in his tracks and turned around to look back at the arches where he saw another tramp, an old boy, had already nicked his place where he'd been kipping, on the earth below the curve of brickwork up against one wall, had even nicked the plastic carrier bag of grass that had been Freddy's pillow. It was bloody typical. He'd walked back a few steps towards the archway so that he could see just who the bugger was, so that he'd know him later. It had taken Fred a minute before he could recognise the nasty-looking piece of work, but once he had he knew he'd never get his spot back now. There was no point in even trying. He'd been moved on, and he'd have to just get used to it.

And Freddy had got used to it, after a time or in no time at all, depending how you saw it. How things were now, it weren't such a bad existence, whatever his friend might try and tell him who lived in the bottom corner house on Scarletwell Street. They meant well, he knew that, telling him he should move up to somewhere better, but they didn't understand that he was comfortable the way he was. He hadn't got the worries that he'd had when he was in the life, but Freddy didn't think they'd understand that, given what their situation was at present. You didn't have the same perspective, living down there, as what Freddy had got now.

Now was a Friday, May the 26th, 2006, according to the calendar behind the bar in the Black Lion where he'd called in just to see if there was anyone about. He'd just been up a bit in the twenty-fives or twenty-sixes, up round there, in the St. Peter's Annexe where that coloured woman with the bad scar who was famous up the way worked with the prostitutes and them on drugs, and all the refugees come from the east. He liked it up that way, the people all seemed more constructive and just getting on with things, but there was never anybody there that Freddy knew and so he'd come down to this bit where he was sitting now, with Mary Jane across the table from him. Both of them were sat there with their chins propped in their hands and looking down, a bit glum, at the empty glasses on the laminated tabletop between them, wishing there was some way they could have a proper drink but knowing as they couldn't, knowing that instead they'd have to have a proper conversation. Mary Jane lifted her always-narrowed and suspicious eyes to look at him across the empty glasses.

"So you were saying you'd been up there in the twenty-fives, then? I've not been up there meself, now, 'cause I've heard as there's no pub up there. Is that right?"

Mary Jane had got a gruff voice like a man, though Fred had known her long enough to tell it was put on. She'd quite a light voice underneath but made it deeper so no one would think she was a push-over, though why she thought they'd think that, Freddy hadn't got a clue. One look at Mary Jane with that face and them scabs all on her knuckles, most folk would know well enough to keep away. Besides, her opportunities to get into a scrap had all been over ages back. There wasn't any need for her to keep on scaring people off. Freddy supposed it was the habit of a lifetime and that Mary Jane was never going to change if she'd not changed by that point.

"No, no pub. Just the St. Peter's Annexe what they call it, where they're looking after people. Tell the truth, I shouldn't think you'd like it much. You know how there's some areas where the weather's always bad? It's one of them. The people up there are all nice enough, some real good sorts like in the old times, but there's never anybody that you know goes up there. Well, except the gangs of kids and that, but they get everywhere, the little buggers. I expect that everyone's like us, stick in the muds what never leave their own bit of the Boroughs and don't go much higher than the fourteens or fifteens."

She listened to what Freddy had to say and then she screwed up her expression, like a face a kid had drawn upon a boxing glove, and glared at him. That was just how she was with everyone. You couldn't take it personal with Mary Jane.

"Fifteens be fucked. I'm not even that fond of how they've got it here."

She waved one scabby-knuckled hand around to indicate the pleasant little bar-room with its other bit down a short flight of steps from where they sat. There were two men stood talking to the girl behind the bar, just while she served them, and a couple in their twenties sitting chopsing in one corner, but nobody Mary Jane or Freddy knew. The Black Lion, this bit of it, was a decent little place still, but there was no arguing with Mary Jane when she was in a mood like this, and she was always in a mood like this so there was never any arguing.

"If you want my opinion, these new places are a waste of fucking time. You're better off down in the forty-eights and forty-nines where there's a better class of individual, with more go in them. Or if that's not what's to your liking, why don't you come up the Smokers of a night, above the Mayorhold? There's the old crowd in there still, them as would know you, so you'd not go short of company."

Freddy just shook his head.

"It's not my kind of place that, Mary Jane. They're a bit rough for me, the crowd up there with Mick Malone and that lot. I'm not being funny, but I'm just more used to keeping to meself. Sometimes I go down Scarletwell to see a chum I've got down there, but I keep off the Mayorhold, mostly, as it is now."

"I'm not talking about now, I'm saying in the night-time. We have a good laugh, up in the Jolly Smokers. 'Course, I've always got the Dragon just across the way there, if I'm feeling in the mood."

A dirty and lascivious grin broke out across Mary Jane's face while she was saying this, and Freddy felt relieved to have the woman from behind the bar come out and interrupt by clearing off the dirty glasses, so they wouldn't have to follow up that line of thought. The barmaid moved that fast that she was like a blur, just whipped the glasses from their table then shot back behind the bar, not paying them the least bit of attention. That was how it was for ones like him and Mary Jane, for the rough sleepers. People hardly knew that you were there. They just looked through you.

Mary Jane, when she picked up the thread of talk again, had moved on from the subject of the Dragon and her love life, which was just as well, but in the absence of a drink to shut her up was reminiscing, still within the general subject of the Mayorhold, on the fights she'd had there.

"God, do you remember Lizzie Fawkes, how me and her went at it outside the Green Dragon in the street, right on the Mayorhold there? We had a set-to over Jean Dove what was so bad that the coppers daredn't bust us up. I'll say this for old Lizzie, she was tough all right. She'd got one eyelid hanging off and couldn't talk for where I'd knocked her jaw out, but she wouldn't let it lie. Meself, I weren't much better, got me head split open and it turned out later that I'd broke a thumb but it was such a great fight neither of us wanted it to end. We went up to the Mayorhold the next morning and we carried on with it a while, but then she'd got a bolt hid in her hand so when she clouted me around the head I went out like a light. That was a fucking beauty, all right. Makes me want to go back down there so I can relive it. Should you like to come along now, Freddy? I can promise you, it was a fucking treat."

There'd been a time when Freddy would have gone along with Mary Jane for fear of how she'd take it if he should refuse, but those days were long gone. She was all bark now and no bite, no harm to anyone. None of them were, not these days. It had been a long time since the coppers took an interest in any of them, Freddy, Mary Jane, old Georgie Bumble, any of that lot. Mind you, the coppers had no jurisdiction in the areas where Fred and Mary Jane spent all their time these days, and it was very, very rare you'd see a bobby round there, not one who'd got any interest in the likes of them. The only one who Freddy knew to say hello to was Joe Ball, Superintendent Ball, and he was all right. An old-fashioned copper out the olden days what had long since retired, though when you saw him he still had his uniform. He'd spend a lot of time talking to villains of the sort he'd once have locked up in the jail, including Freddy, who'd once asked Joe why he wasn't spending his retirement somewhere nicer, somewhere like where Freddy's pal down Scarletwell Street said that Freddy should have gone. The old Superintendent had just smiled and said he'd always liked the Boroughs. It would do him, and you sometimes got the chance to do a bit of good. That was enough for old Joe Ball. He wasn't after anyone, not Freddy and not even Mary Jane. She'd been a holy terror but she'd had the fight go out of her when her old way of life ended abruptly after she'd been struck down by a heart attack. She'd had to reassess things after that and change her ways, so Freddy wasn't worried now as he declined, politely, her kind invitation to revisit scenes of former glories.

"I'd as soon not, Mary Jane, if it's the same to you. That's more your cup of tea than mine, and I've got old affairs meself I should be getting back to. Tell you what, if you'll keep old Malone and all his bloody animals away from me, I'll break the habit of a … well, of a long while it seems to me … and I'll perhaps come by the Smokers when I've been to watch me billiards tonight, how's that?"

This seemed to please her. She stood up and stuck one callused hand out so that Fred could shake it.

"That'll do me. You mind how you go now, Freddy, though I s'pose the worst has all already happened for the likes of us. I'll tell you how I got on in the fight if I should see you up the Smokers. You make sure you're there, now."

She released his hand, then she was gone. He sat there on his own a while eyeing the barmaid. It was hopeless, Freddy knew that. He was older with his hair gone now, and though he still had what he could retain of the good looks he'd had when he was young, as far as the blonde barmaid was concerned he might as well not be there. He picked up his hat from where it rested on the seat beside him, crammed it on his bald spot and got up to leave himself. As he went through the door and onto Black Lion Hill, just from politeness and from habit he called to the barmaid, wishing her a good day, but she took no notice, as he'd known she wouldn't. She just kept on drying glasses with her back to him, acting as if she hadn't heard. He stepped out of the pub and turned right, up to Peter's Church, where all the clouds were moving by so fast above that light was flickering on the old stonework as though from a monster candle.

As he passed the church he glanced in at its doorway, just to see if any young chap or young woman ... they were always young ones these days, with as many girls as there were boys ... was sleeping underneath the portico, but there was no one there. Sometimes, if he felt lonely or just needed human company he'd sneak in with them while they slept, which didn't do no harm, just lying there beside them face to face and listening to them breathe, pretending he could feel their warmth. They were all drunk or too pie-eyed to know that there was anybody there, and he'd be up and gone before they were awake in any case, just on the off chance one might open up their eyes and see him. The last thing he'd want to do was frighten them. He wasn't doing any harm, and he would never touch them or pinch nothing from them, not a one of them. He couldn't. He weren't like that anymore.

From Marefair, Freddy drifted up Horsemarket. As he crossed St. Mary's Street that ran off to his left he glanced along it. You could sometimes see the sisters still up there, a proper pair of dragons who'd been widely-known and talked about when in their prime: wild, shocking and exciting. Famously, they'd once raced naked through the town, leaping and twirling, spitting, running along rooftops, all the way from here to Derngate in about ten minutes, both so dangerous and beautiful that people wept to see them. Freddy sometimes spotted them in Mary's Street, just moping wistfully around the piles of dried-out leaves and litter drifted up against the sunken car park's wall, drawn back here to the place where they had once commenced their memorable dance. The glitter in their eyes, you knew that if they had the chance, even at their age, they'd still do it all again. They'd do it in a minute. Blimey, that would be a sight.

Today, St. Mary's Street was empty save a scroungey-looking dog. Freddy passed on, not for the first time he reflected, to the top of Castle Street where he turned left and headed down to where the flats were now.

It was when Mary Jane made that remark about what she got up to at the Dragon – the Green Dragon on the Mayorhold – which was where the lesbians gathered. As unwelcome as the thought of it had been, it had set Freddy off, set him off thinking about sex again. That's why he'd eyed the barmaid down at the Black Lion. To be quite honest sex was a frustration and a nuisance now as much as anything, but once it came into his head it rattled round until he'd satisfied its nagging voice and all its wearying demands. Now that he thought about it, though, it had been much the same for him while he was in the life. It wasn't fair of him to blame his circumstances now for all the things that made him feel fed up. He'd had a fair shake, Freddy thought, all things considered. No one was to blame but him for how he'd handled his affairs, and he could see that there was justice in the way he'd ended up. Justice above the streets.

He was just thinking that he'd not seen any of that area's clergymen around as yet today, the brothers or whatever they preferred to call themselves, when who should there be struggling up the street towards him than one of that very lot: a stout chap looking hot under his robes and all of that lark, making hard work of an old sack what he'd got across his shoulder. Freddy had a little chuckle to himself, thinking that it was more than likely nicked church candle-sticks or the collection plates or else the lead from off the roof inside the sack, it looked that heavy.

As they neared each other, the old priest chap lifted his flushed, sweating face and noticed Freddy, giving him a big warm smile of greeting so that from the offset Freddy liked the man. He looked like that young actor off the telly who played Fancy Smith in *Z-Cars*, only older, how he'd look if he were in his fifties or his sixties, with a beard and all grey hair. Their paths met halfway down the bit between Horsemarket and the path or ramp or stairs, whatever it was called, that led into the houses there, the flats. Both of them stopped and said hello politely to each other, with this ruddy-faced old Friar Tuck chap having a great rumbling voice and something of an accent Freddy couldn't place. It sounded a bit backwards, like a country accent could if you weren't used to them, and Freddy thought the bloke might be from Towcester or out that way, with his thees and thys.

"It is a hot day to be out, I was this moment saying to myself. How goes the world with thee now, my fine, honest fellow?"

Freddy wondered if this chap had heard of him, his nicking all the loaves and pints of milk back in the old times, and if all this 'honest fellow' stuff was just a parson's manner when he took the mickey out of someone. By and large, though, he seemed a straightforward sort and Freddy thought that he should take him at face value.

"Oh, it looks like a hot day, all right, and I suppose the world goes well enough. What of yourself? That bag of yours looks like a burden."

Setting his rough sack down on the ground with a small groan of gratitude at the relief, the parson shook his wooly head and grinned.

"God bless thee, no ... or if it is it's not a burden I begrudge. I have been told I am to bring it to the centre. Dost thou know where that might be?"

Freddy was stumped just for a moment, thinking that one through. The only centre that he knew of was the sports and recreation centre, where they played the billiards there halfway down Horseshoe Street, where Freddy would be going later on if all were well. Deciding that must be the place that the old feller meant, Freddy proceeded to give him the right directions.

"If it's where I'm thinking of, then you must turn right by that tree along the end there." Freddy gestured to the end of Castle Street. "Go down that way until you reach the crossroads at the bottom. If you go straight over and you carry on downhill, it's on your left across the road, just halfway down."

The old boy's face, already bright with sweat, lit up to hear this news. He must have walked a long way, Freddy thought, dragging that sack. The Holy Joe thanked Freddy thoroughly, he was that grateful to hear that the billiard hall was only down the street, then asked where Fred himself was bound. "I trust that your own journey is towards some pure and godly ending" was the way he put it. Freddy had been thinking that he'd go down in the dwellings just off Bath Street and give Patsy Clarke a poke for old times' sake, but it weren't right to say that to a man of God. Instead, Freddy made out that he'd been off to see an old mate, an old pensioner who'd not got any family, down at the bottom end of Scarletwell Street. This was true enough, though Freddy had originally intended to go down there after his regular rendezvous with Patsy Clarke. Ah, well. It wouldn't hurt to have a change from the routine. He wished the stout priest well, then set off at a jaunty pace, straight past the opening of Bath Street flats and down to Little Cross Street. On the way down, Freddy paused and looked back at the clergyman. He'd lifted up his sack again and had it back across one shoulder, staggering off up Castle Street towards Horsemarket, leaving quite a trail behind him. Everybody left a trail, Freddy supposed. When he'd been in the life, that's what the rozzers always told him when they caught him, anyway.

He could have doubled back to Bath Street flats once the old chap was gone from sight, but that would make him feel dishonest after what he'd said. No, he'd go on down Scarletwell, where they'd be glad to see him. Truth be told, they were the only ones still living down there, when it came to seeing Freddy, who would make the effort. Realising that you couldn't get down Bristol Street without a lot of difficulty these days, Freddy went instead up Little Cross Street to where it joined Bath Street on the flats' far side, then turned left and went on down Bath Street to its bottom as it veered round to the right and into Scarletwell Street.

He was in a sort of fog as he rolled round the corner to his right, and passed the place where Bath Row had run down to Andrew's Road once, years back. There was just the opening to the garages, near where Fort Street and Moat Street had once been. As he passed by it, Fred peered down the tarmac slope that led to the enclosure, a rough oblong that only the closed grey garage doors looked onto. Something of an oddity for blokes of his sort, Freddy didn't hold with premonitions and the likes of that, but there was something down there, down them garages where Bath Row's terraces once were. Either there had been something happen there a long time back, or there was something going to happen there. Suppressing the first faint ghost of a shiver he'd felt in a long time, Freddy carried on to Scarletwell Street, crossing to its other side there at the bottom, down below Spring Lane School's playing fields. You could still see some of the cobbles of the jitty mouth, where it had run behind the terrace down on Andrew's Road, but it was pretty much all gone. It looked to Freddy as if the thick shrubs down at the bottom border of the field had pushed into the space where once the jitty was, with their black foliage covering its smooth grey stones. At least, Fred thought they were still grey, but almost everything down here was grey or black or white to Fred, like an old photo where its all clear and the light's just right but there's no colours. Freddy hadn't seen a normal worldly colour now in forty-something years, as people who still made a living judged such things. The colour-blindness was just part of his condition. Freddy didn't mind it much, except with flowers.

He walked down a few steps to where the house was, standing all alone there on the corner by the main road, nothing but a patch of grass behind it running off towards Spring Lane, where once had stood the terrace where a lot of them that Freddy knew had lived, Joe Swan and them. He stepped up on the doorstep and went in. The doors were never closed down there to Freddy, and he knew he'd always got an open invitation, so he just went through and down the passage to the door what led into the living room, in which the corner house's tenant was sat at the table by one wall and browsing through a picture-album, full of seaside snaps and everything, looking up with surprise as Freddy came in unannounced, but then relaxing upon realising it was only him.

"Hello, Fred. Blimey, you give me a turn. A right old jumping Jack I'm turning into, no mistake. I thought it was the old man. Not that he's a trouble to me, just a bloody nuisance. Every week he's round here saying sorry this and sorry that. It's getting on me nerves. Here, let me put the kettle on."

Fred occupied the empty chair across the table from the photo album, and called to the kitchen while his pal went out to make a cup of tea.

"Well, he's a rogue, old Johnny. I expect he feels he needs forgiving."

His friend's voice came from the kitchen, talking loud above the boiling of the kettle, one of the electric ones that's bubbling in a minute.

"Well, I've told him, like I've told you over other matters, it's himself he should be asking the forgiveness of. It's no good coming round to me. I bear him no hard feelings and I've told him that. For me it was all a long time ago, although I know for him it must seem like just yesterday. Ah well."

The steely-eyed septuagenarian came back out of the kitchen with a steaming mug of tea in one bony-but-steady hand, and sat down opposite to Freddy by the open photo-album, setting down the teacup on the faded tablecloth.

"I'm sorry I can't offer you one, Freddy, but I know it's no good even asking."

Freddy shrugged disconsolately in agreement.

"Well, my innards in the state they are these days, it goes right through me. But I'm very grateful for the offer. How are things with you, mate, anyway? Have you had anybody call by other than old Johnny since I saw you last?"

The answer was preceded by a noisy slurp of tea.

"Well, let me see. I had them bloody kids break in here, ooh, some months ago it must have been. They were most likely trying to cut through into Spring Lane Terrace as was up the back there years ago. The little beggars. It's like all the kids these days, they think that they can get away with anything because they know that you can't touch them."

Freddy thought about the last tea he'd enjoyed, not too much milk, two sugars, wait until the first flush of the boiling heat has gone off of it, then it's right for gulping. Not a drink for sipping, tea. Just gulp it down and feel the warmth spread through your belly. Ah, those were the days. He sighed as he replied.

"I saw 'em earlier, when I was up the twenty-fives in Peter's Annexe, where they've got this darky woman with a scar over her eye who's treating all the prostitutes and them, amongst the refugees. It was that gang of little devils Phyllis Painter's got. They'd broke in through the old Black Lion when it was opposite the cherry orchards, back round there in Doddridge's rough area, then climbed up to the twenty-fives just like a pack of little monkeys. Honestly, you should have heard their language. Phyllis Painter called me an old bugger and her little pals all laughed."

"Well, I expect you've been called worse. What's all this about refugees, then, in the twenty-fives? Have they come from some war? That's a bit close for comfort, that is. That's just up the road."

Freddy agreed, then said how it weren't war but flooding, and how from their accents all the refugees came from the east. His old friend nodded, understanding.

"Well, we can't make out we weren't expecting it, though like I say, we all thought as it would be further off. The twenty-fives, eh? Well, now. There's a thing."

There was a pause to take another swig of tea before the subject changed.

"So tell me, Freddy, have you seen old Georgie Bumble lately? He used to call in here for a chat so I could tell him that he should move somewhere better off, and so that he could take no notice, like all you old ruffians do from time to time. It's just I haven't seen him for a year or more. Is he still in his office on the Mayorhold?"

Freddy had to think about it. Could it really be a year, or even years, since he'd seen Georgie? Freddy tended to lose track of time, he knew, but surely it weren't that long since he'd looked in on the poor old blighter?

"Do you know, I really couldn't tell you. I suppose he's still there, though I don't go up that way much. To be honest, it's a dirty hole up there now, but I'll tell you what, I'll look in on old Georgie when I leave here and see how he's getting on."

Fred could have kicked himself, although not literally. Now as he'd said he'd do it, he would feel obliged to see it through, which meant he'd not be getting round to Patsy Clarke's until much later than he'd planned, sometime around the middle of the afternoon. Oh well. She'd wait. It weren't like she was going to run off anywhere.

Their conversation turned, as Freddy knew it would, to his own stubbornness in staying down here in the lower reaches of the Boroughs.

"Freddy, if you lot only thought better of yourselves you could move up a bit. Or if you did what my great-grand-dad did you could move up a lot. The sky's the limit."

"We've been through all this before, pal, and I know my place. They don't want me up there. I'd only have the milk and bread away from off the door-steps or be getting up to trouble with the women. And besides, the likes of me, I couldn't stand with hand on heart and say I'd earned it, could I? Never earned a thing in all me life. What have I ever done to prove me worth, or where I could at least say as I'd made a difference? Nothing. If I had, if I could hold me head up with the better folk, perhaps I'd think again, but I don't reckon as that's very likely now. I should have had a go at acting decent back when I still had a chance, because it's hard to see how I shall have the opportunity again."

His host went to the kitchen for more tea, continuing their conversation in a loud voice so that Fred could hear, which wasn't really necessary. Freddy noticed that no trail was left behind between the living room and kitchen, contrary to what the coppers had once told him. Obviously, for people like Fred's mate that's what one would expect, but Freddy sometimes found himself so caught up in their conversations that he would forget the one big difference that there was between them: Freddy was no longer living there in

Scarletwell Street. That's why he'd leave scruffy traces in his wake, and why they wouldn't. Several moments passed, and then Fred's chum came back out of the kitchen to sit down again, across the table from him.

"Freddy, you can never tell what twists and turns affairs will take, one minute to another, one day to the next. It's like the houses that there used to be down here, with unexpected bends and doors that led off Lord knows where. But all the pokey little nooks and stairways had their purpose in the builders' plan. I sound like Fiery Phil giving a sermon, don't I? What I'm saying is, you never knew what's going to turn up. There's only one chap knows all that. If ever you get tired of your rough sleeping, Freddy, you know you can always come round here and just go straight upstairs. In the meantime, try not to be so hard upon yourself. There were far worse than you, Fred. The old man, for one. The things that you did, in the final reckoning, none of them look so bad. Everyone played their parts the way they had to, Freddy. Even if they were a crooked stair-rail, it might be that they were leading somewhere. Oh. I've just thought!" This was said springing up from the chair as though in startlement. "I can't make you a tea, but we can go out back and you can look to see if there's new sprouts since last time, so that you could have a bite to eat."

This was more like it. Talking about past crimes always got him down, but that was nothing that a bit of grub wouldn't put right. He followed his long-time companion through the kitchen and into the small bricked-in back yard outside, where he was pointed to the juncture of the north and west walls.

"I caught something moving from the corner of my eye when I was out here putting rubbish in the ashbox just the other night. I know what that's a sign of, and so you might want to take a gander in between the bricks, see if there's any roots there."

Freddy took a close look at the spot to which he'd been directed. It was very promising. Poking up onto Freddy's level from a crevice in the mortar was a stiff and spidery protuberance he knew to be the root bulb of a Puck's Hat, though of what variety he couldn't tell as yet. It wasn't one of the dark grey kinds, he at least knew that much. From behind him came his mate's voice, high and quivery with age but still with backbone to it.

"Can you see one? You've got better eyes for it than me."

"Aye, there's one here. It was its blossoms what you saw the other night. Hang on a minute and I'll prise it out."

Fred reached into the crack with grubby fingertips and pinched the bulb off at its thick white stem, where it led down into the brickwork. One of a Puck's Hat's peculiarities was that it had the root bulb up above, and then the individual shoots grew down into whatever spaces they could find. There was that faint squeal as he plucked it, more a tinny hum that swelled up for a moment then was gone. He fished it out so he could take a closer look at it.

Big as a person's hand, it was a mostly white variety, with the stiff radi-ating outgrowths, each a different length, all sprung like spokes out from the centre. Cupping it beneath his nose he was delighted to discover that it was a type that had a scent, both delicate and sweet, one of the only things that he could really smell these days. Up close like that, he even saw its colours.

What it looked like from above was about thirteen naked women, all two inches tall with all their crowns joined up together in the vegetable's centre, where there was a tuft of orange hair, a small bright spot to mark the mid-dle with the tiny heads grown out of it like petals. The small females sort of overlapped, so that there were three eyes, two noses and two little mouths for every pair of faces. How it worked, around the centre orange spot there was a ring of minuscule blue eyes, like flecks of glass. Spaced out beyond these were the gooseflesh bumps that were the rings of noses, then the dark pink slits, almost too small to see, that were the mouths. The individual necks branched out, then grew into the shoulders of the next girl-shape in line, leaving a little hole between their fused-together shoulders and their fused-together ears. Again, there were three arms for each two bodies, these again arranged to form an outlying concentric ring, each slender limb dividing into tiny fingers at its tip. The women's bodies from the neck down were the longest sections of the plant, with one per head, forming the outmost band of petals, each one bifurcated into tiny wavering legs, small dots of red fluff at their junctions forming yet another decorative circle in the exquisite symmetrical design.

He turned it over so that he could see the ring of buttocks and the clus-ter of transparent petals like the wings of dragonflies arranged around the pinched-off stalk there in the centre. From behind, his friend enquired again.

"I know that you can't show it to me, but if you could let me know what sort of Puck's Hat that it was I'd be obliged. Is it a spaceman one, a fairy one or something else?"

"It's fairies, this one. It's a beauty, too, a good eight incher, one side to the other. This will keep me going for a while, and you won't have to worry about boiling a four-minute egg then finding half a day has gone. You know what these can be like when it comes to missing out a lump of time. It's all because of how they grow."

He took a bite. It had the texture he remembered pears as having, but its taste was wonderful, a perfumed flavour much like rosehips but with more dimension to it, waking taste buds that he hadn't known were there before. He felt the energy, the sort of uplift that they gave you, running into him with the delicious juice. Thank heavens it had been a fairy Puck's Hat, nice and ripe, and not the ashy-coloured spaceman ones that were all hard and bitter, and that should be left to sweeten into fairies, which were more mature. It was a lovely meal, assuming that you didn't mind spitting a couple dozen of the hard and tasteless little eye-pips out. Given a bit of luck and if the pips should lodge in the right place you could have a whole ring of Puck's Hats here in six months' time, although he thought he'd best not tell his friend that.

They went back inside together, one to make another cup of tea, the other one to finish wolfing down his Puck's Hat. They went on with chatting about this and that, and Fred was shown the photo album. Some of the old snapshots with their small black corner hinges were in colour, but Fred couldn't tell which ones. There was a nice one of a young girl in her twenties standing on a lawn looking a bit depressed with buildings in the background like a hospital or school. They talked until the wall-clock in the hallway struck the hour for two, when Freddy thanked his host for sparing him the time and for the bite to eat, then went through the front door again, back into Scarletwell Street.

Feeling much the better for a bit of lunch, Fred fairly shot up Scarletwell Street, past the unbelievably tall flats up at the top there and towards the Mayorhold. A Puck's Hat the size that one had been would keep Fred feeling perky and invigorated for a fortnight. With a certain swagger he ignored the crossing barrier surrounding the wide traffic junction and strode out across it, through the hurtling cars. Motors be blowed, he thought. He was too old to stand there hesitating at the curbside like a little kid, although he stepped back when Jem Perrit's horse and cart went by towards Horsemarket, because that was leaving trails behind like Fred himself was, fading pictures of itself in different stages of its motion as it trotted heedlessly amongst the trucks and four-wheel drives. The horse and cart was part of Freddy's world, and though collision with it could not possibly cause a fatality, there might be other complications that were best avoided. Freddy stood there in the middle of the vehicle-flow and watched the carthorse saunter off downhill towards Marefair, Jem Perrit drunk and fast asleep there at its reins, trusting his horse to get him home to Freeschool Street before he woke. Shaking his head in admiration and amusement at how long Jem Perrit's horse had been performing that trick now, Fred carried on towards the corner where the widened sweep of Silver Street ran down to form part of the junction.

Where the Mayorhold's major shops and stores had been, the Co-op and the butcher's, Botterill's newsagent's and all of those, was one of those new car parks that had all the layers, with its concrete painted ugly yellow, or so Fred had heard. Around the place's bottom down the Mayorhold side was a great bank of thorn-hedge, just there on the corner where poor Georgie Bumble's office was once visible. There was a lot of overgrowth built up since Georgie's time, and Fred would have to roll his sleeves up if he wanted to get stuck in and dig back to it. Stepping out of the busy road into the thicket with the wedding-cake tiers of the car park looming up above him Freddy started pushing all the present stuff to one side so he could get through. First there was hedgerow which you could just shove away like smoke, and then machinery, compressors and cement mixers and diggers you could squash and bend to one side as though made of coloured modelling clay. At last, after he'd dug through all of this Freddy uncovered the big open granite doorway leading into Georgie's office, with the name of the establishment carved elegantly in the stone above the entrance: GENTLEMEN. Brushing away the smears of stale time from his coat-sleeves that he'd picked up unavoidably while rooting through the stuff, Fred wandered in over the chessboard of the cracked wet floor tiles, calling out into the smelly echo.

"Georgie? Anybody home? You've got a visitor."

There were two cubicles that ran off from the main urinal area with its trickling walls and peeling V.D. warning poster that portrayed a man, a woman and those feared initials in black silhouette against what Fred remembered was a sore red background. One of the two cubicles had its door closed, the other open to reveal an overflowing bowl with turds and toilet paper on the floor. That was the way that people dreamed these sorts of places, Freddy knew. He'd dreamed of awful brimming lavatories like this himself when he'd been back there in the life, on one of his Twenty-five Thousand Nights, looking for somewhere he could have a wee and finding only horror-holes like this. It was the way that people's dream-ideas built up like sediment across the years that made the place the mess it was, as far as Freddy was concerned. It wasn't Georgie's fault. From behind the closed door there came the sound of someone spitting, then that of the toilet flushing, then the rattling of the sliding lock on the zinc door as it was opened from inside.

A monk emerged, gaunt, mournful and clean-shaven with the bald patch on the top, the tonsure. From where Fred was standing he looked like one of the Clooneys or whatever they were called from up St. Andrew's. He marched straight past Fred without acknowledging his presence and out through the public toilet's entrance into all the tangled years and instants blocking off the opening like briars. The monk had gone, leaving still pictures of himself in black and white behind that faded into nothing within moments. Fred glanced back at the now-open cubicle the man had just vacated, to see Georgie Bumble shuffling out in the monk's wake with an apologetic half-a-smile, trailing his own plume of self-portraits.

"Hello, Freddy. Long time no see. Sorry about all that, by the way. You caught me just when I was doing business. Well, if you can call it business. Have you seen this, what he give me? Tight-fisted old bugger."

Georgie held his hand out, opening the stubby fingers with their chewed-down nails to show Fred a small Puck's Hat, three inches across at most. It was nowhere near ripe yet, with the circle made from blue-grey foetus shapes that folk said looked like spacemen from another planet barely formed. The large black beads that were the eyes were an inedible and glittering ring around the central dimple, where no tuft of coloured hair as yet had grown, a bad sign when it came to judging higher plants of this type. It was how you knew if they were ready to be eaten yet. If Georgie had done that old monk a favour for a morsel this size, he'd been had more ways than one.

"You're dead right, Georgie. It's a titchy little thing. Still, they're all Frenchies, that St. Andrew's crowd, so what can you expect? If they were half as godly as they made out then they wouldn't still be down here with all us lot, would they?"

Georgie looked down mournfully with his big watery eyes at the unappetizing delicacy in his palm. There was the plaintive dripping of a cistern, amplified by the unusual acoustics with the echo racing off in more directions or else bouncing back from greater distances than were apparent in the dank, restricted space.

"Yes. That's a good point, Freddy. That's a very good point. On the other hand, they're all the trade I get these days, the monks."

Dressed in his shiny suit with rope run through its loops to make a belt, the shabby little moocher bit a stringy gobbet from the sour grey higher vegetable and made a face. He chewed for a few moments, with his rubbery and doleful features working comically around the bitter mouthful, then spat out a hard black glassy eye big as an apple seed into the trough of the urinal. Lazily, it drifted down the foaming channel to bring up against the round white cakes of disinfectant nestling beside the drain, where it gazed up indifferently at Fred and Georgie.

"But you're right, though. Bleeding hypocrites, they are. This is the vilest Hag's Tit as I've ever tasted." Georgie took another bite and chewed it, made another face and spat another bead of jet into the glazed white gutter. Hag's Tit was a different name by which Puck's Hats were sometimes known, along with Bedlam Jenny, Whispers-in-the-Wood or Devil Fingers. They were all the same thing, and however bad it tasted Freddy knew that Georgie Bumble would make sure to eat the whole affair and not waste any, just because the things were such a pick-me-up. Why that should be, Fred didn't know. He had a notion that it was connected to the way the bulb's shoots seemed to interfere with time, so people would miss out whole hours or days while they were dancing with the fairies or whatever they imagined they were doing. Just as lower vegetables sucked up goodness from the substance of whatever they were growing in, perhaps the Puck's Hat also sucked up time, or at least time as people knew it? And if that were true, perhaps that was what gave rough sleepers like Freddy himself or Georgie such a boost. Perhaps to their sort, human time was like a vitamin they didn't get enough of these days, since they left the life. Perhaps that was why they were all so bloody pale. Fred thought about these things during spare, idle moments, of which he had clearly known more than a few.

Georgie had chewed and swallowed his last bite, expectorated his last spaceman's eyeball and was now wiping his rosebud lips, already looking livelier. Freddy was starting to feel cooped up in the twilight lavatories, and could see faint blurred images of modern cars in rows beneath tube-lighting through the V.D. poster. He decided to bring up the reason why he'd called at Georgie's office, so he could discharge his duties and get out of there the sooner.

"Why I dropped by, Georgie, was I'd just been round to visit them on Scarletwell Street corner, and they mentioned they'd not seen you in a while and were concerned, so I said I'd pop in and make sure everything was hunky-dory."

Georgie pursed his lips into a little smile, a twinkle in his liquid eyes as he began to feel the mild effect of the unripe Puck's Hat that he'd ingested.

"Well now, bless the both of you for thinking after me, but I'm all right, same as I ever was. I don't get out much anymore, because of all the traffic on the Mayorhold these days. It's a nightmare to me now, out there, but with a bit of luck in a few hundred years or so the lot of it will be a wasteland or a bombsite. You'll get Rose Bay Willow Herb and that come up where it's all bollards and keep-left signs now, and then perhaps I'll get out a bit more. It's good of you to look in, Freddy, and send my regards to them what keeps the corner, but I'm fine. Still sucking off me monks, but other than that I've got no complaints."

There didn't seem much Fred could say to that, so he told Georgie that he'd not leave it so long next time before he paid a visit, and they both shook hands as best they could. Fred pushed his way out of the toilet's entrance through the pliable machines and dump-trucks, through the bramble months and years with thorns made out of painful moments, out into the fuming thunder of the Mayorhold and the shadow of the multi-storey car park at his back. With the remembered reek of Georgie's office still about him, and despite the fug of vehicle exhaust that hung above the junction, Freddy wished that he could draw a good deep breath. It got you down, seeing the way some of them muddled through these days, just sticking in their little dens or in the shadow-places where their dens once were. Still, that was Freddy's duties finished with, so now he could keep his appointment down in Bath Street. He'd see Patsy, and put Georgie Bumble and the day as it had thus far been behind him. But you couldn't, he reflected, could you? No one could put anything behind them, draw a line beneath it and pretend that it had gone away. No deed, no word, no thought. It was still there back down the way, still there forever. Fred considered this as he strode out into the stream of motorcars, dragging grey snapshots of his previous several seconds like a tail behind him, off to get his how's-your-father.

On the Mayorhold's far side, at its southwest corner, he went through the barrier and straight down Bath Street, feeling stirrings in the phantom remnants of his trousers that were brought on either by the Puck's Hat or the thought of Patsy. As he reached the entrance to the gardens he slowed down, knowing that if he were to get back to the place where she was waiting for him, further digging was required. He glanced up the deserted avenue between the two halves of the flats, with its grass verges and brick walls with half-moon openings to either side, towards the path or steps or ramp or whatever it was at present, up there at the top. The scroungey-looking stray that he'd seen in St. Mary's Street a little earlier that day was still around, sniffing the curbing bordering the grass. Fred steeled himself in preparation, then began to shoulder his way into all the rubbish piled up right back to the fifties. He pushed through the glory days of Mary Jane and further still, back through the blackout and the sirens, folding pre-war washing lines and cockle-sellers to one side like reeds until the sudden stench and lack of visibility told Freddy that he'd reached his destination, back in the high twenties where somebody else's wife was waiting for him.

What the smell was, just as with the veil of smoke so you could barely see your hand before your face, all that was the Destructor, just downhill to Freddy's right and towering up above him so he couldn't bear to look at it. Keeping his eyes fixed straight ahead, Freddy began to walk across the patch of designated recreation area with its swings, its slide and maypole, that extended where the central avenue of Bath Street flats had been moments before, or where it would be nearly eighty years from now, depending how you saw things. This grim playground had been called 'The Orchard', Freddy knew, but always with a certain irony and bitterness. Off to each side of him the blocks of flats in dark red brick had disappeared, and where the border walls with half-moon holes had been were now two scatterings of terraced houses facing one another from across the intervening scrub-ground with its choking pall of smoke.

Approaching him through this, along the beaten path that ran across the middle of the hard, bare ground from Castle Street to Bath Street was the vague shape of a figure walking, pushing a perambulator. Freddy knew that when this had come closer to him through the sooty air it would turn out to be young Clara, Joe Swan's missus, lucky bugger. Fred knew that it would be Clara because she was always here, pushing her baby carriage down between the swings and wooden roundabout, when he came to see Patsy. She was always here because she'd been here on that afternoon the first time when this happened between him and Patsy Clarke. The only time it happened, come to think of it. As she stepped from the acrid fogbank with her baby carriage, pushing it along the packed dirt path towards him, Clara Swan and Clara's baby daughter in the pushchair left no images behind them. No one did down here. This was where everyone was still alive.

Clara was beautiful, a lovely woman in her thirties, slender as a rake and with long auburn hair that Joe Swan had once said his wife could sit on when it wasn't wound up in a bun as it was now, topped with a small black bonnet that had artificial flowers on the band. She brought the carriage to a halt when she saw Fred and recognised her husband's pal, dropping her chin and looking up at him from underneath her lowered brow, eyes disapproving and yet still compassionate. Fred knew that this was only partly something she put on for his and her amusement. Clara was a very upright woman and would have no nonsense or tomfoolery. Before she'd married Joe she'd worked in service, like a lot of them lived down the Boroughs had before they were let go, at Althorp House for the Red Earl or somewhere of that sort, and she'd picked up the manners and the bearing that the better-off expected of her. Not that she was snooty, but that she was fair and honest and sometimes looked down a bit on those who weren't, though not unkindly. She knew that most people had a reason for the way they were, and when it came to it she didn't judge.

"Why, Freddy Allen, you young rogue. What are you up to round here? No good, I'll be bound."

This was what Clara always said when they met here, towards the Bath Street end of the dirt path from Castle Street, upon this smoky afternoon.

"Ooh, you know me. Trying me luck as always. Who's that in the pram you've got there? Is that young Doreen?"

Clara was smiling now despite herself. She liked Fred really and he knew she did beneath all that Victorian disapproval. With a bird-like nod of her head to one side she summoned Freddy over to the pram so he could take a look within, where Doreen, Joe and Clara's year-old daughter, lay asleep, her mouth plugged by her thumb. She was a lovely little thing, and you could tell Clara was proud of her, the way she'd called him over for a look. He complimented her upon the baby, as he always did, and then they chatted for a while, as ever. Finally they reached the part where Clara said that some folk had got jobs at home that needed to be done, and that she'd wish him a good afternoon and let him get on with whatever shady business he was up to.

Freddy watched her push the pram away from him into the smoke that, naturally, was thickest over Bath Street where the tower of the Destructor stood, and then he turned and carried on along the path to Castle Street, waiting for Patsy to call out to him the way she had that first time, how she called out to him every time.

"Fred! Freddy Allen! Over here!"

Patsy stood at the entrance to the little alley that ran down by one side of the right-hand houses near the Bath Street end, and led through to the back yards of the buildings, all in a big square there to the rear of the Destructor. In so far as Fred could see her through the rolling billows, Patsy looked a treat, a curvy little blonde lass with a bit of meat on her, the way Fred liked them. She was older than what Freddy was, not that it put him off at all, and had a sort of knowing look as she stood smiling in the alley mouth. Perhaps because it was so smoky or because the further back you went the harder it was keeping it all straight, but Freddy could see a faint flicker around Patsy, where the alley would change for a second to a railed brick archway, its black iron railings passing down through Patsy's head and torso, then change back again to the rear garden walls of houses, with their bricks a brighter orange yet far dirtier than those comprising Bath Street flats had been. He waited for his view of her to properly solidify, then walked towards her jauntily, his hands deep in his raggedy-arsed trouser pockets and his hat jammed on his head to hide his bald patch. Here in 1928 some of his other flaws had been alleviated ... he'd no beer belly down here for instance ... but his hair had started going during Fred's mid-twenties, which is why he'd worn the hat since then.

When he got near enough to Patsy so that they could see each other properly he stopped and grinned at her, the way he had that first time, only now it had more meanings to it. That first time, it had just meant "I know you fancy me", whereas it now meant something like "I know you fancy me because I've lived this through a thousand times and we're both dead now, and it's actually quite funny how the pair of us keeping coming back down here, here to this moment." That was how it was with every part of the exchange between them, always just the same and word for word, yet with new ironies behind the phrases and the gestures that had come with their new situation. Take what he was just about to say, for one example:

"Hello, Patsy. We'll have to stop meeting like this."

That had been a bit of fun, first time he'd said it. Truthfully, they'd seen each other once or twice across a pub lounge or a market stall, but putting it like that and saying that they must stop meeting, as if they were having an affair already, that had been a way of joking with the subject while at least bringing the idea up into their conversation. Now, though, the remark had other connotations. Patsy beamed at him and played with one dishwater lock as she replied.

"Well, suit yourself. I'll tell you this much though, if you sail past me one more time then you'll have missed your chance. I shan't be waiting here forever."

There it was again, another double meaning that they'd both been unaware of the first time they'd said these words. Fred grinned at Patsy through the smoke.

"Why, Patsy Clarke, you ought to be ashamed. And you a married woman, with your 'til death do us part and all of that."

She didn't drop her smile or take her eyes from his.

"Oh, him. He's out of town, working away. It's getting so I can't remember the last time I saw him."

This had been exaggeration when she'd told Fred that originally, but it wasn't anymore. Frank Clarke, her husband, was no longer drifting round the lower levels of the Boroughs in the way both Fred and Patsy were. He'd moved on to a better life, had Frank. Climbed up the ladder, so to speak. It was all right for him. He'd nothing troubling his conscience that was keeping him down here, whereas Fred had all sorts of things holding him back, as he'd explained down Scarletwell Street. As for Patsy, she had Fred, along with several others from those parts. She'd been a generous woman with that generous body, and her countless sticky afternoons with all their guilty pleasures were like millstones that had weighed her down, preventing her departure. Looking up at Freddy now she wiped her smile away, replacing it with a more serious expression that was almost challenging.

"I've not been eating right, with him not here. I've not had a hot meal for ages."

This, with its unwitting irony, was possibly a reference to the Puck's Hats, staple diet for lower Boroughs residents like Fred and Patsy. She went on.

"I was just thinking how long it had been since I'd had something warm inside me. Knowing you, you're probably feeling peckish around now yourself. Why don't you come through to me kitchen, just up here? We'll see if we find anything to satisfy our cravings."

Fred was on the bone now, good and proper. Hearing steps on the dirt path behind him he craned round his head in time to see young Phyllis Painter, all of eight years old, skip past across the recreation ground towards its Bath Street end. She glanced at him and Patsy and smirked knowingly then carried on along the pathway and was gone into the rolling sepia clouds, off to her house down Scarletwell Street, just beside the school. Fred couldn't tell if the girl's smile had been because she knew what him and Patsy would be getting up to, or if little Phyllis was a revenant revisiting the scene like he was, and was smiling because she knew how this was a loop that Fred and Patsy Clarke were trapped within, however willingly. Phyll Painter and her gang ran wild across the Boroughs' length and breadth and depth and whenth. They scampered round the twenty-fives where that black woman with the golly hairdo and the nasty scar above her eye did all her work, the one they called a saint, or else her and her hooligans cut through his mate's house up to Spring Lane Terrace in the dead of night on their adventures. They might well be scrumping Puck's

Hats all the way down here around the twenty-eights, but on the other hand Phyll Painter would be eight years old in normal living time around this year and hadn't had her gang with her when she went skipping past just then. It was most likely Phyllis Painter as a living child, or at least as his memory of her upon that bygone afternoon, rather than as the little troublemaker she'd turned into since she got out of the life.

He turned back towards Patsy, his face pointing now the same way as his cock was. He delivered his last unintentionally slanted line … "I never say no, you know me" … before she dragged him up the alleyway, both laughing now, and through into the back yard of the third house to their right, with next to it the slaughter-yard behind the butcher's, Mr. Bullock, his shop situated down by the Destructor. From the sound of it, some pigs were being hung and bled next door which would, as ever, cover up the noises he and Patsy made. She flung the back door open and pulled Fred into the kitchen, reaching down and tugging him along by his stiff prick through his rough pants and trousers once they'd got inside, away from prying eyes. They went through like this to the cramped-up, lightless living room, where Patsy had a coal fire burning in the fireplace. It had been a brisk March day as Fred remembered it.

He went to kiss her, knowing that she'd say his bad breath smelled like something died. It wasn't just that some things that they'd said that afternoon turned out to have another meaning. It was all of them. At any rate, Patsy was firm about the kissing, as she had been all the other times.

"Don't take it personal. I never can be doing with a lot of soppy stuff like that. Just get it out and stick it in, that's what I always say."

They were both breathing harder, or at least appearing to be doing so. Fred had known Patsy since they'd both been grey-kneed kids at Spring Lane School together. Lifting her skirts up around her waist she turned to face the fireplace, looking back at Fred across her shoulder, her face flushed. She wasn't wearing any knickers underneath the skirt.

"Go on, Fred. Be a devil."

Fred supposed he must be. Look at where he was. She turned her face away from him again and placed her hands flat on the wall to each side of the mirror that was hung above the mantelpiece. He could see both her face and his, both in the glass and both of them excited. Freddy fumbled with his fly-buttons a moment, then released his straining member. Spitting a grey substance out into his grubby palm he rubbed it on the gleaming, bulbous tip then pushed the length of it up Patsy's pouting fanny, drenched already with ghost-fluids of its own. He clutched her roughly by her waist for leverage then started slamming himself into her, as forcefully as he could manage. This was just as wonderful as Fred remembered it. No more, no less. It's just that the experience had faded with each repetition until almost all the joy was gone from it, like an old tea towel that had been wrung out time after time until the pattern on it disappeared. It was better than nothing, just. At the same moment that he always did he took his right hand off of Patsy's hip and sucked the thumb to make it wet before he shoved it up her bumhole to the knuckle. She was shouting now, above the squealing from the yard next door.

"Oh, God. Oh, fuck me, I'm in heaven. Fuck me, Freddy. Fuck the life out of me. Oh. Oh, fuck."

Freddy glanced down from Patsy's straining, labouring face caught in the mirror to where his thick bristling organ ... these had been the days ... was glistening grey like wet sand in a seaside photo, thrusting in and out of Patsy's slurping, fur-fringed hole. He didn't know which sight he liked the best, not even after all these years, and so kept looking back and forth between them. He was glad that from this angle he could never see his own face in the mirror, since he knew that he'd look daffy with his hat still on, and that he'd laugh and that would put him off his stroke.

It was just then that Freddy noticed something from the corner of his eye. He couldn't turn his head to look straight on because he hadn't done so on that first occasion. Whatever this was, it hadn't happened then. This was some novelty that might spice up the old routine.

He soon determined that it was the flickering effect he'd noticed back when Patsy had first greeted him, stood in the alley that kept turning to an arch with railings. It was something that would happen sometimes when you'd dug your way back to the past. It was as if the present had you on elastic and kept trying to pull you back, so that you'd see bits of it breaking in to interrupt whichever time it was you'd burrowed back to. In this instance, out the corner of his eye, Freddy could see a pretty, skinny little brown girl sitting in an armchair where the straps had busted underneath. She had her hair in ridges that had bald stripes in between, and had a shiny sort of raincoat on although she was indoors. What was the strangest thing was that she sat there staring straight at him and Patsy with a little smile and one hand resting casually down in her lap, turned inwards, so it looked as if she could not only see them, but as if she was enjoying it. The thought that they were being watched by a young girl gave Freddy a mild extra thrill, although he knew it wouldn't bring him off too soon, before they'd got to the appointed time. Besides, a guilty feeling that related to her age offset the slight jolt of excitement that the coloured lass had given him. She looked about sixteen or seventeen, despite her rough condition, and was barely yet out of her childhood. Luckily, the next time Fred had rocked back far enough in fucking Patsy so that he could catch a glimpse out of the corner of his eye, the girl had gone and he could concentrate on doing the job properly.

Where had he seen her recently, that girl? He'd known her face from somewhere, he was sure. Had he bumped into her earlier today? No. No, he knew now where it was. It had been yesterday, round dinnertime. He'd been under the portico at Peter's Church. There'd been a boy in there, a living one, asleep and drunk, so Freddy had crept in and got down next to him. It was a young lad, mousy-haired, with a big baggy woollen jumper and those shoes what they called bumpers on his feet, and Freddy thought the sleeper wouldn't mind if he lay down beside him just to listen to him breathe, a sound Fred missed. He'd been there for an hour or two when he heard the high heels approaching down Marefair and past the church-front, getting closer. He'd sat up and seen her walking past, the girl he'd just seen sitting in her phantom armchair, watching him and Patsy. She weren't looking at him as she walked along, her bare brown legs just swinging back and forth, but something told him that she might have been, and he decided he'd best leave before she looked again. That's where he'd seen her. Yesterday, and not today.

His moment was approaching. Patsy started screaming as she had her climax.

"Yes! Oh yes! Oh, fuck, I'm dying! Fuck, I'm going to die! Oh God!"

Freddy was thinking of the brown girl with her long legs and her scandalously tiny skirt as he shot three or four cold jets of ectoplasm into Patsy. For the life of him, or at least so to speak, he was unable to remember what he had been thinking about when he'd shot his load that first time, when his juice had still been warm. He took his thumb out of her arse and slid his dripping and deflating penis out of her, reflecting as he did so that while what he squirted from his cock these days was a much cooler liquid than his seed had been, it looked about the same. He tucked the gleaming, sagging weapon back inside his pants and trousers, buttoning the fly, while Patsy pulled her skirts down and composed herself. She turned towards him from the mantelpiece and mirror. There were only one or two more lines of dialogue to be said.

"God, that was nice ... although you needn't think that you can come round every afternoon. That was a one-off opportunity. Now, come along, you'd best be getting off before the neighbours start their nosing everywhere. Most likely I'll be seeing you round and about."

"See you around, then, Patsy."

That was that. Fred went out through the kitchen and the back yard, where the noise of all the slaughter from across the high brick wall had ended. Opening the back yard's gate he stepped into the alleyway, then walked along it to the smoke-screened recreation area, the Orchard. This was where he always stepped out of his memories and into his existence in the present, standing here outside the alley-mouth and looking at the hazy children's playground with its slide and maypole looming dimly through the churning smog. Freddy's own maypole wasn't as impressive now as it had been just a few minutes back, when he'd been out here last. When he looked down he noticed that his beer belly was coming back. With a resigned tut, Freddy let the scenery around him snap back to the way it was upon May 26th, 2006. There was a giddy rush of melting walls and swings, of sooty brick that foamed up out of nothing to construct the flats, then Freddy stood once more beside the gated archway, looking out across the grass and empty central avenue to where the scruffy dog that he'd seen earlier was still about. To Freddy it looked agitated, trotting back and forth, as if it hadn't moved its bowels in quite a time.

Fred sympathised. That was, surprisingly, one of the things he missed the most, that blessed feeling of relief when all the smelly poisons and the badness in a person just fell out in a great rush and could be flushed away. What Fred had, he supposed, was like a constipation of the spirit. That's what kept him down here and prevented him from moving on, the fact he couldn't let it go like that and just be rid of the whole stinking lot of it. The fact that Freddy carried it around inside him, all his shit, and with each decade that went by it made him feel more sluggish and more irritable. In another century, he doubted he'd feel like himself at all.

He moved across the grass and floated up the avenue towards the ramp, passing the scabby dog, which jumped back and barked twice at him before deciding that he was no danger and resuming its uneasy trotting back and forth. Entering Castle Street up at the ramp's top, Freddy went along towards where the no-entry joined it with Horsemarket, then turned right. He might have promised Mary Jane he'd call by at the Jolly Smokers later on, but that could wait. He'd go and watch his billiards first, along the centre down in Horseshoe Street where he'd sent that old chaplain earlier.

He glided down Horsemarket and remembered, with a pang of shame, how once before the present dual carriageway was here it had been fancy houses, owned by doctors and solicitors and all the like. The shame he felt now was occasioned by the lovely daughters that some of the gentlemen who lived down there had raised. One in particular, a doctor's girl called Julia that Freddy had developed quite a thing for, never talking to her, only watching from a distance. He'd known that she'd never talk to him, not in a million years. That's why he'd thought of raping her.

He burned, to think about it now, although he'd never seen it through. Just the idea that he'd considered it, had gone as far as planning how he'd wait until she'd crossed Horsemarket on her way to her job in the Drapery one morning, then would grab her as she took her customary route up by St. Katherine's Gardens. He had even risen at the crack of dawn one day and gone up there to wait, but when he saw her he'd come to his senses and had run off, crying to himself. He'd been eighteen. That was one of the hard and heavy stools he kept inside him that he couldn't pass, the heaviest and hardest.

He crossed over Marefair at the bottom, waiting for the lights to change from grey to grey so he could walk across with all the other people, though he didn't need to. He went over Horseshoe Street's continuation of the growling metal waterfall that ran down from Horsemarket, then turned right and headed for the centre and its billiard hall. As Freddy did so he passed by and partly through a tubby chap with curly white hair and a little beard, with eyes that seemed to shift continually from arrogance to furtiveness and back behind his spectacles. This was another one that Freddy recognised and had call to remember. It had been some nights ago, about four in the morning. Freddy had been swirling lazily along a pre-dawn Marefair, just enjoying the desertion when he'd heard a man's voice calling out to him, afraid and trembling.

"Hello? Hello there? Can you hear me? Am I dead?"

Freddy had turned to find out who was interrupting his night's wanderings and seen the little fat man, the same one he'd just this moment brushed through in broad daylight up on Gold Street corner. The bespectacled and bearded fifty-something had been standing, in the small hours, on the traffic-free deserted hump of Black Lion Hill, dressed only in his vest, his wristwatch and his underpants. He'd stood there staring anxiously at Freddy, looking lost and frightened. Fred had thought, just for a moment, that the man had only lately got out of the life and that's why he seemed so confused, stood there amongst the lamplight and the shadows with the street and buildings curdling in and out of different centuries around him. Then, when he'd took note of how the little berk was dressed, in just his under-things, Fred knew that this was someone dreaming. The rough sleepers that you got down here were all dressed how they best remembered themselves dressing, and even the ones who'd not been dead ten minutes wouldn't waddle round in old stained underpants. If they were in the nude or in their pants or their pyjamas then it was a safe bet they were folk still in the life, who'd stumbled accidentally on these parts in their dreams.

Fred, at the time, had took a dislike to the bloke who'd interrupted his nice solitary stroll, and thought he'd put the wind up him. You didn't often get the chance to make a real impression on the ones still down there in the strangles of existence and, besides, the self-important little pisspot had been asking for it. Giving this consideration as he trickled down the slope of Horseshoe Street towards the billiard hall, he knew it had been mean, the prank he'd pulled upon the dreaming man that night, rushing towards the fellow in a flailing, terrifying cloud of after-images, though it still made him chuckle when he thought about it. That was life, he finally concluded. People shouldn't just go launching into it if they can't take a joke.

He slipped into the billiard hall unnoticed and then found his way out back and went upstairs to the top floor. From here he went upstairs again, went properly upstairs, using what types like him referred to as a crook-door which in this case, unbeknownst to the establishment's living proprietors, was hidden in the corner of an upstairs lumber room. Just past the crook-door's four-way hinge there was a Jacob Flight with tired old wooden steps that Fred knew, ultimately, led up to the landings. He began to mount it anyway, knowing the place he wanted would be only halfway up. He wouldn't have to venture within shouting distance of the higher balconies, the Attics of the Breath. He wouldn't have to feel he'd got above himself.

The Jacob Flight, a seemingly deliberately inconvenient construction somewhere in between a boxed-in staircase and a roofer's ladder, was as awkward and exhausting to ascend as ever. All the treads were no more than three inches deep while all the risers were a good foot-and-a-half. This meant you had to climb the stairs just as you would a ladder, sort of upright on all fours, using your hands and feet. But on the other hand you were enclosed by rough white plaster walls to either side, the stairway being no more than four feet across, with just above your head a steeply sloping ceiling, also in white plaster. The ridiculous impracticality of such an angle to the stairway made it seem like something from a dream, which Fred supposed it was. Someone's dream, somewhere, sometime. On the ledge-thin wooden steps beneath his toes and fingertips, again a dream-like detail, an old stair-carpet was fitted, brown with the dark writhing of its floral patterns faded nearly to invisibility and held in place by worn brass stair-rods. Puffing from what he assumed was spiritual exertion, Fred climbed up and on.

At last he reached the enterprise's true top deck, the upper billiard hall, and clambered through a trapdoor up into the cluttered, dusty little office room that was to one side of the main floor with its single giant snooker table, extra wide and extra long. From all the footprints through the faintly phosphorescent moon-dust on the dirty floorboards, and the hubbub that he heard beyond in the main hall while opening the creaky office door, it sounded as though he was late. Tonight's game had already started. Freddy tiptoed round the edges of the huge dark games room, trying to put no one off their shot, and joined the small crowd of spectators standing at the room's top end in their allotted area, watching the professionals at play.

That was the way it worked. Those were the house rules. The rough sleepers such as Freddy were quite welcome to come there and be supporters, but not play. Quite frankly, none of them would want to, not with stakes like that. It was sufficiently nerve-wracking just to gaze between your fingers at the contest going on at the vast table over there, in the bright pillar of white light that fell from overhead. Around the baize, the builders who were taking part strode back and forth with confidence, chalking their alabaster cues and warily inspecting tricky angles, pacing up and down along the borders of the table, twenty-five feet long and twelve feet wide. Only the builders were allowed their game of snooker, or whatever the queer version that they played was called. Riff-raff like Freddy simply stood there in a quietly shuffling mob at the far end and made an effort not to gasp or groan too loudly.

There were several in the crowd of onlookers tonight that Freddy recognised. Three-fingered Tunk who'd had his stall up in the Fish Market for one, and Nobby Clark, all got up in the 'Dirty Dick' gear that he'd worn when he was in the bicycle parade, and holding his old placard with the Pears Soap advert on: "Ten years ago I used your soap, and since then I have used no other". How had Nobby ever got that up the Jacob Flight, Fred wondered? He could see Jem Perrit standing at the crowd's perimeter and looking on with relish at the snooker. Freddy thought he'd slide across and join him.

"Hello, Jem. I saw you on the Mayorhold just this dinnertime. Your Bessie was just taking you off home, and you were snoring." Bessie was Jem's spectral horse.

"Aa. I'd bin up the Smokers for me Puck's 'At Punch. I 'spect it was the work as I'd bin doin' as 'ad wore me ayt. That's when yuh seen me on the Merruld."

Jem spoke with the real Northampton twang, the proper Boroughs accent that you didn't really hear no more. Wood-merchant had been how Jem made his living back when he still had a living to be made, a wiry tinker-looking chap with a hook nose, his dark and doleful shape perched up there on his horse and cart behind the reins. These days, Jem's line of work, if not his living, was as an unusually enterprising and phantasmal junkman. Him and Bessie would roam round the county's less substantial territories, with Jem picking up such apparition-artefacts as he should find along his way. These might be old discarded wraith-clothes, or a vivid memory of a tea-chest out of someone's childhood, or they might be things that made no sense at all and were left over from a dream somebody had. Freddy remembered once when Jem had found a sort of curling alpine horn fashioned to look like an elongated and intricately detailed fish, but with a trunk much like an elephant's and things that looked like glass eyes in a stripe down either side. They'd tried to play it, but its bore was stuffed with tight-packed sawdust that had funny plastic trinkets buried in it. It had no doubt joined the other curios there in the front room of the ghost of Jem's house, halfway down the ghost of Freeschool Street. Right now, whenever that might be, because you never really knew up here, the fish-horn was most probably displayed in Jem's front window with the phantom Grenadier's dress jacket and the reminiscences of chairs.

The Puck's Hat Punch that Jem had mentioned was just what it sounded like: a kind of moonshine that could be distilled out of the higher vegetables and ingested. Fred had never fancied it and had heard tales of how it had sent some ex-lifers barmy, so he left it well alone. The thought of being all in bits and barely able to hold any real identity together for the rest of your near-infinite existence sent a shudder up the spine that Fred no longer had. Jem seemed all right, though. Possibly, if Fred was in the mood, then later on when he went up the Jolly Smokers as he'd promised Mary Jane he would when leaving here, he'd give the punch a sniff, see what he thought. One glass would do no harm, and until then he could relax and watch the game.

He stood there in the shadows next to Jem and all the others, sharing in the ragged congregation's reverent silence. Freddy squinted at the house-wide table in its shaft of brilliance and could see immediately why the spectators seemed unusually rapt this evening. The four players gathered round the table weren't just ordinary builders, as if there could be such things as builders that were ordinary. These lads were the four top men, the Master Builders, and that meant tonight's match was important. This was championship stuff.

As they progressed around the massive billiard tale in their bare feet and their long white smocks, the senior builders all left trails behind, though not as Freddy and his friends did. Fred and them had faint grey photos of themselves in an evaporating string they dragged behind them, while the builders left these burned-through white bits in the air where they'd been standing, blazing after-shapes like when you glimpse the sun or stare up at a light-bulb filament, then close your eyes. That was the way that 'ordinary' builders were, but this quartet tonight were ten times worse, especially around their heads where the effect was more pronounced. To tell the truth it hurt to look at them.

The outsized table they were playing on had just four pockets, one up in each corner. Since the table was aligned so it was parallel with the club's walls, Fred knew the corners lined up with what might be seen, approximately, as the corners of the Boroughs. Set into the heavy varnished woodwork of the table just above each pocket was a separate symbol. These were roughly carved into the centre of the wooden discs that decorated the four corners of the table, gouged in a crude style that looked like tramp-marks, yet inlaid with gold as though it were the most adored and cherished holy manuscript. The symbol at the southwest corner was the childish outline of a castle-turret, while there was a big prick such as you might find drawn on a toilet wall up to the north-west end. A loose depiction of a skull marked the northeast, and Fred could see a wonky cross inscribed at the southeast, the corner nearest to where he and Jem were standing. Since it was a bigger table, there were lots more balls in play, and it was lucky that the builders would call out the colour of the ball that they were going for, since all of them were grey or black or white to Freddy and his friends.

If he were honest, Fred had never really understood the game the builders played, not intellectually so that he could explain the rules or anything, although he knew emotionally, down in his stomach so to speak, what it entailed. You had four players taking part at once, and each had their own corner pocket, with the idea being to knock all the balls you could in your own hole while trying to make it difficult for your opponents to pot all the ones they wanted to. Part of the thrill of watching it was all the trails the balls would leave behind them as they rolled across the baize or else collided with each other, ricocheting from the table edge in sharply pointed pentagrams of overlapped trajectory. The other, more anxiety-provoking part of the enjoyment was the way each ball had its own aura, so you knew it stood for someone, or something. It would just come to you inside your thoughts, what each ball meant, while you stood watching as they bounced and skittered round the table. Freddy focussed on the game in hand.

Most of the action seemed to be down to the east side of the table which, as luck would have it, was the side that Freddy and his fellow audience members were all standing on. The western builders, standing near the cock and castle pockets didn't seem like they had much to do just at the moment and were leaning on their cues watching intently as their colleagues at the eastern corners fought it out between them. As Fred watched with permanently bated breath, the builder playing to the southeast pocket, with the cross on, was about to take his shot. Of the four Master Builders that were playing there tonight (and in so far as Freddy knew there were just four in that league anywhere), this one to the southeast was the most popular with all the locals, since the other three apparently came more from out of town and usually weren't seen much hereabouts. The local favourite was a solid, powerful-looking chap who had white hair, although his face was young. His name was Mighty Mike, or so Fred thought he'd heard the fellow called. He was so famous for the way he played a game of snooker that even the lads below down in the life had heard of him, had even put a statue of him on their Guildhall's gable roof.

He leaned across the baize now, low above his cue and squinting down its length towards what even Fred could see was a white ball. This white ball represented, Freddy understood, somebody white, somebody that Fred didn't know who more than likely wasn't from round here. The white-haired builder known as Mighty Mike now called out "Black into cross corner", and then punched his cue once, hard, into the white ball, sending it at high velocity across the breadth of the tremendous table with its trail behind it like a tight-packed string of bright white pearls. It hit the west side of the table ... Freddy thought that it might represent all them what left here for America after the Civil War with Cromwell ... then rebounded into a collision with the black ball that the white-haired artisan had actually been aiming for, a sharp smack ringing round the dimly-lit hall as they hit. The black ball, Freddy understood with sudden clarity, was Charley George, Black Charley, and he felt a great relief that he could not explain when it shot neatly to drop into the south-eastern pocket, where the sloppy, gold-etched cross was carved into the round boss on the table's edge.

The local hero with the chalk-white hair did that thing all the builders did whenever any of them pulled off a successful shot, throwing both fists up in the air above his head, the cue still clutched in one of them, and shouting an exultant "Yes!" before he let them drop once more down to his sides. Since both arms left their hot white trails as they ascended and descended through the space to either side of him, the end effect was that of burning pinions fanning up to form the shapes of brilliant full-spread wings. The odd thing was that all the builders did this every time one of them pulled off a success-ful shot, as though the nature of their game did not involve them being in a competition with each other. All of them, at all four corners of the table, threw their hands up and cried "Yes!" in jubilation as the black ball dropped into the southeast corner pocket. Now it was apparently the builder at the northeast pocket's turn to take his shot, into the corner decorated with a skull.

This builder was a foreigner, and nowhere near so well liked by the home crowd as what Mighty Mike had been. His name was Yuri-something, Fred had heard, and in his face there was a hardness and determination that Fred thought might very well be Russian. He was dark, with shorter hair than the home favourite as he took the long walk round the table's edge to the most favourable position, bent above his cue and sighted down it at the white ball. As with all the builders' voices, when he spoke it had that funny echo on it that broke into little bits and shivered into ringing nothing.

"Grey into skull corner" was a fair approximation of what he'd said.

This was getting interesting. Freddy didn't know quite who the grey ball made him think of. It was someone bald, balder than Freddy, even, and was also someone grey, grey in a moral sense, perhaps even more grey than Freddy was as well. The grim-faced Russian-looking builder took his shot. The white ball streaked with its pale comet-tail across the table to clap loudly up against another ball that Freddy couldn't tell the colour of. Was it the grey one Yuri-something meant to hit, or something else? Whatever colour it might be, this second ball shot off towards the skull-marked corner.

Oh no, Fred thought suddenly. It came into his head just who the hurtling ball was meant to represent. It was the little brown girl with the lovely legs and the hard face who he'd seen by St. Peter's Church the other afternoon and then again today, sat watching him and Patsy at their Bath Street assignation. She was going into the skull pocket, and Fred knew that this meant nothing good for the poor child.

A hand's breadth from the death's-head drop, the hurtling ball impacted with another. This one, Freddy thought, must be the grey ball that the Russian-looking player had declared to be his target. It was knocked into the pocket Yuri-something had intended, whereupon he and the other Master Builders all threw up their arms into a dazzling spread of feathered rays and shouted out in unison their "Yes!" with all its splintering, diminishing reverberations. Just as suddenly, however, all the uproar died away when everybody noticed that the ball Yuri had used to knock the grey into the hole was now itself perched at the northeast pocket's rim. This was the ball that Freddy had associated with the brown girl he'd seen earlier. This wasn't looking good. The grim-faced player who'd just made the shot looked down towards the ball now teetering upon the brink of the skull-pocket that he'd chosen as his own, then looked across the table and at Mighty Mike, the white-haired local champion. The Russian-looking fellow flashed a chilly little smile and then began to pointedly chalk up his cue. Fred hated him. So did the crowd. He was like Mick McManus or a wrestling villain of that nature, someone who the crowd would hiss, except of course they wouldn't in this case, however they might feel. Nobody hissed at builders.

It was now the sturdy white-haired favourite's turn to take his shot, but he looked worried. His opponent clearly planned to knock the threatened ball into his own skull corner pocket with his next go, unless Mighty Mike could somehow move it out of danger. It was so close to the hole, though, that the slightest touch might send it tumbling in. It was a bugger. Fred was so wound up he almost fancied he could feel his heart pound in his chest. The local hero slowly and deliberately walked round the monstrous snooker table to a spot on its far side, where he crouched down to make his fraught and crucial play. Just as he did so he looked straight across the baize and into Freddy's eyes, so that it made him jump. The look was sober, hard and obviously intentional, so that even Jem Perrit, stood beside Fred, turned and whispered to him.

"Watch ayt, Fred. The big man's lookin' at yuh. What are yuh done now?"

Fred numbly shook his head and said that he'd done nothing, at which Jem had cocked his head back and regarded Fred suspiciously and cannily.

"Well, then, what are yer *gunner* do?"

When Fred did not know how to answer this, both men turned back to watch the builder take his shot. He wasn't looking now at Freddy, with his eyes instead fixed firmly on the white ball he was lining up. Amongst the crowd of onlookers you could have heard a pin drop. This is all to do with me, Fred thought. The way he looked at me just now. This is to do with me.

"Brown in cross pocket," said the white-haired Master Builder, although what he really said was a fair bit more complicated.

Straight away his cue shot out – a boxer's jab – and sent the white ball slamming up the table with its after-images a stream of bursting bubbles in its wake. It whacked explosively into a ball whose grey seemed slightly warm so Freddy thought it might be red, and sent it like a rocket so it struck between the brown ball and the death-trap pocket with a noise that sounded like it hurt, so all the rough-shod audience winced at the same time. The brown ball shot into the southeast pocket at the cross-marked corner of the table like a thunderbolt, and everybody in the room, not just the robe-draped foursome that were playing, threw their arms above their heads and shouted "Yes!" all with one voice. The only difference that there was between the players and spectators was that the fanned shapes the former made when they threw up their arms were blinding white, while those the audience made were grey and looked more like the wings of pigeons. Having pulled off this spectacular accomplishment, the white-haired builder looked once more across the table and directly into Freddy's eyes. This time he smiled before he looked away, and an exhilarating shiver ran through Fred from one end to the other.

With the possibilities for play apparently exhausted on the east side of the table, it was now the turn of the two Master Builders on the west side to pick up the game. Freddy had no idea what had just passed between him and the frost-haired player, but he felt excited anyway. He'd watch to see how the remainder of this championship event turned out and then head up the Jolly Smokers on the Mayorhold so that he could keep his word to Mary Jane. Fred grinned and looked around him at the other down-at-heel departed, who were grinning too and nudging one another as they whispered their amazement at the stunning trick shot they'd just seen performed.

This looked like it was going to turn out to be quite a night.

X MARKS THE SPOT

On his return, from the white cliffs he'd walked the Roman road or bumped along on carts where he should be so fortunate. He'd seen a row of hanging-trees like fishing poles set out beside a river, heavy with their catch. He'd seen a great red horse of straw on fire across a murky field, and an agreeable amount of naked teats when herlots mocked him from an inn near London. At another inn a dragon was exhibited, caught in a mud-hole where it sulked, a kind of armoured snake that had been flattened, having dreadful teeth and eyes but legs no longer than a footstool's. He had seen a narrow river dammed by skeletons. He'd seen a parliament of rooks a hundred strong fall on and kill one of their number in amongst the nodding barley rows, and had been shown a yew that had the face of Jesus in its bark. His name was Peter but before that had been Aegburth and in France they'd called him Le Canal, which in their tongue meant channel, for the way he sweated. This was in the year of our Lord eight hundred and ten, about the Vernal Equinox.

He'd ventured half a world and back, stepped on the skirt's edge of Byzantium and walked in the dazed wake of Charlemagne, had sought the shade of heathen domes in Spain with their insides a myriad blue stars and not a cross in sight. Now he was come again to these close and encircling horizons, to this black earth and grey sky, this rough-made land. He was returned to Mercia and to the Spelhoe hundreds, though not yet to Medeshamstede, to his meadow home there in the bogs of Peterboro, where they must by this time think him dead and would already have allowed his cell to pass on to another. He'd get back there soon enough, but in his travels he had taken on an obligation that must first be properly discharged. The content of the jute-cloth bag slung over his right shoulder, where there was a callus grown he had been bearing it so long, must be delivered unto its precise and rightful destination. These were his instructions, given to him by the friend he'd met when in another place, and it was his resolve to see them now fulfilled that led him up this dry mud path, with spear-sharp grass and weeds on every side, towards a distant bridge.

The morning's dew was cold upon his toes, lifting the smell of wool fat from his habit's damp and dragging hem. He went on uncomplaining up the track, amongst the busy hum and flutter, through the green stink of the chest-high vegetation that surrounded him. Ahead, the wooden crosswalk that would bring him to the settlement at Hamtun by its southern end grew slowly closer, slowly bigger, and he spurred his blistered feet, clad in their coarse rope sandals, onward with the notion that their journey was so near its finish, his ten little soldiers with their faces red and raw on this forced march, advancing by one ordered phalanx at a time, step after step, mile after mile. Beneath low cloud the day was close so that inside his robes he streamed, a salty glaze that covered all his back and belly, lukewarm ribbons trickling in the creases of his groin and spooling down the inside of each meaty thigh. A roasted-looking man basting in his own juice he slowly rolled towards the river's edge, grey as a stone against the greens surrounding him.

Not far before the bridge there was a raised-up square of ground with the remains of a square ditch about it, all its lines and edges softened by some centuries of turf and overgrowth. The banked earth seemed a comfy bed where he might rest a while, but he denied himself this idleness. It was, thought Peter, thereabouts of five and twenty paces on each side, and looked to him as though it had once been the footings of a river fort, perhaps as long ago as Roman times when strongholds of that like were strung like pendant charms along the necklace of this River Nenn. Collected in the bottom of the trench was a variety of rubbishes all in a winding seam, such as a ram's skull and a small split leather shoe, some pieces from a broken barrel and a cheap brooch with its clasp gone, here and there amongst the tares, the stagnant pools. Thus passed away the glories of this world, Peter observed, but doubted in his heart that the new Holy Roman Empire would, despite its aspirations, last so long as its more earthly counterpart had managed. One day, it was his opinion, there'd be gilt-worked manuscripts and princely vestments down there with the splintered staves and beaded rabbit shits, when time had worked the world down to its mulch of sameness.

Passing in between its tall oak end-posts he stepped out onto the bridge's hanging logs, one hand clasped tight about the thick rope rail to make him steady and the other clutched as ever on the neck of his jute bag. Out on the sway and creak of the construction's middle span he stood a moment looking off along the slow brown river to the west, where it curled round a stand of drooping willows at a bend and out of sight. What seemed like several boys were playing on the bank there at the river's elbow, the first people that he'd sighted in two days of walking, but were too far off to hail and so he raised a hand to them instead and they waved back, encouragingly as it seemed to Peter. He went on with mygge-flies gathered in a spiteful halo at his brow that only scattered when he'd passed the far end of the bridge and was some way off from the water's edge, upon a path that led between a scattering of homes towards the settlement's south gate.

Dug down into the earth, each with its wattle roof heaped to a point above the cosy trench, these were submerged in dirty clouds that billowed from their chimney holes so that they seemed more built from smoke than sticks

and clay. Come out into the world above from one such nest of fume was an
old woman, grinning round the few teeth that were left her when she saw him,
climbing painfully the three or four flat stones on hard dirt steps that led up
from the covered hole. Her skin was cracked as pond-bed mud in drought, and
ashen plaits that hung down to her waist recalled the sagging willows, so that
she appeared to him a very river-thing, more like to live beneath the bridge
itself than in her dwelling up this dusty path. The voice too, when she spoke,
was thick with phlegm and had the sound of water dragging over stones. Her
eyes were wicked little snail-husks, wet and glinting.

"Eyyer brung et?"

Here she nodded, twice for emphasis, towards the sack he carried slung
across his shoulder. Something jumped in the pale tangles of her hair. He
was perplexed and thought she knew by some means of his mission; then he
thought again that she'd mistaken him for one appointed to bring something
to her lowly hut, or else that she be mad. Not knowing what to make of her
he merely stared and shook his head in puzzlement, at which she showed her
awful toothless smile again, finding amusement here where he found none.

"What thing there is by all four corners as yet marks the middle. Eyyer
brung et?"

He could make no sense of what she said, could only summon a vague picture that meant nothing to him, of a page of manuscript where all the corners
had been folded in towards the centre. Peter shrugged uneasily, and thought
he must seem dull.

"Good woman, I know not the thing of which you speak. I am come here
across thy bridge from far away. I have not been about these parts before."

It was the crone's turn now to shake her head, the rank plaits swinging
like a beaded Moorish curtain and her ruined grin still fixed in place.

"You are not come across my bridge, not yet. You are not even past my
fort. And I know thee of old." With this she reached one hand out like a brittle
claw and slapped him hard about his rosy, glistening cheek.

He sat up.

He was resting on the banked verge of the ditch that ran around the relic
river fort, the bridge's southern end some distance off upon his left. A beetle
or a spider in the grass had bitten him on one side of his face where he had
dozed with it pressed to the turf, and he could feel a swollen lump beneath his
finger when he raised it to inspect the source of the insistent throbbing. He
was frightened for a moment when he realised he no longer held the jute cloth
bag but finding it upon the slope beside him he was reassured, though still
bewildered by what had occurred. He struggled to his feet, his robes all sodden down the back from the damp grass, frowning at first the fort's remains
and then the nearby bridge, until at length he laughed.

So this was Hamtun, then. This was its character, its notion of a jest with travellers who thought they had the place's measure. In the country's ancient heart this curious essential nature hid and made itself a secret, slyly marvellous and dangerous in its caprice as if it did not realise its frightening strength or else pretended it did not. Behind the madman glitter of its eye, behind its rotted smile, he thought, there was a knowledge it had chosen to conceal with mischiefs, frights and phantoms. At once monstrous and playful, antic even in its horrors, there was something in its nature Peter found he might admire or fear, yet all the while still chuckling in wonderment at its defiant queerness. Shaking now his curly, greying head in good-natured acknowledgement of how amusingly he had been tricked he shouldered once again his sack and made towards the bridge, his second try at it, or so it seemed to him.

This time the structure was all made of wood, a sturdy hump that curved above the muddy flow, supported by stout beams beneath rather than hung from ropes as in his dream. He could console himself, however, that there were still mygge-flies all around him in a droning cloud, and when he paused out on the middle section and looked west there were yet willows stooping at the water's bend, although no children played beneath them. Overhead the great disc of the heavens turned, a grubby fleece that frayed to streaming rags at the horizon, and he carried on across the river with his trailing beard of gnats plumed out behind him.

At the edges of the trodden path that stretched between the bridge and the south gate there were no sunken homes, but only turnip fields to either side, with elms and birches in a fringe beyond them. These were interrupted here and there by rotted stumps so that the tree-line called to mind a ghostly likeness of his dream-hag's smile, her knowing ridicule insinuated now within the landscape that encircled him, or at the least such was his fancy. Peter thought it better he did not indulge this inward shadow play and so turned his attentions from it, noticing instead the true substantial meadow, plain and without mystery, through which he passed. On trembling sprigs there nodded cowslips, green-gold as the cattle-slimes from which they took their name, and he heard skylarks trilling in the grasses bordering the planted crops. It was a fine day to conclude his journey, and there were no apparitions here save those that he himself had dragged along for company.

This patch of earth was where the west-east river made a sudden bend towards the south, leaving a hanging bulge of land before its proper course was once again resumed, a swelling like that on his bitten cheek. Four narrow ditches had been cut through the promontory, perhaps for irrigation, forded by stout logs that he was forced to teeter over awkwardly, one hand clutching his precious burden to his bosom with the other stretched out at the side and waving up and down to balance him, before he came to Hamtun's southern

gate. This stood a little open from the fence of tall and sturdy posts that made
the settlement's south wall, and had a single thin and gloomy-looking man
who held a spear stood by it for a guard. There was perhaps but one day's
growth of beard in a grey blot about his mouth, so that he had in some ways
the appearance of a threadbare and indifferent dog. He did not call a greeting,
but leaned idly there against the gate and watched the monk's approach with
listless gaze, obliging Peter to announce himself.

"Hail, fellow, and good day to thee. I am a brother of the blessed Benedict
whose order is at Medeshamstede near to Peterboro, not far off from here. I
have gone many leagues over the sea and am now sent to Hamtun, where I
bring a token ..."

He was fumbling within the sack, about to take the thing inside out into
daylight as an illustration, when the watchman turned his head to one side,
spitting out a gob of bright green jelly in the paler straws beside the gate, then
looked again at Peter, bluntly interrupting him.

"Es et un axe?"

The guard's voice was at once flat and without real interest, spoken partly
down his long beak of a nose. Peter looked up from the jute bag's dark mouth
at his interrogator, puzzled and surprised.

"An axe?"

The gateman sighed elaborately, as though one wearily explaining to an
infant.

"Aye. Un axe. Un ef I let yer en, shell yer go smashen people's eds wuth et,
un fucken boys un wimmen fore yer sets us all on fire?"

Here Peter merely blinked uncomprehendingly, then noticed for the first
time how the wall and nearer gatepost both had wavering tongues of soot
extending raggedly from near their base to almost at the top. He looked back
to the languid guardian and shook his head in vehement denial, reaching once
again into his sack to bring his treasure forth, this time as reassurance.

"Oh, no. No, it's not an axe. I am a man of God and all I seek to fetch
here is – "

The sentry, with a pained expression, closed his doleful eyes and held the
palm not wrapped about his spear towards the pilgrim, waving it dismissively
from side to side as he declined to view what was contained in Peter's bundle.

"I em not minded ef et be the left leg o' John Baptist for so long uz et's not
put about the smashen o' men's eds, nor that ets ragged end be lit un made a
torch fer burnen. Not last month were one like thee uz ad the skull-bone of the
Lord, un when I asked em ow et were so small, e sed et were the skull o' Christ
from when e were a babe. I erd uz the good folk as dwell beside Saint Peter's
Church ad depped ez cods en tar un sent em cryen ome."

His eyes were open now to stare unblinking at the monk as though his words were no more than plain fact, requiring no response of Peter save that he pass on and leave the sentinel to his bored watch over the turnip patch.

"Then am I thankfully advised. I shall be sure to sell no relics here, whilst in the same wise making certain that I smash no heads, nor yet put anyone to rape or fire until I am past Hamtun, e'en in genuine mistake. I bid thee well."

The guardsman pointedly stared off towards the distant elms and muttered something indistinct that ended with the words "away und melk a bull", so Peter hung his bag once more across his callused shoulder and went on, in where the gate was open, to the hill-path that climbed from the bridge towards the settlement's high reaches. Here he could see thatch-topped homes dug into rows beside the slanting street not very different from the witch's burrow in his dream, though not he thought so palled with smoke. Nor did those several people that he spied who were the huts' inhabitants appear to have a strangeness to them in the way that she had, with instead the semblance of ordinary men and maids, in cap or shawl, that pulled their children, carts and hounds behind them through the lanes, else travelled on shit-spraying mares. He was yet mindful of the sleeping vision gifted him, however, and resolved he would not judge the gentles here as common until he was safely come among and through them all. He plodded on and up along the track, skirting a sump close to its bottom where both recent rain and passing horses had conspired to make a filthy slurry there. Off to his right not very far, beyond some huts, the posts that made the settlement's east wall climbed up the hill abreast with him towards the high ground in the north.

Beside the sunken houses further up the unmown slope were taller dwellings also, though not many, and not far inside the gated wall he passed some ground that had a pox-barn set aside where there lay ones who moaned and worse ones who did not, betwixt small fires that had been set to clean the poison humours from the air. Some of the figures were made incomplete by parts decayed or some of them perhaps hewn off in accident, and back and forth between their mats crept old wives tending them, with faces marked by ailments they had in their time survived and now were proof to. He was grateful that the wind today came from the west, but turned his face off in precaution from the pest field when he passed it by and carried on uphill, where there thronged fellow beings in their dozens such as he'd not known in a great while. The slow climb made him puff, on this close day with all its warmth held in beneath the sky's low quilting, raising sweat upon the sweat already there, yet was he joyous to be once more in the company of men and went amongst them gladly in good spirit, marvelling as though one unaccustomed at their great diversity.

Old men whose parsnip noses almost met their jutting chins pulled sleds with cords of oak-bark piled upon them that were dark red and alive with pismires on their undersides. Peter was made to wait idly upon the corner with a cross-path, by an ale-yard that had high stone walls, until a horse-pulled cart weighed down with troughs of new-worked chalk had rumbled past and aged those in the billowing suspensions of its wake by ten years in as many instants. As at last he made his way across the side street to continue up the hill, he ventured to look down it after the departing horse and wagon. There were not a few mean dwellings at its borders and then black briar hedgerow further down, where Peter saw a mother and her flock of children picking diligently at the brambles, with their findings stuffed into a bag the woman carried. He supposed they were wool-gathering, and that it might be they were family to a woolmonger living hereabouts, so busy and so enterprising did the hill town seem to him.

Indeed, he was surprised to find it so, as he strode up the incline to a crossroads at its top. When he had been a lad named Aegburth growing up at Helpstun near to Peterboro and then later been a monk named Peter cloistered in that place itself, he had heard tell of Hamtun, but not often. It had always been there, he had the impression, though not very much there, and remarkable only in that it never was remarked upon. It was apparent there had been some Roman presence in these parts and he thought savage settlements perhaps before those times, but there was never more to Hamtun than the airy rumour of a place where no one ever went. To see it now with all its barter and its bustle one might, with good reason, ask whence it had come. It was as if, when finally the night and winter after Rome's demise was lifted from the land, Hamtun was simply found here, thriving in its present form, come out of nothingness to occupy this prosperous vantage ever since. And still no person spoke of it.

He knew King Offa, when not building his great ditch at Mercia's edge with Wales, had planted new towns in these territories that were doing well, though Hamtun was not one of them, and had the markings of some earlier vintage. Offa kept a Thorpe as well, a country dwelling off the town's north end, with Hamtun as the nearest port of trade, though Peter was of the opinion Hamtun's prominence had come before the time of Offa. He recalled his grandfather at Helpstun making mention of the place as though of some importance when it had been Offa's predecessor Aethebald who'd reigned, and further still, back in the mists of lost antiquity there'd been a place here that men knew of, yet did not know what it was they knew. Perhaps it was as with a circle, drafted by a knob of chalk upon a string, where only the perimeter was noticed with the centre that the shape depended on not seen at all, or thought to be a hole, like through a ring-loaf. How, though, in an empty hole, was there such furious activity?

When he had lately passed through Woolwych to the east of London he had met a drover of those parts who said he'd heard of Hamtun, once he had been told that it was Peter's destination. This man mostly knew it for the sheep flocks herded down from there, but said that one of Offa's kin was at a manor in the settlement, which had a fine church of its own built near to it. If this were true, Peter supposed it to be in some far part of the town that he was yet to see, although it might be that the dwellings all about him were in lease to such a place, that they would likely pay some small part of their keep unto the manor through the agency of what was called a Frith Borh, who was like a tithing-man. His intuition had been well, he thought, to bring him to this spot, when all he had been given for direction were instructions in a foreign tongue he was not certain that he'd understood, urgent and vague entreaties that the object in his bag should be delivered "to the centre of your land". He knew that Mercia surely was the heart of England and, to see the crowds at work and leisure now about him, was convinced that he had come to Mercia's heart in turn. Yet where, he wondered, was the heart of Hamtun?

He'd by now achieved the crossroads of his path that led up from the bridge, an area where the slope was somewhat levelled out before continuing to climb straight on and to the north. He set his baggage down and looked about him here, that he might get his breath and bearings both, and wiped the drench from off his forehead with one woollen sleeve. Ahead of him, after a mostly flat expanse, the track that he was on resumed its steep ascent past huts and yards where there were mainly tanners from the smell, while at his left and down the hill that was the crossroads' other leg were sheds with smoking forges from where came the clamour of hot metals being wrought. Upon his right, past houses that had fields of pigs and hens and goats attached there stood the open east gate of the settlement, with off beyond its timbered yawn a church of sorts, outside of Hamtun's limit, built from wood. He smiled to greet a woman who was passing and, when she smiled back, asked if she knew about the church and if it was the one that had the manor near. He saw about her throat a pendant stone, this with a rune on that he recognised as sacred to the demon Thor, although he thought there to be no more in this than a peasant charm to ward off thunderstorms. She shook her head.

"Yer wud be thenken o' Sunt Peter's, dayn away there."

Here she gestured back the way that she had come, along the crossing's other path up by the sparking, belching forges, then looked back towards the building just beyond the eastern gates that Peter had enquired of.

"Thet one there's All Hallows what wur only belt when my mam was a child. Ef et's a church yer arfter we've Sunt Gregory's near by Sunt Peter's, or else the old temple ayt upon the sheep trail, not far up ahead und en the way as yer be gooen."

Peter thanked the wife and let her pass on by, while he stood at the corner there considering if this might be the centre he was seeking, thinking that a crossroads or its like might suit the crucial item carried in his sack. He asked, below his breath that those about him did not think him lunatic, "Is this the place?" When there came no response he tried again yet louder, so that idle boys across the street from him all laughed.

"Is this the centre?"

Nothing happened. Peter was not sure by what signs he expected the location that he sought would be made known to him, if signs there were to be, only that nothing in his instinct found such signals here. With people looking at him in bemusement now he felt his cheek made redder yet, and so picked up his bundle and went on, over the crossroads in a hurry that he might avoid its rumbling carts and next straight up the hill, where did the tanners and drape-makers of the town conduct a goodly trade.

Here was a fantasy of things to be remarked on following those long legs of his pilgrimage where novelty was scarce or not at all. Beside the noisome tanning-pits he'd caught the reek of from downhill were boards set out that were all over shoes and gloves and boots and leather leggings, of more styles and hues and sizes than he'd previously thought were in the world entire. The brothy scent of them alone was an intoxication as he struggled up the gradient between the trading posts and stalls, bearing the weighted bag that bumped on his stooped-over backbone now and then. His eyes and ears alike were near to overwhelmed by all the sights and noises that there were, the chatter and the conversation. People gathered in a breathless huddle at a stand where garments were displayed, having the items that were meaner and more easily afforded set about a show-piece, black-tanned leather armour in a full dress outfit decorated by a trim of bird skulls worked with silver. Peter doubted that this suit should ever find a buyer or be worn, yet estimated from the crowd about it that it must already have repaid its workmanship in countless smaller purchases. Having this opportunity to look upon the locals whilst they were distracted so that he might not offend, he saw more plain or ugly faces in the throng than he saw fair, and was surprised to find how many of the men had wild designs of pigment dug into the skin upon their arms, where had they stripped their clothes off on this humid day and these were visible. Not only patterns were there, drawn this way on flesh, but likewise images in crude, of herlots or the saviour or else both at once, together there on the same shoulder, wearing but a single loin-cloth 'twixt the two of them. He chuckled to himself at this and went on up the path where men with dye-stained hands were selling cloth, a richer red than any he had glimpsed in Palestine.

After a time he passed beyond the market street to higher ground, though not the highest, with superior rises still in the southeast. The settlement's east wall, that had breaks in it now and then, continued to climb up the slope beside him, not far off and to his right, while on his left side there were many lanes and passages run off downhill. While he would own that there was little aim to his meander, Peter thought perhaps that if he walked the town's wall in this way then he would have a sense of its extent and its dimension, so that he might more exactly plot its middle being thus informed. His plan, then, was so vague and slight as hardly to be there at all, and now he felt a pressure in his bladder and a hunger in his belly both, distracting him still further from it. He was still on the same northward path that he'd been walking since he crossed the bridge, but had again reached meadows where the ground was flattened out, atop the slope that had the drapery. Here was a fleecy multitude steered into pens by silent and stem-chewing men with noisy dogs, so that he was reminded of the dame who wore the Thor-stone who had counselled him, and what she'd said of an old temple on a sheep-trail, further up along his way. Though he was still to see a church up here, he was yet certain this must be the trail of which she'd told him, as judged by its traffic.

Bleating beasts were everywhere about him as he walked now down into a gentle hollow, creatures driven here in great hordes beggaring imagination with the land made white, horizon to horizon, this in summer and not winter-time, come from the west of Mercia and Wales beyond. Now that he reckoned it, Peter had known since boyhood that the western cattle-trail was ended somewhere not far off from Helpstun or else Peterboro, in the middling hamlets of the country, though he had not thought its ending was in Hamtun. Out of here the drovers would take on the herds to other parts, along the Roman road that brought him hence from London and the high white coast, or else out past the district of Saint Neot on to Norwych and the east, delivering the mutton in this way throughout the land. Were all of England's tangling lines met here, he wondered, tied into a knot at Hamtun by some giant midwife as it were the country's umbilicus? Peter waded in a wool-tide, on and down the broad street pebbled with black turds, still headed north, his bag now hanging in one hand there at his side so that his aching shoulder might be rested.

When he had come almost through the great stupidity of animals, he saw up on a mound towards the right of him a kind of mean church, built from stones, that Peter hoped to be the temple that the woman had informed him of, although it seemed unused and no one was about it. Thinking to have pause there for a pissing-while and eat the cheese and bread hid with some coins in a tuck-pocket of his smock, he turned east from the foul mires of the sheep-path and went up a brief walk overhung by boughs that blossoms fell from in a pretty pepper, to the church-house as he thought it, at the slant's top end.

Some of the flat-faced and incurious woollen-backs were grazing here in shelter of the spreading trees, where Peter set his baggage down and drew aside his habit to unleash less of a stream than he'd expected in the puddled rain that was between a beech's knuckled roots. His water had a strong and orange look about the little that there was of it, and he supposed the greater measure of its fluids had been lost already through his gushing pores. He shook the meagre trickle's last few droplets from his prick-end and arranged his dress, looking about for somewhere he could eat his food. At last he was decided on the green, luxuriant sod about an aged oak that he would sit and lean his back against, but a few paces from the temple's weathered pile.

Now that he looked at this, sat rested on the sward with sack at rest alike beside him, chewing on the crust he had retrieved from its compartment in his robe, he was less certain of the low construction's Christian provenance and was made more alert to its peculiarity. He settled back against his oaken throne and slowly worked the bread and goat-cheese to a sodden, undistinguished lump between his teeth as he considered what the lonely building was or once before had been. The old stone posts to each side of its door had winding round them graven dragon-wyrms, much longer than the poor thing he had seen caught in its muck-hole out near London. If it were indeed a home of Christian worship, Peter knew it for a Christianity more old than his and come from the traditions of three hundred years before, when the forebears of Peter's order had been forced to seek appeasement with the followers of peasant gods by mixing in Christ's teachings with their rude and superstitious lore, preached from the mounds where shrines to devils were once raised. The carvings snaking down the pillars were a likeness of the serpent wound about the world's girth in the old religions where our mortal realm was held to be the middle one of three, with Hel below it and the Nordic heaven built across a bridge from it above.

Leaving the detail of the bridge aside, this was not so unlike his own faith in a life that was beyond this brief span and in some means over it, at a superior height from which the traps and snares of this world were more clearly seen and understood. Though he had never said this while about the monastery of Saint Benedict, he did not think it much a matter if it were a bridge or flight of steps that led to paradise, or by what names the personages dwelling there were known, or even if the gods were made with different histories. It was, he thought, a failing of the Christianity that was in England now that people were so taken with the truth or otherwise of writings that in other lands should be admired as only parables, and nothing held amiss. From what he knew of the Mohammedans, their bible was a book of tales meant only to illuminate and teach by an example, and was not to be confused with an historical account of things. This too was Peter's understanding of the Christian Bible, which he had read all there was of, just as he had likewise read Bede's history and so too, secretly, had heard a telling of the Daneland monster yarn then being talked about by all, yet when he tried to teach the Christian doctrine he would find himself confronted by a narrow-mindedness, by dull demands to know if truly all Creation was accomplished in six days.

The faith that Peter had was in the value of a radiant ideal, with this ideal embodied in the Christ, who was a figure of instruction. Faith, to his mind, was a willed asserting of the sacred. If it were made more or less than this then it was mere belief, as children will believe the goblin tale they hear for just so long as it is being told. To hold belief in a material fact was only vanity, easily shattered, where the ideal was a truth eternal in whatever form expressed. Belief, in Peter's private view of things, counted for little. The eternal, insubstantial ideal was the thing, the light that orders like his own had shielded in the night and sought now to extend across the fallen, overshadowed world. He did not have belief in angels as substantial forms, and as ideals had no need to believe in them: he knew them. He had met with them upon his travels and had seen them, though if this were with his mortal eyes or with the ideal gaze of vision he cared not at all. He'd met with angels. He did not believe. He knew, and hoped his creed would in a hundred years from that time not be foundered in a quagmire of believers. Was this what befell the old gods, near whose temple he was squatted now to eat his bread and cheese?

His ruminations done, he brushed the crumbs from out his beard, where they would do for all the pigeons that there were about the ruin. Standing up and shouldering his bag once more, he made off down the little hill that led back to the sheep-track, with his drab rope sandals kicking through a fallen frost of blossoms from the trees that reached above. The cattle path by now was emptied saving for its carpet made with dung, and for the patterning of hoof-print everywhere upon it like a pricked pot. He went on along it but a trifling distance until he was come upon the town's north wall and the pitch-painted timbers of its northern gate, which stood a little open as its counterpart down by the river in the south had done.

There was a different air about this quarter of the settlement that had a quality of harm and malice, and to which he thought those several severed heads set onto spikes above the gate may have contributed. With such fair hair as yet remained upon the melting skulls worn in the long style, he supposed them to be butchers come from Denmark or nearby, that looked surprised to have discovered there were butchers here in Hamtun just the same. One of the heads was blurred, that made him think his eyes were wrong, though it were only meat flies in a swarm about the remnant, hatched from out its hanging mouth.

He'd walked, then, from the settlement's south end up to its north. It was not very far. Confronted by the barrier of posts he turned towards the west there at his left and started off downhill, to find an edge of Hamtun he had not yet seen. Descending on the valley's side, once more towards the river as he found, he saw the glorious spread of land that stretched away towards where twirls of smoke rose up to mark a district reaching out on Hamtun's west and to the far side of the Nenn. This was a grey and silver braid that wound through lime or yellow fields beneath the distant trees, and had a bridge across it in a wooden arch that by his reckoning would be where all the sheep came in from Wales. He saw a high wall too, not far off from the river on its nearer bank, built out of posts like the town's wall. It mayhap was a cloister or a lord's land, where its east wall served to mark the western limit of the town.

The thought, however slender, that there may be monks near brought to mind his monastery in the quiet fields by Peterboro, which he had not visited now in three years or more. Remembering his cell and cot at Medeshamstede brought a pang, as too did his recall of those among the brotherhood that were his friends, so that he was resolved to travel back there when his work in Hamtun here was over and his obligation was discharged. That would not be, he told himself, until the centre of the settlement was found and Peter's jute-wrapped talisman had been delivered there. This longing to be once more in his meadow home should bring that thing no nearer, and served only to delay its quick accomplishment.

Upon the left of him there were now narrow entries running off in strings of close-together houses, twisting round their turns and out of sight to tangle in a knot that Peter now suspected was the guts of Hamtun, rank and of surprising colour, where upon his walk around its walls he had seen nothing more than Hamtun's patterned and pigmented outer hide. He was sore tempted by an urge to venture deep amongst the labyrinth of lanes, trusting that he could find the spot he searched for by no more than instinct, yet his wiser self prevailed. He here recalled the drover he had met at Woolwych who had known of Hamtun, and another thing that man had said to him: "It is all paths and cross-tracks like a nest of rabbits. It may be that you will find it not so easy getting in, though I can tell thee that it is more hard than murder getting out again." Peter might lose his way among the narrow lanes, and would be better first to tread the limits of the settlement as he had planned, that he should have its measure. He continued therefore down the hill until he had come almost to the wall that he had seen while at its summit, noting to himself that Hamtun did not seem a half so far from east to west as it were south to north, so that he thought its shape was like a narrow piece of bark or parchment. If there were a message writ on this, or if he yet would have the wits to make it out, these things he could not say.

The wall of posts, which ran along the near side of the river, ended by the bridge that led out from the settlement to Wales. Once underneath the wooden span the Nenn bent into this direction also, and the wall between him and the river's edge that wound off likewise westward was replaced by great black hedges serving as fortifications. Having thus come to another one of Hamtun's corners, Peter turned again and set off down what he now knew to be the longer walk before he'd reach its southern boundary where he'd arrived some hours ago. Up to the right of him there was the silvery quarter of the low grey sky where hid the sun, that was about to start its long fall into night. It was a while by noon as he conceived it.

Trudging south he saw there were not many houses here down on the settlement's low flank, but only crofts, each with its humble cottage. Off and up the easy slopes ahead, thin yarns of smoke were raised and knit into a pall, so that he thought these higher pastures were more densely settled. Down towards the riverside where Peter walked, though, he could only see a single dwelling in his way that seemed built near the corner of a track, the further one of two that led up from his route and eastward, side by side with empty cattle fields between them.

He approached the nearer of lanes, to pause and peer along it. As it rose away from him it was well-walked and had an ancient look, as did the ditch beside it where a small stream gurgled, come as he supposed out of a fount or spring up near the top. He crossed the bottom of the path, bag dangling at his back, and carried on in way of the stone croft-hut by the corner where the second side-track met his road. The lowly building seemed as though deserted, all alone here on the west hem of the settlement, without the sign of any fires burned in its hearth. Across the muddy thoroughfare from this, to Peter's right, there was a goodly mound of stone made up, with built above it out of wood a winding-shaft that had a rope and bucket hanging down. He'd had no drink since a freshwater pond he'd passed round daybreak, some leagues south of Hamtun, and so veered from his straight line towards the wellhead, whistling an air he part-recalled from somewhere as he went.

When he was come upon this it was bigger than he'd thought, high to the middle of him where the stones were built up in their ring, which was perhaps two paces over it from side to side. He turned the hand-hold on the winder so that more rope was unrolled, at which the brightly painted wooden bucket dropped away from him down its unfathomable hole. After some moments doing this there came a faint splash from below, and soon thereafter he was hauling up a cup far heavier than was the one that he'd let down. The wetted cable squeaked, and he could hear and feel the slosh against the swaying vessel's sides as it was pulled up from the dark bore, into daylight. Tying off the rope he drew the bucket to him and looked in, thirsty and eager.

It was blood.

The shock of it was like a blow and set the world to spin, so that he knew not his own thoughts. It felt as if a very cavalry of different understandings were stampeding through him, trampling reason with their dizzy, frightful rush. It was his own blood, where his throat was cut that he'd not known. It was the blood of Hamtun come from generations of its people, poured down-hill to drain into this buried reservoir. It was the blood of saints that Saint John the Divine said should be quaffed at the world's end, when in two hun-dred years from now it did occur. It was the Saviour's blood, and by this sign it was announced to Peter that the land and soil itself were Jesu's flesh, for like the barley and the things of earth was he not cut down to grow up again? It was the heart-sap of a fearsome Mystery and richer red than holly-fruit, a marvel of such magnitude that Christians of an era not yet come should know of it, and know of him, and say that truly in God's sight he had been favoured, that he had been shown this miracle, this vision ...

It was dye.

How was he so complete a fool? He'd seen the vivid cloths that were for sale upon the street of drapers, yet had minded not from where they must have come. He'd let the bright red bucket down the well, yet thought that it was painted for a seal and not that it was stained with its unceasing use. These signs had been as plain as daylight, saving to an idiot, yet in his fervour he was blinded to them and had almost thought himself to be already sainted. He resolved he should not tell his brethren back in Medeshamstede of this shameful error, even as a jest against himself, his puffed-up folly and his van-ity, lest they should know him for a prick-head.

Laughing now at how he had been tricked by Hamtun for this second time, he poured the contents of the pail back down the black and gargling throat whence they had been retrieved. Reminded of his brother Matthew back near Peterboro, who had made illuminations onto manuscripts and spo-ken of his craft with Peter, Peter thought it likely that the water's colour was achieved with iron rust from out the soil. While this would not have harmed him greatly, he was still uncommon glad that he had not quaffed deep without he looked. Red ochre, after all, was not the only thing that might produce red colouring. There was, for instance, rust of Mercury, and at the Benedictine brothers' meadow homestead he had heard of monks who'd sucked the bris-tles of a brush where was red pigment still, to make them wet and form them to a point. Day after day, unwittingly, the monks had done this until they were poisoned by it. It was said of one his bones were made so brittle that when he lay dying and the merest blanket was put onto him for comfort, every part of him was broken by its weight, that he was crushed and killed. If this were a true story, Peter did not know, nor did he think it likely that the water in this present well would be thus tainted, but he was yet happy that he had not put it to the test, lest his half-wit mistake had proved instead a deadly one.

Now that the startlement of the event was passed and he reflected, Peter did not judge himself so foolish as he had done. Though the holy blood as he'd supposed had turned out naught but dye in its material truth, was there not an ideal truth to be considered also, where the earthly stain was but a figure made to stand for that which was unearthly, and so without worldly form? Could not a thing have aspects more than one, in that it might be rust of iron when reckoned with the stick of reason, and yet be the very wine of Christ according to the measures of the heart? A well of dye this shade he'd never heard about before, so that it was not much less of a wonder than it were the liquid he had thought at first. Whatever may have been its source it was a sign, to be made out.

As once again he hefted up his sack, it came to him that he had been too plodding and too careful in his thoughts and in his search alike. In walking cautiously about its edge, Peter had but considered Hamtun as a shape or like a flat sketch mapped on parchment, where he now saw it was more like to a living thing that had its humours and its mortal juices, less a territory to be paced than like a stranger he had joined in conversation. Might it warm to him if he were not so rigid and constrained in his approaches to it? Headed back towards his southbound rut he thought of this and so instead decided to go east, up past the solitary dwelling by its hill-path and into the proper settlement, that maze of crouching homes above and on the right of him whose open hearths had made the grubby hanging clouds more grubby yet.

He passed the stone shed on one side as he began the climb, and when he did there came upon him the sensation that he'd heard once called "newly familiar", as when some novel circumstance should bring the outlandish conviction that it had been lived before. It was not, he observed, merely that he had somewhere known a moment that was of a kind with this, passing a single hut alone while making up the grade and in an unaccustomed site. It was instead this instant in its finest detail that he felt he passed through not for the first time: the pale and little shadows that were on the grass thrown by a shrouded sun not far beyond its zenith, and the moss grown to the shape of a man's hand beside the door frame of the silent croft-house; birdsong ringing out from the dark hedgerows in the west just now that was three sharp sounds and a plaintive fall; the souring pork smell that his sweat had where its vapour was escaped from in his robes; his aching feet, the unseen distant river's perfumes and the hard knobs of the sack that jolted on his bended spine.

He shrugged the feeling from him and went by the piled up limestone of the place and up the hill. He could see nothing in the darkened cavities that were its window-holes, but so uncanny was the sense it gave him that he yet half-thought that he was overlooked. A wicked part within his mind that meant to scare him said it was the snail-eyed hag from out his dream, resided by herself there in the shadow of the silent hut and watching what he did. For all he knew this to be no more than a phantom he had conjured whereby to torment himself, he shuddered still and made good haste to put the stead far at his back. Breaking now from the eastward lane that he was climbing, Peter struck out at an angle up a lesser path to the southeast that was a mere discolouration in the thigh-deep weeds.

What had unnerved him mostly at the croft-house was the notion that his passing of it was no sole event, but only one within a line of repetitions, so that there was called unto his mind an image that was like an endless row of him, his separate selves all passing by the same forsaken nook but many times repeated, all of them within that instant made aware of one another and the queer affair of their recurrence, that the world and times about them were recurring also. It was like a ghostly sentiment he had about him, as though he were one already dead who was reviewing the adventures of his life, yet had forgot that this were naught save for a second or indeed a hundredth reading, until he should stumble on a passage that he recognised by its description of a hovel stood alone, a blackbird's song, or else a clot of lichen like a hand. These thoughts were new to him, so that he was not yet convinced he had their full entirety. As though a blind man he groped at their edges and their strange protrusions, though he knew the whole shape was beyond his grasp.

Labouring up the slope, his path bending again towards the east, it seemed to Peter as if the peculiar notions come upon him were an air or a miasma that was risen up in this locality, with its effects become more strong as he went deeper in. It brought a colour to his mood he could not name, as it were like a shade that had been mixed from several such, from fear and also wonderment, from hopeful joy, but sadness too and a foreboding that was difficult to place or to describe. The duty represented in his jute-cloth bag seemed both at once to make his soul all jubilant take flight, and be a matter of such heaviness he should be broke and flattened quite beneath it. In these contradictions did the feeling in him seem all human feelings rolled to one, and he was filled with it so that he thought to burst. This thrilling yet uncomfortable sensation, he concluded, must be that encountered by all creatures when they act the works of God.

He'd waded through the long grass and was on another dirt path now that rose straight up the hillside in the same way that the lane up from the dyer's well had done, but further off from it. This new track had ahead of him a sprawl of dwellings that were covered holes to either side, where dogs with matted coats were sniffing in the midst of laughing men or scolding women that trailed babies. At its top end he could see raised up the roofs of higher buildings and below a traffic made of many carts, and so presumed this place to be a kind of main square to the settlement. Not so far off uphill and on his lane's right side where were the lower houses and their populations, Peter saw that a great fire was builded up, there on a plot of bare and blackened land. Here people came with things that were too many or too vile to burn about their homes, on sledges and in bags. He saw dull piles of cloth, plague-rags as he supposed, unloaded from their barrow with a harvest-fork. There was a midden-wagon that its driver backed with many cries and halts toward the flames, so that the dung was shovelled from it to the furnace with a greater ease by the old men who made their work about this burning-ground. The stench and haze boiled in a filthy tower up from the blaze, for there was little wind, though Peter knew that different weather would see all the dwellings clustered here lost to a stinking fog.

Thinking to skirt the worst part of this foulness he turned off his east-bound way, along a little cross-street when he came to it. There were some huts built on each side of this, yet not so many people and not fires. Some distance down the sloping path ahead of him he saw a broad thatched roof that he supposed was that of a great hall, which had the walled grounds on its rear side turned to him. The lighted region of the sky was once more to his right, that meant he was gone south again, although not far before he had another hindrance blocking him. A distance on along in his direction was a yard that had a great cloud risen up about, as had the yard where wastes were burned, yet as those billows had been black, these were all white. He saw a carriage from behind which loads of chalk were put down on a little hill within the fenced-out patch, and thought how such a cart had crossed his path up from the southern bridge that morn, its dusts and its deposits on his hair and in the creases of his garment still. It was his preference that he remain the colour he had been when first he came to Hamtun and be not turned red by dyes else smoked to black or white, so that he now stood still and took a stock of things to better know where he might turn.

He was once more about a sort of corner, with a path run up from it and to the east again off from the lane where he at present trod. To mark the joining of the tracks there was a mound like to a square that had one of its sides squeezed shorter than the rest. Around this was a trench, dug out so long before it was grassed all across it now, as with the Roman river-fort that he had seen. The tufted hillock kept a sense about it that it was of import or had once been so, although it had no buildings on and only golden clumps of piss-the-bed that were not yet gone into misty balls of seed.

While he stood gazing at the hump, Peter became aware of an alarm enacted at its lower boundary, upon the side where Peter was and so between him and the chalk-yard. Pulled up by the trackside were a horse and drag that had an ugly man sat at its reins. His face was wide with eyes set far apart, and he looked strong yet squat, as though he were compressed. Perched on the low seat of his cart he was in converse with a child, a girl of no more than a dozen years who hesitated on the turf beside the circling ditch and looked up at the fellow all uncertain. She seemed fearful of the man as if she did not know him, shaking now her head and making as though she would move away, whereat the stocky carter made a lunge and caught her fast about a plump wrist that she might not flee.

Peter had but a moment wherein to decide what he should do. If this were a dispute 'twixt a vexed father and his wilful child then he was loath to interfere in it, although he did not think that it were so, and on his travels he had seen enough of rapes that he could not in conscience turn aside and merely hope that all were well.

When he were wont to use it Peter had a voice that boomed, so that his brothers off in Medeshamstede, though they liked him, did not like him making chant with them. This was the bellow that he now employed as he called to the man who held the maiden, with it rolling like a thunder off across the fallow grass between them.

"You there! Stop a moment! Fellow, I would talk with thee!"

He struck towards the cart at a long pace and had his sack now swinging heavy in his hand down by one side of him, so that one could not look upon it without thinking what a fearsome club could be made out of it were it whirled round at any speed. He was a peaceful man, yet knew how he could seem with his thick limbs and his red face when he'd a mind to: he had not come safely half across the world and back without using that baleful semblance knowingly and to his own advantage. On the wagon now the man whose body seemed squashed-down turned his head sharply round to stare at Peter, barrelling straight for him through the sedge with a skull-smasher hanging in one ruddy fist. Releasing the young girl, the rogue was startled and looked eager to escape. Giving a cry to rouse his mare he raced her off, his transport rattling down the raised ground's short side and away around its bend, where at the corner he glanced back in fear towards the monk, then carried on and out from sight.

The maid he had released stood at the edge of the ringed trough and watched as her tormentor made away, then turned instead to Peter who was stopped halfway towards her, bent in two and puffing loud with his exertion, holding up one hand in her direction as he thought to reassure the frightened child. She was an instant while she took the measure of her rescuer, his dripping face like beetroot and the monstrous noise his wheezing made, before she made her mind up to run off another way from the direction her attacker had just taken, scampering away downhill as though to the south road that had the lonely hut and bloody well. He saw her go while he was there recovering among the drowsing stems, and thought it not a slight that she should be afraid at her deliverer. Not all monks were as he, and though he knew

the bawdy songs of rutting friars to be a falsehood in the main, he likewise
had met brothers of unpleasant appetite who would contrive to make such
slanders true. The child was wise to be away with her and trust to no one in
these worrisome new times, so that he found in her departure no offence and
was but glad that by God's grace he'd happened here in good time to prevent
a wrong.

He was in some fine humour, then, when he determined to take once again
the eastward path he'd left to skirt around the waste-fire and its vapours. With
his breath returned to him he started on the lane that went up by the north
side of the lifted mound, and while he walked he dwelled upon what had just
then occurred. Had he not come by his decision at the well that he would take
a different way into the settlement, then it might be that before long the girl
would have been victim of a murder and found ghastly in a hedge. Who knew,
now, of the children and grandchildren she might sire, or all the changes in
the circumstances of the world that might be wrought from this result? If all
else he had come here for should prove but his delusion, brought by too much
foreign sun, then there was this to say that he had yet worked to the purpose
of the Lord. Though it were beating like to a loud drum, his heart had joy in it
as he strove onward up the stony climb, his sack across his shoulder and the
sweat in a cascade upon his brow.

He was remarking inwardly upon how even closer the day had become
when he looked up and saw another rough-shod pilgrim coming down the way
towards him, one not quite so old as Peter was, who made a comic sight where
he was dressed so queer. He had a cap atop his head sat like an upturned pudding
bag that had a spreading rim, and all his garments were an oddment as though
cast away by others, yet what others Peter could not tell, the bits and pieces were
so strange. There was a little coat and some loose britches fashioned from light
cloth, while on the stranger's feet there were small leather boots made in a way
that Peter had not seen, not even at the tanners' stalls set out near Hamtun's
eastern gate. So antic was the aspect of this sorry wayfarer, the monk could not
but smile when they came closer to each other. Though the man possessed an air
about him that was pale and grey, he did not have the look of one with harm in
him, as did the rider of the drag that made to carry off the child some moments
since. This was a poor man who mayhap had his small mischiefs but seemed
good at heart, and when their paths met and they stopped both were already
grinning at each other, although if this were through amity or else because each
found the other one's appearance humorous, neither could say. Peter was first to
make his hellos and to speak.

"'Tis a hot day to be out, I was just this moment saying to myself. How
goes the world with thee now, my fine, honest fellow?"

Here the other man cocked back his head and squinted up his eyes to peer at Peter, as it were he thought that Peter mocked him, but at last decided he did not and answered in a cheery manner.

"Oh, it looks like a hot day, all right, and I suppose the world goes well enough. What of yourself? That bag of yours looks like a burden."

This was spoken with a roguish wink and nod at the jute sack that Peter had upon his shoulder, just as though it might be stolen valuables concealed within. Smiling at this, the monk put down his baggage on the rough track at their feet. He gave a great sigh of relief and shook his head.

"God bless thee, no ... or if it is it's not a burden I begrudge."

The fellow lifted up one brow as though with interest, or as if he invited still more comment, at which Peter thought that here there might be opportunity for guidance to the place he sought. It seemed that his chance meetings thus far on this afternoon were as directed by a higher power, and so perhaps was this one also. Much emboldened after these considerations, he came out and asked the question that he'd thought none but himself might answer, gesturing towards his set-down bundle as he did.

"I have been told I am to bring it to the centre. Dost thou know where that might be?"

There was much thoughtful humming and lip-tugging brought about by Peter's query, where his new-met comrade tipped back the outlandish cap to show a balded pate and looked up to the skies this way and that as though the place he had been asked for were somewhere aloft. At length, just when the monk thought that he should be disappointed, he was given his reply. The other man turned off from Peter and made indication down the lane that was behind him, in the way that Peter was already headed. Here the hill he'd climbed was flattened off, so that his track now led between some dug-in homes and pastures to a broader street ahead, that cut across to run downhill from north to south and was alive with distant carts and animals. A thick elm stood there at the join where met the pathways, and it was to this the monk's attentions were now called.

"If it's where I'm thinking of, then you must turn right by that tree along the end there." Sniffing back some snot the man here spat, in place of punctuation, as it seemed. "Go down that way until you reach the crossroads at the bottom. If you go straight over and you carry on downhill, it's on your left across the road, just halfway down."

Peter was overcome with joy and was likewise amazed at the great providence of God, that his riddle had found so swiftly and so simply its solution. All that had been in the end required of him, so things turned out, was that he ask. He gazed with gratitude upon the ragged pauper who had given him deliverance, and it was then that he first truly saw what was not usual in the man. He was not merely grey or pale as Peter had upon the outset thought him, but was rather without colouring of any kind, more like an image made with charcoal than a living and warm-blooded thing. He was also not only pale, but like to cloudy water so that when the monk made closer study he discovered he could see dark blurs moving across the figure that were traffics on the downhill path that cut across behind it, as if the poor man was made so that he could be seen through, though not clearly. With a tingling that was like an icy brook that trickled down his aching backbone, Peter knew he chattered to a spectre.

He was careful that the sudden fright he felt not show upon his face, lest he affront one who until then had been kindly and most helpfully disposed. Besides, the monk was yet uncertain what the being was he had the conversation of, although he thought it not an evil thing. Perhaps it was a lost soul, neither blessed nor else condemned and so residing in another state, here in its haunts of old. He wondered if it were eternally required to wander thus, or if the spirit knew some further destination, be it heaven or a different place, and to this end he asked where it was bound.

"I trust that your own journey is toward some pure and godly ending?"

Now the ghost looked guilty first, then sly, and in the end composed. Peter made private observation that the wraith's expressions were as easy seen through as its form. The creature hesitated somewhat as it made reply.

"I'm ... well, I'm off to see a friend now, if you want the honest truth. A poor old soul it is, lives all alone on Scarletwell Street corner and without a family to visit 'em. I'll bid you a good day now, Father, or whatever you'd prefer I call you. Good luck carrying your swag-bag to the centre, now."

With that the apparition went by Peter and on down the hill, towards where Peter had just intervened between the knave upon his cart and the young girl. The monk stood on the spot and watched him leave, and while he did so wondered what strange chance had made it so the tattered spirit should be gone about the lonely croft-man's shed near to the dye well, for from how he'd spoken it could be no other place. Since Peter had come here to Hamtun, nothing had occurred that was to his eye only aimless fortune. Rather, it seemed that events had been already set into their place and time, with all their joints and decorations long ordained. While he had felt, upon the corner near the well, that he but viewed again a narrative read many times before, he now thought it more like a plan on parchment that a carpenter had made. His every footstep traced the lines by which he was made part to a design he could not guess. The wandering phantom that had helped him was now some way off and made more difficult to see, so Peter lifted once again his load and hung it on his back, then went along the lane to where the elm tree was. There he turned south and headed down beside the wide street where were many horses led, towards the crossroads that lay near its low end, as he had been told.

About him in their pens that bordered on the path or else come trotting out to join its filthy downhill skid were colts and mares and foals of every kind, so that he thought this must be where the horseflesh dealers made their truck. The smell of all the dung was sweet or like a fruited mash, although it was not pleasant in its sweetness and black flies were everywhere about in whispering thunderheads. The rank air here and the increasing closeness of the day brought out salt floods upon his legs and arms and made his heart fast and his breathing hard, or such was his conclusion. Looking up, he saw the blanketing of cloud above seemed nearer and, more than this, that it was now darker. Peter hoped his quest might soon be done, so that he could the sooner find some lodgings and be indoors if it rained.

The crossroads, when he came to it, had once again the sense that it was seen before, and Peter's head felt light now with a kind of ringing echo in his ears. For all he'd pissed or sweated, there'd not been a drop of water past his lips since dawn. He stood there on the crossing's northwest corner, and looked up along the new street he stood on the brink of, to its east. Here he beheld a scene he recognised that was all smokes and lights, and on the instant understood where he must be. This was the far end of the street where were the forges, that he'd seen the top of on that morning when he'd just arrived and come up from the bridge. If near the place where he stood now were truly England's centre, then how many hours ago had he been just a little walk from it? But then, had he come straight here he should not have seen the relic temple on the sheep track, nor the bloody well, nor should he have been there to save the child from harm. He stared as though made dumb along the sparking, smouldering lane and marvelled at where fate had brought him.

Peter saw there sooty men who worked in melted gold and old men, almost blinded by their years, stooped over silver filigrees. A man that seemed a dwarf stood with his straining cheeks puffed out and lips pursed tight upon the stem of a long pipe or trumpet, from the end of which there came a swelling bubble that was like one made of soap but all on fire, so Peter knew it for a ball blown in hot glass. He saw the smiling traders who had eyes more bright than all the gems kept in their purses, which they'd spill as glinting droplet-streams into an upturned, spidery palm. He saw the riches of the world fresh from their foundry and knew that, among these splendours, what he carried in his jute bag was a pearl without compare.

He turned the other way and looked instead off to the west, along a street where many of the horses from uphill behind him were now being led. Some fair way further down it on the side where Peter stood, he saw there was a mighty thatched roof risen up, and thought that this was the great hall he'd seen the back of when he was up near the smothering chalk-merchant's yard. Across from this and on the way's far side there was a church tower he could see above the building-tops. It might be that the thatched hall was the manor he had heard of, where a prince that was the kin to Offa lived and had a church built for him there upon his land. The good wife he had talked to up the far end of the metal-workers' street had said there was a church here called Saint Peter's, that he thought might be the building he saw now.

Go down until you reach the crossroads, so the ghost had said, then pass straight over, where if he continued down the place he sought should be across the street and on his left. Heart hammering still and in a failing light thrown from the rain-clouds gathering above, he went across the hectic byway haltingly, so that he might avoid its trundling wagons until he was safely on its further side. From this new vantage he gazed anxiously across the downhill road towards the east, to see if he might make out by some sign where was the centre that the pauper soul had told him of. Nothing was there saving more pasture and a fenced-out yard that from its din he thought to be a smith's, although not even this was halfway down the tilt, as he'd been made to think the centre should be. With a sinking worry in his gut he went on down the hill, his tired eyes darting back and forth expectantly about the grounds that were across the way.

The smith's yard, as he thought, was near the bottom, while up by the crossroads at its other end, there on the corner with the street of metal workers was a smith's yard also. Nothing was between them and their blackened forges saving only empty and untended mede, and on his cheek now Peter felt an early rain-spot, fat and cold.

He came upon what seemed to him the middle of the sloping way, and stopped to stand upon its edge and gaze across it, to where there was only wilderness. The thudding in his chest was louder, and he knew that he had once or many times before arrived here to find nothing. He was ever in the action of arriving here and finding nothing. Naught but all the drivers and their mounts gone up and down the broad path through a rain that now was spitting heavier. Naught save the idle man who stood outside the smith's yard, up about the corner this lane had with the gold-workers' street. Nothing but thistles and a tree and some bare ground, where he had thought to find the soul of all his land enthroned. He did not know if it were tears or sweat or rain that poured now down his face as he inclined it hopelessly toward the gravid sky and asked again what he had asked when at the other cross-path, only now his voice was angry and was tired, as if he did not care who heard.

"Is this the centre?"

All was in that moment stopped to him. Inside his ears the echo had become what was a humming of a kind, as if the halted instant were itself reverberant and rang with all the jewels of circumstance that made for its components. Rain hung motionless or else fell only slowly, with its liquids like to countless studs of opal that were everywhere fixed on the air, and in the coats of horses each hair was a blazing filament of brass. A shine was on the very dung that made it seem the prize of all the earth, and of the fields their bounty, that the flies set there about it were raised up on wings like to the windows of fine churches. On the waste-field there across the halted treasure-slide that was the street, midst weeds become like emerald flame, a man was standing all in white and in one hand he held a polished rod made from fair wood. His hair was like to milk, as was his robe, so that he stood as if a beacon in the scene and was the source of all its light, which painted an exquisite glint on every creature's eye. His kindly gaze met with the monk's, and Peter knew it was the friend who had appeared to him in Palestine, who'd charged him with his task and set him on his way. His journey's alpha was become its omega and in his hearing now there was a roar, as though the pounding of great wings, that Peter thought but his own pulse made amplified. The answer of his question was announced.

Across the stilled enchantment that was on the street, the burning figure threw aloft its arms for joy, whereupon there were bright and blinding pinions opened out to either side. Exultant it called out as in a mighty voice amid tall mountains, that the sounds of it whirled off a thousand ways all at one time. It was the foreign speech that Peter had once heard before, with words that burst as though they were puff-toadstools on his thoughts, to scatter new ideas like drifting spores.

"Iyeexieesst."

Yes! Yes! Yes, it is I! Yes, I exist! Yes, it is here in this place of excess that with a cross the centre shall be marked. Yes, it is here where is the exit of your journey, where both ye and I are come together. Yes, yes, yes, unto the very limits of existence, yes!

The being now held out his rounded rod as if he pointed it at Peter. Long and pale as though made out of pine, he saw its closer end had been worked to a point, where at the tip for decoration was a blue like cornflowers. Here the monk was puzzled and knew not why he was indicated thus, then saw that it was not at him the staff was aimed, but at a place that was behind him. Now he turned, and as he did it was as though his motion made the spell undone. The rushing sound he heard was not abated, yet the world was moved again, and rain dropped swiftly all about where it had only crawled before.

Behind him, set between what was a horse-shed and the premise of yet one more smith, he saw a wall of stone that had some violets grown out from its cracks, and let in to it was a wooden gate with iron trims that was a little open. Through this Peter saw a glade with swollen graves and tomb-stones raised up from its sods, and past it was a humble building made from dun and craggy stones by which two monks stood talking to each other. He was come upon a church. The dame who wore the Thor-stone and advised him earlier had said there was another church close by that of Saint Peter, which was called Saint Gregory's. His arm upon the left that held the sack was aching now and so he changed the weighted baggage to his right, although this did not make the aching cease. As though struck dumb he stumbled through what had become a downpour and went in the church-yard's gate, a little way along its path. The clerics broke off with their discourse and had seen him now, whereon they came towards him, slowly first then quickly, wearing faces of concern. Peter was fallen on his knees, though it were not in grateful prayer at his deliverance but more he found he could not longer stand.

The two friars, who soon came upon him, did their best to help him up and out of the deluge, but they were young and slender men who found he was too heavy. All they could accomplish was to set him on his back for comfort, with his head propped up against the bulged-out siding of a grave. They crouched above him with their habits spread out as they thought to keep the rain from off him, though it made them seem like crows and did not shield him much. Above them Peter saw the underbelly of the brewing storm, like darkened pearls that seethed and boiled and were become a changing and fantastic swim of wrinkles.

Everything was in that moment made alight, and then a frightful thunder boomed so that the monks who nursed him cried out and became more urgent in their questions, asking him where he was from and what it was that brought him here. The lightnings came again to drench the whole sky with their flash and Peter lifted up his arm, though not the left one that was numb, and made a gesture to his bag upon the soaking grass beside him.

When they understood him they pulled wide the jute-cloth neck and took what was inside out in the wind and wet. It was the hand-span of a man and half again across in both directions, roughly hewn from brownish stone so that it was too heavy to be lifted easy in one hand. The silvering rain dripped from its angles and its corners and the priests were now made mystified, as too were they amazed.

"What is it, brother? Can you tell us where you found it?"

Peter spoke, though it was hard, and from their faces had the sound of a delirium. From how they heard it, this was one who'd travelled far across the sea and had been near a place of skulls when he had found his treasure buried there. Unearthed, it was as though an angel had appeared to tell him he must take the relic and deliver it unto the centre of his land. It seemed to them as though he said he had a moment since met with this angel yet again, who had confirmed their small church as the pilgrim's destination. Much of what the poor man said was lost amongst the rumble of the heavens, and at last they begged that he should tell them where the land was he had been, that had this place of skulls, and where were holy tokens jutted up from out the soil.

Their voices had become a part of the almighty fluttering that filled him, as though come from far away so that he barely heard them. He was dying. He would not again see Medeshamstede, and he knew it now. Above, the rolling banks of sodden sky were a black silk of Orient that had been crushed into some fissured complication full of crease and shifting crack. He saw now what he had not seen before, that clouds were of a grotesque shape by reason that they were tucked in and had been cunningly compressed. He saw that were they but unfolded they should have a form at once more regular and yet more difficult to be encompassed by the gaze. He did not have the slightest understanding what this odd idea might mean, nor why the feeling was upon him that his years of journey had been naught except a single, briefly-taken step that was now done.

He thought that he had in the last few moments closed his eyes and yet it seemed still that he saw, perhaps mere dreams or memories of sight that were inside the flickering lids. He looked upon the worried brethren squatting over him and at the little church behind them. Just as with his new-found comprehension of the churning, pelting firmament above, so too he noticed for a first time how the corners of a building were made cleverly, that they could be unfolded in a manner whereby the inside of them was out. What he had earlier mistook for carvings over ledges on the church he saw now to be people small like unto mygge-flies, yet then knew that they were large as he but somehow far away. They waved and reached at him, the little men. It seemed to him that he had always known of them. The two monks by his side he could no longer see, although he heard them speaking with him yet, and asking him again whence he had come, his perfect sign to bring.

The last word that he said, it was Jerusalem.

MODERN TIMES

Sir Francis Drake leaned up against a wall of printed bills outside the Palace of Varieties and let his oiled bonce settle back against the giant names in black and red. According to his pocket watch there was a good half-hour before he had to draw his face on with burnt cork for the Inebriate. He could afford to kick his boots here on the corner until then and watch the horse-carts and the bicycles and all the pretty girls go by, with possibly another Woodbine for a bit of company.

He'd been a six-year-old at school in Lambeth when the other boys called him Sir Francis Drake. That had been at the outset of his mother's slide to poverty, when he'd been forced to wear a pair of her red stage-tights that had been cut down to look like stockings, although being pleated and bright crimson hadn't looked like that at all, accounting for the name. In many ways, he thought, he'd got off lightly. Sydney, his big brother … or his 'young 'un' as they'd called big brothers at the Hanwell School for Destitutes … had been obliged to wear a blazer, previously a velvet jacket of their mother's, which had red and black striped sleeves. Aged ten and therefore more self-conscious than his younger sibling, Sydney had been known as 'Joseph and his coat of many colours'.

Standing at the junction of the high-street now he found that he was sniggering at the nicknames, or at least at Sydney's, though they hadn't seemed so funny at the time. Still grinning, he consoled himself that Francis Drake had cut a famously good-looking and heroic dash, while Joseph had been dropped down a deep hole and left to die by brothers outraged at his dress-sense. Anyway, Sir Francis Drake was better than the other names he'd had across the years, which had endured far longer. Oatsie, that was one of them, just rhyming slang from oats and barley. He put up with it, but didn't like it much. He always thought it made him sound as though he was a yokel, and that wasn't quite the picture of himself that he was trying to present to people.

Up the hill towards his corner came a brewer's dray in the Phipps livery, a snorting dappled shire horse with its mop-head hooves as big as dinner plates, dragging its clinking, rattling cartload to a halt in front of him when it came to the crossing where he was. A weathered, chained-off tailboard kept its load in place: old ale-crates that had been stacked empty outside pubs come rain or shine, their damp wood dusted lime with mould, now filled again by brown and glinting cargo headed for some other hostelry, some other windswept corner of a beery cobbled yard. The cart was pulled up at the crossroads, waiting for a moving van and young lad on a bike to go across the other way, before it carried on uphill. He stood there leaning up against the posters, staring at it while it idled, and just for a laugh he thought he'd slip into his character as the Inebriate.

He screwed his eyes up, lowering the lids so he looked half asleep, and made his cake-hole into a lopsided smirk. Even without the cork this creased his face so he appeared some ten years older than his real age, which was twenty. Gurgling deep down in his throat with incoherent lust, he fixed his bleary gaze upon the brewer's wagon and began a veering but determined drunkard's walk in its direction, as though he were trying desperately to affect a normal swagger but with legs that barely functioned. He made three steps sideways off downhill but then recovered and took squinting aim again toward his prize, staggering off the curb and out into the mostly empty cobbled road as he approached the booze-truck standing on its far side. Reaching out his hands as if for all the chiming bottles, he slurred "I must be in Heaven", whereupon the startled driver looked round at him once then geed the horse on, swerving her around the rear end of the moving van that hadn't yet got quite across the street, and went on jingling up the hill as quickly as the vehicle could manage. Walking casually back across the highway to resume his place propped up against its corner wall he watched the cart go and felt half proud at his act's success and half ashamed for the exact same reason. He was far too good at doing drunks.

Of course, the drunks were all his father, Charles, who he'd been named after and who had died from dropsy just a decade earlier, in 1899. Four gallons. That was how much liquid had been drained out of his father's knee, and that was why the better the Inebriate went down, the guiltier he felt. He watched as the September sun fell slanting on the dirty old Northampton buildings hunched around the crossroad's corners, turning brickwork flocked with soot to orange fire, and thought about the last time that he'd spoken to his dad. It had been in a pub, he noted without much surprise. The Three Stags, hadn't it been, down Kennington Road? The Stags, the Horns, the Tankard, one of those at any rate. It had been round about this time of day, late afternoon or early evening, on his way back home to where he lived with Sydney and his mother along Pownall Terrace. Passing by the pub he'd had the strangest impulse he should push the swing-door open and look in.

His father had been sitting up one corner on his own, and through the two-inch crack by which he'd opened up the barroom door he'd had a rare chance to observe the man who'd sired him without being seen in turn. It was an awful sight. Charles Senior sat there in his drab upholstered nook and nursed a short glass of port wine. He'd one hand resting in his waist-coat as if to control his ragged breathing, so he'd still looked like Napoleon as mother always said, but bloated as though puffed up with a cycle-pump. He'd previously had a rather sleek, well-fed look, but had turned to an enormous, sloshing bag of water with his former handsomeness submerged and lost somewhere within it. The appearance he'd had once was smoothly oval-faced like Sydney's, although Sydney's father had been someone else entirely, some displaced Lord out in Africa, at least according to their mother. Even so, his brother still looked like Charles Senior much more than Charles Junior ever had, the latter favouring their mother more, with her dark curls and beautiful expressive eyes. His father's eyes had been sunk in the risen dough that was his face that afternoon in the Three Stags, but they'd lit up with what he'd realised with a start was joy when they'd alighted on the small boy peering in towards him through the partly open doorway and the lapping tides of smoke that hung suspended in the air between them.

Even now, stood at the bottom end of what was it called, Gold Street, in the dead-end venue of Northampton, halfway through another disappoint-ing tour with Karno's *Mumming Birds*, even today he couldn't quite get over just how pleased his dad had been to see him on that last occasion. Lord alone knew he'd not shown much interest in his son before then, and Charles Junior had been four years old already when he'd realised for the first time that he had a father. In the Stags that evening, though, the once-arresting vaudevillian had been all smiles and fond words, asking about Sydney and their mother, even taking his ten-year-old offspring in his arms and, for the first and last time, kissing him. Within a few weeks his old man was dying in the hospital, St. Thomas's, where that bloody Evangelist McNeil had offered only "as ye sow, so shall ye also reap" as consolation, heartless dog-faced bas-tard that he was. 'Old man'. Charles Junior chuckled ruefully and shook his head. His father had been thirty-seven, out at Tooting Cemetery in that white satin box, pale face framed by the daisies that Louise, his fancy woman, had arranged around the coffin's edge.

Perhaps his father knew, there in the fug and mumble of the Three Stags, that he held his son for the last time. Perhaps in some way everybody had a sense before it came, as if it were already all set out, of how their end was going to be. He glanced up at a speckled cloud of birds that dipped and swung and flattened out like a grey flame against the sunset, as they flocked above the local inns and hardware shops before returning home to roost, and thought it was a pity that you couldn't tell beforehand how your life was going to be, and never mind about your death. Things could go either way for him at present, and it was as unpredictable and random as the movements of those roosting pigeons, how events would finally fall out. Without a break of some sort he'd be spiralling around these northern towns until his dreams had all leaked out of him, had proven to be nothing but hot air from the beginning. Then there would be nothing for it but to live up to his mother's bleak prediction, every time he'd come home with a whiff of drink upon his breath: "You'll end up in the gutter like your father." He knew he was standing at a crossroads in a lot more ways than one, put it like that.

There were more carts and vans about now and a few more people crossing back and forth over the intersection as the town made its way home from work to have its tea. Women with prams and men with knapsacks, loud boys playing vicious, agonizing games of knuckles with each other while they waited for the conker season to commence, all jostling along the streets that led to the four compass points and crossing over where they joined, doing a hurried trot between the coal trucks and the atolls made of horse muck and, just at that moment, a red tram with an advertisement for Adnitt's gloves across its front. This came up from the west, along the road that he stood facing down with the inflated, sagging sun behind it, and continued on its iron rail past him on his right to hum away up Gold Street. He was living in a modern world all right, but didn't always feel like he belonged here, in the first years of this new and daunting century. He thought most people felt as jittery and out of place as he did, and that all the optimistic new Edwardians you heard about were only in the papers. Looking round him at the passing people, from their faces and the way they dressed you wouldn't know the Queen was dead eight years, but then when everyone was poor they tended to look much the same from one reign or one era to another. Poverty was timeless and you could depend upon it. It was never out of fashion.

And it never would be, not in England. Look at all the business with the People's Budget as they called it, where they'd made provisions for some money to be taken from the income tax and spent upon improvements in society, but then the House of Lords had thrown it out. Somebody ought to throw them out, he thought, and fumbled in his jacket for his pack of snouts. England was going down the plughole and he didn't reckon that this twentieth century was going to be as kindly to the country as the nineteenth had been. There were all the Germans, for a start, making their ugly noises and their ugly ships. Last year they'd bragged about how much ammonia they'd managed to produce, while now they bragged about how many bombs. Then there was India kicking up a fuss and wanting their reforms. Not that he blamed them, but he thought it was a sign there might not be so many pink bits to school atlases in years to come. The British Empire looked as if it was decaying, inconceivable as that might seem. It had most likely died, to his mind, with Victoria, and now was in the long slow process of accepting its demise and falling quietly to bits.

Thinking about the old days, watching while a junkman cursed a grocer's lad whose bike had shot across before his horse and cart, he was reminded of the first time that he'd come here to Northampton. He'd been nine, so it had been, what, 1898? Taking the box of ten Wills's Woodbines from his pocket, he extracted one of the remaining six and balanced it upon his lower lip while he returned the narrow packet to his coat. It was this very same theatre that he'd been appearing at, that first time more than ten years back, with Mr. Jackson's troupe of child clog dancers, the Eight Lancashire Lads. He'd stood on this corner with his best friend from the outfit, Boysie Bristol, and they'd talked about the double act that they were going to make it big with, as the Millionaire Tramps, decked out in fake whiskers and big diamond rings. This place had been the Grand Variety Hall back then, and Gus Levaine had still been running it, but otherwise it didn't seem so different. There they'd been, Boysie and Oatsie, cutting off from their rehearsals to waste time here on this spot and think about the fame and fortune they could see stretched out before them, much the same as he was doing still today, all these years later. Contrary to what he'd thought about his father knowing he was soon to die, it seemed more likely to him now that people just made mostly hopeless guesses at how things would work out. While he couldn't speak for Boysie Bristol, who he'd not seen in five years, for his part he was fairly certain that whatever roles the future held in store for him, Millionaire Tramp would not be one of them. He took a box of matches from his other pocket, turning to one side and pulling his lapel up as a wind-shield while he lit his fag.

Exhaling a blue plume, the west wind he was facing caught the smoke and dragged it back across his shoulder, off up Gold Street. He was looking at a little patch of wasteland halfway down the hill across the road from him and thinking vaguely of the Eight Lancashire Lads – four of them were from outside Lancashire and one of them had been a short-haired girl, but it was true that there were eight of them – when out of nowhere he remembered. This was where they'd met the black man, the first one he'd ever really seen except for pictures in encyclopaedias.

Him and Boysie had been skulking here, debating the logistics of their double act, deciding that their diamond rings should be made out of paste until their turn had made them into actual millionaires, when down the hill he'd come upon his funny bike, over the crossroads and towards them. The chap's skin was black as coal and not a shade of brown, with salt-and-pepper showing up already in his hair and beard so that the boys had thought he must be getting on for fifty. He was riding a peculiar contraption of a sort that neither lad had previously come across. It was a bicycle that had a two-wheeled cart fixed on the back, but what made it an oddment were its tyres, the two on the machine itself and those upon the trolley that was dragged behind it.

They'd been made of rope. Fitted around the bare iron rims were lengths of the same formerly-white hawser that had been employed to tie the trailer to the bike, now ridden through so many sooty puddles that their colour wasn't noticeably lighter than that of the cyclist himself.

The Negro, seeing that the boys were gaping at him as he came over the crossroads, smiled and pulled his bicycle-and-cart up to the curb a little past them down the hill. He did this with small wooden blocks that he had strapped beneath his shoes for brakes, taking his feet from off the pedals so that they hung down and scraped over the cobbles of the road until the wagon was brought in this manner to a halt. Its rider had looked back across his shoulder, grinning at the two boys who had been regarding him so rudely, and called out a friendly greeting to them.

"Ah hope you two youngsters ain't bin gittin' up tuh any trouble, now."

The man's voice had been marvellous, like nothing that they'd ever heard before. They'd trotted down the hill to where he was and told him they were waiting their turn to perform as clog dancers, which almost was the truth, then asked him where he'd come from. He'd be too self-conscious now, he thought, to just come out and say that to a black man, but when you're a kiddie you just speak what's on your mind. The fellow had black skin and had a foreign accent. It was only natural that they should ask where he was from, and naturally was how he'd taken it, without offence or anything. He'd told them he was from America.

Of course, that had set both boys off on a great stream of questions about Indians and cowboys, and if all the buildings in the cities were as tall as they'd been told. He'd laughed and said New York was "purty big", though looking back he hadn't seemed half so impressed about his origins as the two boys had been. He'd told them how he'd lived here in Northampton for about a year now, "down on Scarlut Well", wherever that was, and then after some more chat had said he ought to be about his work. He'd winked at them and told them to keep out of trouble, then he'd lifted up his wood-blocks and careered away downhill, towards where the ornate grey drum of a gas-holder reared against the sky. After the man had gone, the two of them had enthused for a time about America, and then had imitated how the black bloke talked, his own impression knocking Boysie's into a cocked hat. Then they'd gone back to all their Millionaire Tramp pipedreams, and he'd never thought about the curious encounter from that day to this.

He took a drag that was more like a sip off of his Woody and then blew the smoke out down his nose, the way that he'd seen others do and thought it looked quite stylish. There was now a fair old bunch of people heading back and forth over the crossroads, either riding or on foot, and he stood wondering what else there might have been from those times that he'd just forgot about. Not skull-faced Mrs. Jackson, wife of the Lancastrian former teacher who'd set up the company, sat suckling her baby son while overseeing the clog dancing troupe's rehearsals. He'd remember that sight if he lived to be a hundred. Now he thought about it, there were more than likely very few things like that Negro chap, things he'd forgot about by accident, although he knew there were a multitude of things that he'd forgot about on purpose, as it were.

It wasn't that he was ashamed of where he'd come from, but a lot of what this business was about was how things looked. He had an eye to how he wanted things to be reported if he ever managed to make something of himself. It didn't hurt to come from a poor background: 'rags to riches' was a story everybody loved. The rags part of it, though, that had to be depicted in a certain way, touched up and made more picturesque with all the nasty little details painted out. Nobody would have shed a tear for Little Nell if she'd expired in childbirth or from syphilis. The public had an appetite for sadness and for sentiment, and what they saw as all the colour of the worse-off classes, but nobody liked the taste of squalor. The Inebriate went down a treat for just so long as he was hanging round a lamppost, talking to it like a pal. The skit was cut off long before he shit his trousers or went home and put his wife in the infirmary by belting her until she couldn't walk.

That was another element that needed getting rid of if you wanted to present your tale of poverty in the right light, all of the fights and beatings. If at some uncertain point in the uncertain future he was asked to reminisce, say for some little magazine on the theatre, why, then he'd talk about *Mumming Birds*, he'd talk about *The Football Match* where he'd appeared with Harry Weldon, and he'd even talk about the Eight Lancashire Lads. The years that him and Sydney spent as the performing mascots of the Elephant Boys, though, they wouldn't get a mention. Not a dicky bird.

A sudden gust along the west arm of the crossroads blew the cigarette smoke back into his eyes so that they watered for a second and he couldn't see. He waited for a bit then wiped them with his cuff, hoping that all the people passing wouldn't think that he was crying; that a girl had stood him up or anything like that.

There had been nothing else but gangs all over London back when he was growing up. You didn't strictly have to be in one of them, and if you wanted to stay out of trouble it was better if you weren't, but there was something to be said for being friendly with a gang and sort of on its edges. If you picked a mob to hang around who'd got a reputation that was terrible enough, then with a bit of luck the other gangs would see that you were left alone. There hadn't been a crew in all the city or its boroughs half as frightening as the boys from Elephant and Castle, which was how come him and Sydney pallied up to them.

Him and his elder brother could both sing and dance by that age and had often done turns on the street to earn a penny when their mother's luck was going badly, as it often was. The Elephant Boys, who'd think nothing of disfiguring or robbing adult men, had been impressed by him and Sydney, shrewdly noticing the brothers' obvious entertainment value. They'd be called on as the gang's performing monkeys, either as a means of bringing in some coppers when the funds were low or else to lift morale before and after some hair-raising punch-up with a rival bunch of lads, perhaps the Bricklayer's Boys from Walworth, somebody like that. His speciality had been to jam his dainty feet into the handles on a pair of dustbin lids, then tap-dance on a metal grating just for all the deafening racket it would make. They'd called it Oatsie's Stamp. In fact, the Elephant Boys were the first to call him Oatsie, now he thought about it.

It had been a horror. He'd be doing Oatsie's Stamp with Sydney joining in on spoons or comb and paper, just whatever was about, and there the biggest thugs from out the gang would be, sat by the roadside, studiously sharpening their market-worker's hooks up on the curb-stones, sometimes looking up and whistling or clapping if they thought that him and Stakey were performing well. Stakey was what they'd called his brother in those days, from steak and kidney. There they were, Stakey and Oatsie, hiding round the corner, watching while the scrap or massacre was taking place, then afterwards they'd both be called back on so he could do the victory dance with a white face at all the business he'd just seen – boys running home with one ear hanging from their head, a lad of fourteen screaming with the blood all down his legs from where a hook had caught him up the arse – and he'd be thinking about all of this while he was stamping on an iron grid, the dustbin tops wedged on his plates of meat making a noise like Judgement Day, with hot sparks shearing from the clattering metal up round his bare knees. He'd been what, seven, eight years old?

If he'd learned anything from all of that it had been that he couldn't bear the thought of being hurt, of having something permanent done to his body or especially his face. They were the things he hoped would lift him out of all this grubbing round to make a crust. If anything should happen to them, that should be the end of it. Of him. He'd stood and watched once, sick with shame, while Sydney got a thumping from an older member of the gang who'd taken umbrage over something Syd had said. He'd known, and Sydney had assured him later, that there wasn't anything he could have done to help, but all the same he'd felt a coward over the affair. He could have said something, at least, but then that might have meant that he was next, so he'd just stood there and watched Stakey have his cheek split open. If, unlikely as it seemed, he ever wrote a memoir, none of this would be included.

Arguments or shouting matches, those he was all right with, but a fight was something he'd try anything he could do to avoid. Some of the older entertainers that he knocked about with on the circuit reckoned things were looking bad between England and Germany and thought sooner or later there might be a war. He'd be just twenty-one next April and then he'd have the key of the door, never been twenty-one before and all of that, but he'd still be of army age if anything should start. He didn't fancy that idea at all, and still hoped there was some way he could be safe in another country, if and when it happened. He'd been booked in for a month to play at the Folies Bergère for Karno earlier that year and he'd enjoyed it so much that he hadn't wanted to come home. He'd seen more lovely women than he'd ever dreamed of, which was saying something with *his* dreams. He'd met Mr. Debussy, the composer, and he'd had the only real brawl of his life with the prize-fighter Ernie Stone in Stone's hotel room after too much absinthe. Stone had won, of course, but he'd not done too bad considering and had surrendered only when the lightweight boxer hit him in the mouth so that he'd thought that he might lose his teeth. Returning to the old routines of *Mumming Birds* and touring gloomy north-ern towns after all that had been a disappointment, and he hoped it wouldn't be too long before he got to go abroad again, preferably not in a tin hat as a conscript of the army. Karno had been going on about America, but then Fred Karno talked about a lot of things and only some of them would ever come to fruit. He'd keep his fingers crossed and see what happened.

Oatsie took a few more quick puffs on his fag, then dropped it on the floor and ground it out beneath a swivelling boot before he kicked it off the curb. The crossroads' gutters brimmed with empty cigarette packs, Woodbines, Passing Clouds, and an unappetising salad of dead leaves. He had to squint about a bit before he caught sight of the trees that these had evidently fallen from, some way along the crossroads' westward route so that he only saw the tops of them, gold in the setting sun. Now that he looked he saw that there were also saplings sprouting from a couple of the chimneys closer to him, rooted in the dirty brickwork, like the one he could see growing up above the roofline of the public house across the street, the Crow and Horseshoe. Notic-ing a street-sign bolted up on the far corner and made near unreadable by soot and rust, he saw the slope he stood on was called Horseshoe Street, which helped explain at least the second part of the pub's name. And if those further trees whose tops he could just glimpse were standing in a graveyard then that might explain the first part, he supposed. He pictured chubby carrion birds all perched there screeching on their tombstones where the names had been erased by moss, and then he wished he hadn't.

He was only twenty after all. He didn't need to think of all that morbid business for a long time yet, although there'd been lads killed in the Boer

War a good sight younger than what he was now. For that matter, there had been kids in Lambeth who'd not got to their tenth birthdays. He wished he could still believe in God the way he had that night in Oakley Street, down in the basement where he was recovering from fever, when his mother had performed the most dramatic scenes from the New Testament to keep him occupied. She'd put all of the talents from a stage career she'd only recently abandoned into the performance and had almost done too good a job, with him left hoping that he'd have a relapse in his fever so that he could die that night and meet this Jesus who he'd heard so much about. She'd been that passionate, he'd never doubted any of the stories for an instant. Mind you, that had been before him and his brother were dragged through the workhouse with her, and before she had been put in the asylum for a spell. He wasn't quite so sure today about the heaven that he'd heard described that night, so vividly he couldn't wait to touch it.

These days, though, he'd lowered his sights and if he thought about what might be after death at all it was in terms of how he'd be remembered, or else how he'd be forgotten. What he wanted was his name to live on after him, and not just as a character from pubs around Walworth and Lambeth, how his father had been posthumously labelled. What he wanted was to be well thought of and well spoken of when he was dead, the way that someone like Fred Karno would be. Well, perhaps that was a bit ambitious, given Karno's stature in the business, but at least he'd like to be recalled as someone in the same division, even if he was a fair sight lower down in people's estimation than what Fred would be. Considering the future, when there'd be more people everywhere, he could see how the Music Hall would be much bigger and much more important than it was today, and Oatsie thought there was a chance that he'd get written up somewhere as a contributor to the tradition's early days, at least if he could manage not to get killed in a war before he'd got his break.

The ideas he was entertaining had begun to get him down. He swept his long-lashed girlish eyes across the passing throng in hope of spotting a big bust or pretty face that might distract him from his own mortality, but he was out of luck. There were some women who looked nice enough, but not what you'd call notable. As for their bosoms it was much the same tale. There was nothing that stood out, and so he drifted back to his uneasy contemplations.

What it was with death that worried him was that it made him feel like he was trapped upon a tramline that was only going to one place, that the iron rail was set already in the road in front of him, that it was all inevitable, although actually that was the thing that worried him with life as well, upon consideration. It was how life seemed sometimes like a skit that had been written out beforehand, with a punch line that was set up in advance. All you could do was try and keep up with its twists and turns while the momentum of the story dragged you through it, one scene following another. You were born, your father ran away, you sang and danced on stage to keep your family out the workhouse but they went there anyway, your brother got you a position with Fred Karno, you went off to Paris, came back home, missed out on Harry Weldon's former star role in *The Football Match* because of laryngitis, you got stuck with *Mumming Birds* instead and ended up back in Northampton, and then some time after that, a long time hopefully, you died.

It was all the "and then and then and then" of it that scared him, one scene following another, its events determining how all the acts thereafter would unfold, just like a great long line of dominoes all falling, and it didn't seem you could do anything to change the way they fell, the prearranged precision of it, regular as clockwork. It was as if life were some great big impersonal piece of machinery, like all the things they had in factories that would keep rolling on whatever happened. Getting born was just the same as getting your coat lining caught up in its wheels. Life pulled you in and that was that, you were enmeshed in all its circumstances, all its gears, until you reached the other end and got spat out, into a fancy box if you were lucky. There seemed very little choice in any of it. Half his life had been dictated by his family's financial situation, and the other half dictated by his own compulsions, by his need to be adored the way his mother had adored him, by his frantic scrabble to get somewhere and to be somebody.

But that wasn't the whole story, was it? Oatsie knew that was what everybody thought about him privately, all of his so-called pals from in the business, how they saw him as a climber, always chasing something – chasing women, chasing any scrap of work he had a sniff at, chasing fame and fortune – but he knew they'd got him wrong. Of course he wanted all those things, wanted them desperately, but so did everybody else, and it was never really the pursuit of recognition that propelled him through his life so much as the great black explosion of his background rumbling behind him. Mother starving her way into madness, father swelling up into a stinking, sloshing water-bomb, all of the pictures flickering past to a percussion made by fists on flesh and dustbin lids on gratings, hammering and clanging in the rising sparks. What kept him on the move, he knew, was not the destiny that he was chasing but the fate that he was running from. What people saw as climbing was no more than him attempting to arrest his fall.

The flow of vehicles and people at the crossroads moved like shuttles on a loom, first shunting back and forth from north to south, up and downhill in front of him, then rattling from west to east along the road that had the Crow and Horseshoe in and Gold Street. All the day's smells mingled there upon his corner, cooked by the unseasonably sunny afternoon and now condensed with sunset to a dog-blanket that hung above the junction. Horse manure was the most prevalent among the mixed aromas, giving the perfume its base, but there were other essences stirred into the bouquet: coal dust that faintly smelled of electricity and pepper, stale beer wafted from the ale-yards and another sweet yet noxious fragrance somewhere between death and pear drops that at first he couldn't place but finally decided that Northampton's many tanneries, most probably, were where the odour came from. Anyway, he put all this out of his mind because just then, ascending Horseshoe Street on his side, there was something that he definitely wouldn't turn his nose up at.

She'd never be mistaken for a classic beauty, not the type he'd witnessed on the Champs-Élysées, he could see that even at this distance, yet there seemed to be a radiance she carried with her. Strolling up the slope towards him from down near its bottom he could note a plumpness in the girl that might be more pronounced when she grew older, but which at that moment manifested in an irresistible arrangement of well-balanced and voluptuous curves. Her contours were as generous and as inviting to the eye as a lush garden, with a little of the garden or the orchard also in the sway her walk had underneath the cheap, thin fabric of a flapping summer skirt, her thick thighs tapering to sturdy calves and tiny china feet, which lazily swung back and forth below the fluttering hem as in her own good time she climbed the hill.

Her clothes were drab and mainly brown but complementary to the palette of the landscape she was sauntering through: the leaves that choked the gutters with a fire and chocolate medley and the faded sepia handbills peeling torn from the façade of an antique rival theatre, down there at the foot of Horseshoe Street. Setting the composition off, though, was the woman's hair. Deep auburn as a bowl of polished chestnuts and like lava where they caught the early evening light her curls fell round her rose cheeks in a jiggling spill of brandy snaps. A little more than five feet tall, a pocket goddess, she burned like a lamp flame that was low yet still illuminated the smoke-cured enclosures that it passed amongst.

As this young bit of stuff came closer, he could make out that she carried something up near her left shoulder, one hand underneath it as she leaned whatever it was on the slope of her full breast, the other wrapped around the lump to hold it to her, as you would a shopping bag if both the handles had come off. Still only halfway up the steep climb to where Oatsie stood, she stopped now to adjust her grip upon the bundle, shifting it up higher in her arms before she carried on. A fluffy outcrop on the top end of the item seemed to suddenly come loose and swivel round to point straight at him, whereupon he realised that it was a baby girl.

To be more accurate, despite its size and age it was perhaps … no, not perhaps … it was most certainly the loveliest human creature he had ever seen.

She seemed to be not much more than a year old, with her white-gold locks that dropped down in a shower of wedding rings and her enormous eyes the reassuring blue of police lanterns on a risky night. The infant girl was like a cygnet angel as she met his gaze unblinkingly, perched there in the embrace of the approaching woman. If he'd ever thought that his own beauty might one day lift him above the quagmire of his origins, here was a glory that they'd surely come to talk about the way they spoke of Helen. Nothing would prevent this child from growing to a diamond of her age, a face that stared out of a poster at you once and haunted you forever. She would never in her life go unappreciated or unloved and you could see it in the level, unassuming look that she already had, the inviolable confidence of a celestial orchid grown amidst the clovers and the weeds. If he knew anything, he knew the tot would end up as a bigger name than him and Karno put together. It was unavoidable.

The fact that the small girl was being carried by the shapely little woman didn't necessarily mean they were child and mother, he reflected, looking on the bright side, although even from this far away you couldn't help but notice a resemblance. Still, there was a chance this chickabiddy was the tiny vision's aunt, minding the baby while its parents were at work, and that therefore she might be unattached, despite appearances. It didn't really matter in the long run in that all he wanted was to while away ten minutes with some pleasant and flirtatious talk, not scarper off to Gretna with her, but it somehow always made him feel uncomfortable if he was chatting up a married girl.

Climbing the hill, the woman gazed towards its far side and the patch of wasteland that he'd noticed earlier, dreamily contemplating the gone-over buddleia erupting from between its tumbles of collapsed old brick, seemingly unaware of his existence. He already had the baby's eye, however, so he thought he'd work with that and see how far he got. He dipped his chin until it touched his collar and the fat knot of his tie, then looked up at the toddler from beneath his curling ostrich lashes and the jet-black hyphens of his brows. He gave the gravely staring little beauty what he knew was his most impish grin, accompanied by a brief, bashful flutter of his eyelids. Suddenly he broke out with a clattering burst of expert tap dance on the worn buff flagstones, lasting no more than three seconds before it was over, at which juncture he stopped dead and looked away uphill, pretending to disown his terpsichorean interlude as if it hadn't happened.

Next, at intervals, he darted shy and furtive glances back across his shoulder as though to establish whether the cherubic child was looking at him, though he knew she would be. Every time he met her look, which now seemed slightly more delighted and amused, he ducked his face away as though embarrassed and stared pointedly towards the opposite direction for a moment before letting his gaze creep, as though reluctantly, back round across his shoulder for another glimpse of her, like in a game of peek-a-boo. On the third time he did this, he saw that the pretty woman carrying the waif had been alerted by her charge's gurglings and was looking at him too, wearing a knowing smile that seemed one of appraisal yet was at the same time somehow challenging, as if she weighed him up according to a measure he was unfamiliar with. The breeze was lifting more now as the day cooled off, smashing the dandelion clocks that grew upon the scrap-ground and then scattering their drifting cogs along the street. It shook the woman's curls like burnished catkins as she studied him, deciding whether she approved of what she saw.

It seemed she did, although perhaps not without reservations. Only several paces from him now she called out cheerfully to Oatsie over the remaining distance.

"You've got an admirer." Obviously, she meant the baby.

In a funny way her voice was like blackcurrant jam, which he was passing through a fad for at the time. Both hearteningly commonplace and fruity with suggestive undertones, its sweetness had a quality of darkly dripping plenty and, as well, the hint of a sharp bite. Her accent, though, was not the strange Northampton intonation he'd expected. If he'd not known better, he'd have sworn that she was from South London.

By then, she'd got to the corner where she stopped, a foot or so away from him. Up closer, now that he could see the woman and her baby in more detail, they were certainly no let-down. If the child had been more beautiful or perfect he'd have wept, while the adult companion, who he'd got his eye on, had a glow and warmth about her that if anything enhanced the first impression that she'd made on him from further down the hill. She looked to be about his age, and the hot summer that was drawing to its close had raised a crop of freckles on her face and arms that were like smaller versions of the specks on lilies. He became aware that he was staring at her and decided that he'd better say something.

"Well, just as long as my admirer knows that I was standing here admiring her before she was admiring me." This wasn't quite so obviously about the baby, necessarily, but he was happy with the ambiguity. The woman laughed and it was music, more that of a pub piano on a Friday night than of Debussy, but still music just the same. The western sky was being daubed in other colours now, in melancholy piles of gold like lost exchequers over the gasholder, pastel smudges of pale violet and bruise mauve on its peripheries as she replied.

"Ooh, get away with yer. You'll give 'er a big 'ed, then she'll be spoilt and no one'll want anything to do with 'er." She changed her hold upon the infant here, switching its weight onto her other arm so that he now saw her left hand

and the plain ring on its third finger. Oh well. He found that he quite enjoyed the bit of company, and didn't mind much that it wouldn't lead to anything. He changed his line of complimentary spiel so it was now directed solely at the baby and, freed from the need to make a good impression on the woman, Oatsie was surprised to find that he meant every word of it for once.

"I don't believe it. She looks like it'd take more than flattery to spoil her, and I'd bet five bob that she'll have people flocking round her everywhere she goes. What do you call her?"

Here the brunette turned her face towards that of the small girl in her arms, to smile fondly and proudly as she let their foreheads gently touch together. There were geese above the gasworks.

"'Er name's May, like mine. May Warren. What's yours, anyway, stood out 'ere on Vint's Palace corner with yer pimpy eyes?"

Oatsie was so shocked that his mouth fell open. No one had described what he still thought of as his smouldering gaze in quite that way before. After an instant of stunned silence, though, he laughed with genuine admiration at the woman's insight and her brutal honesty. What served to make the slur much funnier was that at just the moment it was said, the woman's baby turned her head and gazed straight at him with a puzzled, sympathetic look, as if the child echoed her mother's query, also wondering what he was doing out here on the corner with his pimpy eyes. This made him laugh longer and harder, with the woman chuckling deliciously along and finally her tiny daughter joining in as well, not wishing to appear as if she didn't understand.

When they'd eventually stopped, he realised with a certain wonderment how good it felt after the months and years of scripted comedy to have a real, spontaneous laugh, particularly at a joke against himself. A joke that told him he was getting too big for his boots, and that the serious career concerns that were upsetting him not five minutes before were likely to be just as puffed up and inflated. It had put things in perspective. He supposed that was what laughs were for.

He nodded, with as little smugness as he could, towards his name up on the poster he was leaning on, but told her she should call him Oatsie. All his friends did, anyway, and he thought Charles would sound too stuck-up to a girl like this. When him and Sydney had been small their mother had been doing well at first, and would parade her boys along Kennington Road in outfits that she knew nobody else around there could have possibly afforded in their wildest dreams. That had made the collapse to poverty and pleated crimson tights for stockings more unbearable, of course, and ever since he'd had a fear of people thinking that he was above himself, so that they'd be less cruel if he should fall. Oatsie would do, he thought. Their two names even had a sort of harvest supper ring to them. Oatsie and May.

The woman looked at him, eyes narrowed quizzically, miniature fans of decorative wrinkles opening and closing at their corners.

"Oatsie. Oats and barley. Yer a Londoner."

She cocked her head a little back and to one side, regarding him with what seemed like a frown of deep suspicion, so that for a minute he was worried. Had the girl got something against London? Then her face relaxed into a smile again, except that now the grin had something of a knowing, cat-like quality.

"From Lambeth. West Square, off St. George's Road in Lambeth. Am I right?"

The baby had lost interest in Oatsie now, and entertained herself by bunching her small fists, painfully from the look of it, within the copper tangles of her mother's hair. He felt his jaw drop open for the second time in just about as many minutes, although this time was no prelude to hilarity. Frankly, it rather put the wind up him. Who was this woman, who knew things she couldn't know? Was she a Gypsy? Was all this a dream that he was having at the age of six, about the funny world there'd be when he was older, sleeping fitfully, his shaved head rasping on the rough cloth of a workhouse pillow? There and then he felt as if he'd let his hold on what was real slip from his fingers, and a momentary vertigo came over him so that the crossroads' arms seemed almost to be spinning like the needle of a broken compass, chimney smoke and gilded clouds whirled into streaming mile-wide hoops, caught by the centrifugal tug of the horizon. He did not know, any longer, where he was or what was going on between him and this startling young mother. Even at a distance he'd known that she'd turn out to be lively, but the actuality of her went far beyond what he'd foreseen. She was a shocker, her and her unearthly daughter both.

Seeing the panic and confusion in his eyes she laughed again, a throaty bubbling that was shrewd and faintly lewd as well. He had a sense that she enjoyed putting a scare in people now and then, both for her own amusement and to show her power. While his respect for her was mounting by the second, the desire he'd felt when he first saw her was evaporating in direct proportion. This was someone who despite her modest stature was a bigger person than he knew himself to be. This girl, he thought, could eat him, then burp raucously and be upon her way without a second thought.

At last, though, she took pity on him. Disentangling her ringlets from the baby's fingers while the younger May was suitably distracted by another gliding, jingling tram, she proved that she was no professional magician by explaining just how her mind-reading turn had been accomplished.

"I'm from Lambeth, just off Lambeth Walk in Regent Street, that little terrace. Vernall. That's me maiden name. I can remember 'ow our mam and dad would take me out around there when I was a little girl. There was a pub they went to, up the London Road, and when we come 'ome we'd cut back across West Square. I see yer there a time or two. You had a brother what were older, didn't yer?"

He was relieved, though hardly less amazed. The woman's feat of memory, although far past his own capacity, was not untypical amongst those who'd grown up in crowded little neighbourhoods, where everyone appeared to know the names of everybody else within a two-mile radius, along with all their children's and their parents' names and all the mystifying quirks and threads of happenstance that linked the generations. Having never learned the trick of it himself, perhaps because he'd always hoped he wouldn't be stuck in those places very long, he'd been thrown off his guard when it was played upon him, here in this improbable location, in this far-flung town. Unlike the woman, he could not remember any childhood meetings for the life of him.

"Yes. You're right, I had a brother Sydney. Still have, for that matter. When were you around there, then? How old are you?"

She raised, at this point, a reproachful eyebrow at his lack of manners, asking her about her age, but finally replied.

"Old as me tongue but older than me teeth. I'm twenty, if you must know. I was born the tenth of March in 1889."

The more she reassured him that there was a natural explanation for her knowing his childhood address, the eerier the incident of their chance meeting struck him. This surprisingly imposing woman had been born within a month of him and lived perhaps two hundred yards from him while he was growing up. Now here they both were, sixty miles and twenty years away from where they'd started out, stood at one of a hundred corners in one of a hundred towns. It made him think again about his previously held opinions as regards predestination, and if people ever really had an inkling of the path ahead of them. He could see now that it was actually two separate questions that required two different answers. Yes, he thought that probably there was a pattern in how things occurred that had been drafted out beforehand, or at least it sometimes seemed there was, but then again he also thought that if there were such a design it would be far too big and too outlandish to be read or understood, so no one could predict how all its curlicues were going to be resolved, except by accident. You might as well attempt to forecast all the shapes a purple sunset-cloud would make before it burned away, or which cart would give way to which when they met at the crossroads' corners. It was all too complicated to make sense of it, whatever all the prophets and the tea-leaf readers might pretend. He shook his head, replying to her, muttering something inadequate about it being a small world.

The lovely baby was now squirming restlessly, and Oatsie was afraid her mother would use this excuse to take her home and end their conversation, but she asked instead what he was he was doing at the Palace of Varieties, or the Vint Palace as she seemingly insisted upon calling it. He told her how he generally did a bit of this, a bit of that, but how tonight he was appearing with Fred Karno's *Mumming Birds* as the Inebriate. She said it sounded proper funny, and said how she'd always thought it would be nice to be someone who worked in entertainment.

"Mind you, it's our kid, our Johnny. 'E's the one who's always going on about the stage. This is me youngest brother. Reckons that 'e's gunna end up in theatre or else playin' music in a band, but 'e's all talk. 'E wunt 'ave lessons, wouldn't even if we could afford 'em. Too much like 'ard work."

He nodded in response, watching a milk cart headed back towards its depot at the bottom of the street, downhill behind her. From where he was standing it appeared about an inch high, dragged by its disconsolate and shrunken mare along the girl's right shoulder, losing itself in the autumn forest of her hair for quite some time before it re-emerged upon her left and then slunk wearily from sight.

"Well, if your brother doesn't want to put the hours in, he won't get too far as a performer. Mind you, he could still make money as a manager or impresario, and then he could be as bone idle as he liked."

She laughed at this, and said she'd pass on the advice. He took advantage of the pause to ask her why she'd called the venue the Vint Palace.

"Oh, it's 'ad lots of names over the years. Our dad's 'ad family in Northampton ever since I can remember, always going back and forth from here to Lambeth, so 'e's kept up with the changes. It began as the Alhambra Music Hall, from what 'e said, and then they changed it to the Grand Variety around the time what I was born. Accordin' to our dad there was a bad patch sometime after then, when it weren't even a theatre for a while. For getting on five years it weren't the same place one month to the next. It was a greengrocer's and then it was a place where they sold bikes. It was a pub they called the Crow before that moved across the street to be the Crow and Horseshoe, and I can remember when I was a little girl ten years back and it was a coffee house. All the free-thinkers as they called 'em used to go in there, and they were some right 'Erberts, I can tell yer. Anyway, the year the Queen died, that was when they done it up and christened it the Palace of Varieties. Old Mr. Vint, he bought the place a year ago, but still ain't 'ad the sign changed."

Oatsie nodded, looking at the old establishment in a new light. Because he'd come here as a Lancashire Lad all those years ago and it was a variety hall then, he had assumed that it had been one ever since, that it had always been one and, in every likelihood, it always would be. The young woman's casual listing of the purposes to which the premises had been put in the meantime made him feel uncomfortable, although he couldn't put his finger on the reason why. Oatsie supposed it was because the world he'd been brought up in, horrible and suffocating as he'd reckoned it, at least stayed where it was from one year, often from one century, unto the next. Even this shabby corner of Northampton here, a place about as run down as the Lambeth he'd been born to, you could see most of the buildings standing round you were still housing the same businesses they'd housed a hundred years before, even if names and management were different now. That's why the girl's account of the hall's changing fortunes had unsettled him, because the story was a relatively rare one still, although you heard more like it every week. What should it all be like, he wondered, if these here-today-and-gone-tomorrow fleapits came to be the rule, not the exception? If he were to come back here in, say, forty years time and found it was a place that sold, he didn't know, electric guns or something like that, and no longer a variety hall? Perhaps by then there wouldn't even be variety halls. Well, that was an exaggeration, obviously, but it was how May's off-hand narrative had made him feel, uneasy with the way that things were going these days, in the modern world. He changed the subject, asking her about herself instead.

"You sound as if you know the place, gal, anyway. How long is it you've lived here now?"

She cast her eyes up thoughtfully at scraps of lilac cirrus on a field of deepening blue, while her astonishingly well-behaved and patient offspring sucked a gleaming thumb and stared, it seemed indifferently, at Oatsie.

"Ninety-five, I think it was, when I was six we come up 'ere, although our dad, 'e's always goin' back and forth, to get the work. 'E walks it, the old bugger, all the way to London and then back. Many's the time when we've not seen 'im for six weeks, not 'ide nor 'air, then 'e comes waltzing in 'alf-cut with presents, little bits and bobs for everybody. No, it's not a bad old place. This bit round 'ere's a lot like Lambeth, 'ow the people are. Sometimes I 'ardly feel as if we've moved."

Some of the narrow shops across the other side of Horseshoe Street were putting lights on now, a dim glow tinged with green around its edges that crept out between the sparse and shadowy displays in their front windows. Lowering her gaze from up among the chimneybreasts, the elder May looked proudly down now at the younger, cradled in her sturdy, tiger-lily arms.

"I think I'm 'ere for good. I 'ope I am, at any rate, and 'ope the little 'un shall be, too. They're a straightforward lot round these parts, in the main, and there's some real old characters. It's where I met me chap, my Tom, and we got wed up at the Guildhall. All 'is people, they're all local, all the Warrens, and we've lots of family up 'ere on the Vernall side as well. No, it's all right, Northampton is. They do a good pork pie, and there's some lovely parks, Victoria, Abington, and Beckett's. That's where I've just took this one, down by the river there. We saw the swans and went out on the island, didn't we, me duck?"

This was directed at the baby, who was finally beginning to show signs of restlessness. Her mother stuck out her own lower lip and turned her brows up at a tragic angle, mimicking her daughter's glum expression.

"I expect she's 'ungry. Goin' down the park I stopped at Gotcher Johnson's for two ounce o' rainbow drops, but I 'ad one or two as well, so they were finished up some time ago. I'd better get 'er 'ome up Fort Street for 'er tea. It's potted meat, 'er favourite. It's been nice to meet yer, Oatsie. 'Ope yer skit goes well."

At that, he bade goodbye to both the Mays, and said it had been similarly nice to meet the pair of them. He shook the baby's damp, minuscule hand and told her that he hoped to see her name on a big hoarding one day. To her mother he just said "Take care of her", then as the woman chuckled and assured him that she would, he wondered why he'd come out with it. What a stupid thing to say, as if suggesting that she wouldn't look after a child like that. The babe and parent waited until there was nothing coming, then they crossed the foot of Gold Street and went up the hill towards the north. He stood there on his corner and admired the woman's bum, moving beneath her swinging skirt as she mounted the slope, with her imagined buttocks like two faces pressed together as their owners acted out a vigorous two-step. Or perhaps two wrestlers full of muscles in a crush, each one in turn gaining an inch on their opponent who immediately takes it back, deadlocked so that they merely seem to heave from side to side. He noticed at this point the baby, staring soberly across the woman's shoulder at him as she was borne off into the distance. Feeling oddly mortified to think the child had caught him looking at her mother's bottom he glanced rapidly away towards the plot of scrubland halfway down the hill, and when he looked back just a minute later they were gone.

He looked to see what time it was, then fished another Woody from his dwindling pack and lit it. That had been a funny conversation, now he thought about it. It had made an impact on him that was only just now starting to sink in. That woman, May, born just a few weeks after he was, raised not half a dozen streets away, and somehow they'd both met up on a corner in another town twenty years later. Who'd believe it? It was one of those occurrences that he supposed were bound to happen now and then, despite the odds, yet when they did it always felt uncanny. There was always the suggestion of a pattern in the way things worked that you could almost understand, but when you tried to pin down what the meaning or significance might be it all just fizzled out and you were left no clearer than you were before.

Perhaps the only meaning that events had was the meaning that we brought to them, but even knowing this was probably the case, it frankly wasn't that much help. It didn't stop us chasing after meaning, scrabbling like ferrets for it through a maze of burrows in our thoughts and sometimes getting lost down in the dark. He couldn't help but think about the woman he'd just met, how the encounter had stirred twenty-year-old sediments up from the bed of him, and how that made him feel. The root of it, he thought, was how the similarities between his background and the woman's had made all their differences stand out in just as sharp relief.

For one thing he was on the verge, or so he hoped, of an escape from the soot-smothered prison of his and the woman's common origins, from poverty, obscurity and streets like this, where now the sky was cut to rich blue diamonds by the iron struts of the gas-holder. Escape from England, even, if he could. In the event of a forthcoming scrap with Germany, Sir Francis Drake hoped to be in his hammock and a thousand miles away. As for the spirited young mother, May, she didn't have those opportunities. Without the talents he'd inherited or learned from both his entertainer parents, she had lived a life more limited in terms of both its expectations and its possibilities, and its horizons, which she did not feel compelled to cross, were that much closer than the boundaries around his own. She'd said herself she thought she'd live here in this district all her life, and that her gorgeous little daughter would as well. There were no hopes or dreams that she was chasing, Oatsie knew. In neighbourhoods like this, such things weren't practical, were only ever burdensome and painful liabilities. That lively young girl was resigned to live and die, it would appear, within the small cage of her circumstances; didn't even seem to know it was a cage or see its grimy bars. He thanked whatever guardian angel he might have for giving him at least the slim chance to avoid a lifelong penal sentence like the one that she existed under. Every woman, man or baby passing by him through the tannery-infused slum twilight was to all intents and purposes a convict, serving out their time in harsh conditions without any likely prospect of reprieve or pardon. Everyone was safe in lavender.

But May had seemed content, and not resigned at all. May had seemed more content than Oatsie felt himself.

He thought about it, blowing out a wavering slate-and-sepia fern of smoke through pretty, puckered lips. Some of the carriages that moved across the junction had by now fired up their lanterns, as the lapis of the skies above grew gradually more profound. Chandelier snails, they crawled uphill and sparkled in the dead-end dusk.

He saw there were two sides to being poor, to having nothing, not even ambitions. It was true that May and all the others like her didn't have his drive, his talents or his opportunities for betterment, but then they didn't have his doubts, his fears of failing or his nagging guilt to deal with, either. These were people, heads down, crunching through the pavement's autumn garnish, who weren't on the run from anything, especially the streets they'd come from, so they didn't have to feel as if they were deserters all the time. They knew their place, the worst-off, in more ways than one. They knew exactly where they were in so far as society should be concerned, but more than that they knew their place; they knew the bricks and mortar that surrounded them so intimately that it was like love. Most of the poor souls sluicing through this crossroad's floodgates hailed from families, he knew, that would have lived around these parts for generations, just because the distance you could travel was more limited before there had been railway trains. They trudged these byways in the knowledge that their grandparents and great-grandparents had done just the same a hundred years before, had let their troubles soak in the same pubs, then poured them out in the same churches. Every mean and lowly detail of the neighbourhood was in their blood. These knotted lanes and listing pie-shops were the sprawling body they'd emerged from. They knew all the mildewed alleys, all the rain-butts where tin waterspouts had rusted paper-thin. All of the area's smells and blemishes were as familiar to them as their mothers' moles, and even if her face were lined and dirty they could never go away and leave her. Even if she lost her mind, they …

Tears were standing in his eyes. He blinked them back and then took three quick puffs upon his cigarette before he wiped away the excess moisture with his fingertips, pretending that the smoke had blinded him. None of the passers-by were looking at him, anyway. He felt abruptly angry with himself for all the sloppy sentiment that he still harboured and for just how easily the waterworks came welling up. He was a man now, he was twenty though he felt like thirty sometimes, and he shouldn't still be blubbing like a little kid. He wasn't six. He wasn't weeping over his cropped curls in Lambeth Workhouse and it wasn't 1895. Although he knew he hadn't yet completely taken in the fact, this was the twentieth century. It needed people who were bright and up-to-date and forward-looking in the way they thought, not people who got tearful dwelling on the past. If he were to make anything out of his life he'd better pull himself together, sharpish. Drawing deep upon his fag he held it in and looked around him at the slowly darkening intersection, trying to regard it from a modern, realistic viewpoint rather than a maudlin and nostalgic one.

Yes, you could come to look upon this haphazard array of weather-beaten hulks as like a mother, he could see that. At the same time, like a mother, it was not a thing that would eternally endure. Old age had ravaged it with change, and wasn't done yet by a long chalk. Just as he'd been thinking a few moments back about how previous generations were restricted in their chances to go travelling, he understood that things should be much different in this new, enlightened age. The steam engine had altered everything, and on the streets of London now you could see motor-carriages, of which he thought there should be more in time to come. Communities of countless decades' standing like the one around him would perhaps not seem as well-knit if the inmates stood a chance of easily and cheaply getting out, of going where the work was better without walking sixty miles like that girl's dad had done. Even without a war to decimate its young, he doubted that the bonds connecting people to a place like this would last another hundred years. Districts like this were dying. It was no betrayal, wanting to leap out of them to somewhere safe before they finally went under. Anyone who'd seen the world, who felt that they were free to come and go just as they pleased, why would they want to be stuck in a dump, a town, a country even, that was like this? Anyone with any sense who had the means would be off like a shot, soon as they could. There wasn't anything to keep them here, and …

Coming through the settled gloaming up the hill was an old black man, on a bicycle that had ropes fastened to its rims instead of tyres, pulling a cart with the same kind of wheels behind it, juddering like a ghost-tale skeleton across the cobbles.

Oatsie wondered, for the second time within a half an hour, if he were dreaming. It was the same man, riding the same outlandish boneshaker, as on the afternoon twelve years before when he'd stood here with Boysie Bristol, here on this same corner, saying "Yes, but if they're millionaires why do they act like tramps?"

The Negro paused his strange contraption at the top of Horseshoe Street, there on the corner opposite to Oatsie's, waiting for a horse-bus to go by the other way. Of course, he'd aged across the intervening years so that his hair and beard were now a shock of white, but it was without question the same man. He didn't, upon this occasion, notice Oatsie but sat there astride his saddle waiting for the bus to pass so that he could continue up the hill. He had a faraway and faintly troubled look upon his strong, broad features and did not seem in the same expansive mood as when they'd last met, back when the old queen was still alive and it had been a different world. Even if Oatsie had still been an eager, gawping lad of eight he doubted that the black man would have noticed him, as pensive and distracted as he now appeared to be.

The omnibus having by this time rumbled past, the man lifted his feet, which still had wood blocks strapped beneath the shoes. He set them on the pedals, standing up and leaning forward as he pushed down strenuously, gradually acquiring the momentum that would take him and his trailer past the crossroads and away uphill through the descending gloom, in which he was soon lost from sight.

Watching the black chap disappear, he sucked upon his cigarette without account of how low it had burned, so that it scorched his fingertips and made him yelp as he threw the offending ember to the ground, stamping it out in angry retribution. Even as he stood there cursing, waggling his fingers so the breeze would soothe the burn, he had a sense of wonderment at what had just occurred, at the whole atmosphere of this peculiar place where it would seem that such things happened all the time. To think that in the dozen years since he'd last been here, while he'd roamed the length and breadth of England and had his Parisian adventure, all those different nights he'd spent in all those towns and cities, all that time the black man had been still here, going back and forth along the same route every day. He didn't know why he found this so marvellous. What, had he thought that people disappeared because he didn't happen to be looking at them?

Then again, a fellow such as that, who'd already seen the America that Oatsie longed for and despite that had decided to stay here … it might not be a marvel, but it was a puzzle, certainly. Raising his eyebrows and his shoulders at the same time in a theatrical shrug of overemphasised bewilderment aimed at nobody in particular, he took a last glance at the crossroads as it drowned in indigo then walked the few steps to the Palace of Varieties' diminutive front door. He pushed it open and went in, where it was slightly warmer, walking past the ticket office with a nod and grunt to the uninterested portly type inside. He wondered if it would get busy, if they'd get much of a crowd tonight, but you could never tell. Things didn't rest so much in the gods' laps as in how many laps they could entice into the Gods.

The whitewashed storage shed that was his dressing room was down a short but complicated series of bare-boarded corridors and then across a cramped and ancient-looking yard that had a water closet running off from it and stagnant puddles, which had taken up a permanent position in the sinks of the subsiding flagstones. He'd popped in the changing room a little earlier to stow some of his props and gear, but hadn't really had a good look round yet. Much to his surprise the uninhabitable-looking quarters had a gas mantle set halfway down one flaking wall, which he was quick to put a match to so that he could shed some light upon the subject.

He'd seen worse. There was a yellow stone sink in the corner, with its brass tap bent to one side all skew-whiff, and dribbling spinach-coloured verdigris in veins shot through the metal so it looked like putrid cheese. He found a cracked and book-sized mirror in a wooden frame hung by a bent nail from the inside of the door and stood himself before it while he groped in the inside breast pocket of his jacket for a piece of cork. With this produced he struck another match and held the stopper's end that was already blackened in the flame so that it would be freshly charred and not too faint to see from the back row. Waving away the smoke and waiting just a mo for his impromptu stick of makeup to cool down, he gazed into the broken looking glass. Ignoring the black fissure that ran in a steep diagonal across the face of his reflection, he allowed his features to relax into the bleary bloodhound sag of the Inebriate, his sozzled and lopsided grin, with rheumy eyes that he could just about keep open.

First he crushed some of the greasy cork-ash to a dust between his fingers and began applying it beneath his jaw-line, working the black powder in around his tightly compressed mouth and up across his jowls to just below the cheekbones, where it was the shadowy grey stubble of a chap out on a binge who'd been without a wash and shave for some few days. Using the stub of cork itself he emphasised the creases underneath his tucked-in jaw until he had the onset of a double chin, then went to work around the sockets of his eyes to get the wastrel's haggard look before progressing to the heavy, rakishly-arched brows. He daubed a drooping and fatigued moustache on his top lip where there was none, letting the ends trail down beside the corners of his mouth in straggling lines. Just about satisfied with how he had the face he wiped the charcoal from his fingers straight into his greasy hair, messing it all around on purpose so that bits of it stuck up and curls went everywhere like oily breakers on a choppy sea.

He checked his image in the fractured mirror, holding his own gaze. He thought that it was almost there. He started in on the fine detail, deepening the wrinkles at the corners of his mouth and eyes, his whole face starting to take on a greyish pallor from the liberal application of the cork. It could be eerie sometimes, sitting in a silent, empty, unfamiliar room and staring into your own eyes while you changed into someone else. It made you realise that what you thought of as yourself, your personality, the biggest part of that was only in your face.

He watched as the persona that he'd carefully constructed for himself sank out of sight. The animated gaze that he used to get women's sympathy or to communicate his eagerness and his intelligence, all that was gone into the drunk's befuddled squint. The careful way he held his features to convey the breezy confidence of a young fellow of today, in a young century, this was rubbed out, smudged by a sooty thumb into the slack leer of Victorian Lambeth. All the hallmarks of his cultivation and the progress he had made in bettering himself, in struggling up from the ancestral mire, were wiped away. In the divided countenance that stared back at him from the split glass, his restricted present and big future had subsided to the sucking, clutching sludge that was his past. His father and the thousand barroom-doors he'd popped his head round as a child when sent to find him. Small blood vessels ruptured in the cheeks of lushingtons, pressed on the chilly pillow of a curb. Gore rinsed from hooks in horse-troughs. All of it, still waiting there if he were to relax that cheeky, cheery smile for just an instant, just a fraction of an inch.

There was a scent of damp and dereliction draped about the room. Beneath the smeared and ground-in ash he had no colour to his face at all now in the wan, uneven light. Black hair and eyes stood out from a complexion that was silver-grey. Contained within the mirror frame, it was the fading photograph of someone trapped forever in a certain time, a certain place, in an identity that could not be escaped. The portrait of a relative or a theatre idol from a lost time when your parents had been young, frozen eternally within the pale emulsions.

He put on the outsized, wrinkled jacket that he wore as the Inebriate, and filled his green glass 'San Diego' bottle from the tap. Somewhere not far away, he hoped, an audience was waiting. The gas mantle hissed a dismal premonition.

BLIND, BUT NOW I SEE

The mark of a great man, way Henry figured it, was in the way he'd gone about things while he was still living, and the reputation that he left behind when he was gone. That's why he weren't surprised to find out that Bill Cody would be represented to Eternity as a roof-ornament made out of grubby stone that birds had done their business on.

When he'd glanced up and seen the face raised from the orange brick-work on the last house in the row, carved on some sort of plaque up near its roof, at first he'd took it for the Lord. There was the long hair and the beard and what he'd thought to be a halo, then he'd seen it was a cowboy hat if you was looking up from underneath the brim, and if the feller had his head tipped back. That's when he'd cottoned on that it was Buffalo Bill.

The row of houses, what they called a terrace, had the street out front and then in back you had a lot of acres of green meadow where they held the races and what have you. There was this short little alley running from the front to back what led out on the racetrack grounds, and it was up on one of the slate rooftops overlooking this cut-through you had the face carved on the wall up there. Henry had heard how Cody's Wild West Show had come here to these race grounds in Northampton, maybe five or ten year earlier than he'd arrived here in the town himself, which was in ninety-seven. Annie Oakley had been doing her performance, and some Indian braves was there by all accounts. He guessed one of the well-off people living in these houses must have took a shine to Cody and decided how he'd look good stuck up on they roof. Weren't nothing wrong with that. Way Henry saw it, people could like what they wanted to, so long as it weren't nothing bad.

That said, the carving weren't that much like Cody, not as Henry recol-lected from the once or twice he'd met the man. That was a long time back, admitted, up in Marshall, Kansas, out the back room of Elvira Conely's laun-dry what she had. That would have been seventy-five, seventy-six, something like that, when Henry was a handsome young man in his middle twenties, even though he said it all himself. Thing was, he hadn't paid that much attention at the time to Buffalo Bill, since it had been Elvira he'd been mostly there to look at. All the same, he didn't think the William Cody what he'd knowed could be mistook for Jesus Christ Our Lord, no matter how much you was looking up at him from underneath or how much he was standing with his hat tipped back.

He'd been a vain man, or at least that had been Henry's own impression, if the truth were to be told. He doubted that Elvira would have hung around with Cody if it hadn't been important to the way how she was seen in Marshall. Coloured women couldn't have too many well-known white friends.

Henry pushed his bicycle and cart along the cobbled alley from the race-track, with the ropes he had around the wheel-rims crunching through the leaves what was all heaped up in the gutters. He took one last glance at Colonel Cody, where the smoke from out a nearby chimney made it look as if he'd got his hat on fire, then climbed up on the saddle with his brake-blocks on his feet and started back through all the side-streets for the big main road what went way out to Kettering, and what would take him back to the town centre of Northampton.

He'd not wanted to come up this way today, since he was planning for to ride around the villages out on the south-east side of town. There was a man he'd met, though, said there was good slate tiles in an iron-railed back yard off the racetrack where a shed was all fell in, but he'd turned out to be a fool and all the tiles were broke and weren't worth nothing. Henry sighed, pedalling out of Hood Street and downhill towards the town, then thought that he'd do well to buck his ideas up and quit complaining. It weren't like the day was wasted. In the east the sun was big and scarlet, hung low in a milky fog that would burn off once the September morning woke itself up properly and went about its business. He'd still got the time to strike out where he wanted and be back down Scarletwell before the evening settled in.

He didn't need to do no pedalling, hardly, heading into town along the Kettering Road. All Henry needed do was roll downhill and touch his brake blocks on the street once in a while, so that he didn't get up too much speed and shake his trolley what he pulled behind him all to bits upon the cobble stones. The houses and the shops with all they signs and windows flowed by on each side of him like river-drift as he went rattling down into the centre. Pretty much he had the whole road to himself, it being early like it was. A little further on there was a streetcar headed into town the same way he was going, just a couple people on its upstairs there, and coming up the hill towards him was a feller had a cart as he was pushing got all chimney brushes on. Besides that, one or two folks was around, out with they errands on the sidewalk. There was an old lady looked surprised when Henry cycled past her, and two fellers wearing caps seemed like they on they way to work stared at him hard, but he'd been round these parts too long to pay it any mind. He liked it better, though, down where he was in Scarletwell. The folks there, plenty of them, was worse off than he was so he'd got nobody looking down on him, and when they seen him riding round they'd all just shout out, "Hey, Black Charley. How's your luck?" and that was that.

There was a little breeze now, strumming on the streetcar lines strung overhead while he went under them. He rolled round by the church there on the Grove Road corner to his right and swerved to miss some horse-shit what was lying in the street as he come in towards the square. He made another bend when he went by the Unitarian chapel on the other side, and then it was all shops and public houses and the big old leather warehouse what they had in back of Mr. Bradlaugh's statue. Leather was important to the trade round here and always had been, but it still made Henry shake his head how otherwise the town was mostly bars and churches. Could be it was all that stitching shoes had folks so that they spent they private time in getting liquored up or praying.

Somebody was even drunk asleep in the railed-off ground that was round the block the statue stood on when he pedalled past it on the left of him. He didn't think Mr. Charles Bradlaugh would approve of that if he was looking down from Heaven, what with him being so forthright in his views on alcohol, but then since Mr. Bradlaugh hadn't had no faith in the Almighty it was likely that he'd not approve of Heaven neither. Bradlaugh was somebody Henry couldn't get to grips with or make up his mind about. Man was an atheist there on the one hand, and to Henry's mind an atheist was just another way of saying fool. Then on the other hand you had the way he was against strong drink, which Henry could admire, and how he'd stood up for the coloured folks in India when he weren't standing up for all the poor folks here at home. He'd spoke his mind and done what he considered the right thing, Henry supposed. Bradlaugh had been a good man and the Lord would possibly forgive the atheism when all that was took into account, so Henry figured how he ought to let it go by too. The man deserved his fine white statue with its finger pointing west to Wales and the Atlantic Sea and to America beyond, while in the same sense you could say that Buffalo Bill deserved his shabby piece of stone. Just 'cause a feller said he weren't no Christian didn't stop him acting like one, and although he didn't like to think it, he could see how sometimes the reverse of that was true as well.

He went on past the shop what had the Cadbury's chocolate and the sign for Storton's Lungwort painted on the wall up top. He'd had some trouble coughing lately and he thought it could be he should maybe try a little of that stuff, if it weren't too expensive. Next you'd got the store what had the ladies' things, then Mr. Brugger's place with all the clocks and pocket-watches in its window. Up ahead of him he'd nearly caught up to the streetcar, which he saw now was the number six what went down to St. James's End, what they called Jimmy's End. There was a paid advertisement up on the rear of it for some enlarging spectacles, with two big round eyes underneath the business name what made it look as though the backside of the streetcar had a face. It reached the crossroads they were nearing and went straight across with its bell clanging, staring back towards him like it was surprised or scared as it went on down Abington Street there, while he turned left and coasted down York Road in the direction of the hospital, touching his wood blocks on the cobbles every now and then to slow him down.

There was another crossroads by the hospital down halfway, with the route what went on out towards Great Billing. He went over it and carried on downhill the way what he was going. On the corner of the hospital's front yard as he went past it, near the statue of the King's head what they had there, some young boys was laughing at his wheels with all the rope on. One of them yelled out that he should have a bath, but Henry made out like he didn't hear and went on down to Beckett's Park, as used to be Cow Meadow. Ignorant was what they were, brung up by ignorant folk. Paid no attention they'd move on and find some other fool thing they could laugh at. They weren't going to string him up or shoot him, and in that case far as Henry was concerned about it, they could shout out what the heck they liked. So long as he weren't bothered none then all they did was make they own selves look like halfwits, far as he could see.

He took a left turn at the bottom, curving round by the old yellow stone wall and into the Bedford Road just over from the park, where he touched down his wooden blocks and fetched his bicycle and cart up at the drinking fountain what was set back in a recess there. He climbed down off his saddle and he leaned the whole affair against the weather-beat old stones, with all the dandelions growed out from in between, while he stepped to the well and took a drink. It weren't that he was thirsty, but if he was down here then he liked to take a few sips of the water, just for luck. This was the place they said Saint Thomas Becket quenched his thirst when he come through Northampton ages since, and that was good enough for Henry.

Ducking down into the alcove, Henry pressed one pale palm on the worn brass spigot, with his other cupped to catch the twisted silver stream and scoop it to his lips, an action he repeated three or four times 'til he'd got a proper mouthful. It was good, and had the taste of stone and brass and his own fingers. Henry reckoned that amounted to a saintly flavour. Wiping a wet hand on one leg of his shiny pants he straightened up and climbed back on the bicycle, stood in his seat to get the thing in motion. He sailed south-east on the Bedford Road, with first the park and all its trees across from him and then the empty fields stretched to the abbey out at Delapre. The walls and corners of Northampton fell away behind like weights from off his back, and all he had was flat grass between him and the toy villages off in the haze of the horizon. Clouds was piled like mashed potato in blue gravy, and Black Charley found that he was whistling some Sousa while he went along.

The marching music made him think of Buffalo Bill again, sounding all puffed up like it did, which led him back to thoughts of Kansas and Elvira Conely. Great Lord, that woman had some spirit in her, setting up her laundry there in Marshall way ahead of the great exodus and doing as well as she did. She'd knowed Bill Hickok too, but Hickok had been in his grave by the late eighteen-seventies when Henry and his parents got to the Midwest. From how Elvira spoke about the feller, you got the impression that Wild Bill had had a lot of good in him, and that his reputation was deserved. Mind you, in private and among her own kind, she'd admit that Britton Johnson, who she'd also knowed and who was also dead by that time, could have shot the pants off Wild Bill Hickok. It had took a bunch of twenty-five Comanche warriors to bring Britton Johnson down, you never mind about no lone drunk and no lucky shot in some saloon. Yet even little children over here, they knew of Buffalo Bill and Wild Bill Hickok but nobody ever heard of Johnson and you didn't have to think about it long to figure why that was. Looked like a Pharaoh, how Elvira spoke of him. Looked fine without his shirt on was her exact words.

Uphill and on the left of him, across the fenced-off grass and the black spreads of woodland, Henry could about make out the rooftops of the fancy hospital they'd got up there for people who was troubled in they minds and could afford the rent. For them what couldn't, there was what you called a workhouse in the old Saint Edmund's parish, out the Wellingborough Road, or else the Berry Wood asylum round the turn there on the way through Duston. Leaving it behind him, Henry pedalled harder where a bridge bulged up above a river tributary, and had a tickle in his belly like he'd got no weight when he shot down the other side and on towards Great Houghton. He was thinking of Elvira still, admiring her in a more understanding and respectful fashion than the way what he'd admired her in his younger days.

'Course, she'd been only one of the outstanding gals they had in those parts round that time, but she'd been first, upping to Kansas on her own in sixty-eight, and Henry thought a lot of them good women was just following Elvira's lead, not that it took away from what they did. There was Miss St. Pierre Ruffin helping folks with cash from her Relief Association. There was Mrs. Carter, Henry Carter's missus, talked her husband into walking with her all the way from Tennessee, him carrying the tools and her the blankets. Thinking of it, it had mostly been the women was behind the whole migration, even when their men-folk shrugged it off and made out they was just fine where they was. Henry could see now what he hadn't seen back then, how that was 'cause the women had the worst of it down in the South, what with the rapes and having to bring up they children with all that. Henry's own momma had told Henry's poppa how if he weren't man enough to get his wife and son to some place safe and decent, then she'd just take Henry and light out for

Kansas on her own. Said how she'd walk there like the Carters if needs be, although when Henry's pa had finally relented they'd gone in a wagon same as everybody else. Considering those times made Henry's shoulder itch the way it always did, so that he took one hand from off the handlebar to scratch it through his jacket and his shirt the best he could.

A watermill went by him on his right, ducks honking as they took up from a close-by pond where all the morning light from off it was too bright to look at. Sheridan near Marshall had been where Elvira Conely had made her home after she broke up with the soldier feller she was married to out in St. Louis. Back in them days Sheridan had been considered worse than Dodge for all its gambling and murders and loose women, but Elvira carried herself like a queen, straight-backed and tall and black as ebony. When later on she took up as the governess for rich old Mr. Bullard and his family, Bullard's children put it all about how she was kin to royalty from Africa or some such, and Elvira never said or did a thing what could be held to contradict that. Last he'd heard she was in Illinois, and Henry hoped that she was doing fine.

He went on with the climbing sun before him and the roadside puddles flashing in his eyes. The shadows from the moving cloud-banks slipped across the shaggy fields a little at a time as though the summer was on its last legs, unshaved and staggering like a bum. Weeds in the ditches had boiled up and spilled into the road or swallowed fence-posts whole, where dying bees was stumbling in the dying honeysuckle, trying to drag the season out a little longer and not let it slip away. Upon his right he passed the narrow lane what would have took him down to Hardingstone and pedalled on along the top side of Great Houghton, where he met a couple farm carts going by the other way all loaded up with straw. The feller on the box of the first wagon looked away from Henry like he didn't want to let on he could even see him, but the second cart was driven by a red-faced farmer what knew Henry from his previous visits to those parts and reined his horse up, grinning as he stopped to say hello.

"Why, Charley, you black bugger. Are youm come round here to steal us valuables again? Ah, it's a wonder we'm got two sticks to us name, with all that plunder what youm 'ad already."

Henry laughed. He liked the man, whose name was Bob, and knew as Bob liked him. The making fun of people, it was just a way they had round here of saying you was close enough to have a joke together, and so he came back in kind.

"Well, now, you know I got my eye on that gold throne o' your'n, that big one what you sit in when you got the servants bringing in the venison and that."

Bob roared so loud he scared his mare. Once she was settled down again, the two men asked each other how they wives and families was keeping and such things as that, then shook each other by the hand and carried on they individual ways. In Henry's case, it wasn't far before he made a right turn down Great Houghton's high street, past the schoolhouse with blackberry hedges hanging over its front wall. He went along beside the village church then steered his bicycle into the purse-bag close what had the rectory, where the old lady who kept house would sometime give him things she didn't want no more. Climbing down off his saddle, Henry thought the rectory looked grand, the way the light caught on its rough brown stones and on the ivy fanned out in a green wing up above its entranceway. The close was shaded by an oak tree so that sun fell through the leaves like burning jigsaw pieces scattered on the cobbles and the paths. Birds hopping round up in the branches didn't act concerned or stop they singing when he lifted up the iron knocker with a lion's head on and let it fall on the big black-painted door.

The woman, who he knew as Mrs. Bruce, answered his knock and seemed like she was pleased to see him. She asked Henry in, so long as he could leave his boots on the front step, and made him take a cup of weak tea and a plate of little sandwiches there with her in the parlour while she looked out all the bits and pieces what she'd put aside. He didn't know why when he thought of Mrs. Bruce he thought of her as an old lady, for the truth was that she couldn't be much older than what Henry was himself, that being near on sixty years of age. Her hair was white as snow, but so was his, and he believed it might be how she acted with him made him think of her as old, with something in her manner like to that of Henry's mother. She was smiling while she poured him out his tea and asked him things about religion like she always did. She was a churchgoer like him, except that Mrs. Bruce was in the choir. She told him all the favourite hymns she'd got as she went back and forth about the room and gathered up the worn-out clothes there were what he could have.

"'The Day Thou Gavest, Lord, Is Ended'. There's another one I like. Did they sing hymns back where you come from, Mr. George?"

Lowering the doll-house china from his lips, Henry agreed they did.

"Yes, ma'am. We didn't have no church, though, so my folks would sing while they was working or else round the fireside of an evening. I sure loved them songs. They used to send me off to sleep at night."

Smoothing the doilies or whatever they was on her chair-arms, Mrs. Bruce peered at him with a sorry look upon her face.

"You poor soul. Was there one that you liked better than the others?"

Henry chuckled as he nodded, setting down his empty cup in its white saucer.

"Ma'am, for me there ain't but one tune in the running. It was that 'Amazing Grace' I liked the best, I don't know if you heard it?"

The old lady beamed, delighted.

"Ooh, yes, that's a lovely song. 'How sweet the sound, that saved a wretch like me.' Ooh, yes, I know that. Lovely."

She looked up towards the picture rail a little down below the ceiling there and frowned like she was trying to think of something.

"Do you know, I think the chap who wrote it lived not far from here, unless I've mixed him up with someone else. John Newton, now was that his name? Or was it Newton who chopped down the apple tree and said he couldn't tell a lie?"

After he'd let that one sink in a while and puzzled it all through he told her that to his best understanding, it had been a man named Newton who sat underneath an apple tree and figured out from that why things fell down instead of up. The feller who'd said how he couldn't tell a lie, that was George Washington the president, and far as Henry knew it was a cherry tree what he'd cut down. She listened, nodding.

"Ah. That's where I'd got it wrong. His people came from round here somewhere, too, that General Washington. The one who wrote 'Amazing Grace', that would be Mr. Newton. As I heard it told, he used to be the parson up the road at Olney, though I shouldn't swear to it."

Henry felt stirred up by this in a manner what surprised him. He'd been sincere when he'd said it was his favourite song, and not just trying to sweeten the old lady. He recalled the women singing it out in the fields, his momma there amongst them, and it seemed like half his life had been caught up in its refrain. He'd heard it sung since he'd been in his cradle, and he'd thought it must have been a black man's tune from long ago, like it had always been there. Finding out about this Pastor Newton fair made Henry's head spin, just to think how far he'd come since he first heard that song, only to wind up quite by accident upon the doorstep of the man what wrote it.

He'd never been exactly sure why him and his Selina had felt such an urge to settle in Northampton and raise children, after they'd come here on that big sheep-drive out from Wales, working their way in a grey sea of animals more vast than anything what Henry ever heard of in the land where he was born. His life had taken him all over, and he'd never thought no more than it was the Almighty's plan, and that it weren't for him to know the purpose of it. All the same, the feeling him and his Selina had when they'd first seen the Boroughs, what was down from Sheep Street where the two of them arrived and reached right to the place in Scarletwell Street where they'd finally make their home, when they'd seen all the little rooftops it had seemed to them as though there was just something in the place, some kind of heart under the chimney smoke. It made a certain sense to Henry now, with learning about Mr. Newton and "Amazing Grace" and all. Perhaps this was some sort of holy place, what had such holy people come from it? He felt sure he was making too much out of things as usual, like a darned fool, but the news made Henry feel excited in a way he hadn't known since he was small, and he'd be lying if he said it didn't.

Him and Mrs. Bruce talked over this and that there in the parlour while they finished up they tea and bread, with dust-specks twinkling in the light through the net drapes and a grandfather clock making its graveyard tick from up one corner. When they'd done she gave him the unwanted woollens what she'd sorted out and then walked with him to the front door, where he put them in the trailer box he towed behind his bicycle. He thanked her kindly for the clothes, and for the tea and conversation, and said he'd be sure to call again when he was coming through that area. They waved and wished each other well, then Henry rattled back along the high street on his rope-rimmed wheels, "Amazing Grace" sung out of tune trailing behind him through the tumbling leaves and bright rays of the afternoon.

When he'd come out the high street and was back once more upon the Bedford Road he rode on down it to the east. The sun was pretty much above him now so that he barely cast a shadow as he went along, puffing while he was pedalling and singing while he coasted. On his right as he departed from Great Houghton he could see the village cemetery with the white markers lit up bright like pillowcases, there against a blanket made from sleeping green. A little after that he passed upon the left of him the lane what would have took him up to Little Houghton, but he didn't have no business there and so went on a distance, following the south-east bend the road made out to Brafield. There was hedgerows rearing up beside his route, sometimes so high that he was riding through they shade when he went down a hollow, holes low in the walls of bracken here and there what led most probably to dens, them made by animals or village boys or something wild like that. Blood on its snout and black dirt on its paws, whichever one it was.

The land out here was mostly farming property and pretty flat, too, so you'd think it would look more like Kansas, but that weren't the way of it. For one thing, England was a whole lot greener and it seemed there was more flowers of different kinds, maybe because of all the gardening what folks here liked to do, even the kind as lived down Scarletwell Street with they little bricked-in yards. Another thing was how they'd had a lot of time here to get fussy and ingenious about the simplest matters, such as how they built they hay-stacks, how they lay down straw to make a roof, or how they fitted chunks of rock without cement to raise a wall would stand three hundred year. Across the whole sweep of the county he could see, there was these details, things what someone's great-great-great-grandpappy figured out how they could do when Queen Elizabeth was on the throne or somebody like that. Bridges and wells and the canals with lock gates, where men wearing boots up round they thighs trod down the clay to mend the waterways if they was split. There was a fair amount of learning evident, even out here where you might think there weren't a man-made thing in sight. The lonely trees he passed what looked like they was struggled up from nothing else but blind, wild nature had been planted by somebody years back for a well-considered reason, Henry knew. Maybe a windbreak to protect a crop weren't there no more, or little hard green apples for to make the pigs they mash. A quilt of fields was spread about him, and each ragged line of it was there on purpose.

He passed through Brafield when the bell in the St. Lawrence Church struck once for one o'clock, and he was held up for some minutes just outside of there by sheep what filled the road, so that he'd got to wait while they was herded up the lane and in they field before he could go by. The man who walked along with all these bleating critters didn't speak to Henry, not as such, but gave a kind of nod and raised the peak up of his cap a touch, to show how he appreciated Henry being patient. Henry smiled and nodded back, as though to say it weren't no inconvenience, which was the truth. The feller had an English collie helping him control the animals, and Henry thought they was a joy to watch. He couldn't help it, he'd been soft about them hounds since he'd first seen 'em when he got to Wales in ninety-six. That one blue eye they'd got and how they understood what you was saying had amazed him. They'd not had no dogs like that where Henry come from, which was New York and before that Kansas, and before that Tennessee. He scratched his shoulder while he stood and watched the last few sheep hauling they shitty asses out his way and through the pasture gate where they belonged, and then he carried on. There weren't nobody living there in Brafield he could say he knowed, and he was keen besides to ride down the long road to Yardley, a much better prospect to his mind, before the day wore on.

The clouds went by above like ships would if you steered your bicycle and cart across the bed of a clear ocean and somehow you was immune from drowning. Henry had the zinging rhythm of his wheels beneath him and the regular, reassuring click of that stray spoke. The road was pretty much straight on past Denton so he didn't have to think about his riding none and could just listen to the gossip of the trees when he went past, or to a crow some distance off, laughing at something nasty with a voice like rifle-shots.

He hadn't liked his spell upon them ocean waves, aboard the *Pride of Bethlehem* set out from Newark, bound for Cardiff. Henry was a man in his late forties even then, and that weren't no age to go running off to sea. It was the way things had worked out, was all. He'd stayed in Marshall with his momma and his poppa while they was alive, used up what some would say was Henry's best years looking after them and not begrudged one day of it. After they'd gone, though, there weren't nothing keeping him in Kansas, when he'd got no family and nobody he had feelings for. Elvira Conely, by that time she was working for the Bullards, on vacation with them half the time so Henry didn't see her round no more. He'd drifted east in screeching, shuddering railroad cars out to the coast, and when he'd had the opportunity to work his passage on the dirty old steel-freighter what was headed out for Britain, he'd jumped at it. Hadn't given it no second thought, though that weren't on account of bravery so much as it was on account of him not understanding how far off this Britain place would prove to be.

He didn't know how many actual weeks it was he'd been afloat, it may have been no more then just a couple, but it seemed like it went on forever, and at times he'd felt so sick he thought he'd die there without ever seeing land again. He'd stayed below the decks as best he could to keep the endless iron breakers out of sight, shovelling coal down in the boiler room where his white shipmates asked how come he didn't take his shirt off like they'd done and weren't he hot and all? And Henry had just grinned and said no sir, he weren't too hot and he was used to places plenty warmer, although obviously that weren't in truth the reason why he wouldn't work in his bare chest. Somebody put the rumour round he had an extra nipple what he was ashamed of, and he'd thought it better that he let it go at that, since that had put an end to all the questions.

On the *Pride of Bethlehem* you had sheet steel, with anything from candy-bars to chapbooks and dime novels making up the ballast. By then, the United States was turning out more steel than Britain was, so that it meant as they could sell it cheaper, even with the cost of shipping it across. Besides, on the way back what they'd be bringing home was wool from Wales, so that the owners saw a handsome profit both ways on the journey. When he'd not been either hard at work or sicking up, Henry had passed his time in reading Wild West tales on the already-yellowed pages of pamphlets intended for the five-and-ten. Buffalo Bill had been the hero in a number of the stories, shooting outlaws and protecting wagon trains from renegades, when all he ever did was play the big clown in his travelling circus. William Cody. If there'd ever been a man more fit to be a stone face with just chimneys blowing hot air for companionship, then Henry didn't know of him.

Black fields what had but lately had they stubble burned was on his right now, as he knew belonged to Grange Farm, just ahead. The white birds hopping from one scorched rut to another Henry thought was gulls, although these parts was just about as distant from the sea as you could get in England. Up ahead of him the road forked into two, where what they called Northampton Road branched off towards the village square of Denton. Denton was a nice place, but there weren't much in the way of pickings. It was best if Henry only went there once or maybe twice a year, to make it worth his while, and he stuck on the right-hand track now so that he could skirt the village to its south and carry on for Yardley – Yardley Hastings what they called it. He was just past Denton when he cycled through a rain shower was so small that he was in one side of it and out the other without feeling more than one or two spots on his brow. The clouds above him had a couple towers of smooth grey marble floating in amongst the white now, but the sky was mostly a clear blue and Henry doubted if the downpour would amount to anything.

Way off on Henry's left he could make out the darker patchwork of the woods round Castle Ashby. He'd been out there one time when he'd met a local feller couldn't wait to tell him all about the place, how back in ancient London when they'd wanted two wood giants to stand outside they city gates, what was called Gog and Magog, it was Castle Ashby where they'd got the trees. The man was proud of where he lived and all its history, how a lot of folks round here was. He'd told Henry how he thought this county was a holy place, and that's how come that London wanted trees from here. Henry weren't sure about Northampton's holiness, not back then and not now, not even after hearing what he had about the Reverend Newton and "Amazing Grace". It seemed like it was someway special sure enough, though holy weren't a word what Henry would have used. For one thing, holiness, as Henry saw it, it was a mite cleaner than what Scarletwell Street was. But on the other hand, he'd thought the feller had been right, too, in a way: if there was anything about this place was holy, then it likely was the trees.

Henry remembered when he'd first arrived with his new wife in these parts and the tree what they'd seen then, after he'd been in Britain no more than six months. When he'd come off the ship in Cardiff and decided there weren't no way he could face another sea voyage home, he'd got himself a lodging at a place called Tiger Bay what had some coloured people living there. That hadn't been what Henry wanted, though. That was too much like it had ended up in Kansas, with the coloured folks all in one district what was let to fall in pieces until Kansas was too much like Tennessee. Yes, he liked his own people good enough, but not when they was kept away from other folks like they was in a gosh-darned zoo. Henry had struck out for mid-Wales on foot, and it was on the way there that he'd met Selina in a place, Abergavenny, what was on the River Usk. The way they'd fell in love and then got married was that quick it made his head spin, thinking of it. That, and how they'd right away gone up to Builth Wells, for the droving. First thing Henry knowed he'd been wed to a pretty white girl half his age, lying beside her underneath a stretched out piece of canvas while the hundred thousand sheep what they was helping herd to England cried and shuffled in the night outside. They'd been upon the road for near as long as it had took the *Pride of Bethlehem* to get to Britain, but then at the end of it they'd come across what he knew now was

Spencer Bridge, then up Crane Hill and Grafton Street to Sheep Street, which was where they'd seen the tree.

Henry had waded through the herd that milled about there in the wide street, meeting the head drover at the gates of what they called Saint Sepulchre's, which was the oldest and the darnedest church he'd ever seen. The boss had given him his ticket and told Henry he should take it to a place they called the Welsh House in the market square, where Henry would be give his wages. Him and his Selina had set off up Sheep Street for the centre of the town, and it was in an open yard off on they right there that the tree was standing: a giant beech so big and old that they could only stop and marvel at it, even with the ticket for his pay burning a hole in Henry's pants like it was doing. It was that far round, the tree, it would have taken four or five men easy to link up they hands about it, and he'd later heard how it was seven hundred year or more in age. You thought about a tree as old as that one looked, you couldn't help but think of all what it had seen, all what had happened round it in its time. The horseback knights they used to have, and all them battles like in England's Civil War, which had took place a powerful while before America's. You couldn't stand there staring like him and Selina had without you started wondering where every mark and scar had come from, whether it was from a pike or maybe from a musket ball. They'd only looked at it a while, and then they'd picked up Henry's pay before they poked around the town and found they place in Scarletwell, what had its own amazing sights, but he believed that tree had played as big a part in Henry and Selina thinking they should settle here as any practical consideration. There was something in it made the town seem solid and deep-rooted. And there weren't nobody hanging from it.

It was coming on for some while after two he got to Yardley. He went up the first turn on his left, called the Northampton Road just like in Denton, up into the village square, there where they had the school. It was a pretty building what had butter-colour stones and a nice archway leading to its playyard, and he could see children through a downstairs window busy with they lessons, painting onto sheets of butcher's paper at a long wood table. Henry's business what he had was with the caretaker, so he pulled up his bicycle across the street from the main schoolhouse, near where this caretaker lived. It was a feller Henry had a good few years on, although he'd had the misfortune to lose nearly all his hair so he looked older than what Henry was. He answered Henry's knock but didn't ask him in, although he'd got a bag of things he'd saved what he brung through out on the step and said as they was Henry's if he wanted them. There was two empty picture frames made Henry wonder what was in them once, a pair of old shoes and some pants made out of corduroy ripped down they backside so that they was near in half. He thanked the caretaker politely, putting it all in his cart alongside what he'd picked up from

Great Houghton, and was just about to shake hands and be back upon his way when it occurred to him that he should ask how far it was to Olney.

"Olney? Well, you're nearly there."

The caretaker wiped dust from off the picture-frames onto his overall, then pointed back across the village square towards they left.

"See Little Street there? What you want to do is go down that onto the High Street where it takes you back onto the Bedford Road. Keep on it out of Yardley, and you'll not go far before you reach a lane that drops off from the main road to your right. You get on that, what's called the Yardley Road, it's all downhill to Olney. I should say it's three mile there and five mile back, considering how steep it is."

That didn't sound too far at all, not seeing how he'd made such good time getting out here. Henry was appreciative of the directions and said how he'd see the caretaker again 'fore Christmas while he climbed back on his bicycle. The two of them said they goodbyes and then he stood hard on his pedals and was sailing off down Little Street between the women stood outside its shops and such, dark bundles topped by bonnets, rustling across gold sidewalks through the afternoon.

He turned right onto High Street and it took him back down on the Bedford Road, just like the caretaker had said. He went out of the village past the Red Lion public house what they had near the turn there, where farm workers who was coming in already off the fields with mighty thirsts looked at him silently as he went by. That could have been his rope tyres what he had, though, and not nothing was related to his skin at all. It tickled Henry how folks here with all they clever ways of building walls and tying hedges and all that, how they all acted like rope on a feller's wheel-rims was the most outlandish thing they ever seen. He might as well have had trained rattlesnakes instead of tyres, to hear folks going on about it. All it was, it was a trick he'd seen some other coloured fellers use in Kansas. Rope was cheaper, didn't wear like rubber did or else get punctured, and it suited Henry fine. Weren't any more to it than that.

Across the Bedford Road right opposite the High Street turn, the land all dropped away, and where the river tributary did too there was a waterfall. The spray what got flung up from this caught in the slanted light and made a rainbow, just a little one hung in the air, whose colours was so pale that they kept fading in and out of sight. He turned left on the main road and rode on about a quarter mile from Yardley, where he found the steep lane running down upon his right what had a sign said Olney, only saying it was steep weren't doing it no justice. He flew down it like the wind, sending up glassy sheets of water where he couldn't help but splash through puddles, such as on the soft ground near a third of the way down where there was ponds with gnats in a mean vapour hanging over 'em. Speed he was going at, it didn't seem five minutes before he could see the village rooftops down the way ahead of him. He let his brake-blocks skim the dirt road, slowing down a little at a time so that he didn't have no accidents before he'd gotten where he wanted. Back of Henry's mind there was the thought that it was going to be an effort getting up this hill again, but he put that aside in favour of the great adventure he was shooting into like a bottle rocket, with his rope tyres sizzling in the dried-out cowpats.

Olney, when he got to it, was bigger than he'd thought it would be. Only thing he saw looked likely it might be a church spire was off down the other end of town, so that's what Henry headed for. All of the people what he passed by on the street was staring at him, since he hadn't come this way before and was no doubt to they mind a ferocious novelty. He kept his head down, looking at the cobbles what he pedalled over, being careful not to give offence. The streets was quiet, without much horse-traffic that afternoon as he could see, so that he was embarrassed by the noise his cart was making when it thundered on the stones in back of him. He looked up once and caught a glimpse of his reflection, racing by across the window of an ironmonger's shop, a black man with white hair and beard upon a strange machine who passed through all the pots and pans hung on display like he was no more solid than a ghost.

When in the end he reached the church, though, it was worth it. Way down on the bottom edge of Olney, with the Great Ouse River and its lakes spread to the south it was a towering and inspiring sight. It being Friday it weren't open, naturally, so Henry propped his bicycle against a tree and walked around the building once or twice, admiring its high windows with they old stained glass and squinting up towards that spire, what was so high he'd seen it from the village's far end. The clock that was up on the tower there said as it was getting on for half-past three, or 'five-and-twenny arter' like they said on Scarletwell. He reckoned he could look around here for a while and still be home before it got too dark out and Selina started worrying.

He guessed that he was kind of disappointed there weren't nothing on the church what told of Pastor Newton or "Amazing Grace". It was just Henry's foolish notion of how folks in England done things, he was sure, but he'd expected they might have a statue of the man or something, maybe standing with his quill pen in his hand. Instead, there wasn't nothing. There weren't even a bad likeness hung up near a chimney. Right across the street, though, Henry saw there was a graveyard. While he didn't know if Pastor Newton had been buried here as well, he thought there was at least a chance and so he crossed the road and went into the cemetery by its top gate, off from a little path ran down beside a green. Things jumped and scuffled in the long grass near his feet, and just like in the Boroughs he weren't sure if it was rats or rabbits, but he didn't care much for it either way.

Excepting Henry and the village dead the churchyard seemed about deserted. It surprised him, then, when he turned round a corner in the paths what led between the headstones, right by where there was an angel what had half its nose and jaw gone like a veteran from some war, and kneeling there beside a grave to pull the weeds up from it was a stout man in his waistcoat and his shirtsleeves, got a flat cap on his silver head. He looked up, more surprised by seeing Henry than what Henry was by seeing him. He was an old man, Henry realised, older than himself and maybe close to seventy. He was still sturdy, though, with great white mutton chops to each side of a face sent red by sun. Below his cap's brim he had small wire spectacles perched on his nose-end, what he pushed up so that he could take a better look at Henry.

"Good Lord, boy, you made me jump. I thought it was Old Nick who'd come to get me. I've not seen you round these parts before, now, have I? Let me get a look at yer."

The man climbed to his feet with difficulty from the graveside, Henry offering a hand what the old feller gratefully accepted. When he was stood up he was around five and a half feet, and a little shorter than what Henry was. He'd got blue eyes what twinkled through the lenses of his spectacles when he looked Henry over, beaming like he was delighted.

"Well, now, you look like a decent chap. What's brought you here to Olney, then, if you don't mind me asking? Were you looking for somebody buried here?"

Henry admitted that he was.

"I come from Scarletwell Street in Northampton, sir, where mostly I am called Black Charley. I was hearing just today about a reverend what once preached here in Olney, name of Newton. It seems like he was the man what wrote 'Amazing Grace', which is a song as I admire. I was just looking round the church across the way there, hoping for some sign of him, when it occurred to me as he might be at rest someplace nearby. If you're acquainted with this cemetery, sir, I'd be obliged you could direct me to his grave."

The older feller set his lips into a pushed-out frown and shook his head.

"No, bless your heart, he's not here. I believe the Reverend Newton is in London at St. Mary Woolnoth's, which is where he went when he left Olney. Here, I'll tell you what, though. As it happens, I'm churchwarden here. Dan Tite, that's me. I was just tidying the plots to give myself something to do, but I'd be happy to come back across the church with you and let you in so you could have a look. I've got the key here in my waistcoat pocket."

He produced a big black iron key and held it up so Henry could inspect it. Sure enough, it was a key. Weren't no disputing that. Out the same pocket, the churchwarden took a clay pipe and his pouch what had tobacco in. He filled the pipe and lit it with a match while they was walking back towards the gates, so a sweet coconut and wood smell drifted out behind them through the yew trees and the tombs. Dan Tite puffed hard on its clay stem 'til he was sure the pipe was going good enough, and then resumed his talk with Henry.

"What's that accent that you've got, then? Can't say as I've heard its like before."

He nodded while Dan closed the gate behind them and they started up the footpath back to Church Street. He could see the movements in the grass was rabbits now, they noses poking in and out of all the holes was dug into the green and all they ears like babies' slippers left out in the dew.

"No, sir, I don't expect you would have done. I come here from America just twelve or thirteen years back now. It was in Tennessee where I was born, then after that I lived in Kansas for a time. To me, it sounds like I talk pretty much the same as folks around Northampton now, although my wife and childrens, they say as I don't."

The old churchwarden laughed. They were just walking back across the cobbled lane towards the church, where Henry's bike and cart was propped against a tree.

"You want to listen to 'em, then. They're right. That voice you've got, that don't sound nothing like Northampton, and to my mind it's the better for it. They're some blessed lazy talkers, them round there. Don't bother with the letters on the ends of words or even most of 'em what's in the middle, so it all comes out like mush."

The warden took a pause here, halfway up the path towards the big church door, and pushed his glasses back where they'd slipped down again so's he could study Henry's bicycle and barrow what it drug behind it, leaned up on that poplar there. He looked from the machine to Henry and then back again, then he just shook his head and went on to unlock the door so they could go inside.

First thing you noticed was the chill come up off the stone floor, and how there was the slightest echo after everything. There in the room out front the church they called the vestibule, they'd got a big display of flowers and sheaves of wheat and pots of jam and such, what Henry figured as the children had brung for they Harvest Festival. It put a kind of morning smell about the air there, even though the place was cold and grey with shadows. Hung up in a frame above the spread there was a painting, and soon as he saw it Henry knew who it was of, it didn't matter that the picture was a dark one hanging in a darker room.

Man had a head looked near to square and too big for his body, although Henry owned that could have been the painter's fault. He'd got his parson's robes on and a wig like what they had in eighteenth-century times, all short on top and with grey plaits of wool wound round like ram's horns down to either side. One of his eyes looked sort of worried and yet full of what you might call cautious hope, while on the side of his face what was turned away out from the light the eye seemed flat and dead, and had the look of someone carrying a mournful weight they know they can't put down. It might have been his parson's collar was too tight so that the fat under his jaw was plumped out over it a little in a roll, and up above that was a mouth looked like it didn't know to laugh or cry. John Newton, born seventeen hundred twenty-five, died eighteen hundred seven. Henry stared up at the portrait with his eyes he knowed was the same colour as piano ivories, wide and near luminous there in the gloom.

"Ah, yes, that's him. You've spotted him, the Reverend Newton. Always thought meself he looked a tired old soul, a bit like a poor sheep put out to grass."

Dan Tite was up one corner getting something out a stack of hymnals what was there while Henry stood and gazed at Newton's murky image. The churchwarden turned and waddled back across the ringing, whispering slabs to Henry, dusting off the cover on some old book as he come.

"Here, have a look at this. This is the *Olney Hymns*, that they first printed up 'fore eighteen hundred. This is all the ones he wrote with his great friend the poet Mr. Cowper, who perhaps you've heard of?"

Henry confessed as he hadn't. Though he saw no need to say it there and then, it was a fact his reading weren't so good saving for street signs and for hymns in church what he already knowed the words to, and he'd never learned to write none for the life of him. Dan weren't concerned, though, that he weren't acquainted with this Cooper feller, and just went on flipping through the yellow-smelling pages 'til he'd found what he was looking for.

"Well, I suppose it doesn't matter, except Mr. Cowper was another one from Olney and they wrote all these together, although Mr. Newton did by far the greater part. This one, the one that you like, we're almost completely certain that it's Newton's work alone."

The warden gave the book of hymns to Henry, who reached out and took it careful with both hands like it were some religious relic, which he guessed it was. The page what it was open at had got a heading took him some time to make sense from, where it didn't say "Amazing Grace" like he'd expected. What it said instead, he finally figured out, was "Faith's Review and Expectation", and then under that there was some lines from out the Bible in the first book of the Chronicles, what had King David ask the Lord 'What is mine house, that thou hast brought me hitherto?' At last, below where it said that, there was the words all printed from "Amazing Grace". He looked them over, kind of singing them inside his head so's he could make 'em out more easy. He was doing fine until he got down to the last verse, which weren't like the one he was familiar with. That one, the one he knew, said about how when we'd been here ten thousand years in the bright shining sun, singing God's praise, we'd not have hardly started. This one in the book here didn't sound like it expected no ten thousand years, and weren't anticipating anything was shining or was bright.

The earth shall soon dissolve like snow,
The sun forbear to shine;
But God, who called me here below,
Will be forever mine.

Upon consideration, Henry thought the last verse what he knew was best, although he understood it weren't one what the Reverend Newton writ himself. Most likely, he supposed, the one with the ten thousand years and shining sun was writ out in America, which was a country what was younger than what England was, and with a brighter view of everything. Here where the land was older and they'd seen all manner of great kingdoms come and go, this was a country where World's End looked close by, where the ground below your feet might crumble all to dust with age, the sun above your head burn out at any minute. Henry liked the song how he'd been taught it better, with the sense it give how everything was going to be all right, but in his heart he felt the way that Mr. Newton had it here was possibly more true. He stood there for some minutes while he finished up the reading of it all, and then he give the book back to Dan Tite, mumbling how Mr. Newton was a great man, a great man.

The warden took the *Olney Hymns* off Henry and then put it back where it had been before. He looked at Henry quizzically a moment, as though he were trying to figure something out, and when he spoke it had a softer tone what was more intimate, like they was really talking about things what was important now.

"He was. He was a great man, and I think it's very Christian you should say so."

Henry nodded, though he weren't sure why he did. He didn't rightly understand how paying simple compliments was seen to be a Christian act, but didn't want Dan Tite should think of him as an uneducated black man, so he didn't say a word. He just stood shuffling while the warden weighed him up through them round little spectacles. Dan looked in Henry's shifting and uncertain eyes and give kind of a sigh.

"Charley ... it was Charley, wasn't it? Well, Charley, let me ask you something. Did you hear much about Mr. Newton where you came from, of his life and that?"

Henry admitted, to his shame, that he'd not heard of Newton's name before that afternoon, nor that he'd writ "Amazing Grace." The churchwarden assured him as it didn't matter, and then carried on what he was saying.

"What you have to understand with Mr. Newton is he didn't come to his religious calling until he was nearly forty, so he'd knocked about a bit by that age, if you take my meaning."

Henry weren't sure that he did, but Dan Tite went on anyway.

"You see, his father was commander of a merchant ship, always at sea, and young John Newton was a lad of just eleven when he went there with him. Made a few trips with his dad, as you might say, before his dad retired. I think he wasn't twenty yet when he got press-ganged into service on a man-o'-war, where he deserted and was flogged."

Henry scratched at his arm and winced. He'd seen men whipped. Dan Tite went right on with his tale, its echo muttering up the corner of the vestibule like some old relative touched in they mind.

"He asked if he could be exchanged to service on another ship. It was a slave ship, sailing for Sierra Leone on the western coast of Africa. He became the trader's servant and was treated in a brutal fashion, as you can imagine would be likely with a lad of that age. He was lucky, though, and a sea captain who had known his father came along and saved him."

Henry understood now, why Dan Tite was telling him all this, as painful as it was. He'd been surprised when he found out it was a white man wrote "Amazing Grace". He'd always thought only a black man could have knowed the sorrow what was in that song, but this made sense out of it. Mr. Newton had been captive on a slave boat, just like Henry's momma and his poppa was. He'd suffered at the hands of fiends and devils, just like they'd done. That was how he'd come to write them words, about how sweet it was to have relief within the Lord from all that suffering. The churchwarden had wanted he should know how the convictions in "Amazing Grace" was come of Mr. Newton's hard experience, that much was plain. Henry was grateful. It just give him all the more respect for the good man behind the writing. When he sung "Amazing Grace" now he could think of Pastor Newton and the trials he'd overcome. He grinned and stuck his hand out to Dan Tite.

"Sir, I'm real grateful for that information, and for letting me take up your time in telling it. It sounds like Mr. Newton had some troubles, right enough, but praise the Lord that he lived through 'em all and wrote a song that beautiful. It only makes me think the better of him, hearing what you said."

The warden didn't take his hand. He just held up his own, the palm turned out to Henry like it was a warning. The old man had got a look on his pink face now was real serious. He shook his head, so that his white side-whiskers flapped like sails.

"You haven't heard it all."

A church clock somewhere struck for half-past four, either in Yardley up ahead of him or Olney back behind him, when he'd finally walked his bicycle and wagon all the way back up the steep slope of the Yardley Road, now trudging through the puddles what he'd skimmed on his way down.

Henry was all in pieces, didn't know what he should think. He'd walk a little then he'd stop and rub the fat part of his hand across his eyes, wiping the tears off down his cheeks so's he could see where he was going and it weren't all just a fog of brown and green. Up at the top there of the lane, just when the clock was striking, he climbed back onto his saddle and begun the long ride back to Scarletwell.

John Newton had become a slave-trader. That's what Dan Tite had told him. Even when he'd just got rescued from a slaver, even when he knowed what it was like aboard they ships, he'd gone and got a vessel so as he could ply that trade himself. He'd got rich off it, he'd got rich off of slaving and then later on he'd made his big repentance and become a minister and done "Amazing Grace". Dear Lord, dear sweet Lord on the cross it was a slaver wrote "Amazing Grace". He had to put his wood blocks down upon the ground so's he could wipe his eyes again.

How could that be? How could you get flogged as a boy nineteen years old, have Lord knows what done with you as a slaver's servant, how could you go through all that, then see it done to someone else for gain? He knew now what that look had been, what he'd saw in the portrait's eyes. John Newton was a guilty man, a man with blood and tar and feathers on his hands. John Newton was a man most likely damned.

He'd got his feelings under some control now, so he started up his bicycle and carried on, back up the Bedford Road and past the Red Lion what he'd seen before, saving that it was on his right this time. It sounded full, the public house, with all the noise was coming from it, fellers laughing, singing bits from songs what floated out across the empty fields. Upon his left, the rainbow what had been above the clattering waterfall weren't there no more. The sun was getting low down in the west ahead of him as he went by the second Yardley bend and made for Denton with all manner of considerations turning over in his heart.

Henry could see, after he'd chewed upon it for a time, that it weren't just a matter of how Newton could have gone from one side of the whipping-post straight to the other. Now he'd thought about it, Henry would allow that there most likely had been plenty other folks had done the same. Why, he himself knowed people what was treated bad, then took it out on others in they turn. That weren't the thing what was exceptional about John Newton, how he'd started out no better than a slave and then took up that business for himself. That weren't no puzzle, or at least not much of one. The thing what seized on Henry's mind was more how Newton could have been in work so evil and then writ "Amazing Grace". Was it all sham, them lines what had moved Henry and his people so? Was it no more than Buffalo Bill's Wild West Show, 'cept for it was in a church and had fine sentiments where Cody had his redskins?

Right of him and way off to the north a spray of roosting birds was rose in black specks over the dark woods by Castle Ashby, looked like ashes blowed up from the burnt patch where a fire had been. He carried on along the Bedford Road, hunched like a crow over his handlebars. From up above he figured how he must bear a resemblance to one on them tin novelties he'd seen, them where you cranked the handle and a little feller sitting on a bicycle rode inch by inch on a straight wire with only his knees moving, going up and down there on the pedals.

Even knowing what he knowed now about Newton, Henry couldn't see how words what was so heartfelt could have been pretence entire. Dan Tite had said how most folks figured as the song was writ about a dreadful storm what Newton and his slaving-boat had come through on a homeward journey what he made in May, seventeen hundred forty-eight. Called it his great deliverance and said it was the day God's grace had come upon him, though it weren't 'til near on seven years had passed afore he give up slaving. Treated his slaves decent from what the churchwarden said, though Henry didn't rightly know how you could use a word like decent up against a word like slaves. It was about the same as saying spiders was considerate to they flies, how Henry seen it. All the same, he would concede how just because a feller weren't converted all at once or overnight the way he said he was, that didn't mean how his conversion couldn't come to be sincere. Could be how by the time what Newton wrote "Amazing Grace" he was regretful of a lot of things he'd done. Could be that's what he meant when he said how he'd been a wretch. Henry had previously supposed as how the song had meant a poor wretch just like anybody was, but he could see now how John Newton might have possibly intended for the words to have a stronger meaning, what was personal to him. A wretch like me. A fornicating, drinking, whoring, cussing, slaving wretch like me. Henry had never thought about the song like that before, had only heard the bright things what was in it and heard nothing what was savage or was painful. Previous to this day he'd never heard the shame.

He was approaching Denton now, his shadow getting longer on the track behind of him. The road was forked here, like it was upon the village's far side, and Henry took the route most to his left so as he could pass by the place. He went on by the side path what run down to Horton and then passed the thatched humps of Grange Farm what was just slightly further on. The ploughed black ruts what filled the fields was powdered gold along they tops where the low sun's rays touched them. All the little springs and fiddles in his back was acting up so that he felt his age now as he pedalled on for Brafield, horses watching him across the hedgerows, unconcerned.

According to Dan Tite, John Newton had give up his seafaring and slaving some years after he got married, which was in seventeen hundred fifty. Even then, it sounded as though it was illness made him mend his ways, and not conviction. Then, seventeen sixty or near to, he got ordained as a church minister at Olney where he met up with the poet feller Mr. Cooper what was spelled as Cow-per, who'd come to the village some years after he'd done. From the little what Dan Tite had said of Cowper it had seemed to Henry that the poet was a troubled man within his heart and mind, and he could see how that was maybe why John Newton had took such a shine to him. They'd writ songs for they services and prayer meetings and such, with Newton putting in the best part of the labour, writing four for every one of Cowper's. Seems how Pastor Newton was a great one for his writing, not just with his hymns but also in his diaries and his letter-writing. The churchwarden said how if it weren't for Newton's writings, nobody would know a thing today about how slaving was in eighteenth-century times. Henry expected as he meant nobody white.

Newton had writ "Amazing Grace", they reckoned, maybe late as eighteen seventy when he was forty-five or thereabouts. Some ten year after that he'd gone from Olney up to London, where he was the rector at a place they called Saint Mary Woolnoth. Here he'd give some sermons what was well regarded, then went blind afore he died when he was eighty-two. Maybe he thought as he'd atoned, but Henry didn't know a crime was worse then selling others into slavery. Even the Lord in all his mercy had sent plagues on Egypt when the Hebrews was they slaves, and Henry weren't sure what it took to make atonement for a sin that grievous.

He was so caught up in all his thoughts he'd gone by Brafield 'fore he knew it and was riding on due west towards the Houghtons with the red sun lowered like a firebrand, just about to set light to the trees on the horizon up ahead of him. Henry was thinking about Newton and of how peculiar it was he should go blind when in "Amazing Grace" he wrote of just the opposite. He was also turning over something else Dan Tite had said about when Newton was in London at Saint Mary Woolnoth, giving all his sermons. The old churchwarden had said how in the congregation there was Mr. William Wilberforce, who'd gone on as an abolitionist and done a lot to put an end to slav-

ery for good. It seemed in this regard as he'd found Pastor Newton's sermons
generally inspiring. Maybe if it weren't for Newton and his great repentance,
never mind if it were genuine or not, then slavery might not have gotten over-
turned as early as it did, or maybe even not at all. The rights and wrongs of it
went back and forth as Henry pedalled by the turns for Little Houghton on his
right and then, about a mile past that, the one down to Great Houghton on his
left. The sky above Northampton was like treasure in a bed of roses.

Henry knew it was the Christian thing, forgiving Mr. Newton what he'd
done, but slavery weren't just a word, out from them history books he couldn't
read. He scratched his arm and thought about what he remembered from them
days. He'd been around thirteen years old, he thought, when Mr. Lincoln won
the Civil War and set the slaves all free. Henry was marked up as a slave six
year by then, although from that event, when he was seven, he recalled not
one thing save his momma crying, saying hush. What come back most to him
was how scared everybody was, the day they heard they was emancipated. It
was like within they hearts they knowed it was the coloured folk would be in
trouble about getting freed, and that was how it proved to be. The old plantation bosses liked to say how all the slaves was happier before they got set loose,
and it was the plantation bosses and they friends made sure as that was true.
The ten year Henry and his folks had spent in Tennessee before they went
to Kansas, they was nothing else but rapes and beatings, hangings, killings,
burnings; it made Henry sick to think of it. They was all being punished 'cause
they'd been let go, that was the honest truth.

The flames was dying down upon the cloud-banks in the west and darker
blues staining the heavens up behind him when he come along beside Midsummer Meadow in the way of Beckett's Park. Cow Meadow, that was what
the folks down Scarletwell still called the fields round here, though they said
Medder 'stead of Meadow. Henry had been told how it was here another of the
English Wars got settled. This one weren't they Civil War, although that had
its last big battle pretty close to here. This was a war they had before that what
they called the Rose War, although Henry couldn't say what it had been about
or rightly when it was. He couldn't help but think if England was America,
and if you had a place where both the War of Independence and the Civil War
had finished up, then there'd have been a bigger thing made out of it. Perhaps
that was just more the way here, talking things down, although it had always
seemed to Henry how the English liked to puff they past times up as much
as anybody, and considerably more than most. It was as if the folks what writ
them history books just couldn't see Northampton somehow, like it had a veil
across it or like they was horses wearing blinkers with the whole town on they
blind side.

When he reached the crossroads, with the hospital upon his right and what they called the Dern Gate up ahead of him, he stopped there by the drinking fountain at Saint Thomas Becket's well and set his bicycle against the rugged wall while he stooped down and took a drink, the way what he'd done earlier. The water didn't seem to taste as sweet as how it had that morning, although Henry owned as his own feelings may have had an influence on that. It had a bitter tang now after it was swallowed. You could taste the metal in it.

He got on his bike again and at the crossroads he turned left, along Victoria Promenade what went down by the north side of the park there. He rode in amongst the carts and trolley cars and such, where everyone was making they way home under a sky near purple, skimming through the leaves fell in the gutters as he left the meadowlands behind him and went on through the good-natured stink beside the cattle yards. The pens what held the animals was off on Henry's left, where now and then you heard some lowing or some bleating coming through the gloom. As he rolled by he thought about how when he'd viewed it in the daylight you could see how all the sheep, cows and what have you was all marked with dye, got little splashes of it on they backs, both red and blue. He'd never seen one branded, now he thought about it, not in all the time what he'd been over here. He let that notion settle in while he continued past the Plough Hotel, what was there at the Bridge Street crossroads on his right, and carried on towards where the gas-holder's iron frame rose up against the grey light over Gas Street. Here he stuck out his right hand to signal he was going to turn, and then went north up Horseshoe Street, heart heavy in his chest.

It was still Pastor Newton was upsetting Henry. He weren't certain as he could enjoy "Amazing Grace" quite the same way again, not knowing what he knowed. Why, he weren't even sure if he could bring himself to worship in a church again, not if them churchmen could have made they money doing Lord knows what. It weren't that Henry had been made to doubt his faith, for that could never be, but more like he had come to doubt the ministers proclaiming it. Could be that in future Henry might go back to saying prayers in sheds and barns, wherever it was quiet, the way him and his folks had back in Tennessee. When you was kneeling in a barn you knew as God was there, the same like you was in a church. The difference was that in a barn you could be sure you didn't have a devil in the pulpit.

Henry knew as it weren't fair to judge all reverends by the sins of one, but it was just his trust in that profession had got shook. He wasn't even rightly sure as he could fairly judge John Newton, what with all the contradictions as there was about his story, but he felt as all the same he had a right to be real disappointed in the man. The standard by which Henry weighed such things was that of ordinary folks, and he knew neither he nor anybody as he knowed had ever sold another living person into slavery.

'Course, nobody he knowed had ever writ "Amazing Grace" or been no influence on Mr. William Wilberforce and all that neither. There was that to think of. Rattling on the cobbles as he made hard work of climbing Horseshoe Street, the arguments swung to and fro inside of him without they come to any real conclusion you might call. Up at the top there where his route crossed over Gold Street was a big old horse-bus coming out of Marefair so's he had to put his wood blocks down upon the street and stop while it went by.

Out one side of his eye while he stood waiting there he could see this young skinny feller, idling on the corner where they had the Palace of Varieties. The man was staring hard at Henry who, seeing as he was of a downcast turn of mind, decided that this was most likely on account of Henry being black or having rope around his wheels or some fool thing like that. He made out as he didn't notice the young feller gawping at him, and then when the horse-bus had drug itself by and on up Gold Street, Henry stood upon his pedals and continued past the crossroads and uphill, by what they called Horsemarket. Dark was settling on the Boroughs like fine soot as Henry cycled up along its eastward edge, and there was gaslights burning in some windows now. The wagons was all firing up they lanterns, so that he was glad at least his hair and beard was white, and folks would see him so he didn't get run down.

Horsemarket seemed to him more steep than usual, got all the doctors' houses looking cosy to his left there and across the road it was all overhung with trees grew out the gardens of Saint Katherine's. When he got up to Mary's Street he turned along it. Clattering and creaking he made off into the greying tangle of the real old neighbourhood, what used to be all of the town there was.

As much as Henry liked the district where he lived, he couldn't say as he much cared to see it in the twilight. That's when things all lost they edges and they shapes, and what you knew weren't real by daylight seemed a lot more possible. Hobgoblins, fiends and such as that, this was the time you seen 'em, when the paint peeled off a wood gate made a shape like someone standing there, or all the shadow-patches in a clump of nettles was a big face shifting in the wind, eyes narrowing with poison. Dusk played tricks like that all over, Henry knew, though sometimes it would seem to him as if the Boroughs was built crooked specially so's it could harbour all the gloom and haunts up in its corners: nests where poor and ragged ghosts was bred. His rope tyres juddered on the stones as he squeaked through the evening lanes, where there was ugly fairies squirming in the water butts and ghouls crouched in the guttering for all what Henry knew. The bent-backed shops and houses leaned all round him, pale against the dusk like they was spikes of limestone growed up in a cave. Sweet in the mornings, lazy in the afternoons, come dark this was another place entire.

It wasn't on account of this was somewhere you might get attacked and robbed, like Henry knew was the opinion of the Boroughs held by folks in better parts of town. To Henry's mind there weren't no safer place than here, where nobody robbed nobody 'cause everybody knew they was the same, without a penny to they names. As for attacks and beatings, there weren't no denying they went on, but it weren't nothing like it was in Tennessee. For one thing, what you had around the Boroughs was a lot of people who was all so angry on they insides, what they liked to do was just get drunk and fight each other so as they could let it out. That weren't a pleasant thing to watch and it was hard to sit by while young men, and women too, they just destroyed themselves like that, but it weren't Tennessee. It weren't one bunch of folks got all the power taking they vengeance on a lot of helpless people what got nothing. This was poor folks who weren't going to hurt nobody 'cept they own selves, although Henry owned as they could hurt they own selves something awful.

No, it wasn't like the Boroughs was all full of cut-throats. It weren't that what made it kind of frightening after nightfall, it weren't nothing near as reasonable as that. Unearthly, that was what it was after the daylight went, the daylight what was holding back another world where anything might just about be possible. Children, of course, they loved it and you'd always have big squealing gangs of 'em run up and down the dim streets in the gaslight doing hide and seek or some such. Henry didn't doubt the little boys and girls knew that this place was haunted, just like all the growed-ups did. The thing was, children was all at a time of life when ghosts was just about as natural as was anything in they experience. Ghosts was just part of the excitement, to a child. When you was older though, was nearer to the grave yourself and you'd had time to think on life and death a little, well, then ghosts and what they signified, that was all different somehow. That, to Henry's mind, was why no one went out much in the Boroughs after it got dark, 'cept they was drinking men or little kids, or else police. The older people got, then the more phantoms what there was around, the shades of places and of people what weren't here no more. These lanes run back to ancient times, as Henry was aware, so that he shouldn't be surprised if all the spooks was built up pretty thick by now, like some variety of sediment.

He cycled up Saint Mary's Street, where the Great Fire broke out a couple hundred year ago, past Pike Street on to Doddridge Street, where he dismounted his contraption so it could be pushed across the lumpy burial ground what run downhill from Doddridge Church. He manhandled his bicycle over the weedy mounds and wet black hollows of the wasteland, wondering not for the first time why it was they called this stretch a burial ground, and not a graveyard or a cemetery. He could see how possibly it was because there weren't no headstones or no markers, although why that should itself be so when far as he knew it was human people what was buried here, that was what puzzled him. Best he could figure it, it was to do with Mr. Doddridge who had been the minister on Castle Hill, and was what people called a Nonconformist. Henry had heard tell of Nonconformist graveyards was elsewhere in England, where they also put they mass graves for the poor folk, them as was unable to afford a proper burying or tombstone. Could be that was just what happened here. Could be he wheeled his pedal-cart right now above bones was all jumbled up from people didn't even got they names no more. Mindful of ghosts as he was feeling in the wasting light, he muttered some apologies to any skeletons he might be disrespecting, so's they knew as it weren't nothing personal.

When Henry was across the rough ground and in Chalk Lane, near the houses set back from the street they called Long Gardens, he climbed back up on his saddle and rode up the slope in way of Castle Terrace and of Doddridge Church itself, on his right hand there. Passing by the chapel, noticing that funny door set halfway up its old stone wall and leading nowhere, he considered what he knew of Mr. Doddridge, which of course made him in turn consider Mr. Newton.

Mr. Philip Doddridge, now, how people round here told it, was a man in poor health who was wanting that the worse-off folks could feel they had a Christian faith what was they own. When he come here to Castle Hill and started up his ministry, it seems like he took on the English Church by saying folks should have a right to worship as they pleased, and not just how they Bishops and that wanted it. He'd come here to Northampton when he was a young man in his twenties, this was round seventeen hundred thirty, and he'd stayed just over twenty years before his health took him away. He hadn't lived long after that, but in his time he'd changed the whole way how folks thought about religion in this country, maybe in the Christian world all over. All of it done on the little raised-up mound of dirt what Henry was now riding past. Doddridge had writ hymns, too, just not so famous as "Amazing Grace", and in the one old drawing of the man what Henry had once seed his eyes was clear and bright and honest as a child. There weren't no shame, there weren't no guilt. There weren't no anything like that, save for a kindliness and great determination.

Henry could imagine Mr. Doddridge out here strolling of an evening, taking in the same air, looking up at the same early stars, most probably wondering just the same what that fool door was doing halfway up the wall. He'd probably felt, like all men do, as he'd been living for a long time, and like all men he most likely found it hard imagining things any other way than how they was, with him alive so as he could appreciate it all. Yet here we was, with

Mr. Doddridge dead more'n a hundred-fifty years, and with the church what they named after him still stood here, and still doing good for all the poor folks what there was. John Newton never got no church commemorating what he done, and William Cody only got his plaque up by the chimneypots. Henry considered this, and thought it might be that things worked out fairly after all. It was most probably better to assume as the Almighty knew what He was doing in such matters, that was Henry's general conclusion.

He propelled himself up Castle Terrace, over where was Castle Street and Fitzroy Street and Little Cross Street knotted up together, rolling straight across and on down Bristol Street, what was his most direct route home. Ahead and on the left of him he saw what was a woman in a long skirt, walking on her own as Henry thought until he see the baby she was carrying. In the gaslight, all the curls around the child's head was just shining like a goldmine got blowed up, so that he knowed it was May Warren and her momma, who was called May Warren also. He put down one foot to drag his block across the cobbles, slowing down as he drawed up 'longside of 'em.

"Why, Mrs. May and Missy May! You ladies been off gallivanting all around the town, I bet, you only just now coming home!"

The elder May stopped and turned round, surprised, then laughed when she seen it was Henry. Was a deep laugh, rumbling down there in what Henry would admit was sure some big old chest that girl had got.

"Black Charley! Blummin' 'eck, you made me jump, you silly bugger. They should 'ave a law made you lot carry sparklers after it got dark. Look, May. Look who it is, come frightening your Mam. It's Uncle Charley."

Here the little girl, who was without a doubt a child more beautiful than any white child Henry ever saw, looked up towards him and said "Char" a couple times. He grinned down at the baby's mother.

"It's an angel what you got there, May. An angel what's fell down from Heaven."

Young May Warren shook her head, dismissive like, as if she'd heard the compliment that many times it had begun to trouble her.

"Don't say that. Everybody always says that."

They went on to talk a while, then Henry told May as she'd best get her small daughter home and in the warm. They all said they goodbyes, then the two Mays went off down Fort Street, where they lived next door to big May's father, who was Snowy Vernall. Story was, as Henry had been told it, how May's grand-pappy whose name was Ernest had his hair turn white from shock one time, and that had been enough to do the same thing for his young son. Snowy's hair was whiter than what Henry's was, and there were them said he was touched besides, though Henry only knowed him as man liked drinking and who'd got some talent in his hands for making drawings and the like. The momma and the baby, they went off down Fort Street, where there weren't no proper road but only paving, and where it was generally held there'd been a fort in ancient times. The street had got a kind of dungeon look, at least to Henry's eye. It always seemed like a dead end, no matter that you was aware it had an alley running down the back.

Henry continued on where Mr. Beery, who was what they called the lighter-man down in the Boroughs, he was just then reaching up on his long pole to light the gas-lamps what they had in Bristol Street. He called to Henry, cheery like, and Henry he called back. He hoped the children round there wouldn't shin right up that post and blow the flame out soon as Mr. Beery was gone by, although there was most definitely a chance as that might happen. Henry pedalled past and on down Bristol Street where it run into Bath Street. He went left around the bend that took him past Bath Row and onto Scarletwell Street, where he lived. The dark was pretty thick here, on account of Mr. Beery hadn't worked his way down this far yet. It was like all the night was trickled down the hill to make a big black puddle at the bottom. Lamps what you could see was shining through the pulled-to curtains, could be they was all glow-in-the-dark bulbs hanging off the heads of them great ugly fish what people seen, brung up by deep sea trawling boats and similar.

Henry had come out from Bath Street onto Scarletwell just opposite the alleyway what folks here called a jitty, as run down behind Scarletwell Terrace there. The big Saint Andrew's Road was on his left side a short distance, but he got down off his bike and wheeled it up the hill the other way. The house he lived in with Selina and they children was a little way up, opposite the public house was called the Friendly Arms they had across the way. He recollected how when him and his Selina was first come from Wales, after collecting Henry's pay up at the Welsh House in the market, how they'd come down here and took a look around. They wasn't sure how folks round here would take to having a black feller married to a white girl, not if they was living hereabouts. Could be as there weren't no place would accept two different colours, side by side. That was when they'd first come on Scarletwell Street and the Friendly Arms, where they'd been give a sign. Tied up outside the pub and drinking beer from out a glass was what they'd later learned was Newt Pratt's animal. The sight had so amazed them both, unlikely as it was, that they'd determined there and then as this was someplace they could set up home. No matter how unusual they was, two races wed to live as man and wife, nobody down in Scarletwell Street would look twice at 'em, not with Newt Pratt's astounding creature roped up getting drunk across the street like that.

He smiled to think of it, pushing his bicycle and cart on up the slope, his wood blocks slipped off from his feet and in his jacket pockets, where they always was when he weren't wearing 'em. He reached what was a little alley run off on his right there, what would take him round directly to his own back yard. He thumbed the iron latch on his gate, then made an awful racket getting his contraption in the yard, the way he always did. Selina come out on the step, with they first daughter, Mary, who'd got white skin, hanging round her skirts. His wife weren't tall, and she'd got all her hair brushed down so that it reached near to her knees as she stood there on they back doorstep, smiling at him with the gaslight warm behind her.

"Hello, Henry, love. Come on inside, and you can tell us all how you've got on."

He kissed her cheek, then fished all of the stuff what folks had give him from inside his cart, which would be safe out in the yard there.

"Heck, I been all over. Got me some old clothing and some picture frames. I reckon if you got some water boiled up I could use a wash, though, 'fore we has our supper. Been a tiring day, all kinds of ways."

Selina cocked her head on one side, studying him while he went by her, taking all the things what he'd collected in the house.

"You've been all right, though, have you? Not had any trouble, like?"

He shook his head and give her a big reassuring grin. He didn't want to talk just yet with her about what he'd found out in Olney, with regard to Pastor Newton and "Amazing Grace". He weren't sure in his own mind just what his opinions on the matter was, and figured as he'd tell Selina later, when he'd had a chance to think on it some more. He took the picture frames and that through to they front room what looked out on Scarletwell, and put them with the other items what he'd got there, then went back into the living room where Mary and Selina was. They baby boy, what was called Henry after him and was black like his daddy was, he was asleep upstairs and in his crib by now, though Henry would look in on him afore they went to bed. He left Selina brewing up a pot of tea there on they dining table and went back through to they little kitchen so as he could have himself a wash.

There was still water in the copper boiler what was warmish, and he run himself some in a white enamel bowl what he set down into they deep stone sink. The sink was stood below they kitchen window, looking out on the back yard where everything was black now so's you couldn't see. He took his jacket off and draped it on the laundry basket what was by the door, and then commenced unbuttoning his shirt.

It was still Pastor Newton he was thinking of. The man had done tremendous good, to Henry's mind, and had committed likewise a tremendous sin. Henry weren't sure as he was big enough to judge a man whose vices and whose virtues was of such a size. But then, who was it would call men like that to they account, if it weren't Henry and his kin and all them others what was treated so unfairly? All the men what was important, with they hymns and statues and they churches living after them and telling folks for years to come how good they was. It seemed to Henry as these monuments was all like Colonel Cody's rooftop plaque what he'd seen early in the day. Just 'cause a feller was remembered well, that didn't mean as he'd done something to deserve it. Henry wondered where the justice was in all of this. He wondered who decided in the end what was the mark of a great man, and how they knew as it weren't just the mark of Cain? His shirt and vest was off by now, hung with his jacket on the basket down beside the kitchen door. Out in the black night, through the steam rose up from his enamel bowl and past the window panes, he seen his own reflection standing in the dark of they back yard, stripped to its waist and looking in at him.

His own mark was just there on his left shoulder, where they'd branded him when he was seven. Both his momma and his poppa had one just the same. He'd got no proper memory of the night the iron was put on him, and even after all these years he'd still got no idea the reason why they done it. Weren't like there was nigger-rustling going on, as he could recollect.

It was a funny thing, the mark, no better than a drawing what some little child had done. There was two hills, looked like they got a bridge between 'em, else like they was pans hung on a scale for weighing gold. Down under this you'd got a scroll, or could be that it was a winding road. The lines was pale and violet, smooth like wax there on the purple flesh of Henry's arm. He lifted up his other hand and run his fingers over the design. He waited for the wisdom and the understanding what would answer all the questions in his heart, about John Newton, about everything. He waited for the grace so he could put aside all his hard feelings, though he owned as it would truly have to be amazing.

Outside in the royal blue heaven over Doddridge Chapel, stars was coming out and night birds sang. His wife and child was in the next room, pouring out his tea. He cupped warm water with a little soap there in his palms, dashing it up into his face and eyes so everything was washed away into the grey, forgiving blur.

ATLANTIS

Foul fanthoms five his farter lies, and office bones are cobbles made. Ah ha ha ha. Oh, bugger, let him stay down here and underwater in the warm, the sweaty linen currents drefting him away, aweigh in anchor chains and scrabble crabs and mermaids mermering to their slowmile phones, their fishbone combs, don't make him swim up to the light just yet, not yet. Five minutes, just five minutes more because down here it isn't any time at all, it could be nineteen fifty-eight and him a five-year-old with all his life uncoiled unspoiled before him, down here in the warm and weeds and winkles, with his thoughts bright-coloured tetras streaming in amongst the tumbled busts, the dead men's chests, but it's too late, already it's too late. A mattress-spring is poking through the ocean bed-sands, up into his back, and he can feel his jellyfish-limp arms and legs trailing around him in a salty sprawl as he reluctantly floats up through dream-silts in suspension, back towards the dappled dazzle of the surface, where his mother's got the wireless on down in the kitchen. Bugger. Bugger it.

Benedict Perrit half-opened his eyes into their first wince of the day. It wasn't 1958. He wasn't five. It was May 26th, 2006. He was a coughing, farting wreck of fifty-two, a piece of nineteen-hundreds royalty in exile, traipsing back and forth along the shores of an unfriendly foreign century. Ah ha ha ha. Wreck was a bit strong, actually. He was in better shape than most his age, to look at. It was more that he'd just woken up, and he'd been on the ale the night before. He'd pick up later on, he knew, but morning always came as something of a shock to Benedict. You hadn't had a chance yet to get your defences up, this time of day. The thoughts that later on you could avoid or brush aside, they were all on you like a pack of dogs when you were just woke up and hadn't had your breakfast yet. The cold unvarnished facts of his own life, by morning's light, were always like a straight punch in the face: his lovely sister Alison was dead, a bike smash more than forty years ago. His dad, old Jem, was dead. Their house they'd lived in, their old street, their neighbourhood, those were all dead as well. The family he'd started for himself with Lily and the boys, he'd messed that up, that was all finished now. He was back living with his mam in Tower Street, what had been the top of Scarletwell Street, up behind the high-rise blocks. His life, in his opinion, hadn't really worked out how he might have hoped, and yet the thought that in another thirty years it would be over horrified him. Or at least it did when he'd just woken up. Everything horrified him when he'd just woke up.

He let his demons chew on him a minute or two more, then threw them off along with the top sheet and blankets, swinging down his knobbly, hairy legs onto the bedside floor as he sat up. He ran his hands over the mountainous relief-map of his face and back into the still-black tangles of his hair. He coughed and farted, feeling vaguely disrespectful to be doing so while in the presence of his bookshelves, up against the room's end wall. He could feel Dylan Thomas, H.E. Bates, John Clare and Thomas Hardy staring at him pointedly, waiting for him to own up and apologize. He mumbled a "beg pardon" reaching for his dressing gown, hung on a chair beside the ancient writing desk, then stood and padded barefoot out onto the landing, farting once more to assert his independence just before he closed the bedroom door and left the pastoral poets to discern the romance in his flatulence. Ah ha ha ha.

Once in the bathroom he took care of his evacuations, which, thanks to the drink the night before, were wretchedly distressing but concluded fairly quickly. Next he took his dressing gown off while he had a wash and shave, stood at the sink. The central heating, that was one thing from the modern world that he was glad of. Down in Freeschool Street where he'd grown up it had been much too cold to wash more than your face and hands each day. Perhaps you'd have a proper scrub in a zinc bath on Friday nights if you were lucky.

Benedict ran some hot water in the basin – he would grudgingly admit hot water could be seen as an improvement, too – then splashed himself all over before lathering up with his mum's Camay, utilising his abundant pubic hair as an impromptu soap-pad. For the rinse he dragged a towel down from the rail to stand upon, so that he wouldn't soak the bathroom carpet, leaning forward so his genitals hung down into the white enamel basin while he scooped the water up and let it pour across his chest and belly, sluicing off the suds. He used a sponge to wash away the foam beneath his arms, then gave his legs and feet a mostly-soapless rubdown before drying off upon another, larger towel. He put his dressing gown back on, then took his dad's old shaving brush and straight-edge razor down out of the bathroom cabinet.

The bristles – hog or badger hair, he'd never known for sure – were soft and soothing, slathering the white froth on his cheek. He stared into the bathroom mirror, met his own sad gaze, then drew the open razor in a line across the throat of his reflection, some two inches from the windpipe, gurgling mortally, rolling his eyes and sticking out his long and only slightly furry tongue. Ah ha ha ha.

He shaved, washing the blade clean underneath the cold tap and depositing a scum of tiny hairs around the basin's tide-line. It was like a tea-leaf residue, but smaller, and he wondered if the future could be seen amongst the random specks. They always used to say down in the Boroughs how if, for example, you had tea-leaves that looked like a boat it meant a sea voyage was in store, only of course it never was. Putting away the shaving kit he patted dry his face and risked a palm-full of Old Spice. He'd thought the fruity smell was girlish when he'd slapped it on the first time as a teenager, but nowadays he liked it. It smelled like the 'Sixties. Looking in the glass at his clean-shaven face he gave a suave, matinee-idol smile and jiggled his thick eyebrows up and down suggestively, a sozzled gigolo attempting to seduce his own reflection. God, who'd want to wake up next to that, next to Ben Perrit and Ben Perrit's nose? Not him, that was for sure. If Benedict had only got his looks to go on, he presumed that he'd be sunk. It was a stroke of luck, then, that he was a published poet too, on top of all his other charms and virtues.

He went back into his bedroom to get dressed, only remembering the fart when it was too late. Bugger. He pulled on his shirt and trousers breathing through his mouth, then grabbed his waistcoat and his shoes and bolted for the landing, finishing adjusting his apparel once he was outside the room and back in a terrestrial atmosphere. He wiped his watering eyes. By Christ, that was the kind that let you know as you were still alive.

He clopped downstairs. His mam, Eileen, was in the kitchen, hovering by the gas-stove, making sure his breakfast didn't burn. She'd have begun it, scrambled eggs on toast, when she'd first heard him stumbling to the bathroom overhead. She pulled the grill-pan out an inch or two to check the tan on the sliced white, and poked at the yolk-coloured cumulus congealing in the saucepan with her wooden spoon. She glanced up at her son with old brown eyes that were as loving as they were reproachful, tucking in her jutting little chin, pursing her lips and tutting as if after all these years she was no wiser when it came to Benedict, or what to make of him.

"Good morning, Mother. May I say that you're particularly radiant this morning? There's some sons, you know, who wouldn't be so gallant. Ah ha ha."

"Yiss, and there's some mothers as do 'ave 'em. 'Ere, come on and 'ave yer breakfast 'fore it's cold." Eileen retrieved the toast, skimmed it with marge and dumped the steaming, scrambled mass upon it, seemingly in one continuous movement. She pushed back a grey strand that had worked loose from her bun as she gave Benedict the plate and cutlery.

"There y'are. Don't get it dayn yer shirt."

"Mother, behave! Ah ha ha ha."

He sat down at the kitchen table and began to wolf his way into what he perceived as necessary stomach-lining. He'd got no idea why everything he said came out as if it were a punchline or a previously unknown comic catch-phrase. He'd been that way as far back as anyone remembered. Perhaps it was just that life was easier to get through if you thought of it as an unusually long instalment of *The Clitheroe Kid*.

He finished breakfast, swilled down with the cup of tea his mam had meanwhile made for him. He gulped the brew ... I can't talk now, I'm drinking ... keeping one bright, hedgehog-baking Gypsy eye upon the coat pegs in the passage where his hat and neckerchief were waiting, while he sat there plotting his escape. Escape, though, except into poems or fond memories, was the one thing that Benedict had never been successful with. Before he'd set his empty teacup down into its saucer and commenced his dash for freedom, Eileen shot him down.

"Shall yer be lookin' out fer work today, then?"

This was yet another aspect of the mornings, quite apart from thinking about death the moment you woke up, that Benedict found problematic. It was two things, actually, that he was largely unsuccessful with. Escape, and finding work. Of course, the biggest stumbling block he had with finding work was that he wasn't looking, or not very hard, at any rate. It wasn't all the actual work that put him off, it was the job: all the procedures and the people who came with it. He just didn't think he had the heart to introduce himself to a collection of new faces, people who knew nothing about poetry or Freeschool Street and wouldn't have a clue what Benedict was all about. He couldn't do it, not at his age, not to strangers, not explain himself. To be completely frank, he never had been able to explain himself at any age, to anybody, or at least he'd never managed to explain to anybody's satisfaction. Three things, then. Escape, and finding work, and then explaining himself adequately. It was just those areas he had trouble with. Everything else, he was all right about.

"I'm always looking. You know me. The eyes that never rest. Ah ha ha ha."

His mother tipped her head to one side while regarding him, with fondness and bone-tired incomprehension at the same time.

"Ah, well. It's a pity that yer eyes can't pass the trick on to yer arse, in that case. 'Ere. 'Ere's summat fer yer dinner. I expect I'll see yer when yer get back in, if I'm still up."

Eileen pressed ten Benson & Hedges and a ten-pound note into his hand. He beamed at her, as if it didn't happen every morning.

"Woman, I could kiss yer."

"Yiss, well, you do and you'll get this." This was his mam's fist, thrust upwards like a haunted Aboriginal rock outcrop. Ben laughed, pocketing the tenner and the fags, then went into the hall. He fastened his burnt-orange neckerchief across the swallowed Carlsberg bottle of his Adam's apple, squinting at the daylight filtered through the frosted panel by the front door and deciding it looked bright enough to leave his coat behind, though not so bright that he need bother taking his straw hat. His waistcoat looked like brothel curtains as it was. He didn't want to over-do it.

He transferred the ciggies from his trouser pocket to his canvas satchel, where he'd also got some Kleenex tissues and an orange, with a copy of *A Northamptonshire Garland* edited by Trevor Hold and published by Northampton Libraries. It was just something he was dipping into at the moment, just to keep his hand in. Bag across one shoulder, Benedict called goodbye to his mam, drew in a fortifying breath before the hallway mirror and then, flinging wide the front door, he launched himself valiantly once more into the fray, and the frayed world it was conducted in.

Spit-coloured clouds moved over Tower Street, formerly the upper end of Scarletwell. The street had been renamed after the high-rise, Claremont Court, that blocked out half the western sky upon his right, one of two brick stakes hammered through the district's undead heart. On recently refurbished crab-paste brickwork were the words or possibly the single word NEWLIFE, a sideways silver logo, more a label for a mobile phone or for an everlasting battery than for a tower block, he'd have thought. Benedict winced, attempting not to look at it. For the most part, he found it comforting to still reside in the beloved neighbourhood, except for those occasions when you noticed that the loved one had been dead for thirty years and was now decomposing. Then you felt a bit like someone from an item out of *Fortean Times*, one of those lovelorn and demented widowers still plumping up the pillows for a bride who's long since mummified. Newlife: urban regeneration that they'd had to literally spell out because of its conspicuous absence otherwise. As if just bolting up the mirror-finish letters made it so. What had been wrong with all the old life, anyway?

He checked to see the door had locked behind him, with his mam now being on her own in there, and as he did he saw the big fat druggy with the bald head, Kenny something, lumbering down Simons Walk that ran along the end of Tower Street, at the back of Claremont Court. He had grey slacks and a grey sports-top on, which from a distance looked all of a piece, like one big romper suit, as if the dealer were an outsized baby who'd exceeded the safe dose of Calpol. Benedict pretended he'd not seen him, turning left and walking briskly up towards the street's far end, a confluence of sunken walkways tucked away behind the traffic vortex of the Mayorhold. How could anybody get that fat on drugs, unless they ate them in a fried bread sandwich? Ah ha ha ha.

Yellow leaves were plastered in a partial lino on the wet macadam at his feet as he passed the Salvation Army building, a prefabricated barracks that he didn't think he'd ever been inside. He doubted they went in for tambourines these days, much less free cups of tea and buns. The twentieth century had been a better time to be a washout. Back then poverty had come with a brass band accompaniment and a cheek full of scone dissolving in hot Brooke Bond; kindly bosoms heaving under navy blue serge and big golden buttons. Now it came with flint-eyed teenage death-camp supervisors in the no-hiding-place glare of the Job Centre, and whatever soundtrack happened to be playing in the shopping precinct outside, usually "I'm Not In Love". The short street ended as it met the footpath to the underpass, where a high wall reared up to bound the robot shark tank of the Mayorhold. Patterned with a bar-code stripe of ochre, tangerine and umber, it was probably intended to provide a Latin atmosphere, whereas instead it looked like an attack of vomiting restaged in Lego. Benedict stopped walking for a moment so that he could take it in, the ground where he was standing, with its full historical enormity.

For one thing, it was near here that one of his father's favourite pubs had been, the Jolly Smokers, although this was by no means the full extent of the locale's historic pedigree. This spot was where Northampton's first 'Gilhalda' or Town Hall had stood back in the thirteenth and the fourteenth centuries, at least according to historian Henry Lee. Richard the Second had declared it in his charter as the place where all the bailiffs and the mayor were situated. Bailiffs were still seen down here from time to time, though mayors less often these days. Late on in the thirteen-hundreds all the wealth and power had shifted to the east side of the town, and a new Guildhall had been raised down at the foot of Abington Street, near where Caffè Nero stood today. That was the point from which you could most likely date the area's decline: for more than seven hundred years the Boroughs had been going steadily downhill. It was a long hill, evidently, though as he stood there regarding the emetic tile-work Benedict believed the bottom was at last in sight.

Although the first Town Hall had been located here, that wasn't why the former town square had been named the Mayorhold, or not as Ben understood things, anyway. His theory was that this had happened later, in the 1490s, at a time when Parliament had placed Northampton under the control of an all-powerful mayor and council made up of four dozen wealthy buggers, sorry matron, wealthy burghers that they called the Forty-Eight. Benedict thought that this was when the people of the Boroughs, like the folk of nearby Leicester, had begun their grand tradition of electing a joke mayor, to take the piss out of the processes of government from which they'd been excluded. They'd hold mock elections in the square here, hence the name, and would award a literal tin-pot chain of office made from a pot lid to whoever they'd randomly appointed, often somebody half cut, half sharp, half missing from a war wound, or, in extreme cases, all of the above. Benedict had a notion that his own paternal grandfather, Bill Perrit, had been one such appointee, but that was based on no more than the old man's nickname, which had been "the

Sheriff", and the fact that he'd sit there all day blind drunk outside the Mayorhold Mission in an old wheelbarrow that he treated like a throne. Benedict
wondered briefly if he could claim office based upon being descended from
the Sheriff and on living where the first Town Hall had stood? He fancied
himself as a Titchbourne Claimant, as a Great Pretender, one of those who'd
put more forethought into getting crowns on heads than keeping heads on
shoulders. Lambert Simnel, Perkin Warbeck and Benedict Perrit. Names to
conjure with. Ah ha ha ha.

He turned along the sunken footpath, with ahead of him the steps that
led up to the corner where the upper end of Bath Street met the top of Horsemarket. Even from this low vantage he could see the higher storeys of both
tower-blocks, Claremont Court and Beaumont Court, where they poked up
above the Spanish-omelette tiling of the dyke wall hulking on his right. The
towers, for Benedict, had always marked the real end of the Boroughs, that
rich, thousand-year-long saga that had been concluded with these overly-
emphatic double exclamation marks. Newlife. It made you want to spew. Two
or three years back there'd been calls to tear the barely-habitable monsters
down, acknowledgements that they should never have been put up in the first
place. Benedict had briefly thought he might outlive the bullying, oppressive
oblongs, but then Bedford Housing had made some deal with the Council – still
four dozen of the wealthy buggers, still the Forty-Eight after five centuries –
and purchased both blocks for what was reputedly a penny each. The urine-
scented ugly sisters had been tarted up and then turned out, supposedly, as
fit accommodation for "Key Workers" that it seemed Northampton needed,
mostly siren-jockeys: nurses, firemen, policemen and the like. Newlife. New
life that had been parachuted in, in order to contain the previous inhabitants
when they got sick or stabbed or set themselves on fire. As things worked out,
though, what the tower blocks had been filled with was a stream of human
leftovers ... outpatients, crack-heads, refugees ... not obviously different to the
people who'd been living there before.

The leftie Roman Thompson from St. Andrew's Street had once shown
him a list of Bedford Housing's board, which had included former Labour
councillor James Cockie in the roster. This might possibly explain the penny
price tags. Benedict turned left before he reached the steps to Bath Street corner, taking the pedestrian tunnel under Horsemarket that was sign-posted for
town centre. Here the bilious orange-brown mosaic was all round him, rising
to the arched roof of the tunnel where dim sodium lights at intervals emitted
their unhelpful amber glow.

Ben's gangling, insufficiently-lit shape sloped through the queasy cata-
comb that seemed to rustle with the ghosts of future murders. An abandoned
shopping trolley rolled towards him menacingly for perhaps a foot, but then

thought better of it, creaking to a sullen standstill. Only when he passed beneath a ceiling-lamp did his heroically-proportioned features or his tired, resigned smile flare into existence, like a head-and-shoulders sketch by Boz that somebody had put a match to. The unwelcome thought of Councillor Jim Cockie, possibly in combination with these subterranean surroundings, would appear to have unlocked a previously forgotten dream in which the councillor had featured, which Ben suddenly remembered from the night before, if only as a fuzzy string of cryptic fragments.

He'd been wandering through the generic terraces of elderly red brick and railway-arch-bound wastelands that appeared to be the default setting for his dreams. Somewhere within this eerie and familiar landscape there had been a house, a teetering old Boroughs house with stairs and passageways that never quite made sense. The streets were dark. It was the middle of the night. He'd known that family or friends were waiting for him in the building's cellar, but he'd suffered all the usual dream-frustrations finding his way in, picking his way apologetically through other people's flats and bathrooms, navigating laundry-chutes that were part-blocked by antique wooden desks he recognised from Spring Lane School. At last he'd reached a kind of boiler-room or basement that had blood and straw and sawdust on the floor, as if the space had been used as a slaughterhouse just recently. There was an atmosphere of squalid horror, yet this was somehow connected to his childhood and was almost comforting. He'd then become aware that Councillor Jim Cockie, someone that he barely knew, was standing in the gory cellar next to him, a corpulent, bespectacled and white-haired form dressed only in his underpants, his face a mask of dread. He'd said "This place is all I dream about. Do you know the way out?" Ben had felt disinclined to help the frightened man, one of that Forty-Eight who had historically destroyed the Boroughs, and had answered only "Ah ha ha. I'm trying to get further in." At this point, Benedict had woken from what still seemed like somebody else's nightmare. He emerged out of the tunnel, shaking off the bad dreams with the darkness of the underpass, and puffed up the steep gradient to Silver Street.

Across the other side of the dual carriageway that Silver Street now was, there rose the five-floor municipal car park, red and mustard yellow like spilled condiments. Somewhere beneath its stale Battenberg mass, Benedict knew, were all the shops and yards that had once backed onto the Mayorhold. There'd be Botterill's the newsagent's, the butcher's, Phyllis Malin's barbershop, the green and white façade of the Co-operative Society, Built 1919, Branch Number 11. There'd be the grim public toilets on the corner that his mam and dad had for some reason known as Georgie Bumble's Office, and there'd be the fish and chip shop and Electric Light Working Men's Club in Bearward Street and fifty other sites of interest ground to an undifferentiated dust beneath the weight of four-by-fours and Chavercrafts now piled above. The backside of the old Fish Market stood upon his right, itself erected on the synagogue attended by the silversmiths who'd lent the street its name. He added stars of David in a glittering filigree to the imaginary landfill languishing beneath the multi-storey motor show. Ford Transit Gloria Mundi. Ah ha ha ha.

Growing from the brick wall near the Chinese restaurant where Silver Street joined Sheep Street was a solitary wildflower, mauve and flimsy like a mallow though he didn't think it could be. From the pallid institution green of its limp stem stood gooseberry hairs, almost too fine to be distinguished by the adult eye. Whatever its variety, it was of humble, prehistoric stock, like Benedict himself. However delicate and dangling it seemed, it had pushed through the mortar of the modern world, asserted itself ineradicably in the face of a deflowered and drab MacCentury. He knew it wasn't much of a poetic insight, not if you compared it to "The force that through the green fuse drives …", but then these days he'd take his inspirations where he found them, like his wildflowers. Turning into Sheep Street he made for the Bear, where he intended to take up once more the burden of his daily challenge, which was trying to get hammered for a tenner.

Loud despite the relatively small number of customers that time of day, the Bear was simmering in sound from its own fruit machines: electric fairy-wand glissandos and the squelch of crazy frogs. Luminous tessellations rearranged themselves in the blurred corners of his vision, golds and reds and purples, an Arabian Nights palette. He remembered when a morning bar-room was a place of careful hush and milky light decanted through net curtains, not so much as a triumphal click out of the dominos.

The barman was a young chap half Ben's age, a lad he vaguely recognised but whom he nonetheless addressed as "Ah ha ha. Hello, me old pal, me old beauty", this delivered in a fair approximation of the voice associated once with now-forgotten *Archers* mainstay Walter Gabriel, neatly camouflaging, as he thought, the fact that he'd forgotten the bloke's name.

"Hello there, Benedict. What can I get you?"

Ben looked round appraisingly at the establishment's half-dozen other clients, motionless upon their stools like ugly novelty-set chessmen, sidelined and morose.

He cleared his throat theatrically before he spoke.

"Who'll buy a pint of bitter for a published poet and a national treasure? Ah ha ha."

Nobody looked up. One or two half-smiled but they were a distinct minority. Oh well. Sometimes it worked, if there was someone in who knew him, say Dave Turvey hunched up gentlemanly in one corner with his feathered hat on, looking like an autumn day in the bohemian quarter of Dodge City, somebody like that. On this particular Bad Friday morning, though, Dave's usual seat was empty, and with great reluctance Ben dredged up the ten-pound note out of his pocket to deposit on the bar, as a down payment on the pint of John Smith's that he one day hoped to call his own. Farewell, then, sepia Darwin. Farewell green and crimson 3D hummingbird transfixed by swirling patterns in the Hypnoscope. Farewell, my crumpled little friend of this half-hour now gone for good. I hardly knew ye. Ah ha ha.

Once served, he let himself be drawn into the plush curve of the side-seats, taking with him in one hand his filmy, frosted fistful, getting on eight quid in change balled in the other. Hello to slate-blue Elizth. Fry and what looked like a nineteenth-century battered woman's refuge except for the disapproving spectre of John Lennon, sneering from the left of frame. This was quite possibly a fancy-dress campaigner representing Dads For Justice. With the fiver were two pound coins and some shrapnel. Grimacing, he shook his head. It wasn't just that Benedict missed the old money, all the farthings, half-crowns, florins, tanners, though of course he did. But what he missed more, though, was being able to refer to pre-decimal coinage without sounding like an old dear who'd confused her bus pass with her kidney donor card. He was surprisingly self-conscious on the subject of self-parody.

He swigged the first half of his pint, plunging indulgently in the olfactory swim of memory and association, cheese and pickled onions, Park Drive packs of five pink in a green pub ashtray, standing next to his old man at the Black Lion's diseased and possibly Precambrian urinal trough with a six-year-old's sense of privilege. The rapidly successive mouthfuls were diluted gulps of vanished fields, the high-tech recreation of fondly imagined but extinct rusticity. He put down the half-empty glass, trying to kid himself that it was still half full, and wiped almost four decades of oral tradition from his smacking lips onto his pinstripe cuff.

He lifted up the canvas satchel's flap, where it was set on the warm cushioning beside him, and pulled out *A Northamptonshire Garland* from within. Lacking Dave Turvey and a poetry discussion with the living, Benedict thought that he might as well strike up a conversation with the dead. The cheap and chunky hardback came out of the bag with its rear cover uppermost. In an ornate gold frame against a deep red background rubbed with cobblers' wax was Thomas Grimshaw's 1840s portrait of John Clare. The picture never looked quite right to Benedict, especially the outsized moonrise of the brow. If not for the brown topiary of hair and whisker fringing the great oval, it might be a man's face painted on an Easter egg. A Humpty Dumpty with his mess of yolk and shell spread on the lawns of Andrew's Hospital, and no one there to put him back together.

Clare stood posed uncomfortably before a non-specific rural blur, a leafy lane at Helpston, Glinton, anywhere, just after sunset or conceivably just prior to dawn, one thumb hooked statesmanlike upon his coat's lapel. He looked off to the right, turning towards the shadows with a faintly worried smile, the corners of the mouth twitched up in an uncertain greeting, with the slightest wince of apprehension already apparent in those disappointed eyes. Was that, Benedict wondered, where he'd got it from, his own characteristically amused, forlorn expression? There were similarities, he fancied, between him and his enduring lifelong hero. John Clare had a fair old beak on him, not wholly different from Ben's own, at least to judge from Grimshaw's portrait. There were the sad eyes, the faltering smile, even the neckerchief. If someone were only to shave Ben's head and feed him up a bit, he could be stepping out of the dry ice fumes on *Stars In Their Eyes*, one thumb snagged in his jacket, madhouse burrs caught in his sideburns. Tonight, Matthew, I will be the peasant poet. Ah ha ha.

Beneath the owlish likeness in the cover's lower right was pasted a discoloured slug, fired from a price-gun fifteen years ago: VOLUME1 BOOKSHOPS, £6.00. To his consternation, for a moment Benedict could not even remember quite where VOLUME1 had been located. Had that been where Waterstone's was now? There'd been that many bookshops in Northampton once, you'd be hard pressed to get around them all within a single day; mostly become estate agents and wine-bars. In Ben's youth, even big stores like Adnitt's had their book departments. There'd been trays of one-and-thrupenny paperbacks in both the upper and the lower branch of Woolworth's, and there'd been a rash of second-hand dives shading into junkshops with invariably consumptive elderly proprietors, with yellow-covered 1960s pornographic classics glimpsed through dusty glass in unlit windows. Jaundiced Aubrey Beardsley nudes enrobed with Technicolor slapped Hank Janson sluts, a bit of sauce to liven up the casserole of Dennis Wheatley, Simenon and Alistair MacLean. Those grubby, spittle-lacquered archives, where had they all gone?

He raised his glass for a commemorative sip, a sip being approximately half a gill with eight sips to the pint. Taking the pack of Bensons and a street-bought three-for-a-quid lighter from his shoulder bag he gripped one of the cigarettes between eternally-wry lips, lighting it with the stick of liquid-centred amethyst. Ben squinted through the first blue puffs of smoke across the lounge bar. This had filled up, although not with anyone he recognised. Off somewhere to his left, a burbling audial cascade of virtual coins was punctuated with stabs from a science-fiction zither. Sighing non-specifically, he opened the anthology of local poets to its John Clare section, where he hoped that "Clock-a-Clay", written from the perspective of a ladybird, might prove an antidote to the contemporary flash and jangle that he felt so alienated from.

The miniaturist imagery was certainly transporting, though disastrously he couldn't help but read on to the poem that was reproduced immediately after, which was Clare's asylum-penned "I Am".

Into the nothingness of scorn and noise,
Into the living sea of waking dreams,
Where there is neither sense of life or joys,
But the vast shipwreck of my life's esteems;
Even the dearest that I loved the best
Are strange – nay, rather, stranger than the rest.

That was entirely too close to the nerve, instantly sinking Benedict's half-decent mood, already holed below its waterline. He shoved the book back in his satchel, downing the three sips remaining in his pint and purchasing another one before he knew he'd done it. This relieved him of his small-change buffer and exposed his queen, Eliz[th]. Fry, precariously. Her rainy turquoise eyes stared out of the remaining note into his own, with something of his mother's look of worried resignation when she gazed appraisingly on Ben and Ben's unjustly punished liver.

The next thing he knew, it was mid-day. He was emerging from the narrow barroom of the Shipman's, basically a passageway that had a pub where most people have coatpegs, into Drum Lane. Down the alley on his right he could see All Saints' Church across the road, with on his left the waning bustle of the Market Square. Eliz[th]. Fry, apparently, had left him for another man, most probably a landlord. He lugubriously noted that he still had custody of several little ones, silver and copper orphans to the sum of eighty-seven pence. A bubbling protest from his long-drowned instincts for self-preservation told him he should probably invest this in a pasty. Turning right he made his way down the perpetual shadow-channel of Drum Lane, towards the bakery opposite All Saints' in Mercer's Row.

Ten minutes later he was swallowing the last of what he thought was more than likely lunch, tongue probing optimistically in the mysterious ditches of his mouth for any lingering mince, tenacious pastry or recalcitrant potato. Blotting his lips in what he thought might well be the manner of a nineteenth-century dandy on the serviette the snack had come with, Benedict screwed up the tissue with its gravy kiss-print, dropping it into one of the litter bins in Abington Street, which he'd by now reached and was ascending. He was roughly level with the photographic shop close to the mouth of the most recent shopping arcade, Peacock Place. This crystal palace had taken the place of Peacock Way, an open precinct leading to the Market that had cake-shops and cafés where he'd munch gloomily through teenage comfort teacakes, mooning over whichever heart-stopping Notre Dame or Derngate schoolgirl had just told Ben that she liked him as a friend. Originally, this had been the Peacock Hotel, inn or coach-house for five hundred years. People still talked about the lovely stained-glass peacock, one of the establishment's interior decorations, which had more than likely fallen prey to salvage men during the hotel's senseless demolition in November 1959. Up on the glasswork of the arcade's entrance these days was a pallid stick-on imitation, stylised craft-kit product from an overpaid design team.

Passing Jessop's, the photography equipment shop, he wondered if they still had Pete Corr's photograph of Benedict, framed and for sale up on their wall. Corr was a local shutterbug now married, living somewhere out in Canada by all accounts, under the mock-Dutch moniker of Piet de Snapp. Formerly just plain Pete the Snap, he'd specialised in portraits of the town's outlandish fauna: Ben's old Spring Lane schoolmate Alma Warren, posing moodily in sunglasses and leather jacket, mutton dressed up as Olivia Newton-John; the Jovian mass and gravity of much-missed local minstrel-god Tom Hall in customary daywear, individually-engineered playschool pyjamas and a tasselled hat swiped from the Ottomans; Benedict Perrit sat in state amongst the snaking roots of the eight-hundred-year-old beech in Sheep Street, smiling ruefully. As if there were another way to smile. Ah ha ha ha.

He carried on through Abington Street's pink, pedestrianised meander. Without curbs to bound and shape all the frenetic motion that had poured along this main drag for at least five hundred years, it seemed as if these days the street mainly attracted those who were themselves similarly unfocussed and directionless. As Benedict himself was, come to think of it. He'd no idea where he thought he was going, not with only twenty-seven pence remaining in the wake of his impulsive pasty, gone now save for the occasional flavour-haunted burp. Perhaps a long walk up the Wellingborough Road to Abington would do him good, or would at any rate not cost him anything.

Continuing uphill, pleasantly numbed against existence in a warm cocooning fog, the entrance to the Grosvenor Centre crawled past on his left. He tried to conjure the thin mouth of Wood Street, which had occupied the spot some thirty years before, but found his powers of evocation blunted by the beer. The half-forgotten terraced aperture was too feeble a spectre to prevail against the glass wall of swing doors, the sparkling covered boulevard beyond where the somnambulists somnambled, lit like ornamental crystal animals by the commercial aura-fields they passed through. Everyone looked decorative in the all-round illumination. Everyone looked brittle.

Twenty-seven pence. He wasn't even sure that would still buy a Mars Bar, though he could still savour the self-pity. Benedict picked up his pace a little passing by top Woolworth's, these days more precisely only Woolworth's, hoping the increased velocity would straighten out his veer. He gave this up for lack of a result after approximately thirty seconds, lapsing to a melancholy trudge. What was the point in walking faster when he wasn't going anywhere? More speed would only bring him to his problems quicker, and in his state might lead inadvertently to crossing the blurred line between a drunken stumble and a drunken rampage. The unbidden vision of Ben gone berserk in Marks & Spencer's, running nude and screaming through a hail of melting-middle chocolate puddings, should have been a sobering one but only made him giggle to himself. The giggling didn't help, he realised, with his tactic of not looking pissed. This still made only four things he was useless at, namely escape, finding a job, explaining himself adequately and not looking pissed. Four trivial deficiencies, Ben reassured himself, and as naught in the sweep of a man's life.

He tacked against the east wind, chortling only intermittently as he traversed the wide-angle Art Deco front of the Co-op Arcade, abandoned and deserted, windows emptied of displays that stared unseeing, still stunned by the news of their redundancy. The retail parks outside the town had drained the commerce from Northampton's centre, which had been an increasingly ugly proposition for some years now, anyway. Rather than try to stop the rot, the council had allowed the town's main veins to atrophy and wither. Spinadisc, the long-established independent record shop that Benedict was now approaching on the street's far side, had been closed down to make way for a rehab centre, something of that kind. Predictably, there were considerably less substance-users on the premises now that the music and ephemera were gone.

Around the public seating outside the dead jukebox of the former pop emporium, small crowds of black-clad teenagers still congregated in school holidays and at weekends. Ben thought they might be skate-goths or gangsta-romantics. Happy-stabbers or whatever. He had difficulty keeping up. Shifting his doleful gaze from the murder of hoodies flocked on Abington Street's further edge, he looked back to the side along which he was walking. A vague drift of people flowed towards him past the still-magnificent façade of the town library, and there came a synaptic jolt, a minor judder and resettling of reality as Benedict realised that one of them was Alma Warren. Ah ha ha.

Alma. She always took him back, a walking memory-prompt of all the years they'd known each other, since they'd been together in Miss Corrier's class at Spring Lane School when they were four. Even back then, you'd never have confused her with a girl. Or with a boy, for that matter. She was too big, too single minded, too alarming to be anything but Alma, in a gender of her own. Both of them sideshow novelties in their own ways, they'd been inseparable throughout long stretches of childhood and adolescence. Winter evenings shivering in the attic up above the barn in his dad's wood-yard down in

Freeschool Street, Ben's telescope poking into the starlight through an absent windowpane when they were both on flying saucer watch. The tricky post-pubertal stretch when he began his poetry and she her painting, and when Alma would get furiously angry and stop speaking to him every other fort-night, over their artistic differences as she insisted, but most probably when she'd just fallen to the communists. They'd both made idiots of themselves in the same pubs, in the same stencil-duplicated arts-group magazines, but then she'd somehow managed to talk up her monomania into a prosperous career and reputation, while Ben hadn't. Now he didn't run into her much, nobody did, except upon occasions such as this when she came flouncing into town dressed like a biker or, if she were wearing her pretentious cloak, a fifteenth-century nun who'd been defrocked for masturbation, more rings underneath her eyes than on her ostentatiously embellished fingers.

These were currently raised up in an arterial spatter of nail gloss and gemstones, pulling the distressed fire-curtain of her hair back from the pan-tomime that was her face. Her kohl-ringed and apparently disdainful gaze described a measured arc across the precinct as if Alma were pretending to be a surveillance camera, dredging Abington Street's fast-deteriorating stock of imagery in search of inspiration for some future monsterpiece. When the slow swivel of her so-unblinking-they-seemed-lidless fog lamps got to Bene-dict, there was an anthracite glint suddenly alight deep in the makeup-crusted sockets. Carmine lips drew taut into a smile most probably intended to look fond rather than predatory. Ah ha ha ha. Good old Alma.

Benedict went into a routine the moment that their eyes met, first adopt-ing an expression of appalled dismay then turning sharply in his tracks to walk away down Abington Street, as if frantically pretending that he hadn't seen her. He turned this into a circular trajectory that took him back towards her, this time doubling up with silent laughter so she'd know his terrified attempt at flight had been a gag. He wouldn't want her thinking he was really trying to run away, not least in case she went for him and brought him down before he'd got five paces.

Their paths met outside the library portico. He stuck his hand out, but Alma surprised him with a sudden lunge, planting a bloody pucker on his cheek, spraining his neck with her brief one-armed hug. This was some affec-tation, he concluded, that she'd picked up from Americans with galleries who put on exhibitions. Exhibitionists. She hadn't learned it in the Boroughs, of that Benedict was certain. In the district where they'd both grown up, affec-tionate displays were never physical. Or verbal, or in any way apparent to the five traditional senses. Love and friendship in the Boroughs were subliminal. He flinched back from her, wiping at his stained cheek with the back of one long-fingered hand like an embarrassed cat.

"Get off! Ah ha ha ha ha ha!"

Alma grinned, apparently pleased at just how easily she had unsettled him. She ducked her head and leaned a little forward when she spoke, as if to best facilitate their conversation, although really she was just reminding him how tall she was, the way she did with everyone. It was one of what only Alma thought of as her range of subtly intimidating mannerisms.

"Benedict, you suave Lothario. This is an unexpected treat. How's things? Are you still writing?"

Alma's voice wasn't just deep brown, it was infra-brown. Ben laughed at her query on his output, at the sheer preposterousness of her even asking.

"Always, Alma. You know me. Ah ha ha. Always scribbling away."

He'd not written a line in years. He was a published poet in the transitive and not the current sense. He wasn't sure that he was any sort of poet in the current sense, that was his secret dread. Alma was nodding amiably now, pleased with his answer.

"Good. That's good to hear. I was just reading 'Clearance Area' the other day and thinking what a smashing poem it was."

Hum. "Clearance Area". He'd been quite pleased with that himself. "Who can say now/ That anything was here/ Other than open land/ Used only by stray dogs/ And children breaking bottles on stones?" With a start he realised that had been almost two decades back, those writings. "Weeds, stray dogs and children/ Waited patiently/ For them to leave./ The weed beneath;/ The dog and child/ Unborn inside." He tipped his head back, unsure how he should receive the compliment except with an uncertain smile, as if expecting her at any moment to retract her praise, expose it for the cruel post-modern joke it doubtless was. Eventually, he risked a tentative response.

"I weren't bad, was I? Ah ha ha."

He'd meant to say *It* weren't bad, as a reference to the poem, but it had come out wrong. Now it sounded as though Benedict thought of himself in the past tense, which wasn't what he'd meant at all. At least, he didn't think that it was what he'd meant. Alma was frowning now, it seemed reproachfully.

"Ben, you were always a considerable way beyond 'not bad'. You know you were. You're a good writer, mate. I'm serious."

This last was offered in reply to Benedict's plainly embarrassed giggling. He really didn't know what he should say. Alma was at least Z-list famous and successful, and Ben couldn't help but feel as though in some way he were being patronised. It was as if she thought that a kind word from her could mend him, could inspire him, raise him from the dead and make him whole with just the least brush of her hem. She acted as though all his problems could be solved if he were just to write, which only showed, in Benedict's opinion, just how shallow Alma's understanding of his problems really was. Did she have any idea, standing there with all her money and her write-ups in *The Independent*, what it was like having only twenty-seven pence? Well, actually, of course she did. She'd come from the same background he had, so that wasn't fair, but even so. The troubling notion of his present finances, or at least relative to Alma's, had bobbed up from the beer sediments currently settled at the bottom of Ben's mind, and wouldn't bob back down again. Before he even knew that he was going to do it, he'd broken the habit of a lifetime and tapped Alma up for cash.

"'Ere, you ain't got a couple o' quid spare, 'ave yer?"

It felt wrong as soon as the words left his mouth, a terrible transgression. He immediately wished that he could take it back, but it was too late. Now it was in Alma's hands, and she would almost certainly find some way she could make it worse. Surprised, her flue-brush lashes widened almost imperceptibly, but she recovered with a deadpan look of generalised concern.

"Of course I have. I'm fucking loaded. Here."

She pulled a note ... a note ... out of her drainpipe jeans and, pointedly not looking to determine its denomination, pressed it hard into Ben's open palm. See, this was what he'd meant, about how Alma always made things more uncomfortable, but in a manner that obliged you to be grateful to her. Since she hadn't looked to see how much cash she was giving him, Ben felt that it would be *déclassé* for him to do otherwise, slipping the crumpled note without a glance into his trouser pocket. He was feeling genuinely guilty now. The centres of his beetling eyebrows had crept up involuntarily towards his widow's peak as he protested her undue beneficence.

"Are you sure, Alma? Are you sure?"

She grinned, dismissing the uneasy moment.

"'Course I'm sure. Forget it. How are you, mate, anyway? What are you doing these days?"

Benedict was grateful for the change of subject, though it left him grasping hopelessly for something that he could legitimately claim he'd done.

"Oh, this and that. Went for an interview the other day."

Alma looked interested, although only politely so.

"Oh yeah? How did it go?"

"I don't know. I've not heard yet. When they interviewed me, I kept wanting to come out and tell them 'I'm a published poet', but I held it in."

Alma was trying to nod sagely, but was also clearly trying not to laugh, with the result that neither effort was what you'd call an unqualified success.

"You did the right thing. There's a time and place for everything." She cocked her head on one side, narrowing her black bird-eating eyes as if she'd just remembered something.

"Listen, Ben, I've just thought. There's these paintings I've been doing, all

about the Boroughs, and I'm having a preliminary viewing of them down at
Castle Hill tomorrow lunchtime, in the nursery that used to be Pitt-Draffen's
dance school. Why don't you come down? It'd be great to see you."

"Perhaps I will. Perhaps I will. Ah ha ha ha." Deep in his bitter-sodden
heart, he knew he almost definitely wouldn't. To be honest he was barely listening to her, still trying to think of things he'd done, beside the interview,
that he could mention. Suddenly he thought about his visits to the cyber café
and perked up. Alma was widely known to never venture near the Internet,
which meant, astoundingly, that here was someone who, at least in this one
area, was less adapted to the present day than Benedict. He beamed at her,
triumphantly.

"Do you know, I've been going on the Internet?" He ran one preening hand
back over his dark curls, while with the other he adjusted an imaginary bow tie.

Alma was now laughing openly. By mutual consent they seemed to both
be disengaging from the conversation, starting to move slowly off, him uphill,
Alma down. It was as if they'd come to the predestined end of their encounter
and must both now walk away, whether they'd finished talking yet or not.
They had to hurry if they wanted to remain on schedule, occupying all the
empty spaces in their futures they had yet to fill, all at the proper predetermined times. Still visibly amused, she called back to him over the increasing
gap between them.

"You're a twenty-first-century boy, Ben."

Laughter tipped his head back like a well-slapped punch-bag. Several
paces off, he was half turned away from her, towards the upper end of Abington Street.

"I'm a Cyberman. Ah ha ha ha."

Their brief knot of hilarity and mutual incomprehension was unravelled
into two loose, snickering ends that trailed away in opposite directions. Benedict had reached the precinct's topmost limit and was crossing York Road at the
lights before he thought to reach into his pocket and retrieve the screwed-up
currency that Alma had bequeathed him. Pink and plum and violet, the note
sported a blue angel from whose trumpet fell a radiating shower of notes.
Worcester Cathedral was bombarded by them in a joyous cosmic ray-storm,
St. Cecilia reclining in the foreground as she soaked up the UV. A twenty.
Welcome to my humble pants, Sir Edward Elgar. We've been only fleetingly
acquainted previously, and you wouldn't remember, but can I just say that *The
Dream of Gerontius* is an outstanding work of pastoral vision? Ah ha ha.

This was a gift from God. Thanks, God, and do pass on my thanks to
Alma who you've clearly made your representative on Earth. I hope to God
that … well, I hope to You that you know what you're doing there on that one,

so be warned. But still, this was fantastic. He resolved he'd take his healthy walk up Wellingborough Road to Abington Park anyway, despite the fact that he no longer needed to, having sufficient funds to dally where he wanted. Benedict could dally with a vengeance when the mood was on him, but for now he stuffed the note back in his pocket and began to whistle as he walked towards Abington Square, only relenting when he realised he was giving a rendition of the theme music from *Emmerdale*. Luckily, nobody seemed to have noticed.

This had once been the east gate of the town, the strip that Benedict was pacing now, what they'd called Edmund's End back in the eighteen-hundreds, named after St. Edmund's Church, which had been slightly further out along the Wellingborough Road until it was pulled down a quarter century ago. Ben liked the buildings here, on the approach to the main square itself, if one ignored the tawdry transformations of their lower storeys. Just across the road there was the gorgeous 1930s cinema, at different times the ABC or the Savoy. He'd been himself a dead shot with a flicked ice-lolly stick at matinees, although he'd never once had someone's eye out despite all the warnings to the contrary. These days, like getting on a quarter or a third of the town's major properties, the place was owned by a commune of Evangelicals known as the Jesus Army, who had started out as a small nest of rescued derelicts in nearby Bugbrooke and then spread like happy clappy bindweed, until you could find their rainbow-liveried buses organising tramp-grabs almost anywhere in middle England. Still, it wasn't like Northampton and religious mania had been strangers to each other in the past. Benedict sauntered on towards Abington Square, reflecting that the last time that these parts had seen a Jesus Army it was Cromwell's, and instead of pamphlets they'd been waving pikes. It was a kind of progress, Ben supposed.

The square looked almost handsome in the light of early afternoon, unless you'd known it in its youth and could make the painful comparison. The slipper factory had gone in favour of a Jaguar showroom called Guy Salmon. The old Irish Centre had been turned into the Urban Tiger. Benedict had never been inside the venue since the name change. He pictured the clientele as ranks of angry Tamils learning martial arts.

Charles Bradlaugh stood there dazzling white upon his plinth, directing traffic. It had never looked to Benedict as though the great teetotal atheist and equal rights campaigner was just pointing westwards, more as if he was in a saloon bar trying to start a fight. Yeah, that's right. You. Fuck features. Who'd you think I'm pointing at? Ah ha ha ha. Ben passed the statue on his left, with on his right an uninviting new pub named the Workhouse. Ben saw what they'd done there: further up the Wellingborough Road, across from the wall-bounded space where Edmund's Church once stood was what remained of

Edmund's Hospital, which in Victorian times had been Northampton's workhouse. It was like putting a theme pub called the Whipping Post in a black neighbourhood, or Eichmann's in a Jewish one. A touch insensitive.

Ben found that he was travelling at quite a pace, even against the wuthering headwind. In what seemed like only moments the abandoned hulk of Edmund's Hospital itself loomed up on his left side, a haunted palace smothered in a creep of weeds, its smashed eyes filled with ghosts. Ghosts, and if rumours were to be believed, with failed asylum seekers, refugees who'd been denied that status and had chosen to camp out in former terminal wards rather than risk being sent home to whatever despot or electrode-happy strongman they were fleeing in the first place. Home is where the hurt is, that was very true. It struck him that the workhouse, though dilapidated, must feel blessed in its old age. It had its huddled, frightened outcasts back, could take a secret comfort from their secret fires.

There on the other side, across the wall he was now walking past, was the palpable absence of St. Edmund's Church, an empty yawn of green with intermittent tombstones jutting, carious, discoloured, suffering from built-up birdshit plaque, the green and grassy gums beginning to recede. Upon the plus side, Benedict could make out lark song underneath the grumble of the main road's traffic, bubbling notes erupting in a brilliant effervescence to distract cats from the fledglings hidden low down in the graveyard grass. It was a nice day. The eternal was still there, a promising suggestive bulge concealed behind the present's threadbare drapes.

Heading on eastwards out of town along the strip of pubs and shops, he thought of Alma. At the age of seventeen she'd been a glaring giant schoolgirl up at the Girl's Grammar, giving the impression her resentment was occasioned by the fact that she was really twenty-nine and couldn't find a uniform that fit her. She'd been involved in an arty student magazine called *Androgyne*, providing wonky stencil illustrations for a curate's egg of fifth-form verses. Benedict had been at the Boy's Grammar School by that time, and despite the distance that there was between the two establishments, fraternization did occur. The two had seen each other now and then, and Alma, who'd been going through a period of lofty futurist disdain for Ben's romanticism, had asked grudgingly if he might submit something to their alternately simpering and foul-mouthed rag.

Encouraged by this half-hearted solicitation, Benedict had written several movements of what had turned out to be an epic piece of juvenilia, only the shortest parts accepted by a clearly disappointed Alma, who dismissed the rest as being, in her critically mature opinion "fucking sentimental girly rubbish". He was mortified to think that he could still remember the rejection, word for word, some thirty-five years later. At the time, with even less sense of proportion than he currently possessed, he'd been incensed and had resolved to patiently exact a terrible revenge. He'd take the off-cuts Alma had discarded from his poem cycle and he'd build them into a new edifice, a work to shudder the foundations of the ages. Then, when he was welcomed up to literary Olympus, he'd reveal that she had lacked the insight to appreciate his magnum opus and her reputation would be shot. She'd be a laughingstock and a pariah. That would learn her, her and all her Andy Warhol Bridget Riley migraine art. This grand endeavour would be a heartbroken hymn to conjure the departed world, the rustic landscape of John Clare, the golden-lighted lanes that Benedict was born too late to walk outside of reverie. He'd strung it out almost two years before he'd realised it was going nowhere and abandoned it. It had been called "Atlantis".

Benedict glanced up to find that he was some way out along the Wellingborough Road from the last place he'd noticed, which had been the peeling shell of the Spread Eagle, on the corner past St. Edmund's Hospital. Now he was getting on for Stimpson Avenue and that end, starting to think twice about his planned walk in the park, already feeling footsore. Clare, who'd hobbled eighty miles from Essex back home to Northamptonshire, would probably have laughed at him. They'd built their lyric nutters sturdier in his day. Ben thought he might wander round Abington Park some other time, contenting himself for the moment with a visit to the Crown & Cushion, a short distance further up the busy street. He'd only taken to the notion of a leafy stroll when there was nothing else to do, before he'd met with Alma, but now things were different. Now he had a business plan.

He'd not been in the Crown & Cushion for a while, although at one time, just after he'd broken up with Lily, it had been his regular dive. He supposed that his relationship with the pub's clientele was at its best ambivalent, but then the place itself was somewhere he felt comfortable. Largely unchanged, the hostelry at least still traded under its historically appointed name, hadn't become the Jolly Wanker or the Workhouse or the Vole & Astrolabe. Benedict could remember, with a twinge of mixed embarrassment and pride, how he'd once stormed into the bar demanding satisfaction when he'd felt his fellow drinkers weren't taking his claim to be a published poet seriously. A poem of Ben's had just been printed in the local *Chronicle & Echo*, and when he'd burst through the Crown & Cushion's swing door like a piano-stopping gunfighter he'd thrown the thirty copies of the paper that he happened to be carrying into the air with a victorious cry of "There! Ah ha ha ha!" They'd naturally barred him on the spot, but that was years ago, and with a bit of luck that era's staff and customers would all be dead or memory-impaired by now.

Even if not, traditionally the pub had always shown tremendous tolerance and even fondness for the various eccentrics passing through its portals. That was another reason why Ben liked the place, he thought as he pushed open its lounge door and stepped into the welcome gloom from the bright, squinting dazzle of the day outside. They'd had far worse than him in here. There was a story from back in the very early 1980s which insisted that the great Sir Malcolm Arnold, trumpeter and orchestral arranger of such hits as "Colonel Bogey", had been living in the room above the Crown & Cushion's bar, mentally ill and alcoholic, guest in some accounts, virtual prisoner in others, dragged down almost nightly for the entertainment of a drunken and abusive crowd. This was the man who'd written *Tam O' Shanter*, that delirious accompaniment to Burns' inebriated night-sweat, the carousing highland hero chased by a Wild Hunt of fairies through the brass and woodwind dark. This was Sir Malcolm Arnold, who Ben thought had once been the Director of the Queen's Music, a musical equivalent to Poet Laureate, banging out tunes on the joanna for a herd of braying and pugnacious goons. Old and tormented, ambisextrous, in his early sixties then, who knew what imps and demons, djinns and tonics, might have been stampeding through his fevered skull, glistening with perspiration and tipped forward over pounding yellow ivories?

Benedict stood there just inside the door until his pupils had sufficiently dilated to locate the bar. The staff and decor, he observed, were new since his last visit. This was just as well, especially about the bar staff, since as far as Ben knew he'd done nothing to offend the decor. Some, of course, might not agree. Ah ha ha ha. Benedict stepped up to the rail and bought a pint of bitter, slapping down his twenty on the freshly wiped and moisture-beaded bar-top with a certain swagger. This was undercut, though, by his deep regret at having said goodbye to Elgar. Some of this regret was purely on Ben's own account, but mixed with this there was a genuine concern about Sir Edward, an uneasiness at leaving the composer in the Crown & Cushion. Look at what they'd done to Malcolm Arnold.

Taking his glass to an empty table, of which there were an unseasonable number, Ben fleetingly entertained a morbid fantasy in which, as punishment for the newspaper incident, he was incarcerated here in the same way that Arnold had reputedly been held. Each night intoxicated thugs would burst into his room and herd him down to the saloon, where he'd be plied with spirits and made to recite his earnest and wept-over sonnets to a room of jeering philistines. It didn't sound that bad, if he was honest. He'd had Friday nights like that, without even the benefit of being plied with drink. Now that he came to think about it, he'd had entire years like that. The stretch just after Lily told him he should find another billet, when he'd lived in a house broken into flats along Victoria Road, had been like *Tam O' Shanter* playing on a loop for months. Arriving home at 3.00am without a key, demanding as a published poet that he be let in, then playing Dylan Thomas reading *Under Milkwood* at top volume on his Dansette until all the other residents were threatening to kill him. What had that been all about? Creeping downstairs to the communal kitchen one night and devouring four whole chicken dinners that the surly and abusive tattooed couple in the flat above had made for the next day, then waking up another of the building's tenants so that he could tell them. "Ah ha ha! I've ate the bastards' dinner!" Looking back, Ben realised he was lucky to have come through those dire days unlynched, and never mind unscathed.

He sipped his bitter and, taking advantage of the sunlight falling through the window that he sat beneath, removed *A Northamptonshire Garland* from his satchel and began to read. The first piece his eyes fell on was "The Angler's Song", a work by William Basse, seventeenth-century pastoral poet with disputed although likely origins here in the town.

> *As inward love breeds outward talk,*
> *The hound some praise, and some the hawk,*
> *Some, better pleased with private sport,*
> *Use tennis, some a mistress court:*
> *But these delights I neither wish,*
> *Nor envy, while I freely fish.*

Ben liked the poem, though he'd never really done much fishing since his first youthful attempts, which had involved the accidental hooking of another child during the back-swing when he'd cast off. He recalled the blood, the screams, and worst of all his total inability to keep from giggling inappropriately with shame during the subsequent first aid. That had been it for Benedict and fishing, pretty much, though he approved of it as an idea. Along with fauns and shepherdesses it was part of his Arcadian mythology, the angler drowsing by the stream, the riverine crawl of the afternoon, but like the shepherdesses it was something he'd had little practical experience of.

On reflection, that was probably why Ben had let "Atlantis" go unfinished all those years ago, the sense that it was inauthentic, that he had been barking up the wrong tree. When he'd started it, he'd been a schoolboy from a dark house down in Freeschool Street, deploring all the grimy factory yards the way that he thought John Clare would have done; lamenting the bucolic idyll that, in his imagination, the contemporary mean streets of the Boroughs had displaced. Only when those slate rooftops and tree-punctured chimney breasts had been themselves removed had come belated recognition that the narrow lanes were the endangered habitat he should have been commemorating. Bottle-caps, not bluebells. He'd thrown out his central metaphor, the droning, drowning hedgerows of a continent that he'd reported lost but in all truth had never really owned, and written "Clearance Area" instead. After the neighbourhood as Benedict had known it was no more, at last he'd found a voice that had been genuine and of the Boroughs. Looking back, he thought that later poem had been more about the bulldozed flats of his own disillusion than the demolition site his district had become, although perhaps the two were ultimately the same thing.

He lit a cigarette, noting that this left six still rattling loose in the depleted pack, and flipped on through the alphabetically arranged compendium, skipping past Clare this time to light on the inarguably authentic Boroughs voice of Philip Doddridge. Though the piece was called "Christ's Message" and based on a passage from the Book of Luke it was essentially the text of Doddridge's most celebrated hymn: "Hark the glad sound! The Saviour comes!/ The Saviour promised long!" Benedict liked the exclamation marks, which seemed to couch the second coming as a gravel-throated trailer for a movie sequel. In his heart, Ben couldn't say that he was confident concerning Christianity ... the ton-up accident that took his sister back when he'd been ten put paid to that ... but he could still hear and respect the strong Boroughs inflection in Doddridge's verses, his concern for the impoverished and wretched no doubt sharpened by his time at Castle Hill. "He comes the broken heart to bind, The bleeding soul to cure,/ And with the treasures of his grace T' enrich the humble poor."

He'd drink to that. Lifting his glass he noticed that its ebbing tide-line foam was at half-mast. Just four sips left. Oh well. That was enough. He'd make it last. He wouldn't have another one in here, despite the seventeen-odd pounds he still had left. He thumbed his way on through the book until he reached the Fanes of Apethorpe: Mildmay Fane, the second Earl of Westmorland, and his descendant Julian. He'd only really settled on the pair through being taken with the names 'Mildmay' and 'Apethorpe', but soon found himself immersed in Julian's description of the family pile, as admired by Northampton fan John Betjeman. "The moss-grey mansion of my father stands/ Park'd in an English pasturage as fair/ As any that the grass-green isle can show./ Above it rise deep-wooded lawns; below/ A brook runs riot thro' the pleasant lands ..." The brook went babbling on as he sipped dry his pint and bought another without thinking.

Suddenly it was ten minutes after three and he was half a mile away, emerging out of Lutterworth Road onto Billing Road, just down from what had once been the Boy's Grammar School. What was he doing here? He had the vaguest memory of standing in the toilets at the Crown & Cushion, of a ghostly moment staring at his own face in the mirror bolted up above the washbasin, but for the life of him could not remember leaving the pub premises, much less the fairish walk he'd evidently taken down here from the Wellingborough Road. Perhaps he'd wanted to head back to the town centre but had chosen this admittedly more scenic route? Chosen was probably too strong a word. Ben's path through life was governed not so much by choice as by the powerful undertow of his own whimsy, which would on occasion wash him up to unexpected beachheads like this present one.

Across the street and some way off upon his left was the red brick front of the former grammar school, set back from the main road by flat lawns and a gravel forecourt where a naked flagpole stood, no ensign showing which side the establishment was on. Benedict understood the reticence. These days, targets were what schools aimed at, not what they aspired to be. Stretching away behind the calm façade and the aloof gaze of the tall white windows there were classrooms, art rooms, physics blocks and playing fields, a spinney and a swimming pool, all trying to ignore the gallows shadow that league tables cast across them. Not that there was any cause here for immediate concern. Though relegated from a snooty grammar to a red-eared comprehensive in the middle 1970s, the place had used its dwindling aura and residual reputation as brand markers in the competition-focussed marketplace that teaching had become. Invoking the school's previous elitist status and the ghost of poshness past would seem to have succeeded, making it a big hit with the choice-dazed well-off parent of today. Apparently, from what Ben heard, they even made a selling point of the monastic single-sex approach to education. Anyone applying for their son to be accepted had to first compose a modest essay stating why, precisely, at the most profound ideological and moral level, they believed their child would benefit from being tutored in an atmosphere of strict gender apartheid. What did they expect people to say? That what they hoped for little Giles was that at best he'd grow into somebody awkward and uncomprehending in all his relationships with women, while at worst he'd end up a gay serial murderer? Ah ha ha ha.

Benedict crossed the road and turned right, heading into town, putting the school behind him. He'd once been a pupil there and hadn't liked it much. For one thing, having squandered his first decade on the planet in what his mam called "acting the goat", he'd not passed his eleven-plus exams that first go-round. When all the clever kids like Alma went off to their grammars, Benedict attended Spencer School, on the now-feared Spencer estate, with all the divs and bruisers. He'd been every bit as smart as Alma and the rest, just not inclined to take things like examinations seriously. Once he'd been at Spencer for a year or two, however, his intelligence began to shine from the surrounding dross and only then had he been transferred to the grammar school.

Here he'd felt stigmatised, even among the vanishingly small minority of other working-class boys, who'd at least been bright enough to put the ticks in the right boxes when they'd been eleven. With the middle-class majority, especially the teachers, Ben had never felt he stood a chance. The other boys had in the main been nice enough, acting and talking much the same as him, but they'd still snigger if somebody stuck their hand up during class to ask the master if they could go to the lav and not the toilet. On reflection, Benedict supposed, such prejudice as he'd experienced had been relatively minimal. At least he'd not been black like David Daniels in the year above, a serene and good natured lad that Ben had mainly known through Alma, who'd shared Daniels's fondness for American science-fiction paperbacks and comics. Ben recalled one maths teacher who'd always send the only non-white at the school into the quadrangle outside the classroom window, so that in the full view of his classmates he could clean the board erasers, pounding them together until his black skin was pale with chalk dust. It was shameful.

He remembered how unfairly the whole learning process had been handled then, with kids' lives and careers decided by an exam that they'd sat at age eleven. Mind you, wasn't it just this last year that Tony Blair had set out his performance targets for the under-fives? There'd be established foetal standards soon, so that you could feel pressurized and backwards if your fingers hadn't separated fully by the third trimester. Academic stress-related pre-birth suicides would become commonplace, the depressed embryos hanging themselves with their umbilical cords, farewell notes scratched onto the placenta.

Benedict became aware of railings passing in a strobe on his left side to vanish at his back, dark conifers beyond them, and remembered he was walking past St. Andrew's Hospital. Could that have been the reason why he'd taken this route home, as an impulsive pilgrimage to where they'd kept John Clare for more than twenty years? Perhaps he'd muddily imagined that the thought of Clare, his hero, having been more of a hopeless circus-turn than Ben himself, would somehow be uplifting?

Instead, the reverse was true. As with his earlier envy of pub-prisoner Sir Malcolm Arnold – who had also been a former grammar school boy and a former inmate of St. Andrew's, now he thought about it – Benedict found himself visualising the extensive institution grounds beyond the rail and envying John Clare. Admittedly, St. Andrew's hadn't been so lush back in the 1850s when it was Northampton General Asylum, but it had still been a gentler haven, in all likelihood, for lost and bruised poetic souls than somewhere like, say, Tower Street. What Ben wouldn't give to trade his current circumstances for those of a nineteenth-century madhouse. If somebody asked why you weren't seeking work, you could explain that you were already employed as an archaic mental. You could wander all day through Elysian meadows, or else take a stroll downtown to sit beneath the portico of All Saints' Church. With your expenses paid for by a literary benefactor, you'd have time to write as much verse as you liked, much of it on how badly you felt you were being treated. And when even the exertion of poetics proved too much (for surely times like that afflicted everyone, Ben thought), you could abandon your exhausting personality and be somebody else, be Queen Victoria's dad, or Byron. Frankly, if you'd lost your mind, there were worse places to go looking for it than beneath the bushes at St. Andrew's.

Clearly, Ben was not alone in this opinion. In the years since Clare's day, the asylum's tittering and weeping dayroom had become a hall of damaged fame. Misogynist and poet J.K. Stephen. Malcolm Arnold. Dusty Springfield. Lucia Joyce, a child of the more famous James, whose delicate psychology had first become apparent when she worked as chief assistant on her father's unreadable masterpiece, *Finnegans Wake*, then titled *Work in Progress*. Joyce's daughter had arrived here at the pricey but quite justly celebrated Billing Road retreat in the late 1940s, and had evidently liked the place so much she'd stayed for over thirty years until her death in 1982. Even mortality had not soured Lucia on Northampton. She'd requested she be buried here, at Kingsthorpe Cemetery, where she was currently at rest a few feet from the gravestone of a Mr. Finnegan. It was still strange to think that Lucia Joyce had been here all the time Ben was a pupil at the grammar school next door. He wondered idly if she'd ever met with Dusty or Sir Malcolm, picturing abruptly all three on stage as a trio, possibly for therapeutic reasons, looking melancholic, belting out "I Just Don't Know What To Do With Myself". Ah ha ha ha.

Benedict had heard that Samuel Beckett was one of Lucia Joyce's visitors, here at St. Andrew's and then, later, at the cemetery in Kingsthorpe. Part of Lucia's madness had been the belief that Beckett, who'd replaced her as assistant on the *Work in Progress*, was in love with her. Disastrous as this misunderstanding must have been for all concerned, the two had evidently remained friends, at least to judge from all the visits. Ben's good chum Dave Turvey, cricketing enthusiast companion to the late Tom Hall, had informed Benedict of Beckett's sole entry in Wisden's Almanac, playing against Northampton at the County Ground. Amongst the visiting team, Beckett had distinguished himself not so much upon the pitch as in his choice of entertainment afterwards. He'd spent that evening in a solitary trawl around Northampton's churches while his colleagues had contented themselves with the other things the town was famous for, these being pubs and whores. Benedict found this conduct admirable, at least in theory, though he'd never cared for Beckett as an author much. All those long silences and haunted monologues. It was too much like life.

He was by now beyond St. Andrew's, crossing over at the top of Cliftonville as he continued his fastidiously measured stumble, onward down the Billing Road to town. This was the route he'd take each weeknight as a schoolboy, home to Freeschool Street astride his bike, riding into the sunset as if every day had been a feature film, which, very often in Ben's case, it had been.

Duck Soup, usually, with Benedict as both Zeppo and Harpo, playing them, innovatively, as two sides of the same troubled personality. A drift of generally pleasant and only occasionally horrifying recollection, like a fairground ride through Toyland but with horse intestines draped at intervals, conveyed him on into the centre. Where the Billing Road concluded at the crossroads with Cheyne Walk and York Road, near the General Hospital, Ben waltzed over the zebra crossing and along Spencer Parade.

Boughs from St. Giles churchyard overhung the pavement, off-cut scraps of light and shadow rustling across the cracked slabs in a mobile stipple. Past the low wall on Ben's right was soft grass and hard marble markers, peeling benches scored with the initials of a hundred brief relationships and then the caramel stones of the church itself, probably one of those inspected on Sam Beckett's lone nocturnal tour. St. Giles was old, not ancient like St. Peter's or the Holy Sepulchre, but old enough, and here as long as anybody could remember. It was clearly well-established by the time that John Speed drafted the town map for 1610, which Benedict owned a facsimile edition of, rolled up somewhere behind his bookshelves back in Tower Street. Though state-of-the-art technical drawing in its day, to modern eyes its slightly wonky iso-morphic house-rows looked like the endeavour of a talented though possibly autistic child. The image of Northampton poised there at the start of the seventeenth century, a crudely drawn cross-section of a heart with extra ventri-cles, was nonetheless delightful. When the modern urban landscape was too much for Benedict to bear, say one day out of every five, then he'd imagine he was walking through the simple and depopulated flatland of Speed's diagram, the vanished landmarks dark with quill pen hatch-work scribbling themselves into existence all around him. White streets bounded by ink curbs, devoid of human complication.

Benedict continued down into St. Giles Street, passing the still-open lower end of the half-destitute, half-empty Co-op Arcade, its redundant upper reaches gazing bleakly onto Abington Street which ran parallel, a short way up the gentle slope of the town's southern flank. Some distance further on, past Fish Street's gaping cod's mouth, was the Wig & Pen, the disinfected and rebranded shell of what had once been called the new Black Lion, as distinct from the much older pub of that name down on Castle Hill. Back in the 1920s, the St. Giles Street Black Lion had been haven for the town's bohemians, a reputation that the place had suffered or enjoyed till the late 'Eighties when the current renovations were afoot. Another reputation that the dive endured, according to authorities including Elliot O'Donnell, was as one of the most haunted spots in England. When Dave Turvey had been landlord here, around the time when Tom Hall, Alma Warren and indeed the greater part of Piet de Snapp's outlandish portrait gallery had been the Black Lion's customers, there had been footsteps on the stairs and items moved or rearranged. There had been presences and scared pets throughout Turvey's tenure, just as there had been with all the previous proprietors. Ben wondered idly if the apparitions had been made to undergo a makeover, been themed along with the surrounding pub so that if rattling chains or mournful shrieks were heard one of the spectres would put down his ploughman's lunch and reach inside his jacket, muttering "Sorry, guys. That's mine. Hello? Oh, hi. Yeah. Yeah, I'm on the astral plane." Ah ha ha ha.

Upon Ben's right now, broad imperial steps swept up towards the soaring crystal palace that resembled a Dan Dare cathedral but was where you had to go to pay your council tax. Because of this, the place would always have the feeling of a place of execution, like the old Labour Exchange in Grafton Street, no matter how refined and stately its design. Bills and assessments and adult responsibilities. Places like this were faces of the whetstone that ground people down, that shaved a whole dimension off of them. Benedict moved on hurriedly, past the adjoining Guildhall where he wasn't certain if the building had been lately cleaned or if its stones were simply bleached by countless flashgun fusillades from countless civic weddings. Geologic strata of confetti, matrimonial dandruff, had accumulated in the corners of its grand stone stairs.

This was the third and very possibly the final place that the town hall would find itself located, after the forgotten Mayorhold and the intermediary position at the foot of Abington Street. Ben looked up, past all the saints and regents decorating the elaborate façade, to where on his high ridge between two spires stood the town's patron saint, rod in one hand, shield in the other, wings folded behind him. Benedict had never been entirely sure how the Archangel Michael had been made one of the saints, who, unless Ben had got it wrong, were human beings who'd aspired to sainthood through hard work and piety and pulling off some tricky miracles. Wouldn't an archangel have an unfair advantage, what with being quite miraculous already? Anyway, archangels outranked saints in the celestial hierarchy, as any schoolchild knew. How had Northampton managed to recruit one of God's four lieutenants as its patron saint? What possible incitements could the town have offered to perk up a posting so much lower down on the celestial scale of reimbursement?

He went on across Wood Hill and down the north side of All Saints, where John Clare once habitually sat within a recess underneath the portico, a Delphic Oracle on day release. Ben crossed before the church, continuing down Gold Street in a soar of shop fronts as if he were still sixteen and riding on his bike. Down at the bottom, while he waited at the lights to cross Horsemarket, he glanced to his left where Horseshoe Street ran down towards St. Peter's Way and what had previously been the Gas Board yards. Local mythology suggested that it was around where the old billiard hall stood, a few yards

from the corner Benedict now occupied, that some time previous to the Norman conquest there had come a pilgrim from Golgotha, from the ground
where Christ supposedly was crucified, off in Jerusalem. Apparently the monk
had found an ancient stone cross buried at the crucifixion site, whereon a
passing angel had instructed him to take the relic "to the centre of his land",
which had presumably been England. Halfway up what was now Horseshoe
Street, the angel had turned up again, confirming to the traveller that he had
indeed lucked onto the right place. The cross he'd born so far was set into the
stonework of St. Gregory's Church which had been just across the road in
Saxon times, the monk's remains interred beneath it, to become itself a site of
pilgrimage. They'd called it the rood in the wall. Here in this grimy offshoot
of the Boroughs there resided England's mystic centre, and it wasn't only Benedict who thought that. It was God who thought that too. Ah ha ha ha.

The lights changed, with the luminous green man now signifying it was
safe for workers in the nuclear industry to cross. He wandered over into
Marefair, heading down what had for Benedict always been the town's main
street, westward in a bee-line for St. Peter's Church. He was still thinking
vaguely about angels, after the archangel perched up on the Guildhall and
the one who'd shown the monk where he should plant his cross in Horseshoe
Street, and Ben recalled at least one other story of seraphic intervention that
involved the thoroughfare along which he was walking. At St. Peter's Church,
just up ahead, there'd been a miracle in the eleventh century when angels had
directed a young peasant lad named Ivalde to retrieve the lost bones of St.
Ragener, concealed beneath the flagstones in the nave, unearthed in blinding
light to an accompaniment of holy water sprinkled by the holy spirit who had
manifested as a bird. A crippled beggar woman witnessing the incident had
risen to her feet and walked, or so the story went. It all tended to foster Ben's
distinct impression that in the Dark Ages one could barely move for angels
telling you to go to Marefair.

Benedict had reached the top of Freeschool Street, running off Marefair
on the left, before he realised what he'd done. It had been his excursion to the
Billing Road, no doubt, that had inclined him to take his old cycle route from
school back to a home here that had been demolished ages since. Blithely propelling a leak-shot canoe along his algae-smothered stream of consciousness,
he'd somehow managed to blank out the previous thirty-seven years of his
existence, adult feet reverting effortlessly to the trails worn in the pavement
by their former, smaller selves. What was he like? Ah ha ha ha. No, seriously,
what was he like? Was this the onset of damp pantalooned senility and trying
to recall which was his ward? Frankly, for all that it was taking place upon
a sunlit afternoon this was quite frightening, like finding that you'd sleep-
walked to your dad's grave in the middle of the night.

He stood there staring at the narrow lane, Marefair's foot traffic bifurcating to flow round him like a stream with Benedict as its abandoned shopping trolley, utterly oblivious to all the babbling movement he was in the midst of. Freeschool Street was, mercifully, barely recognisable. Only the tiny splinters that you could identify still snagged upon the heart. The paving stones that had gone unreplaced, their moss-filled fractures subdividing to an achingly familiar delta. The surviving lower reaches of a factory wall that dribbled down as far as Gregory Street, ferns and young branches shoving past the rotted frames of what had once been windows, now not even holes. He felt a certain gratitude for the street's bend that blocked his view of where the Perrit family once lived, the company forecourt stretching where they'd laughed and argued and peed in the sink if it was cold outside, together in that single room with the front parlour used entirely as a showcase for the family's more presentable possessions. This, he thought, this was the real Atlantis.

Teenaged and pretentious, he'd bemoaned the loss of byres and furrows that he'd never known, that were John Clare's to mourn. Benedict had composed laments to vanished rural England while ignoring the fecund brick wilderness he lived in, but as things turned out there was still grass, there were still flowers and meadows if you looked for them. The Boroughs, on the other hand, a unique undergrowth of people's lives, you could search for it all you wanted, but that one particular endangered habitat was gone for good. That half-a-square-mile continent had sunk under a deluge of bad social policy. First there had been a mounting Santorini rumble of awareness that the Boroughs' land would be more valuable without its people, then came bulldozers in a McAlpine tidal wave. A yellow foam of hard hats surged across the neighbourhood to break against the shores of Jimmy's End and Semilong, the human debris washed up in a scum-line of old people's flats at King's Heath and at Abington. When the construction tide receded there'd been only highrise barnacles, the hulks of sunken businesses and the occasional beached former resident, flopping and gasping there in some resurfaced underpass. Benedict, an antediluvian castaway, became the disappeared world's Ancient Mariner, its Ishmael and its Plato, cataloguing deeds and creatures so fantastic as to be implausible, increasingly even to Ben himself. The bricked up entrance to the medieval tunnel system in his cellar, could that truly have been there? The horse that brought his dad home every night when Jem was passed out at the reins, could that have possibly existed? Had there been real deathmongers and cows on people's upstairs landings and a fever cart?

Somebody narrowly avoided bumping into Benedict, apologising even though it was quite clearly Ben's fault, stood there staring into nowhere and obstructing half the street.

"Ooh, sorry, mate. Not looking where I'm going."

It was a young half-caste girl, what they called nowadays mixed race, a pinched but pretty thing who looked to be in her mid or late twenties. Interrupting as she was Ben's daydream of a submerged Eden she took on an Undine gloss, at least in his imagination. The faint pallor that her skin retained despite her parentage seemed a deep-water phosphorescence, hair brushed into stripes with twigs of coral and the wet sheen on her plastic coat all adding to the submarine illusion. Frail and exotic as a sea horse, Ben recast her in the role of a Lemurian sultaness, her earrings dubloons spilled from foundered galleons. That this rock-tanned siren should be saying sorry to the weathered, ugly reef where she'd fetched up through no fault of her own made Benedict feel doubly guilty, doubly embarrassed. He replied with a high, strangled laugh, to put her at her ease.

"Aa, that's all right, love. You're all right. Ah ha ha ha."

Her eyes grew slightly wider and her painted liquid lips, like two sucked pear-drops, went through some suppressed contortions. She was staring at him quizzically, a rhyme scheme and a metre in her look that Ben was unfamiliar with. What did she want? The fact that their chance meeting was occurring on the street where Ben was born, and where he found himself this afternoon through no more than a drunken accident, began now to smack dangerously of kismet. Could it be … ah ha ha ha … could it be that she recognised him, saw by some means all the poetry that he had in him? Had she glimpsed his wisdom underneath the nervousness and beer breath? Was this the predestined moment, loitering across from Marefair's ibis hotel, caught in shafts of timeless sunshine with pale stars of ground-in bubblegum around the Dr. Martens, when he was to meet his Sheba? Tiny muscles at the corners of her mouth were working now as she prepared to speak, to say something, to ask him if he was an artist or musician of some kind, or even if he was Benedict Perrit, whom she'd heard so much about. The glistening Maybelline-drenched petals finally unstuck themselves, peeling apart.

"Fancy a bit of business?"

Oh.

Belatedly, Ben understood. They weren't two kindred spirits pulled together inexorably by fate. She was a prostitute and he was a drunk idiot, simple as that. Now that he knew her trade he saw the drawn look that her face had and the dark around the eyes, the missing tooth, the twitchy desperation. He revised his estimate from mid/late twenties down to mid/late teens. Poor kid. He should have known when she first spoke to him, but Ben had grown up in a Boroughs that was something other than Northampton's red light district; had to consciously remind himself that this was its main function now. He'd never used a pro himself, had never even thought about it, not through any notion of superiority but more because he'd always thought of street girls as a middle-class concern, predominantly. Why would a working-class man, other than through incapacity or unrelenting loneliness, pay to have sex with a working-class woman of the kind that he'd grown up amongst and had to some degree therefore been de-eroticised towards? Ben thought it was more probably the Hugh Grants of this world who treated adjectives like "rough" or "dirty" as arousing concepts, whereas he'd grown up in a community that generally reserved such terms for nightmare clans like the O'Rourkes or Presleys.

He felt awkward, having never previously experienced this situation, with his awkwardness yet further complicated by his lingering disappointment. For a moment there he'd been upon the brink of a romance, of an epiphany, an inspiration. No, he hadn't really thought that she was a Lemurian sultaness, but he'd still entertained the notion that she might be someone sensitive and sympathetic, somebody who'd glimpsed the bard in him, had seen the villanelles and throwaway sestinas in his bearing. But instead, the opposite was true. She's taken him for just another needy punter whose romantic yearnings stretched no further than a quick one off the wrist in a back entry. How could she have got him so completely wrong? He felt he had to let her know how badly she'd misread him, how absurd it was for her to have considered him of all people as a potential client. However, since he still felt sorry for the girl and didn't want her thinking he was genuinely offended, he elected to communicate his feelings in the manner of an Ealing comedy. He'd found this was the best approach for almost any delicate or sticky social circumstances.

Benedict contorted his sponge-rubber features into an expression of Victorian moral shock, like Mr. Pickwick startled by a mudlark selling dildos, then affected an affronted shudder so vociferous that his fillings rattled, forcing him to stop. The girl by this point was beginning to look slightly frightened, so Ben thought he'd better underline that his behaviour was intended as comic exaggeration. Swivelling his head, he glanced away from her to where the television audience would be if life were actually the hidden camera prank show he'd occasionally suspected, and supplied his own canned laughter.

"Ah ha ha ha. No, no, you're all right, love, thanks. No, bless your heart, you're all right. I'm all right. Ah ha ha ha."

It seemed that his performance had at least removed her certainty that Ben was a potential customer. The girl was staring at him now as if she genuinely didn't have the first idea what Benedict might be. Apparently disoriented, forehead corrugated into an uncomprehending frown, she tried again to get his measure.

"Are you sure?"

What would it take before this woman got the message? Was he going to have a do a full routine with plank, paste-bucket and banana skin to make her understand that he was too poetic to want sex behind a rubbish skip? One thing was certain: subtlety and understatement hadn't worked. He'd have to spell it out for her with broader gestures.

He tipped back his head in a derisive guffaw that he fancied was in the John Falstaff mode, or would have been if Falstaff had been best known as a gangly tenor.

"Ah ha ha ha. No, love, I'm all right, ta. You're all right. I'll have you know that I'm a published poet. Ah ha ha."

That did the trick. From the expression on her face, the girl no longer harboured any doubts concerning what Ben Perrit was. Wearing a fixed grin she began to take her leave, keeping her wary eyes upon him as she backed away down Marefair, clearly scared to turn her back on him until she was some distance off, in case he pounced. She tottered off past Cromwell House in the direction of the railway station, pausing when she reached St. Peter's Church to risk a glance across her shoulder back at Benedict. She evidently thought he was a psychopath, so he let out a carefree high-pitched cackle to assure her that he wasn't, whereupon she took off past the church front, disappearing into the homecoming crowds on Black Lion Hill. His muse, his mermaid, vanished in a tail-flip and a shimmer of viridian scales.

Five things, then. Just five things that Ben was unsuccessful with. Escape, finding a job, explaining himself properly, not looking pissed, and talking to a woman if you didn't count his mum or Alma. Lily, she'd been an exception, been the one who'd genuinely seen his spirit and his poetry. He'd always felt that he could talk to Lily, although looking back it pained him to admit that most of what he'd talked was drunken rubbish. That was largely what had finished it between the two of them. It was the drink and, if he were entirely honest, it was Ben's insistence that the rules in his relationship with Lily be those that had suited his own parents, Jem and Eileen, thirty years before, particularly those that suited Jem. Back then Ben hadn't really taken in that everything was changing, not just streets and neighbourhoods but people's attitudes; what people would put up with. He'd thought that at least in his own home he could preserve a fragment of the life he'd known right here in Freeschool Street, where wives would tolerate constant inebriation in their husbands and consider themselves blessed if they'd a man who didn't hit them. He'd pretended that the world was still that way, and he'd been stunned right to the core of him when Lily took the kids and demonstrated that it wasn't.

Ben's uncomfortable meeting with the prostitute had faded now to a faint, wistful pang. His gaze had drifted back to Freeschool Street, his boyhood paradise drowning in its own future with the water level rising day by day, moment by moment. He wished he could dive into the cladding of the mostly vacant office buildings and apartments, red brick droplets splashing up from where he'd pierced the surface. He'd dog-paddle down through forty years on one lungful of air. He'd swim through his dad's woodyard gathering up whatever souvenirs he could retrieve to take back to the surface and the present day. He'd tap upon the window of the living room and tell his sister "Don't go out tonight". At last he'd emerge gasping, up from the meniscus of contemporary Marefair, his arms full of sunken treasure, startling the passers-by and shaking beads of history from his sopping hair.

He was beginning to feel distantly in need of food. He thought he might walk back up Horsemarket to home, perhaps visit the chippy in St. Andrew's Street. He suddenly remembered he had slightly more than fifteen pounds left, Darwin and Elizth Fry entangled in a crumpled ball of passion somewhere in the deep recesses of his trousers. That would be enough to get some fish and chips and also go out for a drink tonight if he should want to, though he didn't think he would. The best thing he could do would be to get some food and then go back to Tower Street for an inexpensive evening in. That way he'd still have nearly all the money left tomorrow and he wouldn't have to go through the humiliating pantomime of taking charity from Eileen in the morning. That was settled, then. That's what he'd do. Preparing to vacate the spot and head off up Horsemarket, Benedict attempted to rein in his wandering attention, which was off somewhere at play amongst the gutted ruins of Gregory Street. Stranded dandelions were perched on the remains of ledges twenty-five feet up, hesitant suicides with golden hair like Chatterton …

It was eleven thirty-five. He was emerging from the Bird In Hand on Regent's Square into the grunting, shouting dark of Friday night. Arterial spills of traffic light reflected from the paving slabs of Sheep Street, where there had apparently at some point in the evening been a shower of rain.

Girls in short skirts in gangs of four or five leaned on each other for support, a multitude of 15-denier legs all holding up one structure, turning inadvertently into components of a single giant giggling insect or a piece of mobile furniture as beautifully upholstered as it was impractical. Boys moved like chess knights with concussion, waltzing mice with Tourette's, wandering clusters of them suddenly erupting into murderous bonhomie or well-intentioned bottlings and it wasn't even closing time. There was no closing time. Licensing hours had been extended to infinity by government decree, ostensibly to somehow cut down on binge drinking but in fact so that disoriented visiting Americans would not be inconvenienced by funny English customs. Drunken binges hadn't been eradicated, obviously. They'd simply had their lucid intervals removed.

Ben could remember having plaice and chips a few hours earlier and a few dimly lighted pub interior moments in between – had he been talking to someone? – but otherwise it was as if he had been newly born this instant, squatted out onto this windy street, into these gutters, wholly ignorant of how he came to be here. At least this time, Ben observed with gratitude, he wasn't sobbing and he wasn't naked. Underdressed, perhaps, with evening's chill beginning now to permeate the riotous sunset of his waistcoat, striking through the insulating beery numbness to raise goose-bumps, but at least not nude. Ah ha ha ha.

A rubber-fingered fumble in his pocket reassured him that the treacherous whore Eliz[th] Fry at least this time had not left Benedict for some ill-mannered publican who'd simply use her, wouldn't love or need her the way Ben did. That said, finding her immediately raised the tempting possibility of popping back into the pub to get a carry-out, a few cans, but no. No, he mustn't. Go home, Benedict. Go home, son, if you know what's good for you.

He turned right, shuffling up Sheep Street to the lights where it met Regent Square, the ugly cross-hatching of carriageways that centuries ago had been the north gate of the town. This was where traitors' skulls were placed on spikes like trolls on pencils, as a decoration. This was where the heretics and witches had been burned. These days the junction at the end of Sheep Street was marked only by a nightclub painted lurid lavender from when it had been a goth hangout called Macbeth's a year or two ago, attempting to create a gothic atmosphere upon a corner deep in severed heads and shrieking crones already. Coals to Newcastle, wolfbane to Transylvania. Ben lurched over the various crossings that were needed to convey him safely to the top of Grafton Street, which he proceeded to descend unsteadily. A short way further down blue lights were circling, sapphire flashes battering like moths on the surrounding buildings, but he was too dulled by drink to lend them any great significance.

He glanced up to the higher reaches of the car repair place just across the road, where you could see the solar logo of the Sunlight Laundry still raised in relief, even through the piss-yellow sodium light that everything was bathing in. Fixed in its place, it shone down happily upon a day of 24-hour drinking finally arrived, when it need never sink again below the yard arm. Benedict turned his attention back to the uneven paving slabs immediately in front of him, and focussed for the first time on the lone police car pulled up on the curb ahead, the source of all the dancing disco lights. There was a wreck recovery going on, with a smashed vehicle of uncertain make being winched up on its surviving rear wheels by a tow truck. Grim men in fluorescent vests were sweeping shattered windscreen fragments from the busy road, with the police car evidently flashing there behind them to alert the other motorists to what was going on. A baffling spray of random items such as children's toys and gardening gloves were spread across the tarmac where presumably they had been flung from a burst-open boot. Plant-misters, shower caps and a single flip-flop. Standing by his car and strobe-lit by its beacon, the attending officer was staring down morosely at a melted tyre-print where the now-disintegrated automobile had apparently swerved up onto the pavement, possibly avoiding something in its path, before it crashed into the wall or lamppost or whatever it had been. At Benedict's approach the plump young copper looked up from his contemplation of the burned-in tread mark, and to Ben's surprise he realised that he knew him from around the neighbourhood.

"Hello, Ben. Look at all this fucking mess." The officer, pink choirboy cheeks now red with aggravation, gestured to the pulverised glass and assorted oddments that were carpeting the street. "You should have seen it half an hour ago, before the medics pulled the poor cunt off his steering column. Worse thing is, it's not even supposed to be my shift tonight."

Benedict squinted at the workers sweeping up the debris. There was no blood he could see, but then perhaps the gore was all inside the mangled wreck.

"I see. A fatal accident. Ask not for whom the bell tolls, eh? Ah ha ha ha. Joy rider, was it?" Bugger. He'd not meant to laugh, not at a tragic death, nor had he meant to ask for whom the bell tolled right after delivering Donne's admonition not to. Luckily, the copper's mind appeared to be on other things, or else he was accustomed to and tolerant of Ben's eccentric manner. In a way he'd have to be, with his own sherbet lemon police-issue waistcoat more flamboyant than Ben's own.

"Joy rider? No. No, it was just some bloke in his late thirties. He was in his own car, far as we could see. A family car." He nodded glumly to the bright, trans-generational litter, strewn across the road from the sprung-open trunk. "He didn't smell like he'd been drinking when they cut him free. He must have swerved to miss something and gone up on the path." The young policeman's downcast air briefly appeared to lift a little. "Least I wasn't sent to tell his missus. Honestly, I fucking hate that. All the screaming and the blubbering and that's just me. I'll tell you, the last time I went to one of them I nearly – hang on – "

He was interrupted by a burst of static from his radio, which he unclipped from his coat to answer.

"Yeah? Yeah, I'm still down the top of Grafton Street. They're finishing the cleanup now, so I'll be done here in a minute. Why?" There was a pause during which the cherubic officer stared into space expressionlessly, then he said "All right. I'll be there soon as I get finished with the crash. Yeah. Yeah, okay."

He reattached his radio receiver, looked at Benedict and pulled a face that signified resigned contempt for his own woeful luck.

"There's been another tart done over down on Andrew's Road. Somebody living down there's took her in, but they want me to get a statement from her before she gets taken up the hospital. Why is it always me this happens to?"

Benedict was going to ask if he meant getting raped and beaten up, but then thought better of it. Leaving the embittered constable to supervise the tail-end of his clean-up duties, Ben continued downhill, curiously sobered by the whole offhand exchange. He turned along St. Andrew's Street, thinking about the prostitute who'd been attacked, about the man who'd been alive and driving home to see his family an hour ago with no suspicion of his imminent mortality. That was the whole appalling crux of things, Ben thought, that death or horror might be waiting just ahead and nobody had any way of knowing until those last, dreadful seconds. He began to think about his sister Alison, the motorcycle accident, but that was painful and so Ben steered his attentions elsewhere. Doing so, he inadvertently arrived at a blurred memory of the young working girl who had approached Ben earlier, the one who'd had her hair in rows. He knew it wasn't her specifically who'd been the latest girl to be assaulted at the foot of Scarletwell Street, but he also knew that in a sense it might as well have been. It would be one just like her.

How could this have happened to the Boroughs? How could it have turned into a place where somebody who could have grown up beautiful, who could have grown to be a poet's muse, is raped and half-killed every other week? The spate of sexual abductions and attacks over a single weekend during that last August, the majority of them had happened in this district. At the time they'd thought a single 'rape gang' was responsible for all the crimes, but ominously it had turned out that at least one serious assault was wholly unconnected to the others. Benedict supposed that when events like that occurred with the alarming frequency that they appeared to do round here, it would be natural to assume concerted action by some gang or some conspiracy. Although a menacing idea it was more comforting than the alternative, which was that such things happened randomly and happened often.

Still disconsolately dwelling on the probably doomed girl he'd met in Marefair and the fatal accident whose aftermath he'd witnessed just five minutes back, Ben turned right into Herbert Street, deserted on the slope of midnight. Silhouetted on the Lucozade-toned darkness of the sky behind them, Claremont Court and Beaumont Court were black as Stanley Kubrick monoliths, beamed down by an unfathomable alien intelligence to spark ideas amongst the shaggy, louse-bound primitives. Ideas like "Jump". You couldn't even see what little there was left of Spring Lane School from this specific viewpoint how you once could, not for all the NEWLIFE standing in the way. Ben shambled down as far as Simons Walk beneath a night made tangerine and starless. Turning left along the strip of turf-edged paving that would lead him to his mam's house he felt irritated, as he always did, by Simons Walk and its absent apostrophe. Unless there was some benefactor to the area named Simons that Ben hadn't heard of, he assumed the street's name was a reference to church-and-castle-building Norman knight Simon de Senlis, in which case there should be a possessive ... oh, what was the point? Nobody cared. Nothing meant anything that couldn't be turned instantly into its opposite by any competent spin-doctor or spoon-bender. History and language had become so flexible, wrenched back and forth to suit each new agenda, that it seemed as if they might just simply snap in half and leave us floundering in a sea of mad Creationist revisions and greengrocers' punctuation.

Staggering along past Althorpe Street he could hear screams of laughter and discordant weirdo music made still more distorted by its volume, issuing from slaphead Kenny Something's drug den down at the walk's end. Off in the ochre gloom car engines vented jungle snarls across the darkening cement savannah. Turning into Tower Street he walked up as far as Eileen's house, then spent five minutes giggling at himself while he attempted to unlock the front door without making any noise by trying to fit his key into the doorbell. Ah ha ha.

The house was quiet with everything switched off, his mam having already gone to bed. He passed by the closed door to the front room, still filled with heirlooms and for show rather than use, the way things used to be in Freeschool Street, and went through to the kitchen for a glass of milk before he went upstairs.

His room, the one space on the planet that he felt was his, awaited him forgivingly, prepared to take him in once more for all that he'd neglected it. There was his single bed, there was what he still laughingly referred to as his writing desk, there were the ranks of poets that he'd earlier tried to gas. He sat down on the bed's edge to untie his shoes but left the action uncompleted, trailing off across the carpet with the unpicked laces. He was thinking of the accident in Grafton Street, which meant that he was thinking about Alison, her ton-up boyfriend trying to overtake that lorry that had no wide-load lights. He was thinking about dying, how he did each morning soon as he woke up, but now there was no hope the morbid thoughts would vanish with the day's first drink, not when its last drink was just then expiring horribly beneath Ben's tongue. He was alone there in his room with death, his room, his death, its inevitability, and there was nothing to defend him.

One day soon he would be dead, reduced to ashes or else feeding worms. His entertaining funny mind, his self, that would just simply stop. That wouldn't be there anymore. Life would be going on, with all its romance and its thrills, but not for him. He would know nothing of it, like a splendid party at which he'd been made to feel he was no longer welcome. He'd have been crossed off the guest list, he'd have been erased, as if he'd never been there. All that would be left of him would be a few exaggerated anecdotes, some mildewed poems in surviving copies of small-circulation magazines, and then not even that. It would have all been wasted, and ...

It hit him suddenly, the bleak epiphany, and knocked the wind out of him: thinking about death was something he habitually did as an alternative to thinking about life. Death wasn't what the problem was. Death wasn't asking anything of anyone, except for effortless decomposition. Death wasn't the thing with all the expectations and the disappointments and the constant fear that anything could happen. That was life. Death, fearsome from life's frightened point of view, was actually itself beyond all fear and hurt. Death, like a kindly mother, took the worrisome responsibilities and the decisions off your hands, kissed you goodnight and tucked you underneath the warm green counterpane. Life was the trial, the test, the thing you had to figure out what you should do with before it was over.

But then, Benedict had done that. He'd decided, rashly, back in his romantic youth, that he'd be nothing if he couldn't be a poet. At the time, he hadn't really thought about the lesser of those two alternatives, the possibility that he might well end up as nothing. It had never happened for him, the success he'd thought he might achieve when he was younger, and he'd gradually lost heart. He'd pretty much abandoned writing, but it was so much a part of his identity that he could not admit, not even to himself, that he had given up. He would pretend his inactivity was only a sabbatical, that he was lying fallow, gathering material, when he knew deep inside that he was only gathering dust.

He saw, as through a fog, the grave mistake he'd made. He'd been so anxious for success and validation that he'd come to think you weren't really a writer unless you were a successful one. He knew, in this unprecedented patch of clarity, that the idea was nonsense. Look at William Blake, ignored and without recognition until years after his death, regarded as a lunatic or fool by his contemporaries. Yet Benedict felt sure that Blake, in his three-score-and-ten, had never had a moment's doubt that he was a true artist. Ben's own problem, looked at in this new and brutal light, was simple failure of nerve. If he had somehow found the courage to continue writing, even if each page had been rejected by each publisher it was submitted to, he'd still be able to look himself in the eye and know he was a poet. There was nothing stopping him from picking up his pen again except Earth's easily-resisted field of gravity.

This could be the night that Ben turned it all around. All that he had to do was walk across and sit down at his writing desk and actually produce something. Who knows? It might turn out to be the piece that would secure Ben's reputation. Or if not, if his abilities with verse seemed flat and clumsy with disuse, it might be his first faltering step back to the path he'd wandered from, into this bitter-sodden and immobilising bog. Tonight might be his chance to mend himself. The stark thought struck him that tonight might be his last chance.

If he didn't do it now, if he came up with some excuse about it being better to approach it in the morning when his head was fresher, then it seemed quite likely that he'd never do it. He'd keep finding reasons to put all his poetry aside until it was too late and life called time on him, until he ended up as a statistic at the top of Grafton Street with an indifferent police constable complaining that Ben's death had messed up his night off. Benedict had to do it right now, right this moment.

He got up and stumbled over to the writing desk, tripping upon his dangling laces on the way. He sat down and pulled out his notebook from a rear shelf of the bureau, pausing to ashamedly wipe thick dust from the cover with his palm before he opened it to a clean sheet. He picked the ballpoint pen that looked most viable out of the jam jar standing on the desk's top ledge, removed its cap and poised the sticky, furry ball of indigo above the naked vellum. He sat there like that a good ten minutes, coming to the agonizing realisation that he couldn't think of anything to say.

Six things, then, that Ben Perrit was completely useless at: escape, finding a job, explaining himself properly, not looking pissed, talking to girls and writing poetry.

No. No, that wasn't true. That was just giving up again, maybe for good. He was determined to write something, even if it was a haiku, even if it was a line or just a phrase. He searched his cloudy memory of the uneventful day that he'd just had for inspiration and was startled by how many images and idle notions drifted back to him. The workhouse, Clare's asylum, Malcolm Arnold and the mermaid girl, clover motifs worked artfully into the head of foam upon Ben's dark and swirling consciousness. He thought about the aching crack of Freeschool Street and the drowned continent, the landscape that was gone. He thought about just packing all this drunken nonsense in and getting into bed.

Off in the blackness there were sirens, techno thumps, bear-baiting cheers. His right hand trembled, inches from the snow-blind, empty page.

DO AS YOU DARN WELL PLEASEY

Inside him, underneath the white cake-icing of his hair, there were bordello churches where through one door surged the wide Atlantic and in through another came a tumbling circus funfair burst of clowns and tigers, girls with plumes and lovely lettering on the rides, a shimmering flood of sounds and images, of lightning chalk impressions dashed off by a feverish saloon caricaturist, melodrama vignettes fierce with meaning acted out beyond his eyelids' plush pink safety curtain, all the world with all its shining marble hours, its lichen centuries and fanny-sucking moments all at once, his every waking second constantly exploded to a thousand years of incident and fanfare, an eternal conflagration of the senses where stood Snowy Vernall, wide-eyed and unflinching at the bright carnival heart of his own endless fire.

Within the much pored-over, fondly re-examined picture book that was his life, the narrative had reached a page, an instant, an absorbing incident which, even as he was experiencing it, he knew he had experienced before. When other people spoke about their rare, unsettling spells of déjà vu he'd frown and feel that he was missing something, not because he'd never known such feelings, but because he'd never known anything else. He'd not cried over cut knees as a child because he'd been almost expecting them. He hadn't wept the day his father Ernest was brought home from where he worked with all his hair turned white. Though it had been a shocking scene, it had been one out of a favourite story, heard so many times that its power to surprise was gone. Existence was for Snowy an arcade carved from a single frozen jewel, a thrilling ghost-train wander past beloved dioramas and familiar sideshow frights, the glitter of the distant exit door's lamps clearly visible from his first step across the threshold.

The specific episode that he was now involved in was the famous sequence that found Snowy standing on a roof high over Lambeth Walk on a loud, radiant morning in the March of 1889 while his Louisa gave birth to their first child in the gutters far below. They'd been out walking in St. James's Park in an attempt to hurry up the big event with exercise, the baby being some days late and his wife tearful and exhausted from the weight that she'd been carrying so long. The ploy had worked too well, Louisa's waters breaking by the lakeside with the sudden spatter startling the ducks into a momentary sculpture, a fanned blur of brown and grey and white that spiralled up to make a shape half helter-skelter, half pagoda, beaded diamond droplets paused about it in a fleeting constellation. They'd attempted to get back to East Street with a hurried hobble down the length of Millbank, over Lambeth Bridge and into Paradise Street, but they'd only got as far as Lambeth Walk before there were contractions every other step and it became clear that they wouldn't make it. Well, of course they wouldn't make it. The chaotic childbirth onto the South London cobbles couldn't be avoided; was embedded in the future. Getting home to East Street without incident was not a verse in his already-carven legend. Shinning up the nearest sheer wall when the baby's crown engaged, leaving Louisa screaming at the centre of a gathering clot of gawpers, on the other hand, that was amongst the saga's many memorable highlights and was bound to happen. Snowy could no more prevent himself from climbing up an unseen ladder made of cracks and tiny ledges to the blue slate rooftops than he could prevent the sun from rising in the east tomorrow morning.

He stood straddling the ridge now like a chiselled Atlas with the double chimney breast behind him, balancing the huge glass globe of luminous and milky sky upon his shoulders. His black jacket with its worn sheen hung plumb-straight around him even in the March breeze, weighted by the heavy crystal doorknobs that he had in either pocket, picked up earlier that morning as requirements for a decorating job the Tuesday following. Down in the street below the dark-clad passers-by clustered into an anxious, bustling circle round his splayed and howling wife, moving in sudden and erratic bursts, like houseflies. She sprawled there upon the chilly pavement with her crimson face tipped back, staring up angry and incredulous into her husband's eyes as he looked down at her from three storeys above, indifferent as a roosting eagle.

Even with Louisa's features shrunken by the distance to a flake of pink confetti, Snowy thought that he could still read all the various conflicting feelings written there, with one impassioned outburst scribbled over quickly and eradicated by the next. There was incomprehension, wrath, betrayal, loathing, disbelief, and underlying these there was a love that stood and shivered at the brink of awe. She'd never leave him, not through all the ruinous whims, the terrifying rages, the unfathomable stunts and other women that he knew were waiting down the way. He knew that he would frighten her, bewilder her and hurt her feelings many, many times across the decades still to come, although he didn't want to. It was just that certain things were going to happen and there was no getting out of them, not for Louisa, not for Snowy, not for anyone. Louisa didn't know exactly what her husband was, though nor did he himself, but she had seen enough to know whatever he might be, he was a curiosity that didn't happen very often in the normal human run of things, and that she'd never in her lifetime see another like him. She had married a heraldic beast, a chimera drawn from no recognisable mythology, a creature without limits that could run up walls, could draw and paint and was regarded as one of the finest craftsmen in his trade. Despite the fact that there'd be times when Snowy's monstrous aspect made it so that she could not bear to set eyes on him, she'd never break the spell and look away.

John Vernall lifted up his head, the milk locks that had given him his nick-name stirring in the third floor winds, and stared with pale grey eyes out over Lambeth, over London. Snowy's dad had once explained to him and his young sister Thursa how by altering one's altitude, one's level on the upright axis of this seemingly three-planed existence, it was possible to catch a glimpse of the elusive fourth plane, the fourth axis, which was time. Or was at any rate, at least in Snowy's understanding of their father's Bedlam lectures, what most people saw as time from the perspective of a world impermanent and fragile, vanished into nothingness and made anew from nothing with each passing instant, all its substance disappeared into a past that was invisible from their new angle and which thus appeared no longer to be there. For the majority of people, Snowy realised, the previous hour was gone forever and the next did not exist yet. They were trapped in their thin, moving pane of Now: a filmy membrane that might fatally disintegrate at any moment, stretched between two dreadful absences. This view of life and being as frail, flimsy things that were soon ended did not match in any way with Snowy Vernall's own, especially not from a glorious vantage like his current one, mucky nativity below and only reefs of hurtling cloud above.

His increased elevation had proportionately shrunken and reduced the landscape, squashing down the buildings so that if he were by some means to rise higher still, he knew that all the houses, churches and hotels would be eventually compressed in only two dimensions, flattened to a street map or a plan, a smouldering mosaic where the roads and lanes were cobbled silver lines binding factory-black ceramic chips in a Miltonic tableau. From the roof-ridge where he perched, soles angled inwards gripping the damp tiles, the rolling Thames was motionless, a seam of iron amongst the city's dusty strata. He could see from here a river, not just shifting liquid in a stupefying volume. He could see the watercourse's history bound in its form, its snaking path of least resistance through a valley made by the collapse of a great chalk fault somewhere to the south behind him, white scarps crashing in white billows a few hundred feet uphill and a few million years ago. The bulge of Waterloo, off to his north, was simply where the slide of rock and mud had stopped and hardened, mammoth-trodden to a pasture where a thousand chimneys had eventually blossomed, tarry-throated tubeworms gathering around the warm miasma of the railway station. Snowy saw the thumbprint of a giant mathematic power, untold generations caught up in the magnet-pattern of its loops and whorls.

On the loose-shoelace stream's far side was banked the scorched metropolis, its edifices rising floor by floor into a different kind of time, the more enduring continuity of architecture, markedly distinct from the clock-governed scurry of humanity occurring on the ground. In London's variously styled and weathered spires or bridges there were interrupted conversations with the dead, with Trinovantes, Romans, Saxons, Normans, their forgotten and obscure agendas told in stone. In celebrated landmarks Snowy heard the lonely, self-infatuated monologues of kings and queens, fraught with anxieties concerning their significance, lives squandered in pursuit of legacy, an optical illusion of the temporary world which they inhabited. The avenues and monuments he overlooked were barricades against oblivion, ornate breastwork flung up to defer a future in which both the glorious structures and the memories of those who'd founded them did not exist.

It made him laugh, although not literally. Where did they think that everything, including them, was going to go? Snowy was only twenty-six at this point in the span of him, and he supposed that there were those who'd say he hadn't yet seen much of life, but even so he knew that life was a spectacular construction, more secure than people generally thought, and that it would be harder getting out of their existence than they probably imagined. Human beings ended up arranging their priorities without being aware of the whole story, the whole picture. Cenotaphs would turn out to be less important than the sunny days missed in their making. Things of beauty, Snowy knew, should be wrought purely for their own sake and not made into elaborate headstones stating only that somebody was once here. Not when no one was going anywhere.

Across a tugboat-hooter's reach of river the unblinking birdman smiled at his miraculous domain, while from below Louisa's shrieks were punctuated intermittently with snatched-breath cries of "Snowy Vernall, you're a cunt, a little fucking cunt!" He looked out over Westminster, Victoria and Knightsbridge to the sprawl of blurring burr-green that he knew to be Hyde Park, where there was represented still another aspect of unfolding time, embodied in the shapes of trees. The planes and poplars barely moved at all in their relationship to those three axes of the world that were immediately apparent, but the record of their progress in relation to the hidden fourth was frozen in their form. The height and thickness of their boughs were to be measured not in inches but in years. Moss-stippled forks were moments of unreached decision that had been made solid, twigs were but protracted whims, and deep within some of the thick trunks Snowy knew that there were arrowheads and musket-balls concealed, fired through the bark into the past, lodged in an earlier period, an earlier ring, entombed forever in the wood-grain of eternity as all things ultimately were.

If Mr. Darwin were to be believed, then it was from the timeless dapple of the forest's canopy that men had first descended, and it was the forest's roots that drank men's bodies when they died, returned their vital salts back to the prehistoric treetops in gold elevator cages made of sap. The parks, their Eden swathes of olive drab amongst the tweedy tooth of residential rows, were outposts of an emerald aeon, pools of wilderness left stranded by a swaying ocean now receded that would one day foam again across the urban beach-head, silencing its trams and barrel-organs under rustling hush. He flared his nostrils, trying to catch the scent of half a million years from now above the present's foundry reek. With all of London's people gone, erased by some as-yet-unborn Napoleon, Snowy imagined that the buddleia would swiftly prove itself to be the city's most enduring conqueror. From whispering marble banks and ruptured middens perfumed bushes would burst forth with friable white tongues of flower, where Julius Agricola had raised but a few fluttering standards, and Queen Boadicea naught but flames.

The heavy brothel sweetness would lure butterflies in watercolour blizzards, parakeets escaped from zoos to eat the butterflies and jaguars to eat the parakeets. The rarities and gorgeous monsters of Kew Gardens would break loose and overrun the abdicated town to its horizons, eucalyptus pillars railing off the shattered boulevards and palaces surrendered to colossal ferns. The world would end as it began, as beatific arbour, and if any family crests or luminary busts or graven names of institutions were yet visible between the droning hives and honeysuckle, they would be by then wiped clean of any meaning. Meaning was a candlelight in everything that lurched and shifted in the circumstantial breezes of each instant, never twice the same. Significance was a phenomenon of Now that could not be contained inside an urn or monolith. It was a hurricane entirely of the present, an unending swirl of boiling change, and as he stood there gazing out towards the city's rim, across the granite fields of time towards the calendar's far tattered edges, Snowy Vernall was a storm-rod, crackling and exultant, at the cyclone's dangerous and brilliant eye.

From fifty feet beneath, Louisa's gush of alternating anguished bellows and incensed tirade came floating up to him, a commonplace but awesome human music, where the full brass notes of torment seemed now more insistent and more frequent, dominating the arrangement, drowning out the piccolo abuse, the effing and the blinding. Looking down he noticed an impromptu band convened about his wife, providing an accompaniment of soft and sympathetic strings for her, a rumbling kettle drum of disapproval for her husband straddling the roof above them as they cooed and booed the pair in strict rotation. None of them appeared to be of any more practical use to the distressed and labouring woman than Snowy himself would be, even if he were still down there on the pavement at her side. The milling bystanders were an unpractised orchestra in a continual state of tuning up, their muttered scorn and soothing ululations striving painfully to reach some sort of harmony, their wheezing discords drifting off down Paradise Street, off down Union Street to join the background cymbal-roll of Lambeth, building gradually across the ages as if to some clarion announcement, rattling hooves and drunkards' songs and rag-and-bone men's lilting calls combined into a swell of everlasting prelude.

Like a hurried stage-assistant, the brisk wind wound on the painted cumulus above, and from the angle of the daylight's sudden downpour Snowy judged it to be not far off midday, the sun high overhead and climbing with increasing confidence up the last few blue steps to noon. He let his leisurely crow's-nest attentions wander from the well-attended birth throes of his child below and out into the intestinal tangle of surrounding alleyways, where dogs and people wrapped up in their own experience went back and forth, threads of event that shuttled on the district's loom, either unravelling from one knot of potential circumstance or else unwittingly converging on the next. Across the Lambeth Road, just visible above some low-roofed buildings to his right, a pretty, well-dressed pregnant woman was emerging from Hercules Road to cross the street between the plodding drays and weaving bicycles. A little nearer to him several boys of twelve or so were batting at each other with their caps, play-fighting as they made their way unhurriedly along the grimy seam of a rear-entry passage, cutting through between the smoking housetops and the nappy-flagged back yards from Newport Street. Snowy's eyes narrowed, and he nodded. All the clockwork of the minute was in order.

Judging from the light and from Louisa's escalating uproar he appeared to have another thirty minutes of just standing here, and so allowed his senses to resume once more their phosphorous evaluation of the city. London spun about him like a fairground novelty with Snowy as the ride's attendant, standing balanced there amongst the painted thunderbolts and comets of its central pivot. Turning his head to the northeast, Snowy looked out over Lambeth, Southwark and the river to St. Paul's, its bald white dome that of a slumbering divinity professor, all unmindful of its misbehaving charges, sinning everywhere about it as it drowsed and nodded. It was while employed restoring frescoes on the dome's interior that Snowy's father Ernest Vernall had been bleached by madness, near two dozen years before.

Snowy and sister Thursa went to Bethlehem Asylum when they visited their dad, which wasn't often. Snowy didn't like to think of it as Bedlam.

Sometimes they'd take Ernest's other children with them, Appelina and young Mess, but with their father being put away when those two were still small, they'd never really got to know him. Not that anyone, even their mother Anne, had ever known Ern Vernall through and through, but John and Thursa were still somehow close to him, particularly after he'd become insane. With little Messenger and Appelina there was never that communication, and their visits to the stranger in the madhouse only frightened them. When they'd grown older and were more robust sometimes they would accompany Snowy and Thursa, although only from a sense of duty. Snowy didn't blame his brother or his youngest sister. The asylum was a horror, full of piss and shit and screams and laughter; men who'd been disfigured with a spoon during their dinners by the person sitting next to them. If he and Thursa hadn't been so caught up in the rambling lectures that their father saved exclusively for them, they'd never have gone near the place themselves.

Their dad had talked to them about religion and geometry, acoustics and the true shape of the universe, about the multitude of things that he had learned while touching up the frescoes of St. Paul's during a thunderstorm, one morning long ago in 1865. He told them what had happened to him on that day, as well as he was able, with admonishments that they should never tell their mother or another living soul about Ern Vernall's holy vision, that had cost his mind and all the hot bronze colour in his hair. He told them he'd been by himself up on his platform a great distance over the cathedral floor, mixing his tempera and getting ready to begin his work when he'd become aware that there was now an angle in the wall. That was the way he'd said it, and his children had eventually come to understand that the expression had at least two meanings, an example of the word games and invented terms that peppered Ernest's conversation since his mental breakdown. Firstly it meant just what it appeared to mean, that Ernest had discovered a new angle that was somehow *in* the wall and not in the relationship between its surfaces. A second, more obscure interpretation of the term related it specifically to England and its ancient past, when "Angles" were the people of a tribe that had invaded England, giving it its name, after the Romans left. This second meaning had connected to it by association a quote from Pope Gregory ... "Non Angli, sed Angeli" ... uttered while inspecting English prisoners in Rome, a punning play on words that led Ern's eldest children to a gradual realisation of just what their father had encountered in the upper reaches of St. Paul's on that eventful day.

His father's lunatic account, even the memory of it now as Snowy stood there over Lambeth Walk and his poor wailing wife, conjured the smell of cold cathedral stone, of powder paint, of pinion feathers singed by lightning and Saint Elmo's Fire. The marvellous thing had slipped and slid around the dome's interior, as Ernest told the story to his offspring in the bowels of Lambeth's infamous asylum. It had spoken to their dad in phrases more astonishing than even the extraordinary countenance that was intoning them, its voice reverberating endlessly, resounding in a type of space or at a kind of distance that their father was not able to describe. This, Snowy thought, had been the detail that had most impressed his sister Thursa, who was musically inclined and whose imagination had seized instantly on the idea of resonance and echo with an extra fold, with new heights and unfathomable depths. John Vernall, with his own red hair already turning white by his tenth birthday, had been more intrigued by Ernest's new conception of mathematics, with its wonderful and terrifying implications.

In the street below the clutch of boys had now emerged out of their alley in a shunting, shouting shove and flooded onto Lambeth Walk. Attracted by the furiously inactive crowd around Louisa they had wandered over to stand goggling and jeering at its margins, clearly desperate for a glimpse of quim and never mind the bloody grey corpse-football that was threatening to burst out of it. The twelve-year-olds catcalled excitedly and tried to get a better view by capering this way and that behind the adult bystanders, who were all studiously pretending that they couldn't hear the ignorant and vulgar banter.

"Gor, look at the split on that! It looks like Jack the Ripper's done another one."

"Gor, so 'e 'as! Right in the cunt! It must 'ave been a lucky blow!"

"You dirty, worthless little beggars. Why, what sort of parents must you have, to bring you up like this? Would they think it was brave of you to bray and swear like sons of whores, around a woman in more pain than you have ever known or ever will do? Answer me!"

This last remark, delivered in authoritative cut-glass tones, came from the well turned-out and heavily expectant woman Snowy had seen coming from Hercules Road, crossing the Lambeth Road and, by an indirect route along alleys, entering Lambeth Walk only a pace or two behind the group of rowdy lads. Strikingly pretty, with a bound-up bundle of black hair and a dark, flashing gaze, everything from her costly-looking clothing to her bearing and enunciation marked her as a gal from the theatrical professions, her arresting manner that of one who brooked no hecklers in the audience. Shuffling round to face her both bewildered and surprised, the boys seemed daunted, looking sidelong at each other as if trying to establish without speaking what gang policy might be in novel situations such as this. Their stickleback eyes darted back and forth around the nibbled edges of the moment without lighting on a resolution. From his high perspective, Snowy thought they might be Elephant Boys from up Elephant and Castle, who, between them, were quite capable of meting out a thumping or a knifing, even to a constable or sailor.

This diminutive and therefore even more conspicuously pregnant woman, though, appeared to represent a challenge against which the louts could muster no defence, or at least not without an unrecoverable loss of face. They looked aside, disowned themselves and their own presence there on Lambeth Walk, beginning to drift silently away down various side-streets, separate strands of a dispersing fog. Louisa's saviour, actress or variety performer or whomever she might be, stood watching them depart with deadpan satisfaction, head cocked to one side and slim arms folded on the insurmountable defensive barricade of her distended belly, thrusting out before her like a backwards bustle. Reassured that the young miscreants would not be coming back, she next turned her attentions on the loose assortment of spectators gathered round the pavement birth, who'd witnessed all of the foregoing whilst stood in a shamed and ineffectual silence.

"As for you lot, why on Earth are you all standing round that poor girl if there's none of you prepared to help her? Hasn't anybody knocked upon a door to ask for blankets and hot water? Here, come on and let me through."

Abashed, the gathering parted and allowed her to approach Louisa, gasping and spread-eagled there amongst the cigarette-ends and the sweepings. One of the admonished onlookers elected to take up the newcomer's suggestion of appealing for hot water, towels and other birth accoutrements at doorsteps up and down the street, while she herself stooped by Louisa's side as best as she was able given her own cumbersome condition. Wincing with discomfort, she reached out and brushed sweat-varnished strands of lank hair from the panting woman's forehead as she spoke to her.

"Let's hope this doesn't set me off as well, or we shall have a right to-do. Now, what's your name, dear, and however have you come to be in this predicament?"

Between gasps, Snowy's wife responded that she was Louisa Vernall and had been attempting to get home to Lollard Street when the birth process had begun. The rescuer made two or three tight little nods as a response, her fine-boned features thoughtful.

"And where is your husband?"

Since this question coincided with her next contraction, poor Louisa was unable to reply except by lifting one damp, trembling hand to point accusingly towards the sky directly overhead. At first interpreting the gesture as a signal that Louisa was a widow with a husband now in heaven, the expectant Good Samaritan eventually cottoned on and raised her own dark, long-lashed eyes in the direction that the moaning girl was indicating. Standing straddling the roof-ridge, statue-still above the scene save for the blizzard flurry of his hair, even his jacket hanging oddly motionless in a stiff breeze, John Vernall might have been a whitewashed weathervane to judge from the expression that was in his face as he returned the woman's startled gaze with one that was unflinching and incurious. She stared him out for only a few moments before giving up and turning back to speak to his distressed young wife, thrashing and breathing like a landed fish there on the paving stones beside the crouching would-be midwife.

"I see. Is he mad?"

This was delivered as a straightforward enquiry, without condemnation. Snowy's wife, then resting in a too-brief trough between the waves of pain, nodded despairingly while mumbling her affirmation.

"Yes, ma'am. I fear very much he is."

The woman sniffed.

"Poor man. The same could happen, I suppose, to any one of us. However, I propose that for the moment we forget him and attend to you instead. Now, let's see how we're getting on."

With this she shifted to a kneeling posture so that she might minister with greater comfort to her more immediately needy sister in maternity. By now the fellow who'd gone door-to-door in search of blankets and warm water had returned bearing between both hands a steaming wide enamel bowl, towels draped across one arm as if he were a waiter at a posh hotel. Despite the greater frequency of poor Louisa's screams the situation seemed to be under control, although of course in actuality it never had been any other. Just as John had known it would do, everything was happening in time. Smiling at his own unintended wordplay, no doubt picked up from his father, Snowy tilted back his head and reappraised the sky. More threadbare bed-sheet clouds had been snatched up in haste and dragged halfway across the naked sun, which, judging from such flinching and contracted shadows as remained, was now precisely at its zenith. There was a good twenty minutes left before his daughter would be born. They'd name her May, after Louisa's mum.

He was the snow-capped pole of Lambeth and the borough whirled beneath his feet. Up to the north, beyond the chimneypots, was sooty Waterloo. Down on his left and to the south, he thought, was Mary's Church, or St. Mary's-in-Lambeth as it was more properly called, where Captain William Bligh and both the flora-cataloguing Tradescants were buried, while due west in front of him stood Lambeth Palace. Not far to the east, of course, not far enough for him at any rate, was Bedlam.

He'd not seen the place in seven years, not since he was a lad of nineteen with their Thursa two years younger, which was when his father Ern had finally passed away. There'd been a notifying letter come from the asylum, at which he and Thursa had made the short journey up the road to see their parent prior to burial. A trip of at the most ten minutes' walk, it had become apparently more lengthy and more difficult to make with every passing year, dwindling from a monthly to an annual occurrence, usually at Christmas, which for Snowy ever since had seemed a dreadful season.

That wet afternoon in the July of 1882 had been the first time Snowy or his sister had seen someone dead, this being some few years before their father's mum, their grandmother, had gone as well. The two unusually quiet and dry-eyed youngsters had been shown through to a rear shed where the corpses were laid out, a cold and overcast place in which Ernie Vernall's alabaster body seemed almost the only source of light. Face upward on a slab of pale fishmonger's marble with his eyes still open, John and Thursa's dad had the expression of a military recruit stood to attention on some ultimate parade ground: carefully neutral, focussed resolutely on the distance, trying hard not to attract the scrutiny of an inspecting officer. His blanched skin, now a hard and chill veneer beneath John's cautiously exploring fingertips, had turned the colour of his hair, had turned the colour of the sheet with sculpted, dropping folds that covered the nude form to just above its navel. They could no longer determine, quite, the point at which their father's whiteness finished and that of the mortuary plinth supporting him began. His death had chiselled, sanded down and polished him, transformed him to a stark and beautiful relief.

This was their father's end. Both of them understood that, though not in the same sense that most other people would have done, with 'end' as a mere synonym for death. To John and Thursa, tutored by the late Ern Vernall, it was no more than a geometric term, as when one talked about the ends of lines or streets or tables. Side by side they'd looked in awe on his arresting stillness, knowing that, for the first time, they saw the structure of a human life end-on. It had been wholly different from the side-on view one usually had of people while they were alive, while they were still caught up in the extension and apparent movement of their selves through time, along Creation's hidden axis. Snowy and his sister stood regarding their dead father, both aware that they were gazing down the marvellous and fearful bore of the eternal. Thursa had begun to hum, a fragile little air of her own slapdash and impromptu composition, rising strings of notes left hanging with unnaturally long intervals, during which Snowy knew his sister heard an intricate cascade of subdivided echo filling in the gaps. He'd cocked his head and concentrated until he could hear the same thing she did and then taken Thursa's warm, damp hand, the two of them together in the morgue-hut's whispery pall and thrilling to an implied music that was both magnificent and bottomless.

As Snowy thought about it now, high in the eaves of Lambeth, he and Thursa always had been differently disposed towards the worldview that their father had impressed upon them. For his own part, Snowy had elected to immerse himself entirely in the storm of the experience, to plunge into this new exploded life the way that, as a child, he'd plunged unhesitatingly into the iron-green wall of each oncoming wave upon the yellow shore at Margate. Every moment of him was a roaring gold infinity with Snowy spinning giddy and resplendent at its whirlpool heart, beyond death and past reason.

Thursa on the other hand, as she'd confessed to him not long after their dad's demise, saw in her brother's glorious tempest a devouring force that could mean only the disintegration of her more frail personality. Instead she'd chosen to block out the broader implications of Ern Vernall's madhouse lessons and to fix all her attention on one narrow strand, this being how her father's new conception of geometry applied to sound and its transmission. She had trained herself to hear a single voice in the arrangement rather than risk being swallowed by the fugue of being in which Snowy was consumed. She hung on to herself for dear life, clinging tightly to the mooring of her piano accordion, a scuff-marked veteran beast of fawn and tan which Thursa carried with her everywhere. At present both she and her skirling instrument were lodged with relatives at Fort Street in Northampton, while her eldest brother wore a pendulum track between there and Lambeth, hiking three score miles and back from one location to the other.

Down below the woman with the stagy accent urged Louisa to push harder. Snowy's wife, her thick limbs and broad features glistening with perspiration, only bellowed.

"I am fucking pushing, don't tell me to fucking push! Oh no, I'm sorry. Please, I'm sorry. I don't mean it. I don't mean it."

He adored Louisa, loved her with his every fibre, with each strange and convoluted thought that passed, like party streamers in a gale, through Snowy's frost-crowned head. He loved her kindness, loved the thick-set look of her, at once as plain and pleasing to the eye as fresh-baked bread. Her mass of personality ensured that his wife was a creature of the earth, one grounded in the solid world of streets and bills and childbirth, of her body and biology. She did not care at all for spires or sky or the precarious, preferring hearth and walls and ceiling to her husband's altitudes, the steeplejack obsessions he'd inherited from his late father. She cleaved to the gravity that Snowy knew he'd spend the whole of his unusual existence trying to overcome, and doing so became his counterweight, a vital anchor that prevented him from bowling off into the heavens like a lost kite.

In return, Louisa could enjoy the more remote and somewhat safer thrills of the kite-handler, watching heart in mouth or cheering with delight as he negotiated each fresh updraft, shivering and squinting sympathetically in the imagined gust and glare. He knew that fifty years from now, after his death, she'd hardly venture out of doors again, shunning a firmament into which, by that time, her painted paper dragon would have long since blown away and left her only with a memory of the wind that tugged with such insistence on his string, an elemental force that would at last have won its battle and pulled Snowy Vernall from her empty, reaching fingers.

That, of course, was all in the now-then, while down beneath him in the now-now he could hear, behind Louisa's screams and the bystanders' muffled mutter, the low storm-front rumble of his daughter's coming life as it approached this worldly station. Snowy thought about the cross of whispered rumours that his child would always carry with her, all the talk of madness in the family like something from a gothic novel. First her great-grandfather John, who Snowy had been named for, then poor Ern, the grandfather that she would never know, both locked away in Bedlam. Snowy knew that such was not to be his fate, but that his reputation as a madman would be none the less for this, and neither would the heavy legacy his soon-born daughter should be made to carry. Looking down towards the square of paving where his and Louisa's baby would be shortly making her appearance, he recalled the eerie splendour that had spoken to his father in St. Paul's Cathedral all those years ago; the words with which, according to Ern Vernall, that extraordinary conversation had commenced. Snowy was smiling with amusement and yet felt the hot tears pricking in his eyes as he repeated the phrase softly to himself, while overlooking all the furious activity in Lambeth Walk below.

"This will be very hard for you."

He meant his child, his wife, himself, meant everyone who'd ever struggled from the womb to somewhere that was brighter, colder, dirtier and not so loving in its ways. This, THIS, this place, this eddy in the soup of history, this would be very hard for all of them. You didn't need an angel to come down and tell you that. It would be hard for everybody else because they lived within a moving world of death, bereavement and impermanence, a world of constant seeming change that bubbled with machine-guns, with the motor-driven carriages that he'd heard talk of, with smudged paintings, smutty books, new things of all kinds all the time. It would be hard for Snowy because he lived in a world where everything was there forever, never ended, never altered. He lived in the world as the world truly was, as his late father had explained it to him. As a consequence of this he had become, despite his various acknowledged skills, both lunatic and unemployable. He had become the kind of man who stands about on rooftops with glass doorknobs in his pockets.

Even given this, on balance Snowy felt that he was blessed rather than blighted. There was no point feeling differently, not in a world where every instant, every feeling carried on forever. He would sooner live a life of endless blessing than one of undying curse, and after all, it was in how you chose to see things that the narrow border between Hell and Paradise was traced. Though his condition, part inherited and part acquired, had many drawbacks

in material terms these were outnumbered by the almost unimaginable benefits. He was entirely without fear, able to scale sheer walls without regard for
life or limb, simply because he knew that he was not destined to perish in a
fall. His death would come in a long corridor of rooms, like the compartments
on a railway train, and Snowy's mouth would be crammed full of colours. He
had no idea yet why this would be so, but only that it would be. Until then, he
could take risks without anxiety. He could do anything he pleased.

This freedom was at once the aspect of his state that he valued most highly,
and its greatest contradiction. He was free to do the most outrageous things
only because these actions were already fixed in what to others was the future,
and because he had to. When he looked at it objectively, he saw that the real
measure of his freedom was that he was free of the illusion of free will. He
was unburdened by the comforting mirage that other men took faith in, the
delusion that allowed them to take walks or beat their wives or tie their shoes,
apparently whenever they should wish, as if they had a choice. As if they and
their lives were not the smallest and most abstract brushstroke, a pointillist
dab fixed and unmoving in time's varnish, there eternally on an immeasurable
canvas, part of a design too vast for its component marks to ever glimpse or
comprehend. The terror and the glory of John Vernall's situation was that of a
pigment smear made suddenly aware of its position at the corner of a masterpiece, a dot that knows that it is held in place forever on the painted surface,
that it's never going anywhere, and yet exults: "How dreadful and how fabulous!" He knew himself, knew what he was and knew that this advantaged
him in certain ways above his fellow squiggles in the picture, who were not so
conscious of their true predicament, its majesty, nor of its many possibilities.

Magical powers were his, besides the fearlessness that lifted him amongst
the slate slopes of the skyline. He could easily accomplish an unbearably long
walk, or any other lengthy undertaking for that matter, by the application of
techniques learned from his father. Ernest had explained to him and Thursa
how there was a way of folding our experience of space as easily as we might
fold a map to join two distant points together, say the Boroughs of Northampton and the streets of Lambeth. These two places were in fact unusually easy
to bring into close proximity, due to the numerous others who had made
the trip before and, doing so, had worked the fold into a worn and whitened
crease. Snowy exploited it whenever he was called upon to travel between
Thursa in the Boroughs and his mum's in Lambeth with young Messenger and
Appelina. All he had to do was set off on his journey and then, as his dad had
taught him, lift into a different sort of thinking that moved like the passage
of events in dreams, outside the realm of minutes, hours and days. Time then
would settle easily into this old, familiar wrinkle and the next thing Snowy
knew he'd be arriving at his destination, having sore feet but without fatigue,

without the memory of a moment's boredom and, indeed, without a memory of any kind at all. As Ernest had expressed it to his children, it was easier when travelling to move one's consciousness along the axis of duration rather than the one of distance, though your boot-heels would wear down as quickly either way.

Nor was this all of Snowy's learned abilities. He knew the future, cloudily, not in a sense of prophecy but more in that he recognised the future when he saw it, knew how things would work out in the instant that he came upon them, as with scenes found written in a book embarked upon without recalling that it has been read before, in some forgotten summer, where there comes a tantalizing premonition of what waits beyond the next turned page.

He also had the trick of seeing ghosts. He saw the ordinary sort that were the spirits of past buildings and events embedded in the unseen temporal axis, spectral structures and scenarios which other people thought of as their memories. He furthermore had been a witness to the rarer but more famous kind of wraiths that were the restless dead: pained souls who shirked the repetition of their painful lives and yet who felt unready or unwilling to move on to any further state of being. He would sometimes apprehend them in the corner of his eye, smoke-coloured shapes endlessly circling their old neighbourhoods in search of ghostly conversations, ghostly ruts, in search of ghost-food. Just a year ago he'd seen the shade of Mr. Dadd, the fairy-painter who'd gone mad and murdered his own father. Dadd had died himself early in 1886 at Broadmoor Hospital, an institution for the criminally insane. On the occasion Snowy saw the artist's phantom form it stood, looking regretful, at the gates of Bedlam wherein Dadd had previously been incarcerated. Snowy had observed the faint peripheral blur while it plucked something similarly indistinct from the asylum's worn stone gatepost and proceeded, seemingly, to eat it. The dead painter, from the vague suggestion of his posture and demeanour, had appeared to be not so possessed nor so maniacal as when in life, but rather now clear-sighted and suffused by a profound remorse. The doleful apparition had persisted for some several seconds, glumly chewing its mysterious findings while it stared at the bleak edifice, then melted to a patch of damp discoloured brickwork on the madhouse wall.

The artist William Blake, who'd lived up Hercules Road getting on a century ago, had also seen and spoken with the creatures of the other world, with the deceased, with angels, devils, with the poet Milton who had entered like a current through the sole of Blake's left foot. The Lambeth visionary's notions of a fourfold and eternal city seemed at times so close to Snowy's own view, right down to the exact number of its folds, that he had wondered if there were some quality in Lambeth that encouraged such perceptions. There may be, he'd often thought, some aspect of the district's shape or placement when considered on more planes than three that made it most especially conducive to a certain attitude, to a unique perspective, though he knew that in his own case there had also been heredity as a prevailing influence. He was a Vernall, and his father Ern had taken pains that Snowy and his eldest sister should both know precisely what that meant.

"Nomen est omen", that was how their dad had put it, an illiterate somehow quoting Latin proverbs. This had been the stated rationale, if such it might be called, behind the naming of his youngest children Messenger and Appelina, with one moniker suggestive of a herald angel and the other of our fallen mother Eve. Nomen est omen. The name is a sign. Ern had explained to John and Thursa that there was a place "upstairs" where what we thought of down here as our names turned out in many instances to be our job descriptions. Vernalls, as their father had defined the term, were those responsible for tending to the boundaries and corners, to the edges and the gutters. Though a lowly post in the ethereal hierarchies it was a necessary one that carried its own numinous authority. In Snowy's understanding, by the odd linguistic laws of the superior plane that Ernest had referred to, Vernall was a word with connotations similar to "verger", both in the old sense of one who tended verges and of one who bore the verge, or rod of office, as in the ecclesiastical tradition. But the language of "upstairs", according to Ern Vernall, was a form of speech that were as though exploded, every phrase uncrumpling itself into a beautiful and complicated lacework of associations. Rods were wands of government and yet were also rulers made for measurement, which was presumably how rods of land beside a property were first called verges: grassy strips erupting into life with Spring, the vernal equinox, which also led back to the family name. This aspect of fertility was echoed in Old English, wherein the expression "verge" or "rod" was slang for what men kept inside their trousers, or at least thus was the etymology as passed on by their father, who could neither read nor write. In sum, a Vernall ministered to borderlines and limits, to the margins of the world and the unmowed peripheries of worldly reason. This, Ern had insisted, was why Vernalls tended to be raving mad and penniless.

As he looked down on the arrival of the latest baby to be thus afflicted, he allowed his consciousness of time to crystallise around the quarter-inch of the duration axis that the moment represented so that things slowed to a crawl, the progress of events barely perceptible. It was another talent or disease that he and Thursa had inherited, the means to charm the universe unto a standstill. "Pigeon eyes", their dad had called this gift, without explaining why. The clouds were stopped and curdled in the sky's blue juice, masking a sun that had moved on a little past its peak and was just fractionally behind him, its scant warmth upon his shoulders and the rear top of his head.

Below his parapet in Lambeth Walk the thoroughfare was now become a sculpture garden, all its mid-day rush and bustle rendered motionless. Litter and dust snatched up by the March breeze was frozen in its blustering ascent, suspended in the air at distinct intervals, so that the unseen currents of the wind were speckled with debris and thus made visible, a grand glass staircase sweeping up above the street. A pissing horse produced a necklace-string of weightless topaz, tiny golden crowns formed where the droplets were caught in the process of disintegrating on the slimy cobbles. The pedestrians who had been captured halfway through an action were now posed like dancers in outlandish ballets, balancing impossibly on one foot with their weight thrown forward in an uncompleted stride. Impatient children floated inches over hop-scotch squares and waited for their interrupted jumps to finish. Young men's neckerchiefs and women's unpinned hair flew sideways in a sudden gust and stayed there, sticking out as stiff as wooden flags from railway signal-boxes.

Noise was also slowed, the chorus-voice of Lambeth Walk now born by sluggish waves as though through a more viscous medium, become a dark bass slur, an aural bog. The seamless clattering of hooves was turned to endlessly reverberating single anvil beats sounded at lengthy intervals by a fatigued and unenthusiastic blacksmith, while the rapid trills of indecipherable birdsong had a cadence reminiscent now of trivial and pleasant conversation between old boys playing dominoes. Street vendors' cries from down on Prince's Road creaked like ghost story doors that opened with excruciating languor on some fettered horror. Two dogs fighting down in Union Street mimicked a background rumble of industrial machinery, their barks extended to the snarl of buried engines, to a humming undertone of violence, a continuous vibration in the pavements that was seldom noticed, always there. Amidst it all there swelled the wavering soprano counterpoint of poor Louisa's latest scream, drawn out into an aria. The pregnant midwife kneeling on the filthy street beside her had been halted halfway through a further exhortation for his wife to push, and was emitting a protracted minotaur-like bellowing that Snowy took to be a vowel inflated to the point of bursting.

Snowy's wife seemed similarly puffed up and upon the brink of an explosion. Almost half the baby's head was out, a bluish rupture greased with blood emerging from the stretched lips of Louisa's privates, now impossibly distended to a painful circle, a pullover neck. A torus.

In the dreadful halls of Bedlam, Ernest Vernall had leaned in towards his children, his remaining clumps of hair unkempt and white as hedgerows on a drovers' path. His voice descending into a dramatic whisper both conspiratorial and urgent, he'd impressed upon them the supreme importance of this previously unheard word, a term most usually employed in either architecture or solid geometry. A torus, as their father had explained it to them, was the rubber-tyre shape generated by the revolution of a conic disc around a circle drawn on an adjacent plane, or else the volume that would be contained by such a spatial movement. Tori, at least as their dad defined them, were the single most important forms in all the cosmos. All Earth's living creatures that had more than one cell to their names essentially were tori, or at least they were when looked at from a topographical perspective; irregular tori with their mass arranged around the central holes provided by their alimentary canals. In its fixed orbit round the sun, if this should be considered without the illusion of progressing time, their world described a torus. So did all the other planets and their moons. The stars themselves, rotating with the swirling vortex of the galaxy, were tori of stupendous magnitude that had diameters one hundred million years across from side to side. Ernest had intimated that the glittering universe in its entirety revolved about a point in uncreated nothingness (although there were no means by which we might detect this motion, being relative to literally nothing), and that should both space and time be seen as one undifferentiated substance then the whole of God's creation might be held to be toroidal.

This, apparently, was why the humble chimneypot was such a potent and unsettling configuration. This was at least partly why Ern Vernall's eldest son spent so much of his time on rooftops, in amongst the reeking stacks: you had to keep your eye on them.

The chimneypot ... essentially a stretched-out torus when considered topographically ... was a materialisation of the form in its most dreadful and destructive aspect, was the great annihilating void that it contained made manifest, its central hole become a crematorium pipe up which things deemed no longer necessary to requirements might be easily disposed of; corpses, broken bedsteads and outdated newspapers belched as a foul miasma from these stone or terracotta death-mouths into an insulted sky. The blackened smokestacks thus served also as a social oubliette, as vents that whole swathes of the lower classes had been stuffed up, children first. They smouldered with the awful breath of nothing. The banked chimneypots that Snowy knew stood four abreast behind him on the ridge were fragile shells surrounding empty pits of that same non-existence men came out of and eventually went into, were a grim inversion of that other torus gaping currently between Louisa's thighs that spilled out life where they spilled out its opposite.

Below, although the woman helping to deliver Snowy's child had not yet reached the end of her command to push, being at present caught up in a windy rush of sibilants, the baby's head was now emerged completely. Snowy's wife had the appearance of those peg dolls you could buy that were reversible and had a head on each end at the junction of the limbs. As he stared down through the resplendent treacle of the moment at the half-born infant's gory scalp, he understood that this perspective was a converse to the end-on view of their dead father that he and his sister had once shared in an asylum mortuary. This was life seen, for the first time in his own experience, from its other terminus. It was, if anything, an even lovelier and more terrible thing when looked at through this end of its breathtaking telescope.

He gazed along the long jewelled tube that was his daughter's enviable mortal span, and saw how bright and beautiful the near roots of the coral structure were compared to the gnarled darkness at its distant further tip. He saw the furling sub-growths that were her own children, half a dozen of them budding forth and branching from her mother-stem about a quarter of the way along its length. All six of the gem-crusted offshoots had a handsome lustre that would make her proud of them, but when he saw the closest and thus first-born sprout, both its exquisite burnish and its brevity, he felt the heartbreak aching in his throat, saltwater burning in his eyes. So precious and so small. Now Snowy noticed that a later branch, the next to last, was also cut short some few decades sooner than his girl-child's own demise, and wondered if these losses might account for the deep melancholic colouration he could make out at the human tunnel's furthest end.

His daughter's life reached more than eighty years into what most would call the future, but which he thought of as 'over there'. The murky and discoloured far extremity of her lay in an England that to Snowy was unrecognisable, a place of blocks and cubes and glaring lights. She'd die alone upon the outskirts of Northampton in a monstrous house that seemed to be the whole street pressed into one building. He could see her face down in a too-bright hallway, jowly, liver spotted, features blackening with settled blood. She would be struggling to get to the front door and the fresh air, but the determined heart attack would get there before she did and would have her legs away from under her. His and Louisa's gorgeous little girl. A bundle of old rags, that's what she'd look like, dumped there in the passage inches from a doormat that was bare of letters, undiscovered for two days.

He couldn't bear this. This was too much. Snowy had assumed that by surrendering to the mad splendour of his father's theories he would be in some way made divine, made wise and strong enough to cope with his perceptions, would become immune to the assaults of ordinary feeling. It appeared that this was not the case. He now seemed to remember, as if from before, that this experience, standing on a roof and witnessing May's gutter birth-throes with her lonely death already there, embedded, would turn out to be the first occasion where he'd truly understand the weighty rigours of a Vernall's occupation. This appalling vista of a life foreshortened was simply the viewpoint from the corner, and he'd best become accustomed to it. After all, he was not in reality more gifted nor more cursed than any other man. Did people not speak often of how time would seem to slow for them when in a dangerous situation? Were there not accounts of premonitions, lucky guesses, the uncanny sense that things have happened just this way before? Wasn't it true that everybody had these feelings but elected for the most part to ignore them, perhaps sensing where such notions might eventually lead? *Everyone knows the way there, hey there, hey there!* Surely all parents knew that in their child's birth was its death also contained, but made inside themselves, perhaps unwitting, a decision not to look too deep into the marvellous and tragic well that Snowy was now gazing down.

He didn't blame them. From the customary standpoint, birth must seem a capital offence with an unvaried sentence. It was only natural that people should attempt to dull their comprehension of so terrible a circumstance, if not with drink then with a comfortingly warm and woollen vagueness. Only enflamed souls like Snowy Vernall could be reasonably expected to endure the blizzard of existence without shielding wraps and without merely peeping at its brilliance through smoked glass, stood naked in the stark immortal roar of everything. He there and then resolved he should not pass the Vernalls' rarefied awareness to his daughter in the way that their own dad had handed it to him and Thursa once. The almost-born child had some two decades of happiness and carefree beauty before life would start to load her with its burdens. He would let her have the good years that were due to her without the fore-cast shadow of their ultimate result. Though his condition came with limitations and constraints so that he could not change what was in store for either of them, he at least could give his first-born this, the blessed balm of ignorance.

He now allowed his own unflinching focus to relax, loosening his grip on the lapels of time so that the instant might move on, the horse conclude its piss, the boys continue with their hopscotch. All the frozen clamour of the instant was now of a sudden thawed so that the vulgar bawl of Lambeth Walk accelerated from its droning torpor much like a wax cylinder recording that has slowed and stopped then been rewound, its din spiralling drunkenly back to its usual tumult and crescendo.

"... sh!" the midwife cried. "Push hard! It's coming now!"

Louisa's final wail climbed to a jagged pinnacle then swooned exhausted into its relieved fall. Slippery and silver as a fish, the baby girl was effortlessly poured into the world, the makeshift midwife's arms, the waiting towels and blankets. A warm murmur of appreciation moved across the bystanders like rippling breeze on a still reservoir, and then his child announced her own arrival with a rising, hiccoughing lament. Louisa wept in sympathy and asked the woman kneeling by her was it all right, was it normal, reassured in soft tones that it was a lovely little girl, that she had all her fingers and her toes.

The sun parted its curtain cloud-bank and was on his neck now, some degrees behind him, with a wide stripe of cool shadow thrown down on the slabs of Lambeth Walk below, a flattened triangle with the black cut-out shape of a perspective-stunted Snowy Vernall at its apex. Casually, as if the action were not timed to its last fraction of a second, Snowy reached into both weighted, hanging pockets of his jacket and took out the heavy cut-glass doorknobs, one held by a chill brass stalk in either fist.

He raised his arms on each side, in the way his dad had told him that the angels did when they wished to affirm or else rejoice, a motion like a pigeon lifting up its wings to take off on the downbeat. Sunbeams plummeted from overhead and were cut into ribbons on the edges of the crystal globes. Shavings of varicoloured brilliance, rays sliced thin enough to see their tinsel strata, blue and blood and emerald, fell in paint-box drips on Lambeth Walk, feathers of dye-dipped light that trembled on its curbs and cobbles, brightest in the band of shade now covering his wife and child. Passing the wiped and swaddled newborn to her anxious mother, the still-crouching woman who'd assisted with the birth frowned with bewilderment at one such iridescent jaguar-blotch that was then gliding down over the baby's wrappings and across the midwife's dainty fingers. Stained with jewel she tipped her head back, peering to identify the source of the phenomenon and gasping with amazement once she had, whereon Louisa and those gathered round the birth-slabs followed her example, turning up their faces in the peacock rain.

John Vernall, mad John Vernall was a faceless silhouette stood on the roof-ridge with the sun behind his head and white hair like St. Elmo's Fire or phosphorus, his arms flung up to heaven, a gaunt storm-bird come after the flood with rainbows shredded in its lifted claws, radiant streamers leaking from the cracks between clenched fireball talons. Spectra splashed over the silenced throng in luminous and vivid moth-wings, shed and yet still fluttering on drainpipes, doorsteps, people's cheeks and drooping chins. The fresh-delivered child stopped crying, squinting mystified up into her first glimpse of being, and his wife, released from her ordeal and giddy with reprieve, began to laugh. Others amongst the gathered crowd joined in, one man even beginning to applaud but trailing off embarrassed and alone into the general hilarity.

At length he let his arms sink to his sides, returning the glass doorknobs to his jacket pockets. From the street below he heard Louisa tell him to stop buggering about, to come and see their daughter. Fishing from behind one jutting ear a stub of yellowed chalk secreted there, he turned his back upon the rooftop's edge and took three careful steps along its ridge towards the tall brick chimney breast that now loomed up before him. In a generous and looping hand he scribbled "Snowy Vernall springs eternal" on the brickwork, standing back a moment to admire his work. It would not be washed off by the next rain, which would come from the east, but by the shower immediately thereafter.

Snowy sighed, and smiled, and shook his head, and then went down to face the endless music.

THE BREEZE THAT
PLUCKS HER APRON

The Fort Street deathmonger was Mrs. Gibbs, and on that first occasion when she called her pinafore was starched and spotless white with butterflies embroidered on its hem. May Warren was then just nineteen years old, scared stiff in her confinement's final stage, but even through the unexpected pain and scalding tears she was aware that she had never known this woman's like before.

It was still freezing and the outside lav was blocked with ice, which meant these last two days they'd had to burn their business on the fire. The living room still stank but Mrs. Gibbs made nothing of it, taking off her coat to show the splendid apron underneath, white as a lantern in the downstairs gloom, with summer moths in pink and orange thread ascending her stout thighs and winter paunch.

"Now then, my dear, let's see what we're about." Her voice was like bake pudden, thick and warm, and while May's mam Louisa made fresh tea the deathmonger produced a tin of snuff, small as a matchbox, with upon its lid the late Queen in enamel miniature. Thumb curled back so a hollow was produced between the bones where they met with her wrist, next Mrs. Gibbs, with great precision, tipped a measure of the pungent russet dust into the shallow cavity thus formed. Hand lifted and head lowered she swept up the heaped gunpowder in two fruity snorts, half in each barrel, which she then discharged explosively into a handkerchief, something of a brown study in itself. Beaming at May she put the tin away and got down to her work between May's knees.

The young mother-to-be had never seen a woman taking snuff before and was just going to ask about the habit when contractions drove the question from her mind. May growled and moaned and at the kitchen door her mam appeared with tea for Mrs. Gibbs. She eyed her daughter sympathetically yet could not keep herself from pointing out that May's own birth had been a worse ordeal.

"You think that's bad, gal, you've got no idea, all of the trouble that I had with you. You're not abed because we've got no fire upstairs, so you're down here on the settee, but you be glad you're not on Lambeth Walk, like I was, with your dad up on that roof."

May huffed and glared and turned her face away towards the wallpaper behind the couch, smoke cured so that its pimply rose designs had each turned with the faltering indoor light into a sad-faced tawny lioness. She'd heard it told that many times before – the tale of how she'd come into the world on cobbles flecked with phlegm and orange peel, her dad perched like a gargoyle up above – as if it somehow made her mother proud to start a family tree that had its roots sunk in the poorhouse and the madhouse both.

She heard a muffled bump from the front room: her brothers or her sister playing up, most probably because they were all vexed to be shut in the parlour out the way. May's sister Cora, lately turned sixteen, was keen to know what pregnancy entailed, while their Jim was as keen that he should not. Young Johnny, having reached the dirty age, just wanted to look up a woman's frock.

Her mother, who had heard the noise as well, went tutting from the room to find its source, which left May on her own with Mrs. Gibbs. The death-monger explored May's private parts as though a fragile ledger of accounts, careful as a solicitor or judge. She seemed to be above the meat and mess the way May thought a druid might have been, unmoved while cutting a lamb's throat at dawn. The hearth flames, greenish when they'd burned the shit, did not so much illuminate the scene as lend it a dull torture-chamber scowl and startle shadows from beneath its chairs. Fire-lit down one already florid cheek the older woman glanced up now at May. Ceasing her intimate inspection she next rinsed her hands and dried them on a rag, a tight smile signifying all was well.

"Let's have some light in here, shall we, my dear? It wouldn't do to have a baby born into a world without a bit of cheer."

Taking an oil lamp from the mantelpiece and lifting off its milky covering, the deathmonger produced and struck a match. Touched to the limp black caterpillar wick it yielded a small flame of mystic blue, an engineer smell, safe and workmanlike. The lamp's tall chimney, tiger-striped with soot around its base, flawed by a ghostly crack, was set back into place so that the room was steeped now in a pale, warm yellow glow. The worn-out curtains looked like velvet wine. The room's glass surfaces shone like doubloons, a splendid glitter everywhere upon the mirror and barometer, the face of the slow-thudding Roman-numbered clock. May's dark red hair burned bright as gorse at dusk, even where it was plastered to her brow or slicked down on her damp and gleaming mound. The dismal birthing-pit was quite transformed into a paint-ing done by Joseph Wright of Derby, like his air-pump or his forge. May started to make comment on the change but halfway through was interrupted by her next contraction, the most wrenching yet.

When finally her scream broke like a wave into a shingle hiss of trickling sobs the frightened girl slowly became aware of Mrs. Gibbs close by, holding her hand, hushing and humming sympathetically, as natural and comforting as bees. Her fingers had a dry and papery feel, cool at least in comparison with May's. Her voice took May back to the nursery.

"My goodness, dear, that sounded like it hurt. You've not long now, though, if I'm any judge. Just try to rest while I nip out the room and have a little conference with your mam. I think it's better if she stays through there and keeps your sister and your brothers quiet, then we can manage things between ourselves without nobody sticking in their nose. Unless of course you'd rather she be here?"

It was like Mrs. Gibbs had read May's mind. May loved her mam in the fierce, angry way that she loved all her family and friends, but just that minute she could do without Louisa's tales of greater suffering, of waters broken far more copiously, as if pain and embarrassment were just a competition her and May were in. May looked up eagerly at Mrs. Gibbs.

"Ooh, no, keep her through there, if you don't mind. If I hear her tell anybody else about how I popped out on Lambeth Walk with our dad watching from the bloody roof, I swear to God I'll wring her bloody neck."

Mrs. Gibbs chuckled, a most pleasant sound, like several apples rolling down the stairs.

"Well, now, we shouldn't want that, should we, dear? You just sit tight and I won't be two shakes."

With that the deathmonger slipped from the room, removing with her a faint pepper scent of snuff, unnoticed until it was gone. May lay there on the settee, breathing hard, and heard the muffled chat from the front room. A single yelp of protest that May thought was probably their Johnny sounded, then the voice of Mrs. Gibbs raised sharp and clear despite the bricks and plaster in the way.

"If I was you, my dear, I'd learn my place. If a deathmonger says to do a thing, then you be sure that you do what she says. We shoulder life. We know its ins and outs. We've felt the draft at either end of it. What you're most frit of, that's our bread and jam, and none of us ain't got no time to spare on ignorant, bad-mannered little boys. Don't you dare leave that spot while I'm at work."

There was a subdued mumble of assent, footsteps and doors closed in the passageway, then Mrs. Gibbs came back into the room, all crinkling smiles with Punch and Judy cheeks as if she hadn't just that moment scared a cheeky twelve-year-old out of his skin. Her voice, severe with frost a minute back, was sweet and oak-matured as a liqueur.

"There, now. I think we've got things straightened out. Your youngest brother didn't like it much and started on at me, but I was firm."

May nodded. "That's our Johnny acting up. He's always full of talk and big ideas of him on stage or in the music hall, though doing what, he hasn't got a clue."

Mrs. Gibbs laughed. "He knows already how to make a show of himself, right enough."

It was just then the pain-tide came back in, smashing her bones like driftwood, she felt sure, before receding with an undertow May knew could drag her off, out of this world. One in five mothers died in childbirth still, and May grew faint to think how many times these agonising straits had been the last of life that countless women ever knew. To pass from this delirium to death, knowing the babe you'd carried for so long would in all likelihood be joining you, knowing your family's lineage was crushed to nothing in the hard gears of the world, that bloody millstone grinding till time's end. She clenched her teeth upon the dread of it. She whined and strained until her face went red, the freckles almost bursting from her cheeks, which earned a stern rebuke from Mrs. Gibbs.

"You're pushing! You don't want to push just yet. You'll hurt the baby and you'll hurt yourself. You breathe, girl. You just breathe. Breathe like a dog."

May tried to pant but then burst into tears as the contraction drew back from its edge, subsiding to a mere residual ache. She knew that she would die here in this room, pretty May Warren, not turned twenty yet, breathing incinerated excrement. She had a terrible presentiment of some awesome occurrence bearing down – of the uncanny, hovering close by – and took it for her own mortality. She only gradually became aware that she was holding the deathmonger's hand as Mrs. Gibbs crouched there beside the couch, wiping away the dew of May's ordeal, crooning and whispering to her soothingly.

"Don't fret. You're doing well. You'll be all right. My mam was a deathmonger before me, and her mam and grandmother before her. I wouldn't like to swear in all that time we've never lost a mother or a child, but we haven't lost many. I've lost none. You're in safe hands, my dear, safe as they come. Besides, you're from old-fashioned healthy stock. I understand you're Snowy Vernall's girl."

May winced and shrugged. Her dad embarrassed her. He was half-barmy, everyone knew that, at least since he'd been took to court last year, had up for standing on the Guildhall roof after he'd spent all morning in the pub, drunk as a lord with one of his arms round the waist of that stone angel what's up there, declaiming rubbish to the puzzled crowd that had collected down in Giles Street. What he'd been thinking of nobody knew. He'd worked at the town hall not long before, up by its ceiling on a scaffolding retouching the old frescos round the edge, but since his escapade up on the roof had been in all the papers it was clear he'd never have employment there again. Folk loved his high jinks, but it wasn't them that his behaviour kept in poverty.

The stunts ensured he seldom had a job, but that was not what May resented most. The pranks weren't half the obstacle to wealth that her dad's principles had proved to be, principles nobody could understand except her father and her barmy aunt. Two years before, in nineteen hundred six, a fellow who'd admired her father's skills had offered him a business partnership, a glazier's firm that he was starting up. He'd gone on to make thousands, but back then he'd promised May's dad half-shares in it all, with one condition he insisted on: if Snowy could just keep out of the pub for two weeks the directorship was his. Dad hadn't given it a moment's thought. He'd said "I won't be told what I should do. You'll have to find your partner somewhere else." The bloody fool. It made May want to spit, to think that she was lying giving birth in Fort Street, while the glazier had a house stood three floors high up on the Billing Road. If ever Dad walked past it with May's mam he'd get an earful over what he'd done, cursing his family with impoverishment for generations after, more than like. May muttered some of this to Mrs. Gibbs.

Still smiling, the deathmonger shook her head.

"He's thought of very well around these parts, though I can see he might get on your nerves if you were living with him all the time. The thing is, he's a Vernall. So are you. Like deathmonger, that's not a term you hear nowhere 'cept in the Boroughs. Even then, half them as says it don't know what it means. They're old names, and they'll soon be gone, my dear, with all us what gets called them gone as well. Respect your father, and respect your aunt, her what you see with her accordion. They're of a type I doubt we'll know again, especially turning all that money down. Yes, you could be a rich girl now, but think. You'd have been too well off to wed your Tom, and then where should this little baby be? Things are for reasons, or they are round here."

The mention of May's husband got to her. Tom Warren treated May with more respect than any other man she'd ever known. He'd courted her like she were royalty, as if she were the daughter of a king and not that of a village idiot. The deathmonger was right. If May was rich she'd have thought Tom was after all her cash. If she'd been living up the Billing Road he'd not have got within ten yards of her. This child, that May wanted so desperately, would be one more unwritten human page.

Not that these facts let Snowy off the hook. He hadn't acted for May's benefit, but simply out of bloody-mindedness. He couldn't have known that she'd marry Tom unless he was a fortune-teller too. As always, he had pleased his bloody self with not a thought for anybody else. It was like when he'd vanish up the Smoke, walk all the way to Lambeth, gone for weeks, and what he'd done was anybody's guess. Oh, certainly he'd been doing his work and always had a pay-packet to show, but May knew that her mam Louisa thought that he had other women there as well. May thought her mam was very likely right. He was a lecherous old so-and-so who could be stood hobnobbing with his pals while looking goats and monkeys at their wives. May hoped none of it rubbed off on her Tom, who got on great shakes with his dad-in-law. That morning, as it happened, they were both off up the pub together, out the way. It had been May insisted that they go. She didn't want Tom seeing her like this.

The light was sweet as butter on the hearth, spread thick on the brass knobs that topped the grate. The hunching shadow cast by Mrs. Gibbs across the rose-papered end wall seemed vast, that of a giantess or of a Fate. Made dreamy with exhaustion May could sense some great approach, some presence drawing near, but then the brute fist clenching in her womb tore out each flimsy thread of thought like hair.

This time, although the agony was worse, May did at least remember to breathe out, panting and gasping the way she recalled she had when this pain-bundle was conceived. The thought was comical and she began to laugh, then settled for another scream. Mrs. Gibbs murmured soft encouragements. She told May she was brave and doing well, and squeezed her hand until the flood had passed.

The upset jigsaw pieces of May's thoughts were strewn across her mental carpeting, a thousand coloured, slightly different shapes she was compelled to sort and pick among, establishing each corner, then each edge, distinguishing the blue bits that were sky from those that were the Easter-speckled ground. She patiently restored her picture of herself, of who and where she was and what was going on, but the rhinoceros of childbirth came stampeding through the place again when she'd not been expecting it so soon after its previous foray, and with a rough toss of its horn undid all of her efforts to compose herself. The deathmonger released her hand and moved down to the sofa's end, between May's knees. Mrs. Gibbs's voice was firm and military, conveying urgency without alarm.

"Now you can strain and push. It's almost here. Bear up, dear, and bear down. We shan't be long."

May sealed her lips upon her bubbling shriek and forced it down instead into her loins. She felt like she was trying to shit the world. She pushed and shoved although she was convinced that all of her insides were coming out. The hurt swelled up, inflating to a rim far wider than May knew she was down there. She'd burst, she'd rupture, she'd be split in two, need stitches from her gizzard to her arse. The howl she caged behind her gritted teeth was singing like a kettle in her ears, released to fill the cramped and golden room as she boiled over in a foaming rush.

There was a stifled gasp from Mrs. Gibbs. The baby's head was out and if May looked down over the horizon of her waist she could just make out slicked-down ginger curls that were like flames, much brighter than her own.

Mrs. Gibbs stared wide-eyed, as if she'd been briefly transformed to stone. Recovering, the deathmonger snatched up a folded towel and leaned in ready to receive the birth. Why did she look so pale? What could be wrong?

The moment seemed to shimmer in and out of focus, slide from real to dream and back. Did strong wind at one point blow through the house, though all the doors and windows were shut fast? What stirred the curtains and the tablecloth and the embroidered butterflies that swarmed on the deathmonger's flapping apron hem? Mrs. Gibbs's voice, heard as if through a storm, was saying one last grunt should do the trick, then the discomforts of the last nine months just melted out of May into the couch, into relief more blissful and complete than any she'd imagined in this world. Mrs. Gibbs took the sharp knife that she'd stuck blade-down into the fresh brown garden soil around the roots of a geranium, wilting and potted on the window sill. With one determined slice, she cut the cord.

May struggled to sit up, remembering the look that was on Mrs. Gibbs's face when just the baby's head was sticking out.

"Is it all right? What's wrong? Is something wrong?"

May's voice was ragged, an enfeebled squawk. The deathmonger looked sombre and held up the towel-wrapped shape she cradled in her arms.

"I'm very much afraid there is, my dear. You have an awful beauty in this child."

As she reached for her baby May daren't look, squinting against the lamp and firelight both, the infant edge-lit copper down one side, the other cream. What had the woman meant? She realised with a sudden panicked lurch the baby hadn't cried, then heard it mew. She felt the swaddled weight move in her hands and, flinchingly, risked opening her eyes, as on a furnace or the glare of noon.

Its head was like a rosebud: though scrunched tight May knew it would be glorious unfurled. Its eyes, the ghostly blue of robins' eggs, were big as brooches, focussed on May's own. Their colour was a perfect complement to the new-born child's blazing orange hair, clear summer sky down at the terrace end, framed by Northampton brickwork set alight in the last rays of a descending sun. The baby's skin was dove white, glistening as if beneath a talcum of ground pearl, dusted with highlight on the thighs, the toes, a canvas primed awaiting the soft brush of time and circumstance and character. The wonderstruck young mother's drifting gaze lighted on her first-born's extremities, always returning as though mesmerised to those eyes, that extraordinary face. It was as though the universe had shrunk down to the tube of a kaleidoscope, a gleaming well along the length of which, from each end, child and mother's glances locked, adoring, mirrored and suspended in the amber of the moment for all time. May watched the pink purse of the hatchling's lips work round the shapes of its first burbling sounds, quicksilver spittle in a glinting bead spilt from one corner, lowered on a thread. An aura seemed to hang round the event, lending a burnish, a renaissance glaze. She kissed the russet crown that had a scent like warm milk drunk in bed last thing at night, and knew that she possessed a treasure here. She realised that somehow she'd brought forth a vision of unearthly loveliness so exquisite it unnerved Mrs. Gibbs.

Belatedly, as though an afterthought, May also realised it was a girl.

"What shall you call her, dear?" asked Mrs. Gibbs. May looked round blankly, having quite forgot that there was anybody in the room save for her tiny daughter and herself.

She had agreed with Tom that, if a boy, their offspring should be Thomas, after him, whereas a girl would be named after her.

"We thought we'd call her May, like me" she said. The child's ears seemed to prick up at her name, her round head rolling, shifting restlessly on the lamp-yellowed halo of the towel. Mrs. Gibbs gave a nod, a subdued smile, seeming to be not quite recovered yet from the new baby's petrifying charm, its beautiful Medusa radiance. Was she afraid? May pushed the thought away. What, in a precious blossom such as this, was there to be afraid for? It was daft, just May's imagination running wild, all of the superstitious tommyrot surrounding birth she'd picked up off her mam. It hadn't been that many hundred years since them like Mrs. Gibbs were made to swear an oath they'd not do magic on the child, say any words while it was being born, or swap it for a fairy in its crib. That was before they'd called them deathmongers, back when such women were called other names. But that was then. This was 1908. Mrs. May Warren was a modern girl, who'd just produced a wonder of the world. She'd feed it, keep it clean, look after it, and that would do more good than paying mind to old wives' tales and reading omens in a teacup or a midwife's tone of voice.

The baby, cradled at May's ample bust, was half asleep. May turned to Mrs. Gibbs.

"She's quite a sight, my daughter, don't you think?"

Mrs. Gibbs chuckled, tidying up her things.

"She is at that, my dear. She is at that. A sight I shall remember all my life. Now, cover yourself up before they all come trooping in to see her for themselves."

The deathmonger reached down between May's thighs where with a single move, deft and discreet, she pulled the afterbirth out with a tug of the cut cord, whisking it off before May even realised that it was there. While Mrs. Gibbs got rid of it somewhere May sorted herself out as best she could. Then, just as Mrs. Gibbs had said they would, the family crowded in to take a look.

May was surprised how well-behaved they were, tiptoeing in and talking in a hush. Her mam Louisa cooed and fussed about while Jim was bright red with embarrassment or joy, beaming and nodding in delight. Cora was dumbstruck by the baby's looks, her face much like the deathmonger's had been. Even their John was at a loss for words.

"She's lovely, sis. She's grand" was all he said.

Louisa made another cup of tea for everyone, and May had one as well. It was hot nectar, strong, with sugar in, and while her mam and sister carefully passed the baby round, May sipped it gratefully. The atmosphere, the low and murmuring talk with baby May's infrequent drowsing cries, was like a church event, not even jarred when her Tom and her father came back home.

Dad smelled of beer, but Tom had nursed a half all morning long, which meant his breath was clean. May put her tea down so that they could kiss and cuddle before Tom picked up their child. He seemed amazed, kept looking back and forth between his two Mays. His expression said that he could not believe his and May's luck at turning out this painting of a child. He gave her back, then went to buy May flowers.

Her dad, half cut, declined to hold the babe, which saved the trouble of forbidding him. He'd had six pints before noon, two for lunch, bought with caricatures and rude cartoons, the funny-looking drawings Snowy did of folk, insults for which they paid in ale. Even with a prolific morning's work, May thought it odd her father had been sent on such a bender by his grandchild's birth. Just as rare for her dad, the booze appeared to have brought on a melancholy mood. He couldn't take his eyes from little May, although he viewed her through a quivering lens of tears, the soppy bugger. She'd not known her dad had got a sentimental bone in all his wide-eyed, staring, scrawny frame. She found she liked him a bit more for it. If only he were like it all the time.

Snowy now looked toward the elder May. By this time both creased lids had overflowed and wet was running down her father's cheeks.

"I didn't know, m'love. I never dreamed. I knew she'd be a smasher like your mam and you, but not a precious thing like this. Oh, this is hard, gal. She's that beautiful."

Snowy reached out and placed one hand upon May's arm, a poorly-hid crack in his voice.

"You love her, May. Love her with all you've got."

With that her father bolted from the room. They heard him clump upstairs, most probably to sleep off all the beer he'd put away. Throughout all this Mrs. Gibbs had sat quiet, drinking her tea, speaking when spoken to. May's mam Louisa slipped the deathmonger two shillings, twice the usual going rate. Firmly, Mrs. Gibbs gave one of them back.

"Now, Mrs. Vernall, with all due respect, if she'd been ugly I'd not charge half price."

Stooped by the couch she said farewell to May, who thanked the death-monger for all she'd done.

"You've been a godsend. When I have me next I'll make sure that they send for you again. I've made me mind up that I want two girls, then after that I'll stop, so I suppose you'll be back when me second daughter's due."

May got a wan smile in response to this.

"We'll see, my dear. We'll see" said Mrs. Gibbs.

She said her goodbyes to the family, the lengthiest her one to baby May, then said no one need show her from the room. She put her hat and coat on. They could hear her as she stamped along the passageway and, after fumbling briefly with the catch, went out, leaving the front door on the latch.

———

The tuneless wail of an accordion moved on the river's surface with the light and rippled the September afternoon. From where May stood upon the wrought-iron bridge between the river island and the park, her eighteen-month-old daughter in her arms, she could make out Aunt Thursa, far away, a small brown dot that walked the green's far edge towards the cattle market further up.

Although too distant to be clearly seen May could imagine all too vividly every distressing detail of her aunt, who, next to her dad Snowy, May believed to be their family's worst embarrassment. She could just picture Thursa's bird-like head with its proud beak, its pale and staring eyes, its grey hair that erupted up in tufts and looked as though her brains were smouldering. She'd have her brown coat on and her brown shoes, bloody accordion slung around her neck, an ancient mariner with albatross. Both night and day she'd wander through the streets extemporising, fingers fluttering on the grey keys of her weighty instrument. May's sense of shame would not have been so great if Thursa had displayed the faintest sign of any musical ability. Instead, her aunt made an unholy row, short stabs of falling or ascending chords all smudged into a skirling banshee wheeze, which stopped dead at the sudden precipice of Thursa's frequent random silences. From noon till midnight seven days a week you'd hear her frightening cacophony, winding amongst the yards and chim-neypots, that scared cats and woke babies in their cribs, that scattered birds and showed the Vernalls up. Stood there upon the bridge, May watched the speck of noisy sepia that was her aunt as, like a heron, the madwoman picked her way along the shore of Beckett's Park, where leaves frothed up against Victoria Prom. When Thursa and her grim accompaniment both faded in the distance, May turned back to the blonde infant cradled in her arms.

The red hair that May's daughter had at birth had fallen out and come back as white-gold, luminous catkins in a halo blaze that looked, if anything, more glorious than the hot copper with which she'd been born. Looked even more unearthly, certainly. The younger May grew lovelier each day, to May and Tom's uneasy wonderment. She'd hurt to look at if it carried on. Both parents had at first merely assumed their child was only marvellous to them, that friends were being complimentary, but gradually had come to realise from the reaction everywhere she went that this was beauty without precedent, beauty that startled up a flock of gasps, a nervous awe, as if onlookers saw a Ming vase or the first of a new race.

May purred and drew her baby close to her so that their foreheads touched, pebble to rock, and so that their eyelashes almost beat against each other's like two courting moths. The child gurgled with unrestrained delight, her sole response to nearly everything. She seemed that pleased to simply be alive and evidently found the world at large just as astonishing as it found her.

"There. All that nasty racket's gone away. That was your auntie Thursa who's half sharp, out with her squeeze-box kicking up a fuss. But she's cleared off now, so that me and you can get on with our visit to the park. Out on the island there might be some swans. Swans. Should you like that? Here, I'll tell you what, let your mam get into her pocket here, and you can have another rainbow drop."

Fumbling in a side vent of her skirt her fingers found the small brown paper cone, top twisted, that she'd bought at Gotch's shop in Green Street on their way down to the park. One-handed, with her other full of child, May unscrewed and then opened up the bag, reaching in to retrieve three chocolate drops, hundreds-and-thousands speckling their tops, one for her infant daughter, two for her. She held the first sweet to her baby's lips, which opened with a comic eagerness to let May place it on the minute tongue, then pressed the two remaining chocolate discs together into one, shaped like a lens, the coloured flecks now beading the outside in little dots like the French painters used. She popped it in her mouth and sucked it smooth, her favourite way of eating rainbow drops.

With little May against one shoulder like a set of bagpipes not in current use she sauntered from the slight hump of the bridge onto the island's sparse and yellowed grass. The isle, two or three acres all in all, had the Nene forked around it to its north, continuing as two streams that re-joined to form one river at the land's south tip. A foot-worn path ran round the island's edge, enclosing at the centre marshy ground that was sometimes a pond, but not today. Once off the railed bridge May turned to her right, starting an anti-clockwise circuit of the riverside, breeze in her dark red hair, her daughter slobbering chocolate on her neck. Some clouds slid through the azure overhead so that May's shadow faded then sprang back, but otherwise it was a perfect day.

She walked now with the water on her right and the broad swathe of Beckett's Park beyond, its old pavilion tinted lime by moss, its benches, bushes, and its public lavs, trees scorched by autumn starting to catch fire. The river's mirror-ribbon ran below the dark reach of the overhanging boughs, reflecting shattered umber, cloudy sage, torn scraps of sky in peacock blue beneath the medalled shimmer of its rippled breast.

If today was a Sunday, there'd have been chaps renting boats out from the peeling hut propped up between the crowding elms there on the bank towards its cattle-market end. Most weekends, if the weather was all right, you'd find half of the Boroughs down the park in their best bonnets, walking arm in arm, shrieking and laughing as they rowed upstream through trailing willow fingers for a lark. The chimney-sweep from Green Street, Mr. Paine, who'd got one of them wind-up gramophones, would take it out with him on his hired boat. It was nice, hearing music out of doors; nice seeing Mr. Paine play sweet old songs while he cruised down the river in amongst the lovebirds and the splashing families. It made it seem as if times weren't so bad.

May got on well with Mr. Paine. He'd once shown her the flowers he'd grown in his back yard, which was just down from Gotcher Johnson's shop. Crammed into the brick rectangle there'd been more colours than she'd ever seen before, sprouting from a bewildering array of makeshift flowerpots. Pinks bloomed from tins. Apothecary jars spilled marigolds. Cracked pisspots brimmed with fragrant jasmine sprays. May liked the Green Street crowd in general. She'd often thought that one day her and Tom might find a decent house to rent down there, away from Fort Street and her mam and dad, perhaps not far off from the chimney-sweep who'd got Eden in saucepans out the back, whose murmuring Victrola charmed the crowds out strolling on the Sunday riverbanks. And he loved little May. Who didn't, though?

The riverside path curved round to the left, its grass a threadbare carpet, pile rubbed flat by strolling old men, lovers, truant boys. May followed it towards the isle's far side, her pace unhurried and her skirt's thin hem billowing at her ankles in the breeze. Head on her mother's shoulder, little May was chattering fluently, unhindered by irrelevant concerns like sense or words.

Of course, May understood that while her child was almost universally admired, some people's admiration might be shown in ways that were intolerably cruel. There'd been that afternoon some months before when her and Tom were walking in this park, having a Sunday outing with young May. They'd carried her or let her trot a while between them, holding one of her hands each, lifting her up for slow suspended leaps to skim the puddles and the buttercups. There'd been a well-dressed couple marching by, keeping their distance from the Boroughs types, keeping at nose's length, the way they do. The woman with her gloves and parasol stared at the Warrens and their little girl, remarking to her husband as they passed, "You know, it does upset me when I see a tiny child as beautiful as that being brought up by people of their sort."

The bloody cheek. The bloody, bloody cheek that woman had, to say a thing like that. Tom yelled "You what?" at their retreating backs but they just walked on like they hadn't heard. May could remember how she'd cried herself to sleep that night, face hot and red with shame. You'd think that her and Tom were animals, not to be trusted with a baby girl. May knew, just from the woman's tone of voice, that if the couple could have found some means to have May's daughter took away from her, then they'd have done it without thinking twice. The incident had sparked a fierce resolve, a fire that scorched her throat and stung her eyes. She'd show them. She'd look after little May better than some posh woman could have done.

Mother and child had by now wandered round the island's northern, cattle-market end, dawdling along beside the river's edge towards Midsummer Meadow and the south. The baby's eyes, clear blue like winter sky, gazed fascinated at the central bog where ducks with heads beer-bottle emerald still pecked and fussed near almost emptied nests. Far off, a factory horn made brief complaint.

Around May's snub-nosed shoes were ghost-green leaves with queer pods bulging from their fallen stems. Split with a thumbnail they'd have grubs inside, the offspring (or so May's dad had once said) of small black flies who'd lay eggs in the bud, deforming it to what was called a gall. It was a nasty thought, but better than the first conclusion she had drawn, which was that worms and maggots somehow grew on trees, signs of death blossoming unnaturally from leafy boughs that represented life. The bank was strewn, beside the blighted leaves, with other bits of litter here and there: dog muck blanched by a diet of well-gnawed bones, an empty packet of ten Craven 'A' that had the black cat mascot on its box in sodden cardboard and a half-inch tall, now at the mercy of the island's birds.

Apart from this there was a pair of pants, a set of ladies' bloomers in the grass between the tree roots, white and crumpled up. Some couple had come here to have it off far from the gaslights on Victoria Prom, the river's tinkle lost beneath their groans, then not cleared up behind them when they'd done. May tutted, though she'd done the same herself with Tom before they'd married, here at night beside the river, him on top of her, then afterwards they'd sit here and they'd talk, propped up together underneath a tree. Head resting on Tom's breast she'd heard his heart, both gazing off towards the stream's

far side, the scrublands and the railway tracks that stretched off to the abbey
out at Delapre. She'd listened to him, quiet and wonderstruck, while he told
her his tales from history, the subject that had been Tom's best at school. The
whole Wars of the Roses, he'd explained, the wars between the Lancasters
and Yorks, had been decided on the soil across the river from where May was
walking now. The King was captured on the waste-ground that the Boroughs
thought of still as its back yard. She'd sprawled there, half asleep and marvelling at the important things these fields had seen, at the low voice of her
husband-to-be, whose spunk hung cooling from the dandelions. The memory
made May warm between her thighs so that she had to stop and shake her
head to clear it before she could concentrate on her and young May's Friday
afternoon. She went on, curving round the isle's south end and back in the
direction of the bridge.

Re-entering the main grounds of the park she peeped to see if Thursa
was nearby. Her aunt, however, was by then long gone, as were the other sorts
who'd been about. Perhaps her aunt had led them dancing off Pied Piper fashion with a cockeyed tune on her accordion, brown coat a-flap, her grey hair
streaming like a chimney fire. May laughed and so did young May, joining in.

The only other people she could see were up near Derngate and the hospital, mothers or governesses pushing prams by Becket's Well at the park
corner there. Snobs. Why, even their servants put May off, looked at her like
they thought she'd steal their purse, despite being no better born than her …
although that wasn't strictly speaking true. Being hatched in a gutter full of
shit, near everyone was better born than May.

That didn't make her a bad mother, though. It didn't mean that woman
had been right. She took more care of her own little girl than all the la-di-da
types did of theirs. May looked after her daughter to a fault, at least if what
the doctor said was right. What that had been, young May kept getting colds,
just coughs and sniffles how most babies do. The doctor came to see her, Dr.
Forbes, annoyed he'd been called out so many times, and they'd had words,
him and the older May. He'd led her out onto her own front step and pointed
further off down Fort Street's length to where the simple girl from down the
way was sitting on the cold, uneven flags with a toy tea-set spread out all
around, sharing black puddle-water with her dolls.

"You see? That child is healthier than yours, because her mother lets her
play outside. Your baby, Mrs. Warren, keeps too clean to build up a resistance
to disease. Let her get dirty! Don't they say you've got to eat a peck of dirt
before you die?"

It was all very well for him to talk, him up Horsemarket in his doctor's
house. Nobody would accuse him or his wife of being unfit to bring up a child,
the way that old cow had with her and Tom. His children, May knew, could

have mucky knees and nobody would think the worse of him. It wouldn't be him that got talked about, or be his wife what cried herself to sleep with the humiliation of it all. Having some money spared you all of that. The Doctor didn't know what it was like.

Here young May shifted in her mother's arms and pulled a face. It was her ugliest one, although it would have shamed a work of art. If the wind changed and she'd been stuck like that, May's baby would still knock spots off Miss Pears. The reason for her daughter's restlessness was more than likely want of rainbow drops. She reached in her skirt's pocket for the bag, discovering they'd only got three left. Giving May one she pressed the other two into another sandwich for herself. With her miniature vision in the crook of one arm, so May senior went on beside the railings and the lavatories towards the dung-chute of Victoria Prom. The sun was lower. Time was getting on. She didn't want to keep her little girl outdoors too long, despite old Forbes's advice. With little May not long rid of one cough some fresh park air had seemed a good idea, but there was no sense overdoing things. They'd best get home and in the warm while there was still some bright, and it was quite a walk. Stepping from under tea-leaf coloured trees they turned left on the curving promenade and carried on through cattle market musk towards the iron gas-holder's rotund bulk.

May passed the Plough Hotel across the road at Bridge Street's mouth, continuing until the pair had reached the foot of Horseshoe Street where they turned right, beginning the long trudge uphill along this eastern boundary line into the Boroughs' grubby, glad embrace, into its welcoming and soot-streaked arms. The sun was a Montgolfier balloon descending on the railway station yards. Breeze stirred the pale curds of her daughter's hair and May was pleased she'd brought her out today. There was a feeling in the air, perhaps brought on by sunset or the autumn's cool, as if these hours were a last precious glimpse of something, of the summer or the day, which made them twice as flawless and as fair. Even the Boroughs, with its bricks rubbed raw, seemed to be trying to look its very best. A wealth of newly-smelted golden light slicked its slate rooftops and its guttering, spread blinding scum on the rainwater tubs. The scraps of lilac cloud over Bellbarn were handbill fragments, torn, left pasted up on the great awning's deepening blue above. The world seemed so rich, so significant, like an oil painting May was walking through with her Gainsborough baby on her hip.

Across the trot and creak of Horseshoe Street, its cobbles greased with fibrous olive smears, was wasteland where St. Gregory's once stood, or so May's dad had told his daughter once. There'd been some tale about an old stone cross a monk had brought here from Jerusalem, so as to mark the centre of his land. They'd set it in an alcove at the church, and for some centuries it was a shrine where folk made pilgrimages and all that. "Rood in the Wall" they called it. 'Rood' meant cross, though in May's mind she mixed it up with 'rude' and thought of the stone cross as plain or coarse, chipped ruggedly with rudimentary tools from hard grey rock, rough-cut and biblical. The monk was sent by angels, so he'd said. Angels were common in the Boroughs then, gone now unless you counted little May. The church itself was also long since gone, with only nearby Gregory's Street to mark the fact that it was ever there at all. Now buddleia and nettle ruled the plot, the first with fallen petals thick as meat, the latter thrusting white and senile heads up into the last spare rays of the sun, lit with a burning citrine at their tips. To think it was the centre of the land.

The baby chuckled, clutched against May's side, so that her mother turned to see what for. Some way uphill, where Gold Street and Marefair cut across Horsemarket and Horseshoe Street to form a crossroads, on the corner there outside Vint's Palace of Varieties a slim young fellow leaned against the wall, looking away then slyly looking back as he played peek-a-boo with little May.

Her daughter seemed enchanted by the man, and an inspection forced May to admit that there was much to be enchanted by. He wasn't tall but had a slenderness, a litheness, not a wiriness like Tom. The fellow's hair was blacker than his shoes, a springy nest of unwound liquorice whips. His girlish, long-lashed eyes were darker still, batting flirtatiously to tease the child. Fancied himself, May thought. And fancied her.

She knew the type, their baby strategy: strike up a conversation through the tot, so your advances won't seem obvious. She'd had that quite a bit when she'd been out with little May in this last year-and-half. With such a lovely offspring, it was nice to sometimes get attention of her own. May didn't mind a whistle and a wink, so long as it weren't from a lush or thug. Or if it was, she could soon brush them off, was tough enough to look after herself. But if the lad should be presentable, like this one was, she didn't think it hurt to flirt a bit, or pass five minutes' chat. It wasn't that she didn't love her Tom nor had her eye on anyone but him, but she'd been quite a smasher as a girl, and sometimes missed the looks and compliments. Besides, as they drew closer to this bloke May had a feeling that she knew his face, though for the life of her she couldn't think where it was that she recognised him from. If it weren't that, then it was déjà vu, that feeling like something's happened before. Also, May's daughter seemed to like the chap, who had the knack for making children laugh.

The next time that he turned, mock-shyly, round to sneak a peek at little May he found her mother gazing back at him as well. May spoke first, taking the initiative, saying he'd an admirer in her child, and he came back with something daft about how he'd just been admiring little May. He knew as well as she did this was tosh, and that he'd had his eye on big May too, but they both played along with the pretence. Besides, he could see now that she were wed.

He made an awful fuss of little May, but seemed for the most part to be sincere, saying as how she'd end up on the stage and be a famous beauty of her time and all that. He was on the stage himself, appearing at Vint's Palace later on and only idling on the corner while he had a fag or two to calm his nerves. And look at women, May thought to herself, but let it pass since she enjoyed his talk. She introduced herself and baby May. He said to call him "Oatsie" in return, which was a nickname she'd not heard for years, not since she'd lived down Lambeth as a girl. This set wheels turning in May's mind until she worked out where she'd seen Oatsie before.

He'd been a small boy of about May's age who'd lived in West Square off St. George's Road. She'd seen him, when out with her mam and dad, and recognised him by the pretty eyes. He'd had a brother, older than himself as she recalled, but when she told him this he looked at her as if he'd seen a ghost, out of a past he'd thought behind him now. He looked at her as if he'd been found out. The man's confusion and pop-eyed surprise made May laugh. He'd not been expecting that. He'd bit off more than he could chew with her. She played him on in this way for a while, then, taking pity, let him off the hook, confessing that she too was Lambeth born. He looked relieved. He'd evidently thought she was a Sybil or an oracle, not just an escaped cockney like himself.

Put in his place like this it was as if he didn't need to go through such an act, and their street-corner chat grew more relaxed and warm, without the need for any show. They nattered on discussing this and that, her brother John's ambitions on the stage, the history of Vint's Palace where they stood, and so on, him and her and little May in cheery conference while the Boroughs sky turned from brocade to sapphire overhead. At last, her daughter squirming in her arms, and mindful there were no more rainbow drops, May knew she'd better get the baby home to have her meat-paste sandwiches for tea. She said her farewells to the handsome clown and wished him good luck with his show that night. He told her to take care of little May. She didn't think it odd, not at the time.

The climb up Horsemarket didn't take long although, after some hours of walking round, the child seemed heavier in May's tired arms. Ascending past the lofty houses there, the doctors' residences, lit up warm, she wondered which belonged to Dr. Forbes. Past open curtains children home from school sat on plump sofas next to roaring fires, ate muffins, or else read improving books. She felt briefly resentful at her dad. If he'd not sniffed at that director's job, if just once her old man had spared a thought for someone other than his wilful self, that could be her and little May in there, well-fed and snug, May's daughter on her knee and being read to from a picture book with embossed covers and bright tipped-in plates. She snorted, and turned up St. Mary's Street.

The heavens in the west ahead of her showed bruises from the roughhouse of the day, purpling into dark above the roofs of Pike Lane and Quart Pot Lane further on. It startled May, the way the nights fell in when you got close to this end of the year. St. Mary's Street looked haunted in the gloom. Its alcove doorsteps sucked the shadows in, and splintered work-yard gates clanked on their chains. May strode on with her child held up in front like a blonde candle through the crowding dusk.

She'd have to say she weren't at all surprised that this was where the great fire had broke out, back two hundred and something years ago. There was a simmering feel about the place, as if it could boil over into harm at any time, quick as you could say 'knife'. No doubt it went back to the Civil War with all the Roundheads bivouacked near here, Cromwell and Fairfax kipping over-night in Marefair, parallel to Mary's Street, before they went to Naseby the next day and sealed King Charlie's and the country's fate. Wasn't it Pike Lane where they'd made the pikes? That's what May's dad had said, at any rate. She carried on and over Doddridge Street, continuing across the burial ground that ran from Doddridge Church down to Chalk Place. The Reverend Dodd-ridge, who had preached down here, while not a terrible destructive force like old Oliver Cromwell or the fire was as incendiary in his own way, fighting for Nonconformists and the poor, and suited the spot's troublemaker air. May pressed on through the bone-yard's overgrowth and hoped her daughter wasn't getting cold.

In Chalk Lane, by the chapel's western wall, little May started kicking up a fuss and pointing to that queer door halfway up, as if wanting to know what it was for.

"Don't ask me, love, I haven't got a clue. Come on, let's get you home and lay the fire for when your dear old dad comes back from work."

Except a burp, young May made no reply as Castle Terrace led to Bristol Street. The lamps were going on at the far end which meant that Mr. Beery was about, walking from post to post with his long pole, angling it up towards the gaslight's top, flame held beside the jet until it caught. He looked like he was fishing for the dark, using his little glow-worm light as bait. May's child cooed at the distant, greenish gleams as though they were a Roman candle show.

They went on, heading for the Fort Street turn, when from the unlit terrace at May's heels there came a washboard clatter drawing near, a rattling sound as someone dragged a plank across the bumping cobbles to their rear. A voice as rich as broth called out "Why, Mrs. May and Missy May! You ladies been off gallivant-ing all around the town, I bet, you only just now coming home!"

It was Black Charley, him from Scarletwell who had the rag-and-bone cart and the bike with ropes all round their wheels instead of tyres. The sound she'd heard had been the blocks of wood he had strapped on his feet to use as brakes. May laughed to see him, but then told him off for scaring them, although in truth he'd not. He was a local marvel, who she liked. He brought a touch of magic to the place.

"Black Charley! Blummin 'eck, you made me jump!" She told him there should be a law that forced black men to carry sparklers after dark, so you could see them creeping up on you, then thought it was a silly thing to say. For one thing, there weren't black men round these parts. There was just him, Black Charley, Henry George. Also, she knew her quip made no more sense than if he'd said white people should black up so he could see them coming at midday. He didn't take offence though. He just laughed and made the usual fuss of baby May, saying she was an angel and all that, a compliment May briskly swept aside. Angels were mostly a sore point with her, part of the madness in the Vernall clan. Her dad and granddad and her barmy aunt had all insisted that such things were real, which, in May's own opinion, said it all. Nobody took stuff like that seriously, or at least nobody who was all there. They hadn't since the times of that old monk who'd brought the cross here from Jerusalem. The only angel, little May aside, was that white stone one on the Guildhall roof her dad had cuddled with when he'd been drunk. Besides, May found thoughts like that frightening, great winged chaps watching over people's lives and knowing what would happen 'fore it did. It was like ghosts or anything like that, it made you think of death, or else that life was a big, foggy, overwhelming place you knew would kill you going in the door. She didn't dwell upon unearthly things. Anyway, angels would be snobs, May knew, judging her like that pair in Beckett's Park.

She chatted to Black Charley for a while, and little May, God bless her, tried her best, calling him Char-Char and grabbing the beard that grew in a white frizz around his chin. Eventually, they let him cycle on, shouting goodbye in his deep Yankee voice, down Bristol Street back home to Scarletwell, which was a street May didn't like to go. It just gave her the willies, that was all, although there was no reason why it should. There was that funny creature of Newt Pratt's, on Sundays, drunk outside the Friendly Arms, but that weren't what frit May about the street. Perhaps it was the bloody-sounding name, or else that up round Scarletwell they kept the fever cart, high windows, leaded glass, that let in light but wouldn't let you see the poor buggers inside that it took off, with scarlet fever or that other one whose name May wasn't sure how to pronounce, to camps out on the edges of the town. Whatever it was that got on her nerves about the old hill, you could safely say as Scarletwell Street weren't May's favourite place. That might change, she supposed, in a few years when she was traipsing up there every day and taking little May to Spring Lane School, but until then she'd give it a wide berth.

May turned left into Fort Street where there was no cobbled road, just flagstones wall to wall. Although she knew it bent round to the right at its far point and ran along the back of Moat Street, sloping down into Bath Row, her home street always looked like a dead end where vehicles couldn't go, that led nowhere of very much importance anyway. Her daughter was now bouncing up and down with shrill excitement in May's freckled arms, the child having by this point recognised the dear, familiar row down which they walked. May clacked on over the rough tilting slabs and past her mam and dad's house, number ten. Gaslight was shining from their passageway out through cracks round the poorly hung front door; the parlour dark, empty save ornaments.

Johnny and Cora and her mam and dad would at this time of night most likely be round the tea-table in the living room, having their bread and jam and bit of cake. She went on to her own house, number twelve, and opened its unlocked door with one hand, not putting May down 'til she was inside. She lit the mantle first, then lit a fire, sticking her daughter into the high chair while she went to retrieve the potted meat from the tin safe atop the cellar stairs. She made the baby's tea and served it up after she'd carefully trimmed off all the crusts. Little May slowly ate her sandwiches, taking her time, making a lot of mess, while her mam took the opportunity to do a nice liver and onion roll, then put it in the stove for her and Tom.

The evening nigh on flew by after that. Tom got home from the brewery where he worked, his Friday night pay-packet in his hand, in time to say goodnight to little May before she got took off upstairs to bed, up the apples and pears to Uncle Ned. Next her and Tom had dinner by themselves, then chatted until they retired as well. They cuddled once the candle was blown out, then May asked Tom to pull her nightgown up and get on top so he could put it in. It was their favourite time, a Friday night. No need to get up early the next day, when with a bit of luck their little girl would sleep in long enough for May and Tom to have another fuck when they woke up. Beneath her man, May hardly spared a thought for that chap by Vint's Palace earlier on.

By Saturday, their daughter's cough was back and it seemed like she had a job to breathe. They called old Forbes out, Sunday afternoon, when they'd meant to be walking in the park. The doctor turned up, as he always did, moaning about them spoiling his weekend, then shut up after he'd seen little May. The child's skin had took on a yellow cast which they'd both hoped they were imagining.

He said their baby had diphtheria.

The wagon from the top of Scarletwell was summoned. Little May was placed aboard and off it went, windows of leaded glass placed too high up its sides to see in through. The hooves and coach-wheels hardly made a sound, rolling away down the uncobbled lane as the one ray of light that lit May's heart was taken off inside the fever cart.

———

The second time that Mrs. Gibbs called round she had a different coloured apron on, black where the previous one was pristine white. When May recalled it afterwards she thought that it had had a decorated hem, Egyptian beetles in viridian embroidered there instead of butterflies. That was just her imagination, though. The apron was an unadorned plain black.

May was sat by herself in the front room. The half-sized coffin, resting on two chairs like a mesmerist's audience volunteer, was by the window at the room's far end. Her baby's sleeping face looked grey, suffused by dusty light decanted through the nets. She'd no doubt look all right when she woke up. Oh, stop it, May thought to herself. Just stop. Then she began to shake and cry again.

The cruellest thing was that they'd brought her home. After a week May's child had been sent back to Fort Street from the remote fever camp, so May and Tom had thought she'd be all right. But what did they know of diphtheria? They couldn't even say it properly and called it 'Dip' like everybody else. They didn't know that it came in two parts, or that most people got over the first only to have the next stage take them off. Weakened by the onset of the disease, they'd got no fight left when it stopped their hearts. Especially young children, so they said. Especially, May thought, the ones whose mams had kept their little boys and girls too clean. Whose mams had been concerned lest people say that they weren't fit to take care of a child, and then gone on to prove those people right.

It was her fault. She knew it was her fault. She'd been too proud. Pride came before a fall, that's what they said, and sure enough it did. May felt as if she'd fell out of her life, the lovely life she'd had two weeks before. She'd fell out of her dreams, her hopes. She'd fell out of the woman that she thought she was into this dreadful moment and this room, the coffin and that bloody noisy clock.

"Oh, my poor little darling. My poor lamb. I'm here, my love. Mam's here. You'll be all right. I shan't let anything bad ..." May trailed off. She didn't know what she'd been going to say, hated the sound of her own useless voice making a promise she'd already broke. All of the times she'd comforted her child and told her she'd always look after her, sworn sacred oaths like every mother does then let her daughter down so wretchedly. Said she'd always be there for little May but didn't even know, now, where 'there' was. Just eighteen months, that's all they'd had with her; that was as long as they'd kept her alive. They'd joined that tragic and exclusive club folk whispered sympathetically about and yet preferred to keep their distance from, as though May were in quarantine for grief.

She wasn't even thinking, sitting there. Thoughts wouldn't stick together anymore, led nowhere that she was prepared to go. What filled her was a wordless, shapeless hurt, and the enormity of that small box.

There were black holes burnt in the hearthside rug that she'd not noticed, prior to today. The wicker footstool was unravelling. Why was it such hard work to keep things new?

The door being as usual on the latch, May didn't hear the deathmonger come in. She just glanced up from studying the rug and Mrs. Gibbs was stood beside the chair, her apron showing up the dust flecks like the powdered, folded wings of a black moth. It was as if the previous eighteen months had never happened, as though Mrs. Gibbs had never even truly left the house that first time. There'd just been a change of light, a change of apron, butterflies all gone, embroidered summer's day replaced by night. It was a 'spot the difference' picture game. The baby had been switched on May as well. Her lovely copper cub had disappeared and in its place was just this hard blonde doll. And May herself, that was another change. She wasn't who she'd been when she gave birth.

In fact, upon closer inspection May realised that the whole picture was now wrong, with nothing else but differences to spot. Only the deathmonger remained the same, although she'd put on a new pinafore. Her cheeks, like Christmas stocking tangerines, weren't changed a bit, nor her expression which could mean whatever you supposed it meant.

"Hello again, my dear," said Mrs. Gibbs.

May's "hello" in reply was made from lead. It left her lips and thudded on the mat, a lump of language, blunt and colourless, from which no conversation could be built. The deathmonger stepped round it and went on.

"If you don't feel like talking, dear, then don't. Not lest you need to but you don't know how, in which case you can tell me all you want. I'm not your family, and I'm not your judge."

May's sole reaction was to look away though she conceded, at least inwardly, that Mrs. Gibbs had hit on something there. She'd had no one to talk to properly these last two days, she thought, except herself. She couldn't speak above two words to Tom without she'd weep. They set each other off, and they both hated crying. It was weak. Besides, Tom wasn't there. He was at work. May's mam, Louisa, that was useless, too, not just because her mam wept easily. It was more May had let her mother down. She'd not been a good mother in her turn, not kept up the maternal tapestry. She'd dropped a stitch and failed the family. She couldn't face them, and they couldn't help. Her aunt's attempt had been an awful scene that May was keeping shut out of her mind.

As a result, May had been left cut off. It was her fault, along with all the rest, but she was stuck with nobody to tell about all that was going on inside, the frightening thoughts and ideas what she had, too bad to say out loud to anyone. Yet here she was, and here was Mrs. Gibbs, a stranger, outside May's immediate clan or any clan as far as May could see, except that of the death-mongers themselves. Mrs. Gibbs seemed outside of everything, as carefully impartial as the sky. Her apron, deep and private like a night, or like a well, was a receptacle that May could empty all this horror in without it ringing round her brood for years. May raised her sore red eyes only to find the other woman's grey ones gazing back.

"I'm sorry. I don't know what I shall do. I don't know how I shall get over it. They're burying her tomorrow afternoon and then I shan't have nothing left at all."

May's voice was rusty, cracking with disuse, a crone's voice, not a twenty-year-old girl's. The deathmonger pulled up the fraying stool, then sat down at May's feet and took her hand.

"Now, Mrs. Warren, you listen to me. You're not to tell me you've got nothing left. You're not to even think it of yourself. If nothing's left, what was your child's life worth? Or any of our lifetimes, come to that? It's all got value, else none of it has. Or do you wish you'd not had her at all? Should you prefer that you'd not seen me once if you were going to have to see me twice?"

She took it in and found it was all true. Put like that, asked in such straight-forward terms if little May were better never born then she could only dumbly shake her head. The lank red strands, uncombed, fell on her face. She'd not got nothing, she'd got eighteen months of feeding, burping, going down the park, laughing and crying, changing tiny clothes. The fact remained, though, that she'd not got May. She'd got her memories of her little girl, favourite expres-sions, gestures, favourite sounds, but they were painful in the knowledge that there'd be no new ones added to the list. And that was just her sorrow's selfish part, her pitying herself for what she'd lost. It was her baby should be pitied more, who'd gone into the dark all on her own. May looked up hopelessly at Mrs. Gibbs.

"But what about her? What about my May? I want to think she's up in Heaven but she's not, is she? That's just what you tell kids about their cat or dog when all the time you've found it with its back broke in the street."

At this she wept again despite herself and Mrs. Gibbs gave her a handker-chief, then squeezed May's hand between her papery palms, a bible closing on May's fingertips.

"I don't hold much in Heaven, personally, nor in the other place. It sounds like tosh. All I know is, your daughter's upstairs now, and whether you believe me or you don't is none of my concern and none of hers. That's where she is, my dear. That's what I know, and I'd not say it if I wasn't sure. She's upstairs, where we all are by and by. Your dad's told you already, I dare say."

The mention of May's father made her start. He had said that. He'd used that very word. "She's upstairs, May. Don't fret. She's upstairs now." In fact, now that she thought, she'd never heard him speak of death in any other way. Not him, her kin, nor anyone round here. They never said "in Heaven" or "with God", nor even "up above". They said "upstairs". It made the afterlife sound carpeted.

"You're right, he did say that, but what's it mean? You say it's not like heaven in the clouds. Where is it, this upstairs, then? What's it like?"

In May's own ears her voice was sounding cross, angry that Mrs. Gibbs was so cocksure about a thing as terrible as this. She hadn't meant it to come out that way and thought the deathmonger would take offence. To her surprise, Mrs. Gibbs only laughed.

"Frankly, it's very much like this, my dear." She gestured, at the armchair, at the room. "What else should you expect it to be like? It's much like this, only it's up a step."

May wasn't angry now. She just felt strange. Had someone said those words to her before? "It's much like this, only it's up a step." It sounded so familiar and so right, although she'd got no idea what it meant. It felt like those occasions, as a girl, when she'd been let in on some mystery, like when Anne Burk told May the facts of life. "The man puts spunk on the end of his prick, then puts it in your crack." Though May had thought spunk would be soap-flakes in a little pile, spooned on a flat-topped cock-end into her, she'd somehow known that the idea was true; made sense of things she'd previously not grasped. Or when her mam had took her to one side and gravely told her what jamrags were for. This was like that, sat here with Mrs. Gibbs. One of those moments in a human life when you found out what everybody else already knew but never talked about.

May glimpsed the coffin at the room's far end and knew immediately it was all junk. Upstairs was heaven with a different name, the same old story trotted out again to console the bereaved and shut them up. It was just Mrs. Gibbs's atmosphere, the way she had, that made it sound half-true. What did she know about the hereafter? She was a Boroughs woman, same as May. Except, of course, she was a deathmonger, which gave the rot she talked that much more weight. Mrs. Gibbs spoke again, squeezing May's hand.

"As I say, dear, it doesn't matter much if we believe these things or if we don't. The world's round, even if we think it's flat. The only difference it makes is to us. If we know it's a globe, we needn't be frit all the time of falling off its edge. But let's not talk about your daughter, dear. What's happened can't be helped, but you still can. Are you all right? What's all this done to you?"

Again, May found she had to stop and think. No one had asked her that, these last two days. It wasn't something that she'd asked herself, nor dared to in the wailing, echoing well her private thoughts had recently become. Was she all right? What had this done to her? She blew her nose on the clean hand-kerchief that she'd been given, noticing it had no butterflies, just one embroi-dered bee. When she was done, she screwed the hanky up and shoved it in one jumper-sleeve, a move that meant Mrs. Gibbs letting go May's hand, although once the manoeuvre was complete May slid her fingers voluntarily between the digits of the deathmonger. She liked the woman's touch; warm, dry, and safe in the wallpapered whirlpool of the room. Still sniffing, May attempted a reply.

"I feel like everything's fell through the floor and dropping down a tun-nel like a stone. It doesn't even feel like I'm meself. I sit and cry and can't do anything. I can't see any point in doing things, brushing me hair or eating, anything, and I don't know where all of it shall end. I wish that I was dead, and that's the truth. Then we'd be put together in one box."

Mrs. Gibbs shook her head.

"Don't say that, dear. It's both a cheap and silly thing to say, you know it is. And anyway, unless I'm wrong, you don't wish you were dead at all. It's just that you don't want to be alive because life's rough and don't make any sense. Those are two very different things, my dear. You'd do well to be sure which one you mean. One can be put right and the other can't."

The clock ticked and the tumbling dust motes stirred in sunbeams that fell slanting on the floor while May considered. Mrs. Gibbs was right. It wasn't that she truly wanted death, but that she'd lost the reason for her life. Worse than this, she had started to suspect that life, all life that walked upon the earth, had never had a reason from the start. This was a world of accident and mess without a divine plan that guided things. It weren't that God moved in mysterious ways, more that you never saw him move at all. What was the point of going on with it, the human race? Why did everyone keep on having babies, when they knew they'd die? Giving them life then snatching it away, just so you'd have some company. It was cruel. How had she ever seen things differently?

She tried conveying this to Mrs. Gibbs, the senselessness that was in everything.

"Life don't make sense. It's not made sense to me since Dr. Forbes said May had got the Dip. The fever horse come trotting up the street over the paving slabs where there's no road, when generally carts wait along the end. Just like that, she was gone. They took her off in that dark wagon, off and down Bath Row, and that was that. I stood there in the road, roaring, and chewing on me handkerchief. I shan't ever forget it, standing there ..."

Cocking her bun-crowned head upon one side, Mrs. Gibbs silently renewed her grip on May's hot hand, bidding her to go on. May hadn't realised until now how much she'd needed to recount this to someone, get it all into words and off her chest.

"Tom was there. Tom had got me in his arms to stop me running off after the cart. Me mam, at number ten, she stayed inside to keep our Cora and our Johnny quiet, so that they'd not come out and join the fuss."

Mrs. Gibbs pursed her lips enquiringly and then chimed in with what was on her mind.

"Where was your father, dear, if I might ask?"

May seemed to ponder this, and then went on.

"He was just standing out on his front step and ... no. No, he were sitting. Sitting down. I hardly noticed him, not at the time, but thinking now, he was sat on that step as if it were a Sunday in July. As if there wasn't an emergency. He looked glum, but not upset or surprised like everybody else. To tell the truth, he seemed more rattled back when she were born."

She paused. She squinted hard at Mrs. Gibbs.

"And come to think about it, you did, too. You went white as a sheet when she came out. I had to ask if anything was wrong, and you said that you were afraid there was. You said it was her beauty, said she'd got an awful beauty, I remember it. Then later on, when you were leaving you took ages over your goodbyes to her."

The penny dropped. May stared in disbelief. The deathmonger, impassively, stared back.

"You knew."

Mrs. Gibbs didn't even blink.

"You're right, my dear. I did. And so did you."

May gasped and tried to pull her hand away, but the deathmonger wouldn't let it go. What? What was this? What did the woman mean? May hadn't known her child was going to die. The idea hadn't crossed her mind. Although ...

Although she knew it had, a thousand times, scaring her in a score of different ways. The worst was feeling it was a mistake, this gorgeous child being given to her when it was clearly meant for royalty. There'd been some error, been some oversight. Sooner or later, it would get found out, like a large postal-order that had been delivered to an incorrect address. Somebody would be round to take it back. She'd known she wouldn't get away with it, not with a child what shone like hers had done. Somewhere inside her, May had always known. That was the real reason, she now saw, why she'd took that woman's remark so bad, that time in Beckett's Park. It was because it told her something she already knew and yet was keeping from acknowledging: her daughter would be took away from her. They'd hear a knock upon the door one day, someone come from the council or police, or a Barnardo's woman, looking sad. She'd just not thought it would be Dr. Forbes.

The clock ticked, and May wondered fleetingly how much time had gone by since its last beat. Mrs. Gibbs watched until she was convinced that May had took her point, then carried on.

"We know a lot more than we tell ourselves, my dear. Some of us do, at any rate. And if I'd said back when your May were born what I'd foreseen, then should I have been thanked? There's no point served in saying things like that. If you yourself had taken notice of such premonitions as you might have had, it wouldn't have prevented anything except for eighteen months of happiness."

The deathmonger sat forward on the stool, her crisp black apron almost crackling.

"Now, you'll forgive me saying this, my dear, but it appears you've took this on yourself. You think you're a bad mother, and you're not. Diphtheria don't pick and choose like that or come to people 'cause of how they live, although the poor are very vulnerable. It's a disease, dear, not a punishment. It's no reflection on you or your bab, nor a result of how you brought her up. You'll be a better mam for this, not worse. You'll have learned things not every mother learns, and you'll have learned them hard, and early on. You lost this child, but you shan't lose the next, nor them that likely follow after that. Look at you! You're a mam by nature, dear. You've got a lot of babies in you yet."

May glanced away, towards the skirting board, at which the deathmonger narrowed her eyes.

"I'm sorry if I've spoken out of turn, or said something I shouldn't ought have done."

May blushed and looked back up at Mrs. Gibbs.

"You've not done nothing. You've just hit upon one of the things been going through me mind. Them babies in me, like you said. It's daft, but I keep thinking one's already there. There's nothing what I've got to base it on, and half the ruddy time I think it's just something I've dreamed up, to make up for May. I've had no signs, but then I wouldn't do. If I'm right in this feeling what I've got, then I fell pregnant just two weeks ago. It's all a lot of nonsense, I'm quite sure, just something I've come up with that it's nice to think of, 'stead of crying all the while."

The deathmonger began to stroke May's hand, between caress and therapeutic rub.

"What is it, if it's not too personal, that makes you think you're in the family way?"

May blushed again.

"It's nonsense, like I say. It's just that ... well, it was that Friday night, before they sent the fever cart for May. I'd been out round the park with her all day and she was wore out, the poor little thing. We put her to bed early, then we thought, it being Friday, we'd go up ourselves. So then we ... well, you know. We had it off. But it was special, I can't say just how. I'd had a lovely day, and I loved Tom. I knew how much I loved him on that night, when we were in bed getting up to it, and knew as well how much he loved me back. We lay there afterwards, and it were bliss, talking and whispering like when we first met. Upon my life, afore the sweat were dry I thought "there'll be a baby come from this". Oh, Mrs. Gibbs, whatever must you think? I never should have told you all of that. It's nothing I've told anybody else. You only come round here to do your job, and here I'm dragging all me laundry out. You must think I'm a proper dirty cat."

Mrs. Gibbs patted May's hand, and she smiled.

"I've heard worse, let me tell you. Anyway, it's all included in my shilling, dear. Listening and talking, that's the biggest part. It's not the birthing or the laying out. And as for if you're pregnant or you're not, you trust your instincts. They're most likely right. Didn't you say to me you'd have two girls, and then you'd stop and not have any more?"

May nodded.

"Yes, I did. And laying there that night I thought 'here's daughter number two'. Although it's not, now, is it? It's still one."

She thought about this briefly, then went on.

"Well, it don't make no difference. I still want two little girls, same as I said before. If it turns out I've got one on the way, I'll have one more and then that shall be it."

May marvelled, hearing herself saying this. Her darling girl was cold and lying in a half-pint box down at the parlour's end, not six foot from where May was sat herself. How could she even be considering a baby, let alone one after that? Why wasn't she just sitting here in tears and trying to get herself under control, the way she had done for these past two days? As though she'd found some stopcock in her heart, the waterworks had been at last shut off. She felt like she weren't falling anymore, May realised with surprise. It wasn't like she was filled up with happiness and hope, but at least she weren't plunging down a hole that had no bottom, or light at the top. She'd hit some bedrock where she'd come to rest, a floor that didn't give beneath her grief. There was a faint chance she'd get out of this.

She knew she owed it to the deathmonger. They handled death and birth and everything that come as part of that. It was their job. These women – always women, obviously – had got some place to stand outside it all. They weren't rocked by the mortal ebb and flow. Their lives weren't those arrivals would upend, nor would departures leave them all in bits. They stood unmoved, unchanged, through all life's quakes, invulnerable to joy and tragedy. May was still young. Her daughter's birth and death had been her first exposure to these things, her first instructions in life's proper stuff, its gravity and frightening suddenness, and frankly it had all knocked her for six. How would she get through life, if life did this? She looked at Mrs. Gibbs and saw a way, a woman's way, of anchoring herself, but the deathmonger had begun to speak again before May could pursue the thought.

"Anyway, dear, I'd interrupted you. You were just telling me about the day the fever cart took off your little girl. I butted in and asked about your dad ..."

For just a mo, May looked at her gone out, and then remembered her unfinished tale.

"Ooh, yes. Yes, I remember now. Our dad, sat on the step while it were going on, like he already were resigned to it, while I stood roaring in the street with Tom. I barely noticed him, not at the time, and can't hold it against him even now. I know that I go on about our dad, how he's an old fool and he shows us up with all his climbing round the chimneypots, but he's been good to me since our May died. Me mam, the others, I can't talk to them without the whole lot ending up in tears, but our dad, it turns out, he's been a brick. He's not been down the pub or on his jaunts. He's been next door in earshot the whole time. He don't intrude. He pops in now and then to find out if there's anything I want, and for once in me life I'm glad he's there. But on that day, he just sat on the step."

May frowned. She tried to go back in her mind to Fort Street on that Sat'day dinnertime, shuddering in her husband's arms while they watched little May go trundling off inside the fever cart, across the listing flags. She tried to conjure all the sounds and smells that single moment had been made up from, sausages burning somewhere on a stove, the railway shunts and squeals come from the west.

"I stood and watched the fever cart roll off, and it come welling up inside of me, just losing her, losing my little May. It all come welling up and I just howled, howled as I haven't done in all me life. The row I made, you've never heard the like. It was a noise I hadn't made before, fit to break bottles and curdle the milk. Then, from behind me, I heard the same sound, but changed, an echo with a different pitch, and just as loud as my own screech had been.

"I broke off from me wailing and turned round, and standing there, down at the street's far end, there was my aunt and her accordion. She was stood there like ... well, I don't know what, her hair like wool from hedgerows round her head, and playing the same note as what I'd screamed. Well, not the same note, it were lower down. The same but in a lower register. A thunder roll, that's what it sounded like, spreading down Fort Street. Smokey, like, and slow. And there was Thursa, holding down the keys, her bony fingers and her great big eyes, just staring at me, and her face were blank like she were sleepwalking and didn't know what she were doing, much less where she was.

"She didn't care what I were going through, or that my child was being took away. She was just off in one of her mad dreams, and I hated her for it at the time. I thought she was a callous, useless lump, and all the anger what I felt inside for what had happened to my little girl, I took it out on Thursa, there and then. I drew a breath and yelled but it weren't grief like it had been the first time. This were rage. I hollered like I meant to eat her up, all bellowed out in one long snarling rush.

"My aunt just stood there. Didn't turn a hair. She waited until I were done and then she changed her fingers' placement on the keys, holding them down to strike a lower chord. It was like when I'd first screamed, done again: she hit the same note lower down the scale as though she thought she was accompanying me. Again, it was a rumble like a storm, but one that sounded nearer, nastier. I give up then. I just give up and cried, and blow me if that silly ruddy mare weren't trying to play along with that as well, with little trills of notes like snuffling and sounds like that noise you make in your throat. I'm not sure quite what happened after that. I think old Snowy got up off the step and went along to quiet his sister down. I only know when I turned and looked back the other way down Fort Street, May were gone.

"That was the worst, Thursa's accordion. It made me feel like none of it made sense, like all the world was barmy as my aunt. It was all pointless. None of it were fair, had no more scheme or reason than her tunes. I still don't know. I don't know why May died."

She lapsed here into silence. Mrs. Gibbs released May's hand and raised her own to place them on May's shoulders with a soft, firm grip.

"Neither do I, dear. Nor does anyone know what the purpose is in anything, or why things happen in the way they do. It don't seem fair when you see some of them mean buggers living to a ripe old age and here's your lovely daughter took so soon. All I can tell you is what I believe. There's justice up above the street, my dear."

Where had May heard those same words said before? Or had she? Was that a false memory? Whether the phrase was ever spoke or not, it seemed familiar. May knew what it meant, or sort of understood it, any road. It had the same ring to it as "upstairs", the ring of somewhere that was higher up and yet was down to earth at the same time, without all the religious how-d'you-do and finery, what just put people off. It was one of those truths, May briefly thought, that most folk knew but didn't know they knew. It hovered in the background of their minds and they might feel it flutter once or twice but mostly they forgot that it was there, as May herself was doing even then. Just an impression of the warm idea remained, the bum-dent left in an armchair, a fleeting sense of high authority that was summed up somehow in Mrs. Gibbs. May's earlier notion now came back to her, of the deathmongers as a breed apart who'd gained their ledge within society where they could stand above the churning flood of life and death that was their stock in trade, unmoved by the fierce currents of the world that, these last days, had nearly done for May. They'd found the still point in a life that seemed, alarmingly, to have no point at all. They'd found a rock round which the chaos dashed. Barely afloat upon a sea of tears, in Mrs. Gibbs May caught sight of dry land. She knew what she must do to save herself, blurted it out before she changed her mind.

"I want to know what you know, Mrs. Gibbs. I want to be a deathmonger like you. I want to be stuck into birth and death so I'm not frit by both of them no more. I've got to have a purpose now May's gone, whether I have another child or not. If kids are all the purpose what you've got, you're left with nothing when they're took away by death, policemen, or just growing up. I want to learn to do a useful task, so's I should be somebody for meself and not just someone's wife or someone's mam. I want to be outside of all of that, to be someone who can't be hurt by it. Could I be taught? Could I be one of you?"

Mrs. Gibbs let May's shoulders go so she could sit back on the stool and study her. She didn't look surprised by May's request, but then she'd never looked surprised at all, except perhaps when little May was born. She breathed in deep and exhaled down her nose, a thoughtful yet exasperated sound.

"Well, I don't know, my dear. You're very young. Young shoulders, though you might have an old head. You will have after this, at any rate. What you must understand, though, is you're wrong. There isn't any place away from life where you can go and not be touched by it. There's no place where you can't be hurt, my dear. I'm sorry, but that's just the way things are. All you can do is find yourself a spot that you can look at all life's turmoil from, the babies born and old men passed away. Take a position close to death and birth, but far enough away to have a view, so you can better understand them both. By understanding, you can lose your fear, and without fear the hurt's not half so bad. That's all deathmongers do. That's what we are."

She paused, to be sure May had took her point.

"Now, bearing all of that in mind, my dear, if you think you've a calling to my craft, there's no harm in me showing you a bit. If you're in earnest, then perhaps you'd like to be the one what brushed your daughter's hair?"

May hadn't been expecting that at all. It had been all conjecture up to then. She'd not thought she'd be called upon so soon to put her new ambition to the test, and not like this. Not with her own dead child. To pull a comb through those pale, matted locks. To brush her daughter's hair for the last time. She choked, even upon the thought of it, and glanced towards the box at the room's end.

A cloud had pulled back from the sun outside and strong light toppled at a steep incline into the parlour, strained through greying nets, diffused into a milky spindrift fog above the coffin and the child within. From here, she could just see her baby's curls, but could she stand it? Could she brush them out, knowing that she'd not do it anymore? But then equally daunting was the thought of giving someone else that sacred job. May's child was going away, and should look nice, and if she could have asked she'd want her mam to get her ready for it, May was sure. What was she scared of? It was only hair. She looked back from the box to Mrs. Gibbs and nodded until she could find her voice.

"Yes. Yes, I think as I can manage that, if you'll bear with me while I find her comb."

May stood up, and the deathmonger did too, patiently waiting while May sorted through the bric-a-brac heaped on the mantelpiece until she'd found the wooden baby-comb with painted flowers on she'd been searching for. She gripped it, drew in a determined breath and made to walk towards the parlour's end where the small coffin waited. Mrs. Gibbs placed a restraining hand upon May's arm.

"Now then, dear, I can see you're very keen, but first perhaps you'll join me in some snuff?"

Out of an apron pocket she produced her tin with Queen Victoria on its lid. May gaped at it and blanched, and shook her head.

"Ooh no. No, thank you, Mrs. Gibbs, I shan't. Excepting for yourself I've always thought it was a dirty habit, not for me."

The deathmonger smiled fondly, knowingly, continuing to hold the snuff-box out towards May, its enamel lid flipped back.

"Believe me, dear, you can't work with the dead, not lest you take a little pinch of snuff."

May let this sink in, then held out her hand so Mrs. Gibbs could tip a measure of the fiery russet powder on its back. The deathmonger advised that May should try to sniff half up each nostril if she could. Gingerly dipping her face forward May snorted raw lightning halfway down her throat. It was the most startling experience she'd ever had. She thought that she might die. Mrs. Gibbs reassured her on this point.

"Don't fret. You've got my hanky up your sleeve. Use that if you've a need to. I don't mind."

May yanked the crumpled square of linen from the bulge it had made in her jumper's cuff and clutched it to her detonating nose. Down at one corner the embroidered bee was smothered by royal jelly in result. There were some minor tremors after this, but finally May could control herself. She cleaned herself up with a dainty wipe, then stuffed the ruined rag back up her sleeve.

Mrs. Gibbs had been right about the snuff. May couldn't now smell anything at all, and doubted that she ever would again. Upon the spot she made a firm resolve that if she took up this deathmonger lark she'd find another way to mask the scent. Perhaps a eucalyptus sweet might work.

Unhurriedly, and walking side by side, the women went down to the room's far end and stood a moment there beside the box just gazing at the luminous, still child. The clock ticked, then they both got down to work.

Mrs. Gibbs first took off the baby's clothes. May was surprised how supple the child was, and said as how she thought it would be stiff.

"No, dear. They have the rigor for a time, but after that it all goes out of them. That's how you know when they're best in the ground."

Next they dressed little May in her best things, what were laid out already on a chair, and the deathmonger did her hands and face with some white powder and a bit of rouge.

"Not too much. You should hardly know it's there."

At last, May was allowed to brush the hair. She was surprised how long it took to do, although it might be as she dragged it out and didn't want it to be finished with. She did it gently, as she always did, so that she didn't tug her daughter's scalp. It looked like spun flax by the time she'd done.

The funeral next day went off all right. For saying, there were a big crowd turned up. Then everyone got back on with their lives and May discovered she'd been right about the second child she'd thought was on the way. They had another girl, 1909, little Louisa, named after May's mam. May was determined, still, to have two girls, but rested after having baby Lou just for a year or two, to get her breath. The next child was put off for longer than intended when an Austrian Duke got shot so everybody had to go to war. May and a five-year-old Lou waved Tom off at Castle Station, praying he'd come back. He did. That First World War, May got off light, and afterwards the sex was better, too. She had four babies, straight off, on the trot.

Though May thought one more girl and then she'd stop, their second child, in 1917, turned out to be a boy. They named him Tom, after his dad, the way that little May, their firstborn girl, was named after her mam. In 1919, trying for a girl to go with Lou, she had another boy. This one was Walter, and the next was Jack, then after that was Frank, then she give up. By that point her and Tom and their five kids had moved to Green Street, down along the end, and all this time May was a deathmonger, a queen of afterbirth and of demise who took both of life's extremes in her stride. She was thick limbed by then, and dour, and stout and all her youthful prettiness was gone. Her father died in 1926 and then her mother ten years after that, in 1936, after a score of years where she'd not come outside her house. May's mam had trouble walking by that time, but that weren't really why she stayed indoors. The truth of it was, she'd gone cornery. May's brother Jim got her a wheelchair once, but they'd not reached the end of Bristol Street before she'd screamed and pleaded to go home. It was the cars, which were the first she'd seen.

Her husband Tom died two years after that, and that took all the wind out of May's sails. Their daughter Lou was grown and married now, and May had grandchildren, two little girls. May wasn't a deathmonger anymore. All that she asked for was a peaceful life, after the upsets and the scares she'd had. It didn't seem much, though that was before they started talking of another war.

HARK! THE GLAD SOUND!

A spidery piano music picked its way in cold mist from the Abington Street library to the workhouse in the Wellingborough Road. His feet like ice inside his work boots, Tommy Warren took a last pull on his Kensitas then flicked the glowing dog-end to the ground, a tiny fireball tumbling away in marbled dark, smashed into sparks on frosted paving stones.

The distant, tinkling notes were creeping from Carnegie Hall above the library and out through this November night, their sound a string of icicles. Its source was Mad Marie, marathon concert pianist, booked at the hall that evening, giving one of her recitals which might last for hours. Days. Tom was surprised that he could hear her right up here outside St. Edmund's Hospital, the former workhouse, where he stood while waiting for his wife Doreen, somewhere inside the institution, to give birth to their first child. Though faint and unidentifiable, the veering tune was audible despite the distance and the muffling fog.

There wasn't much traffic to speak of in the Wellingborough Road that time of night … it was about one in the morning as he reckoned it … so it was very quiet, but Tommy still couldn't make out which number Mad Marie was at that moment grinding through. It might have been "Roll Out The Barrel" or conceivably "Men Of The North, Rejoice". Considering how late it was, Tommy supposed that Mad Marie could well be suffering from lack of sleep, swinging from one piece to the other without any real idea what she was playing, or of which town she was in.

It all reminded him of something, standing here in swirling blackness listening to an old song come from far away, but he was too preoccupied just now to think what it might be. All that was on his mind was Doreen, back there in the hospital behind him, halfway through a labour that looked set to carry on for ages yet, like Mad Marie and whatever the racket was that she was bashing out. Tom doubted that it had been music swelling his wife's belly for these last few months, though from the bagpipe skirl that Doreen had been making when he heard her some ten minutes back, it might as well have been. The row Doreen had made was probably more tuneful than the swerving jangle Mad Marie was currently accomplishing, but it made Tommy wonder what kind of a melody had been composed inside his wife during her pregnancy, a soppy ballad or a stirring march: "We'll Gather Lilacs" or "The

British Grenadiers"? A girl or boy? He didn't mind as long as it weren't one of Mad Marie's bizarre improvisations, where nobody had the first idea what it was meant to be. As long as it weren't the men of the north rolling out barrels, or the British Grenadiers gathering lilacs. Just as long as it weren't a conundrum. There'd been far too many of them in the Warrens and the Vernalls as it was, across the years, a great deal more than their fair share. Just this once, couldn't him and Doreen have a normal kid who wasn't mad or talented or both? And if there were a certain number of such problem children to be divvied out by fate, couldn't some other family somewhere take their turn at shouldering the burden? People who had ordinary relatives just weren't pulling their weight, as far as Tommy was concerned.

A solitary big grey car shoving piss-puddle headlight beams before it surfaced briefly from the big grey cloud beneath which all Northampton seemed to be submerged, and then was gone again. Tom thought it might have been a Humber Hawk, but wasn't sure. He didn't really know much about motors, except to his way of mind there were too many of the things about these days, and he could only see it getting worse. The horse and cart was on its way out, and it wasn't coming back. Where Tommy worked in Phipps's brewery at Earl's Barton they still kept the old drays, all the great big shire mares steaming, snorting – more like sweaty railway engines than they were like animals. But then you'd got the bigger companies like Watney's, they'd got lorries now and were delivering right across the country, whereas Phipps's was still local. Tom could see them getting squeezed out given ten more years of it, if they weren't careful. There might not be much of work or horseflesh by then to be found around Earl's Barton. Tom supposed it wasn't what you'd call the best or most secure of times for him and Doreen to have brought a kid into the world.

He screwed his Brylcreemed head round to regard the workhouse forecourt he was standing in and thought that, to be fair, it was a long shot from the worst of times as well. The war was finished, even if there was still rationing, and in the eight years since VE Day there'd been hopeful signs that England was back on the up again. They'd voted Winnie Churchill out, almost before the bombs had finished dropping, so Clem Atlee could get on with putting everything to rights. Granted, at present they'd got Churchill back again, saying as how he wanted to de-nationalise the steelworks and the railways and all that, but in them years after the war there'd been a lot of good work done for once, so things could never be rolled back the way they'd been. They'd got the National Health now, National Insurance, all of that, and kids could go to school for nothing until they were, what, seventeen or eighteen? Or longer, if they passed exams.

It wasn't like when Tommy had won his mathematics scholarship and could have theoretically gone to the Grammar School, except that Tommy's mam and dad, old Tom and May, could never have afforded it. Not with the books, the uniform, the kit, and most especially the big gap in the family income that Tom's staying on at school would have entailed. He'd had to leave at thirteen, get a job, start bringing a pay packet home with him on Friday night. Not that he'd ever for a minute been resentful, or had even idly wondered what life might have been like if he'd taken up the scholarship. Tommy's first duty had been to his family, so he'd done what he had to and got on with it. No, he weren't brooding over his lost chances. He was just glad that things would be better for his little lad. Or lass. You never knew, although if he were honest Tom was hoping it would be a boy.

He paced a little, up and down outside the hospital, and stamped his feet to make sure that the blood was circulating. Every breath became an Indian smoke-signal on meeting the chill air, and just across the street the black bulk of St. Edmund's Church thrust up like a ghost story from the fog. The tilting headstones in its walled yard poked above the mist, stone bed-boards in an outdoor dormitory, with damp and silvery eiderdowns of vapour spread between them. The tall midnight yews were line-posts where the wringing grey sheets of cold haze had been hung out to dry. No moon, no stars. From the direction of town centre came a faltering refrain that sounded like a Varsity Rag waved at an Old Bull and Bush.

The reason he'd prefer a boy was that his brothers and his sister all had boys already that would carry on the name. His older little sister Lou, six years his senior and nearly a foot his junior, had got two girls as well, but her and her chap Albert had produced a youngest boy, it must be getting on twelve year ago. Their Walt, Tom's younger brother and the pride of the black market, he'd got married not long after the war's end and had two lads already. Even young Frank, he'd beat Tommy to the altar and had had a son only the year before. If Tommy, who was after all the eldest brother, hadn't had a kid of some kind by the age of forty, then he'd never hear the last of it from May, his mam. May Minnie Warren, leathery old so-and-so who'd got a voice like a dockworker's fist, with which she'd no doubt pummel Tom to death if him and Doreen didn't get a shift on and extend the Warren line. Tommy was frightened of his mam, but so was everyone.

He could remember, on Walt's wedding night in 1947 or round then, the way their mam had cornered him and Frank out in the corridor at the reception, which was at the dance hall up in Gold Street. She'd stood there by the swing door, with people going in and out so that she'd had to shout over the music that kept blasting forth – it was the band May's youngest brother managed, Tommy's uncle Johnny – and his mam had read the riot act to him and Frank. She'd got half a pork pie held in one hand what she'd had off the buffet table and the other half of it was in her mouth part-chewed while she was talking, flakes of lardy pastry, ground pink pig-bits and yellowy jelly mashed together by her few remaining teeth or in a meat spume, spraying over Tom and his young brother as they stood there quaking in their boots before this strychnine Christmas pudding of a woman.

"Right, that's Walter and our Lou both married off and out from underneath me feet, so you two better buck your ideas up and find yourselves a gal who'll have yer, toot sweet. I'll not have everybody thinking I've brought up a pair of idiots who need their mother to take care of 'em. You're thirty, Tommy, and you, Frank, you're nearly twenty-five. People are going to ask what's up with you."

That had been getting on six years ago. Tommy was thirty-six now, and until he'd met Doreen two or three years back, he'd been starting to ask what was up with him himself. It wasn't like he'd never had a girlfriend, there'd been one or two, but there'd been nothing that had come to much. Part of it was that Tom was shy. He wasn't impish or adventurous like Lou, his sis. He couldn't charm the birds down out the trees then sell them shares in cloud-apartments like their Walter did, nor could he manage all the easy, near-the-knuckle sauciness that Frank would dish out to the girls. Tom was, in his own private estimation, the most knowledgeable of his siblings. He weren't wise like Lou, ingenious like Walt or even crafty like their Frank, but Tommy knew a lot. About the only thing he didn't know was how to set that learning to his own advantage, and when it had come to women he'd been lost and couldn't put a foot right for the life of him.

Another car swam from the fogbank, possibly a snub-nosed Morris Minor, this one headed west and travelling in the opposite direction from the previous vehicle. Its watery headlights splashed across the rough, dark limestone of St. Edmund's bounding wall when it went spluttering past him, and then there were only the bright rat-eyes of its rear reflectors as it seemed to back away from Tom into the shrouded corner represented by Northampton's centre. Mad Marie struck up a bold rendition of "O Little Town of Burlington", or possibly "Bethlehem Bertie", as if welcoming the new arrival.

Tommy was still thinking of his previous luck with girls, or lack of it. When Tom had been a lad back in the 'Thirties, not that long before his dad died, he'd been briefly smitten by the daughter of Ron Bayliss, who was at the time Tom's captain in the Boy's Brigade. It was the 18th Company, who'd met up for drill practice once a week in the big upstairs hall of the old church in College Street. Since Tom had always been not just the shyest but the most quietly religious member of his family, the regular attendance at the church and the band marches once a month suited him fine, and when he'd first clapped eyes upon Liz Bayliss it was just one more incentive. She'd been very pretty and a cut above Tom socially, but he knew he was a good-looking chap himself, and round where he came from in Green Street he'd been thought of as a snappy dresser, too. So he'd worked up the nerve and, after church one Sunday morning, asked her if she'd come to the theatre with him.

Lord knows why he'd said "theatre". Tom had never been to a theatre in his life, had simply thought it sounded cultured and impressive. Anyway, he'd not expected her to say she'd be delighted, and had only stuttered, "Oh, good. Then I'll see you there on Thursday", without any idea what was on the bill that night. As it turned out, it had been Maxie Miller, and it hadn't been his white book the comedian had been performing from on that particular occasion.

Bloody hell. It had been both the funniest and most embarrassing half-hour of Tommy's life. As soon as he'd seen Miller's name up on the posters, Tommy had been horrified, had known that this was the last place on earth that he should take a fervent Baptist like Liz Bayliss, but by then he'd bought the tickets and there wasn't any way he could back out. Besides, he'd heard Max Miller did a clean night now and then, so thought there was a chance he'd get away with it. At least, he'd thought that until Max had come out on the stage in his white suit with big red roses in brocade all over it, his wicked cherub face grinning up at the audience from underneath the brim of his white bowler hat.

"D'you like the seaside, ladies? Yes, I'll bet you do. I love it, me. I was down Kent the other week, ladies and gents, lovely down there it was. I took a stroll, I took a stroll along the cliff-tops it were such a smashing day. Walking along this narrow little path, I was, with a sheer drop down to one side of me and ooh, it was a height, ladies and gents, the waves all crashing round the rocks hundreds of feet below. This path, well, it weren't very broad, just wide enough to have one person on it but without the room for two people to pass, so just imagine, gents and ladies, just imagine my alarm when who should I see coming down the path the other way but a young lady in her summer frock and what a lovely thing she was, ladies and gents, I don't mind telling you. Well, now, you can see my dilemma. I stopped in me tracks, I looked at her, I looked down at the rocks below and didn't know what I should do. I'll tell you, I weren't sure if I should block her passage or just toss meself off and be done with it."

In her seat next to Tom, Liz Bayliss had turned white as Miller's hat. As the theatre all around them had erupted into laughter, Tom had struggled to compose his face into a look as mortified as that of his companion while preventing himself rattling like a boiler with suppressed hilarity. After a further twenty minutes, when the tears were running down Tom's cheeks into the corners of his desperate rictus grimace, Liz had asked him in a voice like graveyard marble if he would escort her out and take her home. That had been more or less the last he'd seen of her, since he'd felt far too awkward to keep up his Boy's Brigade or church appearances much after that.

The Wellingborough Road stretched out to either side of him, its weak electric lamps suspended in the churning dark at lengthy intervals, like lanterns hung from masts on quayside fishing boats. They weren't much use for lighting up a stretch of road like this, not on a foggy night, but they were better than the gas lamps that were still in use in some parts of the Boroughs, such as Green Street where his mam lived on her own with no electric. Tommy pictured her, a scowling boulder in her groaning armchair by the fireside shelling peas, with her cat Jim down at her still-small but carbuncled feet, the hissing gaslight dyeing the room's shadows to a deep dead-nettle-green. Next time he saw his mother, Tom was hoping he'd be able to hold up a grandson like a shield in front of him to stave off her attack. Or a granddaughter, obviously, although a son would probably be bigger and thus slow Tom's mother down for longer.

From across an empty main road the St. Edmund's bell chimed once, although if it were for one or half past he wasn't sure. He squinted at the church tower through the intervening billows and reflected how he wasn't sorry that he hadn't been to church so much since the Liz Bayliss incident. Tom still believed in God and in the afterlife and all of that, but in the war he'd come to the conclusion that it wasn't the same God and afterlife they talked about in church. That sounded too stuck up and fancy in the way that everybody dressed, behaved and talked. What Tom had first liked, as a kid, about the Bible was how Jesus was a carpenter, who would have had big callused hands and smelled of sawdust and said "bugger" just like anybody if the hammer caught his thumb. If Jesus was God's son, it made you think his dad had very likely acted much the same when he was knocking up the planets and the stars. A working bloke; the hardest working bloke of all, who favoured working men and paupers throughout all the best loved stories in the Bible. The same rough and ready God that Philip Doddridge used to preach about on Castle Hill all of them years back. Tommy didn't hear that cheery gruffness in the pious tones of vicars, didn't feel that coarse warmth striking from the polished pews. These days, though Tom's faith hadn't budged an inch in its conviction, he preferred to worship privately and at a ruder altarpiece, alone inside his thoughts. He didn't go to church except for funerals, weddings, and, if this went well tonight, for christenings. He didn't let his lips move when he prayed.

That was the war, of course, a lot of that. Four brothers setting out, three coming home. It still upset him when he thought of Jack, and at the time he hadn't seen quite how the Warren family would get over it, although you did,

of course. You had to. It was like the war itself. It had been inconceivable to
everybody while they were still getting through it that there'd ever be another
way of living, that they could recover from it, all the bombs, all the dead relatives. Nobody could imagine much beyond more of what they were suffering
already, only worse. The future, back then, it had been something that Tommy
couldn't think about, a place he'd never honestly expected he should see.

Yet eight years later here he was, a married man stood waiting for the birth
of his first child. As for the future, Tommy thought of nothing but. Things
weren't the way they'd been before the war. Nothing meant quite the same as
what you'd thought it did, and England was a different country now. They'd
got a pretty young queen that the papers likened to the previous Good Queen
Bess, and even ordinary working people had got televisions so as they could
watch the coronation. It was all like something out of *Journey into Space*, how
quick the onslaught of this modern world had been, as though the war's end
had removed a great impediment and finally let the twentieth century catch
up with itself. Tom and Doreen's first child – and they'd talked already of
another one – would be one of these New Elizabethans everyone was going
on about. They might grow up to live a life that Tom could never dream of,
all the things that scientists would have discovered and found out about by
then. They might have all the chances that Tom hadn't had, or else had been
compelled by circumstances to forgo.

Off in the curdling greyness, Mad Marie still serenaded him with "My Old
Man Said Onward Christian Soldiers", her piano sounding small and far away,
a broken music-box that had been set off accidentally in another room. Tom
thought of his maths scholarship again, the one that he'd passed up to take
the brewery job instead. While it was true he'd not resented missing out on
education if it meant that he could help his family, he still missed all the fun
he used to have with sums and numbers, when it was all new to him.

It was his granddad, Snowy, who he'd got the skill with figures from.
Although the old boy had passed on in 1926 when Tom was nine (gone mad
and eating flowers out of a vase according to Tom's mam), the pair had got
on well and in those last two years of his grandfather's life Tom had spent
most Saturday afternoons at his grandparents' house in the grim, narrow
crack of Fort Street. While Tom's granny Lou had fussed around in the dark
kitchen, Snowy and young Tom had chanted their way through all the multiplication tables, sitting in the living room. Geometry, that was another
thing that Tommy's granddad had instructed him upon: rough circles drawn
around milk-bottle bases with a titchy stub of pencil, sheets of butcher's paper
covering the tea-table until you couldn't see the wine-red tablecloth. Snowy
had told his grandson that most of the know-how came from his own father,
Tom's great-granddad Ernest Vernall, who had once worked touching up the

frescoes of St. Paul's Cathedral in Victorian times. Snowy said him and his sister, Tommy's great-aunt Thursa, had been given lessons by their dad while he was at a rest home. Only some years later, after badgering his mam, had Tommy found out that the rest home had been Bedlam, the original asylum what they'd had in Lambeth.

He recalled the afternoon, fumbling now in his mac pocket for the pack of Kensitas, when they'd been working on the eight- and nine-times-tables. His granddad had pointed out how all the multiples of nine, if you just totalled up their digits, always added up to nine: one plus eight, two plus seven, three plus six and so on, for as high as you could go. The memory smelled of fruitcake, from which Tom assumed his gran had been out in the kitchen baking, that particular occasion. It had tickled him, the thing about the number nine, and for a lark he'd added up the digits in the answers to his eight-times-table, too. The first was just eight, obviously, while the next, sixteen, was one plus six and therefore added up to seven. The next, twenty-four, was two plus four and added up to six, while thirty-two reduced in the same way to five. Tommy had realised with a growing sense of intrigue that his column of additions counted down from eight to one (eight eights were sixty-four, in which the six and four thus added up to ten, the one and nought of which totalled just one), and then began the countdown all again commencing with the number nine this time (nine eights, seventy-two, the seven and the two of which made nine). This run of numbers, nine to one, was then repeated, on and on, presumably unto infinity. That had been when Tom's grandfather had pointed out that this was the same sequence as the one-times-table, only in reverse, and that had set both of them thinking.

Taking one short untipped cigarette out of the pack, with its sleek, smarmy butler mascot in red, black and white, Tom lit it with a Captain Webb's and threw the spent match in the vague direction of an unseen gutter, lost somewhere in the cold smoulder down around his feet. The fag-pack with its butler and the matchbox with its bold, moustachioed channel swimmer both went back into his raincoat pocket. He'd a Fry's Five Boys bar in there, too, with a quintet of lads at various emotional extremes upon its wrapper. All this advertising and this packaging that you got nowadays, it meant that he was carrying seven tiny people in his pocket, just so he could have a smoke and possibly a square of chocolate if he should feel peckish later on.

Upon that memorable afternoon getting on thirty years before, Tom and his grandfather had swiftly reckoned up the digits in the answers to the rest of the multiplication tables. He remembered the excitement that he'd felt, the giddy, sheer thrill of discovery now come back to him in a fruitcake rush of allspice, candied peel and Snowy Vernall's rubbing liniment. The two-times-table, if you added up the figures of the products, it transpired, resulted in a number-pattern that first ran through all the even numbers, two, four, six, eight, then all of the odd ones, one (one plus nought), three (one plus two), five, and so on up to nine (eighteen, or one plus eight). Remembering the way the one- and eight-times-tables had both yielded up numerical progressions that were backwards mirror-versions of each other, Snowy and young Tom had looked at the seven-times-table, where they'd learned that first the added answers counted down through the odd numbers, seven, five (one plus four), three (two plus one), one (two plus eight, which made the ten, the digits of which added up to one), and then went on to run down through the even numbers. Eight (three plus five), six (four plus two) and so on until the count-down of odd numbers started up again. The number seven seemed to work exactly like the number two, but with the sequence running back to front.

The number three, which just went three, six, nine, three, six, nine, unend-ingly if you made sums out of its multiples, appeared to be twinned with the number six, which went six, three, nine, six, three, nine, if you did the same thing. The number four produced a pattern that seemed complicated at first sight, in that it counted down from two numbers in parallel, and alternated in between the two. Thus, what you got was four, then eight, then three (or one plus two), then seven (one plus six), then two (two plus nought), six (two plus four), one (two plus eight, adding up to ten, or one plus nought), five (thirty-two, or three plus two), et cetera, et cetera. The five-times-table, unsurpris-ingly by now, did just the same thing in reverse. It alternated in the same way between two progressions, this time counting up instead of down, so that the sequence in this case was five, one, six, two, seven (two plus five), three (three plus nought), eight (three plus five) and so forth. Tommy and his grandfather had looked at one another and just burst out laughing so that Tom's grandma Louisa had come out the kitchen to see what was up.

What had been up was that there seemed to be a hidden pattern in the sums that could be generated by the answers of the one- to eight-times-tables. They were all symmetrical, one mirrored eight, two mirrored seven, three worked just the same as six, four was like five. Only the number that had sparked off their investigations, nine, remained alone out of the single figures in that it did not possess a twin, a number that no matter how much it was multiplied would yield the same unvarying result.

Tom, eight years old, had been attempting to explain all this to his uncom-prehending gran, when out of nowhere his granddad had yelped with glee, snatched up the midget pencil and, in faint lines on the thin and shiny butch-er's paper littering the table, had inscribed two circles, one inside the other. With one Capstan-yellowed index finger, Snowy had jabbed meaningfully at the drawing, looking up at Tommy from beneath the winter hedgerow of his brow to ascertain whether his grandson understood or not. The old man's eyes were shining in a way that had reminded Tommy, there amidst the fruited oven-fug and camaraderie of the maths game which they'd been working out together, that his grandfather was said by many to be mad, including Tommy's mam. And everybody else, now that he'd thought of it. His granddad had just grinned and once again poked at his mystifying scribble with an urgent finger. All that there had been to Snowy's drawing was just two concentric circles, like a car tyre, or an angel's halo standing on its side. Tommy had squinted at the simple shape for what seemed minutes before he'd become aware that he was looking at the figure nought.

It had been just as if the lights had been switched on. Nought was the only number, other than the number nine, that didn't change if it were multiplied. All of the single digit figures between nought and nine made sequences by adding up their multiples that had a perfect symmetry. As if to underline this, Tom's granddad had once more taken up his pencil, and had written those ten numbers in, all in a ring between the zero's innermost and outer circles, like the numbers round the edges of a clock. The number nought was roughly where the one would be upon a normal timepiece, with the numerals proceeding clockwise round the dial and leaving spaces where the six and twelve were usually positioned. The effect of this was that each number was now set at the same horizontal level as its mirror-twin, the nine up at the top left face now lined up with the nought at the top right. The eight and one were opposite each other at both ten-to and ten-past, the seven and the two were diametrically opposed, each at the quarter-hour mark, with the six and three below that, and the five and four facing each other down the bottom, one at five-and-twenty-to, the other one at five-and-twenty after. It was lovely. In one simple flash a hidden pattern that had been there all the time, concealed beneath the surface, was revealed.

Neither Tom nor his grandfather had had the first idea what their discovery might mean, or could conceive of any useful application for it. Indeed, it was so blindingly obvious once you'd first seen it that they'd both assumed that someone, or more likely a great many people, had stumbled across the notion previously. It didn't matter. In that moment Tom had felt a sense of triumph and sultana-scented revelation that he'd never known before or since. His grandfather had smiled a cracked smile that looked rueful rather than elated, and had stabbed once more with one black fingernail at the blank space enclosed by the big number nought's interior ring.

"The nought's a torus. That means, like, a lifebelt shape what's got a hole in. Or it's like a chimneypot, looked down on from above. And at the middle of the nought here, down the barrel of the chimney, that's where all the nothing's kept. You've got to keep your eye on nothing, lad, or else it gets all over everything. Then there's no chimneypot, there's just the hole. Then there's no lifebelt, there's no torus. There's no nothing."

With this, Snowy Vernall had seemed to get angry or unhappy, just like that. He'd screwed the piece of paper with the altered clock face drawn upon it up into a ball and thrown it on the fire. Tom hadn't comprehended any of what his granddad had just been going on about, and must have looked scared by the old boy's sudden change of disposition. Tommy's gran Louisa, who looked like she'd seen these swings of mood before, had said "Right, that's enough sums for today. Young Tommy, you run off back home before your mam gets worried. You can see your granddad Snowy on another Sat'day afternoon." She hadn't even shown Tom out, perhaps because she'd known that there was an explosion imminent. Tommy had barely shut the worn front door behind him and stepped outside into Fort Street when he heard the furious bellowing and, shortly after, breaking glass. Most probably it would have been a window or a mirror, mirrors being something that Tom's grandfather was known to have become suspicious of. Tommy had scarpered off down Fort Street which, although it had been barely the mid-afternoon, Tom pictured now as having then been ominously dark. However, he recalled that this had happened in the 'Twenties, long before the Borough Waste Destructor had been pulled down to make way for flats in Bath Street, so that was one mystery solved.

Tom pulled upon his Kensitas and blew an unintended smoke-ring, almost instantly made indistinguishable from the chilly, writhing fumes surrounding him there in the Wellingborough Road. He wished he could blow one like that when somebody was watching. When Doreen was watching.

Drifting up from the town centre, to the west and on Tom's right, the jingling and meandering performance of the marathon concert recitalist was still continuing, notes hung on the infrequent threads of breeze like the glass lozenges that dripped from chandeliers. It still reminded him of something, of some other night like this, perhaps, some other music drifting from some other fog? The memory, much like fog, was elusive, and he let it go and instead wondered how Doreen was getting on. She probably would have been in no mood to have appreciated Tommy's smoke-ring, even if she'd seen it. She'd most likely other things upon her mind right now.

He'd go back in. Another fag or two, he'd go back in and sit there in the small beige waiting room close to the front doors of the decommissioned workhouse, where at least it would be warm. He'd sit and drum one foot upon the varnished floorboards, in his mac and his demob suit, just like both the other blokes whose wives were having babies this same night, the seventeenth, who were already sat expectantly inside. Tommy had waited in there with them for a while, just after he'd brought Doreen to the hospital and she'd been took to the delivery room, but he'd not been there very long before the silence had begun to get upon his nerves and he'd made some excuse to quietly slip outside. Nothing against the other chaps, it was just that they hadn't much in common past the fact that nine months earlier they'd had a lucky night. It weren't like they were going to sit and talk about their hopes and fears and dreams, like actors might do in a film. In real life, you just didn't. In real life, you didn't really have much in the way of hopes and fears and dreams, not like a character who's in a film or book had got. Things like that, in real life, they weren't important to the general story in the way they had to be in literature. Dreams, hopes, they weren't important, and if someone were to bring them up then everyone would say he thought that he was Ronald Colman, looking sensitive with his long eyelashes in black and silver through the cigarette smoke at a matinee.

The Wellingborough Road felt like a riverbed, with grubby lamb's-wool vapour rushing down it in a flood of murk, eastwards to Abington, the park, and Weston Favell. The benighted shops and pubs were vole-holes dug into its banks below the waterline, hiding dark merchandise. As Tommy watched, a lone Ford Anglia came darting like a pike out from the grounded cloud then swam away in the direction of town centre, battling upstream against the current of the mist and in the face of Mad Marie's continuing recital. The Ford Anglia was one car Tommy recognised by what he thought of as its sharp italic tilt, a term he'd picked up from his penmanship at school and which had stuck with him. Its cream and cornflower paintwork vanished in the oyster drifts beneath which Abington Square and Charles Bradlaugh's statue were submerged, and Tommy was alone again, scuffing his boots against the rolling torrent's stone and tarmac bed-sands, sucking in the fog through the last half-inch of his Kensitas and blowing it out suavely down his nose.

He knew that thirty-six was late, comparatively, to be starting off a family, but it weren't too late. Tom had known blokes a good sight older than what he was, siring a first child. But then, with both his younger brothers having kids already, he'd not felt that he could leave it any later. If he wasn't a grown man and fit to raise a son by now, after the things he'd been through, then he'd never be one. While the war had took their Jack away from him, the whole affair had given Tom a sort of confidence he hadn't felt before, a sense that if he'd managed to survive all that then Tommy Warren was as good as anybody else. He'd come back home from France with a new twinkle in his eye, a different swagger there in every well-dressed step. Not flashy or expensive, mind you. Just well-dressed.

He could remember his homecoming, pulling into Castle Station on a train packed full of children, matrons, business people, and scores of returning men in uniform like him and Walt and Frank. Standing room only, it had been, all of the way from Euston Station, Tom and his two brothers stuck out in the corridor with getting on two dozen other people, swaying and complaining straight through Leighton Buzzard, Bletchley, Wolverton. As far as Tommy could recall, he'd been stood trading stories with their Walter, which as always was a contest that you couldn't hope to win. He'd been halfway through telling Walt about the night when all the idiot British officers got pissed and drove a tank over the front gate of the ammo dump that Tom was guarding, so he couldn't even shoot the overpaid guffawing twits for fear of setting off the shells. It was at that point in his story, just past Wolverton, that a big Yank, a GI who'd got on the train at Watford and was going on to Coventry, had joined them in the crowded, lurching corridor.

Sometimes, the Yanks, they were all right, and you could have a laugh with them, but by and large they got right up Tom's nose, the way they did with most people he knew. On the front line they'd always used to say that when the Luftwaffe went over, all the English ran, and when the RAF went over, all the Germans ran. When the Americans went over, everybody ran. The cocky buggers had backed Hitler until 1942, then come into the war late and took all the credit, even after they'd walked slap into a Jerry trap and probably delayed the war's end with their 'Battle of the Bulge', or Operation Autumn Mist as Fritz proudly referred to it. The soldiers over here, though, were the worst, or anyway the white ones were. The darkies were as good as gold, you couldn't meet a nicer bunch of chaps, and Tommy could remember being home on leave and seeing the Black Lion's landlord slinging out some white GIs when they'd complained about the black ones they were forced to share a 'barroom' with. "Them niggers in the back there," as they'd called them. Some Americans could be right Herberts, and this fellow who'd come up to Tommy and his brothers on the train was one of them.

Right from the get go, he'd been mouthing off about how much more pay the Yanks got than the English, how they'd give them bigger rations, all of that. Walter had nodded sagely and said "Well, that's only fair, you've bigger mouths to feed", but the GI went on as though he hadn't noticed that their Walt had made a dig. He'd started telling them, in a low whisper on account of all the ladies that were in the corridor, about how many rubber johnnies his lot had been issued by the US army. Seeing as this chap was stationed over here in England this was just as good as saying they'd been given them to use with English girls, which wasn't something British chaps were likely to take kindly to. Tommy had seen the look come in his brothers' eyes, the same as he supposed had been there in his own. Walter had smiled a great big smile, eyes sparkling, which wasn't usually a reassuring sign, and Frank had just gone quiet with a tight little grin on his lean face, which meant the Yank, big as he was, was looking for a swift punch up the bracket if he didn't watch himself.

It was the Warren boys that he was talking to, who'd made a decent name for themselves liberating their small piece of France, who'd lost their brother, the best-looking out the lot of them, and who'd been given in return a lot of medals that they didn't want. Taking their dangerous silence for respect or awe, the GI had elected to back up his brag by fishing out the US army-issue tin he kept his condoms in, prising its lid up to reveal perhaps two dozen prophylactics. Tom had wondered idly if Americans wrote chirpy slogans on the sides of rubbers, like they did with bombs. "Here's looking at ya, Princess Liz!" or something of that nature. Walter had peered down into the open tin and said "I see you've a lot left, then." Frank had ground his teeth and bunched one fist up, ready to kick off, and it was just then that the train had gone over a bump, so that their carriage clanked and rocked.

The johnnies had all shot into the air like sparks out of a Roman candle, falling in a rubber rain on bankers' shoulders, into schoolboys' satchels and on ladies' hats. The Yank had gone as red as Russia, crawling round on all fours gathering them up, apologising to the women while he fished the little packets from between their heels and stuffed them back into his tin. Walter had started singing "When johnnies come marching home again, hurrah" and everybody in the carriage but the Yank had had the best laugh that they'd had since 1939.

Tom risked a burned lip with a last drag on his fag then flipped the ember end of it away into the invisible gutter with its predecessor. That had been a rare old time, back then when they were fresh home from the war. Out every Friday night they'd been, the famous Warren lads all in their suits, but only eldest brother Tommy with the matching handkerchief in his breast pocket. Sauntering from pub to pub, the shunt and jingle of the one-armed bandits strewing fruit and bells before them as they went, the busty landladies' admiring smirks, war heroes, such a shame about your handsome brother. Free shots from the optics, Walter telling jokes and selling knocked-off nylons, only used once previously, miss, and that were by a nun. Frank leering, Tommy going red and trying not to laugh when they were stepping over brawling lezzies on the Mayorhold, and a head-of-Guinness moon cut free to sail above the Boroughs like a pantomime effect.

That snowy Christmas Eve when Walt had found an apple crate up on the market, harnessed Frank and Tommy to it with some string then jammed his tubby arse inside so they could pull him round town centre like two reindeer towing Father Christmas. "Ho ho ho, you buggers! Mush!" They'd gone into the Grand Hotel and bought a round of drinks, just for the three of them, and they'd been charged more than a pound. With Walt directing, Frank and Tom had gone to either side of the big hotel lounge and started rolling up the huge expensive carpet, asking people to lift up their chairs and tables so that they could roll it under them. The manager or someone had come storming out and asked Walt what the devil they thought they were playing at, to which Walt had replied that they were going to take the carpet, since they'd paid for it. They'd had to make a quick escape, without the rug, but luckily their apple crate was still roped to a lamppost outside the hotel. They'd jingled all the way down Gold Street, faces flushing blue and yellow in the fairy lights, along Marefair, back home to Green Street and their waiting mam. Hitler was dead and everything was ruddy marvellous.

Except for Jack, of course. Tommy recalled, with a queer shudder of appalled nostalgia, how the Warren family's Christmas ritual had been that first year after Jack was gone. The family had gathered in the front room, just as they'd done for as long as anybody could remember. Tommy's mam had leadenly retrieved the fancy China piss-pot – easily a foot across, having been manufactured in a time of bigger arses – from its perch atop that old glass-fronted cabinet they used to have. While Frank and Walt and Lou and Tommy had looked on, their mam had filled the guzunder up to its rim with a grotesque and undiscriminating mix of spirits; drainings from the staggeringly varied complement of bottles to be found around their heavy-drinking household. Brimming with a shimmering pale-gold aggregate of whiskey, gin, rum, vodka, brandy and possibly turpentine for all that anybody knew, the glazed white chalice, hopefully unused, had been solemnly passed around the family circle, this accomplished only with both hands and some degree of difficulty. It was obviously impossible to drink from a receptacle that had quite clearly never been designed with that function in mind, at least without a certain drenching of the shirtfront, and this spillage had been worse with every circuit of the front room and of the increasingly incapable and uncoordinated individuals gathered there. On all the previous occasions when this ritual had been enacted there had been a kind of glory in its wretchedness: it had been somehow comical, and brave, and as if they were proud of being the uproarious and filthy monsters that their betters saw them as. There'd been a kind of horrid grandeur to it, but not after Jack was gone. That had been proof that they weren't mighty and immortal ogres after all, invincible in their inebriation. They'd just been a crew of vomiting and tearful drunks who'd lost their brother; lost their son. Tom couldn't now remember if they'd bothered with the Christmas ritual after that unhappy year of victory.

Across the Wellingborough Road, St. Edmund's clock struck twice for two and must have scared a roosting bird awake and into some state of activity, at least to judge from the plump tear of pigeon muck that silently dropped from the mists above him, splattering his mac's lapel with liquid chalk and caviar in its descent. Tom growled and swore and fished out his clean hanky from the pocket with no matches, fags or chocolate bars, wiping the white smear hurriedly away until only a faint damp stain remained. Making a mental note that he must have it washed before he blew his nose on it again, he shoved the used rag back into his coat.

Of course, all that post-war exhilaration hadn't lasted. Not that things had gone bad, not at all. Times had just changed, the way they always did. First Walt had met a little beauty and got married, which had prompted their mam's laying down the law to Tom and Frank at the reception, shouting at them over all the noise that Uncle Johnny's band were making at the dancehall there in Gold Street, telling them they'd better find themselves a pair of girls or else. Frank, wry and wiry with his line of saucy banter, had been quicker off the mark than Tommy in responding to their mother's ultimatum. He'd gone out and found a ginger lass as near the knuckle as what he was and they'd wed in 1950, which had just left Tom to bear the brunt of their mam's grunted disapproval.

Tommy could remember seeking refuge and advice during that period with his big little sister, popping up to see Lou and her husband Albert and their children out in Duston at the least excuse. As always Lou had been a darling, bringing him a cup of tea in her nice, airy little front room, listening to his troubles with her head on one side like a soft toy of an owl. "Your trouble is, bruv, that you're backward coming forward. I'm not saying as you should be a smooth talker like our Walt, or else a dirty little bugger like our Frank, but you should put yourself about, or else the girls won't know you're there. It's no good waiting for them to find you, that's not what girls are like. I mean, you're a good-looking chap, you're always dressed a treat. You're even a good dancer. I can't see as anything's the matter with you." Lou's voice, low and chuckling, had a lovely croak to it, almost a buzz or hum that, with his sister's compact shape, made Tommy think of beehives, honey, and, continuing with the association, Sunday teatime. She could always be relied upon to set you straight and have a laugh while she were doing it. Tom sometimes saw in Lou a glimpse of what their mam must have been like when she were young, before she lost her first child to diphtheria and started getting bitter, back before she were a deathmonger.

The only incident Tom could recall relating to his mother's trade in birth and death concerned an isolated morning in his childhood which had none-theless left an impression. Mr. Partridge, a big, portly chap who'd lived only a few doors from their house in Green Street, had passed on but was too fat to get out through the door of the front bedroom where he'd died. Tommy had watched from down the Elephant Lane end of Green Street while his mam had stood there in the road directing the removal of the house's upstairs win-dow and the lowering of an immense and almost purple Mr. Partridge, with a winch and trestle, down into the horse-drawn hearse that waited patiently

below. Of course, with all the Co-op funeral schemes they had these days
there weren't much work for deathmongers about. Tom's mam had packed it
in, the end of 1945. With Jack gone, he supposed she'd had enough of death by
then, and with the National Health on the horizon, then perhaps she'd reckoned that the birth end of the racket would be gone too, before long.

These days, most women having a first child would come and have it here,
in hospital. There were still midwives, naturally, for later children or for people
stuck out in the country, but these were all midwives working for the National
Health. They weren't freelancers like his mam, and no one called them deathmongers these days. Tom thought it was a good thing, by and large. He was a
modern bloke, and he for one was glad that his wife was just now having her
child delivered in a modern ward, with proper doctors gathered round, not in
a dark back bedroom with some cackling old horror like his mam bent over
her. Doreen had enough reservations about Tommy's mam as things stood,
and if May had stuck her nose into the birth of their first child then that would
have put the tin hat on the occasion good and proper. Tommy shivered, even
thinking of it, though that might have just been the November night.

It was Doreen who'd rescued Tommy from his bachelor state and his
mam's approbation. That had been a bit of luck, his finding her. It was just like
his Lou had said, he was too reticent with girls and couldn't turn the charm
on like their Walt or Frank. Tom's only hope had been to find somebody even
shyer than what he was, and in Doreen that's just what he'd found, his perfect complement. His other half. Like Tom, she wasn't shy as in the sense of
cowardly or weak. There was a backbone under her reserve; she just preferred
a quiet life without a lot of fuss, the same as he did. She, like him and every
other bloke who'd seen the inside of a trench, preferred to keep her head down
and get on with things, to not attract attention. It was something of a marvel
that he'd spotted her at all, stood shrinking back behind her louder, gigglier
mates from work, as if for fear that anyone should see how beautiful she was,
with her big watery blue eyes, her slightly long face and her bark-brown hair
curled up into a wave. With her theatre glow, that mistiness she had about her
like a lobby card. He'd told her, soon after they'd met, that she looked like a
film star. She'd just pursed her lips into a little smile and tutted, telling him
he shouldn't be so soft.

They'd wed in 1952 and though it would have made more sense, in terms
of room, for them to go and live in Green Street with his mam, no one had
wanted that. Not Tommy's mam, not Tommy, and particularly not Doreen.
She was the only person Tom had ever met who, even though she had a timid
and retiring nature, wouldn't put up with May Warren's bullying or her intimidating manner. Tom and Doreen had instead decided to reside down in St.
Andrew's Road with Doreen's mother Clara and the other members of her

family that lived there, or at least had lived there until recently. Though the idea of him and Doreen living with Tom's mam had been like something from a nightmare, these last two years living down the bottom of Spring Lane and Scarletwell Street hadn't been much better.

Now, this hadn't been because of Doreen's mam, the way it would have been with Tommy's, round in Green Street. Clara Swan had worked in service and remained a very proper and religious woman in her own quiet fashion, and though she could be both strict and stern if things should warrant it, she was in almost every way completely different to May Warren, thin and upright where his mam was short and stout. No, Tommy got on fine with Doreen's mam, just like he did with both her brothers and her sister, their respective spouses and their children. It was just that there had been so many of them, until recently, and it was such a little house.

Admittedly, the eldest brother, James, he'd married and moved out before Tom got there, but it had still been a tight fit, packing everybody in. First there was Doreen's mam herself, whose house it was, or at least it were her name on the rent book. Next was Doreen's sister, Emma, and her husband Ted, with their two children, John and little Eileen. Emma, older than Doreen, was the first woman railway guard in England, and it had been on the railway that she'd met her dashing engine driver husband, Ted, who cleaned his teeth with chimney soot. Then there was Doreen's younger brother Alf, the bus-driver, his wife Queen and their toddler, baby Jim. With Tommy and Doreen as well that had made getting on ten people crammed in a three-bedroom terraced house.

Doreen and Tom had started out with a few months of sleeping best they could upon the couch in the front room. Emma and Ted and their two kids had the front bedroom, Clara had the smaller bedroom next to that, which was above the living room, then Alf and Queen were in the smallest room, right at the back above the kitchen. Baby Jim slept in the wardrobe drawer. The nights, then, had been cramped-up and embarrassing, but early evenings had been worse, just after tea with everybody home from work and gathered in the living room to listen to the wireless. Ted and Emma would have hostile silences between them that could last for days, just glaring at each other over the tinned salmon sandwiches and *ITMA* catchphrases: "Dis iss Funf speaking". "Mind my bike", and, "Don't forget the diver". Alf would come home every night exhausted after being up so early with the buses, and would flake out snoring on the mat before the fire, just like a cat big as a man and dressed in a bus driver's uniform. His wife Queen, who was also by coincidence the sister of Ted, Emma's husband, would, on most nights, just sit by the fire and weep. You couldn't blame her. Upstairs, baby Jim would have climbed from his wardrobe drawer and started banging on the bedroom door, sometimes

for hours on end. You couldn't blame him, either, the poor little sod, not living in a wardrobe. If that wouldn't send you cornery, Tom didn't know what
would. Baby Jim's difficulty was, he was too clever. No one in the Swan or
Warren families was what you'd call a dim bulb, but baby Jim was the next
generation and you could see from the outset that they'd be as sharp as knives,
particularly baby Jim. By three years old he'd managed to escape twice from
the house and get four blocks away before the police apprehended him and
brought him back. Mind you, given how hazardous a child's life could be
down St. Andrew's Road, he'd probably have been a good sight safer if they'd
left him where he was.

Again, it wasn't that the adults in the house were negligent, it was just
there were seven of them and three children, getting on each other's wicks
and underneath each other's feet, so accidents were bound to happen. Ted and
Emma's eldest, John, had liked to sit up on the back of the armchair before the
day he lost his balance and tipped over, falling backwards out the window of
the living room into the back yard in a shower of broken glass. Then Ted and
Emma's youngest, pretty Eileen, had fell face down in the fire with all the red
hot coals, necessitating an immediate race up to the family doctor, Dr. Grey in
Broad Street, his Doreen and her big sister Emma running frantically across
a darkened Mayorhold holding the miraculously unscarred child wrapped in
a blanket.

Mercifully, this last year things had fallen right. First Ted and Em had
moved out, to a house further along St. Andrew's Road, in Semilong. Then Alf
and Queen had gone as well, up to the Birchfield Road in Abington. They'd
taken baby Jim with them, of course, but for some reason, at the age of five,
he'd broken out of his new home as well and managed to negotiate about two
miles of busy roads, finding his way back to the Boroughs and his gran's house
unescorted. Tom supposed it might have been that Jim, in the same way that
new-hatched ducklings sometimes got confused, had mixed up his attachment to his mum with an attachment to the wardrobe. Anyway, the upshot of
it was that there were only Clara, Tom and Doreen living down St. Andrew's
Road at present. Tom and Doreen had the big front bedroom Ted and Emma
had vacated, and with fewer people milling round, this baby that the two of
them were having would be born into a safer house. Into a safer world, or at
least that's what everybody hoped.

Tom tucked his bristly chin in, squinting down at his lapel. He could still
see the stain left by the bird-muck and glumly resigned himself to scrubbing
it with Borax after he got home.

He thought that by and large it was a safer world, although not when it
came to bird-muck, obviously. The war was finished, this time, and he didn't
think even the Jerries would be keen to kick it off again, especially not after

losing half their country to the communists. There'd been Korea, obviously, but his lad, if it was a lad, wouldn't be growing up to be conscripted off like Tommy, or to spend nights shivering beneath the table in the living room when there were air raids, which was how Doreen had spent the war, her being ten years Tommy's junior. And anyway, after the A-bomb what the Yanks had dropped onto Hiroshima, didn't they say that if there was a third world war, then it would all be over in about five minutes? Not that this was a cheering thought, admittedly. Tom felt the craving for another Kensitas, but since he'd only got five left and didn't know how long he'd have to stretch them out, he thought he'd better wait.

Churchill had seen to it that Britain let off its first bomb last year, and France was keen to have one too. The Russians and the Yanks had both got hundreds, but Tom couldn't say it worried him that much. To his mind, it would turn out to be like the gas that everybody was so scared of in the war, poor little Doreen having to run back home to St. Andrew's Road from Spencer School when she'd forgot her gas mask. In the end, nobody had been mad enough to use it, even Hitler, and these atom bombs would turn out just the same. Nobody would be mad enough. Although, of course, the Yanks already had, but Tom was standing waiting on the birth of his first child with quite enough to fret about already, and so he decided that he'd let that idea go.

The faint wind from the west at this point made an unexpected push and briefly rattled Tommy's mac. It shoved the fog to one side for a second from the shuttered pub, the Spread Eagle, just past the workhouse front on Tommy's left. The toucan's orange bill on the tin Guinness advert what were bolted up outside poked from the mist and then was gone again. The breeze brought also a renewed burst of cascading notes from Mad Marie down at Carnegie Hall, her mongrel melodies sliding about like nutcase furniture on casters, juddering off along the Wellingborough Road. The music was the usual mishmash; don't sit under the old rugged cross with anybody else but me, no no no, and then suddenly she was just playing one tune, clearly and distinctly, even if she only held it for a few bars before it collapsed into the general piano soup.

The tune was "Whispering Grass".

That did it. Tommy knew at once what the peculiar music in the swirling dark had been reminding him of all along: five, nearly six years back now, in the early months of 1948 not long after their Walter had got married, that time Tommy had gone drinking in the old Blue Anchor up Chalk Lane. It all came back to him in a great sepia wash of beer-blurred snapshot pictures, captured moments from his drunken stumble to the wild accompaniment of a fogbound piano and accordion, and Tommy marvelled that he hadn't thought of it before. How had he forgotten that strange, startling occasion, all the fears and questions it had thrown up in the face of Tommy and his family? He supposed in his defence he'd been preoccupied, what with the thought of Doreen and the bab, but even so he'd not have thought a night like that would slip so easy from his mind.

Tom lit another fag before remembering he'd planned to stretch them out, then turned his collar up as if he was a crook or haunted lover in a film, which was the ambiguous mood the mist and memories had put him in. The collar's stiff edge rubbed on the ear-level stubble of Tom's once-a-week short, back & sides, the haircut that he'd stuck with since his army days. Tommy could take the silver paper from a fag pack, wrap it round a plain brown penny and then burnish it against the bristles there behind his skull until it looked just like florin, which was something Walt had showed him how to do. Unlike their Walt, though, Tom had never had the nerve to pass off his nape-minted two bob bits as the real thing. He'd never had the nerve or was too honest, one or other.

On that evening several years before Tom and his youngest brother Frank had been to the Blue Anchor, which had stood just up past Doddridge Church there on Chalk Lane, almost in Bristol Street. The pub was something of a family favourite as its previous landlord and landlady had been Tommy and Frank's great-grandparents on their mother's side. Their gran Louisa who'd died back in the late thirties, as a girl she'd been the busty landlord's daughter serving drinks at the Blue Anchor in the 1880s when young Snowy Vernall had called in on one of his long walks from Lambeth. If Tom's grandfather had been less thirsty or had strolled the extra twenty yards up to the Golden Lion then there'd have been no May, no Tommy and no baby struggling towards existence right now in the hospital behind him. This explained his family's fondness for the place before it had been torn down a few years ago. Anyway, him and Frank had been in there putting the pints away, and while it had been all right it had all felt a bit lifeless and subdued, to Tom at any rate. Part of it, obviously, was they were missing Walt who'd gone and married six months earlier, which meant that their three musketeers act had been whittled down to two. And without Walter's inexhaustible supply of gags, there was more time to sit and mourn for their fourth musketeer, their Jack, their dead D'Artagnan with his grave in France and with his name down on the monument at Peter's Church.

Whatever the real reason, Tommy had been out of sorts with things that night in the Blue Anchor. Him and Frank had run into some chaps Frank knew from work but who Tom weren't so chummy with, so he'd begun to feel a bit left out and thought perhaps he'd try another pub. Tom had made his apologies to Frank then left him chatting with his mates while he'd put on his coat and stepped out through the pub's front door into Chalk Lane. It had been very like tonight, with all the fog and everything, but being down there in the Boroughs as opposed to up here on the prosperous Wellingborough Road, it had been a lot eerier. Even St. Edmund's Church with all its looming tombstones just across the street didn't give you the shivers, at the stroke of midnight, how some places in the Boroughs could do even by the light of day.

Cut loose and on his own, Tom had decided to head for the nearest hostelry where he'd be sure to know someone, which was the Black Lion down on Castle Hill. Although the place had no direct familial associations such as was the case with the Blue Anchor, in a way it had been a more constant focus of the Warren clan's attentions down the years. Or anyway, it had since Tommy's mam and dad had moved to Green Street, with their house just downhill and across the green from the back gates of the Black Lion's cobbled yard. Being stood since time immemorial there beside St. Peter's Church, it had provided a convenient venue to retire to after family funerals and christenings, and, being just two minutes' walk away, was ideal for a swift half almost any time of day or night. In summer the old gates were opened to the buttercups-and-grass slope at the ale-yard's rear behind St. Peter's, where Tom's mam would often sit out on a creaking bench dusted with emerald mould to have a drink with her surviving friends: old women with black bonnets, coats and dispositions like herself. His mother's best pal, Elsie Sharp, had died before May's eyes on one such sweet, long-shadowed evening after she'd knocked back a swig of stout straight from the bottle and had in the process swallowed a live bumble-bee, which was just then crawling about within the brown glass neck. Stung from the inside Elsie's throat had swollen up and closed, and after an unpleasant minute she'd been dead there in the birdsong and the lemon cordial light diffusing up above the railway station.

Once outside of the Blue Anchor, Tommy had turned left and headed down Chalk Lane to Castle Hill. There'd been a window lit in Doddridge Church, perhaps some group that met up in its rooms, and glancing up across the high stone wall Tom had been able to make out the set of loading doors, positioned halfway up the church's side. As well as an abiding love of mathematics, one of the things Tom had picked up from his barmy grandfather was a deep fascination for the facts of history, especially that subject's local aspect. Even so, he'd never had a proper answer for what those impractically high doors were doing there. The nearest he could get was that before the Reverend Philip Doddridge had arrived at Castle Hill and made the building there into a Nonconformist meeting-house, it had perhaps been used for something else, some business that required off-loading and delivery of goods by winch and pulley up to the first floor. Something about that explanation, though, had never rung quite true to Tom, which left the doors as an enduring question mark on his internal map of the location and its cloudy past.

Doddridge himself, Tommy had thought as he'd gone down beside the chapel and its burying ground, had been as big a puzzle as his church. Not in the sense that anything about him was unknown, but more that he'd been able to achieve such a long-lasting change in how the country thought about itself religiously, and that he'd done it from this tiny plot of land deep in the rat-runs of the Boroughs.

It had been Queen Anne's death during 1714 that had prepared the ground for Philip Doddridge, then a lad of twenty-seven, to come here to Castle Hill one Christmas Eve fifteen years later to take up his ministry. Anne Stuart had, during her reign, attempted to stamp out the Nonconformists. When she'd died the minister who had announced it had said, quoting from the Psalms, "Go, see now this cursed woman, and bury her; for she is a king's daughter." That was a signal for all the Dissenters and the Nonconformists to start celebrating as it meant that George the First, who was a Hanoverian and had vowed to support their cause, would soon be on the throne. All of them little groups – hangovers from the Independents, the Moravian Brethren, that tradition come down from John Wycliffe's Lollards in the thirteen-hundreds – they must have been popping wine corks at the thought of all that they'd be able to do now to shake things up, and Doddridge coming to Northampton had been part of that. Looked back on from the present day, you could say it had been the biggest part.

Sauntering past the unkempt burial ground that evening, Tommy had supposed the town would have been an attractive proposition to a young dissenting minister back then, what with its long tradition as a haven for religious firebrands, insurrectionists and the plain mad. Old Robert Browne who formed the Separatists in the late sixteenth century was buried in St. Giles churchyard, and the town was filled by Nation of Saints puritans and Ranters with their fiery flying rolls during the century that followed. There'd been fierce radical Christians shouting heresies from every rooftop, saying there was no life other than this present one, that Hell and Heaven were nowhere save here on earth and, worst of all, suggesting that the Bible showed God as a shepherd of the poor and not the wealthy. By the time that Philip Doddridge stepped out of the snow that Christmas Eve, 1729, rubbing his hands with frostbite and with glee, Northampton's reputation as a hotbed simmering with spiritual unrest would have been well established.

Doddridge's Evangelism, nine years earlier than that of the more widely-sung John Wesley, was the force that by Victoria's reign had transformed almost all of the Dissenting sects and the whole ruddy Church of England in the bargain. He'd accomplished this from what was even then one of the humblest places in the land, and done it in a little over twenty years before the TB took him when he hadn't yet turned fifty; done it all with words, his teachings and his writings and his hymns. To Tom's mind, "Hark! The Glad Sound!"

was about the best of them. "The Saviour comes, the Saviour promised long." Tommy had always thought of Doddridge writing that sat looking out from Castle Hill, perhaps imagining the last trump sounding in the heavens up above St. Peter's Church just down the way, or picturing a ragged, resurrected Jesus walking up Chalk Lane towards the little meeting house, his bloodied palms spread wide in universal absolution. During the more-than-a-thousand years this district had existed it had seen its fair share of extraordinary men, what with Richard the Lionheart, Cromwell, Thomas Becket, all of them, but in Tom Warren's estimation Philip Doddridge could be counted with the worthiest. He was the Boroughs' most heroic son. He was its soul.

St. Edmund's clock struck once for half-past two and snatched Tom back to where he was, stood outside the converted workhouse with his Kensitas burning away forgotten there between his nicotine-stained fingers. That had been a waste. He flung the smouldering end into the broader smoulder that surrounded him and let his mind return to February 1948 and to a night just as opaque and grey.

He'd come out of Chalk Lane past the newsagent's where he sometimes bought his paper of a Sunday morning; that had once been part of Propert's Commercial Hotel, and crossed the tarmac-smothered cobbles and disused iron tramlines of Black Lion Hill towards the pub the hill was named after. Pushing inside through its front door Tommy had been hit by a near solid wall of chatter, scent and warmth, the captured body heat of everyone who was crammed into the Black Lion on that chilly night. Before he'd took his coat off and stepped through the press of people to the bar, Tom had been feeling glad already that he'd chosen to come here tonight, rather than to have stayed with Frank at the Blue Anchor. There were always more familiar faces at the Lion.

Jem Perrit had been there, whose dad The Sheriff had run a horse-butcher's business in Horsemarket, and who lived himself with his wife Eileen and their baby daughter by the wood-yard that Jem kept in Freeschool Street, just round the corner from the Black Lion and off Marefair. As Tom now recalled the scene, Jem had been playing ninepins at the skittle table up one corner with Three-Fingered Tunk – who had a stall in the Fish Market up on Bradshaw Street – and Freddy Allen. Fred had been a moocher who you sometimes saw around the Boroughs still, who slept beneath the railway arches in Foot Meadow and who got along by pinching pints of milk and loaves of bread off people's doorsteps. The tramp had been narrowing his bleary eyes as he took aim and threw the wooden cheese, but it had looked to Tom as though Jem Perrit or Three-Fingered Tunk would probably be trouncing him. Propped up against the heaving bar there had been Podger Someo, locally famous former organ grinder, now retired, and everywhere that Tommy looked there had been grimy area legends nursing mythic grudges, a run-down Olympus full of sozzled titans spluttering

filthy jokes through mouthfuls of foam-topped ambrosia, fishing clumsily as
minotaurs inside their crisp bags for the blue wax paper twist of salt.

Tommy's own family, at least the Vernall side of it, had been well represented in the pub that night. Tom's uncle Johnny – his mam's younger
brother – had been there with Tom's aunt Celia, and sat up one corner by
herself with a half pint of Double Diamond and her battered old accordion
across her lap there had been Tommy's great-aunt Thursa, in her eighties by
that point and even harder to get any sense from than she'd previously been.
Tommy had said hello to her and asked if he could get her a fresh drink, at
which she'd looked alarmed as if she weren't sure who he was, but then had
nodded in acceptance anyway. Thursa had always liked to play on her accordion al fresco, trudging round the Boroughs, although some years earlier
during the war she'd taken to performances that were exclusively nocturnal.
More specifically, she'd only gone out in the street to play her instrument
during the blackouts, with the German bombers droning overhead and the
ARP wardens threatening to arrest her if she didn't stay indoors and stop that
bloody racket. Tom had never heard, at first hand, his great-aunt's Luftwaffe
sing-alongs, having been stationed overseas. His older sister Lou, however, had
described them to him with the tears of laughter running down her cheeks.
"They sent me out to fetch her in, and honestly, I swear that she was standing
there in Bath Row, looking up at all the big dark planes against the sky and
playing little tootles and long drones on her accordion, as if the bombing raid
was like a silent film and she was its accompanist. It was that awful engine
noise, the way it echoed right across the sky, and there was Thursa doing little
bits that fitted in with it, these little bits that sounded like somebody whistling or skipping. I can't properly describe it, but her little tra-la-las sounding
above the frightening thunder of the aeroplanes, it made you want to laugh
and cry at the same time. Laugh, mostly." Tom had pictured it, the skinny old
madwoman with her mushroom cloud of white hair standing caterwauling in
the blacked out street, the vast might of the German air force overhead. It had
made Tommy laugh too.

With the drinks arrived and Tommy's dotty great-aunt taken care of,
he'd sat down with his quiet auntie Celia and his lively uncle Johnny, who he
got on well with and could be relied upon to keep Tom company till closing
time. Tom could remember, back before the war, being with Walt and Jack
and Frank one night in the Criterion up King Street when their uncle Johnny
Vernall had come in and had a drink with them. He'd kept them all enthralled
with tales of what the almost empty pub had been like in its heyday, with a loaf
of bread, a ham, a jar of pickles and a wedge of cheese provided free on every
table. The increase in custom, Uncle Johnny said, had more than paid for the
comestibles, and you'd had no one getting drunk or rowdy since they'd all got

something in their stomachs to soak up the booze. To the four brothers it had sounded like an Eden, a lost golden age.

Sitting down with his aunt and uncle in the Black Lion's snug, Tommy had asked them how they were and also asked after his cousin Audrey, who just about everybody in the family had a soft spot for, and who played piano accordion in the dance band that her father, Uncle Johnny, managed. This was the same band that had performed so well at Walt's wedding reception up in Gold Street just a few months previously, when Tom and Frank had both been lectured by their mam and where, in Tom's opinion, his young cousin Audrey hadn't ever played so well or looked so lovely as she did upon that night, belting out swing and standards to the lurching celebrants who packed the dance-floor. Audrey was a little smasher, all the family thought so, but on that particular night in the Black Lion, Tom's uncle had just shook his head when Tom enquired about her, and said Audrey was at home and going through a lot of young girl's sulks and moods at present. Tom had been surprised, since Audrey had always seemed such a sunny little thing, but he'd supposed that this reported tantrum was to do with women and the changes that they went through, which at that point, mercifully, Tommy had known almost nothing of. He'd nodded and commiserated with his aunt and uncle, and had told them he was sure their daughter would get over it and be back to her old self in a day or two. On that count he'd been wrong, as it turned out.

Hobnobbing with his relatives, Tom had reflected on how much he liked his uncle Johnny, who he thought added a touch of colour to the family with his loud ties and his jacket's mustard check, his showbiz flair. There was just something up-to-date about the bloke, the way he ran a band and talked of dates and bookings, as if he were rising to the challenge of the world and future we'd got now, after the war, bursting with energy and eager to get on with a new life. According to Tom's mam, her younger brother Johnny had since childhood talked of nothing except going on the stage, of being part of all that sequinned razzmatazz, although he'd got no talent of his own to speak of. That was no doubt why he'd hit on managing a dance band if he couldn't play or sing in one. When his young Audrey had turned out so talented with the accordion, a taste for which she'd evidently picked up from her great-aunt Thursa, Johnny must have been as pleased as Punch. Tommy had often thought that when his uncle Johnny hovered in the wings and watched adoringly while Audrey played, it must have been like he was seeing his young self out there, all of his hopes and dreams at last parading in the footlights. Well, good luck to him. Perhaps the baby boy that Tom was waiting on now in the Wellingborough Road would end up good at something Tom himself had always had a hankering for, like, let's say, football. Tommy couldn't swear that if that happened he'd not be stood on the touchlines cheering, just like Uncle Johnny beaming proudly in the dark and tangled wires offstage.

Tom's auntie Celia was a different matter in that she was quiet where Johnny made a noise, and didn't fuss over their Audrey quite so much as Johnny did. Aunt Celia was always friendly, even cheerful in her way, but never seemed to have a lot to say for herself about anything. She weren't stuck up or toffee-nosed, but if Tom's uncle Johnny should crack one of his blue jokes she'd only smile and look away into her bitter lemon. Tommy's mother didn't care much for her sister-in-law, and said that she thought Aunt Celia had got no gumption, but then Tommy's mam didn't care much for anyone.

He'd kept his aunt and uncle company, that February night five or six years ago, until the landlord called out for last orders and they'd said that they'd not have another one. They'd finished up their drinks while Tommy was just starting his last pint, then got their coats on ready to go home. They hadn't far to go. Johnny and Celia lived with Audrey down in Freeschool Street, just uphill of Jem Perrit and his family, so it was only round the corner past the church. Tommy remembered Uncle Johnny standing up from his chair in the snug and settling his titfer on his head, what made him look as if he were a bookie. Helping Auntie Celia to her feet, Johnny had sighed and said, "Ah, well. I 'spect we'd better goo back 'ome and face the music", meaning Audrey and her bad mood, which was no more at the time than just an innocent remark.

They'd said ta-ta, and Tom had watched their exit from the smoky pub, with its interior as clouded as the foggy street revealed outside when Celia and Johnny had shoved open the Black Lion's door and stepped into the night. Tommy had taken his time finishing the half of bitter what were left out of his pint, eyes roaming idly round the bar on the off chance there might be a half-decent-looking woman in there. He was out of luck. The only female still remaining in the Black Lion other than the landlord's dog was Mary Jane, the brawler who was found more often up the Mayorhold at the Jolly Smokers or Green Dragon, one of them. One of her eyes was closed and violet, puffed up to a slit, and her whole face looked like it had once been a very different shape. She sat there staring into space, shaking her head occasionally as if to clear it, though you couldn't tell if that was because she were punchy, or if it were from the drink she'd put away. Even Tom's great-aunt Thursa had slipped out the pub while he weren't looking. Tommy was alone in an entirely masculine, predominantly broken-nosed domain, even including Mary Jane in that appraisal. While he was used to having mostly men around him from his work, and while he found that much less nerve-wracking than an extended company of women, it was much duller in the bargain. Tommy had knocked back the thin dregs of his pint, said goodnight to the people that he knew, and headed for the door himself while fastening his coat.

Outside the Black Lion, with the cold burning his throat, he'd been in two minds as to which way was the quickest home, back to his mam's in Green Street. Finally he'd opted to walk up by Peter's Church and cut along the alley there to Peter's Street, that marked the top edge of the green. It was just slightly longer than if he'd gone down around Elephant Lane, but being drunk and sentimental Tom had thought he'd like to head up by the churchyard so that he could say goodnight to Jack, or to the monument at any rate. What had been left of Jack was still out there somewhere in France.

Leaving the pub behind, Tommy had gone up Black Lion Hill and onto Marefair, with the mist now snagging on the iron churchyard railings to his right. He'd nodded, half-embarrassed, to the war memorial that poked up from the bed of drifting cotton wool around its base, and wondered who'd struck up the tune that he could hear, come from the inn that he'd just left. It had took Tommy several moments, beer-befuddled as he was, to work out that there wasn't a piano to be found at the Black Lion, and anyway, the noise hadn't been coming from behind him but instead was faint and shimmering, emerging from the Marefair shadows that were curdling up ahead.

Intrigued, Tom had walked past the narrow alley that ran down between the church and Orme's, the gent's outfitters, where he'd been intending to cut through to Peter's Street. He'd wanted to know who it was, making a row at this hour of night, and to make sure that there was nothing untoward trans-piring in the neighbourhood. Besides, as he went on past Cromwell House, Tommy could hear the slightly frantic-sounding tune more clearly, and could almost make out through his middling stupor what it was. It had appeared to be emerging from the neck of Freeschool Street just up ahead of him, the tumbling refrain flowing across the pavement with the fog and tangling round Tom's half-cut feet to trip him up.

He'd paused, outside the brown stone building where the Lord Protector had been billeted the night before he'd gone to fight at Naseby field, and stead-ied himself with one hand on the rough wall to check his wavering balance. That was when he'd seen his uncle Johnny and his auntie Celia come reeling out of Freeschool Street into Marefair, clutching their mouths, holding their hands across their faces as though they were weeping, hanging on each other's sleeves like two survivors of a train wreck clambering up the embankment. What on earth had happened?

What he should have done, he thought now, blowing in his hands to warm them up outside the hospital, was simply to have called out to his aunt and uncle, asking what was wrong. He hadn't done that, though. He'd stood there hidden in the mist and watched the couple, looking like they'd aged ten years within the last ten minutes, as they'd stumbled off into the damp miasma clinging to each other, lowing like maimed animals. They'd headed off in the direction of Horsemarket, the wet noises of their misery becoming fainter. Tom had watched them go from his place of concealment and had burned with shame to think that he'd seen family in distress and simply stood there doing bugger all, not even offering to help.

It had just seemed so private, Uncle Johnny and Aunt Celia's grief. That was all Tom could say now in his own defence. He'd been brought up to help people when things were going rough for them, but then he'd also been taught not to poke his nose in others' private business, and it sometimes felt like a fine line between the two. That was the way that it had been with Uncle Johnny and Aunt Celia that night. It looked as though their lives had just that moment fell to bits, as though they'd fallen in upon themselves, as though whatever had upset them was so personal and so humiliating that to have someone intrude upon it would have only made it worse. Thinking about it now, perhaps what he'd picked up on was that Celia and Johnny weren't seeking assistance with whatever had occurred. They weren't out banging on the neighbours' doors and asking somebody to fetch a fire engine or ambulance. They hadn't gone just down and round the corner to Tom's mam's in Green Street, Johnny's own big sister. They'd not sought help in the Boroughs, but had made for Gold Street and town centre. Tom had later learned that Uncle Johnny and Aunt Celia had sat till dawn both huddling devastated on the steps of All Saints, underneath its portico.

Upon the night itself, he'd watched his aunt and uncle until they were gone, then wandered into Freeschool Street to find out what was going on. He'd stumbled haltingly down the black crevice, where the Free School had been situated in the fifteen-hundreds, walking in the face of all the mournful, stirring music that rang from the haze more loudly with Tom's every cautious step. All the low notes had resonated in the lightless window-glass of the soot-dusted manufacturing concerns to Tommy's right and left, making the panes buzz like trapped flies. It had been round about then that he'd first caught on what tune was being played over and over, being banged out on an old joanna somewhere in the gloom towards what used to be Green Lane. He'd started singing it, inside his head, familiar words all coming back to him before he'd even hit upon its title, though he'd recognised it as a song that he knew well. How did it go? "Why tell them all your secrets ..."

Tommy had progressed hesitantly down the unlit street, as much for fear of tripping over something in the fog and knackering himself as of what he might find when he got further down towards the bottom end. He'd known already that it would be Uncle Johnny's house the tune was coming from, that it would be their Audrey playing it. Who else down Freeschool Street could trot out such a lovely piece as that? "They're buried under the snow ..." Ever so well he knew it, he just hadn't at that time been able to remember what the thing was called. The missing title nagging at his mind, Tommy had staggered further down into the invisible harmony.

In twenty paces, by the time he'd reached the junction with St. Peter's Street, it had become clear that the old song was indeed emerging from his cousin's house across the road, down near the Gregory Street corner. He had also realised that Freeschool Street was utterly deserted save for he himself and for one other: standing rooted in the crawling vapour that was boiling over Uncle Johnny's doorstep, rigid and stick-thin with her wild head tipped back to gaze up at the lit-but-curtained parlour window that the music came from, had been Tommy's great-aunt Thursa. In her arms she'd cradled the accordion like a mute and monstrous child, the waxy and translucent fingers of one hand stroking distractedly across the keyboard, back and forth as if to calm the silent instrument and to allay its fears at this alarming situation. Thursa hadn't make a sound herself, but she'd been listening so intently to the music leaking from inside the house that you could almost hear her doing it. It carried on, the tune, stitching its thread of half-remembered lyrics on the blanket of the mist. "Whispering grass, don't tell the trees ..."

Of course, by that point Tommy had recalled the title he'd been grasping for. "Whispering Grass". That had been an old favourite for years by then, had even worked its way into the language as the slang for an informer, or at least that's where Tom thought that the expression "grass" had come from. Prior to that point it had been Tom's opinion that the song, though haunting, was too soppy and too whimsical, with its idea of grass and bushes talking to each other, just like something that Walt Disney might have done. Hearing it from the creeping fog in Freeschool Street though, on that February night, it hadn't sounded whimsical at all. To Tom's ear, it had sounded terrible. Not terrible as in the sense of bad or badly played, but more as if it spoke of something terrible, of some great hurt too terrible to mend, or of some terrible betrayal. It had sounded angry in the way its chords crashed out, notes almost splintering beneath the impact of the unseen fingers. It had sounded like an accusation and, as well, like an unburdening, an agonized confession that could never be retracted, after which things couldn't be the same again. It had been music for the end of something.

"... 'cause the trees don't need to know." Ashamed. That had been, Tom thought now, another quality apart from hurt and anger that the tune had brought to the dank evening air: an overpowering sense of shame. Even the awful jollity into which the refrain would sometimes break sounded sardonic, sounded vengeful, sounded wrong. Tommy had been disturbed, mostly because he hadn't for the life of him been able to imagine such an unexpected torrent of confused emotions pouring from so self-effacing and demure a vessel as his cousin Audrey. What can have been going through her mind for it to have emerged in the spine-tingling, feverish way it had? What had she been feeling that produced a reeling, stomach-dropping noise like that?

God knows how many times she'd played the tune already before Tom or anybody else had ventured into Freeschool Street to hear it, but as he and his great-aunt had stood there separately listening in the fog he'd heard the song repeated at least four more times, all the way through, before it had eventually ended in a sudden yawning silence that had been in some way even more upsetting than the row preceding it.

A tense few moments had elapsed, perhaps to make sure the recital was completely over, and then great-aunt Thursa had, from nowhere, pressed just four notes from the squeeze-box slung on its worn leather strap around her stringy neck, four grave and trudging tones that Tom had recognised with a mild tingle of alarm as the beginning of "The Funeral March", or at the time he'd thought that's what it was, at any rate. But with only that mournful opening completed his great-aunt had fallen silent and allowed her parchment fingers to drop from the keys. Abruptly, Thursa had turned round and marched away down Freeschool Street as if, aside from her own brief musical contribution, there was no more to be done. Within a moment her gaunt figure had dissolved into the cold seethe of the night.

Tom realised now, stood shuffling in the forecourt of St. Edmund's Hospital, that it had been the last time he'd encountered great-aunt Thursa, who'd took ill with bronchial troubles and had died some two months afterwards. The mental picture of her walking off into the fog, into the roiling mystery, was the last image of her he could call to mind. Perhaps her short rendition of "The Funeral March" had been a prophecy, though as he thought about it now he saw that those four notes could just as well have been "Oh Mine Papa", or probably a dozen other tunes.

After his great-aunt had departed, Tom had stood there for perhaps five minutes more, just staring at the now-hushed house across the way with the soft gaslight filtered through drawn curtains from its parlour window. Then he'd stumbled off down Freeschool Street, along Green Lane to his mam's house in Green Street. May had been abed already by the time that he got in, and Frank hadn't come home yet from the Anchor. Tom had lit the mantle, lit a fag from the same match, then had a sit in the armchair for a few minutes, just before he went to bed.

Across a small room shrunken further by the gaslight, up against one wall had stood the family piano, black and polished like a coffin. Perched on top of it had been an empty vase and a big, glossy eight-by-ten inside a prop-up frame. The photo had been taken for the purpose of publicity, clearly by a professional, and was a group shot of the outfit Uncle Johnny managed. Standing front and centre of the picture, no doubt with an eye to showing off the dance band's most attractive asset, there had been Tom's cousin Audrey with her piano accordion almost bigger than what she was. Resting on its keys her slender hands were placed so elegantly you could tell that it was artificial; she'd been told to hold the pose and the accordion in just that way by the photographer. Tom could imagine it, the chat and patter while he'd took the shot, with the flirtatious manner blokes like that seemed generally to have about them. "Right, that's lovely, let's have a big smile now from the ravishing young lady." And then Audrey would have cast her eyes up, just as she was doing in the picture, looking comically exasperated as she laughed away the compliment – "Oh, honestly!" – but flattered, pleased he'd said it even if he'd done so just to make her smile. Her head was tipped back slightly as if she were making an appeal to heaven, asking for deliverance from men and their smooth, silly talk, and you could see the strong line of her chin, the straight slope of her nose, the finely sculpted head with her dark hair cascading down onto the shoulders of her ironed white blouse. His cousin at that time had been around eighteen years old, and Tommy had thought that the photo looked as if it had been taken two or three years earlier, when Audrey had been fifteen or sixteen. She'd looked so lively and so wry that Tom had sat there in the gas-lit living room a good half hour just trying to fit together the young woman in the picture and the frightening performance he'd just heard in Freeschool Street.

Of course, over the next two or three days, Tom had learned more of what had happened on that night. According to his mam, who by that time had heard her younger brother's full account of things, Tom's uncle Johnny and his auntie Celia had got back home to Freeschool Street from the Black Lion to find their only child had locked them out the house while she sat there inside and played the same lament repeatedly on the piano, pointedly ignoring all their poundings on the door and their demands to be let in. As the demands had swiftly turned to worried pleas, his cousin Audrey had apparently made vocal interjections of her own, shouting above the avalanche of her own playing: "When the grass is whispering over me, then you'll remember." Finally her parents had just given up and slunk away into the mist, away up Gold Street where they'd sheltered under All Saints' portico all night, crushed by the realization of the dreadful thing that had just happened. Their one daughter, their bright, pretty, talented young daughter who they'd hoped would carry all their dreams into the future had gone off her head, gone round the corner. That next morning doctors had been called and Audrey Vernall had been taken up the Berry Wood turn to St. Crispin's mental home, struggling and kicking, screaming out all manner of fantastical delusions as Tom's uncle Johnny had recounted it. She'd been in the asylum ever since, would very likely be there all her life, a shame and a disgrace upon the family. Her name was only mentioned rarely now.

The general consensus, naturally, had been that Audrey's problems were inherited, part of the curse passed down amongst the Vernalls, as displayed in both Tom's granddad Snowy and his great-aunt Thursa.

There it was. The madness in the family. That was a cheery thing to think about while you were waiting for your first child to arrive, but Tom supposed there was no hiding from it. It was just a fact, part of the complicated lottery of birth that would decide whether the baby had brown hair like Doreen or black hair like Tom, whether its eyes were blue or green, if it was to be tall or short, well-built or skinny, sane or insane. Nobody had a say in how their children would be born, but then nobody had a say with most of the important things in life. All you could do was make the best of what you had. All you could do was play your cards as they'd been dealt.

He glanced around at his surroundings, at the gauze fog bandaging the blackness, at the crumbling church across the street, its weight and presence felt rather than seen. On Tommy's left a necklace of dim streetlamps wound away through the dark miles to Wellingborough. To his right the mongrel rhapsodies of Mad Marie were tangled round town centre in haphazard strands of flimsy tinsel and behind him loomed the rehabilitated workhouse, like a thuggish bailiff who'd been given a new job and uniform and swore he was a reformed character. Tom realised with a start that they were more than halfway through the twentieth century already.

Tom also began to see that it weren't just the blood and the heredity that would determine how a child developed. It was everything. It was the aggregate of all the planet's parts and all its history, of every fact and incident that made the world, that fashioned the child's parents, all of these components leading up to that specific baby floating there in that specific womb. With his own offspring brewing now inside Doreen's distended belly waiting to be poured out, Tommy understood that there would be no element of his or his wife's lives that would not influence their baby, just as every circumstance of their own parents' lives in turn had made its mark on them.

The job as a director Snowy Vernall had turned down, for an example, played its part as to what kind of family and upbringing their newborn could expect. Tom's mother's first child dying of diphtheria had meant that she'd not stopped with just two girls but had gone on to have four boys as well. Had it been otherwise, then neither Tommy nor his own forthcoming child would have existed in the first place.

Then there was the war, of course, and all the politics that had come both before and after it. All those things that decided how this coming generation should be educated, what the streets and houses would be like where they grew up and whether there'd be any jobs about once they were grown. And these were just the obvious things that anyone could see would have effects upon a kiddie's chance in life. What about all the other things, events so small they were invisible and yet which added up to someone choosing one path rather than the other, added up to something that might have an impact on the world, upon his child, for better or for worse?

Tom wondered at the whirlpool of occurrences, of lives and deaths and memories that were at present being funnelled into Doreen's each contraction, pressing out an imprint on their baby as it writhed towards the light: the air raid nights, the dole queue days, the wireless programmes and the demolition sites. Glimpse of a woman's legs with fake seams drawn in eyebrow pencil down the calf, of rubber johnnies raining on commuter's hats. Grave of a fifteen-year-old German sniper by the road in France. Tom's granddad crumpling up his careful ring of numbers in a rage to throw it on the fire, the black hole spreading from the centre of the paper as it burned. The photograph of Audrey standing framed on the piano, with her posed hands and her blithe smile and the grinning band members behind her in their bow ties, holding their guitars and clarinets. The fog, the pigeon-shit and Mad Marie all somehow filtering into the new arrival who'd be drawing its first breath and making its first wail within an hour or two, all being well.

St. Edmund's clock struck three times from the higher storeys of the mist. His toes were so cold in his boots he couldn't feel them anymore. Bugger this for a game of soldiers. With his hands thrust deep in his mac's pockets, Tommy Warren turned round on his heel and started walking back along the hospital's long drive towards the blurred and distant lights of its maternity wards, twinkling faintly in the gloom. Doreen couldn't have had it yet, or someone would have been sent out to fetch him. Walking up the path he noticed that the wavering piano was no longer audible, though Tommy didn't know if that meant Mad Marie had stopped at last, or if it merely meant the wind had changed directions. Humming absently to fill the sudden silence, breaking off when he became aware that he was humming "Whispering Grass", Tom changed his tune to "Hark! The Glad Sound!" and then carried on. The bulb-lit porch outside the waiting room was drawing gradually nearer. Picking up his pace and perking up his ideas, Tommy went to welcome in his first-born baby boy.

Or girl.

CHOKING ON A TUNE

Whatever his big sister had implied across the years, or had indeed at one point written on his forehead using magic marker while he was asleep, Mick Warren wasn't stupid. If there'd been a hazard label on the drum, perhaps a yellow death's-head or a screaming stick-man with his face burned off, then Mick would almost certainly have realised that hitting it quite hard with an enormous fuckoff sledgehammer was not the best idea he'd ever had.

But for some reason there'd been no fluorescent stickers, no white government advisory, not even the insipid kind that warned against skin ageing or low birth weight. Mick had blithely hefted the great hammer back just over his right shoulder and then swung it down through its familiar and exhilarating arc. The satisfying clang when it connected, ringing off into the windswept corners of St. Martin's Yard, was only marred by his own startled bellow as the whole front of Mick's head, which he had always thought of as his better side, was sandblasted by poison dust.

His cheeks and brow had instantly been blistered into bubble-wrap. Dropping the weighty hammer, Mick had tried to run off from the toxic cloud his mystery drum had just exhaled as if it were a swarm of bees, swatting his hands around his face and roaring angrily, not "squealing like a girl" as one close relative had later claimed. The relative in question, anyway, had got no cause to talk. At least he'd only looked the way he had for several days as a result of an industrial accident, whereas she'd looked that way since birth and had no such excuse.

Blinded and howling, this according to the subsequent colourful witness statements of fellow employees, Mick had charged round in a semicircle and, with all the slapstick timing of a radiation-scarred post-nuclear Harold Lloyd, had run head first into a bar of steel protruding from the outsize scales on which the flattened drums were weighed. He'd knocked himself out cold, and looking back congratulated himself on the speed with which, in trying circumstances, he had improvised a painkiller that was both total and immediate in its effect. Hardly the actions of a stupid man, he'd smugly reassured himself after a day or two, by which time the worst bruises weren't so bad.

He must have only lay sprawled on his back there in the dirt unconscious for a second before Howard, his best mate down at the reconditioning yard, caught on to what was happening and had rushed to Mick's assistance. He'd turned on the tap that fed the business's one hosepipe, training the resultant jet into Mick's comatose and upturned face, sluicing away the caustic orange powder covering the blistered features like a minstrel make-up meant only for radio. From what Howard reported afterwards, Mick had come round at once, his bloodshot eyes opening on a look of absolute confusion. He'd apparently been mumbling something with great urgency as he recovered consciousness, but far too softly for his concerned workmate to make out more than a word or two of what he'd said. Something about a chimney or perhaps a chimp that was in some way getting bigger, but then Mick had seemed to suddenly remember where he was and also that his blistered and rust-dusted face was now an agonising bowl of Coco Pops. He'd started hollering again, and after Howard had washed off the worst of the contamination with his hose he'd got permission from the anxious management to drive Mick over Spencer Bridge, up Crane Hill, Grafton Street and Regent Square, across the Mounts, then take a complicated set of turns to Billing Road to Cliftonville, this being where the casualty department of the hospital was now. Despite the fact that Mick had spent the whole duration of this journey swearing forcefully into the wet towel that he'd held pressed to his face, something about the route they'd taken had felt queasily familiar.

He'd been lucky, happening to hit a quiet patch at the hospital, and had been treated straight away, not that there was a lot that they could do. They'd cleaned him up and put drops in his eyes, told him his eyesight should be back to normal the next day, his face within a week, then Howard ran him home. All the way there Mick had gazed silently from the car window at the blur of Barrack Road and Kingsthorpe through his swollen, leaking eyelids and had wondered why he felt a sense of creeping and insidious dread. They'd given him the all-clear down at casualty. It wasn't like he had to fret about the accident's long-term effects, and with the few days of paid sick leave that he'd get off work from this you could say he'd come out on top. Why did he feel, then, as if some great cloud of doom was hanging over him? It must have been the shock, he'd finally concluded. Shock could do some funny things. It was a well-known fact.

Howard had dropped him off in the pull-over spot down at the foot of Chalcombe Road, barely a minute's walk from Mick and Cathy's house. Mick said goodbye and thanked his colleague for the ride then mounted the short lane that led to his back gate. The rear yard, with its patio and decking and the shed he'd built himself was reassuring in its tidiness after the chaos and confusion of his day thus far, even seen through the bleary filter of his current puddle-vision. The interior with its gleaming kitchen and neat living room was every bit as orderly and comforting, and with Cath off at work and both the boys at school he had it to himself. Mick made himself a cup of tea and sank into the sofa, lighting up a fag, uneasily aware of the precarious normality of everything.

Although Mick did his fair share of the work, the driving force behind the pristine smartness of their home was Cathy. This was not to say that Mick's wife was obsessed with cleanliness and order. It was more that Cathy had a deep aversion to untidiness and grime and what they represented to her, a conditioning instilled by having grown up in the Devlin family den. He understood that what to him might seem a barely-noticeable minor carpet stain, to Cathy was a crack in the high wall she'd built between her present and her past, between their current comfortable domestic life and Cathy's not particularly happy childhood. Children's toys left scattered on the rug, if not picked up at once, could mean that the next time she looked there'd be her late dad and a gang of drunken uncles sprawled about the place, what looked like a scrap metal business opening in the back yard, and more policemen coming to the door than milkmen. This fear wasn't rational, they both knew that, but Mick could see how growing up a Devlin could impress it on a person.

Mick got on with all his in-laws, very well with some of them, and thought that by and large they were a lovely crowd, at least the ones he knew. Cath's sister Dawn, for instance, was a social worker down in Devon, where Mick and the family had taken lots of holidays as a result. Dawn's youngest daughter Harriet, at the tender age of four, had said about the funniest thing that Mick had ever heard from any child or adult when her dad had asked her if she knew why crabs walked sideways and she'd moodily replied, "Because they're arseholes." Perhaps because there were a lot of similarities in background with the Warren family, Mick had always felt very comfortable about being related to the Devlins.

Mind you, they were still the Devlins. Bulletins through Cathy from the wilder reaches of the massively extended clan still had the power to startle or alarm. There'd been a funeral some weeks before that Mick had not been able to attend thanks to his work. Cathy had gone, and it had been by all accounts the spirited affair that Devlin funerals usually turned out to be. At one point in the service, Cathy's sister Dawn had nudged her and said, "Have you seen our Chris?" This was a distant cousin Cathy had already spotted, standing in the crowd towards the chapel's rear, and so she said that, yes, she'd seen him. Dawn, though, had persisted. "No, but have you *seen* him? Have you seen the chap that he's got with him?" Cathy had glanced back across her shoulder and there stood her cousin, next to someone just as tall as he was who seemed to be struggling to control his feelings at the sad occasion. It was only later, at the wake, that Cath had realised why he'd been standing so close to Cousin Chris. The two of them were handcuffed to each other. The emotionally overwrought man, who'd embarrassed everybody at the do by going on about how wonderful the Devlin family were and just how much he'd been moved by the ceremony, was the plain-clothes prison officer responsible for supervising Chris's day release. Armed robbery, apparently.

Mick's wife's kin were a colourful and various bunch grown from the same black, soot-fed Boroughs earth as were the Warrens. No doubt this was why Cath wouldn't tolerate that self-same native soil if it got tracked across her fitted carpets. The pastel walls and polished dining table were a barrier against the mud that hung in clumps round Cathy's roots, but Mick enjoyed the neatness, the predictable serenity. The only problem with it at the moment came when Mick caught sight of his reflection in the glass doors of the cabinet. Sat there with his erupting face sipping his tea amongst the decorous furnishings he looked like something from a George Romero film, a wistful zombie trying to remember how the living did things.

This stray thought brought with it the return of Mick's unfocussed, inexplicable anxieties from earlier. He still didn't know where they were coming from. Had something happened in his head while he was out? A stroke or something, or perhaps he'd had one of those dreams that you can't quite remember but which leave a nasty atmosphere all day. What had been going through his mind in those first seconds when he came round flat out in St. Martin's Yard, babbling nonsense with volcanoes in his eyes? What had his first thought been upon awakening?

With a lurch he realised that it had been, simply, 'Mum'.

His mother, Doreen Warren who'd been Doreen Swan, had died ten years before in 1995 and Mick still thought about her fondly almost every day, still missed her. But he missed her as an adult misses people, and he didn't think about her with the tone of mental voice he'd heard in his first thought upon recovering consciousness. That had been like a lost child calling for its mother, and he hadn't felt like that since ...

Since he'd woken up in hospital when he was three.

Oh God. Mick stood up from the sofa, then sat down again, unsure of why he'd risen in the first place. Was that what this simmering unease was all about, a chance event of no lasting importance that had happened more than forty years ago? He stubbed his cigarette out in the ashtray that he'd brought through from the kitchen then stood up again, this time to crack a window open and allow the smoke time to disperse before the kids and Cathy came home from their days at school and work. This task accomplished he sat down and then stood up again, and then sat down. Shit. What was wrong with him?

He could remember what it had been like when he was three, opening up his eyes to grey ward walls and the pervasive smell of disinfectant, having no idea of where he was or how he'd got there. He'd been forced to put the

missing incident together one piece at a time from scraps of information that
he'd wormed out of his mum over the next few days, how they'd been sitting
in the back yard when a sweet had got itself stuck in Mick's throat so that
he couldn't breathe, and how the man who lived next door to them along St.
Andrew's Road had driven Mick all limp and lifeless to the hospital, where
they'd unblocked his windpipe, taken out his swollen tonsils for good measure
and returned him to his family as good as new by the weekend. He knew, then,
what had happened to him but he only knew it second hand. When he'd first
woken up with a strange nurse and doctor looming in above him he'd had
no recall of anything from earlier that day at all, not sitting in the garden on
his mother's knee, not choking and not being rushed to hospital. For all he'd
known, the bleak and pungent ward with all the Mabel Lucie Attwell posters
tin-tacked to its walls might have been his first moment of existence.

That, though, had been then. This time, on waking from his accident
at work, there'd been a moment when Mick's mind was far from blank; a
moment in which Mick had suddenly remembered quite a lot. The problem
was that in those first few panicked seconds of recovered consciousness, his
sudden rush of memories had not been those belonging to a forty-nine-year-
old. He hadn't even known that was his age, had not straight away understood
what he was doing in this open yard with steel drums everywhere. He hadn't
thought immediately of Cathy, or the kids, or of the many other reference
points to which, in normal circumstances, he had anchored his identity. It
was, in those befuddled instants, just as if the last four-decades-plus-change
of his life had never happened. It was as though he were once again a three-
year-old awakening in 1959 down at the General Hospital, except this time
he'd been a three-year-old who could remember what had happened to him.

All the details of the incident in the back garden that had been wiped
from his memory as a child had, after more than forty years, been given
back. Granted, they'd been returned in a compressed and jumbled form that
mainly manifested as a vague uneasy feeling, but if Mick just sat and thought
it through he felt convinced that he'd be able to untangle it, to pick this sense
of being haunted that he had apart like so much yarn. He closed his eyes, as
much to stop them stinging as to aid his reverie. He saw the yard, saw the old
stable that was visible across a five-foot-high back wall, its roof with the black
gaps where slates were missing like a crossword puzzle blank. The sofa's cush-
ions underneath him were Doreen's lap, and its hard and bony wooden edge
her knees. He sank into the warm ancestral dough without the slightest difficulty or resistance as the spacious living room surrounding him contracted to
a narrow brick enclosure, with the backsides of the terraced houses rising up
to right and left, a ragged patch of washed-out blue sky overhead.

The Boroughs had been an entirely different place back then, that smelled and looked and sounded nothing like the abattoir of hope and joy it was today. Admittedly, the odour of the neighbourhood had been much worse in those days, or at least in the most literal and obvious sense. There'd been a tannery just north along St. Andrew's Road, with great mounds of mysterious turquoise shavings piled up in its yard and a sharp chemical aroma like carcinogenic pear drops. This came from the noxious blue substance painted on the sheepskins to burn out all the hair follicles and make the wool coats that much easier to pull, and wasn't half as bad as the smell coming from the south, which issued from a rendering plant, a glue factory on St. Peter's Way. The west wind brought a perfume of scorched engine oil blown from the railway with an iron aftertaste of anthracite from the coal merchants, Wiggins, just across the road, while from the opposite direction when the dawn sun rose above the stable's leaking rooftop it would lift the rich scents from the Boroughs' streets themselves, wafting them downhill from the east in an olfactory avalanche: the steamy human essence piping from a hundred copper boilers, good food, bad food, dog food and dog carcasses, brick dust and wild flowers, rancid drains and someone's chimneypot on fire. Hot tar in summer, the astringent smell of frosty grass in winter, all of this and then the River Nene on top, its cold and green bouquet drifting from Paddy's Meadow just along the way. These days the Boroughs had no distinct fragrance that the nose could ascertain, and yet in the imagined cilia of the heart it reeked.

As for St. Andrew's Road itself, or at least as far as their little strip of it had been concerned, that was just gone, replaced by a grass verge that harboured a few trees and the odd ornamental shopping trolley, stretched between the foot of Spring Lane and the foot of Scarletwell. There'd been twelve houses there, two or three businesses, God knows how many people on a plot that now seemed to be the sole province of the upturned mobile birdcages, the cold and hard providers of three generations' packaged sustenance sprawling there in the weeds like obsolete wire mummies that the lab chimps had at last lost interest in.

Sitting there on the sofa in his Kingsthorpe living room he let his mind trickle away down vanished conduits and lost lanes to soak into the past. He saw the narrow jitty that ran parallel with Andrew's Road, up past the back yards of the row, a solitary disused gas lamp halfway down its length. For some years after all the houses were demolished you could still make out the cobbles of the obsolete back alley as they bulged up through the turf; the sawn-through base of the old lamp standard, a ragged-edged iron ring inside which the cross-section bores of smaller wires and pipes had still been visible, the neck-stump of a buried and decapitated robot. This was gone now, swallowed by the grass, or by the bulging fence that ran along the bottom of Spring Lane School's playing field, this boundary having crawled a little to the west within the thirty years or so since his home street had been pulled down and its inhabitants strewn to the wind. There was nobody left who could object or halt the playing field's encroachment. In another twenty years Mick thought the wandering chain link barrier might have got down to Andrew's Road itself, where it would have to wait beside the curb for a few centuries before it crossed.

The road, named after the St. Andrew's Priory that had stood along its northern, Semilong end long before, had once been the town's western boundary. This was in the twelve-hundreds, when the area called the Boroughs now was then Northampton, all there was of it. The locals and the Bachelerie di Northampton – the notoriously radical and monarch-baiting student population of the town – had sided with Simon de Montfort and his rebel barons against King Henry the Third and the four dozen wealthy burgesses who had been governing the place for fifty years since Magna Carta, creaming off its profits, and were forerunners of the still forty-eight-strong council that was running things today, in 2005. Back then in the 1260s, an irate King Henry had sent out a force of soldiers to quell the revolt with extreme prejudice. The prior of St. Andrew's, being of the Cluniac order and thus being French, had sided with the Norman royal family and let the King's men enter through a gap within the priory wall, probably more or less across the street from where the Warrens' house had later stood. The troops had sacked and burned the previously prosperous and pleasant town, while in reaction to the rabble-rousing students it had been decided that it would be Cambridge that became a seat of learning, rather than Northampton. As Mick saw things, that was where the punishment and disenfranchisement of his home turf had started, kicking off a process that continued to the present day. Refuse just once to eat the shit that you've been served up and the powers that be will make sure there's a double helping steaming on your plate at every supper for the next eight hundred years.

That day in 1959 the district had been spread out like a musty blanket on the summer, stalks of bleaching grass poked through its threadbare weave. The factories clanged at intervals or sprayed acetylene sparks in brief, shearing arcs behind smoked Perspex windows. Martins chattered in the baking eaves to either side of tilting streets where women in checked headscarves trotted stoically along beneath their panniers of shopping; where old men at ten past three were still attempting to get home, dizzy with dominoes, from their quick lunchtime half down at the Sportsman's Arms. The school uphill across the yellowed playing field, deserted for the holidays, was deafeningly silent with the non-shrieks of two hundred absent children. It had been a harmless, pleasant afternoon. The tower blocks hadn't been erected yet. The sand-blonde film of demolition dust coating the neighbourhood evoked only the season and the beach.

The whole front of the terraced house had been deserted, Mick's dad Tommy being off at work over the brewery in Earl's Barton and the other family members out in the back yard taking advantage of the weather. From the smooth-worn pavement of St. Andrew's Road, three steps led up into the alcove cowling the tired red of their front door, a black iron boot-scrape, which Mick hadn't fathomed the intended function of until he was approximately ten, set back into the wall beside the bottom doorstep. To the door's right, as seen by a visitor, there was the framed wire grid at pavement level ventilating the pitch-dark coal cellar, and above that was the front room window with the china swan gazing disconsolately out at Wiggins's yard, the rust-and-bind-weed railway sidings stretched beyond and the occasional passing car. Left of the front door was a mutual drainpipe and then the front door and windows of Mrs. McGeary's house, which had a frayed and peeling wooden gate beside it giving access to the cobbled yard and the dilapidated stables at the rear.

Once up the steps and inside number seventeen, there was the plain coconut doormat and the passageway, with ghostly ochre flowers fading into oblivion on its wallpaper and a flypaper-coloured light falling upon its worsted-burdened coat pegs. The first door upon the right led to the then-evacuated front room with its ponderous grandfather clock, its horsehair settee and its easy chair, its paraffin stove and its polished cabinet of fancy crockery that no one ever used, its table mat-sized rented television with a cabinet-style set of doors that closed across the screen. The second offshoot from the passage led into the similarly empty living room, while straight in front of you the stairs rose to the upper floor, carpeted with a writhing brown design that looked like catkins made from Christmas pudding. The top storey of the old house had got his and Alma's room towards the rear up at the stair-way's top, then up one sideways step onto the landing where their gran's room likewise overlooked the narrow L-shape of the semi-tiled back yard, with Tom and Doreen's room, the biggest in the house, being along the landing's end, its windows overlooking Andrew's Road above the ones downstairs with the resigned white china swan. This upper level, being mostly uninhabited by day, he'd thought of as his home's night-storey, lending it a slightly sinister and creepy air. Whenever he'd had childhood nightmares that had used his own house as their set, the scariest bits had always taken place upstairs.

The ground floor was too cosy to be frightening, despite the shadows in the generally sunless kitchen and those in the living room, just off the gloomy hall. Here space was at a premium, occupied by the drop-wing din-ing table with two matching seats, a stool and rugged wood chair making up the set. Two comfy armchairs (one of which Mick's cousin John had fallen back out through the window from years earlier) flanked the meteoric-looking iron fireplace (into which John's sister Eileen had plunged face first at around the same time), with the tiny room also accommodating the large junk-sarcophagus that was the sideboard. A stepped plaster beading, once presumably intended to be decorative, ran round the edges of the ceiling and conspired to make the roof seem even lower than it did already. Hanging from the picture rail of the wall opposite the hearth were washed-out portrait photographs in heavy frames, beige and white images depicting men with knowing grins and bright eyes gazing from beneath the thickets of their brows: Mick's great-grandfather William Mallard, and his gran's late husband, Mick's maternal grandfather Joe Swan with the moustache that appeared wider than his shoulders. There was a third picture also, of another man, but Mick had never bothered asking who it was and nobody had ever bothered telling him. Instead, he called to mind the face of the anonymous chap in the picture as a stand-in if somebody mentioned a dead relative he hadn't known. One week the man might be Gran's brother, Uncle Cecil, and the next he could be Cousin Bernard, drowned during the war whilst trying to rescue others from a sinking battleship. For a bewildering fortnight he'd been Neville Chamberlain before Mick had worked out that the Hitler-appeasing former premier wasn't a close relative.

Cut into the dividing wall between the front and living rooms there was a recess which contained a single panel of stained glass, a floral emblem in bright yellow, emerald green, and red like ruby port. Some evenings around teatime, when the sun was going down behind the railway yards across St. Andrew's Road, an almost-horizontal shaft would strike in through the parlour window, glance across the dipped head of the china swan and blaze through the connecting pane of coloured glass into the dim-lit living room to splash its marvellous and trembling patch of phantom paint upon the bland-faced wireless, wall-mounted between the back-yard window and the kitchen door.

The poky kitchen with its white distempered walls and chilly blue and red slabs making up its floor was down a short step from the living room. Descending this, you had the cellar door on your immediate left, a rusted meat-safe stood behind it there atop the cellar stairs. Upon your right was the back door which led out to the top half of the yard, with just beyond a coarse stone sink sporting a single brass cold-water tap, inlaid with verdigris, beneath a solitary window. Opposite had stood the gas-stove, the old woodworm-riddled kitchen table and the treacherous mangle, and above them, from a nail, had hung the one-size-fits-all zinc bath that the family used for its various ablutions. When required this would be half-filled with hot water from the copper boiler, a gunmetal-coloured cylinder pimpled with condensation at the room's far end, next to the boarded-up and unused kitchen fireplace. Mick remembered the short wooden pole that would be propped beside the copper for the purposes of stirring up the simmering laundry, one end waterlogged and blunted by perpetual use, its grain and fibres turned to corpse-pale slime and given a cyanic tinge by the deployment of excessive Reckitt's Blue, a small cloth bag of sapphire dye dropped in amongst the washing to ensure that shirts and sheets looked iceberg-white. He could remember shelves that weren't much more than grubby planks on brackets, bowing with the weight of saucepans, iron frying pans, the pudding basin that contained a cloudy amber puddle of solidifying dripping in its rounded depths with their mosaic craquelure.

Upon the day in question, Mick's gran Clara had been working quietly and methodically out in the kitchen, juggling several tasks at once the way that she'd been taught to when she worked in service. Clara Swan, who'd died not far into the 1970s, would have been in her early sixties then, but to her grandchildren had always seemed as ancient and authoritative as a biblical papyrus. What she lacked in height she made up for in bearing, upright to the point where no one noticed that she wasn't tall. She stood straight like an ivory chesspiece, scuffed by years of tournaments; was as impassive and as patient and as purposeful. Always a spare and slender woman in her iron-eyed youthful photographs, by 1959 she'd been more stick-like, the long silver hair that hung below her waist bound up in a neat bun. The broomstick spine topped with grey wool gave her the aura of a mop, if mops were seen as things of simple dignity, as endlessly reliable in their utility, were as revered as sceptres and not treated as a lowly household object found most often in the kitchen.

Number seventeen was Clara's house, with her name on the rent-book, and she ruled it unobtrusively. She never laid the law down and she didn't need to. Everybody knew already where her lines were drawn, and wouldn't dream of crossing them. Her power was a less obvious and ultimately more impressive kind than that wielded by May, Mick's nan, his other grandmother. May Warren had been an intimidating rhino of a woman who would get her way through warning growls and threatened slaps and what in general was a bullying demeanour. Whip-thin Clara Swan, by contrast, never raised her voice, and never threatened. She just acted, swiftly and efficiently. When Alma at the age of two, already more foolhardy and impetuous than anybody else within the household, had decided to try biting Clara, Mick's grandmother hadn't shouted or announced a smacking. She'd just bitten Alma's shoulder, hard enough to pierce the skin and hard enough to ensure that Mick's sister never, ever tried again to kill someone by eating them. If only, he reflected, she'd cured Alma of the strangling as well. Or the attempts with poison gas, as when Alma persuaded her young brother to stay with her in the kitchen while she lit a mustard-yellow shard of sulphur. Or her pygmy head-hunter approach, like when she'd shot him with that blowpipe dart. No, really. Mick supposed, in fairness, that even his granny's methods of behaviour modification had their limits. Clara had been in the kitchen on that drowsy afternoon, been shredding suet, baking a bread pudding, boiling handkerchiefs and shuffling back and forth from one task to another uncomplainingly, alone there with the aromatic bogey broth. The badly-fitting back door, hanging open on this fine day to air out the house, allowed the chat and babble of her daughter Doreen and the children to come floating in to Clara from where they'd been sitting just outside, on the slim draughtboard strip of cracked pink and blue tiles that formed the upper level of the house's cramped back garden.

Sitting now in his still, relatively spacious Kingsthorpe parlour, stinging from his honourably-withdrawing-not-retreating hairline to his dimpled chin, he tried to reconcile the cluttered confines of his childhood with the streamlined *TV Century 21* surroundings of his current middle-age. Mick looked once more at the reflection of his raw face in the glass front of the cabinet, deciding on the strength of his disaster-struck complexion that he must be Captain Scarlet. He tried fitting the mostly contented adult he'd become with the unspeakably contented three-year-old he'd been and found that the connection was surprisingly smooth and continuous, Mick's recollection of his young self neither clouded by unhappiness nor tainted by that sorry wistfulness he sometimes heard in others' voices when they talked about their boyhood days. Life had been good then, life was good now. It was just that life was different, in that it was being seen through different eyes, being experienced by a different person, almost.

The most striking thing about the past, at least as Mick remembered it, was not the obvious difference in how people dressed, or what they did, or the technology they did it with. It was something more difficult to grasp or put a name to, that by turn delightful and unsettling sense of strangeness that came over him on handling forgotten photographs, or suddenly recalling some particularly vivid reminiscence. It would come to him as the weak flavour of a fleeting atmosphere, an unrecoverable mood, as singular and as specific to its place and time as the day's weather or the shapes its clouds made, just that once, never to be repeated. He supposed that the peculiar quality that he attempted to describe was no more than the startling texture of the past, the way it might feel should you brush your memory's fingertips across its nap. It was the grain of his experience, composed from an uncountable array of unique whorls and bumps, from almost indiscernibly protruding detail. The string netting of the decomposing dishcloth hung by the back door, stiffened and dried into a permanently tented elbow shape, perfumed by dirty water and warm ham. The finger-sized holes in the blocks that edged Gran's yard-wide flowerbed, beside the faded red and blue check of the path. A secret ant-nest gnawed into the crumbling cement between two courses of the kitchen wall, beside the steps that led down to a lower level of their closed-in yard. That afternoon there'd been the smell of sun-baked brick, black soil, the tinny scent of recent rain.

Now that he thought about it, not without a faint vestigial flicker of resentment, the entire life-threatening incident that had occurred in the back yard that day had been as a direct result of being poor. If he'd not been one of the offspring of the Boroughs then he wouldn't have been sitting on his mother's lap in the sunlit back yard sucking the nearly-lethal cough-drop in the first place.

Mick – or Michael as he'd been then – had been suffering from an inflamed gullet for about a week before that point. When Doreen's homemade remedy of butter-knobs that had been rolled in caster sugar failed to work, she'd wrapped him up and taken him down Broad Street, off the Mayorhold, to the surgery of Dr. Grey. Though neither Mick nor any of his family had thought about it then, he understood now that the doctors who had tended to his neighbour-hood must have resented every minute of their unrewarded, undistinguished toil in ministering to such a lowly and benighted area. They'd almost certainly be working harder than their more illustrious colleagues, just by virtue of the Boroughs being what it was and having more ways people could get ill. They must have come to hate the sight of all those over-anxious mothers wearing toffee-coloured coats and tea-towel scarves, parading half-baked snot-nosed children through their practices at the first sneeze. It must have been all they could do to feign an interest in the wheezing brat for the five minutes that it would be in their office. That was clearly the approach that Dr. Grey had taken with Doreen and Mick that time. He'd shone a torch down Michael's carmine and inflated gullet, grunted once and made his diagnosis.

"It's a sore throat. Give him cough-sweets."

Mick's mum would have no doubt nodded gravely and compliantly. This was a doctor speaking, who'd had training and could write in Latin. This was someone who, by just a glance at the small child she'd brought in with a poorly throat in which it was experiencing soreness, had seen straight away that this was a near-textbook case of Sore Throat that required immediate intervention from a bag of Winter Mixture. Nineteen-fifties social medicine: it must have seemed a step up from the days when laryngitis would be driven out by exorcism. Mick and Alma's parents had been grateful for it, anyway, and Doreen would have thanked the general practitioner for his advice with touching earnestness before she'd wrestled Mick into his duffle-coat and carried him back down St. Andrew's Road, possibly stopping off at the newsagent, Botterill's on the Mayorhold, to buy the medicinal confectionery that had been prescribed.

And that was how he'd come to be in their back yard, in his pyjamas and his scratchy tartan dressing gown, squirming on Doreen's lap while she perched on the curve-backed wooden chair brought out into the garden from the living room. His mum sat just beneath the kitchen window with her back to it, the rear legs of her seat against the edging of the kitchen drain, a foot or so of gutter running from below the window to a sunken trap close by the ant-nest, hidden near the garden's three rough steps. The kingdom of the ants had been the property of Mick's big sister, and, as she'd explained it to him at the time, was hers by legal right of being eldest child. When she was playing Sodom and Gomorrah with the insects, though, to give Alma her due, she'd let Mick be a kind of work-experience avenging angel to her merciless Jehovah. He'd been put in charge of rounding up escapees from the Cities on the Plain, until Alma had fired him for preventing one of his six-legged charges running off by hitting it with half a brick. His sister, who'd been at that moment either drowning or incinerating ants herself, had turned upon him with a look of outrage.

"What did you do that for?"

Little Mick had blinked up at her guilelessly. "It kept escaping, so I stunned it."

Alma, half-blind even then, had squinted at the ant in question, which had lost a whole dimension, and then squinted at her brother in appalled incomprehension before stamping off to play alone indoors.

Alma had been at home that afternoon by virtue of it being the school holidays, probably wishing she could be out in the park or meadow rather than stuck there in the back garden with her mum and useless croaking bundle of a baby brother. While Doreen and Mick had sat there on the upper strip of path, Mick's elder sister, then a tubby five- or six-year-old, had batted energetically around the yard's brick confines like a moth trapped in a shoebox. She'd run up and down the garden's three stone steps a dozen times, her white knees pumping back and forth like juggled dumplings, then raced in a circle round the nine-foot-by-nine-foot enclosure, half brick paving, half compressed black dirt, that was the bottom of the garden. She'd hidden from nobody in particular, twice in their outside toilet and once in the narrow rectangle of dead-end concrete alleyway that ran along its side, the left-hand side if you were sitting on the bowl and facing out.

That little shed with its slate roof – their outdoor lavatory down at the bottom of the yard without a cistern or electric light – had been most notable to Mick amongst the Warren family's various anti-status-symbols. Their back toilet, he had realised at the age of six or so, was an embarrassment even within a neighbourhood not known for its amenities. Even their nan, who lived on Green Street in a gas-lit house that had no electricity at all, at least she had a cistern in her lav. Trips to the loo after the sun went down didn't require a stuttering Wee Willie Winkie candle or a big tin bucket filled near to its brim with water from the kitchen tap, the way they did along St. Andrew's Road.

As a small child, he'd hated their outside lav after dark and wouldn't use it, far preferring either just to hold it in or else use the pink plastic chamber pot stuck under his and Alma's bed. For one thing, he'd been slightly built back then, rather than a great hulking lummox like his sister. Whereas she could confidently clomp off down the garden path with a huge sloshing bucket in one hand and flickering night-light in the other, he could barely lift the bucket using both his hands; would only have been able to affect a comic stagger as far as the garden steps before he'd spilled the ice-cold water down his leg and/or set his blonde curls alight with the incautious flailings of his candle.

Anyway, even if somehow back then in his larval cherub stage he could have managed to successfully transport the heavy pail, their yard by night was altered, unknown territory, too eerie to negotiate alone. The gap-toothed stable roof across the bottom wall was a mysterious slope of silver slate where rustling night-birds came and went through the black apertures. Its grey, ramshackle incline with the dandelions and wallflowers struggling from between its cracks was a steep ramp that led up into night. The tiny five-by-three-foot stretch of alleyway between the toilet and the garden wall was plenty big enough to hold a ghost, a witch and a green Frankenstein, with lots of room left over for those black and spiky imps like charred horse-chestnuts that there used to be in *Rupert*. Mick had always had the feeling, during childhood, that the back yards of St. Andrew's Road by night were probably a bustling thoroughfare of ghouls and phantoms, though that may have just been something that his sister told him. Certainly, it had that ring about it.

It had been all very well for Alma. Not only had she been big enough to lift the bucket, but she'd always been much, much too comfortable with the idea of spookiness. It was a quality, he thought, that she had actively aspired to. Nobody could end up like Mick's sister had unless it was on purpose. He remembered when, aged eight, he'd had a passion for collecting boxed battalions of minuscule Airfix soldiers: British Tommies just two centimetres tall in ochre plastic, ant-sized snipers sprawling on their bellies, others posed on one leg charging with fixed bayonets; or Prussian Infantry in bluish-grey, frozen in mid-throw with their funny rolling-pin grenades. You'd get a dozen soldiers sprouting from each waxy stem, fixed by their heads so that you had to twist them free before you played with them, perhaps five stems in every window-fronted cardboard box. He'd been halfway through an elaborate campaign – French Foreign Legion versus Civil War Confederates – when he'd become aware that both his armies were abnormally depleted. Ruling out desertion, he'd eventually discovered that his elder sister had been stealing soldiers by the handful, taking them down to the outside toilet with her (and her bucket and her candle) when she paid it a nocturnal visit. She'd apparently discovered that if you should light the soldiers' heads using the candle-flame, then miniature blue fireballs made of blazing polythene would drip spectacularly down into the waiting bucket, making an unearthly *vvwip – vvwip – vvwip* sound that was terminated in a hiss as the hot plastic met with the cold water. He imagined her, sat there on the cold wooden seat beside the bent nail in the whitewashed wall where scraps of *Tit-Bits* or *Reveille* would be hung for use as toilet paper, with her navy knickers round her swinging ankles and her eager face lit indigo in ghastly flashes from beneath as a diminutive centurion was turned into a Roman candle. Was it any wonder that the thought of lurking back-yard spectres hadn't bothered her? The moment that they'd heard her footsteps and the clanking bucket, they'd be off.

On that particular occasion with Mick, aged three, convalescing on his mother's lap, Doreen had quickly wearied of her eldest child's stampede around the otherwise agreeable and peaceful yard.

"Ooh, Alma, come and sit dayn 'fore yer make us dizzy. Aya got St. Vitus' Dance or what?"

Like Mick, his sister generally did as she was told without resistance, but had obviously learned that if she *over*-did what she was told then it could be a lot more fun than actual disobedience, and was much more difficult to punish or to prove. Obligingly, his sister had skipped up the steps and sat herself down with her legs crossed on the warm and dusty tiles beneath the window of the living room. She beamed up at her mum and ailing baby brother with bright-eyed sincerity.

"Mum, why is Michael croaking?"

"You know why 'e's croakin'. It's because 'e's got a sore throat."

"Is he turning to a frog?"

"No. I just said, 'e's got a sore throat. 'Course 'e's not turnin' into a frog."

"If Michael turns into a frog, then can I have him?"

"'E's not turnin' to a frog."

"But if he does, then can I keep him in a jam-jar?"

"'E's not ... No! No, 'course yer can't. A jam-jar?"

"Dad could use a screwdriver and punch some air-holes in the lid."

There'd come a point in any conversation between Alma and their mum in which Doreen would make a huge strategic blunder and would start to argue in the terms of Alma's logic, whereupon she would immediately be lost.

"You couldn't keep a frog inside a jam-jar. What's it s'posed to eat?"

"Grass."

"Frogs don't eat grass."

"Yes they do. That's why they're green."

"Is it? I didn't know that. Are you sure?"

This was the juncture at which Doreen would compound her previous tactical mistake by doubting her own intellectual capabilities as an adult against those of her infant daughter. Mick's mum didn't think that she was very clever or well-educated, and would endlessly defer to anyone whom she suspected might have a more firm grasp of the facts than she herself did. Ruinously, she included Alma in this category for no more reason than that Alma, even at the age of five, pretended to know everything and made her proclamations with such ringing confidence that it was simply easier to go along with her than to resist. Mick could remember how on one occasion, his eight-year-old sister had come home from school demanding beans on toast, a dish she'd heard her classmates mention but which was a new one on Doreen. She'd asked how Alma's school-friends' mothers would prepare the meal, at which Mick's sister had insisted that cold beans were tipped onto a slice of bread, which was then toasted on a fork held to the fireplace. Astonishingly, Doreen had attempted this, purely on Alma's say-so, and had not thought to employ her own superior judgement until their whole hearth was smothered in baked beans and splashes of tomato sauce with coal dust in suspension. That, or something equally unlikely, was how things turned out whenever anybody took Mick's sister seriously. He could have told his mum that, back there in the shade and sunlight of the upper yard, if he'd been able to say anything through the balloon of sandpaper that was then steadily inflating in his throat. Instead, he'd shifted on her slippery lap and grizzled slightly, letting her get on with the ridiculous discussion that she'd stumbled into. Alma was now nodding in excitement, backing up her ludicrous assertion.

"Yes! All of the animals that eat grass are turned green. They told us it at school."

This was a flat lie, but was one which played on Doreen's insecurities about her own substandard 1930s education. You heard such a lot of marvellous new ideas in 1959 what with the Sputniks and all that, and who knew what astounding and unprecedented facts were being taught in modern classrooms? Decimals and long division, things like that, which Doreen's own school days had barely touched on. Who was she to say? Perhaps this business with green animals all being fed on grass was something new that people had found out. But still she harboured doubts. It had been Alma, after all, who'd told her that lime cordial poured in boiling milk would make a kind of hot fruit milkshake.

"What about the cows 'n' 'orses, then? Why ent they green, when they eat grass?"

Unflappable, Alma had waved aside her mother's hesitant appeal to common sense.

"They are green, some of them. The ones that ent will go green when they've eaten enough grass."

Too late, Mick's mum had realised she was entering the world of quicksand nonsense that was Alma's centre-parted, pigtailed, butterfly-slide-decorated head. She'd made a feeble yelp of protest as reality gave way beneath her feet.

"I've never seen a green cow! Alma, are you making all this up?"

"No" – this in a hurt, reproachful tone of voice. Doreen remained to be convinced.

"Well, then, why ent I seen one? Why ent I seen a green cow or 'orse?"

Alma, sitting beneath the window of the living room, had looked up at their mother levelly, her big grey-yellow eyes unblinking.

"Nobody can see them. It's because they blend in with the fields."

Despite, or possibly because of the dead serious tone in which this was delivered, Mick had been unable to prevent himself from laughing. Luckily, his ragged throat had done this for him, and the laugh came out as an unlubricated squeak, exploding halfway through into a jumping-jack-like string of coughs. Doreen had glared at Alma.

"Now look what you've done wi' yer green cows!"

Surprised by their mum's sudden conversational manoeuvre, Alma had for once been at a loss, unable to come up with a reply. Irrationality: Alma could dish it out all right, but couldn't take it. Doreen had turned her attention to her youngest child, hacking and mewling there upon her knee.

"Ahh, bless 'im. 'Aya got a poorly throat, me duck? E'yar, you 'ave a pep like what the doctor said you should."

"Pep" was the Boroughs' term for sweet, and as Mick thought about it now it struck him that he'd never heard it used outside the district, or outside the homes of people who'd grown up there. Keeping Michael on her lap with one arm round his waist, Doreen had fumbled in her pocket for the square-shaped foil-and-paper tube she'd bought at Botterill's, finally emerging with the pack of cherry-menthol Tunes. Deftly and with one hand, Doreen had carefully opened one end of the packet with her generous fingernails, squeezed out a single cough-drop, then proceeded to unpick the envelope-tucks of its individual wax-paper wrapping, where the tiny word "Tunes" was repeated several times in medicine-red. With a polite " 'Scuse fingers" Doreen had held up the sticky crimson jewel to Michael's lips, which had immediately parted like a hatchling's beak so she could place the square-cut crystal on his tongue. He sucked it slowly, with its blunted corners poking up against his palate and his gums, especially the sore white-tipped ones at the back where teeth were starting to come through.

Doreen had sat there looking down at Michael fondly, her big face obscuring most of the blue Boroughs' sky that had been visible between the leaning housetops. She must have been in her early thirties then, still trim and pretty with long features and dark, wavy hair. She'd lost the ghostly and unearthly silent film-star beauty that she'd had in pictures Mick had seen of her when she'd been younger, with her huge, wet, dreamy eyes, but it had been replaced by something warmer and less fragile, the appearance of somebody who'd at last grown comfortable with being who they were, somebody who no longer wore those painful clip-on button earrings. He'd gazed back at her, the cough-sweet tumbling and turning over in his mouth, losing its edges in his cherry-infused spittle, gradually transformed into a thin rose windowpane. Smiling, his mum had brushed a stray curl from the damp pink of his brow.

And then he'd coughed. He'd coughed until the air was forced out of his lungs and then had drawn a great big sucking breath in order to replace it. Somewhere in amongst this spluttering and confused bronchial activity, Mick had inhaled the Tune. Like a stray sink-plug dragged into the plughole of a draining basin to arrest its flow, the sweet fitted exactly in the small gap which remained in Mick's absurdly swollen windpipe.

With horrific clarity, which made him grip the arm of the settee as he sat in the peaceful Kingsthorpe living room, Mick could remember the appalling moment when he knew his breath had stopped, a memory he had been spared until revived from his concussion earlier that day. He could recall his sudden and uncomprehending shock, his realisation that something was badly wrong and his uncertainty as to what it might be. It was as if he hadn't previously noticed he was breathing, not until he found he couldn't do it anymore.

The terror of the moment had been overwhelming, and he'd somehow drawn away from it, as if to a remote place deep inside himself. The sounds and movements of the garden seemed far off, as did the desperate, frightened tightness in his chest. His eyes must have glazed over, staring up into his mother's overhanging face, and he remembered how her own expression had changed instantly to one of puzzlement and then mounting anxiety. He'd known, from his dissociated vantage, that he was the cause of her concern but couldn't for the life of him remember what he'd done that had upset her so.

"Ooh Guy, ayr mam! Come quick! Ayr Michael's chokin'!"

The receding porthole that was Michael's field of vision had been jiggled frantically, turned on one side and then the other, with his grandma's taut-skinned features suddenly protruding into view, alarm suppressed beneath the glitter of her bird-like eye. Shudders of impact came from far away, hard and repetitive, like someone banging on a television set when the reception went. That must have been his gran or Doreen, thumping him upon the back as they attempted to dislodge the cough-sweet, but it hadn't budged. He could remember the sensation of an animal with a metallic taste like pennies that had tried to climb inside his mouth, so that he'd bitten down reflexively on his mum's fingers as she'd struggled to retrieve the blockage from his throat.

There had been voices in the distance, women shouting urgently or wailing, though he hadn't thought that this had anything to do with him.

The picture of the garden he was seeing had turned upside down at one point, which, from what he'd heard about the incident from Alma and his mum, must have been when Doreen had shook him by his ankles, hoping gravity would do the trick where all her other efforts had drawn blanks. Mick had an image of a red inverted face, an unfamiliar thing between a dog and a tomato that he'd never seen before, a kind of joke-shop devil mask he did not recognise as his distraught and weeping older sister. His short life and all its details, as they'd slid away from him, had seemed like a strange little picture-story that he'd only been half-reading anyway, with all the settings and the characters forgot even before the book was closed and put aside. The sobbing objects in the dwindling illustration, he had dimly recollected, were called people. These were something like a toy or rabbit, in that they were always doing funny things. The bricks surrounding them, piled up in flat or bulky shapes, were something he was pretty sure was known as a back-yarden in the story. Something like that, anyway, although he didn't know what such arrangements had been used for or to do with. On the blue sheet up above were big and drifting shapes of white that you called lions. No, not lions. Cabbages, was that the word? Or generals? It didn't matter. All these things had just been silly bits and pieces in the dream that he was waking up from. None of it was real, nor had it ever been.

He had been floating through the air, presumably borne by his mother, and was gazing up at the unfolding forms of all the lions and generals above. There'd been a gruff voice in amongst the ladynoise, which he assumed now had been that of Doug McGeary from next door, the yard with the big wooden gates on Andrew's Road and the ramshackle stable at the rear. According to what Mick had been told afterwards, mostly by Alma, once the situation had been hurriedly explained to Doug, the fruit and veg purveyor had offered immediately to drive Mick to the hospital in his delivery lorry that he kept parked in the leaking stable. The unbreathing three-year-old, eyes glazed and staring, had been passed by Doreen over the back wall into the sure hands of Mrs. McGeary's eldest son, or so the story went. Now, though, as the event came back to him, he saw that Alma must have got it wrong, at least that bit of it. His mum had merely held him up to show to Doug, not handed him across the wall. That made a lot more sense than Alma's version, now he thought about it. Doreen had been too upset to pass her choking baby to somebody else, and what would be the point, in any case? Doug had to start his lorry up and get it out the barn, to wrangle it around the corners of their L-shaped yard, out through the splintering and distressed front gates onto St. Andrew's Road. He wouldn't need a half-dead toddler in the cab beside him while he took care of all that.

No, what had really happened, Mick decided as he reconstructed the occurrence, was that Doug had told Doreen to meet him out the front in half a minute, when he'd had a chance to get his vehicle into juddering and coughing action. Christ, what would his mum and gran have done if Doug McGeary hadn't been at home? There'd been nobody else along St. Andrew's Road or nearby in the Boroughs who had transport, motorised or horse-drawn, and as far as calling for an ambulance went, well, you could forget it. No one in the district had a phone, there was a single public call box near the old Victorian public toilets nestled at the foot of Spencer Bridge, and anyway, there wouldn't have been time. In Mick's own retrospective estimate, a good two minutes must have passed by that point since the last occasion that he'd drawn a breath.

He remembered floating back up the stone steps into the top half of the yard, carried along in a soft cloud of hands, of red and tear-stained faces he no longer knew, a drift of frightened voices indistinguishable from the background twitter of the rooftop birds, the breeze that strummed the television aerials, the crackling of aprons. All the world he'd had three years to get familiar with was gradually unravelling, its sounds and its sensations and its images all turning back into the flat words of the narrative that someone had been reading to him, which was coming to an end. The person in the tale that he'd liked best, the little boy, was dying in a funny little house upon a street that nobody would ever hear of. He remembered feeling slightly disappointed that the story hadn't had a better ending, because up to then he'd been enjoying it.

A bumpy current that had fingers swirled him from the light and space and blue of the back yard into the sudden grey gloom of the kitchen and the living room. Doreen, he reasoned now, must have been holding him face-up since he recalled a moving frieze of ceiling scrolling by above him, first the flaking and uneven whiteness in the kitchen and then the expanse of beige with the stepped beading round its edge that topped the living room. His mum had carried him between the unlit summer fireplace and the dining table, heading for the passage and the front door and her rendezvous with Doug. But then something had happened. His glazed eyes had been fixed on the decorative trim around the higher reaches of the room, coming to rest within the shadow-drinking recess of an upper corner. And the corner had been ... bent? Reversible, so that it stuck out where you would expect it to go in? There had been something wrong about the corner, he remembered that much, and there had been something else, what was it? Something even stranger. There'd been ...

There had been a little tiny person in the corner, shouting to him a voice that came from far away, and beckoning, and telling him come up, you come up here with me, you'll be all right. Come up. Come up. Come up.

He'd died. He'd died halfway across the living room and hadn't made it even to the passage or the front door, let alone the cab of Doug's delivery truck, of which he could remember nothing. He could not recall the panicked journey to the hospital ... along the same route Howard had taken him today, he realised belatedly ... because he hadn't been there. He'd been dead.

He sat there on the sofa, looking like a gargoyle suffering from sunstroke, and attempted to absorb this fact, to swallow it, but like the Tune he found that it would not go down. If he'd been dead, then what were all the other memories pressing in upon him now, these images and names he half-remembered from a period that was after his demise between the fireplace and the dining table, but before he'd woken clueless and disoriented in the hospital? More to the point, if he'd been dead, how had he woken at the hospital at all? Mick felt a sort of heavy cloud descending on his heart and gut, and noted with detached surprise that in his tidy, sunlit parlour he was very, very scared.

It was at this point that Cath and the kids came home. First from the kitchen and into the living room was Jack, Mick's oldest boy, a glowering and solidly built fifteen-year-old aspiring stand-up comedian who everyone had always said, in worried tones of deep foreboding, was the spit of his aunt Alma. Jack stopped in his tracks, a pace inside the door, and stared expressionlessly at his dad's new acid facial. Looking back across his shoulder, he called to his mother and his younger brother Joe, both in the kitchen still.

"Did anybody order pizza?"

Cathy had leaned round the door to see what Jack was on about, looked blankly at her husband for an instant and then shrieked.

"Aaah! Fucking hell, what have you done?"

She rushed to Mick's side, taking his head gingerly between her hands, turning it gently one way then another as she tried to see how bad the damage was. Their youngest son, Joe, wandered in serenely from the kitchen, taking off his zip-up jacket. Slightly built and blonde and at eleven years old easily much cuter than his older brother, Joe looked quite a bit like Mick had as a child, at least according to the same authorities (including Mick's late mother Doreen, who should know) that said Jack looked like Alma. Joe, like the young Mick, was quieter than his elder sibling, hardly difficult since Jack's voice had not just recently broken but had melted down like a reactor and was heading for the centre of the Earth. With Joe, although he didn't broadcast on the china-rattling frequency or at the volume of his elder brother, you could tell that every bit as much was going on inside, and that most probably it would be every bit as bonkers, if less loudly advertised. Hanging his jacket on a chair, Joe gazed across the room at his dad's altered countenance, then simply smiled and shook his head as if in fond exasperation.

"Did you get your blowtorch and your shaver muddled up again?"

While Cathy pointedly suggested that both Jack and Joe piss off upstairs if they weren't being any help and Mick tried not to undercut the seriousness of his wife's rebuke by laughing, he reflected that this wonderfully protective smart-arsed callousness with which his kids would greet potential disaster was most probably the fault of him and Alma. Alma, mostly. He remembered when Doreen, their mum, was diagnosed with cancer of the bowel and had called her grief-stunned son and daughter into her ward cubicle to have a serious talk about how everything should be arranged. Taller than Mick in her stack heels, Alma had bent down to deliver a conspicuous stage whisper in his ear. "You hear that, Warry? This is where she's going to tell you you're adopted." They'd all laughed, especially Doreen, who'd smiled at Alma and said "You don't know. It might be you who was adopted." Mick believed that in life there were times when the entirely inappropriate was the only appropriate response. Perhaps, though, it was only him and Alma who thought that way. Mostly Alma.

Cathy, once she'd been assured Mick's new complexion wasn't permanent or otherwise life-threatening, had switched her inner thermostat up from compassionate concern to moral outrage. So, why wasn't there a label on that drum? Why hadn't his employers even called to find out how he was since Howard brought him home from casualty? She'd fumed about it for an hour then phoned Mick's boss, who had at least learned first-hand from the chat what it was like to have a drum of poison go off in your face. When at length it was out of Cathy's system and she'd dropped the probably red-hot receiver back into its cradle, they'd decided to have dinner and as ordinary an evening as they could manage. As a plan this worked quite well, despite the fact that Mick's deformity gave things the feeling of an Elephant Man family video reel.

Dinner was tasty and appreciated and passed by without event. During the main course, Cathy turned reproachfully to Jack and scolded him about his eating habits.

"Jack, I do wish that you'd eat your vegetables."

Her eldest son gave her a look of condescending sympathy.

"Mum, I wish women would fall at my feet, but we both know it isn't going to happen. Let's just face it and move on."

Halfway through pudding, little Joe – if only they'd have named his elder brother "Hoss", Mick suddenly thought, ruefully – had broken from his customary introverted silence to announce that he'd decided what he'd like to be when he did Work Experience next year: "A fridge." Mick, Cath and Jack had all looked at each other worriedly, then gone on eating their desserts. It was a fairly normal dinnertime, as those things went.

After they'd done the washing up, Jack said he had the second series of Paul Abbott's *Shameless* which was out on DVD, and asked if they could watch it. Since there wasn't much of interest showing on terrestrial or Sky, Mick had agreed. Besides, he didn't get to view a lot of television, what with getting up so early in the mornings, and although he'd heard Alma and Jack discussing the new sink-estate-set comedy, he hadn't seen it yet. He'd got the rest of the week off from work, most probably as a result of Cathy's phone call, and so could afford to sit back with a beer and take it in. If nothing else, it would be a distraction from the frightening train of thought his family had interrupted by arriving home. Although the sitcom's sense of humour was notoriously grim, he doubted it was grimmer than a memory of dying in the Boroughs at the age of three.

It was the second season's final episode they watched, Jack having seen the others previously. Though Cathy shook her head and tutted, wandering off to get on with some chores around the house, Mick thought the show was pretty good. From what he'd overheard of Jack and Alma's fierce debate about its merits, Alma hadn't liked it, or had liked it only grudgingly, but then Mick's sister would find fault with almost anything that wasn't her own work, as if on principle. "Like *Bread* with STDs", that had been one of her off-hand dismissals. If Mick understood the gist of Alma's doubts about the programme, what she didn't like was the portrayal of the working class as having inexhaustible reserves of strength and humour in adversity, with which they could laugh off the gruesome deprivations of their genuinely dreadful situation. "Families like that," she'd say regarding the show's central clan, the Gallaghers, "in real life the old man wouldn't be such an ultimately loveable disgusting drunk, and every train-wreck that he dragged his family through with him wouldn't end up in a heart-warming group cackle. That thirteen-year-old girl with the supernatural coping skills would have been shagged by half the married blokes on the estate for alcopops. The thing is, people watch a show like that ... and it's well made, well written, funny and well acted, I'm not arguing with that ... and in a funny way it reassures them about something that they shouldn't feel so reassured about. It's not okay that people have to live like that. It's not okay that terms like sink estate are even in the language. And this plucky, mirthful underclass resilience, it's a myth. It's one the underclass themselves are eager to believe so they don't have to feel so bad about their situation, and it's also one the middle class are eager to believe, for the exact same reason." As Mick now recalled, on that occasion Alma's diatribe (which had been vented, it must be remembered, at her fifteen-year-old nephew) had been terminated when Jack ventured his own counter-argument: "Jesus, Aunt Warry, lighten up. They're only puppets."

Mick was more or less on Jack's side there. At least in *Shameless* there was a more honest picture of existence in the lower margins than in shows like *Bread*, with or without the STDs. And how could Alma honestly expect a situation comedy to reproduce her own bleak and consistently enraged view of society? It would be like an episode of *Are You Being Served?* by Dostoevsky. "Mr. Humphries, are you free?" "None of us are truly free, dear Mrs. Slocum, unless it is in the act of murder."

No, the only problem with the show for Mick was that the longer it went on, the more he was reminded of the strange anxieties that he was watching television in an effort to forget. That little figure he'd remembered, calling from its upper corner of the living room at 17, St. Andrew's Road, what could that mean except that he had died, been taken up into some kind of afterlife by some, Mick didn't know, some sort of angel?

Well, it could mean he was going round the corner. Going barmy. There was always that to be considered in the Vernall clan and offshoots, like the Warrens. Hadn't his dad's grandfather gone mad, and his dad's cousin, Audrey? It was in the family, everybody said, and looked at logically was a more likely cause for Mick's peculiar memories and feelings than that he'd been lifted up to Heaven by an angel. Anyway, the more he thought about it, then the less the tiny person that had been perched in the corner seemed like any sort of angel that he'd ever heard of. It had been too small, too plainly dressed, in its pink cardigan, its navy skirt and ankle-socks. A girl. Mick could remember now that the homunculus he'd seen had been a little girl with blonde hair in a fringe. She hadn't looked much more than ten, and definitely hadn't looked much like an angel. She'd had no wings and no halo, though there had been something odd, what was it, draped around her neck like a long scarf? A fur scarf, that was it. All drenched in blood. With little heads grown out of it. Oh, fuck.

He didn't want to be insane, he didn't want his wife and kids and friends to have to see him in that state, to feel bad when they left it longer each time between visits to whatever institution he'd end up in. Madness was all very well if you were Alma and in a profession where insanity was a desirable accessory, a kind of psycho-bling. You couldn't get away with it down Martin's Yard, though. In the reconditioning business there was no real concept of delightful eccentricity. You'd find yourself as the recipient of a pharmaceutical lobotomy provided on the National Health, as a result of which your waistband would expand as your abilities to think, talk and respond to stimuli contracted. This was not an idea that Mick found agreeable, or even bearable, but at that moment it appeared to be a serious possibility. Mick could feel thousands of unlikely details as upsetting and impossible as the girl's blood-soaked fur scarf, bulging from underneath the floorboards of his memory, waiting to burst up from below and overwhelm his happy, ordinary life. Ideas like that just wouldn't fit in Mick's existence. They would bend it out of shape, destroy it. With renewed determination, Mick fixed his attention on the episode of *Shameless* he was watching. Anything in order to avoid the stubbornly persistent vision of that little girl, dressed in her furry necklace made of death.

The hour-long show was almost over, with the Gallaghers all massed in a communal living-room and trying to get the two twin babies they'd been left in charge of off to sleep. The babies' mother, an emotionally-overwrought Seroxat casualty, had left instructions that the twins could be lulled into nodding off by singing hymns to them, their favourite being Blake and Parry's almost universally admired "Jerusalem". The family are croaking their way through another repetition of the much-loved standard, with no obvious effect upon the howling babies, when the mother of the twins at last gets home. Despite her welders' goggles and her OCD, she then proceeds to send the twins to sleep with a surprisingly ethereal rendition of "Jerusalem" delivered in an unexpectedly well-trained and beautiful soprano. "And did those feet, in ancient time ..."

The tears welled up from nowhere in Mick's eyes, so that he had to blink them back before the kids could see. He'd no idea where this was coming from. It was just something in that melody, the simple way its notes marched up and down, that broke his heart. Worse, there was something in the way the hymn was being used here in this episode of *Shameless*, like a ray of light amongst the busted sofas and the Tourette's and the tea-cup rings, its purity and confidence more bright and blinding for the hopelessness of its surroundings. This fierce, blazing sanctity amidst the squalor was what did for Mick. It had a feel about it that chimed perfectly with all of the disturbing memories from his childhood he was at that moment trying to suppress, a sense of crystal vision thrusting up between satanic mills that fitted like a key in all of Mick's internal locks. The cellar door of his unconscious was thrown open from beneath and a great flood of bubbling unearthliness surged up, much more than he'd imagined could be down there, filling him with images and words and voices, with the language of an alien experience.

Destructor, Bedlam Jennies, length and breadth and whenth and linger, Porthimoth' di Norhan', crook doors and a Jacob Flight. "It's an old can of beans, but every bubble that you ever blew is still inside." Mansoul, the strangles and the Dead Dead Gang. Destructor. Trilliards is the proper name for Builders' Marbles. Pay attention to the chimneys and the middle corners. Some call it the five-and-twenty thousand nights. Ghost-seam. Destructor. Spacemen means it isn't ripe. A saint up in the twenty-fives where all the water level's rising. Angles from the realms of Glory. "You all fold up into us, and we all fold up into him." A balance hangs above a winding road. Soul of the Hole, you see it in their furious eyes. The bare girls dancing on the tannin barrels, what a day that is. "We can go scrumping in the madhouse," and Destructor and Destructor and Destructor. Everywhere and everyone he loved, sucked in and gone. The rood is broke, that's why the centre cannot hold. He rapes her in the car park where Bath Gardens used to be and we run off to find the ghosts that we've annoyed. Woodwork and painted stars upon the landings, Puck's Hats sprouting from the cracks ...

Mick rose abruptly and excused himself, pretending that he needed to go to the bathroom. Joe asked if he wanted them to pause the DVD, but he said that they needn't bother, calling back to them from halfway up the stairs. Locking the bathroom door he sat there on the toilet with its lid down for a good five minutes until he'd stopped shuddering. It was no good. He couldn't keep this to himself. He'd have to tell someone.

He stood and lifted up the toilet seat, taking a token piss before he went back down again, and out of habit washed his hands in the small basin nearby when he'd done. He glanced up at the mirror on the bathroom cabinet and started at the raw and peeling face confronting him, having by then forgotten all about his accident at work. His features looked so much like unconvincing make-up from a horror film, that what with all the supernatural visitations crowding in his head right then, Mick had to laugh. The laughter sounded wrong, though, so he packed it in and went downstairs to join his family.

Somehow he managed to last out the evening, acting normal, without giving anything away, though Jack and Cathy both remarked that he was more than usually quiet. It wasn't until he and Cathy were in bed that it came spilling out, disjointed and so mangled in the telling that it made no sense, even to Mick himself. Cath listened calmly while he told her he was scared that he was going mad, then sensibly suggested he phone up his older sister and arrange to go out for a drink with her, so that he could ask Alma what she thought about it all. In any practical concern that was related to the real world Cathy wouldn't trust her sister-in-law's judgement for a second, but with matters of the twilight zone like those afflicting Mick there was no one she trusted more than Alma. Set a thief to catch a thief. Fight fire with fire. Send for a nightmare to arrest a nightmare.

Mick did just as Cathy said. He might be mad, he wasn't stupid. He arranged to meet his sister at the Golden Lion in Castle Street that coming Saturday, though he'd no clear idea as to why he'd suggested this specific venue, a decaying and unprepossessing hostelry smack in the Boroughs' devastated heart. It just seemed like the right place, that was all, the right dilapidated wonder of a place to tell his older sister his dilapidated wonder of a tale, about the little boy who'd choked to death, to actual death, when he was only three.

About the girl in her pink cardigan and stinking, gory neckerchief who'd reached down from the corner with her hot and sticky hands and said "Come up. Come up."

And taken him upstairs.

Book Two

MANSOUL

It moves me most when slanting sunbeams glow
On old farm buildings set against a hill,
And paint with life the shapes which linger still
From centuries less a dream than this we know.
In that strange light I feel I am not far
From the fixt mass whose side the ages are.

−H. P. Lovecraft,
from "Continuity" (*Fungi from Yuggoth*)

UPSTAIRS

G rand, grand, how grand it was. The little boy ascended with the wonder-thunder rumbling all round him like a brass band tuning up and up. This was the sound the world made when you left it.

Michael felt like he was floating in a rubber ring, just underneath the smoky yellow ceiling of the living room. He wasn't certain how he'd got there and he didn't know if he should be alarmed about the corner-fairy who was waving to him from the shady recess only a few feet above. Although she seemed familiar, Michael wasn't sure he ought to trust her. Michael wasn't even sure if corner-fairies were a thing he'd noticed in their house before that moment, or had heard his parents talk about, though he supposed he must have done. The fact that there were tiny people in the corners didn't seem unusual anyway, not in the sparkly dark that he was rising up through, gilded in bewilderment.

He tried to work out where he was, and realised that he couldn't even properly remember who or where he'd been before he'd found himself adrift amongst the glimmer and the cymbals. Even though his thoughts felt cleverer than any that he'd previously had – not that he could remember many previous thoughts at all, if he were truthful – he still couldn't piece together what had happened to him. Had there been somebody telling him a story, one of the old, famous stories everybody knew, about the prince who choked upon a wicked cherry? Or, unlikely as it seemed, had he been someone in the tale itself, perhaps even the prince, in which case all this business with him bubbling up through musicals and murk was just the next part of the story? Neither of these ideas sounded right, but he decided that he wouldn't puzzle over things just then. Instead he'd pay attention to the corner, which he seemed to be approaching. Either that, he thought, or it was getting bigger.

Michael couldn't make his mind up if he'd always known that corners went two ways, like this one did, so that they stuck out and poked in at the same time, or if this was a notion that had just this moment popped into his thoughts. It worked, he could now see, in much the same way as those tricky pictures that you found on school chalk-boxes did, with all the cubes stacked in a pyramid, but so you couldn't tell if they went in or out. He understood, now that he had the chance to see a corner from up close, that they did both. What he had taken for a recess was revealed as a protrusion, less like the indented corner of a living room than it was like the jutting corner of a table, that had fancy carved trim round its edges where the ceiling had a beaded moulding. But of course, if it was like a tabletop then that meant he was looking at it from above, not peering up at it from underneath. It meant that he was sinking down towards it and not rising up to bump his head on it. It also meant the living room had been turned inside out.

The idea that he was descending, coming in to land upon the corner of a giant table, made more sense of how things looked to him just then, especially because it gave the corner-fairy something to be standing on, whereas before she had appeared to be stuck, unconvincingly, somewhere up past the picture rail. Although, if she was lower down than he was, why would she be calling to him in her bee-sized voice and telling Michael to come up?

He peered at her suspiciously and tried to tell if she seemed like the sort who'd have him on or play a nasty trick on him, deciding that, yes, probably she did. In fact, the closer Michael got to her, the more the fairy looked like any ten-year-old girl from his neighbourhood, which meant that she was more than likely vicious, one of those from round Fort Street or Moat Street who would knock you cold with shopping bags full of Corona bottles they were taking back for the deposit.

Like the corner she was standing on or in, the fairy gradually grew bigger until Michael had a better view of her, so that she wasn't just a squeaking, waving dot in blue and pink among the fly-specks covering their ceiling. He saw also that she wasn't a real fairy, but a normal-sized girl who had previously been far away and had, therefore, appeared much smaller than she really was. She had blonde hair with just a taste of ginger hanging down an inch or two below her ears, worn in a fringe as if a pudding basin had been placed upon her head and cut around. If she were from the Boroughs, then it very likely had.

It lazily occurred to him that he was starting to remember bits and pieces of the life or story that he'd been involved in until only a few moments back, before discovering that he was bobbing in the fawn drifts of the upper living room. He could remember pudding basins and the Boroughs, Moat Street, Fort Street and Corona bottles. He remembered that his name was Michael Warren, that his mum was Doreen and his dad was Tom. He'd had a sister, Alma, who would make him laugh or badly frighten him at least once every day. He'd had a gran called Clara who he'd not been scared of, and a nan called May who he most definitely had been. Reassured to have at least these scraps of who he was back in their proper order, he turned his attentions once more to the matter of the little girl, now hopping up and down in agitation a scant inch or two above him. Or below him.

He had guessed her age as being nine or ten, what Michael thought of as an almost-grown-up time of life, and as he neared her then the more he was convinced that he'd been right. She was a bony, sturdy child, a little older and a little taller than his sister Alma, prettier and slimmer with a wide and smirky mouth that seemed continually on the brink of bursting open in a laugh bigger than she was. He'd been right, as well, about her being from the Boroughs, or at least from somewhere like it. She just had that local look about her in the way she dressed and the condition of her scabby knees. Her white skin, only tanned by Boroughs drizzle, had a grey shine rubbed into its creases from the railway dust that covered everything and everybody in the district. Gazing at her now, though, Michael saw it was the same pale grey that storm clouds sometimes had, where you could faintly make out rainbow tinsels trying to break through. To tell the truth, he thought the dirt looked quite nice as she wore it, as if it were an expensive rouge or powder you could only get from rare and distant islands of the globe.

He was surprised how good his eyesight was. It wasn't that he'd ever had a problem with his eyes, the way his mum and sister had, but simply that his vision seemed much clearer now, as if someone had dusted all the fogwebs from it. Every tiny detail of the girl and of the clothes that she was wearing was as sharp as an engagement diamond, and the muted colours of her dress and shoes and cardigan were not so much made brighter but were just more vivid somehow, bringing stronger feelings from him.

Her pink jumper, worn into a threadbare safety-net of faded rose strands round its elbows, had the strawberry ice-cream glow of summer teatimes to it, when the last rays of the sinking sun leaned in through the small stained-glass window set into the west wall of the living room. It looked as right and natural with her frock of navy blue as the idea of happy sailors eating candyfloss from sticks upon a bulb-lit promenade. Her slush-white socks had crumpled into concertinas or shed caterpillar skins, one noticeably lower than the other, and her scuff-toed shoes were dyed or painted in an old, deep turquoise with a faint map of burnt orange cracks where you could see the leather showing through from underneath. The fraying straps with their dull silver buckles looked as full of history as charger-bridles from a knight-and-castle past, and then there was the swanky duchess stole she had around her shoulders. This gave Michael quite a start when he examined it more closely.

It was made from twenty-four dead rabbits hung together on a bloody string, all hollowed out to flat and empty glove-puppets with paws and heads and velvet ears and cotton-wool-ball bums attached. Their eyes were mostly open, black as elderberries, or the backwards midnight eyes that people had in photo negatives. Though he supposed a scarf of furry corpses was quite horrible, something about it seemed excitingly adult at the same time. It was most probably against the law, he thought, or at least something you could get told off for, and it only served to make the little girl appear more glamorously adventurous.

Only the whiff of her pelt-garland put him off, and at the same time told him that it wasn't just his eyes that had been suddenly rinsed clean. The scent of things had never previously made a big impression on him, or at least not when compared with the rich, bitter broth he was experiencing now. It was like having orchestras up both sides of his nose at once, performing symphonies of stench. The girl's life and the four-and-twenty rabbit lives around her neck were stories written down invisibly, in perfume, and he read them through his squinting nostrils. Her skin had a warm and nutty smell, mixed with the ruddy-knuckled odour of carbolic soap and something delicate like Parma Violets on her breath. Wrapped round all this was the aroma of her gruesome necklace with its flavourings of tunnel dirt and rabbit poo and green juice chewed from grass, the sawdust fustiness of all those dangling empty coats, the tinny sniff of gore and putrid fruitiness lifting in warm waves from the meagre, mangy meat. The reek from all of this combined was so intoxicating and so interesting that he didn't even think of it as ghastly, necessarily. It was more like a pungent soup of everything that had the whole world somewhere in its simmering, the good bits and the bad bits both at once. It was the tang of life and death, both taken as they came.

Michael was seeing, smelling, even thinking much more clearly than he could remember doing as a floor-bound three-year-old, when all his senses and his thoughts had been comparatively fuzzy, as though viewed through streaky glass. He didn't feel three anymore. He felt much cleverer and more grown up, the way he'd always thought that he would feel when he reached seven, say, or eight, which was about as grown up as he could imagine. He felt properly adult. This brought with it a sense of being more important, just as he'd expected it to do, but also brought the troubling notion that there were now more things he should worry over.

The most urgent of these new concerns was probably the matter of what he was doing bumbling up against the ceiling with this smelly little girl. What had just happened to him? Why was he up here now, and not down there, where he'd been before? He had the vaguest recollection of a sore throat and the safety of his mother's lap, of fresh air and of puny wallflowers rooted in the soot between old bricks, then there had been some sort of a commotion. Everybody had been running round and sounding frightened like they did on those occasions when his gran let down her bun and, combing out her long and steely hair before the open hearth, set it on fire. This time, though, it had been something much worse, worse even than Michael's grandmother with a burning head. You could tell from the panic in the women's voices. Distantly, it came to him that this was what was causing all the lovely thunder mumbling around him: it was how the high-pitched shrieking of his mother and his grandmother would sound if it was slowed down almost to a stop, with all the different noises just left hanging there and trembling in the air.

It struck him suddenly, an ominous gong sounding in his stomach, that his mum's and gran's distress might be connected with his current puzzling circumstances. It was Michael that they were upset about, a fact so obvious he wondered why he hadn't hit on it immediately. He must have had a shock, so that he'd needed time to put his thoughts in order. It seemed reasonable to assume that what had shocked him was the same thing that had made his mum and gran sound scared to death ...

No sooner had the word entered his mind than Michael, in a rush of helpless terror, understood exactly where he was and what had happened to him.

He had died. The thing that even grown-ups like his mum and dad lived with the fear of all their lives, that's what this was, and Michael was alone in it just as he'd always dreaded that he would be. All alone and far too little, still, to cope with this enormous thing the way that he assumed old people could. There were no big hands that would grab him up out of this fall. No lips could ever kiss this better. He knew he was entering a place where there weren't mums or dads or fireside rugs or Tizer, nothing comforting or cosy, only God and ghosts and witches and the devil. He'd lost everyone he'd had and everything he'd been, all in a careless moment where he'd just let his attention wander for an instant and then, bang, he'd tripped and fallen out of his whole life. He whimpered, knowing that at any moment there would be an awful pain that would just crush him to a paste, and then there'd be a nothing that was even worse because he wouldn't be there, and he'd never see his family or his friends ever again.

He started struggling and kicking, trying to wake up and make it just a petrifying dream, but all his desperate activity served only to make everything more frightening and more peculiar. For one thing, all the empty space around him wobbled like a slow glass jelly as he thrashed about, and for another, all at once he had too many arms and legs. His limbs, which he was slightly reassured to find were still clad in his blue and white pyjamas and his dark red tartan dressing gown, left perfect copies of themselves suspended in the air behind them as they moved. With one brief, wriggling spasm he had turned himself into a lively, branching bush of stripy flannel that had pale pink finger-blossoms by the dozen sprouting from its multiplying stems. He wailed, and saw his outcry travel in a glittering trumpet ripple through the crystal glue of the surrounding air.

This only seemed to make the little blonde girl who was in or on the corner cross with him, when what with finding out that he was dead and all of that, he'd quite forgotten she was standing there. She stretched her grubby hands towards him, reaching up or down depending on which aspect of her chalk-box optical illusion he was focussing upon. She shouted at him, near enough now so that he could hear her, with her voice no longer like that of a beetle in a matchbox. Closer up, Michael could hear the Boroughs creaking in her accent, with its grimy floorboards and its padlocked gates.

"Come up! Come on up 'ere, yer'll be all right! Gi' me yer 'and, and pack up wi' yer fidgetin'! Yer'll only make it worse!"

He didn't know what could be worse than being dead, but since at that point he could hardly see her for a forest full of tartan trees and striped-pants shrubbery he thought he'd better do as she advised. He held himself as still as he could manage and, after a moment or two, was relieved to learn that all the extra elbows, knees and slipper-covered feet would gradually fade away to nothing if you gave them enough time. Once all of his superfluous body parts had disappeared and weren't obstructing his view of the corner-fairy anymore, he cautiously reached out towards the hand that she was holding down or up to him, moving his own arm very slowly so that all the trailing after-pictures were reduced to a bare minimum.

Her outstretched fingers wrapped around his own, and he was so surprised by how real and how physical they felt he almost let them go again. He found that, as with sight and scent, his sense of touch had suddenly been made a lot more sensitive. It was as though he'd taken off a pair of padded mittens that had been tied on his wrists soon after he'd been born. He felt her palm, hot as a new-baked cake and slippery with sweat, as if she'd held it guarding pennies in her pocket for too long. The soft pads in between her digits had a sticky glaze, like she'd been eating ripe pears with her bare hands and had not had time to wash yet, if she ever did. He didn't know exactly what he'd been anticipating, possibly that being dead his fingertips would simply pass through everything as if it were made out of steam, but he'd not been expecting anything as clammily believable as this, these humid crab-legs scrabbling for his wrist and clamping on the baggy cuff of Michael's dressing gown.

Her grip, not only startlingly real, was also much, much stronger than he would have thought to look at her. Yanking him by the arm she hauled him up, no, down towards her, much like someone trying to land a frantic, flapping fish. He suffered an unpleasant moment during this when both his eyes and stomach had to flip from thinking he was being pulled down to a table corner that poked out, and instead see it as a backroom corner that tucked in, with the girl straddling it and reaching down as if helping him up out of a swimming pool, while she stood safely in the dry astride the junction where its edges met. The room lurched outside-in again as he was dragged up through a sort of hinge, where everything you thought was going one way turned out to be actually going in the other, and next thing he knew Michael was standing wobbly-kneed on the same painted wooden ledge as the small girl.

This narrow platform ran around the rim of what appeared to be a big square vat some thirty feet or more across, with their precarious perch being the lowest level of a tiered amphitheatre that sloped up for several steps on all four sides, like a giant picture-frame enclosing the wide fish-tank void he'd just been rescued from. The ten-yard sweeps of stair that led up from the edges of the pool-like area were, even in his confused condition, obviously impractical and ludicrous. The treads were far too deep, being some feet across from front to rear, while at the same time all the risers were too shallow, no more than three inches high, harder to sit on than a roadside curb. The gently-stepped surround seemed to be made of tiered white-painted pine with its sharp corners rounded into curves, covered all over with a thick and flaking coat of paint, a yellowing cream gloss that looked as though it had been last touched up before the war. To be quite frank, the more he peered at them the more the steps resembled the old beaded moulding that ran round the ceiling of their living room in Andrew's Road, except much bigger and turned upside down. As he stood with his back towards the rectangular pit he'd been pulled out of, he could even see a patch of bare wood where the paint had peeled away leaving a shape a bit like Britain lying on its back, identical to one he'd noticed once up on the decorative trim above their fireplace. That one, though, had been no larger than a penny postage stamp, whereas this was an unjumpable puddle, even though he felt sure that the wriggling contour lines would prove a perfect match on close inspection.

After blinking at the woodwork in astonishment for a few seconds, Michael shuffled round in his plaid slippers until he was face to face with the tough little girl who stood beside him on the pine boards with her collar made of rancid rabbits. She was just a fraction taller than he was himself, which, taken in conjunction with the fact that she was wearing proper clothes while he was still dressed in his night-things, made him feel as if she had him at a disadvantage. Realising that they were still holding hands, he let go hurriedly.

He meant to say something along the lines of "Who are you," or "What's been done to me," but what came out instead was "You who," followed almost instantly by "Worlds bent under me." Alarmed, he raised his fingers to his lips and felt around to make sure that his mouth was working properly. Lifting his arm to do so, Michael noticed that he was no longer leaving picture-copies every time he moved. Perhaps that only happened in the floaty place he'd just that moment been fished out of, but right then Michael was more concerned about the rubbish he was coming out with when he tried to talk.

The girl stood looking at him in amusement with her head cocked on one

side, her wide lips pressed together in a thin line so that she could keep from
laughing. Michael made a fresh attempt to ask her where they were and what
had happened to him.

"Ware whee are, wore 'way? And throttles happy tune me?"

Though the stream of nonsense was no less upsetting, Michael was astonished to discover that he almost understood himself. He'd asked her where
they were as he'd intended to, but all the words had come out changed and
twisted round, with different meaning tucked into their crevices. He thought
that what he'd said translated roughly to "Where are we, in this place where I
feel so aware, that makes we want to shout whee, but which makes me wary,
looking all run-down and worn away, the way it does? And what has happened
to me? I was happy where I was, but fear I may have throttled on a Tune that
has choked off my joyous song." It sounded a bit posh and weedy put like that,
but he supposed that it contained the feelings he was trying to convey.

The smirking urchin could contain her mirth no longer and laughed in
his face, loudly, though not unkindly. Minute beads of opal spittle, each with
all the world reflected in it, hurtled from her mouth to break against his nose.
Amazingly, the girl seemed to at least have caught the gist of what he'd meant
to say, and when her giggles had subsided she made what he took for a sincere
attempt to answer all his questions as directly as she could.

"Yoo hoo to you as well. I'm Phyllis Painter. I'm boss of the gang."

Those weren't the exact words she used, and there were corkscrew syllables that made him think of "gasbag" and "bass gong", perhaps a reference to
how much she talked or how deep, for a girl, her voice was, but he could make
out what she was saying without difficulty. Clearly, she'd got her mouth under
more control than Michael had his own. She went on and he listened, both
intently and admiringly.

"What's 'appened is the world's bent under yer and out yer've fell like
everybody does. Yer've chuckled on a sweet." This seemed to say that he had
throttled or had choked to death as he'd suspected, though with comical associations as if neither death nor choking could be taken very seriously round
here. The girl continued.

"So I tugged yer ayt the jewellery and now 'ere we are Upstairs. We're in
Mansoul. Mansoul's the Second Borough. Do yer want to join me gang or
don't yer?"

Michael comprehended almost none of this except the last part. He
jumped back from her like he'd been stung. His spirited refusal of her offer
was spoiled only by not being in a proper language.

"Know eye doughnut! Late me grow black square eyewash be four!"

She laughed again, less loudly and, he thought, not quite so kind.

"Ha! You ent found yer Lucy-lips yet. That's why what yer saying clangs out wrong. Just give it linger and yer'll soon be spooking properly. But as for where you wizzle be before, there ent no go-back. Life's behind yer now."

She nodded past him, and it sank in that her last remark had been intended as more than a turn of phrase. She'd meant his life was currently behind him. With his neck-hairs tingling as they lifted, Michael swivelled carefully to look at it.

He found that he'd been standing with his back turned to the very edge of the huge, square-shaped tank he'd been dragged up from, with a worrying drop beneath him at his slipper-heels. The area he was looking at, while not much bigger than the children's boating lake he'd seen once at the park, was certainly much deeper, to the point where Michael couldn't tell exactly how far down it went. The great flat pool was filled up to its brim with the same wobbly, half-set glass that he had lately been suspended in. The surface was still quivering slightly, no doubt from the violent jerk with which he'd been pulled out.

As Michael peered down through the shuddering substance he could make out still forms that extended through the glazed depths, motionless and twisted trunks of intricately textured gemstone that were wound around each other as they stretched across the space beneath. He thought it might look a bit like a coral garden, though he hadn't really got a clear idea of what those words actually meant. The interwoven strands with all their branches and their surfaces seemed to be made of something you could see through, like a hard, clear wax. These frilly, tangling cables had no colour of their own, but you could look inside them to where lights of every shade swam back and forth. He could distinguish at least three of the long convoluted tubes, each with its own specific inner hue, as they snaked in amongst each other through the rubbery fathoms trembling far below, like an ice-statue of a gorgeous knot.

The thickest and most well-developed of the stems, lit from inside by a predominantly greenish glow, was the one Michael thought looked nicest, though he couldn't have told anyone precisely why. It had a peaceful quality about it, with the sculpted emerald bough stretched right across the massive box of shivering light, from where it entered through a tall rectangle in the vat's far wall, then coiled around the monster fish-tank prettily towards him before curving off to Michael's left and exiting his field of vision through another looming aperture.

He thought it was an interesting coincidence that both these openings were in the same relation to each other as the doors that led out from their living room down Andrew's Road into the kitchen and the passageway, although these entrances were vastly bigger, more like those you'd find in a cathedral or perhaps a pyramid. As he looked closer with his improved eyes he saw that there was even a black tunnel cut low down into the right-side wall halfway along, in the precise location that their fireplace would be if it were huger and if he were staring down at it from a position up above.

While he was pondering this unlikely similarity he noticed that his favourite frond, the green one, had a rippling and attractive ruff along one side up near the top, resembling a stripe of fanning mushroom gills. At the point where the complicated cable of translucent jade bent to the left, which was the point where it was also nearest him, he had the opportunity to view these gills side-on and realised with a jolt that he was looking at an endless row of duplicated human ears. Only when Michael saw that every one was wearing an identical facsimile of his mum Doreen's favourite clip-on button earrings did he understand at last what he'd been gawping at.

The jelly-flooded chamber, weird as any undiscovered planet, was in fact their dear, familiar living room but somehow swollen up to a terrific size. The luminous, contorted crystal shafts laced through it were the bodies of his family, but with their shapes repeated and projected through the chandelier-like treacle of their atmosphere, the way that Michael's arms and legs had looked when he himself was floundering in the viscous emptiness. The difference was that these extended figures were immobile, and the images that they were made from didn't promptly fade out of existence in the way that his spare limbs had done. It was as though while people were still living they were really frozen motionless, immersed in the congealed blancmange of time, and simply thought that they were moving, when in truth it was just their awareness fluttering along the pre-existing tunnel of their lifetime as a ball of coloured light. Apparently, only when people died, as Michael seemed to have just done, were they released from the containing amber and allowed to rise up spluttering and splashing through the aspic of the hours.

The biggest, greenest structure, that he'd already expressed a preference for, was Michael's mum, passing at great speed through the living room, from kitchen door to passageway. He dimly calculated that in normal circumstances this would only take his mother a few instants, which suggested that the slice of time on permanent display in this capacious tank was, at the most, ten seconds thick. Even so, you could tell from the tortuous interweaving of the sunken lumps that quite a lot was going on.

The curling reef of bottle-glass that was his mother – he could now discern her lime-lit features shuffled through the ridge's uppermost protrusion like a stack of see-through masks – appeared to have a bright fault all along the greater part of its extraordinary length. Where it grew into the enclosure on its far side, through the towering gap beneath the waterline that was in actuality their now-enormous kitchen door, the green mass had a smaller form enclosed within, a roughly star-shaped splotch of radiant primrose running through its centre like the lettering in a stick of rock. This inner glow remained inside the gooseberry-toned configuration from the point at which it surged in via the chasm of the doorway, following it as it briefly veered to Michael's right and then resumed its path towards him, a manoeuvre undertaken to avoid the obstacle of a drowned mesa that he reasoned must be their living-room table. It was here, however, right between the table and the yawning cavern of the fireplace, that the yellow brilliance seemed to leak out from the moulded olive vessel that contained it. A diffused gold plume rose smokily through the engulfing negative-space gelatine, a cloudy and unravelling woollen strand of lemonade that trailed up to the gumdrop pane of the vat's surface quite near Michael's plaid-clad feet as he stood on the framing wood surround. It looked like clean bath water somebody had done a wee in. The soft star-shape with its five blunt points was still inside the greater rolling bulk as this swerved to one side and went out by the presently colossal passage door on his far left, but now it was a colourless and empty hole amidst the warm, enfolding green. The summer light had all drained out of it.

After a while it came to Michael that this had been him, this frail five-petal marigold of brightness which at first glance seemed to be inside the larger crystalline arrangement that was Michael's mum. She had been carrying him with both arms in front of her, so that her wider contours seemed to swallow his as she rushed forward in her stream of repetitions. And the point in her trajectory between the table and the fireplace where his smaller light switched off, that was where he had died, where life had cracked and his awareness had seeped into the enveloping consommé of coagulated time. The yellow traces straggling upwards in the prism-syrup were the ones that his pyjama-swaddled consciousness had left behind when he'd dog-paddled up and through the ceiling.

He gazed down into the grotto at the submarine contortions of the other two illuminated ferns, a spiky russet hedge of what looked like refrigerated orange pop and which he took to be his gran, and then a pale mauve tube much closer to the floor that had a violet torch-beam flare dancing inside it. He assumed this was his sister, flickering with all her purple thoughts. With its delicious paint-box tints and its aquatic layers of transparency, Michael could see why the unnerving girl who'd hoisted him aloft had spoken of it as "the jewellery". It was delicate and beautiful, but he thought there was something sad about it, too. Despite its shifting, coruscating sparks the ornamental diorama had the look of a forgotten snarl of river-bottom junk, so that it seemed a common and neglected thing.

The girl's voice issued over Michael's shoulder from behind him, thus reminding him abruptly that she was still there.

"It's an old can of beans, but every bubble that you ever blew wiz still inside."

Oddly, he knew just what she meant. It was a rusty and discarded old container he was looking at, but all his hopes and wishes had been in it, had been born from it. It was a treasure chest that turned into a coal scuttle once you could see it from outside, yet still he couldn't help but miss the slack that he'd mistaken in his inexperience for finery. He mooned down for a moment at the royal carpet river of malachite filigree that was his mother's hair, then looked round at the girl. She sat, kicking her ankles, on the shabby cream steps banked around the sunken living room. Michael was starting to accept that in some way this framing woodwork was in fact the moulding up around their ceiling, but turned inside-down or upside-out and blown up larger. She was looking at him quizzically, so that he felt he ought to say something.

"Wiz this play seven?"

His enunciation was still bungling his tongue, but Michael thought it might be slowly getting easier to communicate. The trick appeared to lie in meaning every word you said in a precise, pure way that left no room for ambiguity. This seemed to be a place where language would erupt in connotations and conundrums without provocation, given half a chance. You had to keep your eye on it. At least this time his new posthumous playmate wasn't sniggering at his speech-defect as she answered him.

"Yiss, if you like. Or 'ell. It's just Upstairs, that's all. It's up the wooden 'ill, the Second Borough, what they call Mansoul. We're in amongst the angles, and it wunt be long afore yer've got the 'ang of it. You're lucky that I wizzle passing, what with you not 'aving family 'ere to welcome yer aboard."

Michael considered this last, casual observation. Now he thought about it, all this being dead and going up to Heaven business did seem rather poorly organised. It wasn't like he'd had a lot of expectations about angels, trumpets, pearly gates or anything like that, but he would not have thought it would be too much trouble to arrange a passed-on relative or two, just as a welcoming committee to this funny, slipshod afterlife. Although, to be fair, all of his dead relatives had died before Michael was born so that they wouldn't really know him, not to talk to. As for all the members of his family that he was closer to, he'd messed that up by dying out of order. He'd assumed that in the normal run of things, people would die according to how old they were, which meant that his nan May would be the first to go, then his gran Clara, then his dad, his mum, his older sister, him himself and finally their budgie, Joey. If he hadn't died before it was his turn, then all of them except the budgie would be here to lift him up out of his life, to clap him on the back and introduce him to Eternity. It wouldn't have been left to just some girl, some perfect stranger who just happened to be strolling by.

As it was now, though, he'd be here all on his own arranging the reception for his terrifying nan. And what if it were years until somebody else died, years with just the two of them waltzing around together on these eerie, creaking boards? With his eyes desperate and darting at the very notion, he attempted to convey some of his musings to the little girl. Wasn't it Phyllis something that she'd said her name was? He spoke carefully and slowly, making sure of the intention of each word before it passed his lips, so that it wouldn't suddenly betray him by exploding into puns and homonyms.

"I've died while I'm still little. That's why no one elf wiz here to meet me yet."

He was improving, definitely. That sentence had been going fine until the bit where he had inadvertently referred to his young, bowl-cut benefactor as a "no one elf." Upon reflection, though, this didn't seem entirely inappropriate, and she herself didn't appear as if she'd taken it amiss. She sat there on the ancient paintwork, straightening the navy linen of her skirt over her grit and gravel-studded kneecaps, idly picking at the brittle, yellowed edges of the flaking gloss. She looked up at him almost pityingly, and shook her head.

"That's not the way it works. Everyone's 'ere already. Everymum's always been here already. It's just dayn there where yer get yer times and chimes mixed up.'

She nodded to the glistening cavity of Michael's former living room, behind him.

"Only when we're reading through the pages wizzle there be any order to 'um. When the book's shut, all its leaves are pressed together into paper inches that don't really goo one way or t'other. They're just there."

He'd absolutely no idea what she was on about. Quite frankly, Michael was still entering a mounting state of panic at the idea of him turning out to be May Warren's escort in this peeling paradise. In fact, the horror-stricken and appalled reaction to this whole state of affairs that he'd been putting off seemed to be creeping up on Michael in a thoroughly upsetting manner. As the awful fact of his demise continued to sink in, just when he thought that he'd accepted all there was of it, he found his hands were shaking. When he tried to speak he found his voice was, too.

"I don't wilt to be dead. This wizzn't right. If all this wizzle right, there'd be somebody that I knew here waiting four me."

Wizzn't? Wizzle? Michael realised he was using words the little girl had used as if he'd always understood them perfectly. For instance, he knew "wizzle" was a term that had "was", "is" and "will be" folded up inside it, as though to divide things up to present, past and future was thought an unnecessary complication in these parts. This insight only served to make him feel even more lost and worried than he was already. He knew that even if he was here until the end of time, he'd never understand the first thing that was going on.

He had an overpowering urge to run away from all of this, and all that kept his feet still was the knowledge that there wasn't really anywhere safe in the world that Michael could still run to.

Sitting on the low steps, toying with her rotten rabbit wrap, the girl was now regarding him with a more wary and uncertain look, as if he'd said something that she mistrusted, or as if some new fact had occurred to her. She squinched her eyes, Malteser brown, to twin slits of interrogation, with the freckled bridge of her snub nose suddenly corrugated as a consequence.

"This wiz a bit of a pecuriosity, now that I come to think. Even the 'Itlers 'ave their granddads waitin' for 'um, and I shouldn't think yer'd 'ave 'ad time to be as bad as that. What wiz you, six or seven?"

For the first time since he'd landed here, he looked down at his body. He was satisfied to find that in this new light, even his old night-clothes were as mesmerising in their tucks and textures as the clothing of the little girl appeared to be. The tartan of his dressing gown, in reds so deep they verged on the maroon, was bursting with the dried-blood histories of proud and tragic clans. His deckchair-striped pyjamas, alternating bands of ice cream cloud and July sky, made sleep seem like a seaside holiday. Michael was pleased to note, as well, that he was bigger than he'd been: still skinny, but a good foot taller. It was more the body of a smallish eight-year-old than that of the mere toddler he had been just moments earlier. He tried to answer the girl's question honestly, even if that meant that she'd think he was a baby.

"I think that I wizzle three, but now that I'm glowed up I'm more like seven."

The girl nodded in agreement.

"That makes sense. I 'spect yer'd always wanted to be seven, ay? That's 'ow we are 'ere, looking as we best think of ayrselves. Most people monger themselves younger, or they're 'appy 'ow they are already, but infantoms like yerself are bound to be an age such as they wizzle looking forward to."

Adopting a more serious expression now, she carried on.

"But 'ow wiz it a three-year-old 'as got no family Upstairs to take 'im in? There's more to you than meets the I, me little deady-boy. What wiz yer name when you wiz in yer fame?"

None of this chat was making him less nervous, but he couldn't see how telling her his name would make things any worse, so he replied as best he could.

"I'm Michael Warren. It might be there's no one here because I wizn't properly supposed to come up yet to Deadfordshire. It might be a missed ache."

He'd meant to say "mistake", and didn't know where "Deadfordshire" had come from. It felt like a kind of slang that he was picking up out of the air, the way that words and phrases sometimes came to him in dreams. At any rate, the girl appeared to have no trouble understanding him, which indicated that his grasp of cemetery Esperanto was improving. With a troubled look upon her face she shook her head so that her blonde fringe shimmered like a midget waterfall.

"There's no missed aches. I might 'ave known I wizzn't skipping through the Attics of the Breath by accident when yer clogs 'appened to pop up. I thought I'd took a short cut from where I'd been scrumping for Mad Apples at the 'ospital, back 'ome to the Old Buildings, but I see now that I'd got super-intentions what I didn't know about. It's like they always say round 'ere, the character don't run a mile before the author's writ a while."

She breathed a drawn-out "hahh" of deep exasperation, then stood up with a decisive air about her, smoothing down the heavy fabric of her midnight-blue skirt out of habit.

"Yer'd better come with me until we can find out what all this wiz abayt. We can call at the Works and ask the builders. Come on. This wiz borin', all this past and plaster what's round 'ere."

She turned and started walking with deliberation up the shallow stairs of painted planking, obviously expecting him to follow her as she ascended from the inlaid cavity of their amphitheatre. Michael didn't know what he should do. On one hand, Phyllis ... Painter, was it? Phyllis Painter was the only person that he'd got for company here in this echoing and lonely afterdeath, even if Michael wasn't sure he ought to trust her. On the other hand, the fifty-foot-wide jelly-cube behind him was his one connection with the lovely and unwitting life he'd had before. Those frilly dragon statues down there in the instant's diamond varnish were his mum and gran and sister. Even if his new acquaintance found it boring, Michael felt uneasy about wandering off and leaving it behind. What if he never found his way back here again, the way that he could never find his way back to the places in his dreams, which this experience resembled? What if this was his last glimpse of number 17, St. Andrew's Road, of his beige living room, his family, his life? He glanced back hesitantly at the yawning tank that had his final moment in it, frozen and electroplated like a pair of baby-shoes. Then he looked up the flattened steps to where his rescuer was climbing past the edge of the concavity and out of sight, without a backward glance.

He called out "Weight", noticing how his cry reverberated in the different sort of architecture that they had up here, the way it whispered in undreamed-of distances, then he chased after her. He bounded up the chipped cream layers of the framing woodwork, desperately afraid that when he reached their summit she'd be gone. She wasn't, but as he emerged out of the square-cut sink and had for the first time an unimpeded view of where he was, he felt the same despair as if she had been.

It was a flat prairie, though that term did not adequately convey its vastness, nor the fact that it was made entirely out of bare untreated floorboards. Or its shape, for that matter. Staggeringly long yet relatively narrow, it was more like an enormous hallway than a sagebrush plain, being perhaps a mile in width but with a length extending both in front of and behind him for as far as he could see, even with his new eyesight. To all practical intents and purposes, the wooden prairie's length was infinite. Also, the whole eye-boggling reach of it was covered with an endless antique railway-station roof, elaborate wrought iron and ghoul-tinged glass a thousand feet above. It looked like there were pigeons nesting on its giant girders, dust motes of pale grey against the dark green of the painted metal. Up above this, out beyond the tinted glasswork's undersea translucency, there was ... but Michael didn't want to look at that just yet.

He stood there in his slippers, teetering and awestruck on the dirty butter-coloured rim of what had been his living room, his dying room, and forced his gaze down from the eyestrain heights back to the great, boarded expanses that surrounded him. These were not, as he'd first thought, featureless. He saw now that the tiered frame he perched wobbling on the edge of was in fact just one of many near-identical wood rectangles enclosing sunken indentations like the one he occupied. These were arranged in an extensive grid with broad blonde boardwalks running back and forth between them, like a kind of mile-wide gingham. It resembled rows of windows that were set into the floor for some unfathomable reason, rather than the walls. Because this regular and neatly-ordered pattern covered all of the terrain between him and the far, invisible horizon, the most distant trapdoor recesses were shrunken to a screen of close-packed dots, like when he'd held his eyes close to the printed pictures in the comics from America his sister saved.

He thought he'd probably be stricken with a headache if he stared for too long at the vanishing extremities of the preposterously big arcade that he was in. "Arcade", Michael decided, was a term that better conjured up the atmosphere of this immense, glass-covered hall than "railway station", which had been his first impression. Actually, the more that he considered it, the more he came to see that this place was exactly like the old Emporium Arcade that ran up from Northampton's market square, but realised on a glorious, titanic scale. If he looked right or left, across the sweeping breadth of the huge corridor, he saw the bounding walls were a confusion of brick buildings stacked atop each other and connected by precarious flights of stairs with banisters and balconies. Amongst these he could see what looked like decorated if dilapidated shop-fronts, such as those which ran up either side of the emporium's perpetual twilight slope. The deep-stained hardwood balustrade that edged the balconies appeared to be the twin of that which ran around the upper floor of the terrestrial arcade, but he was much too far away, even from this huge hallway's nearest walls, to tell if that was genuinely the case.

It smelled big, smelled like morning in a church hall where a jumble sale was going on, the air a weak infusion in which stale, damp coats steeped with the crumbling fresh pinkness of homemade coconut ice, the sneeze-provoking pages of old children's annuals and the sour metal lick of cast-off Dinky cars.

Training his eyes upon some of the nearer dots, and bearing in mind that even the further ones were apertures some hundred square feet in dimension, Michael saw that here and there massively enlarged trees were growing up through one or two of the more distant rectangular openings. He counted three of these, with possibly a fourth much further off along the endless bore of the arcade, so distant that it might have been another tree but could as easily have been a pillar formed by rising smoke. A couple of the leafy outgrowths, boughs and branches greatly magnified, reached almost to the glass roof, dizzyingly far above. He could see ash-fleck pigeons swirling up and down the huge and jutting trunks from perch to perch, with their size having not apparently been increased in the same way as that of the foliage, so that they now looked less like fowl and more like pearl-grey ladybirds. So small were they, compared with the immense arboreal structure they were roosting in, that some sat sheltered comfortably within the corrugations of its bark. Their ruffling coos, echoed and amplified by the unusual acoustics of the glass emporium roof that curved above, were audible despite the gaping distances involved, a kind of feathered undertow of murmur he could hear beneath the general background rustle of this extraordinary space. The presence of the trees combined with the sheer scale of everything around him meant that Michael couldn't tell if he felt like he was inside or out of doors.

Since he already stood with his eyes lifted to the topmost tablecloth-sized leaves of the immeasurable giants, Michael thought that he might risk another cautious squint at the unlikely firmament that lay beyond the curling ironwork and Coca-Cola bottle panes that formed the covering of the great arcade.

It wasn't quite as bad as he'd expected but, once looked at, it was very difficult to look away. Its colour, or at least its colour over that giant stretch of passage where he found himself, was a more deep and priceless azure than he could have previously imagined. Further off along the mighty hall and at the limits of what he could see from where he stood, the regal blue appeared to have ignited, to have melted down to furnace reds and golds. Michael glanced back across his shoulder, looking down the stunning corridor the other way, and saw that at its most remote extremes the boundless sky, which could be seen through the glass panels of the arcade's ceiling, was on fire. As with the blue above, the hotter hues he could see flaring in the distance seemed almost fluorescent in their brilliance, like the unreal shades you sometimes got in films. However, though the sizzling colours of the heavens were most certainly arresting, it was the unearthly bodies drifting through that vista that had seized Michael's attention. It was these that made the sight almost impossible to tear his gaze away from.

They weren't clouds, although they were as variously sized and just as graceful and unhurried in their motion. They were more, he thought, like blueprint drawings that someone had done of clouds. For one thing you could only see their pallid silver graphite lines and not their contours. For another, all those lines were straight. It was as if some very clever student of geometry had been assigned the task of modelling every crease and convolution of the drifting cumuli, so that each cloud's shape was constructed from a million tiny facets. The effect was more like haphazardly crumpled balls of paper, albeit paper he could see through to discern the lines and angles of their every inner complication. This meant also that the blazing background colours of the sky were visible between the intricate and ghostly limning of the floating diagrams.

Beside their gradual drift across the mile-wide ribbon of celestial blue that he could see through the emporium's roof, he noticed that the forms were also moving and contorting slowly in themselves as they progressed across the sky, the way that real clouds did. Instead of languid and unfurling tongues of vapour, though, the movement here was that, again, of badly crinkled vellum as it gradually unfolded from its scrunch in the recesses of a wicker paper-basket. Faceted extrusions crept and crackled as the towering heaps of blueprint-weather lazily unpacked themselves, and there was something in the way that the interior lines and angles moved which he found fascinating, though he struggled to define exactly what it was.

It was a bit like if you had a cube of paper but were looking at it from end on, so that you couldn't see it was a cube with sides, and all you saw was a flat square. Then, if you turned the cube or changed your viewpoint slightly, all its true depth would swing into view and you would understand that you were looking at a solid shape, not just a cut-out.

This was like that, only taken a stage further. In the shifting of the geometric tangles he surveyed, it was as if he gazed directly at something he took to be a cube, but then it was rotated or his vantage somehow altered, so that it turned out to be a much more complicated form, as different from a cube as cubes were from flat squares of paper. It was a lot cubier, for a start, with its lines running in at least one more direction than there really were. He stood there balanced on the framing edge of the square vat behind him, head tipped back so he could goggle at the spectacle above, and tried to think it through.

The strange new solids blossoming within the crenellations of the diagram-clouds were ones that Michael had no names for, though he found he had an inkling of the way in which they were constructed. Thinking of the paper cube that he'd imagined earlier, Michael realised that if you unfolded it then you'd have six flat squares of paper joined together in a Jesus-cross. The shapes that crawled across the endless strip of skylight overhead, however, were more like what Michael thought you'd get if you could somehow take six or more cubes and fold them all up neatly into one big super-cube.

How long had he been standing frozen on the tank's rim, gaping up into the churning mathematics? Suddenly alarmed, he looked down to the wooden plain of windows stretching all around him and was pitifully relieved to find that Phyllis Painter was still standing patiently a yard or three away across the smooth-planed planks that were the arcade's floor, close to another of the inlaid holes. She looked at him accusingly, as did four dozen of the dead and gleaming rabbit eyes that sequined her repulsive stole, like shotgun pellets blasted into velvet.

"If yer've finished gawkin' at the gret big 'ouses like yer've just got 'ere from Bugbrook, then perhaps we can be on ayr way. I've better things to waste me death on than just showing shroud-shocked little kids abayt."

Flinching at the sharp edge her voice had taken on, Michael jumped down obediently from the raised edge of his former living room's tiered framework, to the smooth pine floorboards she was standing on. He padded dutifully across to her, the sash-tie of his tartan dressing gown undone and trailing round his slippers, then stood looking up at her as if awaiting fresh instructions. Phyllis sighed again, theatrically, and shook her head. It was a very grown-up mannerism that belied her years, but then that was how all the little girls around the Boroughs acted, much like Russian dolls that had been taken from inside their unscrewed mothers and were just the same, but smaller.

"Well, come on, then."

She turned with a maypole swirl of dangling rabbit hides and started to walk off across the width of the titanic corridor, towards the bounding wall on Michael's right with all its balconies and shops and buildings piled higgledy-piggledy, perhaps a half-a-mile away. After a moment's hesitation Michael trotted after her and, as he did so, happened to glance down into the great square vat that she'd been standing near, the next one up the line from that which Michael had himself emerged from.

It was almost perfectly identical, down to the details of the beaded moulding, enlarged and inverted, that made up the tiered steps from the tank's sides down to the sunken jelly-cube that was its centrepiece. Michael could even see the patch of flaking paint that looked like Britain sprawling on its back, playing with Ireland like a deformed kitten with a ball of wool. This was his living room again, but when he peered down at the central tableau's depths Michael discovered that the jewellery was altered. The green mother-shape that had contained his yellow child-shape was now gone, and only the extended gem-fern caterpillars representing Michael's gran and sister still remained. The amethyst Swiss roll that was his sister trailed across the room's floor, up onto some sort of raised plateau which Michael reasoned must be the armchair that stood to one side of the fire. Here it curled into a stationary loop in which the violet sparks looked dull and sluggish, like a disconsolate Catherine Wheel. Meanwhile the bigger, spinier glass animal that was his gran, lit from within by autumn bonfire lights, coiled back and forth in tight loops through the mammoth kitchen door. It was as if his sister was slumped still and sob-bing in the fireside armchair while their grandmother kept popping from the kitchen to the living room to see if the unhappy infant was all right. Michael concluded that this was the next brief time-slice in the continuity of their back room, some moments after his mum Doreen had rushed out into the passage, carrying in her arms the child she did not realise was already dead. All of the sunken window-frames in this particular unending row, he thought, must open down upon the same place but at different points in time. He had an urge to run along the file of apertures and follow the sequential glimpses of his living room as if they were a story in the *Dandy*, but his escort, draped in dead things, was already some way off, heading across the endless corridor and not along it. Stifling his curiosity, he hurried to catch up with her.

As he fell into step beside her, Phyllis Painter cast a sidelong look at him and sniffed, as though in reprimand for Michael having lagged behind again.

"I know that it's a marvelation to yer, but yer've got fourever to explore and see the sights. All this'll still be 'ere when yer get back. Reternity ent gooin' anywhere."

He more or less knew what she meant but still wanted to understand as much of this new territory as he could while he was passing through it. This was not as far as he could see unreasonable, and he decided to risk irritating his corpse-hung companion further with what seemed to him entirely natural questions for an expired lad in his position.

"If the longways rows wiz all our living room over again, then what wiz all these wideways ones?"

He gestured, with one little hand protruding from a too-large tartan sleeve, towards the framed vat they were walking past. Rather than wooden edging, all the inlaid rectangles in this specific row seemed to be bordered with white plasterwork, at least for nearly three of their four sides, with pointed blue brick capstones constituting the remainder of the frame. The girl nodded disinterestedly at the enclosure closest to them on their left as they strolled down one of the mile long avenues that led between the tanks, towards the heaped-up jumble of the arcade's nearest side.

"See for yerself, so long as you don't dawdle over it."

He scampered extra quickly to the raised edge of the thirty-foot-square vat, just to convince her that he wasn't dawdling, and peeped over its side. It took him a few seconds to work out what he was peering down at, but eventually he understood that it was an expanded overview of the top floor of 17, St. Andrew's Road, or the back section of the house, at any rate. Banked plaster steps with what looked like wallpaper carpeting replaced the peeling, painted woodwork that had framed the elevations of their living room, but only for two-and-a-bit sides of the oblong's tiered perimeter. This was because the greater portion of the open-topped space that the frame enclosed was taken up by a big L-shape made from bedrooms, stair-head, and a section of their landing as glimpsed from above. The vertical bar of the L was formed by his and Alma's bedroom, with the top of their stairs and some of the landing visible down at the bottom, where it met the horizontal line that was their gran's room. This indoors-part of the roughly-square area contained within the frame was what accounted for the wallpaper-and-plaster trim that he could see along at least two of its sides, while the remainder of the shape was taken up by a view straight down from the level of the guttering into the higher part of their back yard. It came to Michael that the slate-blue capstones edging the rightmost upper corner of this tank were an expanded version of the stones that topped their garden wall.

There were none of the frilly, crawling jewels that Michael knew to be his family apparent in the scene below him, neither upstairs in the empty bedrooms nor down in the yard below. He could, however, still make out the wooden chair that he and his mum had been sitting on before he'd choked. This must, he thought, be a few moments after everyone had rushed indoors out of the yard and left the chair behind. All the human activity was going on down in the kitchen and the living room, the scene that he'd just witnessed with his sister sitting weeping and his gran keeping an eye on her, so that the bedrooms were both empty here. The only living thing that flickered through the crystallised scenario was an amazing iridescent column that appeared to be made out of beautifully crafted ladies' fans. This seemed to plunge into the clarified time-gravy from a point close to the rooftop's rim, and then described a breathtakingly elegant trajectory down into the far depths of the back garden. It occurred to him that it was probably a pigeon, with its moving wings transforming it to an exquisite glass-finned ornament.

Aware that if he wasn't careful he would break into a dawdle, Michael turned away from this enchanting still life, though reluctantly, and hastened to re-join the little girl. The trouble with this place, as far as Michael was concerned, was that there wasn't anything that didn't fascinate him. Its most minor detail seemed to be inviting him to stare entranced at it for hours. Why, probably even the plain pine floorboards he was walking on, if he were only to look down at them, would ...

... would envelope him within a flowing tide-map universe of grain, with near-invisible striations rippling from the knothole's vortex eye into a peacock feathering, the frozen pulse of a magnetic field. The engraved hearts of hurricanes, reverberating outward in concentric lines of vegetable force; the accidental faces of mad, decomposed baboons trapped snarling in the wood; trilobite stains with legs that trailed away to isotherms. The sweet and fatherly perfume of sawdust would completely overwhelm him with its atmosphere of honest labour, would immerse him in long, silent histories of dripping forest and time measured out in moss, if he were only to look down beyond his stumbling slippers and ...

Michael snapped out of it and hurriedly fell into step with Phyllis Painter, who'd not broken stride while he inspected the new aperture, and who was clearly finished with indulging Michael in his tardiness. They carried on along the wooden avenue between the vats towards the heaping side-wall of the grand arcade gradually getting bigger up ahead of them, a teetering hodge-podge pile of mismatched buildings, taller than a town. He wondered what ungraspable new shapes the folded paper clouds were making up beyond the see-through ceiling overhead, but prudently decided that he wouldn't look to see. Instead, he thought he'd better concentrate upon his ragamuffin tour-guide before she lost interest in him altogether. To this end, he plied her with fresh questions.

"Wiz this all Northampton what we see here, open for Upstairs-men to look down on?"

She spared him a faintly condescending sideways glance, letting him know she thought he was an idiot.

"'Course not. This wiz just the Attics of the Breath above your bit of Andrew's Road. In the direction what we're gooin' now, the attic doors all open dayn on different rooms and floors and whatnot of the 'ouses in your street. The line we're walking dayn, that's all them different places laid ayt in a row, so it goes on a mile or two but don't goo on forever. Now, the other way, along the overhall ..."

She pointed with her skinny left arm here, down the immeasurable length of the vast corridor, to where the thirty-foot vats were close-stippled dots beneath the bloody, golden forge-light beating down through the glass roof high up above.

"That's the direction what up here we call the linger or the whenth of something, and it *does* goo on forever. What it is, if this way what we're walking now is all the different rooms along your bit of Andrew's Road, then that way, lingerways, that's all the different moments of those rooms. That's why the sky above this bit what were in now is always blue, because it's 'alf-way through a summer's day. The bit along the far end where it guz all brass and fireworks, that's the sunset, and if yer went further on there'd be a stretch where it was purple and then black, and then yer'd 'ave tomorrow morning goo off like a bomb, all red and gold again. If yer get lost, then just remember: west is future, east is past, all things linger, all things last. Ooh, and be careful if yer ever in the twenty-fives, because they're flooded."

She appeared to find this a sufficient answer to his query, and they marched on side by side across the springy floorboards without speaking for a while, until he'd thought of something else that he could ask. He sensed it wasn't quite as good a question as his previous one had been but posed it anyway, if only because he was finding that the lapses in their conversation gave him time to think about what had just happened to him, his new status as a dead kid, and that only made him scared.

"How wiz it that our bedroom and downstairs wiz all on the same floor up here appear?"

He'd been right. It had obviously been a stupid question. Phyllis rolled her eyes and tutted, hardly bothering to disguise the weariness and the annoyance in her voice as she replied.

"Well, 'ow d'yer think? If yer'd got plans made for a cellar that was drawn on the same bit of paper as plans for an attic, should yer think as that was queer, that they was on the same sheet, the same level as each other? 'Course yer wouldn't. Use yer flippin' loaf."

Chastised but none the wiser, Michael scuffed along in silence there beside the slightly older, slightly taller girl, running a few steps now and then in order to make up the difference in their strides. A glance into the wooden-edged recess they were then passing on their right revealed a view down to an unfamiliar living room, with different furnishings to number 17 and with its doors and windows round the other way like a reflection in a mirror. Extending through the depths of the enlarged room were more glassy gorgon tentacles with lights inside, but these were different colours – dark reds and warm browns – clearly from a quite separate palette to Michael's own family. Perhaps these were the living quarters of the Mays or possibly the Goodmans, further down the terrace?

He walked on with Phyllis Painter, briefly entertaining the not-utterly-unpleasant notion that if anyone should see them out together for a stroll like this then Phyllis might be taken for his girlfriend. Having never, as a three-year-old, experienced this enviable state, the thought put quite a swagger into Michael's step for a few paces, until he remembered he was clad in slippers, baggy dressing gown and his pyjamas. The pyjamas, now he thought about it, might have a small yellow wee-stain on the fly, although he wasn't going to check and call attention to it. Someone seeing them would be more likely to take Phyllis for his junior nurse than for his girlfriend. Anyway, they were both dead, which made the whole idea of being someone's boyfriend less romantic and attractive.

Up ahead the variegated tumble of walls, ladders, balconies and windows was much nearer and much bigger than when he'd last looked. He could see people moving on the higher fire-escapes and walkways, although he and Phyllis were still too far off from these to make them out in any detail. This was probably just as well, he thought, since some of the parading figures didn't seem entirely normal, being either the wrong size or the wrong shape. It struck him that the place in which he found himself was not like anything he'd been expecting to be waiting for him after his demise. It wasn't like the Heaven that his parents had once sketchily described to him, which was all marble steps and tall white pillars like the adverts Pearl & Dean did at the pictures. Nor was it the Hell that he'd been warned of, not that he had been expecting to be sent to Hell. His mum had told him that he wouldn't go to Hell except for something really bad like murder, which had seemed to him like manageable odds, assuming that he could get through his whole life without killing anybody. Luckily he'd died when he was three, and hadn't had to put this to the test for very long. If he'd lived to be older, he consoled himself, he might have murdered Alma once he had the strength. Then he'd be burning in the special kind of fire his mum had muddily depicted as not ever killing you or melting you away to nothing, even though it was more hot than you could possibly imagine.

He was glad, all things considered, not to be in Hell, although this didn't help with finding out where else this place might be. He thought that enough time might have elapsed since his last hesitant enquiry for him to attempt another one.

"Does this Upstairs have a religature? Has it got Pearl & Deany gates, or toga-gods with chess and peeping-pools like at the pictures?"

Though her eyes did not light up at his renewed interrogation, at least this most recent question didn't seem to make her more annoyed with him.

"All the religatures are right in parts, which means none of 'em are 'cause they all thought as it was only them knew what wiz what. It doesn't matter, anyway, what yer believe when yer daynstairs, although it's best for yer that yer believe in something. Nobody up 'ere's much bothered what it wiz. Nobody's gunner make yer say the password, and nobody's gunner throw yer out because yer didn't join the right gang dayn below. The only thing what really matters wiz if you wiz 'appy."

Michael thought about this as he walked beside her down the row of floor-doors. If the girl was right and all that mattered in life was one's happiness, then he'd done relatively well, having enjoyed three years during which time he'd hardly managed to stop giggling. But what about if people had been happy doing things that were unpleasant, even horrible? There were such people in the world, he knew, and wondered if the same criteria applied to them as well. And what about those who through no fault of their own led lives that were continually miserable? Would that be held against them here, as if they hadn't had a rotten enough time already? Michael didn't think it sounded fair, and was about to chance his arm by asking Phyllis to explain herself when movements on one of the elevated balconies they were approaching caught his eye.

The pair had almost reached the near side of the cavernous arcade, and thus were close enough for Michael to make out the various people strutting back and forth along its levels in more detail. On the platform that had captured his attention, a railed walkway two or three floors up, two grown-up men were standing talking. Both seemed very tall to Michael and he judged them to be quite old, in their thirties or their forties. One of them had whiskers and the other had white hair, though, so he couldn't really tell.

The white-haired and clean-shaven man was dressed in a long nightshirt, and he looked as if he'd just been in a fight. One of his eyes was closed and blackened, and some blood from a split lip had stained his otherwise completely spotless robe. His face was frighteningly angry and he gripped the wooden rail with one hand – in his other hand he held a long staff – as though he'd stepped out onto the balcony in order to calm down, although it didn't look as though his whiskery companion standing next to him was helping much in this attempt. This second person, dressed in a great bush of dark green rags, appeared to be in fits of laughter over the first chap's predicament. With his forked beard and with a mass of chestnut curls beneath his broad-brimmed leather hat, it looked like he was prodding the white-robed man in the ribs and clapping him upon the back, neither of which activities seemed likely to alleviate his black-eyed comrade's filthy mood.

Just then a gust of breeze must have blown down the walkway, with the bearded man's confusion of green pennant rags all fluttering wildly as a consequence. Michael was startled to discover that each flapping scrap was lined upon its underside with silk of brilliant crimson. As the wind disturbed the laughing figure's tatters they flared upwards, rippling in abandon, so that the effect was like a leafy shrub that had spontaneously and suddenly burst into flame. It was a wonder, Michael thought, that the man's leather hat had not blown off as well. Probably it was held in place with cord tied underneath his whiskered chin much like the headgear worn by Spanish priests, which it resembled.

Michael realised that he was in danger of becoming engrossed in this place's details once again, and lowered his gaze from the crow's-nest perches overhead back down to Phyllis Painter. She was by now quite some way in front of him and Michael felt a surge of panic as he ran to catch her up. He knew that if he lost sight of her it would be the way it was in dreams, where he could never find the people that he'd promised he would meet.

He overtook her just as she was coming to the end of the long board-walk, with the last line of the inset vats reaching away on either side of her. A quick peep into one of these revealed another aerial view of a back garden not his own, despite some superficial similarities. Since it was right at one end of the mile-long row, he wondered if it might be the back garden of the corner house, where Andrew's Road ran past the foot of Scarletwell Street. Michael had no time to ponder this idea, since Phyllis Painter was already marching out beyond the endless grid of apertures to where the wooden floorboards ended, somewhat startlingly, in a raised curb made of worn grey brick and then a broad strip of distressed and fractured paving slabs, just like the ones along St. Andrew's Road.

Across these flagstones, facing Michael and the bunny-collared little girl, the lowest level of the monster arcade's bounding wall confronted them, a lengthy terrace made from disparate brick buildings that were clearly not intended to be standing side by side with one another. Two or three of them resembled houses from his street but changed, as if they'd been remembered incorrectly, so that one had got its front door halfway up the wall on the first floor, with almost twenty stone steps rising to it rather than the normal three. Another had the nettle-fringed earth entrance of a rabbit hole where the brick hollow of the boot-scrape should have been, at pavement level down to one side of the doorsteps. In amongst these hauntingly familiar yet distorted house-fronts there were other almost-recognisable constructions, though the places they reminded Michael of did not belong in Andrew's Road. One of them bore a strong resemblance to the school caretaker's house up at the top end of Spring Lane, with black iron railings fencing off a downstairs window that was set perhaps a foot back from the street. Beside this was a section of the school wall which enclosed the always-locked arched entranceway that led into the juniors' playground.

Set between this odd assortment of locations, which at least were all from the same neighbourhood, was one half-glass door with a display window next to it that Michael thought more properly belonged in the town centre. More precisely, it belonged in the real-life Emporium Arcade, that dim-lit incline rising from the fancy scrolling ironwork of its gateway on the Market Square. The shop that he was looking at, nestled incongruously amongst the displaced houses, was an almost perfect duplicate of Chasterlaine's Joke, Novelty & Toy Shop, halfway up the right side of the arcade's slope as you ascended. The wide window with the shop's name in antique gold lettering above it, as he saw it now, was bigger than it should be and the words upon the sign seemed to be wriggling into different orders as he watched, but it was definitely Chaster-laine's, or at least an approximation of the place. "Realist chanes" was what the shop appeared to be called at the moment, though when he looked back it seemed to read "Hail's ancester". How long had he been able to read, anyway? Regardless, Michael was so taken by surprise at this familiar store in such an unfamiliar setting that he thought he'd ask the girl about it as they walked the last few yards of floorboards to the boundary of the massive passageway.

"Are we in the Euphorium Arcade, like on the market? That place there looks like the Choke & Joy Shop."

Phyllis squinted in the vague direction that one baggy sleeve of Michael's dressing gown was pointing.

"What, yer mean The Snail Races?"

Michael looked back at the shop in question and discovered that "The Snail Races" was indeed the name that the establishment was trading under at that instant. He and Phyllis were mounting the curb that edged the wooden Attics of the Breath, as she'd referred to the huge hall, so that Michael was close enough to see the merchandise on show within the 40-watt-bulb-lighting of the window. What he'd taken to be Matchbox cars all standing on a podium of the red-and-yellow cardboard boxes that they came in, such as would have been displayed at the real Chasterlaine's, were in fact life-sized painted repli-cas of snails. Each stood upon its little individual box, the way that the toy cars and lorries would have done, but now the packaging had got a picture label showing the specific model snail resting on top of it. The reproduction mol-luscs all had shells that had been customised or painted in the style of actual Matchbox cars that he had seen, so that one was in navy blue with "Pickford's" in white lettering across it, while another had the snail itself in pillar-box red with a tiny curled-up fireman's hose set on its back where normally the spiral shell would be. Looking back up at the sign above the window, Michael saw that it still read as "The Snail Races", so perhaps he had been wrong about the letters changing. Probably that's what the sign had said the whole time he'd been scrutinising it. Still, all this made no difference to his basic point, which had been that the place resembled Chasterlaine's Aladdin's cave of novelties, up the Emporium Arcade. Michael turned back to Phyllis Painter – they were walking over the broad ribbon of cracked pavement now – and stubbornly restated his assertion.

"Yes, The Snail Races. It looks like the shy-top in the arcade on the market. Wiz that where we are?"

Venting a heavy sigh that sounded put-upon and obligated, Phyllis halted in her tracks and gave him what her tone of voice made clear would be her final explanation.

"No. Yer know it's not. The arcade what you mean, that's Daynstairs. Lovely as it wiz, it's a flat plan compared with this one."

Phyllis gestured to the plane of floor-bound windows stretching off behind them and the high glass ceiling overhead where origami clouds unfolded mystifyingly against a field of perfect iridescent blue.

"In fact, the 'ole of Daynstairs wiz a flat plan of what's Upstairs. Now, this arcade what we've got up 'ere, over the Attics of the Breath, that's made from the same stuff as these Old Buildings what we're coming to."

She swung her stick-thin arm around so that her trophy-necklace swished repulsively and indicated the long, muddled terrace facing them across the fissured paving slabs.

"All this wiz made from people's dreams what 'ave built up. All of the people what lived hereabouts Daynstairs, or all them what passed through, all 'avin' dreams abayt the same streets, the same buildings. And all of 'um dream the places a bit different, and each dream they 'ave, it leaves a kind of residue up 'ere, a kind of scum what forms a dream-crust, all made out of 'ouses, shops and avenues what people 'ave remembered wrong. It's like when all the dead shrimps build up into coral reefs and that. If yer see someone up 'ere who looks hypnotised, walkin' abayt in just their underpants or night-things, it's a safe bet that it's someone who's asleep and dreamin'.'"

Here she paused and looked down thoughtfully at Michael, standing there in his pyjamas, dressing gown and slippers.

"Although I could say the same thing about you, but I just saw yer choke to death."

Oh. That. He'd almost put that whole unpleasant business from his mind, and frankly wished that Phyllis wasn't quite so blunt about the fact that he was recently deceased. It was a bit depressing, and the fact of it still frightened him. Ignoring his distressed wince, Phyllis Painter carried on her morbid monologue.

"I mean, if yer wiz dead, then I'd 'ave thought yer'd 'ave been in yer favourite clothes what yer remembered. Unless yer pyjamas wiz yer favourite clothes, yer lazy little bugger."

He was shocked. Not by her implication that he was bone idle – indeed, his pyjamas were his favourite clothes – but by the fact that she had sworn in Heaven, where he'd not have thought that this would be allowed. Phyllis continued, blithely unconcerned.

"But then, if yer wiz dead, why wiz nobody there to pull yer up and dust yer dayn except for me? No, yer a funny little fourpenny funeral, you are. There's summat about yer what's not right. Come on. We better get yer to the Works and let the builders 'ave a look at yer. Keep up and don't get lorst in all the dreamery-scenery."

Lorst. The same way Michael's mum pronounced the letter 'o' in lost or frost or cost or any word remotely similar. "Don't get lorst." "We've 'ad some frorst." "'Ow much is all that gunner corst?" Not only was his escort definitely from the Boroughs, she was almost certainly from down the bottom end of it, near Andrew's Road. He'd never heard of any Painters round where he lived, unless Phyllis had lived long before his time, of course. Michael was not allowed a breather to consider this, however. True to her word, Phyllis Painter was already skipping off across the moss-seamed paving stones without a backward glance to see if he was following. He shuffled dutifully in her wake, not able to run properly without the danger of his slippers coming off.

As he slapped awkwardly across the slabs he saw that there were openings let into the terrace on the far side of the bounding pavement, passages that he presumed led deeper into the heaped-up confusion of dream architecture. His companion, with her hydra-headed rabbit stole flailing about her, was about to disappear into one such dark chink, an alleyway that ran off from the house-fronts right between the place with its front door positioned halfway up its wall and the façade of the refigured Joke Shop. Picking up his pace Michael trailed after her, her pink-and-navy banner fluttering ahead, leading him on.

The alley, when he reached it, was exactly like the narrow jitty that ran from Spring Lane to Scarletwell Street, all along the back of Michael's house-row. It was cobbled just the same and edged with weeds, and he could even see the grey roof of the stable with its missing slates in next door's yard, the place that Doug McGeary kept his lorry, but viewed from the back. The major difference was that on his right, where there should be the wire fence and hedgerow at the bottom of Spring Lane School's playing fields, there was now a whole row of houses with their latch-gates and their back-yard walls with the rear windows of the red brick dwellings looming up beyond. "Scarletwell Terrace" came into his mind, but was as quickly gone again. Already Phyllis Painter was some distance down the transformed alleyway and showed no sign of slackening her pace or caring much if he got left behind. He padded after her over the cobbles of the shadowed crevice that in real life or in dreams had always made him apprehensive.

On each side a corridor of back walls hemmed him in, the ones on Michael's right completely unfamiliar to him and even the ones upon his left much altered from their counterparts along the rear of Andrew's Road. He ventured a glance upward at the sky above the alley and discovered that this was no longer the unearthly picture-postcard blue that he'd admired through the glass roof of the arcade, nor were there clouds of rarefied geometry uncrinkling as they slid across it. This, instead, was a grey slice of Boroughs firmament that made the spirits sink, fulfilling as it did the usual pessimistic forecast. Michael was alarmed at just how suddenly this colour-change had altered the whole mood of his experience. Instead of being someone on a dazzling adventure, he felt orphaned and bereft, felt pitiful and lonely like a lost child out in his pyjamas past his bed time, trudging down a miserable back entry and expecting drizzle. Except he was worse than lost. He was already dead.

Anxiously, Michael cast his eyes back down from the bleak heavens visible between the rainspouts and the chimneypots and found that, to his horror, he'd been dawdling. The little girl was now much further off from him along the alley than she'd been before, shrunken by distance to the size she was when he'd thought of her as a corner-fairy, which now seemed like hours ago. He reassured himself that if he just ran faster and could manage not to take his eyes off her again, then he'd inevitably catch up with her.

Running with his gaze fixed straight ahead, however, meant that Michael wasn't looking properly where he was going. He caught the plaid toe of his slipper in a sudden hole from which a cobblestone had been prised loose and pitched abruptly forwards on his hands and knees. Although the rounded stones felt hard and solid through the thin material of his pyjamas, Michael was agreeably surprised to find that his fall hadn't really hurt him. It had scared him and upset him slightly, but he felt no pain, nor were there any injuries that he could see. One knee of his striped trousers had got rather wet and dirty, but the fabric wasn't torn and, all in all, he thought he'd got off lightly.

Phyllis Painter, though, was gone.

Even before he'd lifted up his eyes to find the alley empty save for him he'd known she wouldn't be there with the certain fatalism that he'd felt before in nightmares, in those dreams where the one thing you're most afraid of is the one thing that you know is guaranteed to happen.

All around him was the sooty, weathered brickwork of the jitty, with on Michael's right what seemed to be the rear wall of a factory or warehouse interrupting the long run of washing-line-festooned back yards. Was this "the Works" the girl had mentioned as their destination? A black wire mesh could just about be seen through the thick dust of this establishment's high, isolated windows, and a rusting pulley-wheel stuck out beside the gated wooden platform of what Michael thought must be a loading-bay. The empty alley stretched before him, a much greater distance than he could recall its mortal counterpart extending, and he didn't think that Phyllis Painter would have reached the far end of it before he'd looked up, even allowing for his clumsy tumble. It seemed much more likely to him that she'd turned off from the dismal passageway into a door or gate that opened in the factory's rear on his right side.

Keeping this hopeful notion in his mind he stole a little further down the alley's pathway, like a cobbled streambed in the overcast grey light, until he was around the point he thought the girl had been when he'd last sighted her.

Between the blunt stones of the alley floor sage-coloured grass poked up and there were the same minute scraps of refuse that he would have ordinarily expected to be there: an untipped cigarette end, a beer-bottle cap that had been dented in its middle by a bottle-opener, some chips of broken glass. The bottle-top had "Mask-Mask" printed on it where there should have been the brewery's name, and the glass fragments seemed on close inspection to be shards from broken soap-bubbles, but Michael doggedly refused to pay these things attention. He trod slowly onward, looking for an opening in the wall, a door or gap that Phyllis might have vanished into, and at last he found one.

Set into the rear face of the factory or warehouse was a covered stairway, made of old and foot-worn stone that ran up from behind a barred iron gate that stood ajar, half open on the otherwise deserted alleyway. The odd arrangement seemed familiar, and reminded Michael of a gated flight of steps that he'd once seen in Marefair, opposite St. Peter's Church. He'd asked his mum about it and she'd recollected with a shudder how, during her girlhood, Doreen and her best friend Kelly May had climbed the old stone staircase for a dare, only to find a tower-room that was empty save for dead leaves and "a gret big nest of earwigs". Michael wasn't fond of earwigs, since his sister had once told him how they got in people's ears and ate straight through their brains until they reached the warm pink daylight filtering through the other eardrum. Alma had provided helpful sound effects to illustrate what he would hear during the week or so it took for the determined bug to tunnel through his tousled infant head: "Munch, munch ... creep, creep, creep ... munch, munch, munch ... creep, creep, creep."

On the other hand this daunting stairway seemed like his best chance of catching Phyllis Painter, who, although he didn't really like her much, was the one person in this run-down paradise that Michael knew the name of. If he couldn't find her, he'd be lost *and* dead. With this in mind he summoned all his pluck and pulled the iron gate a little further open so that he could slip inside. The bar he wrapped his fingers round was gritty and abrasive to the touch and had a kind of mild sting to its texture. Opening his hand he found that it had left a toilet-smear of rust across his palm. It smelled of stewed tea.

Sucking in his tummy so as not to get the rust and muck on his pyjamas he slid through the gap that he had made between the gate and its brick frame. Once Michael was inside he pulled the railed gate shut behind him without really knowing why. Perhaps it was to cover up the fact he'd broken in and he was trespassing, or possibly it just made him feel safer knowing nothing could creep up the stairs behind him without Michael hearing the gate grating open down below. He turned and peered uncertainly into the darkness that began just six steps up. In normal circumstances he supposed his breathing would be tremulous and shallow, his heart hammering, but Michael realised belatedly that his heart wasn't doing anything at all and he was only drawing breath when he remembered to, more out of habit than necessity. At least he didn't have a sore throat anymore, he told himself consolingly as he began to mount the stairs. That had been really getting on his nerves.

He had been climbing in the dark for a few minutes when it struck him that this foray up the staircase had been a disastrously bad idea. His slipper-shod feet crunched, with every rising step, through a detritus that felt like dead, brittle leaves but could as well have been black drifts of earwig-husks. To make things worse, the stairs that he'd expected to be straight turned out to be a winding spiral, forcing Michael to proceed more slowly in the blackness, with his left hand resting on the turret wall and following its contour as he stumbled upwards, resting lightly, in case there were slugs or other crawling things he didn't want to accidentally stick his fingers in.

Hoping he'd soon get to the top, Michael continued his ascent beyond the point where the idea of turning round and going back became unbearable. Five minutes more of crunching upwards through the darkness, though, convinced him that there wasn't any top, that he had seen the last of Phyllis Painter and that this was how he was condemned to spend Eternity, alone and climbing through an endless blackout with the possibility of earwigs. Munch, munch. Creep, creep, creep. What had he done, in his three years, to merit punishment like this? Was it when him and Alma killed those ants? Did an ant-murder count against you when it came to the hereafter? Worried now, he carried on his halting progress upward, having no idea what else to do. His only other plan was to start crying, but he thought he'd save that until later on, when things got desperate.

As it turned out, this was roughly nine steps later. Michael missed his mum, his gran, his dad. He even missed his sister. He missed 17, St. Andrew's Road. He missed his life. He was just trying to decide which step he should sit weeping on until the end of time when Michael noticed that the pitch black up ahead of him appeared to have a greyish quality about it. This might be, he thought, because his eyes were gradually adjusting to the dark, or it might mean that there was light a little further on. Encouraged, he renewed his clamber up through pearly gloom where there had previously been only opaque black. To his delight he could soon even see the spiral stairway he was climbing, and was much relieved to find that the crisp forms he had been crunching through were neither leaves nor earwigs. They were the wax paper wrappers that you got on individual cough-sweets, hundreds of them, littering the steps. Each one had the word 'Tunes' in tiny, cherry-coloured writing, this repeated several times on every crumpled scrap.

Turning a final bend he saw a door-shaped opening through which weak morning light was falling, only a few steps above. With the medicinal pink blossoms of the cough-sweet wrappers fluttering up around his heels he broke into a run up these last stairs, eager to be on level flooring and able once more to see where he was going.

It was a long interior corridor, painted pale green to halfway up its high walls and with stained and varnished boards forming its floor. It was the sort of passageway that Michael thought belonged inside a school or hospital, only much loftier, so that even an adult would feel child-sized by comparison. Along each of its sides the hall had windows which were letting in the washed-out daylight, though these were positioned too far up for Michael to see out through. Those upon his right, if he looked up through them, revealed only the same drab, leaden sky that he had seen outside over the alleyway. The row of windows on his left, alternatively, seemed to look in on some sort of ward or classroom. Somewhere indoors, anyway, of which Michael could only glimpse the beams and boards that formed its pointed ceiling. The hallway was empty save for two or three big metal radiators, painted in the same dark green you saw upon electric junction boxes, spaced out down the length of the hushed corridor. There was the smoky, biting scent of rubber and the smell of powder paint, like toxic flour. Whatever this place was, it didn't seem to be the factory or warehouse he'd presumed it to be when he was outside, although after the twists and turns of the unlighted stairway Michael wasn't even certain that he was in the same building anymore. The only thing he knew for sure was that there wasn't any sign of Phyllis Painter.

Probably the best thing that he could have done would have been to descend the lampless steps back to the alleyway, to see if he could find her there, but Michael found he couldn't face the prospect of another hoodwinked fumble through the darkness, and especially not one that entailed going downstairs this time, with a greater risk of tripping up and falling. There was nothing for it except to continue onwards, down the silent and puncture-repair-kit-perfumed corridor to its far end.

Along the way he thought of whistling to keep his spirits up, but realised that he hadn't yet learned any tunes. Besides, he couldn't whistle. As another way of interrupting the oppressive quiet he trailed his fingernails across the chunky upright bars of the huge radiators when he passed them. Icy to the touch, they indicated that the heating system they were part of had been turned off for the summer. Furthermore, to his surprise, Michael discovered that each hollow shaft of metal had been tuned by some means to produce an individual note. Each radiator was equipped with seven bars, and when he let his fingers wipe across the first such row of pipes it played the opening part of "Twinkle, Twinkle, Little Star", one of the only melodies familiar in his thus-far limited experience of music. Both intrigued and charmed by this he hurried on to the next radiator, further down the hall, which turned out to be tuned so that it played the "How I wonder what you are" part when he brushed it.

By the time he'd got to "Up above the world so high" Michael was at the passageway's far end where, having reached a corner, it turned sharply to the left. As cautious and as stealthy as an Indian scout he peered around this bend and saw only another stretch of empty landing without anything to differentiate it from the first. It had the same wood floorboards and the same walls, pale green at the bottom, chalky white above. The row of high-set windows on his right looked up onto a dreary fleece of sky while those upon his left looked up into the rafters of the ward or schoolroom that he wasn't tall enough to see into. On the plus side, however, there were three more radiators, and this length of corridor appeared to end not with another corner but with a white wooden door, closed shut but hopefully not locked.

The first of the three radiators that he came upon played "Like a diamond in the sky" when Michael drew his taut and stiffened fingertips across it, as if he were strumming an industrial harp. The next two, as he had by then anticipated, clanged out the last couplet that completed the refrain by echoing its opening lines, with the concluding "How I wonder what you are" only a dozen paces from the closed door in which the long passage terminated. Nervously, he tiptoed over to it then reached up his hand to turn the plain brass knob and find out what existed on the far side. How he wondered what it was.

It wasn't locked. That much at least was in his favour, but he still reeled back from all the unexpected brightness and fresh air that rushed in through the open door to overwhelm him. Blinking, he stepped out into a faint refreshing breeze and found that he was on a balcony, its black wood railing running left to right in front of him, coloured as if with a protective coat of pitch. Walking across to this and gazing out between its rails, Michael was looking down on a vast hall, its many-levelled far wall a full mile away. The hall's floor was divided up into a sprawling grid of sunken apertures that looked like windows that had been erroneously installed in the wrong surface. Up above this plain of holes, out through the glass tiled roof of a Victorian arcade, faceted clouds unfolded languidly into impossibility against the background of an unsurpassable azure. He was back in the Attics of the Breath, or at least on the balustrade-edged walkways overlooking them. Could that be right? He didn't think he'd made enough turns to have come almost full circle, but then that long spiral staircase had confused him so he didn't know in which direction he was heading.

Looking to his left along the elevated walkway he could see a distant figure who was striding resolutely off across the boards away from him. He hoped for a brief instant it was Phyllis Painter, but no more than that. For one thing, the retreating person was much taller than the little girl had been. Also, despite the longish hair and long white frock that they were wearing, they were clearly male. The man stalking away along the balcony was powerfully-built and barefoot, and held one hand to his face as though he nursed some injury. In his other hand he held a slender rod or staff that thudded on the planks at every step. With a slight start, Michael recalled the angry-looking man with the split lip and the black eye who he'd glimpsed from the floor below when he was crossing it with Phyllis. This was the same person, surely? Him, or someone very like him.

Michael then remembered that there had been someone else standing in conversation with the white-robed brawler, someone who had whiskers and a coat of green rags with a bright red lining. From the prickling of his neck he knew that this was who would be behind him when he turned around, even before the cracked brown leather voice spoke from just over Michael's tartan shoulder.

"Well, now. It's a ghostly little fidget-midget."

Michael shuffled round reluctantly, with his plaid slippers moving like the hands of a disoriented clock.

The ruddy and bewhiskered giant, who clearly had a good foot-and-a-half on even Michael's strapping dad, was leaning with one elbow on the pitch-stained railing, smoking a clay pipe. His broad-brimmed priest's hat threw a band of blackness over deep-set crinkly eyes that Michael noticed with a grow-ing feeling of uneasiness were two entirely different colours, one like inlaid ruby and the other a reptilian green. They glinted like impossibly old Christ-mas baubles from the shadows of a heavy, straggling brow, above a hooked nose with a bend that turned almost straight downwards, like an eagle's beak. The man's skin, on his lower face and his bare arms where they protruded from his coat of rags, was sunburned and smeared here and there with blotches of what looked like tar or motor oil. He smelled of coal and steam and boiler-rooms, and underneath his flapping rags were dark green britches and stitched boots of well-tanned leather. Though his mouth could not be seen amongst the brassy tangles of his beard and his moustache, you could tell he was grinning from the way his cheeks bunched into shiny balls of sun-scorched flesh and broken veins. He puffed on his clay pipe, which Michael saw now had the fea-tures of a screaming man carved on its bowl, and let a wisp of violet smoke twist upward from the balcony before he spoke again.

"You look lost, little boy. Oh dear, oh dear. We can't have that, now, can we?"

The man's voice was worryingly deep and creaked like some great pre-historic monster opening its wings. Michael decided that he'd better act as if this were a normal conversation with somebody who was offering directions.

Noticing that on his right were more of the high windows that he'd seen when in the corridor, he feigned an interest in them with a voice that was embarrassingly high and piping after the man's grown-up growl.

"That's right. I'm lost. Can you see in those windows for me so that I'll know where I am?"

The bearded fellow frowned in puzzlement, then did as he'd been asked and glanced in through the windows that looked out onto the balcony. Having thus satisfied himself, he once more turned to study Michael.

"Looks like it's the needlework-room that's upstairs at Spring Lane School, only a fair bit bigger. I hang out round here because I'm very fond of handicraft. It's one of my great specialities. I'm also rather good at sums."

He cocked his curly, bushy head upon one side so that his hat-brim tipped down at a slant and sucked once more upon his pipe, a grey fog brimming from his fleshy lips as he opened his mouth to speak.

"But you don't quite add up to anything that I'm familiar with. Come, little chap. Tell me your name."

Michael was not completely certain he should trust this stranger with his name, but couldn't think of a convincing alias in time. Besides, if he was found out in a lie he might get into trouble.

"My fame's Michael Warren."

The tall man took a step back with his mismatched eyes widening in what seemed to be honest surprise. The trailing triangles of cloth that formed his coat suddenly fluttered upward to reveal the red silk lining of their undersides so that he looked as though he had been briefly set on fire, although Michael had felt no gust of wind. With an increasing sense that all of this was going badly wrong, he understood that it had not been breeze that moved the old man's coat, but more an action like a peacock ruffling its feathers in display. Except that this would mean the two-toned scraps of cloth were part of him.

"*You're* Michael Warren? You're the one to blame for all this trouble?"

What? Michael was stunned, both that his name was known up here and that already he had been accused of something which, from how it sounded, was quite serious. Briefly, he thought of trying to run away before the man could grab him and subject him to some punishment for his unknown transgression, but the big bloke just threw back his head and started laughing heartily, which rather took the wind from Michael's sails. If he'd caused trouble like the tattered man had said, how was that funny?

Breaking off his gale of laughter for a moment, he gazed down at Michael with what looked like dangerous amusement flashing in his jade and garnet eyes.

"Wait 'til I tell the lads. They'll be in fits. Oh, this is good. This is extremely good."

He once again began to roar with mirth, but this time, when he tipped his head back in a guttural and hearty guffaw his broad leather hat slipped off to hang down on his shoulders by the cord that he had knotted underneath his chin.

The man had horns. Brown-white like dirty ivory they poked up from the curls and ringlets of his hairline, thick, stubby protuberances only a few inches long. This was the time, Michael decided, to start crying. He looked up at the horned apparition with tears welling in his eyes, and when he spoke it was with an accusing snivel, sounding wounded by the mean trick that the man had played upon him.

"You're the devil."

This seemed to choke off the coarse, uproarious laughter. The man looked at Michael with his eyebrows raised in almost comical bemusement, as if he was dreadfully surprised that Michael should have ever thought that he was anybody else.

"Well … yes. Yes, I suppose I am."

He crouched down on his haunches until his unnerving gaze was level with that of the little boy, who stood there rooted to the spot with fear. The horned man leaned his head a little closer in to Michael with a lazy smile and narrowed his jewelled eyes inquisitively.

"Why? Where did you think you were?"

AN ASMODEUS FLIGHT

The devil couldn't call to mind the last time he'd enjoyed himself as much as this. This was a great laugh in the greatest sense of the word great: great like a war, a white shark or the Wall of China. Oh, my sweethearts in damnation, this was priceless.

There he'd been, just leaning on somebody's old dream of a balcony and puffing on his favourite pipe. This was the one he'd whittled from the spicy, madness-seasoned spirit of an eighteenth-century French diabolist. He fancied that it made his best tobacco taste of Paris, sexual intercourse and murder, somewhere between meat and liquorice.

Anyway, there he'd been, loafing around above the Attics of the Breath, close to the crux of Angle-land, when up had come this builder, *Master* Builder mind you, with a split lip and a shiner like he'd just been in a fight. I mean, the devil thought, how often do you get an opportunity to take the piss on such a sewer-draining scale as that?

"My dear boy! Have we walked into a pearly gate?" Not too bad for an opening remark, all things considered, dripping as it was with obviously false concern, as if enquiring on the health of an obnoxious nephew you transparently despised. The thing with builders, *Master* Builders in this instance, was that while they were quite capable of levelling a city or a dynasty, they hated being patronised.

The Master Builder – the white-haired one who'd made something of a name for himself playing billiards; held his cue in one hand at that very moment, for that matter – stopped and turned to see who was addressing him. Scowled like a fondled choirboy when he found out, naturally; that thing the builders did to make their eyes flash a split second before they incinerated you. My word, he *was* in a bad mood, was Mighty Whitey.

To be honest, this made a refreshing change from the unasked-for pity and the bottomless forgiveness that was usually in their gaze. Builders would order you at snooker cue-point to inhabit depths that were unspeakable, lower than those endured by syphilitic tyrants, and then add insult to injury by forgiving you. It was a treat to come across one in the throes of a demeaning temper tantrum. The rich possibilities for some inflammatory satire made the devil's ball-sack creep.

The builder, sorry, *Master* Builder, sounded entertainingly slow-witted, with his speech slurred by the swollen lip as he replied.

"Murck naught mye shamfall strate, thyou dungcurst thorng ..."

It was the same profound, exploded rubbish all the builders talked, the strangely resonant and blazing words reverberating off to whisper in the extra set of corners that there were up here. Delightfully, however, even phrases of world-ending awesome fury, spoken through a split lip, were quite funny.

Unaware that everything he said sounded hilariously punch-drunk, the indignant Master Builder had gone on to justify his woebegone condition by explaining that he'd just been in a fight with one of his best mates over a game of snooker. It seemed that this chum had wilfully endangered a specific ball that everyone had known the white-haired Master Builder had his sights on. Technically this was permitted, but was thought of as appalling form. As was invariably the case this ball had got a human name attached to it, but it was somebody the devil hadn't heard of. Not at that point, anyway.

It turned out that the builders had got into an unseemly row across the billiard table, and that the white-haired one had eventually called his colleague something dreadful and suggested that they step outside to settle it. They'd left the shot unplayed, gone out and had their brawl, and were now skulking back towards the game-hall to continue with their uncompleted competition. Talk about showing yourself up. All the scrounging Boroughs ghosts had stood round in a ring shouting encouragements, like boot-faced school-kids at a playground punch-up. "Goo on! Give 'im one right up the 'alo!" Talk about ruffling your feathers. It was all so wonderfully wretched that the devil had to laugh.

"It's not your fault, old boy. It's just competitive sports, in a neighbourhood like this. Brings out the hooligan in everybody. I've seen people have their throats cut over games of hopscotch. What you ought to do is drop the snooker and go back to organising dances on the heads of pins. Not half so violent, and you'd have a good excuse for wearing ball gowns all the time."

The devil nudged the builder in the ribs good-naturedly, then laughed and clapped him on his back. The one thing that they hated more than being patronised was people being over-intimate, especially if that went as far as someone touching them. All of those pictures that depicted builders holding hands with wounded grenadiers or sickly tots, in the opinion of the devil, were just mock-ups for the purpose of publicity.

Slow as the builders generally were in understanding jokes, the white-haired chap had finally caught on to the fact that he was being made fun of, which they hated almost as much as they hated being condescended to or touched. He'd spouted some blood-curdling holy gibberish which more or less boiled down to "Leave it out, Tosh, or I'll 'ave yer", but with extra nuances involving being bound in chests of brass and thrown into the lowest depths of a volcano for a thousand years. Whips, scorpions, rivers of fire, the usual rigmarole. The devil raised his thorny eyebrows in a look of hurt surprise.

"Oh dear, I've made you cross again. I should have known this was your ladies' special time, but I barged in making insensitive remarks. And right when you were no doubt trying to calm down in order to take this important shot. I should be inconsolable if just as you were lining up your cue you thought of me and ripped the baize or broke your stick in half. Or anything."

The Master Builder reared up with a sudden sunburst of St. Elmo's Fire around his snowy head and bellowed something multi-faceted and biblical, essentially refuting that this was his ladies' special time. The second part of what the devil had just said then seemed to sink in, about ruining his game by being in the throes of rage. He checked himself and took a deep breath, then exhaled. There followed a celestial burst of nonsense-poetry where a gruff, unadorned apology would have sufficed. The devil thought about a further goading, but decided not to push his famous luck.

"Think nothing of it, old sport. It was my fault, always taking jokes too far and spoiling things for everybody else. You know, I worry privately that deep inside I'm not a terribly nice person. Why am I aggressive all the while, even when I'm pretending to be jovial? Why do I have all these unpleasant defects in my personality? Sometimes I convince myself it's work-related, as if having been condemned to the unending torments of the sensory inferno was an adequate excuse for my regrettable behaviour. Good luck with the snooker tournament. I've every confidence in you. I'm sure that you can put this unimportant fit of murderous rage behind you, and that you won't irrevocably mess up somebody's only mortal life by having acted like a petulant buffoon."

The fellow seemed uncertain how to take this, narrowing his sole functioning eye suspiciously. Eventually he gave up trying to work out who, precisely, was at fault here and just grimaced as though indicating that their conversation had been satisfactorily concluded. With a curt nod to the devil, who had gallantly tilted his leather hat-brim in reply, the Master Builder carried on along the walkway, lifting up one hand occasionally to tenderly explore the purple flesh around his pummelled brow.

You could tell from the stiff way that he held himself as he was flouncing off that the white-robed chap was still fuming. Anger, as with handicrafts and mathematics, was amongst the devil's fields of expertise. All three things were exquisitely involved and intricate, which sat well with the devil's admiration for complexity. He could have hours of fun with any of them. Oh, and idle hands. He liked those too. And good intentions.

He'd relit his pipe, striking a spark off of a thumbnail like a beetle carapace, and watched the builder as he stalked off grumpily towards the vanishing point of the lengthy balcony. Poor loves. Walking around all day looking Romantic, feeling like the very spinning clockwork of the fourfold Universe with everybody singing songs about them. All those Christmas cards they were expected to live up to and the work that it must be to keep those robes clean all the time. How did they cope, the precious poppets?

He'd been leaning on the pitch-stained balustrade and wondering what he should do next to amuse himself when suddenly, as if in answer to his seldom-answered prayers, a door creaked open in the long wall of accumulated dreams that was behind him and a little boy clad in pyjamas, dressing gown and slippers padded hesitantly out onto the bare boards of the balcony. He was adorable, and secretly the devil had a weakness for small children. They were scared of absolutely everything.

With blonde curls and with eyes song-lyric blue, the little sleepwalker had not at first appeared to realise that he was in the presence of the devil, with the door that he'd emerged from being some yards off from where the fiend was standing. Looking apprehensive and with eyebrows lifted in perpetual startlement, the youngster slippered over to the blackened railings of the walkway and gazed out between them at the stretching Attics of the Breath. He'd kept this up for a few moments, looking puzzled and disoriented, then had turned his head and glanced off down the landing to where you could just make out the battered builder vanishing into the distance, dabbing at his eye.

The kid still hadn't noticed that the devil was behind him, but then people never did. The devil wondered if the boy were dead or merely sleeping, dressed up in his night-clothes as he was. Conceivably, it might not even be a human child at all. It could have been a figment wandered off from someone else's dream or possibly a character out of a bedtime storybook, a fiction given substance here by the built-up imaginings accreted over many readings, many readers.

In the devil's judgement, though, this lad seemed to be real. Dreams and the characters from stories had a tidy quality to their construction, as if they'd been simplified, whereas this present nipper had a poorly-thought-through messiness about his personality that smacked of authenticity. You could tell from the way he stood there, rooted to the spot and gazing after the retreating builder, that he didn't have the first clue where he was or what he should do next. People in dreams or stories, to the contrary, were always full of purpose. So, this little man was definitely mortal, although whether he was dead or dreaming was a matter harder to determine. The pyjamas indicated that he was a dreamer, but of course small children generally died in hospital or in their sickbeds, so infant mortality was still a possibility. The devil thought he'd enquire further.

"Well, now. It's a ghostly little fidget-midget."

There. That hadn't been an over-terrifying opening remark in his opinion. While he might from time to time enjoy a bit of fun with helpless humans, even to the point of driving them insane or killing them, that didn't mean that he was undiscriminating. Children, as he'd noted, were already frightened as a natural consequence of being children. Burst a crisp-bag and they'd jump. Where was the sport or the finesse in that?

The small boy turned around to face him, wearing a ridiculous expression on his elfin face, eyes goggling and his mouth stretched at both sides into a rubber letterbox. It looked like he was trying to conceal his real expression, which was probably pure dread, in order not to give offence. His mum had more than likely taught him it was rude to scream at the deformed or monstrous. Quite frankly, the child's blend of paralysing fear and genuine concern for other people's feelings struck the devil as being both comical and rather sweet. He thought he'd try another pleasant conversational remark, now that he had the lad's attention, so to speak.

"You look lost, little boy. Oh dear, oh dear. We can't have that, now, can we?"

Even though the devil's tone was clearly that of an avuncular child-murderer, the tousled moppet seemed to take it at face value, visibly relaxing and assuming he was out of danger at the first sound of a sympathetic voice. This trusting little dickens was a find, and no mistake. The devil wondered how he'd lasted for five minutes in the unforgiving mechanisms of the living world, and then reflected that most probably he hadn't. Actually, the longer that he spent in the tyke's company, the likelier it seemed that this was someone dead rather than someone dreaming, someone who'd been lured into a stranger's car or an abandoned fridge dumped on an out-of-earshot wasteland.

Watching the boy's features you could almost see what he was thinking, almost see the cogs turn in his as-yet undeveloped mind. He looked as though he thought that he was trespassing, but that if he kept up an act the devil wouldn't realise this was the case. He looked like he was trying to come up with an excuse for being here, but, being young, had not yet had a great deal of experience in telling lies. As a result of trying to construct an alibi, when he eventually piped up he sounded tremulously guilty, even though his flimsy story was most probably the truth.

"That's right. I'm lost. Can you see in that window for me so that I'll know where I am?"

The boy was nodding to the glinting memories of windows set into the dream-wall he'd emerged out of. He clearly couldn't care less what was on the other side but, once told, would pretend to have his bearings and then thank the devil nicely before running off as fast as his short legs would carry him, getting as far away as he could manage, the direction unimportant. He was obviously frightened but was trying not to show he was afraid, as if the devil were no more than an uncomfortably big dog.

Frowning in mild bemusement, the arch-enemy of mankind shot a casual glance through the glass panes the child had indicated. Nothing of much interest lay beyond, just an exaggerated phantom of a local schoolroom plucked from someone's night-thoughts. It was a location that the devil knew, that much went without saying: there were no locations that the devil didn't know. The world of space and history was big, no doubt about it, but then so was *War & Peace*, yet both were finite. Given enough time – or, if you liked, given no time at all – then you could easily attain a detailed grasp of either of them. There was no great trick about omniscience, the devil thought. Just read the story through enough times at your near-infinite leisure and you'll be an expert. He looked back towards the apprehensive toddler.

"Looks like it's the needlework-room that's upstairs at Spring Lane School, only a fair bit bigger. I hang out round here because I'm very fond of handicraft. It's one of my great specialities. I'm also rather good at sums."

This was all true, of course. One of the ways in which people continually misunderstood the devil, woundingly so in his own opinion, was that they thought he was always telling lies. In fact, though, nothing could be further from the case. He couldn't tell a lie if he was paid to, not that anybody ever paid him to do anything. Besides, the truth was a far subtler tool. Just tell people the truth and then let them mislead themselves, that was his motto.

What the truth was with regard to this small boy, however, wasn't really clear. Assuming that the child was dead and not just dreaming, he did not appear to have been dead for long. He looked like someone who had only just that moment found themselves here in the Second Borough, in Mansoul, somebody who had yet to get their bearings. If that was the case, what was he doing scuttling round here in the dream-sediments? Why hadn't he just automatically dived back into his short life at the point of birth, for one more go-round on his little individual carousel? Or if, after a million turns on the same ride, he felt he'd finally absorbed all that it had to offer and elected to instead come up to the unfolded town, why was he unaccompanied? Where were the beery crowds of celebrating ancestors? Even if there were some unprecedented circumstance in play here, you'd still think that management would have arranged an escort. In fact, management was so efficient that an oversight was quite unthinkable. Actually, the devil thought, that was a good point. It suggested more was going on here than immediately met the eye.

The devil puffed his pipe and contemplated the intriguing half-pint specimen that shuffled nervously before him, who was visibly attempting to compose an exit-line and end their conversation. That would never do, and so the devil plucked the pipe-stem from his smouldering maw and made sure he got his two penn'orth in before the infant did.

"But you don't quite add up to anything that I'm familiar with. Come, little chap. Tell me your name."

That was the point at which the foundling child made his astounding revelation.

"My name's Michael Warren."

Oh, my dears, my cousins in the sulphur, can you possibly imagine? It was better than the time when he tricked self-important, brooding Uriel into revealing where the secret garden was located (it was in a fizzy puddle in Pangaea). It surpassed, in terms of comedy, the look on his ex-girlfriend's perfect features when her seventh husband in a year died on their wedding night, the devil having stopped his heart a second prior to the intended consummation. Why, it even beat that moment of hilarity during the Fall, when one of the low-ranking devils, Sabnock or some other marquis, who'd been consequently pushed down further into the excruciating quagmire of material awareness than the others, had called out "Truly this sensate world is one beyond endurance, though I am delighted to report my genitals have started working", whereupon the builders and the devils they were using as a form of psychic landfill all put down their flaming snooker cues for a few minutes until they'd stopped laughing. This dazed baby trumped all that though, knocked it into a cocked hat: his name was Michael Warren. He'd just said so. He'd just come straight out with it as if it was of no significance, the modest little beggar.

Michael Warren was the name attached to the precariously-balanced billiard ball that had kicked off the fight between the builders.

And they hadn't had a fight since, what, Gomorrah? Egypt?

The events that were in orbit around this unwitting child had an intoxicating whiff of intricacy to them, complex as a clockwork anthill, complex as the mathematics of a hurricane. The possibilities for convoluted entertainment that this clueless little soul presented to the fiend were such an unexpected gift that he took an involuntary step backwards. All the dragon frills that edged the image he was wearing rippled in anticipation, flaring up in a display of his heraldic colours, red and green, bloodshed and jealousy.

"*You're* Michael Warren? You're the one to blame for all this trouble?"

Oh, the way his little jaw dropped, so that you could tell it was the first he'd heard about his sudden notoriety. This whole thing was becoming more delicious by the moment, and the devil laughed until he thought he'd burst a testicle. Wiping the hydrochloric tears of mirth from his peculiar eyes, he focussed them once more upon the boy.

"Wait till I tell the lads. They'll be in fits. Oh, this is good. This is extremely good."

That set him off again, the thought of how his fellow devils would respond when he informed them of his latest stroke of undeserved good fortune. Belial, the toad in diamond, would just blink his ring of seven eyes and try to make out that he hadn't heard. Beelzebub, that glaring wall of porcine hatred, would most likely cook in his own rage. And as for Astaroth, he'd simply purse the lipstick-plastered mouth upon his human head into a vicious pout and would be looking daggers for the next three hundred years. The devil really had the giggles now. He laughed so hard his broad-brimmed hat fell back around his neck, at which point the already nervous child abandoned all the manners that his mother had instilled in him and screamed like an electrocuted aviary. The infant's eyes began to well with frightened tears.

Ah, yes. The horns. The devil had forgotten he had horns in this particular ensemble. Horns, for some unfathomable reason, always made them jump when actually they should consider themselves lucky. Horns were nothing. Horns were just his work-clothes. They should see him when he was in fancy dress, for state occasions and the like, wearing one of his more finely-tailored robes of imagery. The coruscating spider/lizard combination, for example, or the gem of infinite regress. By Jingo, then they'd have something to cry about.

Blubbing profusely now the lad looked up with that expression of mixed accusation and outraged betrayal with which people generally seemed to greet him. He had seen it on the faces of Renaissance alchemists and Nazi dabblers alike. The message it conveyed, in essence, was 'This isn't fair. You're not meant to be real.' That was the main thrust of what the aggrieved and weeping cherub was now saying to him.

"You're the devil."

Children. They're so wonderfully perceptive, aren't they? Probably the horns were what had given him away. He felt a flicker of mild irritation at the fact that while people continually identified him as a devil, nobody was ever sure which one he was. It would be like somebody greeting Charlie Chaplin in the street by shouting "You're that bloke out of that film". It was insulting, but he didn't let it get him down. He was in much too fine a mood for that. He'd broken off his laughing-jag and glanced down at the tot, good-humouredly.

"Well ... yes. Yes, I suppose I am."

Poor mite. He looked like he was getting a stiff neck from craning up to keep his brimming gaze upon the demon regent. Out of pure consideration and concern, the devil squatted down upon his haunches and leaned forward so that he and the small boy were eye to eye, the child's blue puddles staring earnestly into the devil's traffic-lights. He thought he'd tease the kid, just for a bit of mischief. What could be the harm in that? He spoke in puzzled tones of the most innocent enquiry.

"Why? Where did you think you were?"

That, thinking back, would seem to have been the remark that finally undid the little scamp. He'd shrieked something that sounded like "But they were only ants" and then had taken off along the endless landing, going nineteen to the dozen, holding his pyjama bottoms up with one hand as he ran to stop them falling down around his ankles.

Oh dear. Him and his big mouth. Despite the wholly innocent intent behind the devil's harmless query, it appeared that Michael Warren had inferred from it that he'd been sent to Hell, possibly for a crime involving ants. Wherever did these jumped-up monkeys get all their ideas from? Not that he was saying that this *wasn't* Hell, mind you. More that the actual situation was far less simplistic than that word implied, and where this devil was concerned one over-simplified at one's own risk.

So there he was, watching the famous Michael Warren running full tilt down the walkway, trying to hold his pants up, squeaking like a fresh-hatched banshee. Was it any wonder that the devil couldn't call to mind the last time that he'd had such fun?

He straightened up out of his crouch and flexed his two-tone rags to straighten them. The fleeing boy was some way off along the monstrously extended balcony, slippers flapping comically against the floorboards underfoot. The devil wondered where the child thought he was going.

Leisurely, he knocked his screaming, man-faced pipe against the balustrade to empty it, and then put it away into a pocket of himself. His smoke-break was now evidently over, and he couldn't stand round here all day. He eyed the by-now tiny figure of the child as it continued its disorganised retreat into the distance of the elevated boardwalk. It was time to get on with some work.

The devil took a short unhurried step, putting his boot down on the boards, heel first and then the ball of his foot in a soft, percussive double thump a little like the beating of a heart: *bump-bump*. He took another step, this time a longer one that swallowed up more ground, so that it seemed like a protracted pause before the double footfall came again: *bump-bump*. He took a further pace. This time the pause went on and on. The twin thud that would signify the step's end never came.

The devil floated a few feet above the floor, still carried slowly forward by the slight momentum of the step or two he'd taken when he launched himself. He narrowed his mismatched eyes, like malefic 3D spectacles, fixed on the dwindling form of the escaping child along the balcony's far end. He grinned and let his scarlet and viridian pinions snap like stormy flags behind as he began to gather speed. He crackled and he burned. He did his trade-mark chuckle.

Comet-arsed and showering coloured embers like a Roman candle in his wake, the devil sizzled down the walkway, screeching after the small fugitive, closing the gap between them effortlessly. In a way, the boy's intuitive attempt to treat the fiend as an uncomfortably big dog had not been so far off the mark. Certainly, you should never run from devils. Your retreating back will simply lend you the appearance of absconding prey, which, when it comes to dogs and demons, only tends to get them going.

Hearing from behind him the approaching firework rush, mixed as the sound was with that of the devil's escalating cackle, the boy glanced back once across his shoulder and then looked as if he wished he hadn't.

Whoosh. The devil reached down with both scorched and blistered hands to grab the squealing escapee beneath his armpits from the rear, snatching him fast into the whistling air, across the balustrade and up into the glass and ironwork altitudes above the Attics of the Breath. The child's scream rose as they did, spiralling aloft with them to ring amongst the giant painted gird-ers, startling the pigeons nested there into a brief ash-flurry of activity. With his slipper-clad feet pedalling frantically, the kid first pleaded for the fiend to let him go, then realised how high up he was and begged instead not to be dropped.

"Well, make your mind up," said the devil, and considered dropping Michael Warren a few times then catching him before he hit the floor, though on reflection he thought better of it. It would over-egg the lily. It would gild the pudding.

They were hovering there, treading air, a thousand feet or more between them and the vast checked tablecloth of square holes spread below. Having considered all the aspects and angles of this novel circumstance, the devil opted for a gentler approach in his communications with the boy. You caught more flies with honey than you did with vinegar, and you caught more with bullshit than you did with either. Tipping forward his horned head he whis-pered in the lad's ear to be heard above the flap and flutter of his banners, red and green, hot coals and absinthe.

"Something tells me that we've got off to a bad start, haven't we? I'm sens-ing, from the screaming and the running off, that I've said something to upset you without meaning to. What do you say we put it all behind us and begin afresh?"

With frightened, pin-prick eyes still fixed upon the hideous drop beneath his kicking slippers, Michael Warren answered in a wavering falsetto, manag-ing to sound scared witless and indignant at the same time.

"You said this wiz Hell! You said you wiz the devil!"

Hmm. Good point. The devil had at least implied both of those things, but took care to sound pained and woefully misunderstood in his response to the boy's accusation.

"Come now, that's unfair. I didn't claim that this was Hell. I merely asked you where you thought you were and you jumped to your own conclusions. As for me being a devil, well, I am. There's no escaping it. I'm not *the* Devil though, or at least, not the one that you were probably expecting. I'm not Satan, and besides, he doesn't look like this. You'd be surprised what Satan looks like, and I promise you you'd never recognise him in, ooh, what, nine billion years?"

By now more confident that his small body would not be allowed to fall, the dangling darling tried to twist his head around, to face the fiend across his shoulder as he spoke.

"Well, if you're not him, who are you, then? What's your name?"

That was a tricky one. The rules that governed what he was – essentially, a field of living information – meant that he was more or less compelled to answer any direct question and to do so truthfully. It didn't mean, of course, that he was under any obligation to make matters easy for the questioner. Given that devils were reluctant to reveal their names, which could be used to bind them, he would generally employ some form of code, or else engage human interrogators in a guessing game. With Michael Warren, he decided to provide his answer in the manner of a crossword clue.

"Oh, I've been given dozens of old nicknames, but in truth I'm just plain, mixed-up Sam O'Day. Why don't you call me Sam? Think of me as a roguish uncle who can fly."

Oblivious to the anagram, the child seemed to accept this, albeit grudgingly. Young as he was, he was already obviously acquainted with the concept of the roguish uncle, and yet was still of an age where he was probably uncertain as to whether they could fly or not. He ceased his futile struggling at any rate, and simply hung there acquiescently. When the boy spoke again, the devil noticed that he had his eyes shut to block out the horrid plunge beneath his tingling toes.

"Why did you tell me that I wiz in trouble?"

All these bloody questions. What had happened to the days when people either exorcised you or else haggled with you for a good price on their souls? The devil sighed and once again took on the same slightly offended tone he'd used before.

"I didn't say you were in trouble. I said that you'd caused some trouble. Quite unwittingly, of course, and nothing anybody's blaming you for. I just thought you'd like to know, that's all."

The kid persisted. That was a big problem these days: everybody knew their rights.

"Well, if I'm not in trouble, wizzle you please put me down? You'll make my arms fall off holding me up like this."

The fiend clucked reassuringly.

"Of course I won't. Why, I'll bet they're not even aching. I don't know how you could possibly mistake this place for Hell. Bodily pain's unheard of up here."

Agonizing torments of the heart and spirit, though, were well known everywhere, but naturally the devil didn't think to mention this. Instead, the fiend glossed smoothly on with his persuasive patter.

"As for me putting you down, are you quite sure that's what you want? I mean, your arms aren't really hurting, are they? And you didn't look as if you knew where you were going when you *were* down on the ground. Putting you back and leaving you alone would just mean you were lost again. Besides, I'm quite a famous devil. I can do all sorts of things. Dismiss me, and you're passing up a deathtime's opportunity."

The lad's eyes opened, just a crack.

"What do you mean?"

The devil glanced down idly at the Attics of the Breath below. Some of the wandering ghosts and phantasms down there were looking up at Michael and the devil, hovering just beneath the green glass ceiling of the grand arcade. The fiend could see a group of urchins, dead or dreaming, who seemed to be paying him particular attention. No doubt they could see he'd caught a child and wondered if they might be next. Have no fear, little children. For today, at least, you're safe. Perhaps another time. Returning his gaze to the back of the suspended boy's blonde head and breathing hot upon the nape the devil answered his last query.

"I mean there are things that I can tell you. There are things that I can show you. It's well known. I'm practically proverbial. I get a mention in the Bible … well, in the Apocrypha, but that's fairly impressive, don't you think? And I was Adam's first wife's second husband, though that got left out of Genesis. It's like with any adaptation, really. Minor characters omitted to speed up the story, complex situations simplified and so forth. You can't blame them, I suppose. And I was very close to Solomon at one point, though again, you wouldn't guess that from the Book of Kings. Shakespeare, however, bless him, Shakespeare gives me credit where it's due. He talks about a kind of trip I can take people on. It's called 'Sam O'Day's Flight', and it's more wonderful and thrilling than the biggest fairground ride you ever dreamed of. Do you fancy one?"

Dangling limply in the devil's arms, the Warren kid seemed unenthusiastic. "How do I know if I'd like it? I might not. And if I didn't, how do I know you'd stop when I wanted to?"

The Fifth Infernal Duke, noting that this was not quite a refusal, bent his head close to the lad's pink ear as he moved in to make the sale.

"If I hear you ask me to stop, I'll stop at once. How's that? And as for payment for the ride, well, I can see that you're an offspring of the Boroughs, so I don't expect that you get pocket money, do you? Doesn't matter. Tell you what, because I've taken quite a shine to you, young man, I'll do this as a favour. Then, at some remote point in the future, if there's ever something useful you can do for me, we'll call it quits. Does that sound fair to you?"

The child's eyes were wide open now, at least in the most literal sense. Still trying not to look directly downwards, he was tilting back his curly head to stare up through the arcade roof at the unfurling geometeorology. The devil could see an enchantingly baroque arrangement of some several dozen tesseracts that were engaged in folding up to form something resembling a ten- or twenty-sphere. No wonder the small boy looked mesmerised and sounded far away when he eventually replied.

"Well ... yes. Yes, I suppose so."

That was all that the fiend needed. True, a minor's spoken affirmation couldn't technically be called a binding compact, nothing written down, nothing in red and white, and yet the devil felt that it could be interpreted as an agreement to proceed.

He dived.

Dived like a crippled bomber, the descending engine drone, dropped like a stone or like an owl that's sighted supper, plunged like the astounding cleavage of his ex-wife, fell out of the vaulted heights above the Attics of the Breath as only he could fall, his coloured streamers rustling in a deafening cacophony. The child was screaming something, but above the wind of their descent you couldn't make it out. As a result of this the devil could say, in all honesty, that he had not yet heard the infant ask to stop.

At the last moment, barely fifty feet above the boarded floor with its enormous vats, the devil pulled out of his plummet in a sharp, right-angled swerve that took them soaring off along the length of the immense emporium. The scruffy little Herberts who'd been rubbernecking at the devil and his captive only a few moments back were now running for cover, probably convinced that he'd been swooping down to gather them up in his claws as well. He seared down the gigantic corridor, a dangerous gobbet of ball-lightning shedding sparks and keening with the process of its own combustion, scattering those few scant souls who were about the Attics at that precise juncture of the century, the year, the afternoon, holding a baby in his sweltering arms.

The toddler's howl was stretched into the Doppler wail of an approaching train by the velocity of his blurred transit, streaking yards above the pale pine boards which were lit briefly by the demon's passage, red and green, poppies and putrefaction.

They were heading west towards the blood-burst of that day's specific sunset, where the light poured in like smelted ore through the glass panels of the arcade roof. The devil knew the nipper's eyes would be wide open during all of this. At speeds like these, with all the spare flesh on one's face rippling towards the rear side of the skull, it was impossible to close them. Saying anything, even a single syllable like 'stop', was quite out of the question.

The boy's head was angled down, watching the huge square vats flash by beneath them. The experience, the devil knew, was very much like viewing a surprisingly engrossing abstract film. The files of apertures that ran along the length of the great attic each allowed a view into a single room at different stages of its progress in the fourth direction. Living beings in those rooms appeared as static tentacles of gemstone, inner lit and still as statues as they wound amongst each other, only the elusive darting lights that were their consciousnesses lending the illusion of mobility and motion. Zooming down a row of tanks from just above them, though, the vats became like single frames on an unreeling spool of celluloid. The winding, frozen shapes appeared to move in the unchanging confines of the endlessly repeated room containing them, sometimes withdrawing altogether for brief stretches when the space was empty, flickering into view again a moment later to resume their strange, fluorescent dance. The fluctuations of the coloured forms mapped random mortal movement through these worldly chambers in a way that was hypnotic and, at times, hauntingly beautiful. The little boy, at least, appeared to be absorbed, in that his high-pitched shriek had sunk to a low moan. This probably meant it was time to step on the accelerator, since the devil didn't want his passenger to nod off out of boredom. He'd his reputation to consider.

A reverberating peal of layered thunder marked the point where they surpassed the speed of sound, and then a little after that there was a pocket of unearthly stone-deaf hush when they exceeded even the velocity of silence. The resplendent devil and the scamp that he was baby-sitting roared down the unending throat of the arcade, the sky beyond the hall's glass roof changing its colours every other moment as they dashed through days and days. The sunset red became first violet and then purple, deepening to a profound black in which the construction lines of the unfolding hyper-weather were picked out in silver. This was followed by more purple and then the cerise and peach of dawn. Blue mornings and grey afternoons smeared past in stroboscopic washes. Long and sleepless nights were gone in seconds, swallowed in the brief flare of another molten sunrise. Faster still they hurtled until neither of them could distinguish the exact point at which one hue turned into another. Everything became a tunnel of prismatic shimmer.

Swerving on a sixpence and without reducing speed, the devil veered all of a sudden so that they were locked on a collision course with one of the enormous trees that thrust up through its fifty-foot-square hole on the far side of the emporium: an elm expanded to an ancient redwood by the variation that there was between dimensions. The ear-piercing screech that came from Michael Warren indicated to the devil that at least his charge had shrugged off the ennui from which he'd earlier seemed to be suffering.

The stretch of corridor that had the giant elm erupting through its floor was in the night-miles that provided punctuation along the vast Attics' length at measured intervals. The firmament seen through the darkened glass above was lustrous ebony. Chrome traceries of snail-slime were delineating the evolving contours of the supra-geometric cumuli outside, the radiance from those huge bodies lending these benighted reaches of the never-ending hall a moonlit and crepuscular appearance. Mixed-up Sam O'Day, the King of Wrath, the groom-slayer, the devil, he scorched through the shadows and the cloudlight, heading for the leafy wooden tower that swelled up terrifyingly out of the silvered murk before them.

Pigeons, rendered almost microscopic in comparison with the huge boughs that sheltered them, awoke from their slow-motion dreams and flapped up in alarm at the loud, spitting pyrotechnics of the fiend's approach. The devil knew that this most special family of birds were more or less unique in their ability to pass between the Upstairs and the Downstairs world, and often would take refuge in a tree's higher dimensions where they knew that they'd be fairly safe from cats. Cats, it was true, could sometimes scrabble through an aperture into the Attics of the Breath – the fiend assumed they'd learned this trick originally by climbing after pigeons – but the higher realm was petrifying for a living feline. Usually, they'd noisily evacuate their bowels and leap straight down the nearest window back into the world. The whole manoeuvre was so stressful for them that they seemed to only use it when they needed to move straight from one room to another without passing through the intervening space. The talent wasn't any use, though, when it came to hunting, so the roosting birds were safe. Not from the devil, obviously, but from practically every other predator that they might reasonably expect to whiz out of the dark towards them, coughing fire. The flock had just been woken unexpectedly from sleep and taken by surprise. There isn't much, the devil thought, which takes a pigeon by surprise. That was no doubt the reason for their agitation.

A split second before he and Michael Warren would have smashed into the thirty-foot-wide trunk the devil executed one of his most showy moves, a sudden spiral swoop that cleverly combined the Golden Section and the Fibonacci sequence, blazing in a corkscrew-tight trajectory that took them down around the tree, just inches from the elephant-hide of its enlarged bark. The zip and zing of it, the helter-skelter swish, was wickedly exhilarating. They looped five times round the wood Goliath, and somewhere in the hair-raising rip of their descent the devil felt his inner compass flip into the new orientation that attended the inferior, three-sided world. He and his passenger were now immersed in the tenebrous gelatine of Time, careening on a left-hand thread around an elm that now appeared to be of normal scale. They came out of their circling nosedive only feet above the tufted knuckles of its roots, then shot up and away into the intermittent twinkle of the overcast night sky above. Swimming as they now were in the sequential soup of minutes, hours and days, they left a Technicolor mess behind, an afterburn procession of spent images trailing flamboyant in their wake. Predominantly these were in the devil's signature array of reds and greens, a wild rose-garden stripe bursting from nowhere that wound down around the tree and then fired itself up into the dark and starlight

Thirty feet above the ground the devil slammed the brakes on and stopped dead, hanging there in the brisk night breeze and summer-scented shadows with his rag-flags spread around him in a rattling carnation cluster. Still clutched in the demon's sooty grip, the bug-eyed little boy sucked in his first breath of the last half-minute and yelled "Stop", rather unnecessarily, as they just had. On realising this, the child twisted his head around as far as it would go, so that he could look up across his shoulder at the devil. It was one of those looks kids put on when they're pretending to be traumatised, the wobbling lower lip, the haunted eyes and obvious affectation of a shell-shocked twitch.

"I never said! I never said I wanted to go on your Flight. I only wanted to go home."

The devil did his best to sound surprised.

"What, that? That little jaunt that we've just been on? That wasn't my Flight. That was a warm-up lap. Give me some credit, my dear fellow. That was only fast, it wasn't fabulous. The real ride is much slower and much more mysterious. I promise you you'll like it. As for wanting to go home, perhaps you ought to take a look around and find out where we are before you start complaining."

There. That shut the little blighter up.

They were suspended in the night air up above the intersection formed where Spencer Bridge and Crane Hill crossed St. Andrew's Road. Beneath them as they hung there facing roughly south there was the meadow where the old Victorian slipper-baths had been converted to a public toilet. A broad tarmac pathway stretched diagonally across the swathe of grass below, from Spencer Bridge to Wiggins's coal yard further up the road. Amongst the trees that fringed the patch of ground there stood the inconspicuous elm down which the fiend and his reluctant cargo had swirled recently from the superior to the lower realm. Upon their left a scattering of headlights crawled up Grafton Street, mounting the valley slope between the factories and pubs on one side and the wasteland sprawl of earth and bricks that had ten years before been people's homes upon the other.

Up ahead and to their right was the illuminated cobweb knot of Castle Station, strings of light running towards it and away through the surrounding blackness. This site was perhaps the devil's favourite of the many ruined vistas that the Boroughs had to offer. He recalled the castle that the railway station had deposed with an abiding fondness. Several hundred years back down the line the devil had obtained a ringside seat for King Henry the Second's spiritually ruinous betrayal of his old chum Tommy Becket, summoning the fledgling saint here to Northampton Castle only to surprise him with a hanging jury of intemperate barons bellowing for the Archbishop's head (and also for his land, although the fiend could not remember any of them saying this out loud upon the actual occasion).

Sideways Sam O'Day – a name he was becoming gradually more pleased with – also had warm recollections of the castle from the time when he'd stood unseen at the elbow of Richard the Lionheart and tried to keep from sniggering as the King set off on his crusade, the third crusade and thus one of the Christian world's first major contacts with the world of Islam, which would set the tone for some side-splitting high jinks further up the road. Oh my word, wouldn't it just, though? It had been at the castle, too, where the fiend had the opportunity to sit in on the western world's first parliament, the National Parliament raised in 1131, and smirk at how much difficulty that was going to cause. And please, don't even get him started on the poll tax that had so upset Walter the Tyler and his peasant army back in 1381. The convoluted nature of the troubles that had blossomed here, close to the country's crux, made it one of the devil's favourite picnic spots, not just in Angle-land but in the wider 3D world.

Cradled there in the devil's tender arms above the crossroads, Michael Warren stared down at the streets that he had known in life with an expression of astonishment and longing. For the infant's benefit the devil executed a slow aerial pirouette, rotating counter-clockwise to show off the glittering nocturnal panorama that surrounded them. By moving slowly, the distracting trail of after-images they left behind them was reduced. Their gaze crawled lovingly across the Boroughs, past the southeast corner that the builders signified upon their gaming-table with a cross of gold. Progressing, Grafton Street climbed east towards the squinting cafeteria- and shop-lights set like a tiara at its top on Regent Square. Then, as the demon monarch turned, the parallel tarmac toboggan-runs of Semilong came into view, slate rooftops with a graphite sheen crowning the rank of terraces as they descended to the valley's bottom, to St. Andrew's Road and to the river winding by on its far side. Continuing their lazy swivel, Michael Warren and the fiend next overlooked the dark grass sprawl of Paddy's Meadow with the Nene a nickel ribbon that unravelled through it, the reflected trees like black and tangled salvage in the river's cloudy depths.

It was along here to the north, if scrambled Sam O'Day remembered rightly, that the wall of the St. Andrew's Priory had once extended. Back upstream in the 1260s, King Henry the Third sent out a punitive platoon of mounted troops to quash unrest and insurrection here in this pugnacious little town, the army let in through a breach in the old priory wall by a French Cluniac prior who sympathised with the French monarchy. They'd pretty much destroyed the place, raped it and robbed it and set fire to it, marking this northwest corner of the Boroughs as the point of penetration. On the builder's billiard table – or their trilliard table as it was more accurately called – this spot was represented by the pocket with the golden penis etched into the wood beside it. Regent's Square in the northeast, conversely, that was the death corner where the severed heads of traitors were displayed once, and its corresponding snooker pocket was emblazoned with a golden skull.

They twirled above the traffic junction, looking out across the business premises just over Spencer Bridge, the new estates of Spencer and King's Heath beyond. Spencer. Another local name, the devil noted, that had interesting repercussions up and down the track. Like figures circling on top of a dilapidated music-box, the devil and his passenger revolved unhurriedly to take in Jimmy's End and then Victoria Park, pretty and melancholy as a jilted bride, arriving finally at the far lights of Castle Station where their orbit reached its end. Clanking and shunting in the dark, the railway terminus was at the Boroughs' southwest corner, with a gilded turret scratched into the grain of the appropriate pocket on the builder's table, representing stern authority. Fidgeting in the devil's grip, the small boy at last found his voice.

"That's it. That's where I wiz. That's where I live."

One midget hand protruded from his dressing gown's capacious sleeve to point towards the part-lit terrace on their left, a little further south along St. Andrew's Road. The devil chuckled and corrected him.

"Not quite. That's where you lived. Until you died, of course."

The child considered this, and nodded.

"Oh. Yes. I'd forgotten that. Why has it all got dark so quick? It wiz all sunny earlier, and I've not been away for very long. It can't be night already."

Obviously, the fiend observed, his young friend needed setting straight on that one, too.

"Well, actually, it can. In fact, this isn't even the same day as that of your departure. When we flew along the Attics of the Breath just now we must have passed three or four sunsets, which means that we're presently at some point later on in that same week. From all the cars in Grafton Street, I'd say it looks like Friday night. Your family are probably right in the middle of their teatime about now. How would you like to see them?"

You could tell from the protracted silence that the kid was thinking about this before he answered. Naturally, he'd want to see his loved ones one more time, but seeing them in mourning for him must have been a daunting prospect. Finally, he piped up.

"Can you show them to me? And will they be shapes with lights in, like they were when we wiz back Upstairs?"

The devil issued a good-natured snort, so that wisps of blue smoke like car-exhaust leaked from his flaring nostrils.

"Well, of course I'll show them to you. That's the main part of Sam O'Day's Flight, in fact. It's what I'm famous for. And as for what they'll look like, it won't be the same as how they seemed from up above. Do you know what the word 'dimension' means?"

The infant shook his tousled head. This would, the devil thought, be a long night.

"Well, basically, it's just another word for plane, as in the different planes a solid object has. If something has length, breadth and depth we say that it has three dimensions, that it's three-dimensional. Now, in truth, all things in this universe have more than three dimensions, but there's only three that human beings seem to notice. To be honest, there are ten, or at a pinch eleven, but there are just four of them that need concern you at the moment. These are the three planes that I just mentioned plus a fourth that is as solid as the others, but which mortal men perceive as passing time. This fourth dimension, viewed in its true light, is how we see it from Mansoul, the realm Upstairs, which is a higher-up dimension still. Looked down on from up there, there is no time. All change and movement are just represented by the snaking crystal forms with lights inside that you saw earlier, winding along their predetermined paths. That's when you're looking from up there, remember."

"As for where we are now, we're not up there anymore. We're down in the three-sided world where time exists, but we're still seeing it with higher eyes. That minor detail, by and large, is the whole basis of my fabled Flight, which, if you'll now permit me, I shall demonstrate."

The babe in arms, who'd listened to the devil's monologue uncomprehendingly for the most part, made an ambiguous whining sound that had a slight upward inflection and could thus be taken as conditional assent. Taking his time so as not to alarm the child unnecessarily, and also to restrict their streaming image-trail, the fiend began to float towards the short and semi-darkened row of houses that the boy had indicated, opposite the coal-yard further up St. Andrew's Road. They drifted over the converted slipper-baths, the devil's emerald and ruby tatters crackling like a radio of evil, and across the unmowed triangle of meadow, moving south. Upon their left as they approached the corner of Spring Lane they passed the looming tannery, its tall brick chimney and its gated yards with dyed skin-shavings heaped in turquoise treasure-mounds, the bald white stumps of tails left on the cobbles and dissolving into soap and gristle. From this height, the puddles near the pulling-sheds were mother-of-pearl fragments, bright and flaking.

Michael Warren and the devil came to rest suspended up above the yard of the coal-merchant, facing east and looking down at a slight angle on the stretch of terraced houses opposite that ran between the bottom openings of Scarletwell Street and Spring Lane. Dipping his horned and auburn head, the devil whispered in the youngster's ear.

"You know, whenever they describe this ride I can provide, they always get it wrong. They tell how the great devil slippery Sam O'Day, if asked, will bear you up above the world and let you see its homes and houses with their roofs gone, so that all the folk inside are visible. That's true enough, for as far as it goes, but it misunderstands what's really going on. Yes, I bear people up above the world, but only in the sense that I can lift them, if I choose, into a higher mathematical dimension such as those we've been discussing. As for my supposed ability to vanish all the rooftops so that sorcerers can spy upon their neighbours' wives at bath-time, how am I expected to do that? And if I could, why would I bother to? This Flight is my most legendary attribute, apart from all the murders. Don't they think I might have something to impart that's rather more important than a glimpse of nipple? Here, you look down at the houses for yourself, and tell me what you think you're looking at. Have I made all the rooftops disappear, or haven't I?"

Of course, the devil knew that this was far from a straightforward question. That was largely why he'd asked it, just to watch the puzzled and conflicted look upon the child's face when he tried to answer.

"No. All of the rooftops are still there and I can see them, but ..."

The boy paused for a moment, as if inwardly debating something, then went on.

"... but I can see the people in the rooms inside as well. In Mrs. Ward's house on the end I can see Mrs. Ward upstairs putting a stone hot-water bottle in the bed, and Mr. Ward's downstairs. He's sitting listening to the radio. How can I see them both when they're on different floors? Shouldn't there be a ceiling in the way? And how can I see either of them if the roof's still there?"

The devil was, despite himself, impressed. Children could sometimes take

you by surprise like that. You tended to forget amidst the chatter and inanity
that their perceptions and their minds were working much, much harder than
those of their adult counterparts. This infant had just posed a more incisive
question, with more honest curiosity, than mangled Sam O'Day's last fifteen
hell-bound necromancers put together. Thus, he did his best to furnish this
intelligent enquiry with a suitable reply.

"Oh, I should think a bright young spark like you could answer that one
for himself. You take a closer look. It isn't that you're looking *through* the roof
and ceiling, is it?"

Michael Warren squinted dutifully.

"No. No, it's more like I'm looking round the edge of them."

The devil hugged the boy until he yelped.

"Good lad! Yes, that's exactly what you're doing, peeping into a sealed
house around an edge you normally can't see. It's like if there were people who
were flat, what they call two-dimensional, who lived on a flat sheet of paper.
If you were to draw a box round one of them, then that flat person would be
sealed off from the rest of the flat world and its inhabitants. They wouldn't see
him, since he would be out of sight behind the line-walls that you'd drawn
around him, nor would he be able to see them, enclosed in his flat box.

"But you're the one who drew the lines, and you have three dimensions.
In comparison to all the little flat folk, you have one more whole dimension you can work with, which gives you a big advantage. You can look down
through the open top side of the square you've drawn, look down through a
dimension that the flat folk cannot see and do not know about. You can look
down upon the flat chap in the box by looking at him from an angle that, to
him, does not exist. Now do you understand how you can see your upstairs
and your downstairs neighbours both at once, despite the roof and ceiling in
the way? It's just a matter of perspective. Doesn't that make much more sense
than me conspiring to hide all the rooftops in some unimaginable manner?
What am I supposed to do with all the slates?"

The child was staring down towards the row of houses with a dazed
expression, but was slowly nodding as if he had taken in at least the bare
bones of what he had just been told. Kids had a flexibility and a resilience
to their ideas about reality that grown-ups didn't, in the main. In scrambled
Sam O'Day's opinion, trying to break the spirit or the sanity of children was
more effort than the task was worth. Why bother with it? There were adults
everywhere, and adults snapped like twigs. Warming reluctantly towards his
sickeningly likeable and picture-postcard pretty passenger, the devil went on
with his tour-guide's monologue.

"In fact, if you were to look closer at your neighbours, you'd discover that
you can see their internal organs and their skeletons around the edges of their

skin. If you got closer still you could look round a hidden corner of their bones and see the marrow, though I wouldn't recommend it. That's the major reason why I keep my flight to up above the house-tops, if I'm honest. If we were much closer, you'd be too distracted by the blood and guts to properly take in the more important aspects of this educational experience. Would you like to look at the house that you once lived in?"

Michael Warren peered back up towards the fiend across one tartan shoulder. He looked eager, apprehensive, and quite sad. It was, the devil thought, a very adult, complicated look for such a youthful face.

"Yes please. Only, if everybody's crying, can we go away again? That wizzle make me cry as well, if they're unhappy."

Shifty Sam O'Day refrained from pointing out that Michael's family were hardly likely to be wearing party hats and blowing paper squeakers so soon after his demise, but simply carried the dead child a few doors further down the terrace, heading south. A breeze out of the west brought the perfume of iron and weeds from off the rail-yards where forgotten tenders peeled and rusted, and the white lights were a rationed, sparing sugar frosting on the blustery Boroughs dark. The devil halted over number 17.

"There, now. Let's see what's going on."

The devil gasped at the same moment that the little boy did. What they could glimpse going on inside the house was, frankly, the last thing that either of them had foreseen. If anything the fiend was more astonished than the kid, being much less accustomed to surprises. This one was a shock and no mistake, like when they'd driven him from Persia all those centuries ago by burning fish livers and incense. He'd not been expecting that, and neither had he been expecting this.

The upstairs floor of number 17 was currently deserted, as were the front room and passageway. Only the living room and kitchen were lit-up and occupied, containing half a dozen people by the devil's estimate. A thin old lady with her smoke-grey hair pinned up into a bun stood in the small back kitchen, waiting while a dented kettle on the gas stove reached the boil. Everyone else was loitering in the adjacent living room around a table set for tea. At one end, near the open kitchen door, a little girl of five or six was sitting in an infant's high chair, which was much too small for her. An upturned pudding basin had been placed atop her head so that the man who stood behind her chair, a dark-haired fellow in his thirties, could cut round it as he trimmed her fringe. Another woman, also in her thirties, was positioned in between the table and the fireplace. She was in the act of moving a small plate of butter from the hearthside where it had been melting into golden oil and placing it towards the centre of the spread white tablecloth. As she did this she was glancing up towards the door that led out to the passage, which was opening as someone entered. This was a tall, solid-looking chap who had a red complexion and the leather-shouldered donkey-jacket of a labourer. In his arms he held …

"It's me," said Michael Warren in a startled tone of disbelief.

It was, as well. There was no getting round it, even in the fourth dimension.

Coming through the door into the living room with a broad grin across his rosy face, the burly working man was carrying a child, perhaps three years of age, a boy with elfin features and blonde curls that were quite unmistakeable. It was a slightly smaller version of the little spirit that the fiend was currently suspending up above the rooftops. It was Michael Warren, evidently very much alive and unaware that he was at that moment being studied by his own bewildered ghost.

"Well, I'll be damned," predicted screwed-up Sam O'Day with confidence.

How had the white-haired builder managed it, especially with a black eye and mild concussion? How had he escaped the snooker that his colleague and opponent had ensnared him in? The devil tried imagining a trick shot that would furnish the unprecedented outcome he was at that moment witnessing, but found to his embarrassment that he could not. The trilliard ball that represented Michael Warren must at some point have been knocked into the pocket that was decorated with a golden skull, the death-hole at the table's northeast corner. Otherwise his soul would not have been careening round the Attics of the Breath in its pyjamas. Just as obviously, the ball had then somehow bounced out again, or in some other fashion been returned to play, returned to life. If not, who was the rascal with the white-gold ringlets being welcomed back into the bosom of his family, down below in the unfolded pop-up book of number 17, St. Andrew's Road? This merited, the devil thought, closer investigation.

"This is certainly a turn-up for the books. Up here you're dead, yet down there you're alive again. I wonder why? Are you by any chance some kind of zombie from a voodoo film? Or, more remotely, I suppose you might be the messiah. What do you think? Were there any signs or omens coinciding with your birth, clouds shaped like crowns, rays of unearthly light or anything like that?"

The youngster shook his head, still gaping at the cheery scene being played out beneath him.

"No. We're only ordinary. Everybody's ordinary on Andrew's Road. What does it mean, that I'm down there? Does it mean that I won't be dead for very long?"

The devil shrugged.

"It certainly appears that way, though I confess that for the life of me I can't see how. There's something very complicated going on with you, young man, and I'm a devil for complexity. Perhaps your background might provide some sort of clue? Come, tell me who those people are, the ones squealing with joy at your return and milling round the room down there. Who's that old lady in the kitchen?"

Michael Warren sounded both cautiously proud and touchingly protective as he ventured his reply.

"That's Clara Swan, and she's my gran. She's got the longest hair of anybody in the world, but it's all tied up in a bun because when it hangs down it catches fire. She used to be a servant for some people in a great big house."

The devil raised one bristling eyebrow thoughtfully. There were a number of big houses round these parts. It wasn't likely that this toddler's grandmother had served the Spencers out at Althorp, but you never knew. The boy continued his inventory.

"The other lady is my mum, who's called Doreen. When she wiz just a little girl they had a war, and her and my aunt Emma watched a bomber crash in Gold Street from their bedroom window. That man carrying me, coming through the door, that's my dad. He's called Tommy, and he rolls big heavy barrels at the brewery. Everybody says he dresses very well, and that he's good at dancing, but I've never seen him doing it. The other man's my uncle Alf who drives a double-decker bus and rides a bicycle when he calls in to see our gran on his way home from work. He cuts our hair for us, the way he's doing for my sister Alma. She's the bossy girl in the high chair."

Unseen by his small passenger, the devil's irises turned black for several seconds with surprise, then faded back to their initial colours, red or green, the stains of war or else the stains of outdoor love. His young charge had a sister, and her name was Alma. Alma Warren. Reconstructed Sam O'Day had heard of Alma Warren. She'd grow up to be a moderately famous artist, doing paperback and record covers, who had intermittent visionary spasms. During one of these she would, in thirty years or so, attempt a portrait of the Fifth Infernal Duke in his full dress regalia, the reptile and arachnid image-wrap with the electric peacock-feather trim. The picture wouldn't be much of a likeness, and she wouldn't even bother trying to depict the lizard lining of his tailored aura, but the devil would feel vaguely flattered all the same. The artist clearly found her subject beautiful, and if he'd felt the same way about her it might have been his Persian passion all over again. Unfortunately, Alma Warren would grow up into a frightful dog, and switchback Sam O'Day was very picky when it came to women. Back in Persia, Raguel's daughter Sara had been luscious. Even Lil his ex-wife, who had fornicated with abominations, hadn't let herself go to the same extent that Alma Warren would do. Though the devil would admit that he quite liked the woman, he would also quickly point out that he didn't like her in *that* way, just in case anybody got the wrong idea.

So, Michael Warren was the pretty brother of alarming-looking Alma

Warren, who could somehow entice fiends to sit for her. And then there was that strange event of cryptic import that would take place nearly fifty years from now, in 2006, with which the woman artist would be heavily involved. Within the trillion-fragment jigsaw of the demon-king's elaborate mind, the pieces started tumbling into intriguing new arrangements. Something positively Byzantine was going on, the devil was more certain by the moment. He reviewed what he could pre-remember of the labyrinthine pattern of events that would surround the early years of the next century, looking for clues and for connections. There was all that business of a female saint in the twenty-fives, with which the devil had a personal involvement. That affair had tenuous links with the occurrences in 2006, links that related to the ancestry of Alma Warren ...

And her brother.

Oh, now, this was interesting. They were siblings, and so had their ancestry in common.

That meant Michael Warren was a Vernall too. It didn't matter if he knew it, and it mattered less whether he liked it. He was tied by blood-bonds to the old profession, to the ancient trade.

The fiend knew that the greater part of Mansoul's unique local terminology came from the Norman or the Saxon, phrases such as Frith Bohr, Porthimoth di Norhan and the like. Vernall was older, though. The devil could recall hearing the word around these parts since, what, the Roman occupation? And he had a notion that it might derive from earlier traditions still, from Druids or the antlered Hob-men that preceded them, weird figures crouching in the smoke-drifts of antiquity. Though Vernall was a job description, it described an occupation that was based in an archaic world-view, one which had not been in evidence for some two thousand years and one which did not see reality in terms the modern world would recognise.

A Vernall tended to the boundaries and corners, and it was in the mundane sense of a common verger that the term came to be understood throughout the Boroughs during medieval times. The ragged edges that comprised a Vernall's jurisdiction, though, had not originally been limited to those weed-strangled margins of the mortal and material world alone.

The corners that a Vernall had traditionally marked and measured and attended to were those that bent into the fourth direction; were the junctions that existed between life and death, madness and sanity, between the Upstairs and the Downstairs of existence. Vernalls overlooked the crossroads of two very different planes, sentinels straddling a gulf that no one else could see. As such they would be prone to certain instabilities, yet at the same time often were recipient to more-than-normal insights, talents or capacities. In just the recent lineage of Michael Warren and his sister Alma, shook-up Sam

O'Day could think of three or four striking examples of these odd hereditary tendencies. There had been Ernest Vernall, working on the restoration of St. Paul's when he fell into conversation with a builder. Snowy Vernall, Ernest's fearless son, and Thursa, Ernest's daughter, with her preternatural grasp of higher-space acoustics. There had been ferocious May, the deathmonger, and the magnificent and tragic Audrey Vernall, languishing at present in a run-down mental hospital abutting Berry Wood. Vernalls observed the corners of mortality, and watched the bend that all too often they would end up going round themselves.

Hanging above St. Andrew's Road with Michael Warren's tiny essence held between his claws, the devil counted all the aces in the hand of information he'd been dealt. This clueless child, currently dead but in a few days time apparently alive, had been the cause of a colossal brawl between the Master Builders. More than this he was a Vernall by descent, related to a woman artist who was central to the crucial business that would take place in the spring of 2006. This forthcoming event was known, in Mansoul, as the Vernall's Inquest. Much depended on it, not least the eventual destiny of certain damned souls that the fiend had a specific interest in. There might be some way slipshod Sam O'Day could tweak the dew-dropped strands of interwoven circumstance to his advantage. He would have to think about it.

Though excited by the tingling web of possibilities, the devil managed to sound nonchalant as he addressed the captive boy.

"Hmm. Well, your family all seem very pleased to have you back with them, but it appears there's been a dreadful mix-up here. At some point over the next day or so you obviously come back to life, so probably you're not meant to be running round Upstairs at all. I'd better end my flight and take you back up to the Attics of the Breath until I can decide what's to be done with you."

The astral toddler shifted in the devil's grip. It seemed as if, once reassured that being dead would not be permanent in his case, Michael Warren was beginning to enjoy this ride the fiend had promised him and was reluctant to see it concluded. He conceded with a heavy sigh, as if doing the devil an enormous favour.

"I suppose so, but don't go so fast this time. You said you'd answer questions for me, but I can't ask any if my mouth's all full of wind."

The devil gravely tipped his horns in the direction of the infant dangling beneath him.

"Fair enough. I'll take it nice and easy, so that you can ask me anything you like."

He turned in a great spiral fan of red and green and started drifting north along St. Andrew's Road towards the meadow sheltering at the foot of Spencer

Bridge. They'd barely reached the fireside-flavoured heights above the coal merchant's before the lad had formulated his first irritating query.

"How does it all work, then, life and death?"

How nice. He'd got a little Wittgenstein for company. Unseen behind the kiddy's back, the devil opened wide his fang-filled jaws and mimed biting the baby's head off, chewing it a time or two, then spitting it into the bays of heaped up slack below them. Relishing this fleeting fantasy, he let his features settle back into their customary insidious leer as he replied.

"There's really only life. Death's an illusion of perspective that afflicts the third dimension. Only in the mortal and three-sided world do you see time as something that is passing, vanishing away behind you into nothingness. You think of time as something that one day will be used up, will all be gone. Seen from a higher plane, though, time is nothing but another distance, just the same as height or breadth or depth. Everything in the universe of space and time is going on at once, occurring in a glorious super-instant with the dawn of time on one side of it and time's end upon the other. All the minutes in between, including those that mark the decades of your lifespan, are suspended in the grand, unchanging bubble of existence for eternity.

"Think of your life as being like a book, a solid thing where the last line's already written while you're starting the first page. Your consciousness progresses through the narrative from its beginning to its end, and you become caught up in the illusion of events unfolding and time going by as these things are experienced by the characters within the drama. In reality, however, all the words that shape the tale are fixed upon the page, the pages bound in their unvarying order. Nothing in the book is changing or developing. Nothing in the book is moving save the reader's mind as it moves through the chapters. When the story's finished and the book is closed, it does not burst immediately into flames. The people in the story and their twists of fortune are not disappeared without a trace as though they'd not been written. All the sentences describing them are still there in the solid and unchanging tome, and at your leisure you may read the whole of it again as often as you like.

"It's just the same with life. Why, every second of it is a paragraph you will revisit countless times and find new meanings in, although the wording is not changed. Each episode remains unaltered at its designated point within the text, and every moment thus endures forever. Moments of exquisite bliss and moments of profound despair, suspended in time's endless amber, all the hell or heaven any brimstone preacher could conceivably desire. Each day and every deed's eternal, little boy. Live them in such a way that you can bear to live with them eternally."

The pair were floating in amongst the treetops of the darkened meadow, heading in the rough direction of the public lavatories that had once been a slipper-baths, at the far end. A plume of fading snapshots smouldered in their wake. The dangling child was silent for a while as he digested what the devil had just said, but only for a while.

"Well, if my life's a story and when I get to the end I just go back and live it all again, then where wiz that Upstairs place that you found me in?"

The devil grimaced, by now starting to get bored with the responsibilities of parenthood.

"Upstairs is simply on a higher plane with more dimensions than the three or four that you're familiar with down here. Think of it as a sort of library or reading room, a place where all of you can stand outside of time, re-reading your own marvellous adventures, or, if you should choose, move onward to explore your further possibilities in that remarkable and everlasting place. Speaking of which, the elm that we're approaching is the one we can ascend into the Attics of the Breath. If you'd prefer I'll go up slowly so that you can understand what's happening."

Hanging there in a breeze perfumed by coal and chlorophyll, suspended like the undercarriage of some gaudy pirate zeppelin, Michael Warren uttered a mistrustful murmur of assent. As they sailed closer to the designated elm the devil savoured the small boy's bewilderment at the perceptual changes he was no doubt going through. The tree seemed to be getting larger as they neared it, just as one would usually expect, except that this was not accompanied by a sensation that the pair of them were truly getting any nearer to their destination. It felt more as if the further they progressed towards the tree, the smaller they themselves were getting. In an effort to pre-empt a flood of questions from his passenger, the fiend instead elected to explain the process to the lad.

"You're probably wondering why we appear to be becoming smaller, or alternatively why that elm there seems to be becoming monstrously enlarged as we get closer to it. It's all on account of a discrepancy between the way dimensions look to one another. We talked earlier about the notion of flat people who had only two dimensions, living hypothetically within the limits of a sheet of paper. Well, imagine that the sheet of paper they were living in had actually been folded up to form a paper cube. They would be living in a world of three dimensions, but with their perceptions limited to only two dimensions, they could never see or understand it to be so. That's quite like human beings, things with three dimensions living in a universe of four dimensions that they cannot properly perceive.

"Now, you've been taken up onto a loftier plane yet, as if our little flat chap had been moved into a space where he could overlook not only his flat world of two dimensions, but could also see the cube that it in fact was part of. How would a shape with three dimensions translate in the thoughts and the perceptions of a being who had only two? Without the concept of a cube, might not our flattened fellow see it as much like the flat, square world he was familiar with, but bigger somehow, in some way that he could not define? That's the effect that you're experiencing now, that you experienced if you looked back into whichever portal you climbed up through to the Attics of the Breath. Didn't the room in which you'd died look so much vaster than it had in life? In fact, I don't know if you ever suffered from a fever or delirium when you were still alive, in which the bedroom walls seemed to be frighteningly far away? You did? That sometimes happens when a human's wandering in the clammy territories between life and death. They get a glimpse of their environment's true scale, as it will seem to them when they've moved up a plane or two. I mean, look at the elm now. It's enormous."

And indeed it was, as was the formerly small meadow that surrounded it. The devil tipped into a spiralling trajectory around the vertical and craggy landscape of the trunk, reprising the manoeuvre he'd adopted when he'd carried Michael Warren here into this world, except at greatly reduced speed and heading up instead of down. As they described their first slow circle round the tree and doubled back upon themselves, the phantom ribbon of stop-motion images that they were leaving in their wake became more evident, predominately red and green, winding across the grassy plot to wind itself around the now-gigantic elm. They spiralled up towards the hidden point at which shambolic Sam O'Day knew there to be a crook-door that would let them back into the Attics, but before they'd reached it his increasingly infuriating cargo had thought up another tiresome question.

"How do trees grow up into the Upstairs place, when they've got roots down here next to the public lavs? And what about the pigeons that wiz sitting in the branches higher up? How can they all go back and forth without them being dead like me?"

Anagram Sam was glad that his and Lil's relationship had borne no offspring. Well, she'd given birth to a great ooze of monsters, obviously, things like dogs turned inside out and things like flattened yard-wide crabs that were the lurid pink of bubble gum. Such horrors, though, did little more than babble senselessly or howl until their mother got fed up and ate them during her post-natal blues. They barely had awareness of their own grotesque existence, much less the ability to formulate an irritating question, and were thus preferable to human kids like this one was, for all that he had two blue eyes and they had either none at all or several red ones clustered at the centres of their faces as is the arrangement with tarantulas. The devil tried to keep a civil tone as he replied.

"My, aren't you the enquiring little scholar? Well, the answer is that in the case of trees and certain other forms of plant life, they already have a structure that expresses perfectly a timeless life in more than three dimensions. Being motionless, the only movement is that of their growth, which leaves a solid trail of wood behind in much the same way we ourselves are leaving a long stream of ghostly images. The tree's shape *is* its history, each bough the curve of a magnificent time-statue which I can assure you that we folk Upstairs appreciate just as enthusiastically as do you humans.

"As for pigeons they are not at all as other birds, and different rules apply to them. For one thing, their perceptions are five times as fast as those of people or most other animals. This means they have a very different sense of time, with all things in the world save them slowed to a crawl in their quicksilver minds. More interesting still they are one of the only birds, in fact one of the only living creatures not a mammal, which can feed its young with milk. I don't pretend to know exactly why the pigeon should be favoured over all the other beasts in its relation to the higher realm, but I imagine that the business with the milk has got a lot to do with it. It probably enhances their symbolic value in the eyes of management, so that they have a special dispensation to behave as psychopomps and flutter back and forth between the pastures of the living and the dead, something like that. I'm not sure what they're for, but mark my words, there's more to pigeons than most people think."

They circled upward at a stately pace around a trunk now some ten yards across and getting on a hundred feet in its circumference. Aware now that the crook-door which gave access to the Attics of the Breath was only one twist further up the spiral, well-spun Sam O'Day decided that he'd best inform his bothersome young fellow traveller exactly what the doorway was before he took him through it, to forestall the high-pitched inquisition that inevitably would accompany such an initiative.

"Before you ask, just up round the next bend there's something called a crook-door. It's a kind of four-way hinge between dimensions that will take us back Upstairs into Mansoul. Most earthly rooms have got a crook door in at least one upper corner, and most open spaces have as well, although with open spaces you can only make out where the corners are when you're Upstairs and looking down. Unless, of course, you happen to be something that has made the journey countless times, like, say, a demon or a pigeon, and you know by heart where every entrance is located. Be prepared, now. There's a crook-door just ahead of us, and as we go through you'll feel something flip inside you as we switch from the perspective of this lower world to that of the superior plane above."

The fiend increased his speed a little, soaring up towards the occult corner he could sense, invisible, not very far above. As they and the red-green procession trailing after them swirled closer to the unseen aperture, like paint-stained water circling an inverted sky-drain, all the noises of the neighbourhood were stretched and elongated to the escalating din of a string-heavy orchestra. The cars on Spencer Bridge, the goods-train rattling beneath it and the murmur of the nearby river, all these sounds were pulled into a cavernous bass drone by the acoustics of the Upstairs world that waited overhead.

As the syllabic salad that was Sam O'Day had just predicted, when they shot out through the crook-door and traversed the juncture of two planes there was a moment when it felt as if their stomachs had turned over, but inside their heads. Then, in a flurry of bright apple colours they exploded from a fifty-foot square aperture framed with a trim of bark that had been greatly magnified, zipped one more time round the titanic elm and splashed amidst a pillow-fight of pigeons up into the ringing heights above the Attics of the Breath.

Beyond the glass roof, silver lines on black mapped out the facets of a splendidly unfurled dodecahedroid that was moving slowly, like a becalmed galleon of lights, through the unbounded darkness outside the immense arcade. The devil hovered for a moment with the dressing gown-clad child clutched tight against his breast, against the clanging of his mighty anvil heart, and then commenced a leisurely flight back along the vast emporium's length towards the purple and vermillion of sunset in the east. He'd take the boy back to the stretch of that colossal corridor, the early afternoon of some few days before, where they'd first happened on each other. Once there, he'd decide what should be done about this little puzzle, who was dead one minute and alive the next, whose plight had got the very builders worked up into a stupendous slapping match.

He hoped to pass the journey privately reviewing all his options, all the moves that might be made in the trans-temporal chess game that was his elaborate existence, his bedizened web. Ideally, he'd have time to carefully consider every way in which his opportune encounter with this bonny lad, this Vernall that he'd met upon their customary corner between here and the hereafter, could be turned to shuffling Sam O'Day's future advantage. Sadly, his anticipations proved unduly optimistic and they'd barely sailed a hundred yards before the pendant tyke struck up another round of Twenty Questions.

"So, then, why is this place called Mansoul?"

The devil was beginning to chew through his famously short tether. Yes, he'd promised that he'd answer any queries that the kid might put to him, but this was getting past a joke. Didn't this squeaking ferret ever take a break from his interrogations? Suspect Sam O'Day was modifying his appraisal of the manner in which Michael Warren's life had ended. Where he'd earlier supposed that the boy's trusting nature might have led him into murderous hands or an abandoned fridge, he now thought it more likely that the infant had been done away with by his relatives in an attempt to shut the little blighter up.

Although obliged by all the rules of demonology to furnish a reply, the devil couldn't keep a bitter edge entirely from his tone as he complied.

"It's called Mansoul because Mansoul's its name. It's like somebody asking you why you're called Michael Warren. You're called that because that's who you are, and Mansoul's called Mansoul because that's what it is. I mean, you couldn't give a thing a plainer label. It's entirely self-explanatory and anyone with any sense would just accept it, although I can see you're not included in that category.

"One of your better human poets, footsore Bunyan, jailbird John, he used to wander through the earthly township of Northampton from his home in nearby Bedfordshire, and at the same time he was wandering in his poetic vision through this higher aspect of the place. Some passing spirit must have told him the location's name, and by some huge fluke he was able to remember it when he returned to mortal consciousness, or at least long enough to jot it down and use it in his pamphlet *Holy War*."

They soared down the eternal hall, while up above the colours of the firmament outside wound back through time, from midnight jet to violet dusk and sundown like a burning slaughterhouse. Below, the dizzying row of vats went flickering by, punched holes on the unreeling music-roll of an old Pianola. As they passed beneath the blue-grey heavens of the previous day and on towards the glistening oyster-shell of dawn, the devil felt sure from the quality of Michael Warren's thoughtful silence that the child was formulating yet another fatuous enquiry, and at least in that one sense he wasn't disappointed.

"Why did you say that it wiz a fluke how that man could remember anything? And wizzle I remember all of this when I come back to life?"

The devil snarled his answer, spitting inadvertent beads of caustic venom on the collar of the infant's dressing gown and bleaching out the tartan fabric in a trail of smouldering white-yellow burns.

"No, sonny Jim, you won't. It's one of the immutable conditions that attends the way in which the thing you see as time is really structured. Nothing that occurs here, in this place outside of time, truly has time to be committed unto mortal memory. If you pass through the narrative that is your life a thousand times, still every thought and deed shall be exactly as it was upon the first such passage. You'll have no recall of having said or done these things before, save for those momentary lapses of forgetfulness that people know as déjà vu. And save such fragments as you may retrieve from dreams, or rarities such as John Bunyan's vision, no one ever has the faintest recollection of what happens to them in these elevated climes. So, really, there's no point in asking me these bloody stupid questions, is there? You'll forget the whole experience once you're returned to life, and that will mean that it has been a waste of your time, and, more woefully, my own. If you'd got any idea what a devil has to go through in the normal course of its existence then you wouldn't plague me with these ultimately useless trivialities."

They were then travelling through the pearl and raspberry atmosphere of Friday's dawn, onward and into the black thread-lit tunnel that was Thursday night. Craning his neck to look back at the fiend across one drool-scorched shoulder, Michael Warren's cherub face was such that you might think he was attempting to be sly as he responded to the devil's outburst, if his slyness hadn't been so clumsy and transparent.

"Well, why don't you tell me what a devil has to go through, then? What are you, anyway? Are you somebody who wiz very bad, or have you always been a devil? You said that you'd answer anything I asked you, so you answer that."

The devil ground his fangs to glistering pumice, although looking on the bright side, if he absolutely had to chat to this insufferably perky young pyjama-piglet, then it might as well be about something that he never shied from speaking of at length, namely himself.

"Well, since you ask, no. No, I haven't always been a devil. When the luminescent halo that is space-time rippled out from non-existence, all at once, then I saw the entirety of my immortal being, which included this benighted period that I must spend in service as a lowly fiend. But how I am now is not how I was back at the start of things, nor is it how I shall be when I'm further down my road. Back at my outset, I was but a glorious part, one of a myriad comprising a far greater entity that basked in simple being, there before the advent of both world and time. I was a builder back then, if you can believe that. Had the white frock and the billiard cue and everything.

"You have to bear in mind that this was back before there was time as we know it now, or a material universe of any sort. There wasn't any trouble. Naturally, that didn't last. It was decided higher up that part of the great being of which I was one component should be pushed down two or three dimensions to create a plane of physical existence. In effect, some of us were demoted from a world of naught but light and bliss into this new construction, this new realm of bodily sensation, of emotions and the endless torrent of delights and torments that those things entail. I'll grudgingly admit that this disastrous reshuffle might well have been necessary, in some way that we who laboured in the lower ranks were not aware of. Even so, it bloody hurt.

"I'm not complaining, mind you. There were others far worse off than I. You might recall I mentioned Satan earlier, and said you wouldn't recognise him if you saw him. That's because he was the first and greatest to be cast down into emptiness, his fiery energies cooled and condensed to matter, that sublime magnificence reduced to backfill. Take a peek beneath us at the tanks we're flying over, at the apertures that look down on the mortal plane.

In their depths you can make out the contorted coral stems that are in fact the living as seen without time. Their luminous and gem-like qualities have earned these growths, amongst the spirit population of Mansoul, the name of 'jewellery'. That's not, however, what we devils call them. We refer to them as 'Satan's Guts'. That's him, in every shuddering, mysterious particle of the corporeal universe. That's what became of him, of his immortal blazing body. Like I say, I got off light, comparatively speaking."

Unstuck Sam O'Day, an oriental fighting kite of threatening device, fluttered in silence for a moment down the Attics of the Breath, along the starlit stretch of passage that was Wednesday night, towards its sunset end. He'd quite upset himself with all that talk about the shining hero who'd become the solid world, become the Satan, the great obstacle, the stumbling block. Still, the distressing tale had kept his paying passenger from kicking up a fuss ... and Michael Warren would at some point pay his fare as they'd agreed, the devil would make sure of it. He hadn't made his mind up as to how yet, that was all. Mindful in case too long a pause should launch a fresh barrage of questions and complaints, the fiend resumed his narrative.

"So there we were, in a dawn world constructed from the living substance of our former governor, still reeling from the onslaught of new feelings and perceptions, left entirely to our own devices, or as much as anybody can be in a predetermined universe. Those were great times to be alive in, I can tell you. They still are, if I fly eastward far enough along the temporal axis of my being. All of those tremendous days still going on, back where we're all still young and angry and invincible.

"We soon found out, from one of the more easily-duped builders, what this whole new earthly plane had been created for. It turned out it was something called organic life. This, in our eyes, was an exceptionally tricky form of muddy puddle, though in your terms it was probably your trillion-times-great-grandmother. But long before anything even faintly like a human being turned up, we realised that this fleshy business was the only game in town. However, credit where it's due, it wasn't until people scrambled wet and shivering from the gene-pool that we knew we'd hit the jackpot. Naturally, by then we'd seen a preview of the whole thing played out on the symbol-level, with the man and woman in their garden and all that, but actually, if anything the squalid mess of the reality was even better.

"Due respect to the symbolic version, though. It had its high points. The young lovely cast initially as Adam's wife before Eve got the part was a real shocker by the name of Lil. I later married her myself, after she'd walked out on her husband in the first celebrity divorce, with incompatibility as the main reason cited. What had happened was that Adam, being up here on the symbol plane, had eyesight that perceived the world with four dimensions. It was like when you were looking down upon your house just now, and you could view your home's interior by peering round the walls, around an edge that isn't usually there. That's how it went with Lil and Adam. His first glimpse of her was a disaster. He could see around her skin, around the muscles underneath, around her bowels to where the slow chyme moved within them. He was sick all up the Tree of Knowledge. Lil was understandably offended, and went off to copulate with monsters, of which, luckily, I was amongst the very first."

The King of Wrath and Michael Warren glided down the length of Wednesday, with the sky beyond the curved glass canopy an overcast and nacreous grey, the lines and angles of its hyper-cumuli limned in a ghostly pink. The tartan package slapdash Sam O'Day was carrying appeared to be absorbed in the unfolding of the fiend's autobiography and, grateful for the silence, the infernal eminence decided to continue with his deadtime story.

"Back near the beginning, there's a patch where me and Lil are married, but it doesn't last. She was too clingy when she could get suction, and I was too headstrong with too many heads. Besides, the human race was waiting just a little further up the line, with all those comely beauties. Human women were a revelation to me, I can tell you, after Lil. Once you've had vertebrate there's no return, and once you look at something with a backbone, there's no looking back. You're only young, so you won't understand about all this, but trust me. I'm the devil, and I know whereof I speak.

"Of all the fiends in Hell, I like to think I was the most romantic and the most appreciative of female charms. In Persia, long ago, there's an occasion where I fall horns over tail in love with an exotic flower named Sara, daughter of a chap named Raguel. You should have seen how shy I was when I was courting her. I'd give her precious gifts and hardly let her get a glimpse of me, just leave some sign to tell her I'd been there: a necklace resting on a silken cushion, possibly, while part of the room's carpet was on fire nearby. When finally and bashfully I introduced myself to her, as I thought in the manner of the Beauty and the Beast, her overwrought reaction was no idyll from a fairy tale, I can assure you. Barely were the words 'I love you' spoken by one of my mouths than my beloved suffered what I think you humans call a stroke. It wasn't serious, and after a few days she could speak properly again, at which point she began describing her encounter with me in the most unflattering of terms.

"I was castigated as a horror, a destroyer, when the woman hardly knew me. She completely overlooked all of the admirable things there are about me, and instead portrayed me as some violent and inhuman stereotype. What's worse, she really rubbed it in by suddenly announcing her forthcoming marriage to another suitor. Naturally, I choked the life out of him on their wedding night, but that's only what anyone would do in such provoking circumstances.

And besides, despite what she claimed later, I could tell that she was only flirting with these other men because she liked to see me angry. Why else would she have proceeded to announce her marriage to a second groom before her first was buried, if she wasn't trying to lead me on and make me jealous? So I killed him too. I threw him off a balcony. To cut a tedious story short, I did the same with her next five. That's seven men in all that I despatched by choking, falling, drowning, burning, straight decapitation, an internal haemorrhage, and finally a heart attack. I almost thought of it as sending her bouquets. I thought she must be interested in me. Why else would she constantly be trying to attract my murderous attention by announcing yet another marriage? Any normal woman, surely, after number five's head had gone bouncing off down the bedchamber stairs, would have just given up on matrimony and enshrined herself within a nunnery.

"Well, anyway, it turned out I was wrong. She wasn't playing hard to get. She genuinely didn't like me. Off she goes to see some conjuror ... a class of people, incidentally, that I despise ... and gets him to enact what these days would be known as a restraining order. He burned certain substances upon a brazier, preventing me from going near her, in effect deporting me from Persia into Egypt. The ingratitude! Where did those people think they had acquired their grasp of numbers and exquisite patterning if not from me? So, knowing where I wasn't wanted, I decamped to Egypt and took all the mathematics with me. That, I thought, would teach them, or to be more accurate, it wouldn't."

Up beyond the glass roof, Wednesday's dawn flared briefly before giving way to the black miles of Tuesday night. The hanging toddler was still listening intently to the devil's monologue.

"In Egypt, though, I got into a spot of bother. Egypt had a reputation as a demon hotspot back at that point of its history, and there were dozens of us hanging out down there. You talk about associating with the wrong crowd. It was trouble waiting quite demonstrably to happen.

"Things came to a head when one of the more lowly devils was tormenting mortal builders in nearby Jerusalem. When the unsettled victims sought King Solomon's protection, he was able to use magic to ensnare the demon that had been responsible. Now, Solomon, he was a clever bugger, no mistake. This devil that he'd captured was then pressurized and threatened until he gave up the names of everybody in the gang, the whole six dozen of us, from Bael to Andromalius. I was about the only one who put up any sort of fight, but it was ultimately pointless. Solomon had got us dead to rights and set us all to work building his temple for him, in a sort of community service scheme. We got our own back though. There's troubles that we built into that temple and its site that people wouldn't understand the scale of for three thousand years or more.

"Since then we've roamed the lower and the upper worlds unsupervised, having adventures, dooming occultists, pursuing various hobbies and that sort of thing. In mortal terms, we're probably best seen as living patterns made out of distinct and different urges, different energies. We're also a dimension down from the three-sided human realm, in that compared to you we're flat like parquet flooring, although naturally our tessellations are much more elaborate.

"We've had the time, since we were first cast down, to come to terms with our condition and to understand our place in the divine arrangement. We believe that we, like all created things, have the capacity to change and grow. It is our hope that in a thousand or so mortal years we shall again attain the limitless, exalted state that we were born to. Mankind is the sole impediment to our ambitions. If we are to reach the highest realm from our current location in the lowest, then the middle realm must first be pushed up from below, ahead of us. If not, our one alternative is clawing our way through you, I'm afraid, should we desire to ever see the sun again."

Outside, the heavens changed from black to mauve to gold, from gold to grey, from Tuesday night to Tuesday morning. As non-standard Sam O'Day flapped backwards down the days with Michael Warren in his rustling arms, he was in one compartment of his Chinese Box intelligence still calculating means by which he might exploit his meeting with the boy. There was somebody in the Boroughs, waiting unsuspectingly some decades down the line, that the arch-demon wanted killed, and someone else he wanted saved. There might yet be some way he could persuade this trusting child to help with one or both of these endeavours.

Tacking against the cold drafts of the unending corridor, they swooped through pale dawn into blacked-out small hours and the miles of Monday midnight. In the east, the sunset of the afternoon on which his passenger had died was looming. Evidently having realised that the devil's narrative was over, his dependent with the bright churned-butter locks had rapidly devised another pointed question.

"Well, what I don't understand wiz what you're doing in the Boroughs when you're so important. Why aren't you off somewhere famous like Jerusalem or Egypt?"

The sky above the arcade was now molten as they came out of a graded lilac dusk. Though faintly riled by the young whippersnapper's disbelieving tone, the fiend conceded that the point raised was a fair one, which deserved an answer.

"Frankly, I'd have thought it would be fairly obvious, even to you, that someone who has access to these timeless higher reaches can quite easily be almost everywhere at once. I'm not *just* in the Boroughs, and on this specific day in 1959 I'm up to mischief all over what people used to call the Holy Land, and in a lot of other volatile and sunny spots as well. But if I'm honest with you, as indeed I'm forced to be, I have grown very fond of this half-a-square-mile of dirt across the centuries.

"For one thing, well over a thousand years ago the Master Builders chose this town to site their rood, their cross-stone, marking out this land's load-bearing centre. There, down on the lowly district's southeast corner, there is England's crux. Out from this central point extends a web of lines, connective creases on the map of space-time linking one place with another, paths imprinted on the fabric of reality by multiple human trajectories. People have journeyed to this crucial juncture from America, from Lambeth and, if we include the monk who followed the instructions of the builders in delivering their cross-stone, from Jerusalem itself. Though all these regions be remote one from another upon the material plane, seen from these higher mathematic reaches they are joined in the most gross and obvious of ways. Indeed, they're almost the same place.

"The destinies of these locations are entangled in a way that living people cannot see. They act upon and so affect each other, but remotely, at a distance. If the monk I mentioned hadn't come here from Jerusalem in the eighth century, come here from hallowed ground near where the lads and I built Solomon his temple, then there would have been no channel for the energies of the Crusades when they went crackling back from this site to Jerusalem some three hundred years later. And of course, after one of the earlier Crusades, one of your Norman knights was good enough to build a perfect replica, in Sheep Street, of the temple that King Solomon had made us put up for him in the Holy City. In the lattice of event and consequence, your meagre borough is a vital crossroads whereat war and wonder meet to shake each other by the hand. No, mark my words, this neighbourhood has fights and fires that make it fascinating to things such as I, and also less ignoble presences.

"Beyond all that, though, do you know, I've rather come to like the people here as well. Like is perhaps too strong a word, but let us say I feel a certain sympathy and kinship. Destitute and dirty, drunk as often as they can afford, avoided with revulsion and distaste by anyone of breeding, they, like me and mine, know what it is to be cast down and made into a demon. Well, good luck to them. Good luck to all of us disreputable devils."

From the lodestone heights of sundown, Michael Warren and the fiend began a slow sycamore-pod descent into the languid summer atmospheres of Monday afternoon. Over the see-through arcade ceiling up above them, lines of polar white described the jewel-faced contours of an algebraic cirrus that unfolded against breathtaking cerulean. Below, the Pianola-music of the Attics' floor was coming closer with its rows of great square spy-holes opening onto world and time, onto the gemstone snarl of Satan's Guts.

Upon the corridor's north side, dismembered Sam O'Day could see the pitch-sealed woodwork of the balcony where he'd first apprehended the small dressing gown-wrapped pilgrim, and, a little further down, the lower storeys where accreted dreams had risen up like stalagmites of psychic guano, forming a long terrace of surreal house- and shop-fronts. One of these establishments, a jumble of unconscious nonsense called 'The Snail Races,' had an alley-mouth not far away from it where a rotund old woman who was either dead, or dreaming, or else being dreamt, had set up a night-watchman's brazier on which it seemed that she was roasting chestnuts. Other than the crone, hunched over her hot coals and utterly oblivious to the devil or his youthful hostage, there was nobody about the Attics of the Breath, at least in the vicinity of this specific moment of the day. Most gratifyingly, there were no black-eyed builders stalking back and forth with trilliard cues to set about the child-abducting Duke of Hell on his return. It looked like a safe place to put the boy down until spiral Sam could work out what to do with him.

Like settling vicious blossom with his streamers rippling up above him in Meccano colours, green and red, the devil touched down lightly on the sprung pine floorboards. He made a great show of setting Michael Warren safely back on terra firma in one piece, so that the infant would feel bad for ever having doubted his infernal benefactor's honourable intentions.

"There! We're right back where I found you, and without a blonde curl out of place. I'll bet you're starting to appreciate just what a decent fellow I can be. As well, I'll bet you're worrying about exactly how you're going to pay me for the marvellous excursion we've just been on. Well, you needn't fret. I've got a tiny errand you could do for me in mind. Then we'd be quits, like we agreed. You do remember our agreement, don't you?"

The tot's eyes were darting back and forth as he in turn considered and ruled out escape routes. You could almost see the miniature cogs turning in his head before he came to the discouraging conclusion that there wasn't anywhere that he might run to where the devil couldn't snatch him up before he'd gone three paces. With his gaze still fluttering about evasively, he nodded with reluctance in response to the fiend's question.

"Yes. You said if I did you a favour sometime then you'd take me on your ride for nothing. But that wiz only a little while ago. You made it sound as if I wouldn't have to pay the favour back until a long time had gone by."

The devil smirked indulgently.

"I think you'll find that what I said was you could do a favour for me further down the line, which is to say at some point in the future. As it happens, that's exactly where my little errand's going to take you. There's a person living forty or so years due west of here, in the next century, who I'm not very happy with. What I'd be very much obliged if you'd arrange for me is to have this unpleasant person killed. Specifically, I want their breastbone smashed to flakes of chalk. I want their heart and lungs crushed into an undifferentiated pulp. Just carry out this simple task for me, and I'll magnanimously cancel all outstanding debts between us. How's that for a handsome proposition?"

Michael Warren's jaw fell open and he mutely shook his head from side to side as he began to back uncertainly away from slinky Sam O'Day. The devil sighed regretfully and took a step towards the boy. Perhaps a livid and perpetual scar across his spirit-belly would convince him that there wasn't really much room for negotiation here.

It was at this point that the sharp voice of the chestnut lady rang out from behind the demon's back.

"Not that way, dear. You come towards me. Don't let that old fright tell you what's what."

The fiend wheeled round indignantly upon the source of this ill-mannered interruption. Standing upright now beside her smoking brazier, the dream or ghost of the old biddy had pink cheeks and iron eyes that were fixed unwaveringly on the fiend. Dressed in black skirts she wore an apron that was also black, with iridescent scarabs and winged solar discs embroidered on its hem. The woman was a deathmonger, and something told the devil that her presence here did not bode well for his immediate intentions with regard to Michael Warren. She called out again, not taking her dark, beady eye from the arch-demon for an instant.

"That's a good boy. You go round him and you come to me. Don't worry, dear. I'll see he doesn't hurt you."

From the corner of his red left eye he saw the child run scampering past in the direction of the brazier's sulking glow. Incensed, the devil turned his most bone-melting glare on the old relic as he spoke directly to her.

"Oh. You'll see that I don't hurt him, will you? And how will you manage that, exactly, from the septic depths of my digestive system?"

The old girl's eyes narrowed. Stepping timidly out of the shadows of the alley-mouth behind her were a gang of dirty and delinquent-looking children, possibly the ones he'd dive-bombed earlier when him and Michael Warren had been setting off upon their flight. As the deathmonger spoke again she did so slowly, in a tone of cold deliberation.

"I'm a deathmonger, my dear, and we know all the oldest remedies. We've even got a remedy for you."

Taking one small hand from behind her back she hurled a fistful of some viscous substance on the greying coals. She then took from a pocket of her apron a small bottle of cheap scent which she upended over her night-watchman's brazier. Stale perfume hissed upon hot embers where the rancid fish-guts were already cooking, and the devil screamed. He couldn't ... aah! He couldn't stand it. An allergic spasm shuddered through his substance and his rags stood up stiff as he retched. It was the cursing conjuror in Persia, it was stinking Persia all over again and like then he could feel his very semblance starting to unravel. He boiled up into another body, an enormous brazen dragon with a bellowing three-headed man astride its back and snorting through his bull's head, lowing though his head like a black ram and stamping, stamping until all the timbers of the timeless Attics shook like straw, like water. Down below him he could see the scuttling tartan form of Michael Warren as the toddler ran to hide in the deathmonger's skirts.

He was swallowing his own volcanic spit, the nausea and wracking torment threatening to shatter him. He coughed, and down his human nose came burning snot, black blood and a confusion of exotic sub-atomic particles, mesons and anti-quarks. The devil knew he couldn't hold this form together for much longer before it collapsed into a pyroclastic flow of rage and rue. He focussed all eight of his stinging, swollen eyes upon the cowering infant, and his voice was like an atom bomb in a cathedral, cracking five of the glass panes above the Attics of the Breath.

"WE HAD A DEAL!"

Both of his hides, the man-like skin and dragon scales alike, erupted into giant blisters that had surfaces like dying bubbles, swimming with a spectrum of slick petrol colours just before they burst. Rapidly losing an entire dimension, he leaked shape and modelling into the ether. Realising that he only had sufficient power left for a flat display, the devil squirmed into a monstrous borealis, shimmering spider-lizard curtains made of light that seemed to fill the stupefying whole of the emporium. For a few moments it was as though all the boards and rafters were on fire with him, and his bird-eating eyes in headlamp clusters glared from every twisting flame, now red, now green, fire engines and gas chamber doors.

Then there was nothing left of him save a few sparks, bowling along in a fish-flavoured breeze down the eternal hallway.

RABBITS

O h, and weren't they all the talk Upstairs, the Dead Dead Gang, their muckabout and mischief round the everlasting drainpipes, famous exploits that had dished out scabs for medals? They were much loved in the shitty gutters of Elysium, wanted for questioning in four or five dimensions and admired by boys and girls throughout the whenth and linger of this shiny, well-worn century. They were a pack of quick and dirty little animals and there were far too many of them, running up and down the world all day.

They trespassed upon babies' dreams and took short cuts across the thoughts of writers, were the inspiration and ideal for every secret club and Children's Film Foundation mystery, for all the books, for every Stealthy Seven, every Fearless Five. They were the mould; they were the model with their spit oaths and their tramp marks, their precarious dens and their initiation tests, which were notoriously tough: you had to have been buried or cremated before you could join the Dead Dead Gang.

Their boss was Phyllis Painter, partially because she said so but, as well, because the gang she'd been in while alive had got a better pedigree and reputation than the mobs that all the others had to brag about. Although she'd lived on Scarletwell Street, Phyllis had been in the Compton Street Girls, who'd been several cuts above the Green Gang or the Boroughs Boys or any of that scruffy lot. It weren't that they were better scrappers, obviously. More that they thought about things for a bit before they did them, which was more than could be said for all the lads. *We are the Compton girls, We are the Compton girls, We mind our manners, We spend our tanners, We are respected wherever we go, We can dance, We can sing, We can do anything, 'Cause we are the Compton girls!* Of course, all that had been some time ago, but Phyllis could still be relied upon to take command if there was trouble.

Therefore, as she stood now a safe distance back behind the stern deathmonger and her brazier, watching an important demon come to pieces brilliantly like a Guy Fawkes Night accident, there was a measure of grim satisfaction in her pursed lips and her narrowed eyes. It was a pity, Phyllis thought, that this high-ranking devil would soon sputter out of visible existence altogether. If he only left a smoking length of his barbed tail, or, better still, a skull with horns, Phyllis could nail it to the ghost of the old town's north gate. Then all six dozen demons, which she thought of as a rougher and more grown-up rival crew, would know to leave this district of Mansoul alone, would know it was the hallowed, yellowed turf of the Dead Dead Gang. And then all the devils round here would be little ones like her, her young 'un Bill, and Handsome John; like Reggie Bowler and Drowned Marjorie. Then they'd have nothing else to do except play out until a bedtime that would never come, above the drowsy days in their decrepit, sweet forever.

Phyllis had been out of the long dream-jitty's far end and halfway up Spring Lane before she'd realised Michael Warren wasn't following behind her anymore. She'd pondered for a moment over whether it was really worth the effort which would be entailed in going back and finding him, eventually deciding that, most probably, she better had. That business with there being no one in the Attics of the Breath to greet him when he died smacked of suspicious circumstances if not outright funny business. You could never tell. This pipsqueak in pyjamas might turn out to be important or, if not, he'd be at least an entertaining novelty and a potential new recruit. With this in mind she'd whistled up the other members of her crowd, and they'd set out to scout the shifting neighbourhood for the post-mortem toddler. Her and Bill had searched the memory of shops. The other three had scoured the Attics in case he was acting up and hiding.

Finally Drowned Marjorie had spotted the lost child up near the curved, transparent roof of the arcade, apparently a prisoner to one of the more spiteful fiends that were upon occasion to be found about the area. When the flaming horror had appeared to see them and had dived, they'd run like Billy-oh until they could be sure he wasn't following and then regrouped at The Snail Races to discuss what they should do. Phyllis herself had favoured visiting the Works to notify the builders, as she'd planned originally, but then her Bill pointed out that being builders they'd already know. Taking his hat off so that he could scratch his black curls in the search for inspiration, Reggie Bowler had suggested that they wait in ambush for the demon-king. However, when Drowned Marjorie had sensibly enquired as to the next part of the plan, asking what they would do if the arch-devil actually showed up, Reggie had put his hat back on and turned moodily silent.

At last Handsome John, who Phyllis secretly admired, had said that they should find a deathmonger. If builders weren't available to deal with this or were too busy elsewhere, and if there weren't any saints around then a deathmonger would be the next-highest figure of authority. Drowned Marjorie had timidly suggested Mrs. Gibbs who had, in life, made such a lovely job of Marjorie herself when the bespectacled and tubby six-year-old had been pulled from the cold brown river under Spencer Bridge. Both Handsome John and Phyllis had said that they'd also heard of Mrs. Gibbs during their mortal days down in the Boroughs, which made the decision more or less unanimous.

The five of them had then spread out to comb the nearer reaches of Mansoul for the respected senior deathmonger, eventually locating her inside a fusty dream of the Green Dragon's lounge bar, near the Attics of the Breath above the Mayorhold in the early 'Thirties. Mrs Gibbs had looked up from her ghostly half of stout and not-exactly-smiled at them.

"Well now, my dears, what can I do for you?"

They'd told her about Michael Warren and the fiend, or more precisely Phyllis had, being the only one involved in this adventure since its outset. Handsome John and Mrs. Gibbs alike had both looked startled when they heard the child's full name, with the deathmonger suddenly becoming very grave and serious as she asked Phyllis for the details of the devil that they'd seen abducting the small boy. What was his colouration like? What did he smell of? What could they remember of his general disposition? Having next received, respectively, the answers 'red and green', 'tobacco' and 'extremely cross', the deathmonger had swiftly reached a diagnosis.

"That sounds like the thirty-second spirit, dear. He's one of the important and ferocious ones, who'll give you more than just a nasty bite. He's wicked, and it's just as well you've come to me. Take me to where you saw him with this little lad and I'll give him a talking to, tell him to pick on somebody his own size. I shall need a brazier or some sort of stove, and other things that I can pick up on the way. Come on. Look lively, now."

In Phyllis Painter's estimation there were few things more impressive than a deathmonger, alive or otherwise. Of all the people in the world, these fearless women were the only ones attending to the gates at either end of life, were in effect doing the timeless business of Mansoul while they were still amongst the living. No other profession had a link so seamless between what folk did when they were down in the twenty-five thousand nights and what their jobs were afterwards, when all of that was done. Deathmongers, living, always had an air about them that suggested they were half-aware of simultaneously having an existence on a higher floor. Some of them, posthumously, would return to funerals they'd arranged during their lifetimes so that they could be the one to welcome the deceased on their disoriented arrival in the Upstairs world, a continuity of service and a dedication to one's job that Phyllis thought was awesome. Taking care of people from their cradles to their graves was one thing, but to take responsibility for how they fared beyond that point was quite another.

They'd found Mrs. Gibbs a smouldering brazier left over from a market-trader's nightmare, which both Handsome John and Reggie Bowler carried carefully between them, old rags wrapped around their hands. The deathmonger had called in at the ghost of the fishmonger's, Perrit's in Horsemarket, and had obtained fish-guts from a man that she referred to as "the Sheriff".

Handing the malodorous parcel, wrapped in newspaper, to Mrs. Gibbs across his counter, the fishmonger with the hook nose and the huge moustache had simply grunted "Devils, wiz it?", to which Mrs. Gibbs responded with a nod and with a faintly weary "Arr" of affirmation.

When the Dead Dead Gang and Mrs. Gibbs had made their way back to the section of the Attics that was the specific afternoon in 1959 where Phyllis had first chanced on Michael Warren, there was hardly anyone about. They saw the dream-self of a hard-faced woman in her forties, standing staring out in puzzlement across the endless sea of wood-framed apertures before she shook her head and wandered off down the arcade. She had red hands that looked like boiled bacon, so that Phyllis thought she might be somebody who did a lot of laundry. Also, she was in the nude. Her Bill and Reggie Bowler started smirking about this last detail until Phyllis told them to grow up, knowing full well they never would.

Meanwhile, the deathmonger instructed the two bigger lads to set their pot of hot coals down within the entrance of the cobbled alley that led from the Attics off into the lanes of jumbled memory beyond, that Phyllis and her pals called the Old Buildings.

"You can put it there, my dears. If this is where that awful creature stole the child from, you can bet that this is where he'll bring him back to when he's done with him. I've got me fish's innards from off the Sheriff, and I think I've got a drop of scent tucked in a pocket of my apron, so that we'll be ready for him when he comes."

Mrs. Gibbs's aprons were almost as famous in Mansoul as was the death-monger herself. She owned a pair of them, just as she had when she was still Downstairs: the white one with embroidered butterflies around the hem, for hatches, and the black one, for despatches. In this upper realm she wore her blinding pinafore adorned with butterflies if she were welcoming some just-departed soul up gasping through a floor-window into the Attics of the Breath, into a bigger life outside of time. Her black apron, in life, had been a plain one without any decoration, though from how it looked at present it would seem that Mrs. Gibbs had always thought of it as something more elaborate. Around its edge were scarab beetles picked out in green iridescent thread, Egyptian styli and Kohl-cornered eyes stitched in metallic gold. She only wore this one when someone needed seeing off, and Phyllis wondered how the deathmonger had known to put it on today. Most probably it was just something she'd felt in her water, in her dust, her atoms. You could always sort of tell when devils were about. There was that smell, and everyone felt quarrelsome and fed up with themselves.

The six of them had waited there a while, lurking around the alley-mouth. Drowned Marjorie and little Bill had burgled a few lumps of slack out of the nearby dream of Wiggins's coal-yard so that Mrs. Gibbs could keep her brazier going until Michael Warren and the fiend showed up, if they were ever going to. Phyllis and Handsome John stood leaning up against the window of The Snail Races, staring up at the unfolding diagrams of weather over the emporium, out through the glass panes of the arcade roof. Faceted clouds crumpled impossibly, traced in white lines upon a perfect, shimmering blue. Neither of the two youngsters spoke, and Phyllis wondered for a moment if John might not take her clammy hand. Instead he turned away and peered through the shop window at one of the decorated model snails, a white one with a red cross painted on its metal shell to make it look like a toy ambulance. She tried to keep the disappointment from her voice when John asked what she thought of it, and said she thought it wiz all right. Sometimes she wondered if it was her scarf of rabbits what put people off.

They'd not been standing there for very long when Reggie Bowler, who'd gone wandering on his own along the hallway to the west, came haring back down the arcade excitedly, dodging between the fifty-foot-square apertures with one hand raised to hold his dented hat on and his long Salvation Army overcoat flapping about his ankles as he ran.

"They're comin' out the sunset! I just seen 'em! Bugger me, that devil's big."

Phyllis was squinting down the length of the great hall in the direction Reggie's flailing sleeve had indicated, at the tangerine and bronze eruption of that evening's sunset going on above the glass roof in the west. She could make out a flickering dot in silhouette against the riot of bloody light, a blackened paper scrap high in the upper reaches of the Attics that appeared to be becoming larger as it flew towards them from the future. Reggie had been right. She'd been too busy running when it dived towards them earlier to get a proper look at it, but this was certainly no minor imp.

Reasoning that the devil might have had more time to study Phyllis and her friends than they'd had time to study it, she ordered everyone into the jitty so that they should not be recognised and give the game away.

"Come on. Get in the alleyway and behind Mrs. Gibbs, so 'e don't see us. Just leave everything to 'er."

Nobody seemed inclined to argue with this eminently sensible idea. By now the fiend had drifted closer so that its alarming size was more apparent and likewise its colouring of flashing red and green, as if a cup of salt had been thrown on a bonfire. Even Reggie Bowler made no protest when instructed to take shelter behind Mrs. Gibbs. He'd evidently reconsidered his original idea, which had been to somehow leap upon the demon's back from hiding.

Handsome John, surprisingly and gratifyingly, took Phyllis by one skinny arm and steered her to the safety of the jitty. He was looking back, the pink glow from the west upon his lean face and his wave of sandy hair. He frowned and creased the sooty and poetic smudge of shadow round his pale eyes, luminously grey like torch-beams playing over water.

"Bloody hell, Phyll. It looks like a Jerry biplane coming down to buzz the trenches. Let's get in the alley where it's safe."

They sheltered breathless in the jitty entrance with their backs so flat against the red brick wall that Phyllis thought they might leave all their colours and their lines behind like tattoo transfers when they peeled themselves away. Her Bill was nearest to the corner, circumspectly poking out his ginger head and then retracting it, keeping an eye on the approaching demon's progress. Mrs. Gibbs, positioned at the centre of the alley mouth and in full view of the enormous corridor, calmly continued tending to her fire with a bent poker, which had been inside the brazier when they'd found it. As she let the air between the sullen coals a blacksmith glow flared up to under-light her face, impassive, with its skin like autumn fruit. Bill called out from the row of children's far end, trying to keep the nervousness out of his voice.

"He's circling in to land, and he looks horrible. He's got horns, and his eyes are different colours."

Phyllis lifted one small hand and made the rabbit sign, her middle- and ring-fingers touched against her thumb to form the nose, her first and little fingers raised like ears. As quiet as rabbits in the grass the whole gang tiptoed forward stealthily to join Bill near the corner, from which vantage they could see more of the mile-wide Attics' floor. Despite their advance warning, all of them except for Mrs. Gibbs jumped visibly when the infernal being finally came into view, drifting down slowly from above like an immense and lurid parrot-coloured blossom, the pyjama-clad child held fast in its sunburned arms.

One of the creature's legs uncurled beneath it with the leather boot's toe pointed dancer-fashion, nimbly alighting on the pine boards in between the rows of sunken vats. For all of its apparent mass the monster landed almost silently, facing away from them with its bright tatters fluttering upward from the draught of the descent, in cockscomb red and poison apple green.

The glamour that it wore was very like a man, albeit one some eight or nine feet tall. A leather priest's hat hung between its shoulders from a cord tied underneath its bearded chin, revealing a long mane of curling russet hair from which protruded two horns, like a goat's. From where she stood beside John, Phyllis couldn't see its face, for which she was immensely grateful. She had never seen a devil this close to before, and frankly she was having enough trouble trying to cope with its upsetting atmosphere, without the added stress of thinking what she'd do if it should turn and look at her.

With a surprising gentleness, the ragged fireball of coagulated ill intentions set down Michael Warren on the Attics' floor before it. The poor little bugger stood there quaking in his striped pyjamas and his dressing gown, which looked the worse for wear since Phyllis had last seen it. There were small tears in the tartan fabric where the monster's claws had evidently snagged, and on the collar and the shoulders were discoloured patches where it looked as if somebody had dripped battery acid. One spot was still smoking faintly. Poor kid, he looked scared to death and then scared back to life again. Although he stood so he was facing towards Phyllis and the jitty-mouth he clearly couldn't take his eyes off of the devil looming over him, and so was yet to notice her.

The thing seemed to be talking to the little boy, stooping towards the trembling infant with an air that looked as menacing as it was condescending. It was speaking in a voice too low to hear from where she stood, the gas-jet roaring of a forest fire ten miles away, but its intentions were transparent. Phyllis recognised the hunched, intimidating bully posture from a dozen Boroughs bruisers, although unlike them and contrary to everything her mother had once said to her, this bully didn't look as if he'd turn out to be secretly a coward. Phyllis doubted that there could be anything much worse than him for him to be afraid of, and she wondered for the first time whether Mrs. Gibbs would be enough to deal with this.

It had appeared to Phyllis, at that point, as though the rustling horror had suggested something awful to the toddler, who'd begun to back away, shaking his flaxen head. Whatever the proposal had involved, it didn't look as though the fiend was in a mood to tolerate refusal. With its variegated foliage shivering threateningly it took one crouching step forward pursuing the retreating child, one callused hand raised to show off the sharpened ivory of its fingernails as if it meant to open Michael Warren like a pea-pod made of flannelette, and Phyllis Painter closed her eyes. She had expected the next thing she heard to be a bubbling scream, like a coursed hare. Instead, it was the reassuring cradle-creak of Mrs. Gibbs's voice.

"Not that way, dear. You come towards me. Don't let that old fright tell you what's what."

Cautiously, Phyllis let her eyelids part to feathered, blurry chinks.

She'd been surprised to find that Michael Warren was not dead, or, anyway, no deader than he had been a few moments back. The little boy had by now noticed Phyllis and the gang, alerted by the interjection of the deathmonger. He'd ceased to back towards the far wall of the vast arcade and was now edging to one side in an attempt to come towards them and the alleyway, while still giving the fiend as wide a berth as possible.

The devil stood stock-still for an exaggerated instant, then turned slowly until it was facing Mrs. Gibbs and the five cowering children. Every one of them except the deathmonger had drawn a sharp breath at this first glimpse of its archetypal features, in which utter evil was expressed so perfectly that it became a horrible cartoon, grotesque and terrifying to the point where it was almost comical, although not quite. Its face was a boiled mask on which the red-brown brows and whiskers drifted in a thick chemical steam. Its ears rose up to curling points but, unlike those of elves in picture-story books, in real life this looked sickening and deformed. The horns were dirty white with rusty smears around the base that might have been dried blood, and, as her Bill had pointed out, its eyes were different colours. They had different stories in them, almost different personalities. The red one radiated torture-chamber interludes, thousand-year grudges and campaigns of merciless attrition, while the green one told of doomed affairs, bruised childhoods and of passions fiercer, more exhausting, than malaria. Together they were like a pair of painted bull's-eyes and were fixed, unwaveringly, on Mrs. Gibbs.

The deathmonger did not appear to be impressed. She held the creature's gaze while speaking almost casually to Michael Warren.

"That's a good boy. You go round him and you come to me. Don't worry, dear. I'll see he doesn't hurt you."

Clearly very much afraid despite the deathmonger's encouragements, the little squirt (who, Phyllis Painter had already made her mind up, was a bit soft) nonetheless heeded her cue to make a break for it. He scampered in a wide arc to the devil's left and everybody else's right, so scared of getting close to his tormenter that his route would take him up as far as The Snail Races before he came doubling back towards the alley and his rescuers. Phyllis and her four cohorts had unpeeled themselves off of the jitty's red brick wall and shuffled timidly to form a ragged semi-circle, some feet safely back from Mrs. Gibbs. Fiddling in nervous agitation with her rabbit necklace, Phyllis's attention darted between Michael and the demon, so she'd caught the moment when the fiend's appalling glare swept sideways to take note of the escaping toddler and then returned with a renewed vindictiveness to settle once again on the old woman in the scarab apron, standing prodding at her brazier. The things the creature's gaze had promised Mrs. Gibbs were things that Phyllis didn't want to name or think about. Its viscous voice was like a burning sulphur treacle when it spoke, purple and toxic.

"Oh. You'll see that I don't hurt him, will you? And how will you manage that, exactly, from the septic depths of my digestive system?"

Phyllis, if she'd still been able to, would almost certainly have wet herself. It had said it was going to eat them, though not in as many words. Not only eat them but digest them, their immortal essences still conscious in the scalding darkness of a monster's bowel. At just that moment Phyllis had been on the verge of telling the arch-devil that it could have Michael Warren and do what it wanted with him, if it didn't wolf them down and turn them into demon-poo. The deathmonger was made of sterner stuff, however. She had stared into whatever abattoir-cum-jungle chaos seethed behind the nightmare's mismatched irises, and as yet had not even blinked. Her voice was level, unaffected as she answered.

"I'm a deathmonger, my dear, and we know all the oldest remedies. We've even got a remedy for you."

What happened next was one of those things which occurred so fast that nobody could tell the precise order of events until much later, when they'd all gone over it a dozen times. Mrs. Gibbs had been holding a soft handful of fish-offal out of sight behind her back, and now she brought it forth to fling on the hot coals in a dramatic, spraying arc. The rancid hearts and lights and livers hissed and sizzled as they melted, but the deathmonger was already at work retrieving from her apron a small tear-shaped bottle of what looked like cheap scent bought from bottom Woolworth's, or the wistful dream of some. Removing first its cap with practised ease, the deathmonger inverted this above her brazier so that its contents rained down on the glowing stones. Steam billowed up in an expanding column that smelled absolutely vile, like wild flowers growing in a filthy toilet bowl. Even for Phyllis, who had long since ceased to notice the perfume of her own rabbit-garland, this was an eye-watering experience. The fiend's reaction to the rich and singular bouquet, though, was much worse.

It arched, spine rippling like a nauseous cat, and all its coloured rags stood up on end in flattened triangles, as though they were the spines of a toy hedgehog. The infernal regent spat and shuddered, and the edges of its image started curdling biliously, blotched molten white as with a ruined photograph, afflicted by an acne of burning magnesium. On contact with the noxious fumes from the deathmonger's brazier, the devil's substance seemed to become vaporous itself, crumpling to a dense and heavy gas in writhing billows that retained the creature's basic shape yet had about their texture something of the intricate and craggy look you found in cauliflower. As if a gas-main had been burst, this nine-foot cloud of poison fog erupted upwards suddenly, became a red-green pillar of smoke hundreds of yards high. Phyllis had watched with ghastly fascination as the towering cumulus had seemed to knit itself together in a new configuration, so enormous and so complicated that she couldn't tell at first what she was looking at.

Oh blimey. Flippin' heck, it had been terrible.

It had been a gigantic dragon, gaudy red and green glints flashing from a million scales as big as high-hat cymbals. Sitting lewdly naked there astride the broad back of the roaring, stamping juggernaut there was a being which, despite its horrifying size, had the proportions of a baby or a dwarf. A snake-tail thrashed behind it, although Phyllis couldn't tell if this belonged to the infuriated mount or to its rider. She supposed that they were both the same thing in the end. Its heads, for it had three of them, were left to right those of a maddened bull, a raging homicidal tyrant in a ruby crown, and a black ram with rolling eyes as if in rut. It held in one fist an iron lance, high as the Eiffel Tower and caked thick with dried blood and excrement, as if it had run something through from bum to brain. A banner flew from this, green with a red device that was all arrows, curls and crosses, and the agonised and furious fiend pounded the lance's hilt against the Attics' floor in screeching, bellowing exasperation. Worst of all, in Phyllis's opinion, had been the thing's feet as it crouched there on its prismatic, smouldering steed. The hell-king's calves and ankles tapered gruesomely to pink and bristling stalks, from which sprouted the webbed feet of some monstrous duck. The webbing, stretched between the yellowed digits, was an unappealing grey with white discoloured patches as though from some waterfowl-disease, and it made Phyllis queasy just to look at it.

The Attics of the Breath were shaking from the dragon's footfalls and the unrelenting thunder made by that appalling lance, crashing repeatedly against the wooden floorboards until Phyllis had thought that the whole Upstairs was going to collapse, all of its dreams and ghosts and architecture tumbling through a great hole in the sky upon the startled mortal world below. From where she'd stood, huddled near Handsome John and peeking out between her parted fingers, Phyllis had distantly taken in the tartan blur of Michael Warren hurtling into view from somewhere to her right, his terrified wail rising like the horn of an approaching train as he came stumbling into the alley-mouth and hid behind the black, capacious skirts of the deathmonger. Phyllis barely noticed him, all her attention fixed on the jaw-dropping spectacle that loomed above them with its three heads almost brushing the glass canopy which covered the immense arcade.

Its anger and distress were hideous to behold. A great convulsion seized it and it seemed to cough or vomit through its central, nearly-human mouth, a blazing spew of fire and blood and tar along with other more unfathomable debris that trailed scribbled lines of light behind its fragments as they spiralled into nothingness. The devil looked as though it were about to fall apart and, what's more, looked as if it knew it. Summoning what Phyllis hoped might be its last reserves of strength and concentration it had focussed all its bleary eyes ... those of the bull, the ram, the howling tyrant and the dragon that they rode ... upon the small boy in pyjamas peering currently in dread around the black-draped bulge of the deathmonger's hip. The demon pointed down at Michael Warren with the claw-tipped index finger of its lance-free hand, and when it screamed its farewell curse it was the worst noise Phyllis Painter ever heard, alive or dead. It sounded like a lot of big jet aircraft taking off at once, or like the whole world's elephants in one berserk stampede. A mighty *whuff* of blue flame belched out from the central crowned head as it opened its vast mouth to speak, and as one Phyllis and the Dead Dead Gang all took their hands off of their eyes where they'd been using them as blind-folds, clapping them across their ears instead. It didn't do much good, and everybody could still hear exactly what the devil shouted at the infant as he quaked there behind Mrs. Gibbs.

"WE HAD A DEAL!"

This was about what Phyllis would expect from Michael Warren. All she'd had to do was take her eyes off him for half a second and he'd evidently gone and signed a compact with a thing from the undying furnace. Was the kid half-sharp, or what? Even her little Bill, who could be silly as a bag of arse-holes, even Bill would never do a stupid thing like that. She'd had to forcibly remind herself that Michael Warren had been only three or four when he'd expired and even younger than he looked at present, whereas her and Bill had both been a bit older. On the other hand, you couldn't just excuse the boy because of youthful inexperience: the fact that Michael Warren wasn't five years old and yet had somehow managed to not only die but also to enrage one of the great biblical forces within minutes of his death suggested that the child was not just clumsy but was bordering on the catastrophic. How could someone who looked so much like an Ovalteeny have upset a horror from the pit so badly, in so short a time? She should, she thought, have heeded her first instincts and just left the dozy little bugger wandering round the Attics of the Breath in his pyjamas.

But she hadn't. She had always had a soft spot for the genuinely pathetic, that was Phyllis Painter's trouble. It was one of her worst failings. She remem-bered when she'd been alive, playing down Vicky Park with Valerie and Vera Pickles and their younger brother Sidney. All three kids came from a family of fourteen at the bottom end of Spring Lane, just down past Spring Gardens, but three-year-old Sidney Pickles was the ugliest of the family by far. He was the ugliest kid that she had ever seen, poor little beggar. No, she shouldn't laugh, but, honestly, Sid Pickles. He'd a face with hardly any features on it, like he'd drawn it on himself with a wax crayon. He'd got bow legs and a lisp, short-tongued was what they called it then, and when he'd waddled up to where her and his elder sisters were constructing tents from bits of sacking by the stream there in Victoria Park, they'd realised from the smell exactly what his problem was, even before he'd proudly told them all.

"I'm thyit methelf."

Vera and Valerie had both refused point blank to go with Sidney on the long walk over Spencer Bridge back to Spring Lane, which meant that Phyllis felt she'd got no option but to take the boy herself, although he stank. Stank to high heaven. What made matters worse was that he'd catch the eye of every passer-by between the park and Spring Lane to triumphantly announce "I'm thyit methelf", even though Phyllis begged him not to and despite that fact that his confession, from the looks on people's faces, clearly told them nothing that they hadn't by then worked out for themselves. She'd only volunteered to walk him home when it became apparent no one else was going to do it, which was more or less the reason she'd helped Michael Warren up out of his life onto the boardwalks of Mansoul. That, and the fact that he'd seemed troublingly familiar. Even if since then he'd somehow incurred a demon's unrelenting wrath, at least he didn't have a squinting turnip for a head like Sidney Pickles and at least he hadn't shit himself, as far as Phyllis knew.

She tried now to draw some slim consolation from these dubious benefits while staring up transfixed at the enormous demon, which had boils and welts as big as tractor wheels erupting from its hide, standing there writhing in the noxious fug from the deathmonger's brazier. These blisters popped and sprayed their hot gold pus in a fine aerosol, like bursts of burning pollen or like puffball detonations. Looking closer with the deeper vision of the afterlife, she saw that the infinitesimally tiny droplets were in actuality a spray of blazing numbers, mathematic symbols and illuminated letters from a wriggly foreign alphabet that Phyllis thought was Arabic. This churning tumble of notations flared like sparks for just an instant, then were gone. It was as if all of the devil's facts and sums were leaking out of it. It almost seemed as though the demon were deflating, although Phyllis knew that didn't quite describe what she was seeing.

More precisely, as the neon characters and numerals escaped, the fiend appeared not so much to be going down like a flat tyre as it did to be something that had in reality always been flat. Perhaps because it had a bull's head and a ram's, she found herself reminded of the toy farm animals she'd played with as a little girl. These had been lovely painted illustrations of fat roosters, pigs and cows, printed on shiny paper and then glued to sheets of wood cut to the right shape with a jigsaw. Standing on their slotted wooden bases, they'd been absolutely realistic if you only looked at them side-on. You barely had to change the angle of your view, though, and they'd start to flatten out and look all wrong. Seen from behind their permanently raised and swishing tails, the solid-looking beasts were hardly there. This was the same thing that was happening now to the colossal, many-headed monster as it spewed out phosphorescent algebra from yard-wide pimples and collapsed into a detailed and painstakingly embellished drawing of itself.

From the expressions on its four vast faces, even this reduced condition was a struggle to maintain. Venting a final booming snarl of loathing and frustration, the huge apparition shattered into countless tongues of Christmas-coloured radiance that seemed to lick from every board and rafter in the Attics of the Breath, as though the whole emporium were on fire with the unravelled fiend's dispersing imagery. In every flare there was the same repeated pattern, intricate and squirming in a filigree of what looked now like lime-green newts, now like a scarlet lace of murderous tarantulas. Multiple lizard or else spider shapes at different scales knitted themselves into the most deranging wallpaper design that Phyllis could conceive of, all of this reiterated in each twist of flame throughout the echoing arcade.

Then it was over and all of the fiend's spent fireworks fizzled into nothing, leaving only the pervasive stench of perfumed fish-guts and an atmosphere of slapped shock in that monumental corridor. The devil-king was gone.

Mrs. Gibbs merely bobbed her chin once in a quiet and workmanlike display of satisfaction, then produced a handkerchief that had a bee embroidered on one edge to wipe the haddock sheen from her pink fingertips. Politely, she instructed Handsome John and Reggie Bowler to lift the no-longer-smouldering but still offensive brazier and lug it to some far remove along the jitty where, if no one dreamed about it for a week or two, it would break down into the homogeneous mind-residue from which the avenues and alleys of Mansoul, the Second Borough, were constructed. As the bigger boys wrapped rags around their palms again and grudgingly bent to their task, the death-monger fastidiously folded her now-fishy hanky, tucking it away into whatever obscure corner of her funeral pinafore it had emerged from. Having cleaned and tidied herself thus, she turned her head and peered as best she could at Michael Warren who, in spite of the arch-demon's disappearance, was still sheltering behind the black Niagara of her skirts.

Phyllis was still recovering from the events of the past several minutes. It occurred to her that, frightening as the visitor from Hell had been, this rosy-cheeked old lady was the terror everybody should watch out for. Death-mongers alive were nothing else if not formidable, but dead they were a good sight more impressive. Mrs. Gibbs was a rotund black skittle shape sporting a bonnet, almost seen in silhouette against the dazzling blueness over the arcade as Phyllis, Michael Warren and the other titches in the gang looked up at her. She seemed to be considering the little blonde boy as he stood there and regarded her uncertainly in his pyjamas, slippers and plum tartan dressing gown, which had been stained by something yellow and sulphuric, more than likely demon-slobber.

"So, now, you're this Michael Warren that I've heard so much about. Don't shuffle round behind me when I try to talk to you, my dear. Come out where I can see you proper."

Nervously, the toddler sidled from behind the deathmonger and stood in front of her, as he'd been bidden. His blue doll-eyes darted everywhere, from Mrs. Gibbs to Phyllis Painter, then to her Bill and Drowned Marjorie.

He looked at everyone as if they were his firing squad, with not a word of thanks for saving him from hellfire and damnation just a moment back. As he returned his apprehensive gaze to Mrs. Gibbs he tried to give her an engaging smile, but it came out like a peculiar wince. The deathmonger looked pained.

"There's no need to be frit of me, my dear. Now, did that brute do anything to hurt you when he had you in his claws? What was that business that he mentioned about how you had a deal with him? I hope you've not made any promises to a rough chap like that."

The freshly dead child moved his weight from one plaid slipper to the other, fiddling with the sash cord of his dressing gown uneasily.

"He tolled me he wiz glowing to snake me four a raid, and shed that I could prey him back by dooming him a fever."

Her Bill guffawed rudely at the boy's derailed pronunciation, which revealed him as a new arrival in Mansoul as surely as a country twang would have betrayed him in a city. Phyllis noticed that the Warren kid's ability to make sense when he talked had taken a step backwards since she'd seen him last. When she'd escorted him across the Attics to the jitty where they were now standing, he'd appeared to be finding his Lucy-lips and was beginning to speak clearly without mangling every phrase as it was born. From his performance now, however, it seemed as though witnessing the giant fiend's extraordinary fit of pique had set him back a bit. His sentences went everywhere, like matchsticks from a box that had been opened upside-down. Luckily, Mrs. Gibbs, by virtue of her work on either side of death's sharp corner, was conversant with the diction of the recently deceased and could take Michael Warren's gibberish in her stride.

"I see. And did he take you for this outing that he'd promised you, my dear? Where did he fly you to, if I might ask?"

At this the nipper's face lit up, as though a grown-up had just asked him to describe which ride he'd liked best at a funfair that he'd visited.

"He shook me down into nixed Fraidy night, to where my hours wiz instant Andrew's Road. Eyesore myself, and I wiz back true life again!"

Now everyone was staring in bewilderment at Michael Warren, and not on account of his exploding elocution. Everybody was too startled by what he'd just said to take much notice of the way he'd said it. Could it possibly be true? Could the arch-devil have transported the boy into the immediate future, where he'd glimpsed himself restored to life? Barring a miracle this made no sense at all, and Phyllis tried to find a more feasible explanation for the child's unlikely story. Possibly the fiend had carried him into the past and not into next Friday night, as the lad obviously believed. The devil had cold-bloodedly deceived the kid by giving him a glimpse of himself back within the bosom of his family, then had told him this was something that would happen in a few days time, rather than something which had already occurred, a week or two before the toddler had choked to death. It was a cruel and spiteful hoax, intended to crush Michael Warren's infant soul by offering false hope. While Phyllis much preferred her cynical interpretation to the more miraculous alternative, something about it didn't ring entirely true.

For one thing, Phyllis and her gang had seen the demon streaking off with Michael into the red west with their own eyes, the same direction that they'd just seen him returned from. *West is future, East is past, all things linger, all things last.* Not only that, but it was well known that a devil had no more capacity to lie than did a page of hard statistics. Like statistics, they could only seriously mislead. Moreover, although Phyllis hated demons generally, she had to grudgingly admit that they were seldom petty. Playing heartless tricks on three-year-olds was probably beneath them, or at least beneath the more high-ranking fiends, such as the one who'd stolen Michael Warren had appeared to be. Of course, this line of reasoning led to the plainly unacceptable conclusion that the boy was right, and that within a day or two he'd be alive again, back with his family in St. Andrew's Road. Phyllis regarded Mrs. Gibbs and saw from the deathmonger's manner as she scrutinised the little chap that the old girl had independently arrived at the same impasse in her thinking.

"Well, now, there's a fine kettle of fish. And why, I wonder, did that old snake take an interest in you in the first place? You think hard, my dear, and tell me if there's anything he said as might give me a clue."

The child in nightclothes, who was evidently unaware of the tremendous import of what he was blithering about, tried to look thoughtful for a moment and then beamed up helpfully at Mrs. Gibbs.

"He tolled me that hide claused sum trouble here Upscares."

The deathmonger looked blank at first, then slowly corrugated her age-spotted brow as if with dawning comprehension.

"Oh, my dear. You're not the little boy who's caused the falling-out between the builders? Someone told me earlier as they was having a big scrap up at the Mayorhold, on account of one of 'em had cheated in their trilliard game, but I'd not dreamed as it was you was at the bottom of it."

What was this? A fight between the builders? Phyllis gaped incredulously, and to judge by the sharp gasps that came from her Bill and Drowned Marjorie, it was the first they'd heard of it as well. Wouldn't a fight between the builders mean that the whole world would fall in half, or something terrible like that? Sounding excited by the prospect, Bill relayed his obvious enthusiasm to the deathmonger.

"Cor! Whenabouts are they having it, the angles' punch-up? I'd like to be there for that."

Not for the first time, Phyllis felt embarrassed that her kid was such an unapologetic little ruffian. Mrs. Gibbs clucked at young Bill disapprovingly.

"It's not a game, my dear, and if the builders are at odds it would seem disrespectful to be stood there goggling at them. And of course it would be very dangerous, and not a place for little children, so you put that idea right out of your head."

Though Phyllis knew he hadn't put the idea from his thoughts at all, Bill pulled his glum and reprimanded face to make the deathmonger think that he had. Mrs. Gibbs turned away from him and carried on with her appraisal of the hapless Michael Warren.

"Well, my dear, it sounds to me as if you're at the middle of some funny goings-on. I'm not surprised, given the things I know about your people and the family you come from. Even so, I've never heard the like of this. You've drawn attention from a fiend ... the thirty-second devil, who's a bad un ... and done something that has made the builders have a falling-out. On top of that, you're dead one minute and alive the next, if you're to be believed.

"Now, as regards that devil, when it said it wanted you to do a favour for it in return for giving you a ride, did it say what the favour wiz, at all?"

The little boy stopped beaming and turned pale enough to stand out in the present company of ghosts.

"He said I'd got to help him kill somebody."

Phyllis thought it was a measure of how shaken-up the thought made Michael Warren, that he'd managed to get through a sentence without garbling any words. Mind you, it was a dreadful thought, one frightening enough to cure a stutter. Bill said "fucking hell" and Phyllis slapped him hard on his bare lower leg where it stuck from under his short trousers, before Mrs. Gibbs did. With a withering sideways glance at Bill, the deathmonger turned her attention back to the suddenly worried-looking younger lad.

"Then that was very wrong of it, my dear. If it wants someone killed, then it can do it by itself. From what I hear about it, it's had more than enough practice. Frankly, I'm surprised it was allowed to snatch you up and say such awful things to you ..."

The deathmonger broke off, and cocked her head upon one side. It looked to Phyllis as though Mrs. Gibbs had just been struck by the full implications of the words that she had said, which prompted Phyllis to consider them herself. Allowed: that was the word on which the matter rested. Why had all of these outlandish breaches of the normal regulations, in the first place, been allowed? As Phyllis had observed when she was helping Michael Warren up into the Attics of the Breath, nothing in Mansoul was by accident, neither the issue of there being no one there to greet the child, nor Phyllis happening upon the scene while she was skipping homeward from a scrumping expedition. Phyllis felt the soft touch of a larger hand in these affairs, so that the memory of her flesh crawled briefly in response. From Mrs. Gibbs's face, it looked as though the deathmonger were having many of the same considerations. Finally, she spoke again.

"To be quite honest, dear, I don't know what to make of you. I have a feeling there's a lot more to all this than meets the eye, but if the builders are involved then it's too much for me to puzzle out all on my own."

At this point Handsome John and Reggie Bowler sauntered back along the jitty, brushing off their hands as they re-joined the gang, having responsibly disposed of the dream-brazier somewhere in the alley's depths. Mrs. Gibbs noted their return with a curt nod, then carried on with what she had been saying.

"As I say, my dear, I'm out my depth. What I suggest is that you don't go running off all by yourself again, or who knows what could happen? You stick with these older children, and I'm sure they'll see you don't get into any mischief. In the meantime, I intend to have a word with someone higher up than me, who knows what's going on. I think I'll call on Mr. Doddridge, and see what he's got to say. You do as you've been told, and keep safe with these boys and girls. I'll see you later on, when I've found out what's what, so you be good until I do."

With that, the deathmonger turned on her heel and glided off along the great emporium, heading east, dawnwards over the strip of flagstones bordering the Attics' mile-wide sea of wood and windows. Standing mutely in the jitty-mouth the children watched her go, a big black pillow dwindling to a pin-cushion as she receded into the arcade's far reaches, into yesterday and out of sight.

Surprised by the abruptness of the deathmonger's departure, Phyllis wasn't sure what she should think. On one hand, Phyllis understood that Mrs. Gibbs was simply getting on with things that needed doing in her usual brisk, efficient way, but on the other hand she couldn't help but feel a bit abandoned. Other than keep Michael Warren out of trouble, what were her and the Dead Dead Gang going to do with him? From what the deathmonger had said, it sounded like this moppet in a dressing gown was turning out to be a much thornier problem than he'd first appeared. If Mrs. Gibbs, who'd just stared down the worst that Hell had got to throw at her without so much as blinking, if she'd said that Michael Warren was too big a quandary for her alone, then how were Phyllis Painter and her gang expected to look after him? She fiddled agitatedly with one frayed end of the two-stranded sisal where her rabbit pelts were hung, deliberating over it.

After a moment's thought, though, Phyllis saw more sense in what the deathmonger had done by making the boy Phyllis's responsibility. There was

that feeling of a higher hand in all of this, and Phyllis knew that Mrs. Gibbs
had felt it too. In Mansoul, nothing was by accident, and given that she'd
been the first to greet the child on his arrival, this meant she was already
involved in the unfolding of events. This clingy, helpless little lad was evidently meant to be with Phyllis, not because he'd thyit himthelf and not
just because Mrs. Gibbs had said so. This was more like something designated higher up, by management, and Phyllis knew that her and her four
cronies would just have to make the best of it. Looked at in one way it was
quite an honour, and she there and then resolved that the Dead Dead Gang
would prove worthy of the task that they'd been set. She wouldn't have it
said around the Attics of the Breath how they weren't up to it, how they'd
turned out to be no better than the little hooligans that everyone already
thought they were. Between them, they'd pull off this babysitting job a treat,
and they'd show everybody. All their varied talents would be brought to
bear upon the matter, and those were considerable.

The Dead Dead Gang could be whatever they desired in the great liberty
that waited beyond life and substance. They could scurry in the bushes and
the alleys of Eternity and be the scourge of ghosts and devils, or they could
be valiant myrmidons, or stealthy savages, or master criminals. In Michael
Warren's case, with all the mysteries surrounding him, she thought that they
could be secret detective spies as easily. They'd find out who he was, and find
out what this bother was about, and ... well, they'd make sure everything
turned out all right by some means Phyllis hadn't had a chance to think of
yet. She knew that this was going several steps past the strict outline of the
babysitter role that Mrs. Gibbs had had in mind for her, but felt that she was
acting in accordance with the spirit of the deathmonger's instructions, rather
than the letter of them. If the powers that be hadn't intended Michael Warren
to get mixed up with a crowd of scruffy kids, then Phyllis wouldn't have been
skipping back across the Attics when he'd crawled up through the afterlife
trapdoor. That so unlikely an event had happened was as good as saying Phyllis Painter had been placed in charge of the pyjama-clad boy and the grand
adventure that apparently surrounded him. The parting comments Mrs.
Gibbs had made only confirmed it. Phyllis was still boss of the Beyond, and
knew the Dead Dead Gang were all depending on her to come up with some
sort of a plan, as she'd be called upon to do in all their other dead, dead games.

By now the figure of the deathmonger was lost from view in the wet
salmon light that bathed the dawn-end of the everlasting corridor. Phyllis
turned round to look at Michael Warren, wondering not for the first time who
she'd been reminded of when she'd first seen him and he'd seemed so tantalisingly familiar. She'd thought at first that there might be a faint resemblance to
Handsome John despite the five-year difference that there was in their appar-

ent ages, Michael Warren being an apparent seven and John being an apparent twelve, but looking at them now she couldn't really see it. The blonde toddler lacked the sculpted and heroic gauntness that there was about John's face, and didn't have the deep-set eyes with shadow round them in a sad, romantic soot like John did. No, she was convinced that she recalled the little boy from somewhere else, but couldn't for the death of her think where. Possibly it would come to her, but for the moment she had more important matters to attend to. Michael Warren was now looking back at Phyllis, staring up at her forlornly in his demon-distressed dressing gown with its drool-blemished collar. She returned his gaze with a no-nonsense look, then softened.

"Well? How are yer diddling? I'll bet that put the wind up yer, that devil carrying yer orf like that."

The infant nodded, gravely.

"Yes. He wizzn't very nice, although he wanted me to think he wiz. Thank you for coming back to find me and rescape me."

Phyllis sniffed and ducked her head once, modestly, dismissively. Her rotten rabbits rattled with the movement. She was pleased to note that Michael's capabilities with language were once more progressing steadily after the relapse his encounter with the demon had brought on. Perhaps he'd find his Lucy-lips yet, after all.

"Yer welcome. Now, what are we going to do with yer? What do yer say we take yer to ayr 'ideout until we can all decide on what comes next?"

The child gave a delighted beam.

"Wizzle that mean I'm in your gang?"

Oh, *now* he wanted to be made a member, did he? Well, he'd changed his tune since earlier, then. Despite the fact that Phyllis was at last beginning to develop a degree of sympathy for her pyjama-sporting stray, she had to take a firm line with him. She was leader, and if Phyllis were to bend the rules for everybody that she'd felt a pang of pity for, where would they be? She pulled a serious face and shook her strawberry blonde fringe decisively, though not unkindly.

"No. I'm sorry, but yer can't join now. Not with what yer just said about 'ow yer'll be back to life again by Friday. In the Dead Dead Gang we've got initiation ceremonies and all things like that. There's tests what yer just wouldn't pass."

Hurt and a bit indignant, Michael Warren looked as though he thought that Phyllis was just being nasty.

"Howl do you know? I might be the bestest in the test. I mighty be a champernaut."

At this point, much to Phyllis's surprise, Handsome John intervened on her behalf, placing a chummy and consoling hand upon the infant's tartan shoulder, which was flecked by fiend-foam.

"Come on, kid. Don't take it personal. She's only telling you the way things are up here. To be in the Dead Dead Gang, in the rules it says you've got to be cremated or else buried. Very nearly both in my case as it turned out, but the point is, if you're going to be alive again on Friday, then you're neither. Here, I'll tell you what, we'll let you be an honorary member for the time you're up here, like a sort of mascot or a regimental goat. Then, if one day you manage to die properly, we'll take you on full time. How's that?"

The toddler tilted back his head to scrutinise John carefully and seemed partially mollified, prepared to trust the sterling look John had about him and his reasonable tone of voice. Only a faint trace of uncertainty remained, most probably because the new boy didn't know who John was and had not been introduced to him. Phyllis decided to take care of this last oversight.

"I wiz forgetting that yer don't know anybody in the gang. This 'ere is John, and over there that's Reggie, in the 'at. Reggie's been in the gang longer than anybody, aytside me and ayr Bill, because 'e's been cold the longest. This is Marjorie, who drayned dayn Paddy's Meadow, and this is ayr Bill. We're the Dead Dead Gang, so we play ayt after dark and after death, and won't goo 'ome until we're called. Now, should you like to see ayr den? It's only dayn the jitty 'ere and up Spring Lane a bit."

Without agreeing vocally to anything that had just been proposed the little boy fell into step with the loose gaggle of dead children as they started to meander down the alleyway and left the Attics of the Breath behind them. Michael Warren trotted dutifully along over the damp, fog-coloured cobbles, in between Phyllis herself and Handsome John. The kid would first peer up at one of them and then the other, frowning slightly and still with a lot of questions clearly on his mind.

"Why did you scrawl yourselves the Dead Dead Gang? It's funny when you say it twice like that."

John chuckled, with a lovely toasty sound that Phyllis would have ate for breakfast if she could.

"Well, when we wiz alive we wiz in different gangs. Me and my brothers used to hang out in the Green Gang, Phyllis here wizzle be in the Compton Street Girls, while old Reggie wiz a member of the Gas Street Mob and then the Boroughs Boys. Drowned Marjorie, I think, wiz in a secret club from Bellbarn. Just about the only one of us who didn't grow up in the Boroughs was Phyll's little Bill, and he was in a bunch of kids up … Kingsthorpe, was it, Phyll?"

Casting an eye to where Bill walked ahead of them along the jitty's gloomy urban crack with Marjorie and Reggie Bowler, Phyllis piped up briefly in correction.

"Kingsley. 'E wiz in the Kingsley Lads."

"Kingsley, that's right. So, anyway, rather than argue over whose old crowd we'd take our name from, Reggie said we ought to call ourselves the Dead Dead Gang. From what I can remember, it wiz from a dream he'd had while he was still alive. He'd dreamed he wiz in school, having his lessons, and the teacher held a book up what he said that they wiz going to read from. It had got a green cloth cover with a line drawing embossed in gold what showed a load of kids, and one of them had got a bowler hat on and an overcoat down to his ankles like what Reggie wore. The book was called *The Dead Dead Gang*. Reggie suggested that was what we called ourselves, and we all thought it sounded snappy so we went along with him."

Wandering down the narrow alley with brick walls on one side, back gates on the other and a memory of leaden sky above, John grinned at Michael.

"As for what it means, I couldn't tell you. All that I could think of was, some people are dead lucky and some people are dead clever, but not us lot. We're dead dead."

A little further down the alleyway, young Bill had evidently made some smart remark that had upset Drowned Marjorie. A pushing match had then ensued, and Phyllis was alarmed to note that Marjorie, who'd set her mouth in a determined line, had taken off her spectacles and handed them to Reggie Bowler for safekeeping. This was never a good sign with Marjorie, and Phyllis thought someone had better intervene before affairs got out of hand.

"John, go and see to them. Tell Marjorie to put 'er specs back on and tell ayr Bill that if he dun't behave I'll smack his arse so 'ard 'e'll end up in another cemetery."

John smiled and nodded, ambling ahead of Phyllis and the toddler on his long legs with the grey socks pulled up smartly. Reaching Bill and Marjorie he draped a friendly arm around each of their shoulders, walking in between them so that neither one could take a wild swing at the other, steering them along the cobbled jitty as he steered their conversation into calmer waters. Handsome John could always be relied upon to sort things out so that nobody was left feeling in the wrong, Phyllis observed with a faint glow of second-hand pride, just from being in the same gang as what he was. He was such a natural peacemaker that Phyllis found she couldn't picture him at war, for all she knew how fearless he could be.

Walking beside her, Michael Warren pointed suddenly towards the recessed entrance of a staircase, dark behind an iron gate set in the alley wall upon their right.

"That's where I thought you'd gone to when I lost you, up them stairs. The steps wiz dark and there wiz crunchy things on them I thought wiz earwigs, but they turned out to be wrappers off of Tunes. There was a horridor up at the top that had a radigator what played 'Twinkle, Twinkle, Little Star', then after that the devil caught me."

Phyllis nodded as they passed the gated alcove. As the leader of the Dead Dead Gang she knew all of the secret passages and the hereafter shortcuts.

"Yes. It leads up into someone's dream of Spring Lane School, if I remember right. Spring Lane's a lovely school if yer still down in the Twenty-five Thousand Nights, but if yer find yerself there in yer dreams it's a bit frightening, and frightening things can 'appen. Specially at night, but even in the day it's never very bright inside. I'm not surprised that bogey found you there."

They were just scuffling past the beautiful imaginary gas-lamp standard that in Phyllis's opinion was the nicest thing about the jitty. What, down in the solid world, was only a plain cylinder and stem had been transformed, up here, to sculpted bronze. An oriental-looking dragon that had tarnished to a pale sea-green with glinting golden flecks of metal showing through from underneath wound down the tall post to coil sleepily in low relief about the base, where a nostalgia for grass thrust up in tufts out of the summer grit and puddle gravy. Up atop the serpent-circled shaft, the lamp itself had stained-glass panes in its four tapering windows. Of these only three were visible, the panel at the rear being continually out of sight, and since the lamp was not alight at present even these three weren't that easy to make out.

The leftmost one, as looked at from the front, was decorated by the portrait of an eighteenth-century gentleman who had a blunt and thuggish face yet wore a pastor's wig and robes and collar. Over on the right-side pane was the translucent image of a coloured chap with white hair, sat astride a bicycle contraption that had rope, not rubber, fastened round its wheel-rims. Phyllis knew that this was meant to be Black Charley, who had lived in Scarletwell Street while he was alive and who you sometimes saw still, pedalling around Upstairs. The central pane between these two was without colour and had only black lead lines on its clear glass. It showed a poorly-rendered symbol rather than a proper picture: the loose ribbon of a road or pathway and above it a crude balance, little more than two triangles joined by two straight lines. This, Phyllis knew, was the town crest of Mansoul and you saw it everywhere, although she wasn't sure what it was meant to represent.

Beside her, Michael Warren wasn't taking any notice of her favourite lamppost, but from his expression was engaged in brewing up another silly question.

"What's that what you said, Twenty-five Thousand Nights? It sounds like stories about skying carpets or a turban genie-bottle."

Phyllis looked at the dishwater sky above the alleyway and pushed her lips out while she thought about it for a moment.

"Well, I s'pose it *wiz* a lot of stories abayt wondrous things that 'appened once and then never again, but it's *ayr* stories that folk mean when they say that, Twenty-five Thousand Nights. It's just the number of nights, roughly speaking, that most people get, seventy years or so. Of course, there's some get more, and then there's some ... especially raynd 'ere ... who got a good sight less. Poor Reggie Bowler froze to death when 'e wiz sleeping rough on the old burial ground by Doddridge Church, that wiz some way back in the eighteen-sixties or the seventies, and 'e wiz no more than thirteen. Four thousand nights, give or take a few 'undred. Or there's Marjorie, who went into the river dayn at Paddy's Meadow when she wiz nine, trying to get 'er dog ayt, silly little sod. 'E got ayt right as rain, but Marjorie didn't. She washed up where it gets shallow under Spencer Bridge. They didn't find 'er till next day. Three thousand nights or thereabouts, that's all she 'ad. When they say twenty-five, that's just the average."

The little boy appeared to think about this for a while, perhaps attempting to work out how many nights he'd personally had. As Phyllis calculated it, it was a bit more than a single thousand, which was in itself no reason he should feel hard done by. There were those who'd died when they were tiny babies and had only a few dozen or few hundred days ... and, unlike Michael Warren, they would not be coming back to life again to notch up who knew how many more thousand nights before they finally and permanently passed away. He didn't know just how well off he was. The ghost-kids these days, Phyllis thought not for the first time, they don't know they're died.

Over against the jitty's left-hand wall ahead of her and Michael, Phyllis noticed Mrs. Gibbs's brazier, that she'd got John and Reggie to dispose of. It was already beginning to break down into the dream-mulch that collected at the curbs and corners of Mansoul, starting to lose its form and function as the rusting fire-basket curled back in corroded petals from the spent coals resting at the blackened centre. Its three tripod legs were buckling together, fusing to a single stalk so that the whole thing looked like it was turning to a metal sunflower, charred from having grown too near the sun. It didn't pay to sit still for too long here in the Second Borough, where things slid and shifted and you never knew what you'd end up as.

Stumbling along beside her, Michael Warren gave her what was probably as close as he could get to an appraising look.

"How old wiz you, then, befour yew wiz dread? Did you get many nights?"

Phyllis gave him a look that could have fried an egg.

"Don't be so cheeky. Yer should never ask a lady when it wiz she died. Old as me tongue and a bit older than me teeth, I wiz, and that's as much as yer'll get ayt of me."

The child looked mortified and slightly scared. Phyllis decided that she'd let him off the hook.

"Now, if yer'd asked when I wiz born, that'd be different. I wiz born in 1920."
Obviously relieved to find he hadn't irrecoverably overstepped the mark, the little boy moved onto safer ground as he resumed his questioning.

"Wiz that round here, down in the Boroughs?"

Phyllis gave a little hum of affirmation.

"I wiz born in Spring Lane, up the top. When I wiz late for school I could climb over ayr back wall into the playground. Dayn ayr cellar, yer could pull a board away and look dayn in the dark upon the spring itself, what Spring Lane wiz named after. There wiz never any money, but my childhood up there wiz the happiest time I ever 'ad. That's why I'm like I am now. This is me 'ow I remember me when I wiz at me best."

Ahead of them, the other four had reached the alleyway's far end, where it emerged into Spring Lane. Her Bill and Reggie Bowler were already out of sight, having apparently turned right and started trudging up the hill, but Handsome John and Marjorie were hanging back to make sure Phyllis and her small companion knew where they were going. John waved to her from the jitty's mouth and pointed up Spring Lane to indicate that was where him and Marjorie were heading next and Phyllis grinned, raising one thin arm in reply. The infant shuffling beside her in his slippers was still seemingly preoccupied by her last statement, about how she looked now being what she thought of as her best.

"Well, if this wiz your best, why wiz them niffy raggit-thins all round your neck?"

If she'd have wanted, Phyllis could have took offence at having the rank odour of her garland raised in conversation, when to her it was a smell she hardly noticed anymore. However, she was starting to find Michael Warren at least tolerable company and didn't want to bust things up when they were going well. She kept the faint affront out of her voice as she replied to him.

"There's lots of reasons. Rabbits are the 'oly magic animal raynd 'ere, along with pigeons. There are some who say that's why they call this place the Boroughs, that it should be 'Burrows' 'cause of 'ow the streets are tangled in a maze and 'ow folk dayn there breed like rabbits. That's not really why it's called the Boroughs, naturally, but it just shows yer 'ow some people think. One of the reasons why I wear them is because, up 'ere, the rabbit stands for girls just like the pigeon stands for boys. Abington Street up town wiz what they used to call the Bunny Run because of all the factory girls went up and dayn it and yer'd have the chaps stood at the edges, whistling and winking. I wiz told that Bunny wiz an old Boroughs expression for a girl, by reason of another name for rabbit being coney, what wiz also called a cunny, and ... well, it involves bad language what I shouldn't say, so yer'll just 'ave to take my word for it. And then, of course, they say that Chinamen can see a lady in the moon where we can see a man, and that she's got a rabbit with 'er, so there's one more reason rabbits are to do with girls.

"As for the Boroughs, rabbits sum it up, the life down 'ere. There wiz so many of them on the wastelands and the bits of meadow what we 'ad about, we thought of 'em as vermin, just like all the people as lived at the better end of town would think of us: all 'opping raynd between the weeds and looking for a scrap to eat, all in ayr grey and brown and black and white, all 'aving lots of children because we knew nature would take some of them away. We thought of them as vermin, rabbits, or we thought of them as supper, and ayr dad would go ayt 'unting them, then bring 'em 'ome and skin 'em by the fire. We'd eat the meat and 'ang the skins up on a string, and when we'd got enough, ayr mam would send me up the rag-and-bone yard where the man would give me a few coppers for them. They'd be in a great long necklace, just like they are now.

"One time I 'adn't gone straight to the junkyard with them, because I wiz 'aving fun pretending that I wiz a duchess with me fur coat raynd me shoulders. I wiz playing with the other Compton Street Girls, up Bellbarn and Andrew's Street and all raynd there, and in St. Andrew's Church there wiz a wedding gooin' on. Of course, we thought all that wiz very glamorous and so we slipped into the chapel and we took a pew together at the back, so we could watch.

"The smell from off my rabbit skins wiz so bad that they 'ad to stop the wedding while the ushers chucked us ayt. I didn't care. I liked 'em, and I still do. After all this time I've got so I can't smell 'em anymore. Give it a while and yer won't notice them yerself."

They were now almost at the alley's end, where it met Spring Lane's slope in a T-junction. Phyllis noticed Michael Warren peering up at the old metal street-sign bolted to the jitty wall, black painted letters on a white ground specked with faecal orange, the plaque's edges oxidised to friable iron wafer. Neither of the two words on the sign was wholly visible, obliterated by the rust so that only the cryptic message SCAR WELL RACE remained. Phyllis translated, for the toddler's benefit.

"Scarletwell Terrace. It wiz what the jitty wiz before it wiz a jitty. That's what all these back gates are that we've been passing on ayr right. Daynstairs in the three-sided world, all this 'as been pulled dayn by your time and there's just the bottom playing-field of Spring Lane School, but up 'ere in the dream-crust it's still standing."

Michael didn't comment on what Phyllis had just said, but seemed to understand. They traipsed around the corner, turning right into Spring Lane and facing up the hill. The view stopped Phyllis's diminutive companion in his slipper-slapping tracks and made him gasp, so that she had to forcibly remind herself that all of this was new to him. Beyond the Attics of the Breath and the back alley they'd just left, the toddler had seen nothing of Mansoul itself. Watching the feelings and reactions wash across his upturned face as he gazed up the sloping lane, she tried to put herself back to when she was fresh arrived here in the Second Borough, tried to see the dream-hill as the child was seeing it.

It clearly wasn't an abundance of the customary phantasmagoria you found around Mansoul that had so taken the small boy aback: Spring Lane was very much as it had been in life when Phyllis had been living down here, only more so. There were hardly any dreamlike touches of the kind that typified the upper world, no cellar grids with blackened teeth instead of bars, no fur upon the paving slabs. Instead there was no more than the familiar incline, but on fire with itself and shimmering with identity, with its own foot-worn history, with all the lights it had been saturated by across the thousand years of its existence.

Spring Lane burned with a mythology of chipped slates, pale wash-water blue and flaking at the seam. The summer yellow glow of an impending dawn diffused, diluted in the million-gallon sky above the tannery that occupied this low end of the ancient gradient, across the narrow street from where Phyllis and Michael stood outside the alley-mouth. The tannery's high walls of browning brick with rusted wire mesh over its high windows didn't have the brutal aura that the building had down in the domain of the living. Rather it was softly iridescent with a sheen of fond remembrance – the cloisters of some mediaeval craft since disappeared – and had the homely perfume of manure and boiled sweets. Past the peeling wooden gates that lolled skew-whiff were yards where puddles stained a vivid tangerine harboured reflected chimney stacks, lamp black and wavering. Heaped leather shavings tinted with corrosive sapphire stood between the fire-opal pools, an azure down mounded into fantastic nests by thunderbirds to hatch their legendary fledglings. Rain-spouts eaten through by time had diamond dribble beading on their chapped tin lips, and every splinter and subsided cobble sang with endless being.

Michael Warren stood entranced and Phyllis Painter stood beside him, sharing his enchantment, looking at the heart-caressing vista through his eyes. The district's summer sounds were, in her ears, reduced to a rich stock. The lengthy intervals between the bumbling drones of distant motorcars, the twittering filigree of birdsong strung along the guttered eaves, the silver gurgle of a buried torrent echoing deep in the night-throat of a drain, all these were boiled down to a single susurrus, the hissing, tingling reverberation of a cymbal struck by a soft brush. The instant jingled in the breeze.

Uphill, the other four official members of the Dead Dead Gang were climbing through a tentative prismatic haze that seemed to fog – deliciously – each windowsill and curbstone in the slanted lane. Making hard work of it, their slogging forms looked every bit as marvellously typical as the scrubbed doorsteps they were trudging past, looked just as indispensable to the beguiling composition of the scene. Phyllis's Bill and Reggie Bowler were the closest to the top, with Handsome John and Marjorie sharing a joke as they ascended past the entrance to Monk's Pond Street, opening to their left on Spring Lane's other side. Trading a glance in which they both acknowledged what a marvel this all was, Phyllis and Michael started dawdling up the perfect street after their comrades.

Fastening the wine-red dressing gown more tightly round his waist the little boy took big steps to keep up with Phyllis, staring all the time in wonderment at the long terrace reaching from the hill's foot to its crown, the row of painted wooden doors almost uninterrupted on their right as they went up. At last he could contain his curiosity no longer.

"What are all these houses? Spring Lane wizzn't like this when I wiz alive still."

Placing one blue shoe before the other on the pink and weathered pavement as she struggled up the hillside, Phyllis glanced towards the homes that they were passing with a wistful look upon her fair-skinned face.

"Yer right, it wizzn't, but it wiz when I wiz little. Most of these got knocked dayn right before the war, and then it wiz just wasteland for the kids to play on until it got turned to the school playing field. That little row of 'ouses where your house wiz, on St. Andrew's Road, that's all that's left of a big block of 'ouses. They wiz all up Scarletwell Street and Spring Lane, all along Crispin Street up at the top, and there wiz whole streets in between what ain't there now. Scarletwell Terrace, what we've just come ayt of, that wiz one, and a bit further up on this side of the lane there's Spring Lane Terrace."

Michael Warren was still listening, but he was letting his gaze wander to the road's far side where now the entrance to Monk's Pond Street opened up, running off north from Spring Lane's east-west line. Phyllis reflected that this side-street would look vastly altered, too, from the small boy's perspective. Closest to them, on the left-hand side as they looked down Monk's Pond Street, stood the east wall of the tannery, which would be recognisable from Michael's lifetime. Opposite and on the right, however, some two dozen well-kept doorsteps stretched away north to connect with Crane Hill and the bottom end of Grafton Street. Two dozen sprawling families, perhaps two hundred people in their proudly-maintained row, which would, by Michael Warren's day, become a patch of rubble that the local children called 'The Bricks' or else be factory property fenced off by walls of corrugated tin. Only up here, in the magnetic fields of dream and memory, were the old homesteads manifest.

Along the thoroughfare's far end upon its leftmost, western side there was the feature that had evidently captured the youngster's attention. The expansive pond from which the street derived its name, dried up down in the timely world since the late sixteen-hundreds, glittered in the sourceless sunlight. Two or three unhurried figures in dun-coloured habits stood conversing by the waterside, one of them carrying a fishing pole.

"They're monks," Phyllis explained to Michael. "They're monks who lived a long while back at Andrew's Priory, which wiz up near where St. Andrew's Church wiz now, that I got booted ayt of when me rabbit skins wiz causing such a stink. They're Frenchies most of them, I think, and it wiz one of them who let the King's troops in to ransack everything, eight 'undred year ago. Up 'ere that's all forgiven, by and large, but mostly they don't mingle wi' the local ghosts and still keep to themselves. Or sometimes the more boozy ones will 'aunt a pub, just for the company. There's several of the inns round 'ere 'ave got a ghostly monk in the back cellar or the snug, though I can only think of one by name and that's Old Joe who floats araynd the Jolly Smokers on the Mayorhold. Old Joe's not his real name, 'cause that would be something French, but it's just what the people Daynstairs call him."

Michael Warren looked at her, perplexed.

"Can people who are still aliveable see ghosts, then?"

Phyllis shrugged.

"Some of them can, but only if they're a bit funny in the 'ead, like mystic people are, or people who've gone mad. People who drink a lot or who smoke opium or things like that, they can see ghosts as well. That's why yer get more 'aunted pubs than any other sort of building, because dead folk like a place where there's a chance someone wizzle be drunk enough to notice them. But even the few people what are able to see ghosts can only see them when they're wandering abayt dayn in the ghost-seam."

Monk's Pond Street was vanishing behind them on their left as they continued up the fond and sparkling daydream of the hill. The tartan-shrouded toddler's attention was now wholly fixed on Phyllis.

"What's a ghost-seam?"

Phyllis couldn't help herself from saying "Funny, till yer get to know 'im," which was an old joke up in Mansoul and which the baffled infant clearly didn't get. She answered him again, more seriously.

"The ghost-seam's what it saynds like. It's a ragged seam what joins the Upstairs to the Dayn-below, and it's where all the real ghosts 'ang ayt, all the ones what don't feel comfortable up 'ere. It's like the Second Borough's on the top with the First Borough underneath, and in between them there's the ghost-seam, like when yer go in a pub and all the fag-smoke's 'anging in the air like a grey blanket, wobblin' abayt when people move and cause a draught. That's what the ghost-seam's like. 'Ere, look 'ere on the right. It's Spring Lane

Terrace, what I said abayt, one of the streets what got pulled dayn to make the playing field."

They were just walking past the corner where the terrace trickled off due south, towards their right, with house-fronts in a line to either side of dusty flagstones that were smeared with a thin margarine of morning light. Rather than peering down the tributary street, however, Michael Warren was more interested in the corner of it that was opposite the one which he and Phyllis had just passed, the corner they were now approaching as they walked across the mouth of Spring Lane Terrace. In the stead of doorways and net-curtained downstairs windows like the ones that started further down the side street, up this end was only plain brick wall supporting low slate roofs, which Phyllis knew to be the backside of a row of stables. As the pair of them continued up Spring Lane, leaving the offshoot terrace in their wake, they passed the gated yard upon their right out onto which the stables opened. There was the warm, hairy Bovril scent of horses and the stronger smell of disinfectant, which, though Phyllis didn't like it, always made her nose excited.

The small boy gazed pensively at the closed gate as they walked by it, carrying on uphill. The deep fire-engine red that its gnawed woodwork had once been was faded by forgotten decades to the colour of a kiss. Phyllis explained, before the kid could ask.

"I think this yard's still 'ere while yer alive, but it's part of a factory by your time. Back when I was living dayn 'ere, though, it wiz the place they kept the fever cart."

It made her ghostly substance shiver, even to pronounce the words. The fever cart, to Phyllis, had since she was small seemed to be from the night-side of the Boroughs. Rattling down the huddled byways it had been one of those sinister phenomena, like deathmongers or phantom monks, which she'd believed to be peculiar to the area. Such things spoke of the neighbourhood's relationship with death, a tiger-trodden foreign land to little girls enjoying a relationship with liquorice-whip and dandelion-clock life.

The baby in his night-things, trotting there beside her, just stared at her blankly.

"What's a fever cart?"

She sighed theatrically and rolled the memory of her childhood eyes. She'd obviously been right in her assumption that this nipper had been brought up soft. Phyllis supposed that most of those born in the 'Fifties had things cushy, what with all the science and medicine they had by then, at least compared with how things were when she was young.

"Yer don't know nothing, do yer? What the fever cart wiz, it wiz a big wagon what they put the kids in when they 'ad the smallpox and diphtheria and that. It took 'em to a camp near the stone cross what's ayt near 'Arding-stone, that's there to mark the spot where Queen Eleanor's body wiz put down when she wiz being taken back to London. In the fever camp, ayt in the open air with all the other children what were ill, they'd either die or they'd get better. Usually they'd die."

The child was gazing at her now with a new look in his blue, long-lashed eyes. Above them, the remembered Boroughs sky graded from Easter yellow into watery rose.

"Wiz there a lot of things what made you poorly, when you wiz down here? Wiz that what made you dead?"

Shaking her head, she put him straight.

"No. There wiz a lot of bad diseases, right enough, but none of 'em put paid to me."

She rolled one pink sleeve of her jumper up, wearing a gruff and business-like expression as though Phyllis were a pint-sized stevedore. Thrusting her bony arm out under Michael Warren's nose she showed him two blanched areas the size and shape of sixpences, close to each other on her pale, soft bicep.

"I remember I wiz playing raynd the Boroughs with ayr sister. Eight, I must have been, so this wiz still back in the 'Twenties. We saw this big queue of people leading ayt the door of Spring Lane Mission over there, where we'd go for ayr Sunday School."

She gestured to the far side of the lane that they were climbing, where the tan stones of the mission's plain façade wore their humility and lowliness with a pride that was almost luminous.

"Seeing the queue I thought as they wiz giving something ayt, so I got on the end of it and made ayr sister do the same. I thought it might be toys or something good to eat, 'cause back in them days sometimes yer'd get parcels give by better-off folk, what they'd distribute around the Boroughs. Anyway, it turned out it wiz vaccinations they wiz lining up for, against smallpox and diphtheria, so we got given 'em as well."

She rolled her jumper sleeve back down again, concealing once more the inoculation scars. Her young companion glanced behind him at the yard that they'd just passed, and then returned his gaze to Phyllis.

"Did the other places in Northamstrung all have their own fever carts as well?"

On this occasion Phyllis didn't snort or role her eyes at his naivety, but merely looked a little sad. It wasn't that the boy was stupid, she decided. Just that he was innocent.

"No, me old duck. Only the Boroughs 'ad a fever cart. Only the Boroughs needed one."

They went on up the hill in silence. On their left across the lane they passed the mouth of Compton Street, which ran off north towards a recollected Grafton Street with hazy Semilong beyond. The burnished lustre of Mansoul hung over everything, lovely and slightly wrong, as with hand-tinted postcard photographs: the doors that stretched away to each side of the street looked like they'd just been painted, apple red or powder blue, and faced each other in two ranks like guardsmen with their chests puffed out, stood waiting for inspection. Doorknobs seemed more gold than brass, and in the dusty fawn meniscus of the summer roadway flecks of mica winked the promise of a jewel mine. *We are the Compton girls, We are the Compton girls ...*

Phyllis remembered every one of them. Cath Hughes. Doll Newbrook. Elsie Griffin. The two sisters, Evelyn and Betty Hennel, and Doll Towel. Phyllis could see their faces sharp as anything, recalled them far more clearly than the people that she'd sat with in church congregations and school classrooms while she was alive. That was the thing with gang allegiances. You made them when your soul was pure and so they counted for much more than your religion, or the party what you voted for when you wiz old enough, or if you joined the Freemasons or something. She suppressed the urge to run off up the ghost of Compton Street to number 12 and call on Elsie Griffin, and instead turned her attentions back to Michael Warren. He was, after all, the job she had in hand.

The other four, ahead of them, had by now reached the summit where the north-south line of Crispin Street and Lower Harding Street ran straight across the top end of Spring Lane. Reggie and Bill were halfway round the factory corner on the top left, disappearing into Lower Harding Street, with Marjorie and Handsome John some way behind them. Phyllis knew that John was hanging back to keep the drowned girl company, since she'd got shorter legs than him and couldn't climb the slope as fast as he could. Phyllis thought that Handsome John was wonderful.

A little further up the hill and on their right the sacred slab of Phyllis's own bottom doorstep jutted out an inch or two into the street. When they drew level with it, Phyllis put her hand on Michael's tartan-covered arm and stopped him so that they could look at it. She couldn't pass the place unless she paused to offer her homage, silent or otherwise. It was a habit with her, or a warmly-harboured superstition.

"This wiz where I used to live, back when I used to live."

Up four stone steps the door of number 3 Spring Lane was olive green bleaching to grey, like stale sage, in the sun. The house was narrow and had clearly once been one half of a somewhat larger place along with number 5, next door and downhill on the right. Still further down in that direction were the rear wall and back gate of Spring Lane School, so that on mornings when she'd woken up too late, Phyllis could pull her trick of popping out of the back door, down to the bottom of the back yard that they shared with number 5 and climb over the wall to drop straight into the school playground. This had meant that Phyllis's report card always had high marks for punctuality, although both Phyllis and her parents were aware that she didn't deserve them, strictly speaking.

Phyllis knew that past the weathered door, where brittle paint peeled back from blisters to reveal imaginary continents of plain wood underneath, beyond the door there was no passageway or hall. You just stepped without preamble into the Painter family living room, which was the house's only room downstairs. A twisting flight of stairs ran from it to the single chamber up above, her parents' bedroom, with the attic in which Phyllis and her sisters slept directly over that. On Friday nights when it was warm they'd sit out on their window-ledge and watch the fights outside the pub across the street at chucking-out time. Shouts and shatterings would waft up to them through warm air that smelled of hops and copper, blood and beer. It was the 1920s, and they'd not had television then.

With only the one space downstairs there'd obviously been no room for a kitchen, and the nearest that they'd had was the cold water tap and old tin bucket, standing on a glistening-wet concrete block atop the flight of blue brick steps that led down to their cellar. This was shared, like the back yard, with number 5 next door and consequently it was cavernous with lots of twists and turns and alcoves that you could get lost in. Up one corner of the cellar, under number 5 and therefore technically a part of next door's house rather than Phyllis's, there was a stone slab in the ground what you could move if there were two of you. Lying there with your belly pressed into the chill and coal-dust of the cellar floor you could peer down a short black chimney-well, with pallid silver rings and ripples dancing on its sides, to where the spring that gave the lane its name roared downhill through the dark below. Although the secret torrent had foamed white as spit, Phyllis had always felt as if she were a doctor, gazing spellbound down an aperture into a rushing open vein, part of the Boroughs' circulation system that would link up with the Monk's Pond and the Scarlet Well. There was a lot of water hidden underneath the neighbourhood, and it was Phyllis's conviction that the water was where all of the emotions and the memories collected as trace elements that gave the stream its biting, reminiscent tang; the cold, fresh spray which damped the cellar air.

Phyllis glanced down and to one side at Michael Warren, standing next to her.

"Do yer know, when I wiz alive, if I wiz very ill or very troubled for some reason, it would always be the same dream what I 'ad. I'd be stood in the street 'ere, in Spring Lane where we are now, and it would just be getting dusk. I'd be the age what I am now, a little girl, and 'stead of going in the 'ouse I'd just be stood 'ere, mooning up at 'ow the gaslight in the living room wiz made all green and pink as it fell through the coloured curtains what were drawn across the daynstairs window, ayt into the twilight. In the dream, I'd always 'ad the feeling that no matter where I'd been, no matter 'ow long or 'ow rough the journey wiz, when I wiz standing 'ere and looking at the light shine through the roses on those curtains, I'd come 'ome at last. I always felt sure that when I wiz dead, this place would still be waiting 'ere for me, and everything would all be 'unky-dory. As it turned ayt, I wiz right, as usual. There's not a minute of ayr lives is ever lost, and all the pulled-dayn 'ouses what we miss are 'ere forever, in Mansoul. I don't know why I ever got so worried in the first place."

Phyllis sniffed and took a last look at her former residence for now, then they continued up the hill. The next door on their right and to the left of number 3 was that of Wright's, the sweetshop, with the stout bay window that displayed its wares behind small, thick panes of myopic glass just past the bell-rigged door as you went up. Because this higher landscape was accreted from the husks of dreams, the row of glinting chandelier-glass jars that the shop wore like a best necklace in its window were not filled with actual sweets, but with the dreams of sweets. There were small Scotty dogs made out of amber barley-sugar that had twisted middles, many of them fused to nine-dog lumps by the warm day, and in the jar of rainbow sherbet (which you could make kali water out of) there were extra strata of the different-coloured powders which, unlike the ordinary ones, fluoresced. There was a purplish layer that you couldn't really see up at the top, and at the bottom of the jar a pinkish layer that was similarly difficult to look at, but which made your tongue feel cooked if you ate any of it. Only chocolate rainbow drops seemed anything like normal, or at least until she noticed two or three of them were climbing up the inside of their jar and realised they were outsized ladybirds that had shells coated with hundreds-and-thousands, pink and white and blue. Though their mobility put Phyllis off, the pretty beads of sugar on their backs meant that they still looked as though they'd be nice to eat. She didn't blame the toddler she was escorting for the way he lingered by the sweetshop, staring longingly in through its panelled window until Phyllis tugged the cuff of his pyjama top and made him hurry up.

Before they knew it, they were at the peak and gazing back down the long street that they'd just climbed. She knew that in the living world Spring Lane was nowhere near as long, nor yet as steep, but knew that this was how small children would remember it, hanging annoyingly onto their mother's coat-tails as they tried to trick her into towing them up the demanding slope. Phyllis and Michael, standing at the top end of Spring Lane, looked west across the bottom of the valley over memories of the coal yard on St. Andrew's Road, striped as though by the rays of a low sun. Beyond were railway yards where spectral drifts of steam like spirits of departed trains followed the lost, dead tracks on into nettle-beds, and past these the green daybreak of Victoria Park suffused the wide sky's far edge with a lime blush that looked drinkable. After admiring the soft radiance of the deadworld panorama for a moment, both of them turned left and followed Handsome John, Bill, Marjorie and Reggie into Lower Harding Street.

Running along to Grafton Square where once the Earl of Grafton had some property, the resurrected Lower Harding Street was different in its atmosphere to the surrounding thoroughfares of the dream neighbourhood. It had not been remembered in its pristine state, with all the brickwork and the pointing good as new in brilliant orange that appeared to have been painted on. Instead, it had been fondly recollected from some later point, during the street's decline. Where once two rows of terraced houses faced each other without interruption save the opening to Cooper Street which sloped off on the right, here there were breaks along the left-side row where dwellings had been emptied prior to demolition. Some of the abandoned buildings were already half knocked-down, with roofs and water services and upstairs floors conspicuously gone. Halfway up one sheer wall, which had become a palimpsest of several generations' wallpaper, a former bedroom door hung on its hinges, opening no longer to the promise of a good night's sleep but on a sudden plummet into rubble. Some half-dozen houses opposite the lower end of Cooper Street were barely there at all, their lines merely suggested by a few remaining outcroppings of brick shaped like stray jigsaw pieces, poking from the grass and weeds that had supplanted a beloved front-room carpet.

With the elegiac glow of Mansoul over everything, the dereliction did not seem forlorn or ugly but was more like sad and stirring poetry. To Phyllis, the effect was strangely comforting. It seemed to say that, in somebody's dreams or memories, even the moss-bound stages of this slow deterioration were held dear. The sight of Lower Harding Street confirmed her feeling that the Boroughs had still been a thing of beauty throughout its undignified and gradual surrender. Though by 1959 and Michael Warren's time this area's downstairs counterpart would be a wilderness, Phyllis was confident that it would still retain its place in local hearts, or at least in the younger ones.

Beside her, Michael's blonde head was tipped back to stare up at the partially demolished house-fronts that they were approaching as they followed their four dead confederates along the revenant terraces. The boy seemed taken by the exposed edge of a dividing wall, or with an ornate fireplace stranded in an upper room that had no floor. He turned and offered Phyllis a confiding look, so that she stooped towards him with one hand cupped at her ear to find out what he had to say.

"These houses look a bit like how my house down Andrew's Road did when that dervlish showed me it, and I could look round all its walls to see what wiz on the inside."

Phyllis herself had never undergone a ride like that on which the fiend had taken Michael Warren, and she'd only heard tenth-hand accounts from those rare individuals who had. As a result she only had the sketchiest idea of what the kid was going on about, and so responded with an indeterminate-yet-knowing grunt. Deterring further comment, Phyllis turned away from Michael and towards the rest of her Dead Dead Gang, who were gathered on the sun-baked slabs outside the broken houses opposite the mouth of Cooper Street and obviously waiting for the pair of stragglers to catch up. Reggie and Bill were playing a profoundly painful-looking game of knuckle-rapping with each other as they passed the time, while Handsome John stood there with folded arms and grinned as he looked back along the road at her and her pyjama-boy. Drowned Marjorie sat by herself upon the pavement's edge and gazed up the incline of Cooper Street towards Bellbarn where she'd resided, before, unable to swim, she'd plunged into the Nene to save a dog who evidently could.

With Michael Warren pottering along behind her, Phyllis marched up to the others and asserted her authority.

"All right, come on, then. 'Ow's this going to be ayr secret 'ideout if we're always stood raynd in the street aytside and letting on to everybody where it wiz? Go through to the back yards where nobody can overlook us, and then if it's safe we'll let the lad 'ere see the den. Bill, you and Reggie pack that up and do as yer've been told before I give yer a good 'iding. And Marjorie, buck yer ideas up. Yer'll get piles from sitting on the curb like that."

With varying degrees of muttered insubordination, the dead children stepped through a mere absence in the brickwork where the door of number 19 Lower Harding Street had previously been and creaked in single file across the debris – colonised by snails – that had at some point served as the home's parlour, living room and kitchen. The rear kitchen wall was gone entirely, so that it was hard to tell where what was formerly indoors came to an end and the back yard began. The only demarcation was a tide-line of domestic rubbish, which had drifted up against the single course of bricks that still remained, a band of refuse that was touchingly familiar and intimate. There was a doll's head made of hard, old-fashioned plastic, brown and brittle, one eye dead and closed, the other open wide as though the undertaker's penny had slipped off. There was a broken beer-crate and the undercarriage of a pram, along with solitary shoes, the deadly throat of a milk-bottle and one sodden and disintegrating copy of the *Daily Mirror* with a headline that referred to Zeus although the story underneath was all about the crisis in Suez.

Having negotiated the precarious obstacle-course of the roofless home's interior, the gang collected in what there was left of the communal back yard that had once been shared by numbers 17 to 27, Lower Harding Street. It was an area some ninety feet in width, which slanted in an avalanche of tall, parched grass towards a crumbling bottom wall, a little under sixty feet down-hill. The remnants of two double-privies stood against this lower boundary, which was at intervals collapsed into a scree of salmon-coloured brick, and here and there across the overgrown enclosure there were piles of junk com-posting down to dream-dross in amongst the yellowed shoots. Phyllis allowed herself a tight smile of self-satisfaction. If you didn't know already it was there, then the Dead Dead Gang's hidden den could not be seen.

She led the gang and Michael Warren down the slope, past a haphazard pile of corrugated iron sheets, discarded cupboard doors and flattened card-board boxes. At a point approximately halfway down she stooped and ges-tured proudly to the bushy gradient itself, for Michael's benefit.

"What d'yer think?"

Bewildered, Michael squinted at the screen of wilted stalks, and then at Phyllis.

"What? What do I think about what?"

"Well, abayt our den. Come on. Get closer up and have a proper butcher's at it."

Hitching his pyjama-bottoms up self-consciously, the little boy leaned further in, as he'd been told. After a while he gave a faintly disappointed yelp as he discovered something, although from the sound of it, it wasn't anything much good.

"Oh. Wiz this what you meant, this grabbit-hole?"

He pointed to a minor burrow, only a few inches wide, and Phyllis laughed. "Not that! 'Ow would we get dayn that? No, look a bit more to yer right."

She let him root round in the empty region on the left side of the bur-row for a moment and then told him which his right was. He resumed his search and found what he was meant to find almost immediately, although he sounded none the wiser as to what it was.

"Is it a clockpit from an aeroplane what's gone down underground?"

It wasn't, obviously, but you could see where he'd got that impression. In fact, what the boy was looking at was the green-tinted Perspex windscreen of a motorcycle sidecar that had been embedded in the slope, then smeared with ochre mud to cut down any telltale glints. That had been Handsome John's idea, that clever military touch.

"No. It's the window of ayr den. When we wiz playing 'ere one day we found the 'oles and thought they might all lead to a big burrow further back. The boys fetched shovels, and we dug dayn under where them sheets of metal are, back up the 'ill. It took some time, but we broke through into what 'ad been an old rabbit-warren but was empty now. We kicked all the old tunnel walls dayn and we dug it ayt some more until we'd got a massive pit, looked like a shell 'ad 'it it. Then we widened ayt the biggest rabbit 'ole so we could 'ave a window, where we put this windscreen off a sidecar what we'd faynd. We dragged old doors and that from 'ere-abayts and fitted them across ayr pit to make a roof, but so that it would look like rubbish somebody had dumped."

She gave a nod and Reggie Bowler scrambled back a few feet through the tall grass, up the slanted yard to where the seeming pile of refuse was located. Bending forward far enough so that his battered hat fell off, he grubbed around amongst the scrap until his fingers found the edge of a dilapidated plywood screen. Grunting with effort – Phyllis thought that he was overdoing it a bit if truth be told – he dragged the mud-stained wooden sheet back, scraping over corrugated iron, until he'd revealed the pitch-black entrance of a tunnel. Stooping to retrieve his fallen bowler, Reggie sat down on the hole's rim with his pale legs dangling away into the darkness and then, with a slithering motion very like a stoat, he disappeared from sight.

Giving Reggie time to find and light the Dead Dead Gang's sole candle, Phyllis next sent her Bill and Drowned Marjorie into the subterranean lair, with her and Michael Warren following while Handsome John brought up the rear, since he was tall enough to reach and slide the plywood sheet back into place above them once they were all in.

The pit was roughly circular, perhaps eight feet across and five feet deep with a flat floor and sides of hard-packed soil. The curved wall had been dug to form a ledge just under halfway up so everybody had somewhere to sit, although not comfortably. The same shelf, running all around the den's perimeter, also provided alcove space, which had been hollowed from the southern section of its arc. Here all the gang's possessions were kept safe, not that there were a lot of them: two water-damaged copies of *Health and Efficiency*, black-and-white blondes with beach-balls on their cockled covers, which both Bill and Reggie Bowler had insisted be included in the treasury; a pack of ten Kensitas cigarettes that still had three fags left inside, although the picture on the box had been remembered wrong so that the pompous butler mascot had one gloved hand raised to hold his nose and it said 'Sea Stink' where the Kensitas name should have been; a box of matches that had Captain Webb the channel-swimmer on the front, and, finally, their candle. This stood fused by wax to a cracked saucer and supplied the underground den's one source of illumination, if you didn't count the greenish underwater radiance that filtered in through the mud-plastered windscreen set into the western wall.

They sat round in a ring there on the narrow and encircling ledge, the candle-glimmer fluttering across their grinning mugs, with only Michael

Warren's legs too short to reach the ground. His slippered toes swung back and forth scant inches from the mouldy carpet-remnant that concealed most of a trodden black-dirt floor. He looked so little Phyllis almost felt a twinge of fondness for him, smiling reassuringly as she addressed him.

"Well, then? What d'yer think?"

She didn't wait for him to answer, since there was no doubt what he would think, what anyone would think. This was the best den in Mansoul, and Phyllis knew it. Why, they hadn't even showed him the most thrilling thing about the place yet, and already he looked mesmerised. She carried on with her enthusiastic, bubbling tirade.

"It's not bad, wiz it, for a gang of kids? For saying it wiz us who made it, like? Now then, I'd better call this meeting of the Dead Dead Gang to order so we can decide what's to be done with yer. I reckon yer a mystery what needs solving, what with all this getting carried off by devils, starting fights between the builders and then being back to life again by Friday nonsense. So yer lucky yer've fell in with us, since we're the best detectives in the Boroughs, 'igh or low."

Drowned Marjorie said "Are we?" in a startled tone which Phyllis just ignored.

"Now, what we've got to find ayt first wiz who you are. Not what yer name wiz, yer've already told us that, but who yer people are, and where yer come from. And I'm not just talking about coming from St. Andrew's Road, but where the stuff what made yer come from before that. Everything in the world what happens, everybody who wiz ever born, it's all part of a pattern, and the pattern stretches back a long way before we wiz 'ere, and it guz on a long way after we're all gone. If you want to find out what life's abayt you have to see the pattern clearly, and that means yer've got to look at all the twists and turns back in the past that made yer pattern what it wiz. Yer've got to follow all the lines back, do yer see? Years back, or centuries in some cases. We might have to goo quite a long way before we find out what yer about."

The little boy already looked disheartened.

"Have we got to walk all back along that big arcade for years? It's lots of miles for even just a day."

Drowned Marjorie, who sat the other side of Michael Warren on the packed dirt shelf, turned round to reassure him with the leaping candlelight smeared over each lens of the girl's unflattering National Health spectacles. Her boggling, earnest eyes were lost in puddles of reflected flame.

"That wouldn't be no good. Up in the Second Borough here, it's not like how it wiz back down below. It's just a sort of dream of how things used to be, so we could walk back down the Attics for as far as they went on and never find out anything worth knowing. It would all be thoughts and fancies, without much to do with anyone's real life."

You could almost hear the clockwork turning in the infant's head as he considered this.

"But couldn't we look down through all them big square holes and see all what wiz really going on below?"

Here Handsome John leaned forward, thrusting his heroic face into the halo of the candle as he butted in.

"All that we'd see is jewellery, the solid shapes what people leave behind them when they move through time. I'll grant you, if you study them a long while you can more or less make out what's happening, but it takes ages and you're often none the wiser at the end of it."

The little boy was clearly thinking so hard now that Phyllis feared his blonde head might inflate and blow to bits.

"But what if we went down the attic-holes like I did with that devil? We could see things normal then."

Phyllis, at this point, snorted with derision.

"Oh, and seeing people with their guts and bones on the aytside wiz normal, wiz it? Anyway, it's not just anybody who can take you for a ride above the daynstairs world like that. There's magic powers what only fiends and builders 'ave. No, if we want to find ayt all the clues and bits of evidence that are to do with yer, there's only one thing for it. We shall 'ave to use one of ayr special secret passages, that runs between Mansoul and what's below. You do the 'onours, Reggie."

Climbing to his feet in a half-crouch but with his bowler scraping on the hideout's corrugated tin roof anyway, the gangly Victorian urchin cut a weird, fantastic figure in the candlelight with his Salvation Army overcoat swinging about his white and bony knees. He squatted on his haunches in a posture very like that of a jumping spider and began to roll the mouldering patch of carpet up from one end. It had had a pattern once, something with diamonds in two shades of brown, but through the gloom and rot only the barest rumour of design was visible as Reggie Bowler rolled it back. While he was thus engaged, Phyllis became aware that Michael Warren and the other members of her gang were edging gradually away from her along the hard black ledge where they were seated. Realising after a few moments that it was the odour of her rabbit pelts in this confined space that was driving them away she tossed her head dismissively and threw one end of the fur necklace back across her shoulder like an actress with a stole. Let them put up with it a minute or two longer. Soon enough they'd all be in a place where no one could smell anything.

The carpet remnant was now rolled into a damp cigar at one end of the rounded pit, exposing the distressed mahogany of an old wardrobe door apparently pressed down into the dirt beneath and which had been previously hidden by the mildewed rug.

"Give us a hand, John." This was Reggie speaking as he worked his filthy fingernails down into the loose soil up at one end of the embedded door, fumbling for purchase. Handsome John stood up as best he could with the low ceiling and then got down on one knee at the far end of the scuffed wooden rectangle, pushing his fingers down into the crack between the door and its surrounding dirt like Reggie had. Upon the count of three and with a mutual grunt of effort, John and Reggie Bowler lifted the door clear and to one side.

It was as if someone had switched a television on in a dark room. A flood of nacreous grey light burst in to fill the cramped den, shining in a fanning hard-edged ray up through the ragged hole that had been underneath the wardrobe door, which had itself been hidden by the sodden carpet. Michael Warren gasped, beginner that he was. All the dead children's faces were now under-lit as if by buried starlight and the candle was no longer necessary. Phyllis pinched it out, so's not to waste it, and received a second skin of hot wax on her thumb and index finger for her pains. The Dead Dead Gang and their pyjama-sporting honorary member climbed down from their packed dirt perches, kneeling in a ring around the pearl blaze of the aperture as they stared mutely down.

The void, about three feet across, was like a peephole that spied down upon a luminescent fairy kingdom underneath the ground, a detailed landscape kept safe in a magic music box on which the lid had just been lifted. Nothing was in colour. Everything was black or white or one of several dozen finely-graded neutrals.

They were looking at a silvery patch of waste ground from above, with gouged clay soil from which grew buttercups and rosebay willowherb in vibrant monochrome. Tin grass shoved up its spears between a fallen sprawl of wet grey bricks, and the rainwater gathered in an upturned hubcap was reflecting only bands of quivering smoky shadow and the leaden clouds above. It was exactly as if somebody unpracticed with a camera had accidentally clicked the shutter while the box was pointed at the ground beneath their feet, had taken a fortuitously-lit and detailed photograph of nothing much at all. The snapshot world that they could see, though three-dimensional, had even got white creases running back and forth across it like a wedding picture left forgotten in a cluttered sideboard drawer, although on close inspection Phyllis knew that these would prove to be trajectories left in the wake of ghostly insects, which would fade from sight in moments.

Michael Warren glanced up from the landscape of burned platinum, its photo-album glow lighting his upturned chin from underneath as he gazed questioningly at Phyllis. He looked from her to the silent film view through the blot-shaped hole, and back again.

"What wiz it?"

Phyllis Painter hung her bloody bandolier of rabbit hides more comfortably around her skinny shoulders and was unable to keep from grinning smugly as she answered. Was there any other bunch of cheeky monkeys in the whole of Heaven had a bolt hole half as good as the Dead Dead Gang?

"It's the ghost-seam."

There below the grey breeze blew a sheet of blank, grease-spotted chip-wrap into view across one corner of the scene. Overexposed at its far edge the grainy and nostalgic image bled out to a flaring white, and one after another all the boys and girls went down into the zebra-and-Dalmatian dapple of the ghost-seam, down into the bleached Daguerreotype of a remembered world that was death's mezzanine.

THE SCARLET WELL

Straight down the rabbit hole, and through the wardrobe door: it seemed to Michael as if this was a completely proper and time-honoured way to get into another world, although he couldn't for the death of him have told you why it felt like that. Perhaps he just remembered something similar from an old story that he'd once had read to him, or else he was becoming more accustomed to the way things happened in this curious new place that he was lost in.

After all the fuss and fireworks of his kidnap by the horrifying Sam O'Day and then his rescue by the eerie ragamuffins of the Dead Dead Gang, he had decided that the best thing he could do would be to treat the whole thing like a dream. Admittedly, it was a dream that seemed to carry on for an uncomfortable length of time, a bit like going into your back yard and finding half a dozen soap bubbles you'd blown three days before still rolling round there in the drain-trap, and in Michael's heart of hearts he knew that this was not a dream at all. Still, with its colours and its strangeness, it was easy to pretend that he was dreaming, which was better than reminding himself every moment of his actual situation, of the fact that he was dead and in a shabby-but-familiar afterlife with devils and ghost-children everywhere, or anyway, that's where he was for the time being. Treating it all like a nightmare or a fairy story was a lot less bother.

Mind you, that was not the same as saying it was effortless. He found that he was having to work quite hard to ignore all of the things that told him this was more than just a dream that had outstayed its welcome, such as how real all the people seemed to be. Dream-people, he had found, were nowhere near as complicated as real people were, nor half as unpredictable, in that they generally did what you expected them to do. There never seemed to be much to them, not in Michael's estimation. All the people he had met in Mansoul, on the other hand, seemed just as messy and as genuine as his own family or neighbours were. The lady who had saved him from the demon, Mrs. Gibbs, who'd called herself a deathmonger, she'd been as real to him as his nan May. In fact, when Michael thought about it, out of the two women, Mrs. Gibbs was probably the most believable. As for the Dead Dead Gang they were every bit as real as a grazed knee, along with all their special signals and their shortcuts and their secret den, all of the funny bits and bobs that made them what they were. Even if all of this did somehow still turn out to be a dream he thought that he'd be best off sticking with the dead kids, who at least appeared to know what they were doing and who clearly knew their way around.

This ghost-seam though, the light from which blazed upwards through a wardrobe door-sized hole in the den's floor, that felt a bit like trespassing. It felt like something older children might get you to do just so's you'd get in trouble. Didn't all the phantoms down there mind having a gang of hooligans running around and bothering them even after they were dead?

On Phyllis Painter's orders they all climbed down through the glowing rectangle, with the good-looking older boy called John being the first one to descend. Michael supposed that this was probably because John was the tallest and could drop more easily into the black-and-white world underneath. Once John had found his feet below, he would be able to reach up and help the smaller members of the gang to clamber down beside him. The old-fashioned-looking boy with all the freckles and the bowler hat went next, and then the sober-sided little girl with glasses that they called Drowned Marjorie. The kid with ginger hair who Michael thought was more than likely Phyllis Painter's little brother followed Marjorie, which left just him and Phyllis in the television flicker of the hideout, with the colourless light shining up out of the earth to make the ladies on the cover of *Health & Efficiency* look grey and chilly.

Michael thought he might be warming to the bossy little Dead Dead girl, especially since she'd come back and saved him from that rotten devil, and not just abandoned him like he'd expected her to do. She was all right, Michael decided, for a girl. However, although she'd gone up in his opinion over the last hour or so, and even though he'd gradually been getting used to how her scarf of rabbits smelled, he found that being in a closed-in space such as the den with her was a bit much. Because of this, he didn't make a fuss when Phyllis told him that he was the next man down the hole. It would be a relief, quite frankly, to be out in the fresh air again, even if Michael didn't really need to breathe it quite as urgently as he might once have done. Being inside the hideout with her was like being buried in a coffin full of weasels.

Phyllis told him to get down upon his tummy and to let her gradually lower him backwards, holding tight onto his tartan sleeves in case he slipped. When he was halfway down and had his upper half still poking up into the den he felt strong hands supporting him from underneath. He trusted them enough to let his head sink down below the level of the hideout's floor, still clinging to the hard dirt of the hole's rim with his sweaty palms.

It was a bit like going underwater suddenly. The light looked different and it changed the way you saw things, so that everything was sharp and crystal-clear but hadn't got its colours in it any longer. This new level of the afterlife felt different, too, as though it were a little colder, although Michael didn't think that was the proper explanation. It was more as if when he'd been in the world Upstairs there'd been a sticky memory of summer warmth, whereas down here there wasn't any temperature at all. It wasn't hot, it wasn't cold. It just felt a bit numb. The same was true with how things smelled. The dreadful niff of Phyllis Painter's rabbits vanished at the moment Michael's nose dropped down below the level of the hideout floor, and he discovered that he was unable to smell anything at all. The realm that he was being dangled into had no more scent than a glass of tap-water. Even the background noises of the ghost-seam, swelling up around him, sounded just like his gran's wind-up gramophone might do if it were being played inside a cardboard box.

The firm grip of what proved to be John's hands moved up and around Michael's ticklish midriff, and the next thing that he registered was being set down on the off-white grass that grew there in the country of the ghosts. Everything looked as though it had been drawn in Indian ink or charcoal, and to his surprise he found that he was once more leaving trails behind him as he moved, though these weren't the fancy wine-red tartan plumes he'd sprouted when the devil took him on his flight. The fading pictures he was leaving in his wake now looked as soft and grey as pigeon feathers. Blinking, he peered all around at the odd place in which he found himself, trying to make his mind up if he liked it much. Colourless dandelions, he learned, looked quite upsetting, while the white wasps striped like flying humbugs left him feeling slightly queasy.

Phyllis Painter, meanwhile, made a big display of holding onto her plain navy skirt, now simply black, as John lifted her from the den down to the hilly wasteland where the rest of them were standing, with his eyes averted throughout in a gentlemanly manner. As she came down, Phyllis dragged one corner of the carpet remnant into place across the gap above her, with the wardrobe door itself being presumably too heavy for a single person. Since the carpet's underside already had an indistinct and murky hue, the entrance to the den was neatly camouflaged against the cloudy Boroughs sky that it appeared to be suspended in, a jagged hole cut in the air a few feet up above the sparse turf and uneven ground. As John helped Phyllis find her feet, Michael continued to inspect the startling newspaper-coloured kingdom that was all around them.

Michael and the other children seemed to be in the same spot as the Dead Dead Gang's den had been up in the dreamy, colour-drenched world of Mansoul that they'd just climbed from, but the version of the place that Michael looked out over now was very different, and not just because it was all black and white and sounded flat and hadn't got a smell. The thing that made the most impression on him was the difference in the place's atmosphere. It made it near enough impossible for him to keep up the pretence that he was dreaming, because this felt nothing like a dream. The landscape running off down-hill before him was far too let-down and sad not to be real.

The houses that had stood there between Monk's Pond Street and Lower Harding Street were gone; all of the fond and shining memories of homes they'd passed while they were trudging up Spring Lane and all the dwellings that were half pulled down and that they'd had to pick their way through to the derelict communal yard where the Dead Dead Gang kept their hidden den. All gone. Now there were just bleached weeds and straggling, sooty bushes rising from the heaps of rubble. Michael couldn't even see the faintest lines to show where all the former walls and boundaries had been.

The whole of Compton Street, which had been roughly halfway down the sloping wasteland, had completely vanished. In its place was an unsurfaced track of grey and glistening mud that ran across the wilderness from left to right as he gazed down the hill. He recognised the area now, whereas the glowing streets of Mansoul had seemed unfamiliar: this was how the place had been in Michael's lifetime. These were the demolished bombsite outskirts of the Boroughs where his older sister Alma played, and that he'd heard her call 'the Bricks'.

He had a funny feeling, as if he were in a blurry photograph from this year, 1959, a creased old picture that was being looked at by somebody in a century from now, when he and everyone he knew would all be gone. It almost made him want to cry just thinking of it, of how quickly everything was finished and how everyone's lives were as good as over with already, from the minute they were born. The colour-blinded landscape dropped away from him towards the west, where stands of nettles that were almost black rustled and swayed on slides of sunlit mud that flared with dazzling white. Uneasy, Michael turned back to the members of the Dead Dead Gang, who were all down on solid ground by now.

To Michael's left stood Phyllis Painter, who looked like she thought she was Napoleon or somebody, stroking her chin as she surveyed her troops. Her small hand, raised up to her face, left grey and white shapes through the air behind it in a fan of ostrich plumes.

"Right, you lot. Back to Spring Lane and across it into Crispin Street. We'll take ayr 'onorary member for a walk dayn Scarletwell Street to 'is 'ouse in Andrew's Road. John, you walk up the front and keep an eye ayt for rough sleepers. Bill and Reggie, you 'ang back and do the same so that we dun't get any mad ghosts come upon us from behind. Remember, there's a lot of 'em what we've played tricks on, up and dayn the years, and they don't like us. Most of 'em are 'armless, but if yer see Mary Jane or old Tommy Mangle-the-Cat then run like billy-oh. We'll meet up later on the Mayorhold, where the Works wiz, if we should get separated."

Michael thought this sounded more alarming than the pleasant stroll he'd been expecting. What, he wondered, were rough sleepers? Also, why would anyone be called "Mangle-the-Cat"? Nevertheless, he fell in with the other children as they climbed the slanting wasteland with its test-card tones, back up towards all that was left, by 1959, of Lower Harding Street. He tried to haul himself up a particularly steep bit of the slope by clutching at a clump of bind-weed, but discovered that his fingers passed through the white trumpet blossoms and the thick grey veins of creeper as if he was made completely out of cigarette smoke, rather than just being the same colour as it at that moment. He supposed it made sense if the weeds were real and he was ghostly, but then what about the ground that he was clambering on? Why didn't he and his new dead friends sink down through it to Australia or somewhere? He decided to ask Phyllis, who was struggling up the hill ahead of him.

"What makes the flaw be solid when the rest of everything is mistreous?"

He pulled a face, dismayed to find his tongue was playing up again. It seemed to happen most when he was nervous, and he thought that it was very likely all this talk of mad ghosts and cat-manglers that was upsetting him. Phyllis scowled back at Michael over one pale woollen shoulder of her jumper, which looked warm grey even though he knew that it was really milkshake pink. Smudged after-images were smoking from her back.

"Yer don't 'alf ask some silly questions. All them things grown ayt the land, all of the 'ouses and the people and not just the plants and trees, they're only 'ere a little while. It's only like a month, a year, a century or what-not, and they're gone. The linger of 'em 'ardly 'as a chance to make a real impression on the worlds what are all up above. Some places, like St. Peter's or the 'Oly Sepulchre what 'ave been there for ages, it can be a struggle walkin' through the walls of 'em because they're thickened by 'ow long they've been there. There's a beech tree up in Sheep Street what's been there eight 'undred years, so yer can give yer 'ead a nasty smack on that, an' all. Compared with that, gooin' through factory walls or them in people's 'ouses wiz a piece o' cake. You just pass through 'em like yer made from steam. This slope we're walkin' up, though, that's been 'ere for like a million years, so it feels solid even to a ghost. Now, keep yer trap shut 'til we're up the 'ill."

They climbed on for a moment or two more, and then the whole gang reassembled on the cracked stone paving slabs of Lower Harding Street. Michael was pleased to see that all the houses on the street's far side had people living in them and were being kept in good condition, with the gentle rise of Cooper Street still running up to Belbarn and St. Andrew's Church, although the near side of the street where he stood with the other ghost-kids had all been pulled down. Above the street, the polished silver pot-lid of the sun was blazing from a wide expanse of cool grey sky, which Michael thought might be a summer blue if it were looked at by the living. Little white clouds stood out from the background here and there, as if drops of peroxide bleach had fallen onto blotting paper.

In a trailing throng the gang of phantom children made their way down the old-fashioned crackling newsreel of a street and back towards Spring Lane, each with a row of fading look-alikes that streamed along behind them. As they'd been instructed, little Bill and Reggie what's-his-name brought up the rear, while Phyllis and Drowned Marjorie walked side by side towards the middle of the line, engrossed in giggling female conversation that was punctuated by swift, furtive glances at the unsuspecting tall lad, John, who paced along in front of everybody.

Michael tried to walk with Marjorie and Phyllis so that he'd have somebody he knew to chatter with but Phyllis tossed her fringe, causing her rabbit necklace to swing back and forth, and told him that it was "a private matter" what they were discussing. Given that he wasn't sure yet what to make of the mischievous Bill or the tough-looking Reggie, Michael hurried to catch up with John, who strode with a heroic bearing at the front of their ragtag parade. This oldest member of the Dead Dead Gang appeared to Michael to be a dependable and decent sort of lad. He glanced round and grinned amiably as the pyjama-clad child scampered from behind to trot along beside him.

"Hello, nipper. Phyllis given you your marching orders, has she? Never mind. You keep me company instead. You never know, it might be we could learn a thing or two off of each other."

Michael did a sort of double skip in order to keep up with John's long legs and greater stride. He liked the older boy a lot. For one thing, John was the first person that he'd met up here who seemed as though he wouldn't get annoyed if Michael asked him things. Michael decided that he'd put it to the test.

"What wiz that Phyllis said about rough sleepers? Are there bad ghosts going to come and get us? Wiz that what you're looking out for?"

John smiled reassuringly.

"They're not bad ghosts, not really. They're just people who aren't sleeping soundly in their afterlives because of one thing or another. They don't fancy running through their lives again, and they don't feel right going upstairs to Mansoul. Some of 'em don't feel like they're good enough, and some of 'em just like it here where everything's familiar, even if it's all in black and white and there's no smell or anything."

The handsome boy's face took on a more serious look.

"They're harmless for the most part, that sort, but there's one or two of them who ain't. There's ones who've been down here a long time and it's sent them funny, either that or they were funny to begin with. Then there's ones who've got too fond of ghost-booze, Puck's Hat Punch they call it. They're the worst to look at. They can't hold themselves together properly, so they get shapes and faces that are mixed up like a jumble sale, and they're forever flying into rages. Old Mangle-the-Cat, he's one of them, and I'll tell you for nothing, if a ghost gives you a thick ear then you'll feel it."

John gave Michael a soft prod in his left shoulder with one finger as a demonstration, and although it didn't hurt, the younger boy could see it would have done if John had put more force behind it. Satisfied he'd made his point, John next untucked his phosphorescent shirt tails from the waistband of his knee-length trousers, pulling up the garment and the pullover he wore above it to reveal his belly. Just below the ribcage on John's right-hand side there was a dull grey light that seemed to pulse at intervals beneath the skin, as if John had a tiny road-lamp flashing in his stomach.

"That's where Mary Jane put in the boot when we'd been playing tricks on her, some while back now. A ghost-bruise like this, it'll fade away eventually, but I dare say that if you got enough of 'em at once, your spirit might be done some damage that'd be a job to fix."

John rolled his shirt back down and tucked it in. The action left a churning storm of ghostly hands and cuffs around his waistband that dispersed after a moment.

On the other side of Lower Harding Street a front door opened with a muted squeak and a disgruntled-looking woman in her forties came out through it, as did a brief burst of wireless-music playing from somewhere inside the house. It was a song that Michael recognised, by an American. He thought it might be called something like "What Did Della Wear", but it was cut off as the woman shut the door behind her and then bustled down the terrace a short distance, with arms folded truculently and her dark permed hairdo bobbing like a feeding blackbird. Calling at a neighbour's some doors down she knocked upon the door and was let in almost immediately by a tall lady whose short hair was either blonde or grey. Neither of the two women left a trail behind them as they moved, nor spared the gang of children wandering by upon the street's far side a second glance.

"They're still alive, so they can't see us," John remarked conspiratorially. "The way that you can tell wiz that they don't have streamers following behind 'em, like what we've got." Here he waved one arm so that it fanned out like a hand of cards, the extra limbs persisting for an instant before disappearing.

"If you see somebody without streamers and it looks like they can see you, chances are it's someone who's asleep and dreaming. You don't get as many of 'em hanging round the ghost-seam as you do Upstairs, but every little while you'll get a couple of 'em what have blundered down here and are having all their dreams in black and white. Most of 'em, they'll be wearing just their vest and pants or they'll be in the nude. If you see someone dressed who's looking at you, and they don't leave any pictures when they move, it's one of them few characters what are alive but can still see things. If they're drunk or dosed with drugs, or if they're a bit barmy, then they'll glimpse you some-times. Barmy or poetic, either one will do. Most of the time they won't be sure they've really seen you, and they'll look away."

Walking along by Michael's side with Michael hurrying to keep up, John gazed down at the pavement reeling by beneath their feet and frowned, as if he was recalling something that he didn't like.

"The psychics and the swamis, they're all tosh. They'll look straight through you while they tell your mum how happy and how comfortable you look, and how you didn't suffer. You can stand there screaming 'Mum, I got blew up and it wiz bloody horrible', but she won't hear. Nor wizzle they, the phoney buggers.

"Mind you, once I went round to a séance this old girl wiz throwing, in her parlour. She wiz faking everything and telling people that their loved ones wiz beside her when they wizn't. It was only me, I wiz the only ghost there, so I went and stood in front of her and blow me if she couldn't see me! She just looked at me and she burst into tears. Right there and then she called the séance off and sent the people home. She packed the table-tilting in just after that. She never held another meeting, and she wiz the only one I ever met who I'd call genuine."

Ahead of them the top of Spring Lane was approaching and the ancient street ran off downhill upon their right, where Lower Harding Street turned into Crispin Street once it had crossed the lane. The waste-ground that they walked beside had been fenced off with criss-cross wire, beyond which they could see the early stages of some building work. A big sign stood behind the wire, propped on a steel-pipe scaffolding, with words to the effect that all the fenced-in ground belonged to somebody called Cleaver, who was putting up a factory sometime soon.

John strolled along by Michael's side, keeping him company, thoughtfully taking shorter strides so that the youngster could keep up with him more easily. He kept on glancing down at Michael with a faint smile, as if he was privately amused by something but was for the moment keeping it all to him-self. At last he spoke again.

"They tell me your name's Michael Warren. So, whose lad are you, then? What's your dad's name? Is it Walter?"

Michael was confused by this, and wondered if the bigger boy were mak-ing fun of him in some way that he was too young to understand. He shook his head.

"My dad's called Tom."

John beamed, giving the smaller boy a disbelieving look that was at the same time admiring and delighted.

"What, you're Tommy Warren's son? Well, I'll be blowed. None of us ever thought that Tom would marry, with him being a late starter like he wiz. How wiz he, Tom? He's happy, wiz he? Settled down and that, not living with his mam round Green Street anymore?"

Michael was flabbergasted, looking at the big lad in bewilderment, as if John had produced a flock of parrots out of thin air.

"Did you know my dad?"

The older boy laughed, swinging one leg idly as if to kick a bottle-top off of the pavement, though his foot passed through it.

"Blimey, I should say so! I hung round with Tommy and his brothers on the green, when we wiz kids. He's a good bloke, your dad. If you should get took back to life like everybody round here seems to think you wizzle, don't you play him up too much, ay? It's a decent family what you come from, so don't let 'em down."

Here John broke off and gave the fenced-off area that they were walking past a thoughtful look. Grey rain hung trembling on the grey weave of the wire.

"You know, your granddad ... no. No, it's your father's granddad, your great-granddad. He wiz an old terror they called Snowy. He turned down an offer from the man whose company wiz putting up this building here. This feller said that he'd make Snowy a half-partner in the business, on condition Snowy kept out of the pub for the next fortnight. 'Course, he got told where to stick his co-directorship and that wiz that. He wiz a mad old bugger, Snowy Vernall, but he'd got the power in him, right enough. However poor he wiz, he'd got the power to throw away a fortune just like that."

From Michael's point of view this didn't seem much of a power, not when compared to flying, say, or turning to a giant. He'd have asked John to explain, but by that point they'd reached the corner of Spring Lane, unreeling down from where they stood towards the coal-yard and the west, where John suggested that they wait until the others had caught up a bit. Michael gazed off and down the hillside as he whiled away the time.

Even without its dusty, faded colours, this was the Spring Lane that Michael recognised, Spring Lane as it was in the summer months of 1959 and not as it had been in the bright-tinted memories of Phyllis Painter or the other people who had lived here long ago. For one thing, nearly all the houses on the lane's far side had been pulled down. The homes that had been near the upper end were gone, including Phyllis Painter's and the sweetshop that had stood next door, demolished to make room for a long patch of grass that ran along the top Crispin Street edge of Spring Lane School, just a few stone steps up from the school's concrete playground. This was silent and deserted on account of the school holidays.

The houses lower down the hill, the ones that had been standing in between Scarletwell Terrace at the bottom of the slope and Spring Lane Terrace halfway up, these had all disappeared, as had the terraces themselves. The lower playing field of Spring Lane School now reached from the old factory where the fever cart had once been kept, down to the jitty-way that ran along behind the houses on St. Andrew's Road. Although the view was cosy and familiar, Michael found that he was looking at it in a different way, as somebody who knew what had been there before and knew how much was gone. The gaps between the buildings didn't look as if they had been planned, the way they'd looked to him before, but seemed more like reminders of some great disaster.

Michael understood for the first time that he'd been living in a country that had not had time yet to get over being in a war, although he didn't think that many German bombs had fallen on Northampton while all that was going on. It just looked like they had, or as if something every bit as bad had happened. It was funny. If he hadn't seen Mansoul and seen how Spring Lane looked in people's hearts, then all of this would seem normal to him, instead of being bare and broken-looking. It would look like it had always been this way, with all its holes and empty bits.

The other children had by then caught up to him and John, with Phyllis and Drowned Marjorie still smirking slyly as they whispered to each other. The boy Reggie, in his dented bowler hat, had once more started up the game of knuckles he'd been playing earlier with Phyllis's young brother Bill, as they lagged back behind the rest of the Dead Dead Gang. Ginger Bill was blonde like Michael in the ghost-seam, which was colourless as a new Magic Painting book before you'd brushed the water on. As Bill and Reggie's clenched hands hurtled down to smack each other on the knuckles, the two boys were blossoming with fists like angry monsters or like funny gods that people from another country might believe in. Michael wondered briefly if this was the reason why so many things in legends had got extra heads or arms, but just then his attention was seized by a passing bright grey ladybird, so that the idea trailed off uncompleted.

Once they had regrouped, the ghostly urchins crossed Spring Lane and carried on down Crispin Street, beside the woven wire boundary that fenced off the grubby white fur of the school's top lawn. It wasn't until Bill and Reggie plunged straight through the fence to rough-and-tumble there upon the pale and poorly-looking grass that Michael was reminded how he now had the ability to pass through walls and things. He wondered why he and the others kept so strictly upon one side of the wire partition. He supposed that it was habit, and decided not to test it out by joining Bill and Reggie. If he wasn't walking through things all the time then it was easier to pretend that everything was normal, if you didn't count the lack of colour or the burst of twenty hands he now apparently required to quietly pick his nose.

As they got nearer to the scuffed and silvery metal hurdle of the crossing-barrier that stood outside the school's top gate, Michael gazed over Crispin Street to Herbert Street; there it ran off uphill between two patches of tall grass and rubble where it looked like there had once been houses. In his ordinary life, wheeled past it in his pushchair by his mum Doreen, Michael had thought that Herbert Street looked like a run-down sort of street where run-down people lived, although it might have been the name that gave him that impression. Herbert Street, he half-believed, was where the Herberts started out, including not only the Scruffy Herberts and the Lazy Herberts that his dad had often mentioned, but also their more successful-sounding relatives, the Crafty Herberts. This was an idea which more than likely had been passed on to him, like an eyeless teddy bear, by his big sister.

Thinking idly about families and where they started out, including all the things that John had said about his dad and his great-granddad, he was startled when the big boy grabbed him by the collar of his dressing gown and pushed him face down on the grass-seamed paving stones. John did this with such force that for a second Michael's face was shoved below the surface of the street, which was alarming until he discovered that it wasn't really a great inconvenience, although there wasn't much to look at except worms. Bobbing his head back up he caught the tail-end of what John was shouting, with the bigger boy himself down on the ground now, next to Michael.

"... body get down! It's Malone at ten o'clock, up over Althorp Street! Were the same grey as what the path wiz, more or less, so if we stay still he won't see us, being right up in the sky like that."

Although afraid to move a muscle, Michael slowly tipped his head back so that he could peer into the firmament above them.

At first, he mistook it for a smear of dirty smoke, a drifting stain of factory black above the chimneypots that rose between here and the Mayorhold, uphill to the east. It scudded over the slate rooftops like a small but viciously determined thunderhead, and Michael was just wondering why anyone would name a cloud "Malone" when he first noticed the two yapping terriers that it was carrying beneath its arms.

It was a man, a dead man judging from the smudge of picture-portraits stuttering behind him in his wake as he progressed across the off-white heavens. He wore hobnail boots, a shabby suit and long dark coat, the outfit topped off by a bowler hat like Reggie wore, though a much smarter one that looked more business-like. It was the fading plume of after-images from this drab clothing that had looked like smoke when Michael first set eyes on it, a filthy airborne blemish caused by someone burning tyres. However, as he studied it more closely with the better eyesight that he'd had since he'd been dead, more and more horrid details became readily apparent.

There was the chap's face for one thing, a white mask suspended in the churning black steam of his head and body. Pale, with small grey wrinkles where the eyes should be, the ghostly countenance was smoothly shaven, almost rubbery, that of a well-kept sixty-year-old man with absolutely no expression. Michael thought the deadpan features looked more frightening than droll. They didn't look like they'd react to anything, no matter how sweet, terrible or sudden it might be. The colour of the fellow's hair was hidden underneath a stream of bowler hats, but Michael thought that it was more than likely white and oiled, like feathers from an albatross.

Not very tall yet wiry in his build, the man was upright as he moved across the sky, legs pedalling as though he sat astride an unseen bicycle, or as though he were treading air. Each sweep and swing of his long coat hung there recorded on the space behind him in a tongue of tarry vapour. Underneath his arms he clutched his pair of dogs, one black, one white, like on the label of Gran's whiskey bottle, while up from his jacket pockets boiled the writhing heads of what the horror-stricken Michael first took to be snakes then realised were ferrets, not that this was any less distressing. He could hear their distant cheeps of threat and panic, even in amongst the startled barking of the terriers, despite the ghost-seam's soundproofing that sucked the echo out of every note.

"What wiz he?" Michael asked John in a whisper as the two of them lay face down, side by side upon the tiles of Crispin Street. The older boy kept his poetic-looking eyes fixed watchfully upon the smouldering figure passing overhead as he replied.

"Him? That's Malone, the Boroughs' ratter. He's a fearsome man, make no mistake. They say he does a party trick where he'll catch rats and kill 'em with his teeth, although I've never seen him do it. Phyllis stole his bowler once and put it on a great big rat. All you could see was this hat with a rat's tail scuttling down the street, and old Malone grey in the face as he went running after it. Malone wiz furious. He said that he'd hang Phyllis with her rabbit-string if he caught up with her, and sounded like he meant it. From the way he's headed, I'd say he's just come out of the Jolly Smokers. That's the pub they haunt, up on the Mayorhold, so he might have had a drink. At any rate, you're best off steering clear of him, whether he's drunk or sober. With a bit of luck he's heading home to Little Cross Street, where he lived, and he'll be passed by in a minute.'

As it turned out, John was right. Although he moved as slow as treacle, the dead rat-catcher progressed in a south-westerly direction through the

ashen Boroughs' sky, cutting across the corner of the school's top lawn from
Crispin Street to Scarletwell Street, floating off above the maisonettes, past
Bath Street to the tangled courts and passages beyond. The whining of the
hounds grew fainter as their master's blot-like shape was shrunken to a smut,
a breeze-borne speck like something in your eye, no different from the other
black flakes carried from the railway station.

Cautiously, the Dead Dead Gang climbed to their feet once they were
sure he wasn't going to come dog-paddling back through the still summer
air and pounce upon them. Bill and Reggie were both giggling as they remi-
nisced about the rat-and-bowler incident that John had mentioned, although
Phyllis had a faintly worried look and fiddled nervously with her long scarf of
putrefying rabbit pelts. Only Drowned Marjorie seemed unconcerned by the
experience, dusting her skirt down with a brisk efficiency and brushing bits of
ghost-grit from her chubby knees as she stood up. Michael was starting to see
the bespectacled girl as the gang's most stoic member, taking every new experience in her stumpy stride without complaint. He thought that this might be
an outlook that came naturally to someone drowned before the age of seven.
Things would probably seem relatively unsurprising after that, even if they
were flying rat-catchers.

Although the sighting of Malone had evidently rattled Phyllis, she still
managed to maintain a tone of calm authority as she addressed her men.

"Come on. If we're to find ayt all the clues an' evidence abayt ayr regimental mascot then we better get dayn Scarletwell, before somebody else comes
sailin' past."

Michael fell into step beside the gang as they continued along Crispin
Street. In the square holes where paving-tiles had been prised up were pud-
dles, shimmering like chips of mirror on a pantomime princess's ball-gown.
Shuffling in his slippers to keep up with John, Michael was unable to put
Malone the ratter's recent aerial stroll out of his mind.

"How wiz he flying, right up in the air like that?"

The older boy frowned quizzically at Michael, so that Michael thought he
must have said his words the wrong way round again.

"What do you mean? Malone's a ghost. Ghosts don't have any heaviness,
what they call mass, so here in the three-sided world the pull of things don't
make no difference to 'em. Not much, anyway. It's just the same for us lot.
Here, give me your hand and jump as if we're in the long-jump."

Michael did as he was told. To his astonishment he found that he and John
were sailing through the air in a slow arc which, at its summit, took them
higher than the fencing of the school yard to their right. As light as dandelion
clocks they drifted back to earth again a few yards further down the street,
their after-images like kite-tails settling behind. Michael was speechless with

delight at this exciting new discovery but nonetheless resumed his normal walking style there next to John, who had by now let go of Michael's hand.

"There's lots of things like that what you can do. You can jump off a roof and fall so slowly that you don't get hurt. Or you can fly like old Malone, although there's lots of different ways of doing it. Most people pick their feet up off the floor until they're sort of lying in the air, then do a breast-stroke like they're swimming. Others do a doggie-paddle like Malone, and some just swoop about like bits of paper in the wind. You'll find with the majority of ghosts, though, that they can't be bothered flying everywhere. For one thing, it's too bloody slow. The air's as thick as marmalade. You're faster walking, or else running in the special ways that ghosts can run: there's skimming like you're on a frozen slide that's just an inch above the pavement, or there's what we call the rabbit run, on all fours so that just your knuckles graze the ground. That's a good laugh, if everybody's in the mood for it, but by and large it's safer walking. You've got time to spot all the rough sleepers before they spot you."

They were now at the end of Crispin Street, where it ran over Scarletwell Street and turned into Upper Cross Street. John insisted that they wait again at this new junction for the others to catch up, so Michael practised jumping on the spot, achieving altitudes of several feet before John asked him, genially, to pack it in. From where they stood upon their corner, Scarletwell Street was unrolled down to St. Andrew's Road upon their right, while on their left it sloped up in between the facing terraces towards the cosy oldness of the Mayorhold. Michael always thought of this familiar enclosure as a sort of town square that was meant for just the people of the Boroughs, even though he knew that the real Market Square was further off uptown.

Standing there in his drool-scorched dressing gown, there in the draught-board-coloured copy of his neighbourhood, the little boy looked at the weathered brickwork of the houses at the top of Scarletwell and had a sense, for the first time, of how long everything had been here before he'd been born. There was what John had told him about playing on the green behind St. Peter's Church with Michael's dad when they'd been boys. He hadn't really thought before about his dad having once had a childhood, although now it struck him, shockingly and suddenly, that everyone must have been little once. Even his dad's mum, his nan, May, she'd have begun life as a tiny baby somewhere. Then there was her dad, Michael's great-grandfather, who John had mentioned, who was mad and had the power to not have any money. Snowy, had John called him? Snowy must have been a boy of Michael's age once, long ago, who'd had a mother and a father, and so on and so on, back to times he'd heard about "when we were living in the trees", which he'd assumed were probably the ones down in Victoria Park. Michael stared off down Scarletwell, between the modern maisonettes or flats on one side and the playing fields of Spring Lane School upon the other, feeling as if he were peering down a real well, one that dropped away beneath him, down through all the mums and dads and grandmas and great-granddads, back through all the days and years and hundred-years into a smelly, dark place that was damp and echoey, mysterious and bottomless.

Once all the other dead kids had caught up and joined them on the corner, John and Michael carried on down Scarletwell Street. From the hill's top, gazing down across the squeaking railway yards towards Victoria Park and Jimmy's End, the view was much the same as it had been up in Mansoul, except that here it looked like an old silent film, silver like fish-skin, without all of the remembered warmth and colour. It was only when he thought about the way things would have been only a little while back, in his parents' day, that it occurred to Michael how much change the district must have seen in those few years.

Judging from how he'd heard his mum and gran describe it, the whole big oblong of ground, which stretched from Scarletwell Street to Spring Lane and from St. Andrew's Road to Crispin Street, had been much simplified. Where once the block had been a maze of homes and yards and businesses, now there were just the classrooms of Spring Lane School sheltered in a concrete hollow at the hill's crest and a single row of houses at the bottom on St. Andrew's Road, the terrace that Michael had lived in when he was alive. All of the land between was now banked playing fields, with the exception of a sole surviving factory over on Spring Lane. A hundred warehouses, sheds, pubs, homes that had served for generations, alleyways for kissing couples, outdoor toilets and lamplighter's shortcuts had been swept away to leave grey meadows where the whitewash margins of the football pitch stood out like old scars. Although this was Scarletwell as Michael knew it, somewhere that seemed always to have been the way it was and where his own house still stood safe and sound, he had a sudden tingling sense of all the names and stories that had been rubbed out to make a place where school-kids could have sack races on sports day. All the people that were gone, and all the things they'd known.

Michael was walking beside John, still, as they sauntered down the washed-out reproduction of the hill. Not far behind them, Phyllis and Drowned Marjorie were sniggering conspiratorially again and Michael wondered if it was at him, but then he always wondered that with girls. Or boys. Following at the rear, Phyllis's little brother Bill conferred in hushed tones with the bowler-clad boy, Reggie, telling him what Michael thought was probably a dirty joke, then having to explain the modern parts of it that the Victorian boy obviously didn't get. Michael could hear him saying "Well, okay, the woman in the gag's not Elsie Tanner, then. What if it's Mrs. Beeton?" Michael didn't know the first name, but he thought the second had something to do with either cookery or nursing, or perhaps she'd been a murderer. He strained to hear the finish of the story, which appeared to involve either Elsie Tanner or else Mrs. Beeton answering the door to a delivery boy when she was nude and straight out of the bath, but Phyllis Painter turned round to her younger brother and told him to knock it off before she clouted him. There was a tightness in her voice that Michael didn't think had been there before they'd had their near run-in with Malone. She sounded a bit scared, and in the light of what he'd heard about the fearless pranks that Phyllis played on ghosts, this puzzled him. He thought that he'd ask John.

"So, if ghosts frighten Phyllis, why does she play tricks on them? If she wiz to leave them alone, perhaps they wizzle do the same."

John shook his head, so that for a brief instant he had three of them. He and the younger boy were just then strolling past the south side of the school's top lawn, towards the stone posts of its main gate, further down.

"It's not Phyllis's nature, to leave ghosts alone. I'll tell you, she knows how to bear a grudge, does Phyllis, past the grave if necessary. What it wiz, when Phyllis wiz a living girl, she wizn't scared of nothing except ghosts. Even if the ghosts wizn't really there, they played upon her nerves so bad that she made up her mind to one day have revenge. She swore that if she ever got to be a ghost herself, then she'd give all the other ghosts what for, for scaring little children. She'd be such a terror that the ghosts would all end up afraid of kids and not the other way around. I have to say, she's done a good job so far, even if there's places in the Boroughs we can't go in case they lynch her."

John and Michael neared the entrance of the schoolyard, with its own iron crossing barrier stood there in front of it, the gates locked for the summer holidays. Across the road from this the mouth of Lower Cross Street opened, running south along the bottom of the maisonettes to cut across the slope of Bath Street, heading towards Doddridge Church in the blurred snapshot of the distance. Down this side-street, rumbling towards the junction where it met with Scarletwell, there came a baffling assortment of fused body parts and cycle-wheels that Michael couldn't come to terms with for a moment. It appeared to be a man in a dark trilby, riding on a bicycle, but all the images that he left trailing after him had got their black and white reversed, like when you saw the negatives of photographs. This, Michael thought, was surely a notorious and perhaps dangerous rough sleeper. He tugged hard upon John's sleeve and stammered the alarm, although the tall lad didn't seem unduly worried by the apparition. After a few moments Michael understood the reason why, or, at least, he began to understand it.

The gruff-looking fellow in the trilby turned left at the corner and free-wheeled away down Scarletwell Street on his bicycle, a creaking old contraption that looked pony-sized to Michael. As the man rolled off downhill he left no pictures of himself behind, which meant that he was still a living person. The peculiar thing that Michael had at first mistaken for a string of after-images in negative remained, unmoving, at the end of Lower Cross Street.

This turned out to be a coloured man with white hair, also sat astride a bicycle, who appeared fleetingly familiar to the little boy. Had Michael glimpsed a picture of this old chap somewhere recently, an image on a circus poster or a stained-glass window or something like that? The black man changed his grip upon the handlebars, and Michael noticed a brief flurry of too many fingers, from which he deduced this cyclist was the ghost, and not the other one. When Michael had first noticed him approaching Scarletwell Street, he must have been riding his ghost-bicycle so that he occupied the same space as the trilby-sporting white man, which explained how they'd seemed all mixed up together. Looking closer, Michael also realised that the black man's bike (which pulled a two-wheeled cart behind it) had white tyres made out of rope, rather than the black rubber ones that had been on the living rider's vehicle. This had probably helped give him the impression that one cyclist was a reversed copy of the other, now he thought about it.

As they both approached the school gate and its finger-worn gunmetal crossing barrier, John ducked his head to whisper an aside to Michael, who was diligently shuffling along beside him.

"That bloke who just rode off down the hill, the living fellow with the trilby on, he wiz the one you should be scared of out of them two. He's George Blackwood, who rents half the houses in the Boroughs out, and half the women too. Bit of a gangster, Blackwood wiz, collecting rent and his cut of the takings from the prostitutes. He's got a lot of hard men who he pays to back him up. 'Soul of the Hole', we call his type up here. He's one of them where you can see the first signs of a kind of emptiness that gets into a place and turns it rotten."

Michael didn't have the first idea what John was on about. He merely nodded wisely so that his pale ringlets bloomed double-exposed into a lamb-white catkin-bush, and let the older lad continue.

"Everybody's scared of Blackwood. The exception, funnily enough, wiz your nan, May. May Warren treats him just the same as she treats everybody else, which wiz to say she tells him off and scares him stiff with a right ear-ful and then asks him if he wants a cup of tea. Old Blackwood likes her. He respects her, you can tell. And I'd not be surprised if him and his young ladies hadn't needed a good deathmonger at times over the years, if you know what I mean."

Though Michael didn't, he tried hard to look as though he did. The bigger boy went on.

"The coloured feller, on the other hand, he's good as gold. His name's Black Charley and you won't find anybody more well-liked throughout Mansoul. The Mayor of Scarletwell, that's what they call him. If you look close you can see he's got his chain of office on, around his neck."

Michael looked closer, as instructed, and saw that the black chap had indeed got something like a rough medallion hanging down to his white shirt-front. In its way, it was as memorable a piece of neckwear as the scarf of rabbit-hides that Phyllis had got on. It seemed to be a tin lid hanging from a lavatory chain, but with the pale grey metal polished so that it was blinding when it caught the silver of the sunlight. The old coloured bloke was gazing, not unkindly, at the gang of kids as they approached the junction, obviously waiting there upon his funny-looking bicycle so he could talk to them. Michael spoke from the corner of his mouth to John, in much the way that tough Americans talked in the films you saw on telly.

"Wiz he a rough sleeper?"

John dismissed the notion with a wave, a dozen hands in grey-white like the pages of a fanned-through book.

"Nah. Not Black Charley. The rough sleepers, for the most part, hang about here in the ghost-seam because they don't think they'd like it in Mansoul, up in the Second Borough. I've heard some say as the ghost-seam's purgatory, but if it wiz, it's one that people chose themselves. It's not like that with Charley. He's like us, he comes and goes exactly as he pleases. He's as happy Upstairs as he wiz down here, and if he's passing through this layer it's because he wants to, just like us. What's more, he's one of the few ghosts, along with Mrs. Gibbs, that Phyllis shows respect for, so there's no bad blood between Black Charley and the Dead Dead Gang, just for a change."

They were now down beside the crossing barrier, outside the padlocked gates of Spring Lane School. John raised one hand and called across the road to the old black man on the other side. He had to shout a bit to get his voice to carry in the deadened atmosphere of that unusual half-world, where there wasn't even any colour to the sound.

"What ho, Black Charley. How's death treating you, then?"

All the other children had by this point reached the school gates, catching up with John and Michael, and were calling their own greetings to the phantom cyclist. The black rider laughed and shook his tight white curls into a phosphorescent blur, as though in amiable resignation at the sight of the dead urchins. Easily distracted, Michael noticed that a windborne sheet of newspaper was leaving a whole magazine of after-images behind it as it tumbled off down Scarletwell Street. He supposed it must be a ghost-newspaper, ghost-rubbish snatched up by the faint ghost of a breeze he thought he felt on his bare neck and ankles. Putting it out of his mind he turned his full attention back to the old coloured man who sat across the street astride what looked like home-made transport.

"My eternal life be treatin' me just fine, thankin' you kindly, master John. I'm just here carryin' out the duties what I got as Mayor o' Scarletwell, warning the local dead folks about this bad weather we got comin' up and tellin' 'em to get theyselves indoors, but now I'm more concerned about you little outlaws, gettin' up to trouble all the time. Miss Phyllis, don't you play no stunts on any o' them gentlemen what takes their liquor at the Jolly Smokers. They's a rough crew, so take my advice an' keep away from 'em."

He glanced around at all the other children, as if counting heads and making sure they were all present and correct.

"Miss Marjorie and Master Bill, hello to you, and to old Reggie Got-His-Hat-On I can see stood up the back there. And who's this young feller what you're no doubt leadin' into wicked ways?"

Michael realised belatedly that the good-natured ghost was talking about him. Phyllis chimed in on his behalf and introduced him to Black Charley.

"This wiz Michael Warren and 'e choked upon a pep, or so 'e says. I faynd 'im in the Attics of the Breath with no one there to meet 'im, so I took 'im underneath me wing. He's been nothing but trouble ever since. First 'e got kidnapped by a devil, then we faynd ayt that 'e'd started a big fight between the builders, and now it turns ayt 'e'll be come back to life by Friday. It's a lot of bother, but the Dead Dead Gang are looking into it. We've brought him dayn 'ere, where 'e lived, so that we can investigate 'is murder-mystery."

Michael piped up here in protest.

"I coughed on a choke-drop, so I wizzn't murdered."

Phyllis turned to stare at him. She clearly didn't much like being interrupted.

"'Ow do you know? What with all the bother what yer cause, I'd be surprised if *somebody* weren't planning to get rid of yer. If I were yer mum, I'd be shoving cough-sweets dayn yer throat without unwrapping 'em or even bothering to take them ayt the packet! Anyway, we're the detectives and yer only the dead body what we're trying to solve the killing of, so you keep quiet and don't get in the way of ayr enquiries, or we'll 'ave you booked for wasting police time and you'll be put in prison."

Michael, even though he'd died this morning, hadn't been born yesterday and was beginning to catch on that almost all of Phyllis's authority was just a game and a pretence. He took no notice of her, his attention caught instead by what he thought must be a whole flock of ghost-pigeons that were passing overhead towards the foot of Scarletwell. Each of the dead birds drew a fluttering queue of grey potato-prints behind it, dozens of long smoky threads unravelling towards the west, where the blanched sun was slowly settling above a burnished steel-engraving of the railway yards. Michael was more intrigued by the idea that birds and animals went Upstairs when they died than he was in replying to what Phyllis had just said, and anyway, it was at that point that Black Charley intervened, replying for him.

"Now, Miss Phyllis, don't you tease the child like that. Did you say how he'd started a big ruckus in between the builders?"

The black ghost was staring hard at Phyllis now. She nodded. Something with veined wings that looked like an enormous bat sailed past, bouncing in short hops down the hill and leaving pictures of itself behind it, making Michael jump until he realised it was just the ghost of somebody's umbrella. Satisfied that Phyllis wasn't having fun with him, Black Charley carried on.

"Then this boy is the one what I've been hearin' about. Michael Warren, did you say? The way I heard, he plays some part in that big capstone ceremony what the builders talk about, their Porthimoth di Norhan like they calls it. That's how come the players at the table got upset when this child's trilliard-ball got placed in dreadful danger, and that's how come two of 'em wiz fightin'. It's their battle what they have up on the Mayorhold causin' all this wind what's comin', what I'm warnin' folks about."

All of the ghost-kids except Michael suddenly looked worried. Reggie took his bowler hat off as if he were at a funeral, questioning Black Charley anxiously in his peculiarly-accented and twangy voice.

"Gawd love us. There's not gunna be a ghost-storm, wiz there?"

Charley nodded, gravely and emphatically.

"I fear so, master Reggie, and you bin round these parts longer'n what I have, so you know what happens when them ghost-winds start up blowin'. My advice is get yourself inside and get Upstairs, or up to sometime where the weather ain't so bad. And you make sure as you look after master Michael here, because if this wiz what the builders do when he's just put in danger, I don't wanna think about the way they'd take it if'n you should get him hurt."

A black cat skittered yowling past, pulling behind it a half-knitted sock of trailing images and followed by the tinkling ghost of a pale ale bottle. Buzzing shoelace threads stitched themselves through the air that Michael finally concluded were a pair of phantom flies. Black Charley picked one foot up off the ground decisively and set it on a pedal. Michael was surprised to notice that the coloured man had blocks of wood strapped underneath his shoes.

"I got me dead folks I should warn about the storm in Bellbarn and around St. Andrew's Church, so I can't wait around here anymore. You get yourselves out of harm's way, and look after that little boy. He's got important wagers ridin' on him."

With that, the determined-looking ghost trod down upon his upraised pedal and the bicycle-and-cart rolled over Scarletwell Street and away uphill, with fading likenesses of its white wheels bowling along behind it in a long

string of Olympic hoops. Black Charley rode away from them, into the wind
that was now clearly rising, ruffling the ghost of everybody's hair. To Michael
the old coloured fellow seemed strangely heroic, pedalling his rope-wheeled
junk-cart like a crow-black herald of the coming storm. The Dead Dead Gang
seemed to stand rooted to the spot for several moments after his departure,
goggling at each other with wide, anxious eyes. Above them all, a squawking
static-pattern of dark stripes that might have been a phantom budgerigar blew
past, as did a ghostly undertaker's top hat with a dove-grey hatband ribbon
rippling in its wake amongst the rush of after-pictures. At last, Phyllis Painter
broke the silence with a panicked but commanding yelp.

"Ghost-storm! You 'eard 'im! Everybody rabbit-run, dayn to the 'ouse
what's on the corner!"

With a suddenness that frankly startled Michael, Phyllis dropped onto
all fours and raced off down the hill with the most puzzling gait that he had
ever seen. Taking advantage of the slow, treacle-like quality that ghost-seam
air possessed, Phyllis was able to skim lightly down the slope with just her
scampering knuckles grazing on the surface of the road, propelled by circling
back legs that barely needed touch the ground themselves. It was a sort of
rabbit-movement, he supposed, explaining the manoeuvre's name, although
to Michael it looked more like how he though baboons might run, except for
all the trailing reproductions that made Phyllis look like a long locomotive
that had wheels made out of skinny little girl's legs. To his great alarm, first
Marjorie then Bill and Reggie followed Phyllis's example, crouching down
then bounding off downhill with a surprising speed. He was just starting to
get worried about being left behind by all the dead kids when he noticed John,
who'd hung back to look after him and who was now encouraging the smaller
boy to try the rabbit-run himself.

"Come on, it's easy. You'll soon get the hang of it. Just get down on all
fours then lift your feet up so you're walking on your hands."

Michael squinted uphill into the gathering wind. The sky above the Mayorhold at the top of Scarletwell was speckled by what Michael realised with
a lurch of horror was ghost-debris, some of it comprised of flailing animals
and people, and all of it blowing rapidly towards them. He needed no further
urging. Dropping down onto his haunches and then lifting up his feet as he'd
been told, Michael soon found himself bowling along like stripy flannel tumbleweed. Only his hands were scrabbling across the gritty surface of the road
beneath him as he scuttled down the hill after the other children, heading for
the corner at the bottom where St. Andrew's Road met Scarletwell Street.

John had been correct. This method of getting around wasn't just easy, it
was also massive fun. It seemed like such a natural way to travel, effortlessly
rushing through the streets with your back legs sizzling along behind you like

grey Catherine Wheels, kicking up ghost-grit in a shower of welding-sparks. He took to it so readily and found the form of movement so surprisingly familiar that Michael wondered if he had an instinct for it. Was this how his family had walked once, back when they'd reportedly been "living in the trees", possibly in Victoria Park? It certainly made his descent of Scarletwell into a thrilling ride, the off-white flats flickering by on one side with their rounded balconies that made him think of going to the pictures, and the bleak school playing fields that smeared past on the other.

He was starting to enjoy it when the ghost of an old busted armchair spoiled all that by somersaulting through the air above him, followed by two stony-faced but obviously embarrassed phantom monks and a whole shower of ghostly bird's-nests, broken deckchairs, pencils, fag-ends, ants, books that had pictures of bare ladies in, chipped bathroom tiles and spectral bars of soap, each hurtling object with a fuming trail of after-images behind it, like a swarm of angry burning bees. The prospect of this wave of haunted shrapnel overtaking him reminded Michael, forcefully, of the ghost-squall that surged behind them and which they were trying to get away from. He decided that he'd better take this rabbit-running business far more seriously, redoubling his efforts as he tore downhill towards the other dead kids, who were gathering near Scarletwell Street's bottom corner.

As he slowed and stumbled to a halt beside them with ghost cinders, toffee wrappers and lost plimsolls whistling past his ears, he noticed that they hadn't congregated at the junction with St. Andrew's Road, the terrace where he'd lived and died, but were instead a house or two up from the corner, huddling beside the long brick wall of a back yard belonging to one of the homes in the short row between the jitty-mouth and the main road. The dead gang's hair and clothing flapped and rippled like grey signal-flags and they were clutching at each other's jumpers as they tried to keep from being blown away.

Buckets and boaters cart-wheeled by above them; afterlife coal-dust in a cloud that turned the sky black even though you could still see the calm and sunny mortal afternoon behind it all. Through the miasma, Michael could make out scores of uprooted ghost-seam residents, cursing or wailing, struggling or hanging there limp and resigned as the ferocious wraith-wind blowing from the Mayorhold hurled them through the darkening heavens overhead, all dragging their last several instants in their wake like advertising banners, cheap ones where they couldn't afford colour. He saw several monks, all holding hands and gliding in formation, and a cross old lady in a district nurse's outfit who tried to arrest her flight by grabbing at the television aerial of the end house as it whizzed by below. Her insubstantial fingers passed straight through the metal letter H without effect and she was whipped away by the ethereal hurricane towards the overexposed photo of the train yards and the de-greened park beyond. Standing in front of Michael with her string of rotten rabbits being tossed about in an impossible confusion of repeated ears and tails and eyes, Phyllis was shouting something at him through the dead acoustics of the ghost-seam and the howling wuther of the gale.

"... in through the wall! We've got to get inside the corner 'ouse so we can all get 'igher up, ayt of this wind!"

The blustering force behind him was propelling Michael haltingly in Phyllis's direction, his plaid slippers slithering upon the paving slabs beneath them. Reaching blindly he clutched on to something solid, only realising afterwards that it was John's arm, with the tall lad having stood protectively at Michael's back to shield the youngster from the eerie blizzard. With his forward slide thus halted, Michael gaped at Phyllis in bewilderment. Just past her he could see Drowned Marjorie as the bespectacled and tubby little girl threw herself headlong at the wall that they were sheltering beside, only to disappear into or through the mother-of-pearl sheen upon the brickwork and be gone from sight. Phyllis's younger brother Bill went next and then the gangling and freckled Reggie, clutching his hat tight against his chest so that it wasn't ripped away from him by the typhoon as he ducked through the wall into whatever back yard was presumably beyond. Michael was still confused, and called to Phyllis over the ghost-tempest.

"But that's knot the corner house. That's slumboggy's back-yarden. There's the corn ear just downhill behive you."

Phyllis glinted at him, something in between glaring and squinting, as she faced into the flickering thunderstorm of distressed apparitions that were gusting straight towards them down the ancient hill.

"That dayn there's where the corner wiz. We're climbing up to when the corner wizzle be in ten or twenty years, where 'opefully we'll be above this weather. Now, come through the wall with us or get blown dayn to Vicky Park with all them other silly buggers. I'm not got the time to stand 'ere and debate wi' yer."

With that she jumped into the jigsaw pattern of grey bricks and whitish mortar, vanishing into the wall. Michael stood hesitating for a moment even then, before John grabbed him by the spit-scorched collar of his dressing gown and hurried him towards the very solid-looking boundary.

"Do as she says for once, ay, Tommy's boy? It's for your own good."

John shoved Michael at and through the wall. Although he closed his eyes instinctively just prior to the expected impact, this did not shut out a brief glimpse of exactly what bricks looked like from within, with all the little cylinders of nothing where the vent holes were. Emerging spluttering and gasping on the other side with John stepping unhurriedly out of the wall immediately after him, Michael discovered he was in a large though fairly plain and bare

rear yard, with just a garden shed, a single narrow flowerbed and a washing-line with wooden prop and hanging sheets to occupy the mostly cob-
ble-stone enclosure. The high brick walls, having stood in that spot for some
eighty to a hundred years, served to keep out a fraction of the raging ghost-tor-
nado boiling through the Boroughs, though not all of it by any means. Revenant grime and litter spun in frantic eddies at the back yard's corners, the
attendant after-images smudged into solid doughnut shapes by the rotation.

Phyllis Painter was already organising the Dead Dead Gang into what, for
Michael, was unfathomable action. Reggie stood there at the centre of the yard
with Phyllis perching balanced on his shoulders like they were both in a circus act. Drowned Marjorie held Reggie's bowler hat while he had both hands
clasped around Phyllis's ankles, steadying her. The plucky little dead girl in her
scarf of rancid rabbits stood there wobbling with both her cardigan-clad arms
raised up above her head, where she made pawing motions with her hands as
if attempting to dig upwards into empty nothing like a mole with no sense
of direction. Looking closer, Michael noticed that the air around her clawing
fingers seemed to bend and quiver. He could make out moving bands of black
and white like television interference patterns, glimmering stripes squeezed
together, pushed to one side by the ghost-child's frantic burrowing. He dimly
understood from what Phyllis had said a moment or two previously that she
was climbing up through time to "when the corner wizzle be in ten or twenty
years", and he supposed the strips of wavering white and black might be the days
and nights that she was forced to tunnel up through, vellum mornings interleaved with carbon-paper darkness. Clearing away minutes, hours and years
like layers of onionskin her flickering hands were grey anemones of fingers.
Michael realised that the more he got to know the often bossy and unfriendly
self-appointed leader of the Dead Dead Gang, the more he came to like her and
admire her. She was someone you could count on, someone with resources.

In the windswept yard the other members of the outfit looked on agitatedly as Phyllis teetered there on Reggie's shoulders, excavating thin air, while
above a howling torrent of unearthly jetsam seethed and skittered through the
rectangle of sky over their brick refuge. There were uncanny ironing-boards
with their crossed legs leaving a string of fading kisses through the afternoon
behind them, a whole set of dominoes stretched into spotted liquorice sticks
by the array of visual echoes that each one was dragging, several million splinters of ghost-wood or ghost-glass, whole spook-trees with wraith-soil raining
from their exposed roots in wispy picture-streamers, toppling tattered pets
and men and women, a confetti of careening and complaining shadow-shapes,
all the torn phantoms of Northampton.

Meanwhile, Phyllis's young brother Bill appeared to have discovered
something nestling in an obscure corner of the brickwork.

"Bingo! There's mad-apples over 'ere!"

His voice was faint, damped by the ghost-seam and submerged beneath the banshee chorus of the roaring storm. Peering into the juncture of the yard walls that the previously ginger but now ashen scamp was pointing to, Michael could see what looked like two small slate-grey flowers sprouting from a fissure in the crumbling mortar. On further inspection he was slightly unnerved to discover that each petal was a nasty-looking little figure with a big head and a pair of glittering jet eyes. Balancing awkwardly on Reggie's shoulders, Phyllis frowned down angrily at Bill and his discovery.

"Leave 'em alone, you nit! They're elf-ones, so they'll gi' yer bellyache. Yer've gotta leave 'em until they can ripen into fairies. Anyway, I reckon I've broke through up 'ere, so you can climb up Reggie's back and 'elp me."

Bill abandoned the grey horror-blossoms and went grudgingly to do his sister's bidding, and yet Michael found it hard to take his eyes off of the things once they'd been called to his attention. From the shadowed angle of the back yard's corner he could feel the man-buds watching him and sensed they were unpleasantly aware in their own way. Michael could not imagine what kind of awareness that might be, what murky thoughts or vegetable desires might pass through all those joined-together heads, and found upon reflection that he wasn't really that keen on imagining it anyway. Reluctantly he tore his gaze away from the disturbing corner-fruit and tried instead to concentrate on what the Dead Dead Gang were up to.

As the essence of a sideboard turned elaborate pirouettes through the junk-peppered maelstrom shrieking above Scarletwell Street, young Bill was obeying Phyllis's instructions and was clambering up Reggie's back while shedding picture-copies in a smoky squirrel-tail behind him. Michael noticed that just over Phyllis, at the point where she'd been scraping at the air so frantically, there was now a round patch of solid blackness slightly wider than the circle of a dustbin. Bill shinned onto Reggie's shoulders and then started climbing Phyllis, who was standing there as well. Michael was wondering how the pug-nosed Victorian urchin could support the load when he recalled what John had said about how ghosts weighed hardly anything. Upon consideration, he supposed that this was how the fierce winds blasting downhill from the Mayorhold could uproot seemingly heavy things like – he glanced upwards at the square of rushing sky above them all – like prams and tramps and double beds and the bewildered spirits of inverted horses, sending them all spiralling away across the burnished railway yards into the soot-smudged whiteness of the sunset. Michael watched as Bill hauled himself up onto his sister's back and, in a squirm of after-images, continued crawling upwards through the dark hole in the air, completely vanishing from sight.

Swaying on Reggie's shoulders, Phyllis Painter craned her neck to look down at the other dead kids on the cobblestones beneath her.

"Marjorie, you're next, and then the new boy."

The whole yard was resonating now, making the mournful sound milk-bottles make if someone blows across the neck of them, this plaintive tone mixed with the deafening bellow of the ghost-squall so that Phyllis's commands were hardly audible. Nevertheless, Drowned Marjorie obediently scrambled over lanky Reggie and up Phyllis, holding Reggie's bowler hat between her clenched teeth as she did so, vanishing into the same black aperture that had claimed Bill just moments earlier. Now it was Michael's turn.

Casting a doubtful look at John, who gave merely a tight nod in reply, he started his ascent of Reggie and discovered it was all much easier than he'd anticipated. The near-weightlessness meant that there wasn't any need to haul himself laboriously up, hand over hand, and that his grip on Reggie's damp jumble-sale coat was only necessary to keep him from floating off into the screaming flood of spectres being dashed across the district by this supernatural tempest. As he climbed on over Phyllis with his small hands clenched in her ghost-cardigan, he saw that from close up the black space overhead was not completely black, just dark, as if it led into an unlit attic. Round the edges of the sky-hole he could see the pattern of the black and white lines that he'd spotted earlier, the bands of night and day now squeezed into a luminous grey trim of shimmer at the aerial excavation's rim. More startlingly, as he reached Phyllis Painter's summit and stared up into the lightless opening, he could see a quartet of hands emerging from it, reaching down to grab him in a flurry of repeated cuffs and thumbs and filthy fingernails.

Before he'd had a chance to work out what was going on he was dragged upward through a wriggling and kicking outburst of himselves and pulled across the sparkling threshold into blackness. Suddenly he found that he was sitting on the upstairs landing of a dark and unfamiliar house, between Drowned Marjorie and Bill. Before them in the landing's faded carpet was a hole, up through which flared the pewter-coloured radiance of the ghost-seam, shining up to glint on wooden banisters and crowded wallpaper that writhed with roses, under-lighting the three children's faces as they knelt or sat around the blazing well-mouth gaping in the floor. Drifting up out of this came the faint voice of Phyllis Painter.

"Pull me up next, then all of us can 'elp with John and Reggie."

Following Bill and Drowned Marjorie's lead, Michael leaned over the hole's rim and squinted down into the glare. Beneath him was the cobbled yard, with Phyllis swaying as she stood on Reggie, reaching up towards them with both hands and an aggrieved look on her face. The trio of ghost-infants crouching on the silent midnight landing took her by the wrists and pulled her gossamer-light form up through the shimmering gap, onto the carpeting and floorboards they were crouching on.

Phyllis peered into the gloom about them.

"Bugger. I've dug up too 'igh. This is up in the nothings. Ne' mind, ay? Let's 'elp up John and Reggie and we'll work ayt what to do from there."

Down in the yard beneath them, John had now taken his place upon the shoulders of the uncomplaining Reggie. With a still-surprising lack of effort, the four smaller members of the dead gang whisked him up onto the boards beside them. Next, all five of them caught hold of Reggie as the freckle-faced Victorian boy, lacking a human ladder, was compelled to burst up through the radiant opening from a standing jump.

Once they were reunited on the strip of grey and mottled carpeting they stopped to catch their wistful memory of breath. The old dark of the unknown house about them ticked and creaked and bumped at intervals with muffled sounds of habitation on a lower floor, and Phyllis Painter raised a stream of fingers to her lips, shooting a warning glance at her companions. When she spoke, it was an urgent whisper.

"Don't make any noise. I've dug us up into the nothings by mistake, when there's a watcher livin' at the corner. Let's just cover up this 'ole, then we can plan ayr next move."

With a frown of concentration, Phyllis started scrabbling her sudden multitude of fingers at the shimmering edges of the aperture. She teased long strands of carpet-coloured fume out from the hole's perimeter and combed them carefully across the gap in space, through which the walled enclosure down in 1959 could still be seen, its flickering Laurel and Hardy light erupting through the landing floor to make the ring of children's faces glow like weird theatre masks. Below, the ghost-typhoon still raged in the deserted yard, flinging its multiple-exposure phantom debris through the air in a bewildering profusion that included fishing tackle, wailing stillborn kittens in a wicker picnic hamper, a collection of diversely decorated beer-mats and the angry spirit of a swan that hurtled past beneath them in a hissing pinwheel tumble of exploding white rosettes. Drowned Marjorie and John joined in with Phyllis's attempt to spread the smouldering fibres from the rim over the opening, so that in moments the illumination from below was broken into triangles and misshapes by the crisscross web of smoky filaments they'd dragged across it. Instants more and these remaining chinks were also covered over, with the thin spindles of brilliance that shone up into the landing's darkness snuffed out one by one. At last the six of them were crouched around a patch of carpet upon which the rudimentary floral pattern was uninterrupted, just as if it hadn't been a mass of vaporous tendrils only minutes earlier. Nobody would have known the tunnel into 1959 had ever been there.

Though the only source of light had been obliterated by the matted substance of whatever present day this was, Michael discovered that he could still see the looming banisters and his companions in surprising detail even through the unrelenting gloom, as if the scene were picked out in fine silver stitches on black velvet. He supposed that since ghosts mostly seemed to venture out at night, it followed that they probably could see well in the dark, along with all their other strange abilities. Phyllis was talking now, her voice low and conspiratorial, her crafty face and dangling rabbit stole drawn with thin tinsel lines upon the blackness.

"Right. I reckon as we're up in nothing-five or nothing-six. We can dig dayn again into the fifties if we want to, but I don't think we should do it 'ere, not in the corner 'ouse. This is a special place, and there's somebody livin' daynstairs who's bin put 'ere to take care of watchman duties, so remember: they can see us, they can 'ear us. They can get us into trouble what's so bad it sets me teeth on edge to even think abayt it."

Most of this was said with Phyllis's eyes fixed unwaveringly upon Michael Warren, as if it were mainly for his benefit. He felt he ought to say something, or at least whisper it.

"Whine wiz this corner-how a spatial plays?"

His syllables were acting up again, perhaps because the ghost-storm the Dead Dead Gang had so recently escaped had literally rattled him, but everybody seemed to catch his general drift, particularly Phyllis. Mumbling an aside to the effect that he still hadn't found his "Lucy-lips" yet, she replied in a dramatically hushed version of the scornful tone that he was starting to imagine was affectionate.

"It's a special place because it's like an 'inge between the First and Second Boroughs. It's to do with this 'ouse being on the corner at the bottom left of Scarletwell Street, while the Works where all the builders goo wiz up on the top right, where the old Tayn 'All used to be. In the four-sided world, they're folded up so that they're the same place. From 'ere yer can goo straight up to Mansoul. This is where the rough sleepers sometimes come, if they ever get up the nerve to leave the ghost-seam and to make their way Upstairs."

Seeing the answering look of blank incomprehension upon Michael's face, she gave a subdued sigh and then climbed to her feet in a profusion of repeated knees and ankle-socks. The other gang-members obediently followed suit, with Michael getting the idea and also standing up, a moment or two after all the rest. There in the curiously see-through shadows of the landing, Phyllis seemed once more to be addressing only him. Around her mouth the shiny pencil tracings on the blackness that were very likely dimples flickered in and out of being with the movement of her whispering lips.

"I s'pose that since yer 'ere, yer might as well see 'ow it works. If I remember right, they've got a Jacob Flight in the end bedroom, just along the landin'. We'll be right above the front room, where the look-out's more than likely sittin' watchin' telly, so be extra quiet and goo on tiptoes. We'll just take a quick peek, then we'll goo daynstairs and ayt the front door before anybody knows we're 'ere."

With this the little ghost-girl turned away and started heading for the far end of the landing, walking with a comically exaggerated tiptoe motion like a cat in a cartoon. As he fell in with the four other members of the Dead Dead Gang behind her, Michael looked about him, taking note of his surroundings. Reaching from the stair-head that was somewhere to his rear, the upstairs passageway led to a closed door at its further end, towards which Phyllis was now stealthily advancing. Upon his right were banisters that overlooked the darkened staircase, while upon his left the wallpaper was now adorned with a gorgeous gilt filigree of twisting roses, which was just the way its faded pattern looked to Michael's ghostly new nocturnal vision. Up ahead of him, Phyll Painter walked on tiptoe at the head of a short, slowly disappearing column of Phyll Painters. Without breaking step, she walked into the closed door, disappearing through it with her queue of duplicates pulled after her like a grey tail. Drowned Marjorie was next to stride into the panelled wood and out of sight, followed by Bill and Reggie. With a gentle shove from John, who walked behind him, Michael stepped into what turned out to be a brief vision of whorled grain, a fraction of a second in duration, before he emerged into the room beyond. Most probably the door had only been there a few years, which would explain why he had barely noticed passing through it.

On the other side, there were faint colours to the wavering light that fell in curtains, dappling the room, delicate pinks and greens and violets that were the first hues he'd seen since entering the ghost-seam. Only as he stood there with the other phantom children, gazing awestruck in the painted underwater shimmer, did he realise how much he'd missed blue and orange whilst he'd wandered through the black and white streets of this half-world. They were like best friends he hadn't met in ages.

Michael and the ghost gang were now obviously in a bedroom, not unlike his mum and dad's back down in 1959, except that all the furnishings and fittings looked a bit wrong and he couldn't see a chamber-pot beneath the bed. There was a dainty bedside table, although where you might expect to find a tin alarm-clock ticking reassuringly there was instead a flat box. It was roughly book-sized and upon its black front edge had numbers made of straight white lines, a little like the numerals that he'd seen people fashion from spilled matchsticks during idle moments. 23: 15 was how it read at present, with the two dots in the middle blinking on and off, and ... no. No, it was 23: 16. He'd evidently been mistaken. After staring at this cryptic message for a while and wondering what it meant, Michael at last thought to look up towards the source of the pale rainbow light that bathed the room where he and his dead friends were trespassing.

Up in the far right corner of the ceiling was an opening, perhaps the entrance to a loft and roughly four feet square. This blazed with pure and undiluted colour like a jazzy modern painting, splashing a pale echo of its vivid shades onto the grey and upturned faces of the spectre-children gathered there below. Immediately beneath this dazzling panel an impossibly cramped flight of steps descended to the bedroom floor, with both its angle and its shallow tread more like a ladder than a staircase. Michael thought that both the window to another world and the strange rung-stairs underneath it looked like they were made from something different to the ordinary room that these were situated in. They looked like they were made from ghost-stuff, and he doubted that they would be visible to ordinary people. Standing next to him with shivering bands of watery rose and turquoise slipping over the sharp contours of her face, Phyllis explained what the fluorescent trapdoor was in tones so hushed that they were barely audible.

"It's what they call a crook-door, and that stairway underneath it wiz a Jacob Flight. It leads straight to the Works, up in Mansoul. That's why yer can see all the colours everywhere. It's been in place 'ere on this corner or nearby since Saxon times, ever since 'ere-abayts became a proper settlement. It's an important entry to the Second Borough, and that's why there's always been somebody 'ere to sit watch on the gate and keep it safe. The ones what mind the corner between one world and the other, they're a scary bunch of customers what we call Vernalls. They're like deathmongers: they're 'uman, but they're half-Upstairs even before they've kicked the bucket."

Michael, gazing up entranced into the bright-dyed portal of Mansoul, ventured a dreamy interjection here.

"My dad's mum was called Vernall befour she got weddled."

It was as if somebody had dropped a snowball down the back of Phyllis's grey cardigan. Forgetting all her admonitions to keep quiet she yelped in sheer astonishment.

"You *what?* Well, that's why all of this is 'appening, then! That's why yer die and then come back to life. That's why the builders 'ad a fight, that's why the devil picked on yer, that's why Black Charley said abate the Porthimoth di Norhan, and that's why yer family wiz down 'ere near Scarletwell! It's in your ancestors. It's in your blood. Why wizn't I told all this sooner?"

Standing absolutely still in the weirdly-illuminated bedroom with confetti-

coloured light falling around them, the Dead Dead Gang were all staring nervously at Phyllis now. Looking a little sheepish for some reason, John reached out
in an array of pullover-clad arms and placed one hand upon Phyllis's shoulder.

"Don't blame him, Phyll. To be honest, I knew that his nan had been a Vernall, but I never thought to bring it up. Besides, it's not like everybody who's
related to that family shares their calling, wiz it? Most of them are ordinary
people."

Phyllis glared at John indignantly and was apparently about to answer
when Drowned Marjorie hissed urgently from where she stood beside the
bedroom's dressing table. Michael noted that neither the tinted radiance nor
the bespectacled and tubby ghost-child were reflected in its mirror.

"Shush, the pair of you! I think I just heard something move."

In the tense and exaggerated hush that followed Marjorie's announcement, they could all make out the rhythmic grunt of floorboards as somebody
slowly crossed the room beneath. There came the rattle of an opening door
and then a voice came drifting up the stairs, reedy and high with age yet still
spine-tingling in its effect.

"Is there somebody up there? Woe betide if it's all you dead little buggers
treading ghost-mess round my house!"

Footsteps, slow and deliberate, began to mount towards the landing from
the passageway downstairs, the squeak of every tread attended by the sound
of laboured breathing. Michael had no flesh to creep or blood to run cold,
but as he stood with his new friends in the pastel light that drizzled from the
opening above, he felt an afterlife equivalent to both of those sensations, a
sick ripple in the phantom fibre of his being. The unearthly presence climbing ever closer on the other side of the closed bedroom door was the strange
corner-keeper, not entirely human, who could get them into difficulties that
set plucky Phyllis Painter's teeth on edge to even think about. Though he had
often heard his parents or his gran use the expression 'woe betide' before,
he'd never previously heard it uttered with an intonation that conveyed so
clearly what it meant: a sea of woe, a churning tide of troubles reaching to
the grey horizon. Michael thought that he was probably about as scared as he
could get, and then belatedly remembered that the stairs and landing along
which the eerie watchman was approaching had been the Dead Dead Gang's
planned escape-route. *Then* he was about as scared as he could get.

It looked like Phyllis and the other kids had realised their predicament
at roughly the same moment that it had occurred to Michael. Phyllis's eyes
darted round the bedroom with its settling rainbow-sherbet light, looking
for hiding places or an exit of some sort, finally narrowing to slits of stern
determination.

"Quick! Ayt through the wall!"

Rather than bothering to say which wall she meant, the ghost-gang's self-appointed boss led by example, running full tilt at the pulled-to curtains of a window opposite the bedroom door, a fading trail of little girls with flailing rabbit-scarves pursuing her. Without an instant's hesitation Phyllis flung herself out through the hanging drapes, which didn't even tremble as she vanished into them and out of sight. Michael remembered, with a start, that they were upstairs. There'd be no floor on the far side of that outer bedroom wall, only a drop to Scarletwell Street down below. Phyllis had just as good as jumped off of the roof. More worryingly, everybody else was following her lead. First little Bill, then Reggie and Drowned Marjorie, charged at the curtained window or at the dull wallpaper to either side of it, hurling themselves out through the wall into the sheer drop and the night beyond. As usual, it was John who'd hung back to make sure that Michael was all right.

"Come on, kid. Don't be frightened of the drop. I told you, things don't fall as quickly here."

Out past the bedroom door, the creaking footsteps were now coming down the landing, drawing closer with the ragged breathing that was their accompaniment. Clearly deciding there was no time to let Michael reach his own decision, John scooped up the night-clothed infant underneath one arm and ran towards the wall that their companions had already disappeared through. Stretched into a many-legged tartan centipede of blurring motion, Michael thought he heard the doorknob turn behind them as John leapt towards the curtains.

There was a brief flash of insubstantial linen, vaporous glass, and then they were both tumbling like smouldering blossom through a lamp-lit darkness. As the older boy had promised it was an unusually slow descent, as if submerged in glue. Although the other children had all plunged out through the wall into the night moments before, Michael could see that Marjorie, the last to jump, had not yet reached the ground. She fell on Scarletwell Street in a waterfall of spoiled and streaky snapshots, stout legs bending in a bulge of chubby knee as she touched down upon the paving slabs below. Michael supposed that he and John must have the same spent-firework plume of pictures dribbling behind them as they sank down through the viscous shadows, John's long limbs already bracing for the negligible impact.

From the moment that they'd left the bedroom with its haze of colour they had been once more immersed in the black, grey and ivory landscape of the ghost-seam. Even so, to Michael there appeared to be a sickly tinge about the lamplight, giving the impression that it wasn't the clean white electric gleam that he was used to. He and John were almost at the end of their languid trajectory, about to bump down on the gritty slope of Scarletwell where their four friends were waiting, gazing up at the descending pair with eager,

anxious eyes. There was the faintest shudder as John's scuffed-toe shoes connected with the ground, and then Michael was being set down on the pavement with the other children. Still a little dizzy from the breathless pace of
their escape he hadn't had a chance to get his bearings yet, and Phyllis Painter
didn't seem inclined to give him one.

"Come on. Let's get away from 'ere in case they come ayt after us. We'll
'ave time to think over all this Vernall business later. We can 'ead towards the
Mayorhold through the flats and alleys, so we shan't be spotted struggling
back up Scarletwell Street if the watcher steps aytside to 'ave a nose abayt."

She fixed on the disoriented Michael by one tartan sleeve and started
dragging him across the street towards the 'PRESS KNIVES' factory on Bath
Street's blunted corner (although the familiar sign was for some reason missing), with the other ghost-kids shuffling along in a loose cluster that had him
and Phyllis at its centre. Something wasn't right.

He peered across the midnight street in the direction they were headed
and for a brief moment he was lost. Why was this bottom end of Scarletwell
Street suddenly so wide? It seemed to just fan out unbounded, and Michael
was wondering why he could see so far up the dark length of Andrew's Road
towards the station when he realised that the terraced houses opposite the one
that they were fleeing had completely disappeared. Only a swathe of turf was
stretched between the main road and a long blank wall some distance further
up the hill. The unexpected grassy emptiness, where things that looked like
monstrous birdcages on wheels lay toppled miserably on their sides at intervals, was somehow horrifying. Michael started to ask Phyllis what was going
on, but she just marched him over the deserted street with greater urgency.

"It's nothin' need concern yer. You just 'urry up and come with us ... and
don't look back in case the watcher's peerin' ayt their window and they see
yer face."

This last bit sounded like an over-clever afterthought, which meant it
sounded like a lie, or as though Phyllis had some other reason why she didn't
want him to turn round. Together with the way that the Dead Dead Gang
crowded in about him as if shielding something from his sight, her blustering
tone made Michael more convinced than ever that something was wrong. In
mounting panic, he pulled free from Phyllis's tight grip upon his arm and
wheeled around so that he could look back towards the house near Scarletwell
Street's bottom corner, from which they had just escaped. What could there
be about the place that was so dreadful no one wanted him to see it?

Looking solemn, Reggie and Drowned Marjorie fell back to either side
so that Michael could gaze between them at the building they'd so recently
vacated. It stood silent, with a weak light filtering through the curtains pulled
across its downstairs window. If you didn't count the fact that it seemed big-

ger, like two houses knocked together into one, then other than the detail of it being situated in a space where Michael knew an empty yard had been in 1959, it looked completely normal. There was nothing odd or terrible about the residence itself that he could see. It was just everything except the house that was all odd and wrong and terrible, that was all gone.

The terraced row along St. Andrew's Road between Spring Lane and Scarletwell, where Michael and his family and all their neighbours lived, had vanished. There was just the bottom fence and hedges of Spring Lane School's playing fields and then another patch of empty grass before you reached the pavement and the road immediately beyond. Save for a few small trees the double-sized house near the corner stood alone on the benighted fringe of ground, a single eye-tooth still remaining when the jaw itself had rotted down to nothing. From where Michael stood amongst the other phantom children, halfway over Scarletwell Street, he could see the little meadow on the other side of Andrew's Road, which nestled at the foot of Spencer Bridge ... or rather, he could see the place the meadow had been, the last time he'd looked. Save for a bordering fringe of trees there were now only rows of giant lorries hulking in the dark, much bigger than the vegetable truck that the man next door had tried to take him off to hospital inside. These each looked like two tanks piled up on top of one another, or perhaps a mobile branch of Woolworth's. Spaced out along the main road into the twinkling blackness of the distance there were things that looked like streetlights in a dream, impossibly tall metal stems each flowering at the top into two separate oblong lamps. The sickliness Michael had noticed in the lighting earlier seemed concentrated round these lanterns in unhealthy halos, which suggested that they were its source. Their wan rays fell upon the slumbering trucks and on the glistening tarmac of the empty roadway, on the whispering carpet that had grown across the floorboards of his missing birthplace, his evaporated street. The place he'd lived. The place he'd died.

This was what Phyllis and the others hadn't wanted him to see. His holy ground, except for the one single household that incongruously remained, had been razed flat. His devastated wail could be heard blocks away by those who weren't alive, despite the stagnant sonic currents of the ghost-seam. Filled with endless loss the wrenching cry unlaced the night, splitting the dead world end to end, while all around the living Boroughs slept on unaware and dreamed the troubled husks of its disgraceful future.

FLATLAND

Reginald James Fowler was the beautifully-written name upon the only two certificates he'd ever been awarded, which were the same two that everyone got, just for turning up.

He'd been called Reggie Bowler ever since Miss Tibbs had got his name wrong, reading out the register on his first day at school. The actual hat had come much later, and he'd only started wearing it to fit in with the name. He'd found it, with his much-too-big, perpetually-damp overcoat, amongst the rubbish on the burial ground near Doddridge Church, when he'd been sleeping there just after his twelfth birthday. He'd already had the dream by then, of Miss Tibbs holding up a book called *The Dead Dead Gang* with an overcoat-and-bowler-sporting urchin in gold inlay on its front, but when he'd come across those articles of clothing in real life this premonition was forgotten and was quite the furthest thing from Reggie's mind. He'd just been overjoyed to find the free apparel, the first bit of luck he'd had since losing both his parents.

At the time he'd tried to jolly himself up by looking on the hat and coat as presents, kidding himself that his dad had come back and had left them there for him, hung on the brambles growing in the crook of a stone wall already peppered green with age. If he was honest with himself he knew the garments were more likely those of an old man named Mallard, who'd lived in Long Gardens off Chalk Lane and who had killed himself in a depression. Probably his son, who'd very soon thereafter taken up employment as a slaughter-man in London, had got sick of looking at the suicide's old clothes and thrown them out. That would have been, by Reggie's reckoning, around 'Seventy-one or two, about a year before the bad frost that had finally seen Reggie off.

There'd been a lot of people do away with themselves in the Boroughs down the years. Old Mallard only stuck in Reggie's memory because he'd been a man, when nearly all the others had been female. It was harder for the women, or at least that's what he'd heard their husbands tell each other over beer in a pub garden, if the subject should arise.

"It's something that's in them old houses," was the general opinion. "For the chaps it's not so bad, because they're out to work. The women, though, they're left indoors with it and they can't get away."

He'd often wondered, in his idle moments, what "it" was. If it was something somehow "in" the houses, then it could be damp or dry-rot, some miasmal presence seeping from the beams and brickwork that could make a person so ill that they'd want to take their life, although he'd never heard of such a thing. Besides, the way that grown-up fellows talked about the matter, nodding solemnly over their pints of watery pale ale, had given Reggie the impression they'd been speaking of a living creature, something that had wandered in one day to take up residence and then refused to leave. Something so upsetting and so miserable that you'd be better dead than stuck at home with it, trying to do your housework with it sitting in the corner wriggling and clicking, looking at you with its knowing little black eyes. Reggie always pictured "it" as a giant earwig, although part of him knew full well it was only ordinary despair.

This was the nesting horror that had done for Reggie's mother, so he thought about it quite a lot. She'd tried to kill herself so many times that by her third try even she could see the funny side. Her first attempt had been at drowning, in the Nene where it ran through Foot Meadow, but the river wasn't deep enough at that point to accommodate her and she'd given up. Next she'd jumped from the bedroom window of their house in Gas Street, which resulted only in a pair of broken ankles. On the third occasion she'd tried kneeling with her head inside the oven, but the gas ran out before she'd finished and she didn't have a penny for the meter. It was that, being too poor to even gas herself, which in the end made Reggie's mother laugh about her troubles. So surprised were Reggie and his dad to see her chuckling again that they'd joined in, laughing along with her there in the freezing kitchen, with its windows open to dispel the rubbery and acrid fumes. Reggie himself had giggled most, although he hadn't really understood the situation and was only laughing because everybody else was. Also, he supposed that he'd guffawed out of relief and gratitude, convinced that a dark chapter of his family's story was now over.

In a sense, of course, he'd been quite right: some few weeks after the hilarity in the cold, smelly kitchen, Reggie's mother once more threw herself out of the upstairs window, this time managing to hit the ancient and indifferent paving stones of Gas Street with her head, which finally seemed to do the trick. A chapter certainly had been concluded, but the ones that followed it were even darker, even worse.

Following his wife's successful fourth and final stab at self-destruction, Reggie's dad had started drinking heavily, chucking the ale back for dear life, and then had started fights. Night after night he'd carried on like that, blood jetting from smashed noses up against a privy wall, teeth spat into the Gas Street drains like miniature bone rockets with a shower of red sparks behind them, and inevitably the constabulary would be called. His first offence, they beat him up. His second one, they locked him up and Reggie hadn't even known which gaol his dad was in. Abandoned, Reggie had lived in the Gas Street house alone for getting on a week, eating and sleeping in his parents' big bed for the luxury of it, not answering the door the first time that the rent-man called. On his next visit, though, the rent-man had a bailiff with him, who had simply kicked the door in, by which time Reggie was scarpering through an untended back yard, hurdling the bottom wall and making off along the alleyway.

His subsequent address had been the wasteland that they called the burial ground, opposite Doddridge Church. He'd been pleased with himself about the little house he'd built there, up against the bounding wall that overlooked Chalk Lane. Even though it had only been a plywood packing crate, Reggie was proud of his own ingenuity in turning it into a home. He'd tipped it on its side, swept out the snails and tacked someone's discarded curtain up across the opening as a sort of door. He camouflaged it with dead branches, thinking that this sounded like the sort of thing an Indian scout would do, and made a spear with which he could defend himself by sharpening a long stick with his rusty penknife, before realising the knife itself would make a better weapon. He'd been a bit dim back then, but then, he'd only been eleven.

That said, finding food and getting by, which in the circumstances you might well expect to be a hardship, these were things that Reggie found he took to naturally. He'd haunt the edges of the square on market night and find squashed fruit and veg thrown out amongst the tissue paper, straw and empty boxes. The back doors of baker's shops at closing time would often yield a loaf that was no longer saleable though not entirely stale, and from the butcher's there were sometimes bones for soup.

He'd realised, after trudging through the streets with a bowed head for one long afternoon, how many small coins people lose, especially in the larger shops. Other than what he found, Reggie would sometimes beg a ha'penny or two, and had once tossed off an old tramp who'd promised him a thrupenny bit but then reneged. That had been in the jungle of unused riverside land between Victoria Park and Paddy's Meadow, inaccessible except by paddling under Spencer Bridge, a wilderness where the damp-scented vagrant had a modest campfire made from bits of cardboard, wood and cut-off ends of car-pet. Reggie still remembered with a shudder how the whiskery chap's spunk had sizzled, following a slippery liquid arc into the yellow flames, and all for nothing, not a farthing. Still, despite such disappointments, Reggie managed to survive. He wasn't hapless, wasn't weak, not in his body or his mind. It hadn't been a lack of sustenance that killed him, it had been an English win-ter, and however strong or clever or resourceful Reggie was there'd been no getting round it. When they'd found him curled up in his packing crate after a day or two, one of his eyelids was still frozen shut and sticking to the ball. That had been that, the end of Reggie's life, though obviously not of his existence.

To be honest, he'd turned out to be better at death than he had ever been at life, taking to the new medium like a duck to water. Even so, he still remembered how surprised and lost he'd been, those first few hours after he'd passed on. It had been on a Sunday morning when it happened. He had woken to the sound of oddly-muffled church bells and the somehow worrying realisation that he was no longer cold. He'd tried to pull the curtain remnant serving as his door aside, but something puzzling had happened and he'd found himself crouching on hands and knees outside his makeshift crate-house, where the rags tacked up above its entrance were still hanging motionless and undisturbed.

The first thing that had struck him, thinking back, was that the grass upon which he was kneeling was now oyster-grey instead of green, although its rime of frost remained a granulated white. On climbing to his feet and looking round he'd seen that everything was black and white and grey, including the faint floral pattern on his tacked-up curtain, which he'd known should actually be an insipid blue. It made him smile now to recall how, with the subdued chiming of the bells, the black and white of everything had led him to the frightening conclusion that at some point in the night he'd been sent deaf and colour-blind, as if those were the worst things that could happen to you on a winter's evening. It was only when he'd noticed all the pictures of himself that he was leaving every time he moved that Reggie had suspected there was something badly wrong, wrong in a way that spectacles or hearing trumpets would not remedy.

Of course, soon after that he'd started to experiment with touching things, discovering that he no longer could. Attempting to draw back the curtain from the mouth of his crude shelter, he'd found that his hand now passed through the material as if it wasn't there and disappeared from sight until he'd pulled it out again. At that point Reggie had decided that to see inside the crate he'd have to push his face in through the fabric of the entrance, in the same way that he'd just done with his fingers.

He'd been pitiful, the little boy inside the box. Frozen into the same position in which he'd fallen asleep, bald knees drawn up and one hand welded to a flattened ear, his eyebrows had been frosted white. A crystal dusting glinted off the fine hairs of his freckled cheek and from one nostril there depended a grey icicle of snot. Unlike a lot of ghost-seam residents that he had subsequently met, Reggie had recognised his own corpse straight away. For one thing, the dead child was dressed in a long coat and bowler hat identical to those that he himself appeared to still be wearing. For another, it had Reggie's tea-stain birthmark, roughly shaped like Ireland, on the left calf above the stiffened folds of its refrigerated ankle-sock. The leaping commas that he'd glimpsed out of the corner of his eye had turned out to be sober and pragmatic fleas abandoning their host. He'd screamed, a curiously flat sound that had little resonance, and jerked his head back through the hanging curtain, which had not so much as trembled as he'd done so.

Reggie had then sobbed for some time, the unsalted globs of ectoplasm rolling down his face, more like the memory of tears than tears themselves. At last, when it became apparent that however much he wept no one was going to come and make it better, he'd sniffed loudly and had stood up straight, resolving to be brave. His lower lip and chin thrust out, he'd marched determinedly across the burial ground heading for Doddridge Church, with the frost-hardened soil feeling somehow springy and giving underneath his insubstantial tread, like sphagnum moss. Grey replicas peeled from his back, pursuing him in single file over the January wasteland, hindmost figures fading out as more were added to the front end of the queue.

It having been a Sunday, Reggie had seen a few individuals and couples making their way through the slanting Boroughs streets towards the church, although since it was also perishingly cold these were less numerous than they might otherwise have been. Striding across the burial ground towards the old church and its gathering congregation, he'd become aware that no one else was shedding pictures of themselves behind them in a trail the way that he was. He'd had an uneasy intimation as to what this meant, but had tried calling out to the churchgoers anyway, bidding them a good morning. This had come out as "God mourning" by mistake, although he didn't think it would have made a difference to the pious throng's response, however he'd pronounced it. They'd ignored him as they exchanged pleasantries with one another, bundled in their winter clothes and shuffling towards the building's worn iron gates. Even when he'd danced round in front of them and called them names – queer jumbled-up names that had sounded wrong even to Reggie – they just looked straight through him. One of them, a tubby girl, had even *walked* straight through him, giving him a brief unwelcome glimpse of squirting veins and bones and flickering stuff that he'd thought might be her brains. Reggie had been at last convinced of his condition by this incident, had finally accepted that these people neither saw nor heard him, being still amongst the living whereas he was now apparently amongst the dead.

It had been while he'd stood there by the gate allowing this dire fact to sink in that he'd heard the tiny, chirping voices from above him and looked up towards the eaves of Doddridge Church.

Since he'd passed over Reggie must have had the whole phenomenon explained to him a thousand times, how all of it made sense according to some special version of geometry, but for the life of him he couldn't get to grips with it. He'd never really fathomed ordinary geometry, which meant this new variety was bound to be beyond his grasp. He doubted he would ever truly understand what he had seen when he'd glanced upwards at the higher reaches of the humble structure.

All the buttresses and things that you'd expect to poke out from the upper walls had looked instead like they were poking in, as if they'd all turned inside out. In the apparent cavities and indentations caused by this effect there had been little people perching, no more than three inches high, all waving frantically at Reggie as they called down to him with their twittering bat-like voices.

Back then, at the age of twelve, he would have probably been just about prepared to accept that they might be pixies, if they hadn't been so drab and scruffy in their dress or homely in their features. In minute flat caps and baggy trousers hoisted by minuscule braces, wearing aprons and black bonnets, they'd milled back and forth along miniature balconies formed from inverted recesses. They'd beckoned and gesticulated, mouthed at him through lips that were infinitesimal, their faces marked by all the warts and lazy eyes and strawberry noses that you'd find in any ordinary pauper crowd on market day. The women's coats had microscopic brooches, cheap and tarnished, pinned to the lapels. The fellows' waistcoat buttons, those that weren't already missing, verged on the invisible. These hadn't been the sharp-eared fairies from the picture-books in all their gaudy finery, but had instead been normal folk in all their plainness and their ugliness, somehow shrunk to the size of horrid, chittering beetles.

As he'd stood and gaped in mingled fascination and revulsion at the capering homunculi, he'd noticed that nobody else amongst the scattering of worshippers converging on the church was doing so. No one had looked up at the strangely concave ledges where the slum-imps gestured, trilled and whistled, and it had occurred to Reggie that live people could not see them. He'd concluded that only the dead could do that, displaced souls like him who left grey pictures in their wakes rather than the faint puffs of fogging breath that marked the living on that bitter January day.

He'd not known what the creatures were and, back then, hadn't wanted to find out. It had been slowly dawning on him, ever since he'd seen what was inside the crate, that he was dead yet didn't seem to be in heaven. That, in Reggie's limited grasp of theology, left only one or two more places that this ghostly realm might be, and neither of them sounded very nice. In mounting panic he had backed away, passing between or through oblivious Boroughs residents arriving at their place of worship, all the while keeping his eyes fixed firmly on the scuttling apparitions in the eaves, in case the rat-like men and women suddenly teemed skittering down the church walls and surged towards him.

Finally he'd turned and run away with his pursuing trail of after-pictures hurrying to keep up, haring around the left side of the church and into Castle Terrace, where an even more bewildering sight awaited. It had been that old door, halfway up the western face of Doddridge Church. In life he'd often puzzled over this and tried to guess its purpose, but as he'd dashed round the corner and stopped dead with all his phantom doubles piling up behind him, Reggie had at last been furnished with an answer, even if he had no way of understanding it.

Although he looked back with amusement now at his uncomprehending first glimpse of the Ultraduct, if he was honest Reggie wasn't that much clearer as to what it was or how it functioned even after all these years, whatever meaningless immeasurable number that might be. He just recalled the breathless awe with which he'd reeled, dazed, through the spaces of its marvellous white pilastrade, his head tipped back to goggle at the glassy underside of the impossibly-constructed pier above him. Beyond the translucent alabaster of its planking, phosphorescent patches had moved purposefully back and forth, over his head and over Castle Terrace, fugitive light falling through the chiselled struts to settle on his upturned features like the snow that everyone had said it was too cold for.

Passing underneath the glorious eye-straining structure in a dazzled trance he had eventually stumbled out the other side, with his evaporating replicas all stumbling after him. Freed from the Ultraduct's transfixing glamour, Reggie had let out a great moan of perplexity at the sheer overwhelming strangeness of his situation. Without looking back he'd raced off in a funk down Bristol Street, his ghost-hat clapped tight to his head, his spectral greatcoat flapping around his bare knees. Blindly he'd charged deeper into the sallow echo of the Boroughs that had seemed, then, to be his new home for all eternity, the awful place he'd been condemned to. He'd roared down the colourless coal-chute of Bath Street like a steam-train, towing look-alikes instead of carriages and tenders. Down there in the district's pallid guts he'd trickled to a halt, then sat down in the middle of the road and taken stock of things.

Of course, it hadn't been long after that when he had come across his first rough sleepers: a small crowd of what had looked and talked like drinking men from several different centuries. They'd put him straight about the nature of the ghost-seam or, as they had called it, purgatory. Like many of the Boroughs' wraiths they'd been at heart a sentimental crew and taken him beneath their wing, instructing him in a variety of useful skills. They'd taught him how to scrape away accumulated circumstance and dig through time, then told him where to find the sweetest Bedlam Jennies, growing in the higher crevices that people with a heartbeat couldn't see. They'd even found the ghost of an old football for him, although his first kick-around had underscored the limitations of the game, or at least this posthumous version of it: for one thing, the football didn't bounce so high, in much the same way as sound didn't resonate so clearly. For another, being insubstantial, the ghost-ball would be forever sailing through the house-walls of the living. Constantly retrieving it from underneath the table or inside the armchair of a family eating dinner unaware had rapidly become far too much of a bother.

Reggie had been grateful for the old revenants' help and camaraderie, and yet with hindsight he could see they hadn't really done him any favours. While they'd helped him to adjust to his new state they'd also fostered in him the belief that this bleak half-world, this unsettling ink-wash purgatory, was all that he deserved. He'd taken on their disappointed, self-defeating outlook as his own and looked to them for all his cues. They'd told him he could have his life over again if that was what he wanted, although there was something in the way they'd said it which implied that this would be a very bad idea. Back then, he'd been inclined to share this view, and in a sense was still of that opinion. Living through his mother's suicide attempts again was nothing he looked forward to, and neither was the prospect of reprising his dad's drunken rages. Nor did a repeat of wanking off the tramp or being once again frozen to death inside a packing crate seem to provide much real incentive. Now he was outside his life he could at last admit to himself what a nightmare and a torment it had been. The thought of going through it all again, a thousand times or even just the once, was more than he could bear.

The broken-hearted mob of ghosts who had been Reggie's mentors in the afterlife had also counselled against going "Upstairs" to a place they called "Mansoul". That, they'd explained, was for a better class of dead folk who had led respectable and carefree lives, not for the sorry likes of Reggie and his new-found friends. Their poor opinion of themselves had chimed with his own faltered self-esteem, and it occurred to Reggie that he might still be one of their company, to this day shambling through the joyless alleys of the ghost-seam with them, listening to their complaints and their regrets there in that muted landscape where each sound and every hope fell flat. He'd almost certainly still be amongst that wretched fellowship, he realised soberly, if it had not been for the great ghost-storm of 1913.

That had been like the Almighty trumping, in that it was deafening and unexpected. It had been much worse than the comparatively minor squall that Reggie and the Dead Dead Gang had just affected their escape from, down in 1959. Both had been caused, though, by the same phenomenon: by the violent activity of higher supernatural forces in the region of Mansoul that corresponded to the Mayorhold, where there was a place they called the Works. In 1913 these superior powers, be they the builders or the former builders who had been reclassified as devils, were in uproar over something that was said to be connected with the coming war. Their outraged flailings had provoked a wind of terrible ferocity that had torn through the phantom neighbourhood and had blown all of Reggie's fatalistic chums away to Delapre. That was the reason it had put the wind up Reggie, so to speak, when him and all the other kids had heard Black Charley say there was a ghost-storm on its way: Reggie had been through one before.

There'd not been any warning, just a sudden rush of phantom dust and debris bowling down the middle of St. Mary's Street, and then a ghostly rubbish bin had come careening out of nowhere and hit Reggie smack between the shoulder blades, so that he fell flat on his face. That, looking back, had been what saved him. Toppling forward, with his bowler somehow landing pinned and flattened underneath him, he'd instinctively put out both hands to break the fall and found himself embedded past his elbows in the ancient and thus partially substantial Boroughs soil. His scrabbling spectral fingers, out of sight a foot or two beneath the ground, happened upon a tree root that was also of sufficient age to get a grip on, and he'd thus been anchored more or less securely when the main sledgehammer blow of the ghost-gale had hit them only instants later.

Old Ralph Peters, a bankrupted grocer from 1750-something who'd looked like John Bull, had voiced a startled and despairing cry when he'd been lifted up into the air, as weightless as a feather, and had been sent soaring off in the direction of St. Peter's Church. They'd all been rummaging about amongst the trees and overgrowth between the burial ground where Reggie had passed over (and had subsequently been interred), and Marefair. As the fierce north-easterly had torn poor Ralph into the sky he'd clutched in desperation at the topmost branches of an elm in hope of finding purchase, but the twigs had been new growth and had passed through the portly spirit's hands like they weren't there. Ralph had been snatched away arse-first towards the south horizon with the frightening velocity and dreadful noise of a deflating grey balloon, the after-pictures of his shocked face spiralling behind him like a hundred John Bull posters gushing from a printing press.

While Reggie had sprawled there screaming inaudibly above the tempest, clinging to the buried tree root for dear death, he'd watched as one by one the rest of the threadbare assembly – Maxie Mullins, Ron Case, Cadger Plowright, Burton Turner – had careened away into the clouds, passing through factory chimneys, fences made of rusty tin and the brick walls of people's houses as they went. He'd heard Ron Case's shriek of agony as the stooped little ghost with the perpetual sniffle had collided at high speed with the nine-hundred-year-old spire of Peter's Church, a building venerable enough to have accumulated solid presence even in the ghost-seam. From what Reggie had been told a few years later, Ron had hit the church tower and been bent around it, caught upon it like an airborne ribbon hooked upon a nail. The raging winds had pulled his insubstantial body out as if it were a paper streamer, with the outcome being that by all accounts he'd ended up as something twice the height and much too thin to look at without shuddering. As for the others, Reggie didn't have the first idea where they'd eventually been set down: from that appalling day to this, he'd never met with any of the kindly but dejected bunch again. For all that he knew they might still be up there, moaning and complaining as they twirled and flapped, caught in the planet's jet-streams for eternity.

He'd been alone, then, in the spiritual hurricane, face down and shoulder-deep in Boroughs rock with his feet lifted off the ground and trailing in the churning air behind him, a whole football team of after-image boots and darned socks kicking helplessly. As he recalled he'd been debating whether to keep clutching at the root until the storm abated, if it ever did, or whether to let go and join his colleagues. He had just about decided on the latter of these options when he'd noticed that something peculiar was happening to the wasteland turf about a yard in front of him. There'd been concentric bands of black and white that seemed to ripple outwards from a dark spot in the middle, and it had been from this shimmering central point that Reggie had seen what he'd at first taken to be plump and ghastly worms but had then understood were a child's fingers, wriggling up from underneath the earth. As there were at least thirty digits visible at one point, he had realised that the owner of the hands must be a ghost-child like himself, which had provided cause for cautious optimism.

Scraping back the wavering Liquorice Allsort stripes to either side with movements like the shovelling front paws of a mole, the mystery hands had very quickly made the portal wide enough for larger body-parts to be pushed through. Thus it had been that he had found himself with arms sunk in the earth, cheeks fluttering and eyes watering in the fierce wind as he'd stared disbelievingly at the small girl whose head and shoulders had suddenly poked up from the waste-ground a few feet in front of him. Around her neck had been a ruff of rabbit skins that made it look like she was surfacing out of a barrel of dead animals. Her bowl-cut hair had whipped about all round her head in the still-raging tempest, every loose strand dragging after-image curtains of itself to veil her scowling features in a mask of matted steam. That had been his first meeting with ferocious, mouthy, brave, infuriating Phyllis Painter.

Verbally abusing him throughout and treating him as if he were an idiot, Phyllis had managed to reach out and grab him by the wrist once he'd unearthed one of his arms. With what had turned out to be her kid Bill holding her ankles from below, she'd somehow hauled both Reggie and his squashed hat through the opening she'd dug, yanking him down into the glittering see-through darkness of a tunnel that had run from Peter's Church up to St. Sepulchre's, or at least had done in the thirteen-hundreds, which was the time period that Phyllis had been digging her way up from when she'd happened upon Reggie. They'd all landed in a heap on top of Bill, struggling on the packed dirt floor amidst dropped Saxon coins and Norman dog-bones, giggling and yelling as if the whole dire predicament had been enormous fun. After the untold years of his association with resigned old men who hadn't even had death to look forward to, Reggie had known once more the spirit-lifting thrill of being a daft little lad unburdened by regret. They'd finally stopped laughing and sat up, there in the fourteenth-century gloom, to shake hands and make proper introductions.

Him and Bill and Phyllis had been more or less inseparable from then on, organising games of hide and seek in heaven, playing ghost-tag, sliding on their bottoms down the dusty decades. As he'd got to know them better, Reggie had picked up the odd fact here and there, such as how they were both from the same family and had both lived and died a good while after he had. He'd found out that Phyllis's last name was Painter, which was more than Reggie knew about his other young pals. He assumed that Bill must be a Painter too, but he'd got no idea as to the surnames of Drowned Marjorie or John, whom Reggie and the Painters had encountered some time after the three of them had first met, in medieval times, beneath the burial ground. As with living kids, dead ones preferred to deal almost exclusively in Christian names, or so it seemed to Reggie.

Bill and Phyllis had before long disabused him with regard to the forlorn philosophy he'd picked up second-hand from Maxie Mullins, Cadger Plowright and the rest. They'd taken him up to Mansoul, up to the Second Borough on the floor above the mortal realm, where the reverberant sound and overwhelming colour had brought Reggie to his knees, as had the smell of Phyllis's dead-rabbit scarf once they'd climbed from the odourless dominion of the ghost-seam. Having met the down-at-heel but glorious individuals who resided mostly in that upper world, people like Mrs. Gibbs, old Sheriff Perrit or Black Charley, Reggie had revised his idea of himself. The afterlife – which was in some ways also the before-and-during life – had not turned out to be the snooty and judgemental place that Burton Turner and the others had described. It had instead been both a wonder and a terror, the most thrilling playground for a child that Reggie could imagine, and he'd understood that all its shining residents were only people who had lived their lives and done the things they'd had to do, the same as Reggie had. All the disheartened spirits that he'd previously knocked about with, he had realised, were not condemned to purgatory by anything except their own shame and a mercilessly low opinion of themselves.

It had been at some point during the early days of their association, possibly just after the Adventure of the Phantom Cow and just before the Mystery of Snow Town, that the three of them had first decided that they were now an official gang. This would have been about the time that Reggie had remembered his old dream about Miss Tibbs and had suggested that they call themselves the Dead Dead Gang, which everybody had seemed tickled by. They'd stuck together ever since then, although Reggie had got no idea how long ago the founding of their happy throng had been, nor even how you'd calculate a thing like that on the time-free plane of Mansoul.

Time being what it was up in the Second Borough, Reggie kept things straight by reckoning events in the same order he'd experienced them, the way most people did. He had a notion that the builders and the devils saw things differently, but that was somehow tied up with the business about special geometry and mathematics and dimensions, so he tended not to dwell upon it very much. For Reggie, keeping track of years and dates had always been a headache, and the best that he could manage was to maintain an internal list of big occasions in their proper sequence. For example, following the naming of the gang they'd pretty soon embarked upon the Snow Town business, when the three of them had gone exploring in the twenty-fifties, and right after that there'd been the Case of the Five Chimneys. Their next exploit, The Dead Dead Gang Versus the Nene Hag, had been the one where they'd picked up Drowned Marjorie, and eight or nine adventures later they'd encountered John, with his boy's-paper hero looks, during the Subterranean Aeroplane Affair. Though weeks, years, decades or possibly centuries had passed since then, to Reggie it seemed like one endless afternoon in much the way that children think of their school summer holidays, measured in games played or best-friendships forged.

That period, with its Riddle of the Crawling Arm and Incident of the Delirious Blackshirt and the rest, had been a largely calm and happy one for Reggie. Now, though, with their current operation ("The Enigma of the Soppy Little Kid"), he wondered if those carefree times were drawing to a close, the way his days with the rough sleepers had done. First there'd been that trouble with the devil, the first really famous fiend that Reggie had bumped into in his time Upstairs, and then there'd been that stuff about this nipper kicking off a scrap between the Master Builders. Throw in the unsettling ghost-storm and in Reggie's estimation this whole latest escapade was turning into a complete disaster. He had previously thought that having died inside a packing crate would be the worst thing that could ever happen to him, and that relatively speaking the remainder of eternity would be a pushover. This Michael Warren business, though, with all its demons and its dangers, made that notion look too optimistic. Privately, he was of the opinion that the sooner they dumped the new blonde kid down the scarlet well and into the fifth century, the better.

Look at the fuss he'd made just now, when he'd turned round and noticed that his house and street had gone, Reggie thought scornfully. The lucky little beggar had already found out he'd be coming back to life again, and then he goes and throws a fit about some buildings that had been demolished. He should try freezing to death inside a crate. As Reggie saw things, all these sissy little modern kids should try freezing to death inside a crate. It'd be good for them.

Reggie stood with his comrades and the new boy at the junction of Bath Street and Scarletwell, sometime in nothing-five or nothing-six, up in the twenty-somethings. Michael Warren was still blubbering and pointing to the place his home had been while big John tried consoling him and Phyllis told him not to be so daft. Contemptuously, Reggie hawked some ectoplasm up and spat it out into the gutter. Tilting down his bowler's brim to what he thought might be more of a tough chap's angle, he looked off downhill towards St. Andrew's Road and the lone house, there near the corner, that they'd just escaped from. In all fairness to the wailing toddler, Reggie didn't much like being this far up the ladder of the decades either. His own century, the nineteenth, was all right, despite it having treated him so poorly, and he thought the first half of the twentieth was reasonably presentable if you ignored the wars. Time periods much after that, though, and it all went funny. This one that they were in now, the twenty-first, was somewhere that he'd kept away from ever since the Snow Town episode. Despite the fact that Reggie was a ghost, this present century gave him the willies.

What was worst were all the houses they had here: the flats. Where Reggie could remember tangled lanes crowded with individual homes now there were only great big ugly blocks, a hundred residences crushed into a cube, like when they squash old cars in a machine. And naturally, having to live a new way had made everybody different. These days families were all divided up like eggs in cartons, one to a compartment, and folk didn't hang together in the way they'd done when their untidy streets and their untidy lives had all been knotted up in one big ball. It was as if society had finally caught up with Reggie Bowler, so that now the vast majority of people were content to live and die alone, inside a box. Aimlessly gazing at the single red-brick structure jutting from the night grass near the junction with St. Andrew's Road, he realised with a start that up here in the twenty-somethings, this peculiar relic was the only proper house still standing in the Boroughs. All the rest had been replaced by concrete lumps.

Behind him, Michael Warren was berating Phyllis, between sobs and gulps for breath, over the way she'd brought him here to this upsetting place. He said he didn't think that she was really looking after him at all, and that she was just doing what she wanted to and being selfish – which from Reggie's point of view there may have been some truth in, but he knew it was a bad idea for the new kid to point it out to Phyllis like that. Sure enough, the Dead Dead Gang's girl boss immediately got on her high horse, and then got that to balance on the saddle of an even higher horse as she turned her ferocious approbation on the sniffling little boy, loudly recalling how she'd helped him in the Attics of the Breath and how she'd saved him from the clutches of the devil-king. Letting the whole debate sail past him Reggie spat again into the dark, the wad of ghost-phlegm leaving pale dots on the darkness as it arced towards the pavement, like a perforation line. Returning his attention to the faded ribbon of St. Andrew's Road as it spooled through the night towards the north and Semilong, Reggie inspected its infrequent motor traffic that passed back and forth beneath the craning streetlamps with their sickly grey coronas.

Cars had frightened Reggie when he'd first encountered them while playing tiggy-through-the-wall with Bill and Phyllis in the 1930s, and had then amazed and fascinated him as he'd become increasingly familiar with them. Reggie fancied that he had turned into something of a connoisseur of motor vehicles across the timeless time since then, being particularly fond of those you came across down in the 1940s and the 1950s. Double-decker buses were his favourite, especially after Phyllis had informed him that as living people saw them, they were a bright red. He liked the transport of the twentieth century's middle decades largely for its pleasing shapes, its mudguard curves and bumper bulges. Also, Reggie thought the cars you saw around those years had cheerful faces, the arrangement of the headlights, bonnet mascot and the radiator grill that Reggie couldn't help but see as eyes and nose and mouth.

The intermittent modern cars that hummed and hurtled through the night along St. Andrew's Road were, like so many of this current era's trappings, less to Reggie's liking. They had either the sleek bodies of malicious cats advancing rapidly on something through tall grass, or they resembled trundling military tanks that had been geed-up to go faster. Worst of all, in his opinion, were the cold, mean-spirited expressions of their features, crowded in beneath the forehead of the bonnet like the blunt and vicious masks of fighting fish. The headlamps were now lidded and inscrutable above the radiator's surly overbite, the entire four-wheeled metal skull now that of a belligerent bull-terrier. He'd once remarked to Phyllis that they looked like they were out hunting for something in the dark, and she'd just sniffed and said "Round 'ere, it's girls."

The row between Phyllis and Michael Warren was still going on, back over Reggie's greatcoat-shrouded shoulder. Phyllis said, "I oughter just abandon yer, if that's the way yer feel abayt it", and then Michael Warren said, "Glow on and see a fakir", which to Reggie's ear made very little sense. But then, that was the way the newly dead found themselves talking before they were used to the expanded possibilities of language that there were in Mansoul, along-side the richer sounds and colours. Before they had found their "Lucy-lips", as the expression went. Reggie remembered his own early gibberish tirade at the unwitting members of the congregation filing into Doddridge Church down in the 1870s, and felt a pang of sympathy for the disoriented youngster, though not much of one. As there were no cars passing by at present, Reggie was about to turn back to the other ghost-kids squabbling behind him and resume his part in their discussion when he noticed something odd emerg-ing from the featureless brick wall bounding the enclosed garages belonging to the flats, a little further downhill from where they were standing, nearer to where blacked-out Scarletwell Street joined the sodium-lit ribbon of St. Andrew's Road.

It was a patterned smear extruded from the high wall of the garages, extending itself down across the dark grass like a line of dribbled paint or, more exactly, like a squirt of that astounding toothpaste with the stripes in that Phyllis had shown him in the novelty-filled reaches of the 1960s, except that the rolling globule here was checked rather than striped. Also, to judge from the subdued sounds that at intervals would issue from it, it was weeping. After a few baffled moments, Reggie saw that it was a rough sleeper, a stout fellow in a loud checked jacket that left a predictably eye-popping streak of after-images behind it. The ghost's hair was black, as was the pencil mous-tache on his upper lip, though Reggie thought that both looked dyed, as if the spirit best remembered himself as an older man still trying to look young. He wore a grey bow-tie with a white shirt that bulged out like a flour-sack at his midriff and from his trajectory as he streamed down across the rustling weeds towards St. Andrew's Road, Reggie suspected that he might have just emerged from Bath Row at some juncture several decades further down into the past, when the constricted cut-through was still standing. Setting his bowler hat more tightly down around his ears because he privately believed this made his thoughts more disciplined, Reggie observed the weeping phantom as it stumbled down the slope and realised belatedly that it was headed for the sole remaining residence that stood near Scarletwell Street's corner, the same heaven-haunted house they'd just escaped from. He decided that he'd best alert his comrades to this new development, just in case it should turn out to be anything significant. When he spoke, it was in an urgent whisper.

"'Ere, look at this chap. 'E's makin' fer the corner 'ouse, and 'e looks in a right state."

Everybody turned to see what Reggie was referring to, then gazed in silence as they watched the tearful spectre in the snazzy jacket make his way across the turf that had replaced dozens of houses, lifting chubby hands to hide his face and blubbering more volubly as he approached the lonely edifice that loomed there on the other side of Scarletwell. Presumably able to see despite his ectoplasmic tears and pudgy fingers, the Dead Dead Gang stared as the ghost made a sudden detour in a semi-circle from the straight path that he'd previously been following.

"That'll be the scarlet well that he's avoiding. 'E don't want to fall through a few 'undred years of dirt and find 'imself splashin' about in bloody-lookin' dye."

In grunts and nods, the rest of the dead children quietly concurred with Reggie's explanation. Only big John actually spoke up.

"You know, I think I know him. I think that's my uncle. I've not seen him since I passed on, and I never dreamed that he'd end up as a rough sleeper, but I'm sure that's him. I wonder what he's got to feel so down upon himself about?"

"Why don't yer ask 'im?"

This was Phyllis, standing at John's side with her truculent features picked out in the dark in silvery needlepoint. The tall good-looking boy, who Reggie somehow managed to resent, envy and like tremendously at the same time, peered off into the gloom towards the sobbing snappy dresser and declined, shaking his head.

"I wizn't really close to him back when we were alive. Nothing he'd done, just something in his manner that I never cottoned to. Besides, he looks like he's got enough on his plate already. When someone's roaring their eyes out like that, generally all they want wiz to be left alone."

Still covering his tear-stained face, the chequered wraith slid over Scarletwell towards the doorstep of the street's single remaining house. Wiping one garish sleeve across his dark-ringed eyes the plump man hesitated for a moment on the threshold, and then melted into the closed front door and was gone.

And when they looked round, so was Michael Warren.

"Oh my giddy aunt, 'e's run orf! Quick, which way's 'e gone?"

Reggie was mildly startled at how panicked Phyllis sounded. She was turning round in anxious circles, squinting anxiously into the silvered darkness for some sign of the absconded toddler. Settling his bowler hat to what he thought was a more sympathetic angle, he did his gruff best to reassure her.

"Don't worry, Phyll. 'E'll soon be back, and even if 'e's not, it's not our business. Everybody says 'e's going back to life soon, anyway. Why not let all that take care of itself? Then we can just get on with scrumping Puck's Hats from the madhouses, and our adventuring and everything. What about Bill's plan to dig a big 'ole all the way down to the Stone Age, so that we can capture a ghost woolly-elephant and tame it for a pet?"

Phyllis just stared at him as if appalled by his stupidity. Reggie adjusted his hat to a more defensive slant as she replied in an explosive shower of double-exposed spirit-spit.

" 'Ave you gone orf yer 'ead? You 'eard what Mrs. Gibbs an' old Black Charley said about the builders and their punch-up! And there's all this to-do with the Vernalls and the Porthimoth di Norhan that we 'aven't sorted ayt yet! You goo and catch mammoths if yer like, but I'm not gunna be in the Third Borough's bad books, not if I can 'elp it!"

With that, Phyllis turned and raced towards the gated lower Scarletwell Street entrance of Greyfriars flats, which was about the only place that Michael Warren could have disappeared into while they weren't looking, rabbit-scarf and pictures of herself trailing behind her in a string of grimy flags. The other members of the Dead Dead Gang stared after her for a stunned instant, shocked as much by Phyllis's bold reference to the Third Borough – Reggie hardly dared to even think the name – as they were by her desperate flight. Gathering themselves up from their gaping stupor they rushed after her, a clattering mob of four, twelve, sixteen, eighty phantom children pouring down the brief and narrow passage leading to the inner courtyard of Greyfriars, pushing their smoky substance through the black iron railings of a gate that had been there for only a few years and thus provided no impediment. Hot on the multiplying heels of Phyllis Painter they burst out into the lower level of a large two-tier concrete enclosure ringed by silent 1930s flats, where everybody paused to take stock of their suddenly alarming situation.

From the gilt-trimmed shadows of the upper courtyard came the frightened cries of cats and dogs, who were no fools when it came to detecting ghostly presences, and the cross shouting of their human owners, who quite clearly were. Along with his deceased companions, Reggie peered into the gloom of the split-level quadrangle. Down at the lower end where they were, half-dead vegetation rustled on a small patch of neglected ground originally intended as a modest arbour. Up three granite steps, on the top deck of the communal yard, a single pair of lady's tights dangled forgotten from the washing line and brick dustbin-enclosures guarded black bags, split and spilling the unfathomable prolapsed waste of the twenty-first century, the slimy plastic trays and rinds of unfamiliar fruit. Of Michael Warren there was not the slightest trace.

Seeming to summon fresh resolve out of adversity, a steely and determined look came into Phyllis's pale eyes.

"Right. 'E'll 'ave either 'eaded up the 'ill and over Lower Crorse Street to the maisonettes, or 'e'll 'ave cut along the bottom 'ere and come ayt into Bath Street. We'll split up in two groups so we've got a better chance of findin' 'im. Marjorie, you and John and me wizzle search through the maisonettes. And as fer you two ..."

Phyllis turned a somewhat frosty gaze on Bill and Reggie.

"You two can search Bath Street and Moat Place and all round there ... or yer can goo and look fer woolly elephants, fer all I care. Now, 'urry up and piss orf, or there's no tellin' 'ow far away the little nuisance might 'ave got."

With that, Phyllis and John and Marjorie swirled up the stone steps and away into the tinfoil glitter of the Greyfriars darkness, leaving Bill and Reggie on the murky path that cut across the courtyard's lower reaches from Bath Street to Scarletwell. Bill laughed, the laugh of a much older and much lewder individual, despite the little boy's high voice.

"The dirty old tart. She just wants to be off in the dark with Johnski, and she's letting poor old Drowned Marge tag along for cover. So, it looks like it's just you and me then, Reggie me old mucker. Where d'yer fancy lookin' first?"

Reggie had always got on well with Bill. The lad had substance but it was a substance with rough edges to it; less intimidating than the burnished aura of nobility that hung around big John in a heraldic sheen. The ginger nipper was approachable and funny, with a repertoire of more rude jokes than Reggie had imagined could exist, and was astonishingly knowledgeable for an eight-year-old, even a dead one. Reggie shrugged.

"I reckon we'd be best to do as Phyllis says fer once, so we're not in worse trouble with 'er. We can catch that woolly elephant another time. Let's 'ave a look in them new flats where Moat Street was and see if we can spot the little blighter. Then we can be shot of this whole bloody century and get back down where it's more comfortable."

The two of them were walking side by side, their hands deep in their pockets, following the path along the bottom edge of the night-steeped enclosure, wandering unhurriedly towards another gated passage that led out to Bath Street. Bill was nodding in acknowledgement of Reggie's last remark, the after-images stretching his face into a sort of carrot shape to match his carrot top, albeit only momentarily.

"You're not wrong, Reg, much as it pains me to admit it to a fuckin' dead Victorian bugger like yerself. Now, me, I lived into this fuckin' century we're in now, lived for a lot longer than I was expecting, and I'll tell yer, even I think it's a load o' shit. Give me the 'Fifties or the 'Sixties any day. I mean, I know places like this wiz run-down even then, but look at all this. This wiz just taking the fuckin' piss."

Bill's sweeping many-handed gesture took in the wide, litter-strewn tarmac expanse upon their left, the patch of dying hedges to their right side and, by implication, the whole devastated neighbourhood surrounding them. As they passed through the black bars of the Bath Street gate and left the shadow-crusted yard behind them, Reggie studied Bill appraisingly and wondered if he could confess his ignorance of almost the entire world they existed in without appearing stupid or inviting ridicule. Despite the fact that Bill appeared a great deal younger than did Reggie, Reggie thought he'd very likely lived to be much older and much wiser than Reggie himself had managed, with his wretched twelve years. In a strange way, he looked up to the much shorter boy as if Bill were an adult of considerable experience, and Reggie was reluctant to expose his own humiliating lack of knowledge by bombarding Bill with all the questions that he'd dearly love to know the answers to: the basic details of their puzzling afterlife that he had never had explained to him and had been too embarrassed to enquire about. His policy had always been to maintain a façade of knowing, worldly silence so that no one could make any smart remarks about him being an unschooled and backward half-wit from a backward century, which secretly he feared he was. Still, Bill had never seemed like the judgemental sort and as they ventured out onto the dark incline of Bath Street, Reggie thought he'd chance his arm while they were both alone together and he had the opportunity.

"Wiz you expecting it to be like this once you wiz dead? With all the builders and the black and white, and all the leaving pictures of yourself behind yer?"

Bill just grinned and shook his briefly-multiplying heads as the boys drifted over the benighted street in the direction of the Moat Place flats.

"O' course I wasn't. I don't reckon anybody thought that it'd be like this. None o' yer main religions sussed it, and I don't remember any of the Mahari-shis or whatever talking about after-images, or Bedlam Jennies, or just living the same life time after time, with all yer fuck-ups coming back to 'aunt yer and fuck all that you can do to change 'em."

They were starting to head down a drive that dipped into a hollow, with the garage doors of the flats' basement level on their left and on their right a stretch of featureless grey brickwork. Bill was looking thoughtful, as though reconsidering his last remark.

"Mind you, 'avin' said that, there wiz this bird that I used to knock about with, and fuck me, she knew all sorts of stuff, and she'd go on about it if you let 'er. I remember 'er tellin' me once 'ow she thought we 'ad the same lives over again. She said it 'ad to do with stuff about the fourth dimension."

Reggie groaned.

"Oh, not the ruddy fourth dimension! I've 'ad everyone try and explain it to me and I'm none the wiser. Phyllis said the fourth dimension was the length of how long things and people last."

Bill wrinkled up his nose into an amiable sneer.

"She don't know what she's on about. I mean, she's right in one way, but time's not the fourth dimension. As this bird I knew described it to me, pass-ing time's just 'ow we see the fourth dimension while we're still alive.

"She used to talk about these blokes who first went on about the idea of the fourth dimension, chaps from not long after your time. There was this bloke 'Inton, who got in the shit over a threesome with his missus and another bird and 'ad to leave the country. He said what we saw as space and time wiz really one big fuck-off solid block with four dimensions. Then there wiz this other feller, by the name of Abbott. He explained it all with kinda like a children's story, in this book called *Flatland*."

As they floated up the concrete steps to one side of the wall that blocked the hollow's far end, Reggie wondered if a "threesome" was the racy episode that he imagined it to be, but then forced his mind back with some reluctance to the subject that Bill was discussing. Reggie felt sure that if he was ever going to understand this special geometric business, then an explanation told so that a child could understand it was, in every likelihood, his last, best hope. He did his best to concentrate upon what Bill was saying, listening intently.

"What 'e did, this Abbott geezer, was instead of goin' on about a fourth dimension nobody could get their 'eads round, Abbott talked about the whole thing as if it was 'appenin' to little flat things what wiz in a world with two dimensions, as if they wiz livin' on a sheet o' paper. How he told it, these flat fuckers, right, they've just got length and breadth, and they can't even picture depth. They've got no idea about up and down. It's all just forwards, backwards, right and left to them. The third dimension what we live in, it makes no more sense to them than what the fourth dimension does to us."

This was already sounding promising to Reggie. He could easily imagine two-dimensional things, flatter than the wrigglers you could sometimes see if you got right down near a pool of rain and squinted with the vastly improved vision of the dead. He pictured them as shapeless little blobs going about their forwards-backwards-sideways lives on their flat sheet of paper, and the image made him smile. They'd be like draughts manoeuvring around a board, though obviously much thinner.

At the top of the stone steps there was a car park, open to the night sky and hemmed in by high black hedges on its southern side, though Reggie had a notion that when him and the Dead Dead Gang had passed through here in the 1970s, while on their way to Snow Town, it had been a queer and ugly playground for the bafflement of children. Now a dozen or so modern cars, snub-nosed and predatory, were hunkered down in darkness as though snoozing between kills. The Warren kid was nowhere to be seen.

The car park had been built where Fitzroy Street was situated, half a century beneath them in the past. Reggie and Bill streamed up its slope beneath the black quilt of a sky patched with grey cloud and a few isolated stars, almost too faint to see. The sprawl of square-cut buildings they were leaving, the drab, peeling blocks of Fort Place and Moat Place with their railed balconies and sunken walkways, had been put up in the 1960s on the rubble of Fort Street and Moat Street, and to Reggie's eye looked even more disheartening than the neglected 1930s hulk of Greyfriars, which at least had some curves to its concrete. As their likenesses went stuttering up the darkened car park's exit ramp towards Chalk Lane and the raised hillock at the foot of Castle Street, Reggie could make out lumpy children's drawings stuck up in the windows of the single-storey building on the mound. He had an idea that the place was once a dancing-school of some sort, but across the flickering passage of the years had been transformed into a nursery. Still, there were worse fates. In the silver-threaded murk beside him, Bill continued his description of the little flattened people in their squashed world that they thought was the whole universe.

"So, if a little flat bloke wants to be indoors, away from everybody, all 'e's gotta do wiz draw a square on 'is flat sheet o' paper, and then that's 'is 'ouse, right? Fuck the other flat blokes. If 'e wants to, our chap can just go inside 'is square and then 'e's shut away so none o' them can see 'im. Now, 'e don't know there's a third dimension up above 'is, where there's us lot looking down and *we* can see 'im, sitting there all safe and sound inside 'is four lines what 'e's got as walls. 'E can't even imagine nothin' up above 'im, 'cause 'e can't even imagine *up*, just forwards, backwards, right and left.

"Poor little cunt, 'e might be sitting there and we just, like, reach down and pick 'im up, then put 'im down again outside 'is 'ouse. What would 'e make o' that? To 'im it would be like some fuckin' weird shape just appearing out o' nowhere and then draggin' 'im out through the wall or something. It'd do 'is 'ead in. It's like us, when we're up in the Attics of the Breath and lookin' down into somebody's gaff. We're up above 'em in a way what they don't know about and can't even imagine, because their world's flat compared to ours, just like the piece-of-paper world is flat compared to theirs."

The wraith-boys were emerging onto the deserted roadway at the join of Little Cross Street and Chalk Lane just opposite the nursery, and off in the Northampton night there was a muffled uproar of drunk cheers and angry bellows, startled squeals, the constant wheeze from a catarrh of distant motor traffic or protracted and nerve-shredding bursts from eerie, unfamiliar instruments that Bill said were alarms or phones or sirens, every sound damped into a peculiarly urgent murmur by the dead acoustics of the ghost-seam. It struck Reggie that in nothing-five or nothing-six they had a lot more jangling and unnerving noises and a lot less starlight than in the decades below, where Reggie found the ratio between these two phenomena more to his liking.

As their ambling path began to gradually veer towards the left and Little Cross Street, Bill continued chattering about the fourth dimension and to Reggie's great surprise he found that he was following the drift of it, despite the bits of slang he didn't recognise and couldn't work out for himself. "Bird", for example, sounded like another way of saying "girl" or "woman", and Reggie supposed it was a bit like "chickabiddy", which he'd heard men use while he was still alive, down in the eighteen-hundreds. On the other hand, he'd no idea what a "gaff" was, not unless it was a sort of street fair or the yells and outcries that a fair like that would raise, and Reggie didn't reckon Bill meant that by it at all. The way he'd used it, it had sounded more like it meant "room" or something like that. Reggie let it go and concentrated on what Bill was saying at that moment.

"Anyway, this bird said 'ow people like Abbott and this 'Inton kicked off all the fuss about the fourth dimension in the 1880s or around then. Come the 1920s, though, and everybody's into it. All of the artists and the cubists and Picasso and all them, they were just tryin' to think 'ow it would look if, say, somebody turned their 'ead towards yer and yer could still see 'em side-on. I mean, that's 'ow us lot see each other all the time."

To demonstrate, Bill whipped his head around and grinned at Reggie. Reggie didn't really know what cubists or Picassos were, but he could see what Bill had meant: the after-image of the ginger nipper's profile was still hanging in the air even though Bill now faced him, a translucent ghost-ear superimposed fleetingly on Bill's right eye. Perhaps that was the sort of thing that the Picubos painted.

"And it wizn't just the artists. All the spiritualists and the dodgy séance types wiz celebratin'. They wiz well chuffed, 'cause they thought the fourth dimension would explain all of the weird things ghosts wiz s'posed to do, like seeing inside boxes and all that old bollocks. For a time down in the 1920s, even all the boffins and the scientists an' what-not thought the table-rappers might be onto somethin' with this fourth dimension business. Then I 'spect they 'ad a war, or summat else come up, and everybody just forgot about it."

Reggie silently absorbed this. Though he couldn't say that any of it was the revelation he'd been hoping for, it made at least a bit more sense of Reggie's circumstances. He'd not realised that the trails of pictures following the dead about were tied up somehow with this fourth dimension, having previously considered the phenomenon merely a random nuisance. Now he knew that it was scientific, it might not be so much of a bother.

As he listened to Bill ramble on – something about a chap called Einstein, probably another painter – Reggie scanned the unlit neighbourhood about them, part of his attention still fixed doggedly upon the task of finding the ghost-runaway. Glancing across his shoulder to the right he saw the nursery on the mound and, just across the mouth of Castle Hill, the blunt age-rounded corners on the sandstone mass of Doddridge Church. From where he stood with Bill he couldn't quite see the queer doorway stranded halfway up the

church's wall, nor the appalling, vision-straining splendour of the Ultraduct
that sprouted from it, curving off unfathomably to the south, towards the
madhouses on Mansoul's outskirts and beyond that London, Dover, France,
Jerusalem. Although the structure was itself invisible from Reggie's current
angle, he could see the falling chalk-dust light it scattered as it settled on the
ragged end of Little Cross Street.

Just across the road, in front of the two phantom boys and to their left,
there loomed the gaunt west face of Bath Street flats, their bruise-dark 1930s
brickwork glistening like snail slime in the intermittent lamplight. Although
Reggie doubted that there had been more than a few years between the raising
of their Greyfriars counterparts and these somehow forbidding residences,
there was an immense dissimilarity in their respective atmospheres. Greyfriars had seemed no more than miserably disappointed, but the soulless and
disinterested windows of the Bath Street buildings wore a genuinely dreadful
look, as though they'd seen the worst and were just waiting now to die.

Though in the ghost-seam's monochrome the flats' bricks were a charred
grey, almost black, Reggie had heard they were the brownish-red of dried
blood, each one like a block of corned beef slithered from its tin, with yellowed
lard for mortar. At a point halfway along the west wall, double doors more
suited to a closed-down swimming-baths stared menacingly from beneath the
sagging hat brim of their portico. The only glass pane that remained intact
was cracked, the other three replaced by speckled plasterboard. Two low brick
walls, on one of which white moss was crawling, bordered a thin concrete passage, running from the hooded doorway and across a grass verge to the paving
slabs of Little Cross Street. Unreadable words were scrawled in pale paint on
the stout brick end-posts, and accumulated in the angle between wall and turf
was a dismaying silt of rubber johnnies, dead birds and dead fag-ends, hinged
and gaping square-cut oysters made of plastic foam that haemorrhaged cold
chips, a single child-sized buckle shoe, six flimsy beer-tins crushed in rage or
boredom, several ... Reggie brought himself up short. Moss didn't crawl. He
looked back at the clump of ashen tufts which even now appeared to be progressing slowly, like a great albino caterpillar, as it crawled along the flat top
surface of the nearside wall. Except it wasn't really something fluffy balancing
upon the wall, but was instead the blonde hair of somebody crouching down
and shuffling along behind it.

"Bill! I see 'im! Look, 'e's over there!"

No sooner had the words left Reggie's mouth than he regretted them and
wished he'd thought to try a subtler approach. Over upon the other side of
Little Cross Street, Michael Warren stood up from behind the wall where
he'd been hiding and gaped, horrified, at Bill and Reggie as their multiplying
images began to blur across the road towards him. Venting a brief yelp of

panic, the pyjama-clad child whirled around and plunged into the plaster-board and glass of the closed doors, without the least trace of his earlier hesitation with regard to passing through substantial objects. Reggie dashed over the empty roadway in pursuit with Bill swearing beside him, both of them aware that the new kid had only run away because their roughness frightened him. If John or even Phyllis had been present, Michael Warren would have probably just given up the chase and gone along with them, grateful to be no longer lost in this unfriendly century. By shouting out the odds the way that he just had, Reggie had possibly scared off the little boy for good. If he should dig into another time, even a half-hour back or forward, they would very likely never find him and then all the dire consequences everyone had promised if they lost the hapless tot would come to pass.

In this eventuality, he couldn't bear the thought of facing Phyllis and explaining to her how he'd messed things up. Frantic lest Michael Warren should escape again, the boys and their attendant images charged in a conga-line of hooligans, diagonally across the grass and straight in through the western wall of Bath Street flats, not bothering to enter by the double doors as the blonde fugitive had done. Reggie and Bill dived recklessly through the blood-pudding bricks into the startling, unexpected realm beyond.

The first apartment that they rushed through was unlit save for the hissing radiance of a television set tuned to an empty channel. Sitting in the room's sole chair, a middle-aged man stared into the incoherent static, weeping while he clutched a woman's straw hat to his face. The two ghost-boys smeared past him, passing through the rear wall and the empty kitchenette beyond into another flat, this one blacked out save for the spidery chrome lines of their nocturnal vision. Picked out as if by metallic thread, Reggie could see a filthy baby sleeping fitfully in its dilapidated cradle, the place otherwise unoccupied save for five underfed cats and their droppings. Him and Bill moved on, a ruffian wind that bowled down passageways and under doors, through hovel after hovel: three excited black men playing cards while in one corner lay a fourth, bloody and whimpering; a plump and vacant-eyed old woman in her underwear, patiently counting and arranging tins of dog-food in a pyramid without the least trace of a dog in sight; a skinny young dark-skinned girl with her hair in plaited stripes, who alternated between sucking smoke out of a dented tin and pasting cut-out photographs of a blonde woman into an already-bulging book.

At last the pair of junior apparitions flowed through an exterior wall, emerging gratefully into what, if they'd still been capable of breathing, would have been fresh air. They were now in the central avenue that split the flats, effectively, into two halves. A straight path with a strip of lawn to either side, bounded by walls with strange half-crescent arches, Reggie knew that getting on for ninety years beneath them this was the bleak recreation ground known as the Orchard. The whole place was greatly changed since then, of course. In fact the place was greatly changed, at least by night, since Reggie last remembered passing this way, on a short-cut through the 1970s. Although the basic structure of the buildings had not altered, Reggie was amazed to see that every grimy balcony or stairway visible through the brick arches bordering the path was lit up from beneath, so that these features floated in the dark and made the flats seem like some fabulous abandoned city of the future, full of blazing lanterns but devoid of people. At the central path's south end, before it got to Castle Street, it turned into a broad and brick-walled concrete stairway. On the bottom step towards its middle sat the ghost of Michael Warren, narrow tartan shoulders shaking as he wept into his lifted hands.

This time, Reggie and Bill approached the clearly frightened kid more carefully, moving so slowly that they hardly left a single duplicate behind them. Not wanting the child to glance up suddenly and think that they were creeping up on him, Reggie called out in the most soft and reassuring tone that he could manage.

"Don't be scared, mate. It's just us. Yer not in any trouble."

Michael Warren looked up, startled, and for just a moment you could see he was debating whether to run off again or not. Evidently he finally decided 'not', lowering his head again as he resumed his sobbing. Bill and Reggie walked up and sat down on the stone step to either side of him, with Reggie draping one long coat-clad arm around the spectral infant's heaving shoulders.

"Come on. Blow your nose and pull yerself together, ay? It's not so bad."

The little boy looked up at Reggie, ectoplasm glistening on his cheeks.

"I just want to glow home. This wizzn't the place I leaved in."

Reggie couldn't really argue there. The angular black masses with their hovering islands of illumination looming up around them weren't the place that he had lived in either, or the place he'd left. And what was more, in Reggie's case the glow of home was some hundred and fifty years beneath them, down there in the Boroughs dirt. He gave the troubled ghost-child's arm a brief squeeze through the tartan fabric of his ghostly dressing gown.

"I know. Tell yer the truth, me and Bill don't much like it up here in the nothings either, do we, Bill?"

On Michael's other side Bill shook his head into a scruffy, momentary hydra. "Nah. It's pants, mate, and the further up yer go, the worse it gets. I mean, there's cameras stuck up everywhere around 'ere as it is – that's why there's all these lights – but if you go up into nothing-seven or round there, the fuckin' things start talkin' to yer. 'Pick that fuckin' litter up'. I'm serious. Old Phyllis only dug 'er way up 'ere by accident, to get us out that storm. I bet when we meet up with 'er, she'll want to tunnel back down to sometime a bit more civilised. So don't go runnin' off again, ay? We're yer mates. We want to get you out of 'ere as much as you do."

Michael Warren sniffed and wiped a mollusc-trail of ectoplasm on one tartan sleeve.

"Where hag our how's gone?"

From the note of piping query in the toddler's voice, it sounded as though he was cautiously prepared to be consoled. Reggie attempted to address the infant's question sympathetically, putting aside his earlier opinion that the Warren kid should simply grow up and get over it. Everyone had their cross to bear, Reggie supposed, and Michael Warren had been very young when all this happened to him. He deserved a chance.

"Look, Phyllis dug up nearly fifty years, and nothin' lasts forever, does it? Nearly all the 'ouses what us lot grew up in are pulled down before the twenty-somethings, but they're all still standing somewhere underneath us in the bygone, so don't worry. We can dig you back to 1959 again before you can say knife."

This did not appear to reassure the lad as much as Reggie might have hoped. He shook his blonde locks ruefully.

"Blub I don't want all this to be here. Ebonything's all nasty, and I used to like it when my mum cut through these flats to take us home. I remumble once when I wiz in my plushchair, and she bumped me down these stairps. It took a long time and my hisster sat on that wall there and read her comet-book. She said it was about forbidden worlds, and there were planets on the letters ..."

As if realising that his ramblings were not conveying his great sense of loss, the ghost-boy let his reminiscences trail off and simply gestured to the dark aisle they were sitting in, its under-lit verandas flaring as they hung suspended in the night to either side.

"I just don't like what's magicked all that into this."

With a deep sigh and a pistol-like report from the ghosts of his knee-joints, Reggie stood up from the step and signalled Bill to do the same. Realising that the other lads had risen to their feet provoked the Warren kid to follow them. When they were all standing, Bill and Reggie each took Michael by one of his hands, both hoping that they didn't look like sissies, and proceeded to walk with him down the grass-fringed avenue between the two halves of the flats, heading for Bath Street in a three-strong column of pursuing pictures like a marching band. Reggie looked down towards the little boy.

"None of us like it, mate, the thing what's made this place the way it is. Soul of the 'ole, that's what we call it. If we walk down further this way, you'll see why."

Having reached the north-most end of the long walkway, they stepped into Bath Street. The two older children paused here, and when Michael War-

ren looked up questioningly Reggie nodded grimly to a spot a little further
down the lamp-lit hill.

It was such an unprecedented sight, a little like one's first glimpse of the
Ultraduct, that Michael Warren wouldn't know at first what he was looking
at, Reggie felt certain from his own experience. Unlike the Ultraduct, however, the phenomenon that hung there swirling in the night air down by Little
Cross Street did not inspire overwhelming awe so much as crushing dread.

It was a scorched and blackened hole burned in the supernatural fabric
of the ghost-seam. Roughly twenty yards in its diameter it hung there a few
feet above the listing and subsided Bath Street paving slabs, spinning unhurriedly. Quite clearly not a thing of the material world, its furthest edges passed
straight through the bacon-coloured brickwork of the flats' north side, seeming to make the walls transparent as it did so. Reggie could see through into
the inner chambers, where the cindered edges of the gradually revolving discus reached into one of the rooms that he and Bill had passed through a few
moments back, in which the dark-skinned woman with her hair in stripes sat
sucking smoking melted grains of glass out of her tin and pasting pictures in
her scrapbook. The hole's turning rim cut through the girl's translucent body
like a black circular saw, the charred flakes of its millstone passage fluttering
down to settle in her exposed inner workings, all without her knowledge. On
the other side of Bath Street the gyrating aperture's far edge was doing much
the same thing to an upper corner of the maisonettes in Crispin Street. A
see-through fat man sat upon a see-through toilet, ground unwittingly on the
monstrosity's sooty perimeter as it rotated through his bathroom. A terrible
seared cog that had oblivious anatomic specimens caught on its teeth, the
horror wheeled with a dire inevitability there at the night-heart of the unsuspecting neighbourhood, as though it were the works and movement of some
huge and devastating timepiece. Michael Warren gaped at the infernal spectacle for some few moments and then he glanced up, appalled and lost, looking
to Bill and Reggie for some explanation.

"What wiz it? It smells cackrid, like old guttercats."

The kid was right. Even here in the ghost-seam where Phyll Painter's
rotten rabbits had no odour, you could smell the crematorium perfume of
the slowly-whirling abyss, biting and unpleasant on the membrane of your
phantom throat, behind the cringing spectral nostrils. Tightening their grips
on Michael's hands, Reggie and Bill propelled him swiftly over Bath Street,
past the yawning maw of the black nebula languidly spiralling only a dozen
paces down the street. They didn't want him getting scared again and running
straight into the bloody thing.

"It's like the wraith of a big chimney what they 'ad down 'ere for burnin' all Northampton's muck. In the three-sided world, the smokestack wiz pulled down seventy years ago, but nobody could put its fires out down 'ere in the ghost-world. It's been burnin' ever since, and gettin' bigger. If you think it looks and smells bad 'ere, you ought to see it from Upstairs. We call it the Destructor."

Simply to pronounce the word, for Reggie, felt like smashing both fists down upon the keys to the left side of a piano, and appeared to have the same effect upon the trio's spirits as they soldiered on in silence over Bath Street to the square of army haircut-mown grass on its further side. Michael kept looking back across his dressing gown-clad shoulder at the levitating maelstrom. Reggie knew the nipper would be asking himself the same question everybody did the first time they set eyes on the Destructor: what about the mortal spaces and the living people that it intersected with? What was it doing to them when they didn't even know that it was there? The simple truth was that nobody knew, although you didn't have to be a brain-box to conclude that in all probability it wasn't doing anybody any good. Now, ghosts who accidentally got too close to it, this was another matter. Everybody knew what happened then: they were incinerated and next pulled to pieces, pulverised to atoms by its vortex currents with their residue dragged into the remorseless onyx swirl. For all that anybody knew, the essences of these unfortunates might still be living and aware within that frightful, endless turning. Reggie didn't want to think about it and urged Michael Warren on across the light-less swathe of lawn.

Just when the older boys were starting to believe that their young charge would never again tear his eyes away from the Destructor, then, as is often the way with smaller children, his attention was seized suddenly by something that he evidently found still more remarkable, the soul-destroying whirlpool hovering in Bath Street there behind them instantly forgotten.

It was the two tower blocks, Claremont Court and Beaumont Court, that had entranced the kid. The twelve floors of each monolith soared up towards the torn cloud and the mostly-absent stars above, postage-stamp rectangles of curtain-filtered light gummed here and there upon the buildings' tall black pages. Although Reggie smirked a little at how easily impressed the infant was, in fairness he'd had longer to grow blasé with regard to the colossal head-stones. The first time he'd chanced upon them he'd been every bit as dumb-struck as was Michael Warren now. They'd been the tallest houses that he'd ever seen, truly gigantic packing crates dumped on a truly vast expanse of scrubland. The big metal letters up towards the top of each huge block, recent additions spelling NEWLIFE, had been put up sideways for some clever modern reason, making the two towers seem to Reggie even more like packaging that had been turned onto its side. Around the concrete base of the dual edifices, scattered scraps of litter shone like funeral lilies in the silver-threaded darkness. Michael was as much perplexed as awed.

"I thought it wiz all pawed-down houses here. Where did these thingers come from?"

Reggie laughed, not in derision. It was true. He'd never thought of it before, but the towers did look like two great big fingers raised in a titanic V-sign to the Boroughs. Letting go of Michael's hand he ruffled the boy's milky hair instead.

"That's a good question, little 'un. When wiz it, Bill, these ugly bastards wiz put up?"

Bill screwed his face up pensively.

"Down sometime in the early 'Sixties, I'd 'ave thought. When yer took back to life in 1959, yer'll probably be seeing these things go up in a year or two. So what yer getting now's a preview, but yer won't remember it when yer alive again."

Reggie inclined his bowler, nodding in solemn agreement. That was well known. You could no more take a memory back from the ghost-seam or Mansoul than you could bring a treasure-chest back from an avaricious dream to waking life. Returned to the three-sided mortal domain, Michael Warren would be utterly unable to recall the slightest detail of his exploits Upstairs with the Dead Dead Gang except perhaps as fleeting instances of déjà vu, quickly forgotten. Reggie was still pondering this vaguely disappointing fact when Phyllis, John and plucky little Marjorie burst from the pebble-dashed wall of the maisonettes in Crispin Street and streamed across the road towards the wide grass verge where Reggie and the other two were standing, lightning sketches of the newcomers peeling as though out of an artist's sketchpad in their wakes.

"Yer found 'im, then. Yer slippery little beggar. What d'yer think yer doin', runnin' orf like that?"

Phyllis looked very cross as she stood towering over Michael Warren, albeit only by about four inches, buckled shoes planted apart and bunched fists resting on her skinny hips. Even the glassy black eyes of her rabbit stole seemed to be glaring disapprovingly at the poor kid. Having somewhat revised his own opinion of the little ghost-lad, Reggie didn't think that Phyll was being fair. He was about to intervene, although reluctant at the thought of facing up to Dead Dead Gang's self-appointed leader, when big John stepped in and saved Reggie the trouble.

"Take no notice of her, titch. She's just relieved we've found you and that you're all right. You should have heard her a few minutes back when she thought that you'd been done in by the rough sleepers and your remnants flung in the Destructor. She wiz getting so upset, her lip was wobbling."

Phyllis turned and scowled at John. She tried to stamp hard on the tall, good-looking ghost's toes, but he laughed and whipped his foot back just in time. Phyllis attempted to sustain her indignation in the face of John's hilarity as it began to spread amongst the other spectral children. Even Reggie sniggered at how vexed she looked, but turned it to a cough in case she heard him.

"I wiz not! I wiz just worried that 'e'd 'ave an accident or get grabbed by another devil, and then we should be in trouble! As if I give tuppence if 'e falls base over apex dayn the scarlet well, or gets et up by Malone's terriers so all we find is dogshit with 'is blonde curls stickin' out of it!"

Disastrously for her composure, this last bit even made Phyllis giggle. They all stood there laughing on the night lawns, and soon everyone was pals again.

While Michael Warren and the others made up and swapped tales of their adventures since they'd split up at the bottom end of Scarletwell Street earlier, Reggie and Bill amused themselves by playing idly in the shadows on the cropped grass. Bill suggested they play knuckles, but when both of them inspected their own hands they found the finger-joints still weakly pulsed with dull grey bruise-lights from their previous session, and decided to do something else instead. At last they settled down to running in tight circles round a piece of chip-wrap that was crumpled on the turf, to see if they could make it flutter. Sometimes you could do that, if there were enough of you. You just ran round and round an object like a toy train circling a little track, fast as you could, and if you could get up enough speed it would wear a temporary groove into what Reggie had heard others call the time-space or the space-time of the mortal plane. Eddies of wind would funnel down to fill these small depressions, and if you ran quick enough for long enough you could start miniature tornados in the little car park between Silver Street and Bearward Street down in the 1960s, or make tiny whirlwinds blossom from the straw and orange-peelings at the corners of the market square. On this occasion though, with only him and Bill contributing to the effect, they couldn't do much more than make the litter shift a half inch. When Phyll told them to stop playing silly buggers and get ready to move on, they gave the dizzying pastime up with quiet sighs of concealed relief, grateful for the excuse to quit their unproductive efforts.

The six ghostly children and their mob of trailing look-alikes made their way up the gentle grassy incline bordering the tower blocks and parallel with Bath Street, heading for the row of homes that ran along the lawn's top edge beside a path that Reggie thought was possibly called Simons Way. It looked like Phyllis had decided they should cut behind the hulking NEWLIFE flats to Tower Street, which was what the former top end of Scarletwell had been renamed. Most likely she was making for the Works, though Reggie hoped she didn't plan on visiting it here in nothing-five or nothing-six, or wherever the ruddy heck they were.

Although Reggie judged it to be in the morning's early hours, one or two living people were about their business, unencumbered by the strings of replicas that Reggie and his posthumous ensemble dragged behind them. A small-eyed and porky fellow with a smooth-shaved head emerged from a front door in Simons Walk to leave a pair of filmy milk-bottles on his front step before retiring back inside again. Although the children all slapped their grey, insubstantial hands through his bald cranium as he stooped to put the bottles down, he didn't show the least awareness of their presence, which was as it should be. This was not the case with the nocturnal stroller that they next encountered as they turned right into Tower Street, with the looming concrete monuments now at their back.

It was a tall skinny feller with black curly hair, who looked to be somewhere around his forties or his fifties, and who'd obviously had more than a few too many. He was veering slowly down the length of Tower Street towards the phantom kids, having presumably descended to this level via one of the flights of steps at its top end. He was reciting something in a slurred voice to himself that sounded like a poem, something about people being "strange, nay, rather stranger than the rest". Reggie and Bill both had a laugh at that, and were starting to take the mickey out of the half-cut chap when he stopped dead in his tracks and looked straight at them.

"I can see yer! Ah ha ha ha! I know where you're hiding, round the bend and up the flue. Ah ha ha ha! I see yer, all right. I'm a published poet."

The dead kids stood rooted to the spot, gaping in disbelief. There was always a chance, of course, that someone living might occasionally glimpse you, but they'd almost always look away, concluding that they hadn't really seen what they had thought they'd seen. For them to try and speak with you was practically unheard of, and as for a living soul who greeted your appearance with amusement, well, it never happened. Even Phyllis and big John were looking at the sozzled bloke gone out, as if they'd no idea what to do next.

Fortunately, the serious predicament this could have led to was averted by the timely opening of a bedroom window on the top floor of the first house in the row, behind the ghost gang and up to their left. An ancient but incredibly resilient-looking little woman in a dressing gown leaned out and hissed down sharply at the drunk chap swaying in the lamp-lit street.

"Yer silly 'ape'orth! Are yer crackers? Come in 'ere before I clock yer, standin' talkin' to yerself when it's the middle of the night!"

The clairvoyant lushington looked up towards the window with his generous eyebrows rising in surprise. He called out to the woman with the same distinctive cackle that he'd just greeted the children with.

"Mother, behave! Ah ha ha ha! I was just chatting with these … oh. They've gone. Ah ha ha ha!"

The man had dropped his gaze once more to Tower Street and stared directly at the ghost-kids, but he blinked and looked uncertain now, squinting his eyes as if he could no longer see them. Further admonitions from the woman, who appeared to be his mother, prompted him to stumble forward, laughing to himself and fumbling for his house-keys as he passed unheedingly through the half-dozen junior apparitions standing in his path. The dead gang turned to watch him struggling with the Yale lock on the door of the end house, all the while giggling to himself, the muttering old woman having loudly pulled her bedroom window shut by now, leaving her drunken offspring to his own devices.

Phyllis shook her head as the gang turned away from the sloshed feller trying to open his front door, resuming their ascent of Tower Street.

"Flippin' Nora. What the devil wiz 'e, when 'e wiz at 'ome? And to think livin' folk are frit of us!"

She made her shoulders ripple in a comically exaggerated shudder to imply that living beings were much stranger and a great deal spookier than ghosts. Reggie agreed. In his experience, dead people were a lot more down to earth.

The gang came to a halt outside some sort of modern undertaking owned by the Salvation Army that was closed up for the night. These premises were on the children's left, while up ahead of them there loomed the ugly grey-on-grey mosaic of the wall bounding the traffic junction that the Mayorhold had become. Sneaking a glance at Michael Warren, Reggie realised that the youngster couldn't get his bearings amongst all this unfamiliar architecture, and thus had no idea where he was. Considering what had happened to the Mayorhold, this was probably as well. Look how the kid had taken it when it was just one row of houses that had disappeared.

The raised-up intersection blazed with sodium lamps that Reggie had been informed were the yellow of stale piss when seen by mortal eyes. This was what lent the ghost-seam's monochrome such an unhealthy tinge, the sick light spilling from the elevated motor-carousel to splash upon the streets and underpasses down below, where the Dead Dead Gang gathered in a ring about their leader. Phyllis was explaining what she thought would be the best thing to do next, mostly for Michael Warren's benefit so that the toddler didn't suffer any more ghastly surprises.

"Right. I've 'ad a think abayt all this. We know that titch 'ere is a Vernall, who are people with great works to do, what very orften they don't know nothin' abayt. We know 'e's gooin' back to life again, and that it's all summat to do wi' this big job the builders 'ave got on, the Porthimoth di Norhan. Now, 'e's so important to this contract that the builders 'ave 'ad a big dust-up over 'im, back dayn in 1959. I reckon we should goo back Upstairs to Mansoul and watch the fight. We might find ayt a bit more abayt 'ow 'is nibs 'ere wiz involved in it."

Shifting uncomfortably inside his outsized overcoat, Reggie protested.

"Don't go Upstairs 'ere, Phyll. Not 'ere in the nothings. 'E's already seen 'ow the Destructor looks, just 'angin' there in Bath Street ..."

Phyllis bristled.

"Do I look 'alf sharp? 'Course I'm not gunna goo Upstairs from 'ere! Fer one thing, we'd be traipsing miles along the Attics of the Breath to get to where the builders 'ad their scrap. We're gunna dig down inter 1959 first, then we'll make ayr way Upstairs from there."

Bill, standing on the outskirts of their circle, kicking pointlessly at dandelions and pebbles that he could not touch, frowned in concern.

"That'll just drop us straight back in that ghost-storm, won't it?"

Flinging her long stole around her neck in what would have been a dramatic film-star gesture had it not been for the putrefying rabbits and their after-pictures, Phyllis fixed her younger relative with an unnerving glare.

"Oh, use yer loaf fer once, ayr Bill. Not if we dig back to an 'our or two before all that kicked orf it won't! If we goo careful, we'll know when we've reached the stripe where all the wind wiz, so it's just a layer or two down past there. Now, anyone 'oo wants to 'elp me can, and anyone 'oo don't can clear orf ayt the way."

With that, she marched across towards the fabricated wall of the Salvation Army building in a single file of glowering schoolgirls and began to scrape at its accumulated time with both hands. Shimmering bands of black and white that Reggie knew were days and nighttimes interleaved began to gather in a loose whorl round her pawing fingertips, as, grudgingly, the other members of the gang walked over to assist her. Only Michael Warren and Drowned Marjorie were excused tunnel duty, Michael on the grounds of probable ineptitude and Marjorie because they were all frightened that the small boy would run off again if he had nobody to sit and keep him company.

After a minute or two's dedicated scrabbling at the wall, Phyllis announced that she could feel the ghost-storm slicing into windy ribbons on her fingernails. Progressing with more caution, she rolled back the tissue edges representing the duration of the squall, dragging them out into the wavering Belisha-beacon stripes around her tunnel's widening mouth. A moment more and she reported that she could feel through into a place without a breeze, inviting her confederates to help enlarge the aperture, now that she'd done all of the hard work for them.

Pitching in with everybody else to haul the hole's rim further out and make it bigger, Reggie was surprised to see that there was just more blackness on the portal's other side, and not the 1950s daylight that he'd been expecting. When the opening was sufficiently distended for the gang to climb through, though, he found that they were in a cellar, which accounted for the dark. Boxes that turned out to be filled with racy magazines and paperbacks were stacked up by one wall and a great heap of coal and slack reclined against another, the whole scene delineated in the silverpoint of the dead children's night-sight. One by one the kids climbed through the entrance into 1959, with Phyllis herself bringing up the rear while ushering Drowned Marjorie and Michael Warren through in front of her. Once everyone was in the darkened basement Phyllis got them to seal up the hole behind them, that led out to nothing-five or nothing-six. Diligently they combed the smoky fibres of the present day across the gaping vent until no sign of Tower Street or its blocks of flats against a star-deserted sky remained. Having observed the ghost-seam protocol about shutting the gate behind you, Phyllis next turned to address the gang. She wasn't whispering, so evidently there were no watchmen here with second sight, the way there'd been in that lone house down at the bottom end of Scarletwell.

"In case yer wonderin' where we are, it's 'Arry Trasler's paper-shop, just orf the Merruld 'fore yer get to Althorp Street. We're in 'is cellar. All we've gotter do is goo upstairs and we'll be just araynd the corner from the entrance to the Works."

They found the cellar stairs beyond a string-bound stack of *True Adventure* magazines, which looked American and had almost-bare ladies on their covers, nude save for their underwear and Nazi armbands, who were menacing manacled men with uniformly gritted teeth by brandishing hot irons and bullwhips. Going up the steps one at a time the children passed out through a closed and bolted cellar door into a daylight passageway that led to the newsagent's shop itself: a former front room that had comics, paperbacks and magazines hanging from great iron bulldog clips in a bay window given over to display. Here, behind an old and black-grooved wooden counter that divided the small room in two along its length, a balding and pot-bellied man with sallow skin and dark-ringed eyes stood calculating the returns upon the morning papers during a brief intermission between customers. Reggie presumed that this must be the Harry Trasler that Phyllis had mentioned as the shop's proprietor. Morose and seemingly preoccupied, he didn't even look up from his jotted column of additions as the ghost-kids melted through his countertop, which was apparently not old enough to stop them doing so despite appearances, and drifted out into the July sunshine that was just then painting the serene enclosure of the Mayorhold.

It did Reggie's phantom heart good to see once again that passably rectangular expanse where eight streets ran together, hemmed in by various tradesmen's yards, five public houses, getting on a dozen cosy-looking little shops and the imposing pillar-decorated façade of the Northampton Co-operative Society. This outfit had first started out down Horsemarket in Reggie's day as the West End Industrial Co-operative Society, and he was pleased to see the worthy venture was still doing nicely more than seventy years later. Flanked on one side by a butcher's shop and on the other by the old Victorian public toilets curving round and into Silver Street, the Co-op seemed to be the busiest area of the Mayorhold on this summer morning. Women laden down with raffia shopping bags and wearing headscarves chatted in the recess of the shop's front doorway, stepping back occasionally to let some other customer pass in or out of the establishment.

Pleasingly dusty light was sprinkled on the hard-faced women who were going at that moment into the Green Dragon by the mouth of Bearward Street, and on the motor-coaches sleeping near the Currier's Arms here on the western side of the forgotten former town square. Just emerging from the sweetshop that was next to Trasler's, three young lads in knee-length grey serge trousers held up by elasticated belts with S-shaped buckles shared what seemed to be a bag of acid-drops as they barged through the ghost-gang without noticing that they were there.

Reggie and company continued on past the Old Jolly Smokers on their right, mindful that in the astral upper reaches of the pub where the rough sleepers congregated, Mick Malone the ratter would be knocking back his Puck's Hat Punch and thinking about heading home across the sky to Little Cross Street with his ferrets in his pockets, as they'd seen him doing earlier. The ghost-kids almost tiptoed past the saloon bar's swing door, crossing the top of Scarletwell Street where it ran into the Mayorhold.

Opposite the Jolly Smokers on the other corner of the run-down thoroughfare was a three-storey building, old and derelict, its timbers and its stonework so dark they looked almost smoked. The windows of the place were boarded up within their weathered, splintering frames and up above the similarly-boarded door were remnants of what seemed to be a shop-sign, too few painted letters still remaining to make out the former owner's name, or what it had once sold. Although Reggie remembered the place being open once, back in the early nineteen-somethings, he still couldn't for the death of him recall what kind of shop it was. He only knew that a good while before that, right back in the 1500s before Reggie had been born, this ruin had once been the Town Hall of Northampton.

The kids entered through the front wall, finding themselves in a stripped and shadowy interior where wands of sunlight fell through chinks between the nailed-up lengths of wood across the window. Wallpaper that was four generations thick in places sagged and separated from damp plaster, hanging like loose skin, while a far corner had been decorated by some empty Double Diamond bottles and what looked to be a human bowel movement. They ascended a collapsing staircase to the first floor, floating over mildewed voids where steps were rotted through, and then continued on to the top storey. Here, a dozen or so missing slates had made the building open to both birds and rain, transforming it into a maze of dismal chambers carpeted with stalagmites of pigeon shit and clouded puddles.

The crook-door and its attendant Jacob Flight were in the end room, coloured light falling in party streamers through the radiant portal, settling on the children's upturned faces, on the sodden planks and rugs and papers that had fused into one substance, on the pitifully narrow treads of the celestial ladder.

Reggie felt a tightness in the memory of his throat, and the spook-fluids welled up in his eyes. This was the place Phyllis and Bill had brought him to that first time, not long after they'd all met in fourteenth-century catacombs while sheltering from the Great Ghost-Storm of 1913. This was where they'd finally convinced him he was just as good as anybody else, with as much right to Hell or Heaven. He had no idea why all these feelings should well up inside him every time he saw these stairs to Mansoul. They just did. He wiped his brimming eyes upon one coarse sleeve of his greatcoat furtively, so no one else should see.

Phyllis was first to climb the Jacob Flight, her rabbit necklace swaying and her after-pictures burnt away like morning fog as she went up into the colours and the brilliance. Michael Warren followed her, with lanky John behind him and then Bill and Marjorie.

Taking a last look round at the smudged pencil-drawing of the ghost-seam, Reggie followed suit. He was a bit scared, he supposed, at the idea of being audience to a brawl between the builders. Having witnessed the resultant howling gale he wasn't sure that he was ready for the fight itself, but that was only nerves and common sense. That wasn't the whole reason for the teary-eyed reluctance that descended on him every time he climbed these rungs and ventured up the wooden hill to Deadfordshire.

He still didn't believe it, that was what it finally came down to. Even after all of these incalculable years, he still couldn't accept that there was somewhere wonderful where he was wanted, where there was a place for him that wasn't just an unmarked plot on Doddridge Church's burial ground. He blinked away the ghostly moisture in his eyes and sniffed back a thick gob of ectoplasm as he manfully composed himself before resuming his ascent, out of the grey into the gold and blue and rose and violet.

Hat tipped at a jaunty angle to disguise the fact that he'd been weeping, Reginald James Fowler clambered through the crook-door up into the Works, where suddenly about him were unfurling sounds and rich painterly tones, the holy smell of planed wood and the honest sweat of builders. He'd pulled back the tacked-up curtain, so to speak.

Reggie was home.

MENTAL FIGHTS

Scrambling up out of the crook-door after Phyllis Painter, all the ringing uproar of the Works – its scale and colour and especially the niff of Phyllis's putrescent scarf – hit Michael Warren squarely in the mush. The factory floor that the Dead Dead Gang had emerged onto, big as an aerodrome and flooded with a pearly light from its improbably high windows, hummed with purposeful activity. Builders were everywhere, on ladders and on gantries, striding back and forth with scrolls and sheaves of documents, calling instructions to each other in a language where each syllable flowered to an intricate and lyric garden.

Clad in wooden sandals, wearing plain robes of soft pigeon-grey that had a hint of green or purple in the folds and shadows, these seemed to be builders of a different rank to the white-haired one Michael had glimpsed earlier, with his bare feet and icy, shining gown. Whereas he'd had the bearing of an artisan, the several dozen individuals industriously employed about the vast enclosure had the look of labourers, albeit labourers who carried themselves with more grace and dignity than any emperor that Michael had seen pictures of, or ever heard about.

One of the builders, a lean, pious type with slightly elongated features and tight ashen curls at his receded hairline, passed the rather cowed gang of ghost-children as he marched across his whispering cathedral of a workplace. Having just come from the ghost-seam, Michael found it odd at first that there were no evaporating duplicates trailing behind this purposeful employee as he walked, but then remembered he was somewhere different now. The long-faced worker paused in his traversal of the large and intricately decorated flagstone tiles to scrutinise the gaggle of dead urchins with eyes that were endless and of brilliant emerald.

"Wvyeo gaurl thik comnsd! Pleog chrauwvy ind tsef!"

These words (if that was what they were), delivered in a voice neutral as breeze and frilled with echo, seemed to put down heavy, lumpy suitcases in Michael Warren's mind which then proceeded to unpack themselves into progressively more compact and ingenious parcels of significance.

"We golden ones, we toilers in this veiled vale, we who tread the vintage in these glorious vineyards of undying wisdom, we grey guardians of the endeavour welcome thee, welcome thee to our wonder, to our world, our wealth, our

ward, where are our Works made! For lo, it doth please us, if it should please you, here to present a plan and a prospectus of our pasture as it was in ages past and so shall endure unto the far ending of eternity, so that it shall serve as thy guard, thy guide and great deliverance within these walls, these halls, these hallowed houses of the endless soul and self!"

As Michael understood it, this boiled down to "Welcome to the Works. Please have a guide." The labourer extracted half-a-dozen leaflets with a single fold from the untidy stack of papers that he carried under one arm, handing copies of the slender booklet to each of the six deceased kids before nodding curtly and continuing across the busy floor towards a boundary wall that was too far away to clearly see, his raincloud-coloured robe glinting with pinks and mauves as it swung near his ankles.

Michael looked down, as did his companions, at the pamphlets they'd been given. Printed in gold ink on thick cream paper, all four pages of the folded sheets were covered in dense text that was apparently composed of small and wriggly symbols from a foreign alphabet. At three years old and having barely learned to recognise more than a word or two of written English, Michael was convinced that he'd have to get someone to explain it to him, but this turned out not to be the case. Upon closer inspection all the tiny, unfamiliar characters seemed to impart their meaning in ideas and words that he could understand – or at least, concepts he could understand now, in his present state. He'd noticed he was getting cleverer since he'd been dead, as if the soul continued to develop to its proper level even when the mind and body were both gone. He gazed down at the teensy, crawling letters with his improved ghostly eyes and he began to read.

THE WORKS

The Works is founded in the lower world during the year 444 AD, where the First Borough is established. Its material manifestation is originally a marker-stone set at the top end of a footpath leading to the scarlet dyers' well. However, in the Second Borough the four Master Angles do contrive to skilfully unfold the single, rough-hewn granite block unto a mighty fortress for the purpose of their wondrous manufacture. For its signboard and its seal, so all might know that Justice Be Above the Street, this being the chief slogan of the enterprise, it is marked thus:

Its situation is about the central point of the First Borough, though offset a little to the East that it should thus more accurately represent the crossways of those lines described diagonally on the district, so as to connect its corners. These four corners are the termini of the arrangement, channelling its four disparate energies, with each distinguished by its emblem. In this way, the southeast corner is emblazoned with the Cross, being the fiery quarter of the spirit, while the southwest corner bears the image of a Castle as the airy quadrant governing material majesty. The northwest corner is adorned by a crude Phallus though it is a watery and female quarter, for this is the site of penetration and invasion. Finally the northeast corner shows a Death's-head, for this is the earthy part of the design and to it is attributed demise. The symbols are initially scratched on the granite keystone, one inscribed by each of the four Master Angles in accordance with their signal temperaments and humours. With these glyphs shall their domains be known:

These premises are presently engaged in the construction of a Porthimoth, or "Worthy point or portal, properly proportioning the hem or trim of the immortal psyche, with this Art our theme, our path, our permit", commonly described as a four-folded capstone to be set upon the summit of a greater chronologic structure, thus to tie together all the moral lines and rafters of event comprising that immense Timearchitecture. While this work is underway, the Management regrets that builders will not be available to escort visitors on tours of the establishment, respectfully suggesting that this guide be kept about the person at all times as a convenient source of reference.

On the ground floor is the main entrance, opening onto the Attics of the Breath above the present Mayorhold. Two quadrivial-hinged ingress-points or 'crook-doors' placed at either end of the 5th century well-path

also offer access to this lowest storey, where specific parts of the endeavour are assembled and where labours are allotted and coordinated.
Visitors may notice that the floor is made from two-and-seventy great
slabs, each one a hundred paces long or wide and set into a nine-by-eight
arrangement. These large tiles, upon inspection, have a tessellate design
to their adornments, this peculiarity occasioned by the ...

Michael looked up in surprise from the engrossing booklet to discover
that his five ghost-comrades were starting to wander off en masse in the
direction of the nearest wall, which was perhaps a quarter of a mile away
towards the east. Rolling the helpful leaflet up into a tube and thrusting it into
one tartan pocket of his dressing gown he hurried after them as quickly as his
flapping slippers would permit. He'd scared himself when he'd run off and left
them at the foot of Scarletwell Street, and he didn't want to become separated
from them anymore.

That, Michael thought, had been a stupid thing to do. It had just been the
shock of suddenly seeing St. Andrew's Road like that: an unused grass verge
where his terrace used to be. It looked so wrong. Worse, it had seemed to say
that nothing would turn out the way that anybody hoped it would; that all his
mum's and dad's dreams ended up in trees and turf and wire carts on wheels.
He hadn't wanted to accept that, and still didn't. He'd not wanted to be looking at that flat ground, with its flat proof, so he'd run away into a midnight
neighbourhood that he no longer recognised.

While all the other children had been looking at the weeping ghost in
the check suit as he'd wandered towards that awful, solitary house that stood
upon the corner, Michael had been overwhelmed by all the strangeness and
the desolation of his circumstances, unable to cope a moment longer with this
eerie and upsetting afterlife, this dreadful and demolished future. He'd slipped
silently away and ducked into the reassuringly familiar folds of Greyfriars flats,
and though the black iron gate across the narrow entrance gave him pause
for thought – why had the former unofficial children's playground that was
Greyfriars courtyard been barred off like this? It hadn't stopped him sliding
through the bars like kettle-steam, into the hushed and shadowy enclosure.

Greyfriars' inner yard had been almost the same as he'd remembered it
from pram-bound shortcuts in the 1950s, although obviously he'd never seen
how it looked in the middle of the night before. The only noticeable difference, other than the gates, had been a sort of tiredness and untidiness, as if
the place had given up. He'd passed along the pathway at the bottom of the
courtyard's lower level, drifting through another locked gate at the far end
and out into Bath Street. Only then had it occurred to him that he'd got no
idea where he was.

The somehow sheltering incline of red brick houses on the street's far side, including Mrs. Coleman's sweetshop and its sugar-dusty jars, had been taken away. Replacing this accustomed view were ugly flats with rust-railed concrete steps, rectangular black windows staring coldly from prefabricated walls that had at some time in the past been painted white, to best show off the Boroughs grime.

Michael had crept disconsolately up the hill with his equally-stealthy duplicates in Indian file behind him. Only when he'd got as far as Little Cross Street, where the row of homes that used to prop each other up like punch-drunk fighters had also been done away with by the white-walled modern buildings, had he happened on a place he knew in the surprisingly consoling bulk of Bath Street flats

Upon closer inspection, even these had turned out to be not all that they'd once been. Rough and mottled lengths of cheap board had been used to patch the double doors beneath their cinema-like portico where someone had kicked in the glass. He'd crouched beside one of the low brick walls edging the path that ran from the dilapidated doorway, had a little weep and tried to think what he should do. That had been when he'd spotted Bill and Reggie Bowler, ambling up the tarmac slope where Fitzroy Street once was, and shortly after that, they'd spotted him.

If they'd not shouted and come scuttling across the road at him like that, with all their extra eyes and arms and legs, he might have just stayed where he sat and let them catch him. As it was though, he had taken flight and run off through the partly-boarded door into the flats themselves. That had been frightening, all of those funny-looking rooms with horrid people doing things he didn't understand. When he'd burst out onto the open central walkway with the steps it had been an immense relief, despite the strange lights floating everywhere.

This time, when Bill and Reggie seeped out through the drab red brick-work and approached him he had more than had enough, was even pleased to see them. Chastened by his unsuccessful stab at ghostly independence, he'd allowed the older boys to take his hands and lead him past the terrifying spectral hole in upper Bath Street, over to the grounds of those two stupefy-ing towers, where they'd been reunited with John, Marjorie and Phyllis. Even though the Dead Dead Gang's girl boss had told him off for his desertion, Michael was beginning to know Phyllis well enough to understand just how relieved she'd been to find him and to see he was all right. He wondered if she was perhaps developing a secret crush on him, the way that he suspected he was starting to develop one on her. Whether or not this was the case, he didn't want to let her or the gang out of his sight again, and scampered hurriedly behind them now across the busy work-space, trying to catch up.

As he drew level with the knot of urchins, big and friendly John looked round and grinned at him.

"Are you still with us, titch? We thought we'd lost you for a minute there. Here, what about all this, eh? It's a picture, wizn't it?"

The tall lad gestured to the bustle and commotion going on around them, the incessant to and fro of the grave builders in their shimmering grey robes, waving just one slim arm where Michael was still half-expecting there to be a dozen. The interior of the Works was, to be sure, a picture. Over giant flag-stones, with complex and colourful designs that seemed to crawl and flicker in the corners of the vision, moved the solemn builders at their diverse tasks, while high above the multitude, on a huge boss raised from the wall that they were nearing, was the queer design that Michael had seen in the pamphlet: a flat scroll or ribbon that seemed to unroll away towards the right, and over that two triangles joined by a double line. Rough and unpractised, it looked more like something that a three-year-old like him might scribble rather than the work of the mysterious 'Master Angles'. Trotting there alongside John, Michael blinked up at him.

"Wiz that big mark up there an advertising sign?"

John chuckled.

"Well, yes, I suppose it wiz. It means 'Justice Above the Street' which wiz a sort of motto here, much like 'Out of the strong shall come forth sweetness' on the treacle tin. It tells you all about it in this guide the builder gave us just now. Have you read it?"

Michael said he'd read a bit of it before he'd stuffed it in the pocket of his dressing gown for fear of being left behind. John smiled and shook his head.

"Nobody's going to leave you anywhere, not after how frit Phyllis wiz when you ran off. You ought to take another decko at that pamphlet. It'll tell you loads of things, like about all the different devils that they've got trapped in these floor-tiles."

Michael stopped dead in his tracks at that and stared down at the hundred-yard-long slab they were then passing over. When you paused to properly examine its involved design it really was an eyeful. The elaborate pattern was ingeniously composed of two repeated shapes that had been artfully contrived to interlock, one of the forms arranged to fit into the empty gaps between the carefully-spaced outlines of the other. Both of the two different figures making up this wallpaper-effect were quite unpleasant, with one having the appearance of a wolf that had a slimy snake-tail where its own should be while gouts of crimson flame belched from between its snarling jaws. The second shape was that of a disturbingly fat raven, its beak open to display the fangs of a big hunting dog.

The means by which the contours of the two dissimilar monstrosities fitted together was a marvel of delineation, aided by the flames erupting from the wolf-snake's maw to wrap its lupine body in an aura of red fire, the scalloped edge of these fitting exactly with the black serrations in the wings of the dog-raven that was set to face the other way. Hypnotically, the ragged lines where the two different pictures intersected seemed to be perpetually moving, as if either the flame-halos around the wolf-snakes licked and leaped or else the dog-ravens were ruffling their feathers angrily. Retrieving the guide-pamphlet from his pocket, Michael resumed reading at the point where he'd left off in hope of learning what this convoluted parquet flooring was in aid of.

> Visitors may notice that the floor is made from two-and-seventy great slabs, each one a hundred paces long and wide, and set into a nine-by-eight arrangement. These large tiles, upon inspection, have a tessellate design to their adornments, this peculiarity occasioned by the comprehensive catalogue of former employees that are both flattened and compacted in their manufacture.
>
> These ex-builders, commonly called devils, are compressed into a two-dimensional plane of existence by the Master Angles and their armies during the foundation of the mortal and material realm. Once subjugated, these are governed by a golden torus worn upon one finger of the Master Angle Mikael as a controlling ring of holy dominance. In the symbolic strata overlooking the substantial world, the Master Angle Mikael then gives this token to King Solomon that he might likewise triumph over the same demons, setting them to build his temple at Jerusalem. This structure is reprised in the First Borough as the round church of the Holy Sepulchre, just as the Master Angle Mikael himself, conflated with Saint Michael of renown, presides over the earthly township from his vantage at the great Gilhalda of Saint Giles.
>
> The full six dozen fiends incarcerated in the tiles, commencing from the southeast corner are in their depictions and their names as follows:
>
> The first Spirit is a King that rideth in the East called BAEL. He makes men to go invisible. He ruleth over six-and-sixty Legions of inferior spirits. He appeareth in divers shapes, sometimes like a cat, sometimes a dog and sometimes like a man, or sometimes in all of these forms at the one time ...

There then followed a long list of these appalling creatures and their attributes, most of which sounded horrible. Realising that the southeast corner of the cavernous enclosure was the one ahead of them and to their left, Michael could count along the massive flagstones to the one that him and the Dead Dead Gang were now standing on, which was the seventh from the end.

Moving his finger down the column of demonic dukes and princes until he'd reached the appropriate spot, he then began to read.

The Seventh Spirit is called AMON. He is a Marquis, great in power and most strong. He appeareth like a wolf that hath a serpent's tail, vomiting out of his mouth flames of fire, yet sometimes he appeareth like a Raven that has dog's teeth in his head. He telleth all things past and present and to come; procureth love; and reconcileth all controversies twixt friends & foes. He governeth full forty Legions of inferior spirits.

That seemed to be it for dog-toothed, serpent-tailed wolf-raven Amon, as the mostly red and black and grey moving design beneath Michael's plaid slippers was apparently addressed. Michael gazed down at the depicted creatures' two visible eyes: one that of the in-profile raven and the other that belonging to the similarly side-on wolf. Now that he knew more of how timeless Mansoul functioned, the ability to "telleth all things past and present and to come" quite frankly didn't seem much of a trick, though he supposed a talent for acquiring love might be seen as impressive if he were a little older. Mind you, since he felt a great deal older as it was, he thought it sounded quite good even at the moment. Rolling up the leaflet once again and putting it back in his pocket, Michael frowned enquiringly at John.

"What wiz it makes the pictures move?"

John offered him a sympathetic look.

"These what we're walking on ain't pictures, titch. These are the gentlemen themselves. You should be grateful they can only move the little that they can."

Michael looked back down at the slab that they were standing on, with its writhing embellishments. He gave a little squawk and then performed a complicated dance in which he seemed to be attempting to lift both his slipper-clad feet from the tile at once, as if afraid of infernal contamination. In the end he stood on tiptoe, which was evidently the best compromise that he could manage. John was trying not to laugh, capping the sound off in a muffled detonation of amusement somewhere up his nose.

"Don't worry, they can't hurt you. When they're flat like this they're no more dangerous than Keyhole Kate or someone else out of a comic. Anyway, we're nearly at the floor's edge as it wiz. We'll soon be on the stairs, where there's no devils."

Just as John had said, the vast wall rose immediately ahead of them and running up across it in diagonals there was a wooden staircase, its great zigzag length connecting four strata of balcony, the highest almost level with the poorly-drawn seal of the Works on its enormous plaque. The steps themselves were broad and sturdy and looked relatively normal in their ratio of tread to riser, unlike those that Michael had experienced a moment back while clambering up the Jacob Flight out of the ghost-seam. Anxious to be off this squirming carpeting of interlocking horrors, Michael didn't risk any more dawdling until he and the gang had safely reached the possessed factory floor's near side.

Seen from close up the stairs were several yards in width, bounded on one side by the sheer and soaring wall and on the other by a masterfully-wrought and polished banister of what was more than likely oak. Each step was cut from some unknown variety of marble, a profound and rich dark blue with mica twinkles seemingly suspended inside the translucent stone at differing depths, rather than simply glinting uniformly from its surface. Every one was like a solid block hewn from the night sky, and amongst the sparking flakes of mica here and there, Michael discovered, there were curdled nebulae and comet smears. It was a fire escape made out of universe, though he supposed they all were really, when you stopped to think.

The Dead Dead Gang began to climb the stairway from the dove-like murmur of the workplace, Phyllis Painter in the lead and striding up ahead of everybody else. As he ascended, somewhere near the group's rear with big John, Michael looked down across the oaken balustrade towards the tiled floor dwindling beneath them. From this raised perspective he could almost see a unifying pattern to the movement of the builders as they hurried back and forth on their inscrutable trajectories, as if each worker were an iron filing caught up in the loops and whorls that radiated unseen from a magnet.

He could also now see clearly, thanks to his ghost-vision, all six dozen of the giant demon-haunted flagstones that comprised the floor, set out like an array of nightmare playing cards. He thought he could remember the death-monger, Mrs. Gibbs, saying that out of all the devils that there were, the one who had abducted Michael, sneaky Sam O'Day, was number thirty-two. If that was right then his specific slab should be against the left-side wall, four rows away. He stood there gazing out over the wooden banister, moving his lips and jabbing at the air with one pink index finger as he counted to make sure. The stone in question, once he'd found it, was quite unmistakeable.

For one thing, it was one of only three or four flagstones in the arrangement that all of the builders seemed to manage to avoid as they traversed their busy place of labour. For another, unlike his confederate Amon, Sam O'Day was only shown in one form on the tile, this being the three-headed thing astride a dragon that had raged above them in the Attics of the Breath, what seemed a day or so ago. This complicated semblance was repeated something like a hundred times across the area of the slab, its contours engineered precisely so that all of the identically irregular shapes fitted perfectly together with an intricacy that was genuinely infernal. Empty spaces in between the creature's many heads, as an example, were placed to accommodate the four legs of the dragon-steed belonging to the duplicate immediately above them in the pattern, while the tapering tail of each such mount was tailored to fit neatly in the open jaws of an identical heraldic dragon waddling behind it. Taking out his guide and scanning down the lengthy roll of hellish eminences until he'd reached number thirty-two, he tried to find out more about the fiend who had both literally and figuratively taken Michael for a ride.

The two and thirtieth Spirit is called Asmoday. He is a great King, strong and powerful. He cometh with three heads, whereof the first is like a bull, the second is like to a man and the third like unto a ram. He hath a serpent's tail and belches noxious gas. His foot is webbed like to a goose. He sitteth upon an infernal dragon, carrying a Lance and Standard in his hand, whereon his ensign is displayed as so:

He giveth of the ring of Virtues, and teacheth the arts of Arithmetic, Geometry, Astronomy and handicraft. He giveth of full and true answers to all questions and can maketh men invisible. He showeth places where is treasure hidden and he governeth a full six dozen Legions of inferior spirits. If requested he may lift the conjuror into a higher place where they may looketh down upon their neighbours' homes and see their fellows at their business as though it were that the roof had been removed.

Of all the eminences here bound and contained, most special caution is advised in all transactions with this Spirit. Of the devils captured by King Solomon on the symbolic plane, the fiercest and most difficult to subjugate is Asmoday. Indeed, in the rabbinical tradition it is said that Asmoday alone is proof against the magic ring of Mikael that he hath gifted to King Solomon. In their encounter, it is Asmoday who triumphs, hurling the defeated King so far into the sky that when he is returned to Earth he has forgotten quite that he is Solomon. Unchallenged, Asmoday assumes the form of Solomon and goeth on in this impersonation to complete the building of Solomon's temple at Jerusalem and next take many wives, and to raise other, lesser temples to the foreign gods that these wives worship.

He is husband to the monster Lilith, Queen of Night and Mother of Abominations. While besotted with a princess in the land of Persia, Asmoday does slay as many of her rival suitors as there are days in the week, for which crimes is he driven out by exorcism into antique Egypt, spitefully removing all his mathematic insights from one kingdom to the other in attrition.

Asmoday, in the arrangement of ten rings or tori by which Hell and Heaven are composed, is the demonic ruler of the Fifth plane and is thus associated principally with Wrath. The flower of this particular domain is the five-petal rose, this being emblem to the mortal township, making it conducive to the fiend. Similarly, the reproduction of Solomon's Temple raised in the First Borough is believed to strengthen the affinity felt by this Spirit for the earthly district. He is the most terrible of all the devils here confined, and in his wrath he is implacable. Asmoday's colours, by which he is known, are red and green, which signify both his severity and the emotive nature of ...

Michael glanced up from his guide-booklet, colour draining from his face until he looked almost exactly as he had done in the black and white expanses of the ghost-seam. Sizzling Sam O'Day, it seemed, was not just any common devil. He had beaten up King Solomon despite the King's almighty magic ring which he'd been given by a Master Angle. He was "the most terrible of all the devils". In his wrath he was "implacable", which Michael thought meant something like "will get you in the end". The small boy squinted hard at the end slab in the fourth row until he realised that the ram's eyes, bull's eyes, dragon's eyes and man's eyes in each picture, multiplied a hundred times across the writhing surface of the stone, were all staring directly at him. It was not a loving look.

Not without difficulty, Michael tore his gaze from the entrancing scintillations of the thirty-second Spirit and fell in with Phyllis and the others as they struggled up the constellated stairs to the first landing where, if he had understood their plan correctly, they intended to serve as spectators in a dreadful and unprecedented fight between the Master Builders. As Michael himself was seemingly the cause of this affray he wondered if attending it in person was the safest thing to do, the doubts he'd had on Scarletwell Street's corner about how well Phyllis and the gang were looking after him resurfacing, if only for a moment. The five Dead Dead children were the only real friends that he'd got round here. Sticking the leaflet back into his pocket, Michael scurried upstairs after them.

A pair of builders passing down the wide and sweeping staircase in the opposite direction seemed to pay particular attention to the gang of ghost-kids, and specifically to Michael Warren. One inclined his head towards the child, at which the other nodded sagely. Both of them then smiled at Michael before walking on down the star-spattered steps, in their long trailing gowns of grey with peacock colours shimmering at the hem. Michael was faintly startled, having not seen this expression on the faces of the other builders labouring below. While they'd seemed fond or even proud of him, which made him feel warm and important, just the simple fact that they'd appeared to know him was a bit unnerving and raised fresh concerns regarding the advisability of turning up to watch the angle-fight.

By now the six of them had reached the first of the three landings jutting out from the east wall. A heavy swing door with a stained-glass panel and brass push-plate, like the ones that he had seen in pubs, led from the stellar marble of the platform out onto the floorboards of a long and relatively crowded balcony with a black railing of pitch-treated wood. It looked a lot like the raised walkway up above the Attics of the Breath where the toddler had met with shifty Sam O'Day, and as big John held the door open for them while they filed out into crystal-perfect daylight, Michael briefly thought that it might be the same place but then realised swiftly that it wasn't.

The most obvious and immediate difference was the sheer amount of people milling back and forth along the endless gallery, or leaning on its rail and chattering excitedly like patrons in the gods, the upper circle at a theatre. By Michael's flailing estimate, along the reach of the veranda for as far as he could see, there must have been perhaps two or three hundred ghosts. He wondered if there was a special word like "pride" or "flock" or "herd" that you should employ when discussing such enormous quantities of phantoms, and asked his five ghost-pals if they'd heard of one. Phyllis insisted with an air of great authority that the appropriate term was "a persistence", while Bill ventured "an embarrassment" as his alternative. Then John ended the speculation by suggesting that the best expression for a spectral multitude would be "a Naseby", which he then had to explain to Michael, although everybody else was nodding gravely in agreement.

"Naseby wiz the village just outside Northampton where they had the final battle of the English Civil War. King Charles wiz captured and the field ran red, with bodies piled up in its ditches. Never visit Naseby while you're in the ghost-seam, nipper. There's dead cavaliers and Roundheads standing thick as rows of corn, chaps with great pike-holes through their jackets, all blood-black and bone-white and brain-grey, dragging maimed photo-trails behind 'em through the mud. You've never seen so many angry dead men. No, 'a Naseby of ghosts': that's the only way to put it when you've got a crowd like this one here."

The ghosts surrounding the Dead Dead Gang on the balcony were certainly diverse, containing representatives from most of the twenty or thirty centuries that there'd been people living in the present town's vicinity. As he and his companions passed along the boardwalk, dodging in and out amongst the swarm of wraiths, Michael saw women clad in mammoth fur and children naked save for their deep blue tattoos. Homesick Danes with long golden plaits rubbed shoulders with jocular infantrymen who'd been casualties of World War One. A haughty-looking man with no chin and a black shirt leaned against the balustrade smoking a coloured cocktail cigarette, glumly discussing Jews with what appeared to be an equally disgruntled lower-ranking Roman soldier. There were even one or two of the ghost royalists and Roundheads John had mentioned, which suggested that they hadn't all remained down in the ghost-seam out at Naseby, wallowing in the black mud they'd died in. Strangely, one man in a plumed hat who was the most obvious cavalier in the assembly stood there at the rail in amiable conversation with a hulking, grey-garbed man who had a cropped head and, even with no distinctive peaked iron helmet to confirm the fact, looked very much like someone who'd fought on the other side back in the 1600s. Puzzled, Michael pointed out the pair to John, who made a sound of mingled admiration and surprise on recognising at least one of them.

"Blimey! Well, I don't know who the long-haired fellow wiz, but I expect you're right and he fought for King Charley. Now, the big bloke with the shaved bonce, he's a different matter. That's Thompson the Leveller and, yes, he wiz on Cromwell's side at first, but it wiz Cromwell in the end who laid him low, as surely as he did that cavalier what Thompson's talking to. Old Cromwell, when he needed everybody he could get for taking on the King, he promised the idealists and the revolutionaries like the Levellers that if they helped him they could make England the place they'd dreamed about, where everyone wiz equal. Once the Civil War wiz won, of course, it wiz a different story. Cromwell had the Levellers done away with, so they wouldn't cause him any trouble when he backed down on the promises he'd made 'em. Thompson – you can yourself see what a fierce-looking sod he wiz – he made his last stand in Northampton, and it looks as though he's hung around here ever since. No, him and the old laughing cavalier there, they've both got a lot in common, I expect. You very seldom see him as high up as this, old Thompson. It looks like this fight between the builders has pulled in a crowd from up and down the linger of the Second Borough."

It was true. As the ghost-children passed on down the length of the veranda, the thick crowd parting before them when they caught the scent of Phyllis Painter's rancid necklace was like a peculiar historical parade or pageant, only one where no one looked as if they knew they were in fancy dress. Of course, most of them weren't. A large majority of the good-natured jostling mob were ordinary Boroughs residents of the nineteenth and twentieth centuries, their clothing hardly different to the togs that Michael and the others had got on. The sightseers who'd turned up from other eras weren't that difficult to spot, and most of them were easy to identify: a sack-clad Saxon drover with a modest herd of half-a-dozen ghost-sheep bleating all around him as they clattered down the timeless boards; innumerable monks of different dates and different orders, all with very little to debate except how wrong they'd got the afterlife; anxious and flinching Norman ladies; angry-looking Ancient Briton prostitutes who'd been sequestered to a Roman legion.

There were also other figures that were hard to put a name or time to. Something very tall was coming down the balcony towards them from the opposite direction, looming up a good two or three feet above the heads and shoulders of the milling horde around it. It looked like a kind of wigwam made of rushes, with a hollow wooden tube protruding from its upper reaches that looked something like a beak and gave the whole thing the appearance of a huge green wading bird. As they passed it, Michael noticed that it walked on stilts that poked out past the interwoven reeds around the hem of its strange gown. He'd got no idea what it was, nor what unheard-of period it had originated from. He watched it stalk away down the long landing, melting into the delirious masses that were gathered there, and was about to ask John for an explanation when his eye was caught by something that, to Michael, appeared every bit as curious.

It was a cowboy – a real cowboy in dust-coloured clothes and a soft hat that had been battered shapeless, old boots with a second sole of dry blonde mud and at least seven guns of different types and sizes, shoved in everywhere they'd fit. Two were in splitting leather holsters hung from a cracked belt with three more jammed into the fellow's waistband. One was stuffed down one side of a boot, another jutting from a trouser pocket. All of them looked ancient and as dangerous accidentally as by intent. The man stood leaning on the rail, gazing across it with a prairie stare, and his smooth, flawless skin was blacker than the pitch with which the balustrade was painted. Slouching there at rest he had the lithe lines of a jaguar, the carved and stylised head of an Egyptian idol in obsidian. He was quite simply the most beautiful and perfect human being – man or woman – that the child had ever seen. The idea of a cowboy being black, though, seemed improbable, as did his presence here amongst the teeming, phantom flow of former Boroughs residents. This time, John noticed Michael gawking and was able to provide assistance without being asked.

"That one, the black chap there, he's not a ghost. He's someone's dream. Somebody from the Boroughs dreamed about this bloke enough for him to have accumulated a fair bit of presence up here."

Bill, who had been listening in on what John said to Michael as the dead gang walked along, put in his own two penn'orth.

"Yeah. I saw the Beatles a few minutes back, dressed in all that 'I am the Walrus' kit they wore. Somebody must have dreamed them 'ere as well."

There then ensued an unproductive several moments in which Bill attempted to explain all about beetles dressed as walruses before he realised he was talking about things that hadn't happened during John's or Michael's lifetimes. This itself seemed to provoke fresh questions from the dressing gown-clad toddler.

"So how wiz there dreams up here that people haven't had yet? Do dreams just queue up round here waiting to be dreamt?"

John seemed quite taken with the thought, but shook his head.

"It's not like that, or I don't think it wiz, at any rate. It's more to do with how time works a different way when we're Upstairs. I mean, the future here, it's only a few miles down that way."

Here he gestured to the west, somewhere behind the ghost-gang as they made their way along the endless boardwalk, before he continued.

"Dreams can walk here from the times to come as easily as they can from the past. The same thing's true with all the ghosts. You must have noticed some of the daft clothes these silly beggars have got on, the puffy coats and things like that girl there."

John nodded to the phantom form of a young woman they were just then passing, who had trousers on that were either too small for her or else were falling down so you could see her bum-crack, which had some kind of elasticated string caught up it. Now that Michael looked around he noticed a few more outlandishly-garbed individuals who, following John's explanation, now looked likely to be spirits from the future of the Boroughs, people who by 1959 had certainly not died yet and in many cases had still to be born. Michael was looking out for other ladies with their bums half showing since these were a fascinating novelty he hadn't seen before, when the whole group of children suddenly stopped dead. Putting aside his search for half-mast trousers, Michael himself shuffled to a halt, wondering what was up.

"Oh, Christ," said Phyllis Painter. "Everybody get over one side, against the rail."

The other ghost-kids did as they were told immediately, to find that almost all the other phantoms on the balcony were trying to accomplish the exact same thing, crowding against the railing in a muttering and fluorescent crush like startled parrots in an aviary. Attempting to see past the human billows and learn what was prompting this unusual activity, Michael could hear John saying, "What the bloody hell wiz that?" and Reggie Bowler gasping. Little tubby Marjorie said, "Oh my Lord. That poor man," to which Bill replied, "Poor man my arse. That cunt's done it 'imself." For once, Bill's older sister didn't reprimand him for his swearing. Phyllis just gravely intoned, "That's right. That's right, 'e has. 'E's ..."

The remainder of whatever she'd been going to impart was drowned beneath a growing thunder-roll which Michael realised had been building up for some few moments, even though he hadn't really been aware that he was hearing it. He craned his ghostly neck, trying to see.

Proceeding slowly down the balcony towards them, taking small and halting steps like a pall-bearer, came a walking flower of noise and fire. It seemed to be a man from the waist down, and yet its upper half was a great ball of light in which small specks of darkness were suspended, motionless. The rumbling noise seemed to be wrapped around the figure in some way, circling round the blinding flare that was his body and increasing to a deafening roar as he approached. When he drew level with the frightened children, flattened up against the balustrade to let him pass along with all the other ghosts, Michael could make out more of his appearance, squinting through the glare surrounding the appalling spectacle.

It was a foreign person, Michael wasn't sure what sort, dressed in a quilted jacket and a little round white pillbox hat or skullcap of some kind. His youngish face was turned towards the sky, his bearded chin tipped back, a smile held wilfully upon his lips despite the fat teardrop evaporating on one floodlit cheek, and eyes filled with a look that might have been salvation but could just as well have been excruciating shock or agony. The padded jacket seemed to have been captured in the moment it was torn to shreds, dark ribbons of material twisting upwards into ragged and fantastic shapes as if attempting to escape the dazzling whiteness flooding from beneath it, where its owner's breast had evidently opened in a spray of phosphorous. Michael could see now that the dark blots hanging there unmoving in the brilliance were some several dozen screws and nails, an asteroid belt of dark specks eternally caught in their rush away from the exploding heart of light and heat behind them. Deafening noise was crawling all around the figure now, unchanging in its pitch as though it was the sound of one brief, devastating instant that had been protracted infinitely, slowed down from the tumult of a second to the drumroll of a thousand burning years. The hybrid creature, half man, half St. Elmo's Fire, continued forward in small painful steps along the landing, hands raised slightly from his sides with palms turned outwards, features still contorted into that ambiguous, uncertain smile. A walking cataclysm it moved past the gaping children, heading on down the veranda with its ball of frozen flash and clamour, with its shrapnel halo of hot bolts and rivets. In its wake, the trans-fixed phantom crowd backed up against the wooden rail began once more to move and mutter, wandering off to occupy the rest of the broad walkway that they'd cleared to let the blazing thing go by.

Michael stared up at John.

"What wiz it?"

John's dark eyes, matinee-idol smudges in repose, were now as big and as bewildered as the toddler's own. Speechless, the older boy just shook his head. For all of John's experience, he'd clearly no more understanding of the spectacle that they'd just witnessed than Michael himself had. Marjorie and Reggie were likewise uncomprehending, mute and quietly horrified, and it was left for Bill and Phyllis to shed light upon the startling incident. The girl leader of the Dead Dead Gang seemed shaken as she tried to take charge of the situation.

"'E wiz what they call a terrorist. Suicide bomber, weren't it, Bill? I never liked to read abayt 'em in the papers while I wiz alive. Gi' me the willies, all that business did. Bill 'ere knows more abayt all that than I do."

Bill, as it turned out, had read the papers and knew quite a bit about the almost mystical incendiary vision that had just passed close enough for them to feel its heat, though even the resourceful red-haired urchin seemed uncer-tain and perplexed.

"Phyll's right. Suicide bombers started cropping up in England around nothing-five, all Moslems with a strop on because us and the Americans had fucked Iraq up past all recognition, and 'cause we wiz crackin' down on rag 'eads generally. It wiz a bit like with the IRA and that lot: you could see they'd got a fair point to start off with, then they went and fucked it up by blowing kids to bits and actin' like a load o' twats. Suicide bombers, what they'd do, they'd 'ave this thing they called a martyr vest, packed full of some home-made explosive, fertiliser or chapatti flour, something like that. They'd get on buses or on tube trains and just blow themselves up, tryin' to take as many people with them as they could."

John looked aghast.

"What, just blowing up civilians, like? The dirty sods. The dirty, evil buggers."

Bill just shrugged, though not unsympathetically.

"It's just what 'appens, ennit? I don't s'pose you were around to see what our lot did to Dresden, or the Yanks did to the Japs. These days, John, me old mucker, it's not like it wiz in your day. There's no country what can stick its 'and up an' say 'No, not us, mate. We're not like that.' Those times are long gone, all that God, King and Country bollocks. We know better now.

"As for old matey-boy who just went sizzlin' past, I reckon as 'e looked the way 'e did for the same reason Phyllis still 'as all 'er fuckin' stinkin' rabbits." Bill ducked nimbly as he dodged a swipe from his big sister before he went on.

"I'm only sayin' that it must be 'ow it wiz for all of us: we look the way we best remember ourselves being when we wiz alive. For bomb-boy what we just saw, that must be the way that he prefers to see 'imself, right at that moment when he pulled the string or whatever they do and took out 'alf o' Stringfeller's or Tiger Tiger. From 'is eyes and from the way that 'e wiz walkin', it looked like he'd shat 'imself, but I suppose it's all part o' the martyrdom, ay?

"What I can't get me 'ead round wiz what 'e wiz doin' up 'ere in Mansoul. At a rough guess, I'd say it must be because 'e grew up around the Boroughs, or because 'e died 'ere. Grew up, or else blew up. But I don't remember anybody like that from my lifetime. 'E must be from further up the line than me an' Phyll."

Everyone thought about that for a while, the idea that the Boroughs would at some point in its future either suffer the attentions of a suicidal bomber, or produce one.

Michael turned towards the pitch-stained balustrade that he and the Dead Dead Gang had not moved from since the passing of the smiling, shuffling explosion. It appeared that the upsetting visitation had produced at least one helpful side effect, in that the six ghost-children now had their own strip of rail, over or through which they could look at the impending fight between the builders without having lots of grown-up ghosts in front of them. He also realised that the reason why the older phantoms hadn't crowded straight back in and jostled the wraith-kids out of the way was more than likely Phyllis Painter's rabbit scarf, which obviously had its uses.

He supposed it was a bit like the one time his mum and dad had taken him and Alma up to see the Bicycle Parade in Sheep Street at the top of Bull-Head Lane. Michael had travelled up there in his pram, but had been unstrapped on arrival to stand by his mum, Doreen, holding her hand. Unfortunately, he'd been so excited that he'd been sick over two whole paving stones where they were standing. This had ensured that he and his family were given lots of room in which they could enjoy the simultaneously thrilling and disturbing cavalcade of marching bands, princesses, clowns on bicycles and horrors with great peeling heads of papier-mâché, Michael's vomit having much the same effect that Phyllis's putrescent stole was having now.

Not being tall enough to see over the rail, he looked between the wooden bars like a surprisingly young jailbird, out across the mesmerising view available from this first-storey balcony that jutted from the Works.

His first impression was that he was looking down upon the Mayorhold, or on something that the Mayorhold might have been a Matchbox toy-scale reproduction of, almost as if the modest mortal square were a page out of a closed pop-up book that had been opened and unfolded here upon this higher plane. Seen from this elevated angle it was very much like being in some giant amphitheatre, peering down into a well that was a mile or so across and seemingly descended through some several layers of reality. The different worlds in slowly undulating bands stacked one upon the other, like trick drinks he'd seen on telly, in a tall glass with the different booze in different-coloured stripes.

The highest level was perhaps on one of the two floors above him, with their balconies protruding from the front wall of the Works directly overhead, or possibly the vast expanse of Mansoul sky that dominated the enclosure, where the funny geometric clouds unfolded themselves in progressively more complicated shapes, pale lines against a singing and celestial blue. However you divided it, the Second Borough was on top of the arrangement, with the buildings ringing this expanded Mayorhold being of the same dreamy immensity that seemed to be a feature of the architecture here Upstairs.

Michael allowed his gaze to slide down the steep lines of the huge structures opposite him, on the far side of the former town square. These appeared to be inflated and flamboyant versions of the humble enterprises that, down in the living world, looked out upon the Mayorhold. Straight across from him there was a sort of layered pyramid composed from two varieties of marble, one white and the other green, arranged in alternating giant blocks. Tall windows interrupted the façade, and round the curve of a high decorative arch that crowned the building, picked out in mosaic letters, was the legend 'Branch 19'. He realised he was looking at a higher version of the Co-op, the same place they'd glimpsed a little while ago when they were in the faded duplicate of 1959 that was the ghost-seam. Having recognised this landmark, he was able to deduce that the austere grey tower just south of the stretched-out Co-op, which he'd taken for a sober-looking church or temple of some kind, was actually a Mansoul-style exaggeration of the public toilets at the foot of Silver Street.

As he continued to inspect the ever-lower reaches of the premises on the Mayorhold's far side, he reached the second trembling and vaporous strata of the piled realities. Here, following a pitch-railed wooden walkway running round the bottom of the higher edifices, the great swooping contours of the Mansoul-made constructions were continued down into the hue-forsaken smoulder of the ghost-seam, their lines narrowing in steep perspective for the necessary fit with the much smaller, more realistically-scaled half-world. As seen from the vantage of Upstairs, this foggy black and white realm of self-denigrating wraiths appeared to be translucent, like a sheet of colourless grey jelly of the type found in pork pies. Burrowing through this viscous medium hundreds of feet below, with streams of tiny after-pictures dissipating in their wakes, were several of the area's rough sleepers, although none that Michael recognised.

He found that if he focussed with his ghost-eyes, he could see down through the level where the sorry apparitions went about their business, and see down into the plateau underneath. This was a plane of writhing, interwoven crystal growths in which moved variously coloured lights, and he assumed that this must be the mortal Mayorhold as seen from the Second Borough, just as he'd looked down upon the jewellery snaking through his human living room when he'd first surfaced in the Attics of the Breath. The tangled intestinal lengths of hematite and opal were, he knew, the ordinary living people of the district, viewed as though they were extended through time into gorgeous and unmoving coral millipedes. These knotted into an elaborate carpeting of vivid gem-strands and apparently provided a ground floor upon which the superior tiers were standing. Michael stared entranced between the pitch-stained bars, down through the onion layers of the world.

As with the normal earthly Mayorhold, its exploded Mansoul counterpart was situated where eight mighty avenues converged, these being gloriously unrestricted complements to Broad Street, Bath Street, Bearward Street, St. Andrew's Street, Horsemarket, Scarletwell Street, Bull-Head Lane and Silver Street. These thoroughfares led off from the enclosure like the plastic legs plugged into the main body for a game of beetle-drive, eight spindly tributaries running to a massive central reservoir. The soaring super-buildings circling this huge expanse were like great cliff-faces with windows and verandas, and pressed up against each pane or perched on every ledge and balcony there were the countless threadbare spectres of the Boroughs, in centurions' cloaks or fingerless wool mittens, here to watch the Master Builders come to blows. The rustle of a thousand ghostly conversations whispered round the auditorium like ebb-tide hissing over shingle. Michael thought it was a bit like being at the pictures in the bit before the lights dim almost imperceptibly and everyone goes quiet.

The children lounged against the balustrade, waiting for the main feature to commence. Reggie and John were tall enough to lean upon the rail itself, chins in their hands, while all the others had to be content to crouch with Michael, peering through the upright bars like four afterlife monkeys. Bill was holding forth about the human firework that they'd just been witness to, John having asked him why these people were prepared to kill themselves for their beliefs.

"It's the beliefs what are the trouble. Far as I can make out, all these nutters reckon that they're gunna be blown up into the sky and land in paradise, where there'll be all these fourteen-year-old virgins to attend their every whim. Fuckin' good luck, mate, that's all I can say. I mean, it's a bit fuckin' weird, 'avin' ideas like that to start with, where you blow up a few dozen blameless individuals and that gets you past the bouncers in nonce 'eaven. That bloke we just saw must wonder where the fuck 'e wiz. Not only that, but where the fuck's 'e gunna find a fourteen-year-old virgin in the Boroughs?"

Bill went on to talk about the fighting in a country called Iraq, which John had never heard of, at which Bill explained that it shared borders with Iran, which John had never heard of either.

"Look, it's not that far away from Israel ..."

"Israel?"

They appeared to be discussing two completely different planets, about neither of which Michael Warren had the faintest clue. He gazed distractedly between the blackened bars and puzzled over other matters, such as how it was that Phyllis Painter could remember so far back into the 1920s and around then, before Michael had been born, and yet appeared to have survived to a much later date than any of her fellow Dead Dead Gangsters, Bill excepted. Michael was deliberating on this thorny issue when he noticed that the background downpour of excited Boroughs' voices had thinned to a drizzle and then stopped. Only an anxious-sounding whisper came from Reggie Bowler, barely puncturing the newly-imposed silence.

" 'Ere they come."

All of the faces crowding on the balconies and at the windows were now turning to peer in the same direction, to the southern end of this projected Mayorhold, where the wide unfolded canyon that was the Mansoul equivalent of Horsemarket surged up the hill from Horseshoe Street and Marefair. Shifting round and angling his head to get a better view out through the railings, Michael's enhanced ghost-sight made it possible for him to take a look at what was happening down at the foot of Horsemarket's steep gradient.

A dust of light was being kicked up to obscure the south end of Mansoul: a desert hurricane with sparks instead of sand that hung a borealis curtain over Gold Street. At the centre of this luminous and roiling cumulus were two dots of white brilliance, so intense that they left coloured shapes of splattered Plasticene inside your eyelids if you stared at them, like when you accidentally looked at a light-bulb filament, or at the sun. The dots, Michael could see by squinting through his lashes, were two men in gowns of blinding white, both carrying slender staffs of some description as they walked with an impatient, angry gait uphill towards the Mayorhold.

A small voice piped up which turned out to be Marjorie's, who never said a lot and thus took Michael a few instants to identify.

"I never knew they did that. Look, they're getting bigger as they come towards us!"

At first, Michael thought that poor Drowned Marjorie must have had time for very little education before jumping in the Nene to save her dog at Paddy's Meadow. Even he knew everything got bigger as it came towards you. Then he took a closer look and understood what Marjorie had meant.

The figures stalking up Horsemarket weren't just seeming to get bigger as they neared the erstwhile town square. They were genuinely getting bigger. What had started at the bottom of the hill as men of roughly normal height, by halfway-up had been transformed to two colossi, twenty feet or more in stature and continuing to grow as they came closer. By the time they strode out into the immense arena of the Mayorhold, they were each at least as large as the twelve-storey NEWLIFE flats that Michael had been so impressed by when he and the Dead Dead Gang had made their eerie detour through the ghost-seam into nothing-five or nothing-six. In Michael's judgement, standing on the balcony with all the other gawping ghosts, he was approximately level with the towering builders' abdomens and had to crane his neck back and look up to see their sphinx-sized faces.

One of them was the same Master Builder that he'd seen talking to shuffling Sam O'Day above the Attics of the Breath, the one with white hair, which, on this scaled-up representation looked quite like the whiteness of a mountain peak above the snowline. The wide ocean-liner planes of the unearthly sculpted face rose up away from Michael, who found himself fascinated by the rippling play of the reflected light trapped in the shadows of the chin's vast underside. The white-haired builder paced around the spacious confines of the unpacked Mayorhold with his blue-tipped rod gripped in one monstrous marble fist, big as a bungalow. His naked feet, a dizzying distance down beneath the children's first floor balcony, appeared to walk upon the writhing coral carpet that was what the mortal world looked like seen from Upstairs. The angle waded through the ghost-seam, with its dirty grey tideline seeming to lap about his redwood thighs, and reared up to the floating mathematics of the sapphire firmament above, spanning three realms of being as he circled the enormous hushed enclosure, fuse-fire crawling in his pale, mill-wheel-sized eyes.

The other builder was a different matter. Not that he was any the less awesome or imposing, simply that he had a very different atmosphere attaching to his monumental semblance. The eye-watering glare of his apparel seemed to only reinforce the air of dark there was about him, from his close-cropped hair – jet black where his opponents was both long and fair – to his green eyes set deep within their sooty sockets. High above the balcony he turned the shadowy cathedral mass that was his head and curled lips long as barges into a blood-curdling snarl of fury and resentment, baring teeth like city gates of polished ivory, glowering poisonously at the other white leviathan, shifting his grip upon the slim and street-length wooden wand he held in hands that could have cupped a village. Stamping round the yawning stage that was an utter realisation of the Mayorhold, every footfall sending shudders through the nearby Mansoul residences that the ragged ghosts assembled on their balconies could feel, two of the four great pivots of the cosmos spiralled fatefully towards each other, as unhurried and inevitable as colliding glaciers.

The tension in the stadium-like corral was like tiptoeing over creaking glass: a dreadful apprehensive hush as several hundred numinous spectators on the balconies held breath that they no longer truly had. Even a deathly silence, Michael noticed, had an echo in the outlandish acoustics of the Second Borough, where even a purely nervous pressure was enough to make your ears pop. Toes curled up and ghost-teeth grinding anxiously, the toddler was just wondering if fainting might be a way out of this unbearably fraught situation when the dam broke, and all of the witnesses like Michael who'd been hoping only moments earlier that it would do just that found themselves desperately wishing that it hadn't.

The dark Master Builder suddenly broke from his wary circling to rush across the three-tiered battleground, the twisting crystals of the mortal bedrock shivering beneath his tread and the grey blanket of the ghost-seam warping and distorting like a murky fluid around the gargantuan form splashing through it. Michael could see colourless ghost-busses bending in the middle and the hapless spectres still down in the half-world washed against the phantom Mayorhold's walls in bath-scum ripples by the churning passage of the angry craftsman. From a throat deep as a railway tunnel came a vengeful howl that sounded like wind keening through dead cities. Furnace doors swung open in the crew-cut giant's eyes as he brought up his staff with both hands clasped around its base, moving the pallid shaft so quickly that its whiteness broke apart into component colours and an arcing rainbow smear was left behind as it sliced through the tingling air.

His white-haired adversary, just in time, brought up his own azure-tipped wand to block the lethal blow, held with a hand towards each end as an unyielding bar.

The two rods smashed together with the sound of a whole continent snapping in two, and in that moment the blue china bowl of Mansoul's sky turned an impenetrable black from rim to rim. Out from the point of impact, jagged threads of lightning crazed the heavens with a spider-web of trickling fire, cracking the sudden darkness to a million spiky fragments. The report of the explosion rumbled off into the over-world's unfathomable distances and it began to pour with something that appeared to be a very complicated form of rain. Each droplet was a geometric lattice, like a snowflake, but in three dimensions so that they resembled silver balls with intricately carven filigree that you could peer through to the empty space inside; these tiny structures somehow built from liquid water rather than from ice. As each bead splashed against the rail or boardwalk it broke into half a dozen even smaller perfect copies of itself, rebounding up into the suddenly dark air. Michael found himself wondering briefly if this was what water really looked like, with the type he was familiar with from Downstairs in the mortal realm being an incomplete perception of an actually four-sided substance. Then the sheer force of the frightening downpour drove all such considerations from his mind as, with the district's other phantom residents, he inched back from the railing, trying to get beneath the meagre shelter offered by the balconies above.

Against a new black sky, the warring Master Builders blazed like two Armada beacons. The white-haired one, having dropped to one knee while he staved off his opponent's blow, now sprang up with a speed borne of his greater leverage and, with his staff held only in one hand now, drove the other fist up from below into the darker angle's face. There was a bubbling spray of what should have been blood but in the current circumstances turned out to be molten gold, the costly gore steaming and hissing, tempered by the pounding wonder-rain to rattle down upon the lower levels of reality as smoking ingots, precious misshapes.

An entire exchequer dripping from his ruined nose, the injured Master Builder reeled back swearing in his own unravelled language. Michael somehow knew that with each curse, somewhere across the world a vineyard failed, a school was closed, a struggling artist gave up in despair. With an afraid, sick feeling mounting in the memory of his heart, he knew this wasn't just a fight. This was all that was right or true about the universe, attempting to destroy itself.

The shaven-headed builder lashed out blindly with his rod in a one-handed scything sweep which, by sheer luck, hit his opponent in the mouth. Lip cut and gushing bullion, his white-haired antagonist gave an ear-splitting bellow, shattering every window in the higher town square. Lightning forked again across the black dome up above them, and the monsoon of unfolded rain redoubled in its onslaught. Both the giants were bleeding treasure now, starting to miss their footing on the crystalline entanglements of the material world beneath them, where the jewel-web and its crawling coloured lights were lost beneath a slick of pelting hyper-water.

Michael realised with a start that when he'd seen the white-haired builder earlier, up in the Attics of the Breath, the Master Angle had been nursing wounds and on his way back from the fight that Michael and the other members of the Dead Dead Gang were watching now. Since on that first occasion Michael had only just died, did that mean that right now down in the mortal world his mum Doreen was carefully unwrapping the red cherry-menthol cough-sweet from its small waxed-paper square with "Tunes Tunes Tunes" all over it? As the snow-peaked colossus cast his turquoise-pointed wand aside and threw himself across the sizzling rain-drenched Mayorhold at his enemy, was the pink lozenge at that very moment sliding into Michael's dangerously restricted mortal windpipe in the sunny yard of 17, St. Andrew's Road, down there in the First Borough? Worse still, somewhere in himself the infant knew that this divine affray and his own deadly choking fit, both terrible events in their own way, were intimately linked and were in some unfathomable fashion causing one another to occur.

Over on the supernal town square's far side now, a mile or two away, the paler of the combatants crashed into his more saturnine foe and the pair of them went over like collapsing skyscrapers. The phosphorescent robes billowing all about them as they fell must have glanced up against the balconies of the ennobled Co-op Branch 19 exactly opposite, since its wood railings burst immediately into flames, these luckily being extinguished by the convoluted and torrential rain almost immediately.

It seemed to Michael, watching from between his parted fingers, that the bloody golden free-for-all occurring up here in the heights of Mansoul must be having repercussive echoes in the stacked-up planes below. Indeed, down in the pearly film of gelatine that was the ghost-seam he could see fights breaking out in sympathy amongst the surly wraiths who were the half-world's occupants. Comparatively minuscule, their monochrome forms paired up into tiny clots of vigorous animosity around the massive warring planetoids that were the Master Builders, intertwined and pummelling each other at the Mayorhold's centre, rolling blood-stained in the hopping, spitting puddles wide as boating lakes. He saw two lady apparitions laying into one another outside the grey ghost of the Green Dragon at the foot of Bearward Street, opening brutal fans of after-image limbs with every swinging punch or kick. One of the brawlers was a squat tank of a woman with an eyelid hanging off, the other smaller and already bleeding worryingly from one ear yet armed with a phantasmal broken bottle that she wielded with both relish and efficiency. Their multiple arms whirling like two murderous windmills, the ghost-women tilted at each other as though they were re-enacting some unsettled feud from when the pair of them were living, blow for vicious blow. Elsewhere in the smoky domain of the rough sleepers, outside the old public toilets at the bottom end of Silver Street, the spirits of two Romany or Jewish market traders were engaged in gleefully kicking the stuffing from the man in a black shirt that they'd got on the floor between them. Everywhere about the ashen shade of the enclosure, abject disembodied souls used strangleholds and tried to gouge each other's eyes, joyously joining in with the ethereal hostility of the titanic Master Angles as they wrestled there amidst the ghost-spite and the hammering deluge.

If Michael focussed on the layer underneath the ghost-seam, where the twining spark-lit fronds of coral that were living people knitted to a glittering foundation for the terraces above, then even here the heavenly aggression that cascaded down from the superior worlds was having its effect. He fancied that in some of the livelier areas of the human pattern, he was looking at the stationary vectors of a mortal punch-up where the green and blue and red glass millipedes seemed more than usually contorted and wound into knots that were fantastic and intractable. One such arrangement, a confused and looping mess of coloured filaments, put him in mind of the three living schoolboys that they'd seen outside the sweetshop next to Trasler's newsagent's in the ghost-seam. Michael wondered if the lads had somehow managed to fall out over dividing up their gobstoppers and had now come to blows down in the mortal shopping-square, unconsciously responding to the unseen skirmish going on above them. Staring in mute dread at the enormous builders as they rolled together in the rain, engrossed in their expensive bloodshed, Michael didn't doubt that there were ants and microbes battling at the mortal school-kids' feet, nor that in the incomprehensible geometries that drifted far above Mansoul there might be abstract formulae at war, fractiously trying to disprove each other. It was like a tower of wrath and violence with the raging builders at its centre, reaching from the very bottom of existence to the unimaginable top, and it was all because of him. He was the reason this was happening, him and his cough-sweet.

As if underscoring this unnerving fact, the white-haired builder was now trying to regain his feet, crouched over in the unrelenting downpour close to the west wall of the enclosure, where the Works was situated. As the Master Angle strived to pull himself up from the muck and wet there came a terrifying instant when one of his huge hands settled on the wooden balustrade, four marble fingers thick as Doric columns clenching suddenly on the pitch-painted railing so that all the ghost-spectators gathered there jumped back and screamed, the adult spectres just as loudly as the phantom kids. The motley audience shrank against the balcony's rear wall and trembled as the giant figure, painfully and slowly, hauled itself erect. As though a monstrous candle had been snuffed, a gasp that split into a thousand skittering echoes went up from the cowering mob as first a forest of white curls and then the stunning face, wide as a circus tent, were dragged up into view over the handrail like a pale and angry sun inching above a flat and black horizon. As the Cyclopean visage drew level with the crowded landing, the ferocious battering that it had taken was horrifically apparent. The carved ship's-prow of his chin was gilded with the angle's priceless blood, spilled from a split lip that had now scabbed over with doubloons and ducats. One of the vast eyes was swollen shut with a bruise-sheen of shimmering opal pigments starting to erupt in the abraded

alabaster flesh. The other, full of weariness and urgent import, fixed its endless stare for several paralysing seconds upon Michael Warren. Nothing was
conveyed by that long glance save powerful recognition, but if Michael had
still had a bladder he would have released it there and then. *I know about you,
Michael Warren. I know all about you and your cherry-menthol Tune.*

Breaking the gaze and straightening up so that his head and shoulders
were once more high overhead above the parapet, the Master Builder wheeled
round in a showering swish of soaked and heavy robes, striding as if with
renewed purpose to the far side of the Mayorhold where his crop-skulled fellow combatant was on his knees in the congealed arterial gold, punch-drunk
and still attempting to stand up. The shining ogre leaned upon his polished
staff, one huge paw fumbling for purchase on the cream and emerald ledges of
Co-op Branch 19, where the ghostly onlookers scattered in squealing terror.

Rushing upon his dazed, downed adversary from behind, the white-
crowned builder voiced a terrible world-ending roar and seized his groggy
former comrade by the gown's damp shoulders. In a petrifying show of
strength that seemed to violate every law of mass and motion that existed,
the dark builder was whipped up into the air as weightless as a scarecrow. His
limp form described a rapid, blurring semi-circular trajectory before he was
slammed down agonisingly onto his back, the impact juddering through the
foundations of Mansoul. So swiftly had the move been executed that its draft
could be felt on the balcony outside the Works, where mangy spirits who had
sidled back towards the balustrade once the pale Master Builder had removed
his hand were now blown back against the landing's rear wall, their red Roman
cloaks and Saxon furs and shiny-kneed de-mob suits flapping frantically. Phyll
Painter looked round at the other children, shouting to be heard above the
moaning of the unexpected wind.

"Ay up! This wiz that ghost-storm gettin' gooin', so we'd best be ayt of 'ere
before it kicks orf proper. Why don't we goo earlier, dayn the billiard 'all, then
we can see 'ow all this started!"

This at least sounded to Michael like some sort of plan, though the details
of its accomplishment seemed vague. As the Dead Dead Gang began heading
back the way they'd come along the walkway, shoving through the gathered
horde, Michael took one last look at the dismaying and yet thrilling spectacle that they were quitting. The white-haired immensity, with effort, lifted
up his by now only semi-conscious foe above his head, no doubt preparing
for another pulverising throw. The ringside mob observing eagerly from their
high walkways now commenced to chant their favourite's name in guttural
encouragement, their mass voice thundering in the acoustic labyrinth of magnified and murmuring Mansoul.

"MIGH-TY! MIGH-TY! MIGH-TY!"

As Michael hurried after his departing colleagues, ducking between adult legs along the busy balcony, there came another dull, earth-shattering boom that shook the timbers underneath his plaid-clad feet and which he thought was probably the crew-cut builder being dashed to the wet, streaming squiggles of the higher Mayorhold's floor again. This squeezed fresh lightning from the crackling jet sky above and wrung new cheers from the excited audience of shabby afterlifers.

"MIGHT-TY! MIGH-TY! MIGHT-TY!"

Following in Phyllis's malodorous and therefore relatively crowd-free wake, the phantom kids retraced their steps, back through the swing doors to the Works' interior then down the starry midnight stairs and gingerly across the wriggling expanse of the demonically-tiled workplace to the crook-door in one corner. From here, backing one by one precariously down the Jacob Flight with its ridiculously narrow treads, they re-submerged themselves within the colourless and muffled fathoms of the ghost-seam, where you almost missed the reek of Phyllis Painter's rabbit wrap and where you found yourself examining the rear of your own head as you climbed backwards down the creaking rungs with grey, proliferating after-images trailing in front of you.

Descending, light as scruffy thistledown, they made their way down through the ruined and soggy storeys of the building that had centuries ago been the town hall, drifting across the gaps in the collapsing stairway to the ground floor, passing out through the warped boards that had been nailed across a once-grand door into the faded memory of the Mayorhold, drained of all its paint and life and perfume.

As they stepped into the half-world's open air Michael discovered that it was still raining hard down in the ghost-seam, although judging from the dry clothes and unhurried gait of the enclosure's living occupants along with the sharp-edged black shadows that they cast, the mortal Mayorhold still luxuriated in a sunny Summer's lunchtime, unaware of the bad weather punishing its higher reaches. On the square's far side, much closer than it had appeared to be up in Mansoul, the two wraith-women were still pummelling each other, spattering the pavement outside the Green Dragon with black ghost-blood. Noticing that Michael had his eye upon the pair of harridans, whose spattering ink and multiply-exposed limbs made them look like brawling squids, John stooped to mutter an aside to him as the dead children made their way along the Mayorhold's western edge towards Horsemarket.

"That's the lezzies, settling scores over who pinched whose girlfriend. That one with the broken bottle there, the little nippy one, that's Lizzie Fawkes. The other one, the monster with a torn eye, that one's Mary Jane. She gave me that bad bruise I showed you earlier, where she'd kicked me in the ribs. This what we're seeing now's a famous fight they had when they wiz living. Nearly killed each other, so I heard, but I suppose they must have both enjoyed it or they wouldn't be down here replaying it all, time and time again."

The Mayorhold's other spectre-fights were all still going on across the breadth of the enclosure. The two hook-nosed market traders by the public lavatories were dragging the black-shirted man inside, across piss-glistening tiles, to mete out further punishment. Michael could also see that there were tempers flaring up amongst the area's live inhabitants. The shoppers who'd been chatting amiably together in the doorway of the Co-op were now hissing accusations, both with arms folded aggressively and heads bobbing from side to side like wobbly toys. He saw too that his intuition with regard to the three mortal school-kids had been accurate: just outside Botterill's, the square's other newsagent, two of the boys were ganging up on the remaining lad, who held the bag of sweets they'd purchased earlier. A nasty atmosphere had settled on the formerly agreeable enclosure, but of the celestial presences that Michael knew to be the cause of this unpleasantness there was no sign at all. He realised that neither the massive Master Builders nor the soaring pinnacles of Mansoul that surrounded them were visible from down here in the ghost-seam, or at least they weren't unless you knew what you were looking for.

After a moment or two's peering through the curtain of unfolded rain, Michael still couldn't see the feuding builders, but he could make out the areas where they weren't. One of the motor-coaches parked down at the Mayorhold's lower end seemed suddenly to swell up like a bubble until one half of its cab was ten times bigger than the other half, deflating back to normal almost instantly as the strange patch of visual distortion moved on to inflate the front of the Old Jolly Smokers, bending both the ghosts and living people who were loitering outside the tavern into bowed and elongated smears. It was as if something were moving a great magnifying lens about the square, or as though an immense glass marble of flawless transparency trundled invisibly around the Mayorhold, curving all its light into enormous fisheye bulges. This phenomenon, he reasoned, must be tracking the unseen moves of the Master Angles as they smashed the gold out of each other in the higher realms above.

The tartan toddler also became anxiously aware of the abrupt and startling gusts of wind that were erupting out of nowhere to cause sudden eddies in the ghost-dust or to send the flat cloth caps of local phantoms bowling off down Broad Street with their after-images and owners in forlorn pursuit. This was quite obviously, as Phyllis had remarked, the onset of the howling ghost-squall that had almost blown them all away down at the foot of Scarletwell Street. Since on that occasion they'd not seen their own forms sailing overhead towards Victoria Park then he supposed this meant that they were going to escape the rising storm in some way, although Michael still kept shooting worried glances at his fellow dead kids, waiting for somebody to suggest something.

Predictably, Phyllis already had a plan. As the ferocity of the ghost-breeze began to mount she led her miniature commando troop across the top of Bath Street where it joined the Mayorhold. Squinting down the sloping lane Michael could just about perceive a slow black swirling in the grey air outside Bath Street flats, but if this was the grinding wheel of the Destructor it was clearly nowhere near the scale it would achieve by nothing-five or nothing-six. Rotating dolefully above the empty road it didn't really seem to pose an actual threat as such, and Michael wondered if he'd made too much of it by coming on the twirling burn-hole suddenly by night when he'd been upset anyway.

Once over Bath Street, the gang congregated by one of the waist-high hedges bounding the top lawn of the distinctly 1930s flats. The wind was really getting up now, lashing the chandelier-crystal droplets of the super-rain across the paving slabs in frilled and spraying sheets of fluid glass. As the drops shattered into even more exquisite copies of themselves against the toes of the tot's slippers, each wet bead trailing an after-image necklace through the ghost-seam glaze behind it, it occurred to Michael that though he could feel the complicated splashes hitting him, he wasn't getting wet. The gems of liquid seemed to keep their rubbery surface tension even after being subdivided into intricately-structured dots no bigger than a pin-head, rolling from his striped pyjama cuffs while leaving nothing of themselves behind. His dressing gown pulled up into a cowl to shield his head while leaving both his legs and bum exposed, he ran bent double through the rain towards the doubtful shelter of the hedging where his ghostly pals were gathered, doppel-gangers scurrying behind him like a pygmy hunting party.

Crouching by the hedge, Phyllis was making the by-now familiar pawing motions with her hands as she began to tunnel into time, although the waver-ing interference-pattern bands of black and white around the widening portal were on this occasion absent. There was a pale, single stripe of luminosity around the hole's edge, and it came to Michael that if Phyllis were just trying to dig an hour or two into the past or future then there'd be no black stripes representing night-times squeezed into the opening's flickering perimeter.

As it turned out, this was indeed the case. Digging the shallow hole unaided in less than a minute, Phyllis wriggled through it and did not appear above the hedge on the far side, an obvious invitation for the other members of the gang to follow her. John indicated with a nod that Michael should go next, at which the infant got down on his hands and knees, rain drumming on his neck and ghost-wind whistling around his ears, to follow the gang's leader through the light-rimmed aperture.

When Michael crawled out on the other side he found that, unsurprisingly, he was still on the hedge-fringed upper lawn of Bath Street flats that ran down by Horsemarket, with Phyll Painter standing some few feet away, tapping her toe impatiently. He stood up and looked back across the top of the low privet wall, noticing with alarm that Bill, John, Marjorie and Reggie were no longer anywhere in sight. An instant after that he realised that there was no wind, and that it had stopped raining. He remarked as much to Phyllis, but she smirked and shook her head into a momentary rosebush of blonde, grinning blooms.

"Nah, titch, it's not stopped rainin'. It just 'asn't started yet."

Meanwhile, the other members of the Dead Dead Gang emerged on all fours through the time-gap in the box-cut foliage. When the six phantom kids stood once more reunited on this much more clement and less windswept side of the trimmed bush, Michael gazed back across the top of Bath Street to the Mayorhold. The enclosure was both dry and sunny, albeit only with the wan grey sunlight of the ghost-seam. There were no rough sleepers fighting on the corner next to the Green Dragon, nor outside the public toilets at the foot of Silver Street. The trio of live boys who'd come to blows over their bag of sweets were nowhere to be seen. Phyllis explained.

"I've dug us back abayt three-quarters of an 'our, ayt o' the wind and rain. Now we can all goo dayn the billiard-'all and see 'ow the scrap started."

With that, drifting through the hedge onto the pavement bordering Horsemarket, the gang started to move down the hill towards Marefair and Gold Street, each one with a dissipating stream of grubby copycats behind them. It occurred to Michael that if this was half an hour or so before the angles had their fight, then it must also be before he'd choked to death in the back yard down on St. Andrew's Road. Was Doreen at this moment taking out her straight-backed wooden chair to set down in the top half of the yard beside the drain-trap, telling Michael that fresh air would do him good? Was Michael's sister Alma getting bored already, starting to charge round the close brick confines of the cramped apology for a back garden? Fretting over these concerns he hurried to catch up with Phyllis Painter, tugging at her foggy woollen sleeve until she turned and asked him what he wanted.

"If this wiz before the sweet-cough croaked me, we could glow drown Andrew's Woad and swap this from unhappyning!"

Phyllis was firm, but not unsympathetic.

"No we couldn't. For one thing, it's all already 'appened, and will never 'appen any different. For another, if we did goo dayn to Andrew's Road then I'd 'ave seen us when I 'auled you up into the Attics of the Breath. I've come to the conclusion that if this wiz 'appenin' then it's 'appenin' for a reason, and it's up to us to see it through and make sense of it all. If I were you, I wouldn't waste time tryin' to change the past. In the Dead Dead Gang, what we've found wiz that it's always best to just get on with the adventure and find out 'ow everythin' ends up. Come on, let's pay a visit to the snooker 'all and see what got them builders into such a lather."

With that, Phyllis took his hand and they spontaneously began to skip together down Horsemarket's incline, every bouncing step taking them both higher and further. Michael was so thrilled to feel the touch of her cool fingers twined with his that he began to giggle with delight and then they were both laughing, bounding down the hill together leaving arcs of after-images behind them that looked like bunched Christmas decorations, only nowhere near as colourful. They only paused when they were almost at the bottom and abruptly realised that they'd raced too far ahead of their companions, who were daw-dling halfway up the slope while they watched Bill and Reggie throw themselves in front of hurtling cars. This looked to be a lethal pastime, although obviously the modern traffic passed harmlessly through the spectral roughnecks, and besides, Reggie and Bill were both already dead. Michael assumed that, viewed from their perspective, dying had just meant they could relax and be a bit more reckless in their play, hurl themselves under trains or off ten-storey buildings with aplomb and things like that. For Boroughs kids, it seemed, death was a marvellous amusement park without the queues or irritating safety regula-tions. Phyllis watched what Michael now believed was almost certainly her younger brother, shaking her head ruefully but smiling fondly as she did it.

"'E's a silly little bleeder. 'Im and Reggie, they both do that all the time, jumpin' in front o' cars like that. 'E says you get to see all o' the complications of the engine in what's like a stack of diagram-slices as you rocket through 'em, but I'll take their word for it. I never 'ad much time for cars, meself."

Phyllis and Michael waited down towards the Horseshoe Street and Gold Street crossroads for the stragglers to catch up. They floated up to sit on a high window ledge together while they waited so that all the living people that there were about the intersection wouldn't keep on barging through them all the time. While Michael knew they weren't aware that they were doing it, he didn't want a lot of blithely unselfconscious strangers showing him their bow-els without a by your leave. Also, it felt nice to be sitting there unseen upon the ledge with Phyllis in the silvery mid-day sun. It felt as if they were invisible tree-pixies, crouched there beaming on their knotted bough in an old grey engraving while woodsmen and peasants passed by unaware beneath them.

When the other four at last arrived, Michael and Phyllis jumped down holding hands in a slow waterfall of after-images, and the Dead Dead Gang carried on towards the bottom of Horsemarket. Heading down the hill, they passed over the east-west axis of the crossroads and continued into the steep tilt of Horseshoe Street, floating across it to the Gold Street side that had Bell's gas-fire showroom on the corner.

Halfway down was a flat-topped, three-storey building that appeared to be of 1950s vintage and thus put up only recently, a drill-hall or a sports and social club of some sort. Slipping through the closed front doors, the ghost-tykes found themselves within a shadowy interior where patches of mosaic light fell through wire-reinforced glass from the high-placed windows. There was hardly anyone about at this time of the morning save for several owners or employees who were tidying up and couldn't see the phantom children, and a marble-coloured tabby that quite evidently could. A grey and furry fireball it streaked yowling off down a rear corridor, leaving the Dead Dead Gang to follow Phyllis, wafting lightly up a white-walled stairway to the upper floors.

These higher levels were, as far as they could tell, deserted. At the very top, hidden away in a spare room where there were stacks of chairs and cardboard boxes full of documents, there was a crook-door and a Jacob Flight. Unlike the previous examples Michael had experienced, down at the foot of Scarletwell in nothing-five or nothing-six and underneath the Works just a short time ago, no ribbon-lights unravelled from this opening in pale fruit-cordial colours, nor were there any rippling Mansoul sounds that filtered from the baffling spaces up above. These stairs, apparently, did not go all the way up to the Second Borough. Either that or it was a good few flights further up.

The children scaled the awkward rung-like steps one at a time, again with Phyllis in the lead and Michael following behind her. Passing through the ceiling of the dusty lumber-room, the Jacob Flight continued as a steeply-angled chute enclosed by flaking plaster walls. The two-foot risers and the three-inch treads beneath them as they climbed laboriously upwards had a covering of distressed brown carpet with an ugly creeper-pattern, held in place by scuffed brass stair-rods. As he clambered on with Phyllis struggling in front of him he tried his best not to look at her knickers, but it wasn't easy with the stream of after-pictures peeling from her back to break like photo-bubbles in his face. At last the gang emerged through a trapdoor into what seemed to be a small back office-room with kippered wallpaper, a polished desk and fancy throne-like chair, these last two made of scarred and ancient wood that might have come from Noah's Ark. Across the dark and varnished floorboards there was a fine dusting of what seemed to be a queerly luminous white talcum with a host of worn-down shoe and boot prints leading through it, from the trapdoor to the office entrance.

Tiptoeing across the room, the floor and furniture of which felt solid to the children being made of ghost-wood, they went through the creaking office door the normal way, by opening it first. This led them out into a cavernous and shady gaming-room that seemed to take up what was left of the three-storey building's unsuspected fourth floor. This huge area was windowless, illuminated only by the chiselled pillar of white light that crashed down on the single monstrous billiard-table in the centre of the black expanse.

Crowding the shadows at the chamber's edges were a horde of fidgeting rough sleepers, abject ghost-seam residents from different periods – although it seemed to Michael that there wasn't such a wide variety of centuries here represented as there had been on the balconies outside the Works. Despite the presence of a few historic-looking monks, the phantom mob appeared to be mostly composed of individuals from the late nineteenth or early twentieth centuries. Some had gabardine macs on, some wore braces, all of them were wearing hats and almost all of them were men. They stood there shuffling in the restless gloom, their dead eyes glued upon the floodlit table in the middle of the yawning hall, and on the dazzling quartet of shapes that moved around it.

Bright as sunlight flashing Morse-code dots and dashes from a pond, these were almost too fierce to look at properly, although Michael persisted. Once his eyes had got used to the glare he realised that two of the figures striding round the edges of the table were the Master Builders that he'd just seen fighting in the Mayorhold, only shrunken to a slightly more realistic size. The white-haired angle seemed to concentrate his game upon the giant table's southeast pocket which was one of only four, though Michael thought that he remembered normal snooker tables having more than that. Meanwhile, the shaven-headed builder with dark eyes appeared to be more focussed on the northeast corner of the grey baize, sighting down his long smooth billiard cue – these were the wands the angles had been wielding, Michael realised belatedly – towards the colourless, undifferentiated multitude of balls spread out across the outsized field of play. He didn't recognise the other two contestants, situated to the southwest and southeast, but thought that they were probably of equal rank. Their robes, at any rate, were just as blinding. Someone's mum used Persil.

Noticing that there were symbols scratched in gold into the wooden discs affixed to the four corners of the table, Michael could recall reading about them in the guide-book he'd been given at the Works, which he remembered was still stuffed into the pocket of his dressing gown. Retrieving it, he scanned its somehow legible-though-writhing pages, finding that his ghostly night-sight made it readable despite the darkness. Michael thought that it must be like Alma reading underneath the bedclothes but without the leaking shafts of torchlight that would usually give her away. He re-read the bit about the four poorly-drawn symbols, then skipped through the lengthy list of seventy-two devils, This was followed by a register of seventy-two corresponding builders, which he also skipped, and then by some material about the billiard hall, which was what he'd been looking for. Peering intently at the squirming silver things that weren't exactly letters as they twinkled on the dark page, he began to read.

At the south-eastern corner of the physical domain, near to the Centre of the Land, is to be found a gaming hall wherein the Master Angles play at Trilliards, this being what their Awe-full game is rightly called. The intricacies of their play determine the trajectories of lives in the First Borough, such lives being subject to the four eternal forces that the Angles represent. These are Authority, Severity, Mercy and Novelty, as symbolised respectively by Castle, Death's-head, Cross and Phallus. The Arch-Builder Gabriel governs the Castle pocket, Uriel the Death's-head, Mikael the Cross and Raphael the Phallus.

"Due to the multiplicity of their essential natures, capable of manifold expressions, the four Master Builders never cease their game of Trilliards, even though they simultaneously may be required and indeed present elsewhere. The single exception to this otherwise unvarying rule is the event of 1959, when two of the four Master Angles leave the Trilliard table to pursue an altercation above the terrestrial Mayorhold, their quarrel precipitated by what is claimed to be an infringement of the rules regarding a disputed Soul named Michael Warren. He ...

Hurling the pamphlet to the billiard-hall floor as if it were a poisonous centipede, Michael let out a yelp of mortal terror. He was a "disputed Soul", the only one there'd ever been if what the guide-book said was true, and Michael didn't for a moment doubt it was, in every last eternal detail. It was only when he looked up from the suddenly disquieting leaflet on the floor that Michael realised everybody else was looking at him, his abrupt shriek having evidently drawn attention in the otherwise tense hush that hung above the contest. Phyllis and the other members of the Dead Dead Gang were shushing him and telling him spectators weren't allowed to interrupt the game, while the rough sleepers lurking by the walls were frowning at him through the murk and trying to work out who he thought he was. Amongst the Master Builders grouped around the table, though, there was no such uncertainty. All four were looking at him, and all of them looked as though they knew him.

The dark, crew-cut builder seemed to pay Michael the least attention, merely glancing up to register the source of the sharp outcry and then smiling chillingly across the room at the ghost-infant before bending once more to the table and his shot. The pair of unfamiliar builders on the table's western side stared first at Michael, then each other, then Michael again, wearing identical expressions of startled anxiety. The most surprised to see him out of the four Master Builders, though, was the white-haired one.

Standing by his southeast corner of the table with a gold cross gouged into its mounted wooden disc, the curly-headed angle stared at Michael with a look of terrible bewilderment that seemed to say, "What are you doing dead?", reminding Michael that although this was the second time he'd seen the builder in the last half-hour or so, from the perspective of the builder this was the first time they'd met. The suddenly alarmed and puzzled-looking angle looked like he was running at enormous speed through a long list of calculations in his head, trying to come up with an explanation for the toddler's presence here in this weird snooker-parlour of the dead. With widening eyes as if he'd just considered an unpleasant possibility, the white-haired builder turned back to the table just in time to see the dark and shaven angle take his shot.

Along with every other spectral presence in the room, including the rough sleepers, the Dead Dead Gang and the other Master Builders, Michael looked towards the billiard table with a horrible presentiment of what was just about to happen.

The crop-haired and saturnine contestant had just jabbed his lapis-tipped cue with considerable force into one of the hundred balls in play upon the table, each a subtly different tone of grey. The sphere that had been hit streaked off across the baize with a long, blurring string of after-images pursuing it. Several shades darker than a large majority of the surrounding balls, Michael thought that it might be a deep cherry-red if seen without the colour-blindness that was a condition of the ghost-seam. In fact, Michael thought it might be the exact same colour as the sticky lozenge he had choked upon. In an instinctive flash that seemed to come from nowhere, Michael knew that this ball somehow stood for Dr. Grey, the Boroughs' doctor up in Broad Street who'd told Doreen that her youngest child was suffering from no more than a sore throat and should be given cough-drops. As he watched the Dr. Grey-ball rocket up the length of the huge table, Michael felt, deep in his sinking stomach, that he knew where all of this was leading.

With a mighty crack the hurtling ball collided with another, a much paler orb that Michael understood with a transfixing clarity was somehow meant to stand for him. This second grey globe spun off from the impact to rebound against the south-side cushion and cannon towards the table's northeast corner, where the raised disc was emblazoned with a childish golden scribble that was meant to be a skull. The Michael-ball, slowed to a trickle after its collision with the cushion, rumbled inexorably towards the death's-head pocket, gradually losing momentum in nail-bitingly small increments to finally stop dead less than a hair's breadth from the corner-hole's dark edge. More than a third of its dull ivory curvature protruded out precariously over the skull-marked miniature abyss like a swollen belly, looking as though the slightest vibration in the billiard hall's floor would send it toppling over the rim into pitch black oblivion. Although he knew nothing about snooker, Michael sensed that with this shot both he and the pale Master Builder had been placed in an almost impossible position.

It appeared that the white-haired contestant had come to the same regrettable conclusion. He stared at the table silent and aghast for some few seconds as though he could not believe that one of his three blazing colleagues had seen fit to snare him in this awful and apparently insoluble predicament.

He looked up from the threatened billiard ball towards the shaven-headed angle who had landed it in such appalling jeopardy, his eyes so filled with fury that the audience of deadbeat Boroughs ghosts all shrank back nervously into the shadows, deeper than they were already. Without blinking and without a flicker of expression on a face that was now statue-like, the white-haired builder carefully pronounced one word in his fourfolded tongue.

"Uoricyelnt."

Everyone gasped, except for one or two who laughed involuntarily then choked it off into a dreadful and embarrassed silence as they realised what the Master Builder had just said, give or take several layers of subsidiary nuances and meanings.

"Uriel, you cunt."

It brought the house down, almost literally. The shaven-headed builder's face appeared to pass through an eclipse, where you could see the swathe of shadowy emotion move across his features from the hairline's stubble down to the bone bulwark of his jaw. He brought the hand that held the cue round in a swift arc, overarm across his shoulder with a sweep of white and molten after-images behind it, burning pinions in a savage, slicing wing, and hurled his cue down on the snooker-parlour floor. It boomed, the very crack of doom, so that the entire building lurched and tilted with a number of rough sleepers staggering and tipping over, ending in a jumbled heap with their associates against the billiard hall's rear wall. Michael was both relieved and mystified to note that throughout all this shaking, shuddering and falling over, not one of the balls on the grey table even trembled.

Dust rained from the ceiling, flakes of plaster settling as if lowered on threads of multiple exposures. Even in the flat acoustics of the ghost-seam, rumbling repercussions from the slammed-down snooker cue still charged like bulls around the premises, while the assembled wraiths who were still on their feet stood rooted to the spot in a religious panic. Surely, time would end now. Stars would be tidied away, put back inside in their jewellery casket, and the sun would pop.

As Michael stood there boggling, he found himself seized by his dressing gown's fiend-phlegm-flecked collar from behind and yanked into activity by somebody who turned out to be Phyllis Painter.

"Come on, 'fore the shock wears orf and everybody's tryin' to get ayt of 'ere at once!"

The Dead Dead Gang moved quickly and efficiently, clearly experienced in ducking out and scarpering from the most unexpected and apocalyptic situations. Streaming with their after-images across the billiard hall as if someone had just turned on an urchin-tap, the children smeared across the small back-office, tumbling down the Jacob Flight and then continuing at speed, descending through the mortal building to the bottom floor by jumping down the stairs twelve at a time, scaring the same grey-marbled cat that they'd upset on their way in.

They reached the lobby of the sports and social centre, with the thunder of the now-stampeding phantom snooker crowd pursuing them down from the higher storeys as the other ghosts belatedly came to their senses and made an attempt to clear the room. Michael and all the others were about to bolt out through the double doors and into Horseshoe Street when Phyllis yelled for them to stop.

"Don't goo ayt there! The 'ole mob'll be pouring through them doors in 'alf a minute! I've a better way!"

With that she closed her eyes and pinched her nose between her thumb and forefinger like somebody preparing to jump from the baking concrete pool edge into the opaque green waters of the lido at Midsummer Meadow. Making a short rabbit-hop into the air, she plunged down through the floor and disappeared beneath the lobby's tiles, leaving the just-mopped surface undisturbed by so much as a ripple. Looking at each other doubtfully then glancing up as one towards the ceiling where the avalanche-roar of escaping ghosts was growing louder as it neared, the children followed Phyllis's example. Shutting eyes and nostrils tight, they did their little jumps and found that they were falling through a foot or so of flooring into damp and all-embracing darkness.

Picking himself up from noticeably hard and therefore very likely ancient flagstones, Michael looked round with his tinsel-trimmed ghost-vision at the sparkling outlines of his five chums, who were similarly rising to their feet and dusting themselves down. They seemed to be in a big unused cellar with brick walls, cobwebbed and black with age. Phyll Painter, having been the first one back up on her feet, was standing at the basement's western end and scraping at a patch of brickwork that looked relatively modern in comparison with its surroundings, possibly a former doorway that had been sealed up. As her companions gravitated to her, gathering in a loose ring at her back, she generously shared the scheme which, of course, they were by then already committed to.

"I reckon that we've seen as much o' why the builders 'ad their barney as we're gunna see. I think it's time we went to meet with Mrs. Gibbs at Dodd-ridge Church, the way that we agreed, an' see if anybody's faynd ayt anythin'."

John, looking baffled, interjected here.

"But surely, Phyll, the quickest way to Doddridge Church is straight along Marefair to Doddridge Street. Why are you digging through the years again?"

At the gang's rear, Michael stood on his toes to see what the tall youngster was referring to. Phyllis was standing with her back towards them, burrowing into the brick wall like one of the rabbits that hung dismally around her neck. Just as the hour-deep hole that she'd dug in the Bath Street hedge had had a rim of daylight only, so the one that she was hollowing out now was bordered by uninterrupted darkness. Heaven only knew how many lightless days or years or decades she was folding back into its black perimeter.

"I'm takin' us along Marefair to Doddridge Street, yer nit. There's nothin' says we 'ave to goo the borin' way. There's tunnels dayn this end o' tayn what goo back to antiquity and link up all the oldest churches an' important buildings. That's where me and Bill faynd Reggie, in the passageway what runs from Peter's Church up to the 'Oly Sepulchre. This cellar what we're in now used to be part of the underground route from St. Peter's, through St. Gregory's and up towards All Saints, what used to be All 'Allows when it wiz still built from wood. Down 'ere it doesn't take much diggin' till yer right down in the twelve- and thirteen-'undreds with the later centuries all over 'ead so that yer can dig up into whatever time yer fancy. There. I think that's done it."

Phyllis stepped back so that everyone could see, although in truth there wasn't very much to look at. She had dragged the midnight edges of the time-gap out to roughly the dimensions of a motor-tyre, with nothing visible upon the hole's far side except more blackness. Still, if Phyllis said that this was the exciting way to travel along Marefair, Michael was prepared to trust her. Her announcement that the gang were at last going to meet with Mrs. Gibbs had done much to dispel his earlier worries that she might be recklessly exposing him to trouble, and as she hitched up her skirt to clamber through the space she'd made he jostled forward past the other members of the crew to be the first one after her.

Only the tunnel's rough and glistening limestone walls betrayed the fact that they were now in medieval times, with total darkness being much the same in any century. The glittering embroidery of Michael's night-sight picked out fragments of archaic debris littered here and there – part of an old stone bottle with a wire-and-marble stopper, lumps of dog-mess that looked fossilised and half a hobby-horse with wooden spine snapped just below the head – but nothing that seemed very interesting. With the remainder of the gang and their attendant images in tow, Michael and Phyllis began walking into the impenetrable blackout, heading roughly west.

They hadn't travelled very far, about the width of Horseshoe Street as far as Michael could make out, before the tunnel widened into what he thought was an abandoned vault of some kind, with a flagged floor on which jigsaw chunks of broken stone were strewn, perhaps the shattered lid of a sarcophagus. Phyllis confirmed the tot's suspicions.

"Yiss, this wiz what's underneath St. Gregory's Church, or under where it used to be, at any rate. This wiz the very spot where one of the four Master Builders told a monk to come, 'undreds of years ago. This builder, it wiz probably your mate the curly chap, 'e made the monk bring a stone cross 'ere, all the way across the deserts and the oceans from Jerusalem, to mark the centre of 'is land, slap in the middle o' the country. That old cross – the Rood, they used to call it – wiz the thing what makes the Boroughs so important. Upstairs, it's the hub of England's structure so it's bearin' all the weight. That's why the nasty burn-'ole what you saw in Bath Street earlier is gunna end up as a flippin' gret disaster if someone ent careful."

Michael chose not to ask Phyllis what she meant as he did not particularly want to think about the nasty burn-hole that they'd seen in Bath Street. The six junior wraiths meandered on along the subterranean passageway, leaving the ruined vault of St. Gregory's behind as they progressed into the antique darkness under Marefair.

After another fifty or so paces, Phyllis called the company to a halt and pointed to the burrow's moist and dripping roof, mere feet above them.

"This is where I reckon we should dig up to the surface. It'll bring us ayt just opposite the mouth o' Doddridge Street in Marefair. Give us a leg up, John, would yer?"

The best-looking member of the ghost-gang did as he was told, cupping his hands into a stirrup so that the near-weightless Phyllis could stand on them and commence her pawing at the tunnel's ceiling. This time there were shifting bandwidths of both black and white around the fringes of the excavation, which suggested that the space above them was at least familiar with the ordinary procession of successive days and nights.

To Michael's eye Phyllis was being much more careful in her digging, wiping patiently away at the accumulated ages like a cautious archaeologist rather than scrabbling frantically, which was the only technique that he'd seen her use before. It looked as if she were attempting to bore through to a specific year or even a specific morning, so precise and delicate were the progressions of her ghostly multiplicity of fingers, scratching in the dark.

At last she seemed to have achieved exactly the degree of penetration she was seeking, with a sizeable breach in the fabric of the tunnel that afforded a restricted view up into what appeared to be the shadowy and laughably low-ceilinged room above. With a delighted and triumphant chortle, Phyllis scrambled up and through the opening she'd fashioned, reappearing moments later crouched beside the time-hole's rim and grinning down towards them from above. She called to Michael, holding out her hand and telling him that he should come up next. Obediently, the toddler hopped up into John's linked hands and allowed Phyllis to manhandle him up through the rend in the stone roof, into the dusky chamber overhead.

He found himself not in a crawlspace with its wooden ceiling only three feet overhead, as he'd believed he would, but underneath a table. As he kneeled with Phyllis by the aperture, helping first Marjorie then Bill to struggle up beside them, Michael noticed that beneath the near side of the tabletop the lower reaches of a seated man were visible. Perched on a stately hardwood chair, his most prominent feature was the pair of high, soft boots with dull iron buckles just below the ankle and a flap of leather rising to obscure each knee. The man was obviously alive, since when he moved one foot it left no after-images behind it, which meant that probably he couldn't hear them. All the same, Michael tried not to make a noise as Reggie and then John were hauled up through the time-trapdoor, whereupon the entire gang crawled like bear-cubs out between the table-legs into a large and quiet room with long slanted rays of afternoon light falling through its criss-cross leaded windows.

Standing there to one side of the high-roofed quarters with his spectral playmates, Michael gazed across the polished oaken tabletop towards the top half of the man whose high boots he'd already seen, sitting at the far end and writing with a quill pen in some sort of log or ledger.

Dark hair, lank and greasy-looking, hung down to the dusty mantle of the man's old-fashioned tunic, and his bowed head, bent above his writings, had a poorly-concealed bald spot. It was hard to judge his stature, seated as he was, although he didn't look to be unduly tall. Despite this, his broad chest and shoulders fostered an impression of solidity and bulk. Skin grey in the drained radiance of the ghost-seam, the man looked like a lead soldier scaled up for the play of giants.

Coming to the end of a long paragraph the fellow sat back in his chair to read what he had written, so that the ghost-children could more clearly see his face. To Michael, the grave countenance looked almost thuggish, even though the general bearing of man suggested rank and prominence. His features were like thick-cut bacon, broad and fleshy and possessed of what might almost be an earthy sensuality if not for the expressionless grey eyes like flattened musket balls that dominated the arrangement, staring down unblinking at the page of cramped but ornate script that he'd just authored. A fat wart jewelled the depression between lower lip and chin, with a much smaller growth just over his right eyebrow. There was a nerve-wracking stillness to him that Michael imagined to be like the stillness of a bomb the moment after it's stopped ticking.

Standing in the silent room beside him, Phyllis nudged him gently in his phantom ribs. She looked pleased with herself.

"There. See 'im? That's the Lord Protector, that wiz."

"That's Oliver Cromwell."

SLEEPLESS SWORDS

That blowing-up bloke on the balcony had rattled John. He liked to think that generally he kept an even keel but the two-legged fireball had upset him, there was no denying.

For a kick-off, John had never seen before what an exploding person looked like, not in all that frozen detail and not from outside. When John himself had copped his lot over in France he hadn't even realised it had happened for a good few minutes. He'd just taken it for a near miss and had gone running up the road with all the other lads. He'd noticed that the shell-fire was now muffled and that he was seeing everything in black and white, but just assumed the bang had made his eyes and ears go funny. Only when he'd realised he was leaving pictures in his wake, unlike his strangely unresponsive squadron-mates, had John begun to take in what had happened.

Once he'd understood his circumstances he'd been overcome by horror, which was only normal: it had been a gruesome way to perish. So to see that fellow on the landings at the Works, inside his lethal halo with that forced smile and the tears turning to steam upon his cheek, remaining in that awful second for eternity because that was the way that he remembered himself best … John couldn't make it out. When Bill had told them that these human bombs were doing it as part of their religion, waging holy war as you might say, that had just made John even more bewildered.

John had been a Christian while he was alive. Never a good one, mind you, nowhere near as serious about religion as his eldest brother had been, but more serious than his sister, mam, or either of his other brothers were. He'd gone to church up College Street most Sundays, where he'd been a member of the Boy's Brigade. That was where John had prayed, sung hymns, been taught to march, and learned to see this combination as entirely natural. Onward Christian soldiers and all that.

There had been no religious books to speak of in the family home where he'd grown up except the Bible, which John was ashamed to say he'd found as dry as dust, and an old copy of *The Pilgrim's Progress*, which he'd fared a little better with. He'd not had much idea, back then, what Bunyan's allegorically-named characters were meant to represent, but found that he enjoyed the tales and fancied that he'd caught their basic moral gist. He'd even got halfway through Bunyan's *Holy War*, the first place that he'd come across the name

"Mansoul", before he'd given up in bafflement and boredom. All of this had only underlined the notion that had been instilled in him by Boy's Brigade – ten minutes' prayer after an hour's drill practice in the upper church hall, blue-black military caps on bowed young heads – the sense that Christianity and marching were bound up together inextricably. He was no stranger, then, to the association between warfare and religion, but that, surely, was a thing for proper wars, with soldiers who had proper uniforms. The fellow on the land-ing, a civilian blowing himself up and taking others with him in the name of God, that was a different matter. That was neither warfare nor religion as John comprehended them.

Also, whatever Boroughs-of-tomorrow the perpetually exploding man had wandered back to 1959 from, that was not a future that John comprehended either. How could his scuffed, peaceful neighbourhood produce something like that in only sixty years or so? Though John had been on various sorties into the twenty-first century with the Dead Dead Gang since first hooking up with them, he realised that he'd no more than the barest understanding of how people felt and thought and lived during those future decades, anymore than he could claim to know much about France simply because he'd died there. All he knew was that the sight of that half-man, half-Roman candle made him fearful for the Boroughs, and the England, and the whole world that was yet to come. Throughout the fight between the builders and the drama in the billiard hall, John had found that he couldn't take his mind off that illumi-nated and fragmenting figure, shuffling on the wooden walkways of a Heaven that it couldn't have conceived of or anticipated, wrapped forever in the flames of its own savage martyrdom.

Indeed, not until John had realised where Phyll Painter meant to take the gang after escaping from the snooker parlour had he started to pay much attention to their present undertaking, unable to banish the compelling vision of the man-explosion from his thoughts. The English Civil War, though, was John's hobby in the afterlife, much in the same way Reggie Bowler had a craze for cars or Marjorie liked books. If anything could stop the image of the walk-ing detonation from preoccupying him, it was the thought of tunnelling into the evening of June 13th, 1645, here in Marefair at Hazelrigg House, or, as locals called it, Cromwell House.

In the brief interlude between his death and his encounter with the Dead Dead Gang, a few subjective years at most, John had pursued his interest inde-pendently. He'd twice been out to Naseby, once an hour or two before the bat-tle and once during, and he'd travelled up the Wellingborough Road to Ecton for a look at how the Royalist prisoners were treated afterwards. He'd never previously paid a visit, though, to the occasion he was currently observing: fresh from his promotion to lieutenant-general, rising Parliamentary star Oliver Williams-alias-Cromwell, bivouacked in Marefair on the night preceding the decisive battle of the English Civil War.

John could remember how alone he'd felt in those years following his death, before encountering Phyll and the gang. His journey back from France had been accomplished with surprising speed. One moment he'd been standing in the shell-pocked mud, staring appalled at his own offal, glistening as it spilled from the burst body at his feet, desperately wishing that he'd lived to see his home again. The next, he'd found himself stood in the middle of the green behind St. Peter's Church, now grey and silvery in the colourless expanses of the ghost-seam. Spilled-milk clouds drifted at anchor in a sky of blazing summer platinum, and John had bounded down the grassy slope towards the terrace at the bottom, leaving a parade of muddy soldiers in the air behind him.

Yes, he'd seen his mam and even seen his sister who was visiting with her two little girls, but since they'd not been able to see John he'd found the whole encounter both frustrating and depressing. What had made it worse was that his mam and sister, obviously, didn't know that he was dead yet. When his sis had started reading out a letter John had sent home to her daughter Jackie, talking about all the fun he'd have the next time he was home on leave, with all of them sat round the family dinner table, tucking into mam's bake pudden, John had broken down. His mam, sat in her armchair up the corner, had smiled fondly as her only daughter read the letter, scrawled in pencil on the tiny pages of a jotter, clearly looking forward to bake pudden with her sons as much as John had been the night he'd written to his niece. She didn't know that the reunion feast would never come. She didn't know that her son's ghost was sitting on the lumpy horsehair sofa next to her, weeping with helplessness for her and for himself and for the entire rotten business of that bloody war. Unable to take any more, John had streamed through the closed front door, away along Elephant Lane towards Black Lion Hill, commencing his short-lived career as a rough sleeper.

Not that John had been as rough as most of that sort were, by any means. He'd always kept himself presentable while he was still alive, and thus approached the afterlife with a Boy's Weekly sense of military discipline. He'd made himself a den in the unused round tower jutting incongruously from condemned Victorian business premises upon the far side of Black Lion Hill. He'd chosen the location partly from a sense that proper ghosts should haunt somewhere that looked appropriately creepy like a turret, and partly because his previous choice, St. Peter's Church, seemed to be overrun by ghosts already. John had met at least fifteen on his first tentative excursion to the Norman-renovated Saxon building. By the gate in Marefair there had been the spectre of a crippled beggar-woman, talking in a form of English so archaic and so thickly accented that John could barely understand a word of it. Around the church itself John had met phantom pastors and parishioners from several different eras, and encountered a geologist named Smith who claimed to have identified the limestone ridge that stretched from Bath to Lincolnshire, called the Jurassic Way. According to the affable and chatty soul, it was the way that this primordial cross-country footpath met the river Nene which had determined where Northampton would be most conveniently situated. Smith himself, coincidentally, had died here in Marefair while passing through the town and was commemorated by a plaque fixed to the church wall, which he'd proudly pointed out to John.

After that limited exposure to the ghost-seam's other occupants, John had decided on a policy of keeping for the most part to himself. He'd watched the wraiths coming and going from the window of his tower-room, but they'd seemed to him peculiar things, some of them monstrous, so that he'd not felt inclined to seek their company. For instance, John had one day spotted the giant wading-bird made out of stilts and rushes that he'd seen again just recently, up on the balconies outside the Works. Upon that first occasion he had watched it striding round St. Peter's Church in a full circuit before struggling through a wall of thousand-year-old stones and out of sight. Back then he hadn't had a clue what it might be, and was no wiser now. The wood-beaked creature that left puddles of ghost-water everywhere it set its spindly legs served only as an illustration of the half-world's oddness, which had prompted John to take an isolated, self-sufficient path in all his dealings with the afterlife.

He'd found that he liked his own company, liked planning expeditions such as those he'd made to Naseby, even though his second visit halfway through the actual battle had been horrible and made him glad that he'd been done in by a shell and not a pike. In general, he'd felt lively and adventurous during those early months of being dead, and it had been around then John had realised that he was no longer wearing his army uniform. He'd just looked down one day and found that he was in black knee-length shorts, a jumper that his mam had knitted and the shoes and socks he'd worn when he'd been twelve. He realised now, of course, that his ghost-body had been slowly gravitating to the form that it had been the happiest with in life, but at the time he'd simply been delighted to discover that he was a lad again, and didn't care to speculate how this had come about.

He'd thrown himself into his solitary escapades with renewed vigour, always choosing the most daring situations to investigate, fancying himself as a dead Douglas Fairbanks Junior. When that British bomber had crashed at the top of Gold Street, John had watched it passing overhead from his tower's window at the foot of Marefair and had straight away gone racing through the sparkling dark along the east-west avenue, chased by a scrum of after-image schoolboys as he'd rushed to see if anyone was dead, if there were any new ghosts stumbling about confused, needing advice.

As it had turned out, nobody was killed by the huge aeroplane's astonishing descent, the crew and pilot having already bailed out and the sole casualty being a late-night Gold Street cyclist who'd sustained a broken arm. The only ghost other than John upon the scene that evening was that of the plane itself. Amazingly, although its substance had been almost totally destroyed on impact, the ethereal framework of the aircraft had been driven down into the misty topsoil of the ghost-seam, so that underneath the surface of the street a phantom bomber was at rest and perfectly intact. It had been while John sat there in its cockpit, shouting out commands to his imaginary crewmen and pretending he was on a bombing-mission that, embarrassingly, he had found himself surrounded by four snickering ghost-children who had introduced themselves as the Dead Dead Gang.

Standing now in Hazelrigg House, watching Cromwell writing in his journal as the long, last rays of the day's sun were spent outside, John smiled as he recalled that first adventure with the other ghost-kids, or "The Subterranean Aeroplane Affair" as Phyllis had insisted that they afterwards refer to it. Larking about there at the controls of the immaterial craft, the spectral urchins had discovered that they could make it move slowly forward by merely pretending they were flying it, provided they pretended hard enough. Although they couldn't get up enough speed to break the surface tension of the streets and take the plane back up into the air, they found that they could glide round underground at a serene and stately pace, and even execute a dive into the geologic strata underneath the town by leaning on the joystick. Travelling through clay and rock, though, hadn't been much fun, and so they'd mostly kept to a flight corridor that was a few feet down beneath the surface. Here they'd droned through tunnels, crypts and cellars and endured a comically disgusting episode while taxiing along a vintage iron sewer-bore. At last, laughing at their own ingenuity, they'd steered their phantom aircraft carefully into the space presented by a subterranean speakeasy, on the corner of George Row and Wood Hill, which, bizarrely, had been built to replicate the fuselage and seating of a passenger plane and so made a perfect parking-place for their ghost-vessel.

John had given up his independent ways upon the spot, throwing his lot in with these hooligans who'd managed to make death into their funfair. He'd not been back to his lonely turret-room since that hilarious night, preferring the nomadic life of the ghost-children as they capered through the decades and dimensions, moving between purgatory and paradise, from hidden den to hidden den. He liked the crew he'd fallen in with a great deal, even if Reggie

Bowler sometimes seemed to squint resentfully from underneath his hat-brim and you seldom heard more than a word or two out of Drowned Marjorie.

He got on best with Phyllis Painter. In a funny sort of way he thought that they might even be in love. He saw the admiration in her bright eyes every time she looked at him and hoped that she could see the same in his, although he knew that what there was between the pair of them could go no further, not without the whole thing being ruined. As John saw it, what he had with Phyllis was perhaps the very best of love in that it was a child's game of love, an infants' school idea of what it meant to be somebody's boy or girlfriend. It was heartfelt and unsullied by the smallest cloud of practical experience. Before he'd died aged barely twenty, John had several girlfriends and had even had it off with one of them. Likewise, although he'd never asked her outright, he got the impression that Phyll Painter had lived to a ripe old age and had at one point even possibly been married. So to some extent they'd both been through the grown-up part of love, the animal delight of sex, the troughs and torments of a passion off the boil.

They'd both known adult love and yet had opted for the junior version, for the thrill of an eternal playground crush, romance that hadn't even progressed to behind the bike-sheds yet. They had elected to taste nothing but the dew upon love's polished skin, and leave the actual fruit unbitten. That was how John felt about it, anyway, and he suspected it was probably the same with Phyll. At any rate, whatever the success of their relationship was due to, they'd loved in their fashion for some several timeless decades, and John hoped they might keep on like that until the very doorstep of infinity.

All things considered, John's death suited him as well or better than his life had. The wayward agendas of the ghost-gang, scampering from one absurd adventure to another, meant that John was never bored. With the grey blush of every phantom morning there was always something new. Or, in the case of Bill and Reggie's plan to tame a spectral mammoth, something very old.

Take all of this to-do over the ghost-gang's latest member, for example. While John felt, as Phyllis did, that being in charge of the temporarily-dead infant was a grave responsibility, he also felt that this was turning out to be their grandest episode to date. In fact, John had good reason to take Michael Warren's plight even more seriously than Phyllis did, and to be even more concerned about the toddler's safety. He was buggered, though, if he'd let that stop him enjoying an extraordinary outing: demon-kings like plunging Messerschmitts! Ghost-storms and deathmongers! This was the kind of dashing spree he'd fondly hoped a war might be, before he'd found out otherwise. This was more what he'd had in mind, the very picture-paper essence of adventure with no scattered entrails and no grieving mums to turn a radio-serial romp into a tragedy. This was the best bits, all the spills and spectacle without

the mortal consequence. John marvelled as he thought of the colossal builders, bleeding gold and lashing at each other with their billiard cues on the
unfolded acres of the Mayorhold, then broke off that train of thought on realising that it led him back to the exploding man, the stumbling phosphorescence on the balcony with his suspended nails and rivets, his soiled trousers,
his evaporating tears.

To rid himself of the recurring apparition, John switched his attention
to their current whereabouts, the downstairs parlour of Hazelrigg House, an
ominous June evening in the mid-seventeenth century. Having emerged from
underneath a gleaming rosewood table, the group stood assembled at the spacious chamber's eastern end, all taking in the monumental presence sitting
at the table's further edge, one side of his great griffin snout lit by the sunset
falling through the leaded windows from outside, his warts in shadow.

John, of course, had recognised old Ironsides from the previous occasions
when the plucky youth had visited the dark days of the Civil War. He'd witnessed Cromwell, riding out with General Fairfax and his major-general of
foot-soldiers, Philip Skippon, on the slopes of Naseby Ridge at first light on
June 14th – or tomorrow morning from John's current point of view. Cromwell
on that occasion had seemed giddy with delight as he inspected the terrain
between the ridge and Dust Hill, getting on a mile off to the north. Cantering
back and forth in his black armour, he had burst out laughing intermittently,
as if by looking at the land he saw the battle in advance and chuckled over the
foreseen misfortunes of his enemies. John had seen Cromwell with another
face as well, a semblance cast from flint, unblinking in the screaming heart
of battle as his cavalry pursued the Royalist horse almost to Leicester, cutting
down the hindmost by the score. Whatever mood they were expressing, he'd
have known those features anywhere.

Phyllis and Bill quite clearly also knew who they were looking at, and so
did Reggie Bowler, who was nodding knowingly with a wide grin across his
freckled face. Although Drowned Marjorie remained impassive, staring flatly
through her National Health spectacles, John had an inkling that somebody
as surprisingly well-read as her might well know more about the lank-haired
man than all the rest of the gang put together. That left Michael Warren –
Michael Warren, son of Tommy Warren, John reflected to himself with an
amazed shake of the head – as the one person in the slowly darkening room
without a clue regarding what was going on. John was about to venture his
own explanation for the nipper's benefit when Phyllis intervened and beat him
to the punch.

"There. See 'im? That's the Lord Protector, that wiz. That's Oliver Cromwell."

It was painfully apparent that the name meant nothing to the little boy, thus giving John a chance to stick his oar in after all and give his expertise an airing.

"Where we are now, it's the 1640s. Charles the First wiz on the throne, and hardly anybody thinks he's making a good job of it. For one thing he's brought in this tax, Ship Money, which wiz paid direct to him and makes him less dependent on the English Parliament. Nobody likes the sound of that, especially since they know Charles wiz matey with the Catholic Church and may be plotting to sneak in Catholicism by the back door. Bear in mind that all of this wiz happening in an England where the rich and poor have grown apart since the beginning of the 1600s, when the gentry had begun enclosing common land and taking people's livelihoods away. You can imagine how cross and suspicious everybody wiz. England wiz like a powder keg, just waiting to go off."

John paused here as an image of the detonating man-bomb shuffled weeping and unbidden through his mind, then carried on.

"In the last months of 1641, the whole of Ireland wiz in flames with a rebellion against English rule. The rebels were destroying or else seizing back the land that had been given to Protestant settlers, killing many of these settlers in the bargain. Back in England, this wiz looked on as a Popish plot that Charles the First wiz in collusion with. Rebels in Parliament published a *Grand Remonstrance* airing all their grievances with Charles, which only served to push both camps further apart. In January, 1642, the King left London to the rebels and began to gather armies for a civil war that by then everybody knew wiz coming. God, that must have been a terror. From one end of England to the other, families must have been on their knees and praying that they'd get through the next years without too many members dying."

That was certainly how it had been for John's clan during 1939. He watched the figure at the room's far end arrest its writings for a moment with quill poised a fraction of an inch above the page, perhaps deliberating over word-choice, before dipping once more to the vellum and continuing its row of Gothic curls and slanting, marching uprights. John supposed that his own family's prayers upon the eve of war must have been heeded, for the most part. Everyone lived through it, after all, with present company excepted.

Looking round, John realised that the other members of the Dead Dead Gang were waiting patiently for him to carry on. Even Drowned Marjorie, behind her jam-jar lenses, appeared interested.

"Anyway, that fellow over there, Oliver Cromwell, wiz born to a fairly well-off family in Huntingdon. Their name wiz Williams, but they were descended from Henry the Eighth's adviser Thomas Cromwell and had taken on his name, grateful for all the good he'd done the family as the bloke who'd managed Henry's great Protestant Reformation, and defiant at the way he'd later been beheaded for his troubles. Ollie over there calls himself 'Williams, alias Cromwell' all the way through life, but I suppose that Cromwell has more of a ring to it than Williams.

"He has a wife, a family and a comfortable life, but I suspect he'd always wanted more than that. In 1628, aged twenty-nine, he entered politics as the MP for Huntingdon, and by the time the Civil War wiz brewing some four-teen years later he wiz one of the King's sternest critics in what they called the Long Parliament. When Charles requested help from Cambridge, Cromwell stormed straight down there with two hundred armed men, bullied his way into Cambridge Castle and grabbed all their armaments. Not only that, he also stopped them from transferring any silver to help out the Royalists – and this was at a time when almost everybody else was dithering about what should be done. By seizing the initiative, Cromwell began to look like good material for the Parliamentary cause, and was promoted from a captain to a colonel.

"He was busy, in them next few years, dealing with Royalists in King's Lynn and Lowestoft and then securing all the bridges on the River Ouse. With that done, he went on to fortify the Nene – we can go outside in a minute, and I'll show you what I mean. Anyway, Cromwell proved himself in scraps like Gainsborough in Lincolnshire, and battles like the one on Marston Moor near Manchester in 1644, where Cromwell led the cavalry. Bouts like that led to Parliamentary General Sir Thomas Fairfax making Cromwell the lieutenant-general of horse at a war-council that took place ..."

Here John paused and pretended, for effect, to search his memory for some venerable date before continuing with, "... ooh, it must have been an hour or two ago. Today, June 13th, 1645. For Mister Cromwell over there, today's the turning point of his whole life. He's finally been given power enough to carry out the task he's got in mind, and straight away he's been sent to Northamp-tonshire to deal with Royalist Forces under King Charles's son, Prince Rupert. Rupert has just taken Leicester by siege from the Parliamentary forces, and when Cromwell turned up at the Roundhead camp near Kislingbury this morning, just a mile or two southwest of here, they greeted him with cheers. Last night a Parliamentary advance guard surprised some Royalists close to Naseby village, five miles south of Market Harborough on the edge of Leices-tershire. Before that happened neither side had realised quite how close their armies wiz to one another, but now everybody's worked out that they're in for an almighty battle come tomorrow morning. That's why all the Roundhead troops wiz overjoyed when Cromwell turned up: he's the only bugger within hundred mile of here that's looking forward to it."

On an impulse, John detached himself from the grey cluster of the Dead Dead Gang and crossed the varnished floorboards to the room's far side, so that he stood behind the seated figure, raven-hunched over its writings. The unusually sharp sight that being dead afforded John detected three or four fat lice that foraged in the greasy undergrowth of the lieutenant-general's thinning scalp. He'd never been as close as this to Cromwell, having only seen him gallop past during his previous visits to the actual field of battle. He could almost feel the thrumming dynamo-vibrations of the future Lord Protector's personality filling the air between them, and wished he could breathe in Cromwell's scent without the odourless encumbrance of the ghost-seam being in the way, just to determine what variety of animal the man might truly be. Bill interrupted John's close-up inspection here by calling from the chamber's far side, where he stood with Phyllis and the others.

"What's 'e writin'?"

It was a good question, and John transferred his attention from the escapades of Cromwell's head-lice to the page across which the man's crow-quill moved. It took John several moments' scrutiny before he had the hang of the peculiar cursive script, then he glanced up as he addressed the gang.

"It looks like it's the first draft of a letter to his wife. I'll read you what I can of it."

Placing his hands on his bare knees John angled himself forward, leaning over Cromwell's shoulder to peruse the missive's contents.

"'My most dear Elizabeth – I write with what I trust is welcome news. Your fond and constant husband is this day appointed to lieutenant-general of horse by Sir Tom Fairfax, and at once despatched to attend some small matter in Northamptonshire, from whereabouts I pen these lines. I am, you may be sure, of a good humour and feel certain we shall have a fair result upon the morrow, but please do not think that this promotion tempts me to vainglory. Any victory is surely that of God alone, nor is my elevation of importance, save in that I am enabled to more vigorously work His will.

"'Now, let us have no more of your unworthy husband's bragging, and instead hear tidings of more estimable things. How fares our humble Huntingdonshire cot, that is forever in my thoughts with you and all our little ones about your skirts, stood at its door? Bridget, I know, will scoff at being called a little one, and so will Dick, but they are as such in my thoughts and ever shall be. Oh, Elizabeth, that I might have you by me now, for your sweet presence lifts my soul more than all laurels and high office ever could. All that I do, I do for God and in the same kind do for you, my pretty Beth, that you and our dear children might live in a godly land, safe from the tyrannies of Antichrist. I know that our young Oliver would say the same, were it not for the cruel camp-fever this last year. Please God that by my efforts shall his sacrifice, with those of many more Parliamentarian lads, be made worthwhile.

"'I should be pleased to hear of how the garden comes along, for it is a fine thing about this time of year, and with the present tumult I am feared I shall miss all of it if you will not describe it for me. In a like vein, tell me of your least affairs, your travels to and fro about the town and your most minor inconveniences, that I may pretend I hear again your voice and its familiar turns of phrase. Tell little Frances that her father promises to bring her a fine pair of shoes back from Northampton, and tell Henry I am confident that he will do his duty and make sure the dogs are exercised. Now that I think on it, I wish that you would send me a good wooden pipe, for all the clay ones to be had about these parts are easy broken and ...' That's more or less how far he's got, and it seems he's just going on about his home and family. To be honest, he don't strike me as a bad bloke, not from reading this."

John straightened up, beginning to view Cromwell with a different attitude. Across the room with its pitch-painted beams and copper ornaments, Marjorie shook her head.

"Well, I don't know. He don't sound as if he's all there to me. I mean, he knows how rough this battle's gunna be tomorrow, and just look at him: as calm as anything, asking her how the garden's getting on. It's like he don't think any of it's real, like it's a play he's watching through to see the end. You ask me, he's got summat missin'."

Everybody gaped at Marjorie, astonished less by the perceptive point she'd made than by the sheer amount of words she'd used in making it. No one had ever heard her say so much before, and nor had they suspected her of harbouring such strongly held opinions. John considered what she'd said for a few moments and concluded that the tubby little girl was more than likely right. In his own letters home, John had sometimes made light of his grim circumstances, it was true, but not to the extent that Cromwell was engaged in doing. John had never written to his mam about attending 'some small matter' off in Normandy, or rattled on about bake-pudden to the point where you forgot there was a war on. Cromwell's writings were those of a normal man in normal times, and on both counts you couldn't help but feel that this was knowing misrepresentation. Gazing at Drowned Marjorie across the chamber through the failing light, John nodded soberly.

"I think you might have something there, Marge. Anyway, it doesn't look like he'll be doing much in the next little while. Why don't we go outside while it's still light and see what's happening?"

There was a mutter of assent. Leaving the statue-still lieutenant-general to his writings, a dark shape losing its definition in a darkening room, the children flocked out through Hazelrigg House's thick walls of coursed rubble to the street beyond, where there was much activity. Marefair, with low but well-appointed buildings to each side of it, bustled with life in a tin sunset. The last drip of daylight glinted from the points atop iron helmets, from the bundled blades of the long pikes that an old man was just then carrying into Pike Lane for sharpening. It flashed upon the bridles of fatigued and steaming horses, sparked from the tall mullioned windows of Hazelrigg House, dotting the ghost-seam's murk with points of brightness, dabs of white relieving thick umber impasto on the day's completed canvas. Delicately beautiful and subtly disturbing; it was the fragile illumination just before a summer storm, or during an eclipse. Tired Roundhead soldiers slogged through the well-trodden mud of the main concourse, looking for a tavern or else stabling their bony mounts, while such few local men and women as there were about Marefair did all they could to keep out of the troopers' way. John saw a dog kicked with a Parliamentary boot; a pock-marked youth cuffed to one side by a stout leather glove.

On every countenance, both military and civilian, was the same look of profound and paralysing dread. It only underlined Marjorie's point about the calmness of the man who still sat writing in the room they'd just vacated, with his face like a heraldic beast and his detachment in stark contrast to the fearfulness afflicting everybody else upon this otherwise serene June evening. These were monstrous times, in which only a monster might feel comfortable. Somewhere behind John, Bill began to sing what sounded like a fragment from a catchy song, although it wasn't one that John had ever heard before.

"... and I would rather be anywhere else than here today."

Bill broke off with a rueful, knowing chuckle. He and Reggie Bowler wandered over to the street's far side where they distracted themselves with the manufacture of small dust devils by racing round in circles. They weren't doing very well until Drowned Marjorie went over to assist them, at which point they raised a whirlwind big enough to make at least one burly Roundhead step back in surprise and cross himself. Meanwhile, Phyllis and John were left in charge of Michael Warren, standing on the funny wooden duckboards outside Cromwell House. The infant turned his curly blonde head back and forth, trying to work out where he was. Finally he looked up at John and Phyllis.

"Wiz this Marefair? I can't tell what bit of it I'm looking at."

Phyllis took Michael's hand – she had a way with kids, John thought, as if she might have had a couple of her own – and crouched beside the infant as she turned him round until he faced due west.

"Don't be so daft. O' course yer can. Look, that dayn on the left wiz Peter's Church. Yer know that, don't yer? And next door, even this long agoo, there's the Black Lion."

John peered in the same direction that the toddler was being pointed to. A little further down Marefair on their side of the street, St. Peter's Church seemed much the way it had during John's life, sombrely overlooking Parliamentary battle preparations with the same impartiality that it would show three centuries later as it watched the unmanned bomber plunging towards Gold Street. Next door to the church on the same side, as Phyllis had just pointed out, stood a two-storey wooden hostelry from which there hung a signboard that declared the place to be the Black Lyon Inne, although the animal depicted on the board looked more like a charred dog.

Only when John allowed his eyes to wander past the tavern, down the slope on which it stood and on towards the town's west bridge, was he presented with a view markedly different from the same scene in the twentieth century. The bridge itself, a wooden structure as opposed to the stone hump that would come later, had been pulled down and rebuilt a year or two ago on Cromwell's orders. It was now a massive drawbridge that had iron chains and winding mechanisms so that it could be pulled up if Royalists should attempt to cross the Nene. As the three young spooks stood and watched, a heavy-laden wagon creaked across its timbers and rolled on towards what looked to be a mill in the southwest while all the day bled from the sky above. As odd as this fortification seemed to modern eyes, however, it was instantly forgotten as the ghost-kids' gaze crept further right, until they overlooked the site on which the railway station would one day be raised. Both John and Phyllis were familiar with the spectacle, but Michael Warren gasped aloud.

"What wiz it? It black-blocks the sky out so I can't see the Victorious Park."

Phyll laughed and shook her head, so that the after-image of her swinging bangs transformed it briefly to that of a wilted dandelion.

"Victoria Park won't be there for abayt two 'undred years, and neither will the railway station. That's Northampton Castle, what they named the station after. Get a good look at it while yer can. It's been 'ere since eleven-'undred, by this bridge for 'alf a thousand years, and in another sixteen it'll be knocked down."

John nodded gravely as he took in the enormity of the dark pile before him, the oppressive bulk of its square towers, the corrugated and judgemental brow of its long, frowning battlements against the silver-lode of the horizon. Sprawling and immense, the brooding structure was encircled by the black scar of a moat, and on the plunging trench's far edge sputtering firebrands that appeared to be as tall as John himself were set to either side of the great gateway, a stone mouth with its portcullis teeth bared, clenched in agony or rage. A curdling mix of light and smoke dribbled up from the torches across high, rough walls where archery-slits squinted out untrustingly into a gathering dusk.

Upon the open land around the edifice's south side, at the margins of the dirt road that continued Gold Street and Marefair's line west past the converted bridge, a hundred or so men of the New Model Army were erecting ragged tents on the parched summer grass. Retrieving deadwood and dry bracken from the copses in Foot Meadow just across the river, the bedraggled troops were lighting campfires, chalk-white smudges flaring here and there about the castle's twilight flank, islands of faint cheer floated on an ocean of approaching night. Despite the muffle of the ghost-seam, on a frail westerly breeze John heard guffaws and curses, a lone fiddle tuning up, the firewood's damp spit or the crack of an exploding knot. Horses were whinnying their anxious lullabies, silenced and hidden by the campfires' drifting smoulder when the wind changed, just as it was changing through the length and breadth of England on this fraught and dangerous night.

Whispering as though awe-struck by the vista, or as though he thought that the foot soldiers shambling past along Marefair could hear him, Michael Warren looked from John to Phyllis as he spoke.

"Why dig they knock it drown?"

John grimaced.

"Well, you see, the battle out at Naseby that they're going to fight tomorrow morning, Cromwell and the Parliamentary army win the day. The Civil War limps on for several months, but after Naseby there wiz no chance of the Royalists coming out on top. Once Parliament has won, Cromwell starts calling all the shots. Within four years, in 1649, he'll have King Charles the First beheaded and turn England into a Republic that will last until his death in 1658. His son Richard succeeds him, but he abdicates within the year. By 1660, you'll have Charles the Second made king and the monarchy restored. This new King Charles will hate Northampton, so as soon as he's had everybody who conspired in his dad's downfall executed, he'll demand Northampton Castle be demolished."

Michael looked perplexed.

"Why wizzle he do that?"

Here Phyllis chimed in from where she was crouching on the toddler's other side.

"Just take a gander at that bloody drawbridge there, yer'll 'ave yer answer. This place wiz a Parliamentary strong'old in the Civil War, and we backed Cromwell all the way. I 'spect that Charles the Second blamed us for the way that we'd 'elped get 'is father's 'ead chopped orf, especially wi' Naseby bein' in this county. Come the restoration o' the monarchy and we wiz on the ayts with England, good an' proper."

John considered this, glancing behind them back up Marefair. Reggie, Bill and Marjorie were still creating pygmy dust-storms, to the consternation of the passers-by in these times where each natural phenomenon was looked on as an omen of unrest, as if omens were needed. Satisfied that their gang-mates weren't causing too much mischief, John turned his attention back to Phyllis and the infant.

"To be fair, Phyll, we were in this country's bad books long before the Restoration. We've been seen as troublemakers here for centuries, at least since all the rebel students during the twelve-hundreds who provoked Henry the Third to sack the place. Then from the thirteen-hundreds we had Lollards here, more or less preaching that ideas of sin were all made up by clergymen for keeping down the poor. During the Civil War this wiz a hotbed of extremists, Muggletonians, Moravians, Fifth Monarchists, Ranters and Quakers – and these weren't the Quakers who are pacifists and own all of the chocolate companies. These were fanatics calling for the overthrow of worldly kingdoms in God's name.

"And all these sects, although they had big differences, they all made much of how Jesus had been a carpenter and all of his apostles lowly working men. The way they saw it, Christianity wiz a religion of the poor and the downtrodden, and it promised that one day the rich and godless would be done away with. Ever since the early sixteen-hundreds, when the gentry were permitted to enclose what had been common land, the rich folk had been doing well, the 'middling sort' like Cromwell had been struggling to keep afloat, and the poor people had been starving. It wiz during these times that you first heard everybody saying how the rich got richer and the poor got poorer, and there wiz more people being turned to beggars every day. Around the century's mid-years, like we're in now, there would be tens of thousands of what they called masterless men roaming round the country, vagabonds and tinkers answering to no one. All it took wiz a bright spark like Cromwell to work out how all these angry paupers could be put to use."

John gestured to the scores of Roundhead soldiers who were trudging along Marefair, or sat baking spuds around their campfires on the grounds beside the hulking castle.

"I suppose one of the reasons why Northampton took to Cromwell wiz that the poor people here wiz as rebellious as you could find just about anywhere in England. This had been the first place to protest the land enclosures, with an uprising led by a chap called Captain Pouch. The uprising wiz quashed, of course, and Pouch wiz chopped to bits, but the resentments that would lead to civil war in fifty years wiz nowhere stronger than here in the Midlands. Now, I dare say a good many round here played along with Cromwell because they were frightened of him, but I bet there were a lot more who'd been praying for someone like him to come along. In 1643 there was a feller from Northamptonshire who'd said 'I hope within this year to see never a gentleman in England'. Around here we thought of Cromwell as, quite literally, a Godsend. It's no wonder that we got the job of kitting out his army with thousands of pairs of boots."

Here Michael Warren put in his two-penn'orth, just to show that he'd been following the conversation.

"Why wiz we so poor, then, if the people who made shoes had all that work?"

John was about to answer this surprisingly sharp question when a cackling Phyllis Painter beat him to it.

"Ha! That's because bloody Cromwell never paid us for the bloody boots! Once we'd 'elped get 'im into power 'e turned on us same as 'e turned on everybody else who'd been 'is mate when times were rough, the miserable old bugger. While we're on the subject, d'yer reckon 'e'll 'ave finished writin' to 'is missus yet? It don't look like there'll be a lot more gooin' on ayt 'ere, other than soldiers getting' sloshed and chasin' after 'ores. We should look in upon old Ironsides before we move on."

John nodded, glancing back along Marefair through a descended gloaming that still clinked with reins and scabbards, the gloom punctuated here and there by a dull pewter gleam from peaked round helmet or iron musketbarrel. On the dusty boards outside Hazelrigg House, Bill had enlisted Marjorie and Reggie's help in manufacturing an even bigger whirlwind than their previous attempts. The three of them were racing furiously in a solid ring of after-images around the knees of an unlucky and astonished broadsheet-seller. Wailing in confusion and religious terror, the poor fellow couldn't see the children and was only conscious of the sudden wind from nowhere, tearing pamphlets from his grasp and spinning them into the dark above him like outsized confetti. John was chuckling despite himself as he replied to Phyllis.

"Yeah, I reckon that you're right. We can leave your Bill and the others to their monkey business, since they look as if they're having fun."

Each taking one of Michael Warren's hands, Phyll and John led the foundling back towards Hazelrigg House amidst a fluttering rain of the dismayed street-vendor's tumbling tracts. Scanning a folded sheet already fallen to the floor, John noted that it was entitled *Prophecy of the White King* and seemingly foretold a violent end for Charles the First, based on astrology and various prophecies attributed to Merlin. Given that the leaflet bore tomorrow's date and was apparently fresh off the printing press, John smiled and gave the publisher ten out of ten for timing, even if the source of his predictions seemed a little flimsy. Out of habit, John made an attempt to kick the pamphlet to one side, feeling like a buffoon as his foot passed straight through it ineffectually and he remembered he was dead. He only hoped that Phyllis hadn't noticed.

As luck had it, Phyllis was at that moment distracted by a rather pretty living man who was approaching the front door of Hazelrigg House just ahead of them. His long hair, girlish to John's way of thinking, fell in curling waves around the high white collar that he wore above black armour, plated on the arms and shoulders so that it resembled a fantastic beetle carapace. A sheathed sword swung at his left hip. The gallant's face, its plumpness offset by a well-trimmed beard and a moustache, was one that John felt he had seen before, perhaps in combat out at Naseby, though a name refused to come to him.

John watched as the chap rapped on the stout wood door and was immediately bidden enter. Not wishing to miss the introductions, John yanked Phyll and Michael through the thick stone wall into the inner chamber, where he noticed that three tallow candles in a branching holder had been lit during their absence. There was something feverish about the tilting shadows as they lurched across the bare white plaster walls and lunged at the complaining black beams that held up the ceiling. Cromwell was still seated where they'd left him on the far side of the table, closing the front cover of his journal now and looking up without expression as the young man entered.

An approximation of a smile twitched briefly into being upon Cromwell's lips and then was gone. Not rising to his feet to meet the newcomer as John might have expected, the new Parliamentary lieutenant-general spoke only the man's name by way of greeting.

"Henry. It does my heart good to see thee."

Henry Ireton. With only a little prompting John had placed the long-haired chap, whom he remembered that he had indeed seen previously, or to be more exact would see tomorrow morning, getting wounded and then captured as he led his regiment up the left flank at Naseby Field. The young man nodded courteously to the still-seated Cromwell.

"As it does mine own to see thee, Master Cromwell. My congratulations upon your appointment as lieutenant-general of horse. I was myself promoted as a commissary-general not a week since. It seems that a man may of a sudden rise or fall amidst the boiling waters of our present conflict."

Ireton's voice was light, at least contrasted with that of the older man, who clasped his hands together on the table and sat back a little in his chair as he responded.

"By God's grace, lad. Only by His grace are we raised up, as by His grace shall our opponent be cast down upon the morrow. Praise be, Henry. Praise be unto God."

In John's opinion Ireton looked a bit uneasy here, even as he was nodding in agreement with the seated general's ardent proclamation.

"Yes. Yes, of course. Praise be to God. Do you believe that we shall have the day? The prince may be spurred on by his late victory in Leicester ..."

Cromwell waved one fleshy hand dismissively, then laced its fingers with the other, resting on the polished tabletop before him.

"I do not believe that we shall have the day, but rather know it in my bones.

It is my destiny that I should win, just as it is King Charlie's destiny that he should fail. I know it just as surely as I know that Christ hath promised our salvation, as He hath so done with all of His elect. I must ask thee how thou dost doubt God's providence, that levelleth the cities of the plain, and bringeth plague upon the house of Pharaoh?"

Looking over-warm inside his armour on this summer evening, Ireton tugged at his starched collar as though in a vain attempt to make it looser. Even though the younger man ranked only slightly beneath Cromwell, John could see the deference and nervousness in Ireton's manner as he struggled for a suitable rejoinder. Phyllis, John and Michael went and squatted on the lower steps of a contorted spiral staircase over in one corner of the room, the better to observe this somehow threatening and yet compelling interview. At last, the bearded man risked a reply.

"Think not that I do doubt the Lord, but only that mine confidence in such predestinations be less sturdy than thine own. Is there not risk that we may be complacent in assurances of our salvation, and in this way be made negligent in our pursuit of faith?"

Now, for the first time, Cromwell curled his meaty lips into a smile that showed his grey teeth and was genuinely dreadful to behold. The midnight marbles of his eyes glittered beneath half-lowered lids.

"Dost thou think me some Antinomian heretic, that sins, and lazes in the sun, secure in his belief that he be saved, no matter whatsoe'er that he be wicked? Though I be convinced that all the times to come are surely writ already, nor do I shirk from my part in bringing them to be. Oh, trust in God by all means, Henry. Trust in God, but do not fail to keep thy powder dry."

Here Cromwell laughed, a startling bark that rumbled gradually off to nothing, like a thunderclap. Ireton, who'd started visibly at the laugh's onset, seemed now to be reassured by his superior's good humour. Smiling forcedly at Cromwell's oft-repeated joke, Ireton apparently thought it appropriate to venture a restrained jibe of his own.

"Good Master Cromwell, truly do I know thou to be neither Antinomian nor heretic of any stripe. 'Tis but the Ranters, that cry out thy praises in the marketplace, who would make their foretold salvation to a license for debauch."

As quickly as they'd been dispelled, the dark clouds rolled back in across Cromwell's broad features. Over on the last step of the spiral staircase, looking in unseen on the exchange, both Michael Warren and Phyll Painter shivered in spontaneous unison.

"Do not concern thyself with Ranters, Henry. When our war is won, then where will be the need for Ranters or their fiery, flying rolls?"

Ireton looked unconvinced.

"Are you so certain of tomorrow's victory?"

The older man's face was as still as a carved sphinx.

"Oh, yes. Our men have not been paid for some few weeks. Their bellies grumble, but I have assured them that a win tomorrow will provide a sizeable exchequer from which we may swiftly make remunerations. I have fashioned of myself a sword for God to wield. He shall not be gainsaid. Naseby shall do the trick, thou may be certain, and then afterwards I shall, that is, *we* shall determine what is to be done about such dross as Ranters, Levellers or Diggers."

Frowning disconcertedly and narrowing his eyes, Ireton appeared mildly alarmed.

"Surely you would not see such men suppressed, that have fought bravely for our cause? Would it not shame us to take rights from those who campaign only that the rights bestowed by Magna Carta be upheld?"

Here Cromwell laughed again, this time a throaty chuckle that was less loud and less disconcerting than his previous outburst.

"Magna Farta, it might with more truth be called. Why, old King John was under siege some six weeks at the castle down the way before he could be made to sign it. Such conventions are by force of arms alone brought into being, and by force of arms may be revoked, and we shall see what we shall see."

The senior general's head, a trundling cannonball, rolled round upon his neck until his leaden eyes were fixed directly upon John. The lanky ghost-boy shrank against the curving staircase wall, convinced for just a second that Cromwell was looking at him before realising that the seated man was merely staring into empty space as he reflected.

"We are come upon a fateful place, which hath oft-times served as a pivot for the swivellings of history. The fortress stood at this hill's foot was where the sainted Thomas Becket was most treacherously brought to trial for doing God's will rather than a king's. Holy crusades were raised up thereabouts, as likewise were our earliest Parliaments. Not half a mile off to the south is the cow-meadow where Henry the Sixth was beaten by the Earl of March in an affray that ended the War of the Roses. Be assured this town, this soil, it hath the matter's heart within it, and it looks not kindly upon kings and tyrants. If I listen, Ireton, up above the hollow sound that the wind maketh in the chimney-tops, I fancy me to hear the grinding and annihilating mills of God."

From his position halfway up the spiral stairs John thought that he could hear them too, but then decided that the sound was more probably that of a big cannon being wheeled along in darkness through the quagmire of Mare-fair outside. Considering what Cromwell had just said, John found himself reminded of the only line from John Bunyan's *The Holy War* that had lodged in his memory: "Mansoul it was the very seat of war." The words rang true, whatever sense you took them in. Northampton, in all its obscurity, was birthplace to an inexplicable amount of conflict and the point of culmination for a great deal more. Crusades, Peasant's Revolt, War of the Roses and the Civil War, all of them had begun or ended here. If, on the other hand, you took the word 'Mansoul' to mean just what it said, to be the soul of man, then that too was a source of warfare, be it Cromwell's fierce Protestant zeal or the religion to which the exploding martyr on the Mayorhold's higher landings had belonged. Mansoul it was the very seat of war, no doubt about it. That had been the message behind every quick march and about turn in that chilly upper hall at College Street, when John was in the Boy's Brigade.

The memorable quote caused him to spare a thought now for the other John, John Bunyan, and to idly wonder what the seventeen-year-old author-to-be was doing upon that momentous night. As a young Roundhead soldier he might be commencing a first watch there in the garrison at Newport Pagnell, where Bunyan was stationed during 1645. Perhaps he smoked a pipe there in his watch-post and gazed up at the abundant stars, trying to read in them some sign that Christ would be returning soon to overturn King Charles and all his kind, then to announce a new Jerusalem here in the English heartlands. To declare a nation of elected saints amongst which both John Bunyan and the figure sitting now across the candlelit expanse believed themselves to be included.

Breaking off from his grim reverie, Cromwell looked up at Ireton.

"Tell me, Henry, do your men find themselves billets near these parts? At first light I must hurry to inspect the ground at Naseby, and wouldst soon be in my bed." Realising that he'd been dismissed, Ireton appeared almost relieved.

"My regiment and I have quarters but a short way off, and will be ready with the dawn. I would not keep you from your rest, yet only ask, Sir, that you should convey my most sincere endearments to your daughter."

John belatedly recalled that Ireton had eventually become son-in-law to the other man by marrying his eldest daughter, Bridget. Cromwell chuckled almost warmly, scraping back his chair as he stood up.

"Pray do not Sir me, Henry. Sooner would I have thee call me father, for so it shall be in time. I have just now been at a writing of a letter to my home, and when I copy it in fair I shall be glad to pass to Bridget your affections. But enough of such things. Get thee to thy regiment and to thy bed, and in the morn may God be with thee."

Stepping from behind the table, Cromwell crossed to Ireton, reaching out to shake the young man stiffly by the hand. Ireton blinked rapidly and swallowed as he answered.

"And with thee, good Master Cromwell. I shall bid thee a good night."

With that the interview appeared to be concluded. Cromwell opened the front door for Ireton, who stepped back into the darkness of Marefair and was immediately gone from sight. His guest having departed, the lieutenant-general sighed and walked towards the spiral staircase in the corner, picking up the flickering candelabra on his way. Kicking unwittingly through the three ghost-kids that were sitting there, he mounted the steps wearily, presumably towards his bedroom on the building's upper floor. Exchanging glances, Phyll and John drifted like vapour up the stairway after him, towing the tiny shade of Michael Warren in between them. Clearly, both of them were eager to learn how the future regicide and Lord Protector slept upon the eve of his most famous battle.

John, though, was still thinking about Henry Ireton. Although he was fated to receive a pike-wound and be captured by the Royalists tomorrow morning, Ireton's captors would release him in the later stages of the battle, fearing for their own lives as the Parliamentary forces moved in for the kill. He would go on to marry Bridget Williams-alias-Cromwell, shackling himself inseparably to the Cromwell family and their fortunes for the rest of his short life. By 1651 Ireton would be stationed in Ireland trying to end the Catholic rebellion by laying siege to Limerick, a rebel stronghold, where he would succumb to plague. His death, however, would not spare him Royal retribution nine years later when King Charles the Second was restored as monarch. Shortly before pulling down Northampton Castle the new king would have the bodies of both Ireton and his father-in-law dug from their Westminster Abbey tombs and dragged through London's streets to Tyburn, where the pair would be somewhat unnecessarily hung, drawn and quartered. As with many wars, holy or otherwise, in John's opinion neither side had much to recommend them when it came to manners.

Phyllis, John and Michael were now on the upstairs landing at Hazelrigg House, pursuing Cromwell as he slouched with candelabra in one hand towards his bedchamber. The hulking hunchbacked shadow that crept after him reminded John of the frontispiece illustration in his childhood copy of *The Pilgrim's Progress*. It had been a funny-looking picture, not at all realistic in the style that John preferred although if he remembered rightly it had been a painting done by William Blake, who was quite famous and respected even though to John's eye he drew like a baby. The wash reproduction had shown Bunyan's Christian with his weighty moral burden strapped onto his back, bent double over the beloved book that he was reading as he trudged along. This was the shape that sidled after Cromwell now along the landing, a devout giant trailing in the future Lord Protector's wake much as the massed horde of poor, godly English people did. Or, it occurred to John, was that pious and down-at-heel shadow-colossus driving Cromwell on before it and not following him after all? Whose will was truly being done in England during this tumultuous and bloody decade? Who was using who?

Cromwell turned from the passageway and through the open door of a room on the children's right, closing it after him. Following his example John and Phyllis poured into the portal's timbers in pursuit, with Michael Warren dragged between the duo and grey chorus-lines of after-pictures shimmering behind them.

The bedchamber turned out to be overlooking Marefair through the diamond grid of the tall windows on the room's far side. Out through the criss-crossed panes John could see pale forms fluttering through the night, strange nightingales accompanied by streams of stop-motion photography and ringing peals of mirth. Only when he'd observed that one of the unusually aerobatic creatures wore a pair of National Health glasses did John realise that Reggie, Marjorie and Bill had got fed up of raising dust-storms and had taken to the air, swooping above the street and shrieking as they played at being proper spectres of the sort you found in horror-stories. John thought that they showed a shocking lack of discipline but probably weren't doing any harm, and so turned his attentions to the hefty wooden bed, like something from Hans Christian Andersen, which was the chamber's centrepiece.

Cromwell sat on its edge, wearily pulling off his boots. Beside the closed door, set out on or near a wooden trunk, John noticed the black-painted armour, pretty much identical to Ireton's, which Cromwell would wear tomorrow morning. Cromwell's suit would do a better job protecting him than Ireton's would, though, John reflected. Unlike Ireton with an ugly pike-wound to his shoulder, his father-in-law to be would come through Naseby and emerge unscathed, no more than winded while defeated cavaliers were being rounded up, or while Fairfax's men were raping and disfiguring the women in a captured Royalist wagon-train. John had seen, or would see, some of that for himself after tomorrow's battle. He remembered that it had been this climactic scene of cruelty, ears cut off and noses slit, that had forced him to tunnel back to his own time on that first visit to the battle, some while prior to meeting the Dead Dead Gang. Of the horrors John had witnessed, both in 1640s Naseby and in 1940s France, the mutilation of the Royalist women, wives and sweethearts labelled "whores and camp-sluts" of "that wicked army", had been easily the most unbearable. For God's sake, they were women.

Cromwell had by now removed all of his clothes, briefly exhibiting a saddle-callused arse before he pulled on the long nightgown that had been left folded up on his top blanket. Kneeling, the lieutenant-general of horse pulled a stone chamber-pot from underneath the bed and piddled into it, at the same moment letting off a lengthy trombone-tuner of a fart that reduced Michael, Phyllis and eventually even John to helpless laughter. When he'd finished urinating and returned the heavy Jeremiah to its hiding place in the below-bed shadows, Cromwell remained kneeling with hands pressed together and eyes closed as he recited the Lord's Prayer. With this completed, he stood up and pinched off the three flames that flickered from his candelabra where it rested upon a plain chest-of-drawers beside the window. In the darkness outside the three corresponding starbursts of reflected brightness winked out one by one, leaving the night to Reggie, Bill and Marjorie whom John could still hear giggling as they sailed through the black heavens over Marefair. Grunting as though with discomfort from stiff joints, Cromwell walked back across the room and climbed beneath the bedclothes. After a surprisingly few moments' grumbling and turning he appeared to fall asleep, apparently not troubled in the least by all the slaughter that awaited him come daybreak.

"Well. I 'spect that's that, then."

Phyllis sounded disappointed, and John was forced to admit that he felt the same way. He felt let down, although he didn't know what he had been expecting. Doubts and tears, perhaps, or evil gloating like a fiend from the Saturday morning pictures down the Gaumont; manic cackling to scare the nippers at the flicks, the tuppenny rush?

As Cromwell snored contentedly, John drifted over to the window so that he could see what capers their three gang-mates had been getting up to. Squinting upwards through the lead-striped glass he saw them swinging back and forth on the night breezes high above the street. They'd evidently startled pigeons from their roosts in Marefair's eaves and were now chasing the bewildered fowl against a cream three-quarter moon and its corona, cast upon the summer haze. John called Phyllis and Michael over from where they were standing by the bed, amusing themselves by inserting ghostly fingers into the black, gaping nostrils of its sleeping occupant.

"Here, leave his nose alone and come and see what your kid and the other silly beggars have been doing while we've been in here."

The ghost-gang's leader and her little charge did as John had suggested. Soon they stood beside him, pointing upwards through the patterned panes and making comments in alternate glee and disapproval as their wayward colleagues herded baffled birds amongst the moonbeams, far above Northampton. Entertaining themselves in this fashion, the three children were engrossed to the extent that for a moment they forgot completely where they were. The deep voice sounding from the dark behind them, then, came as that much more of a shock.

"Who are you, and what is your business?"

Michael screamed and grabbed John's hand. The phantom children wheeled about in startlement to find a sour-faced boy of something like eleven years of age standing there nude beside the bed, in which Cromwell still snored, and glowering at them through the shadows. The lad was afflicted by the most terrible haircut John had ever seen, shaved to grey stubble high up at the back, the bristles ending where a basin cut began. The boy's dark hair looked like a toadstool with his spotty, luminously pallid face and neck providing the black deathcap with its soapy and translucent stem. John's mind raced as he tried to work out just what they were seeing, and a sidelong glance at Phyll confirmed that she was in the same boat. Michael simply stood there, lids peeled back as if attempting to expel both eyeballs from their sockets by sheer force of will.

"I ask again your business in my farmer's house. Be quick to tell me, and not in a frightful way!"

It was a man's voice, John thought, coming from a boy barely in puberty to judge from the one isolated hair on a pudenda otherwise entirely bare. Something about the way the figure framed its sentences, the way that it said "farmer's house" but sounded as if it meant "father's house", suggested someone newly dead who hadn't found their Lucy-lips yet. On the other hand, the nervous movements that the lad made weren't attended by the usual visual echoes, which suggested that he was alive. On yet a third hand, he could see them, when in normal circumstances he would not be able to unless he was deceased.

Or dreaming.

Everything fell into place. John placed the adult tones at the same moment that he noticed the beginnings of a wart between the boy's chin and his lower lip. Turning towards the still-bewildered Phyllis, John permitted himself a smug chuckle.

"It's all right. I've worked out who it wiz."

He looked back at the naked waif standing beside the bed.

"It's all right, Oliver. It's only us. You recognise us, don't you?"

Now it was the youth's turn to seem puzzled. Blinking rapidly he looked from John, to Michael, then to Phyllis, trying to remember where he knew them from, if anywhere.

Cromwell was dreaming. He was dreaming himself in the form he'd had when he was small and vulnerable yet kept the deep voice of an older and more armoured self, perhaps because it had become like second nature and was thus not easily abandoned. John had no idea where the lieutenant-general believed himself to be, or what his dreaming mind thought it was seeing. He just knew that dreamers were suggestible, and if you told them something they'd accept it and would work it in amongst the fabric of their dream as best they could. The younger Cromwell squinted at them now, as if he'd made his mind up.

"Yes. I see you now. You are my little ones, Richard and Henry and dear, pretty Frances. You must not annoy your father now, when he has much to do upon the morrow. Be about your catchy schisms!"

John decided that the last bit was most probably intended to be "catechisms". Evidently, Cromwell now believed they were his children, even though he dreamed himself as too young to have fathered them. Such was the logic that sufficed in dreams. John was intrigued by the bare youngster's comment about having much to do tomorrow, though. Was this some dim awareness of the coming battle that had lingered in the general's sleeping mind? He thought that he'd investigate a little further.

"Father, we've already said our prayers, don't you remember? Tell us what you're going to do tomorrow morning."

The boy nodded gravely, agitating the black mushroom of his brutal haircut.

"I'm going to fight Pope Charles the First, and if I win then I shall make them take his hat off. I shall bring it to your mother, with blood on its feathers, so that she may set it on our mantelpiece above the fire."

Phyllis was snickering. Wondering why, John glanced down at the fledgling Cromwell's groin and realised that the boy's knob had gone on the bone, was pointing to the timbers of the bedroom ceiling with its owner unaware. It made John feel uncomfortable, especially with Phyllis being there. The unfulfilled first blush of love that existed between Phyll and him was harder to believe in with even a crayon-sized erection in the room. He made an effort to divert young Cromwell's dreaming mind to territory that would hopefully prove less arousing.

"Father, what about when you have won your fight? What then?"

Initially, this line of questioning did not appear to have deflated the youth's errant member, and indeed seemed to have made things rather worse. Grey eyes alight with visions of his future glory, Cromwell was apparently becoming more excited by the moment. His gaze glittering with firebrands, fixed on some unguessable horizon, the boy smiled, voice soft with awe at his own majesty as he replied.

"Why, then I shall be Pope instead."

The stripling's wonderstruck expression of self-satisfaction lasted only a short while before the chilly shadow from a cloud of doubt was cast across it. The young Lord Protector suddenly looked frightened, and John was relieved to see that his tumescence was subsiding. When the naked child began to speak again the adult voice was gone, with in its place the tremulous and reedy piping of a scared eleven-year-old boy.

"But if I am become a Pope, shall not God hate me? And the pauple, the poor people that have followed me shall hate me also if I dress in purple. They will find me out and hate me. They will take away my hat from off my shoulders. You must help me! You must tell them that your father was a child, a child like you who did not know what he was doing. You must ..."

Here the boy trailed off, and something of his older self's grey steel once more entered his eyes. The voice was now again the rough growl of a grown-up.

"You are not my children."

Pimply face contorting to a mask of rancour, the bare body started fading in and out of view like something on a television set with faltering reception. Both the picture and the sound seemed to be going at the same time, so that anything the boy said was now punctuated by transmission gaps. Meanwhile the slumbering form upon the bed, a dark mass only visible to the three children's tinsel-trimmed night vision, started mumbling in an eerie counterpoint to the dream-Cromwell's flickering and interrupted speech.

"... fatherless bastards of a low kind, skulking ... half the whores in Newport Pagnell say it was the Holy Ghost who put it in them! Get thee ... or must I be pinn'd like a soot-coloured moth to history and ever ... Father? Leave me be! I have not ... faeries. They are devils, ghosts or faeries and they look upon my ..."

Phyllis nudged John, leaning over Michael as he stood between them.

"'E looks like 'e's wakin' up. Come on, let's goo aytside and see what them daft sods are gettin' up to, 'fore ayr Bill does summat as 'e shouldn't."

Still with Michael dangling between them, John and Phyll turned from the intermittent spectre of the dream-youth and jumped through the front wall of Hazelrigg House, passing through stonework which, in 1645, had been in place less than a decade. Showering down upon the boggy street in a grey snapshot waterfall, the children dusted themselves off then peered into the dark for some sign of the gang's remaining members.

John spotted them first, still scaring pigeons in the upper reaches of a night sky like blackcurrant cordial, darkness thick and settled at the bottom but diluting in the moonlight higher up. He could see trails of after-images dragged back and forth across the milky firmament like grubby woollen football scarves, and could deduce their pigeon-worrying from the abrupt and unexpected rain of bird-shit, spattering in Marefair's mud from high above. In John's opinion, having a bird do its business on your head was even worse for ghosts than it was for the living. Granted, you were spared the fuss of having to wash the repulsive stuff out of your hair and clothes, but on the other hand the droppings fell straight through you and you sort-of felt them, plunging through your skull into your neck, splashing on down to exit through your shoe-soles as a radiating splat of black and white. It came to John that pigeon-shit looked no worse in the ghost-seam's half-tones than it did in mortal life's full Technicolor. It was one of those things like remorse or unfulfilment that would still get on your nerves when you were dead.

Phyllis, who'd suffered from the aerial bombardment just as much as John had, lost her temper and announced that she was "gunna adda goo up there and sort 'em ayt". Making a little hop to get her started, she commenced to swim laboriously up through the seam's thicker and more buoyant air, doing a variation of the breast-stroke. Only after half a minute, when she was perhaps ten feet above them, did John realise that both he and Michael were intently staring up her frock. He thought that he'd strike up a conversation in an effort to divert them both into something more suitable.

"How do you like the Dead Dead Gang, then, nipper, now you've had a chance to get to know us? I'll tell you for nothing, it's a lot more fun than being in the army."

All around them, Marefair was surrendering to blackness. A few couples wandered to and fro between the alley-mouths of Pike or Chalk Lane and the still-lit doors of the Black Lion, soldiers stumbling arm in arm with chortling, whispering women, pressed so close together that they looked like pairs in a licentious, drunk three-legged race. Strewn on the castle's flank downhill the campfires had all burned down to a sullen glow, and other than the lustful mumblings of the stragglers the only other sound was that of bats, needle-sharp voices threaded round the steeple of St. Peter's Church. Michael looked up at John from where he stood beside him, his blonde ringlets multiplying with the motion so that he looked for a moment like a tidier Struwwelpeter or a bleached-out gollywog.

"I like it ever such a lot. I like the clambering about in different days, and I think everybody's nice, especially Phyllis. But I miss my mum and dad and gran and sister and I'd like it if I wiz back with them soon."

John nodded.

"Well, that's understandable. I bet your family are real good sorts, or at least if your dad wiz anything to go by. What you should remember, though, wiz that all these adventures what you're having here are happening in no time at all. Up in the living world you're only dead for a few minutes, if what everybody's saying wiz to be believed. Looked at like that, before you know it you'll be with your parents and this wizzle be forgotten, just as if it hadn't happened. I'd enjoy it while you can, if I wiz you. Besides, I've got an interest in your family and I'm getting quite attached to having you about."

Michael looked thoughtful, narrowing his eyes as he gazed at the older boy.

"Wiz it because you knew my dad and used to play with him?"

John chuckled, reaching out with four or five left arms to scuff up Michael's hair.

"Yes, I suppose it's something like that. I knew all your dad's side of family, back when I wiz alive. How's old May getting on, your dad's mum? Wiz she still a terror? What about your aunt Lou?"

He still wasn't sure why he was keeping the full story back from Michael, when it wasn't really in John's nature to be secretive. He'd wondered, when he'd first heard Michael's surname, if it might be the same Warren family that he knew, but there'd been no point in mentioning that at the time in case he was mistaken. Then, when it had been confirmed, he'd quite enjoyed having a piece of secret information for himself, something than even Phyllis didn't know about – although that wasn't the whole picture, if he was completely honest. What it was, he didn't want to burden Michael with the truth of who he was or their relationship. He didn't want the boy or any of his family to hear first-hand the facts about how John had died in France, how scared he'd been, how he'd been trying to work up the courage to desert when they'd come under fire upon that country road. That was the real reason he'd spent all those years haunting a disused turret after he was dead, rather than going straight up to Mansoul. He'd had a guilty conscience, just as much as Mick Malone or Mary Jane or any of the area's rough sleepers did, because both John and God knew that John was at heart a coward. Better, surely, to let all that rest. Better to keep up his white lie, best to allow the tot who now stood pondering beside him to retain his blissful ignorance of how the world could sometimes be, even in how it treated little boys who came from decent, working families. Michael was still considering John's questions before venturing his answers.

"Well, I like my nan, but sometimes she gets a bit frightening and I have dreams about her where she's trying to catch me. Aunt Lou's like a lovely owl, and when she used to pick me up she'd chortle to me and I'd feel it running through her when she held me. Nan wiz nice, though. If we go round her house she gives me and Alma each an apple and a sweetie from her jar that's on the sideboard."

In the moonlit reaches far above them John could make out a grey comet with a tail of fading photographs that he thought was most likely Phyllis, herding a disgraced triumvirate of similarly pluming spectres back towards the Earth. It looked as if the ghostly kids were playing join-the-dots between the stars. He smiled at Michael.

"No, she's not a bad sort, May. I know there's times when she can put the fear of God in you, but she's had a hard life that's made her that way, ever since she first popped out into the gutter down on Lambeth Walk. You shouldn't judge her harshly."

The four other members of the Dead Dead Gang had by this time floated down far enough to be in hailing distance. John could hear Phyllis regaling Bill as they descended.

"… and if you chase pigeons, the Third Borough knows abayt it! You'll be lucky if 'e don't turn you into a pigeon and then make a pigeon pie out of yer!"

Bill, doing an ostentatious butterfly stroke through the air with after-image arms like spinning wagon-wheels grown from his shoulders, clearly wasn't taking any notice. A broad smirk kept threatening to break out and spoil the usually-ginger troublemaker's penitent expression. Before long Phyllis had guided the three truants in to land and then had settled down upon Marefair herself, an ashen dandelion clock or man-in-the-moon as John had always called them, spilling picture-parasols up into the night sky behind her.

After Phyllis had conducted a brief show-trial for the trio of miscreants and issued what she must have felt were necessary recriminations, the gang had a vote on what route they should take back to the nineteen-hundreds. The resultant show of hands – something like fifty if you counted all the after-images – appeared to be unanimous in favouring a somewhat indirect approach commencing at the Black Lyon Inne a little further down the way. The sole abstention in the crowd was Michael Warren who, as regimental mascot, didn't really get a ballot anyway. John sympathised with Michael in his simply wanting to go home, but it was true enough what he'd said earlier about these exploits taking up no time at all, back in the mortal world that Michael all too soon would be returned to. John had also meant what he'd said about having become quite fond of the nipper, and he didn't want him going back to life and thus forgetting all of this just yet.

The gang moved down Marefair towards the castle, on the slopes of which the soldiers' campfires were all now extinguished. On their left they passed by the bat-sanctuary of St. Peter's Church, where the dog-whistle squeals pierced even the soundproofing of the ghost-seam. In the shadows of the gateway John could make out the slumped shape of the lame beggar-woman's ghost that he'd met on his first posthumous visit to the church, but didn't call the other kids' attention to her. Motionless and silent she watched them pass by, her luminous eyes hanging in the dark, disinterested.

The Black Lion, when the children reached it, still seemed to be serving even though its front door had been closed up. Passing through this, John found himself in a pub that was disturbingly familiar in its basic layout while the people and the pastimes it contained were wildly different. Bleary Roundheads sat and drank a treacly-looking beer as they attempted to forget that this might very well be their last night on Earth, while others who had women on their laps were working their scarred fingers back and forth beneath flounced layers of underskirt. The room, split level as in John's day with three stairs connecting the two tiers, was made almost entirely out of wood. The only metal seemed to be that of the burnished oil-lamps or the heavy tankards, if you didn't count the swords and helmets that were in the place at present, and save for the windows there was no glass to be seen. The lone quartet of bottles that presumably had spirits in, standing upon an otherwise unoccupied shelf at the bar's rear, were all made of stone. John was surprised how much the lack of glinting highlights in a hanging blur altered the feeling of the pub, and there were other things that made an unexpected difference, too.

One of the tables had been set aside for food, a bowl of perished fruit, wedges of cheese and a half-eaten loaf, onions and mustard and a ham that had been sliced down to its stump-end, hovered over by a troupe of pearly-bellied meat-flies. Two or three dogs snuffled round the legs of chairs and the whole sound of the inn seemed subdued to John, even allowing for the way the ghost-seam muffled things. Such chatter as there was, including that between the troopers and their girlfriends, sounded hushed and reverent to modern ears. Apart from an occasional loud clump of boots across the floorboards as somebody went to use the privy in the pub yard, or a faint snort from one of the horses stabled there, then lacking the familiar chink of glass on glass there was no noise at all. It wasn't even modern silence, having no thud of a ticking clock to underline it.

Bill and Reggie seemed intrigued by all the unselfconscious groping that was taking place up in the tavern's darkened corners, but John didn't like it and was pleased to see that Phyllis didn't either. With a military briskness that concealed their mutual embarrassment they organised the gang into another human tower, this time with Reggie on the bottom and Bill standing on his shoulders, scraping with both hands in the accumulated time of the inn's ceiling. Being upwards of three hundred years, the excavation was quite clearly going to take a while, leaving John, Michael and the two girls with no other option than to stand there awkwardly amidst the almost-mute debauchery, trying to find something that wasn't sexual to stare at.

As his gaze shifted uneasily around the half-lit room, John realised with surprise that he and his five comrades weren't the only phantoms frequenting the Black Lyon Inne on that specific evening. On a long and pew-like wooden seat against one wall there sat one of the Roundhead troops, a freckled nineteen-year-old boy who had no chin to speak of, with a hard-faced woman in her thirties grunting softly as she sat astride his lap, her back against his belly. Her long skirts had been arranged in a desultory attempt to hide the obvious fact that the lad had his implement inside her as she surreptitiously moved up and down, trying to make it look like rhythmic fidgeting.

To each side of this not-so-furtive copulating couple sat a pair of middle-aged men in long robes, one chubby and one thin, whom John at first assumed to be the lovers' friends. Granted, he'd thought the friendship seemed unusually close if it permitted their acquaintances to be spectators on such intimate occasions, but then what did he know of the actual moral climate of the sixteen-hundreds, where it was apparently acceptable to have sex in a public bar? Only when one of the two men lifted a fan of several arms to scratch his

eyebrow did John realise that they were both ghosts, peeping-tom spirits that
the whore and soldier didn't know were there. Looking a little closer, John
could make out that the voyeuristic duo were some type of monks, perhaps
the Cluniacs who'd had their monastery a little north of here, three or four
hundred years ago. Each one sat with hands folded piously and resting in his
lap, not hiding the tent-poles that they were putting up under their habits as
they watched the panting trooper and his wanton with wide-eyed attention.
So absorbed were the two friars that they evidently hadn't noticed there were
other ghosts, children at that, just feet away across the room, John thought
indignantly.

All of a sudden, though, the tableau shifted from merely unpleasant to
unspeakably grotesque. One of the spectral monks – the tubby one who sat
upon John's far side of the pair – removed a plump hand from his own lap
and, before John could work out what he was up to, swept it in a stream of
after-images to plunge it through the apron of the mounted woman, thrusting
his arm to the elbow in her labouring body, all while she remained completely
unaware. From the lewd grin that bulged the friar's ample cheeks and from
the sudden increase in both gasps and agitated thrusts between the lovebirds,
it appeared as if the monk had his whole fleshy hand inside the woman's lower
abdomen, grasping the soldier's ... John felt a bit sick and looked away. He'd
never seen a dead man do a thing like that before, had not even imagined it.
Ah, well. You died and learned.

Luckily, no one else seemed to have noticed the repulsive spectacle, and it
was just then that Bill gleefully declared his tunnel up into the twentieth century to be completed. Phyllis was the first to scramble up the ladder formed by
Bill and Reggie, disappearing into the pale gap with twinkling edges dug into
the plaster ceiling, in between the kippered beams. Next Michael made the
climb, multiple photographs extending his short dressing gown into a tartan
bridal train as he ascended. Marjorie went after Michael, followed rapidly by
Bill, leaving first Reggie and then John to leap up through the time-hole from
a standing jump, buoyed by the ghost-seam's viscous atmosphere.

Only when John had rocketed up through the aperture to find himself
in a synthetic habitat where everything had rounded edges, in which Phyllis
was haranguing Bill with more than usual vigour, did he realise there was
something wrong. This wasn't 1959. The room that they were in looked sparse
and sterile, like a kitchen in a super-modern hospital with a steel sink, some
kind of sleek and complicated cooker and two or three other hefty metal
boxes that had dials, the functions of which John was unfamiliar with. Next
to the doorway stood a dozen plastic canisters of bleach, designed to look like
bath-toy buzz-bombs with unscrewing nose-cones, held together in a cube

formation by a skin of laddered polythene that seemed to have been sprayed on. In a cardboard box beneath the chamber's solitary rain-streaked window were what looked like Toyland hypodermic needles, flimsy little items each in its own individual see-through bag. Looking more closely, John saw that there were numerous cartons packed with bottled pills stacked up haphazardly wherever there was space, along with sacks of bulk-bought oats and rice, multiply-packaged tins of baby-food and an incongruous assortment of other mass-purchased medical or culinary supplies. Posters tacked to a sheet of pasteboard on one wall bore names and slogans that were utterly incomprehensible to John: ST. PETER'S ANNEXE; NO GRAZING, NO SLIM; NOISE KILLS; BLINDER AND TASER AMNESTY; DON'T LET C-DIF BECOME C-IMP; SEX TRAUMA INDICATORS; CONFLICT TRAUMA INDICATORS; SPOT A SPARROW; TENANTS AGAINST TREACHERY ... where on earth were they? John was going to ask Phyllis but before he could she turned to him with an exasperated look and answered anyway.

"'E's dug us up too 'igh, the little sod. We're in the twenty-fives, up in St. Peter's Annexe. Look at all that bloody rain!"

John glanced out of the window onto what he thought must be Black Lion Hill, although the view was unfamiliar. Marefair was unrecognisable, paved with a parquet of pale tiling where the cobbled and then tarmac-covered road had been. Through the torrential sheets of downpour he could see a glass-walled overpass that arced above the mouth of a much-changed St. Andrew's Road, connecting the extended sprawl of Castle Station with the raised ground near the bottom of Chalk Lane, right where John's long-demolished turret had once been. Here there were bulging Marmite-pot constructions with designs that seemed to have resulted from a joke or dare, across the lane from older, plainer structures with which they contrasted jarringly. The self-consciously futuristic bridge, a length of transparent intestine ravelling across the scene from west to east, looked like a tawdry, worldly apprehension of the Ultraduct to John, an earthly copy of the sweeping immaterial span that reached from Doddridge Church. Beneath the bridge peculiar traffic hissed amidst the deluge, back and forth along St. Andrew's Road, none of it venturing up into Marefair which appeared now to be only for pedestrians. Most of the flow of vehicles was made up of the brick-shaped cars that John had seen during the ghost-gang's recent foray into nothing-five or nothing-six, but there were also a great many stranger vehicles, near-flat contrivances like armoured skate that were completely silent and a uniform jet-black in colour. Even Reggie Bowler, the gang's car-fanatic, stood beside the window with his hat off, scratching his dark curls perplexedly. Phyllis was fuming, which, if anything, made her look prettier.

"If we were any bloody further up we'd be in bloody Snow Tayn! 'E's done this on purpose, all because I wouldn't let 'im gawp at all them old pros gettin' interfered with down there in the sixteen-'undreds!"

Bill protested.

"Oh, and when you dug us up too 'igh down Scarletwell Street that wiz different, wiz it? You're a bossy old bat, wanting everything your own way. Who's to say we shouldn't have a nose round while we're up 'ere, anyway? It might be educational, which I remember you bein' in favour of when I wiz only a daft kid."

Phyllis sniffed haughtily.

"Yer still a daft kid, and yer still a bloody nuisance. All right, I suppose we might as well see 'oo's abayt, now that yer've dragged us up 'ere. Only fer a minute or two, mind, and then we're gooin' straight back dayn that 'ole to Cromwell's time, so we can take another route to Doddridge Church."

Drowned Marjorie, standing beside a little wooden book-rack stuffed with dog-eared paperbacks and no doubt trying to extend her knowledge of twenty-first-century literature, peered at the others through her spectacles' milk-bottle-bottom lenses.

"Out through that door I think there's a passageway to an extension that pokes into Peter's Churchyard. I remember it from The Return to Snow Town, just after The Dead Dead Gang Versus the Nene Hag and before The Incident of the Reverse Train."

Marjorie was turning into quite the little chatterbox. John was impressed, though, by her cataloguing of the gang's adventures in such careful order, even if they were more kid's games than heroic exploits, truth be told. The six ghost-children filed out through the door of the deserted doctor's surgery or kitchen that they'd tunnelled into, leaving the time-hole uncovered in anticipation of their exit back to the seventeenth century.

Beyond the door, as Marjorie had already predicted, was a corridor. This had an area that seemed to be a children's playroom running off one side, in which perhaps a dozen infants of various nationalities were making an ungodly mess with powder paints under the supervision of a patient-looking bald man in his middle fifties. Even though the light within the room was poor, John thought that this was due more to the weather than the time of day, which he supposed to be mid afternoon. A calendar that John had noticed in the surgery-cum-kitchen – one that had a stout Salvation Army lady posing on it, John remembered suddenly, naked except her bonnet and trombone – had said that this was July 2025, although it looked too cold and wet outside to be mid summer.

An entrance at the passage's far eastern end gave access to a couple of prefabricated dormitories, each subdivided into half a dozen modest cubicles by curtains hung on mobile railings. The first such enclosure that they came to seemed to have been set aside for females only, with a few women of different ages sitting watching an enormous television on which nude young men sat in some species of communal bath or paddling pool and told each other they were "out of order". The bored-looking women who were viewing this unedifying spectacle ventured disdainful comments on the program in what might have been a Norfolk accent. John presumed that a male dormitory must lie beyond the closed doors at the room's far end, and went to stand with Michael Warren who was jumping up and down as he tried to see out of the rear window.

This looked south towards the area behind St. Peter's Church and over whatever was left by this date of the green that John had played upon with Michael Warren's dad when they were boys. John helpfully picked up the hopping infant so that he could see, not that a lot was visible through the incessant rain.

"Not much to look at, wiz there? How d'you fancy jumping through the wall and going for a poke-about outside? We won't get wet because the rain passes right through us."

Michael frowned up dubiously at John.

"Will it feel horrible when it falls through my tummy like that bird-poo did?"

Grinning, John shook his noble, chiselled head so that it double-exposed into an array of film star eight-by-tens.

"No. Rain feels clean when it goes through you. Come on. Phyllis and the others wizzle be mooching around here for a good while yet, so we've got lots of time. Remember what I said about how all of this wiz flashing past like lightning in the living world, and take the opportunity to go exploring while you can."

Michael considered this for a few moments and then nodded in consent. Still holding the tartan-wrapped toddler in his arms, John stepped out through the shell of glass and plasterboard into a shower of silver, falling with the rain and his attendant after-pictures to the churchyard's beaded turf a floor below. Once they had landed John set Michael down upon the sodden ground beside him and then, hand in hand, the two of them drifted around the west face of the church towards its rear. John was agreeably surprised to note that all the funny or horrific Saxon carvings high on the stone wall were still intact, although when he and Michael were behind the church and looking between its back railings at the derelict green his surprise was less agreeable.

Green Street was gone. Elephant Lane, Narrow-Toe Lane, both gone. Free-school Street was transformed into bland forts comprised of offices or flats that looked suspiciously unused. Across the altered landscape in a curving scalpel-swipe was the disfiguring surgical scar of a broad two-lane motorway that ran from Black Lion Hill, away south through grey veils of inundation towards Beckett's Park and Delapre, a distant skyline where the break between tall concrete and descending storm clouds could no longer be discerned. The green itself, neglected and unkempt, had lost its edges and its definition, its identity. It was purposeless grass now, melting in the rain as it awaited the surveyors, the developers. Standing there next to John with his lip trembling, Michael Warren made a disappointed, whining sound.

"The street that wiz down at the bottom of the green wiz gone, just like my street on Andrew's Road. My nan used to live there!"

Keeping up his pretence, John didn't look at Michael as he answered.

"Yes, I know. That's where your dad grew up, as well, with all his brothers and his sister. That where your great-granddad died, sitting between two mirrors with his mouth stuffed full of flowers. All of the things that happened in that little house, and now ..."

John trailed off. There was nothing else that he could say without revealing matters best kept to himself. With copies of the boys trailing behind them through the graveyard like a funeral procession for the neighbourhood, Michael and John went back the way they'd come, towards the two-storey prefabrication jutting into consecrated ground out from the modified Black Lion next door. This meant that they walked past the black stone obelisk that stood some feet west of the ancient church and which John had paid no attention to when they passed by the other way just moments earlier.

Glistening wet like whale-hide in the drizzle, the dark monument appeared to be a war memorial. It hadn't been in evidence when John had paid his one and only visit to the place just following his disembodied homecoming from France, when all the ghosts had put him off from coming back again. He paused to look at it more closely, bringing Michael similarly to a halt. He was just reading the inscriptions when the toddler yelped down at his side and pointed to the needle's base.

"Look! That man there has got the same last name as me!"

John looked. Michael was right. Nobody spoke for a few seconds.

"So he does. Ah well, I s'pose we should be should be getting back to Phyllis and the rest, see what they're up to. Come on, before they go back to 1645 without us."

Hand in hand the two wraiths slid amidst the tippling precipitation, passing through the insulated layers of the pub extension's lower walls into an office where a pretty, burly, coloured woman with a dreadful scar above one eye was talking to what looked like a stamped-on sardine tin held against her ear.

"Don't give me that. The government awarded all this money weeks ago, when Yarmouth had the floods. I've got two dozen people here, and some of them are ill, and some need drugs. Don't tell me that the payments have to go through channels when the fucking cheque is sitting there in your account and earning interest for the council."

There was a brief pause and then the Amazon resumed her fierce tirade.

"No. No, you listen. If that cash is not wired into the St. Peter's Annexe account by next Tuesday at the latest, I'll be at the Guildhall for the meeting on the Friday after with a list of every dodgy deal between you lot and the Disaster Management Authority. I'll strap one on and give your mates a public fucking so rough that they won't be sitting down in council or anywhere else for months. Now, get it sorted."

With a sneer that curled her luscious glistening lips to form a swimming-pool inflatable the woman snapped a lid across the sardine tin, contemptuously tossing it into the innards of a cartoon dog that sprawled there gutted on a work-surface and which John finally identified as some variety of handbag. Tipping back her office chair and flipping through a file she'd taken from a shallow wire tray on her desk, she was magnificent, quite unlike any female John had seen before. Although he didn't hold with women swearing and although he'd never really been attracted to what he thought of as half-caste girls, this one possessed a kind of atmosphere or aura that was absolutely riveting. She had as much intensity about her as Oliver Cromwell had, a short walk down Marefair and getting on four hundred years ago, except that the force burning in her was less black and heavy than the energy that churned inside the Lord Protector.

She was also a much healthier and more attractive specimen. Her ludicrously splendid mane of catkin hair fell to her shoulders which were naked where her thick, masculine arms, those of a lady weightlifter, emerged from the chopped-off sleeves of her T-shirt. This had a man's face printed upon it, his hairstyle almost identical to that affected by the garment's wearer, with above it the word EXODUS and then below it the phrase MOVEMENT OF JAH PEOPLE. The girl looked to be in her late thirties, but the radiance of youth was undercut by the grown-up and very serious-looking ragged seam of flesh just over her left eyebrow. This did not deface her beauty so much as it loaned a strength and gravity to her young countenance. John was just thinking that her powerful, mannish arms and air of resolute nobility gave the impression of a Caribbean Joan of Arc when he put two and two together and remembered where he'd heard about this girl before, blurting the answer out to Michael Warren.

"It's the saint. It's that one that I've heard about who looks after the refugees here in the twenty-fives. I think that I've heard people call her 'Kaff', so I suppose that's short for Katherine. She pioneers some treatment here that wizzle save lives right across the world, folk who are on the run from wars and floods and that. They say that in the nothing-forties people talk about her like a saint. She's the most famous person that comes from the Boroughs in this century, and here we are getting a look at her."

Michael regarded the oblivious woman quizzically.

"Where did she get that nasty cut that's near her eye?"

John shrugged, with briefly multiplying shoulders.

"I don't know. I don't know much about her, to be honest, other than the saint thing. Anyway, we can't stand nattering here. Let's find our way back to the first floor and catch up with Phyllis and the rest."

Walking around the seated goddess as she finished with her scrutiny of the plain folder and replaced it with another from the same wire tray, Michael and John stepped through the office wall and found themselves in a short corridor that had the lower reaches of a stairway leading up from it. As the pair floated up this on their way to rendezvous with the remainder of the Dead Dead Gang, John found himself considering what it would take to get you labelled as a saint.

It all depended, very probably, upon the times that you were in, the background that you came from. In the middle ages it required a miracle, like the one that was said to have occurred here in St. Peter's Church down in 1050-something, where an angel had apparently helped find the body of the man who would become Saint Ragener, the brother of Saint Edmund. Then in Cromwell's day, a hundred years after Henry the Eighth had severed England's ties with Rome, the saints were living people, men like Bunyan who believed that they were destined to be counted with that rank when sinful worldly kingdoms had been swept away and were replaced by an egalitarian society united under God, an entire nation of the saintly that would not be needing either priests or governments.

Just when he thought he'd finally forgotten all about it, John found that he was reminded of the blowing-up man there on Mansoul's landings. Wouldn't he be thought of as a saint, a martyr, by the people who believed what he did? John supposed that one thing that united Bunyan, Cromwell, Ragener, the human bomb – and from the look of that scar near her eye the girl downstairs as well – was that they'd all passed through some sort of fire. That was a factor, clearly, although not the only one, otherwise John would be a saint as well after his own dismemberment in France. John thought that it must be the attitude with which one went into the flames that made the difference. It must be one's courage, or the lack of it, that sainthood rested on. There was much more to being canonised than getting shot at by a cannon.

Just when John and Michael reached the first floor, pandemonium erupted. At its top end, the staircase emerged into a corridor with two doors leading off on the right side, which John assumed must be the dormitories they'd caught a glimpse of earlier. He was about to poke his head into the wall looking for Phyllis when a small and sickly flying saucer sailed out through the nearest of the shut-fast doors with insubstantial doubles of itself behind it, marking its trajectory. Before it hit the floor, a whirling tumbleweed of streaming motion like two Siamese cats fighting followed the disc through the solid door and caught it in mid-hover. Still for just a second, this grey blur resolved into Drowned Marjorie and then ducked back into the presumed dormitory taking the captured object with her. John and Michael looked at one another in astonishment then raced across the passageway to follow Marjorie in through the chamber's flimsy modern wall.

As John had guessed, on the wall's far side was a dormitory, a more or less identical male counterpart to the girl's quarters that they'd passed through a short while ago. As for the frantic action taking place inside, however, John had not predicted that at all.

Four living men sat playing cards, their ages ranging from about eighteen to forty, all completely unaware of the spectral commotion going on around them. In the riot of proliferating ghost-forms hurtling around the room it was almost impossible at first to make out what was happening, but after a few moments John believed that he had grasped the situation: counting John and Michael there were seven ghosts inside the dormitory, six being the assembled Dead Dead Gang. The seventh was an adult phantom, a rough sleeper that both John and Phyll had known of while they were alive, named Freddy Allen. In his mortal day Freddy had been a well-known Boroughs vagrant, sleeping under railway arches in Foot Meadow and keeping alive by pinching loaves of bread and pints of milk from people's doorsteps, slinking off in the deserted and conspiratorial hush of early morning. Since his death, he'd been one of the most anonymous and harmless spirits to frequent the sorry territories of the ghost-seam, much less of a terror than Malone, or Mary Jane, or old Mangle-the-Cat. Unfortunately, this made Freddy a convenient and relatively risk-free target for Phyll Painter's ongoing vendetta against grown-up ghosts.

What must have happened was that Freddy had been up here in the twenty-fives and minding his own business, sitting in upon a mortal hand of three-card Brag, when Phyllis, Reggie, Bill and Marjorie had burst in through the wall and started mucking him about. The 'flying saucer' that John had seen Marjorie retrieving from the corridor a moment or two back was Freddy's hat, plucked from his balding crown by one of the ghost-children, who were now engaged in running round the dormitory and throwing Freddy's battered trilby back and forth to one another while the paunchy and out-of-condition revenant flailed helplessly there at their centre, trying to catch his headgear as it whistled past. As the Dead Dead Gang tossed the ghostly hat from hand to hand, its after-images persisted long enough to leave a looping chain of wan and cheerless Christmas decorations strung around the upper reaches of the room.

Freddy was spluttering and furious.

"You give that 'ere! You give that 'ere, you little tearaways!"

The item of apparel he was after spun in a high arc above his bare grey pate, out of his reach, to be plucked from the air by Phyllis Painter, who was dancing up and down next to the dormitory's windows. Waving the old trilby back and forth above her head until it multiplied into a solid stripe of hats, she grinned at Freddy.

"Come and get it, you old bugger! Serves yer right for 'avin' all them loaves orf people's doorsteps!"

With that, Phyllis hurled the immaterial trophy through the hard glass of the windowpane into the open air outside, where it went sailing down into the rain-lashed churchyard. The ghost-tramp howled in dismay and, with a final angry glare in Phyllis's direction, dived out through the window after it.

Phyllis, already starting to step through the wall into the women's dormitory next door, called for the gang to follow her.

"Come on, let's get back dayn to the Black Lion in Cromwell's times, before the old git finds 'is 'at and comes to look fer us."

The astral-plane adventurers followed their leader back through the adjoining girls' communal bedroom. On the huge, sideboard-sized television one of the chaps who'd been bathing earlier was in a futuristic kitchen having a foul-mouthed exchange with a young woman wearing what John could only assume were artificial joke-shop breasts. The man, apparently, was 'fuckin' mashin'' the girl's 'fuckin' swede', whatever that entailed. The women sitting on their beds and watching the enormous telly tutted and remarked upon the on-screen harridan's augmented bosoms in their flat east-country tones as the ghost-children passed unseen amongst them.

Gliding down the corridor beyond the far wall of the dormitory the gang came to the room with all the bleach, syringes and tinned baby-food, where they had unintentionally emerged into this strange, overcast century. The hole that Bill had made still gaped there in the antiseptic lino-tiling of the floor, but it looked down now into unrelieved and silent blackness, rather than the lamplight and the amorous rustlings that they'd climbed up out of. Reggie Bowler lowered himself into the time-tunnel first, vanishing down into seventeenth-century dark so that he could help the gang's smaller members clamber after him. Phyllis descended next, then Michael, Bill and Marjorie.

Taking a final, mystified look round at all the medicines and the unfathomable posters – THANK YOU FOR NOT SCREAMING; TALKING ABOUT TYPHOID – John let himself down into the black well after his companions.

Below, in 1645, the tavern was deserted and had evidently been closed for the night, its final patrons chucked out into mud and starlight. Phyllis stood on Reggie's shoulders and patiently wove the fabric of the moment back across the aperture that Bill had made, observing an afterlife version of the country code, which John approved of. Although living people couldn't physically pass through a time hole in the way a spirit did, one that had been left open could still pose a threat to them. A mortal person's mind might fall through such an opening although their bodies were not able to, producing the potentially nerve-shattering experience of being in another time. John hadn't ever heard first-hand of this occurring, but he'd been assured by older, more experienced wraiths that such things were a horrifying possibility. Better to close your burrows off behind you, just in case.

When Phyll was done with covering their tracks, the children leaked out through the old inn's bolted door onto a Marefair quite devoid of life or afterlife. The gang meandered in the general direction of Pike Lane, a lightless crack that ran north from the main street, and John turned it over in his thoughts, this business about warrior saints, this death and glory lark.

In John's opinion it was all a fraud, the stuff he'd had drummed into him when he was in the Boy's Brigade, singing "To Be A Pilgrim" while associating being good with church and church with marching; diligently painting Blanco on your lanyard; taking orders. All these things had been mixed up together for John's generation. Ritually blackening the cold brass buckle of a B.B. belt above a candle flame before you polished it led seamlessly into the sense of Christian duty that you felt when you first got your call up papers. "Hobgoblin nor foul fiend shall daunt his spirit. He knows he at the end shall life inherit." The next thing you knew you were in Naseby getting run through by a pike, you were exploding in a shower of nails and brilliance, you were being blown out of your flesh by an artillery shell in France. It wasn't life that you inherited. That was just what they told you so that you'd die in their military campaign without a fuss. All wars were holy wars, which was to say they were all ordinary bloody wars that someone had decided to call holy when it suited them, some king, some pope, some Cromwell who believed he knew what Heaven wanted. As John saw it, if you were engaged in killing people then you very probably were not a saint. Perhaps that coloured girl with the appalling scar was the best candidate for the position after all, unlikely as she looked. Her only weapon had been a sardine tin.

Up ahead of them Pike Lane sloped gently from Marefair to Mary's Street, which led to Doddridge Church, their destination. John was idly musing about Mary's Street and what had happened there when Bill seemed almost to pick up these thoughts, loudly proclaiming his new idea for procrastination as he hopped from one foot to the other in the narrow and benighted side-street, generating extra legs with every bounce. Whatever he'd got on his mind, he seemed excited.

"I know! I know! We could go and see the fire! It's only thirty years up that way!"

Everyone agreed. It would be a tremendous waste to be in Mary's Street during the sixteen-hundreds and not go to visit the Great Fire.

Phyllis began to dig into the midnight air. She said she'd stop when she hit sparks.

MALIGNANT,
REFRACTORY SPIRITS

You see more naked people when you're dead, or at least this was the conclusion Michael was fast coming to. There had been nudes and semi-nudes amongst the crowd on Mansoul's balconies, sleepwalking dreamers in their underpants, and there had been the Cromwell boy only a little while ago in Marefair. In the afterlife, nobody seemed to mind if you'd not got your clothes on. This approach appealed to Michael, who had never understood what all the fuss was over in the first place.

Then there were the two young women Michael was now looking at, capering bare along the drab September length of Mary's Street in the mid-1670s. So beautiful even a three-year-old could see it; they were hardly real women at all and more like something made-up from a film or magazine as they skipped gaily through the cooking steam and refuse in the narrow lane at that time of the bygone morning. These, he dimly comprehended, might just be what the commotion over nudity was all about.

The prancing females were, he thought, a lovely shape, even though one was skinny and the other plump. He liked the extra bits they had upon their chests, and how they didn't have the corners grown-up men had, being rounded like the country was rather than square-cut like a town. As usual, he wondered vaguely what had happened to their willies but was confident that this would all make sense eventually, like jokes or frost-patterns.

Of course, the really striking thing about the two nymphs was the colour of their hair: it had a colour, even in the ghost-seam's unrelenting black-and-white. Tossed up above their heads as if by the strong breezes from the west, billowing out and tangling in the wind, their manes were vivid orange on the half-world's photo-album grey.

The dead girl that he was starting to think of as his secret sweetheart, Phyllis Painter in her rotten rabbit ruff, had dug a tunnel up from midnight Marefair on the eve of battle in the 1640s into daylight Pike Lane only thirty years thereafter. Michael and the gang had clambered through the opening into a side street where two men were arguing about the tallied chalk-marks on a blackboard hanging by the doorway of their ironmonger's shop, and where old women wearing threadbare pinafores emptied the contents of cracked chamber pots into already-brimming gutters. Since there were no other ghosts around, no one could see the children as they conscientiously repaired the hole they'd made arriving here, out of a night three decades gone.

The phantom ruffians had streamed up to St. Mary's Street, where there were jumbled yards and cottages piled up higgledy-piggledy, alive with chickens, dogs and children; not at all like the neat modern flats of Michael's day. From where the six of them were at the upper entrance to Pike Lane they could see only nondescript wood buildings on the mound towards the west where Doddridge Church would later stand. Looking towards the east and Horsemarket, however, they had spied the beautiful bare ladies with their hair in colour, twirling blissfully along the busy morning street, apparently unnoticed by the downcast wagon-drivers and preoccupied pedestrians going about their business. Phyllis had seemed pleased to see the pair.

"That's good. We're 'ere before they've properly got started. We can watch the 'ole thing now, from start ter finish."

Michael had been puzzled.

"Who are those two ladies? I thought we wiz coming here to see the Great Fire of Northampton."

Phyllis looked at Michael patiently, patting his tartan sleeve as she explained.

"They *are* the Gret Fire o' Northampton."

Tall John butted in.

"Phyllis wiz right. That's why nobody else can see 'em, and that's why their hair wiz coloured when the rest of us are all in black and white. If you look closer, it's not hair at all. It's flames. They're Salamanders."

The fire-headed women tripped and laughed amongst the dross of Mary's Street. They looked enough alike for Michael to be sure that they were sisters, with the plumper of the pair being perhaps nineteen or twenty and the leaner one some five years younger, barely in her teens. He noticed that right at the bottoms of their tummies, where their willies should have been, the little patch of hair they had was made of orange fire as well, with stray sparks drifting up around their belly-buttons. They swung lazily around the wooden posts supporting musty barns and tightrope-walked along the duckboards. Neither of them spoke a word – Michael was somehow sure they couldn't – but communicated only in shrill laughs and giggles that were reminiscent of the way that early-morning songbirds talked together. The two didn't seem to have a single thought between them that was not about their laughter or their random, skittering dance. They were so happy and carefree that they looked almost idiotic.

Seeming to guess what the little boy was thinking, Phyllis gently put him straight.

"I know they look 'alf sharp, but that's just 'ow they are. They don't 'ave proper thoughts or feelings like we 'ave 'em. They're all spirit. They're all urge, all fire. Me and Bill saw 'em first, before we started up the Dead Dead Gang. We'd both been dayn to Beckett's Park, Cow Medder, in the fourteen-'undreds at the old War o' the Roses, and we wiz just diggin' ayr way back up through the sixteenth century. Abayt 1516 we broke through into this one day where everything wiz like a bloody gret inferno with the Boroughs burning dayn araynd us, and this wiz when there weren't much more to Northampton than the Boroughs, mind you.

"The two Salamanders, the two sisters, they wiz pirouettin' through the blaze and settin' fire to everythin' they touched. O' course, they wiz both younger by a century or two in them days. The plump girl, the eldest one, she looked abayt eleven and the youngest one wiz only five or somethin'. They wiz trottin' back and forth between the burnin' 'ouses, carrying the fire with 'em in their cupped 'ands and then splashin' it all over everywhere like two kids playin' with a tub o' water. Only it weren't water.

"I've met ghosts who've told me abayt when the two of 'em were first seen araynd 'ere. That wiz twelve-sixty-somethin', when 'Enry the Third ordered the town burned dayn and ransacked as a punishment for sidin' with de Montfort and the rebel students. From what these old-timers told me, when King 'Enry's men were let into the Boroughs through a big 'ole in the priory wall dayn Andrew's Road, the sisters came in through it with them, walkin' naked and invisible beside the 'orses. The big girl looked to be six then, and was carryin' 'er baby sister in 'er arms. Nobody's ever 'eard 'em say a word. They only giggle and set light to things."

The ghost gang watched the trilling, tittering duo as they flounced from house to house along seventeenth century St. Mary's Street, slipping between the traders and the scowling, put-on housewives without anybody knowing they were there. Their hair billowed behind them on the westerly in trailing orange pennants, flickering and hazardous. Seeing them, Michael noticed for the first time just how well grey and bright orange went together, like a bloated morning sun seen through the fog above Victoria Park. In their meandering the women seemed to gravitate towards a single dwelling, a thatched house on the Pike Lane side of the street, a little closer to Horsemarket than the children were.

"Come on. It looks like that's the 'ouse. Let's goo and 'ave a butchers at 'em when they set it orf."

Following Phyllis's suggestion the dead urchins doppelganged towards the ordinary-looking dwelling, just in time to pursue the two sisters in through its front door, a poorly-fitting thing propped open by a brick. Inside, the downstairs of the cottage was a single room, gloomy and cluttered, evidently serving as a front room, living room, kitchen and bathroom all rolled into one. An infant with a dirty nose crawled on the coarse rugs that were spread about a cold brick floor, while by the open hearth a woman who appeared too old to be the baby's mum stood frying scraps of meat in melted dripping, shaking the round-bottomed iron pan she held above the fireplace in one hand. At the same time, using her other hand, she stirred a clay jug of what turned out to be batter with a wooden spoon. The way that the old lady could do both things at the same time impressed Michael. When he'd watched his mum and gran cook in their kitchen down St. Andrew's Road, they'd always split the chores so that each of them only had to do one thing at once. The other members of the Dead Dead Gang were nodding knowingly, all except Bill who was too busy ogling the naked fire-nymphs as they poked inquisitively round the crowded, cosy living space.

"She's makin' a Bake Pudden. When she's stirred the batter up, she'll tip it in atop the meat, then put the 'ole lot in the oven – that's the little black iron door beside the fireplace – until it's done. A lot o' people say as Yorkshire Puddin' is a recipe them northern buggers pinched from us, but were too tight to put the bits o' meat in. It was just a way of makin' up a proper meal from leftovers and odds and ends."

As Phyllis wandered into the specifics of Bake Pudden-making and its history, Michael was watching the two sisters in their progress round the murky, fire-lit room. Surprisingly, they seemed uninterested in the fireplace itself and were converging on a patch of carpet to the far side of the central wooden table, where the crawling infant was investigating a fat garden spider that had probably retreated indoors at the first hint of a chill to the September air. The Salamanders made a great fuss of the baby, stooping down and chuckling in their musical brass wind-chime voices to it while they pulled a lot of silly, grinning faces.

Michael realised with a start that the small child, barely a year old from the look of him, could see the snickering, flickering young women. The tot's gaze was shifting back and forth, tracking the movement of their bonfire beehive hairdos as they wavered in the drafts blown from the open door. The Salamanders winked and smirked and played games, walking their slim fingers back and forth along the table's edge like tiny pairs of legs to catch the babe's attention as it crawled there on the floor below. They marched their digits over the piled apples in a wooden fruit bowl resting on the tabletop, cooing and beaming at their fascinated audience of one. The baby gurgled happily as it watched the two flame-haired women from its spot down near the dangling hem of a slipped tablecloth that looked like it had previously seen service as a lady's shawl. Only when the child's chubby, grubby hand reached for the cloth's fringed edge did Michael realise what the fire-sprites were up to. He called out a garbled warning to the others – "Look! The fieries want to bake the maybe start an appleanch!" – but by the time they'd worked out what he meant, it was too late.

Things came together like the comically elaborate machinery in a cartoon: the baby grabbed the hanging makeshift tablecloth, thus dragging the heaped fruit-bowl to the table's edge, then over it. Missing the child the wooden bowl fell clattering to the rug, although one of its bouncing apples struck the startled mite above his eye and made him wail. Alarmed, the stooped old woman who was possibly the baby's grandmother turned from her cooking to see what was up, at which point the round-bottomed iron pan that she was using tipped up slightly, spilling melted fat into the blazing hearth and setting fire to the pan's contents simultaneously. The hissing gout of flame resulting from this momentary carelessness surged upward to ignite the dusters hanging with the pots and saucepans from the mantelpiece, causing the by-now frightened and confused old dear to reach out with her ladle, batting the offending blazing rags down from the hearthside to the brick floor and, disastrously, one of the dusty rugs. Within about five seconds nearly everything that could be on fire was. The woman stood there staring in stunned disbelief at what she'd done for a few instants, then ran round the table to scoop up the howling tot before she hauled it through the front door, shrieking "Fire!" as they fell stumbling out into St. Mary's Street.

The sisters clapped their hands together in excitement, jumping up and down and squealing as the conflagration spread around the room. Only the tangerine tongues licking from the Salamanders' heads had any colour, Michael noted. All the other flames now roaring in the cluttered cottage were bright white around the outside with profound grey hearts as they ascended like a line of ants towards the ceiling's timber beams. Phyllis grabbed Michael by the scorched, discoloured collar of his dressing gown.

"Come on, we're gettin' ayt of 'ere. We don't wanna be all stuck jostlin' in a burnin' doorway with the two o' them."

The elder of the crackling, spitting females had now hopped onto the table and was executing a variety of cancan, while her younger sister laughed and posed coquettishly amongst the smouldering curtains. The wraith children burst out through the doorway like a spray of playing cards, all Jacks and Queens, all spades and clubs without a splash of red between the six of them.

St. Mary's Street was in the grip of an incredible commotion. Dogs and people ran this way and that, their barks and shouts and panicked screams uproarious despite the ghost-seam's dampening effect. Two or three men were racing frantically to the afflicted home with slopping pails of water in their hands, but only got to within ten feet of its door before what Phyllis had predicted came spectacularly true: the Salamanders leapt together from the house into the street, accompanied by loud peals of hilarity and a great furnace blast of white flame that drove back the would-be firemen and their useless little buckets. It was almost ten o'clock upon the morning of September 20th, 1675.

Michael was asking John why the two easily-amused fire-fairies were called Salamanders when the younger, thinner one began to clamber effortlessly up the front wall of the burning cottage, reaching its thatched roof in seconds with her fleshier and more formidable big sister scuttling immediately behind her. Neither of the young girls moved like people, Michael thought. They moved like insects, or perhaps like ...

"Lizards." This was John.

"A salamander, with a little 's', that's like a lizard or a newt. But people once believed that salamanders lived in flames, so when we talk about a Salamander with a big 'S' then we're talking about what's called elementals, spirits of the fire."

Marjorie interjected here, reflected firelight flaring from her spectacles.

"The ones that govern water are called Undines. The Nene Hag, who almost got me when I had me accident down Paddy's Meadow, she wiz one of them. Snail-shells for eyes, she'd got. Then there's the ones what rule the wind, they call them Sylphs although the only ones I've ever heard of have been horrible old men who stand a mile high. Spirits of the earth, they're what's called Gnomes officially, although round here we call 'em Urks or Urchins. You don't see 'em much above ground, but they ride round the tunnels underneath upon these big black dog-things what are known as ... oh, hang on. Looks like they're off and running."

The drowned girl was pointing up towards the rooftops, where the brace of Salamanders were commencing an outlandish waltz along the ridge of the thatched buildings. The incendiary beauties clung together tight, helpless with mirth, whirling each other round with an accompanying flame-tornado rising from the parched straw at their heels as they progressed from roof to roof. The dozens milling in the lane below watched helplessly as cottage after cottage was consumed by the fire-spirits' unseen choreography. Unwittingly, the mob were following the sisters' dazzling performance as they moved with the west wind along St. Mary's Street towards Horsemarket, kicking up a loud din as they did so. There were curses, groans, despairing cries and several different sorts of weeping. An old man with cataracts was calling up above the clamour in a high and reedy voice, declaring that the fire was punishment from God as a result of papists in the Parliament withdrawing Charles the Second's Declaration of Indulgence for dissenting congregations. A cross-looking youth who stood beside the raving ancient pushed him over in the mud and was immediately set on by two burlier and crosserlooking fellows who'd seen what the boy had done. A fight broke out in the already-distraught byway while, above, the Salamanders danced amongst the chimneypots with sheets of flame rolling and billowing about their bare legs like flamboyant ball-gowns. As the pair approached Horsemarket, people at that eastern end of Mary's Street were already evacuating their doomed dwellings, moving what they could of their meagre possessions out into the frantic and stampeding avenue.

Michael ran hand in hand with Phyllis through the crowd, literally in some instances, as the Dead Dead Gang kept up with the devastating Salamander ballet. By the time the incandescent nudes had reached the wide dirt track of Horsemarket that sloped north-south across the thoroughfare's far end, both sides of Mary's Street were angry walls of fire with burning straws from the disintegrated thatching carried on the wind across the road. Chains of combustion snaked off down the incline towards Gold Street while at the same time the brilliant rivulets trickled uphill into the Mayorhold. Pausing only to squat down in turn over the chimney of the last house in the row and piddle streams of golden sparks into its darkness, the two sisters swarmed face first down the end wall, both snickering like cracking hearth-logs.

Hopping from one burning, bolting wagon to another they crossed Horsemarket and scampered gaily eastwards up St. Katherine's Street, with townsfolk scattering before them, the ghost-ruffians and their after-pictures hurrying behind, not wanting to miss anything. When they were nearing College Street the redheads stopped before the gated entrance of what seemed to be a family-business tannery. The gorgeous monsters gazed towards the premises, then at each other, struggling to keep a straight face as they did so. Each one with an arm draped chummily around the other's naked shoulder, the two giggling sisters stepped through the now-blazing gateway, vanishing from sight into the walled yard. Before Michael, Phyllis and the gang could follow them, the whole establishment blew up. It didn't just ignite in a great rush like all the other buildings had done; it exploded, with a tower of fire erupting up towards the overcast September sky and needle-shards of debris trailing threads of smoke behind them raining for a hundred yards in each direction, falling through the spectral children while they stood there gaping in astonishment.

Michael spoke first.

"Whop wiz all that big clangerbang?"

John shook his head, staring in disbelief as the two Salamanders stepped from the inferno of the flattened workplace with volcanic lava-coloured tears of mirth now streaming down their silvery cheeks, holding each other up to stop themselves collapsing in a quaking, sniggering heap.

"I've no idea. That wiz like an artillery shell. I'd always wondered how the

Great Fire spread from Mary's Street to Derngate in just under twenty minutes, but if there were blasts like that to help it on, I'm not surprised."

Drowned Marjorie's moon face was crumpled by a frown, as if she was
considering some problem, turning the alternatives this way and that inside
her mind. Whatever she was thinking, the bespectacled child didn't seem
to come to a conclusion that she thought worth mentioning. Marjorie kept
her ruminations to herself as Phyllis led the gang along the roaring corridor
after the fire-girls, who were by that time advancing merrily into the tinder-
box of College Street, or College Lane as the incline was currently referred
to, Michael noticed from a signboard that he read without the least surprise
that he could do so. Pyrotechnic trails unravelled from the sisters, bowling
through the slanting lane in both directions, turning everything with which
they came in contact to another glaring torch. Appearing to pick up their
pace, the clearly-tickled creatures sauntered through a charring gate on College Street's far side and disappeared into the long dark passageway that
Michael knew would later on be called Jeyes's Jitty and which cut through to
the Drapery. Chirping and twittering their happy nonsense, the two pretty
engines of destruction wandered off into the alley's blackness with their fiery
tresses sputtering behind them and the grey ghost-children in pursuit.

It wasn't until they stepped out into the Drapery that Michael realised
the full scale of the disaster. People in their hundreds wept and bellowed as
they fled in mortal dread or else charged impotently up and down the busy
high street dragging pointless, slopping buckets as they tried to save their
businesses. Vast flocks of startled birds flowed from one abstract shape into
another under palls of smoke that turned bright morning into twilight. Just
south of the alley entrance, the top end of Gold Street was ablaze and a slow
river of incinerating light was starting to roll inexorably away down Bridge
Street, driving soldiers, sheep and shopkeepers before it. Half the town was
burning down, and it had only been ten minutes since the baby pulled the
fruit bowl from the tabletop.

Across the way, the timber pillars holding up a wooden version of All
Saints Church were on fire. The sisters watched for a few moments until they
were certain that the building had caught properly and then proceeded up the
Drapery, tripping amongst the milliners' and cobblers' stalls and pausing to
inspect some item every now and then, like fussy ladies on a shopping jaunt,
looking for something in particular. On the rough cobbles just outside a pitch
displaying boots and shoes, they evidently found what they were after. Stopping dead they gazed towards some barrels standing in a row against the avenue's east wall, then both threw up their hands and shrilled with glee. Holding
their sides they staggered round in fiery rings, bent double with amusement
and convulsing at some private joke apparent only to the two of them.

Drowned Marjorie gave a tight little smile of satisfaction. Clearly, she'd worked something out.

"So that's it. That's why the whole town burned down in under half an hour."

The younger of the Salamanders, the slim thirteen-year-old with the flat chest and lone curl of pubic flame where her plump older sister had a brush-fire, suddenly sprang into action. From a standing jump she made a ballet dancer's leap through the cascading smoke, her hair in a long orange smear behind her shedding sparks like dandruff, to alight on top of the end barrel, standing on her pointed toes with skinny arms curled up to either side for balance.

She'd just hopped to the next barrel when the first one in the line blew up, smashed from within by a huge fist of liquid fire that sent its wooden staves sailing into the sky and sprayed a burning dew over the as yet untouched properties to either side. The slender little girl danced nimbly onto the lid of the third container as that of the second took off like a rocket: a black, flaming disc that disappeared over the roof into the Market Square beyond. A lake of blazing fluid began crawling down the Drapery. The sprite skipped from one barrel to the next and they exploded like a deafening string of jumping jacks while the performer's older sister looked on and applauded, jigging on the spot in her enthusiasm. Everything in sight was now on fire. Drowned Marjorie gave the assembled phantom kids the benefit of her considered verdict.

"Tannin. It wizn't a strong west wind all on its own what made the town burn down so quick. It was the tannin. As long as there's been a town here, it's been known for gloves and boots, and that's because we had all the right things here to make leather. We had lots of cows, and lots of oak trees. You need oak trees for the tannin, from the bark. The thing is, tannin wiz like aeroplane fuel. It speeds up a fire and makes it worse. That's why the tannery in Katherine Street blew up, and that's what's in them barrels that she's danc-ing on. I mean, you think of all the tannin that wiz in the Drapery, and then over the back there on the Market Square, that was the Glovery – "

The little girl broke off as the whole top end of the street went up with an enormous boom. From the direction of the market came what sounded like the racket of a big jet aircraft taking off until Michael remembered that this was the sixteen-hundreds, realising that the noise was actually that of a lot of people screaming all at once. Squinting between fountains of flame and through a lowering curtain of black, fuming fragments he could see the elementals as they climbed once more towards the rooftops, sticking to the blazing walls, a giggling pair of orange-crested reptiles.

Just uphill the lower end of Sheep Street was now also catching fire. A riderless and burning horse was spat out of the ancient byway's mouth to gallop terrified in the direction of All Saints, rolling its eyes. Nothing was safe and almost everything was flammable. By mutual assent the children raced around the top east corner of the Drapery into the caterwauling nightmare of the marketplace, into the bright core of the cataclysm, which made all they'd seen so far a preamble.

The Salamander sisters, having skittered up to the thatched ridges, had abandoned their pretence at dancing and commenced to race around the upper reaches of the square like two competing sprinters. That, however, was where all human comparisons were swept away: the pace at which the women ran along the roofs was so unnatural as to be genuinely horrid, like the unexpected speed of spiders. The sight would have been upsetting even if it hadn't been attended by the realisation that the people in the square, and there were scores of them, were now contained in a sealed box of fire.

The tradesmen in the premises that ringed the marketplace ran back and forth, arms laden with whatever items they could carry from their threatened shops as they deposited the rescued wares in at least temporary safety on the cobbles of the square. As the extent of their predicament began to dawn on them, however, the trapped townsfolk for the most part became less concerned with saving their possessions than with getting out alive. Not all of them, though. Some were plundering the burning stores, and there were dreadful scenes towards the bottom of the market where an over-greedy looter who'd caught fire was being driven back inside the blazing building he'd been trying to rob by angry market traders armed with poles and meat-hooks. Individual squeals and bellows were inaudible, subsumed within one deafening common shriek as people stormed through the familiar enclosure that had turned into a crematorium, desperately looking for an exit.

Not only were living townspeople attempting to escape. Amongst the various establishments that ringed the marketplace were several taverns, notably the coaching inn there on the square's far side, and these vomited spectres. Gushing from the doors and windows, leaking through the wooden walls in forms inseparable from the surrounding smoke, four or five hundred years' worth of accumulated gentleman spooks, medieval ghouls and shapeless ancient apparitions joined the panic-stricken living hordes who were unfortunate enough to be at market on that fateful day. Dead dogs streaked past with photo-finish images strung out behind them like a greyhound race, and up above it all the lovely human fireworks crowed and leapt and somersaulted as they overlooked their handiwork.

Out from the flaming, overflowing cauldron of the town square, tributaries roared up Newland and through Abington Street, Sheep Street, Bridge Street, Derngate, the whole town turned to a burning cobweb with the market crowd stuck struggling at its centre. Michael started crying at the awfulness of all the people who were going to die, but Phyllis gave his hand a squeeze and told him not to worry.

"Nearly everyone wizzle get out of 'ere all right, you'll see. In the 'ole town only eleven people died, and that most likely wizn't many more than yer'd get on an ordinary day. Ah! There, yer see? Over the market's other side, there at the bottom end of Newland, where the crowd are makin' for ..."

She pointed to the northeast corner of the square, towards which the majority of the great panicked herd seemed to be heading. Men were waving, shouting something as they urged their fellow escapees to follow them. The phantom children drifted in the same direction as the fleeing mob, and as they neared the far side of the market's upper reaches Michael saw that everybody was converging on a single building at the foot of Newland, a place which by his day would have been transformed into a funny little sweetshop that had coats-of-arms and things like that carved in the plasterwork above its door. These decorations, he saw now, had been a feature of the house as far back as the sixteen-hundreds. The trapped people in the square were filing underneath the plaster heraldry as they all tried to cram themselves into the house, like circus clowns attempting to get back inside their too-small car. As the gang stood and watched this almost-comic exodus, Phyllis explained to Michael.

"That's the Welsh House. I dare say it wiz a sweetshop when you wiz alive, same as it wiz fer me. Before that, though, it wiz like the paymaster's office fer the drovers what 'ad brought the sheep from Wales. The 'erds would all arrive in Sheep Street, and the chaps who'd 'erded 'em across the country would all come dayn 'ere to pick their money up. As yer can see, it's mostly stone and it's got slates up on its roof instead o' thatchin', so it doesn't burn as quickly as the 'ouses all araynd it. Everybody's gooin' in its front and comin' ayt the back into the alleys, where they can all get to safety."

It took very little time for the humanity-filled bladder of the burning marketplace to empty itself through the pinched urethra of the Welsh House, flooding with a great sense of relief into the backstreets further east. Most of the square's ghosts also chose this method of escape from their predicament, traipsing invisible along the house's passageways amongst the living. They appeared reluctant to just walk out through the market's flaming walls, perhaps because the way they'd learned to treat fire when they were alive still had a hold on them now they were dead. Michael saw one such phantom looking more confused and frightened than the rest, constantly glancing back over his shoulder in alarm at his own tail of fading images as he fell in with the long, shuffling queue of spooks and citizens who were evacuating the condemned ground. After a brief stint of puzzled peering, Michael recognised him as the looter who'd been driven back into the blazing building by the vengeful tradesmen only minutes earlier. The toddler watched the hunted-looking spirit, stumbling through the crowd-crammed doorway with the other fugitives, until he was distracted by a yell from Reggie Bowler.

"Well, blow me! Where 'ave the Sally-Mandies gone? I took me eye off 'em for just a minute and they've bloody disappeared!"

They had as well. The posse of ghost-children all looked up and scanned the market's fire-fringed skyline, searching for some smudge of orange, some sign of the sisters, but the two torch-headed girls were nowhere to be seen. Although the kids were all privately disappointed to have lost sight of the thrilling elemental arsonists, Phyllis made an attempt to treat the matter philosophically.

"I 'spect they've both got bored and gone orf to wherever they call 'ome, now that they've seen the best of it. I mean, this'll be burnin' for another five, six 'ours or more, but all the biggest spectacles are over, pretty much. We might as well walk back the way we come, dayn to St. Mary's Street. We can make our way up from there to Doddridge Church in 1959, where Mrs. Gibbs is waitin' for us. Then we'll find ayt what she's learned abayt ayr mascot 'ere."

Seventeenth-century Northampton spewed fire from its windows, its scorched timbers cracking and collapsing into cinders everywhere about them. The Dead Dead Gang flickered back like newsreel refugees across the now-deserted square, towards its northwest corner and the passage through into the Drapery. Just like the marketplace this was abandoned to the radiant catastrophe, even the neighbourhood ghosts having given up the ghost. As they meandered on the sputtering, flaring incline of the devastated high street, the six wraith-waifs found themselves looking into the smouldering mouth of Bridge Street further down. The town appeared to be alight as far as South Bridge and the river, and the chilly glass bowl of the early autumn sky arced overhead was soot-black, like an oil-lamp's mantle. Other than those distant uproars carried on the wind, the only sounds were those of the inferno: its deep sighs and coughs that sprayed a sputum of bright sparks across the street; its irritated mutter in the splitting doorframes.

Walking back along the spindly fissure into College Street was a peculiar experience, since this forerunner of Jeyes' Jitty was by now wholly consumed and filled with a blast-furnace blaze from one end to the other. Being made for the most part from ectoplasm, which is naturally a damp and largely fireproof substance, the ghost-children weren't in any danger as they trooped along the narrow pass but, as Michael discovered, they could feel the fire inside of them as they passed through it, just as they had felt the bird-poo and the rain. Deep in his phantom memory of a tummy he could feel the tickle of the flames, developing to an unbearably delightful and insistent itch that felt, if anything, much, much too good. It sort of made him want to do things just on impulse without any thought for whether they were right or not, and he was glad when they were out of the infernal alleyway and crossing over what was left of College Street. The old sign that identified the place as College Lane had been reduced to ashes and the ashes blown away. There were some looters at the top end of the side-street loading goods from an abandoned shop onto a two-wheeled cart, but otherwise the lane was bare.

St. Katherine Street, like all the surrounding byways, looked like Hell, or at least looked the way that Michael had imagined Hell to be before he'd had his run-in with sardonic Sam O'Day and found out that it was a flat place made entirely of squashed builders, or something like that at any rate. In the exploded ruins of the tannery up near the top, a twenty-foot wide scorch-mark bristling with spars of blackened rubble like a giant bird's nest struck by lightning, they found what had happened to the Salamanders.

It was Bill and Reggie, running into empty dwellings on their route simply to nose about, who made the big discovery and called excitedly for Michael, Phyllis, John and Marjorie to come and have a look. Phyllis's little brother and the freckle-faced Victorian were standing in the middle of the flattened yard, next to a pockmark in the dark soil and the smoking wreckage, a small crater that was no more than a foot or so across. They both seemed very pleased with what they'd found.

"I'll eat my hat! This wiz a blessed queer thing. Come and have a look at this, you lot."

At Reggie's invitation, the best dead gang in the fourth dimension gathered round the shallow indentation in a whispering and excited huddle, even though it took them a few moments before they worked out what they were looking at.

The circular depression was a hollow of grey, cooling ashes and curled up within it, silvery skin almost indistinguishable from the powdery bed that they were resting on, were the two sisters. Both of them were sleeping, having been no doubt worn out by their caprice, appearing very different in repose to how they'd looked when they were jigging on the rooftops of the Market Square only a little while ago. For one thing, all the tangled flames sprung from their scalps had been extinguished so that both of them were hairless. For another, neither of them was now taller than eleven inches.

They had shrunken into bald grey dolls, half-buried and asleep there in the fire's warm talcum residue, reclining head-to-toe so that they looked like the two fishes on the horoscope page of the daily paper. You could tell they were alive because their sides were going up and down, and with the better vision that the dead have you could see their tiny eyelids twitching as they dreamed of Lord knows what. Exhausted by their great annihilating spree, the nymphs were evidently dormant. They had eaten a whole town and would now drowse away the decades until next time, shrivelling to cinders of their former selves as all the heat went out them, and slumbering beneath the Boroughs in their bed of dust and embers.

After a brief conference on the merits of attempting to wake up the pair by prodding them, which Bill suggested, the children instead elected to continue with their saunter through the burning lanes towards St. Mary's Street and, ultimately, Doddridge Church. They left the Salamanders snoozing in the ruined tanner's yard with poison fumes for bed-sheets, carrying on down St. Katherine's Street as they headed for the blackened remnants of Horsemarket at the bottom. Michael scuffed along in his loose slippers between John and Phyllis while the other three ran on ahead, their grey repeated shapes soon disappearing in the drifts of smoke that crawled an inch above the cobbles.

"Wiz the Boroughs all barned down, then?"

Phyllis shook her head in a briefly-enduring smear of features, much like when you drew a face in ballpoint pen on a balloon then stretched the rubber out.

"Nah. There wiz a west wind, so all the fire got blew towards the east and burned the Drapery and the Market and all that. Other than Mary's Street, Horsemarket and a bit of Marefair at the Gold Street end, the Boroughs came ayt of the episode unmarked."

Michael was cheered to hear this reassuring news.

"Well, that wiz lucky, wizn't it?"

John, wading knee-deep in a blazing fallen tree on Michael's right, didn't agree.

"Not really, nipper, no. You see, the east part of the town wiz levelled by the flames, so that all got rebuilt with new stone buildings, some of which are still standing around the Market Square in your time. Everywhere else in Northampton got improved, except the Boroughs. That wiz pretty much left as it had been when the fire broke out there in the first place. Should you date exactly when the Boroughs first began to be seen as a slum, you'd have to say that it wiz after the Great Fire, here in the sixteen seventies. If there'd been an east wind today, then all of us might well have grown up somewhere posh, and all had different lives."

Phyllis was sceptical. Michael could tell this by the wrinkles suddenly appearing on the top bit of her nose.

"But that's not 'ow it 'appened, wiz it? Things only work out one way, and that's the way they 'ave to work out. If we'd grown up in posh 'ouses then we wouldn't be us, would we? I'm quite 'appy bein' 'oo I am. I think this wiz 'oo I wiz meant to be, and I think that the Boroughs wiz meant to be 'ow it wiz, as well."

They'd reached the bottom of the street and were confronted by Horsemarket, a charred ribbon that unreeled downhill and where people were diligently working, with some small success, to bring the blaze under control. The spectral children fogged across the road, swirling between the chains of bucket-passing men on whom the sweat and soot had mixed to a black paste, an angry tribal war-paint.

They unwound into the little that was left of Mary's Street like spools of film, only to find the fire was almost out, here in the lane where it had started. People picked disconsolately through a clinging scum of sodden ash or stroked their weeping spouses' hair like doleful monkeys that had been dressed in old-fashioned clothes for an advertisement. Unnoticed, the dead ne'er-do-wells floated amidst the desolation, past the black and cauterised gash that was Pike Street as they made their way to Doddridge Church, which wouldn't be there for another twenty years. Moping along a little way behind the others, Reggie Bowler was beginning to look a bit sad and lonely for some reason, pulling his hat further down onto his head and shooting melancholy glances from beneath its brim towards the wastelands spilling downhill from the as-yet non-existent church. Perhaps something about the place awoke unhappy memories for the ungainly phantom guttersnipe.

Michael, who'd been expecting somebody to dig another mole-hole up into the future, was surprised when Phyllis told him this wouldn't be necessary.

"We don't need to do that, not dayn 'ere. There's summat near the church what we can use instead. Think of it like a moving staircase or a lift or sum-mat. They call it the Ultraduct."

They were now on the low slopes of the mound called Castle Hill, where Michael had thought there were only barns and sheds when he'd looked ear-lier. However, as they neared Chalk Lane – or Quart-Pot Lane as signs pro-claimed it to be called at present – he could see around the west side of the flimsy, makeshift buildings, to what he assumed must be the structure Phyllis had just mentioned.

Whatever it was, it still appeared to be under construction. Half a dozen of the lower-ranking builders that he'd seen going about their business at the Works were labouring upon the pillars of some sort of partly-finished bridge, their grey robes shimmering at the hem with what were almost colours, but not quite. As Michael looked on three old women, who were obviously alive, beetled around the mound's flank from the north, wearing expressions of con-cern to mask their natural morbid curiosity as they came to observe the fire's aftermath. They walked straight through the builders and the posts they were erecting, utterly oblivious to their presence, while for their part the celestial work-gang didn't let the three distract them for a moment from their various tasks. To judge by the intent look on their faces, they were trying to meet a demanding schedule.

The material that they were working with was bright white and translucent, pre-cut planks and columns of the stuff swung into place with ropes and pulleys. The immense span of a bridge that looked like it was more or less completed stretched across the Boroughs from the west, only to finish in mid-air some few feet from the end barn that stood there on Chalk or Quart-Pot Lane. The elevated walkway, which appeared to curve off to the south, away into the grey and misted distance, was supported all along its dream-like length by the same alabaster pillars that the builders were attempting to manoeuvre into place there on the gentle, grassy slopes of Castle Hill. Something about the way the columns were positioned struck Michael as being very wrong.

The bridge was held up by two rows of the semi-transparent posts, one on each side. The problem was that if you trained your eyes on what you thought to be the bottom of a nearside strut and traced it upwards, it turned out to be supporting the far side of the construction. Similarly, if you focussed on the upper reaches of a pillar that was holding up the walkway's closest edge and followed it straight down towards its base, it would invariably end up being in the further row of columns. When you took in the whole thing at once, it looked right. It was only when you tried to make some sense of how it all fitted together that you realised the impossibility of the arrangement you were staring at. As he approached it with the Dead Dead Gang, Michael discovered that just seeing it gave him the ghost of a tremendous headache. Screwing shut his eyes he rubbed his forehead. Phyllis gave his hand a sympathetic squeeze.

"I know. It makes yer brains 'urt, dunnit? It guz all the way to Lambeth, then to Dover, then across the channel and through France and Italy and that, to end up in Jerusalem. From what I 'ear, it's much the same as when the council put a proper street where previously there'd only been a footpath worn into the grass. The Ultraduct began like that, as just a crease that had been trodden into bein' by the men and women gooin' to an' fro, except the Ultraduct wiz a path worn through time and not just grass. It 'ad been there since long before the Romans, but they were the ones 'oo properly established it, as you might say. Then people like that monk who come 'ere frum Jerusalem and brought the cross to set into the centre, they trod it in deeper. Then, o' course, there wiz all the Crusaders, back and forth between 'ere and the 'Oly Land. Around 'Enry the Eighth's time in the fifteen-'undreds, when 'e broke up all the monasteries and forced the split with Rome so 'e could get divorced, that wizzle be about the time the builders started puttin' up the Ultraduct. What we're lookin' at 'ere wiz when it's nearly finished, which'll be in abayt twenty years frum now."

In a concerted effort to stop staring at the eye-deceiving pillars, Michael gazed instead towards the Ultraduct itself, the alabaster walkway sweeping off across Northampton to the far horizon. All along the railed bridge there appeared to be some sort of blurred activity, a sense of constant motion even though you couldn't really see anything moving. Waves of what seemed to be heat-haze pulsed both ways along the overpass and rippled into intricate and liquid patterns where they crossed each other. Even though the structure was unfinished, it was clearly already in use by some person or persons who were travelling too fast to see. Or, Michael thought, they might be travelling too slow to see, although he had no idea what he meant by that.

The gang had by now reached the spot on Chalk Lane where the grey-robed builders were at work. Being the outfit's self-appointed spokesman, Phyllis elbowed her way past her colleagues, dragging Michael in her wake as she approached the nearest of the labourers, one skinnier and taller than the others with a shaved head and a long and mournful face. Phyllis addressed him, speaking slowly and deliberately in the way you would if you were talking to somebody who was deaf or a bit dim.

"This Michael Warren. We the Dead Dead Gang. Can we go on the Ultra-duct and talk to Fiery Phil?"

The builder peered down at the ghost girl in her grisly scarf, and at the dressing gown-clad little boy beside her. His grey eyes were twinkling and he pursed his lips as though to keep himself from laughing.

"Dje banglow fimth scurpvyk?!"

Michael was beginning to get used to how the builders talked. First they would speak the gibberish that was their version of a word or sentence, then that nonsense would unroll itself inside the listener's head into a long speech full of thunderous and ringing phrases. In the current instance, this expanded monologue began with *In the Big Bang's glow we stand, I and thee, child of whim ...* and then seemed to continue in that vein for ages. Finally, as Michael understood it, once you'd listened to them talking and absorbed it all as best you could, you sort of came up with your own translation. If he'd heard the builder right, the tickled-looking chap had just said, "The Dead Dead Gang? Why, I've read your book! So I'm the angle that you met when you were at the Ultraduct in chapter twelve, "The Riddle of the Choking Child", and then again at the end of the chapter. What an honour. Now, let's see, you must be Phyllis, with your rabbit scarf, and this is Alma's brother Michael. I suppose that must be Miss Driscoll herself behind you. Yes, of course you can see Mr. Doddridge. I'll take you myself. Goodness, just wait until I tell the others!"

Looking puffed up fit to burst the builder gently herded them towards a ladder that was propped against the elevated walkway, though as they got closer Michael saw that it had carpeting and was in fact a narrow section of what he'd heard called a 'Jacob Flight'. The cluster of ghost-children all shuffled obediently forward as they'd been directed, with nobody kicking up the usual ruckus. Everyone, in fact, looked too astonished by what the grey-robed beanpole had just said to make a sound. Although the Dead Dead Gang liked to pretend to being famous, you could tell that they were flummoxed by the thought that even builders had apparently read their adventures. Where, though, had they read them? There were no real books about the gang except the one in Reggie Bowler's dream, which clearly didn't count. And who was this Miss Driscoll? As he reached the bottom of the staircase-ladder, Michael could hear Bill and Phyllis whispering excitedly, somewhere behind him.

"'E said about *Forbidden Worlds* when me an' Reggie found 'im up in Bath Street flats, but still I didn't catch on."

"Well, I knew as I'd seen 'im before when I first faynd 'im in the Attics o' the Breath. I just couldn't think where, but now I know. It wiz the show, just up the street there. Well. This changes everything."

It sounded as if they were talking about him, but Michael couldn't really make much sense of it. Besides, he'd reached the bottom of the Jacob Flight with everybody else queued up behind him, so he had to concentrate upon the climb. As usual, this was awkward, with the tiny treads too small for even Michael's feet, but his ascent was much assisted by the ghost-seam's general weightlessness. In moments he was clambering up onto the shining, milky boardwalk of the Ultraduct.

He stood there rooted to the spot and lit from underneath by the white crystal planks of the unfinished bridge, his small form almost bleached out of existence like a figure in a photo that the light had spoiled. As his five comrades and the helpful builder climbed onto the boards behind him, Michael stared transfixed at the changed landscape that was visible from this new vantage point, this overpass that Phyllis said was built upon a path worn into time itself.

Around them, from horizon to horizon, several different eras were all happening at once. Transparent trees and buildings overlapped in a delirious rush of images that changed and grew and bled into each other, see-through structures crumbling away and vanishing only to reappear and run through their accelerated lives over again, a boiling blur of black and white as if a mad projectionist were running many different loops of old film through his whirring, flickering contraption at the same time, at the wrong speed. Looking west down the raised highway, Michael saw Northampton Castle being built by Normans and their labourers, while being pulled down in accordance with the will of Charles the Second fifteen hundred years thereafter. A few centuries of grass and ruins coexisted with the bubbling growth and fluctuations of the railway station. 1920s porters, speeded up into a silent comedy, pushed luggage-laden trolleys through a Saxon hunting party. Women in ridiculously tiny skirts superimposed themselves unwittingly on Roundhead puritans, briefly becoming composites with fishnet tights and pikestaffs. Horses' heads grew from the roofs of cars and all the while the castle was constructed and demolished, rising, falling, rising, falling, like a great grey lung of history that breathed crusades, saints, revolutions and electric trains.

The castle, obviously, was not alone in the transforming flood of simultaneous time. Above, the sky was marbled with the light and weather of a thousand years, while there beside the shimmering edifice the town's west bridge shifted from beaver dams to wooden posts, from Cromwell's drawbridge to the brick and concrete hump that Michael knew. Now standing next to him, Phyllis gave him a slightly funny look, as if regarding him in a new light. At last she smiled.

"What d'yer think, then? How's that for a view? I tell yer what, if yer've got any business you want answered, you just ask away. I know I might 'ave told yer to shut up and not ask questions all the time, but let's just say I've 'ad a change of 'eart. You ask me anything yer want, me duck."

Michael just blinked at her. This was a turn-up for the books, and he'd no idea what had brought it on so suddenly. That said, he thought he'd take advantage of this new spirit of openness in Phyllis while it lasted.

"All right, then. Wizzle you be my girlfriend?"

It was Phyllis's turn now to stare at Michael blankly. Finally she draped a sort of consolation-arm around his shoulder as she answered.

"No. I'm sorry. I'm a bit too old for you. And anyway, when I said about questions, it weren't questions like that what I meant. I meant about the Ultraduct and things like that."

Michael looked up at her and thought about it for a moment.

"Oh. Well, then, why can we see all different times from here?"

The whole gang and the builder who had volunteered to be their guide were by now heading slowly for the walkway's ragged, uncompleted end. Phyllis, who looked immensely grateful for the change of topic, answered Michael's query with enthusiasm as they walked along together.

"This wiz what time looks like when yer up above it, looking dayn. It's a bit like if you were in a gret big city, walking in its streets so yer could only see the little bit what you were in at present, and then yer got taken up inter the sky, so you could look dayn and see the 'ole place with all its buildings, all at once. The Ultraduct is mostly used by builders, devils, saints and that lot, when they're moving through the linger what's between 'ere and Jerusalem. They're used to seein' time like this, so they think nothin' of it, but to ordinary ghosts it still looks funny. 'Ave a decko at the church along the end 'ere if yer don't believe me."

Michael glanced away from Phyllis and towards the jutting and unfinished pier-end that they were approaching. Just beyond the point where the bridge terminated in mid-air was a tremendous visual commotion, churning

imagery somewhere between a speeded-up film advertising the construction
industry and a spectacular Guy Fawkes Night firework show. He saw the naked
prehistoric slope that would be Castle Hill and over this, superimposed, he
saw outbuildings of the Norman castle as they rose and fell, a single stone
retreat encircled by a little moat, the lonely turret crumbling down to rubble,
the surrounding ditch drained and filled in to form a ring of hard dirt lanes
around the mound. A wooden chapel bloomed and crumpled into empty
grass, with burdened plague-carts blurring back and forth as they delivered
human backfill to a briefly-manifested burial pit. The barns and sheds that
he'd seen on the site when he'd been back down in the 1670s a little while
ago were flickering in and out of being and amongst it all an oblong structure
made from warm grey stone was starting to take shape.

At first the building was just walls that knitted themselves into being from
the bottom upward, leaving gaps for three high windows on the southern face
and two long doorways where the bricks swirled out in an extension to the
west, which looked as if they might be loading bays of some sort. Michael
noticed that the luminous white walkway he was standing on seemed to be
leading straight into the top half of the leftmost door, but was distracted by
a slate roof rattling into existence as it unrolled from the eaves, just as a similarly slate-topped porch that had its own brick chimney started to squeeze
itself forward from the block's south side, right under the three windows.
Boundaries sprang up a few yards from the property, enclosing it in limestone
walls that rose to curious rounded humps where the four corners should have
been, only for these to melt into the lower and more sharp-edged forms that
Michael was familiar with. At the same time – and all of this was at the same
time, from the ancient grassy hillock to the Norman turret and the teetering,
ramshackle barns that followed it – he saw the porch with its lone chimney
and its steep slate roof collapse into a broader, grander church-front: a Victorian vestibule that had a flagged and iron-gated courtyard spread before it.
Looking back towards the nearest, western side he saw that the two lengthy
doorframes had been mostly filled in, leaving one small entrance halfway
up the wall of the extension, corresponding neatly with the end-point of the
Ultraduct. This previously uncompleted juncture of the walkway had apparently been finished in the last few seconds and now fitted perfectly against
the chapel, leading smoothly into the suspended doorway. Doddridge Church,
now wholly recognisable, exploded into space and time as modern flats and
houses licked the skyline to its rear with tongues of brick.

Meanwhile, above the forming contours of the building, something else
was going on. Strokes of pale light were sketching in a towering diagram of
scaffolding and girders, an enormous, complicated latticework of luminescent tracings that soared in a square-edged column to the curdling heavens,

with its upper limits out of sight beyond even the range of Michael's ghost-eyes. Matchstick lines of fleeting brilliance scintillated in and out of view, elaborate grids of white against the swirling centuries of sky that fogged and clarified above, suggesting something vast of which the earthly church was merely a foundation stone. He looked up quizzically at Phyllis, who smiled proudly in return.

"And you thought that them tower blocks up in nothing-five or six wiz big, ay? Well, they're not a patch on Fiery Phil's place. It goes straight up to Mansoul and even 'igher, up to the Third Borough's office if the rumours are to be believed."

Michael was puzzled by the name which, even though he thought he might have heard it earlier, had yet to be explained.

"Who's the Third Borough?"

"Well, it's like the normal livin' neighbour'ood, that's the First Borough, like I told yer. Then above that there's the Second Borough, what we call Upstairs. And up above that … well, there's the Third Borough. He's a sort of rent-collector and he's sort of a policeman at the same time. He runs all the Boroughs. He makes sure that there's justice above the street and everythin' like that. You never see 'im, not 'less yer a builder. 'Ere, come on, let's goo in through the crook door and meet Mrs. Gibbs, see if she's faynd ayt anythin' abayt this big adventure what yer on."

The group had reached the point at which the shining walkway ended with the wooden doorframe halfway up the church's western wall. Taking his hand in hers, Phyllis pulled Michael through the door's black-painted boards into rich, sudden colour and ear-popping sound. As bad as or else worse than he remembered it, the reek of Phyllis's pelt-necklace curled into his nostrils before he could clench them shut and made him want to retch. The after-images that had been trailing them on their excursion through the Great Fire of Northampton all abruptly vanished, indicating that they were now up above the ghost-seam. They were Upstairs. They were in Mansoul.

That said, the room in which they found themselves appeared to be of normal size and hadn't been expanded into one of Mansoul's endless, gaudy aerodromes. Its furnishings – its tables, chairs and carpets – were all of an eighteenth century design, and though they glowed with dearness and with presence they did not seem to be those of a rich man, nor one who was extravagant or showy.

As the children and their grey-robed escort percolated into the gold-lit room through its half-sized wooden door they found that Mrs. Gibbs was there already, waiting for them. The rotund and pink-cheeked deathmonger stood at the far end of the chamber, wearing a white apron that had brightly coloured bees and butterflies embroidered round its edges. There beside her

was a man of moderate height who looked to be in early middle age. His chiselled features, with the smooth brow and the curved blade of the nose, were
nonetheless inclined to plumpness, a slight bulge of fat between the rectangle
of his antique starched parson's collar and the firm, cleft chin. His eyes, however, had a somewhat sunken quality, the kindly slate-blue gaze retreated into
wide, round sockets that appeared to catch reflected light around their rims,
a fever-bright shine smeared on the high cheekbones. The cascading golden
curls of what Michael realised belatedly must be a wig fell to the shoulders of
the pastor's long black smock, enclosing the kind, noble features in a fancy
gilded frame, like an old painting. A fond smile haunted the corners of the
thin lips' longbow line. This, Michael thought, must be the man that Phyllis
had called Fiery Phil, although he didn't seem to have the slightest thing about
his manner that was fiery. Fire, as Michael had experienced it recently in the
cavorting of the Salamander girls, was nowhere near as reasonable or considerate in its appearance.

Both Mrs. Gibbs and the somehow imposing clergyman seemed pleased
to see the scruffy phantom children and the builder that accompanied them.
The deathmonger bustled forward, beaming.

"There you are, my dears. And Mr. Aziel, how nice to meet you. Now then,
this wiz Mr. Doddridge who I said I'd have a word with. Mr. Doddridge, this
wiz the Dead Dead Gang, who I dare say you'll have heard of."

Doddridge smiled, although the radiant eyes looked a bit sad to Michael.

"So these are the very terrors of Mansoul! My word, but we are honoured.
My wife Mercy often reads your exploits to our eldest daughter, Tetsy. I must
introduce you to them presently, but for the moment there wiz one amongst
you that I am most eager to encounter."

Michael thought that this would more than likely turn out to be him,
since everybody in the afterlife seemed to be taken with him. At the same
time, unbeknownst to Michael, Phyllis Painter was assuming that the clergyman meant her, as the Dead Dead Gang's leader. Even Marjorie, for her
own reasons, puffed up just a little in anticipation before all three were let
down when Doddridge strode across the diamond-patterned carpet, walking
in between them to clasp Reggie Bowler by the shoulders. None of them had
been expecting that, least of all Reggie.

"By your raiment I can surely tell that you are Master Fowler. When I read
that you had met your frozen end in plain sight of our little church it made me
weep, and Mercy wept as well. You must take time away from your adventures
to attend the ghost academy I am attempting to establish, where those spirits
that are less advantaged may partake of learning even when their mortal term
has been concluded. Tell me that you'll visit us, for that should make my heart
most glad."

Dumbfounded, Reggie nodded and shook the man's proffered hand. The clergyman beamed with delight and then turned his attention to the other children.

"So, then, let us see. This must be Phyllis Painter in her famously offensive scarf, which means that over here we have our little author. The tall fellow at the back must be our dashing solider-boy, and from your family resemblance to young Miss Painter I assume you must be Bill. Be sure that I shall keep my eye on you."

Finally Doddridge turned to smile at Michael, crouching down upon his haunches so that his gaze would be level with that of the dressing gown-clad child.

"By process of elimination, then, this bonny little fellow must be Michael Warren. Poor lad. I imagine that all this bewilders you, the ins and outs of our existence in Mansoul while all the time your earthly body speeds towards the hospital I founded with my good friends Mr. Stonhouse and the Reverend Hervey. And if that wiz not enough, dear Mrs. Gibbs informs me that one of the higher devils has deceitfully ensnared you in some wicked bargain."

Michael's lips began to tremble at the memory.

"He said I'd got to help him do a murder. I won't have to, wizzle I?"

Doddridge glanced down towards the cream-and-chocolate decorations of the carpet for a moment and then once more raised his gaze to look at Michael, his eyes now grave and concerned within the bright-rimmed sockets.

"Not unless it be the will of He who buildeth all things, though it may be so. Be brave, my boy, and know that nothing can occur save by necessity. Each of us has his part to play in the immaculate construction, in the raising of the Porthimoth di Norhan, and none more so than yourself. Your part entails no more than that you carry on with your adventure. See all that you can of this eternal township where we are continued, even if those sights are on occasion dreadful. See the angles and the devils both, fair lad, and try hard to remember all that you experience. Your time here shall provide the inspiration for events that, be they modest, are essential to the Porthimoth's completion."

Phyllis here jabbed Bill hard in the ribs with one sharp elbow, hissing "See? I told yer!"

Michael still had no idea what they were going on about, and anyway was more concerned about something that Mr. Doddridge had just said.

"That Sam O'Day said that I wizzn't going to remember anything when I went back to life again. He said that wiz the rules of Upstairs."

The preacher nodded, trembling the golden ringlets of his wig. He smiled at Michael reassuringly then looked up at the other children, fixing them with his calm gaze.

"It never ceases to surprise me, but the plain facts are that devils cannot lie. We all know what our young friend has just said to be the truth, that all events in Mansoul are forgotten in the mortal realm. I fancy, also, that a couple of you know already why this must not be the case with Michael. You must do all that you can to see that he recalls his time with us. Though this would seem impossible, a way exists by which such things may be accomplished. From what I have read of your most entertaining novel, you should simply put your trust in your own reasoning and be assured that, in the last analysis, all shall be well."

Drowned Marjorie piped up here, sounding peeved as she addressed the minister.

"If you already know the way we're going to sort things out, then why don't you just tell us and save us the bother?"

Rising to his feet, the cleric laughed and ran one hand through the stout little girl's brown hair, ruffling it up affectionately, although Marjorie glowered through her National Health spectacles and looked affronted.

"Because that's not how the tale goes. At no point within the narrative that Mercy read me did it say that poor old Mr. Doddridge intervened and told you how the story ended, so that you could skip ahead and spare yourselves the bother. No, you'll have to work it all out on your own. For all you know, the bother that you're so keen to avoid might be your yarn's most vital element."

Mrs. Gibbs gently butted in.

"Now then, my dears, I'm sure that Mr. Aziel and Mr. Doddridge have got matters what they'd like to talk about. Why don't I take you through to meet with Mrs. Doddridge and Miss Tetsy? I think Mrs. Doddridge said as she'd be making tea and cakes for everybody."

The whole ghost-gang seemed to be inordinately cheered by this announcement, flocking round the deathmonger as she began to shepherd them out through the bright room's further door into the passageway beyond. The mention of refreshments came as something of a shock to Michael, who until that moment had assumed that ghosts could neither eat nor drink. He realised that the last thing past his lips had been the cherry-menthol Tune his mum had given him there in their sunlit back yard down St. Andrew's Road, at least a week ago by Michael's reckoning. Since then he hadn't felt the need for food, but now the memory of how good it had been to chew and swallow something nice was making him feel hungry and nostalgic at the same time, so that both sensations were mixed up together and could not be told apart. He was becoming ravenously reminiscent.

Michael and the other children followed Mrs. Gibbs into the cosy, creaking passageway, leaving the reverend and the tall, bony builder to their conversation. Mr. Doddridge and the man that Mrs. Gibbs called Mr. Aziel were settling themselves into two facing armchairs as the parlour door swung shut behind the children and the deathmonger. The corridor in which the phantom kids now found themselves was short but pleasantly arranged, with pink and yellow flowers in a vase upon the single windowsill, caught in a slanting column of fresh morning light that fell as a white puddle on the varnished floorboards. A framed panel of embroidery hung from the mint-green pinstripe of the wallpaper on Michael's left, with the roughshod design that he had seen already in Mansoul, the ribbon of a street or road unwound beneath a crudely rendered set of scales, picked out in golden thread on plump rose silk. There was the most delicious smell of baking leaking out into the passage from the far end, sweet and fragrant even in its competition with the niff of Phyllis Painter's decomposing rabbits.

Bustling like a black hen, Mrs. Gibbs led the delinquent spectres through the plain oak doorway at the landing's end into the Harvest Festival glow of a cheery and old-fashioned kitchen. This, Michael determined instantly, was where the fruit-pie perfume he'd detected in the passage had originated from. Two very pretty and nice-looking ladies with their raven hair pinned up in buns were standing talking by the black iron stove, but turned delightedly to the deathmonger and her flock of phantom roughnecks as they entered.

"Mrs. Gibbs – and these must be our little heroes! Do come in and find yourselves a chair. Tetsy and I count ourselves amongst your most ardent admirers, and now here we are, right in the middle of your 'Choking Child' chapter, saying all the parts of dialogue that we've already pored over a dozen times. It really wiz the strangest feeling, and tremendously exciting. You must all sit down while I make us some tea."

It was what Michael took to be the older of the women who had spoken. She was slightly built, having a heart-shaped face and kindly eyes, clad in a dress of white damask embroidered with silk blooms and speckled orange butterflies like those around the edge of Mrs. Gibbs's apron. On her rather small feet she wore shoes of soft, pale ochre leather, which had stitches of black thread to look like leopard spots and heels that were perhaps two inches high. Motherliness hung everywhere around her in a warm, toast-scented blanket so that Michael wanted to attach himself to her and not let go. As the nice lady led him to one of the wooden chairs around the kitchen table, over by the beautifully-tiled fireplace, he missed his mum Doreen more than ever. Mrs. Gibbs was making introductions.

"Now then, my dears, pay attention. This wiz Mrs. Mercy Doddridge, Mr. Doddridge's good lady wife, while this young lady standing by me wiz their eldest daughter, Miss Elizabeth. You wouldn't think to look at her, but Miss Elizabeth wiz younger than a lot of you are. You wiz six, dear, wizn't you, back when you turned the corner into Mansoul?"

Miss Elizabeth, a younger and more animated version of her mother, wore a frock that was the delicately-tinted primrose of the east horizon in the minutes before dawn, embellished here and there with tiny rosebuds. She had a mischievous laugh as she responded to the deathmonger's enquiry, shaking her black curls. To judge from their expressions Reggie, John and Bill were already infatuated with the reverend's daughter, hanging on her every word.

"Oh no. I wizn't even five before I came to grief with lots of bother and consumption. I remember that I died the week before the party celebrating my fifth birthday, so I never got to go to it, which made me awfully cross. I think that I'm still buried under the communion table downstairs, aren't I, Mama?"

Mrs. Doddridge gave her daughter an indulgent, fond look.

"Yes, you're still there, Tetsy, although the communion table's gone. Now, be a pet and take our fairy-cakes from out the oven while I make the tea. The over-water surely must be boiled by now."

Sitting beside the fancy fireplace with his slippers kicking idly back and forth, Michael looked up towards the stove. A big iron saucepan steamed upon the hob, seemingly filled with the same balls of liquid filigree that he'd seen raining on Mansoul during the fight between the giant builders. This, to judge from the small intricate beads spat above the pan's rim, must be over-water. Mrs. Doddridge crossed the spacious kitchen to a wooden counter-top on which a lustrous emerald teapot of glazed earthenware was resting. With his ghost-sight he could see a bulbous miniature of the whole room reflected in the ocean-green bulge of its sides before the reverend's wife stepped up to the counter and obscured his view. Taking the lid from off the teapot, she reached up towards the higher reaches of the window overlooking her wood worktop, pulling down one of the oddly shaped things that were hanging from the window-frame on strings as if to dry out. Michael hadn't noticed these before, but once he had they gave him quite a start.

They ranged in size from that of jam-jar lids to that of a man's hand, resembling desiccated starfish or the dried-up husks of massive spiders, albeit spiders with a pleasant ice-cream colouration. This idea was in itself unsettling enough, but peering closer Michael found that the true nature of the dangling shapes was even more disturbing: each one was a cluster of dead fairies, with their little heads and bodies joined together in a ring so that they formed a radiating web that looked like an elaborate lace doily, only plumper. They reminded Michael of the strange grey growth that Bill had found when they'd been digging their way up out of the howling ghost-storm, from the back yard near the bottom end of Scarletwell Street. Those, though, had been horrid things with shrunken bodies, swollen heads and huge black eyes that seemed to stare at you, whereas these specimens were gracefully proportioned and did not seem to have any eyes at all, with only small white sockets like the chambers in an apple core when someone had dug out the pips. They hung down on four knotted lengths of cord, with two or three of the dried fairy-clusters to a string, making a hollow clatter as they knocked together like a set of wooden wind chimes.

Mrs. Doddridge yanked one of the larger blossoms free, breaking a couple of the brittle fairies' lower legs off accidentally as she did so. Briskly and unsentimentally the reverend's wife began to crumble the conjoined nymphs into pieces that were small enough to fit in the receptacle, whereon she hurried to the stove and lifted up the pan of bubbling super-water by its handle so that she could pour the contents out into her teapot, over the crushed fairies. A mouth-watering aroma rose from the infusion, very much like tangerines, if tangerines were somehow peaches and perhaps a bag of aniseed balls at the same time.

Meanwhile, the enchanting Miss Elizabeth was taking a black baking tray out of the oven. Laden with a dozen or more small pink cakes it smelled, if anything, more tempting than the perfumed tea. Setting it on the side to cool, the younger of the Doddridge women fetched a small plain basin from the mantelpiece of the tiled fireplace close to where Michael was seated. As she passed him, he could not contain his curiosity.

"Why are you called Tetsy if your name's Elizabeth and why are you so grown up if you're only four? What's in that basin? My name's Michael."

Miss Elizabeth stooped down to beam at him.

"Oh, I know who you are, young Master Warren. You're the Choking Child from chapter twelve, and I'm called Tetsy because that's how I said Betsy when I wiz a little girl. The reason I've decided to grow up since I've been dead wiz that I never really got a chance to see what growing up wiz like while I wiz still alive. As for the basin, well, see for yourself."

She held the bowl down, tilting it so he could see inside. Heaped at the bottom of it was a midget dune of powdered crystal, quite like granulated sugar except that this substance was the blue and white hue of a perfect summer sky. Elizabeth invited him to take a dab of the cerulean dust upon one fingertip and taste it, which he did. It was a bit like normal sugar though it also had a sharp and fizzy taste, like sherbet. Being taken with the novel flavour, Michael asked her what it was.

"It's all the little blue pips that we pick out of the Bedlam Jennies. Once we've got enough of them we grind them down into Puck-sugar with a pestle so that we can sprinkle it upon our fairy-cakes."

Belatedly, he realised what had happened to the missing eyes from the suspended clusters of dead fairies. Sticking out his tongue as if he didn't want it in his mouth after its dalliance with the eyeball frosting, Michael pulled a face that made the reverend's daughter laugh.

"Oh, don't be silly. They're not really fairies. They're just parts or petals of a larger and more complicated fruity-mushroom sort of thing that's called a Puck's Hat or a Bedlam Jenny. We once had the spirit of a Roman soldier visiting us from Jerusalem, and he called them Minerva's Truffles. They grow in the ghost-seam or the Second Borough, rooting anywhere there's sustenance. When they're still small they look like rings of elves or goblins and you mustn't eat them. You must wait until they've ripened into fairies. People in the living world can't see the blossoms. They can only sometimes see the shoots that the Puck's Hat sends down into the lower realm, where what wiz actually a single growth looks like a ring of separate, dancing fairies – or a pack of horrible grey goblins with black eyes if they're not ripe. They're really all we have to eat up here, although there wiz a sort of ectoplasm-butter you can get from ghost-cows. On its own it doesn't taste of anything, but if you grind the blooms down into flour you can rub in the phantom fat to form a sweet, pink dough. That's what we use to make our fairy cakes, and now if you'll excuse me I believe they must be cool enough for me to spoon the Puck-dust on and serve them up."

The younger Doddridge moved on round the kitchen table, letting all the other children have a lick of the sweet powder, even-handedly distributing the treat. Meanwhile her mother had produced an absolute flotilla of small cups and saucers from a previously unnoticed cupboard and was pouring everyone a measure of the rosy, steaming brew out of the deep green teapot that gleamed like a fat ceramic apple. Mrs. Doddridge fussed between the wooden worktop and her seated guests, dispensing tea to everyone and telling all the younger children to be careful that they didn't spill it.

"And be careful not to scald your tongues. Blow on your tea to make it cool before you drink it down. We have a jug of ghostly milk if anyone requires it, although we find that it rather spoils the taste and gives the tea a chalky flavour."

Meanwhile, Tetsy finished sprinkling powdered fairy-eyes onto the warm cakes, dusting each pink fancy with a twinkling frost of cobalt. Mrs. Gibbs and the six children were allowed to take one each from the large plate on which the freshly-baked confections stood, a flock of sunset clouds against a wintry china sky. Pouring refreshments for themselves, the Doddridge women pulled up wooden stools beside the table, both selecting one of the remaining treats to nibble at and joining in with the soft susurrus of teatime conversation.

Mrs. Doddridge, who had seated herself next to Mrs. Gibbs, was questioning the deathmonger regarding an old bylaw that concerned the gates of Mansoul, of which there were five, apparently. From where he sat beside the fireplace Michael couldn't really follow the discussion, which appeared to draw comparisons between the various entrances and the five human senses. Derngate, from the sound of it, was touch, whatever that meant. Mystified, the little boy switched his attention to vivacious Tetsy, who had sat down next to

Marjorie and was now eagerly interrogating the drowned schoolgirl on some subject even more unfathomable than the talk of taste buds and town gates.

"My favourite chapter wiz the one with that hateful black-shirted fellow blundering around Upstairs whilst suffering from delirium in his mortal body. It made Mama and I laugh so much that I could hardly read it to her. And the passage where the phantom bear from Bearward Street turns out to be pro-Jewish and pursues him through the ghost-seam into the V.E. Day celebrations wiz a marvel."

Marjorie seemed very pleased to hear all this, though none of it made sense to Michael. Further round the table, John and Phyllis sat and talked together as they slurped their tea. They looked as if they liked each other, and although he was still faintly disappointed about Phyllis saying that she didn't want to be his girlfriend, Michael thought they made a lovely couple. Seated opposite him, Bill and Reggie were still making plans to capture a ghost-mammoth, spraying violet crumbs upon each other's faces as they both talked through unsightly mouthfuls of partly-chewed fairy-cake.

Having no one to chat with at that moment, Michael thought that he might take the opportunity to try the dainty pink-and-blue creations for himself. He lifted up the tempting morsel he'd been given, holding it beneath his nose and sniffing its warm perfume. Like the tea, the cake had a delightful yet ambiguous aroma. Michael could tell that it wasn't aniseed, exactly, that was mixed in with the hints of peach and tangerine, but it was something as distinctive and unusual. He bit into the sapphire-sugared topside and almost immediately his mouth exploded with sensations so immense and intricate he felt his tongue had finally arrived in Heaven with the rest of him. The cake tasted as rich and complicated as, say, a cathedral looked or sounded. The elusive tang of unknown fruits from half-imaginary islands rang around his cheeks like organ music and the airy, crumbling texture was like Sunday light through stained glass. As he swallowed he could feel a tingle starting in the centre of him where his tummy used to be and spreading to his toes, his fingers and the tips of his blonde curls. Feeling as if his spirit had been dipped in the rose scent that people sometimes put on birthday cards, Michael luxuriated in an aftertaste that echoed through the toddler like a hymn. It filled him with a fresh vitality and at the same time was so satisfying that it brought a dreamy and delicious drowsiness. It was a very contradictory experience.

He blew upon his tea as Mrs. Doddridge had suggested, and then took a cautious sip. The taste was like the cakes but clearer and more pleasingly astringent, like a hot breeze blowing through his phantom mind and body rather than like anything substantial. Michael thought that he was as contented and relaxed as he had ever been, sitting with friends in this somehow familiar kitchen that he'd never seen before. The chatter of the other people at the table was receding to a distant murmur – Reggie asking Bill what the best bait would be to lure a ghostly mammoth, Tetsy Doddridge wondering aloud to Marjorie if having two gang-members with the surname Warren might not be confusing for the readership – but Michael was no longer bothering to keep up with the various conversations. He munched on his fairy cake and drank his fairy tea, discovering that these were reawakening in him the thrilling sense of marvel that he'd felt when Phyllis had first pulled him up into Mansoul.

Back then, when it had all been new to him, he'd been completely mesmerised by every surface and each texture, getting lost in woodgrain or the worn pink threads of Phyllis Painter's jumper. Though he hadn't noticed it occurring, since then his appreciation of the wonderful displays surrounding him had grown more dull and blunted, as if he were coming to take this extraordinary afterlife and all its finery for granted. Not until his faculties had been enlivened by this vicarage tea-party had Michael realised how complacent he'd become, or how much he was missing. Now he looked around him at the kitchen with its milky morning light and the dear scuffs or marks of wear on its utensils, glorying in all the humble wonders and the profound sense of home that they entailed.

His gaze alighted on the decorative tiling of the fireplace beside him and he saw for the first time its stupefying detail. Each tile had a different scene delineated on it in the graded blue tones of a willow pattern saucer, fine lines of rich navy on a background of an icier and paler shade. After a moment or two, Michael understood that the square panels were arranged in order so that all the separate pictures told a story, like they did in Alma's comics. If that was the case, it seemed to him that the most sensible place to commence the tale would be the bottom left side of the fire's surround, next to where he was sitting.

Looking down, he was immediately absorbed in the depicted episode, his enhanced vision swimming in its deep blue intricacies until with a start he comprehended that it was almost an image of himself, a small boy staring at a story told in painted tiles around a fireplace, pictures in a picture in a picture. Michael was more fascinated by this endless regress than he'd been by all the spectacle and sparkle when he'd glimpsed the Attics of the Breath for the first time. Although the infant in the miniature didn't resemble him, having dark hair styled in a pudding-basin cut and wearing buckled shoes with knee-length britches, Michael felt himself being sucked into the exquisite illustration. He was not sure anymore if he was Michael Warren, sitting in a kitchen eating cake and staring at a tile, or if he was the painted youngster leaning on his mother's lap as she perched by the fire and pointed to the bible stories on the painted tiles around it. The warm room about him and its crowded table melted to a wet ceramic gloss, became a parlour in another century and doing so acquired a lustrous Prussian tint. His own hands were now cyan outlines on a wash of faint ultramarine and he was ...

He was Philip Doddridge, six years old and learning scripture from his mother Monica, her blue-limned right arm round his shoulders as she read from the worn Bible resting on her slippery skirted thighs. She gestured with her other hand towards the Delft tiles round the fire by which she sat, each one emblazoned with a scene from the New Testament, a crucifixion or annunciation to illuminate the passage she was reading to her son. It was a rainy afternoon during the autumn months of 1708 and by the fireside of the drawing-room in Kingston-upon-Thames all things seemed holy. On the mantelpiece a pair of paper fans flanked an ornate brass clock enclosed within a giant bullet of clear glass, and royal blue firelight glistered on a lacquer screen to one side of the hearth. Monica Doddridge's soft voice continued its instruction while her son's glance darted back and forth over the beautiful Dutch tiling. Here an enormous Jonah was regurgitated by a whale no bigger than a chubby pike, while not far off a prodigal son in a periwig was welcomed back into the fold. So entranced was the boy in the beguiling tableaux that he almost felt a part of them, a nearly-turquoise figure underneath the glaze, perhaps an infant Jesus lecturing his dumbstruck elders on the temple steps. Becoming lost among the indigo embellishments, Philip composed himself and pulled back from the biblical scenarios before he was immersed completely. He was ...

He was Michael Warren. He was sitting in a sunlit kitchen in Mansoul, gathered around a table with five other children and three grownups, all of whom were chattering convivially and paying Michael no attention whatsoever. Wondering what had just happened to him, he let his attention creep back to the tile-work, this time peering cautiously towards the second tile up from the bottom on the left. It didn't look ...

It didn't look like much of an occasion, on that August morning in the Congregational Church there at Fetter Lane in 1714. Philly was twelve, a sickly sketch in blue fountain-pen ink, sitting between his father and beloved Uncle Philip in the front pew, listening to Mr. Bradbury the minister delivering his morning sermon. Philly's mother had died suddenly three years before, and the frail, uncomplaining child did not believe his father or his uncle would be with him for much longer. It was not a family that knew rude health, with Philly and his elder sis Elizabeth the only two survivors out of twenty children and the other eighteen all dead before he was even born. A movement in the upper gallery roused Philly from his reverie and looking up he saw a falling handkerchief, a lacy thing with cornflower stippling, caught in its leisurely descent towards the flagged church floor. Everyone gasped except for the boy's father, Daniel Doddridge, who began to cough. The kerchief was a signal, dropped deliber-

ately by a messenger from Bishop Burnet to announce the passing of Queen
Anne, the Stuart monarch who had done so much to harm their Nonconformist
cause. Indeed, her latest effort to discomfit them, her Schism Act, was due to be
made law that very day. It was a clear attempt to undermine the grand tradi-
tion of religious discontent that reached back to John Wycliffe's Lollards in the
fourteenth century or the great radical dissenter Robert Browne two hundred
years thereafter. It attacked the faith of Bunyan and his revolutionary affiliates
the Muggletonians, Moravians and Ranters, but the Schism Act would almost
certainly now be abandoned with the passing of Queen Anne, its instigator.
Shuffling on the hard pew Philly felt extremely nervous but was not sure why.
Alerted by the signal from the gallery, the minister curtailed his sermon hur-
riedly and offered up a prayer for their new King, the Hanoverian George the
First who had already sworn support for Nonconformity. By now the church
was rustling with excited whispers and the thrilling realisation that the hated
Anne was dead at last. Smiling with private satisfaction, Mr. Bradbury led the
singing of the 89ᵗʰ Psalm before once more reading sternly from the text. "Go,
see now this cursed woman, and bury her; for she is a king's daughter." Philly's
ears were ringing as he realised he was present at the dawn of a new age, an era
of religious freedom that the boy could scarcely visualise. He felt ...

He felt the hard edge of the kitchen chair pressing against his thighs, the
sweet and slimy gobbet of unswallowed fairy cake at rest upon his tongue. He
gulped it down and took a hasty swig of tea before inspecting the next tile.
He found that he ...

He found that he was dressed up in a nightgown and a borrowed petticoat,
wearing a pudding-tin atop his dark hair as a helmet. He was twenty-one years
old, performing Rowe's play Tamerlane *with friends and fellow students from the*
Dissenting academy in Kibworth, Leicestershire, acting the part of the illustrious
Sultan Bazajet. All the impromptu cast were laughing until tears rolled down
their cheeks, including good old Obadiah Hughes, whom they called Atticus, and
little Jenny Jennings whom they nicknamed Theodosia, the daughter of the rev-
erend conducting the academy. His own cognomen was Hortensius and as he
flounced his lavender-blue skirts he wished that this hilarity could last forever,
that he could somehow stop time and thus preserve the moment for eternity, a
giggling and joyous fly in amber. The Lord knew that there'd been precious little
laughter in Hortensius's life thus far. An orphan at the tender age of thirteen,
he'd been made ward to a gentleman named Downes who would lose all the lad's
inheritance to ruinous financial speculations in the City. Following a shiftless
and unsettled period living with his big sister Elizabeth and her husband the
Reverend John Nettleton, Hortensius had found a place in the Kibworth estab-
lishment, where by God's grace had been instilled in him the discipline and the
humility that would, he hoped, sustain him all his days. The Reverend John Jen-

nings and his wife had been almost a second set of parents to the boy, so dear were
they and so concerned with his development. It had astonished him to learn that
Mrs. Jennings' father had been one Sir Francis Wingate from Harlington Grange
in Bedford, who'd committed poor John Bunyan unto Bedford gaol. Now, doubled
over in his mirth with his makeshift tin helmet clattering down upon the floor
and all his friends about him, he was stricken by the contrast between this frivol-
ity and the abiding loneliness he felt throughout most other areas of his life. There
was the passion that he felt for Kitty Freeman, his Clarinda as he called her,
though he feared that his affections by and large went unrequited. Tripping on
the lapis line that was his nightgown's edge, thereby provoking renewed squeals
of merriment, he wondered if some perfect partner waited in the future for him.
Was that in God's plan, if God's plan should indeed include Hortensius? Did a
wife and suitable vocation figure in that great, ineffable design? What was his
destiny? What was ...?

What was all this? Michael had the sensation he'd been cut adrift somewhere between this homely kitchen and the fine engraved world of the tiles,
a gleaming china landscape rendered in the hues of billiard chalk with all
of time reduced to thin blue strokes on white enamel. Though he knew that
he was being helplessly pulled into each new image that he gazed upon, he
found he couldn't stop himself from looking. The euphoria that had accompanied the tea and cake surrounded Michael like a deep and fluffy blanket, dulling the anxiety that he would end up trapped amongst the painted
curlicues. He let his scrutiny slide upwards to the next representation in the
sequence. It looked ...

It looked eerie, the diffusing morning mist, white on the sapphire bram-
bles of the country lane; the travelling minister who'd paused to talk with a
young woman clad in cross-hatched tatters, her eyes wide and bright against
an almost imperceptible slate wash in the bucolic byway. Reverend Doddridge,
passing through the villages about Northamptonshire and speaking to those
congregations where he was invited, sat astride his patient mare and mar-
velled at the sallow and unearthly-looking girl who blocked his path. Her name
was Mary Wills, and she was a respected prophetess from nearby Pitsford,
a hedge-seer and a mystic who had called out to the pale, much-in-demand
young preacher as he went upon his way. She seemed a thing assembled from
the fog that trickled in the ditches, built with weeds or sodden deadfall, and she
claimed that in her sight the future was a book already writ, a sculpted form
encased within the iron mould of time. "'And when he would not be persuaded,
they ceased, saying, The will of the Lord be done.' Those are the words of the
first sermon you shall preach in the poor boroughs of Northampton, where it is
that you shall be a pastor." He would meet the ragged oracle again across the
years and would come not to doubt her visions, yet upon this first occasion he

was twenty-six years old and thought her prophecies a sham, though he was not unkindly or offhand to her in his behaviour. It was the business of a ministry here in Northampton, Doddridge thought, that gave the lie to her predictions. He had only just agreed to the entreaties of his colleagues within the Dissenting congregation, Dr. Watts and David Some and all the rest, who'd begged him to take up the running of the Dissenting academy at Market Harborough, a post made vacant by the passing of its former minister, the much-missed Reverend John Jennings. Wagons had already taken Doddridge's belongings to the Harborough residence where Mrs. Jennings would continue managing household affairs, and Doddridge further entertained the hope of an affectionate relationship with Jennings's delightful daughter, Jenny. The idea that he might be prevailed upon to sacrifice such an illustrious position for some draughty shack in the benighted districts of Northampton was therefore a senseless fancy that, he was assured, should never come to be. He thanked the weird child for her warnings and continued with his journey. There was ...

There was no escaping the implacable progression of the tiles once Michael had surrendered to the tale's compelling undertow. Drowning amongst the glassy blue-white breakers he gave up his feeble thrashing and went under, tumbling in the current of the narrative from one scene to the next. He didn't really know ...

He didn't really know why he was doing this, leading his horse through delicate lace curtains of descending snow on Christmas Eve, towards the warm lights of the meeting-house on Castle Hill. He crunched through the crisp drifts over the burial ground, a stew of paupers' ribs and plague-skulls somewhere underneath the ice crust and the frigid, powdery depths that it concealed. He had been settled into his academy at Market Harborough but a month or two when he'd received the earnest imprecations offered by the people of Northampton, that he should take up instead the ministry at Castle Hill here in the lowliest, western quarter of the town. The district was a crumbling eyesore that had been denied the pretty renovations undergone by the remainder of the township after the great fire, and he was anyway committed to his work at Harborough. He'd gracefully declined the offer, but the humble congregation were persistent. Finally the popular young reverend had chosen to deliver his refusal personally, gently conveying to his would-be flock that they should cease from their entreaties, by means of a sermon. This began "And when he would not be persuaded, they ceased, saying, The will of the Lord be done", and yet he had not thought of Mary Wills or her prediction until halfway through his sermon, where he found himself fulfilling it. The folk of Castle Hill, moreover, had seemed filled with such good will towards him that his thoughts were all in turmoil as he'd walked back to his lodgings at the foot of nearby Gold Street. Passing by an open door he'd heard a boy reading aloud from scripture to his mother, as the troubled reverend himself had done so many times, declaring, "As thy days, so shall thy strength be", in a clear, true voice. The sentiment had been impressed upon him in that instant with great force, so that it seemed a revelation: all his days were part of Doddridge, part of his eternal substance, and he was comprised of nothing save those days, their thoughts and words and deeds. They were his strength. They were his all. He had decided there and then to give up his academy in Harborough and to accept instead the less promising post here in Northampton. His fellows, Mr. Some and Samuel Clark, had been outraged at first and begged that he should reconsider but had both reluctantly decided that, so strange were the events, a higher cause than theirs may have decreed the outcome in accordance with its own inscrutable agendas. And so here he was on Christmas Eve, trudging towards his destiny through blue-black shadows flecked with falling white. Only with difficulty could ...

Only with difficulty could Michael remember anything about the kitchen or the cake. The blue-etched episodes were coming thick and fast now. He knew he was ...

He knew he was meant for Mistress Mercy Maris from the moment he set eyes on her, there in the Worcester parlour of her great-aunt, Mrs. Owen. Six years younger than himself at twenty-two, with a good humour and a fresh complexion, she had been the bright jewel that he'd feared he was without the means to purchase. He'd but recently proposed to sixteen-year-old Jenny Jennings, yet upon being rebuffed had raised his siege and had considered himself pleased in her continuing friendship. The impulse that had possessed him, though, on that recent occasion, was as nothing to the passion that he felt towards Miss Maris, which had struck him like a very thunderbolt. He had persisted in his suit, unable to do otherwise, and found to his delight that his affections were reciprocated. They'd been wed upon the 29ᵗʰ day of November in 1730 at Upton-on-Severn, and his new wife had arrived to live with him here at Northampton, joining in enthusiastically with all his works despite the meanness of the neighbourhood. The local people had been models of good cheer and helpfulness, for all the squabbling that would break out between what may have been a dozen different Nonconformist creeds. Indeed, both he and Mrs. Doddridge found their congregation most agreeable despite the reputation it had earned for insurrection and unrest, this quiet nook where the most seditious of the 'Martin Marprelate' broadsides had been pseudonymously writ and published in the previous century. Had not Sir Humphrey Ramsden stated that Northampton was "a nest of puritans" in correspondence with John Lambe, describing the townspeople as "malignant, refractory spirits who disturb the peace of the church."? And yet it was in this shire that churchgoers first insisted, in the reign of Queen Elizabeth, upon hymn-singing at their ceremonies, where before were only chanted psalms. It was a good place, in its way a place holy as any other, and his wife and he were well to be here, although Mary Wills the prophetess had told him that their first attempt to bear a child would end in sadness. Still, perhaps on this occasion she should be proved wrong. After all, regarding his position on determinism, he stood ...

He stood in the darkening church at Castle Hill and wept; gazed through a quivering salt lens at the small gravestone set amongst the floor tiles under the communion table. He'd believed the crying to be done with, and this sudden bout surprised him. It had no doubt been occasioned by the pamphlets, recently delivered from their printing company, one of which he held now in between his trembling hands. "Submission to Divine Providence in the Death of Children recommended and inforced, in a SERMON preached at NORTHAMPTON on the DEATH Of a very amiable and hopeful CHILD about Five Years old. Published out of compassion to mourning PARENTS By P. DODDRIDGE, D.D. Neve Liturarum pudeat : qui viderit illas. De Lachrymis factas sentiat esse meis. OVID. LONDON: Printed for R. HETT, at the Bible and Crown, in the Poultry. MDCC XXXVII. [Price Six-Pence.]" It had been writ more in tears than ink and now the former splashed down, further to dilute and blotch the latter. It was ...

It was not, perhaps, so splendidly appointed as was the academy at Harborough, standing here in Sheep Street with the mouth of Silver Street just opposite, but Doddridge thought that in its practice it was quite the best in England. He and Mercy and their four surviving children had resided comfortably enough down at his previous establishment upon the corner of Pike Lane and Marefair, but with fresh students arriving every week to study scripture, mathematics, Latin, Greek or Hebrew it was evident that the Dissenting institution's newer and considerably larger premises would be required to hold them all. He hoped ...

He hoped it was his tolerance that had acquired for him so many worthy friends. His church enjoyed an amiable acquaintance with the Baptist ministry in College Lane, and in his private life he counted Calvinists, Moravians and Swedenborgians alike among his fellows. He stood now in George Row on a March morn in 1744, with his most valued and unlikeliest companion by his side. Mr. John Stonhouse had led an eventful, reckless life and had at one point even penned a tract attacking Christianity. One evening, on his way to rendezvous with a loose woman, he had stopped to hear the famous Philip Doddridge speaking and upon the spot renounced his former ways, becoming a most steadfast ally of the doctor's cause and helping him inaugurate a town infirmary, the first outside of London, which was the occasion that had called them to George Row upon this blustery morning. From the ...

From the dark November sky above him firework flowers shed burning cream-and-cobalt petals in a rain on the Sheep Street academy, brightly illuminated by a horde of candles that had been arranged to spell out "KING GEORGE, NO PRETENDER". Doddridge had been long aware how lucky the Dissenters were under this Hanoverian monarch, and had warned his congregation to be wary of a Stuart resurgence that might re-establish Catholic oppression. Now, though, in 1745, the threat was more than hypothetical, with Prince Charles Edward Stuart, the pretender to the British Throne, raising his standard at Glenfinnan and then marching south and into England. Doddridge, warned six years before of this eventuality by Mary Wills of Pitsford, was prepared. Enlisting his good friend the Earl of Halifax, he'd galvanised a parliament apparently indifferent to the Young Pretender's threat and raised a force more than a thousand strong that had two hundred cavalry, most of them garrisoned here at Northampton. The Pretender, who had counted on strong Jacobite support that had not been forthcoming, was reputedly further discouraged by the news of armed men waiting just a little further south. He had already started his retreat back towards Scotland and, presumably, eventual ruin, hence these splendid bonfire celebrations. He rejoiced in ...

He rejoiced in God's great providence as he lay dying in the little country house a few miles outside Lisbon. He and Mercy, aided by donations from the kindly folk of Castle Hill, had been sent forth on a recuperative voyage to Portugal when his health, never sturdy, had at last begun to comprehensively decline. That sunlit country, in 1751, was famed for its good weather and for the restorative effects of its environment, though their advisers in Northampton clearly had not known that late October marked, traditionally, the commencement of the annual rainy season. Now it was approaching three o'clock on the black morning of the twenty-sixth. He listened to the downpour drumming on the roof and fancied that the end would not be long. Mercy herself was ill, a victim of the climate, and he knew that she could not assist him though she wanted to with all her heart. He thanked God for that loyal and beloved woman who had so enriched a goodly number of the forty-nine years he had spent on Earth. He thanked God for his life, its every triumph and reversal, for allowing him to further the Dissenting cause to the remarkable extent he had, forcing the church to recognise its Nonconformist brethren, and all this accomplished from the lowly mound where stood his humble meeting-house. Mercy was sleeping next to him. He heard the rain, and felt her breath upon his cheek. He closed ...

He closed his eyes. Michael was under the impression that ghosts didn't sleep, but then he'd thought that about eating until he'd been served the tea and fairy-cake. Sinking into a pinkish drowse he idly supposed that while dead people didn't really need a meal or nap, they probably indulged in both things now and then, just for the simple pleasure of it. He could still hear all the other voices in the sunny kitchen, but they sounded far away and nothing much to do with him. He felt somebody – probably one of the Doddridge ladies – take the cup and saucer from his slackening grip before he spilled it on the floor. He'd either eaten his cake or already dropped it, but he didn't know which and it didn't matter.

Bill and Phyllis murmured to each other somewhere nearby. Bill was saying "Well, we must be gunna work out some way 'e can keep 'is memories, 'cause we've seen the pictures." What did that mean? Were they talking about all the pictures on the tiles that Michael still felt half-submerged in? Elsewhere, Tetsy Doddridge was insisting that Drowned Marjorie should sign her name on something. "Won't you be a sport? It shall take but a moment." He could hear a faint and rhythmic beat that he at first took for his pulse before remembering he didn't have one anymore and realising it must be the ticking of a kitchen clock, counting the moments of that timeless world.

At some point later on he was picked up by someone, one of the two older boys to judge from how it felt, and, judging from the clean and dry smell, probably not Reggie Bowler. That meant it was John who carried him, like a limp sack of flour against the taller youngster's chest and shoulder, from the kitchen into the short passageway and on towards the parlour. Michael heard the other members of the gang clumping and clattering around them and presumed they were all leaving now that teatime was concluded. He was sure that if his mum Doreen were here she'd tell him to wake up, to thank the Doddridge family for having them and say goodbye to everybody properly. He did his best to rouse himself and tried to force his eyelids to creak open, but they wouldn't budge and anyway he was too snug and comfortable in John's arms for the moment. He remained content to let it all slip by him in a luminous and rosy fog.

They were now in the parlour and ahead of them he could hear Mr. Doddridge bringing to an end his conversation with the grey-robed builder chap, who Mrs. Gibbs had said was Mr. Aziel. Michael discovered that it was much easier to understand the strange, spiralling rubbish that the angles spoke if you were half asleep. From what he could make out, the gold-wigged doctor of divinity was still interrogating Mr. Aziel upon the subject of suspicious Sam O'Day, asking the worker how the different entities related to each other, all the devils and the ordinary people and the builders, and how all of these connected up to the mysterious "Third Borough". Doddridge's guest chuckled and said "Te wysh folm updint", which instantly unravelled within Michael's slumbering awareness into something that was only marginally more comprehensible:

"They fold up into you. You fold up into us. We fold up into Him."

This seemed to both intrigue and satisfy the parson, who hummed thought-fully before he ventured one last question to the amiable artisan.

"I see. And might I ask if, anywhere in this ingenious arrangement, any of us ever truly had Free Will?"

The lanky angle sounded somehow mournful and apologetic as he answered with a syllable that was apparently the same in English as in his own tongue.

"No."

After a well-timed pause as if before the punch line of a joke, he went on to pronounce another angle-word that Michael understood almost immediately.

"Dyimoust?"

What this meant was "Did you miss it?"

There was a shocked silence, and then both the reverend doctor and his guest began to laugh uproariously although Michael didn't see what was so funny. As with the majority of grown-up jokes, he evidently didn't get it. Like the one that ended 'If I put a penny in the slot and press the button, will the bells ring?' He'd had no idea what that one was to do with either, eider, duck-down drifting off into the candyfloss of his snug thoughts.

When the amusement shared by Mr. Doddridge and his visitor had died away, the doctor said his farewells to the children, as did Mrs. Gibbs, Miss Tetsy and her mother. Of these goodbyes, Mr. Doddridge's was the most lengthy and effusive.

"Thank you, children, for your visit. I hope I shall see you all again, and not just Master Reggie when he comes to study at my afterlife academy. And as for you, young Phyllis Painter, you should know that you and your associ-ates are being trusted with this child because such wiz the will of the Most High. All the experiences you share with him, even your truant capers and transgressions, are the lessons he must learn. That he recall those lessons shall be your conundrum to unpick, though be assured that we who serve Mansoul have every faith in you. As for the fiend we spoke of earlier, it seems apparent he shall have his way at some point, and when that time comes then my best counsel would be to remind you that even the lowest creatures are but the unfolded leaves of the Third Borough and are in the end subservient to His design. Now, be upon your way with our friend Mr. Aziel. Have faith, and do not fear."

As if from far away, Michael heard Phyllis ask the reverend if what he'd said regarding truant capers and transgressions meant that the Dead Dead Gang could take Michael scrumping for mad apples out at the asylums, without getting into any trouble? Doddridge laughed again, and said that he supposed it did. There followed more goodbyes and Michael felt at least two small, damp kisses on his almost-sleeping cheek, most likely from the doctor's wife and daughter.

Then there was the brief sensation of elaborate wood-grain as they passed through the door halfway up the church's western wall. It wasn't as if Michael suddenly felt cold, simply that he no longer felt the slightest trace of any temperature at all. The smell of Phyllis Painter's vermin stole was shut off like a tap and he could almost hear the crinkling of the ghost-seam's cotton wool, stuffing itself into his ears. He opened eyes gluey with ectoplasm to a world of black and white, just as John gently lowered him onto the phosphorescent planking of the Ultraduct, where time boiled up like scalding milk all round them.

Phyllis asked if anybody was still hungry.

THE TREES DON'T
NEED TO KNOW

Marjorie Miranda Driscoll was amongst the well-read dead. She hadn't been much of a reader when she'd followed her dog India into the dark Nene down at Paddy's Meadow, but she'd caught up in the timeless time since then. She'd loitered, liminal, in libraries, skulked spectrally in sitting rooms and crept, crepuscular, through classes. The bespectacled girl's tubby, weightless form had bobbed unseen at scholars' shoulders like a grey, translucent pillow as she'd followed them through Chaucer, Shakespeare, Milton, Blake and Dickens, into the linguistic hinterlands of Joyce and Eliot with quite a lot of M.R. James and Enid Blyton on the way. She'd enjoyed nearly all of it, particularly Dickens, although she'd remained entirely unimpressed by the demise of Little Nell, who Marjorie considered a theatrical young madam. If she'd written it, somebody would have chucked the whining little bugger in the Thames; see how she handled that.

Not that Marjorie could have written *The Old Curiosity Shop*, if the truth be told. She knew, despite the recent unexpected flattery from Mr. Aziel and the Doddridge family, that she was nowhere near as good as that. It was exciting, she'd admit, to think that somewhere further down the linger of eternity her novel was already finished, somehow published, and apparently quite well received. However, being a realistic sort, Marjorie thought her future popularity was probably more on account of *The Dead Dead Gang*'s novelty than any special literary merit. Hardly anybody wrote books after they were dead and even fewer saw their efforts through to ghostly publication, and so she supposed that anyone who did was bound to get a fair bit of attention.

Marjorie was a beginner, she knew that, with only a beginner's sense of how to craft a narrative or shape a story. She'd worked out a few things on her own – a chapter would seem more complete unto itself if it set up some minor question in the reader's mind right at the start, then answered it, perhaps in the concluding lines – but other than a smattering of similar devices, she felt horribly under-equipped to deal with the demands that writing a whole book had placed upon her.

What was irritating was that nobody would tell her how her novel ended or how she was meant to get it into print. She'd heard that Mr. Blake still published from a glowing workshop in the higher territories over Lambeth, but that seemed like a long hike along the Ultraduct just on behalf of the eleven sketchy and meandering chapters she'd completed thus far. Still, judging from her admirers within Mansoul's upper echelons, the stoic little girl accepted that it was a journey she might one day find herself upon. Then she would have a green-and-gold bound copy of her memoir that she could hide in a century-old fantasy of Spring Lane School for Reggie Bowler to find in a dream, which was the thing that had inspired Marjorie's novel in the first place. When she'd found out where the Dead Dead Gang had got their name from, she'd decided that to write the dream-book whence the name originated would be a dead clever writer's trick. A fine conceit, as she had learned such things were called – not that she'd ever speak the phrase in earshot of her roughneck phantom colleagues, who would only take the mickey. It was fear of ridicule or even being ostracised that had made the otherwise fearless child feel disinclined to read or write much while she'd been alive. Down in the mortal Boroughs – the First Borough – all you really had was other people, all in the same leaky boat that you were in. Start talking posh or walking round with *Portrait of the Artist as a Young Man* underneath your arm and you risked everybody thinking you were trying to get above yourself. Above them. People might just laugh and call you Brains or Lady Muck at first, but then they'd break your glasses. Even though she didn't think that any of her current crowd would act like that, she'd still elected to pursue her literary education and commence work on her novel unannounced, so that she wouldn't look so stupid if she failed.

Although she'd been with her ghost-gang associates for almost every moment since they'd saved her from the Nene Hag, Marjorie had found out that her secret double life as scholar and aspiring author was ridiculously easy to keep up, thanks to the ghost-seam's solid nature. In the ghost-seam, time was something you could dig through. You could leave whatever you were doing, burrow off to somewhere different – say six months haunting a public reading room – and then dig back to half a second after you'd departed, before anyone had noticed you were gone. Marjorie had her own private existence outside the Dead Dead Gang and assumed the other members more than likely did as well. Phyllis had once said something that led Marjorie to conclude that she had another grown-up life, or lives, elsewhere within the simultaneous reaches of the afterlife, perhaps a husband in one region and a boyfriend in another. Nothing wrong with that, of course. Phyll Painter had lived to a ripe old age and it was only natural that there were different periods in that life that would be dear to her in different ways. Marjorie hadn't even had the time to form a crush on anyone before she'd waded after India into the night chill of the river, so she didn't have as many choices. It was the Dead Dead Gang, or the library, or nothing.

That said, Marjorie had been impressed by Tetsy Doddridge. Here was someone who'd been plucked from life at a much younger age than Marjorie, yet who had chosen to grow, posthumously, to a vibrant and attractive woman. It implied that Marjorie could have the same afterlife for herself, if that was what she wanted, and if that was what she dared. She could be taller, slimmer, prettier, without the National Health glasses that she only wore because she'd worn a pair in life. She wouldn't even have to let her comrades know that she was gallivanting round the district's spectral nightspots as a lovely debutante, since when she was with them she'd manifest as a four-eyed and podgy ten-year-old, the same as always. Marjorie imagined herself in the arms of some handsome young wraith or other, maybe Reggie Bowler if he grew a foot and smartened himself up a bit, both twirling round a ghostly Salon Ballroom. Wondering momentarily what sex was like, she felt herself blush a profound grey in the colourless continuum of the ghost-seam. Hoping nobody had noticed, the young author focussed herself on her current circumstances to dispel the clouds of heated speculation that had bothered her at intervals since she'd become a writer.

Marjorie was standing on the brilliant boardwalk of the Ultraduct with the Dead Dead Gang and the builder, Mr. Aziel. Looking out across its alabaster rail, they watched as all the idle moments of the Boroughs piled themselves up into decades: centuries of cobblers and crusaders, with the castle blooming like a huge and heavy granite rose only to wither with its petal bulwarks picked or fallen, one by one. Time steamed, and in its vapour-curls fugitive images and instants flared and melted as the past and future churned together, simultaneously and forever. One of the recycled flickering vignettes in particular caught Marjorie's attention, blazing into being to go through its motions before vanishing, with this cycle repeating every few subjective minutes: on a low stone wall that had sprung up around the southerly front side of Doddridge Church down to her left, she saw a pair of oldish-looking men sitting there side by side, bent over double and convulsed with laughter. One of the two blokes, the tallest one, looked like he might be queer, dressed in a fluffy, girlish sweater with his messy hair down to his shoulders and what looked like make-up on his face. The other one, weeping with mirth beside his freakish friend, was really quite good-looking, even though he'd gone a bit bald at the front. Marjorie had the fuzzy and uncertain sense that she might know this second man from somewhere; that she might have run into him once but had forgotten it. She was just puzzling over this when lanky John distracted her by calling out from where he stood beside the rail, two dead kids and a builder to her right.

"Well, blow me. Come and look what I've found, nipper. Phyllis, hold him up so he can see what's carved onto this railing."

John was talking to the new boy, Michael Warren. Evidently, the tall lad had found something of note inscribed on the translucent balustrade that edged the Ultraduct. As Phyllis Painter followed John's instructions, lifting up the dressing gown-clad toddler so that he could see, Marjorie and the other phantom children crowded round them as did Mr. Aziel, anxious for a peek at the discovery. Marjorie, at the group's rear and herself not that much taller than the Warren kid, had to make do with second-hand descriptions, being unable to look at the graffiti for herself. She made sure she remembered all the details, though, convinced that she would need them when she wrote up her next chapter, or "The Riddle of the Choking Child" as she'd been recently informed that she was going to call it. John was pointing out something scratched on the handrail to the infant.

"See? There, dug into the marble-work or whatever it wiz, right where I'm pointing. 'Snowy Vernall springs eternal'. That's your granddad, that wiz. No, hang on. It's your *great*-granddad. He must have been up here on the Ultra-duct at some point, although Lord knows what he used to carve his name in the stone rail like that … unless he'd pinched one of the angles' chisels."

It was at this point that Mr. Aziel interjected, the lugubrious artisan sounding somehow annoyed, sad and reluctantly amused at the same time as he pronounced his brief burst of cascading gibberish.

"Hevdrin fawgs mobz cluptyx."

This unfolded, in a part of Marjorie's mind that seemingly existed only for the purpose of deciphering builder-talk, into a rolling and fluorescent speech that would have taken a good twenty minutes to read out, and then condensed again into the normal English of the chubby little girl's own summary:

"He did indeed, and it wiz my own chisel that he stole. With his grand-child, beautiful little May astride his shoulders, he has gone exploring to the furthest reaches of the Ultraduct, walking and clambering unto the ends of Time itself. I have myself been up as far as twenty centuries hence and found this same inscription waiting for me, though I have as yet not found my chisel."

After this had sunken in, John vented a low and admiring whistle.

"So that's why I've not seen him or little May since I've been up here. It's like when he used to make his long walks, back and forth from here to Lambeth."

Mr. Aziel nodded.

"Solft minch bwarz kepdug."

After passing through the florid, epic stage of the verbal filtration process, this emerged as something marginally more edifying.

"So it wiz. In fact, his lengthy walks helped form the crease through Time on which the Ultraduct wiz founded and constructed."

Marjorie was memorising all of this with glee. It was such great material, not only as a background detail she could use in Chapter Twelve of *The
Dead Dead Gang*, but as a potential subject for her second novel, if she ever
wrote one. She could see the central image in her mind's eye. White-haired
and eccentric Snowy Vernall, whom she'd heard of – everybody in Mansoul
had heard of Snowy Vernall – trekking through the ages into the far future,
with the supernaturally attractive baby May sat perched upon his shoulder.
Marjorie had heard about the lovely deceased infant, too, although she hadn't
realised until this moment that the tragically young beauty was related to
the mad and fearless steeplejack of legend. From what she'd been told, the
eighteen-month-old had elected to remain in the same gorgeous baby semblance that she'd had before she'd been snatched by diphtheria, although her
mind and her vocabulary had matured into those of what was by all accounts
a wise and eloquent young lady; Tetsy Doddridge if she'd left her infant semblance just as it was. Marjorie imagined all the marvellous exchanges they
could have, the dialogues between the strange old man and the exquisite baby
girl as they paused on their possibly unending quest into futurity and overlooked some unimaginable landmark, perhaps entire cities sculpted out of
insulated ice up in the twenty-second century or tented desert townships in
the twenty-fourth. Realising that her writer's cloud-cover of fervent speculation had crept in once more, she returned her attention to the conversation of
her fellow Dead Dead gangsters.

Phyllis, who'd set Michael Warren down onto the Ultraduct again after
she'd lifted him up so that he could see the words carved on its railing, was
insisting loudly that her colleagues take up the suggestion that she'd made
when she'd first stepped back out onto the shining bridge and asked if anybody was still hungry.

"Come on. We've all 'ung abayt 'ere long enough. We ought to be off
scrumpin' for mad apples ayt at the asylums, like I said. When I faynd titch
'ere in the Attics o' the Breath, I wiz just on me way back from the loony-bins
to tell you lot that all the Puck's 'Ats 'ad turned ripe for pickin'. While we're up
'ere on the Ultraduct we might as well pop out as far as Berry Wood so that we
can collect 'em all. Besides, you 'eard what Mr. Doddridge said. It'll be educational for little Michael 'ere."

Nobody had an argument with that, and Marjorie herself thought that
it sounded like a good idea. She had been tantalised rather than satisfied by
the delicious fairy-cakes and Puck's Hat tea that Mrs. Doddridge had served
up. The prospect, then, of ripe, moist fairy-clusters hanging from the madhouse eaves in bucket loads, dripping with juice, was one she found rather
appealing. She'd discovered that she always had the best ideas for stories when

she'd gorged herself on Bedlam Jennies, and besides was always interested in a musical and literary field-trip out to the asylums. Marjorie had heroines and heroes there.

They all said their goodbyes to Mr. Aziel, who shook everybody by the hand and shook Marjorie's twice, before they set off boldly down the Ultraduct as it curved out to the southwest, leaving the glum and bony builder to re-join his fellow craftsmen somewhere at the bottom of his Jacob Flight, down near the base of the walkway's support posts in the late seventeenth century. As the ghost-hooligans strolled cheerily along they sang the club song that Phyllis had introduced, though Marjorie suspected that it was an old song from whatever mob that Phyllis used to be in, which had seen its lyrics modified.

"We are the Dead Dead Gang! We are the Dead Dead Gang! We mind our manners, we spend our tanners, we are respected wherever we go. We can dance, we can sing, we can do anything, 'cause we are the Dead Dead Gang!"

Even the puzzled-looking Michael Warren picked the words up after a few repetitions and sang lustily, if squeakily, along with all the rest. As Marjorie mumbled in tune with the bold marching air, she mused upon the fact that hardly any of the song was true. They were the Dead Dead Gang, that part was straightforward enough, but it had been some time since any of them minded manners or spent tanners. Neither could they technically be said to be respected wherever they went, not even in the ordinary places where they went most often. Most of the more reputable ghosts thought Phyllis and her crowd were ectoplasmic scum, while most of the disreputable ghosts agreed with them. They couldn't dance for toffee, and as far as singing went Marjorie thought that the ungodly racket they were making at the moment had shot that claim down in flames as well. Other than manners, tanners, dancing, singing and commanding the respect of others, though, the song was right. They could do anything.

She thought about the funny night she'd met them. "India! Come back, you bloody, bloody silly bloody thing!" It was the most appallingly-constructed sentence that she'd ever spoken, and thank God she hadn't written it. She'd waded out and as the freezing river water overflowed into her Wellingtons she'd suffered her first moment of uncertainty, but brushed it to one side as she plunged deep into the crawling darkness of the Nene after her bloody, bloody dog. She could remember thinking, as the coldness reached her knickers and her waist, "This is what a brave little girl would do." In retrospect, Marjorie saw that she would have been better off in thinking "Can I swim?" She must have thought the Nene was shallower than it turned out to be, or possibly she was assuming that swimming was something that came naturally to mammals when they got out of their depth. To be quite honest, she had no idea what had been going through her mind, other than her misplaced concern for India.

The raucous choir of spectral juveniles strode on along the Ultraduct, which hummed and resonated with their sloppy footfalls. Down beneath them, Chalk Lane churned with pubs, dust and fanatics, and as the dead children sauntered down the elevated pier with all their after-images shuffling behind them, they became aware that they were not alone upon the phosphorescent planking. Dull lights streamed towards them from the distant vanishing point where the walkway's parallel rails seemed to meet, resolving briefly into milky and translucent figures as they neared, then passing through the gang to hurtle on towards the church behind them. These, Marjorie knew, were travellers from different times as they moved back and forth along the shining overpass. Some of them were, no doubt, the ghosts of Normans, Saxons, Romans, Ancient Britons, while a few were smouldering demons and the rest were builders. To these other voyagers, the Dead Dead Gang would look as fleeting and as insubstantial, briefly-glimpsed shapes flickering across that vast and timeless span.

By now they'd crossed Chalk Lane and were progressing over the peculiar and unfolded stretch of wasteland that extended to the high wall of St. Andrew's Road. This was a startling feature of the landscape, even by the standards of the ghost-seam, and so Marjorie was not at all surprised when Michael Warren asked the gang to pause so he could take a look at it. From what she'd pieced together from the ghostly conversations that she'd overheard, Marjorie understood the patch of rough ground to be an example of astral subsidence, very like the overlapped asylums that the children were at present heading for. She found the concept of ethereal collapse obscurely frightening, the thought that even the eternal had its breakable and transient components, and yet here beneath her was the evidence.

Part of the higher reaches of Mansoul, made out of congealed dreams and memories, had tumbled through into the ghost-seam, so that the grey half-world was itself pressed down into the mud and puddle-sumps of the material domain. This lowest, earthly level, as seen from the Ultraduct, seemed to have been a wilderness for some considerable time, without the constant rise and fall of mortal dwellings that seethed everywhere about. Only the craggy contour lines of the neglected land were warping, shifting up and down, with straggly trees and bushes flowering briefly into life before they were sucked back into the underlying clay, like transient blooms of algae. On this relatively tiny scrap of physically-existent dirt, the massively expanded and imaginary structures of Mansoul had fallen in, so that the area that they were looking down on seemed in consequence immense: a yawning earthworks where

straight edges were cut into looming cliffs of flint and limestone and compacted soil. What were no more than puddles down there on the bumpy waste
ground of the mortal level were also refracted in the higher spaces that had
caved in from above, the separate spills of petrol-coloured rain unwrapping
into an opaque lagoon that lapped against the towering and irregular mud
walls. Seen from above the excavation looked enormous, prehistoric, like a
monstrous rock pool where the escaped fantasies of Mansoul or back-broken
wraiths from the crushed ghost-seam might be scuttling like awful crabs
beneath the black and silver shiver of the lake's reflective surface. All in all, it
looked like a tremendous place for scruffy little apparitions to have fun in, and
predictably the Warren toddler asked if they could clamber down and play
there for a while. Phyllis refused, of course, though not in an unkindly way.
Something about Phyll Painter's attitude to Michael Warren seemed to have
changed drastically since they'd all been to visit Doddridge Church, at least
in Marjorie's opinion.

"If that's where yer fancy gooin' then we'll 'ave a poke abayt there a bit later,
on ayr way back from the madhouses. We'll goo and do ayr bit o' scrumpin'
first, though, so we won't be playin' on an empty stomach and get shirty with
each other. 'Ow does that saynd?"

This seemed to mollify their mascot, and so they continued on their way,
over the deep plunge of St. Andrew's Road and further still, across the railway
station and the river, which as usual made Marjorie think of her bit of bad
luck, and the Nene Hag.

She had known that she was going to drown the moment that the toecaps
of her scuffed shoes were unable to locate the river bottom and she'd at last
understood the simple physics of her situation. Still, she'd had Victorian stories read to her where heroines slipped peacefully and elegantly to a watery
death, their petticoats billowing up around them, opening like lace anemones,
which all made drowning sound like quite an easy, dignified and above all
poetic way to die. That had, of course, turned out to be a load of shit.

In her post-mortem readings she had learned that the first stage of drowning was what experts called "the surface struggle", which in Marjorie's own
view was a succinct and accurate description of the process, or at least as she
remembered it: the first thing is the frightening realisation that you're having
difficulty keeping your head up where there's still air for you to breathe. Then,
if you can't swim, what you try to do is try to climb out of the river as if you're
caught in a flow of stepladders rather than icy water. When that doesn't work
you thrash around in desperation for a bit and then get tired, and stop for just
a second, and go under. As you sink, you'll hold your breath and wait for the
Victorian swoon to come, so that you won't know anything about what's happening, but it doesn't, and eventually you can't help …

Marjorie was shuddering and squirming at the same time as she thought about it. The idea, the memory of it, set her ghostly teeth on edge and made her phantom toes curl up.

Eventually you can't help opening your mouth and breathing in some water, then that makes you cough so that you inhale a lot more and ... *aarrgh*. She couldn't stand it, the remembered black ache in her chest. That dreadful instant when you understand that you will never draw a breath again, and that your life is finished as the empty, silent darkness at the edges of your sight begins to crowd into the centre and the pain and horror is all happening to someone else; to that fat, specky little girl down there.

It was the next bit, though – the stage of drowning that is talked of everywhere but very seldom written of in reputable journals – that had been the point where everything became all weird and unexpected. This was the supposed juncture of the drowning process where "you see your whole life flash before your eyes", and yes, Marjorie could confirm from personal experience that this was just what happened, although not quite in the fashion that the phrase would lead you to expect. Marjorie had assumed that when your whole life flashed before your eyes it would be like an old Mack Sennett film and full of crackling people flashing through each comical or poignant episode. The actuality of what had opened up inside her mind as she had drifted down towards the river-bottom's rising sediments with her lungs full of freezing green, however, had been nothing like that. For one thing, the Keystone Kops scenario that she'd envisaged would have had its giddy and accelerated incidents all happening in a sequence, chronologically, with one thing following another. This came nowhere near describing the phenomenon that Marjorie had subsequently learned was called "The Life Review".

It had been a mosaic of moments, an arrangement like the Delft tiles Marjorie had lately noticed all around the fireplace at the Doddridge house. Each vital second of her life was there as an exquisite moving miniature, filled with the most intense significance and limned in colours so profound they blazed, yet not set out in any noticeable order. Furthermore, each scene was less a painted vignette than it was a whole experience, so that to look on a depicted instant was to live through it again, with all its smells and sounds and words and thoughts intact, its shockingly strong pleasures and its crystal-sharp ordeals.

The glowing, living pictures weren't a bit like, say, for instance, *The Rake's Progress*, in that firstly they weren't all arrayed as a progression of events, and secondly they didn't have a moral. Some of the illuminated episodes portrayed deeds Marjorie was not particularly proud of, some showed what she thought of as her better side, and the majority appeared to be entirely neutral, even insignificant. Nowhere in any of the glimmering vignettes, though, did she feel a sense of moral judgement, or have the impression that one likeness represented good things she'd accomplished while another signified the bad she'd brought about. Instead, the foremost apprehension that accompanied the tessellated drift of imagery was, overwhelmingly, one of responsibility: these, good or bad, were things that Marjorie had done.

As an example, she remembered now one of what, at the time, had seemed like the more humdrum and less promising scenarios. Amongst the mosaic tableaux spread before her was a study in soft browns and greys, Marjorie and her mother in the unlit kitchen of their house in Cromwell Street. Her mum fussed at the stove, scrawny and woebegone, with an expression of exasperation as her little daughter tugged her skirts and pleaded with her. Studying the moment as it hovered with its fellows in the shimmering curtain honeycombed with moving images that hung before her, Marjorie had lived it all again down to its most minuscule detail. She had smelled once more the nothing-scent of suet off the glutinous bacon-and-onion roll her mother was preparing, and had heard the instantly-familiar rhythm of the dented brass tap as its signature drip-pattern fell into the old stone sink. One of the Bakelite stems of her ugly spectacles was chafing over her right ear, where it had made a sore pink place, and most of all she relived every impulse, every notion that had crossed her mind and every syllable that passed her lips as she'd stood in the gloomy kitchen, badgering her poor mother relentlessly, the same words over and over again. "Can we, mum? Can we have a dog? Why can't we have a dog, mum? Mum? Mum, can we? I'd look after it. Mum, can we have a dog?"

It wasn't good, it wasn't bad, it was just something Marjorie had done. She was responsible. She was responsible for going on and on until her parents finally gave in and bought her India, got the dog that would lead Marjorie out through the rushes and into the chilly, breathless deep. The realisation had been shocking, sobering, and only one among a thousand such small revelations glittering in the supernatural lobby-card display of highlights excerpted from her short life. She'd hung there in a kind of shining nowhere, contemplating all the mysteries of her existence and discovering that their answers had been obvious all along. Marjorie didn't know how long she had remained in this condition – could have been a century or could have been only those final seconds as her heart stopped and her brain shut down – but she could still recall with absolute precision how and when her everlasting reverie had ended.

She'd become aware of subtle movements on the surface of the time-tiles spread out there before her – moving threads of light, luminous flaws that seemed to travel from the heart of the pictorial assembly to its edges – and had understood after a while that they were ripples. It was as though the kaleidoscope view of her life had been made liquid or as if it had been liquid from the start, the still meniscus of a lake that only now was troubled by some unseen movement in its depths beneath the flashing, visionary surface.

That was when the giant face of the Nene Hag had pushed itself in three bulging dimensions into being out of Marjorie's flat, decorated screen of memories.

The pictures broke apart in coloured pond-scum; wet balloon-skin clots of vivid oil-paint slithering like rainbow mucous through the corpse-floss strands of weed that trailed to each side of that awful, sculpted face. The slimy fragments of the drowned girl's recollected life slid down a lunging brow thrust forward so aggressively that it was almost flat; the thuggish, narrow temples of a pike. Gobbets of pink and turquoise reminiscence, still with fluid and distorting scraps of a familiar place or person rolling on their jelly contours, dribbled from the forehead's grotesque overhang to drip across the lightless mouths of the eye-sockets' grotto-caves, or trickled down the threatening scythe-blade of the creature's nose. There in the black depths of its eye-pits was a sticky mollusc gleam and, down beneath a hooked proboscis quite as large as Marjorie herself, a horrid little mouth worked shut and open as if chewing mud or uttering a complicated silent curse. It had dead cats and the corroded skeletons of bicycles between its jutting, rotten, sunken tea-chest teeth.

The shattered Life Review melted away, became diluted pigment-ribbons floating off into the murky soup of the nocturnal Nene, and Marjorie had found herself back under water but no longer inside her own body. This was tumbling away from her, a grey and lumpy parcel that collided slowly with the silted riverbed amid the rising cumuli of muck and rubber Johnnies. Marjorie had found herself adrift in a continuum of black and white that had no temperature and where it seemed she sprouted extra arms and legs with every movement. As alarming as she'd found these strange phenomena, however, they'd not been her greatest worry.

The Undine, the water-elemental that she'd later learned to call the Nene Hag, had been there in the subsurface twilight with her. The monstrosity's enormous face was right in front of Marjorie, half pike and half deformed old woman, the jaw hanging open, the decayed fangs dredging through the bed-sands. The wraith-thing's translucent body trailed away behind it in the river darkness, an indefinitely long affair that had seemed to be mostly neck, a ten-foot thick eel or perhaps a section of the transatlantic cable. Up towards the looming head-end of the creature wizened little arms that sported disproportionately massive and web-fingered claws grew from the trunk to either side. One of these had unfolded, with a brief impression of too many elbows, to grasp Marjorie's confused and helpless ectoplasmic form around one ankle, dragging down the struggling fresh-hatched ghost to its own eye-level so it could take a better look at her.

Suspended there before the horror with its waterweed mane billowing and twisting up around her, eye to snail-shell eye, she'd watched the chewing movements of the ghastly, too-small mouth and had concluded that this wasn't the inhabitant of any hell or heaven Marjorie had ever heard of. This was something else, something appalling that implied an afterlife of endless and unfathomable nightmare. What kind of a universe was everybody living in, she'd thought with mingled fear and anger, when a ten-year-old who'd only tried to save her dog could find herself confronted not by Jesus, angels or a much-missed grandparent, but by this gnashing, slavering abomination with its train-sized head?

The worst thing, though, had been the moment when she'd finally met the apparition's gaze, had stared into the lightless wells that were its orbits and had seen the eyes gleam in their depths like tight-coiled ammonites. In those vile seconds, and although she desperately hadn't wanted to, Marjorie understood the Nene Hag. All the awful and unwelcome details of almost two thousand years alone in cold gloom had rushed flooding through the newly-dead girl's paralysed awareness, filling her with moonlit metal and aborted foetuses, the hateful dreams of leeches, until all the terror came exploding out of her in a long, bubbling scream that nobody alive could hear ...

Marjorie traipsed along the Daz-white Ultraduct behind her chattering colleagues. She knew that she had a reputation for not saying very much, but that was only because she was always thinking, trying to find the right words to convey her urgent memories and feelings so that she could get them down upon a literally ghost-written page. The elevated walkway had now borne them safely far across the river and above the sunken pasture of Foot Meadow, on to Jimmy's End. Once past the reminiscent swirl and slop of the lead-coloured torrent, Marjorie found she could put the business that had happened there behind her, at least for the moment, and turn her attention to their present whereabouts.

St. James's End, bubbling beneath them as they gazed down from the soul-bridge into its contemporaneous flux, seemed to have been possessed since its inception by an air of bleak municipality. Even the Saxon hovels that were building and demolishing themselves down in the deeper time-layers looked to be too widely set apart from one another, with great lonely windswept gaps between them. On more modern levels, coexisting with the mud-and-straw huts of an earlier vintage, cramped Victorian shops burst newly painted into life and then went bust, collapsing to a disappointment of soaped glass and peeling, sunburned hoardings. A bus depot bloomed and died repeatedly, the

double-deckers hunched in a perpetually rain-lashed forecourt, and across
the squirming neighbourhood a kind of shabby, brash modernity was everywhere, spreading and shrinking back across unfathomable store-fronts like a
blight. What was a Carphone Warehouse? What was Quantacom? On slack-
jawed wooden gates and fencing made from corrugated tin, graffiti writhed,
evolving from the neat calligraphy and simple sentiments of 'Devyl take the
King', through BUF and NFC and GEORGE DAVIES IS INNOCENT in blunt,
utilitarian whitewash capitals, into a melted and fluorescent lexicon of arabesques that were illegible and marvellous: inscrutiful. Marjorie wished that
she were seeing it in colour.

The Dead Dead Gang wandered, chatting, whistling and singing down
the brilliant boardwalk as it swept over St. James's End, swooping above the
Weedon Road and out to Duston. Here, on the more recent strata of the simultaneous timescape, there were nicer homes, at least when compared with the
Boroughs' soot-cauled terraces. Semi-detached, these were the homes of families who, through hard work or luck, had managed to put a considerable and
literal distance between themselves and the downtrodden neighbourhoods
their parents had been born in. Houses like the ones in Duston, not the sweet
stone cottages of the original outlying village but the later dwellings, always
looked to Marjorie as if they had expressions of pained condescension on
their big flat faces, probably something to do with the arrangement of those
wide and airy modern windows. They all looked as if somebody had just
dropped one. Marjorie's own view was that those who decried it very probably supplied it.

From her current vantage, looking down upon the architecture of a dozen
centuries occurring all at once, Marjorie couldn't see the people, live or dead,
who must presumably be swarming through the different structures as they
rose and fell. Compared with static streets or buildings, ghosts and living people never stayed still long enough to register in the accelerated urban simmer
that was visible from up here on the Ultraduct. Even so, Marjorie had ventured
out this way before, down in the ordinary ghost-seam, and she knew about the
phantoms who resided in the drained grey cul-de-sacs and crescents that the
gang were passing over, although they were nowhere to be seen at present.

She knew, for example, that the pleasant mews beneath them had a much
more crowded ghost-seam than did the run-down lanes of the Boroughs.
Whereas in the phantom half-world superimposed over Scarletwell Street
you might bump into perhaps another ghost or two at any given time, in this
more well-to-do location there were often dozens of dead doctors, bankers,
office managers and neatly coiffured housewives loitering beside well-tended
flowerbeds or running wistful, immaterial hands over the contours of parked
cars. In the sedate front parlours of homes sold by grown-up children follow-

ing their parents' deaths you would find uncommunicative deceased couples criticising the new owner's renovations, fretting endlessly about whether the value of their former property was going up or down. Sometimes you'd see a crowd of them: an otherworldly civic action group standing there glumly on the edges of some previously rural meadow where they'd used to walk their Labradors and where a new council estate was now under construction. Either that or they'd convene in the back garden of whatever Pakistani couple had just moved into the area, simply to mutter disapprovingly and glare, these demonstrations obviously rendered doubly futile by the protestors' invisibility. That must be, Marjorie concluded, why they never bothered making any placards.

It was funny, now she thought about it, all the differences there were between the spirit world above the Boroughs and the one over this better class of residences. The main difference, paradoxically enough, was that down in the Boroughs there was nothing like the number of rough sleepers, people resting only fitfully in their own afterlives. Moreover, the unhappy spectres of the poorer neighbourhood were for the most part burdened only by low self-esteem, a sense that they weren't good enough at life to dwell up in the higher district of Mansoul. That clearly wasn't what was keeping the successful types below tied to their earthly habitats, however. Was it, then, the opposite? Was the suburban ghost-seam that the gang were passing over occupied by souls that felt they were too good for Heaven?

No. No, Marjorie suspected that it wasn't as clear-cut as that. Perhaps it was more that the poor had fewer things in their material lives that they were reluctant to give up. There wasn't much point, after all, in hanging round the home in which you'd lived your life when it had been demolished or passed on to other council tenants. Not when you were only renting anyway. It was much better to go up into the "many mansions" of Mansoul, the way that the majority of Boroughs people did. The spirits around these parts simply didn't have the same incentives to salvation as they did where Marjorie had come from, but she was still not wholly convinced by her own argument. An inability to let go of material possessions seemed an insufficient reason to forgo the glories of the Second Borough, even if you were ridiculously posh. It didn't ring true. Anyway, there were a lot of lovely people in Mansoul who were by no means working class and yet who'd rushed Upstairs without a second thought the instant that their lives were over. Look at Mr. Doddridge and his family. It must be something else, some other factor that prevented such a lot of these suburbanites from moving up to the eternal avenues above.

It came to her after a moment's thought that it was more than likely status. That was probably the word that her beginner-writer's mind was searching for. The well-off phantoms down beneath her shunned Mansoul because one's earthly status had no meaning there. Other than builders, devils, Vernalls, deathmongers and special cases like the Doddridge family or Mr. Bunyan, Mansoul was without rank. One soul could not be rated superior to another, save for in whatever individual innate virtues they might happen to possess, and even that was in the eye of the beholder. For those people, of whatever class, who'd never really been concerned by status, moving up into Mansoul was not a difficulty. On the other hand, for those who could not bear that radiant commonality, it was to all intents and purposes impossible.

She thought about the few scraps of the Bible that she could recall from Sunday school, the bit about the camel squeezing through the needle's eye and how rich people would find it as hard to enter Heaven. When she'd heard that, she'd assumed there must be some bylaw in paradise prohibiting the posh from getting in, but now she realised it wasn't like that. There was no door-policy in Mansoul. People kept themselves out, rich and poor alike, either because they thought they were too good to mingle, or too bad.

Pursuing the idea – it might turn out to be a poem or short story one day, who could say – Marjorie felt that it could also be applied to the born aristocracy, those who were truly posh and truly rich, the upper classes with their country seats or castles in Northamptonshire's outlying towns and villages. By definition, they'd have more material possessions to relinquish and more status to give up than anyone. No wonder there were so few toffs in Mansoul. Oh, you got the odd one, rarities who'd been born to the purple but had never placed much stock in their position or had even turned their backs on it, but they were in a vanishingly small minority. The vast majority of people Upstairs were the working classes of a dozen or more centuries, with a comfortable rump of middling sorts and then a scattering of isolated Earls, Lords and repentant squires like golden pimples on that rump.

Meanwhile the ghost-seam of the Boroughs was in consequence mostly deserted, and these streets out in the suburbs appeared relatively thick with posthumous professionals and suchlike by comparison. What must the stately homes be like? Packed with innumerable generations' revenants and banshees bearing medieval grudges, everybody claiming seniority and wondering where all the underlings had gone ... Marjorie shuddered even as she sniggered. It was hardly any wonder that such fancy places were notoriously haunted: they were dangerously overpopulated, creaking at their stone seams with ancestral ghouls and spectres, twenty to a parlour, contravening astral fire and safety regulations. It was strange to think of all the regal piles and palaces as overcrowded wraith-slums, heaving ghostly tenements with syphilitic great-great-great-grand-uncle Percy raving about Gladstone in the next room, but in some ways the idea made perfect sense. The first shall be the last, and all of that. Justice above the Street.

Trudging along in front of Marjorie, Phyllis's little handful Bill was earnestly debating all the ins and outs of phantom mammoth husbandry with Reggie Bowler, who seemed unconvinced.

"It'd take ages, that would, digging right back to the ice age so as we could round up a ghost-mammoth. I don't reckon as you've thought this through."

"Don't be a twat. Of course I 'ave, and it'll be a piece of piss, I'm tellin' yer. What does it matter if it takes us ages, you daft bastard? I thought that was what eternity was all about, things takin' ages? We can dig back, find a mammoth, take as long as we want taming 'im, then bring 'im back up 'ere five seconds after we set out."

"How are we gunna tame it, then, and anyway, how do you know as it's a him? It might be, I don't know, a mammothess for all you know."

"Oh, fuckin' 'ell. Look, are we partners in this mammoth plan or ain't we? It don't fuckin' matter if it's male or female. As for 'ow we tame it, we just gain its trust by giving it a lot of what ghost-mammoths like to eat."

"What's that, then, you're so bloody clever?"

"I'm not clever, Reggie, I'm just not as fuckin' thick as you are. Puck's 'Ats, Reg. We'll feed it Puck's 'Ats. Name me one dead thing that would refuse a sack of Puck's 'Ats."

"Monks. Some of the ghost monks, they're not s'posed to eat 'em 'cause they reckon they've got devils in 'em."

"Reggie, we're not going to come across a mammoth who believes that, you can trust me. There weren't any Christian mammoths. Mammoths didn't 'ave religion."

"Well, perhaps that's why they all died out, then, you don't know."

Marjorie tuned the nonsense out and listened to the overlaid dawn choruses of several centuries of birds, a blissful tide of sound that slopped across the sky and sounded wonderful despite the muffling of the ghost-seam. In fact, heard without the half-world's dull acoustics it might well have been unbearable.

The Ultraduct rolled on through Duston, the railed span's magnesium-ribbon brightness running level with the multi-temporal bubbling of the treetops. Marjorie could work out which trees were the oldest and most permanent by how they changed the least, and by the way in which their upper branches seemed alive with a St. Elmo's Fire of muted colours, even in the ghost-seam's Cecil Beaton monochrome. This was because the oldest trees, all fourth-dimensional constructions in their own right, poked up out of the material plane into the Attics of the Breath there in the corresponding regions of Mansoul, with all of the specially-favoured pigeons passing up and down their transcendental trunks, between two worlds.

Marjorie wondered what it must be like to be a tree, to never move unless gripped by the wind but only to grow up and outwards into time, the bare twigs raking at the future, clawing for next season and the season after that. Meanwhile the roots extended down past buried pets or buried people, twisting through flint arrowheads and in amongst the ribs of Bill and Reggie's mammoth, reaching for the past. Sometimes a sawn-through trunk would expose an embedded musket-ball, a deadly little iron meteorite surrounded by the thickening of age and time, the growth-rings spreading out like surf-line ripples to engulf this violent instant from the 1640s in a smothering wooden tide.

Were trees in any way aware, she wondered, of the animal and human flow that rushed so frantically about them in their still longevity? Marjorie thought that trees must have *some* knowledge of mammal activity, if only in the broad historic sense: forested Neolithic valleys razed to black stumps by the first land-clearances and acres of felled timber to erect the early settlements. Wars would leave their reminders – spears and shrapnel sunk into the bark – while hangings, plagues and decimations yielded welcome human compost; nutrients to spark fresh growth. Extinctions brought about through over-hunting, whether by man or by other predators, would change and modify the woodland world in which these timeless giants existed, sometimes in a minor way, sometimes disastrously. The mounting centuries would be accompanied by urban overspill, planning permission, yellow bulldozers and diggers. All of these would have their impact, would send tremors through the hushed continuum of an arboreal consciousness, a vegetable awareness rising and descending with the sap.

She thought it likely, then, that trees knew of the human world remotely. Its large-scale events would filter through eventually, if these were of adequate duration. Those despoliations and depletions that went on for years or centuries would surely register, but what of the more fleeting interactions? Did the forest notice every gouged heart, every lovers' declaration cut deep to disguise any forebodings or uncertainties? Did it maintain a record of each walked dog and its piss-map? Queen Elizabeth the First, as Marjorie remembered, had been sitting underneath a tree when told of her succession to the throne, while Queen Elizabeth the Second, some five hundred years thereafter, had been sitting up one. What about the anecdotal apple tree that Isaac Newton sat beneath while formulating the ideas that would power the machine age, ideas that would set the trundling earth-movers on their implacable advance towards the tree-line? Was there any nervous rustling in the leaves? Did the boughs sigh with weary premonition? Marjorie thought privately that probably they did, at least in a poetic sense, which was certainly good enough for her.

The alabaster walkway that the ghostly kids were on was curving noticeably now in its approach to the asylums, up amongst the simultaneously with-ering and budding treetops. Glancing back across her shoulder, Marjorie could see the children's dissipating after-pictures following them in a rowdy-looking albeit silent crowd. She studied her own dumpy little image, stumping along at the group's rear, and was disappointed at how stolid and expressionless she looked. Almost immediately, though, the trailing multiple exposures caught up with the instant at which Marjorie had turned to look back, and she found that she was squinting without much real interest at the rear of her own head. Observing that from this angle she seemed to have a case of phantom dan-druff she faced forward once more as the Dead Dead Gang slowed to a halt on the celestial viaduct. It seemed that Michael Warren needed something else explained to him.

"Why wiz that place that's in front of us all punny-looking? I don't look the like of it."

The toddler sounded anxious. Marjorie could tell by how he mixed his words up into dream-talk, having not yet settled comfortably into the more flexible vocabulary of the afterlife. She knew exactly what he meant, though, and she fully understood the reasons for the infant's apprehension.

Up ahead of them, the glowing boardwalk passed above an expanse of the ghost-seam that appeared to be much more abnormal than was normal, so to speak. For one thing, there were sudden flares of vivid hue amongst the unre-lenting greyness of the muffled half-world. For another … well, the air itself was sort of creased, as were the faintly eerie structures that you could see through it. Space itself appeared to have been hideously mangled, crumpled up like paper in a giant's fist, with random fold-lines running everywhere and all the grounds and buildings of the place beneath them made into a clumsy, mad collage. This spatial fragmentation and distortion, added to the shift and flow of different times that was already evident, made the asylums an alarm-ing sight. Reality was crushed into a faceted, chaotic tangle of now, there, and here, and then: an indescribable topography that was one moment crystal-line and convex and the next a field of odd-shaped cavities and holes, where black and white inverted forms were drenched at intervals by colour-bursts of frightening hallucinatory blue, or hot and lurid Polynesian orange. Wonder-ing how Phyllis Painter could conceivably make sense of this demented and yet somehow glorious spectacle to wide-eyed Michael Warren, Marjorie was all ears. She might learn something important, and besides, she always made an effort to remember dialogue.

"Well, what we're comin' up to 'ere, it's what we call the mad-'ouses or the asylums. It's a bit like all that funny waste-ground between Chalk Lane and St. Andrew's Road what we saw earlier, where I said we could goo an' play on ayr way back, if yer remember. In both places it's a kind of a subsidence. Fer whatever reason bits of Upstairs 'ave fell through ter Daynstairs. What we're lookin' at, dayn in the world below it's more or less in the same place as Berry Wood, the mental 'ospital. Saint Crispin's, what they call it. But, because most of 'em what are livin' dayn below us are doolally, it's a bit more complicated than it saynds.

"See, up in Mansoul, where I faynd yer in the Attics o' the Breath, all o' the shops and avenues and whatnot are all made from like a crust o' livin' people's dreams and their imaginings. The problem 'ere wiz that 'alf o' the lunatics what places like this 'ave 'ad in 'em dayn the years, they don't know where they are. Some of 'em don't know *when* they are, and that means that the area of Mansoul that's above 'em wiz made out of dreams and memories what are wrong. Thoughts, Upstairs, are builder's materials, and if the thoughts are flawed then all the architecture what's built out of 'em wiz flawed as well, and that's what's 'appened 'ere. A faulty part o' Mansoul 'as fell in and crushed the ghost-seam, and as a result all the asylums in Northampton 'ave collapsed into one place, at least from ayr perspective. It's because the patients don't 'ave much idea which mental 'ome they're in, so everythin' gets all confused up on the 'igher levels too. That what we're looking at dayn there, it's the St. Crispin's 'Ospital at Berry Wood, but bits of it are from Saint Andrew's 'Ospital on Billing Road and other bits are from the mad-'ouse what there used to be in Abby Park, where the museum wiz now. All o' them colours what keep flashin', that's where coloured rubble from Mansoul 'as ended up embedded in the ghost-seam. It's in a right two-and-eight, and you wait 'til we're dayn there in it! Livin' and dead loonies everywhere, and even they can't tell one from the other!"

Marjorie agreed inwardly. It was most probably as succinct an appraisal of the madhouses as she herself could have come up with, and she hadn't previously known that the subsidence in the Second Borough had been caused by the frail, broken minds that were supporting it down in the earthly realm. She'd known that all the different mental institutions overlapped, so that deluded inmates from one place or time could mingle freely with the medicated shufflers of another, but she hadn't fully understood the way that it all worked. Phyllis's explanation made sense of the startling eruptions of pure colour, too: the visual qualities of a collapsed Mansoul reacting with the firework emotions of the mentally disturbed.

With Michael Warren's curiosity now wholly satisfied and with his fears only somewhat allayed, the clutch of latchkey phantoms headed on along the Ultraduct, deeper into the fold and flux of the asylums. Marjorie, who'd had her inner reverie interrupted by the toddler's query, found that she could not recall what she'd been thinking. No doubt it had been some vaguely literary musing about birds or clouds or something, but now it had vanished. Lacking its distraction, Marjorie Miranda Driscoll found her thoughts returning to their customary drift of shadowed memories and images, the very things that she indulged in literary musings to avoid.

The Nene Hag's massive, murky shape had hung there in the river-bottom gloom before the drowned child, with its horrid and incalculable length trailing away behind it into underwater blackness. Brilliant fragments of Marjorie's shattered Life Review were still caught in the strangling tangles of the creature's hair, swirling and curling all about them both. One of the Hag's umbrella-pterodactyl hands was clamped tight on the newly-dead girl's ankle, holding her immobile as it studied her. Right at the bottom of the slimy wells that were its sockets, she had seen the slug-like glisten of the monster's eyes and in them was the mer-thing's whole unbearable, unasked-for story; every terrifying detail of its near two-thousand-year existence leaking into Marjorie like septic drainage from a rusted cistern.

It was of the Potameides, of the Fluviales. Merrow, naiad, Undine, it was all of these and had been called Enula once, when last it had a name; had been called 'She' when last it had some vestige of a gender. That had been during the second century, when what was now the Nene Hag had been then a minor river goddess, worshipped by a crew of homesick Roman soldiers garrisoned at the town's south bridge in one of the many river-forts erected between here and Warwickshire, along the Nene. Those ancient afternoons, the clots of colour that were sodden floral offerings, drifting with the current. The Latin imprecations, half believing, half embarrassed, muttered underneath the breath. Enula – had that really been her name or was it a mishearing, a false memory? The creature didn't know or care. It didn't matter. Enula would do.

She'd started life as hardly anything at all, a mere poetic understanding of the river's nature in the minds and songs of the first settlers; a flimsy tissue of ideas, barely aware of her own tenuous existence. Gradually, the songs and stories that had brought her to the brink of being grew more complex, adding to her bulk with new and more sophisticated metaphors: the river was the flow of life itself, its constant one-way passage that of time, its quivering reflective surface like the mirror of our memory. She'd taken on a fragile substance, at least in the world of fables, dreams and phantoms that was closest to the muddy mortal sphere, and finally had been made spiritually concrete when they'd given her a name. Enula. Or had it been Nendra? Nenet? Something like that, anyway.

Back then she'd been a beautiful young concept, her appearance that of an unusually elongated mermaid, ten or twelve feet prow to stern, her face a fabulous confection. Each eye, then much closer to the surface of her head, was an exquisite violet lotus with its myriad petals opening and closing on the crinkles of her smile. Her lips had been two foot-long curls of iridescent fish-skin where prismatic hues of lavender and turquoise played, and lustrous tresses of deep bottle-green drifted about the polished pebble hardness of her breasts and belly. Both her eyebrows and her maidenhair were of the softest otter pelts and her extraordinary tail was terminated in a fin like an immense jewelled comb, big as a longbow. Her bright scales and her eight oval finger-nails alike were made from mirror, where black bands of shadow rippled like reflected trees.

She'd even had a love, those many centuries ago. His name had been Gregorius, a stranded Roman soldier working out his term of duty at the river-fort, missing his wife and children far away in warm Milan. His floral offerings to the spirit of the waters had been the most frequent and the most profuse, and every other morning he'd bathe naked in her chilly flow, his balls and penis shrivelled to a walnut. She remembered, dimly, the distinct smell of his sweat, the way he'd sweep the water back across his scalp to wash the dark, cropped hair. Her opal droplets trickling down his spine towards the buttocks. Once, during his riverside ablutions, he had masturbated briefly and discharged his seed into the torrent foaming at his knees, the congealed sperm swept off towards the distant ocean. Lovesick, she had followed this most precious offering almost to the Wash before she'd given up and headed back for home, wondering all the way at the ferocity of the obsession that had seized her.

Then one dismal morning her young man had gone, as had his cohorts. The abandoned river-fort became a crumbling playhouse for the local children and, within a few years, had been scavenged and dismantled to the point where it no longer served as anything at all. She'd waited and she'd waited, writhing in frustration down amongst the silt and sediment, but she had never seen Gregorius again, nor any of his kind. There had been no more flowers, but only night-soil flung upon her bosom by the hairy, slouching Britons when they rose each morning. Clearly, she was not regarded as even a demigoddess any longer and, accordingly, down in her cold, resentful darkness she'd begun to change.

She'd been so lonely. That was what had altered her by inches, turning her from lovely Nenet, Nendra or Enula to the Nene Hag, to the mile-long thing she was today. Her simple solitude had fashioned her into a monster, had precipitated all the desperate actions since then. All the drowned souls she'd claimed, all of them taken only for companionship.

She'd held herself back, had restrained her urges for some several centuries before she'd given in and grabbed a ghost as it was struggling to escape its bobbing body. She had been aware that once that step was taken it was irrevocable, a vile crime of the spirit from which there could be no turning back. That's why she'd put the moment off for so long, why she'd hesitated until the idea of an eternal life without love could not be endured another instant. That point had been reached one summer night in the ninth century, almost a thousand years ago. The man's name had been Edward, a stout crofter in his fortieth year or so, who'd tripped and fallen in the river as he'd made his way home through the dark fields with a belly full of ale. Edward had been her first.

These were not pleasant things from her perspective, neither Edward's taking nor their subsequent relationship. She'd never really bothered to consider what the drowned man's own view of such matters might have been. During the years they'd spent together, Edward had appeared to be in a continuous state of shock or trauma anyway, right from the moment when she'd closed her huge webbed hand around his thrashing and disoriented spectral body. In his widening eyes she'd caught her first glimpse of what she must look like now, the way that she must seem to them, the humans. Even if she should be fortunate enough to find a new Gregorius, how would she stop him screaming at what she'd become?

Edward, of course, had screamed at first – long bubbling spirit-noises that were somewhere between sound and light. Eventually, he'd fallen silent of his own accord and had retreated to the glazed and trance-like state in which he'd stayed for the remainder of their courtship. He became a paralysed and staring pet-toy, drifting and inert as Nendra or Enula batted him this way and that between her crab-leg fingers or attempted to communicate with him. Unable to elicit a response that went beyond a moan, a twitch or a convulsion, the Nene Hag had at last settled for a one-way conversation that went on uninterrupted for the full five decades he was with her. She unburdened herself of her many trials and disappointments, several times, and even told him of the day when she had chased Gregorius's clotted sperm to the freshwater limits of her territory. He made no sign that he heard or understood her utterances, and she might have thought that she had no effect upon him whatsoever were it not for the continuing disintegration of his personality, shedding layers of awareness in an effort to escape the unrelenting horror of his circumstances. Finally, when Edward had no more self than a knot of driftwood, Nenet let him go. A piece of ghostly flotsam, used-up and sucked dry of its vitality, she'd watched as he was swirled away towards the east, towards the sea, still silent and still staring.

Then she'd gone and caught another one.

How many had there been since then? Two dozen? Three? The Nene Hag had lost count and had by now forgotten most of her companions' names. She thought of all of them as "Edward", even the half-dozen women that she'd netted down the decades, when she thought of them at all. Some of them had been more responsive to her presence than the first Edward had been. Some of them had tried pleading with her, some had even asked her questions as they'd struggled through their fear to comprehend her and to understand the nightmare they were caught in. All of them, however, would sink into her first suitor's catatonic state, sooner or later. And when there was almost nothing left, when consciousness had shrunken to a numb, insensate dot, she would get rid of them. When their eyes ceased to follow the rare shafts of sunlight filtered from above as through a dirty glass, when their whole souls went limp and did not move thereafter, when there was no longer even Nendra's dreary entertainment to be had from them she sent them off upon her stately and unhurried currents, never wondering what became of them, whether they would remain as mindless husks until the end of time or if they might one day recover. Mute and unresponsive she had no more use for them, and there were always more fish in the stream.

It – for it was most certainly an 'it' by now – had only taken women when no men were to be had, having arrived at the conclusion that ghost females caused more fuss than they were worth. Most of the women, it was true, had lasted longer than the men before withdrawing to a vegetative torpor, but they'd also been more fierce and frightened and had fought harder as well. Combining with Enula's natural antipathy to its own former gender, this resistance had brought out a streak of cruelty in the Nene Hag's nature, where before had only been abiding loneliness and bleak embitterment. One of the female Edwards who'd got on the creature's wrong side had been slowly psychologically dismantled, picked apart in tumbling flakes of astral fish-food and then, after almost ninety winters, had been flung away. The ancient sub-aquatic phantasm had been surprised by the response that this deliberate torture had awoken in it: a dim, distant glimmer of sensation that was almost pleasure. Obviously, once discovered, this new tendency to inflict suffering had rapidly become more urgent, more pronounced, more necessary to the river-monster's equilibrium.

It hadn't caught a child before. It hadn't felt the need, regarding them as minnows, no more than a mouthful when there was a great abundance of more adult sustenance to hand with each new year, all of the accidents and suicides. The nineteenth and the twentieth centuries, however, had been something of a lean stretch on account of the increasing numbers that were learning how to swim. Around the join of the two periods, Nenet had noticed with disdain an old man giving swimming lessons to a flock of nude young boys there on the stretch of it that marked the old town's western boundary. Infuriatingly, from waterside discussions it had overheard, it later learned that the long meadow in the area, near where Saint Andrew's Priory once stood, had been renamed after this irksome Irish lifeguard, an ex-military man named Paddy Moore, and was now known as Paddy's Meadow. Consequently, through the interfering efforts of such people, most of those who entered the Hag's province would climb safely out again. The creature had been without company since it had let the remnants of her last associate go, sometime during the 1870s, but now its dry spell had come to an end. Now it had Marjorie.

This entire tide of dreadful history had rushed into the helpless phantom child, along with a great host of other apprehensions, mysteries and gruesome trivia pertaining to the creature's long, famished existence. Though transfixed by terror, Marjorie had suddenly known all the river's cloudy secrets, known the whereabouts of both the missing and the murdered, had known where the lost crown jewels of Bad King John had ended up, the ones that never did "all come out in the Wash". The little girl had stared into the wet grey spiral of the Undine's eye and understood with absolute conviction what was to become of her: she'd spend unbearably protracted decades, horribly aware of how her very being was unravelling, flinching itself to pieces as it bore the undivided weight of the Nene Hag's attentions, and then in the end when even Marjorie's identity and consciousness were too much to endure she'd be discarded, one more used ghost heading for the east coast, dead twice over.

It was as all this was sinking in that there had been a terrible commotion in the nearby waters. The Nene Hag's glutinous eyes had narrowed and contracted, squinting in surprise at this unwelcome interruption. The huge flattened head had turned, seeking the source of the disturbance, and then it had –

Marjorie bumped suddenly into the back of Reggie Bowler, who had stopped dead on the Ultraduct in front of her. The radiant flyover was evidently passing just above a central point in the web of entangled lunatic asylums, this being where Phyllis Painter had seen an abundance of mad-apples earlier, before she'd got mixed up with Michael Warren in the Attics of the Breath.

"All right, 'ere's where I saw the Puck's 'Ats. There wiz 'undreds of 'em, 'angin' from the trees and from the gutterin'. If we jump dayn from where we are now, we can bag the lot of 'em."

So saying, Phyllis clambered nimbly up onto the alabaster rail that edged the walkway, asking John to pass up Michael Warren so that Phyllis and the toddler could jump from the Ultraduct together, holding hands. The other children followed suit, and soon they were all plunging slowly through the ghost-seam's treacle atmosphere towards the scrunched-up time and space below, grey after-pictures in a smear behind them marking their trajectories. The phantom ruffians fell towards the overlapping madhouse lawns like graceful and unhurried smoke grenades.

Marjorie landed in a crouch upon the shaved baize, with her staggered rain of multiple exposures in accompaniment. The piece of lawn she landed on appeared well tended and was therefore probably a displaced fragment of St. Andrew's Hospital, rather than part of the more lowly nuthouse here at Berry Wood. Upon closer inspection she could even see the seams where neatly-manicured St. Andrew's verges met with the more roughly-shorn grounds of St. Crispin's or Abington Park: irregular trapeziums and wedges of dark or light grass fitted unevenly beside each other like a poorly manufactured jigsaw, different places crumpled up into a single landscape by the cave-in of the higher planes above. Tilting her head and looking up, Marjorie noticed that the sky itself appeared pasted together; distinct cloud types from diverse locations and from wildly varying altitudes clumsily juxtaposed, with only rough torn-paper lines dividing them. From some segments or slices of the heavens, it was drizzling.

As disorienting as the natural features of the view such as the grass and sky might be, the folded-in and mixed up buildings of the various institutions that surrounded them appeared much more peculiar. Stretches of ivy-covered limestone that were clearly part of the asylum-turned-museum in Abington fused jaggedly with pale and stately ship-like buildings from St. Andrew's Hospital, metamorphosing ultimately to the faintly sinister brick edifices of St. Crispin's. These bizarre, Victorian constructions were most prevalent amongst the mix of madhouses, no doubt because St. Crispin's was the actual geographical position in the ghost-seam that these other places had become conflated with, both in the upper territories and the confused inmate dreams those higher realms were founded on.

The architecture of the institution here at Berry Wood had seemed perverse to Marjorie since she'd first learned the word "perverse". It just seemed wrong, housing the mentally disturbed in an unsettling environment such as St. Crispin's, where the high-windowed brick wings huddled together in a whispering conspiracy, peering suspiciously from under the steep brims of their slate hats, and where a spidery tower of no apparent purpose rose obscurely from the already oppressive skyline. Taken as a whole, St. Crispin's Hospital had the demeanour of a strange Bavarian social experiment, left over from a bygone century. There was a gaol or workhouse flavour to its labyrinthine paths, its curfew hush, its isolation. Frankly, having fragments of St. Andrew's or the Abington Park madhouse muddled up with it was rather an improvement.

The ghost-children were progressing cautiously across the variegated lawn towards a hodgepodge of asylum buildings dominated by the purposeless St. Crispin's tower, a thing too slender to make any sense save as a crematorium chimney stack. One of the huddled structures near the turret's base was a prefab extension of its native hospital, a single-storey unit where on previous visits Marjorie had stumbled upon various framed artworks executed by the inmates. In amongst the strangely captivating landscapes on display, the burning orange skies, the metal shrubs trimmed to a dangerous and spiky topiary, she'd been unsurprised to find painted depictions of the way the overlapping madhouses appeared when looked at from the ghost-seam, lumps of Abington Park or St. Andrew's spliced in with St. Crispin's as though by mistake. Even the sudden bursts of higher-space phenomena – like the cascading moiré pattern currently erupting from behind the spindly brick spire ahead of them – were reproduced upon some of the canvasses, a proof that living people in an extreme mental state could sometimes see the upper world and its inhabitants. She'd even found a crayon drawing of a figure that looked the dead spit of Phyllis Painter, with the rabbit skins hung in a rancid garland round her neck. It had been a distorted charcoal sketch that made the ghost gang's leader look a lot more frightening than she was in real life or death.

Marjorie's reverie was interrupted by a sudden loud, indignant outburst from the real Phyll Painter, the sheer vehemence of which made Marjorie think that the unknown mental patient's portrait might have been more accurate than she'd at first supposed.

"Some bugger's 'ad 'em! There wiz 'undreds of 'em earlier, and all these trees wiz nearly creakin' wi' the weight of 'em! If I find out who's come and nicked our Bedlam Jennies before we could nick 'em then I'll punch 'is bloody lights out, even if it's the Third Borough!"

Everybody else, even her presumed younger brother Bill, seemed stunned by the near-blasphemy of Phyllis's incendiary rant. Marjorie glanced towards the nearby trees and madhouse eaves. She noticed that while there were still enough Puck's Hats growing upon them to provide a satisfying meal for the dead youngsters, there were nowhere near as many as Phyllis had led them to expect. Was their infuriated leader right? Was there some other well-informed and highly organised ghost-scavenger at work here, possibly a rival phantom gang attempting to encroach upon their territory? Marjorie hoped that this wouldn't prove to be the case. She'd never previously heard tell of gang warfare in Mansoul, but she imagined that it could get luminously ugly. Wraith-brawls spilling over from the Mayorhold, urchins swinging dreams or memories of pickaxe handles, although how would they distinguish between differing gang colours in the monochrome arena of the ghost-seam? One side could wear black, perhaps; the other white, like violent, scruffy chess. Her wandering thoughts had got as far as revenge doorstep exorcisms when she realised that she wasn't thinking about her real, present circumstances at all but was instead plotting a third book, presumably a follow-up to her forthcoming novel about Snowy Vernall and his beautiful granddaughter hiking through Eternity.

It was as Marjorie was forcing her unruly literary fancies back into their cage that tall John cried out suddenly.

"I can see one of the blighters! Look! He's peeping from behind the tower!"

Marjorie turned in time to see a tiny fair-haired head bob back behind one corner of the edifice's base. You could tell that it was that of a ghost-kid by how it left a grey stream of little heads evaporating in its wake. So, she'd been right. There was a rival gang of spectral ruffians who'd beaten them to the mad apples. There were poachers on their land! Surprised by her own sense of angry indignation, Marjorie joined with the other children as they stormed towards the tower, their half-a-dozen swelled into a shrieking Mongol horde by all the trailing doppelgangers.

Rounding the dark brickwork of the corner they stopped dead and Marjorie once more found herself piling into Reggie Bowler's back. Recovering, she peered between the taller gang-members in front of her, taking her glasses off to polish them upon one sleeve before replacing them, as if unable to believe what she and her confederates were seeing. It was actually a gesture she'd seen someone do once in a film – possibly Harold Lloyd – rather than natural behaviour. As if whatever startling vista you were seeing was a smear of grime to be wiped from the lens. It would, she thought, have to be quite an oddly-shaped and convoluted smear, especially in this current instance.

Some way off, a time-hole had been opened in the air quite near ground level, being almost three feet in diameter by Marjorie's own estimate and bordered by the flickering static bands of alternating black and white that usually attended such phenomena. There were two tough and grubby-looking ghost-boys, one tall and the other short, holding between them what looked like some sort of lettered banner that was sagging under what must have been hundreds of ripe Puck's Hats, all the moist and interlocking fairy figures in their starfish clusters, hints of colour in their glisten, fugitive and delicate, piled up like so many prismatic turnips on the strange flag being used to carry them. Now that she looked more closely through her dead-eyes and her polished spectacles, Marjorie could see the tops of some embroidered letters on the banner that appeared to spell out the word 'union' or 'upiop', most probably the former. Had somebody formed a Union in Heaven, bargaining for better outfits and a shorter working ever-after? Focussing upon the two unlikely union representatives who were about to make off through their warp-window with all the stolen wraith-food, Marjorie could not help noticing that the loftier interloper wore a hat like Reggie Bowler's ...

On a head like Reggie Bowler's. And a body.

It was Reggie Bowler, several yards away from her and from the other Reggie who was standing just in front of Marjorie and moaning in bewilderment as he surveyed his evil Puck's Hat-thieving twin. The Reggie look-alike was holding one end of the heavy-laden banner while the other end was gripped by a precise and vivid reproduction of Phyll Painter's nipper, rowdy little Bill. The real Bill, meanwhile, was stood swearing fluently beside his elder sister, who for once did not admonish him. Marjorie took her glasses off and polished them again, being unable to come up with any more appropriate reaction. This she left to Phyllis, who was after all the gang's titular leader.

"William! What the B– 'Ell d'yer think yer playin' at, you effin' little C?"

Marjorie gasped. She'd never thought that Phyllis Painter would be one to use such coarse and vulgar letters of the alphabet. It was then that big John pitched in, sounding almost as angry.

"That's a British Union of Fascists banner that you're holding! If you've joined the Moseleyites as well as taking all our Bedlam Jennies then I'll knock your heads together!"

By this point the surplus Bill and Reggie towards whom these hostile comments were addressed had managed to manoeuvre their apparently Blackshirt-affiliated makeshift stretcher full of Puck's Hats through the time-hole. They were on the gap's far side, weaving the interference-coloured edges back across the centre as they sealed the aperture behind them. Just before the opening disappeared completely, Reggie and Bill's doubles gazed back through it at their dumbstruck counterparts.

"There's a good explanation for all this, so don't go blamin' me."

"Shut up, Reg. Listen, everybody, just remember that the devil's in the driver's seat. That way it won't be a surprise when – "

It was at this juncture that the final shimmering filaments were drawn across the breach in space, cutting off Bill's twin in mid-sentence. There remained only the fractured view of the conjoined asylums, where a hundred or so years of inmates wandered aimlessly across a differently-toned patch-work of amalgamated lawns, and there was nothing to suggest that the time-hole had ever been there. It had vanished without trace.

Speechless with rage, Phyllis smacked Bill around the ear.

"Ow! Fuckin' 'ell, you mad old bat! What are yer 'ittin' me for?"

"Well, what are you stealin' all ayr Puck's 'Ats for, yer rotten little bugger? And what was that business abayt devils in the drivin' seat?"

"Well, I don't know! Are you completely fucking mental? I wiz standin' over 'ere the 'ole time. That weren't me and Reggie. It just looked like us."

"Looked like! I'll gi' you looked like in a minute! That wiz you! D'yer think as I don't know me own flesh and blood? That wiz just you from somewhere up the linger, from a moment we ent got to yet! You're gunna dig back 'ere and pinch ayr mad apples before we 'ave a chance to 'arvest 'em, you and this silly bastard stood beside yer." Phyllis glared at Reggie here. Disastrously, Bill tried to reason with her.

"Well, 'ow am I supposed to know what it all meant if we ain't got there yet? I'm only fuckin' dead, I'm not clairvoyant. John, mate, can't you reason with her? When she's off 'er HRT like this I might as well not bother."

The good-looking older boy gave both the errant duo a refrigerated look of withering contempt.

"Don't try to creep round me, you pair of bloody Nazis. Come on, Phyll. Let's you and me and Michael go and gather up whatever pickings these two bandits have seen fit to leave us with."

So saying, John and Phyllis each took one of Michael's hands and walked off with the toddler in the direction of a spinney, swinging him between them in the ghost-seam's feeble gravity. Marjorie felt a little disappointed at the way that she'd been casually left with the renegades, but thought that the apparent snub was in all likelihood a thinly-veiled excuse for John and Phyllis to sneak off together, rather than a personal affront. Besides, she'd always got on slightly better with Reggie and Bill than she had with Phyll Painter and big John. Phyllis could be ever so bossy, while John sometimes played upon his war-hero good looks too much. Bill, on the other hand, once you'd got past the lewd remarks about your knockers or your knickers, was surprisingly well-read and well informed, while Marjorie had always had a soft spot for poor Reggie. Reggie bordered on good-looking in a certain light, although she had to privately agree with Phyllis's appraisal of his intellectual faculties: he was a silly bastard.

"What was all of that about, then? Have you got some plan to nick the Puck's Hats and divide 'em up between you two and your new Blackshirt comrades?"

Reggie started to protest his innocence, but Bill grinned ruefully.

"Well, I 'ave now, I'll tell yer that for fuckin' nothin'. If that old cow's gunna bat me 'round the 'ead for summat I've not done yet, then I'm gunna make sure that I fuckin' well deserve it. I don't know so much about joinin' the Nazis, although I've thought very often that I'd look quite rock 'n' roll in jackboots. No, Marge, that was fuckin' weird, seein' meself like that. I wonder what I meant about the devil being in the driver's seat?"

Reggie looked thoughtful, or least as thoughtful as he ever did.

"I reckon as that wiz a trick done with a mirror."

Bill snorted derisively.

"Reggie, mate, you're not the sharpest suit in Burton's window, are yer? How wiz it a trick done with a mirror? They were dragging a great banner full of Puck's Hats whereas we conspicuously ain't. And anyway, how wiz a mirror s'posed to talk to us? It's only light what they bounce back, not voices. Now come on, let's see if we can get back into Phyllis's good books by finding lots of fairy fruit for 'er to scoff, the stroppy bitch."

They were all laughing now at Phyllis's expense as the three of them strolled around the various confused and fused asylum buildings, peering up into the gutter's underhang for any sign of the elusive delicacies. A fountain of almost-fluorescent acid green erupted suddenly into the pieced-together heavens from behind a nearby shed or annex, making them all jump, then giggle in relief as the effect subsided and was gone.

On what appeared to be a misplaced slice of the asylum chapel from St. Andrew's Hospital they found a luscious cluster of ripe Puck's Hats that the other Bill and Reggie must have overlooked, growing there in the shadowed angle underneath a window-ledge. Reggie removed his hat for use as a receptacle while Marjorie and Bill began to harvest the abundant hyper-vegetables or 4D fungi or whatever the peculiar blossoms truly were. Reaching beneath one foot-wide specimen that was especially magnificent, Marjorie pinched off the thick stalk with her ethereal thumbnail and could briefly hear a high-pitched whine like that of a small motor fading into silence, one of those sounds that you didn't know that you'd been listening to until it stopped. She held the splendid trophy up, supported by both chubby little palms, and, with a writer's eye, examined it.

The fairy figures, radiating in their doily pattern like a ring of paper dolls, were in this instance blonde. A golden tassel of their mutual mane grew from the fluffy dot at the thing's centre, where the tiny heads were stuck together in a bracelet loop, while the minuscule tufts of ersatz pubic hair that sprouted from the intersection of the petal legs was also golden. Even in the colourless dominion of the ghost-seam, you could see a rouged blush on their minute cheeks, a sky-blue glitter in the circle of unseeing pinprick eyes. Except the Puck's Hat wasn't really a bouquet of pretty individual fairies, was it? That was only what it looked like, so that it could entice ghosts to eat it and spit out its crunchy blue-eyed seeds. In actuality, the Puck's Hat was one single life form with its own inscrutable agendas. Trying to ignore the winsome female countenances, Marjorie instead attempted to see the true face of the mysterious organism.

Gazed at without thinking of the creature's separate parts as miniaturised people, and without the natural sympathies that this resemblance provoked, the meta-fungus was a truly horrid-looking thing, a candy-tinted octopus with squirm-inducing convolutions that were messy and unnecessary. Ringed around the wrongness of its central honeyed top-knot were at least fifteen or twenty tiny and inhuman eyes, many of them disturbingly inverted, with outside this a concentric band of rosebud mouths like nasty little sores. A band of sculpted pseudo-breasts came next, then navels, then the obscene dimpling of the pudenda where the blonde fuzz grew like blots of penicillin. Looked at as a whole it was a frightening iced cake, decorated with unnerving symmetry by a hallucinating schizophrenic.

Before she could develop an aversion to the things for the remainder of her afterlife, Marjorie shuddered and hurriedly thrust the suddenly-alarming ghost-fruit into Reggie's upturned bowler. What with it being so large, her find immediately took up nearly all the space inside the hat, prompting the boys to improvise by taking off Bill's jumper with its sleeves tied in a knot, converting it into a somewhat more capacious sack. Marjorie watched them for a while as they continued to collect the riper specimens amongst those crowding underneath the window sill, leaving the immature and bluish spaceman-blossoms well alone. The dumpy little phantom girl did not even attempt to see the alien countenance that these concealed behind their individual skinny foetus forms. They were quite horrible enough when looked at in the normal manner. It was possibly the unborn baby look they had to them, with those enormous heads, but Marjorie had always thought they most resembled some extraordinary pre-natal disaster, Siamese octuplets with their skulls fused to become the petals of a hideous daisy. Marjorie knew from bitter past experience exactly what they tasted like, but always found the acrid flavour maddeningly difficult to translate into words. It was a bit like eating metal, but if metal had the soft consistency of nougat and could putrefy in some way so that it went sour like sweaty pennies. She knew some ghosts who would eat an unripe Puck's Hat if the adult fairy fruit were unavailable, but for the death of her she'd no idea how they could manage it. She'd sooner do without until the end of time, which was about how long her memory of that first incautious bite would last. Besides, she got that same sense of a hearty meal and spiritual sustenance provided by the Bedlam Jennies from a good book these days. On the minus side of the equation though, a bad book could be left for decades and would never ripen into something sweeter.

Bill and Reggie gathered all the edible mad-apples from the cluster underneath the window and then wandered vaguely off, looking for more and heatedly discussing what their duplicates might have been up to, pilfering the crop of ghost-fruit before Phyllis and the gang could do so.

"Well, it's gotta be us in the future, ennit? It's somethin' what we've not done yet."

"You don't know that. It might be us in the past."

"Reggie, wiz that fuckin' 'at too tight or somethin'? If it wiz us in the past then we'd remember it, you twat. And anyway, 'ow would we know when all the 'Ag's Tits would be growin' 'ere? We only just found out when Phyllis told us. No, you take my word, Reg, all that business what we saw, that's somethin' what we're *gunna* do. All that we need concern ourselves about wiz why and when we're gunna do it. That, and what the other me meant when 'e said about the devil bein' in the driver's seat."

The two boys had apparently forgotten Marjorie. Engrossed in their discussion they meandered in amongst jaggedly juxtaposed asylum buildings, seeking out fresh pickings. Marjorie wasn't that bothered, to be honest. Having rather put herself off Puck's Hats and their harvesting for a few hours at least, she thought she'd take a stroll across the vast composite lawn in the direction of the copse towards which Phyllis, John and Michael had been headed when she'd seen them last. A rippling fan of brilliant yellow opened suddenly above a prefab observation wing, lasting for a short while before subsiding once more into graded half-tones: to the ghost-seam's different shades of smoke. Marjorie glanced across her shoulder, through the dissipating doubles that were following her, and caught a brief glimpse of Reggie Bowler as he disappeared around a madhouse corner, still stubbornly arguing with Bill.

"Well, I don't see why it can't be us from the past. It might be summat what we did as we've forgot about, for all you know!"

Marjorie smiled as she turned back and carried on along her own path over the inexpert patchwork of the grass, towards the distant trees. She thought about the first time she'd seen Reggie, on the night she'd drowned. He hadn't had his bowler on, on that occasion. Or his coat. Or anything, now that she stopped to think about it.

The Nene Hag had turned its elongated face away from her, revealing a disturbing profile like an alligator with a beak. Its flat brow had been corrugated by a frown of puzzled irritation as it squinted through the underwater shadows, looking for the source of the commotion, the splash that had just distracted it before it could begin its awful soul-destroying work on Marjorie.

Some way off, flailing in the grey murk of the river, there had been a naked boy – or at least, there had been the displaced spirit of a naked boy, with all the extra naked arms and legs that Marjorie would later realise were the mark of someone dead. Still clutched tight in the Hag's webbed claw, she'd felt the Undine's bafflement: after a long drought with no suicides or accidents for the monstrosity to claim, had fate delivered it two offerings in one night?

The boy was long and white and thin, plummeting down towards the silt and pram wheels of the riverbed. While he was not, perhaps, the beauty that her bathing Roman lad had been, he was at least young, probably much younger than the paunchy old drunks that had typified Enula's catches from the outset. Also, most importantly of all, he was a male. In every likelihood the creature had not actually been looking forward to dismantling Marjorie, given its antipathy for females and especially for those too young to have developed a real personality that would be worth taking to pieces. For an instant, the Nene Hag stared at the struggling nude figure through the sub-aquatic gloom while weighing up the options, and then it made its decision. The three pallid crab-leg fingers holding Marjorie were suddenly withdrawn as the Hag lunged against the sluggish current, making an upriver dart towards the clearly helpless youth. It was at this point that things had begun to happen rather quickly, so that Marjorie had only pieced together later what had actually occurred.

Newly released, floating there dazed and frightened in the lightless waters with her incorporeal form gradually drifting up in the direction of the surface, Marjorie had watched the Hag's fresh prey as the bare boy alighted on the muddy river-bottom. She'd had time to notice that he'd landed in a crouching posture which appeared to be planned and deliberate, in contrast to the aimless thrashing that he'd demonstrated up until that moment. As the entire stupefying length of the huge Undine nosed towards him through the blackness, he even appeared to have a grin across his freckled, snub-nosed features.

It was then that something plunging down into the water from above them had grabbed Marjorie beneath the arms and hauled her up into the clear night air, which she'd discovered she no longer needed now she wasn't breathing anymore. She'd known a moment's dread during which she believed herself to now be in the grip of some enormous astral herring-gull when she had had only just escaped the clutches of a massive ghostly eel, but these fears were displaced by genuine bewilderment once Marjorie had truly grasped her situation.

What was dragging her aloft had turned out to be something even odder than the giant phantom bird of her imaginings, in that it had seemed to be a trained trapeze act comprised of two upside-down ghost-children and a lot of eerily-suspended rabbit corpses. A small boy was holding Marjorie beneath the arms, his ankles held in turn by a girl who looked somewhat older and was dangling with her buckled shoes wedged in the forked branch of an ancient tree that overhung the river. Wrapped around her neck was a long piece of string from which swung all the velvet carcasses that Marjorie had noticed. This at least explained why the dead animals had looked like they were floating, but not why the girl was wearing them as jewellery in the first place.

The pair of young aerialists had evidently sliced down through the surface of the water in an arc to snatch up Marjorie, with their momentum carrying all three of them high up into the air as though upon a dangerously stoked-up swing. Right at the peak of their trajectory, the little hands beneath her arms had let Marjorie go and she'd sailed upward, cart-wheeling into the starlight with a dreamy slowness, just as though the air were made of honey. In an instant, her two rescuers came streaking from below her to arrest her tumbling ascent, with this time each child grasping one of Marjorie's outstretched and wildly flapping hands. Linked like a charm bracelet the trio had sailed further up into the night through the thick, gluey atmosphere until they'd hovered, treading nothingness, some fifty feet above the Nene and looking down at its slow silver ribbon, its reflected constellations.

That was when the naked adolescent boy came rocketing up from the river as though fired out of a submarine, with a long stream of photo-reproductions trailing through the dark behind him. Marjorie remembered thinking that this would explain the crouch with which the lad had landed on the riverbed, the better to propel himself up from the depths into those starry altitudes after he'd served as a diversion for the ghastly river-nymph. No sooner had she thought this than the placid Nene below exploded, shattered from beneath by a ferocious impact that had made all of the children scream and not only the relatively inexperienced Marjorie.

Rearing up to treetop level out of the benighted torrent came the first thirty or forty feet of the Nene Hag, as if some hurtling underwater train had jumped the rusted tracks to fling itself into the sky. The creature's long umbrella fingers were extended to their fullest with the grey and blotchy membrane stretched tight in between them as the towering, swaying monster raked the air in an attempt to capture its escaping prey. The nude boy's earlier grin of self-assurance had been swapped for an expression of surprise and terror as he realised belatedly the mer-thing's true extent and reach. Kicking his legs and doing what appeared to be a vertical front-crawl the plucked and plucky youngster shot beyond the swaying horror's grasp, into the safety of the sequinned heavens over Paddy's Meadow, where Marjorie and the other spectral children floated, breathless with excitement and mortality.

The Undine shrieked in its frustration and its rage, its disproportionately tiny forelimbs clutching uselessly at empty space for several seconds before it gave up and, with a disappointed wail that chilled its nervous audience, fell back towards the Nene like a collapsing chimneystack. There was no splash as its great insubstantial length hit the material surface of the water, only an unnerving final moan having the sound of something that had once been very close to human speech but which had turned into a strangled bellow through disuse. For one appalling instant it had sounded as though it were trying to say "Gregorius".

And after that, once Marjorie had been formally introduced to the Dead Dead Gang, they'd all drifted light as thistledown towards the point a little further up the grassy bank where Reggie Bowler had left all his hurriedly dis-carded clothing underneath a squeaking, listing death-trap called a Witch's Hat which was erected in the children's playground there upstream. Along the way they'd passed above a bobbing parcel, turning slowly in the petrol sheen and pond-scum on its way to Spencer Bridge, which Marjorie had scru-tinised for some time without realising it was her; her human envelope, its ugly glasses gone at last, its lungs all filled with water.

She had also spotted bloody, bloody, silly bloody India, who, as it turned out, could swim after all. The dog was scrabbling up onto the bank, where next it shook itself and then commenced to trot beside the water, barking as it kept pace with the drifting body. That had been that. Chapter Seven: The Dead Dead Gang versus the Nene Hag. That had been Marjorie's short life.

She walked now on a patch of crew-cut grass, mown into stripes, which must presumably be part of the better-maintained St. Andrew's Hospital. This was confirmed by the quite evidently better class of lunatics at large upon the broad swathe of grey-greenery, dotted about across the neatly-shorn expanse like chessmen, lost without their grid. As she progressed across the lawn in the direction of the spinney, Marjorie passed by one living inmate whom she thought she recognised, a shuffling fellow in his sixties, dressed in a loose cardigan and trousers stained by breakfast. The poor man was humming something complicated and askew beneath his breath as he made his laborious way past her, unaware that she was there, and she was almost certain that it was the old composer chap, the one who'd made his name long after Marjorie had lived and died. Sir Malcolm Arnold, that was it. Him who'd made wild, delirious music out of Robbie Burns's *Tam O' Shanter* and who'd orchestrated "Colonel Bogey" with a full arrangement of impertinent and farting brass. Bemused and balding, very likely drunk or medicated, Arnold slippered on across the fractured madhouse grounds without acknowledging her presence, crooning his refrain with only ghost-girls and the nearby trees to hear it.

Marjorie, quietly appalled, noticed that the composer had a ripe and thriving Puck's Hat growing from his liver-spotted forehead, just above one eye. She knew that Bedlam Jennies favoured the proximity of people who were mad or steeped in alcohol or both, which she supposed was where they'd got their name from, but she'd never previously seen one with its roots apparently sunken directly into someone's brain. His dreams must be infested, overrun by twittering and mindless pseudo-fairies to the point where Marjorie imagined that fresh compositions would be near impossible. And how could the affliction ever be removed when by the very nature of the 4D fungus, nobody alive could see it? Nobody, including the composer himself, was aware that it was there. Marjorie watched Sir Malcolm tottering away from her towards the riot of mismatched asylum buildings, with the pulchritudinous growth bobbing on his skull at every step. The blank-eyed little nymphs whose naked bodies formed the blossom's petals even seemed to wear miniature knowing smirks upon their ring of overlapping faces.

Marjorie walked on, passing between the optical-illusion pillars of the Ultraduct as it swept overhead on its long arc between Jerusalem and Doddridge Church, its endless alabaster mass casting no shadow on the composite of institution lawns below. When the grass changed from light to dark, from short to shaggy and unkempt beneath her lace-up shoes, she knew that she'd crossed into territory belonging to either St. Crispin's or the older madhouse in Abington Park. The thick and bristling copse was now much closer, and she could see Phyllis, John and Michael sauntering amongst its trees, collecting the few Puck's Hats that the future-Bill and future-Reggie hadn't plucked already. Phyllis waved to her.

"All right, Marge? I expect that them two thievin' buggers are both gloatin' over 'ow they're gunna come back 'ere and pinch our Puck's 'Ats, somewhere up the road."

Wandering up to join the other children in the dapple of the overhanging leaves, Marjorie shook her head.

"Nar. They're as confused about it as the rest of us. Your Bill's filling 'is jumper up with all the Jennies they can find, to make it up to you."

Phyllis appeared surprised by this, and stuck her lower lip out pensively as she considered.

"Hmm. Well, I suppose as I'm not bein' fair, takin' the 'ump with them before they've even done the thing what's made me cross. Besides, we've found enough mad-apples just on these few trees to make the visit worth ayr while. Look – they're all ripe and everything, but they're just little uns."

Festooned with hollow, decomposing bunnies, the Dead Dead Gang's leader held out her white handkerchief for Marjorie's inspection. There at its unfolded centre rested half a dozen tiny Bedlam Jennies, with the biggest being no more than two inches in diameter. As Phyllis had affirmed, the hyper-fruits were ripe, with every fairy-petal fully formed down to the last infinitesimal detail, despite the fact that some of them measured no more than half an inch from toes to crown. Marjorie found that it took both the enhanced vision of the dead and her entirely decorative National Health spectacles to spot the smaller features, such as their near-microscopic navels. With each specimen at most providing one or two good mouthfuls, it was easy to see why this dwarf strain had been overlooked by the two scavengers from some point in the future. Phyllis, John and Michael all had pockets full of coin-sized blooms, adding transportability to the variety's advantages. They also seemed to be abundant, growing in a virtual carpet down the rear sides of the elms and silver birches, where these faced away from the asylum grounds and turned instead to the interior of the bordering woodland. Fighting down her recent self-induced revulsion for the fungal creatures, Marjorie agreed to try a couple, then a couple more.

They really were extremely good. The taste was even sweeter than that of the larger species, and the perfume more evocative, more concentrated. Better still, once swallowed, the immediate benefits were more pronounced. The energising tingle of euphoria pervading every fibre of one's self which Marjorie associated with the full-sized Puck's Hats was more noticeable here and seemed to last for slightly longer. Filling her own jumper-pockets with as many of the things as they would hold, she ate them as though they were a particularly more-ish type of fruit-drop, stuffing one or two into her mouth at once while playing an impromptu game of tag with the three other ghost-kids. Giggling and shrieking they ran back and forth amongst the trees that edged the muddled institutions' equally disjointed lawns and gardens.

Marjorie was first to recognise the living female inmate who appeared to be performing an incomprehensible routine upon the neatly-trimmed St. Andrew's grass not far away, although it was young Michael Warren who was first to notice her.

"Look at that funny lady over there. She's walking like that man does in the films, and doing crossed eyes like that other man."

Marjorie looked, along with John and Phyll, and saw what the pyjama-clad child was referring to. The woman patient skipped or danced or waddled, back and forth, across an area of grass that was approximately the same size as a small repertory stage. Her movements, which seemed to include incongruous ballet-like leaps and twirls, were nonetheless, as Michael had observed, an eerily exact impersonation of the 'little tramp' walk first made popular by Charlie Chaplin, that man in the films. To flesh out her impression, the dark-haired and middle-aged asylum inmate had appropriated a long, slender tree-branch from the nearby vegetation, tucking it beneath one arm like Chaplin's cane as she paced to and fro, continuously muttering long strings of almost-musical nonsense and gibberish to herself: "Je suis l'artiste, le auteur and I live, your plural belle, I liffey laved in Lux, in light, in flight, in fluxury and in flow-motion, gravually unriverling translucid lingo, linger franker in ma-wet streams, ma-salt dreams as I slide see-ward and I've not a limp-bit nor a barnacle to hinder me and it'll come out in the strip-wash, murk my words, about my Old Man of the Holy Roaming Sea when he was on my back or I was, cat-licked and that's how it got my tongue ..."

The insane monologue ploughed on, quite independent of the twirled cane or the Chaplin walk, the twitch-nosed waggling of an imaginary moustache or the occasional surprising pirouette. Though he'd been right about the woman's strange gait, Michael Warren had been wrong when he'd assumed her eyes were crossed in an impression of Ben Turpin or whoever he'd meant by "that other man". Marjorie knew that this was how the woman's eyes looked naturally. She inclined her stout body to one side so that she could speak softly into Michael Warren's ear. She'd no idea why she was trying not to make a noise when the live mental patient couldn't hear them anyway, but thought it might be in response to the deluded woman's strong resemblance to a rare, easily-startled bird. She whispered to the toddler in a probably unnecessary effort not to scare the inmate off.

"You know how when you're dead like us, and sometimes all your words get mixed up so they come out wrong? And Phyllis or somebody else will tell you that it's taking you a while to find your Lucy-lips?"

The infant blinked and nodded, shooting sidelong glances at the mad-woman who jigged this way and that upon the grassy boards of a theatre only she could see. Marjorie went on, still in the same pointlessly low murmur.

"Well, that woman there, that's Lucy."

Even Phyllis seemed astonished by this.

"What, that's wossername, old Ulysses's daughter? 'Im 'oo wrote the racy book?" The ghost-gang's leader had announced her questions at her normal, raucous volume-level, prompting Marjorie to give up on her own subdued tones as she answered Phyllis.

"Yes. That's Lucia Joyce. Her dad was James Joyce, and she used to dance for him when he was writing his great book, *Finnegans Wake*, to give him inspiration. When he took the writer Samuel Beckett on as his assistant with the work, Lucia thought that she'd been elbowed out. She also started think-ing Beckett was in love with her, and began having mental problems generally. She's up there on the Billing Road now, at St. Andrew's, where she's been for a few years. They say that Beckett sometimes goes to visit her there, if he's in the area. Her family, the ones that are alive, they play down her existence in case it should cast a shadow on her father or his works. Poor woman. It's a shame the way that she's been treated."

Phyllis was regarding Marjorie suspiciously.

"Well, 'ow come you know such a lot abayt it all? I never knew you wiz a reader."

The rotund girl peered impassively up through her glasses at her rabbit-wrapped senior officer.

"I'm not. I just keep up with all the gossip."

Phyllis appeared satisfied by this, and after a few moments more of watch-ing Lucia's repetitive and oddly mesmerising act, the four of them resolved to make their way back over the broad sweep of recombined lawns and find Bill and Reggie. Pockets bulging with a hoard of the dwarf Puck's Hats that would more than compensate for the ones stolen by the future duo, everyone agreed that it had been a very nice excursion but that there was no point in extending it now that they'd got the bounty that they'd come for, or at least a reasonable substitute. Once they'd located their two disgraced members – who it seemed that Phyllis was prepared to pre-forgive after her earlier prejudgement – they could head back up the Ultraduct to Doddridge Church and possibly take time to play on the subsided wasteland that they'd passed above when they were on their way here.

Marjorie was thinking about Lucia, thinking about Sir Malcolm Arnold and all the other inmates, past and present, of Northampton's various asylums.

John Clare, J.K. Stephen and the countless others whose names no one save for their immediate relatives and friends would ever know, all of them eventually wandering across the unmarked boundary that separated the acceptable and minor madnesses of ordinary life from the more unacceptable behaviour and opinions that were classed as lunacy. What was it like, she wondered, going mad? Were you aware that it was happening? In the first stages, did you still possess a measure of self-consciousness allowing you to notice that the world surrounding you and your responses to it were markedly different from the way they used to be? Did people fight against it, the descent into insanity? It struck her that, for a great many people, ordinary life itself was something of a surface struggle.

As they made their way along the copse's edge, taking a slow, circuitous route back towards the jumbled madhouse buildings, they stumbled upon two women who sat talking on a weathered bench. Both living, neither of the pair seemed to detect the presence of the phantom children. From the length and colour of the grass where they were seated, Marjorie judged that the two were actually materially present in St. Crispin's Hospital, rather than overlapping from St. Andrew's in the mayhem of the higher world's collapse, as both Sir Malcolm Arnold and Lucia Joyce had been. Marjorie didn't recognise the pair, at any rate. They both seemed to be women in their middle years, one tall and somewhat gaunt, the other shorter but more fully rounded. Marjorie could see that only one of them, the lanky one, appeared to be a patient, while her friend carried a handbag and looked more as if she might be visiting. Other than this, there didn't seem to be much you could call remarkable about them. Marjorie would have walked on if tall, good-looking John had not stopped suddenly and stared from one face to the other in amazement before making an announcement to the group in general and to Michael Warren in particular.

"Well, I'll be blowed. I reckon that I know these two. The littler one, that's your dad's cousin Muriel, nipper, and I think the other one's his and her cousin Audrey. Audrey Vernall. She went barmy just after the war. She used to play accordion in a show-band that her father managed, then one evening when her mum and dad had been out down to the Black Lion, she locked them out and sat there playing "Whispering Grass" on the piano, over and over again. Her parents had to go and sit beneath the portico of All Saints Church all night, there on the steps, and in the morning they had someone come and bring her to the hospital up here at Berry Wood. She's been here ever since, from what I've heard."

Marjorie scrutinised the taller of the seated pair more closely, in the light of John's account. The woman, Audrey, had a strong face and a pair of large and luminously haunted eyes. She seemed to be addressing Muriel, her visitor, with some considerable urgency, her cousin's hand gripped tight in Audrey's long and sensitive accordionist's fingers. Because John's announcement had caused everyone to cease their idle chattering and pay attention to the women's conversation, all four of the ghostly children clearly heard the words that Audrey Vernall said next, after which Phyllis and John had both looked nauseated and embarrassed, and had hurried Michael Warren off before he could hear any more.

Soon after that they found Reggie and Bill, who'd gathered a huge haul of Puck's Hats as an act of penitence for crimes they'd not committed yet. Once Phyllis had officially forgiven them for their impending larceny, the gang ascended back up to the Ultraduct by leaping high into the ghost-seam's thickened atmosphere and then dog-paddling up for the remainder of the distance, John and Phyllis towing Michael Warren in between them.

As they headed back along the dazzling overpass to Doddridge Church they munched upon their mad apples and Phyllis once more made them all strike up the Dead Dead Gang's club song. Marjorie thought that Phyllis was most probably attempting to make lots of noise so everybody would forget what gaunt and wild-eyed Audrey Vernall had said to her cousin when the two of them were sitting on their bench and didn't think they could be overheard. Marjorie, though, could not forget it. It had had a dreadful ring to it, that stark confession there amongst the rustling and eavesdropping boughs, and with her writer's sensibilities she thought that it would make a powerful ending for at least a lengthy episode in her forthcoming Chapter Twelve:

"Our dad used to get into bed with me."

The gang continued, heading east to Doddridge Church and singing as they went.

Oh, and the dog was called that because on its side it had a dark brown blotch that looked a bit like India.

FORBIDDEN WORLDS

I n Bill's experience, being both intelligent and working class was usually a recipe for trouble. In the lower orders – lacking academic aspirations – genuine intelligence most often manifested itself as a kind of cunning, and if Bill was honest with himself he'd always been too cunning for his own good. Just look at the frankly awful current circumstance that his latest scheme had led to, cowering behind the portly shade of Tom Hall while a gang of nightmarish and drunken spectres tortured a bald, weeping man who seemed to be made out of wood. Hardly an ideal outcome, even for a serial optimist like Bill who generally tried to make the best of things.

He could remember the first intimations that had led to his disastrous plan. That had been quite a while ago, just after they'd escaped the ghost-storm by ascending to the isolated corner-house on Scarletwell Street, sometime during nothing-five or nothing-six. On that occasion, upset to discover that his terraced street had been long since demolished, Michael Warren had run off into the haunted night and it had been Reggie and Bill who'd found him, sitting on the central steps of Bath Street flats and whingeing about how he missed his sister and the comics that she used to read. *Forbidden Worlds*, that had been the specific title that the little boy had mentioned, which had sounded vague alarm bells in the cloudy reaches of Bill's less-than-perfect memory.

It hadn't been until the gang's encounter with Phil Doddridge, though, when the great man had casually let slip the Christian name of Michael Warren's sister, that Bill had found all the puzzle-pieces starting to slide neatly into place. The comic-reading sister's name was Alma, Alma Warren. Well, of course. With origins down in the Boroughs and with an enthusiasm for weird fantasy and horror stories from an early age, who else could it have been? Bill had known Alma while he'd been alive, known her quite well. Certainly well enough to be aware that what the moderately-famous artist thought of as her most important work was an arresting and inscrutable series of paintings which she claimed were based upon a visionary near-death experience reported to her by her younger brother. Michael Warren, clearly, was the brother that she'd been referring to, while all the little boy's excursions with the Dead Dead Gang, presumably, must be the visionary near-death experience that he at some point had related to her. Bill, if his legs had been slightly longer in his current child-form, could have kicked himself for having failed

to make the obvious connection between Michael Warren and the Alma Warren that he'd been familiar with in life.

Of course, once Bill had worked out what was going on he'd talked it
through with Phyll, the only other member of the gang who'd have the first
idea what he was on about. Phyll had known Alma too, albeit not as well as Bill
had. Him and Phyllis had agreed between them that this piece of information
pretty much changed everything. For one thing, they'd already learned that
Michael Warren was a Vernall on his father's side, one of that odd, tinker-like
breed who, in Mansoul, were trusted with the maintenance of boundaries and
corners. And if Michael Warren was a Vernall, then so was his sister, Alma.
This brought other factors into the equation, many of them much more large
and ominous than even Alma herself had been, as Phyllis and Bill remembered her.

Most worryingly, there was all this stuff about the Vernall's Inquest to
consider. As far as Bill understood it, "Vernall's Inquest" was a term – like
"Porthimoth di Norhan" and expressions such as "deathmonger" – that was
historically unknown outside the Boroughs of Northampton. Bill thought
this was probably because the phrases all originated Upstairs in Mansoul,
the Second Borough, and had somehow filtered down to enter usage in the
lower territory, the First Borough, this specific mortal district that appeared
to be of such importance to the higher scheme of things. The centre of the
land, apparently, where angles had instructed that eighth-century monk to
put down his stone cross from faraway Jerusalem, right opposite the billiard
hall. The rumour circulating amongst well-informed ghosts and departed
souls was that the top man, the Third Borough (which title or office was itself
found nowhere save Northampton) had something important planned for this
unprepossessing neighbourhood.

The friendlier and more communicative builders even had a name and target date for the completion of this seemingly momentous project, this event:
it would be called the Porthimoth di Norhan, a tribunal at which boundaries and limits would be finally decided, where a judgement would be handed
down once and for all, and this would all take place during the early years of
the twenty-first century. Bill had no clear idea of what that meant, of course, it
was just gossip that he'd heard. Given that the decision would be made upon
the highest level, somewhere above life and time, Bill thought it likely that the
boundaries and limits under scrutiny would be accordingly significant, rather
than hedge disputes brought up by feuding neighbours. Who could say? Perhaps the borders in between dimensions were about to be revised. Perhaps the
boundary line of death would be redrawn. Something of that scale, anyway,
which sounded disconcertingly like some variety of judgement day to Bill.
That was the Porthimoth di Norhan. Before any judgement could be made,

however, there must first take place a full and rigorous inquiry, also instigated by Mansoul's mysterious management, and this preliminary investigation was known as a Vernall's Inquest.

Now, according to the word on heaven's streets, the Porthimoth di Norhan would be held during the first decades of the twenty-first century, before half time, and with the necessary Vernall's Inquest taking place sometime before that, Bill presumed, perhaps during the century's first ten or fifteen years.

He could remember seeing Alma's paintings, a good while before he'd popped his clogs from the effects of hepatitis C, and could remember the impression, albeit fleeting, that they'd made upon him. Those astonishing sur-realist landscapes populated by peculiar entities and full of dazzling colour; the soft charcoal studies of the Boroughs' streets and alleys, trodden by grey figures that left fading after-images behind them – not until Bill had passed on himself did he fully appreciate how closely Alma's pictures had resembled the realities of Mansoul or the ghost-seam. He recalled her telling him of how she'd been inspired by something that her brother Michael had related to her, how after some accident at work he'd found that he was able to remember details from an earlier incident, the aforesaid near-death experience in infancy. The accident had happened, if Bill's recollection was correct, during the spring of 2005. Alma had somehow managed to get all the work completed in a single year, and Bill had first seen the hallucinatory result in 2006. This date was well within the period allotted for the Inquest, for the vital preamble to the forthcoming Porthimoth di Norhan, and as they'd all recently discovered, Alma Warren was a Vernall.

If – and Bill was speculating – Alma's paintings were in any way essential to the Vernall's Inquest, and if they had been inspired by the adventures of her younger brother during his brief visit to the afterlife, then that would explain everything. It would explain why the two Master Builders had considered one child's life or death sufficiently important to provoke a public brawl up on the Mayorhold. It might even explain why that demon who'd abducted the poor kid had taken such an interest in him. It was an illuminating notion that cleared up a lot of things, although as far as Bill could see it left him and the rest of the Dead Dead Gang squarely in the shit.

The worst thing, naturally, was the responsibility. Responsibility, while Bill had never shunned it, wasn't something that he'd ever actively sought out. When Philip Doddridge and that quietly scary and formidable death-monger, Mrs. Gibbs, had told them that Mansoul's authorities were leaving the whole Michael Warren business up to them, Bill's largely metaphorical blood had run cold. It sounded, on the face of it, like adults taking an indul-gent and relaxed view in regard to the inconsequential games of children, but that wasn't it, Bill knew. That wasn't what was going on. The Reverend Dr.

Doddridge and the deathmonger weren't really adults, for a start-off, anymore than the Dead Dead Gang were real children. They were all just ageless, timeless souls suspended in the pyrotechnic linger of Eternity, all dressing themselves in the forms and personalities that they thought they looked best in. And the doctor of divinity's instructions to the gang amounted to something a lot more serious than "run along and play."

If Michael Warren was as crucial to the pending Vernall's Inquest and the Porthimoth di Norhan that would follow it as Bill was starting to believe he was, then the success or otherwise of a divine plan had been left to an unruly mob of phantom ruffians. It was *Mission: Impossible* over again, only without the handy get-out clause of "Your mission, should you choose to accept it ...". The gang didn't really have a choice about accepting it, considering the source the orders came from. Bill hoped, not without a sense of irony, that the Third Borough knew what he or she or it was doing, although given Bill's lifelong mistrust of management, he frankly rather doubted it. The central flaw in the proposal, as Bill saw it, was that they'd been more or less instructed to make sure that Michael Warren was returned to life with at least some recall of where he'd been, so that he could inspire his sister's apparently necessary paintings. And yet all the regulations of Mansoul, which were like laws of physics and could not be broken, stated that it was impossible to retain memory of your exploits in the higher world once you'd returned into your life again. Otherwise everybody would remember from the moment of their birth that this had all occurred a billion times before. Since this was not what everybody had experienced during their own nativity, then for them suddenly to realise it would be to change what had happened, what was happening, what would forever happen. It would alter time, time as a physical dimension, time as a solid component of a solid and changeless eternity. You simply couldn't do it. Even the Third Borough couldn't do it, and as a result what happened in Mansoul stayed in Mansoul.

This was the problem him and Phyllis had been wrestling with for a good deal of their long walk along the Ultraduct to the collapsed and merged asylums. They'd debated how to go about returning Michael Warren to the mortal world without him just forgetting everything, their sense of hopelessness only allayed by the assurance of eventual success that their own memories allowed them. After all, they'd both seen Alma's finished paintings during their own mortal lifetimes, which implied that they were going to find some way to sort this mess out, so that Alma's pictures could reflect her brother's vision of this comical and frightening before-and-afterlife.

The problem was, Bill hadn't really paid that much attention to the artworks when he'd seen them, and could not remember how specific they'd been in depicting Upstairs or the ghost-seam. He recalled a wall-sized board of tiles that looked as if it had been swiped from M.C. Escher, and another terrifying large piece that had been like looking down into a mile-wide garbage grinder that was in the process of devouring everything noble or dear in human history. There had been all the charcoal drawings with their double-exposed figures reminiscent of the half-world's desolate rough sleepers, and those jewelled acrylic studies of immense interiors that may have represented Mansoul, although Bill couldn't remember anything conclusive. The piece that Phyllis and Bill had found the most impressive had been that scaled down papier-mâché model of the Burroughs, which had not had any obviously supernatural elements and which had not eventually been included in the final London exhibition of her work that Alma had put on. Unsettlingly, it had occurred to Bill that just because Alma had done some pictures of an afterlife, it didn't mean they were the right ones. What if the Dead Dead Gang didn't manage to return Michael to life with enough memory of his vision to make Alma's paintings meaningful, make them sufficient to the task required of them? What if the Vernall's Inquest was a failure, and the Porthimoth di Norhan could not then be held? It struck Bill that this current caper, far from being the gang's greatest triumph, could turn out to be a damning failure that would reverberate unendingly throughout the long streets of forever. Him and Phyllis were still chewing all this over when they'd finally reached the asylums and their conference had been interrupted by another Reggie Bowler and another Bill, bewildering invaders from the future, having all the mad-apples away wrapped in a fascist banner.

He'd got no idea what all that was about. It must be something him and Reg were going to do at some point, but with all the other problems he was wrestling with he hadn't really had the time or inclination to consider it. The thing with Michael Warren, that was the main business, and since Phyll had gone all huffy with him after the appearance of his thieving future self he'd had to think it all through on his own. The best that he'd been able to come up with was that they'd be better off in nothing-five or nothing-six, up closer to the time when these events were meant to come about, so that they'd have a better sense of what was going on. He'd mentioned this to Phyllis on their way back from the madhouses, once she'd recovered from her strop and had decided that she was still speaking to him, and she'd grudgingly agreed that it was probably a good idea. She hadn't got a better one, that much was obvious. In fact, Phyllis had seemed a bit distracted and upset after her, Michael, Marjorie and John had re-joined Bill and Reggie up at the asylums. Bill wasn't certain what had happened in the half-an-hour or so that they'd been separated, although it had looked to him like Phyllis now had worse things on her mind than his and Reggie's future theft of a few mad-apples.

The six of them had walked along the Ultraduct, stuffing themselves with

Puck's Hats and attempting to sing Phyllis's "We are the Dead Dead Gang" song through a mouthful of chewed fairies, spraying bits of wing or face or finger when they laughed. Their rowdy after-images pursued each of them like a cheerier, paediatric version of *The Dance of Death*, the jigging figures streaming back along the alabaster boardwalk in their wakes.

Above them, sunsets borrowed from ten thousand years of days and nights competed for attention in the shifting, melting heavens. Bill had marched and sung along with all the others, had allowed the stimulating and invigorating tonic of the Bedlam Jennies to spread through his ghostly system, hopefully inspiring him with some solution to his baffling predicament. As the familiar dreamy and creative glimmer of the meta-fungi gradually enwrapped his thoughts, Bill had gazed down across the blazing causeway's handrail at the bubbling suburban trees and houses they were then passing above, the crofts and cottages and Barratt Homes constructing themselves out of dust and then as quickly disassembling themselves back down to that same substance. Doubting that his cunning would be adequate to the huge metaphysical conundrum facing him, Bill had reviewed the Michael Warren matter inwardly, turning it over in his mind while he and his companions headed back along the glowing overpass to Doddridge Church.

As he'd recalled, it was this accident at work sometime in 2005 that had restored the adult Michael's memory of what had happened following the choking incident when he'd been three or so. Bill could remember Alma telling him, with snarling indignation, how her brother had been at work reconditioning steel drums in Martin's Yard, pounding them flat with a sledgehammer as he was employed to do. Apparently, Michael had flattened an unlabelled drum that had turned out to hold corrosive chemicals. These had exploded out into his face, burning and blinding him, thus causing Michael to run into a conveniently-placed steel bar, knocking himself unconscious in the process. It was when he'd woken up from that, Alma had told Bill, that her brother had been suddenly beset by memories of those few childhood minutes when he'd been technically dead.

It had occurred to Bill, strolling along the Ultraduct while munching upon a particularly flavourful and fragrant Puck's Hat, that if that was what he could remember Alma telling him, then that was almost certainly what happened. It had happened, therefore it would happen, was constantly happening in their fourfold eternal universe where Time was a direction. It would happen, had already happened, whether Bill came up with a solution to the Michael Warren mess or not. Which let him neatly off the hook for perhaps thirty seconds, at which point he'd realised that the "accident" at work might well have only come about because of some as yet undreamed of cunning stunt that Bill himself was going to pull, which of course placed him back upon the same uncomfortable barb. It had all called to mind the snatch of conversation that they'd overheard between that Aziel bloke and Mr. Doddridge, where the minister had asked if anyone had ever really had free will, although Bill couldn't have explained exactly why this brief exchange seemed to be relevant to his present dilemma. He'd just known he'd better come up with an answer to the problem and he'd better do it quick.

So, he had reasoned, if he thought there was a chance that he might in some way end up contributing to Michael Warren's accident perhaps that was the area of strategy that he should focus on. How could he manage such a thing, he'd asked himself? Was it even a possibility? With his imagination perked up by the Puck's Hats, he'd wondered at first if there was some way that he could be instrumental in positioning the iron bar that would knock Michael out, but as with all the profit making schemes he'd once come up with after a few joints, the obvious dead-ends in his blue sky thinking had swiftly revealed themselves.

Foremost amongst these was the issue of how Bill, encumbered by his ghostly state, was going to move an iron bar or, worse, the more than likely heavy mechanism that the iron bar was attached to. How was he going to do that, when the only way that phantoms could affect the physical world was by running themselves dizzy in some corner of a car park, trying to shift a fucking crisp bag? Even then, it would take two of you to generate a tiny dust storm. You'd need a whole continent of ghosts, all running in a circle, before you could shift an iron bar …

It had been then, just as the gang were coming to the Doddridge Church end of the Ultraduct that Bill had first begun to formulate the idea that had led him to his current difficulty, crouching with a clearly-distraught Michael Warren behind the voluminous form of the late Tom Hall, upstairs at the wraith-pub, the spectral Jolly Smokers, watching the horrific floorshow.

Bill had been struck suddenly by inspiration just as Phyllis called a halt, some yards short of the little door halfway up Doddridge Church's western wall which marked the end of that stretch of the Ultraduct. What if there was some object that was much, much lighter than the iron bar, and yet which might have just as great a part to play in Michael knocking himself out? Bill had been thinking about this when Phyllis told them that if they all jumped down from the shining overpass at this point, they could go and play in the collapsed earthworks-lagoon they'd noticed earlier, as she'd promised Michael.

The peculiar little acre of unfolded wasteland, there between Chalk Lane and the brick wall that was the boundary of St. Andrew's Road, had always been one of Bill's favourite places in the ghost-seam. Like the merged asylums, this rough patch had been subjected to astral subsidence and collapse, although unlike the situation with the madhouses, nobody seemed to be sure why this should have happened. At the institutions, after all, were lunatics whose confused thoughts and dreams had led to faults in the foundations of the higher world above. Here, as far as anyone knew, the area had always been a wasteland except for five hundred years or so when it had been an obscure and unpopulated outskirt of the castle grounds. Why should the gaudy floorboards of Mansoul choose this point to fall in, when nothing much had ever happened here and where there were no inmate nightmares or delusions undermining the celestial territories that were overhead? Perhaps, Bill had surmised, this region was the way it was because of its proximity to the end of the Ultraduct, or possibly it had just fallen in because of old age and neglect, the way that most things tended to.

The children had jumped down from the white walkway above history, grey after-pictures in a rubber-stamp trail following behind them, and had landed in the Chalk Lane car park on an evening in the spring of nothing-six. Just over the deserted lane they could see Doddridge Church, with its low outline crouching against the impending dusk and multi-storey flats that loomed around it menacingly. Nearly all of the surrounding district was unrecognisable from when the gang had seen it in the 1600s, or even the 1950s. Phyllis, still seeming a bit distracted by whatever she had overheard or witnessed up at the asylums, shepherded the gang across the hushed enclosure to its northwest corner, where you could climb up onto the piece of land that the collapsed lagoon was coexistent with. Upon the mortal plane, the stretch of wasteland had been designated as a remnant of Northampton Castle, purely for the benefit of hoped-for tourists who had never actually turned up, but everybody local knew that this was pants. Logs had been placed as if to replicate some vanished set of castle steps, when all there'd ever really been in this location was a lot of mud and grass, the same as there was now.

The children clambered up to the raised ground, with Phyllis hurrying them from the rear. Bill was the last but one to make the climb, and having done so he turned round to reach down and give Phyllis a hand up. That was when he had noticed the young living woman making her way up Chalk Lane, across the car park's far side, and had paused to wonder where he recognised her from.

She'd looked like she was on the game with the short skirt and heels, the PVC mac, but Bill hadn't thought this was the context that he'd seen her in when he had noticed her before. In one of those bizarre and tenuous chains of association, he'd found that she called to mind the phrase *Forbidden Worlds*, which was the comic-book the Warren kid had mentioned after Bill and Reggie Bowler found him sitting on the central steps at …

Bath Street flats. That was where Bill had seen the girl before. It had been while Reggie and him were showing Michael Warren the Destructor, the vast, smouldering astral whirlpool emanating from the point in Bath Street where the waste-incinerator chimneystack had stood until the 1930s. Its slowly-rotating radius of obliteration had appeared to intersect with various rooms inside the blocks of flats, including one where this same girl, her hair arranged in corn-rows, had sat doing crack and gluing pictures in a scrapbook, unaware that a great whirling phantom buzz-saw scraped at her insides, her spirit.

It had been just as Bill managed to haul Phyllis up beside him that the woman, a mixed-race girl from the look of her, had turned her head towards them, squinting at them through the shadows of the car park as if not entirely certain whether they were really there or not. He'd pointed the girl out to Phyllis.

"'Ere, Phyll, look at that, her over there. I reckon she can see us."

Phyllis, with her rabbit necklace dangling around her neck, had glanced across her shoulder at the puzzled-looking prostitute before she'd struggled to her feet and carried on into the waste-ground.

"Well, I'm not surprised if she could see us. She looked like a tart, and all o' them raynd 'ere are on the stuff, the crack. I shouldn't be surprised if she'd not seen things a lot worse than us. Yer shouldn't 'ave been looking at 'er, anyway, yer dirty-minded little bugger."

Even buoyed up by the Puck's Hats that he'd eaten, Bill had not been able to muster the energy required for arguing with Phyll. He could have pointed out that he'd been looking at the girl because he thought he'd recognised her, but it would have been a waste of breath. Well, not exactly breath because he'd not had any of that in a long time, but it would have been a waste of something.

As the pair of them had stepped over the grassy crest for their first sight of the lagoon-cum-earthworks, an impressive sunset had been going on in radiant grey and white above the ugly sprawl of Castle Station. Somehow glorious and ethereal despite the lack of colour, this display was beautifully reflected in the dream-lakes bounded by the sheer soil walls of the unfolded earthworks. Down the hunchbacked roller-coaster path ahead of Bill and Phyllis, leading to the edge of the still waters, the four other members of the ghost gang were already playing on the banks and rocky ledges of the vast anomaly. Great granite tablets, biblical in their proportions, jutted at steep angles from the tar-and-chromium dapple of the surface, fused with the inverted mirror-images beneath them into weathered 3D Rorschach blots, and all around the square-cut earthen walls and corners of the quarried landscape rose towards the grey blaze of the sky.

It had been the sheer scale of the environment, at least as looked at from the ghost-seam, which made the astral collapse apparent. The earthworks, as seen from here, appeared to be at least a quarter-mile across, while when observed from the perspective of the mortal realm, the corresponding patch of wasteland – or castle remains if you preferred it that way – measured barely fifty feet. What were unnoticed sumps and puddles in the physical three-sided world had here unpacked themselves into opaque lakes like black looking-glasses, where dream-leeches and imaginary newts wriggled invisible through unseen depths.

He'd known that living people sometimes dreamed about that place. He'd seen them wandering its shorelines in their underpants or their pyjamas, gazing mystified at its black cliffs, perturbed by its beguiling mix of the primordial unknown and the achingly familiar. While he'd been alive, he'd thought he could remember visiting it once himself during some nocturnal subconscious ramble. Both in his almost-forgotten dream and as the place had seemed then, when he'd wandered down towards the waterside with Phyllis, it had had the same haunting and faintly melancholy atmosphere. The locale's rough-hewn contours spoke of something timeless and enduring, something beside which the human lifespan barely registered. "We have been here forever", the great silent bulwarks seemed to say, "and we don't know you, and you'll soon be gone." The sky above its dark cliff edges had a watery clarity, a graded and nostalgic look to it as it had deputised for the receding sunset.

Bill had messed about with all the others, playing chase at the lagoon's edge, leaping from one slanted rock perch to the next, but all the time he had been running through the finer details of his coalescing plan. If where they were at that point was the spring of 2006, then the adult Mick Warren's accident at Martin's Yard must have presumably occurred roughly a year before. Perhaps a spot of burrowing back to the earlier period was called for, though Bill hadn't felt inclined to go through proper channels and consult with Phyllis. Even though she'd sort-of made up with him after all that business with the scrumping doppelgangers from the future, it still hadn't felt to Bill like she completely trusted him. If he were to suggest his plan to her while she was still annoyed with him, he'd thought there was a good chance that she'd veto it, just to be awkward. The best course of action, he'd decided, would be to just bypass Phyllis altogether, though that in itself would take some planning.

Squatting on a flinty outcrop overlooking the hushed rock-bound pools below, he'd spotted lanky John and Phyllis sitting talking earnestly upon a sheltered patch of grass down near the water. He'd thought at the time that they might be discussing whatever it was that had upset them out at the composite nuthouses, not that it had much mattered to his strategy. After Bill had conferred discreetly with Drowned Marjorie and Reggie, just to make sure they were up for an excursion if the opportunity arose, he'd gone and plonked himself down next to John and Phyllis who'd both looked a little irritated by this interruption to their conversation.

"'Ere, Phyll, wiz it all right if we dig about into some of the other times round 'ere? Reg says that back in his day he thought there wiz 'ouses where we are now, but I don't see as that can be right. We could take Marjorie and Michael with us, 'ave a poke about, find out what's what, and all be back 'ere before you knew we wiz gone. I mean, you two could come as well, but I thought that it looked like you wiz talking."

Phyllis had drawn in a breath as she'd prepared to tell him that if he thought she'd trust Michael Warren to a layabout like him he must be crackers, or at least Bill had assumed that this was going through her mind, but then she'd stopped herself and just looked pensive for a moment. To Bill, it had looked as if she was considering who it would leave alone up here if him and Reggie Bowler and Drowned Marjorie and Michael were to tunnel off into the past for half an hour. The answer, obviously, had been her and tall, good-looking John. Once Phyllis had performed the necessary calculations, she'd appeared to change her stance.

"All right … as long as yer not digging back to join the Blackshirts and pinch all ayr Puck's 'Ats."

Bill had struck an attitude of injured protest.

" 'Course we're not. That's why we're taking Michael and Drowned Marjorie along, so they can keep an eye on us, and because you know that they wizn't with us when we saw ourselves out at the madhouses … but, look, if you don't trust us we can all stay 'ere with you. It makes no odds to me."

Probably fearful at the thought of losing her idyllic twilit lagoon interlude alone with John, Phyllis had quickly done her best to smooth what she thought were Bill's ruffled feathers.

"No, no, you goo on and play. Just don't get Michael into any mischief."

Bill had sworn he wouldn't, and then bounded off from stone to stone along the water's edge to tell the others that he'd got permission for a jaunt into the earthworks' past. From their bemused expressions, Bill had received the impression that nobody thought this sounded like much of an outing, but once Reg had loyally agreed to go with Bill, the other two abandoned their resistance.

Scrabbling with their fingertips in empty air, they'd swiftly pulled away the crackling black and white time fibres representing nights and days to make a hula-hoop-sized hole approximately twelve months deep. As he'd followed his three companions through the aperture into last year, he'd even risked a cheery wave to John and Phyllis before climbing through the gap in time and sealing it behind him.

On the portal's far side he'd found Reggie, Marge and Michael all standing about morosely in a flooded excavation that was the dead spit of where they'd been ten seconds earlier, only a little darker. Reg had fiddled with his bowler's angle for a minute and then spat a gob of ectoplasm into the lagoon, a sure sign that the gangly Victorian waif was cross about something or other.

"Well, this don't look like much fun to me. I thought as you'd 'ave something a sight livelier than this place up yer sleeve when you said we could 'ave
an expedition."

Bill had given Reggie an appraising look, and then had asked him what
he'd thought of Oddjob in *Goldfinger*. Reggie, who was good with naming cars but who had barely heard of moving pictures, had just frowned
uncomprehendingly.

"I don't know what odd job you're on about, or what it's doing in a finger.
You're not making sense. 'Ave you gone off your 'ead, lad?"

In reply, Bill had just grinned and deftly plucked the hat from Reggie's curly
locks before flinging it like a Frisbee, up through the descending darkness and
across the gouged-out cliff-top looming to the north, where it completely disappeared from view, rapidly followed by its graceful trail of after-images.

"No, but there's something gone off yours."

With Reggie slack-jawed at the sheer effrontery of what Bill had just done
and Marjorie and Michael Warren both starting to giggle, Bill had scampered
off in the direction that he'd thrown the bowler, pausing halfway up the earthworks' northern wall to shout back down to Reggie.

"And if I get to it first, I'm gunna piss in it!"

As he'd continued up the slope, Bill had heard the three other ghost-kids
whooping as they chased him, Marjorie and Michael both shrieking with
mirth while Reggie was just shrieking that Bill better not piss in his hat. Bill
hadn't really been intending to, of course, and if Reg had just thought about
it for a second he'd have realised that ghosts couldn't piss. Well, they could
squeeze a drop or two out if they wanted to, just like Reggie could spit, but it
was hardly like ghosts had a lot of extra moisture that they needed to unload.
Made mostly out of energy, wraiths were not succulent or sweaty or incontinent. They were as dry as brown October leaves save for the ectoplasm, which
tended to make them a bit chesty.

Reaching the cliff's top, where the unfolded and enlarged zone of the
astral earthworks ended, Bill had sat himself down on the expanse of grey
grass that ran alongside the St. Andrew's Road down to the foot of Scarletwell
Street while he'd waited for the others to catch up. It had been well and truly
dark by then, and other than the odd car purring up or down the main road
on its way to Sixfields or to Semilong it had been pretty much deserted. Reggie's phantom bowler had been lying there upturned, the freckled boy had
noticed, some yards from Bill's sprawling boots, but it had been too far away
to piddle into.

Gazing over the redundant stretch of empty lawn, an unused playing field
where there had once been twenty or more houses, Bill's attention had eventually settled on the solitary building rearing at the bottom end of Scarletwell

Street, the lone terraced house abandoned by its terrace. Even back while Bill had been alive, he'd thought the place an oddity, and that had been before he'd found out about its loft-ladder to Mansoul or its current ghost-sensitive inhabitant, the so-called Vernall that they'd fled from earlier. As it had been related to him, the space occupied by the peculiar remaining house had been owned by an admirably bloody-minded individual, an Eastern European bloke if Bill had heard it right, who had refused to sell his property to the town council just so they could knock it down. Its history since that point had been cloudy, although Bill supposed that the original unbudging owner must be long since dead, the property passed into other hands. He'd heard that at one point the council had been using it as a halfway house, somewhere to stick mental patients who'd been turfed out of their institutions and placed in the largely non-existent care of the community, but that had been some time back and he didn't think that it was still the case. These had been more or less the limits of the information that Bill had concerning the official story of the corner house, and of its supernatural situation he'd known even less.

As far as he'd been able to make out, the lonely edifice possessed its gateway to the realm Upstairs and current eerie resident thanks to its geometrical relationship with what had once been the original town hall, up at the top corner of Scarletwell Street and upon the street's far side, the structure that provided a foundation for the huge builders' headquarters called the Works from which Mansoul was governed. That was all that Bill had known about the place's more ethereal aspects, and, to be quite honest, even that he didn't really understand.

Besides, just at that moment, Bill had been less bothered by the house's history, material or otherwise, than he'd been by its probable effects on Michael Warren. After all, that had been the exact point which the dressed-for-bedtime child had done a runner from the yawning strip of vacant turf where Michael's home and street and family had once been situated. Since Bill could by then hear his three pursuers as they climbed over the cliff-edge and onto the gentle slope behind his back, he'd swiftly made his mind up to avoid the creepy, isolated corner house and take a different route to Martin's Yard, which was the place that he had been intent on reaching all along.

Reggie had run up behind Bill and hurdled him, pouncing upon his fallen bowler and inspecting it at length before he'd crammed it on his head. He told Bill that Bill better not have pissed in it, but he'd been laughing as he said it, as were Marjorie and Michael when they'd finally caught up with the two jostling boys. That was when Bill had come clean as to the true purpose of their outing, or at least as clean as he could comfortably manage.

"Listen, what it wiz, I've had this idea what I reckon could sort out a lot of everybody's problems, but if I told Phyllis it, I'm pretty certain she'd refuse just out of spite. What it involves wiz us takin' a trip to Martin's Yard – that'd be Martin's Fields to you three – and attempting an experiment what I've come up with. I know it don't sound like much, but I thought if we flew there rather than just walking it, it might liven things up a bit."

This last bit, the flying, had been an improvisation that was actually intended to get everyone to Martin's Yard without the added obstacle of walking Michael Warren past the old house at the foot of Scarletwell Street, but the prospect of an aerial manoeuvre had seemed to go down well with the other three, so Bill was glad he'd thought of it.

The quartet had laboriously taken to the air using the method of an escalating series of high lunar-landing leaps and bounces. This had largely been because it was the easiest means of getting novice flyers such as Michael Warren up into the sky. When the beginner had bounced high enough you just encouraged them to either dog-paddle or swim in order to maintain or possibly increase their altitude, helping them with a tow if necessary, as it had been in the case of Michael Warren. Once they'd all ascended to a fair way up above the railway yards on Andrew's Road, Bill had grabbed Michael's hand so that the bright-eyed and clearly delighted youngster could remain aloft. He'd noticed, peering through the darkness with his spectral night-sight, that Drowned Marjorie had been pretending that she couldn't swim or doggy-paddle either, prompting Reggie to assist her by taking her hand. Marjorie's inability had been a con, Bill was convinced. She may have not yet learned to swim when the Dead Dead Gang had first hauled her spirit-body from the Nene all of those years ago, but she'd been managing a competent breast-stroke when they'd been chasing pigeons over Marefair back in 1645. Was Marjorie getting a crush on Reggie, Bill had wondered as he'd climbed with Michael Warren through the Boroughs night towards a lemon-wedge half-moon?

Their as-the-crow-flies journey across railway yards and parked overnight lorries towards Spencer Bridge and Martin's Yard beyond had been exhilarating, even for a frequent flyer like Bill. Perhaps because he'd been accompanied by the wide eyed and relatively speechless Michael Warren, Bill had found that he was able to remember what his own first post-death flight had been like, prompted by the marvelling expression on the toddler's face.

Beneath them, even in these Stygian outer reaches of the town, had blazed a galaxy of lights, all of them rendered white or off-white by the ghost-seam's lack of colour. Interrupting these illuminated clusters were dark masses representing whistle-emptied factories and unlit meadows, with a hundred street-lamp sequins crusting on the edges of these black and cryptic shapes like phosphorescent barnacles. St. Andrew's Road, unrolled beneath them, north to south, was a chrome-studded leather belt that had provoked a comment from the infant struggling through the air beside Bill, even though he'd had to shout above the bluster of the wind.

"This wiz near where that devil took me on his flight, bit it wiz all in colour then."

Bill had called back across the few feet separating them, a distance equal to their clasped-together hands and outstretched arms.

"That wiz because the pair of you had come straight down to the First Borough from the Attics of the Breath, travelling in a special way what only builders, devils and the likes of that can do. Even meself, I've never seen it from up 'ere in colour. I bet it wiz quite a sight."

It had been about then that they'd been passing over Spencer Bridge which drew a bellowed comment from Drowned Marjorie, soaring there hand in hand with Reggie Bowler on Bill's starboard side.

"Look at that bloody bridge down there below us. That's the one they found me under. I can tell you one thing, I'm glad we're up here and not down there walking across it. It gives me the willies still, the thought of that old eel-woman, down there in the dark and damp."

Bill hadn't had an argument with that. He could remember the hair-raising night they'd rescued Marjorie from the Nene Hag, and of all the astounding sights that Bill had seen both in his life and out of it, that glimpse of the seemingly endless creature as it had reared up out of the midnight river, raking at the air with its long foldaway claws and the leprous membrane stretched between them, howling its frustration and its murderous hatred at the stars, had been the most spectacular ... at least until that giant snorting, stamping demon had turned up. Or the two Master Builders fighting. Those had been pretty amazing too, when he had stopped to think about it. Oh, and those two Salamander girls spreading the Great Fire. Those aside, Bill had thought the Nene Hag was absolutely blinding.

With their trailing smoke of after-images, the children had descended gently into the drum-reconditioning premises in St. Martin's Yard like slow, spent skyrockets. As he'd let go of Michael Warren's hand the toddler had retied the dangling tartan sash belt of his dressing gown and had stood for a moment taking stock of his surroundings before looking questioningly up at Bill.

"Where's this place, then?" he'd asked.

This is the place you're going to work when you're a man. This is what all those boring hours at school were to prepare you for. All of the hopes and dreams you're going to have while growing up will all end up here being beaten flat with hammers; being reconditioned. All these answers, honest but too cruel and painful for a child to bear or even understand, remained unspoken at the sore tip of Bill's bitten tongue. He'd felt a sudden surge of empathy for the poor kid, standing there blissfully oblivious to the bleak, disheartening prospects that were all around him, staring him right in the face. Bill, while he'd been alive, had worked in places just as joyless and soul-deadening, but never for more than six months or so. From what he could remember Alma telling him about her brother, Michael would be labouring in this grey, uninspiring place for far too many years. If he'd have murdered his employers in the way that they so patently deserved, he would have been released from his confinement sooner, the poor little bleeder. Trying to conceal these sombre thoughts behind his most impermeable cheeky grin, Bill had looked down at Michael as he'd tried to formulate an answer to the infant's question that he thought the kid could live with. Well, not *live* exactly, but Bill had known what he meant.

"It's a bad place, titch. Spots like this, Soul of the Hole wiz what we call 'em, and they won't do you or anybody else no favours. Never 'ave done, never will do. So, if we were to do something a bit naughty, then we'd not be hurting anybody who didn't deserve it."

This last bit had been an abject lie. The person who'd be most hurt by the "naughtiness" that Bill proposed would be Michael himself, given an acid facial and then knocked out by an iron bar, and Michael certainly did not deserve to undergo such tribulations. On the other hand, of course, his personal misfortune would be in the service of a greater good, or at least theoretically, but Bill had the uneasy feeling that they'd probably said that to all the whippets they'd had smoking eighty fags a day at the laboratories.

By this time Marjorie and Reggie had alighted too, looking self-conscious as they'd let go of each other's hands, and had wanted to know what this wild jaunt to the arse-end of nowhere was in aid of. He'd explained as best he could, with Michael being present.

"Look, you know that stuff that Fiery Phil wiz telling us at Doddridge Church, when he said that us lot had got a challenge on our plates, but that the powers that be were confident as we could 'andle it? Well, 'e wiz talkin' about Willie Winkie 'ere. Apparently, when 'e's brought back to life, we 'ave to make sure 'e remembers at least some of this what's happened to him, even though that's s'posed to be impossible. Now, I think I've worked out a way it can be done, but I can't go into the ins and outs of it in present company. Little pitchers, if you catch me drift."

Here Bill had been staring at Marjorie and Reggie, who'd both nodded almost imperceptibly to signal that they'd understood and were prepared to go along with Bill, despite the fact he couldn't really explain anything with Michael present. As for the toddler himself, he'd nodded wisely too, while obviously having no idea what Bill was on about. Encountering no objections, Bill had pressed on with his scheme.

He had originally been intending to have a poke round in the surrounding days and nights, to make sure that they'd got the right date and the right occasion, but he'd changed his mind. It had been what Phil Doddridge said to them, about how they should feel free to take Michael where they pleased and rest assured that anything that happened would be what was meant to happen. This predestination and free will lark cut both ways, as far as Bill had been able to see. If he'd brought Michael and the others to the yard on this precise night, that was divine destiny at work and it would have been almost rude to double-check. Bill had begun to realise that accepting the idea of Fate could actually remove some of the burden of responsibility. You could delegate upwards.

Having thus decided that they were indeed in the right place at the right time, Bill had next led the foursome on a wander round the reconditioning yard, inspecting stock and searching out likely material for what he'd had in mind.

It really had been a depressing place, that yard. Bill had remembered stories that his mum had told him, about when she'd been a little girl and would come round to Martin's Fields, as this place had then been, when she was out 'May Garling'. This had been something her and her mates did on the first of May. They'd go round door to door displaying a small basket full of wild flowers with a kiddie's doll sat in their midst, and for a halfpenny a turn they'd sing their little Mayday song that they'd all learned: "On First of May, my dear, I say, before your door I stand. It's nothing but a sprout, but it's well budded out by the work of Our Lord's hand." Looking around him at the heaps of dented cylinders, Bill had reflected that the yard, or fields, had sounded a much nicer and more picturesque location in his mother's day.

From Bill's own lifetime, his most striking anecdote about the place had been one that he didn't even feature in himself. It had been there in Martin's Yard, as he recalled, that the police had placed surveillance officers when they were keeping an eye on the land along the far end of St. Andrew's Road belonging to Paul Baker, a notorious villain Bill had known back in the day. The coppers had thought Baker might be hiding loot from some bank job or other on the property, and had their suspicions raised when they'd spotted two shady types who'd appeared to be tunnelling into the fifty-year-old piles of ashes and composted waste that hulked from Baker's territory.

In actuality, these two supposed accomplices had been Bill's old mates Roman Thompson and Ted Tripp. Ted had been an accomplished and discerning burglar who only burgled stately homes, while Rome had been a fearless union fighter and a celebrated all-round nut job. They'd been on Paul Baker's patch of ground with his permission, digging in the mounds of compressed mud and cinders dumped there decades earlier as waste from the Destructor up in Bath Street. Ted and Roman had been on a hunt for old Victorian stone bottles, the kind with the little marble for a stopper, for which they could likely get a few bob up at the antique shops. Rome, who'd always taken reckless courage to the point of death-wish, had been tunnelling into the heap's side, tempted further in and further still by an enticing partial glimpse of the words 'ginger beer' upon a curving surface. In the end, there'd only been his ankles sticking out, which had been when the entire hillock had decided to collapse on top of Roman Thompson.

Ted, a sturdy chap considering his size, had taken hold of Roman's feet and hauled him from the suffocating dirt and clinker in a great surge of adrenaline. It was at this point that some two or three cars full of coppers, who'd been watching the whole episode from up St. Martin's Yard, had roared onto Paul Baker's premises and had come screeching to a halt beside the thoroughly disoriented pair. Bill hadn't known what the police were hoping to achieve by their manoeuvre, but he'd bet they weren't expecting the appalling sight of Roman Thompson, covered head to toe in black filth, hair and beard plastered to muddy spikes and his crazed, furious eyes blazing amidst the soot and mire. It had occurred to Bill, as he'd thought back upon the incident from there in Martin's Yard, nosing around with Reggie, Marjorie and Michael, that if not for Ted Tripp's timely actions, the Destructor would have killed Rome Thompson even after it had been demolished for the better part of forty years. If Bill had been the superstitious type, the sort who readily believed in demons, ghosts and thousand-yard-long river monsters, he might even have concluded that this had been the Destructor's murderous intent.

As they'd continued wandering around the reconditioning yard – Bill hadn't known what time it was, except that it was clearly outside working hours – they'd come at last upon about a dozen drums that had been set apart from all the rest, perhaps to begin work upon first thing the morning following. One of the battered metal cylinders, which stood a yard or two away from its companions, had a strip of tape dangling from it; its fierce warning-notice trailing into grit and oily puddles where it had become detached at one end.

Destiny. Fate. Kismet. Bingo.

Bill, delighted that for once in his precarious existence things seemed to be working out as planned, had organised the other three ghost-children as if for a game of trains. Since Reggie was the tallest, Bill had let him be the locomotive at the front of their impromptu conga line, with Michael, Marjorie and Bill himself playing the coal tender and coaches. With Reg Bowler trying hard to make appropriate train-whistle sounds and puffing noises, they'd set off in a restricted circle round the isolated drum, chugging around their miniature loop of imaginary track as if they were pretending to be a toy train rather than a full-sized one.

Even in the sluggish atmospherics of the ghost-seam they had quickly gathered speed, as Bill had learned would happen if there were enough of you all pushing. Circling faster and still faster, their pursuing after-images had fused into what must have looked from outside like a grey and spinning giant doughnut made of blur: a torus, as Bill had heard this apparently important shape described by Mansoul's brainier inhabitants. About the bottom of the drum, the dust and fag-ends had begun to get caught up in the rotating currents of the mini-whirlwind that the phantom kids had been creating. Glittering metallic toffee-wrappers and spent matches spiralled up into the night, and Bill had shouted above Reggie Bowler's dopey sound effects for the Victorian urchin to run faster. The detached end of the warning tape had started lifting itself from the pool of water, oil, and indeterminate hazardous chemicals that it was draped in, flapping dolefully, with toxic droplets flung out from its snapping, fluttering extremities. Bill had called out to Reg again, to tell him he was running like a girl, which had resulted in the anger-fuelled acceleration Bill had hoped for. Soon the drum had been wrapped tight in a tornado of revolving lolly-sticks and spinning grit, the length of tape standing straight up into the darkness over the container, rattling against the cyclone like a tethered kite.

Eventually the other end had come unstuck as well, at which point Bill had yelled for Reg to stop and they'd all run into each other, falling over in a breathless, laughing heap. The roughneck spectres had sat in St. Martin's Yard and watched while the soiled streamer sailed away, bowling across the property's enclosing fence and off into the sodium-lamp sparkle of the night. Mission accomplished, even if nobody except Bill had known precisely what the mission was.

They hadn't hung about long after that. They'd bounced and swum and doggy-paddled up into the windswept firmament as they'd returned to the unfolded earthworks, back the way they'd come, treading the moonlight over Spencer Bridge and the whore-magnet of the overnight long-distance lorry park. This was tucked in the corner where the bridge met with Crane Hill and the St. Andrew's Road, the transport café that had previously been a public lavatory and, prior to that, a slipper-baths. This had become a major point of trade that had supplied the customers who drew the girls, who brought the pimps, who dealt the drugs, which bred the guns that shot the kids who lived in the house that crack built. Even though Bill had lived a fair way into that current century, the twenty-first – much longer than he'd been expecting to, at any rate – he'd found that visiting the period made him just as uncomfortable as it made Reggie Bowler or, to judge from her expression, Marjorie.

It had been something in the way the streets and factories and houses looked from up above, something that made you think of all the sacrifices and the struggles, the ambitions and the childbirths and the deaths and disappointments that those doll-sized little homes had seen across the years, all of it leading up to what, exactly? Bill had been unable to suppress the melancholy feelings that things had been meant to turn out a lot better than the way they had. The world that everybody had been given hadn't been the one that they'd been promised, that they'd been expecting, that they'd been supposed to get. Although when Bill had thought about the state Mansoul was in during these early reaches of the new millennium, the damage done by the Destructor and its widening arc of influence, he couldn't say he was surprised. The modern streets of heaven were in terrible condition, right here at the divinely appointed centre of the country's fabric. Was it any wonder, Bill had mused, that present-day English society should start to fall to bits, start to unravel, as the burn-hole in the middle of its painstakingly-woven fibres had begun to spread, to gradually unpick the whole of the material?

While Bill had been considering these notions, up there in the haunted sky above the railway yards with Michael Warren, and with Reggie and Drowned Marjorie riding the night breeze hand-in-hand beside them, he'd been struck by his second and, with hindsight, more disastrous idea. Perhaps he'd been encouraged by the seeming unanticipated success of his first scheme, or perhaps it had still been the Puck's Hats that he'd eaten having their enlivening effect upon Bill's consciousness, but he'd all of a sudden made a startling connection. He'd been thinking about the Destructor and the miserable twenty-first century view from there above the Boroughs when he'd made a lateral leap to Alma Warren's paintings, most especially the huge and terrifying one that had looked down into some sort of mile-wide rubbish-grinder or incinerator.

That was the Destructor, he had realised with a jolt. That was the way it looked when seen from the perspective of a semi-devastated Mansoul at this sordid juncture of the century. Since Alma had received all of her images at second-hand from Michael, Bill had understood that at some point they must be going to take the toddler up there, even though it was a dreadful place and time, most usually avoided by all but the Master Builders and those souls who were already damned. Certainly not the place that anyone in their right mind would dream of taking an easily-frightened child, though clearly they were going to have to. He would see to it. He had decided to tell Phyllis all about this latest side-trip that he'd slotted into their itinerary before they took the toddler back to 1959 and his resuscitated infant body. There was no way of avoiding Phyllis's involvement in an expedition fraught with such dismay and danger and besides, he'd reasoned, she'd seen Alma's all-devouring vision of apocalypse as well. She'd understand why it was necessary, what Bill was suggesting.

The four of them had alighted gently on the same deserted stretch of turf that they'd set out from, up towards the railway station end of Andrew's Road. Unhurriedly – they'd had a whole year before they were due to rendez-vous with John and Phyllis, after all – they'd wandered up what seemed to be a grassy incline leading to the modest patch of land on which the 'castle remains' were exhibited. At least, the slope had seemed that way, the way a living person would experience it, until they had reached its top, when they'd found themselves looking down the astral earthworks' plunging walls into the dark collapsed lagoon, rather than staring in disinterest at a few half-hearted plaques and cheaply-recreated castle steps.

Like grubby mountain goats they'd made their way down a meander-ing and narrow cliff track, single file, into the lower depths of the phantas-mal excavation. Here the shadows had appeared to lay around in solid slabs, propped up at eerily suggestive angles on each other, while off in the dripping blackness there were small and sudden sounds. He'd heard a tinkling splash of aural chromium as though some dream-thing, perhaps plated all in iridescent scales and without eyes, had surfaced briefly to devour another dream-thing that had the misfortune to be hovering too close to the midnight meniscus on its lacy tinsel wings. The night was lively with carnivorous imaginings.

When they'd descended to the waterside point where Bill had grabbed Reggie's hat and sent it skimming off into adventure, Bill had started scraping the nocturnal air as he'd begun the time-hole that would take them up twelve months into the spring of 2006. Dragging the alternating black and white onionskin layers representing night and day to one side, he'd soon opened up a yard-wide aperture with a migraine-like flickering on its perimeter. With-out a second thought, he'd clambered through the crackling gap and called a raucous greeting into the surrounding gloom.

"All right? It's us. We're back."

The first thing Bill had seen that indicated there was something funny going on had been the string of rancid rabbit pelts just lying there discarded on a jutting granite outcrop several feet away. His ghostly night-sight, which embroidered every hidden thing with silver stitching round its edges, had leapt instantly upon the fallen carnal garland and his phantom heart had dropped. Phyllis had got so many enemies throughout the mezzanine-realm of the ghost-seam, he'd concluded grimly, that something like this had been bound to occur sooner or later.

Bill had just been in the act of summoning whatever last reserves of cunning he'd had in him to cope with this new and desperate situation when two figures had stood up from an inviting mossy hollow in the rocks nearby: a man and woman who both looked to be in their mid-twenties. The young fellow was a squaddie, hurriedly refastening the gleaming buttons on his army jacket, glaring angrily at Bill throughout with deep and dark matinee-idol eyes. The woman smoothing down her knee-length 1950s skirt as she'd stood there beside him had been a real smasher: a pale blonde with glistening lipstick and strong, finely-chiselled features that had just then been arranged in an expression of dismay, appalled and startled. There had been something so familiar about both of this strikingly handsome pair that Bill had briefly wondered if they might be famous film stars, actors that he'd previously seen in some Ealing production, a repeat shown on a Sunday afternoon during his boyhood. Certainly the grey tones of the spectral half-world, with their whiff of *Brief Encounter*, had done nothing to reduce the post-war cinematic quality that had perhaps created this impression.

It was then that Bill had finally realised who the couple were. More unaccountably embarrassed than he'd ever been during his earthy and robust existence, he'd ducked straight back through the time-vent into 2005, colliding with Drowned Marjorie, Reggie and Michael Warren who'd been just about to step through the hole after him. It had required some rapid thinking.

"Sorry, chaps. Don't mean to hold you up or anything, but I'd got a nice juicy Puck's 'At in me pocket what I'd kept for later, and it's not there now. I reckon as I must 'ave dropped it, stepping through this bloody 'ole. Why don't you be good eggs and help us look for it?"

The four of them had plodded round in circles for a good few minutes, scrutinising the surrounding area with their enhanced afterlife vision until Bill had sighed dramatically and had announced in woeful, disappointed tones that he must have misplaced his cherished Puck's Hat elsewhere, and that they could give up on their search and at last follow him back through the glittering window into a year later.

This time, when Bill had stepped back into the almost identical place on the hole's far side, he'd been relieved to find that everything was back to normal. Tall John was sat perched upon a brick-shaped boulder some way off, chewing a stem of ghost-grass as he idly scratched one knee beneath the hem of his short trousers. He'd not bothered to look round as Bill and the three others had climbed through the time-gap to re-join Phyllis and him. Phyllis herself had been standing not far from the rent in time's fabric when the four adventurers returned, dressed in her dark grey skirt and light grey cardigan, her blunt-toed buckle shoes. She'd stood there primly rearranging her disgusting rabbit necklace, draping it around her shoulders before looking up at Bill impassively, searching his grinning features for some indication as to what he'd seen or what he knew before, at length, she spoke to him.

"So 'ow did yer get on, then? Took yer long enough, whatever you wiz doin'. Up to no good, I'll be baynd, yer shifty little beggar."

Phyllis had been smiling faintly as she spoke, and Bill's own grin had widened in reply.

"Oh, you know. We did all right. And by the way, you needn't worry about 'ow we're gunna make sure the boy wonder 'ere gets back to life with all his memories and what-not. I've took care of it."

She'd looked surprised and slightly angry.

"You've done what? You little sod. Why didn't you tell me?"

Still grinning, Bill had put one arm around her waist and given her a little squeeze.

"I can remember my dear mother saying as 'ow everybody wiz allowed their little secrets, gal. She also used to say that if you asked no questions, you'd be told no lies."

Phyllis had laughed then and affectionately punched him in the gut. For just a moment it had almost been like how they'd used to be together, their relationship when they'd both been alive. She'd always had an eye for a well turned-out gentleman back then as well, Bill had reflected with amusement, even when she'd been a woman in her seventies.

Seeing as she'd appeared to be in a good mood, Bill had taken the opportunity to tell her about where he thought they should next escort Michael Warren, taking a circuitous route before getting to the matter's heart, so that he didn't put her off.

"'Ere, Phyll, do you remember that big painting Alma did? The one where you're above some sort of horrible great waste-disposal unit, looking down, and there's all little terraced streets and little people sliding into a big smoking hole?"

Phyllis had nodded, rattling her rabbits.

"What abayt it?"

"Well, I reckon that I've worked out what it wiz. It's the Destructor, Phyll. It's the Destructor when you look down on it from Upstairs, Upstairs as it is now, in these first years o' the new century."

The Dead Dead Gang's girl leader had turned pale. To call it deathly pale, he'd realised, would be a redundancy given their posthumous condition.

"Oh bloody 'ell. Yer right. I can remember when we saw it, what a funny turn it give me, 'ow it looked as though the world wiz comin' to an end. I 'adn't thought abayt it since I got up 'ere, though, so I 'adn't thought abayt 'ow much it looked like the Destructor. Bloody 'ell. Does that mean as we've gotta take 'im up there so that 'e can see it an' describe it to 'is sister?"

Bill had nodded glumly. Even though it had been his idea, a trip to Mansoul in its current state was nothing that he'd been particularly looking forward to. Now blanching to a shade of what Bill had thought must be infra-white, Phyllis had fretfully continued.

"But you know 'ow bad it's got up there. It's only the fire-fighters what'll go anywhere near it! There's been souls fall in, as well, and not come ayt again. What if we take the nipper up there, before we can take 'im back to 1959 and 'is own body, an' it all guz wrong? What if 'e's damaged and we end up spoilin' everythin'? If the 'ole Vernall's Inquest and the Porthimoth di Nor'an come to nothin' and its all ayr fault? I'll tell yer now, it'll be you explainin' it ter the Third Burrer and not me, if anything should 'appen."

Good old Phyll, as swift as Bill himself when it came to shirking responsibility. Now that he'd thought about it, that was more than likely where he'd got it from.

"Yeah, but you 'eard what Doddridge said, about 'ow we should take 'im where we wanted to and rest assured that it'd be where we were meant to take 'im. I've got an idea that this decision what we're faced with now might be exactly what 'e meant. Perhaps 'e told us that so we'd 'ave confidence enough to make the right choice. This might be really important, Phyll. This might make all the difference as to whether we succeed in doin' what we've been told we should do, or not."

That had seemed to persuade her. Phyllis had marshalled her soldiers with competing terror and determination in her voice and her expression. She'd told them that they'd got one last stop to make before returning their new regimental mascot and most recent member to his own time and his own resuscitated body. She'd explained that this would mean another short trip to the Mayorhold, up to Tower Street where they'd been the last time they were in this century, before they'd dug back down to 1959 so they could go upstairs and watch the Master Builders have their fight. She hadn't spelled it out much more than that, presumably for fear of scaring Michael Warren, but you could see in the eyes of Reggie, John and Marjorie that they'd known something serious was up, just by the strain in Phyllis's tight voice.

She'd led the ghost gang and their trailing duplicates up the same northern earthworks' wall from the collapsed lagoon that Bill and his accomplices had climbed up on their brief trip back to 2005. This brought them out onto the same long slope of grass that ran down alongside St. Andrew's Road to Scarletwell Street and the solitary house that loomed there near its corner. Bill had been just about to point out to Phyllis that this was the spot that had scared Michael Warren into running away earlier – which was why Bill had chosen flying over walking, after all – when Michael himself had piped up and put his own two penn'orth in.

"Is that our street down there, that's got the haunt-head house stood all Malone upon its corner? I shed like to go and have a lurk at it, if that's all ripe. I premise I won't ruin away again, like I dead lost time."

Although you could tell from how he'd mixed his words up that the small boy had been nervous, you could also tell that he'd been serious. He seemed to have matured quite rapidly since he'd absconded earlier, perhaps starting to grow into his timeless and eternal soul the way that people did when they were dead, regardless of what age they'd died at. Anyway, he'd seemed quite keen to go and have a look at the bare turf and young trees that were now presiding where his family home had previously been, and so the gang had all traipsed down the slope with him towards Scarletwell corner. When he'd thought of all the pains he'd taken to avoid the place for Michael's benefit, Bill had been moderately annoyed to think that they'd all been for nothing. Of course, if the four ghost-children had walked over Spencer Bridge then that would have upset Drowned Marjorie, and anyway, the flights they'd taken there and back had both been lovely. Plus, the aerial view had tipped him off as to what Alma's wall-sized Armageddon painting had been all about, so he'd come out on top, whichever way you looked at it. He'd decided to quit all his internal moaning and just get on with the job in hand.

The gang and their pursuing after-images had trickled to a halt halfway along the unattended patch of lawn there just past Scarletwell Street corner and its lonely single house. They'd all stood silently as an unusually sombre Michael Warren had paced in his slippers up and down between the thirty-year-old silver birches that had first been planted sometime after his home street had been demolished. When the ghost-child had at last identified a spot where he seemed satisfied his house had stood he'd simply sat down on the turf and had a private weep, both dignified and brief, before he'd wiped the tears of ectoplasm from his eyes with one sleeve of his tartan dressing gown and then stood up again, re-joining his dead friends who'd all been standing a few feet off, keeping a respectful distance.

"That wiz all I wanted, just to find out how it felt with nothing there, but it wiz peaceful, like it always wiz. We can all go up to the Mayorhold now, if that wiz what you thought we ought to do before you take me home."

They'd all been just about to do as Michael had suggested when the young girl in the mini-skirt and PVC mac that they'd spotted earlier in Chalk Lane had come clicking on her high heels down the hill and started walking back and forth along the strip of pavement between Scarletwell and Spring Lane while the gang had stood there on the grass verge, watching her.

Reggie and Marjorie had both begun to giggle when they'd realised that the mixed-race woman with her hair done up in frizzled corn-rows was a prostitute, while Michael Warren had sniggered along with them without having the first idea what he was laughing at. At this point the young woman had stopped in her tracks and turned her head in their direction, peering puzzled and uncertain through the gloom towards them for a moment before she'd resumed her pacing to and fro along the empty former terrace.

Phyllis had hissed in reproach at Reg and Marjorie for laughing.

"Cut it ayt, you two. Me and me little 'un saw her earlier in Chalk Lane, and we reckon she can see us, with whatever drugs she's on or comin' orf of."

Reggie, peering at the young pro as she got to Scarletwell Street and turned round again to face them, walking back along with her arms folded to suppress a shiver, had removed his hat to scratch his curly head and then had stooped to speak to Phyll in a stage whisper.

"I reckon as I've seen 'er before as well, although I can't think where it wiz."

Bill had chimed in, putting his less quick-witted chum out of his misery.

"We saw 'er up in Bath Street, you big bowler-hatted berk. She wiz sat in 'er flat and we could see 'er through the walls, with the Destructor grindin' at her innards while she did 'er scrapbook. You remember. It wiz just when we were bringin' titch 'ere out the flats, after we'd found 'im on the steps there, talkin' about 'is *Forbidden Worlds* and that."

Reg had grinned amiably.

"Oh, yeah, that's right. I can't remember nothin' about no forbidden worlds, but I remember seein' 'er with that big smoking wheel workin' away at 'er, and her with no idea as it wiz 'appenin'."

It had then been Drowned Marjorie's turn to raise objections.

"Well, what about me, then? I weren't with you when you found him up by the Destructor. I wiz with Phyllis and John, and yet I think I know her from somewhere as well. Haven't we seen her working somewhere, not the work she's doing now, but in a shop or something? Oh, I can't remember. P'raps I'm makin' a mistake."

While the ghost-children had stood talking on the grass, a number of the era's stern and serious cars had hurtled past, narrow-eyed and suspicious, heading for the station or for Spencer Bridge and the attendant lorry-park. Bill had mused idly and perhaps mean-spiritedly that when they'd brought Princess Di back to Northamptonshire for burial, they should have brought her through Spencer Estate and over Spencer Bridge, so that she could have passed at least once over the dilapidated byways that her family had loaned its name to. He'd gone on from this to wonder why the girl was plying her trade here, when not two hundred yards away there was the Super Sausage café and the lorry park with its potential customers, the lonely men away from home nursing their urgent super sausages. He'd watched her shivering and shaking as she'd paced the meagre limits of her territory, most probably quaking from drug withdrawal rather than the cold on such a mild spring night, and it had come to him that unlike in the area near Spencer Bridge, there were no cameras here. That was the likely reason that she'd picked this spot, even though there was much less chance of passing trade.

As if to prove Bill wrong, it had been then that the dark-shelled Ford Escort had come purring down St. Andrew's Road, proceeding northwards from the station end towards them, slowing down and coming to halt beside the curb across the other side of Scarletwell Street, near the buried site of the old scarlet well itself. The by-now shuddering and clearly desperate girl had gazed in the direction of the idling vehicle for a moment, hesitating as she tried to weigh the situation up, before she'd clicked and clacked along the vanished terrace, making for the creepy single building at the path's far end, for Scarletwell Street and the waiting car beyond.

The car, a nondescript affair only a few years old, had been wrapped in an aura of bad news that the ghost-children could pick up from getting on a hundred yards away. "Soul of the hole," Drowned Marjorie had said in a hushed voice, and all of them had known that she was right. They hadn't, from that distance, been able to see how many men there were inside the Escort, even with their enhanced vision. Nonetheless, they'd all sucked in a nervous breath as the young woman bent down from the waist to exchange words through the side-window with the driver and then tottered round the car's front, briefly silhouetted in the headlights, before clambering into the passenger seat by the offside door. The engine had roared into life and the almost-black car had taken off, turning a sharp right as if it intended to head off up Scarletwell Street but then turning right again to disappear into the lower elbow-end of Bath Street, after which the motor noise had suddenly cut off completely.

It had obviously been none of their business, and the six ghost-tykes had all begun to walk along the hidden remnant of the old back alley, up against the wire fence and hedges bordering Spring Lane School's lower playing fields. Reduced to a few cobbles, this vestigial jitty led them onto Scarletwell Street right beside the lonely edifice, apparently without disturbing its clairvoyant resident. Making a left, the six of them had started heading up the battered gradient towards the Mayorhold. They'd barely begun to do this, trudging uphill by the school fields on the far side from the flats, when they'd heard the faint cries, dulled by the ghost-seam's dead acoustics, which had issued from the black and gaping mouth of Bath Street, just across the road.

It hadn't been their business. It had been a matter of the mortal world, already pre-ordained, and had nothing to do with them. It hadn't been as if they really knew the girl and, anyway, they'd been on an important mission. Besides, if it had been serious the screams wouldn't have broken off almost as soon as they'd begun, now, would they? Even if it *had* been something serious, what were they going to do about it? They were just a bunch of kids, dead kids at that, who couldn't touch or alter things in the material world, unless it was a crisp bag or a length of hazard tape. Even if, for the sake of argument, that girl had been in awful, dreadful trouble, then what ... were ... *Shit.*

Phyllis and Bill had both spontaneously begun to run towards the Bath Street opening at the same time, with the four others following a fraction of a second later. Spouting misty after-pictures like a boiling kettle, the Dead Dead Gang had streamed into the bent, crooked lane only to find it empty, simmering in dark and silence. After a few moments' bafflement, as one they'd stared towards the gap in the curved line of Bath Street's further side, the entrance into a secluded walled space that provided garages and parking for the Moat Place and Fort Place developments. If Bill remembered right, the draughty tarmac strip descending into the enclosure had once been a little terraced street known as Bath Passage. The ghost-kids had drifted down it, cautiously, into the absolute night of the parking area.

The stationary Escort had been sitting in the middle of the surfaced rectangle that the row of gunmetal garage doors faced onto, with its snout pointing away from the ghostly ensemble. Muffled yelps, along with bumps and growls, had been escaping from the crouched, unmoving vehicle, sounding as if two boisterous Alsatians had been negligently left locked up inside. The children had approached the car. If they'd had hearts, their hearts would have been in their mouths.

They'd peered into the dark of the posterior windscreen. In the car's rear seat the woman had been on her back, her skirt either torn off or else scrunched up into invisibility. Kneeling between her pitifully thin legs, raping her at the same time as he was punching her about the head, had been a stout and almost babyish-looking man in his late thirties, short black curly hair already greying at the temples. Flushed and, if it were not for the ghost-seam, full of colour, his plump cheeks had wobbled faintly with each thrust that he made into her, each blow he landed on her face or shoulders. Despite the ferocity with which he'd hit her and despite the snarled instructions to just shut up and do as he'd told her, judging from the man's expression, he'd not even seemed to be possessed by uncontrollable rage, or, indeed, by anything. His features had been blank and dead, almost disinterested, as if the whole sordid nightmare was something on television; was a porn-loop he'd already seen too many times to muster any real enthusiasm. As the horror-stricken children watched, the man had smashed one ring-decked fist into the woman's forehead just above her eye. Even in black and white, the blood erupting from the wound had looked appalling. It had run across her face, across her split lips that were opening and closing around noises she was too afraid to make.

There'd been three figures in the car. There'd been a second man, wearing a broad-brimmed hat, who had been sitting in the right front seat behind the

steering wheel, facing away from everybody and apparently entirely unconcerned by what was happening behind him.

Possibly encouraged by the hand-in-hand flight up to Martin's Yard they'd
shared together, Michael Warren had reached out and clutched Bill's mitt,
looking for reassurance. Standing rooted to the spot by the vile moment he
was witnessing, Bill had until then utterly forgotten Michael's presence and
had cursed himself for letting a small child see this abomination. He'd taken
a step or two away, still holding Michael's hand, and they had ended up a few
feet to the car's right, further down the gentle tarmac slant of the enclosure.
Inadvertently, this had meant they could see the hat-clad figure sitting in the
front seat both more clearly and in profile ... or at least, he'd been in profile
until he had turned and smiled at Bill and Michael.

Although every other object in Bill's field of vision was a different tone
of grey, he'd realised that the man's eyes were in colour. One was green. The
other one was red. So that was what his future self had meant, about the devil
being in the driving seat.

The thirty-second spirit, who'd been hundreds of feet high, sporting three
heads and sat astride a dragon on the last occasion Bill had seen him, had
leaned casually through the side-window of the Escort to address the boys.
He hadn't wound the window down or broken it in any way. He'd just leaned
through it. By now, the remainder of the gang had gathered behind Bill and
Michael to see what was happening, but when the fiend spoke it had been
quite clear that his words were meant only for young Michael Warren.

"Ah, my little friend. I knew you wouldn't have forgotten our agreement.
I had faith in you, you see? I knew that you'd remember I'd arranged a job for
you, up in this brash new century, as payment for that lovely trip I took you on.
Specifically, if you recall, I wanted someone killed, their breastbone smashed
to flakes of chalk, their heart and lungs crushed into an undifferentiated pulp.
Do you think you could do that for me, or have you perhaps a hankering to
see again what happens when you make me cross? Hm? Wiz that it? All of my
different heads as big as tower-blocks and all screaming at you, when your little deathmonger, your little hag who stinks of afterbirth wizn't around to save
you? Wiz that what you want?"

The traffic-light eyes glittered. Small blue flames had drooled inconti-
nently from the corners of the fiend's lips as it spoke. There in the rear of the
unmoving car, the fat man in the white shirt and grey windcheater had turned
the by-now bloody girl onto her hands and knees, he and his victim wholly
unaware that something mentioned in the Bible sat there in the front seat
watching them, appreciatively, and with some amusement.

Looking back, the Dead Dead Gang's reaction had resembled some posthumous sequel to *The Goonies* or an episode of *Scooby-Do*: they'd screamed in

perfect unison and then they'd run away, with Bill still holding Michael Warren's hand, both of them shrieking as he'd dragged the infant out of the garage enclosure into lower Bath Street. The whole mob of them had been halfway up Scarletwell Street before they'd ceased howling and had stopped to draw a breath, or at least figuratively speaking. Everyone had been aghast, and no one had known what to do. Phyllis had looked more worried and upset than Bill had ever seen her, in an even worse state than that time she'd come to visit Bill down in the cells, when he was in there for that stabbing.

"What are we all gunna do? We can't just let that poor girl 'ave that done to 'er and not do nothin'. Ayr Bill, can't you think o' summat?"

Bill, still trembling from the run-in with the demon, had been absolutely blank, unable to come up with anything, as if he'd used all of his cunning on the business out at Martin's Yard.

"Well, I don't know! We could go and find some of the bigger and uglier rough sleepers what are round 'ere, see if they knew what to do, except that they all want to kill us because you keep pissing 'em about!"

Phyllis had gone quiet and had stared into empty space for a few moments before she'd replied.

"What abayt Freddy Allen? We've not 'urt 'im, we've just messed abayt with 'im, and 'e's a good sort underneath. 'E'd 'elp us if we asked 'im."

Bill had shook his head in violent disagreement, briefly growing extra noggins like a hydra as he did so.

"What good could 'e do? 'E's no more use than we are. Anyway, where are we gunna find 'im, even if 'e 'as forgiven us for nickin' 'is 'at earlier, when we wiz up there in the twenty-fives?"

Phyllis had thought about it for a moment.

"What abayt the Jolly Smokers? Most o' the rough sleepers goo there of an evenin', and if Freddy wizn't there, there'd be somebody 'oo knew where 'e wiz."

Bill had goggled at her in disbelief, the other children looking on in anxious silence.

"Are you fuckin' mad? The Jolly Smokers, that's where Mick Malone the ratter and all them go! Tommy Mangle-the-Cat and Christ knows who else! If us lot set foot in there, they'll pull our heads off and then stick 'em on the beer pumps!"

Phyllis had just looked at him, a queer and thoughtful look stealing across her pointy little face.

"Yiss. Yiss, I can see that, what yer sayin'. If I wiz to go up there, that's what they'd do to me, yer can be sure. But what if just you wiz to go up there and ask for Freddy Allen? After all, it wiz you what reminded me abayt what Mr. Doddridge said, 'ow we should just go where we please, and rest assured as that was the place we were meant to go."

In retrospect, Bill saw now that this had been when his big ideas had taken a quite definite turn for the worse. Disastrously, he'd made a feeble effort to use logic as a means of extricating himself from the bear-pit of responsibility he'd accidentally dug.

"No. No, what Doddridge said, that was just Michael 'ere who 'e meant, 'ow we should feel free to take 'im anywhere because it would just be part of 'is education. If we're takin' Michael somewhere, that means that it's all been planned by management, and that we'll all most probably come out all right. If it's just me, all on me own, then it's quite likely that I could get slaughtered without it affecting any 'igher plan. No way. No, I'm not doin' that."

Phyllis had cocked her head. She'd looked like she was making quite a big decision.

"All right. Take 'im with yer."

Bill hadn't been sure he'd heard her right. Quite frankly, he'd not been expecting that.

"What? Take who with me?"

Phyllis had remained expressionless.

"Take Michael with yer. If you take 'im, then it wizzle be part of 'is education, like yer said, and both of yer wizzle be okay. If you expect me to take 'im Upstairs, in the state it's in at present, just upon your say-so, then you ought to be prepared to put yer money where yer mayth is."

Bill had floundered, possibly knowing already that his argument was doomed even before he had attempted to express it.

"W-Well, why can't we all go up, in that case? Or why can't just you and Michael go?"

Phyllis had given him an almost pitying smile.

"Well, if we all went up there, it'd look provocative. And if I wiz to go up there, that'd be even worse. All things considered, yer the best one for the job, 'cause yer've 'ad more experience with rough pubs then the rest of us lot put together."

Well, there'd been no arguing with that. She'd had him there, game, set and match. The gang had carried on uphill as quickly as they could, with Bill still holding Michael's faintly sticky hand. They'd swirled around the bases of the ironically-titled NEWLIFE flats and into Tower Street, the short terrace, leading to the raised wall of the current Mayorhold, which had once been the top part of Scarletwell Street.

They walked to the street's end, past the house where they'd seen the pissed-up bloke earlier, the one who'd had the funny laugh and who had seemed to see them, too. With their grey multiple-exposures smouldering behind them they'd moved through the sickly sodium-light which spilled down from the elevated traffic junction that the Mayorhold had become into the underpasses and walkways below. They'd turned left out of Tower Street and there, almost upon the corner, had been the concealed front doorway of the Jolly Smokers.

It had looked like a thin sheet of vapour, door-sized and just hanging in the lamp-accentuated gloom near the Salvation Army hall, across from the ugly mosaic ramparts of the Mayorhold. Absolutely two-dimensional in its appearance, it had been too flat to see at all when looked at from the side and, unless you were dead, nor was it any more discernible when looked at from the front. With wraith-sight you could see the doorway if you stood before it, though why anyone would want to see such a dishearteningly ugly thing had been beyond Bill's comprehension. Even by the miserable standards of the half-realm, the pub entrance had been drab and uninviting. Its ghost paint had peeled, hanging away from the worm-eaten phantom wood beneath in little curls resembling dead caterpillars. Scratched upon its upper timbers as if by a pen-knife in a childish and uneven hand had been the legend *Joly Smoaker's*, and when the Dead Dead Gang listened past the mezzanine-world's sonic cotton-wool they'd made out drunken shouts and bursts of nasty-sounding laughter, seemingly originating from the empty, sodium-tinged night air above the sunken walkway.

Bill, quite frankly, had been bricking it. The last place in the universe that he'd wanted to visit was the most notorious ghost-pub in the Boroughs, the ghost of a long-demolished pub, where all the old-school horrors of the neighbourhood had congregated. Although Bill had always been an anarchist at heart and generally applauded the largely unsupervised conditions of the afterlife, he'd long accepted that rule-free utopias would end up harbouring some complete fucking nightmares, like the Jolly Smokers. Christiana, out in Denmark, the sprawling and well-established hippy free-state that he'd visited while on his mortal travels was a good example, starting out with marvellous and visionary homes, domes made from empty beer-cans that would open to the stars, and ending up at one point, so he'd heard, in games of football played with human heads. No, it was fair to say, for once, that Bill had not been looking forward to the prospect of a session in the pub.

That had been right when the most welcome sight that Bill had ever seen came billowing out of the underpass's mouth which opened from the Mayorhold's bounding wall some distance to their left. The massive figure – it had been a man – had clearly been deceased like they were, judging from the burly medicine-ball after-images that had rolled after it out of the tunnel entrance and onto the lamp-lit walkway.

Even though the large ghost was in monochrome like his surroundings, there'd been no denying that he looked innately colourful. A floppy and vaguely Parisian beret slept like a minimalist cartoon cat atop his shoulder-brushing mullet, or "the hairstyle of the gods" as Bill remembered the voluminous spook once describing it, back when he'd been alive. The hair, in its then-current circumstances, had been smoky grey like the neatly Mephistophelean beard, or the moustache with its ends curling up in two waxed points. Round as the moon, the spirit's awe-inspiring girth was draped in clothing that could only have been manufactured for that very purpose. Sewn-on teddy bears gaily arranged a tablecloth to have their picnic on the slopes of the impressive stomach, under the white fluffy clouds and cheerful sun that had been carefully stitched across the noble bosom of his dungarees. Worn over these was a capacious summer jacket sporting bold vertical stripes, giving the wearer the appearance of an ambulatory deckchair, or at least of something that suggested summer and the seaside. In one hand, the welcome apparition had been carrying a sturdy walking stick, while in the other hand he'd held a leather instrument case like a giant black teardrop, the unusual shape suggesting that it contained a pot-bellied mandolin.

Tom Hall. The glorious spectre rumbling towards them had been Tom Hall (1944 to 2003): Northampton's minstrel, bard and one-man Bicycle Parade – a memorable show each time he'd set foot outside his front door. He'd been the wildly Dionysian and tireless founder of numerous brilliant groups from the mid-'60s onwards, like the Dubious Blues Band, Flying Garrick, Ratliffe Stout Band, Phippsville Comets and a dozen more that Bill remembered seeing play in the back room of the Black Lion. This had been the Black Lion in St. Giles Street, and not the older pub of the same name down there by Castle Station. The St. Giles Street Black Lion, hailed as the most haunted spot in England by ghost-hunters such as Eliot O'Donnell, had been sanctuary to the town's drugged-up bohemians and drunken artists from the 1920s to its sorry end during the 1990s when it had been ruinously improved, converted to a tavern meant for an expected passing trade of lawyers and renamed the Wig & Pen. For all those decades, though, the Black Lion had provided a fixed point about which a great deal of the town's lunacy could orbit, and of all the many legendary titans that had at one time presided over the cacophony of its front bar, Tom Hall was without doubt the very greatest.

The respected revenant, in sandals and carefully clashing socks, had sloshed and sauntered down the walkway with a gait that Bill found reminiscent of a berthing tugboat, stopping in his tracks on sighting the Dead Dead Gang, at which point his trailing look-alikes had piled into the back of him and melted. His calm gaze, continually unsurprised and unshakeably confident, had fallen on the huddle of ghost-children standing there outside the entrance to the Jolly Smokers, hanging in the air before them. Bristling brows had knitted to a frown and for a moment the benign but very tough musician had looked stern and frightening, a bit like Zeus or one of them. And then Tom Hall had laughed, like a delinquent cavalier.

"Haharr. What's this, then? Have they finally found out where all the Bisto Kids were buried?"

Bill had eagerly stepped forward, dragging Michael Warren with him. He'd known that Tom wouldn't recognise him in his current form, nor by his current name. William or Bill, although it was what he'd been christened, was a name only his family had called him during life. He'd thought he better introduced himself to Tom using the nickname that had been bestowed upon him in his youth by a forgetful P.E. teacher in the course of a particularly energetic game of football: "Come on! Pass the ball to … Bert."

Michael and Bill had stood there looking up at Tom from what would have been the site of a full eclipse if the enormous poet, songwriter and multi-instrumentalist had still possessed a shadow. Bill had grinned.

"'Ello, Tom. 'Ow yer gettin' on, mate? It's me, Bert, from Lindsay Avenue."

The brows had risen in a querying expression, with a slightly mocking undertone to it that Bill remembered from their earthly conversations.

"My dear boy! Not Bert the Stab?"

This winning soubriquet, bestowed after the unfortunate teenage incident that night in the back room of the Black Lion – there'd been extenuating circumstances, Bill was reasonably certain – had been Tom's at once affectionate and ridiculing nickname for the young and almost beardless Bill. Acknowledging that he was indeed Bert the Stab, Bill had explained to the deceased performer how this part of him, the part that had loved being eight and playing in the streets, was currently involved in quite a serious adventure with his mates, the Dead Dead Gang. The immense apparition had thrown back his head, somehow without dislodging the beret, and had let laughter like an earthquake ripple through his ectoplasmic bulk so that the stitched-on teddies shimmied on his paunch.

"HaHAAAR! Har HA har! The Dead Dead Gang. I like it."

The compulsive versifier had begun extemporising on the spot.

"The Dead Dead Gang, the Dead Dead Gang, so bad they killed them twice! The Dead Dead Gang were born to hang for paediatric vice! HaHAAAR! How about that? That could be your theme tune, couldn't it? Whaddaya think? Ha HAARR!"

Phyllis had scowled at the lyric leviathan with genuine menace, toying meaningfully with her ribbon of dead rabbits.

"We've already got a theme tune."

Stepping in, Bill had attempted to stop Phyllis alienating yet another otherwise-accommodating spirit by steering the conversation back from theme tunes onto the more pressing matters that were currently at hand.

"Tom, what it wiz, I've got to pay a visit to this place 'ere, to the Jolly Smokers. There's somebody what I'm searchin' for who might be up there, but quite frankly I'm not lookin' forward to it, not at this size, and not with the nutters that you get up there. You couldn't chaperone us, could you, mate? Me and the nipper 'ere?"

The genial colossus had beamed radiantly.

"Your want to go up to the Smokers? Well, you should have said. That's where I'm off to now. I've got a gig up there with me new band, Holes In Black T-Shirts. It wiz Tom Hall's Deadtime Showstoppers for a few years, but then I got fed up and changed it. 'Course I'll take you up there, little Bert the Stab. HaHARRR! I wouldn't leave you sitting out here on the front step with a bottle of Corona and a bag of crisps while I went in like a neglectful dad and had a drink, now, would I? Har har har. Come on."

With that, Tom had placed one palm flat against the hanging 2D tissue of the door, and pushed. The portal had swung inwards and away from them, seeming to gain a third dimension as it did so. It had opened onto a drab, narrow hallway with depressingly dark wallpaper, a space apparently carved into empty air which, when Bill had leaned out round the door's edge to check, had turned out to be utterly invisible if looked at from the side. Tom had already entered and was rumbling away down the grim corridor that wasn't there. With a last anxious glance at Phyllis, and still dragging Michael Warren by one hand, Bill had stepped through the door, pushing it shut behind him. Him and his bewildered infant charge had followed the beloved entertainer into the notorious wraith-pub, listening to the pandemonium above increase in volume as they neared the rotting staircase at the hall's far end.

Without breaking his leisurely, unhurried pace, Tom had looked back and down across the shoulder of his stripy humbug jacket, studying the pair of phantom children, who were dutifully scampering after him, their trailing after-images completely swallowed within the much larger ones that he himself was leaving in his wake.

"So who's the little cherub with you, then? We've not been introduced. Wiz it somebody else I should remember? Christ, it's not John Weston, wiz it? Ha HARR!"

Bill, by now laughing himself at the very thought that Michael Warren might grow up into the mutually-acquainted chemical and human train wreck that the troubadour had named, had shaken his head in denial, briefly growing new ones as he did so.

"No. No, this wiz Michael Warren, and 'e's the same age as what 'e' looks.

'E's technically dead at present, like, but back in 1959 he's in a coma or what-have-you for ten minutes, and then 'e'll be goin back Downstairs and back to life. 'E's Alma Warren's little brother. You remember Alma."

Tom had stopped in his ponderous tracks, close to the foot of the dilapidated stairs.

"Well of course I can remember Alma. I'm cremated, I'm not senile. She read that stuff at my funeral about me being ... manly ... in my stature, and about how I'd bust three of her settees, the disrespectful cow. So this is Alma's brother. Michael. Michael. Do you know, I think I met you when I turned up to play at that birthday party you were holding for your aunt, who'd died the day before and couldn't make it. O' course, you wiz so much older then. You're younger than that now. HaHAAAAR! I'm pleased to meet you, Alma's brother."

Tucking his impressive walking-stick beneath his arm, Tom had bent over and elaborately shaken hands with Michael, the child's tiny paw engulfed in the musician's fist up to the forearm.

"You know, this lot that I'm playing with tonight, Holes In BlackT-Shirts – its Jack Lansbury, Tony Marriot, the Duke and all that lot – I got the name out of a dream I had about your sister. She'd got my three kids all lying on a railway track and said that if a train ran over them, then they'd become invisible. Her idea was that when they were invisible, we'd dress them up in her old shirts and put a show on called "Holes In Black T-Shirts". HaHAAR! Good old Alma. Even in your dreams she was value for money!"

After that ringing endorsement, they'd begun to mount the creaking spectral staircase to the main bar of the Jolly Smokers. Which was where they were now, cringing in the shelter of the mountainous performer, peering nervously between his teddy-decorated legs at the demented horror of the scene beyond.

It wasn't *Texas Chainsaw* horror, lacking both the colour and the blood. This was a *Dr. Caligari* horror shot on hazardous and decomposing film stock, eerie black and white scenarios melting into a rash of supernovas from the heat of the projector. Writhing hieroglyphic filigrees of murderous graffiti were gouged into all the scarred and ancient tables, scrawled on each available bare area of wall in hundred-year-old palimpsests of bile and bitterness. There was a light like rotten silver trickling over every pin-sharp detail of the resurrected alehouse, dripping from pump-handles fashioned out of horse skulls, glinting on the cracked ghost-mirror, hung behind the optics, in which nothing was reflected but an empty, fire-damaged room. In actuality, the front bar of the Jolly Smokers did not appear fire-damaged, but then neither was it empty.

Every badly-varnished barstool, every corner alcove with its threadbare, stained upholstery was fully occupied by the degenerate spectres of a neighbourhood that had been running down for centuries. The place heaved with belligerent ectoplasm and perspired a morbid jocularity that would have made flesh creep if there'd been any flesh around. Upon a mottled carpet that on close inspection turned out to be different strains of mould on bare wood boards; beneath a nicotine-glazed and oppressively low ceiling that was hung with rusted tankards, verdigris horse brasses and a mummified cat swaying up one corner; in an atmosphere that seemed smoke-saturated on account of all their overlapping after-images, the ugly spirits of the Boroughs jostled and cavorted.

In one corner was George Blackwood, gangster and procurer, sprouting extra arms as he dealt cards, properly ghostly now and not a living man like when Bill and the gang had seen him earlier, down in the 1950s. Blackwood sat across a tilted table from the terrifying ratter, Mick Malone, whose many-headed ferrets bubbled from his jacket pockets, sniffing the rank barroom air, and whose black and white terriers snapped and snarled around his polished work-boots. Having been part of the operation when Phyllis had slipped a ghost-rat under Malone's bowler, Bill shrank back behind the ample cover that Tom Hall afforded before the rat-catcher saw him.

Gathered round the bar were other revenants Bill recognised, at least the ones who still had normal faces. Old Jem Perrit stood nursing a shot-glass that contained a double measure of the tavern's home-made Puck's Hat punch, distilled from the fermented fairy-blossoms. He was cackling uproariously, sharing some dark joke with his companion at the bar. This was Tommy Mangle-the-cat, the local wraith who was a casualty to the ferocious brew, mad-apple cider as Bill usually referred to it. Repeated and prolonged exposure to the potent moonshine had affected Tommy's mind, which had of course been all that kept his insubstantial form together, with its various components in their proper order. As Bill watched, the dissolute ghost's bleary eyes were both commencing a slow, slithering trip up one unshaven cheek towards the mostly-toothless mouth that gurned and grimaced disconcertingly slap in the centre of the dead man's forehead, spraying phantom spittle when it laughed. The awful convolutions of a cauliflower ear, upside down, provided an appropriate centrepiece in the position where you might expect the nose to be. Presumably, the other ear and Tommy's actual nose were off upon some expedition to the back of the grotesquely scrambled head and would both be returning presently.

Although Mangle-the-cat's visage was pretty much unbearable to look at, it was not the most disturbing feature of the scene enacted there beside the bar. Along with old Jem Perrit and his carrion laugh, the lesbian bruiser Mary Jane and various assorted Cluniac or Augustan monks, Tommy was having fun watching what was, quite literally, a floor show: somehow struggling in the floorboards at their scuffling feet was an apparently alive and conscious relief-sculpture of a man, made out of living, moving wood. From what Bill could make out through all the whorls of grain and double nail-heads that formed the half-submerged figure's screaming and contorting countenance, it looked to be a young lad, no more than nineteen at most. His scrawny wooden arms flailed in the air, pine fingers with exquisitely-carved bitten fingernails flexing and clawing as though seeking purchase. His puppet legs thrashed, a bent knee made from seemingly supple planking rising briefly from the surface before straightening and sinking back into the filthy, mildewed timbers. Brutally, Jem Perrit ground one heel upon the trapped form's nose, pushing its sculpted face back down beneath the arabesques of mould that carpeted the naked boards, guffawing raucously throughout, mocking the animated figurine while forcing its head under so that it could drown in unswept floor.

"Goo on, yer useless little bugger. Get back dayn where yer belong. We dun't want yer up 'ere!"

The same did not hold true, it seemed, when it came to another apparition made out of unusually limber bits of plank, this one fully emerged and standing sobbing by the bar. This second human marionette appeared to Bill to be a slightly older specimen than his floor-bound and struggling teenage companion, maybe somewhere in his early thirties. Badly overweight and with the loops and knotholes of his carpentry clearly delineated on a shaven skull, the portly doll-thing moaned and wailed, perfectly whittled tears of liquid balsa rolling down his wobbling wooden jowls. This was no doubt because the hairy-arsed butch mauler, Mary Jane, had got him by one lathe-turned forearm and was carving her initials in his splintery and syrup-weeping flesh with a ghost-screwdriver. Wherever the doomed woodentop had come from, Bill observed, he should have known that within a graffiti-smothered dive like this he simply represented a fresh canvas.

All around the yammering and infernal hostelry, walk-ons from nightmares slapped each other on the back or else hawked bronchial ectoplasm up into each other's drinks. In a cleared area against the room's west wall a casually-dressed collection of deceased local musicians that Bill recognised were setting up their crackling phantom amplifiers. There was Tony Marriot, the drummer with the physique of a farmer and the hairstyle of a farmer's scarecrow, grey straw tickling his shoulders at the back though it receded sharply at the front above a stolid, faintly punch-drunk fizzog that looked braced for disappointment. Next to Marriot, Pete Watkin, who they'd called the Duke, stood tuning up his bass and grinning quietly at the supernatural mayhem that surrounded him, shaking his mop of Jerry Garcia curls into a double-exposed pussy-willow bush with amazed disbelief. Meanwhile Jack Lansbury emptied ghost-spit from the mouthpiece of his spectral trumpet and looked disapprovingly at the array of tomb-wights, relics and rough sleepers that comprised his audience. He looked as though he'd played to either a dead crowd or else a rowdy audience in the past, but never both at the same time.

Bill scanned the room between Tom's tree-trunk thighs. The scrounging shade of Freddy Allen, who Bill had been sent up here specifically to find, was nowhere to be seen. Though he supposed that Freddy might be skulking somewhere at the rear of the tightly-packed supernatural inebriates who filled the bar, Bill didn't fancy wandering amongst them so that he could take a look. Not with Mangle-the-cat and Mick Malone and all the rest of the Dead Dead Gang's not-so-mortal enemies about. In this rare if not wholly unique instance, Bill found that he didn't have the nerve.

He looked up at Tom Hall, who had the nerve to dress up in teddy bears' picnic pantaloons, and if he'd got the nerve for that he'd got the nerve for anything. Bill could recall an incident in the front room of the Black Lion, the area where all the older and more serious offenders congregated. Tom had been, as was his custom, cuttingly sarcastic in his treatment of a drug-addicted, truly homicidal patron of the old Bohemian pub, a towering leather-padded skeleton called Robbie Wise. The easily-offended junkie, bridling at Hall's remark, had whipped an open straight-edge razor from his raincoat pocket and had held it up to the musician's face. Tom had just tipped his head back and drawn a straight line across his own throat with one chubby index finger, just below the beard-line. "My dear boy, just cut it here. HahahaHARRRRR!" Robbie Wise had looked almost terrified for some taut seconds before pocketing his blade and rushing from the Black Lion's front bar in a panic, out into the dark and wind of the St. Giles Street night. No, Tom Hall was completely fearless, in his life and no doubt in his death. He was the one Bill should consult about the Freddy Allen situation.

"Tom? Look, we wiz sent up 'ere to look for an old tramp called Freddy Allen. Could you ask if anybody's seen 'im anywhere?"

The corners of the maestro's eyes crinkled with mirth. Bill thought that Tom's admirers had been wrong when they'd said that he was like Falstaff. Rather, he was more the man that Falstaff wished he was. His voice, when he called down to Bill over the hubbub, possessed the endearing creak of honey casks or kegs of mead.

"Hahaar! As if I could say no to little Bert the Stab! I'll see to it immediately."

Turning his personal volume to eleven, the seasoned performer next addressed the bustling room. All conversation stopped as the attendant phantoms paid attention to this noisy soul who seemed to be dressed as a monstrous bag of sweets. Even the wooden torture-victim at the bar and his bull-dyke tormentor stopped what they were doing so that they could listen.

"HahaHAAAR! Lamias and gentlemen, boys and ghouls, can I have your attention for a moment PLEASE! Thank you. You're very kind. You're very gen-

erous for a crowd of unsuccessful coffin-dodgers. Now, does anybody know
the whereabouts of somebody called … Freddy Allen was it? Freddy Allen. Is
he in heaven or is he in hell, that damned elusive pimpernel? Hahaaaar!"

Jem Perrit, pausing for a moment in his trampling of the bulging mask-
face back into the floorboards, raised his black and flapping crow-voice in the
sudden silence.

"Fred Allen's dayn the place along the end o' Sheep Street, Bird in 'And or
Edge O' Tayn or whatever they calls it now. The breather pub. 'E's dayn there
with that 'alf-sharp lad o' mine. When are we gunna 'a' some music, then?"

That was the long and short of it. Bidding a fond farewell to Bill and
Michael, Hall had drifted like some playschool sea-mine through a lapping
scum-tide of the place's patrons, making for the spot where his accompanists
were tuning up. The two ghost-children, their corpulent cover gone, rushed
for the bar door and went down the staircase in one long, slow jump, with Bill
still holding Michael's hand as he had been throughout. The infant hadn't said
a word during their visit to the phantom watering-hole. He'd simply stood
there, rooted to the spot with terror, staring transfixed at Mangle-the-cat and
all the other monsters, the poor little bugger. Bill wished that he hadn't had to
take the toddler up there with him, but it had helped ensure Bill's own safety
and besides, wherever they took Michael would turn out to be where he was
meant to go. That was what Phill Doddridge had said.

They reached the street door, bursting out onto the lamp-lit walkway
where their friends were waiting for them. Slamming the air-door back to
its 2D state behind him, Bill informed Phyll as to the suspected whereabouts
of Freddy Allen, upon which the gang took off for Sheep Street. Swimming
through the air or bouncing upwards from a standing start, the gang ascended
from the underpass and smeared themselves across the busy traffic junction
of the Mayorhold, after-pictures mingling with the exhaust fumes as they
poured into the mouth of Broad Street.

The ghost-kids raced down the grimly functional dual carriageway along
the three-foot high raised concrete wall that was its central reservation, rivers of bright light and metal flowing in opposed directions to each side of
them. They were approaching Regent Square, where Sheep Street and Broad
Street converged, north-eastern limit of the Boroughs that was marked upon
the angle's trilliard table with a crudely-rendered skull, the corner-pocket of
demise, death's quadrant. This was where they'd burned the witches and the
heretics, where they'd stuck heads on spikes, with astral remnants of these
dreadful moments sometimes visible on a clear day, despite the intervening
centuries. It struck Bill forcefully, not for the first time, what an unbelievably
strange place the Boroughs was and always had been.

Bill had not been born down in the area, nor had he lived there, but it was the place his mum's side of the family had come from. Bill, like stately-home-invader Ted Tripp, had been raised a Kingsley boy, but from an early age he'd known about the Boroughs and its alternately wondrous or disturbing aura. The district's split personality was nicely illustrated by that time when Bill had been comparing childhood anecdotes with Alma, the unnerving elder sister of the wee ghost he was just then chaperoning along Broad Street. Alma had described an incident when she'd been visiting her fearsome-sounding grandma, May, who'd lived down Green Street. May had chicken-coops in her back yard, apparently, as did a lot of people during those days of post-war austerity. Alma had dreamily recalled the magical occasion when she'd been called by her dad to have a look at what was happening in her nan's kitchen. Sitting on the top stone step, she'd gazed down at the sunken floor, which was completely carpeted with fluffy yellow chicks, chirping and stumbling against each other on their new legs. That was the idyllic aspect of the Boroughs, while the anecdote that Bill had countered with, though similar in many ways, reflected the old neighbourhood's more startling face.

Bill, too, had been out visiting a grandparent who lived down in the Boroughs, though in Bill's case it had been his granddad's house in Compton Street. He'd been accompanied by a parent, just like Alma had, albeit by his mother rather than his dad, and there had been a miracle of nature in the kitchen, although nowhere near as charming as the Easter vision Alma had remembered. What it was, Bill's granddad used to catch and jelly his own eel. On the occasion when five-year-old Bill and his mum had been visiting, the old man had just brought home a fresh load of elvers, baby eel he'd netted from the wriggling hordes that were then currently migrating up the River Nene. He'd got them in a big iron pot, its lid held down securely, and was taking them into the kitchen so that he could kill and skin them. Bill had only wanted to see all the little eel, and even though his mum and granddad had done their best to dissuade him, although they'd explained that the eel would be released in a sealed kitchen which would not be opened up until the job was done, he'd still insisted. Even at that age, he'd usually had his own way, and even at that age it had all usually ended up as something dreadful. This occasion had been no exception. He'd followed his grandfather into the little kitchen and his mum had shut the door behind him, from the other side. She wasn't stupid, and knew what was coming next. Bill's granddad had then cautiously removed the iron cover from the pot.

The slippery black question-marks had boiled up in a horrifying rush from the receptacle, desperate for liberty, and had gone everywhere. There must have been at least two hundred of the fucking things, slivers of inner-tube with tiny staring eyes, rippling across the worn tiles of the kitchen floor and somehow pouring themselves up the walls, the door, the table-legs, the screaming five-year-old. They'd been all over him, inside his clothes and in his ginger hair, and he had realised too late why no one would be opening the kitchen door to let him out until all this was over. Grim-faced and, with time, completely drenched in eel-blood, Bill's grandfather had beheaded and then skinned the slithering abominations by the handful. It still took a good half-hour, by which time young Bill had been absolutely traumatised, standing there with the shakes, staring and mumbling, nowhere near as pleased with the experience as Alma had been by her lovely little chickens. But then that was what the Boroughs had been like, he thought now: fluffy sentiment next door to wriggling fear and madness.

The ghost-gang had by now reached the end of Broad Street and were flurrying in a smudged arc about the rounded building on the end. This place had once belonged to Monty Shine, the bookmaker, before it had become a nightspot and had undergone so many changes in identity that Bill thought it might be in some witness-protection programme, for its own good. It had been at one point a Goth hangout called MacBeth's, and Bill knew that its curving front wall had been painted a vampiric lilac, although in the ghost-seam this appeared as a cool grey, which looked much better. Bill had often thought that giving this place a Goth makeover was over-egging the blood-pudding or gilding the funeral lily. Heads on spikes, witch burnings ... just how Gothic did these people want it?

Crossing Sheep Street, walking straight through the unwitting mortal punters who were out that evening, the gang slipped in through the front wall of the Bird in Hand. The place was full of rowdies but, being the living, breathing sort, they were no problem when compared with their posthumous counterparts up at the Jolly Smokers. Shimmering through the cigarette smoke in the bar – Bill thought that indoor smoking had been banned later that year – the pint-sized poltergeists located Freddy Allen without difficulty. He was perched upon an empty stool beside a table at which two still-living men sat talking, which was unsurprising in itself: a lot of the rough sleepers liked to knock about in pubs, where there was more chance of a heavy drinker glimpsing them and where they could eavesdrop on mortal conversations for old times' sake. What took Bill and his colleagues aback, however, was that Freddy wasn't merely listening to the chatter of the living. He was joining in.

When Bill examined the two men that the ghost-tramp seemed to be talking to, he recognised the pair of them and had a partial answer to the question of how Freddy could be in debate with anyone who wasn't among the departed. The man Freddy was addressing was the same peculiar individual that the kids had seen arriving home in Tower Street sublimely pissed, before they'd gone up to Mansoul to watch the angle-scrap. He'd been able to see the phantom children then, and so presumably could see and talk to Freddy now. The other chap, sitting across the table from the spectral moocher with his anxious eyes fixed firmly upon the warm-blooded drunk beside him, was a little fat man with curly white hair and glasses who Bill recognised as Labour councillor Jim Cockie. He looked quietly terrified, although Bill quickly realised that this wasn't due to Freddy's presence. Cockie couldn't see the spectre he was seated opposite to, and was instead frightened by his table-mate, the chap with the repeated and demented laugh who was, as far as the plump councillor could tell, conversing with an empty stool.

Phyllis had taken a deep breath, if only for the way it sounded, and marched boldly up to the three seated men, two living and one dead. The moment Freddy spotted her he leapt up from his seat and clutched his weather-beaten hat close to his balding scalp.

"You keep away from me you little buggers! I've had quite enough o' you lot for one day, with all that messin' me about when you were up there in the twenty-fives."

Phyllis had raised her palms towards the angry spirit in a calming and placating gesture.

"Mr. Allen, I know we've been rotten to yer, an' I'm sorry. We wun't do it anymore. I'd not 'ave bothered yer, except by all accaynts yer thought to be a decent sort, and there's this young girl what's in trouble."

From the moment Freddy had stood up, the pissed-up and apparently clairvoyant chap beside him had begun to laugh uproariously, transferring his inebriate attentions to the clearly nervous councillor instead.

"Ahahaha! Did you see that? He just stood up like he'd got piles. He's cross because a load of little blighters just come in." The psychic drunk had turned his head to look directly at Bill and his dead confederates here. "You can't come in! You're underage! What if the landlord asks to see your death-certificates? Ahahaha!"

The rattled councillor glanced briefly in the same direction that the other man was looking, but appeared unable to see anything. Cockie looked back towards the chuckling boozer seated next to him, badly unnerved now.

"I don't understand this. I don't understand you people."

Freddy, meanwhile, had become less furious and more puzzled at Phyll's mention of a young woman in trouble.

"What young girl? And anyway, what's it to me?"

The drunken, giggling bloke was turning to the councillor now, saying "I can't hear 'em. Even when they're right up next to you they sound faint, have you noticed? Ahaha."

Phyllis persisted.

"I don't know if you'll 'ave seen 'er, just around and that, but she's an 'alf-caste girl about nineteen, who's got 'er 'air all done in plaits, like stripes. She wears one o' them shiny coats, an' it looks like she's on the game."

A glint of recognition came into the threadbare apparition's sad eyes.

"I ... I think I know the one you're on about. She lives down Bath Street flats, in what used to be Patsy Clarke's old place."

The ghost gang's leader nodded once, doubling the number of her heads and sending a brief tremor through her hanging rabbit pelts.

"That's 'er. There's some bloke got 'er in that little garage place down where Bath Passage used to be. 'E's got 'is car parked down there an' 'e's doin' you-know-what to 'er. Not as a customer, like, but against 'er will."

From the expression on his face, it looked like an inviolable line had been crossed on Fred Allen's private moral playing-field.

"Bath Passage. I passed by there earlier, visiting me mate. I could feel something bad wiz going to 'appen. Oh my God. I better get down there. I better see what I can do."

With that, the ragged soul of the notorious doorstep-robber streaked straight through five or six customers, a table, and the front wall of the Bird In Hand, gushing into the night outside like angry steam. Bill didn't know if the ghost-vagrant would be able to help that young girl or not, nor if the demon would still be in the front seat when Freddy got there, but it didn't matter. They'd done all they could and now it was out of their hands. Perhaps it always had been.

With the hooked-nosed drunk still giggling as he pointed at the ghostly children only he could see, the dead gang followed Freddy out into the dark gullet of Sheep Street, but the disincarnate dosser had already vanished, off about his urgent business. Phyllis threw her putrid stole across her shoulder like a zombie child-star and announced that they'd head back up Broad Street to the Mayorhold, where they would return to Tower Street and next ascend up to the Works, or what was left of that sublime establishment in 2006. Then they'd take Michael back to 1959, his body, and his life.

This had of course been Bill's idea, but in the pit of his long-vanished stomach he was dreading it, the spoiled Mansoul and the Destructor, most especially the latter. It was what it represented, the annihilating thing in everybody's lives, regardless of what form it took. For Bill, he'd first felt its remorseless turning currents when he'd been alive, a seventeen-year-old freshly expelled from school and trying his first shot of smack in a candle-lit party room, one Friday night after the pub. They'd all been there, all of his mates, or at least a good number of them. Kevin Partridge, Big John Weston, pretty Janice Hearst, Tubbs Monday and about four others that Bill could remember. Tubbs had been the generous supplier of the goods in question, and it had been his works that the rest of them were passing round. And while it had turned out he was himself immune to the disease, Tubbs was the carrier who'd passed on Hepatitis B and C to everybody else.

Bill could remember every daft word of their unimportant chatter as they'd sat handing the spike around, even remembered the chill instant when he'd briefly thought to himself I shouldn't be doing this, almost as if he'd known this was the action that would kill him, forty years or so along the linger of his life. That was the moment when, in retrospect, he'd felt the brush of the Destructor, felt its sobering breeze blown from the future. And yet Bill had done it anyway, as if he'd had no choice about it, as if it was destiny, which he supposed it had been. "Yeah, cheers", Bill had said, and pushed the needle in.

He thought about the chat he'd overheard, between the friendly builder Mr. Aziel and Phil Doddridge, when Doddridge had asked the angle if mankind had ever truly had free will, to which the long-faced Mr. Aziel had responded glumly in the negative, then added "Did you miss it?", followed by unfathomable laughter. Unfathomable at the time, at least, although Bill understood it now. He got the gag. In some ways, it was almost comforting, the notion that whatever you did or accomplished, you were in the end only an actor running through a masterfully scripted drama. You just didn't know it at the time, and thought you were extemporising. It was sort of comical, Bill saw that now, but he still found some solace in the thought that in a predetermined world, there was no point at all in fretting over anything, nor any purpose to regret.

He was still trying to draw reassurance from that when the Dead Dead Gang arrived in Tower Street and began their climb up to the sooty wreck of Heaven.

THE DESTRUCTOR

"*Michael? Ooh Gawd. Michael, can you 'ear me? Please cough. Please breathe ...*"
"*'Old on, we're nearly there. 'Old on, Doreen.*"

The sight of sulphurous Sam O'Day leaning out through the window of that car, the one that had the lady being hurt inside it, that had nearly done for Michael. And the pub full of bad ghosts, with those two screaming wooden people and the man whose features floated round his face like clouds, that had almost been worse. Those things aside, though, he was starting to get used to all this haunting business.

He liked burrowing through time, and being in a gang, and having fallen secretly in love with Phyllis even though she didn't want to be his girlfriend. Being in love was the main thing, after all, and Michael couldn't see that it much mattered if the other person felt the same or even knew you loved them. Surely just that sad and lovely feeling was enough? That was the thing that everyone wrote songs and poems about, wasn't it?

Michael was even growing fond of all the other Michaels that would split off from him every time he moved. It was a bit like having your own home crowd of football supporters following you everywhere, and made you feel more confident and not so lonely. Even though he knew that all his doubles were made out of nothing more than ghost-light, he was getting quite attached to them. He'd even started giving them all separate names, but as these were all variations or diminutives of Michael – Mike, Mick, Mickey, Mikey, Micko and some others that were just sounds he'd made up – it had been pointless and he'd packed it in. Besides, they melted into thin air after only a few seconds, and if you'd made friends with them and given them a name it only made it that much harder.

Actually, there were a lot of things about the afterlife that Michael liked. Walking through walls was fun, and seeing in the dark, and flying through the night was the thrill of a deathtime, but by far the best thing about being dead was eating Puck's Hats. He had been put off at first by the idea of biting into pretty little fairies, but once he'd found out that they had sweet and succulent white fruit inside rather than giblets he had taken to it with surprising gusto. It was only like eating a jelly baby after all, he'd rationalised, even if, as with jelly babies, you still felt a wee bit guilty when you bit their feet off. Anyway, given the phantom blossoms' luscious flavour, Michael thought he might have wolfed down Puck's Hats by the dozen even if the starfish things had kicked and wept and begged him not to. Well, not really, but they did taste wonderful. He'd miss them when he finally got taken back to life again.

From what Phyllis had told him this would be quite soon, although apparently the Dead Dead Gang needed to take him for one last trip to the Upstairs place, Mansoul, before they took him home. That was why they'd just billowed like a thick fog of old photographs across the Mayorhold, letting the cars hurtle through them so that they'd caught blurry glimpses of dash-lit interiors, men muttering to themselves and couples bickering, before the gang had settled once more on the sunken paths of Tower Street. Peering up towards the hulking blocks of flats, the two huge landmarks with the NEWLIFE lettering that loomed over the underpasses and the cowering council houses, Michael thought the massive tombstones looked more worn out than they'd been a short while earlier, before the giant builders had their fight, when Michael had run off from all the others and got lost. The burrowing about through time could get confusing, it was true, but by his reckoning the previous visit to the tower blocks would have been no longer than twelve months ago. How could somewhere start looking so roughed-up and old within a year? His house along St. Andrew's Road, the one that wasn't there up in this draughty century, had been about a hundred years old when he and his family were living in it, and had still looked better-kept and nicer than the tall flats did.

He still wasn't entirely sure what Phyllis and the others wanted him to see up in Mansoul or why they were determined he should see it, but if it was to be his last adventure in the Upstairs world then he was going to make the most of it. He privately suspected that the gang were going to show him something that was even more fantastic than the things he'd seen already, as a sort of special treat or party to commemorate his going away. At three, he'd been through enough Christmases and birthdays to know that when somebody was planning a surprise for you, you had to make out that you didn't know, or else you'd spoil it. That was why he was just quietly smirking to himself while Phyllis and the others sorted out their entrance to the builders' meeting-place, the Works, and all pretended to be worried over something. Michael knew what they were doing. They were trying to throw him off the scent of the amazing pageant they were organising to mark his departure, but he didn't let on that he knew. He didn't want to hurt their feelings.

Michael played along, then, as the gang assembled on each other's shoulders, a manoeuvre he'd seen them perform before. John stood at the bottom of the tower, then Reggie Bowler, balanced with his worn-out boots to either side of John's heroic face. Clambering up the two boys like a mountaineer, Phyllis was perched on top of Reggie, fumbling in the air above her at the summit of the human pile. Since Michael, Bill and Marjorie were littlest and therefore of no great advantage to the height of the arrangement, they just stood and watched from a few paces further up the walkway.

Mildly puzzled, Michael asked Bill what the gang's three tallest ghosts were up to.

"Well, if you remember, the last time we wiz up 'ere in this new century, we dug back down to 1959 and went from there up to Mansoul. We went in through that boarded-up old building that wiz on one corner of the Mayorhold, where the first town hall had once stood, ages back. The thing wiz, this time we don't want to show you Mansoul like it wiz in 1959. We want to show you what it looks like now, in 2006, and up 'ere there's no place left standing we can enter through. But that's all right. When we 'ad all of our adventures in the future, up in Snow Town and all that, we left a hole up in the air around 'ere, covered over with a bit of carpet like the trapdoor of our den on the rough ground near Lower 'Arding Street. That's what our Phyll's looking for now. Oy, Reggie! 'Ere's your chance! Look up 'er frock!"

Teetering above them, Phyllis called down through the sickly sodium light.

"Just you dare, Reggie Bowler, an' I'll piddle on yer 'ead. Now 'ush up an' behave. I think I've found it."

Making pulling motions in the dark above her as if hauling something to one side, the Dead Dead Gang's intrepid leader was uncovering a ragged patch of violet-blue which hung there in an overcast sky that was otherwise completely colourless. Having thus located the gang's route up through the shouts and sirens of the night into Mansoul, Phyllis next went about directing their ascent. She told the crew's three smallest members to climb up the ladder formed by their companions, with Bill going first, then Michael, and then Marjorie. When this was done they helped her up and through the skyhole so that she in turn could help up John and Reggie. After they'd replaced the waterlogged and filthy carpet-remnant that had been used to conceal the aperture, the ghost-gang stood beside it for a moment, taking stock of their ominous new surroundings. Michael was a bit put out, as these did not suggest the special treat he'd been expecting. Probably, he thought, the others were just dragging things out so it would be more of a surprise.

The space that the gang stood in, cavernous and indigo, was nonetheless still recognisable as the same ghost-structure they'd climbed through just before the angle-fight, although in a much worse state of repair. At least one of the phantom floors had fallen in completely, due to what seemed to be water-damage from above. Sodden and broken beams stuck out from halfway up one tall and badly distressed wall like snapped ribs and the bluish light was everywhere, scabbing to purple where the shadows pooled.

Michael remembered that in 1959 this building had been all in black and white, with no apparent hue at all until you went up to Mansoul by that short flight of useless, narrow stairs on the top floor. It looked as if the world Upstairs was leaking colour, amongst other things. Michael couldn't remember all this water being here before, streaming like silver down the derelict and towering walls, or gathering in hollows like carpeted rock pools down amidst the rubble of the floor. It also seemed as if the quality of sound found in Mansoul had percolated down into the usually-muffled phantom realm along with all the wetness and the moody coloured light. Each plip, drip, splash and glassy tinkling reverberated eerily about the echoing, damp-scented ruin, which resembled nothing more than some enormous warehouse after an insurance fire.

Damp-scented? Michael realised that along with sound and colour filtering down from above, his sense of smell had started to improve to something more like the rich, overwhelming faculty that it had been Upstairs, where there were entire stories in the way that something smelled. He was beginning, for example, to detect the stink of Phyllis's fur wrap, along with the perfumes of mould, decay and – what was it, that other thing? He sniffed the air experimentally, confirming his suspicions. It was smoke, the faintest whiff of it, and Michael couldn't tell where it was coming from.

He stood with his five phantom friends, who all seemed genuinely hushed by the thick atmosphere of desolation that had fallen on them – along with the cobalt light and the cascades of water – from above. While he suspected they were only putting on an act to conceal the surprise they had in store for him, Michael was feeling a bit put out by his going-away party so far and sincerely hoped that it would pick up later. He gazed up into the dripping blue gloom overhead and listened to the ringing leaky-tap noises, the gush and spatter, burbling liquid trills that almost had the sound of whispered conversation.

"Ooh, Gawd. Ooh, Gawd, Doug, I think 'e's gone. Whatever shall we do?"

"Just you 'ang on, Doreen. 'Ang on, gel. It's just up over the Mounts. We'll be there in another minute ..."

Still with no one really saying very much, Michael had joined his ghostly playmates as they'd started their ascent of the partly-collapsed building's interior. This proved a lot more difficult than when they'd come this way before. For one thing, the dilapidated staircase they'd used then looked to be long since gone, requiring the six children to climb up the crumbling walls like spiders, but with half as many legs. Brave John went first, pointing out foot and handholds, indentations in the sodden plaster, for the benefit of the five spectral youngsters who were following him.

For another thing, besides there being vestiges of Mansoul's sound and smell and colour down here in the normally sense-stifling ghost-seam, traces of the upper world's increased feelings of weight and gravity were also evident. If they'd have fallen from the sheer face of the wall, they'd probably still have descended slowly enough not to seriously hurt themselves, but flying through the air or bouncing up like lunar beach balls obviously wasn't going to work. All of them felt too heavy and too solid, meaning that they had no other choice but to climb slowly and laboriously up the high wall in a cautious human chain. They still had a few after-pictures peeling from them, but as they went higher these grew flimsier and fainter, and then winked out of existence altogether.

Part of the top storey had not yet collapsed completely, with some areas of floorboards and a few supporting beams remaining, though these sagged and looked precarious. After what seemed to Michael like at least an hour of climbing, the Dead Dead Gang at last reached these creaking islands of comparative security. The temporarily-dead toddler wriggled on his tummy up over the soggy planks that were the platform's edge, with Phyllis pushing from behind and big John pulling from in front. It felt nice, being able to stand up – if only on the sturdier, beam-reinforced parts of the floor – and have a short rest after all that scrambling.

While they all recovered, Phyllis generously passed around some of the dwarf variety of Puck's Hats that they'd found at the asylums, where the little fairies were only a half-inch tall. Michael discovered that when eaten in closer proximity to Mansoul, where your senses all woke up, these tasted and smelled even better than they had down in the ghost-seam. Sweet juice glistening on his chin, he'd sat against a doorframe that was only half there with his slipper-clad feet hanging past the rotted flooring's edges, kicking back and forth above the sapphire-tinted abyss.

He thought about where they'd been, the things they'd seen and heard. They'd gone for tea and cakes at Mr. Doddridge's, and then they'd walked along that funny bridge-thing out to the asylums. The asylums were where they kept people who'd gone cornery, and because people like that were all mixed-up in their heads then the asylums had got all confused and muddled up together too. It had been a peculiar place, with all the firework-sprays of coloured light and then the other Bill and Reggie from the future turning up and stealing most of the mad-apples. What had struck him as the oddest thing, though, was the way that Phyllis, John and Marjorie had acted when they'd happened on that pair of living ladies who were sitting on the bench. These had both looked completely normal and were just having a talk, the way that grown-ups did sometimes. Michael had not been really listening to them, but he thought the taller and more fragile-looking one had said that her dog used to get in bed with her. This sounded like the sort of thing that a pet dog would more than likely do, and on reflection it was probably the reason why his mum had never let him have one, but he couldn't see why that had made Phyllis and John look so upset. Perhaps they had both come from tidier and more fastidious homes than his.

It had been after they'd returned from the asylums, though, when they'd come up into this funny-feeling century which he'd disliked so much the last time they were here, that things had started to turn a bit horrible. When they'd jumped from the Ultraduct down to Chalk Lane in nothing-six or wherever they were, it had just been beginning to get dark, which Michael always found a bit unsettling. When he'd still been alive, if he'd had dreams where it was night-time in the dream, they'd always turn out to be nightmares. For a long while he'd thought that this was the definition of a nightmare: they were dreams where the strange things that happened all took place by night. So when the darkness had begun to settle while the ghost-gang mucked about down in that big lagoon-place, he'd been feeling a bit nervous from the start.

The trip he'd taken with Bill, Marjorie and Reggie – which he hadn't really understood the purpose of – had been a bit of fun, or at least those parts that involved playing at trains or flying through the night sky had been. Michael hadn't liked that draughty yard with all the metal barrels in it much, though. Miserable and uninviting as the enclosure had looked, there'd been something about it that the child had found disturbingly familiar, even though he'd never visited the place before. Perhaps he'd seen it during one of the innumerable run-throughs of his life which Phyllis and the rest assured him he'd experienced already, even if he didn't actually remember any of them. Perhaps the drab yard was somewhere that he would one day become familiar with, although he found that this thought filled him with a heartache that was inexplicable.

It had been after they'd returned through the night sky to the lagoon, however, that events had taken a severe turn for the worse. He'd cried a little bit when Phyllis and the rest had let him go and have a look at the bare grass patch on St. Andrew's Road, with nothing left to show him and his family had ever lived there, but the crying hadn't been a bad thing. It had just been Michael starting to accept the way things were, the way that in the mortal world people and places would just flash by and be done with in an instant. That was how life was, but in the end none of that mattered because death was different. Death and time weren't really happening, which meant that everyone and everywhere were there forever in Mansoul. His house was up there somewhere, with its faded red front door, its china swan in the front window and its largely-unused boot-scrape set into the wall beside the bottom doorstep. He'd been comforted by that and so had wiped his eyes and set off with the rest of the gang for the Mayorhold, which was when the really bad things had commenced.

The first and probably the worst had been the thing that happened in that little walled-in garage place just off the lower end of Bath Street. Everyone had crowded round the parked car as if to stop Michael seeing what was going on inside, but he had glimpsed enough to know that a bad man had got a lady pinned down underneath him and was hurting her, punching her like he was a boxer. Then when Bill, who Michael had begun to like, had led him away from the vehicle and to one side, that's when they'd seen the other person sitting in the driver's seat. That's when he'd seen side-winding Sam O'Day and been so frightened that his heart had almost started beating.

He had known that he was bound to meet the devil at least once more, with the inevitability that a bad dream has, or a frightening program on the telly. He just hadn't been expecting it to be right there and then, nor had he thought the demon would remember all that business about Michael having someone killed. He was at least relieved that he had managed to avoid doing a dreadful thing like that. That stuck-up Sam O'Day had thought he was so clever, but he'd still not managed to turn Michael to an instrument of murder, for which Michael felt he could congratulate himself.

Of course, once they'd thwarted the fiend by the surprisingly successful and simply-accomplished trick of running away screaming, they'd gone to that dreadful pub that Michael didn't even want to think about. Upon the few mortal occasions when he'd been taken into a tavern's yard or garden by his mum and dad, he'd found pubs a bit gruff and grown-up and intimidating for his tastes, but that was nothing when compared with how he'd felt up at the Jolly Smokers. The man with a crawling face, and those poor wooden things that had apparently just surfaced from the barroom floor, he was quite certain that these images would be with him for the remainder of his life, no matter what everyone said about how all of this would be forgotten once they'd got him back inside his body and he'd somehow been reanimated. Michael wondered how all that was going, then remembered he was now in nothing-six, the choking incident over and done with nearly fifty years before, and wondered instead how all that had gone.

"Michael? Come on, Michael. Breathe. Breathe for yer mum."

When everyone had finished the emergency supply of midget Puck's Hats, Phyllis led the way through what remained of the deteriorating building's upper floor, across the safest-looking planks and beams to what upon their previous visit had been a small office at one end but was now an anonymous and open space, squelchy with water. Up against one of the two surviving walls, with a few of its narrow rungs gone since the last time that they'd seen it, was the Jacob Flight which led up to a cloudy-looking crook-door in the ceiling. This, thought Michael, would be when everyone all jumped out and yelled 'surprise' and showed him all the ice-cream and the jellies and the presents at his going-away party.

But there wasn't any special treat awaiting Michael in Mansoul. There wasn't any party. There was hardly a Mansoul.

The crook-door had looked cloudy because the whole ground-floor area of The Works was prowled by huge and rolling billows of white smoke. This was due to the fact that one vast wall of the cathedral-sized hall was on fire, with builders and some larger and more indeterminate forms visible through the thick haze, all working hard to put it out. Arranging themselves into chains they passed gigantic goblets hand to hand, there seemingly being few buckets to be found about Mansoul. The spillage, bouncing Chinese ivory-puzzle droplets of the more-than-3D water Michael had seen earlier, had spread across the massive flagstones of the floor and was presumably responsible for all the flooding and despoliation down below.

The Dead Dead Gang climbed from the dank and doleful blue expanses of the phantom building up into the even worse place that was up above it. Standing huddled round the crook-door set into the flagstone flooring of the Works, the tough crew were quite clearly frightened as they peered into the drifts of smoke that scudded everywhere about them. With a sinking feeling, Michael realised that their anxious glances hadn't been an act to cover up some carefully-planned celebration. They had been exactly what they looked like, terrified expressions on the faces of small children who were going to watch Heaven burning.

Phyllis was holding up her woollen cardigan – which was now ice-cream pink again – to cover both her mouth and nose against the acrid fumes. At least, thought Michael with his blue eyes watering, you couldn't really smell her rabbit necklace when this smoke was everywhere. She gave her orders between coughs.

"All right, let's make a line with everybody 'anging on the coat or jumper o' the kid in front, so as we wun't get lorst. We'll try and get across the floor to where them stairs wiz last time we wiz 'ere, so we can get ayt on the balcony. Come on, you lot. This wun't get any better if we stand araynd from now until the cows come 'ome."

Obediently, Michael gathered the collar of his dressing gown together with one hand, holding it up over his nose and mouth, while with the other hand he grabbed at the rear waistband of John's trousers as the older boy stood in the line ahead of him. Behind him, Michael could feel Phyllis take a

hold upon the tartan belt that he had knotted round his midriff. In this fashion, single file as if they were explorers in a vapour-jungle, they set off across
a floor they knew was vast despite the fact that at that moment everything
more than a yard or so away from them was hidden by the creeping smoke.

The gang had gone only a little way before Michael remembered the
demonic decorations, all the intricate and interlocking devil-patterns that had
writhed with a malign vitality on the six dozen massive flags that formed the
area's floor. He looked down in alarm at the huge paving slab that his plaid
slippers were then scuffling over, half-expecting to see some grotesque design
of jigsaw-fitted scorpions and jellyfish, but what he actually saw was only
cracked and broken stonework, which was somehow worse. Beneath a sliding
veil of grey smoke and a scattering of the discarded leaflet-guides that Michael
had read on his previous visit, there was only the smashed paving, fissured
into monstrous pieces as if broken and pushed up by tree roots or some other
great force from below. The colourful and fiendishly involved depictions of the
seventy-two devils were completely absent. They weren't shattered with the
stones that they'd been painted on, nor were they faded or concealed behind
graffiti. They were simply gone, as if those ghastly and resplendent presences
had seeped out of their portraits once the glaze was fractured. Still holding
his dressing gown over his nose like a cowboy bandanna, Michael glanced
round nervously into the churning billows. If the devils weren't trapped in
their pictures then where were they?

The six children, heading for the huge workplace's south wall in their
stumbling chain-gang line, had not gone far across the smoke-wreathed factory floor before the toddler had an answer to his question: trundling from
the bitter fug ahead of them was an enormous wagon, an immense flat cart
that had eight mighty wagon-wheels on either side. The vehicle was slowly
being towed with numerous stout, tarry ropes towards the building's blazing
northern end by what seemed to be at least thirty of the lower-ranking builders in the pigeon-coloured robes, with more of them grouped to the rear of
the colossal trolley, pushing from behind while their companions pulled and
heaved in front.

These rank-and-file celestial workers all looked much the worse for wear
compared with the brisk, bustling employees that they'd been when last the
Dead Dead Gang came to Mansoul, in 1959 to watch the angle-fight. Their
hands were scratched and callused and some of them wore no sandals. As they
hauled upon their creaking ropes, Michael could see their delicately-tinted
robes were torn and scorched, their melancholy faces smudged with soot and
grease. They kept their downcast eyes upon the splintered flagstones at their
feet, perhaps to avoid dwelling on the mountainous impossibility that they

were trying to move, the behemoth that squatted unconcerned upon their rolling platform.

At first Michael took this for a statue or an idol of some kind, an incalculably large toad carved from what seemed to be solid diamond, bigger than a church or a cathedral. Then he noticed that its dazzling sides were going in and out and realised it was breathing. As he understood that he was in the presence of a living creature, almost certainly one of the missing devils from the flagstones, Michael looked more closely.

Its blunt head, as flat and wide as if it had been squashed, was tilted back imperiously upon several bulging chins, great rolls of diamond fat like layers in a jewel-and-zeppelin sandwich. Seven disproportionately tiny piggy eyes, arranged to form a ring, were set into its precious brow. These would each blink indifferently after unbearably protracted intervals, in no distinguishable sequence, then return to staring loftily into the white or blue-brown clouds that hid the upper reaches of the Works from view. It seemed to regard being dragged upon a trolley as a terrible indignity, and Michael wondered if felt ashamed about its size and weight.

Whatever it was really made from – be it diamond or, for all that Michael knew, cut glass – it was translucent, and Michael got the impression that the monster was completely hollow, like an Easter-egg. What's more, when he peered through its swollen sides he thought that he could see a sort of blurry sloshing motion, as though the leviathan were half filled-up with water. From the way it pursed its wide slash of a mouth the creature looked uncomfortable, and Michael thought that having all that liquid in its belly, turning it into a whopping crystal jug, might possibly explain this.

The great wagon rumbled slowly forward on its way to the north wall of the fire-fogged enclosure, while the line of phantom children passed it as they crept and coughed their way by, heading in the opposite direction. Michael wished he could ask Phyllis why these awful things were happening, but everybody had their coats or jumpers covering their mouths and noses, and so nobody could talk.

Only when the cart and its tremendous burden had almost completely passed the ghost-gang by did one amongst the scores of angles pushing from the rear notice the scruffy throng of dead kids and raise an alarm.

"Wharb mict yel doungs?"

This meant *What are you doing here amongst these ruins and these smoking relics when thou art but children*, and a further paragraph or so in the same vein, translating roughly to "Oy! You lot! Clear off!"

Everyone froze, not sure what they should do, with even Phyllis seeming disconcerted. It was clearly one thing to be generally disobedient and cheeky when it came to ghosts or devils, but if builders told someone to do something, even the lower-ranking builders, then there wasn't any argument. Everyone did what they were told. They just did. Luckily, it was at this point that a second dove-robed labourer detached himself from the main team that strained and pushed at the huge wagon's rear, to intervene upon the gang's behalf. He called to his more bellicose confederate in a convivial and reassuring tone.

"Whornyb delm stiv cagyuf!"

Worry not, my brother, for this is the Dead Dead Gang that I did tell you of some several centuries ago ... and so on. It was Mr. Aziel, the builder who had taken them to visit Mr. Doddridge following the Great Fire of Northampton back down in the sixteen-hundreds. The first angle, who had shouted at the children, now turned round to gape at Aziel in disbelief.

"Thedig cawn folm spurbyjk?"

The Dead Dead Gang we read of in that splendid book? My brother, why did you not say? Is that Drowned Marjorie with all those stinking rabbits round her neck? When all the meanings of the other builder's breathless outburst had subsided, Mr. Aziel shook his head. His long, lugubrious face was still recognisable beneath its mask of sweat and black dust, shaking his head as he replied to his companion.

"Nopthayl jis wermuyc."

No, that is Phyllis Painter. Now, I must accompany them on their journey. It is written. With that Mr. Aziel turned from his colleague and began to walk across the ruined flagstones, heading for the children with a fond smile showing through the inadvertent blacking.

"Herm loyd fing sawtuck?"

Hello, my young friends. Shall I take you to see the great end of all wonders?

All the other children nodded, since consenting verbally would have meant taking down the tents of clothing that they held across their mouths. Though Michael wasn't certain what he was agreeing to, he nodded along with the rest of the Dead Dead Gang, so as not to be the odd one out.

Aziel led them from the front end of their shambling, wheezing queue, with tall John holding tight onto a rear tuck of the artisan's singed green-and-grey-and-violet gown. Although it still took ages to reach the south wall where all the comet-spangled steps were, they made better time than if they hadn't had the builder guiding them. What's more, they were less cowed by all the towering and unnatural shapes that stalked or slithered past them in the mercifully obscuring clouds, going the other way. At last the angle, who was seemingly impervious to smoke, announced that they were at the bottom of the south wall's staircase. Its oak banisters and rail were mostly gone or else reduced to charred stumps, but the night-blue stairs with their embedded constellations were intact. Still clutching at each other's clothing, for they were not yet above the level of the roiling fumes, the ruffians cautiously ascended in the wake of Mr. Aziel.

When they were roughly halfway up the first of the long zigzag flights of stairs ... fifty or sixty feet over the workplace floor by Michael's estimation ... they broke through the surface of the curdling vapour-ocean into something that was more like air. Michael, however, thought he must have accidentally inhaled some smoke since he was still experiencing difficulty in catching his breath.

"Get ayt the way! Get ayt the way, yer silly bugger! Can't yer see we're in an 'urry?"

"Ooh, Doug, 'e's dead. Ayr Michael's dead. What are we gunna do? What shall I tell Tom when 'e's 'ome from work? Ooh, God. Ooohh, God ..."

Once they were clear of the asphyxiating fog by several large and midnight-speckled steps, the builder let the children pause to pull down their makeshift bandannas and take in the sights from their new elevation.

The whole bottom level of the vast celestial warehouse was filled by a cube of smoke some sixty feet deep, and the children's view was as if they were up above the clouds, like people in an aeroplane. The eight-by-nine arrangement of cracked flagstones that had previously kept the devils captive was invisible beneath the shifting, suffocating blanket, as were all the many builders occupied in battling the conflagration threatening the northern wall. The only things that Michael could see poking up above the level of the smog were what he quickly realised must be the smashed floor-tiles' former occupants.

Something that looked either like a dragonfly or a glass skyscraper was picking its way carefully across the vista upon twelve or so impossibly thin crystal legs. Considerably smaller but still big enough to loom out from the fumes was a tremendous spider-thing that had three heads. The nearest one looked like a cat's head, if a cat's head were the same size as a whale, while the one in the middle was that of a tittering long-haired man with lipstick and eye make-up on, who wore a golden crown. The spider's third head was too far away from Michael to see properly, but he thought it might be a fish or frog. Colossal horrors paced this way and that through the grey fields of murk that stretched below his vantage point as he stood there upon the galaxy-stained stairs with their black stumps of banister. To Michael's puzzlement, they seemed to be assisting with the fight against the blaze.

At the enormous chamber's far, north end, Michael could see the diamond toad upon its trolley, or at least could see its head and shoulders where they rose above the smoke. Its priceless cheeks were puffed out like balloons, and with a vehement expression in its ring of piggy eyes it was expelling a great waterspout against the burning wall, so that hot gouts of steam surged

up to join with the surrounding swirl. Michael, quite frankly, would have liked
to look at it for longer, but that was when Mr. Aziel suggested that they should
resume their climb.

They carried on up the star-pimpled stairs. The high-set windows of the
Works above them, which had looked out onto clear blue sky the last time
Michael had been up this way, now glowered a sullen red. Alarmed, he looked
up at the great seal of the Works, the raised disc with the balance and the
scroll on, just to make sure it was still all right, but it seemed more or less
untouched. He wasn't certain why he found the crude design's survival quite
so reassuring, unless it implied that even in all this confusion and distress,
Justice was still above the street.

Somewhat consoled, Michael continued his ascent. None of the gang were
clutching at each other's jumpers now that they could see where they were
going, and Michael made sure that he kept well clear of the stairway's outside
edge, where there were only blackened stumps of balustrade between him and
the long drop to the broken slabs below. At last they reached the building's
lowest landing, where the heavy swing-door that led out onto the balcony was
situated. The thick portal's stained glass, heavily discoloured, had been broken
in one lower corner. The brass plate was now completely jet with soot, save for
the butter-coloured smudges left by Mr. Aziel's fingers pushing on it, opening
the door onto the balcony. A wall of air as thick and warm as gravy rushed
in from outside and dashed itself over the builder and the kids, making them
blink and gasp. Still following the mournful lesser angle, the Dead Dead Gang
filed out through the entrance to the once-majestic walkways of Mansoul.

John crossed himself, while Phyllis groaned as though tormented. Reggie
Bowler screwed his hat down tighter and spat spectral phlegm over the remnants of the pitch-daubed handrail. An infernal torture-brazier light crawled
on the children's faces, on the split boards at their feet and sidled everywhere
in the prevailing darkness. His expression now more melancholy than was customary, Mr. Aziel gently shepherded the ghost-kids out onto the endless landing, steering them towards a section of the wooden railing that was still intact
so that they could see down into the great well of the astral Mayorhold, the
arena wherein the gigantic Master Builders had their fight in 1959. For his part,
Michael didn't want to look, and instead focussed his attention on the upper
balconies surrounding the unfolded former town square, well above whatever
was providing the hell-tinted radiance that was under-lighting everything.

It looked like there was more activity up on the elevated boardwalks
than there had been on the smouldering ground floor of the Works. Angles
conferred with devils as they overlooked the Mayorhold. Demon work-gangs
rasped commands to one another in toe-curling voices that were those of carrion birds or insects, greatly amplified. There were no ghostly throngs of spec-

tators filling the balconies as there had been on Michael's previous visit here, however, and the few lone, wandering phantoms he could make out all looked frightful or a bit mad.

He could see a chubby man who wore old fashioned clothes and had a round, pink baby face, standing upon the walkway opposite and singing an old hymn in a sweet tenor voice above the chittering and buzzing racket of the labouring devils. In the endlessly unravelling acoustics of Mansoul the singer's every word was audible despite the distance: "Yea, though I walk through death's dark vale, yet shall I fear no-oh ill ..." The man's expression, staring petrified into the hell-glow, contradicted the song's lyrics pointedly. He looked as if he feared ill very much. Elsewhere upon the landings, Michael saw a small gaggle of elderly men and women who clung desperately to one another as they screamed and wept and pleaded for deliverance. Judging from the fact that all of them were naked or clad only in stained underwear, Michael concluded that they must be people having a particularly nasty dream.

The most upsetting stroller on the balconies, however, was a solitary figure on the same stretch of the walkway as the children, someone Michael recognised. Coming towards them from the scorched and partly-ruined landing's far end was the rumbling ball of frozen fire that walked upon two legs, the blowing-up man that the children had glimpsed in this very spot the last time they'd been up here, nearly fifty years before. He looked the same as he had then, amid the same wasp-swarm of light and shrapnel, walking with the same stiff-legged and deliberate gait, as if he'd done his business in his trousers. The slowed and protracted sound of the explosion that had killed him, stretching and reverberating as it rolled eternally around his blissfully disintegrating form, was audible even across the distance separating Michael and the walking bomb-burst, a low modulated drone that growled aggressively down at the lower threshold of the small boy's hearing. Tall John, standing next to Michael, had apparently seen the continuously detonating ghost as well.

"Oh. It's that silly sod blowing himself to bits up here as well, then. If he's walking back along the linger of Mansoul, then I expect it must be sometime around now that he set out from. I can't say as I'm surprised, not from the look of things round these parts. If Mansoul itself wiz on fire up in this new century, then wiz it any wonder you've got living people doing stupid bloody things like that?" John nodded to the man in question, who was still some distance off and only very slowly getting closer.

"From what Bill said, they're prepared to get blown up because they think that they'll end up in Heaven. I suppose that's what I thought as well, and that's what all the Jerries thought, and all the Japs. We're all half-sharp, the lot of us. As if there could be any more to us than what we make of ourselves and our lives while we're still living them. The people that we are when we're alive, that's who we are forever, nipper. Like that dibby Herbert all in pieces down the walkway there."

John placed one hand upon the toddler's shoulder, drawing back his fingers when he realised they were touching the discoloured patches where slobbering Sam O'Day had dribbled. Quietly, the taller boy steered Michael over to the fragment of surviving railing where the scorched and sorry-looking builder stood with their four friends.

"Come on. From what Phyll told me while we waited for you and Bill there outside the Jolly Smokers, you've been brought up here so we can show you the Destructor. We might just as well get it all over with, then we can take you home."

Michael felt suddenly afraid and shied back from the landing's edge, protesting fretfully to the determined-looking older boy.

"But obscenic be four, in Birth Street. It wiz like a sinning-wheel, all smokery and dredgeful and choo-chooing heavenlything to grits!"

John's resolved expression softened. He could tell how frightened Michael was by the degree to which the infant's language skills had been derailed by just a solitary mention of the word "Destructor". Firmly and yet sympathetically, he shook his head.

"No, nipper. You've not seen it from up here before, and that makes all the difference, you can trust me. You see, down in Bath Street in the living world, all people see wiz the effects of the Destructor, all the, well, the prostitutes. The drink and drugs and all the fighting, long as anybody can remember but much worse, the way it's got in these times. Then, if you're with the rough sleepers in the ghost-seam, you can see the thing itself, or at least you can see a bit of it: the hub, the big dark whirlpool thing that you saw down in Bath Street. From up here in Mansoul, though, you see a bigger picture. You can see the whole of it."

By now the pair were closer to their friends and Mr. Aziel. Phyllis Painter reached out and took Michael by the hand.

"Look, it's important that yer know abayt this. This'll show yer why things are the way they are. See, yer remember 'ow we told yer all abayt the monk 'oo brought the cross 'ere from Jerusalem, to mark the centre o' the land? Well, this place wiz the centre in all sorts o' ways. It's in the middle o' the country, true enough, and it's the middle of the country's spirit, too. It's where all o' the big religious changes and upheavals are kicked off, and where the wars are finished. But the most important way that we're bang in the middle wiz that we're the centre of the ... what's it called, John? The way things are all fitted together in one piece?"

"The structure."

"Structure, that's the word. The Boroughs is the middle bit of England's structure. It's the knot what 'olds the cloth together, if yer like. And back when everybody sort of understood that, understood it in their 'earts, then even when the times wiz bad they'd still got that big structure, that cloth, like a safety-net they could fall back on. But there come a time – I reckon it was back araynd the First World War meself – when all that started changin'. People started to forget abayt the things that 'ad been so important to 'em fifty years before. They weren't so certain abayt God, or King, or country, and they started pullin' dayn the Boroughs, lettin' it fall into disrepair. Can yer see what I'm gettin' at? It wiz the centre of the land, of England's structure, and they let it come to bits. They put up the Destructor, and for years all of Northampton's shit went up that chimney – 'scuse my French – and there wiz stinking smoke from Grafton Street to Marefair. It become a symbol of the way that people saw the Boroughs, even us what lived there, as a place where all the rubbish went. It wiz that disrespect what done it, if you ask me. It wiz that what give one filthy chimney so much power in people's minds."

Here, Mr. Aziel interjected.

"Bixt vorm fwandyg sulpheck."

It is a torus, is the secret shape of space and time. Tori enclose the necessary holes within the fabric of existence, but their spread endangers all. The man who stole my chisel, Snowy Vernall, had learned from his father that a chimney is a torus. That is why he spent much of his life on roofs, keeping an eye on the infernal things, when all the time it was the chimneystack in Bath Street here that posed the only serious threat.

A rush of sparks erupted from the well-mouth of the Mayorhold, scurrying up into the dark behind the silhouetted builder. Timber was collapsing somewhere lower down. Michael was still attempting to look anywhere but at the view beyond the railings. The old people in their underpants still huddled in a wailing, weeping mass of wrinkled pink and scrubby grey. The baby-faced man was still singing the same hymn, eyes streaming as with mad determination he stared fixedly into the heat-haze. The exploding person further down the balcony seemed to have paused in order to appreciate the view, one spectacle looking admiringly upon another. Somewhere nearby, perhaps on the landing overhead, a team of fire-fighting demons were discussing the logistics of those devils who had wings flying reconnaissance above the fire-pit of the former town square. Michael played for time.

"Gut eye don't blunderstand! How clang one chillery-pot claws all dis turble?"

John sighed.

"Because of where it wiz and what it meant, that's how. It wizn't just Northampton's waste that the Destructor wiz intended to destroy, it wiz the whole community that it wiz built right in the middle of. Destroying people's dreams and hopes about a better future for their kids, that takes a special sort of fire, a fire that people in the living world can't even see, not even when its turning all their houses, schools and clinics into rubble. The thing wiz, a fire like that, you can't just put it out by knocking down the waste incinerator that it started from. By the time the Destructor wiz pulled down, back in the 'Thirties, its effects had spread into the way that people thought about the Boroughs and about themselves. Its special sort of fire had spread right to the heart of things. Down in the half-world all our ghosts and memories were smouldering, until Mansoul itself wiz set alight. It's burning, nipper. Heaven's burning. Come and have a look yourself, then we can all get out of here."

Still unconvinced but prompted by the promise of an early exit from this dreadful situation, Michael took a slippered step towards the landing's edge. He didn't know if it was fear that made his throat so sore and tight or if it was the Guy Fawkes tang the air had, but he almost felt like he was choking.

"Doug, that policeman blew 'is whistle at us."
"I don't care. It's only down York Road now. You just 'ang on."

Almost at the gap-toothed railings, Michael thought he heard his mum's voice over all the clamour of the devils and the high-voiced man who still sang the same hymn, but realised that he must have just imagined it. With John and Phyllis standing to each side of him, he stepped up to the short stretch of remaining balustrade and gazed down, between its pitch-painted bars, into the roaring, swirling mouth of the Destructor.

It was all the dogs, the drain, the smoke that everything was either going to, or down, or up in. It was rack, and it was ruin, and the destination of the handcarts. It was other people. It was where you led apes. It was what you rode for leather and what came in absence of high water.

Pink light broke on Michael's cheeks, his forehead, and below the Mayorhold was a mile-wide maelstrom, all ablaze. Worse, as John had explained, this was not common fire that lit a cigarette or charred a house. This was instead a pure and awful poetry of fire, that set morality and trust and human happiness alight, that turned the fragile threads connecting people into ashes. This was fire enough to burn down decency, or self-respect, or love. Michael looked down into the spitting, crackling chasm. From the flaming debris turning in its magma stir he realised that it was consuming nothing physical, but only a more precious fuel of wishes, images, ideas and recollections. It was as if something had collected up a thousand different family albums full of corner-mounted photographs, remembered moments that had been important to somebody once, and in a fit or misery or rage had thrown them all into a furnace. Blistered incidents and scorching pictures circled sluggishly in the volcanic eddy, in the churning black and red.

He saw terraced houses fall against each other in a run of demolition dominoes, complex spider-webs of jitties and rear-entries simplified to blocks of flats like giant filing cabinets. Hundreds of heirloom prams rolled rattling and squeaking down a smoky gradient into the abyss. Everybody's pets died, countless budgie-cages empty save for shit and sandpaper that tumbled endlessly through ruddy darkness. Everybody's favourite toys were lost. Small girls who wanted to be nurses, show-jumpers or film stars played a skipping game, ageing with each turn of the rope to drudges, inadvertent mothers or hairnets and pairs of hands on a conveyor belt. Small boys who wanted to be football heroes kicked and kicked and kicked and never realised that their goal was unattainable, was only drawn in chalk onto the shabby brickwork. Envelopes fell with a sigh on bristly doormats bringing bad news from the front line, bank or hospital. A desperate landlord murdered a streetwalker with a hammer in the back yard of his pub, and at the head of Scarletwell Street men in black shirts with moustaches and their skulls shaved halfway up the back held rallies, shouted slogans and folded their arms like gods. Everything burned and didn't know it burned. These were the pictures in that frightful, final hearth.

Sheep Street seemed to have broken in the middle, its near end a steep slope that was almost vertical, and toppling down it there were fifty years of Bicycle Parades. Girls dressed as fairies rattling their collection tins, deliberately wonky bikes with oval wheels and men whose papier-mâché heads with leprous, peeling paintwork were much bigger than their bodies – all of these poured down the chute into the gaping conflagration of the Mayorhold and were lost. A marching band assembled by the Boy's Brigade went tumbling after them in a percussion-heavy clattering of drums and cymbals, a lone glockenspiel attempting to perform "It's a Long Way to Tipperary" before it was swallowed in the light, the thunder, the collapse. Eleven-year-old boys with plastered hair that smelled of chlorine and with damp Swiss rolls of towel and swimming trunks inside their shouldered kitbags skittered on the tilting cobbles, trying to arrest their slide. Nothing was safe, the district's sense of safety having been the first thing to catch fire.

A line of butcher's, barber's, greengrocer's and sweetshops all went in, and then a whole church that he thought might be St. Andrew's. Michael watched it as it ground and slithered inexorably towards the glaring edge and then tipped over, limestone buttresses crumbling away from the main structure, falling to the firestorm in a shower of smashed stained glass and smoking hymnals. Pews that still had tiny people kneeling in them spilled out of the plunging buildings through its broken doors and windows, dropped into the all-consuming mortal bonfire like unwanted dollhouse furniture. Eyes stinging, Michael saw his own home on St. Andrew's Road, its windows covered up with corrugated tin, as it sank helplessly into a quicksand of rough grass, its

chimney at length disappearing underneath the patch of turf that was itself
creeping towards fiery oblivion down an upended Scarletwell Street. Horses
pulling tinkling milk floats shied and snorted in distress, dropped steaming
fibrous pancakes, good for roses, which were quickly shovelled up into tin
buckets by the grubby children who were plummeting behind them on the
sudden incline. Everything went on the pyre, went down the flaming pan.

Michael understood that it was meaning that was being turned to ash
here, and was not really surprised that many of the burning, blackening scenarios were only meaningful to him. He saw his stick-thin grandma, Clara,
fall abruptly to a shiny kitchen floor that wasn't red and blue tiles like the
one they had down on St. Andrew's Road. He saw his nan, May, clutching at
her drooping bosom as she stumbled down the passage of a little modern flat
somewhere that wasn't Green Street, trying to reach the front door and fresh
air, collapsing on her face and lying still instead. He saw a hundred other old
men and old women moved from the condemned homes where they'd raised
their families, dumped in distant districts with nobody that they knew and
failing to survive the transplant. By the dozen they keeled over on the well-lit
stairs of their new houses; in the unfamiliar indoor toilets; onto their unprecedented fitted carpets; on the pillows of magnolia-painted bedrooms that they
failed to wake to. Countless funerals fell into the Mayorhold's fires, and furtive teenage love-affairs, and friendships between relocated children sent to
different schools. Infants began to understand that they would probably now
never marry the classmate that they had been expecting to. All the connecting tissue, the affections and associations, became cinders. He became aware
that he was weeping, had presumably been weeping for some time.

In the shifting lava patterns of the hell-well he could see that all of it, the
wasting of his neighbourhood, had been, was, or would be for nothing. The
decline and poverty that marked the Boroughs was a sickness in the human
heart that would not be improved by pulling down its oldest and, inevitably, best-constructed buildings. Scattering the displaced occupants would
only spread the heartbreak and malaise to other areas, like trying to put out
a burning pile of leaves with an electric fan. It was that spread of the Boroughs' condition, Michael knew, that was the worst part of this whole disaster.
Michael knew how it had happened and how it would all work out. He saw
both past and future in combusted rubbish circling the nightmare plughole of
the astral town square.

There were sepia councillors and planners in Edwardian offices changing the way they thought about the poor, from seeing them as people who
had problems to problems themselves, problems of cost and mathematics that
could be resolved by tower-block proposals or by columns in a balance-book.
He saw blue posters with a woman's face on. She had pained eyes like some-

body who's embarrassed by you but is too polite to say, and a nose built only for looking down. Out of the hoardings she gazed condescendingly across a landscape where the clearance areas multiplied, England unravelling from its centre outwards until almost everywhere was drunk and out of work and in a fight, just like the Boroughs. Every region started to descend the same slope that led here, that led to soot, sparks and annihilation. On the posters, background colours altered and the woman's picture was torn down to be replaced by those of men whose smiles looked forced or insincere, if they could even smile at all. Spy cameras flowered from lampposts and the pub names melted into gibberish. People waved their fists, then knives, then guns. He could see money, rustling flows of blue and pink and violet paper bleeding from stabbed schools and gashed amenities. He could see an entire world spiralling down into the incendiary maw of the Destructor.

Over on the square's far side, standing upon one tier of what seemed to be an unfolded wedding-cake of ugly concrete, the pink-faced man started up his hymn again from the beginning. Elsewhere, one by one, the underdressed and weeping pensioners winked from existence as they woke from their appalling dreams to wet sheets, wards or care-home dormitories. Further down the damaged landing that the builder and the phantom kids were perched upon, the walking ball of light and noise and shrapnel broke off from his contemplation of the fall of Mansoul and commenced again his patient, soiled-trouser shuffle down the balcony towards them, weeping steam, with flying nails and rivets as his halo. It was time to go. Michael had seen enough.

They re-entered the Works by the swing door and went back down the carven blocks of firmament that were the stairs, pulling their dressing gowns or jumpers up over their noses long before they reached the level where the smoke began. Above the choppy vapour ocean, Michael could see the upper reaches of the larger devils as they waded through the fuming fathoms to attack the blaze at the north end. Something that had the head and shoulders of an immense camel – if camels were made from dirty bubble-gum – stood squirting spinning globes of hyper-water at the burning northern wall. Forming a line again and hanging on the clothing of the ghost in front of them, the Dead Dead Gang let Mr. Aziel lead them down into the suffocating shroud.

"There it is! There's the 'orspital! Goo faster, Doug. Goo faster."

It took a while for them to make their way back over the smashed, fiend-vacated flagstones to the crook-door in the corner, where the mournful builder shook their hands and said farewell to them, with the farewell alone taking a good five minutes. The gang navigated the disintegrating top floor of the ghost-building below the Works, then carefully descended through the soaked and gaping storeys lower down, hand over hand, the same way they'd gone up. Nobody said much. There was nothing much to say after they'd witnessed the Destructor. Before Michael knew it, he was dropping through the ghost-gang's secret trapdoor in the phantom ruin's waterlogged floor, down onto the lamp-lit pavement outside the Salvation Army place in Tower Street. The six kids assembled with their trailing look-alikes upon the sunken walkway, odourless and colourless again now they were back down in the halfworld, and awaited Phyllis's command.

"Right, then. Let's dig back into 1959, so we can goo up to Mansoul when it's not burnin' dayn. If Michael 'ere's to get back to 'is body, it'll 'ave to be done from the Attics o' the Breath, the same way 'e come up 'ere. Everybody pitch in so we get the 'ole dug quicker, and be careful to stop diggin' 'fore we reach that bloody ghost-storm. If we go back to just after them two Master Builders 'ad their fight, I reckon that should do us."

And that was precisely what they did, scraping away some fifty years of Mayorhold until they were all able to climb through the resultant hole into the bulb-lit cellar of the newsagent's, owned by poorly-looking Harry Trasler there in Michael's native time-zone. They picked their way through all the American adventure magazines, swaggering and salacious mountains that most probably intimidated the neat, nervous stacks of *Woman's Realm* which they were standing next to. Floating up the stairs and through the cluttered shop, where the proprietor and his elderly mother were conducting an entirely silent argument, the gang and their pursuing after-pictures poured themselves onto the grass-pierced pavement bordering the Mayorhold.

It was evidently some time following the previous occasion that they'd been down there, but not by very long. The mortal former town square still enjoyed its sunny afternoon, and the boys with the acid-drops whom they'd seen fighting earlier appeared to have made up. As for the ghost-seam, it too seemed to have returned to something like normality. The super-rain was over, leaving phantom puddles fizzing in the cobbled gutters, unseen by the living, and though Michael's dressing gown was ruffled by mild gusts of an abiding spectral wind he thought the ghost-storm must be finished with by now. The lens-like areas of visual distortion that had rolled around the place and signified the presence of the brawling Master Builders in the world above were gone, and so were the two murderous ghost-women who'd been trying to tear each other into cobwebs outside the Green Dragon. The only remaining indications of the bad mood that had gripped the Mayorhold earlier were the two Jewish-looking ghosts, chuckling and dusting off their hands as they stepped from the public toilets on the square's far side, into which Michael, earlier, had seen them drag one of those men in the black shirts who turned up around here from time to time. Apart from that it was a perfectly agreeable day, there in 1959 at the convergence of the eight streets that had once comprised the ancient township. Phyllis, with one arm draped around Michael's shoulder, took charge of the situation.

"Well, then it looks like it's time to take ayr regimental mascot 'ome. We'll go up through the old Tayn 'All into the Works and then take 'im across the Attics to the 'orspital."

Drowned Marjorie piped up at this point, sounding a bit irritated.

"Phyll, that'll take ages. You know 'ow much bigger everything wiz Upstairs. Why can't we just take him through the ghost-seam and then go Upstairs when we get to the … oh. Oh, right. I see. Forget that I said anything."

Phyllis nodded, satisfied by Marjorie's sort-of apology.

"See what I mean? Dayn at the 'orspital there isn't any Jacob Flight so we can get Upstairs. I know it's a long slog across Mansoul, but there's no other way to do it."

Bill, who had been standing by himself and staring thoughtfully towards the public toilets at the foot of Silver Street, spoke up at this point.

"Yes there wiz. I know a way that we could get there quicker. Reg, you come with me. As for you others, we'll meet you lot Upstairs in five minutes' time."

With that, grabbing the sleeve of a bewildered Reggie Bowler, Bill ran off along the west side of the Mayorhold before Phyllis could forbid whatever he was planning. The two boys turned right just a little way off, vanishing into the upper stretch of Scarletwell Street that had been the sunken walks of Tower Street up in 2006 only ten minutes back. By the time that the gang got to the corner that their pals had disappeared around, the corner where the mortal Jolly Smokers stood, Reggie and Bill had dug a narrow time-hole and squeezed through it. They were on the aperture's far side, hurriedly filling in the gap they'd made by dragging threads of day and night across the opening, so that it winked out of existence altogether before Phyllis and the others reached it.

"Ooh, that aggravatin' little bleeder! You wait 'til I get my 'ands on 'im and bloody Reggie! As if we'd not got enough on ayr plate as it wiz, withayt them clearin' off like that. Well, sod 'em. We'll take Michael 'ome withayt 'em. Come on."

With her string of rabbits swinging angrily she marched across the Scarletwell Street cobbles to the derelict place on the corner opposite the Jolly Smokers. Michael, John and Marjorie trailed after her with the exhaust-fume putter of her after-pictures breaking up against their faces. Michael noticed Phyllis making nervous glances back across her shoulder at the Jolly Smokers as she did so, as if half-expecting Mick Malone or that man with the crawling face to burst out from it and devour her.

Seeping through the boarded-up front door of the forgotten town hall, the quartet of ghost-kids found the place in much the same condition as when they'd come up this way to see the angles fighting. The same wallpaper hung from the plasterwork like sunburn, the same saveloy of poo still curled there in its nest of Double Diamond bottles. The abandoned edifice was still a thing of bricks and mortar here in 1959, where ordinary sunlight fell through slats and carpeted the messy floor in blazing zebra hide. There was no indication of the water-damaged phantom building that they'd recently ascended through, which would be all that stood here within less than fifty years. Michael went with the others up the half-collapsed stairs, grateful that they didn't have to climb like spiders up that treacherous and trickling wall again.

On the top floor they made their way along into the mouldering boxroom at the end, where a confetti of pale hues diffused into the ghost-seam's grey through the crook-door atop a creaky Jacob Flight, fugitive colour filtering from the higher world. The gang mounted the useless shallow steps in single file, taking on pink and blue and orange as if they were outlines in a colouring book. The sounds of Mansoul welled around them like theme music in the last five minutes of a film.

As the children emerged onto the echoing and bustling shop floor of the Works, Michael was pleased to see that it was just how he remembered it from the first time he'd been up here. The lower-ranking builders with their robes tinted like pigeon-necks were hurrying everywhere across the seventy-two massive flagstones that now writhed with painted imagery again, the paving's demon occupants all back in place and scintillating with malevolence. There were no smudge-faced angles or huge diamond toads engaged in battling a blaze and there was no smoke ... or at least, not yet. Not for another forty years or so. The toddler felt haunted, felt all horrible whenever he involuntarily remembered the Destructor; when he thought of that incendiary millwheel grinding Michael's home and world and grandmothers to nothing while it consumed paradise. How could that be? How could this busy realm of enterprise and order go so literally to hell in a few decades, more than likely within Michael's renewed lifetime? How could heaven be on fire unless it was the end of everything, only a few score years into the future? It disturbed him more than any of the frights or freaks he'd witnessed in the ghost-seam, and he really didn't like to think about it.

Deftly, the Dead Dead Gang wove their way into the complicated choreography of the industrious builders, ducking through brief gaps in the continuous processions of these grey-robed workmen, skipping over numerous discarded "Welcome to the Works" books that had been dropped to the demon-decorated flooring. They were heading not for the south wall that had the stellar stairway and the crudely-rendered emblem halfway up it, but towards the eastern side of the enclosure, where it looked as if there were a door that led out to street-level rather than the elevated balconies. Like the exits upstairs, this was a swing portal with a stained-glass panel similar to the ones you sometimes saw in pubs. They pushed it open and the morning breezes of Mansoul washed over them, almost dispelling the aroma of their leader's rancid necklace.

It was a fine day Upstairs, with that smell like burned soil which hung over summer streets after a storm. On the mile-wide expanse of the unfolded Mayorhold there were many brightly-dressed ghosts standing there chatting excitedly about the just-concluded brawl between the builders. Meanwhile other spirits tried to chip off fragments from the solid pools of hardened gold that lay in dazzling splotches round the square which Michael, with some consternation, realised were dried angle-blood. The fight had obviously finished only recently, and Michael found himself considering the combatants and wondering what they were doing now, although somehow he knew.

In his mind's eye he saw the white-haired builder, who would even now be striding angrily along the walkways up above the Attics of the Breath with one eye blackened and his lips split. He'd be on his way back to the trilliard hall to take his interrupted shot when he met with sardonic Sam O'Day there on the balconies over the vast emporium. Right at this moment, Michael knew that elsewhere in Mansoul the two eternal foes confronted one another on the landing while, somewhere below them, he himself looked up and wondered who they were. What if he got the gang to take him to the Attics now, so he could meet himself and other-Phyllis as they made their way across the giant hall of floor-doors? Except he couldn't do that, could he, because that had not been what had happened?

With his three ghost-friends, Michael set out across the Upstairs version of the Mayorhold, the unfolded boxing-ring where the two titan builders had but lately come to blows. Across a sky so blue that it was almost turquoise sailed white clouds much like their earthly counterparts, save that the marble shapes and faces which you saw in them were much more finely chiselled, much more finished: penguins, Winston Churchill, a trombone, perfectly sculpted in the aerial snowdrifts.

Now the Master Angle would be in sight of the trilliard hall, his pace marked by the rhythmic drumbeat of the blue-tipped staff he carried, thudding on the boardwalks of Mansoul with every other step. He'd cross the path of his dark-haired opponent, who'd return to the celestial snooker parlour by a different route, and the two shining entities would nod to one another without speaking as they both made for the outsized table to resume their play. Michael could almost see the crowded solar system of the balls grouped randomly upon the wide green baize, could almost see his own smooth, polished sphere balanced precariously, trembling on the lip of the skull-decorated pocket.

The ghost-children had progressed what seemed barely a hundredth of the distance over the unfolded former town square. Bill, apparently, had been correct. It would take days for them to get down to the hospital at this rate.

Michael's thoughts were just beginning to drift back to the enormous gaming table and the shot upon which everything depended when the strangest sound that he had ever known suddenly issued from behind him, rolling and reverberating in the augmented acoustics of the Second Borough. It was like a thousand oriental monks blowing their thigh-bone trumpets all at once, and, given where they were, Michael was worried that it might be the great blast announcing Judgement Day that he'd heard his gran mention once. The noise rang out again. With Phyllis, John and Marjorie he turned to gape at what was thundering across the square towards them.

It appeared to be some sort of elephant. Against the gloriously decorated hoardings and façades of Mansoul, with their painted circus stars and funfair dodgem swirls, it somehow didn't look entirely out of place.

Whatever it was, it was certainly approaching them at a tremendous lick, eating the ground that lay between them as it cannoned out of what must be the higher version of St. Andrew's Street, carelessly throwing back its trunk at intervals to sound its thrilling and inspiring war-cry along with the cavalry of echoes that immediately followed. As it came within the range of Michael's crystal-clear afterlife vision, he observed that it wasn't much like the elephants that he had seen on posters. For one thing it wasn't grey, but was instead a lovely russet brown. This was because it had either been dressed up in a giant-sized fur coat, or else was covered in a layer of hair. The idea that it might be garbed in clothing of some sort didn't seem very likely, although Michael was prepared to entertain it since the shaggy elephant was also wearing some form of novelty hat atop its massive skull.

This disproportionately tiny headpiece, though, upon closer inspection, was an ornamental plaster garden gnome holding a fishing rod. Then, after a few seconds when the beast had rumbled a considerable distance nearer, it turned out that it was Bill sitting there on the creature's cranium, clutching the makeshift fishing-rod with Reggie Bowler hanging on for dear death just behind him. What in here's name was all this about? And whose voice was that he'd just heard, talking to someone called Doug? Who was Doug?

"Is this the right way what we've come in, Doug? Do they take people with emergencies in at the front like this?"

"They'll 'ave to. Open the door your side, Doreen. I'll goo round and lift 'im out ..."

Michael was hearing things again. He shook his golden head to clear it just as the huge trumpeting behemoth slowed and juddered to a halt barely ten feet away.

Perched there upon the monster's crown, holding a pole from which there hung a string of Puck's Hats, Bill grinned down at Michael and the rest with Reggie Bowler making faces from behind his shoulder.

"There. Wiz this the bollocks, or what? Climb on up and we'll be down the 'ospital in no time."

Phyllis stared up at her reputed little brother blankly, then gazed at the thing that he was riding, equally uncomprehendingly, and then looked back at Bill.

"What wiz it?"

Bill was just about to answer when John did it for him.

"It's a woolly mammoth, Phyll, or rather it's the ghost of one. They've been extinct since prehistoric times. Where did the two of you find one of these so quickly?"

Bill and Reggie were both laughing now.

"Quickly? You're joking. We've spent nearly six months finding Mammy 'ere and training 'er and everything. You want to try it sometime."

As he spoke, Bill was allowing the apparently tame animal to snag a couple of the dangling Puck's Hats with its trunk, tearing the fairy-blossoms from the length of twine that they were strung on. It chewed up the ghost fruit noisily, two or three in a single mouthful, and drooled ectoplasm as it did so.

"What we did, just after we left you, we dug about five minutes up into the future and went over to the public lavs there on the corner of the Mayorhold in the ghost-seam."

Reggie broke in here, unable to contain himself.

"I tell yer, Marjorie, gal, it was a right laugh! We'd seen them two old Jewish fellers coming out the privy looking pleased as Punch, and we remembered 'ow we'd seen 'em drag one o' them chaps with the black shirts in there when the two builders 'ad their scrap. Me and Bill, we goes in, right, and 'e's laying there knocked silly with 'is short-back-and-sides resting in the trough. He's 'aving a good cry, like, and there's that queer feller whose ghost lives there in the toilets, 'e's just standing there taking the mickey out the bloke wi' the black shirt on. 'Onestly, you should have seen 'em."

Reggie, by this point, was laughing too hard to continue, and so Bill took up the tale.

"So, anyway, Reggie and me, we 'elp this Blackshirt to 'is feet and wring the ghost-piss out 'is trouser leg, while 'e goes on about us being fellow Aryans and all that. I didn't tell 'im 'ow our dad threw Colin Jordan in the Tyne once, because we were getting on so well I didn't want to spoil it. Me and Reggie said we'd 'elp him to get back to his own times, back there in the 'Thirties when the Blackshirts 'ad their office on the Mayorhold 'ere and there were a few Blackshirt ghosts for 'im to knock about with.

"Well, we dug him back into the 'Thirties, only when we ran into 'is fascist mates we told 'em 'ow we'd seen two Jewish blokes come out the toilets lookin' satisfied and then gone in to find their chap in conversation with a well-known 'omosexual. They thanked us for tellin' 'em, then while they dragged 'im out to the back yard so they could kick 'is 'ead in, me and Reg 'ere nicked the ghost or dream of their big British Union of Fascists banner, and then we dug our way up to a few 'ours before we all went to the asylums so that we could get there first and grab most of the Puck's 'Ats."

Phyllis, who Michael had thought would go berserk at this point in the narrative, was instead looking from Bill to the munching mammoth and then at the dwindling string of mad apples that were suspended, tantalisingly, above the creature's head. At last a broad smile broke across her pointed, fox-like features as she worked out what had happened.

"Ooh, you crafty little bleeder. D'yer mean to tell me that you took all of them Jennies, wrapped up in the banner, and dug all the way back to – "

Bill looked so smug that he was going to have to grow an extra head to fit his smirk on.

"... all the way back to the Ice Age. It was bloody cold. I tell yer, you could feel the draft from the third century BC and it got worse the further back we went. In the end we 'appened upon Mammy 'ere while she was still alive, and then waited for 'er to kick the bucket so that we could make friends with 'er ghost by feeding 'er the Puck's 'Ats. That's what took most o' the time. Once we'd all got to know each other we led Mammy back along the time-hole into 1959, and then got 'er up 'ere out of the ghost-seam so that she could be our ride down to the 'ospital. Come on, climb aboard. I tell yer, it's like Whipsnade Zoo being up 'ere."

Now everyone was grinning, and especially Michael. This was it. This was the treat, the party, the surprise, the send-off he'd been hoping for. All giggling, Phyllis, Michael, John and Marjorie tried to work out how they were meant to mount the mammoth, finally electing to just climb up its back legs using thick tufts of golden-brown hair for their handholds. Mammy didn't seem to mind. Her small eyes blinked contentedly deep in the wrinkle-vortex of their sockets as she cannily detached another Puck's Hat from the dangling string and wolfed it down. This being the last one, Bill passed the pole and empty line to Reggie, who sat on the bristling hump of Mammy's neck immediately behind him with a half-full fascist sack of Bedlam Jennies in his lap. Swiftly and expertly – he'd had six months to practice, after all – the bowler-hatted urchin threaded eight or nine of the ripe ghost-fruits on the lure and gave it back to Bill.

While this refuelling operation went on, the four other wraith-kids scrambled up into position on their prehistoric steed. Drowned Marjorie climbed up onto the mammoth's back first so that she could sit there behind Reggie, with her arms looped round his middle as if he were taking her out for a ride upon the pillion of his hairy, ice-age motorbike. Michael went next, clinging in the massive ghost's toast-coloured fur, rubbing his cheek against the nap and drinking in the ancient must. Phyllis was snuggled up to Michael's back, which was a lovely feeling but smelled dreadful, while John sat there at the tail-end and held on protectively to the Dead Dead Gang's leader. The perfume of Phyllis Painter's vermin-ermine didn't seem to bother John at all.

The various ghosts about the Mansoul Mayorhold on that radiant blue afternoon had mostly stopped what they were doing to admire the mastodon, this grand, ten-foot high specimen with its sixteen-foot tusks that had so unexpectedly arrived there in their midst. Even the gold-prospectors, who were still trying hard to chisel up a precious fragment of coagulated angleblood from the flat puddles that were everywhere, paused in their labour to inspect this latest novelty. What an extraordinary day, they must have all been thinking, even by the extraordinary standards that applied Upstairs. First two colossal Master Builders smack each other silly, there in the unfolded town square, and now this turns up! Whatever next?

Cosy against the prehistoric plush, Michael was thinking about Mighty Mike, his namesake with the even paler hair, who even at this moment would be pacing on the twenty-five foot margins of the trilliard table, studying the angles and deliberating while the grey mob of rough sleepers looking on all held their breath forever. A nerve ticking at one corner of his damaged eye, he'd grind the cube of chalk with too much force against his cue, gaze fixed unwaveringly on the off-white globe that hung in peril at the death's-head corner, teetering upon the black brink of the pocket's drop. This, of course, was the off-white globe which represented Michael's soul.

There was a sudden lurch that interrupted Michael's reverie, almost dislodging him from his perch on the creature's back and causing him to clutch tight at the rusty fur. Bill clapped his feet against the matted flanks and swung his pole so that the string of Puck's Hats hung a tempting inch or two ahead of Mammy's uncurled woolly caterpillar trunk. The ginger mammoth-jockey called out into the stupendous echo-chamber of Mansoul.

"Hiyo Mammy! Awaaaaaay!"

And they were off. Braying magnificently through her swaying, raised proboscis, the apparently sweet-natured Palaeolithic throwback broke into a trot, and then a canter, then a gallop. Its hairy umbrella-stand feet pounded on the sacred paving, crunching through the gold scabs still remaining from the builders' fracas, fracturing the hardened puddles' bullion sheen into a fine web of ceramic cracks in passing. All the coloured-costume phantoms and the semi-naked sleepers gathered in the astral Mayorhold cheered and waved their caps or bonnets. From the tiered verandas up above a multitude of dreams and ghosts yelled their encouragement. The shaven-headed giant in Roundhead uniform that Michael had been told was called Thompson the Leveller thumped rhythmically and jubilantly on the handrail as he watched, and the ethereally handsome black-skinned cowboy they'd seen earlier fired his six-guns in the air in celebration.

The gang and their wondrous mount rumbled up an unfolded higher surrogate of Silver Street, one of the eight archaic lanes converging there in the original town square. Since Mansoul was built out of nothing more than dreams and poetry and stray associations, the considerably widened street was made wholly from silver. What was no more than a narrow lane down in the mortal realm was here a polished swathe of silver cobbles, with a fish-eye miniature of Mammy and her ghost-child cargo swimming in the bulge of every argent stone as they stampeded by, splashing through pools of super-rain left by the recent downpour, sending sprays of complicated droplets bouncing in the hallmarked gutters. From moon-metal landings overlooking the exalted thoroughfare, Silver Street's ghostly occupants of several different centuries were whooping and applauding as the famous Dead Dead Gang rode past on their pet mammoth.

There were beautifully painted nancy boys from the public convenience at the lane's bottom end, a magnified Mansoul enhancement with its fifty-foot-long trough and endless row of cubicles all fashioned from white marble. Dressed in flouncy, near-fluorescent outfits that they would have never dared to wear while they were still alive, the pretty sissies cooed and shrilled like birds of paradise, and one called out "We love you, Marjorie", brandishing a green-and-gold jacketed book as Mammy passed beneath them. There were Rabbis from the vanished synagogue up at the top end of the passage, where the lofty-windowed cube of brick that was the Fish Market stood, down in the material world. The Hebrew clerics clapped politely and seemed to be nodding in agreement, although Michael didn't know what with. Balcony after balcony of ghostly silversmiths, streetwalkers, publicans, judo instructors, pawnbrokers, resplendent paupers and antique policemen had turned out, it seemed, to watch the temporarily dead infant taken back to life. Michael clung tight to Mammy's fine, luxuriant pelt and felt a bit intimidated by all the attention. He'd had no idea he was so famous. He tried to shrink further down into the musty fur, but found that as upon those bitter winter nights when he'd tried sleeping right down underneath the bedclothes, it was hard to breathe.

"... this lady's little boy. 'E's got a sweet lodged in 'is throat ..."

" 'E ent breathed. 'E ent breathed all this time!"

"Oh, my goodness. Give him here, dear. Nurse, can you fetch Dr. Forbes, please, and tell him to hurry?"

Out from the old metalworker's lane their Pleistocene Express banked to the right, into a yawning plaza that was very like the lower end of Sheep Street, only massively inflated. Mammy blasted out a nasal fanfare as she stormed past the old, stately-looking building that was opposite the mouth of Silver Street, which, although much expanded, Michael recognised as the academy he'd seen in Mr. Doddridge's Delft tiles. Upon its soaring terraces the young and fiery scholars were applauding, shouting their approval in Greek, Latin, French and Hebrew as they celebrated and lit bottle-rockets. On the lower levels of the glorious edifice a hundred thousand candles had been patiently arranged to spell out KING GEORGE – NO PRETENDER in massed choirs of primrose flame. The sky above was grading into violet where the students' fireworks banged or twittered and strewed coloured sparks in great hot handfuls down upon the Dead Dead Gang's parade.

Perched behind Michael as they avalanched down the titanic phantasm of Sheep Street, Phyllis shouted in his ear over the racket of the pyrotechnics and the constant drum-roll of their charger's footfalls.

"'Ere, I just thought. Ask ayr Bill 'ow 'im and Reggie got this bloody great thing up 'ere to Mansoul. I mean, it's 'ard enough for people to climb up a Jacob Flight, so 'ow did they get Mammy to goo up a ladder?"

Michael dutifully passed this on to Marjorie, in front of him, who conveyed it to Reggie sitting just in front of her. Reggie said something back to Marjorie and they both snickered before Marjorie turned round and hissed conspiratorially at Michael.

"They pushed Mammy upstairs through the bottom of our hideout up near Lower Harding Street. Apparently it wrecked the den, so there's only a mammoth-sized hole where it used to be. If you tell Phyllis, she'll go spare. Just say that Reggie can't shout loud enough for Bill to hear him over all this noise. Tell her she'll have to ask him later."

Michael haltingly repeated this white lie to Phyllis, who narrowed her eyes suspiciously but seemed prepared to let the matter rest there for the moment. On they went down Sheep Street, heading for the Market Square and Drapery. Around their pet giant's tree-trunk legs, the toddler noticed that there slopped a white tide made of sheep, all clattering and bleating idiotically as they tried to get out of the rampaging brute's way. He assumed that these must just be part of Sheep Street's poetry, like all the silver lampposts, drains and paving stones that Mammy had just passed in Silver Street. He hoped that they would not be going anywhere near Ambush Street, or Gas Street for that matter.

They passed by an enlarged Fish Market upon their right, the glass-roofed structure somehow fused into one building with the synagogue and Red Lion tavern that had previously occupied the site. Chaps with long ringlets spilling from beneath their skullcaps served dark beer across fishmongers' slabs that were sequinned with scales and wet with highlight. Men in dazzling white coats and hats who wore cleavers or knives like jewellery were repeating Jewish prayers while filleting the cuts of cream or pink or vivid haddock-yellow that were spread upon a varnished public bar-top. Everyone looked up and smiled or raised their foaming tankards as the ghost-gang went galumphing by.

People were everywhere as they continued onward down a huge dream of the Drapery, where towering houses made of leather had been cut into fantastic shapes on each side of the sloping street. Palatial mansions in the form of boots or shoes loomed over them, and dizzy pinnacles like ladies' evening gloves. Adnitt's department store was a tremendous corset with a multitude of jubilant spectators sitting on the stitching of the upper levels as they cried out their support or adulation. There were lower ranking builders in grey gowns that were still pregnant with all sorts of other colours, like a rain-cloud. There were ghosts in party clothing who threw streamers; shabby poltergeists who just gave a thumbs-up and grinned. The women, men and children of the higher township lined its streets in an uproarious throng, accompanied by phantom dogs and smoky spectral cats, by ghostly budgerigars freed from their mortal cages and the brilliant souls of goldfish, without their confining bowls or water, that just shimmered through the air, staring and mouthing silently, occasionally releasing a small bubble to drift upward like a weightless pearl.

Some of the crowd held banners while some carried placards bearing goodwill messages or simply naming favourite members of the Dead Dead Gang. Posthumous teenage girls squealed and held signs up that said merely 'John', but all six children seemed to have their followers. Michael was slightly miffed to realise that the majority of flags and waving notices said "Marjorie", although it looked as though he was the next most popular, which perked him up a bit.

Emerging from the bottom of the Drapery they rocketed around a version of All Saints Church that looked bigger than the Tower of Babel. In the higher world this still had its great portico supported by thick columns, but up here there were at least eight monstrous porticos stacked one atop the other, piling up into a many-layered monolith of brown and yellow limestone that looked like old gold against the shifting blues and purples of the sky. Gathered below the highest porticos were hundreds of onlookers and well-wishers, whistling and stamping as the previously-extinct animal rode by, while underneath the broad sweep of the lowest canopy stood only a few privileged spooks as if this area were reserved for special guests, celebrities or royalty. Behind him, Phyllis dipped her head to whisper into Michael's ear.

"That there's John Bunyan, and the old boy sittin' in the alcove, that's John

Clare. There's Thomas Becket, Samuel Beckett and I think the feller on the
end there is John Bailes, the button-maker who lived until he was getting on
'undred and thirty. Saints and writers, for the most part. Look, they're wavin'
to yer. Why don't you wave back?"

So he waved back. As they swerved into George Row, an appreciative
audience up on the sills and ledges of a swollen alabaster law court threw
down laurel wreaths or floppy garlands of imaginary flowers, some of which
caught on Mammy's frightening tusks to swing and rustle decoratively in the
crystal-clear, invigorating Upstairs air. Right at this instant, Michael knew,
the white-haired Master Builder would be crouching to his crucial shot, be
sighting down the glaring shaft of light that was his cue, closing his blackened
eye and drawing back his elbow. There was everything to play for.

Petals fell upon them from above, and ticker-tape, and even, inappropriately, ladies' pants. A set of these got caught on Mammy's tusk beside the
wreaths and floral tributes but, since they had little daisies on them, didn't
look entirely out of place.

They hammered down St. Giles Street, here a mind-bending boulevard,
and on their left the Guildhall, the Gilhalda of Mansoul, was an immense
and skyscraping confection of warm-coloured stone, completely overgrown
with statues, carven tableaux and heraldic crests. It was as if an archi-
tecture-bomb had gone off in slow motion, with countless historic forms
exploding out of nothingness and into solid granite. Saints and Lionhearts
and poets and dead queens looked down on them through the blind pebbles
of their emery-smoothed eyes and up above it all, tall as a lighthouse, were
the sculpted contours of the Master Builder, Mighty Mike, the local champion. In one hand the great likeness held a shield, and in the other one he
held his trilliard cue. Unfolding from his back were wings of chiselled glass
that spread across the better part of the illuminated town, so that a rippling
aquarium light fell on the countless couples who seemed to be getting married on the Guildhall's greatly magnified front steps. Beautiful brides in virgin white or iridescent green, in shawls or veils or intricate mantillas threw
their bouquets and blew kisses as the Dead Dead Gang, the darlings of the
afterlife, went roaring by.

And, oh, the stamp and shout of it, the showering affection and the shine
soaked into all of them, enflamed them, and was better than a hundred Puck's
Hats. They crashed past a much-ennobled Black Lion, not the pub in Marefair
that they'd passed through on their Cromwell capers but the other one, the
one with all the ghosts. These leaned out of the astral tavern's great increase of
upper windows, cranking wooden rattles and releasing half-a-dozen different
colours of balloon, each with one of the children's faces stencilled on it. The
balloons sailed up into the opal permutations of a peerless Mansoul sky, and

Michael noticed with some satisfaction that the ones which had his features on were powder-blue.

The Black Lion wraiths who'd launched the bright, bobbing flotilla heavenwards, famous haunts who were doubly immortal thanks to the attention they'd received from all the psychic sleuths and the pot-boiling ghost hunters, were by and large a more old-fashioned and traditional variety of apparition, more the kind of spooks you read about in stories. Some had trailing chains and some carried their heads beneath their arms like footballers before the kick-off. Some had torn their garments open to reveal bare ribs that caged a scarlet pumping heart while others, phantoms of the old school, weren't much more than sheets and breezes. They all whooped and whistled, hurling down psychic phenomena upon the passing children as a tribute, séance drums and trumpets, lengths of slimy muslin, disembodied pointing hands cascading down onto the burnished cobbles where accusing bloodstains bloomed mysteriously, indelibly, around the mammoth's padded trundle.

The Dead Dead Gang surged along St. Giles Street upon their one-horse cavalcade and Michael tried hard to burn every detail into his blue eyes. He knew that he must not forget this, ever. He must hold these streets of glory fast within himself, these hordes of roaring celebrants, and know that in Mansoul he was important. In his mind's eye he could see the Master Builders in their monumental trilliard hall, the white-haired champion crouched over the baize sliding his luminous cue back and forth in halting practice-jabs upon the bridge of his spread fingers. The smooth lacquered rod, sweat-lubricated, slipped against the web of cushioning flesh between the almost-diametrically opposing forefinger and thumb. All the potential force and energy was trapped, was held inside the hesitating cue and focussed on the blue-hot tip of it, thrumming and simmering, waiting to burst out.

Lifting her trunk to sound a clarion, Mammy carried them along the great stretch of the St. Giles Street carriageway to where it blurred into Spencer Parade outside the honey-coloured stone spectacle of St. Giles Church. This building, monstrously increased, now had the upper reaches of its castellated steeple lost amongst the beautifully modelled clouds that passed by overhead: a seahorse and a birthday cake; a map of Italy; a bust of Queen Victoria. A sizeable stone badge or emblem was raised from the tower's lower reaches, fish-shaped, with a woman's figure at its centre and the words "FEED LAMBS". The graveyard grass around the hyper-church had become a savannah from which soaring obelisks and headstones rose in cliffs of inscribed marble, and atop the tallest monument danced somebody that Phyllis, whispering to Michael from behind him, said was Robert Browne who'd started the Dissenting movement in the fifteen-hundreds and who'd perished in Northampton Gaol, an eighty-year-old man who couldn't pay his parish

rates. Fizzing around Browne's spirit in the air was a corona of banned sermons, blazing words and excommunications, while the jigging figure capered
as if overjoyed to be in this dissenting heaven, a spectator to this splendid
pageant. Everyone exalted as the phantom kids urged their ghost-mammoth
on towards the crossways of York Road and Billing Road, towards the ashlar-
fronted coliseum of the Mansoul General Hospital that swelled up with its
bays and arches, storey after storey, into the ethereal haze which hung above
the town.

They swerved over the crossroads, with the carnival of Mansoul's traffic
backed up at the junction's other openings in order to let the Dead Dead Gang
through, a honking jam of tarot-decorated caravans, jewelled wagons and festooned palanquins joined in jostling ovation, with their passengers and costumed coachmen waving gaudy pennants or those green-and-golden books
that everybody seemed to have a copy of.

On the opposite corner of the intersection loomed a bust of George the
Fourth, big as a Rushmore head, the monarch's slightly-baffled frown apparently fixed on the bunch of scruffs racing towards him from the mouth of
Spencer Parade, bareback on their woolly mammoth. High on the bald marble
plateau of King George's skull stood three people whom Michael recognised
as Dr. Philip Doddridge, his wife Mercy and their grown-up daughter Tetsy
who had died days short of her fifth birthday. All of them were beaming down
at the six children and their Stone-Age transport, fluttering their freshly-
laundered handkerchiefs. Standing beside the family on the King's head was a
fourth person, droll and rakish in his gait, whom Michael realised was familiar from the moving scenes that tiled the Doddridge hearth. It was the ne'er-
do-well John Stonhouse, who had been converted when he heard the reverend
doctor speak and gone on to become his closest friend, co-founder with him
of the first infirmary to be built outside London, in George Row. Having made
that connection, Michael understood what Stonhouse and the Doddridges
were doing here: this hospital, the old infirmary's second and more capacious
site, would not exist if it were not for the two men who stood above him now.
Doddridge himself was calling down excitedly in the direction of the gang as
Mammy loped around the giant regal cranium and through an arch of cathedral proportions, just below the doctor on his left.

"Wizn't this grand? Everyone's read your masterpiece, Miss Driscoll.
That's why you've got such a crowd turned out to see you. They all want to be
in the last scene of chapter twelve! God speed you, Michael Warren, on your
wild ride back to life! God speed you all!"

They rattled through the archway and into an endless auditorium that
Michael thought looked very like the Attics of the Breath had when he first
arrived Upstairs, except that this was floored with gleaming tiles instead of

planks and had the ringing sound of a colossal public lavatory or swimming baths. Still a bit puzzled by the reverend Dr. Doddridge's remarks, Michael nudged Marjorie who sat in front of him and asked her who Miss Driscoll was. She chortled and said "I am", which left him not much the wiser. In the susurrus and echo of the cavernous infirmary he heard a million anxious voices whispering.

"Now then, what's going on?"
"This little boy is choking, doctor. They've just ..."
"It's a cough-sweet what 'e's choked on. 'E's not breathed this 'ole time. Is 'e dead?"
"All right, calm down. Let's have a look at him ..."

Michael was joggling all over Mammy's hump, holding on tight as she experienced difficulty with the massively-scaled hall's tiled floor, slithering on its polished sheen, the mammoth's inverted reflection struggling to keep up with her as she tobogganed on the slippery porcelain. Around them, just as in the Attics of the Breath, window-like vents were set into the flooring, an eye-boggling grid of them that reached off to the tiered walls of the arcade on either side. Above, through an immense glass canopy, the crystal-facet webs of lines that were the diagrams of clouds glided and changed their shapes against a backdrop of sublime azure. He felt convinced that this was just the section of the Attics that was up above the hospital, its field of trapdoors opening down on earthly wards and operating rooms below. As their mount went into a trumpeting and blaring skid that it could not arrest, Michael felt a sharp shock reverberating through him and knew that down at the trilliard-hall the Master Builder had taken his shot. The tiny blue fist of the cue's tip had just punched the necessary ball so that it racketed across the crowded table with a pearl necklace of after-images trailing behind it. He could almost feel its spin and roll in Mammy's uncontrolled trajectory across the glistening floor. He was in play, and there was nothing he could do about it.

Finally their carom reached a halt, only a dozen yards or so from one of the large apertures that opened down into the floor inside a white tiled frame a little like the raised edge of a paddling pool. A group of getting on for fifteen people were stood gathered round this opening, possibly previously passed-on relatives waiting for somebody now dying in the earthly hospital downstairs. They looked up in alarm as Mammy skittered to a stop with her half-dozen urchin riders toppling from her back, all giggling, down to the treacherous glaze. Michael could understand the worried glances from this afterlife reception-crowd when he considered that if their primordial steed had gone only a little further, then these people's dying loved ones would find themselves trying to get into heaven while a hairy elephant plunged down the other way. Nobody wanted that.

Struggling to their feet and helping their pet mammoth do the same, the Dead Dead Gang set about searching down the rows of tile-rimmed floor-doors as they tried to find the place and time that Michael's lifeless body had been brought to. Everywhere in the unending echo-chamber of the hyper-hospital there was a scent of purity and freshness, which after some several minutes Michael realised was the smell of ordinary pongy disinfectant that had been unwrapped into a new dimension. From horizon to horizon of this great indoors an almost church-like reverential hush hung over everything, and in the distance he could see Crimean nurses in their bonnets and black skirts conferring with staff of more recent vintage who wore perky white caps and blue nylons. There were visitors as well, who'd come to welcome up expiring friends and family, sometimes in thirty-strong committees or sometimes alone, and Michael even saw a deathmonger or two bustling down the eternal aisles upon their mortal missions. And down at the trilliard parlour he could feel the cue-ball hurtling at breakneck speed towards the ivory globe that represented him, balanced upon the death's-head pocket's rim. The gasp of the rough sleepers as they stood transfixed and watched the game merged with the constant murmur of the supernal infirmary around him. *Whisper, whisper, whisper.*

"... God! This child's got the worst case of tonsillitis that I've ever seen. Give me a tongue-depressor so that I can ..."

Michael's reverie was interrupted by a cry from Reggie Bowler, who had taken charge of Mammy and was feeding Puck's Hats to the docile mammoth as he led her down the wide, tiled pathways of the grid arrangement.

"Phyll? I reckon that this 'ere's the lobby, over 'ere. That must be where they bring 'im in, like. Come and 'ave a look, see if the young 'un recognises anybody."

Dutifully, everyone traipsed over to where Reggie and their shaggy mount were standing, next to one of the great thirty-foot long openings that were set into the floor. Leaning across the raised tiles of the edge, the gang peered down into the living world below where motionless and colour-filled transparent coral forms stood woven in a complicated knot, the whole glass-animal array suspended in a jelly-cube of time.

Michael gazed down into the jewellery, the strangles, into the twenty-five thousand nights. The space below appeared to be about the same size as his living room down in St. Andrew's Road had looked when he had seen it from the Attics of the Breath, all of those Mansoul weeks ago and getting on ten worldly minutes back. He guessed that he was looking at some sort of doctor's office or a little side room running off from the hospital lobby. There were four – no, five – distinct shapes intertwining in the chamber's aspic depths, and with a sudden rush of joy the child identified one of the elongated figures as his mum, Doreen. He knew her by the gentle green glow emanating from inside her, not a showy emerald but the deep, sincere green that you found on mallards' necks. With Doreen in the room there were four other fronded gem-forms, their streaming trajectories crossing or intersecting with her own, elaborately. One of the extended see-through statues had a rich, earth-coloured light within it that made Michael think, for no good reason, about nice Mr. McGeary who lived next door to them in St. Andrew's Road, although he wasn't certain why Mr. McGeary should be down there at the hospital, standing near Michael's mum.

The other three jewel-patterns in the mortal room below were also grouped together in a cluster. There was a calm blue one, like a gas flame, that the ghostly infant thought might be a doctor, and a reddish growth of crystal that was possibly a nurse. This rose-tinged structure had translucent frills of arms along its winding flanks, the foremost pair clasping together at the toothpaste-squeezing's front end as though holding something at the level of its chest, where a bust bulged out from the abstract shape's façade as did a plump maternal face a little higher up – both of these features sculpted in pink glass. The final jewel-form, smaller than the rest and a pale, lifeless grey, was clasped at the convergence of the trailing limb-fins and held up before the rubicund extravagance's bosom. Michael comprehended with a start that this was him, this colourless glass starfish at the heart of the display. This was his little human body. The tall blue construction, curled above it like a wave, seemed to be poking something down a tiny hole in the top end of it, of him.

"... can see it. Come on out, you little blighter. Aa! I almost had it. Let me just ..."

His throat hurt, but that might have just been because he was going to have to say goodbye to all his friends, that hot lump that he sometimes felt when people went away. He leaned back from the aperture and turned around to sit instead on its raised boundary, kicking his slippered feet, with the Dead Dead Gang and their mammoth standing round and smiling at him fondly. Well, the mammoth wasn't smiling, but it wasn't glaring at him or looking offended either. Phyllis crouched down on her haunches so that she was at his eye-level, and took his hand.

"Well, then, me duck, it looks like this wiz it. It's time for yer to goo back dayn where yer belong, back in yer own life wi' yer mum and dad and sister. Shall yer miss us?"

Here he started snuffling a little bit, but blew his nose upon his dressing gown instead until he'd got himself under control. Michael was nearly four, and didn't want the older dead kids thinking that he was a baby.

"Yes. I'll miss all of you very much. I want to say goodbye to everybody properly."

One by one, the rest of the gang came and kneeled or squatted beside Phyllis to make their farewells. Reggie Bowler was the first, lifting his hat off when he crouched as though he were in church or at a funeral.

"Ta-ta, then, little 'un. You be a good boy with yer mum and dad, and if yer dad goes off to prison and yer mum chuck's 'erself out the bedroom window, don't go sleepin' in a packing crate, not when it's winter. That's the best advice what I can offer. You take care, now."

Reggie straightened up and went to stand beside the mammoth, who contentedly chewed on her cud of Puck's Hats. Marjorie took Reggie's place, kneeling in front of Michael with her eyes swimming like tadpoles in the jam-jars of her spectacles.

"You look after yourself now, won't you? You look like you'll turn out to be everybody's favourite character, in what seems to be everybody's favourite chapter. I suppose we've solved the Riddle of the Choking Child, and so this is the chapter's ending. Don't go getting knocked down by a car in two years' time and spoiling it so that I have to do a re-write. Although when you *do* die of old age or whatever it wiz, and you come back up here, then don't forget to look us up. We can all get together for the sequel."

Marjorie kissed Michael on one burning cheek and went to stand with Reggie. Michael hadn't got the first idea what any of what she'd just said to him had meant, but felt it was meant kindly all the same. The next in line was Bill. Not much taller than Michael in his current form, the ginger-haired rogue didn't have to kneel or crouch, but just reached out and shook the dressing gown-clad child by his free hand, the one that Phyllis wasn't holding.

"Cheery-bye, kid. Say 'ello to Alma for us when you see the mental bint, and I expect that we'll meet up again in forty year or so, downstairs, when we don't recognise each other. You've got bottle, mate. It's been good knowing yer."

Big John came after Bill, so tall he had to grovel to look Michael in the eye, but grinning in a manner that suggested that he didn't really mind.

"Goodbye for now, then, nipper. You give your dad, your nan and all your uncles and your aunts my love. And you can tell me one last thing: did your dad Tommy ever talk about his brother Jack at all?"

Though puzzled by the reference, Michael nodded.

"He's the one what got killed in the war, I think. Dad talks about him all the time."

John smiled and seemed inordinately pleased.

"That's good. That's good to hear. You have a good life, Michael. You deserve one."

Standing up, John went to stand beside the others, which left only Phyllis crouching there before him with her dangling rabbit feet and faces, with her scabby knees protruding bluntly from beneath her navy skirt's hem as she squatted.

"Goodbye, Michael. And if we'd 'ave met somewhere else in a different life or in a different time, I should 'ave loved to be yer girlfriend. You're a smashin'-looking kid. You've got the same good looks as John 'as, and that's sayin' summat. Now, you go back to yer family, and try not to forget all what you've learned up 'ere."

The infant nodded gravely as Phyllis gently detached her hand from his.

"I'll try. And you must all look after one another and try not to make so many enemies. I shouldn't like it if one of them hurt any of you. And Phyllis, you must look after your little brother and not always be all cross with him like Alma is with me."

Phyllis looked confused for a moment, then she laughed.

"Me little brother? You mean Bill? 'E's not me brother, bless yer. Now, let's get you 'ome before that devil turns up or there's summat else what stops yer gooin'."

Phyllis placed her hands upon his shoulders and leaned forward, kissing him upon the lips. She drew back for a second, smiling impishly at Michael in the aftermath of their first and last kiss, and then she pushed him over backwards, down the hole, before he even had the time to yelp.

Down at the trilliard hall, the cue ball smashed so hard into the globe that represented Michael that it shattered instantly to powder. Michael's ball was slammed across the gaping death's-head pocket, spinning there in empty space above that dark obliterating plunge, and he was dead, dead for ten minutes, cradled by his weeping mother as the vegetable truck rattled through the town towards the hospital, as fast as it could go, dead for ten minutes, hanging there in nothingness then wham! His ball smacks up against the corner-pocket's inner edge, rebounds across the void to shuttle down the baize with all its after-images behind it, heading for the pocket with the golden cross and he's alive again and all the white-robed men around the massive table, even the dark-haired one who'd caused all the trouble, all of them throw up their arms in blinding pinion fans and yell "Iiiiyyyesssss!" and the on-looking phantoms and rough sleepers all go wild.

Michael was falling backwards with a silent splash and into the time-jelly, tumbling through the viscous moments with six little figures standing waving on a sort of corner that was inside out and up above him. With dismay, he realised that he'd already forgotten all their names, the grubby little corner-fairies. Was that what you called them? Or were they called lions, or generals, or cabbages? He didn't know, didn't know much of anything. He wasn't even certain what he was, except that he was something which had lots of tartan arms and legs and which left a bright yellow trail that he hoped wasn't wee behind it through the heavy clock-oil of the breathing world. Down, down he went and in the corner overhead were tiny little creatures, insects or trained mice, waving goodbye to him. Stretched sounds wrapped round him in long humming ribbons, and then something happened that was like a noise or flash or impact and he fell into a bag of meat and bones, a sack of solid sub-stance that was somehow him, and there were fingers in his mouth and wind was whistling down his throat in a long gust that felt like sandpaper and he remembered pain, remembered what a nasty and upsetting thing it was, but nothing else. What was his name? Where was he and who was this woman holding him and why did it all taste of cherry cough-sweets? Then the flat, familiar world rose up about the little boy, and he forgot the marvellous things.

When Michael woke up properly, which was the next day, something felt wrong in his neck and he was told that somebody had taken out his tonsils, which, not having previously known that he possessed such things, he didn't care that much about. At the week's end his dad and mum came in a taxi-cab and took him back home to St. Andrew's Road where everybody made a fuss of him and he was given jelly and ice-cream. He went to bed that night and the next morning he began to grow into a handsome forty-nine-year-old with wife and children of his own who got up every day and beat steel drums flat for a living. One day he was flattening a drum that, curiously, hadn't got a label. Blinded by a rush of chemicals he knocked himself out cold and came round with his head full of impossible ideas that he recounted to his artist sister, on a slow night at the Golden Lion. Naturally, he hadn't retained all the details of his afterlife adventures, but Alma assured him that if he'd forgotten anything it wouldn't be problem.

She'd just make it up.

Book Three

VERNALL'S INQUEST

Now Besso has departed from this strange world a little ahead of me. That means nothing. People like us, who believe in physics, know that the distinction between past, present and future is only stubbornly persistent illusion.

—Albert Einstein,
Letter to Vero and Bice Besso, March 21, 1955

CLOUDS UNFOLD

A lways now and always here and always me: that's what it's like for you.

Now always and here always and me always: this is what it's like for me.

Now. Here. Me.

Now always, even when it's then. Here always, even when it's there. Me always, even when I'm you; even when I'm in Hell and am I fallen, when am I a thousand fiends. They fold up into you. You fold up into us. We fold up into Him.

This will be very hard for you.

————

Above space, over history hovering, genocide and utopia in the downdraught. Whooomff. Whooomff. Whooomff. Bullroarer breath through the white feathers sent to conscientious cowards, blood objectors. Whooomff. Whooomff. Whooomff.

Seeing and being everything, never detached and never distant. Pitying you and admiring you, endlessly angry, endlessly in love. Auschwitz and Rembrandt in the upbeat. Whooomff. Whooomff. Whooomff.

The view from here is fierce. The view from here is final.

From above, the world is a stupendous flayed anatomy. Motionless on its slab of stars it does not move or change or grow, save for the way it is expressed in the concealed direction. Burning gas and vaporised ore spinning into molten balls, the magma crusting over with a thin black rind of elements, and in the heat and poison there is life here even now, microbial seethings in the cyanide drifts and the hydrochloric puddles.

Reading cosmos left to right, from bang to crunch, from germ to worm to glinting cyborg and beyond, the woven tapestry unpicks itself, reorganises into new designs. The marbling of cloud changes its colour. Leaning closer like impassive doctors, mottled planet-meat is visible, exposed, a skin of circumstance pinned back in plump and larded folds. The worms grow backbones and the newts sprout feathers. Bus routes alter and post offices are closed. Perfectly ripe, the scab lifts from the knee intact, reveals a waxy pinkness underneath.

I know I am a text made only of black words. I know you are observing me. I know you, and I know your grandmother. I know the far threads of your family line reading me in a hundred years, reading me now, from left to right, from Genesis to Revelation. Syphilis and Mahler in the wheeling arc, the holding pattern.

Whooomff. Whooomff. Whooomff.

––––––

In my beginnings am I a black word against the blinding white, am I a meaning, staining the ineffable. All my identity is in this quadrant crease, this angle wherein am I folded down from singularity with my three brothers. Each of us, in ninety paces, count the gold degrees of our awareness, our domain. Each of us has his corner, has his pocket. Each of us has his own element to work with and his own direction of the wind. These are our nails, these are our hammers, fire and flood and hurricane and avalanche. We are the strong hand in the nuclear flash, the weak hand in the isotope's decay. We are the hand wherefrom the lightnings bristle, and the hand that flings the apple or the suicide alike to earth. Four Master Builders, we have rods and we have measures. We are crowbars of creation. We are smiling in the hum and harmony before the world starts.

Here am I become a soldier at the Fall, my staff made slippery with the ichors of the fallen as we drive them down into the low geometries, into the hells of substance and sensation, torture-mazes of the intellect, maelstroms of bile and longing. We are loving them and weeping as we run them through and tread them under, out of mathematical necessity. The thirty-second spirit, who is mighty, drags himself towards me down the cue-shaft that impales him, coughing up a blood of logarithms. Rape is in his red eye, murder in his green one. Algebra spills from his punctured breast and he reviles me, saying, "Brother! Fellow builder! How is it you treat us thus, when are we but unfolded leaves of thee? It is thine own selves that are trampled here into this dark, into this worldly muck!" The words he speaks are true. I raise my naked foot and plant it square against him, push his gory weight along my spear's slick length, kick him from its blue-powdered end to plummet howling into stars and calendars and money, into form and passion and regret. Around me in this slaughter-firmament, this massacre of clouds, our painful war rages forever and the maimed djinns are like locusts, raining on parched fields where have we sown a universe.

Now on the sheer plateau of signs and symbols where shall be raised up Hierusalem, where shall be raised up Golgonooza and Mansoul and all the higher townships, am I stooped in conference with fabled Solomon. My language breaks against his leather cheek. Crumbs of mythology flake from our blazing edges and I gift him with the ring, the holy torus whereby may the stumbling blocks, the satans, all be bound to the construction of his temple. Only harm can come of this: Hierusalem, Mansoul, they are the very seat of War, for warring devils fidget in their stones, their architectures. I am but a builder. What am I to do, when rubble and demise are in the diagram?

And in Golgotha now I touch the perspiration-heavy sleeve of Peter that is once called Aegburth, telling him to take the stone cross jutting from the dry earth at his feet; to set it at the centre of his land. I take a step. We are in Horseshoe Street and he is a year older, dying in the marvels; dying in the pigeons and the rain. The lines are all precise. The spot is marked. The rood is in the wall.

In Tennessee I seize a drunk plantation-keeper's hand
Curl it to scrolls and triangles as he designs the brand.

On his cathedral platform Ernest Vernall screams and weeps. The fire burns from his hair to leave white ash as he receives the brunt of an exploded education. My lips, moving in the fresco. He is cowering amidst the tins and dishes, and I am remembering the episode when I am him, how terrible it is to see my giant eyelids blinking from the antic skitter of the paint; how comical it is when I explain the shape of time and drive him mad with chimneys. Thunders roll about the dome, which are my skirts of noise and electricity. I am a builder, and I bang the words and numbers into him so that his children tally different sums or dance to altered music. And now Ernest is in Bedlam. I sit here by his asylum cot, the sheets marked with a dried shit of delusion, where I wait for him to speak out and not only look at me and cry.

My eyes are carved by R.L. Boulton, late of Cheltenham. Unblinking over Guildhall Road, George Row and Angel Lane I stare towards the south. In my left hand is there a shield and in the right I hold the trilliard-cue. The eldest son of Ernest Vernall stands beside me, one arm draped across my sprouting shoulder-blades with an unsettling familiarity as he harangues the gaping crowd beneath us. Even when I turn my granite head to whisper to him he but laughs and does not seem afraid, so foreign is he to mankind, so distant from the habits of the street. His tragedies affect him only as theatre: scenes restaged from a beloved melodrama that still wrench the heart on each fresh viewing, although the experience is aesthetic and the tears no more than a sincere appreciation of the play. In my petrified sight, his final scenes are acted between mirrors: a concluding chorus line of kicking, struggling old men with petals in their beards. Ah, mad John Vernall, furious Snowy; when I'm you, it near to frightens me.

I am in all my images. I watch you through a billion Christmas cards.

———

May Vernall slithers bare into a Lambeth gutter choked with fish-heads, rain-bows, sodden blossom. Bare she copulates upon the grassy shoulder of the river at Cow Meadow. Gasps of joy unfold to screams of childbirth and the green bank, damp with starlight, is become a narrow downstairs chamber still perfumed by excrement recently burned upon its hearth, an offering to winter spirits that have filled the lavatory with ice. The deathmonger is hovering in her white apron, where embroidered moths swarm on the frill. She takes the lovely newborn from its mother's gaping and tormented birth canal, carries it eighteen months and some few steps into the grainy light of a front parlour. Here she sets it carefully in a small coffin, and May Warren brushes out the golden hair her child has grown in its brief passage from the living-room through to this dying-room. Her life comes charging in, sweeps her away into further maternities and air-raid nights, corpse-hoists and fever carts, abortion kitchens, until finally she stumbles in the hallway of her little King's Heath flat, falls dying, and the last thing that she thinks is *Charlie Chaplin! That's who that man was! I talked to–* Now it's two days later and her one surviving daughter, Lou, is peering through the letterbox after receiving no response to her increasingly impatient rapping. Supine, the coagulated blood has settled in May's face and turned it black. For several moments, Lou believes that she is looking at a bundle of old rags, carelessly dropped there in the circular-and-leaflet flooded passage.

I am there in all my words, there in the hymn, there in the lovers' flattering serenade. A bland popular song plays on the radio and for an instant I flare up, albeit vaguely, in a million minds, an angle playing in your heart.

Louisa Warren is amongst the sweetest strokes upon the canvas, mixing lavender and russet, with the vibrant line beginning on the dun and dusty under-colour of the Fort Street labyrinth, born as a consolation prize replacing her diphtheria-departed elder sister, little May. The line continues through four brothers, Tommy, Walter, Jack and Frank, its fine sweep broadening to become plumed and adorable, a twinkling flapper clacking through the Drapery's November mists upon the arm of her intended, Albert Good. Off in the fog a lovelorn beau is shouting "Gloria? Where are you, Gloria?" – so desperate and forlorn that Albert mentions it; wonders aloud who Gloria might be. "Well, I'm sure I don't know," Lou mumbles into her fur collar, although Gloria is the name she's given to the handsome chap who's made an effort to romance her during Albert's lengthy visit to the cloakrooms. Her bright line uncurls as she becomes Louisa Good, with children and grandchildren branching from the vine. Her eldest daughter weds a lighthouse-keeper, while the artistically gifted and bohemian daughter who comes next weds a French communist. The youngest child, a boy, sprouts washboards and a tea-chest bass as he grows through a skiffle band into an airline steward, marrying at first disastrously, then happily. Louisa finds her mother May dead, crumpled up like laundry in the King's Heath hall. Louisa lives with Albert in their Duston home. In his decline he's watching television dramas, afternoon plays that disturb him, even though the set is not plugged in.

At last her lyric contour is alone as it progresses left to right across the masterpiece, in the concealed direction. As she nears her eightieth birthday, her late brother Tommy's kids, her niece and nephew, Mick and Alma, have arranged a party for her. This will be entitled "The Night of the Living Warrens", so they've told her. All of the surviving family have been invited. It's a few days prior to the event and Lou is having tea in the back garden of her nephew Michael Warren's Kingsthorpe home. Michael's wife Cath is there, and his two children, Jack and Joe. His sister Alma's there and has a friend of hers in tow, another lady artist: an American girl called Melinda. At first it's a nice day, but then some light specks of rain begin to fall. Lightnings attend our exits and our entrances.

Black clouds begin to gather and it is suggested everyone retire indoors. Lou finds she can't stand up. As the two manliest amongst those present, Mick and Alma lift her chair between the pair of them, carry her like an empress on their improvised sedan into the living room. Her breathing is becoming difficult. The sudden stark reality of everything is overwhelming. Her niece sitting there beside her with one arm around Lou's quivering shoulders, murmuring reassurances into her ear, kissing her hair. Cathy and Alma's artist friend attend the worried children and then there are paramedics out of nowhere, lifting her up from her chair, calling her love. There is a mighty pounding like an anvil in her ears now. Whooomff. Whooomff. Whooomff.

She's somehow in the ambulance, motionless in the rain-lashed close outside. Her nephew Mick is with her while the funny modern doctor in his green work-jacket presses down repeatedly upon her chest. I can see Alma Warren there beneath me, stood some yards behind the modern fever-cart upon the spattering tarmac drive, soaked through in just her vest and jeans, watching the bobbing medic through the vehicle's rear window. Her messy hair is plastered to her hollow cheeks, to her bare shoulders, and she seems to tip her head back and stare up into my eyes as I strike with my cue's blue tip against the great ball of the world. The black mirror of night is shattered and, for but an instant, in the ravelling cracks and fissures can be seen the sky's half-silvered backing. With this sizzling flourish I conclude Louisa Warren's painted swoop. Seen close it is a mark, a daub, but oh, when we step back and see what it is part of ...

Some leave with the thunder, some with trumpets, some with only mother silence.

And now Michael Warren swings the hammer down through its foreordained arc onto the dented cylinder, a giant metal lung that flattens and expels its final withering breath into his face. The hammer falls upon the drum, the hammer falls upon the drum, this single act relived, resounding endlessly in a reverberant space-time and become an almost musical crescendo, a percussive storm that wells from thin air, a dramatic and hair-raising punctuation in the symphony: BDANK! BDANK! BDANK! The hammer falls upon the drum, the hammer falls upon the drum and from its threaded throat it coughs a tightly-crinkled cloud of orange poison that expands, unwraps itself, unfolds to fill the world of Michael Warren's breath and vision. A cascade of half-dimensions, the unfurling chaos of its shape contains, just for an instant, every fugitive and frail line from his sister's future paintings. He inhales the imagery that he spits back across the table at her now, now in the Golden Lion's Saturday-night limbo and she wipes it from her face and smears it on her canvasses, just like the ambulance-light and the rain upon the night when her Aunt Lou dies in the thunderstruck rear access-way. She wipes it from her face and smears it on her canvasses. The hammer falls upon the drum. I am a builder, and with each new course my swift trowel catches up the surplus flab of mortar squeezed from in-between the bricks. I build the centuries, I build the moments. I am following the diagram. All of the weight is carried at the centre.

I am sighting down my straight cue at a rounded life, precariously at rest on the world's baize, and in its glaze the dancing highlight glint of soul. I knock the reason and the colour both from Ernest Vernall's head. I squeeze May out into a gutter and send fever-carts to carry off her firstborn daughter. I cram Snowy's mouth with flowers and I throw the poison dust in Michael's eyes. I bank, roll into the high thermals. Majesty and rubble in the dive, the tailspin. Whooomff. Whooomff. Whooomff.

Of course we know pain. We know cowardice and spite and falsehood. We know everything. I call my brother Uriel a cunt. We punch and gouge each other in the town square and the wind raised by our feud alone blows ghosts halfway to Wales. The repercussions ring across the Earth. He blacks my eye and China's great leap forward carries it into an economic abyss. I collapse his nose and Castro comes to power in Cuba. From my split lip dribbles struc-turalism, rock 'n' roll, and hovercrafts. We pick the golden clots before they're ready and the Belgian Congo blooms with severed heads.

Of course we stride among you, thigh-deep in your politics and your mythology. We wade through the pink map-scrap petals of your rapidly disintegrating commonwealth. We march in a black tide on Washington. We juggle satellites and Francis Bacon. We are builders. We build Allen Ginsberg, and Niemeyer's cathedral in Brasilia. We slap up the Berlin Wall. Clouds pass across the sun. We're with you now.

Of course we dance on pins and level cities. We deliver up the Jews from Pharaoh, unto Buchenwald. We flutter tender in the first kiss, flap in agony above the last row in a draughty kitchen. We know what fellatio tastes like and how childbirth feels. We climb upon each other's backs in shower cubicles to flee the fumes. We are in the serene molecular indifference of the Zyklon and the dull heart of the man who turns the wheel to open up the ducts. We are forever standing on those bank steps in Hiroshima as the reality surrounding us collapses into an atomic hell. That moment when you reach your orgasm together and it is the sweetest, the most perfect instant that you ever live through, we are both of you. We keep slaves, and we write *Amazing Grace*.

Of course we shout. Of course we sing. Of course we kill and love. We cheat in business and we give our lives for others. We discover penicillin and we dump the children we have strangled in back alleys. We bomb Guernica just to create that painting, and the bursts of smoke and scream beneath us are our brush-marks. We are from the realms of Glory; we are from the nursery, the school, the abattoir, the brothel. How could we be otherwise? You fold up into us. We fold up into Him.

We are in every second of a billion trillion lives. We're every ant, each microbe and leviathan. Of course we're lonely.

Everything swirls in my eye. If I but blink, all of existence breaks down to an alphabet of particles and thence to only numbers, to an endless sea of values circling in radiant symmetry about their axis, which reside between the figures four and five. When multiplied with their resultant digits added, these reflect each other perfectly, as do the three and six, the nine and zero, ten and minus one, sixteen and minus seven, on to positive and negative infinity alike. There at the centre of the numerical hurricane I stand. Its eye is mine. I am between the four and five, where is the pivot of the universe. I am revolving slowly between mercy and severity, between the blue shift and the red. I breathe in and the stars tumble towards me, toppling back into a single white-hot quark, into the minus numbers. I breathe out, an aerosol of black, exotic matter, galaxies and magnetars: positive sums exploding from my lips unto the cold and dark extremities of time.

I am too often angry, cleaving more toward the five, the fingers in a clenched fist, than towards the four, the ones clasped in a handshake, those extended in a stroke or a caress. Too often am I inclined to severity, towards the red, rather than to the cyan of forgiveness. This, then, is the reason that we keep our cue-tips blue: as a reminder of compassion and its weak force, so that even as we smash the balls towards their predetermined pockets we bestow sky-coloured kisses of eternal grace and mercy, made from billiard chalk.

I see Marla Roberta Stiles, aged four, arranging daisy-heads on miniature pink plastic plates for a tea party to which she'll invite her teddy and her mother, the two soft toys that she loves best in the world. She pours a cold infusion of fruit pastilles in tap-water into tiny cups and takes it both ends in a spit-roast with her pimp Keith and his mate Dave just thirteen years later. Marla asks her mother if she'd like a dried sultana as dessert and spits out semen; scolds the glassily impassive bear for falling off his chair as she sucks up the crystal smoke. She calls sultanas "tanas", and a rosy-cheeked father of two punches her in the face and rapes her in the back of his Ford Escort, and I love her.

I see Freddy Allen stealing pints of milk and dying underneath a railway arch. I see him as a younger man, waiting in Katherine's Gardens for the doctor's daughter that he plans to sexually assault upon her way to work. I'm running with him, weeping with him as he flees the scene in horror at himself, the deed undone. I see him sleeping in the weeds, I see the grey trudge of his afterlife, all Freddy feels that he deserves. His guilt has turned to anger, reso- nating through his days so that he has no hope now of release. The loaves and bottles are all gone, with the doorsteps they stood upon. Nothing can ever be put right.

I see Aegburth who is called Peter with his sandal idly scuffing the Golgotha dirt, revealing a protruding corner of grey stone, too obviously chiselled to be natural, its angles right. He claws and scrabbles for an hour to finally unearth the ancient rood, holding it up two-handed in the sun to see it better. Soil rains on his sweaty brow, his slippery cheek, falls into the Sargasso of his beard. He tastes the crucifixion ground and he wears the cold shadow of the cross upon his face. His weak heart sounds a rhythmic blacksmith clang, BDANK! BDANK! BDANK! He totters, unaware, upon the precipice of his mortality. There at the brink he sees me and the meaning of the universe is altered evermore about him. In France, for his mighty perspiration, he is known as 'le canal', which means 'the channel'.

I see Oatsie Chaplin in debate with Boysie Bristol, there outside the Palace of Varieties on Gold Street corner in the first years of the twentieth century. "But if they're millionaires, why do they dress as tramps?" I see him come home to his native Lambeth following the First World War, a famous film star now, returning from America. The cockneys – former neighbours who've lost sons or brothers to the conflict while he batted his long lashes for the camera – dash pints of beer into his face. Rescued by his assistants and wiped down with borrowed towels in a nearby public convenience, he smells his past, he smells his father in the sodden jacket, the damp trousers.

I see Henry George, praying in barns when he no longer trusts the church. Pigeons are cooing in the rafters and the light falls in a twinkling shaft through breaches in the slates, the thatching. On his shoulder flares a brand that is my own design, that is his private shame, that is his holy burning glory: pallid violet lines on purple skin, the balance and the road. Road of the exodus from Tennessee to Kansas, drovers' road from Wales to Sheep Street where he washes up into the Boroughs on a bleating tide of white, all paths are one. The lynch-ropes of his youth are now the tyres that speed him on his way, with the black champions and martyrs of Northampton striding in his wake.

I see Benedict Perrit, writing lines of painful beauty, laughing, drinking, arguing with ghosts. I see him sitting up alone save for the distant sirens, fingers hesitating over his typewriter's dusty keys on the night prior to Alma Warren's exhibition. He stares like a lost explorer at the Arctic whiteness of the empty page, waiting for inspiration, for the least brush of my wing. Three miles away, off in the yellow Whitehills lamplight filtering through the curtains, Michael Warren cannot sleep and thinks about Diana Spencer's funeral procession, all the people on the footbridge as she came into Northampton. All the eyes and silence.

I see Thomas Ernest Warren, Michael's father, digging holes or taking time off work with a bad back which doesn't seem to bother him much after his retirement. Earlier, he's in his twenties, learning how to throw grenades. He's part of a long file of men who one by one leap up onto a platform with their sergeant, pull the stalk from their iron pineapple, count three, and hurl the death-egg over a high wall of sandbags to explode. Tommy is next in line, wanting to do it right. The chap in front of him pulls out the pin and starts to count. Tom, over-eager, has already jumped up on the platform right behind the nervous soldier, who counts up to three, then accidentally drops the lethal fir-cone at their feet. Sighting along my cue, I hit their sergeant so that he streaks forward, knocking Thomas and the other man to either side and simultaneously sweeping the grenade over the barrier; into the death's-head pocket, and we builders at the table all throw up our hands. Iiiiiyyyessssssss!

I see the stipple and the hatch, the filigree and the fine shading. I see Doreen Warren carefully unwrap the cherry-menthol Tune and place it in her infant's mouth. I see the councillor, Jim Cockie, in his bed full of bad dreams. I see the pavement artist Jackie Thimbles, and Tom Hall, the minstrel ghost. I see Fat Kenny Nolan as he contemplates the species of *datura* he has cultivated, and I smile to see it is an Angel's Trumpet with the blossom's white bell hanging down, all rueful. I see Roman Thompson sitting in a borrowed car, silently in the darkened mouth of Fish Street with a snooker cue at rest on the back seat behind him, cold blood coursing through his heart. I see John Newton after his unblinding. I see Thursa Vernall turning German bombers into her accompanists, and the heroic dream of Britton Johnson. I see Lucia Joyce and Samuel Beckett, see him chatting to her in the institution; by her graveside. I see miseries. I see redemptions.

I see Audrey Vernall on the dance-hall stage, her fingers trickling on the keys of her accordion, tossing back her hair, with one small blue shoe keeping time on the worn boards, skirt swinging, *"When The Saints Go Marching In"*. Her tight smile falters in the spotlight and her eyes keeping darting sideways to the wings where her dad Johnny, the band's manager, gives her the thumbs-up, nods encouragingly at her, and then, later on, he's taking off his loud checked jacket, hanging it up on the hook for dressing gowns behind her bedroom door.

I see Thomas á Becket, and I see the brown-skinned woman with the scar who works from the St. Peter's Annexe up in two thousand and twenty-five. I see the saints go marching in.

I see the dog turd on the central walk of Bath Street flats, unbroken on the Friday afternoon, stepped in by midday Saturday when Michael Warren notices it on his way to Alma's exhibition.

I step back before the canvas, reeling in its splendour.

At the very start there are a thousand planets racketing about the solar system, ricocheting and rebounding, pulverising one another in a pinball free-for-all, and this is where we get the idea for our trilliard table. Something hits the fledgling world, with debris from both bodies settling at the edges of Earth's field of gravity, coagulating to a moon, a lucky opening break.

Some short while later a less sizeable projectile makes its impact, and also its contribution to the culling of the thunder-lizards. In the aftermath, amoebic creatures called agglutinated foraminifera clothe themselves within protective tests of meteoric nickel and space-cobalt; plate their unicellular forms in peacock displays of microscopic diamond dust. The ornaments of their miniature cosmos, clad with jewellery from the void they scintillate there in the Late Cretaceous silence, in the very dusk of life. They neither know about nor have concern for the extinctions of the macrocosm. They remain oblivious to the trees and monsters toppling and dying overhead, in the long night that follows the extra-terrestrial collision. In their multitudes they are as various as snowflakes and yet I know each one intimately, know them by their individual coruscations, their signature sparkle. They move with the moon's pull, with the magnet-tides, as do the generations that come after them, migrating on lunar meridians to feed the underwater bugs that feed the fish, that feed the birds and bears and crouching monkey-men.

You will appreciate that our game involves a great deal of strategy.

Sometimes we're on the ball. Sometimes we get distracted, miss the easy shot, but only when we're meant to. I give Solomon the holy torus and he wears it on his index finger when he subjugates the howling djinns that have rampaged through Egypt and the Middle East as an infernal weather-pattern, as a hornet swarm. When he elects that they should build his temple I try to prevent it with a safety shot but I misjudge; I miss.

The binding of the fiends is going well enough until the sorcerer-king gets to the thirty-second spirit, at which point the King is obviously out of his depth. He has failed to anticipate the unbelievable ferocity that senior devils like Asmodeus will resort to if you have them in a corner. The thing takes shape in the pentacle, three-headed and no bigger than a doll astride the cat-sized dragon form that is its steed. The bull's-head lows, the ram's-head bleats, and the crowned human dwarf's-head in the centre lets forth both a flood of terrifying threats and its vile breath alike, to fill the room. It stamps the pommel of its gory lance upon the flagstones and the magus panics, flinching back so that the lamen hung about his neck comes untied at one end and clatters to the floor. By then the chamber is aflame with flickering spider-salamanders and the operation has become a screaming pandemonium, a catastrophe. I close my marbled eyes and turn away.

In consequence of this I do not know what next occurred. It may be that the founder of the temple was possessed by the efreet, or it may be as rabbinical scholars claim, with Solomon flung far away into a desert land and driven from his wits while the triumphant demon steals his shape. It may be that Asmoday merely takes advantage of the King's discomfiture to plant destructive notions in his mind, or it may well be that the thirty-second spirit does nothing at all, and all of the calamities to come are Solomon's alone. I only know that when I look back, the First Temple is completed, with the malice of the seventy-two tempters, flatterers and devastators coded in its columns and its lines. A focus for the world's three most belligerent religions, I see crusade, jihad and retaliatory air-strike circling the pillars of the structure's round. I see a foul and fruity pulp of tortured men, raped women and pulverised children sliding down its ancient walls.

King Solomon. What a colossal idiot.

———

Derek James Warner, 42, works as a driver for one of the big private security providers. Derek's looking forward to the Friday night ahead of him, out scouting for a bit of skirt and confident he'll be successful, even though he's greying at the temples, even though he's put on a few pounds just recently and even though he's married with two children, Jennifer and Carl.

His wife Irene has taken them off to her mother's house in Caister for the weekend. Derek drove them up there, but forgot to unload all the children's rubber rings and beach-toys from the boot before he drove back home again. Irene has given him a bollocking for that over the phone already, earlier this evening. Derek doesn't give a fuck. He can't remember the last time the two of them had sex, the last time that he'd felt any desire for her. That's why he's off out on the prowl tonight, because of her.

He sits on the settee, the one that he's still paying for despite the fact that it's already knackered, perched beside the handset of his son Carl's X-Box as he smokes a crystal chip of methamphetamine. He's picked this up – the habit and the drug itself – from Ronnie Ballantine, another driver at the company that Derek works for. Ballantine's a cocoa-shunter, though you wouldn't know to talk to him. Great big bloke, great big driver's forearms. He'd told Derek about crystal meth, how it would keep you going all night with a hard-on like a ripping chisel. Derek likes the sound of that.

He finishes the rock then goes out jingling his keys impatiently and climbs into the black Ford Escort. He feels like a killer robot or one of the Gladiators that they used to have on the TV. His Gladiator codename would be either Dominator or Tarantula, he can't make up his mind. He's getting movements in the corners of his vision, things that bob up into view but vanish if you look at them directly, like a game of Whack-A-Mole, but overall he's feeling lucky, feeling good.

Look out, girls.

Here he comes.

———

Lucia Joyce is dancing on the madhouse lawn. Her twirling body is a fragile coracle, becalmed there on the still green sea of grass. She circles beautifully without effect, one of her inner oars misplaced. Her crossing has no other side, no harbour, no admirers cheering on the docks and no ships' whistles blowing when her craft at last comes into view on the horizon. The reception crowd have either all died waiting or have given up on her and finally gone home.

Her Da, while living, sees her as a work in progress and perpetually unfinished, an abandoned masterpiece. Perhaps one day he'll have another go at her, fiddle with her a bit and try to sort out the stalled plotlines, all the uncompleted sentences, but then he dies and leaves her stranded there in the excluded information, the ellipses ...

Lucia's family have edited her out, reduced her to a footnote in the yarn, all but excised her from the manuscript. Dear Sam still visits her, of course, but doesn't love her, or at least not in the way she thought he did, the way she wanted him to love her. This too, as she sees it, is her father's fault. By making Sam into the literary son he's always wanted, he's transformed that lovely man into the brother Lucia already has and never asked for in the first place. Beckett loves her like a sister. Nothing can go on between them now without occurring in an atmosphere of incest; in an air that Lucia can no longer bear to breathe. And yet she thinks about the monsoon of his hair, his long and leathery cheek, a sailor's sorry wisdom in his stare.

She dances. She attempts to reduce the complexity of being to a gesture, tries to pull the whole world into every dip and turn, her history, her father's book, the blinding light from the asylum's wet slate roofs. She takes protracted and deliberate paces, planes her open hands as though attempting to smooth wrinkles from the empty space surrounding her. She cranes her neck to strike a perfect hieroglyphic profile so that her imaginary audience won't notice the boss eye. In my sight she is perfect, the slight cast in one orb reminiscent of the ocular deficiency that Michelangelo bestows upon his David, the gaze misaligned deliberately so as to offer the most pleasing views when seen from either side. Such artistry is not intended to be looked full in the face.

Northampton wraps its arms around her, honoured by her presence: she could have gone there-ward but instead washed here-ward in the wake of her unsatisfying tour through European sanatoriums. At last she dances her way out of tempo, out of time into the Kingsthorpe cemetery just up the road from

Michael Warren's house, two or three headstones down from Finnegan himself, with Violet Gibson who shot Mussolini in the nose and was committed to St. Andrew's Hospital not very far away. Lucia pirouettes ecstatic now on the eternal boardwalks of Mansoul. Now she can see straight. She knows what the work progresses to, and knows that not a single step was wasted.

———

I keep up with the continuing argument over 'Intelligent Design', although if one subscribes to late twentieth-century ideas of consciousness as an emergent property, the disagreement vanishes. If self-awareness can emerge from systems that have passed a certain threshold of complexity, then is not the expanding universe of space and time, by definition, the most complex system that can possibly exist? Mark that I do not seek to trespass on the faiths or ideologies of others with this observation. I'm just saying.

———

I glimpse Alma Warren in her early sixties, standing at her easel in the house there on East Park Parade during the year 2016. She steps off from the canvas, squints and curls her lip, mugging for cameras that aren't there. She angles her long body forward as if stooping over prey and slops a thick impasto curl of dirty cream along a splashing wave-top, then leans back again, considering.

The large acrylic image is one of a series that she's working on at present, for an exhibition tentatively titled *Landscapes?* These are scenic views which would at one point have been in the category suggested by that title, but are in the process of transforming into something else, a more ambiguous state. The painting that Alma is currently engaged with shows a public house towards the north end of the Yarmouth seafront, an art-deco structure from the 1930s called the Iron Duke. Though semi-derelict as it's depicted here, the pub retains a grandness and a generosity of spirit, vestiges of the brave, misplaced optimism typifying the decade of its inception.

A decaying beauty, in its salad days it stands adjacent to North Denes, the busy caravan camp where Alma and Michael are brought by their parents for a factory fortnight, almost every summer of their childhoods. They meet all their Spring Lane classmates and their Boroughs neighbours on the salty promenades, in bulb-lit pub yards carpeted with cockleshells, the greater part of working-class Northampton having relocated to the east coast for the same two long-anticipated weeks.

The pub is now positioned slightly right of centre, in the painting's middleground. Its rear-yard walls of dark red brick are listing from the building's central bulk, slowly collapsing, while the glass panes of the higher moulded windows are surprisingly intact. Surrounding the deteriorated edifice are only the North Sea's expanded waters. Wavelets capped with grey detergent suds lap at the fan of steps that lead, beneath a crumbling portico, from the saloon bar to a submerged car park. The deserted terrace with its curving balustrade now looks more like the fo'c'sle of a foundered galleon. Barnacles have colonised the lower reaches of the flaking drainpipes.

Alma has applied a texture to the drowned pub's scabby brickwork, speckling its distressed surfaces with minute dabs of purple that are almost black, so that the walls seem pitted as though by ancient corrosions. This technique, known as decalcomania, is borrowed from the great surrealist Max Ernst, and in this instance is a reference to his jewelled and eerie masterpiece, *Europe after the Rain*. Off in the distance of her painting's background Alma has suggested ruined pleasure-beach attractions, decommissioned roller-coasters, skeletal Big Wheels looming above the waterline, their spidery lines just visible through scumbled morning haze that she's created using a dry brush. She wants the work to be at once serene, sad and unsettling; intends to use the hostelry and its clean Bauhaus contours as a symbol of man's fragile notions of modernity, succumbing to the old simplicities of time and tide. She wants the viewer to hear gulls, infrequent splashes, and an absence of machines or voices.

In the cluttered ground-floor front room that she uses as her studio, books and paintings in various stages of completion are arranged haphazardly. A creased and battered paperback edition of *The Drowned World*, J.G. Ballard's lyric conjuring of watery apocalypse, rests open on one worn arm of an equally distressed leather settee. A hashish smog has gathered under the high ceiling. It's been ten years since her exhibition in the Boroughs. She's more famous, more ungrateful and withdrawn than ever. Alma finds herself identifying with the ruin in the painting, both of them falling to bits and jutting picturesquely and conspicuously from an otherwise flat and unruffled ocean, both of them still decent-looking in a good light, if you like that sort of thing.

She paints until the brink of dusk, then walks to Marks & Spencer's on Abington Avenue to buy a ready-meal. Above the cricket ground the evening sky grades like over-diluted lemon squash.

———

I sit through all of the extinctions, all the species that have reached the natural end of their extension into the concealed direction.

Every other week, a human language dies. Beautiful, unique life forms with intricate skeletons of grammar, delicately hinged by syntax, they grow weaker and fold in their wings of adjectival gossamer. They make their last frail noises and then crumble into incoherence, into silence, no more to be heard.

A stilled tongue, every fortnight. A concluded song. Hark, the glad sound.

———

There is a television channel that is broadcast only to the nearly dead, transmitted on a disinfectant fug through care-home dayrooms, terminal ward twilights. Senile screens provide the best reception, signals sparking in corroded diodes, fraying synapses. The station's logo, white upon closed-eyelid black, depicts a crudely rendered set of balances above the winding ribbon of a stylised path. Accompanying this there is a four-note trumpet flourish, serving as the channel's theme-tune.

Albert Good sits in the armchair at his Duston home, having just woken from a nap to find the telly on and some sort of afternoon play in progress. Even though it's all in black and white, Albert can tell immediately that it's one of those modern dramas that he doesn't care for much, one of those Wednesday-night things where somebody's always either sleeping rough or pregnant. He'd get up and switch it off, but he's been feeling so run-down just lately that he hasn't got the energy, can only sit and watch.

There seems to only be one set involved in the production, with the audience looking at a broad flight of stone steps which rise beneath the huge porch of a church. Giant stone columns, more than likely made from painted plywood, rear up at each side, framing the scene. To Albert, it looks very like the front of All Saints Church here in Northampton, although he supposes that there must be lots of places throughout England that look similar, having been built around the same time and in the same style. Between the Gothic pillars it is night. The only lighting is positioned to resemble that of off-stage streetlamps, filtering into a pearly gloom beneath the portico.

Whichever town the play is set in, it appears to be almost deserted after dark. To Albert's way of thinking this suggests it's taking place some years ago, possibly just after the war, before midnight town centres were lit up like Christmas trees and full of drunken youngsters. All the props and scenery have that cosy post-war feel about them, something Albert only finds these days in local photograph collections or in reprints of the annual *Giles* editions, the authentic flavour of the air back then. He squints uneasily in the direction of the relatively tiny screen and tries to make sense of what's going on.

A man and woman, both in middle age, are sitting on the cold stone steps, stage centre. Albert finds the pair familiar and is almost certain that he's seen both actors previously, in something else. The man, who wears a loud checked jacket, might have been in *Hi-de-hi*, now Albert comes to think of it. The woman, with her coat pulled tight around her neck against the evening's chill and weeping intermittently, is possibly Patricia Haynes when she was younger. Though they seem to be a married couple, there is too much space upon the step between them. When the husband shuffles closer to the wife she flinches and moves further off, away from him. Their dialogue is sparse and cryptic, with long silences between the questions and the answers. Albert can't make head or tail of it.

Even more baffling are the drama's other characters, four or five figures in outlandish clothes who loiter underneath the portico, behind the man and woman in the foreground. Despite the oddness of their clothing and how loudly they are talking, neither of the seated couple seem to be aware of them. Eventually Albert works out that these other players, the ones chatting in the background, are meant to be ghosts of some sort. They can see the living wife and husband sitting on the church steps, and pass comment on them, but the mortal pair can't see the phantoms and presume they are alone. Albert finds this disturbing. It gives the impression of so many ghosts that every paving stone and public toilet in the country must surely be haunted, every human conversation overheard by the eavesdropping dead.

He doesn't want to look at this. He turns away and shuts his eyes. Although he isn't able to determine the exact point at which he nods off again, he later realises that he must have done. When he awakens, Lou has come back from the shops. The television is now silent, from which Albert concludes that Lou must have switched it off when she came in. She asks him how he's feeling, and he tells her about the upsetting play or old film or whatever it was meant to be.

"I watched this thing on telly that had ghosts in it. I didn't like it much, to tell the truth. It put the willies up me. I don't think they ought to show that kind of effort in the afternoons, when you've got kiddies home from school. I think it's shocking. I've a good mind to complain."

Lou cocks her head on one side like a bird and looks at him, then glances at the unplugged television set, which is just as she left it when she went out earlier. She clucks over her husband sympathetically, agrees that all the programmes these days are a waste of license money and then makes a pot of tea for both of them. Within an hour the mystery theatre presentation is forgotten.

When this secret television station of the near dead is off air it cannot be detected, except as a high-pitched and near ultrasonic whistling tone experienced in the inner ear. If you just listen carefully, you'll find that you can hear it now.

———

Hymns are, of course, tremendously important, be they penned by William Blake, John Bunyan, Philip Doddridge or John Newton. An attempted transcendental poetry intended for the common multitude, they fertilise the dreams and visions that shall grow into the very boardwalks of Mansoul. As they delineate Hell or depict Heaven, so too do they build those places, brick by brick, stanza by stanza. Come, lift up your hearts and voices and rejoice. Give me a platform of ideas and harmonies on which to gesture and unfurl my wings. Give me a place to stand.

I know I am a text. I know that you are reading me. This is the biggest difference that there is between us: you do not know that you are a text. You don't know that you're reading yourself. What you believe to be the self-determined life that you are passing through is actually a book already written that you have become absorbed in, and not for the first time. When this current reading is concluded, when the coffin-lid rear cover is eventually shut tight, then you immediately forget that you've already struggled through it and you pick it up again, perhaps attracted by the striking and heroic picture of yourself that's there on the dust-jacket.

You wade once more through the glossolalia of the novel's opening and that startling birth-scene, all in the first person, foggily described in a confusion of new tastes and scents and terrifying lights. You linger in delight over the childhood passages and savour all the powerfully realised new characters as they are introduced, the mother and the dad, the friends and relatives and enemies, each with their memorable quirks, their singular allure. Engrossing as you find these youthful exploits, you discover that you're merely skimming certain of the later episodes out of sheer boredom, thumbing through the pages of your days, skipping ahead, impatient for the adult content and pornography that you assume to be awaiting you in the next chapter.

When this turns out to be less an unalloyed joy, less abundant than you have anticipated, you feel vaguely cheated and you rail against the author for a time. By then though, all the story's major themes are welling up around you in the yarn, madness and love and loss, destiny and redemption. You begin to understand the true scale of the work, its depth and its ambition, qualities that have escaped you until now. There is a dawning apprehension, a sense that the tale might not be in the category you have previously supposed, that of the picaresque adventure or sex-comedy. Alarmingly, the narrative progresses past the reassuring borderlines of genre into the unnerving territory of the avant-garde. For the first time you wonder if you've bitten off far more than you can chew, embarked upon some weighty magnum opus by mistake when you'd intended to pick up only a pot-boiler, holiday reading for the airport or the beach. You start to doubt your capabilities as reader, doubt in your ability to stick this mortal fable out to its conclusion without the attention wandering. And even if you finish it, you doubt that you're astute enough to understand the saga's message, if message there be. You privately suspect that it will sail over your head, and yet what can you do but keep on living, keep turning the calendar-leaf pages, urged on by that cover-blurb that says: "If you read only one book in your life then make it this one."

Not until you're more than halfway through the tome, near the two-thirds mark, do the earlier, seemingly random plot points start to make some kind of sense to you. The meanings and the metaphors begin to resonate; the ironies and the motifs reveal themselves. You're still not certain if you've read all this before or not. Some elements seem awfully familiar and you have occasional premonitions as to how one of the subplots will work out. An image or a line of dialogue will sometimes strike a chord of déjà vu, but by and large it all seems like a new experience. It doesn't matter if this is a second or a hundredth reading: it seems fresh to you, and, whether begrudgingly or not, you seem to be enjoying it. You don't want it to end.

But when it is concluded, when the coffin-lid rear cover is eventually shut tight, you immediately forget that you've already struggled through it and you pick it up again, perhaps attracted by the striking and heroic picture of yourself that's there on the dust-jacket. It's the mark of a good book, they say, if you can read it more than once and still find something new each time.

––––––

If you could view the lone house there on Scarletwell Street's corner from a higher geometrical perspective, you would understand why complex and unlikely circumstances had to come about in order for that edifice to remain standing, even when the terrace that it once was part of had been long demolished. When seen in the light of the events and the chronologies it is supporting, it becomes apparent that the isolated house is a load-bearing structure. It provides the anchor and foundation stone for a specific moment and occasion, and it cannot be pulled down before that date, tonight, Friday, May 26th, 2006. It would have been impossible to do so. Seen from one dimension up, the reasons for this would be obvious: time simply isn't built like that. It was one demolition that was never going to happen, or at least, not until it was ready.

In the yellowed light of the front parlour sits the building's occupant, the Vernall made responsible for that specific corner. Humming a jazz standard, they anticipate the frantic banging at the front door that will herald their celestial visitor. Tonight's the night. It's on the cards, it's in the tea leaves. All they have to do is sit and wait for fate, for destiny, and it will all come marching in.

––––––

I see the world, and, through a lens of prose or paint or song or celluloid, the world sees me.

The emerald bauble of the planet, nested on a sequin-dusted jeweller's cushion of black velvet, this is not the world. The several billion apes with improved posture that cavort across the planet's surface, these are likewise not the world. The world is no more than an aggregate of your ideas about the world, of your ideas about yourselves. It is the vast mirage, baroque and intricate, that you are building as a shelter from the overwhelming fractal chaos of the universe. It is composed from things of the imagination, from philosophies, economies and wavering faith, from your self-serving individual agendas and your colourful notions of destiny. It is a flight of fancy spun to while away those empty-bellied Neolithic nights, a wishful fantasy of how mankind might one day live, a campfire tale you tell yourselves and then forget is just a tale that you are telling; that you have made up and have mistaken for reality. Civilisation is your earliest science-fiction story. You come up with it so that you'll have something to do, something to occupy yourselves during the centuries to come. Don't you remember?

For all that it manifests materially in castles, hospitals, sofas and atom bombs, the world is founded in the immaterial reaches of the human mind, is standing on a flimsy paradigm that has no actual substance. And if that foundation does not hold, if it is based perhaps upon a flawed perception of the universe that does not match with later observations, then the whole confection falls into an abyss of unbeing. Both in terms of its construction and its ideology, the world is far from sound. To be quite honest it's a creaking death-trap, and there are all of these health and safety regulations. I don't make the rules.

I am a builder. You'll appreciate that this entails a lot of demolition work. Your world, the way you think about yourselves and your most fundamental notions of reality are the result of unskilled labour, cowboy workmanship. There's bad subsidence; dry rot in the moral timbers. This will all have to come down, and it's not going to be cheap.

Does the phrase "clearance area" mean anything to you?

———

Ideas of self, ideas of world and family and nation, articles of scientific or religious faith, your creeds and currencies: one by one, the beloved structures falling.

Whooomff.

Whooomff.

Whooomff.

A COLD AND FROSTY MORNING

Alma Warren, barely out of bed and naked in the monstrous bathroom mirror, staring bleary at her sagging fifty-three-year-old flesh and still fancying herself something rotten. She finds her enduring vanity almost heroic in the scale of its delusion. She's prepared to face the facts, safe in the knowledge that the facts will only scream and run away. All things considered, she's a funny piece of work.

The big square bathroom with its plaster-rounded corners is a blunted cube of grey steam rising from the eight-foot chasm of the filling tub, an ostentatious lifeboat made from tide-lined fibreglass. Subjected to this sweltering rain-forest climate every morning for at least ten years the chamber's blue and gold-veined lining paper has begun to droop down from the ceiling's curve, a wilted winter sunrise. At the bottom of the giant bath itself there are the studs of an unused Jacuzzi fixture, gilt flaked off to show the dull grey metal underneath. Alma has never really had the knack of keeping something nice.

She picks a bath bomb from the green glass fruit bowl on the counter, Fairy Jasmine from the fragrant branch of Lush down in the Grosvenor Centre, lobs it casually into the deep hot water and takes childish pleasure from the scum of blue metallic glitter that seethes up out of the fizz and foment. She'll have sequinned cheeks, hands, hair and sheets for a few days but, on the plus side, will be living in the early 1970s. Alma climbs up onto the near end of the boxed-in miniature lagoon and strikes a pose like a high diver, squinting down into the steam until she can imagine that her bathtub is a massive reservoir as seen from several hundred feet above. She makes as if about to execute a swallow dive but then appears to change her mind and steps down carefully into her bath in the conventional fashion. This strange pantomime is something she does each day without having any idea why. She only hopes that nobody ever finds out about it.

With a pig-pink soap-bar redolent of Woolworths' Pick'n'Mix she lathers herself everywhere then sluices it all off, relaxing back into the heat and suds until only her face is visible above the surface as a floating mask. The long hair drifts about her outsized skull like waterweed, becoming sleek and saturated as she listens to the ringing underwater noises that her bath makes inadvertently, the peeling gold tap's rhythmic dripping and the amplified scrape of a toenail on the long tub's moulded sides. Alma feels comfortable, reduced to nothing but a bobbing face with all the rest of what she is concealed beneath the bubbles and the drifting clots of iridescent blue. This is essentially the strategy with which she faces life, believing that it lends her the advantage of surprise: there might be anything beneath the suds and sparkle, mightn't there?

After an amniotic minute of submersion she sits up, hair a lank comma dribbling between her shoulder blades, and scoops a viscous palm-full of her lime and sea-salt shampoo from its pot, rubbing the gritty slime into her scalp. The product promises its user traffic-stopping shine and volume, although Alma is unable to remember the last time that she'd stopped traffic in a good way. Moulding her hair forward in a lather-stiffened quiff that sags towards its dripping tip a good eight inches from her forehead, Alma mumbles "Thang yuh verrah much" into the humid fog, then rinses it all off using a peeling golden shower attachment. She is, she likes to believe, the spitting image of the King if he'd lived to be an old woman.

Once the strands are squeaking like violin strings, she turns off the nozzle and lies back, her sodden head draining into the folded towel that she's forethoughtfully placed on the long tub's pointed end. Stretched out full length and motionless, a dead Egyptian monarch whose sarcophagus has first been flooded and then strewn with glitter for unfathomable ritual purposes, Alma reviews her thoughts, such as they are at this time of a Friday morning. Near the surface, a storm-layer of nonsensical rage and resentment is subsiding gradually into this foamy interlude between her breakfast Shreddies, her sensible daily aspirin and her bio-yoghurt drinks, already wolfed down, and her first joint of the day, which is still yet to come. Beneath this scum-line of residual anger is a tediously efficient secretary-strata, listing everything that Alma has to do today, Friday, May 26th, 2006: finish the *Chain of Office* picture, pay her treacherous bloodsucking council tax, go to the bank, visit the little day-care nursery down near Doddridge Church to see if everything has been delivered safely for tomorrow's exhibition. Oh, and shop for food in town, because there's nothing in the fridge except for weird, exotic relishes and dips she's bought while in an altered state. Perhaps she'll pop her head into the Grosvenor Centre branch of HMV to see if the new season of *The Wire* is out yet; maybe trawl the local-interest shelves at Waterstone's, looking for photographs of sepia barges on a brown-ale river; lemming-waves of kids in 1950s swimming costumes running at the camera, splashing through the shallow end of the Midsummer Meadow lido.

Down below this relatively-tidy organising level are the ceaselessly-rotating cogs and flywheels of creative process. These are anxiously reviewing minor irritations in completed works – the central white-haired labourer in *Work in Progress* for example, looking back across his shoulder at the audience with eyes perhaps too stern and frightening – or else are sifting patiently through possibilities for paintings yet to come. She has a nebulous idea that involves tracking down the sites depicted by great, bygone landscape artists, recreating the same view in the same medium, with all the car-crammed motorways and modern alterations rendered classically in lustrous oils with patient glazes, freezing a degraded present in the unforgiving gaze of a more able past. There's something in the notion that appeals to her, but it's too glib and obvious in its present form. Besides, she'll have had five ideas as good or better before she retires tonight. Alma's attention skitters over this and other fledgling projects pretty much non-stop, even while other areas of her awareness are engaged in pressing matters of their own, such as pretending that whomever she is talking to has her complete attention.

Under this productive and untiring shop-floor of the mind we next encounter the vast, monitor-lit basement complex of a super-villainess, where part of Alma's too-elaborate personality sits in a swivel chair amongst the shifting screens and contemplates deranged agendas. These include affecting the development of culture by the subtle introduction of extreme ideas, which, if pursued, will almost certainly precipitate widespread apocalyptic psychological collapse. This will fulfil Alma's ambition, having first gone mad herself, of taking everyone else with her. Then, of course, there's the ongoing scheme to argue her way out of death, which is progressing rather nicely. She sits swivelling and chuckling in her imaginary lair, but does not stroke a cat, having anticipated that her stature as a villainess would be severely undercut by the predictable and obvious sexual pun. Instead, when circumstance requires, she strokes a raucous and red-crested cock.

Descending further there are Jungian catacombs of alchemy, kabbalah, numerology and tarot, paranormal residues resulting from her still-current preoccupation with the occult. She decodes the day around her in accordance with the correspondence-tables of Cornelius Agrippa, Dr. Dee, Aleister Crowley, all the other occult heavyweights. Today's a Friday, Freitag, Vendredi, day of the planet Venus and the number seven, a good female day in all. Its colours are three shades of green with amber as a complement. Its perfume is attar of rose, its metal copper. This specific zone of Alma's consciousness allows itself to be productively distracted by the tangential idea of roses, following a fragile thread of free-association starting with Diana Spencer, "Goodbye, England's Rose", Taupin and John's camp Monroe eulogy refitted for another blonde girl dead of cameras, misplaced ambition, and betrayal. The funeral cortège that Alma's brother Mick had watched, bringing the body home along the summer motorway, thrown blossoms wilting on the bonnet, vivid on the dull gunmetal of the casket. Utter silence from the crowds beside the road. Northamptonshire, Rose of the Shires. The rose originates in Turkey, only red or white varieties available, and it is introduced in Europe by returned crusaders, many of these coming back here to the town where their crusades had started. Proving popular, the flower, in its two distinct shades, is eventually adopted as a symbol by the Houses of both Lancaster and York, with their subsequent conflict settled at the Battle of Cow Meadow, between Beckett's Park and Delapré across the river. Blood and roses, a repetitive motif across the printed fabric of Northampton's muddy skirt.

A little further down are Alma's feelings, her emotional component, a far sunnier and less nightmarish pasture than appearances might lead one to suppose. In this enclosure, all of Alma's friends and pets and family, alive or dead, frolic amidst enactments of her treasured moments. These might represent a dream, a first kiss, or that funny afternoon when she'd been nine, taking a long-cut home through Greyfriars flats down Scarletwell Street, noticing the bush, the single dangling caterpillar. All of Alma's positive experiences are rerouted here for long-term storage. All her negative experiences are fed to an appalling thing with turquoise eyes, kept in a pen behind the recreation area and only taken out for walks upon special occasions.

Under all of this is Alma's soul, the Real of her that cannot be expressed, which is a lovely and ingeniously fashioned artefact, if possibly a little showy and impractical. Essentially, it is that of a serious-minded yet imaginative and very clever seven-year-old girl, and at the moment is dissolving blissfully into the jasmine-scented, sapphire-dusted currents of a scalding hot bath.

When she starts experiencing pangs of proletarian guilt at her minor-celebrity indulgence, which takes only a few minutes in a tub of this preposterous size, she sits up suddenly and pulls the plug out. Leaping from the bath, she tries to dry herself and get her clothes on before all the water has drained gurgling away, a habit that she used to think of as simple efficiency but has since realised is just part of her quite ordinary individual madness. Finally, triumphantly, having completed dressing while the last few nebulae of foam and glitter are still circling the plug's black hole by the simple expedient of not bothering with any underwear, she slings her robe over the banister and thunders down the stairs. It's half-past seven in the morning and time to commence her hectic and demanding schedule of attempting to intimidate the planet's other occupants. It's not that Alma finds this wholly self-imposed task difficult, especially. It's just that there's so many of them, and so little time.

Downstairs, amidst a clutter of rare book and uncompleted canvas that is only reassuring to Alma herself, she fills her space-age kettle-jug and switches on its eerie blue light before settling into her armchair and beginning the construction of her first jazz cigarette. These ostentatiously long items, accurately labelled as "nine-inch Gauloise dick-compensators" by her one-time visitor Alexei Sayle, are a leftover from her younger days when she still went to parties and contrived a reefer long enough to still have something left for herself after it had circumnavigated a room full of people. When her partial deafness and increasing weariness with alcohol led to Alma foregoing parties and most often smoking on her own while working, she simply forgot to modify the length, that's all. It's not that she's a drug-glutton or anything.

When all ten Rizla papers have been glued into a white flag of surrender and the filling of tobacco added, Alma cooks the blunt end of a bar of hash over her Zippo lighter. This current variety, which as a teenager she would have recognised as coming from Afghanistan or Pakistan, has more than likely been renamed Taliban Black to suit the present situation. She reflects upon this as she crumbles the still-smouldering resin into the tobacco, burning her almost entirely nerveless left thumb and forefinger in the process. Next there comes a scrabbling carpet-rolling motion and a swift pass of the gummed edge across Alma's tongue, a twist at one end and a neat insertion of rolled cardboard at the other, all before her blue-lit orgone-kettle in the kitchen has stopped bubbling. She pours the boiling water, spattering, into a horribly dis-coloured BEST AT EVERYTHING mug, guides the sizzling torrent so that it falls on the centre of the circular grey teabag and inflates it satisfyingly into a pillow of trapped heat. Mashing it up against the cup's side with her spoon to squeeze the last drop of its vital juices out, she flips the spent and steaming carcass into her conveniently open pedal bin. Foregoing milk and sugar – she prefers her beverages "black and bitter, how I like my men" – Alma transports the brimming mug back to her living room, her armchair and her waiting contraband cheroot.

Behind her chair there is an arching stained-glass panel where gold stars mark the positions of the kabbalistic spheres against a deep royal blue grading into aquamarine. The low sun through the room's rear window falls through this and drenches Alma in cobalt and yellow radiance as she lights up the cigarette. The painted stars break eggs onto the cyan glaze of her wet hair. She holds the smoke in for a moment and then sits back and exhales into the gathering indigo, luxuriating in her own identity, in the incessant fun and mostly-pleasant strain of simply being her.

As the cloud-chamber of her consciousness begins to warm up, turbines whirring into life as it approaches normal operating speed, she reaches for the nearest page of print to give her rapidly engaging mental processes a point of focus. This turns out to be the latest issue of *New Scientist*, dated May 4th, open at an intriguing article concerning Alma's favourite science philoso-pher, the beautifully-named Gerard 't Hooft, whose criticisms of string theory she'd been so impressed by. It seems that 't Hooft has formulated a hypothesis which would, if proven, finally resolve the quandaries of quantum indetermi-nacy; would resolve them right out of existence, if Alma is reading it correctly. The philosopher apparently suggests that there's a deeper and more fundamental level, as yet undiscovered, underlying the mysterious quantum world. 'T Hooft predicts that once we have developed tunnelling microscopes that can reveal this previously unsuspected layer of reality we'll find that Heisenberg's idea of particles existing in a wide variety of states until observed is an illusion based upon misunderstanding.

Reading all this between alternating sips of tea and smoke, Alma allows herself the guttural chortle of an ogre who's just realised where the schoolchildren are hiding. She can spot a well-constructed dangerous idea when she sees one, and 't Hooft's proposal strikes her as one of the most ingenious conceptual land mines that she's ever heard of. The idea's attractions are immediately apparent. Quantum indeterminacy is the stumbling block preventing any easy resolution of the vast discrepancies between the quantum worldview and the classically-constructed universe of Einstein, Newton and the rest. If tiny subatomic particles behave according to the Lewis Carroll laws that govern quantum physics, then why do entirely different laws govern the stars and planets? The attempts thus far to reconcile the quantum microcosm with the classic macrocosm have led to such mind-wrenching extravagances as string theory, notions that require extra dimensions, ranging between ten and twenty-six, before the mathematics will make sense.

That's not to say that the string theorists might not be correct, Alma observes, but simply to suggest that to her ear it all sounds rather messy and unnecessary. If 't Hooft is right, however, and there is no quantum indeterminacy, then the problem vanishes to leave a unified field theory which accounts for everything without resorting to exotic explanations that can often raise more questions than they answer. She can see how many scientists would find 't Hooft's hypothesis hard to resist, but then there is that other shoe to fall: if there's no quantum indeterminacy, then there's no free will. That, right there, is the problem, and in Alma's estimation it has the potential to make all the other current disputes between Christianity and science pale by comparison.

That's why she's laughing as she reads. It's all this free will business and the way that everybody gets so jittery about it, even thinkers that she has the greatest of respect for. Alma, having worked all year upon her brother Warry's near-death vision, has grown very comfortable with predetermination, with the idea of life as a great recurrence that we re-experience, unvaryingly and eternally. During this time, though, she's learned that both Nietzsche and one of her idols, the Brixton-based artist and magician Austin Osman Spare, have previously formulated almost the same concept but then shied away from it because of the implied negation of free will.

Alma can't see what all the fuss is over. She's convinced that no one really needs free will as long as there is a sustainable illusion of the same to stop everyone going mad. It also seems to her that our perception of free will depends upon the scale at which we view the issue. Looking at a single individual, it's obviously impossible to accurately forecast what will happen to that person during, say, the next five years. This would seem to support the argument for free will and a future that is not yet written. On the other hand, if we consider a large group of people, such as the few thousand souls inhabiting the Boroughs or an average modern sink estate, then our predictions become frighteningly easy and precise. We can state, near enough exactly, just how many people will get sick, get stabbed, get pregnant, lose their jobs, their homes, have minor triumphs on the Lottery, will beat their partners or their kids, will die from cancer or heart failure or sheer blind accident. It strikes her, sitting in the rich blue light and finishing her smoke, that this is the same quandary faced by the physicists, translated into a context of sociology. Why is free will, like quantum indeterminacy, only evident when we look at the microcosm, at a single person? Where does free will disappear to when we turn our gaze upon the larger social masses, on the populations that are the equivalent of stars and planets?

Stubbing out the joint she puts the magazine aside and starts to roll another one. The mug of iron-black tea, only three-quarters finished, has grown cold with small tan platelets formed upon its surface like a skin. She'll make a fresh cup before she gets down to work in a few minutes, now her hair's not dripping anymore.

Still musing on the subject of Gerard 't Hooft she drifts through the next slice of time to find herself stood at her easel by the window, with a newly-filled and steaming mug upon the high table beside her, near the ashtray and the as-yet-unlit second joint propped on its lip. She holds a double-zero brush in her right hand, dead still and horizontal like the raised spear of a patient jungle hunter, unblinking and confident her prey will make a movement before she does. It will give itself away, the image or the line that she is looking for, and then her short dart will stab forward, tipped with poison colour.

On the easel is the final piece to be completed before Alma's exhibition opens up its playschool doors tomorrow morning. The last-minute nature of the painting is due to the fact that Alma didn't make her mind up to include it until fairly recently. Entitled *Chain of Office*, it's an afterthought, a kind of visual epilogue to the preceding works. It shows a single figure, standing posed as though for an official mayoral portrait, on an indistinct and drifting field of almost drinkable green pointillism, a deep emerald smoulder. The imposing subject, features still unfinished, stands draped in a strange and ornate ceremonial robe that hides the contours of its body, which could just as easily be male or female. Lacking a completed face to rest upon, the eye is drawn to the exotic and cascading fabric of the gown, which, upon close examination, seems to be what the whole picture is about. The intricate design of detailed scenes set in irregularly contoured panels, linked by a gold filigree of branching lines, turns out to be a lavishly illuminated map of Alma's former neighbourhood, from Sheep Street to Saint Andrew's Road, from Grafton Street to Marefair. On the decorated hem is a motif of paving stones, each individually cracked and weathered, fringed with seams of bright viridian moss. The cuff-buttons are glued-on snail-shells. Isomorphic images of Doddridge Church, bulging with ranting puritans, seem to be painted or embroidered on the garment's folds, with Spring Lane School and Scarletwell Street sliding from a hanging pleat into the crease's umber.

The imposing figure stands with both hands raised in welcome or in benediction, draped in its astounding coat of maps. Hung round the neck, in a dull grey that stands out strikingly against the riotous surrounding colour of the vestments, is the dented gong of an old saucepan lid attached to what appears to be a length of lavatory chain.

Alma's one problem with the piece is that she can't decide whose face this splendid Boroughs totem should be wearing. Philip Doddridge's, perhaps? Black Charley's? What about the sweet owl roundness of Alma's beloved and deceased Aunt Lou, lost in a lightning storm? No. No, that will look wrong, perched on an already-completed body that is differently proportioned. She puts down her hovering brush and picks the joint up, lighting the touch-paper twist. After a pull or two, she sets the fuming column back down in the ashtray and retrieves her brush, having arrived at a decision.

For the next two hours she works upon the face until she's satisfied, then spends a further half hour gazing love-struck at the finished painting, basking in her own magnificence. Finally, her vanity starts to exhaust her. Alma feels she's earned a break.

She stands, with a theatrical sciatic groan, and slouches out into the kitchen where she fries up sliced halloumi while a brace of pitta pockets puff and fatten in the oven. When the thick-cut steaks of cheese have taken on a leathery autumnal mottle she retrieves them from the pan; slips them inside the pouches of warm bread with an accompanying spill of mixed leaf salad and some guillotined tomatoes. She can never eat halloumi without feeling a misguided sense of vegetarian guilt. This is because her first taste of the fibrous and salt Greek delicacy, decades earlier, had led her to assume that the halloumi was a possibly-endangered species of Cypriot fish. Even though she knows better now, she still can't shake the frisson of forbidden and delicious flesh that comes with every carefully-chewed mouthful, and in fact she rather likes it that way.

After she's devoured whichever meal her hasty fry-up was supposed to represent – elevenses or brunch or lunkfast (her own coinage) – Alma gets rid of the plate and rolls another smoke. Having completed *Chain of Office*

an hour earlier than she'd anticipated she has time to pick over a couple of
her other projects, maybe make laborious, autistic-looking jottings in block
capitals across whatever unmarked pages she can find in one of several work-
books. She has never mastered joined-up handwriting. Along with tying
shoelaces the ordinary way, it is a skill that she experienced initial problems
with and instantly gave up on, stubbornly resolving that she'd come up with
her own approach to things and stick with it, even if it was obviously wrong.
This is the formative decision, made when she was seven, that has shaped her
entire subsequent existence. In a recent interview, when asked if the political upheaval of the 1960s had caused Alma's fiercely individual approach to
life, her puzzling response of, "No, it was those fucking shoelaces" apparently
became the subject of much speculation on the message boards she never saw
but only heard about.

Settling back into her chair, her nest of curling vapour ribbons, she picks
up the nearest blank-paged and hard-covered exercise book from the cluttered
coffee table on her left, scooping up a blue ballpoint pen that still looks viable
while doing so. She makes a few notes on the possible autobiography that she's
considered writing, which at present isn't much more than a paragraph or two
about her nan, May, and a working title, *We Was Poor But We Was Cannibals*.
Alma composes a few dozen chapter headings, phrases that seem funny, resonant or smugly clever to her, and makes tiny notes beside each one suggesting
what ideas or episodes that chapter might include. The details and the actual
meat of things can all be worked out later, on the hoof, on wings and prayers.

Conveniently satisfied with her half-hour's work just as she is starting to
get bored with it, she puts the workbook down and reaches for whichever
paperback or magazine or comic is closest to hand. As it transpires, this is
a polythene-bagged copy of *Forbidden Worlds*, seemingly issue 110, dated
March-April 1963 and published by the long-since vanished ACG, or American Comics Group. Being both sick and tired of the protracted adolescence
typifying the contemporary comic business, publications of this vintage are
almost the only ones that Alma will allow into the house.

Removing the frail pamphlet gently from the elderly and wilting plastic of
its envelope, Alma examines the admittedly completely crappy covers, front
and back. The rear is an advertisement, in black and white, for an impressive
catalogue of novelties from Honor House Productions, boldly labelled as a
"TREASURE CHEST OF FUN". The fun seems to involve confusing adults
with ventriloquism, frightening them with a cigarette-dispensing lighter
that "looks like a Browning automatic", or increasing their nuclear anxiety
with an Atomic Smoke Bomb: "Just light one and watch the column of white
smoke rise to the ceiling, mushrooming into a dense cloud like an A-Bomb."
These cost twenty cents. Also available are silent dog-whistles, Ju-Jitsu les-

sons promising that YOU, TOO, CAN BE TOUGH, a deck of marked cards
and the snappily-described SEE BEHIND GLASSES that "enable you to see
behind you without anyone knowing you're watching. Really comes in handy
at times." Struggling to imagine on precisely which occasions these wing-
mirrored spectacles would "really come in handy", other than if she should
be compelled to back her massive head out of a cul-de-sac, she turns instead
to the front cover, all in citrus colour with its oversized seal of approval from
the once-important Comics Code Authority and the black "9d" imprint of a
British newsagent stamped on the planet-decorated logo.

The front image, by an artist Alma doesn't recognise, is clearly a generic
piece of cover artwork pulled from the inventory. It shows a thuggish-looking
monk clad in green robe and hood grimacing from within a fortune-teller's
crystal ball. A blue-tinged cover blurb appended to the illustration tries to
justify it by pretending that the sulky-looking figure in the snow-globe is "just
ONE" of various menaces that the anthology's single continuing character,
Herbie, would meet inside. Flicking through two or three nondescript tales of
strange adventure to the Herbie story at the back, the only reason that she's
kept the tattered comic-book, Alma discovers that this is the ruse she had suspected. The green monk is nowhere to be seen throughout the ten-page yarn,
a favourite of Alma's called "Herbie and the Sneddiger's Salad Oil".

Herbie had been created several issues previously in what may have
been intended as a one-off tale. Readers, however, were intrigued by its protagonist, a spherical and solemn schoolboy with a bowl-cut hairdo, horn-
rimmed glasses, unexpected supernatural powers and an unusual obsession
with fruit-flavoured lollipops. Due to this favourable response the character
appeared more frequently from then on, clad in his trademark attire of weirdly
scaled-down adult clothing with blue pants, white shirt and a black tie. While
obviously not a look that everyone could get away with, Herbie would have
bailed out of *Forbidden Worlds* within a year of issue 110 and be established
as the title character in his own comic, of which Alma owns a very-near complete collection.

The main reason for this singular compulsion is Alma's infatuation with
the strip's distinctively obsessive artist, Ogden Whitney. Whitney, working
in the business since the 1940s, had a drawing style that somehow managed
to take smothering suburban blandness to extremes which should have been
the envy of the avant-garde. His tidily-coiffured cast of generic middle-class
Americans might have stepped from a magazine ad for soap-powder, cars
or coffee were it not for a conspicuous lack of grinning toothy confidence.
Instead, his characters wear tight expressions of barely-suppressed anxiety as
they stand hesitating in the kitchens of their uniform white-painted homes or
loiter upon bright green lawns so neatly-shorn as to be utterly devoid of tex-

ture, mere outlines left for the colourist to fill. And then, amidst this twitchy Cold War landscape with its populace of clenched neurotics, there is the still, planetary mass of Herbie Popnecker.

According to the legend, ACG house-writer Richard Hughes, writing under the pseudonym of Shane O'Shea, had become fascinated by the way in which the literal-minded Whitney would draw anything the script required of him in the same blandly realistic style. Possibly to amuse himself, the writer's scripts become more comically surreal as the series progresses, treating the already baffled readership to strange encounters between the impassive levitating dumpling-child and a selection of then-current film-stars and world leaders like the Kennedys, Nikita Khrushchev, Fidel Castro, Queen Elizabeth the Second, or the Burtons. Typically, female celebrities are smitten with the spherical and enigmatic ten-year-old. Ladybird Johnson, Jackie Kennedy, Liz Taylor and Her Majesty the Queen all sigh and heave their bosoms as he walks away into the sky with an expression of supreme indifference, an unlikely fanny-magnet sucking jadedly upon a lollipop as round as he is.

All these real-life luminaries coexist contentedly with things from outer space, broom-riding witches, talking animals, anthropomorphic objects and the supernatural denizens of ACG's distinctive green-tinged afterlife. This occult region, carpeted in limeade-coloured clouds, is a Rod Serling version of Eternity that features intermittently across the outfit's other books and is referred to as "The Unknown" on what looks like a hand-painted sign in its cumulus-strewn reception area. The place is an abode of sheet-clad ghosts, trolls, leprechauns and monsters cribbed from Universal Studios' back catalogue, along with wingless, robed custodians who seem like biliously-hued Frank Capra angels, tubby and avuncular. It distantly occurs to Alma that she may well have been influenced in some way by this secular, fantastical and folksy view of paradise while realising Warry's childhood vision in the paintings and the illustrations she's been working on for this last year. Despite the lack of any similarity between their styles, Alma's elaborate depiction of a higher Boroughs filled with dreams and fiends and phantoms probably owes a great deal to Ogden Whitney's staid surrealism.

On the other hand she is aware that Whitney's merits, many though they be, are merely camouflage to mask the actual nature of her interest in his work. This is entirely based on Alma's extreme identification with the artist's best-known character. She'd been a portly little lump herself before her frankly terrifying growth-spurt and, like Whitney's hero, had endured a pudding-basin haircut. She had also shared Herbie's conviction that the powers and forces of the universe should all know her by name and have the basic common sense to get out of her way. In the adventure that she's holding in her red-nailed strangler's hands, "Herbie and the Sneddiger's Salad Oil", the omnipotent schoolboy scares away a full grown Frankenstein, a barrage of machine-gun bullets that have worried little faces and which swerve from their trajectory on recognising Herbie, lion-headed alien dinosaurs from the beleaguered planet Bertram, and even such astronomical phenomena as an aggressive comet, which veers from its course in panic at its first sight of the lollipop-addicted human bowling ball. As Alma sees it, this is no more than the same polite respect which she expects rampaging elephants, Cruise missiles, werewolves, corporations, bolts of lightning and invading spacemen to extend to her.

Another reason for her empathy is Herbie's eyes, both for the heavy-lidded bored look that she knows from her own baby-photographs and for the ugly spectacles that he's apparently compelled to wear. That's how she could have ended up, what with the almost useless left eye that she has inherited from her mum, Doreen. She had only managed to avoid a pair of National Health face-deformers by the application of her seven-year-old ingenuity. When taken by her mother for a mandatory school eye-test, Alma had glanced at the chart in passing and had memorised it, top to bottom, utilising the extraordinary powers of recall that neither her school-friends nor family had noticed yet, and which she hadn't been in any hurry to inform them of. The school optician had clamped Alma's outsized head in Clockwork Orange goggles, then had pointed to the hovering grey blurs that floated in the fog while she reeled out a list of letters that she couldn't see for toffee. This technique had kept her glasses-free until her teenage years, when the eye-test procedure had been altered unexpectedly and Alma had been caught out as a half-blind fraud with an almost vampiric sensitivity to light. She'd subsequently been made to endure two years of thin frames and blue-tinted lenses that had somehow managed to make her look even more pretentious than she was already. When one lens fell out and shattered, Alma's colour-blind optician had replaced it with pink-tinted glass that made her look like someone from the audience of a 3D film. By then, she'd made her mind up that her vision without glasses was deteriorating, and this latest outrage had just piled insult on injury. She'd thrown the two-tone spectacles away, resolving that if she was going to go blind then she'd do it on her own terms, thank you very much. Later she'd learned that wearing no lenses at all produced what was known as a "negative lensing effect" within the muscles of the eye that actually improves the vision. Or is it a positive lensing effect? It doesn't matter. All that matters is that in Alma's own estimation, she's been proven right. It's Alma one, opticians nil, as far as she's concerned.

Returning her attention to the story she is reading, Alma thinks again of Ogden Whitney, of his sad demise as detailed in *Art out of Time*, the lovely volume that Mike Moorcock sent her as a thank you for her cover illustration on a recently reissued Elric paperback. Within the wonderful collection of neglected and peculiar comic strips from bygone times, Alma had been delighted to see a characteristically demented *Herbie* offering included, with accompanying text about the artist. She'd been touched if unsurprised to learn that Herbie's looks and general physique were based on those of Ogden Whitney as a child, and had filled up with tears to read how he had died, forgotten and insane from booze in an asylum. She imagines Herbie in his sixties, sitting in the day room at the home, white shirt and blue pants traded in for a stained bathrobe and his differently-powered lollipops replaced by bottles. The time-travel bottle-pop would be the only one that worked. His sleepy eyes gazing unfocussed through thick beer-glass lenses and his paunch now drum-tight with the enlarged liver. Greying, bowl-cut head filled with his flat, precisely-drawn dementia, lion-dragons and Sneddiger's Salad Oil, the many ghosts and featured creatures of a green Unknown.

Taking a last pull on the sepia-streaked stub she grinds it out and stands up with another creaking outcry at the dull ache in her back. She's barely consciously aware she makes these noises anymore, so constant and repetitive have they become. Sorting amongst the notebooks, comics, pens and paperbacks Alma locates a hairbrush that has somehow managed to survive its daily skirmish with her head. This one, a sturdy wooden item that is capable of 'MEGA Taming' if one pays attention to the printed promise on its handle, has already lasted for over a year with no more than a dozen or so of its plastic teeth wrenched out. Its predecessors, that have snapped in two or have been otherwise dismantled by their first or second painful drag through Alma's tangled locks, were simpering pansies by comparison.

She's learned early in life that if she doesn't brush her mane once every day it will develop knots that in a week will have turned to impacted rhino horn; bolls of mahogany that it will take tree-surgeons, chainsaws, ropes and ladders to remove. Closing her eyes she starts to pull the brush down from the crown, her face immediately concealed behind a grey-brown safety curtain as the bristles rake excruciatingly through the unyielding snarls. The sound of ripping follicles and snapping vinyl prongs, she has discovered, make the ritual far more upsetting for anyone forced to listen to it than it is for her. Her artist friend Melinda Gebbie, would sit covering her ears and whimpering if she were witness to a brushing, frightened that Alma would yank part of her skull away while Alma was herself apparently oblivious to this self-scalping. Her relationship with pain has largely been one of indifference since she realised that its actual physical component rarely hurt that much, and that it is the psychological and the emotional attached files that do all the harm. As far as she is able, therefore, she has disconnected hurtful physical sensations from accompanying mental reflexes of shock or fear or anger. As a minor by-product of this largely successful process, Alma is no longer even ticklish. She terrorizes those who are with absolute impunity.

The worst part of the ordeal is now over. Alma's giant head is now concealed within a church bell made of hair, so that if they should view her from the shoulders upwards, onlookers would have no clue as to which way round she was standing. Lifting both hands, Alma scrabbles with her scarlet fingernails down what feels like the middle of her Rushmore cranium in order to create a centre parting, dragging back the faded auburn curtains to each side so that she can peer at the mirror hung above the fireplace and weigh up the result. Alma decides that she particularly likes the vagrant ash-and-copper strand that snakes across her almost-blind left eye, which is her scariest one, possibly because it's governed by the mad pre-verbal basilisk of her right brain. Alma's right eye is the humane and twinkling one which understands that it's preferable if people – humans as she calls them – like her and aren't frightened off by her appearance or behaviour. Conversely, Alma's left eye clearly doesn't give a fuck. It glowers, grey and yellow and unfocussed, from beneath an overhanging forehead that swells gently into noticeable bumps, as if she's either growing horns or a new frontal lobe.

Hair sorted, Alma paints a face on in the style pioneered by Mr. Potato Head. Her eyelashes soon sag beneath the weight of the mascara and resemble the deleted giant spider scene from the original *King Kong*. Next, pouting like Mick Jagger before the embalmers got to him, she coats her lips in a bloody impasto of red lippy. She believes that this wards off potential rapists and the like by making her appear to be the more voracious sexual predator. Finally satisfied, she grins at her reflection. Every day is Halloween for Alma.

Pulling on an ancient leather jacket, its lapels hung with a fat crop of outdated causes thick as August blackberries, she's almost ready to confront the yammering planet and stare down reality again, but first she has to put her rings and finger-armour on. A splendidly malevolent array of jointed metal talons, sculpted scorpions and rearing silver snakes alongside a selection of big, colourful and bruising gemstones, these lethal adornments probably contribute more than the carnivorous lipstick to her rape-proofing, she realises upon the rare occasions when she thinks realistically. One slap and an assailant's features would be hanging off in strips of soggy wallpaper. She'd do it, too. She'd once informed her brother Warry that although she almost thought of him as family, she'd open him without a second's hesitation like a tin of Hula Hoops.

Making sure she's got her chequebook and her key, she hurls herself along a cluttered hallway that has swathes of gold stars licking up its walls, out through a specially-carved front door with twin snakes in a caduceus design, down her front path onto East Park Parade. Its York stone paving slabs are bathed in clear blonde sunlight, a presentiment of summer, with the lovely trilobite erosions of an ancient riverbed picked out in sharp relief. Across the busy Kettering Road are the tall trees that edge the Racecourse, a green fringe around the immense parkland's mile-wide lampshade sky. People walk on the broad grey paths in ones and twos or cut an independent course across the rolling sea of grass. Someone is trying to fly a kite, perhaps in an attempt to recreate some cherished illustration from a 1950s kids' encyclopaedia, the washed-out yellow diamond faltering against a faded blue. Suspiciously enormous crows patrol the rippling turf, a bigger and more confident crowd of them every year, too many to be called collectively a murder these days. This is more a Harold Shipman of the fucking things.

Her indoor lungs adjusting rapidly to the cold draughts of breath that she sucks down, Alma turns left as she commences her walk into town. Her Dr. Martens scuff against the pavement's fossil fronds and her mind floods with random ideas and associations, words and pictures snagging on the shop-front scenery that rattles by the other way as Alma hits her stride. She thinks about the flagstones vanishing beneath her tread, the only view afforded to the downcast, irrespective of which century they happen to be in. The old stones, obviously, remain unchanged since the nineteenth, but there are nuances to the discerning eye: deficiencies of dog-shit; chocolate wrappers that have been rebranded so as not to further mystify touring Americans; unfathomable particle-collider tags in whorls and spirals of white spray. Across the road a distant man attempts to steer some kind of sail-powered car across the Racecourse but the wind has dropped and he's becalmed amongst the strutting crows and the abruptly plunging kites. If there's no wind before it gets dark she supposes that the meadow-mariner is doomed. Despite the extra lighting that the vast and, by night, absolutely black expanse has relatively recently acquired, it's still referred to as "The Rapecourse" by a healthy number of the town's inhabitants.

She crosses from East Park Parade over Abington Avenue's tail-end and carries on down Kettering Road. George Woodcock – Alma's Arts Lab crony from her teenage years – had written a long, neon-lighted poem on this crumbling thoroughfare, a jewelled urban lament entitled *Main Street*, just before he'd jacked in all the literary bollocks and become a trucker. She can still see lines and phrases from the since-lost epic, smeared and tangled in the cobbled gutters; on the replaced plastic drainpipes. She can still see all the vanished incidents and nights and people that the lines referred to, former selves from several bygone decades striding up and down the shabby avenue, a noisy nineteen-year-old drunk girl in a posse of small-town bohemians, an angry-looking Gas Board office worker stamping her way home through drizzle on another Friday afternoon, a forty-something mad witch in a black cloak with a horde of Alcopop-emboldened simpletons calling her "Grotbags", "lez" or "minger" from the safety of their passing vehicles if she goes out to do a bit of shopping. The town's streets are like a living palimpsest to Alma, all the layers still intact, everyone still alive and everything still going on, the misguided romances and the rows, the shimmering acid trips, the hasty fucks in doorways.

This perception of a simultaneous eternity, while she's had intimations of it on and off throughout her life, has only flared up into vivid actuality since she's been working on these paintings. The idea, once fully formulated, was so dazzlingly obvious that she remains amazed at having reached the age of fifty-something without clearly understanding it: time as an everlasting solid in which nothing changes, nothing dies. It had been right before her eyes for all those years, and she'd not known what she was looking at until that moment with her brother in the Golden Lion when the penny finally dropped. The moment of apocalypse and revelation, almost like that time in Greyfriars' flats when she'd been dawdling home from Spring Lane School at dinnertime. Down in the little patch of shrubbery at the bottom of the washing-line enclosure there'd been a single translucent grub or caterpillar hanging by a thread from one leaf of a bush that Alma didn't know the name of. She had stood there staring at it for perhaps a minute, and then something strange had happened –

A black cab growls past and honks its horn. Unable to see clearly who the driver is, Alma lifts one metallic claw and waves convivially to his rearview mirror. She gets on with all the local cabbies and they sometimes give her free rides into town if they should see her walking that way in inclement weather. To be honest she gets on with nearly everyone, which somewhat undermines the petrifying gorgon image that she's worked so long and hard to put together. If this situation should persist she'll have to chop up some Girl Guides in order to regain her rep.

Across the street, the mutable and transient hoardings flicker past. Charity outlets with batty proprietors and racks of cardigans that someone's died in, Caribbean grocer-shops all facing north with no sun for the crated yams that languish in pink shadow. Alma sniggers at the name of one establishment, Butt Savouries, although at her age you'd hope she'd be more mature. A little further down the road is a kebab-house, Embers, that makes her feel wistful for the days when it had been Rick's Golden Fish Bar. Not that she had ever been a customer, but she had often entertained the fantasy of going in and being served with mushy peas and chips by Humphrey Bogart, who would eye her ruefully and drawl "Of all the golden fish bars in the world, she has to walk into mine." Somewhere behind her, the rapid staccato beep of the Pelican crossing slides subliminally into her awareness, prompting her to hum the fast bit of "The Donkey Serenade" without having any clue why she is doing so. There is another crossing, back along the Kettering Road in Kingsley, with an even more up-tempo rhythm that can leave her whistling "The Sabre Dance". Susceptible as an eight-month-old baby and invulnerable as a ptero-dactyl made of diamonds, she continues into town.

A skinny boy in modern hair and spectacles stops in his tracks and gapes at her incredulously, face contorting in a rubbery cartoon expression which, if he were not so youthful, might be taken for a paralysing stroke. Remember-ing she hasn't bothered putting on her knickers, Alma glances down to make sure that the zipper on her jeans is still intact then realises that the thunder-struck young man is an admirer. He tells her she's Alma Warren, which she's always grateful for. One of these days, when she's gone wandering from the home, she'll need that information. As he lists his favourite album sleeves, dust-jackets and comic-book covers Alma smiles, attempting to convey a girl-ish modesty but actually delivering the lipstick rictus and unblinking gaze of Conrad Veidt in a lost outtake from *The Man Who Laughs*. She shakes her stage-door Johnny's nerveless mitt and thanks him for his kind words before carrying on down the Kettering Road, privately noting that his handshake had been far less manly than her own. Mind you, he more than likely hadn't practised since the age of ten like she had, red-faced as she squeezed a set of bathroom scales until she could exert her own substantial weight with just the pressure of her thumbs. Before she'd left Spring Lane she'd given two boys a good strangling for picking, ill-advisedly, on her or little Warry. One of them had been left with appalling bruises round his throat like a jet necklace and his mother had come to the school and yelled at Alma. This would seem to have been largely ineffectual in that to this day she hasn't properly absorbed the concept of a measured and proportionate response to anything.

She trots over another crossing, this one with the slow beep of a faltering heart-monitor that doesn't provoke any musical accompaniment on her part, to the street's far side. After a few more grocers' shops with enigmatic indi-vidual atmospheres and an outlet for decent-looking Hip Hop clothing she is crossing Grove Road, with the once-majestic bulk of the Essoldo cinema just up the way. As far as Alma can remember, it was in Grove Road during the 1970s that people had their windows blown out by an IRA bomb at the RAF club that was somewhere in the neighbourhood. The government back then had been reluctant to describe the mess that everybody was involved in as a war of any kind, much less a war on terror. This had been before the war on drugs, of course, when launching military campaigns against abstract emotions or inanimate materials would have been seen as the behaviour of highly-strung and over-reaching Daleks.

On the corner with the Kettering Road is Queensgrove Methodist Church, an impressive nineteenth-century red brick edifice that is today without the posse of nice-looking black guys who in slightly warmer weather decorate its steps. Less than a dozen paces further on Alma walks past the open-plan contemporary phone booth that has played host to a fatal stabbing only a few nights before. What a way to go out, she thinks, in a glass coffin that's been shrink-wrapped with an ad for season two of *Prison Break*. It's good to talk.

The way she heard it, both the victim and the perpetrators had been black, and Alma doesn't care much for the U.S. cop-show ring that has about it. That isn't the way she likes to think about Northampton being stacked. The town's relationship with racial issues is a subtle and a complicated thing that goes back centuries, and simplifying it all down into a criminal profiler's class-skewed vision of society seems both disastrous and highly probable to Alma. She thinks about Black Charley – Henry George – one of the first black faces to be seen about the county and, in 1897, a tremendous novelty. That sense of novelty had lasted up until at least the 1960s, when her mate Dave Daniels had been the first non-white pupil at the Grammar School on Billing Road. They'd run a full-page article about it in the *Chronicle & Echo* at the time, including a large photograph of David looking apprehensive, just in case he wasn't feeling singled out enough already.

Back during the 70s and 80s, all the rudeys and the rastas had set up a club in the magnificent Salvation Army fort that used to stand on Sheep Street, just across the road from where Phil Doddridge founded his academy. Three floors of people with impeccably cool names like Elvis, Junior or Pedro, coming, going, children playing round their ankles and always a pot of bean stew simmering somewhere upstairs, that was the old Matta Fancanta club. Its antique boards had quaked in time with U-Roy or Lee Perry on the sound system, dub beats she'd been convinced were deep enough to make her womb fall out. As she remembers, it had been when vehicles that should have only been affordable to whites began to manifest in the adjoining car park that local authorities began to take an adverse interest in the place. The fort – which should have been, surely to God, a listed property – had been demolished, as if it had proven easier to pull it down than shut it down. There's only the ubiquitous bare grass there now where it once stood, just down from the arse-backwards gargoyle mass of Greyfriars bus station, built wrong way round to start with and more recently voted to rank amongst the most disgusting buildings in the country. That had been that for the public face of genuine black culture in Northampton, or at least until comparatively recently. Now there is a Northamptonshire Black History Association that is setting all the records straight, and Alma has been hanging out with a determined, racially-diverse young bunch of rappers from the Boroughs that are trading under the collective name of Streetlaw, which she thinks is at the very least a cute coincidence. Justice above the street and all that. No, it isn't all gloom for the black community by any means, assuming that it can resist the dead-end role that Hollywood's casting departments and the major record labels are apparently considering it for: let's make the underclass a glamorous and edgy place to be, then people won't mind being stuck there quite so much and we can craft dramatically-lit and well-mastered versions of their struggle to sell back to them for the few quid they've not already spent on scratch cards. Everybody wins.

Alma walks on, past the arched entrance to a cobbled yard, an unmistakeably Victorian construction that has "Dickens Brothers, Ltd" hand-lettered up above the archway. She suspects that elsewhere in the town there stands a black-beamed Tudor premises called "Shakespeare's" and perhaps a "Chaucer & Sons" half-thatched cottage out near Hardingstone. Northampton, after all, is a well-labelled town. Once, from her window, she saw two vans pass each other, travelling in opposite directions on East Park Parade. One, possibly belonging to a mattress company, had the word DREAM stencilled upon its side. The other one, perhaps a television or computer retailer, was blazoned with the word REALITY. She'd noted that REALITY was heading for town centre, which was unsurprising, while DREAM followed a trajectory that would eventually lead it to Kettering. She thought that it was more than likely going there to die.

Picking the pace up, on her right the storefronts melt into her slipstream, into one long smear of shop where you can get a Chinese meal, a drum-kit, a peyote cactus, a tattoo or a tattoo removed. She veers around a quorum of rough-looking blokes with beer-cans, who all nonetheless grin toothlessly and growl a cheerful "Hello, Alma" as she passes. Thirty seconds later a young policewoman in a Day-Glo lemon waistcoat beams and nods in recognition at the former menace to society turned local institution. She's the queen of Kettering Road.

Tacking due west now, Alma executes a smooth curve opposite a shop-soiled Unitarian church and banks into Abington Square, past the unoccupied new properties which have replaced a scruffy row of shops that used to stand upon this rounded corner. She remembers her and David Daniels hiking round the newsagents and second-hand shops on Saturday mornings when they were thirteen, looking for comics or science fiction paperbacks, often paying a visit to the murky enterprise that hung on here, in the perpetual umbra of the church across the street. The owner had been an old lady with a bad cough who was always in her dressing gown and slippers, flecking ragged copies of *Amazing Adult Fantasy* and yellow-jacketed pornography alike with inadvertent sputum.

Alma feels protective of these vanished people, insufficiently noteworthy or attractive for the sepia retrospectives; these anonymous dust-bunnies who got lost forever underneath the huge, immobile wardrobe of the twentieth century. She wants to fill the crowd scenes in her paintings with them, wants to think of them suspended with their hours and habitats in time's huge starry jelly, hanging there forever with their feuds and frailties intact, notes on the stave of a stupendous music.

On her right now is the Jaguar dealership, Guy Salmon, a name that has since become Alma's pet euphemism with which to refer to male ejaculate. Abington Square unfolds around her. Up ahead, Charles Bradlaugh's statue stands upon its traffic-island plinth, facing away from her towards Abington Street. Nice arse. She's always rather fancied Bradlaugh, although more for his moral ferocity than for his physical allure if truth be told. Dishing out contraceptive literature with Annie Besant, knocking round with Swinburne, standing up for subjugated India so vocally that youthful devotee Mohandas Ghandi turned up at his funeral. A riot-precipitating atheist teetotaller and champion of the poor, Bradlaugh is Alma's dream-date. Curiously, whenever she attempts to picture this she always sees herself arriving at the school dance with an animated statue, white stone splinters flaking from its joints with every step. During the slower numbers at the evening's end they'd leave a swirling chalk-dust trail on the gymnasium floor behind them as they clung together for *Wichita Lineman*, and then afterwards he'd conscientiously discuss the need for contraception before trying to feel her up on the way home. She looks up at the chiselled figure with its finger pointing ever westward and can hear him bragging to his mates at the pub afterwards: "Here, Algernon, smell this."

She's giggling to herself as she strides on towards the junction with the Mounts and York Road, where the snarling, swearing horsepower of the trucks and Chelsea tractors is constrained by pretty lights. A small boy towed behind his carrier-laden mother stares at Alma disbelievingly. A man nudges his wife and mutters "Here, that's Alma Warren" as she lollops past them, and outside the Bantam Cock three young lads produce copies of the Moorcock *Elric* book for her to sign. They don't seem to be frightened of her, joking amiably as she scrawls her lazy autograph, and Alma finds she rather likes them. They inform her that they share a private fantasy about her, in which Alma lives on top of the Express Lifts tower and overlooks Northampton from a throne of human skulls. It's an arresting image, and she's beaming fondly as she waves goodbye to them. Before she's reached the traffic lights two pretty girls who look like art students have smiled and nodded at her, she has made another three-year-old look haunted and another cab has chirped its horn as it purrs by, prompting another clueless raising of the silver talons and another jingling rattle of the finger-armour. She reflects that she is fortunate to have been blessed by an inflated self-image since infancy. Anyone else subjected to this much attention would most probably start acting strangely, she concludes while searching for a kabbalistic insight in the sequence of red-amber-green.

Her personality is a long-running radio drama that is broadcast chiefly for her own amusement, much as she suspects is true of many people. Obviously some prefer personas that are tuned into light comedy, while judged by their expressions the few individuals waiting at the lights with her have modelled their essential natures on the weather forecast. Or perhaps Religious Affairs, Alma reasons after a consideration of the Deco edifice that looms behind her while she stands there by the crossing. Opened in the 1930s as the Savoy Cinema and operating as the ABC throughout her back-row dating years, hosting the Beatles once, the place is now amongst the growing number of town properties owned by the Jesus Army, an expanding horde of sometimes-strident evangelicals that had begun recruiting from Northampton's pool of derelicts or drunks back in the early 1970s, whisking them from park benches off to Army headquarters in nearby Bugbrook. She recalls an incident from a few years ago when the group had been censured after traumatising children with an unannounced alfresco re-enactment of the Crucifixion, but apart from that they seemed to be permitted to do what they wanted, pretty much.

Alma is unsurprised by this. The town has been a thriving hotbed of religious nutjobs since the fourteen-hundreds, many of whom Alma feels a certain retroactive fondness for. She likes the poetry, she likes the attitude, the heresy and anarchy that sought to brush aside the King and clergy, sought to recreate society as an egalitarian domain of ranting tinkers, mechanic philosophers, a whole Nation of Saints that answered to no temporal authority but only to a moral vision, to an enflamed state of mind, a level of both spiritual and political awareness that would *be* Jerusalem in England's green and pleasant land. She likes the Lollards and the Ranters and the Muggletonians. She likes the incendiary ravings of the founding Quakers, likes imagining that nice man on the oat-box tearing off his clothes and screaming for the violent overthrow of monarchy. She's even partial to Moravians, albeit mainly for their freak-show value with that mental business about penetrating the messiah in his spear-hole and their influence on her enduring idol William Blake, but Alma doesn't like the Jesus Army very much. She finds herself suspicious of religious zeal that has a business plan.

The lights change and she crosses to an intermediary island in the middle of York Road. Alma reflects that she is standing on the spot that Doug McGeary's vegetable truck had rumbled over nearly fifty years before, transporting her unbreathing brother to the hospital. She realises that today Doug's mercy-dash would have to take a different route, with it no longer being possible to sail down from the Mounts into York Road. He would have had to turn left at the cinema, circle the Unitarian Church and come back at the square the other way, adding some very-likely fatal minutes to his journey. Mind you, by all rights her brother should have been a goner when the truck was still halfway up Grafton Street, so perhaps the diversion wouldn't have made that much of a difference.

Finally she squeezes past the barrier railings at the top of the pedestrian precinct and is in Abington Street, or at least in what's left of it. Back a few hundred years ago this was the town's east gate, called the St. Edmund's End after the since-demolished church across the Wellingborough Road from the converted workhouse in which Alma had drawn her first breath, to voice the first of many furious and unreasonable complaints. Daniel Defoe, writing his guide to English towns, described Northampton as essentially a crossroads, with its north-south axis running along Sheep Street, down the Drapery and into Bridge Street while its east-west axis traced a line through Abington Street, Gold Street and Marefair towards the ruins of the castle. By pedestrianizing one end of this east-west passage, the town council have effectively stitched up a major vein, inviting gangrene. She can see it setting in already, read its symptoms in the plasterboarded windows and the bloom of estate agent shingles. There's no passing trade and the shop rents are all ridiculously high. If this persists, Alma predicts, the town will turn into an economic crater where the money only circulates around the rim, through retail parks and giant chain-stores, while the centre is abandoned to the tumbleweed of repossession notices, transformed into an after-dark arena, to a Walter Hill set with more vomit, more teenagers lying in their own piss, and more incoherent warcries. Incoherent wars. You know it's a bad sign when you see bunches of commemorative flowers taped to lamps on the pink paving, with no road in sight.

Pigeons rise fluttering around her, blissfully oblivious to the mean-spirited poster pasted on a rubbish bin which states that feeding them is a variety of littering and therefore punishable by a fine. It isn't that she thinks this will make any difference to the birds themselves, who after all can't read and don't depend on handouts from animal-lovers to sustain them in the first place, but she feels indignant at the sentiments expressed. What in the name of fuck is wrong with pigeons? If the council were attempting to discourage wasps, attack dogs or the Jesus Army she could see some sense in the campaign, but pigeons? With that green and violet shimmering on the ruff; that wobbling and fluffed-up coo? If the municipal authorities think getting rid of pigeons is their number one priority for the apparently-condemned town centre, then why don't they just plant landmines on all of the window sills and get it over with instead of sticking up their pissy little threatening notices?

She carries on down Abington Street. There are very few other pedestrians but she is wading through a crowd of ghosts and memories, her killer robot hands deep in her jacket pockets like a 1950s badboy, Jimmy Dean after the menopause. She skirts around the dopey Francis Crick memorial erected in the centre of the thoroughfare, a piece of kitsch with silvery double-helix twists supporting what appear to be a pair of nudist superheroes, sexless manikins whose bald and featureless Barbie pudendas clearly won't be passing on inherited genetic traits to anyone. Besides, the only thing connecting Abington Street with the local scientific pioneer is the conspicuous DNA evidence to be found following an average Friday night. Of course, the monument might be a comment on local inbreeding, with the figures diving upwards in a desperate spiral to escape a tiny, stagnant gene-pool, more of a gene-puddle if the truth be told. Alma recalls the rumour of an entire cyclops-village somewhere out near Towcester, full of cyclops postmen, cyclops publicans and cyclops toddlers, then remembers it was her that started it.

By curving round the structure to her left she is now walking down beside the library, the only building in the street that hasn't changed since Alma was a little girl. She'd joined up at the age of five and visited the library several times a fortnight for the next ten years, mostly for ghost-stories and yellow-jacketed Victor Gollancz science-fiction. She'd had haunting, memorable dreams about the institution as a child, walking through winding corridors of wooden shelving with impossible and fascinating tomes propped up to every side, books that you couldn't read because the words would crawl around upon the page if they were opened. Her dream-library had padded flooring covered in red vinyl like a bar stool or a car-seat into which were set round holes that were most probably vaginal, so that the book-browsing clientele could climb from floor to floor.

The actual waking library had been almost as marvellous in its interior – the tiny section like an open wardrobe that hummed with the aura of the books on séances and mesmerism that were kept there – and from the outside it was still beautiful, the busts of benefactors set into the honey-coloured stone. Alma likes showing visiting Americans the library, just so she can point to the carven likeness at the upper right of its façade and ask them who they think it is. They generally assume that it's George Washington, an English gesture of respect for their first president, seeming bewildered when informed that it is in fact Andrew, George's older relative, back from before the Washingtons left Barton Sulgrave for America when the New Model Army were converging on Northamptonshire during the sixteen-hundreds. The family, reputedly, had even pinched the village crest of bars and mullets to provide a basis for the starry, stripy flag of their adopted home. To be quite frank, the only Washingtons she unreservedly respects are Dinah, Booker T. and Geno, whom she feels at least gave something back.

She's just about to cross the precinct to the Co-op Bank on its far side when she becomes aware of an unusually solid-looking ghost from bygone times approaching from the opposite direction, walking up past the dilapidated mouth of the former Co-op Arcade. Dragging her hair back from the soot-ringed blast-sites of her eyes to take a closer look, she realises that the only thing which marks the figure as a ghost is the anachronistic clothing it affects: the pinstripe shirt, the neckerchief and waistcoat. With her spirits lifting out of their default disgruntlement, she recognises the bucolic spectre as perhaps her oldest mate, Benedict Perrit. Ah, Northampton. Just when you've decided that the planners have clubbed her into insensibility, she throws you a bouquet.

The moment Benedict sees Alma, he goes into one of his routines. First the appalled look, then the turning round and going back the way he's come as if pretending that he hasn't seen her, then another sharp reverse to bring him back in her direction, only this time quivering with silent giggles. Good old Ben, mad as a Chinese situation comedy, the only one amongst Alma's associates and former classmates to consistently out-strange her without even trying, and one of the few artists or poets from her teenage years who didn't jack it all in for a comfortable life when they hit twenty-five. Anything but. Benedict's face is creased with lines of verse and looks like it resulted from an ill-judged one-night stand between the masks of comedy and tragedy. He has been killed by poetry, and at the same time poetry is all that saves him and redeems him. Good old Ben.

He sticks one paw out for a handshake, but she's much too pleased to see him and she isn't having it. Dodging around the proffered hand she plants her bloody lips upon his cheek and scoops him up into a python hug. Sooner or later he'll breathe out, which will allow her to constrict him further and then when he loses consciousness she'll dislocate her jaw and swallow him. Before she can accomplish this he flinches back out of her grip, frantically wiping at the Girl-Ebola she has left smeared on his chops.

"Get off! Ah ha ha ha ha ha!"

His laugh is that of Tommy Cooper, left marooned upon a desert island until it has morphed into the seagull-scaring cackle of Ben Gunn. Delighted, Alma tells him he's a suave Lothario and asks him if he's writing these days. When he tells her he's still scribbling, she remarks on reading "Clearance Area" a day or two ago and lets him know what a good poem she thinks it is. He looks at her uncertainly, unsure if she is being genuine.

"I weren't bad, was I? Ah ha ha."

The use of the past tense and subtle shift of subject from the poem to its author registers as a small blip on Alma's radar of concern. It doesn't sound good, like a clichéd western gunslinger retired to the saloon, fondly remembering his cordite-scented triumphs through a haze of redeye. What a load of shit. She sternly reassures him that he'd been considerably better than "not bad", then, realising that she too has used the past tense, she attempts to rectify her blunder by just coming out and telling him without condition that he's a good writer, whereupon he taps her up for a few quid.

This startles her, even as she is fumbling automatically in her jeans' pocket for a piece of crumpled paper that won't turn out to be an old till receipt from Morrison's. Alma has gladly dished out cash to the town's homeless ever since they blossomed in shop doorways during the late 'Eighties, and especially since it became official policy that this was just "encouraging the beggars". Having come from a community of beggars, this only spurs on her bloody-minded generosity, much the same way that she's been idly planning to strew crumbled blueberry muffins up and down the precinct ever since she spotted that annoying pigeon notice at the street's top end. A friend, like Benedict, is always welcome to some spare cash if she has it, but as she presses a note into his palm she's more concerned about the shift in self-esteem that seems to have befallen him since the last time they met. Taken along with the "I weren't bad, was I?" comment, Alma's feeling a bit worried for him. Making matters worse, he's looking guilty now about taking the money, which she brashly brushes over by assuring him she's "fucking loaded", anxious to get on to safer ground. The moment passes. Alma asks him to tomorrow's exhibition, not expecting him to come, and when they're saying goodbye some few minutes later Benedict is telling her that he's a Cyberman and Alma's laughing like a drain. Everything's good again.

Waving farewell while still snickering down her nose at intervals, she wanders a few paces further down the street and then remembers that she had originally been heading for the bank, correcting her trajectory accordingly. She's thinking about Benedict, about how one of the most blazing and important moments in her life had been provoked by Ben's inspiring idiocy. They were both something like ten or eleven and had worked out an ingenious way to climb up to the rooftops of the copper warehouse which stood on the corner that connected Freeschool Street with Green Street. This ascent, which obviously needed to be made at night, had first required a trip to Narrow-Toe Lane, just around the block, where they could wriggle on their bellies underneath the locked gate of a builder's yard. Here they had clambered up a borrowed ladder onto a rear wall of the adjacent Perrit property and scampered giggling along the ridge of Benedict's dad's woodpile in the starlight. This eventually allowed them access to the warehouse outbuildings, from whence it was an easy scramble up to the slate roofs and chimneypots above.

For months it had been their precarious kingdom, only shared with cats and birds. Dangerous games of chase evolved to suit the slanted planes of the new landscape, but these had their limits: dead-end precipices that the two kids couldn't find the nerve to overcome. The worst of these was at the far end of a guttering, a rain channel between the slope of one roof and the upright wall that was the boundary of the next. Their chases would end prematurely at this point, night after night, because of the sheer drop into a narrow alley filled with metal scrap and probable impalement that plunged down into the dark immediately beyond. The threatening passage had been only four or five feet wide and had the angled tiles of a one-storey storage shed on its far side. If it had been a jump between two chalk marks in a sunny playground they'd have made it without hesitation, but to try the same thing on a rooftop in pitch darkness with an abyss full of tetanus junk beneath you was a very different matter.

Then, one moonlit evening, Benedict had upped his game. Alma was chasing him across the blue-grey hills some thirty feet above the street, pursuing him with an unsettling degree of relish through a Caligari world of chimneys, tilts, and shadows. Benedict, only a few paces ahead of her, was giggling with terror that was wholly justified and understandable: most people would get through their lives without being pursued across the skyline by a predatory Alma Warren anywhere save in unusually vivid nightmares, while for Benedict this had been his unenviable reality. Upon the night in question she had herded him into the dead-end fold between the rooftops, knowing that she had him trapped and slavering triumphantly as she moved in upon her shrill and tittering quarry for the kill. It was at this point that Ben's fear of being caught by Alma had at last outweighed his squeamishness regarding getting speared by shards of glass or rusty railings in the alleyway below. Benedict jumped, shrieking with fear and somehow laughing at the same time, hurtling across the lethal gap to land upon the shed roof, five or six feet lower down on its far side.

Alma, still running at full tilt behind him, had just seconds to decide that she preferred the possibility of gory death at age eleven to the utter certainty of someone beating her at something. Having made her mind up, when she reached the edge she just kept going.

In the fraction of a second during which she hung in empty space above the snarl of rusted implements and broken windows down below, Alma had been illuminated. As the instant stretched itself, she realised that she'd accidentally jumped free of all her fears and limitations, fears of injury and death and ruin. Trusting only to the moment she'd propelled herself past doubt and gravity and in that moment had known with abiding certainty that there was nothing she was scared of, nothing that she couldn't do.

Even as an eleven-year-old girl she had, of course, been both considerably bigger and much heavier than Benedict. She sailed across the treacherous alleyway to land on the shed roof beside him and immediately went through it, shattering its slates and ending up embedded in its gradient to her scabby knees. Oh, how they'd laughed, exhilarated and hysterical, once they'd checked to make sure that nobody had lost an eye. The incident had given Alma an important insight into overcoming psychological impediments, which she'd experimented further with. Having a morbid dread of drowning, as a twelve-year-old she'd swum out to the steel partition that divided one end of Midsummer Meadow's lido from the other and had dived down to one of the railed vents that were some feet underwater. She had pushed her arm between the bars then turned it round so that she wasn't certain she could pull it out again. For perhaps thirty long and awesome seconds she had floated at the still heart of her wholly self-inflicted terror, trying to absorb and understand it, and then she had calmly turned her arm the right way round to pull it from between the bars and strike back for the glittering surface. Alma smiles now at the memory as she enters the bank. The critics and sometimes admirers who describe her as eccentric really haven't got the first idea.

She knows all the bank staff by name, the Co-op having been her bank of choice for the last twenty years. She'd started with them solely on the basis of their ethical investment policies, but as the decades had ticked past on her milometer she'd come to notice that whenever there was a financial meltdown caused by banking improprieties, the Co-op's frankly boring logo never featured in the cascade of shamed high-street brands that poured across the tea-time news-screens. In the dizzying casino spin of a roulette economy, inside a threadbare circus tent stuffed with adrenaline-deranged rogue traders, oligarchs, and corporate bosses living beyond anybody's means, the Co-op stood fast. Despite its refusal to invest resources with arms manufacturers, the bank stuck to its guns. Also, when Alma's mum Doreen had died in 1995 they'd sent a big bouquet of flowers with personal messages from everybody at the branch. As far as Alma is concerned, they could be caught providing orphan baby seals for Rio Tinto Zinc to use as sex-slaves after that, and she'd most probably turn her blind eye.

After she's said hello to everyone, Alma inspects herself on the closed circuit television while she waits in line. The camera is over by the Abington Street entrance several yards behind her, and so only gives a rear-view long-shot of the leather-jacketed old woman with the hanging-gardens hairstyle, a good head and shoulders taller than the other people in the queue. This is the nearest that she ever gets to an objective image of herself and finds she doesn't like it very much. It makes her feel obscurely isolated, and besides, she doesn't see herself like that. She sees herself as bigger and a great deal nearer. And not from behind.

She checks her balance and draws out a random wad of cash to stuff in the side-pocket of her jeans. Just yesterday she'd had a chat with the incorrigible serial-sympathiser and unlikely innocent Melinda Gebbie, her best mate from Semilong. The other woman artist had remarked on how she always liked to have some reassuring totem in her pocket, useful Kleenex tissues, dead bees or particularly pretty leaves that she'd picked up. Alma had thought about it for a while and then said "Yeah, well, see, for me that would be money." While she's probably lost several high-denomination notes across the years she still resists the idea of a purse or handbag, reasoning that this would only be a good way to lose everything at once. She thinks it highly probable that she'd eventually leave the handbag in a café, whereas it's unlikely that she'd leave her trousers. Not out of the question, but unlikely.

Exiting the bank she nips next door into the premises of Martin's, the newsagents, so that she can stock up on essentials: Rizla papers, fags, Swan matches, magazines. She pulls the latest issues of *New Scientist* and *Private Eye* down from their upper shelves, wondering if their placement might be part of an entirely sensible campaign to make sure that only the tall receive appropriate intellectual stimulation. One day soon, when she and her kind have grown smart enough to formulate a foolproof plan, then Stephen Fry will give the signal and they'll all rise up and massacre the short-arse numbskulls in their beds. Something like that, at any rate. Let a girl have her daydreams.

Alma takes the two mags to the till where genial, bullet-headed Tony Martin and long-suffering wife Shirley have already got her forty Silk Cut Silver, five packs of green Rizla papers and two boxes of Swan matches waiting for her. Tony shakes his shaved dome ruefully while ringing up the Rizlas.

"Alma, honestly! All o' these Rizla papers! Surely you must 'ave got that scale model of the Eiffel Tower completed ages ago? What's the matter with yer?"

Shirley looks up from re-stocking shelves and tells her husband to shut up and not to be so rude, but Alma's grinning.

"Yeah, I did, but I got bored with it and started on a model of the Vatican. Now, are you going to ring those up, or shall I get my matchstick Pope to excommunicate you?"

It's a running joke between them. Years ago someone who worked behind the counter had asked Alma why she bought so many Rizla papers, to which Alma had replied with a deadpan expression and without a beat that she was building a scale model of the Eiffel Tower out of the flimsy, gum-edged leaves. While this had only been a gag she'd found it an appealing one, an idea she could get a bit of mileage out of. Well, more than a bit as it turned out. She sees ideas much as a farmer sees his pigs, and doesn't even want to waste the squeal if she can help it.

With her purchases inside a flimsy plastic carrier-bag, the national flower, she waves a clattering metallic goodbye to the Martins and steps back out of the shop into the wide pink precinct. She continues her descent of Abington Street, calling in at Marks & Spencer's to pick up some bits and pieces for her evening meal: a couple of long demon-tongue Ramiros peppers, cranberry and orange stuffing, and some feta cheese. She navigates a designated path between the open-plan departments, overlooked by Myleene Klass and a still-lovely Twiggy. Alma never feels entirely comfortable in the conspicuously poncey store, but, having recently boycotted Sainsbury's, lacks for a convenient alternative.

The Sainsbury's episode still makes her smile, though it's the ghastly smile of something that one really should have killed but only wounded. She had been emerging from the Grosvenor Centre branch of Sainsbury's, where she knew most of the ladies at the tills by name, laden down by two bulging store-brand bags-for-life filled with her purchases. A uniformed security guard, shrewdly noticing the lizard-green-with-watermelon-pink-interior hoodie that she happened to be wearing, had deduced she was therefore a member of the underclass (which, emotionally at least, she was) and stepped to block her path, demanding to see Alma's till receipt. Towering above the relatively pint-sized individual she had craned her neck, lowering her massive head to his eye-level as if talking to a woefully underachieving eight-year-old. Explaining that she wasn't in the habit of collecting till receipts, Alma had asked if this was some new policy of random stop-and-search, or if he'd had some other reason for selecting her amongst the dozen or so more conventional-looking shoppers who were then emerging from the supermarket. Looking more and more uncertain by the moment, the guard had then pointlessly requested that she show him what was in her Sainsbury's shopping bags, perhaps suspecting somehow that they'd prove to contain shopping that had come from Sainsbury's.

She had repeated her inquiry, leaving an exaggerated gap between each word so that he had the time to fully comprehend one syllable before being required to struggle with the next. "Why ... did ... you ... stop ... me ... specifically?" By this point other customers were nervously approaching and protesting Alma's innocence, looking more worried for the clearly-new employee, understandably, than they were for the famously belligerent giantess. Attempting to salvage a sense of his authority in this deteriorating situation, the guard had said that Alma must keep her receipts. Alma had duly noted this new Sainsbury's policy but had explained that since she wouldn't be returning to

the store, it wasn't really going to affect her. Smiling anxiously as she'd begun
to walk away, he'd called out a reminder to hang on to her receipt next time,
which had made Alma pause, sigh heavily, and then explain in her best child-
friendly voice what all the long words about not returning to the store in her
last sentence were intended to convey. When she'd got home she'd rung customer services and told them it was Alma Warren calling, at which the young
woman on the other end had chirpily informed her that she'd seen Alma on
telly just the previous night. Alma had told her that was nice and then gone
on to detail what had happened earlier, explaining that she could only interpret the guard's scrutiny as being class-based and how this had prompted her
decision to give Sainsbury's a miss in future. She'd assured the perfectly-nice
woman that she wasn't asking Sainsbury's for an apology, though anyone who
knew her would have heard the implication that it was too late for such a useless trifle to placate her; that she was by now embarked upon a grudge that she
would carry to the grave.

It hadn't been the first time she'd attracted the attention of security in
Sainsbury's, although on the previous occasion she'd been in the company
of her dear chum, the actor Robert Goodman, so she hadn't really blamed
them. Bob, blessed with what a desperate estate agent would call "distinctive features", had during his various career played the Hamburglar, and the
corpse-humping rapist solider in Luc Besson's *Joan of Arc*, while in a number of
advertisements for car alarms, alongside his appearances upon *The Bill*, *East-
enders*, and in *Batman* and *A Fish Called Wanda*, he had made the role of Second Scar-faced Thug his own. Given Bob's murderous demeanour, she wasn't
surprised that they'd been followed round the store. If Alma didn't know Bob
personally, and if he wasn't currently researching stuff on her behalf pertaining to tomorrow's exhibition, then she'd have him taken out by snipers; would
have more than likely done so long ago. This latest incident, however, had no
such extenuating circumstances: she'd been stopped and questioned because
she looked poor. In fucking Sainsbury's, which Alma hadn't realised was now
such an elite concern. By contrast, here in poncey Marks & Spencer's, the one
guard who'd ever spoken to her had just smiled and said he was a fan. Class
prejudice, apparently, is not seen as a major issue, possibly because its victims
are traditionally inarticulate. Alma herself, of course, never shuts up, particularly when it comes to people of her background being demonised. She can
drone on about the subject endlessly, most usually in the two or three media
interviews she does each week, or some more permanent form. No, she won't
be needing an apology.

Back in Abington Street, burdened by two carrier bags now, she carries
on towards the coffee shop down at the bottom, Caffè Nero. Why name a café
after someone like Nero, Alma wonders? You might just as well call it Caffè

Caligula or Caffè Heliogabalus. Or Caffè Mussolini for that matter. The caffeine of Europe.

The café stands roughly on the former site of the town hall, the intermediary model serving as a stepping stone between the first Gilhalda on the Mayorhold and the splendid current Guildhall round the corner in St. Giles Street. It was here on this spot almost ten years before that Alma had crossed paths with then-Prime-Minister-in-waiting Tony Blair, on a pre-landslide walkabout with suited *Reservoir Dogs* minders and the rictus grin and painted eyeballs of a ventriloquist's dummy who's determined not to go gack in the gox. The party had been sauntering down Abington Street just as Alma had been walking up, sunbathing in the awed attention they clearly imagined they were getting from the utterly oblivious passers-by. You could tell that inside their minds they were parading down the recently pedestrianised precinct, all in flattering slow-motion with the faint breeze ruffling their jet-moulded hair attractively.

Scanning the passing faces for a sign of something other than indifference, Blair's eyes had eventually met Alma's grey and yellow hazard lights. Of course, she hadn't known at that point he was going to drag the country into an interminable and disastrous war, buddying up to the Americans with a view to his own retirement prospects, but she'd been aware of him for years and knew that he would almost certainly be doing *something* vile. She'd watched him and his party tacitly support repressive Tory legislation like Clause 28 or the Criminal Justice Bill. She'd watched him 'modernise' the Labour party by excising the last vestiges of the core values that her parents and grandparents had believed in; watched him sell the poor, the disinherited and even the trade unions who'd brought his party into being down the same endlessly rolling opportunist river. On the afternoon of her encounter with him, then, despite the fact he hadn't been elected yet, she'd thought to get in her retaliation early. She hadn't looked daggers at him, she'd looked Daisycutters, with a glare of such intensity that she would only normally employ it if she were attempting to blow up the moon. There had been fields once that had given Alma cause to look at them like that, where now there would be nothing growing for the next few hundred years. She'd held the contact long enough to make sure it had registered, waiting until Blair's grin had frozen to a rictus and his startled eyes had undergone their first-to-see-the-creature moment before she had curled her lip and looked dismissively away, continuing with her ascent of Abington Street.

Entering the café now to grab a cup of hot black tea and slice of Tiramisu, she talks with the Polish girls behind the counter before relocating to a punch-drunk leather armchair by the window, still considering her brief encounter with the man who is at present hanging on to leadership with the desperate tenacity of a hand-chosen lobster clinging to the ornamental castle in the restaurant tank. This is the man who by his own account has felt the hand of history upon his shoulder with such dreary frequency across the years and yet has never realised that it's fastening a label saying "stab me" to his back with Sellotape.

Levering up a forkful of her custard/coffee cake towards the tag team of bright red Mexican wrestlers that are her lips she thinks about the pair of local men, both former Labour Party members, who are currently confined by a restraining order which prevents them leaving England and forbids them talking to each other. One of them, a civil servant by the name of David Keogh who lives just off the Mounts, was a communications officer seconded to the Foreign Office during 2005. While thus employed, Keogh had received the transcript of a conversation between Blair and U.S. President George W. Bush in which the gangster and his moll had discussed the advisability of bombing non-combatant Arab television station Al-Jazeera. Understanding that this was a war-crime in the making, Keogh had panicked and passed on the information to his fellow Northamptonian and Labour Party chum, former political researcher Leo O'Connor, then employed as an assistant to Northampton South Labour MP and erstwhile Inter-City Firm football enthusiast Tony Clarke. Alma has always had a soft spot with regard to Clarke, who seems to her an honourable, decent man. To be fair, she supposes that unless he'd wanted to be in the frame himself as part of a conspiracy the MP would have had no choice but to do what he did upon discovery of the memo, which was putting in the call to Special Branch.

This has led to a minor quandary at the Foreign Office, detailed in the pages of a recent *Private Eye*. Apparently, while one department of that august body had been claiming that the Bush/Blair Al-Jazeera conversation never happened and was the malign invention of Keogh and O'Connor, a completely separate department had announced in its response to an enquiry on the case that although they possessed a transcript of the conversation, they could not release it. Alma wonders how they'll charge the pair for breach of the Official Secrets Act without reminding everyone what the official secret under scrutiny had been. Her guess is that they'll leave it a few months until some new catastrophe or scandal has eclipsed the matter and the overall amnesia of the general public has had time to kick in. Then they'll rush the case through court with a D-Notice on the media, preventing press and television from giving details of the original offence in any coverage. That's what she'd do if she were some pink-faced Magister Ludi in the depths of Whitehall.

Blotting mascarpone from the scarlet crime-scene of her lips, she feels indignant that this Kafka re-run should be happening to people from her town, one of them living on the Mounts just past the northeast corner of the Boroughs, her beloved neighbourhood. Mansoul, it is the very seat of war.

She jingles goodbye to the Polish girls and exits Caffè Nero, crossing the vestigial tarmac stump of Abington Street that's still hanging on past the pink paving, heading for the market square. Alma remembers she'd been going to pay her Council Tax, but realises that she's left the bill at home. Oh, well. Who cares? She'll sort it out on Monday, when the preview exhibition's over. Given how Northampton has responded to Poll Tax demands across the centuries, she doubts that her late payment will present much of a problem. After Margaret Thatcher overreached herself by introducing it back in the 'Eighties, bailiff's wagons had been chased back to their depot by infuriated Eastern District tenants who'd gone on to wreck the repossession company's business premises. A mob of protesters had taken over council offices, holding staff prisoner at fist-point in a day-long siege. Of course, all that was nothing to the fourteenth century when the first Poll Tax had been raised down at the castle at the south end of St. Andrew's Road, precipitating upon that occasion the incendiary orgy that was the Peasant's Revolt. No, they could wait until after the weekend and count themselves lucky that she wasn't going to torch the Guildhall. Probably.

Walking in a diagonal across the market's gentle gradient, stepping between the wooden posts of recently-vacated stalls or dodging under the perpetually wet-looking canopies, Alma is thinking still about Keogh and O'Connor, free will, Gerard 't Hooft, Benedict Perrit and her rooftop leap across the scrap-filled chasm when she'd been eleven. She assumes that all the other people making their way back and forth across the square are similarly occupied with idiosyncratic matters of their own. This is reality, this teeming of illusions, memories, anxieties, ideas and speculations, constant in six billion minds. The actual events and circumstances of the world are just the sweaty and material tip of this immense and ghostly iceberg, the entirety of which no individual being can conceivably experience. For Alma, this raises the question of just whom or what reality is real *to*. You would have to postulate some hypothetic point of absolute omniscience outside the human world, some being constantly engrossed in knowing everything and therefore not having the time to act itself, a still and inert point of utter understanding, utter receptivity.

The nearest Alma can come to conceiving this sole motionless spectator of an ultimate reality is the stone angel that's atop the Guildhall, somewhere to her rear as she strides up across the marketplace towards its northwest corner. The archangel Michael, hopelessly mixed up with Michael, patron saint of corporations, standing with his shield and snooker cue above the town, hearing its every thought yet never opening those birdshit-spattered lips to voice a warning or betray a confidence. Aware of several deaths and several hundred copulations every hour, knowing which of a hundred billion sperm will hit the mark, will end up as a nurse, a rapist, a social reformer or an accident statistic; end up going through divorce, a bankruptcy, a windscreen. Fully cognisant of every Starburst wrapper, every dog turd, every atom, every quark; knows if Gerard 't Hooft's equations of an underlying state beneath the charm and strangeness will turn out to be correct or not; knows if Benedict Perrit will be coming to her opening tomorrow. Every fact and fancy, everything reflected perfectly, exquisitely, upon the dull stone brow. This entire universe, including Alma and her current musings, caught in a synaptic shimmer of the gelid and impartial granite mind.

Halfway across the emptying market, it occurs to her that she is walking through the blossoming iron phantom of the monument, the empty spot where once it stood upon its stepped stone base. Perhaps she even transects an eight-year-old self sat risking piles on the cold pedestal, examining her knees where they extend beyond the pleated hem of her thin navy skirt. The vague, ungathered wool of memory that fills the square is spun into specific strands of yarn upon the monument's ghost-spindle. Shiny, rain-licked cobbles emerge briefly through the pink replacement paving and the empty wooden outlines of each stall are coloured in, filled with dead traders and their long-since perished merchandise. A trestle of unbranded sweets, cartoon confectionery even then unseen outside the pages of *The Beano*, all presided over by a man with heavy black Italian eyebrows and a starched white coat. The stand of comics and used paperbacks that she still sometimes dreams about, Sid's, its proprietor in cap and gloves and muffler, breath and pipe-smoke hanging in the winter air and all around a gaudy flowerbed of *Adventure Comics* and *Forbidden Worlds* held down by flat, round iron paperweights, *Mad* magazine or *True Adventure* with its Nazi temptresses and whipped G.I.s, hanging from bulldog-clips along a spring-like wire connected to the bookstall's upper reaches, just below the green-and-white stripes of its canopy. In the pre-Christmas dark the huddled pitches look like painted paper lanterns from above, the white glare of the storm lamps sieved through coloured canvas. Glowing cigarette ends hover in the black. Magnificent and evanescent, the Emporium Arcade flares on her right, alight with toys and knitting patterns, before once again subsiding to a blank and stone-clad modern wall, the grand wrought-iron Victoriana of its entrance melting to a brutal concrete underpass where teenagers kicked an Albanian man to death a year or two ago.

As she is heading from the open corner of the marketplace towards the indeterminate point where the Drapery meets Sheep Street, Alma glances downhill to her left and notices the Halifax Building Society's confident frontage on the corner of Drum Lane. Caught in the floss of other times, Alma can still see Alfred Preedy's paper shop that occupied the premises forty or fifty years before, the place she'd had the dream about when she was five, the hooded foreman and his midnight crew of carpenters that she'd attempted to describe with *Work in Progress*. Was the job completed to its schedule, or is it still going on, she wonders, somewhere in the dreams of children? A fragmentary idea comes to her, something about the planed wooden boards of the nocturnal workers representing lengths of time or sets of linked events, with every human life a nail, her and her brother Warry, Tony Blair, Keogh and O'Connor, everyone she knows and everyone she doesn't know, hammered into being by their parents' coital rhythms, bang, bang, bang, immovably embedded in the hard grain of eternity, so that –

Her train of thought is interrupted by a genial young fellow in a baseball cap and trainers that are better-looking than her own. All that he wants to do is shake her hand and tell her that her work's amazing while apologising for approaching her, which makes her feel all warm and motherly. Just as she's saying goodbye to him, one of the remaining traders on the market square behind her calls out, "Me too! Well done, Alma!" giving her a brief round of applause. She beams and waves. Sometimes this is all like a dream, too pleasant, a reality suspiciously benevolent to Alma Warren. There are times when she suspects it's all some ludicrously vain and self-regarding compensatory fantasy she's dreaming in some other, less auspicious life. Perhaps she's really sitting, heavily sedated, in a pool of her own piss at an asylum somewhere, or maybe she's in a coma in the 1970s after she drank so much that she stopped breathing at her twentieth birthday party. It occurs to her that her unusually enjoyable existence might be some hallucination happening in the stretched-out instant of her death, a vision of the life she might have had. Who knows? Perhaps she never really cleared that alley full of rusted junk, back when she was eleven.

She passes between the Abbey National's Drapery Branch and the majestic colonnaded front of the old Corn Exchange, its chiselled steps ascending into what had once been the town's other major cinema, called variously the Gaumont and the Odeon. Here she'd been forced to watch *The Sound of Music* three times with her mum Doreen, which she considered to be technically a form of child abuse. She'd been stood up twice, waiting on the cold steps for some acne-stippled tossrag who'd quite evidently only asked her out when dared to by his mates. She'd also come here several years before her teenage trials, when she had been a member of the Gaumont Boys and Girls club. Every Saturday they'd be let in for sixpence and would then be led by an enthusiastic adult, Uncle Something, in the singing of peculiar old songs like "Clementine", "The British Grenadiers" or "Men of Harlech in the Hollow" before they were allowed to watch a short cartoon, a Children's Film Foundation main show that would frequently involve an island, schoolboys and a foreign saboteur, then finally one episode from an ongoing eight-week serial, *King of the Rocket Men* or an old black-and-white *Batman and Robin* where the couple drove around in a completely ordinary 1940s car and Robin pushed his cardboard mask up on his forehead while conversing with his costumed pal in public. The main entertainment had been crawling under people's legs along the rows of seats, or deftly flicking an ice-lolly stick to maybe blind a seven-year-old stranger several rows in front.

These days, of course, the building is another theme pub, a Hard Rock Café, and the town's major cinema is a bog-standard multiplex at Sixfields, out past Jimmy's End and a car-ride away. There's almost a conceptualist brilliance to it all: turn all the cinemas to pubs, get everybody ruinously pissed and then make sure that there's no outlet for the spasms of imagination, fury or libido, nothing to drain off the clumsy fantasies that bob up to the surface of a seventh pint of Wifebeater. The simple-minded plotlines, absent motivation and pointless momentum of the cancelled celluloid will back up and spill out into the Saturday night streets. Before long you'll have fascinating pieces of pure verité on every corner, budget Tarantino stabbings with assailants who hold their knives sideways and debate pop-culture trivia while giving you a Chelsea smile. The Oscars will be going to a flock of scattering shadows on CCTV.

Alma lopes across the woolly, shitty arse of Sheep Street to the gated entrance of the old fish-market, which she notices with some surprise is open. The big covered hall with its glass roof and glistening white slabs is part of Alma's childhood landscape that she thought had been railed off forever. Vanished voices ringing from the wet tiles with an echo like a swimming-baths, and her nan May parting the crowds as she rolled through them like a black iron wrecking ball, lifting a liver-spotted hand and calling out to the fishmongers, all of whom she knew by name. The only one that Alma can remember is Three-Fingered Tunk, presumably so-called in order to distinguish him from all the other men called Tunk who had a different number of remaining digits.

She vaguely remembers hearing something about plans to turn the Fish Market into some sort of exhibition space or gallery, but has dismissed the idea as too fanciful. Not in Northampton; not in this world. It would never happen. The idea that she might have been wrong in her appraisal has, as usual, not occurred to her, which is perhaps why seeing the green metal concertina gates standing unlocked and open seems at first unreal. Feeling as if she's stepping over the tiled threshold of a private dreamtime, Alma and her carrier-bags cross into the white emptiness of the interior.

The daylight falling through the dusty lens of the glass ceiling is diffused and milky, which transmutes the space into that of a realist painting. There are hardly any other figures to be seen about the echoing expanse, as dream-like and deserted as the streets in eighteenth-century prints. It's early days yet, she supposes, with none of the promised art and fashion outlets up and running, but the church-like volume of the place impresses her. She's never previously seen the Fish Market like this, denuded of its mumbling crowds, stripped of its cheery traders calling imprecations into the salt echo.

Now the slabs are bare and bloodless. The establishment is pared back to the bone, the trappings of its recent history sluiced away. Leftover shreds of topaz haddock, the prismatic gutter-silt of scales and staring collar-button eyes, swept off to join the horse-brasses and tankards of the Red Lion Inn that previously occupied this spot; join the menorahs and yarmulkes from the synagogue of a few centuries before. Its past removed, the market is a fertile vacuum waiting to be filled with future, a mysterious quantum void that hums with immanence and possibility. Alma is disconcerted by a sudden surge of hope, a cynicism override. Part of her is gloomily certain that the council will find some way to undo or undermine the venture, probably through sheer indifference rather than hostility, but the mere fact of its existence is a cause for optimism. It suggests to her that there are people in Northampton, people in the country, people in the world who have the will to make things be a different way. It's the same feeling that she gets when she's around her rapper buddies with their Boroughs-esoteric stage names: Influence, St. Craze, Har-Q, Illuzion. It's the sense of social transformation that she sees, at least potentially, in art and occultism, even sometimes on the ragged Roman Thompson fringe of politics. This passionate desire to change reality into a domain more amenable to human beings, this is the ethereal fire that Alma can feel hanging in the brisk Fish Market air.

As if brought into being by her lifted spirits, one of the few blurred forms in Alma's myopic middle-distance suddenly resolves itself on her approach into the unassuming and yet inspirational semblance of Knocker Wood, one of the greatest local antidotes for cynicism since the passing of the sorely-missed lyric barrage-balloon that was the late Tom Hall. Knocker – Alma had known him since they were both teenage hippies without ever learning his first name – had been achingly pretty as a young man, with his long black hair and the wild glitter in his eye that looked like poetry but turned out to be heroin. One of the town's first junkies, Knocker had been part of that mysterious slapstick coterie who took part in their own Narco-Olympics every other Saturday, competitors in the 400-metre dash with stolen television set, haring along the Drapery to the cheers of the flowered-up bohemians gathered on the steps of All Saints Church.

Then everybody had got older. The majority of the long-haired spectators on the steps had straightened up and bailed out of the ailing freak-scene upon turning twenty, getting proper jobs and living up to parents' expectations. This had left only the working-class contingent of the counter culture, who remained committed largely because they had nowhere else to go, and the addicted casualties like Knocker Wood for whom commitment was no longer the real issue. Knocker's middle years had been a horror film, wilfully gothic in the way that only junkies can aspire to. Alma can remember scabby ghouls who held up their collapsing veins with safety-pins, a pre-punk gesture, or who'd ruefully announce that they were "forced" to shoot up in their eyeball or their cock.

While Knocker hadn't been amongst this self-consciously morbid set, for long years he had been a babbling mess that Alma is ashamed to say she'd crossed the street in order to avoid on numerous occasions. He'd lost his wife to an overdose, their daughter to a strain of hepatitis, devastating blows that methadone and Carlsberg Special Brew could not completely muffle. He'd been on a hell-bound train that overshot its destination and ploughed on relentlessly for somewhere even worse when by some miracle he'd managed to leap off the footplate, tumbling helplessly down the embankment towards hard and cold sobriety. No-one had thought that he could do it. Nobody had seen it done before. Knocker had somehow managed to rebirth himself as a hill-walking rural rambler, a drink-and-drug-free boulevardier, a vision of redemption that these days Alma will happily cross several busy motorways to say hello to.

"Knocker! Good to see you. How's it going?"

He's still a good-looking man, beginning to bleach out attractively, worn smooth with age, but the stone-washed demeanour suits him to a T. The short grey hair is in retreat, daily conceding territory to the forehead, while his eyes are still as bright though clear now and engaging fully with the diamond world around him. He's a soothing, peaceful sight, like clean blue pebbles in a stream. He beams and says hello to her, submitting to a hug and genuinely pleased to see her here; pleased to see every dust-mote spinning and illuminated in its Brownian waltz.

He tells her that he's now a counsellor, bringing his own experience to bear on mending others, beating out the world's dents where he can. Alma sees him as one of Bunyan's "mechanick philosophers", dispensing healing words among the other tinkers, a one-man Nation of Saints without the Christianity and bloody pikestaffs. She is overjoyed to hear about his new line of employment, as pleased for herself as she is thrilled for him. Knocker is an important, vital totem in the way that Alma sees the world, proof positive that even in the blackest and most hopeless circumstances things can sometimes turn out wonderful.

She tells him about tomorrow's exhibition, which he says he'll try to get to, and then they discuss the transformed Fish Market, its tundra whiteness stretching all about them. Knocker's eyes light up and flash the way they used to do, though now it's the anticipatory pre-Christmas sparkle of a child rather than the mad hypodermic glint of yore.

"Yeah, they say they'll be having costume balls here and events and things, as well as exhibitions. I think it sounds great. Northampton's never really had a place like this."

About to launch into her usual expectation-lowering list of reasons why it isn't going to work, Alma remembers who she's talking to and brings herself up short. If Knocker Wood can be so bravely optimistic about the Fish Market's prospects, then it's somehow craven for her to indulge in comfy pessimism. She should step up to the mark, and not be such a whining bitch.

"You're right. I like the light here, and I like the atmosphere. It could be really, really good. It'd be nice to see this place filled up again with crowds of people, all in fancy dress. It'd be like the dreams you have when you're a kid."

They talk for a few minutes longer, then they hug goodbye and carry on their individual trajectories. As Alma leaves the market, pushing open the glass swing door at its rear and stepping out into the muddled area at the top of Silver Street, she feels elated both by the encounter and the prospects for her little art-show of the following day. Perhaps her pictures can do what she wants them to. Perhaps they can live up to her unreasonable demands and do something to salve the wounded Boroughs, if it's only by drawing the right kind of attention to the place. At very least she'll have discharged the obligations that she'd taken on after her brother's afterlife experience, and laid some ghosts to rest for both of them, possibly literally. That isn't bad for a year's work.

Alma's descent of the wide road that narrow Silver Street became during the 1970s is her descent into the past, into the Boroughs, and inevitably the cheap pre-war scent of the locale's charisma wells up to surround her, colouring her thoughts and her perceptions. This is the paved-over ground she grew between the cracks of. This is where whatever vision she possesses came from, these thin lanes that trickle downhill to St. Andrew's Road like dirty bathwater. Across the busy road the Multi-storey car park squats upon two or three vanished streets and a few hundred hours of Alma's childhood: the Electric Light Working Men's Club in Bearward Street where she'd go with her parents and her brother on a Sunday night, the Judo club in Silver Street where she'd learned self-defence until she'd realised that she was too big and unpredictable for anyone to pick on. All the memories are crushed beneath the vast weight of the car park and compressed to a prismatic form of anthracite, a fuel that she's been running on for more than fifty years.

The view from this point, high upon the area's eastern slopes, has stayed essentially unchanged for all that time, if by 'essentially' you mean that the fleeced sky is in the same place and the angle of the sweeping incline remains constant. Nearly every other feature of the landscape has been altered or removed. The recently refurbished NEWLIFE buildings dominate the stepped-on vista, the surrounding circuit board of flats and maisonettes, communal cubes that have replaced the terraces of individual homes. Though greatly simplified, the neighbourhood's original main thoroughfares are visible in their archaic tangle, Bath Street, Scarletwell, Spring Lane. Some patches of the panorama are dispirited and overcast while others briefly glory in their sudden spotlight as the afternoon sun pours down through a threadbare sheet of cloud. The graduations of the distance appear much the same as ever, or at least they do to Alma's blurring eyesight. She sees bands of brick or concrete housing giving way to stripes of railway track with overhead wires, and then finally resolving to the grey-green smoulder of Victoria Park in the far west. Despite the shabby overlay of the last half-a-century, she knows the golden template of the district is still there somewhere. The buried heart still beats under the rubble. Forking off from Silver Street into the incline of an underpass below the roaring Mayorhold, Alma draws in a deep breath and ducks her head beneath the mottled surface of the present.

She emerges from the tunnel's orange murk onto a sunken walkway lined with thirty-year-old tiling that suggests to Alma a bulimic Mondrian after a Spanish omelette. Turning left she climbs the ramp towards Horsemarket (West) and makes her way down into the bollard-occluded mouth of Bath Street, past the Kingdom Life building that was erected as a Boy's Brigade Hall in the 60s. Alma's brother had belonged to that peculiar Baptist paramilitary, the Baden-Powell Youth. He had marched with them and their cacophonous percussion-heavy band on Sunday mornings, an eleven-year-old with a brass badge and a lanyard, with a jaunty cadet cap atop his girly golden curls, a happiness and innocence in his blue eyes that Alma thought looked borderline subnormal. He'd have made a perfect paediatric Nazi if he could have carried off a decent goose-step without skipping like a cartoon milkmaid. Alma's fairly certain he attended the odd torchlight rally at the pebble-dashed pavilion across the way, him and his mates all chanting "Arbeit Macht Frei" or "Be Prepared" or whatever their motto was.

She idly wonders if the former Boy's Brigade Headquarters is located near where Moseley's Blackshirts had their offices back in the '30s. This provokes a trailing strand of thought relating to an article by Roman Thompson, which the grizzled lefty veteran had photocopied for her, all about the B.U.F.'s activities around the Mayorhold. There'd been grainy reproductions from newspaper photographs of leading local fascists posing with Sir Oswald while he toured the provinces, with one name in the captions underneath the pictures whited out, presumably by somebody in the archive department. Roman hadn't noticed the deletion and had no clue as to what the missing name might be, though Alma had heard unsubstantiated rumours about Mr. Bassett-Lowkes, the erstwhile local footwear manufacturer and former owner of a house in Derngate with interiors by Rennie Mackintosh. Who knows? If World War Two had gone a different way he might have launched a line of sporty jack-brogues to commemorate the Führer's victory.

Alma carries on down Bath Street with the corned beef-coloured Moseley-vintage flat-blocks on her left, the NEWLIFE towers and their attendant modern terraced houses coming up on Alma's right. Her inner musings still have a large National Socialist component, very like the winter scheduling on Channel Five. She's heard, relatively recently, that Hitler's planned invasion of the British Isles had ended with the capture of Northampton, as if once the centre of the country had been taken then the rest was a foregone conclusion. Alma giggles to herself. Say what you like about the Third Reich, at least they recognised places of historical strategic import when they saw them. And the area has ended up with all the brutal and intimidating Nazi architecture anyway. Albert Speer might have stuck eagles and swastikas up on the tower-blocks, but would that necessarily have made the locals feel more subjugated and discouraged than the cheesy sideways silver lettering that's up there currently? Quite frankly, either way the message would be much the same: tomorrow, most assuredly, does not belong to you.

The further down the hill she goes the more subdued and shadowy her mood becomes, as though Bath Street were an emotional gradient. She's thinking about history's celebrated victims, thinking of the holocaust, the blight of slavery, female suppression and the persecution of sexual minorities. She can recall her own *Spare Rib* days in the 1970s and how she'd briefly entertained the idea that a woman leader might make all the difference. This had obviously been back in the *early* seventies. Her point is that despite the very real continuing abuses born of anti-Semitism, born of racism and sexism and homophobia, there are MPs and leaders who are female, Jewish, black or gay. There are none who are poor. There never have been, and there never will be. Every decade since society's inception has been witness to a holocaust of paupers, so enormous and perpetual that it has become wallpaper, unnoticed, unreported. The mass graves at Dachau and at Auschwitz are, rightly, remembered and repeatedly deplored, but what about the one in Bunhill Fields that William Blake and his beloved Catherine were shovelled into? What about the one under the car park in Chalk Lane, across the road from Doddridge Church? What of the countless generations that have lived poor and have in one way or other died of that condition, uncommemorated and anonymous? Where are their fucking monuments and special ringed dates on the calendar? Where are their Spielberg films? Part of the problem is, no doubt, that poverty lacks a dramatic arc. From rags to rags to rags to rags to dust has never been an Oscar-winning formula.

Across the street a door opens in Simons Walk, one of the modern terraces that crouch beneath the high-rise buildings, and a fat bloke with a shaven head and internet-porn eyes emerges. He looks flatly and dismissively at Alma and quite blatantly hits the 'Delete' key on his Wank Bank before lumbering off along the walkway, probably towards the chip shop in St. Andrew's Street. Alma lets her attention linger for a moment on the tree-walled 'pocket park' that's just over the road, one of the only genuinely nice additions to the neighbourhood. She's got an artist friend called Claire who lives down here in Bath Street flats and makes a point of keeping the small green enclosure litter-free and weeded. Claire had painted an intensely-felt cartoon depiction of her threatened acre with carnivorous tower blocks encroaching on it from all sides which she'd insisted upon giving Alma after Alma fell in love with it, refusing any money and deeply embarrassing the nouveau-riche celebrity, who is forever in her fellow artist's debt. Claire's brave and lovely and a bit bipolar. She makes Alma smile just thinking of her, with a psilocybin mushroom and the legend 'MAGIC' tattooed on one forearm; 'FUCK OFF' on the other. Both of these, to Alma's mind, are worthy creeds to live by.

She considers the made-over bulks of Claremont Court and Beaumont Court, the NEWLIFE towers engaging in their double penetration of the sky. About ten days ago, knowing the renovations for the publicly-loathed swindle that they really were, the council had attempted a stealth opening event. Ruth Kelly's deputy as Minister for Housing, Yvette Cooper, had been ferried in to cut the ribbon early on a Wednesday morning with no prior announcements made, in order to avoid alerting organised protesters. Roman Thompson, obviously, heard all about the covert visit on the night before it happened. Requisitioning a megaphone from local union premises, Roman had turned up bright and early with a hastily convened posse of local anarchists and activists, bringing the sleepy tenants of the maisonettes on Crispin Street out to their balconies by bellowing "GOOD MOOOOOOOORNING, SPRING BOROUGHS" through his borrowed loudhailer. When the pencil-necked Deputy Minister and partner of Brown-aide Ed Balls arrived with the attendant local dignitaries, Roman's vastly-amplified Old Man of the Sea voice had gleefully regaled them with their recent improprieties. He'd sympathetically asked Labour MP Sally Keeble how well she was sleeping these days, after voting for the Iraq War. He'd loudly paid another councillor a compliment upon how smart he looked and speculated that this might be due to all the backhanders he'd recently received. At this point a policeman had rushed up to Roman and informed him that he couldn't say that, to which Roman had replied by pointing out, with logic that was unassailable, that he already had. Alma is grinning. It had been an entertaining morning in the Boroughs, from the sound of it.

Reluctantly she turns her gaze back to the side of Bath Street that she's walking down, the 1930s flat-blocks with the entrance to their central walk-way on her left and just ahead. Alma stares at the spot where she is fairly certain that the hulking chimneystack of the Destructor had once stood and instantly her cheerful mental image of Claire's painting shatters into shel-lac flakes of green and yellow. These immediately scatter on the wind to be replaced by Alma's previous notion of the Boroughs and the other districts like it everywhere across the world as concentration neighbourhoods: zones where the population could be readily identified by prison uniforms of apron or shiny demob suit if they strayed beyond the boundaries, zones where the inmates could be safely worked, starved or simply depressed to death with no fear of a public outcry. Here in Bath Street they'd even provided the contin-ually smoking tower of an incinerator chimney to enhance the death-camp ambience.

Alma, who makes little distinction between internal and external real-ity, doesn't much care if the Destructor in her brother's vision is the awful supernatural force that he described it as, or if it's some hallucinatory and visionary metaphor. As Alma sees things, it's the metaphors that do all the most serious damage: Jews as rats, or car-thieves as hyenas. Asian countries as a line of dominoes that communist ideas could topple. Workers thinking of themselves as cogs in a machine, creationists imagining existence as a Swiss watch mechanism and then presupposing a white-haired and twinkle-eyed old clockmaker behind it all. Alma believes that the Destructor, even as a metaphor, especially as a metaphor, could easily cremate a neighbourhood, a class, a district of the human heart. By the same token then, she must believe that art, her art, anyone's art, is capable of finally demolishing the mind-set and ideas that the Destructor represents if expressed with sufficient force and savagery; sufficient brutal beauty. Alma has no other choice than to believe this. It's what keeps her going. Hardening her eyes to the eroded Bauhaus bal-conies and arches, bricks the colour of dried blood, she turns left and begins to head up the long path that separates the two halves of the flats, towards the walled ramp that leads into Castle Street.

The sun absconds behind a cloud and the green lawns turn grey. The orna-mental stepped edge of the brickwork, grass-cracked and distressed, takes on a different character. The architecture, neat and modern and efficient in its time, now looks its age, a pre-war civil servant who'd once had a promis-ing career ahead of him but now is in his eighties, haunted and incontinent, incapable of recognising his surroundings. Past the flats' drawn curtains are the chambers of a crumbling mind through which the tenants shamble like unfathomable dreams. Outpatients, rock-heads, migrant workers, prostitutes and refugees and transposed flowers like Claire somehow still painting pictures in amidst it all, the way that Richard Dadd had laboured on his tiny fairy visions in the screaming, defecating hells of Bedlam and of Broadmoor.

Alma realises that the place is like a grindstone on which reason, sense of self, and sanity are milled to an undifferentiated flour of madness. Mental illness and depression have been stirred into the mortar of these buildings, or have seeped into the plaster as a type of melancholic damp. Attempting to sustain even the ordinary notion of a purpose to existence in this bleak environment would slowly drive you round the bend, would send you cornery. She realises, wading through the thick air of the central walkway, that insanity occurs most often where a human vision meets the social brickwork. She remembers Pastor Newton's old hymn-writing colleague, madhouse veteran William Cowper, in 1819, addressing William Blake: "You retain health and yet are as mad as any of us all – over us all – mad as a refuge from the unbelief of Bacon, Newton and Locke."

This was a different Newton that the fragile poet was condemning, obviously, not hymn-composing and slave-trading John but Isaac, architect of a material scientific certainty that would supplant the levelling moral apocalypse of his contemporary John Bunyan. Isaac Newton, founding member of the Royal Society and of Freemasonry's Grand Lodge, brutal commander of the Mint and therefore engineer to a financial system rife with Darien Disasters, South Sea Bubbles, Wall Street Crashes and Black Wednesdays. Instigator of the gold standard and thus of Britain's gold reserves, which Blair's chancellor Gordon Brown has quietly sold off just this last year. Sir Isaac, the inventor of an utterly imaginary colour, indigo, and the creator of the modern world's materialistic rat-trap on so many different levels. The great tranquilliser of the spirit, the inducer of what Blake called, accurately, "Newton's Sleep". In Bath Street flats, amongst the destitute and desperate and depressed, she can see all the dreams with which that sleep is troubled.

She breaks from her train of thought to skirt around a recent-looking dog-evacuation that is in her path, a turreted turd-castle that's as yet unbreached by toddler's shoe or teenage trainer, perfect end-product of the material world and also its inevitable monument. It gives at least a semi-solid form to the most frequent word, most frequent thought upon the local modern mind, reiterates the creed of the Destructor: "This is where we send our shit, the things that we no longer have a use for. This means you."

Heading towards the ramp that has replaced the steps that she remembers from her childhood Alma wonders, with a lurch, how many individuals have died down here, how many last breaths have fogged mirrors in unsatisfactory bathrooms or escaped into cramped kitchenettes. It must be hundreds since the flats were put up in the 1930s; all those disappointed souls, their stories worked into the grain of the veneer, encoded in the bar-stripes of the ugly wallpaper. She feels as though she's walking on the bottom of a sea of ghosts, through suffocating fathoms of unruly ectoplasm reaching far above her. Bed-sand memories and voices rise in clouds of silt at every footstep. Poltergeist shells, astral rubbish, rusted ghoul-cans tumbling through the murk of her periphery. Grey ladies drifting on the sluggish phantom current like a strain of supernatural waterweed. An algae of dead monks. She wades with astronaut deliberation up the ramp, a channel-walker slogging up an underwater rise that might with any luck turn into Dover Beach, uncertain how much longer she can hold her breath beneath this sea of misery, this betiding woe.

Under the concrete of the ramp, the steps she sat on as a child must still be there. She can remember walking home once with her mum and little brother, cutting through from Castle Street to Bath Street. Alma would have been, what, nine or ten? She'd bought a comic from Sid's bookstall on the market and had run ahead of Doreen so that she could sit here on the steps and read it for a moment while she waited for her mother to catch up. The comic, unsurprisingly, had been *Forbidden Worlds*. She can't remember if there'd been a *Herbie* story in that issue, but it would have certainly contained the work of Ogden Whitney in one form or other. While she'd sat here on her chilly granite perch and marvelled, Whitney would have been already more than half-way down the boozy path that led to the asylum and the grave. She has a chilly premonition that somewhere in the year 2050 there is someone having much the same thoughts about her, as if Alma and Ogden are already both together in a pallid green Unknown with all the wolf-men and the Frankensteins; as if the whole world and its future were already posthumous and she was looking down on all this loveless folly from a point outside and over time, from the forbidden world. Everything's dead already. Everyone is gone.

She steps out onto Castle Street and pauses, noticing the almost instantaneous shift in mood and light. Well, that was interesting. She turns to gaze back down the ramp, along the central path to Bath Street with the NEWLIFE tombstones rising up beyond, and smiles. Fear of decay and death, she thinks. Fear of depreciation, destitution and decline. Is that the best you've got?

With a refreshing dodgem whiff of new resolve flaring her nostrils, Alma heads down Castle Street towards the point where Bristol Street bleeds into Chalk Lane. Crossing over the deserted road towards its south side, Alma eyes up the dilapidated Golden Lion, the establishment where Warry had poured out his wild phantasmagoria to her only a year ago. A year. She can't remember anything about it except painting, drawing, chewing Rizla papers up and spitting them into a bowl, the shifts of season only noticeable in the change of imagery upon her drawing board or easel, a whole summer spent delineating snotty-nosed dead children in soft pencil. And now here she is.

The junction she's approaching used to have a sweetshop owned by some-one that she and the other children knew as 'Pop', a white-haired portly chap with glasses who sold homemade penny ice lollies and penny drinks. The latter had been half-pint milk bottles filled up with tap water and homeopathic doses of fruit cordial, a water-memory of having once been shown a molecule of rosehip syrup. Still, on thirsty afternoons, even the immaterial concept of a tasty beverage had been enough. They'd paid their pennies and had gratefully gulped down a fluid that looked pinkish if you happened to be drinking it at sunset. Looking back, she realises that she should have automatically mis-trusted anybody who called themselves Pop. Ah, well. You live and learn.

Down at the bottom end of Castle Street, she passes on her left the lit-tle patch of grass, still seemingly unoccupied, where she had almost been abducted as a child. It's one of the few childhood memories that she still can't properly resolve, where she's still not sure what was really going on. Her and some other eight-year-olds had found the rusted shell of an abandoned Morris Minor on the grass and, in an area that offered little in the way of free activ-ities and entertainments, they had treated it as if it were a theme park or at least a proto-bouncy castle. They'd climbed on its bonnet and had sat inside behind its steering wheel. Alma had been on top of the wrecked vehicle, man-ically jumping up and down on its corroded roof, using it as a heavy metal trampoline, when a black car had glided out of Chalk Lane into Bristol Street to pull up suddenly beside the stretch of turf where they were playing.

When the thin young man with Brylcreemed hair and a dark suit climbed from the driver's seat and started striding angrily towards the child-infested Morris Minor, all the other kids had been positioned so they could immedi-ately scarper, leaving only Alma stranded on the creaking roof. The man – whenever she tries to remember what he looked like she gets only a false, superimposed photograph of Ian Brady – had grabbed her from atop the wreck and carried her, screaming and wailing, back to his own motor, shov-ing her inside. There was a youngish woman in the car, with mousy brown hair, although once again Alma's melodramatic memory has pasted in a shot of Myra Hindley, slightly younger and without the bleach or vampire panda make-up. Alma had been pleading, crying, struggling in the back seat. The young man had said that he was going to take her off to the police station but then had suddenly relented, perhaps when he noticed that the woman with him was by now looking almost as frightened as the tubby, weeping little girl. He'd opened the rear door and let her out onto the pavement before roaring off, leaving her standing sobbing by the roadside for her pals to find when they emerged from hiding. What had all that been about?

Part of her is almost inclined to take the story as it comes. She can quite easily see her would-be abductor as a sour-faced and emotionally strangled young churchgoer of the middle classes and the early 1960s, taking his fiancée for a daring spin through the poor quarter, wanting to impress her with his moral rectitude by scaring straight one of the district's infant vermin. That seems much more likely than the lurid child-molester narrative she'd retroactively imposed on the scenario, although it doesn't make her feel a lot less interfered-with, or less angry. She recalls the young man's pasty skin and his cold little eyes. Whatever he'd imagined he was doing and whatever his intent, he'd been no different from the current rash of curb-crawlers, using the Boroughs as their private zoo. She'd been disturbed to learn that during the alarming weekend of apparent rapes that had occurred last year, one of the victims had reported being dragged into a car in Chalk Lane, almost on the same spot where Alma's attempted kidnapping had happened. Walking past the unkempt slope of yellow-green she wonders if the place has some malignant genius loci, something in the soil that gives it a predisposition towards a specific crime, repeated down the decades. She remembers hearing that a skeleton had been found at the site during some excavations in the nineteenth century, but doesn't know if it turned out to be the product of an ancient burial or of a relatively recent murder, doesn't know if it was male or female, child or adult. Lacking any contradictory evidence, she construes the remains as those of an abduction victim, lonely underneath the earth and calling out for company. Whichever way she looks at it, this is a haunted piece of ground. How typical, then, that she's chosen this place for her preview.

She turns left into Chalk Lane where she immediately sees the nursery with people moving round inside it, gingerly transporting canvasses from one side of the small space to another. Alma can't see any obvious signs of damage or catastrophe and feels relieved, although to be quite honest she's not in the least bit nervous about how tomorrow's going to turn out. She's confident that everything will be the way it's meant to be.

Mounting the short flight of stone steps towards the door, she casts her mind back to when this place was the Marjorie Pitt-Draffen dance school, an oasis of refinement that had been incongruously situated in the Boroughs, not known for its Terpsichorean accomplishments, a place where they discouraged having sex while standing up in case it led to dancing. Her distinguished actor pal Bob Goodman has confessed to having often visited the dance school as a child, presumably back in the days before his face had caught fire and been put out with a shovel. She imagines him, a nervous middle-class kid shuffling up these very steps each Saturday to take his hated lessons, dressed up in a kilt. It's probably all for the best that little Bob and little Alma never met back then, not with him in a tartan skirt and talking posh. She'd have well kicked his head in.

Pushing open the swing door, Alma takes in the scene. Other than her there are three people present. Visiting from Wales, Burt Regan is the one officially entrusted with getting the pieces down here and set up in the right place, although it seems he's being helped in this by wiry Roman Thompson. Burt calls out to Alma as she enters.

"'Ello, Alma. 'Ere, was that yer finger-armour that I could 'ear rattlin' when you were comin' down the street, or 'ave you 'ad yer fanny pierced?"

"Yes, actually, I have. I got a length of anchor-chain from the Titanic that I wear as jewellery. That's probably what you could hear. It cost me thousands, and it would have been twice that if I'd have bothered to have all the rust scraped off. Hello, Rome."

Setting *Work In Progress* up against the makeshift gallery's end wall, Rome Thompson grins, crumpling the moth-eaten glove puppet of his face, a distressed Basil Brush after the Pytchley Hunt has finished with him. Crafty wrinkles in a windscreen shatter-pattern radiate from eyes that still burn like gunpowder fuses. Alma thinks that Roman Thompson is quite possibly the most dangerous individual she has ever met, and she means this in an admiring way. Why are the best blokes always gay?

"'Ow are yer doin', Alma? D'yer like 'ow we've set up yer exhibition? I've been supervisin', like. Burt needs a foreman so that 'e don't fuck it up."

"You lying cunt! I've been 'ere since eleven, and this fucker turned up 'alf an 'our back. 'E's refused to lift a fuckin' finger ever since. 'E says 'e's only 'ere in 'is capacity as an art critic. 'E's like fuckin' Sister Wendy, only interested in the ones with cocks."

Leaving the two men to their robust interlocution, Alma sidles over to the nursery's fourth occupant, a pretty, goggle-eyed young woman standing at the room's far end and looking moderately intimidated by Roman and Burt, a pair of nutcase ogres from another century. This is Lucy Lisowiec, a representative of the community association CASPAR, a group that provides one of the few remaining neural networks still holding the senile neighbourhood together. Alma met her through the Streetlaw rappers, for whom Lucy seems to be a combination of street-credible but sensible big sister and benign probation officer. It was Lucy who managed to secure the nursery for Alma's exhibition, which means that it's Lucy's job that's on the line if anything goes wrong. This is no doubt the reason why she's looking nervously at Burt and Roman, who give the impression that there's something going badly wrong simply by turning up, like uniformed Gestapo officers at a pet funeral. Alma attempts to reassure her.

"Hello, Luce. I can see just from that look you've got on your face that these two – well, they're little more than hired thugs, really – that they've managed to offend you. You poor love. You've probably heard things that someone your age shouldn't have to hear, things that will stay with you forever. All I can do is apologise. The man down at the pen said if I didn't give them work, then they'd be put to sleep."

Lucy is laughing, showing off her winsome overbite. She really is a little darling, working on a dozen projects with the Boroughs residents at once, minding their kids down at the CASPAR offices in St. Luke's House on nights when she's there working late, shepherding Streetlaw to their gigs, living alone above MacDonald's in the Drapery, developing a stomach ulcer at the age of twenty-seven – Alma has been recently force-feeding her both Actimel and Yakult – all from trying to cooperate creatively with wonderful, deserving people who are also sometimes utter fucking nightmares, Alma herself certainly included in that category.

"Aw, no, they're all right. They're house-trained. No, I was just looking at the pictures and the model and all that. Alma, this is fantastic. This is really full-on."

Alma smiles politely, but is much more pleased than she lets on. Lucy is an accomplished artist in her own right, mostly working in the risky medium of brick and aerosol. The only female tagger in the county and as far as Alma knows one of the only ones in England, Lucy had been forced to start out working solo as the 1-Strong Crew before an influx of new member meant that she could upgrade to the 2-Strong Crew. Under the nom-de-guerre of CALLUZ, an urchin enunciation of the spectrum or of street-worn calluses, she's beautified a number of unprepossessing premises throughout the years, although she now protests that she's too old to climb and run. Alma suspects, however, that this façade of responsible maturity is liable to evaporate after a second Smirnoff Ice. Lucy, whatever she pretends, is still an active artist, and so naturally her opinion means a lot to Alma. More than this, though, Lucy's young, part of a generation that Alma has very little knowledge of and isn't certain that her work appeals to. If Lucy at least admires her stuff enough not to spray over it in bold metallic Fat Caps with Day-Glo drop-shadow, well, then Alma must be doing something right. She lets herself cast an appraising eye across the works that are already in position, which is to say most of them. She finds, possibly unsurprisingly, that she agrees entirely with Lucy's assessment of her full-on and fantastic show.

Up at the room's north end is the large tile arrangement partly cribbed from Escher, mounted on its backing board and titled *Malignant, Refractory Spirits*. Sharing the same wall as this are a variety of what seem to be illustrations from a children's picture-book, some in soft pencil monochrome and some in gloriously-realised watercolour, like the psychedelic stand-out image *An Asmodeus Flight*. The east wall, the biggest one, is dominated by the overwhelming mass of *The Destructor*, which Alma is pleased to see has been left mostly covered by a hanging cloth: it's too much, too distressing to stand in its naked glare, just as she wanted it to be. It's Alma's *Guernica*, and she doubts that it's going to be hanging in the Mitsubishi boardroom any time this century. Quite frankly, she can't see it hanging anywhere that ordinary decent people who just want to get on with their lives might stumble over it. The painting is so forceful that only the strongest of the smaller pieces can be hung on the same wall. *Forbidden Worlds*, with its infernal hostelry, goes to the left of *The Destructor*. When she brings the final painting, *Chain of Office*, down here to the nursery tomorrow morning, she decides she's going to hang it on the west wall, facing the more devastating piece as some kind of aesthetic counterbalance.

In the middle of the room there are four tables pushed together to support the papier-mâché model that she'd made with all those Rizla papers, chewing them and spitting them into a suitable receptacle. Melinda Gebbie, her best mate, had looked a bit revolted when Alma had demonstrated her technique, which had made Alma try to justify her processes by referencing the book-devouring 1960s visionary John Latham, whom she'd met once and was an admirer of. She'd also tried explaining the importance of using her own saliva, so that in a literal sense her DNA would be part of the complicated structure she was building. In the end she'd given up and confessed that she just liked gobbing.

If she is honest with herself, the model is the only item in the exhibition that she isn't wholly sure about. It doesn't seem as if it's saying much, just sitting there like that, solid and unambiguous. Maybe she'll see how it goes down tomorrow at the preview and then leave it out of the ensuing London show if she's not pleased with the response. There's no point worrying about it now, at any rate. Things tend to sort themselves out, Alma thinks, although she knows that this directly contradicts the laws of physics, common sense, and her political experience of the last forty years.

She looks up from the tabletop display, out through the nursery's front picture-window, where she notices that Chalk Lane teeters on the brink of dusk. A skinny little mixed-race girl with corn-row hair and a fire-engine red PVC mac is clacking through the umbra, her arms crossed defensively across her chest and a preoccupied expression on her face. Alma thinks 'crack whore', then berates herself for her descent into class-profiling and for her lazy and mean-spirited assumptions. By then the young woman has departed, tottering away into the twilight that is gathering in the east, spilling out from Horsemarket and down Castle Street in an obscuring violet avalanche.

Alma stands chatting in the borrowed space with Roman, Burt and Lucy for a little longer. Roman tells her that he's been out door to door, drumming up interest in tomorrow's exhibition from amongst the local populace. She asks him how the cartoon poster that she knocked off for his Defend Council Houses group is selling, and is told that it's still moving steadily. This image, which depicts a Godzilla-sized 'fat cat' looming from behind the NEWLIFE towers to rake through Scarletwell Street's surface with its monstrous talons, while not a well-drawn piece by her usual standards, had provoked some small controversy. With his keen eye for free publicity Rome had involved the local *Chronicle & Echo*, thus affiliating Alma publicly with his extremely worthy cause. In the accompanying article had been some rather piqued, dismissive comments from a Conservative councillor, one Derek Palehorse, who'd insisted that he couldn't see what all the fuss was over when so much was being done to help the neighbourhood already. Alma smiles now at the memory. How nice of him to stick his head above the parapet. She can recall the recent scandal when through Roman Thompson's machinations, the town council's very generous remuneration of a former colleague had been published in the local paper, prompting councillors to protest that their dealings should never have been made public. When the newspaper had polled its readers to see what their feelings were upon the issue, they'd been startled to discover that most of the votes supported the town council's right to secrecy. Then they'd found that almost all of these votes had issued from Councillor Palehorse in one way or other. It was mentioned on the "Rotten Boroughs" page of *Private Eye*, to the deserved embarrassment of everyone concerned. Honestly, Alma thinks. These people. What a bunch of shitclowns. This is a new word that she's picked up from columnist and splendidly ill-humoured television writer Charlie Brooker, whom she wants to marry, and a term which she already can't imagine how she got along without for all those years, for all that endless line of shitclowns climbing out of history's collapsing car. Don't bother, they're here.

Taking a sudden fancy to the thought of walking home through her old neighbourhood, she waves aside the offer of a lift from Burt and kisses everyone goodbye. Rome Thompson hints mysteriously of something that he's got to tell her but first wants to check his facts; something about the stretch of river next to the gas-holder down on Tanner Street. He says he'll let her know tomorrow morning at the show. Leaving the others to arrange the last few details and lock up, she zips her jacket to the neck and exits by the swing door, shuffling down the stone steps onto Phoenix Street. Glancing towards her left and down Chalk Lane she can see Doddridge Church, with that bizarre door halfway up its western wall. Alma imagines the celestial flyover, the Ultraduct, as she's depicted it in one of the works that she's just been looking at, an elevated walkway that seems to be chiselled out of light emerging from the blocked-off loading bay to curve away towards the west, with phosphorescent figures blurring back and forth across its span.

The church itself seems, in her eye, to sum up the combined political and spiritual upheavals that have typified Northampton's history. It occurs to her that most of these have been linguistic in their origins. John Wycliffe had begun the process in the 14th century with his translation of the Bible into English. Right there, by insisting that the English peasant classes had a right to worship in their own tongue, Wycliffe and his Lollards were establishing an element of class-war politics in the religious altercation. In Northampton, Lollards and other religious radicals seem to have found a natural home, so that by Queen Elizabeth's reign in the fifteen-hundreds there are Northamptonshire congregations singing home-made hymns in English rather than just listening to chanted psalms in Latin as the Church demanded. Lacking any earlier examples that spring readily to mind, she wonders if her town is where the English hymn originates. That would explain a lot, now that she thinks about it.

Within fifty years of Queen Elizabeth's demise, of course, the Civil War kicked off with Parliament greatly emboldened by the radical sects that seemed to be clustered in the English Midlands, all the Ranters, Anabaptists, Antinomians, Fifth Monarchists and Quakers, most of them engaged in publishing inflammatory texts or fiery flying rolls. Some of the openly seditious 'Martin Marprelate' tracts had been published secretly here in the Boroughs, and in general it seemed that the Protestant revolution hinged upon the word, with painting and the visual arts perceived as the preserve of Papists and elitists. To become a painter would require materials and means, while writing, strictly speaking, required only the most rudimentary education. Obviously, literature was still seen as the sole preserve of the elite, which is just one of many reasons why John Bunyan's writings, crystal-clear allegories conveyed in common speech, were so incendiary in their day. His hymn, *To Be a Pilgrim*, was the anthem for the disenchanted Puritans migrating for America, while *Pilgrim's Progress* would become a source of inspiration for the New World settlers second only to the Bible, and these weren't the rakish, courtly witticisms or the fawning tributes of contemporaries such as Rochester or Dryden. These were written by a member of that new and dangerous breed, the literate commoner. They were composed by someone who insisted that plain English was a holy tongue, a language with which to express the sacred.

Of course, they'd banged Bunyan up in Bedford nick for getting on a dozen years, while art and literature are still most usually a product of the middle class, of a Rochester mind-set that sees earnestness as simply gauche and visionary passion as anathema. William Blake would follow Bunyan and, closer to home, John Clare, but both of these had spent their days impoverished, marginalised as lunatics, committed to asylums or plagued by sedition hearings. All of them are heirs to Wycliffe, part of a great insurrectionary tradition, of a burning stream of words, of an apocalyptic narrative that speaks the language of the poor. At the stone meeting house in Chalk Lane, Philip Doddridge pulled all the diverse strands of that narrative together. Hanging out with Swedenborgians and Baptists, taking up his ministry here in the poorest quarter, writing *Hark! The Glad Sound!*, championing the dissenting cause, all from this scruffy little mound ... Doddridge is Alma's foremost local hero. It'll be an honour staging her show in the shadow of his church. Alma elects to walk down Little Cross Street and then follow Bath Street round to Scarletwell and her beloved strip of bare grass on St. Andrew's Road.

She lopes down through the failing light with blocks of flats to either side of her, the Bath Street buildings' west face on her right and to her left the 1960s landings and the sunken walkways of Moat Place, Fort Place, outlying features of a long-demolished castle become streets where Alma's great-grandfather Snowy Vernall had lived, getting on a hundred years ago. Mad Snowy, marrying the landlord's daughter from the long-since disappeared Blue Anchor pub in Chalk Lane, which he'd visited on one of his improbably long strolls from Lambeth. All these chance events, these people and their complicated lives, the trillion small occurrences without which she would not be her; would not be here.

Across the street, incontinent lamps stand apologetically in puddles of their own piss-coloured light. She just about remembers when Moat Street and Fort Street were still standing, and when Mrs. Coleman's gingerbread-house sweetshop was down at the lower end of Bath Street, although Alma was no more than four or five back then. A much more vivid memory remains from slightly later, when the maze of red brick terraces had been demolished and there was just wasteland here, before the blocks of flats had been erected. She remembers playing with the first of many best friends, Janet Cooper, on vast fields of rubble and black mud beneath a dirty fleece of Boroughs sky. For some reason there had been industrial off-cuts scattered everywhere and gingering the puddles, L-shaped bits of metal which Alma and Janet had discovered could be plaited into rusty orange swastikas and skimmed across the demolition site like Nazi throwing-stars. Just as with the abandoned Morris Minor, the brick scree and piled-up devastation were regarded as civic amenities, play areas provided for the district's young, tetanus crèches of a kind then common in the neighbourhood. Mind you, this had been back in the Macmillan years, the later 1950s. Alma and her little pals, flying kites into power lines, opening veins climbing through ragged gaps in corrugated tin, had never had it so good.

She turns left at Little Cross Street's end, into the bottom part of Bath Street. Now the 1960s housing blocks are on her left, the shabby 1930s elegance of Greyfriars Flats across the darkening road upon her right. As she

descends the flow of time becomes more viscous, thickened by historic sediments that have collected near the bottom of the valley. In the settling obscurity around her there are windows lighting up, weak colour washes filtered
through thin curtains, faded postage stamps fixed to the night with unseen
hinges. Everywhere is gluey with mythology.

The district's different blocks of flats, which were already crowding out
the terraced houses even forty years ago, had been no different to the district's dumped cars or demolished buildings from a child's perspective. All of
it was landscape, meant to be inhabited and climbed and hidden in, its hulks
transformed by juvenile imagination into frontier forts, unheard-of planets,
a perpetually mutating Gormenghast of slates and splinters. Greyfriars Flats,
being the nearest to their house down on St. Andrew's Road, had always been
a second, more expansive back yard to her for as long as Alma can remember, practically an annex to her tombstone-cold front doorstep. One of her
two almost-murders had occurred here, the attempted strangling in a dustbin
cul-de-sac, and she's had dreams about the place that were more vivid than
her memories. There was the dream where she was dead and confined to the
inner washing-line enclosure of the flats, pursued by a mercury-poisoned and
moth-eaten version of Carroll's Mad Hatter round the overcast and dismal
purgatory until the end of time. There was the dream with a tall, futuristic
tower of blue glass erupting from the flats' top end on Lower Cross Street,
where Alma remembers being shown a quietly humming oblong mechanism
with a small display screen upon which all of the universe's particles were
being counted. And of course, this was where Alma had been visited by her
first life-transforming vision. Smiling to herself in the congealing twilight,
Alma crosses the deserted road to Greyfriars' southwest corner, carrier-bags
swinging from one ornamented fist.

The bottom entrance to the inner rectangle is gated off with black iron
rails and has been for some years. Residents only, which she finds entirely
understandable. She can still stand there at the gate and peer along the path to
where the little patch of shrubbery is partly visible. As she recalls, it had been
on a chilly day in early Spring when she'd been eight or nine, sauntering home
for lunch from Spring Lane School up at the top of Scarletwell Street. On a
whim, she'd taken a diversion through the flats purely because she'd thought
it might make a more interesting view than the plain slope of the old hill, the
empty playing fields that bordered it, the rear windows of their surviving terrace on St. Andrew's Road. Idling down the concrete pathways of the block's
interior amongst the flapping sheets and baby-clothing, she had reached the
triangle where all the bushes grew down at the bottom end. She might have
walked past and paid the familiar vegetation no attention were it not for the
intriguing detail that had caught her junior miniaturist's eye.

Hung from the thinnest needle of a twig, there on a waxy evergreen, was a translucent white grub that appeared to levitate, so fine was the material by which it was suspended, its minute head blind and glistening. Dangling in the cold crystal of the morning air it curled and shimmied like an escapologist, albeit one whose act worked in reverse and hinged upon secreting his own straitjacket. Twisting and contorting it deliberately wound itself up in the near-invisible strands that it was somehow producing. Alma had stooped closer to the bush in awe, her nose only an inch or two from the dependent caterpillar. She remembers wondering if it was thinking anything and making up her mind that probably it was, if only squishy little caterpillar thoughts.

She'd never witnessed this precise form of activity before, and she had puzzled over why the tiny creature was alone in its pursuit. She'd realised that she must be looking at the manufacture of a rice-grain sized cocoon, but hadn't previously understood that this was such a solitary operation. It was then that Alma had observed to her relief that the grub had at least one little friend, another pallid maggot that laboriously inched along a nearby shoot, where there were ...

Alma had gasped noisily and taken a step back. Reality had shivered, reconfiguring itself before her startled eyes. On every branch, on every twig and under every leaf of the coniferous shrub had been a thousand more identical white worms, all patiently engaged in the same task. The bush itself was an immense white cobweb, suddenly alive with writhing threads of alien purpose. How could she have stood there for five minutes and not noticed this spectacular and otherworldly sight? The moment had been an apocalypse, in the sense that the poets of that school might use the term, people like Henry Treece or Alma's favourite, Nicholas Moore. She'd realised in that instant that the world about her was not necessarily the way she saw it, that amazing things might constantly be happening under everybody's noses, things that people's mundane expectations stopped them from perceiving. Watching what she'd later realised must be silkworms colonise what she'd belatedly construed to be a mulberry bush, she'd formed a vision of the world as glorious and mutable, liable to explode into unlikely new arrangements if you simply paid enough attention; if your eye was in.

She stands there, a suspicious figure peering through black bars and evening murk into the Greyfriars courtyard, and feels phantoms swarming everywhere around her. She is always here at this precise location and this moment, her ordained position in the simultaneous and unchanging 4D gem of space-time. Life is on an endless loop, her consciousness revisiting the same occasions for eternity and always having the experience for the first time. Human existence is a grand recurrence. Nothing dies or disappears and each discarded condom, every dented bottle-top in every alleyway is as immortal as Shamballah or Olympus. She feels the unending marvel of a beautiful and dirty world swell to include her in its fanfare music. Lowering her caked lashes, she imagines everything around her wriggling and alive, suddenly made out of a billion glossy organisms that she has not previously noticed, the whole landscape covered in a spectral gauze, a fresh-spun silk of circumstance.

At length she turns away from the locked gate and carries on down Bath Street into Scarletwell Street and on to St. Andrew's Road. The short strip of ancestral grass is still the same. As usual she puzzles over the still-standing corner house and tries without success to work out where the Warren residence had once been situated. Actually, she's pretty sure it was the spot between two young and sturdy trees about halfway along. It feels appropriately eerie, but she can't be certain. Finally it strikes her that to be stood motionless beside the road down in this quarter of the town might possibly be sending the wrong signals and she turns away to walk the long route home, up Grafton Street to Barrack Road and then around the Racecourse back onto East Park Parade.

Crossing the Kettering Road up by the oddly decorative sheltered tram-stop where the town's principal gallows at one time resided she is thinking about art in the Charles Saatchi era; art become mono-dimensional commercial gesturing directed at an audience so culturally lost it feels it has no platform from which it can venture criticism. Only other artists – and then only renegades – seemed confident enough in their opinions to effectively mount a rebuttal. She recalls the last time that she'd had Melinda Gebbie over for a memorable meal during which the expatriate American provided an unanswerable critique of Tracy Emin's work which Alma wishes that she'd said herself: "My God, can you imagine being able to fit all the names of everyone you ever slept with in a *tent*?" Alma had gaped for a few moments and then soberly put forward her suggestions for capacious venues that might just about accommodate Melinda's list. The Parthenon, Westminster Abbey, China, Jupiter.

Making her way along the gorgeously eroded pavement of East Park Parade she at last reaches her own door, fumbling in her too-tight trouser pockets to retrieve a temporarily elusive key before effecting entry. Inside Alma switches on the lights and winces ruefully at all the mess and clutter. Why can't she be tidy like a proper adult? Inwardly, she blames it on the influence of Top Cat. When she and her brother Warry were both growing up they'd both aspired to live in a converted dustbin like their feline hero, somewhere where you could just brush your teeth then switch the nearby streetlamp off with a convenient pull-cord before pulling on the battered lid and bunking down. Only much later had she wondered where he spat the toothpaste.

Alma stuffs her peppers, covers them with feta cheese and sticks them in the oven. As they roast she rolls a joint and smokes it while she makes a start on leafing through her copy of *New Scientist*. After supper she has three or four more reefers while she finishes the science magazine, reads *Private Eye* and then re-watches two more episodes from the last season of *The Wire*. Around eleven she stubs out her final fatty of the day, gulps down her Red Rice Yeast pill and her ineffectual Kalms and turns off all the lights before retiring.

Naked underneath her duvet, Alma rests on her right side and pulls a tuck of quilt between her bony knees. Off in the smash and puke of Friday night are sirens, catcalls, curses from over-relaxed young men and women navigating their ways back and forth along East Park Parade. She rubs her feet together, satisfied by the dry rasp of sole on sole. Mulberry cobwebs creep across the inside of her eyelids.

On the edge of sleep, her mind replays an incidental image from the beautifully-written television drama that she's just been watching: a bandanna-sporting corner-boy sits on his stoop amidst the desolated vacant lots or syringe-carpeted back alleys of West Baltimore. The muddily-remembered snapshot brings her suddenly awake with a deep pang of dread and loss that she does not immediately understand. Something about the Boroughs, some-thing about all the neighbourhoods that are essentially just like it, right across the world. All of the men and women, all the kids inhabiting this universal landscape of cracked pavements, steel-jacketed grocer shops and meaningless corroded street-names from another century, living their whole lives among these sorry dead-ends with the knowledge that the concrete bollard and the chain-link fence will still be there when they are all long gone, long gone.

A bottle smashes, somewhere off along the Kettering Road. She pushes all the haunting thoughts of ghetto and mortality away, and tries instead to let the revelatory silkworms wrap her in a merciful cocoon of anaesthesia.

Alma's got a big day ahead of her tomorrow.

ROUND THE BEND

Awake, Lucia gets up wi' the wry sing of de light. She is a puzzle, shore enearth, as all the Nurzis and the D'actors would afform, but nibber a cross word these days, deepindig on her mendication and on every workin' grimpill's progress. Her arouse from drowse is like a Spring, a babboling book that gorgles up amist the soils o' sleep, flishing and glattering, to mate the mournin' son. Canfind in this loquation now she gushes and runs chinkling from her silt and softy bed, pooring her harp out down an illside and aweigh cross the old manscape to a modhouse brookfast. Ah, what a performance, practised and applausible. She claps her hands, over her ears, to drone out all the deadful wile-ing and the sorey implecations of whor farmlay. With her bunyans all complainin' she escapes the Settee o' Destraction and beguines her evrydaily Millgrimage towar's ridemption or towords the Wholly Sea; to wards, the tranquilisity of night.

Spoonin' the tousled egg into her scrambled head she wells, as iffer, on the past now. Sadly hatched in Triste at seven past the century and seven past the year, born to the clench and stamour of a paupoise warld, she was denied the mummer's teatre. Not a dripple Nora drop was she aloud. The molcow was sucked dry, by George, who went from one mamm to an udder all of his serpenitentine life. Eve'n the girden of her garlhood he had snaken from her, eden then, with him the dirty apple of their Mermaw's eye and allwas raising cain, which Lucia had resistered for as long as she was abel. He'd been furteen, shy was only ten, to pet it baldly. Wristling under milky and transluciant sheets in a suck-session of clamped, crusterphobic rended rooms, the da off summerwhere with all his righting and the mudder rural, pagan in her unconcern, forever standing pisspots on the parlour table where they lifft their venerable beaded halos on the varnish. Giorgio's dragon would rear up, out from the scampy wondergrowth and orgiantly demanding her at-ten shuns while their Moider only smirled, ingently dull, and let her borther press a head with his idventure, up into the little light, the little depth.

Not that she hoydent wellcomed his hardvances, penfull at forst, back then when she still beliffied that he loved her, back there in their papadise when she was tigrish in the milibloom of her youth-ray tease. Setting in the die-room now she chews over her toast, raised two old tines, and wanders if he ova reilly and tooralee was her brooder. Hidn't there once been a scarlet letter, a dismissive from their Further in the Land of Ire? He'd met with Cowsgrope the Invincible who had confleshed to scraping the odd barnacle in nineteen nundread-for, the year that Orgy-porgy-puttin-pie was farst consceptered. Is Dis Nod my sun, her darkglassed da had cried in his tormental angruish, to witch the briny mare durst not deply. The mater had been left unseddled. Woden that expain a Lot, now, about Morma and her Gorgo? How the peer of hum were all-ways clost, unhearthily so in her cestimation, from the grendle to the crave? She maddily recalls her fishermum warmin' up the jung mastur's bait incide her muth on chillywilly ofterrnoons, or thinkshe-thinkshe does. Of curse, it wurd make plaint for alter see why they t'woo had insested she be liplocked with insanatoriums, fear Luci-lippi was heir poppy's seed, his sperkle efferdent in all she set or dit, they way she allwise spoke her wheel, whoreas in Dirgeo was not a wit o' the same subsdance to be scene. Old Gnawer had deicided then and there that her firstbore should carryon the dinnersty, no mutter that he mite halve been an utter mance. As for her lital gill, the da's reel darter, shutter up in lumatrick asylence, like at Pranginstein's or finalee herein Saif Handrue's house-piddle.

Lucia's nicey-nercy, featherly Patrisia, sips besight her while she bibs her searly monin' cuppla Tees and mentalpatiently ensquires jest what the flame-ous rider's cross-i, dot-t doubter well be druin' with hersylph toda.

"Will, I thought I might have a wonder in the ground, now, seeing as it's such a liffley day and all the flawers are in Bloom. I dent mind bein' bi myself, and I dar say you've auther fish to frey. Bee off, and don't you weary about me, Pat. Isle be writer's reign."

With her compinion thus-why's beassured, Lucia blots her nips upon a paper lapkin and excurses herself, skipling out and thistling down a freshly dizzifected carrydor towheres glass D'orways at its fatherst and, light runnin' inter light.

Outsighed, she stunnds and tics it in, from the cerebrulean skullbowl of the fymirment above to the sage cortin of the fir hereyeson, ur the flarebeds close at hand withal their petalsparks and fleurwork sprays o' culeur. Though it's not ideyll she likes displace the best of all she's in-bin. She injoys the handson dictors with their bed's-eye menners, und dien, roughly for o'cock, she aften langours at the gaits to watch the jesslin' squallboys from the Glammar Scruel that stems adjescent to hier pysche-hattrick instinction. Spitty as a pricksure they go scruffling down the Bulling Roude beyond the iron realings, snurchin' up each other's badgered caps an' grubbin' at each other's bawls wit' wilde hel-larity, obliffeyus to her sprying from the foolyage in wishtful, privet larchery.

Bud wort she likes the bestival apout her current reasidance is how it old-ers with the saysongs, nava quit the seam firm one die to the nicht. The weir and wen of it der knot same so influxable as some lockations that hav inter-trained her persence down orcross the docaides. Her, she carn miander reed-ily betwin her pa'stime and her fewcheers; betorn hear an' dare; betwhether wan welt under noxt. Heir at Feint Andruse Cycle-logical Infirmitry it is entimely passible, in Lussye's questimation, to slep from the birthly whelm intru a terrortree o' feary-tell and eld mirthology, where every mutterforth is an immadiate and enternal troth. Wye, summertimes she hurdly gnos whatch finny-form she's in at prisent, or if altimately alder not-houses might nut torn out to bye the selfshame plaice, one vurst istabilismend trance-ending inner-notional bindaries and filt-wit fausty dactyrs tyin' to gut hauled ov hert sole.

The bride-green yawns strich all orerrnd her, wid the poplores, erlms and faroof bildungs all roturnin' in her planetree obit, undherstood still art the cindre like the Son, the veri soeurce of lied. The sauce of her, now! With a gae spring in her stoop, she-sex out on her walk in purgress, on her wake-myop parundulations, on her expermission, heeding oft acrux the do-we grass twowords the poertree-line of the spinny wetting in the da'stance. Iff she flaunces, as veneficent as elled Sent Knickerless hermself, an innerscent ulled lay-die in a wurli cardiagran out strawling on the institrusion lorns.

What the upserver dursn't know, hooever – and there's all-ways en absur-ver, err at list in Lucia's experience – is that she's nu alld woman. En fict, she's no age atoll: she's orl her silves at whence, curdle to gravey, won insight the ether like a sat of Rushin' dirlls. Her Babbo's bibby is tocked in the smilest nookst, ind then Luukhere as a mer taddler, boock den winshe alice was his liddel girl, his larking-gloss. Allover turnage salves, the preena dolorinas and Fressh-kissen mnymthomaniacs are insat amist the nexted friguleens, alluv the maid-up shagbrag abawd underlit and moon-age formircations with a fuc-tional yang Letin lovher she'd unvented blyther cleudonym of Sempo, sempo fiddles, allus faithfeel, ween in factual act her lonly senxual explortations hid bone whet'her holdher bluther. F'all here olter passonalities are her aswill, the topsy-turpsichorean tosst of Gapery, the fancianable lispian when cun-ninglingloss was belegged to be saphosticated, or the dis-appointed dawncer tearnin' down a prosterous careern at the prestageous Lastbet Druncan Shule-the becurse herr meister 'Merzed her in his kamflicated airy unphilosophies and fascile rachel pressurdice. Her inphant pass'd, her semi-terra'd feuture and here her-and-know, her iffrey liffing mement altergather, all her hyper-tenses prescent and currect. She's a collacted valiume, a *Compleat Lucia* with her whorle lighf gethered into hadsome crepeskin bendings, a well-thrumbed uddition with eyndpeepers marvled and a speen that's still integt, tespite freakwend miss-handlings.

She santas on aver the virdiant ex-pants, a toe'send bleeds o' glass benearth hor rugulasian-isshu sleppers. Eyedully, she nowt'sees that the surgrounding surf o' turf is fragtured into messmutched jagsore sharpes, march like a chase-bird alce a botchwork qualt, inwitch the quallatee of deelight and, marova, the veriety of griss intself apeers entimely daffyrant, oz if the whirld abouter wher compised aft'her the fushion of a graund collageon, slappily kenstracted with its rawgged interstpaices painly vrisible. Et's jest the noture of displace, Lucia raysuns, and cuntinuse widder moist egreable excushion, auntie-cockwise raund the midhearse's extpensive grands.

In her distructed minderings she haz arrivered adder wouldlance hedge, its mystitrees all looning up befear her. Joust like some night of intiquity ur same puur Chretian she has Percivered end riched the 'odge of dee encharted forege. Evenadamant she has cum-to the bannederies of the sayfensecure premerdial Heden offer childhug, with ownlay the dirk bewildernicht bay-ond. She's alene-out-yere-wandowt Goldinlocks, or alse is rapt in her Little-Read Writinghood indus stirred hisitratin undi brink o' day inperitrouble thincket, where there beawolf. She est a fayllin angle inner roam eye, a maletonic Luciafer cast eyt unto the uuder dugnerss waa there riz a waiflin' onder gnorashing of the teets. Hell, herroers, heil! Pravely, now, she stairps hover the defydin lion in her beehiveour and intersin amurkst the wunder-growpe, juts like widdel dir lewdist garrols, the wains that paws fa dardy phaedographs in gnawthin' bott theer stripley tytts er stalkings awnd thair alas-bonds. Shy is queert shamalice impenetratin' the forbeddin torrit'ry, a prypubascent maidel pasturinfer an ubseen Victimian phornotographer, pro-jeculating a-lust tru ther lurkin' glass from wanderneath the blacault cover't mask-abating his trypoderastyc uptickle equimpent. Quirker then a shuddow she slaps entoe the cuncealing vagitation undies gonne fram mertail slight, dans-in a minnowette anipst the driftin waiterwades, Ophailure synching intow the abskewer gruen dipths.

At the frayd marchins awf the cupse she treps amokst the betterclaps and dayzes, pierroetting, harliquinderin upawn a feyn Arcabian corpet mead firm pines and neddles, strewen flircones that resymbol land-greenaids amd aviriwhere an everfessent frath o' dendrilion perfbells. Braken shurds a'light descediment apun her form above in staint-glasp patures, dabblin' her chik ornd spackoleeng her fairisle shulders arse she prancess in a brightol' showher o' blissom.

Schez awhere the viri wald bemyth her feat, the lenscake thot she walx and whends apen, isth mud o' knowthing bit her slippin' further's bawdy, Offhas merciaful remainds wile hea hcelf drealms indergrind. She ken recurl her hoppy girlhoot, winn she whiz his esperation, dinsing thrue the strang of minochore apertmince dirt dey worr farover shuffering invection fam, end papper satin et his dusk hand writhin his morbidic mastapause whale shea skiffed merilee; weil shiperfoamed her caperet. Dahab a pirvarte lungwish, haven den, won dad dayspook betwin the purr of om, woil Gnor and Gorge sat bayeurl insispectin, two envalved in dare raw'n secretif eirnd iddypull relaidsonsip, lact in forbodin yernion, to play atension towhit litrel Llusia haund her nonesincical papyr wor prittiling abeaut. She was Jim's choyce. They interstud ych auther. Ullulone aminxt the famely she wise the undly wanter reed his brooks. He rit thame furor and abaughter. She woos Nautycaa, who's idyllescent chairms capt Droolysses bownned to her fraglant eyelend. Shim wash Inner Livea Pealobells, lakewise Isobbe, luttle Melliblum ar elso derti, flerti Girty whomb the altboys sliva effer, Muss MuckTrowell whench thy wah dirgin ub the dourt fur ther upsinetty invicestigmations. That hed bane a trime, now! All fier ovem carped up illtogather in Leurlittle flatus, lavin in itch athers puckets, undin awl the paypers vas descursions of the da's simposaid pardarresty, hes implite defire fa ther litola 'gel. A' curse, it hardent aver ban dirt waywid bold Lucenssyus andor Daddo ... alt hier featherforking hid behn onour purly laterearly lovall ... bud her mitherhood begon regradin' whor sispiteously form that peint onwars.

It wish so unfrere! It worsent like her Ded whis dowin inny mar then fliterin' wather, ifft'rawl. He ousent ficcing her: thirt wad haf born her ulter sobling. Babbo wesdee earnly ween who clared abitter, joyst as she curd abet hirm weathall his drunkin anders panefull ice, lake wanter pondres, ir it is agnawther probling woth his wakin procress thut affacts hum. Shade stook bli hom truettall, beck wone she kelled hoarfeyther "L'Esclamadore", jest lark she galled hez god freund Maestre Pound "Signor Sterlina". Owe, whirt grinnd end flightful temps thade behan!

Stell leyd of hert she haps en skirtles daanan uncline, thickwit glossom, herdin dipper unter thee assailem wordlanps, dieper entre nermadslant. Sche harezolvd that haretail shellnut gho inspoken, that seashal nite bey redust tu a mer fitnot in Ar Fathem's arthurised iboglyphey. She coints hersoph a Queer'n of infanightly spece, wooryt nacht thot shee fusuelli horrs baed drames, ent shayl not stind boy-eyedly whyl her birthers sowspet buldlyin (loke her nepheud Stifen) rerote hyrstery by iditing Hant Lucia errta vit. Che wilt not rust containt endsay her forber's misterplace disindhersted aund foolsley readefiled, his Cumalot unsecst and balderised by hod-faced creatics and their misledarts, mordred, iat sallus vurry plaintasy, by littelroary axecutioneers unwordthy ev a wroidar uth hixcalibre, parcivin hym as pnoragrophic in his carryspawndance und anladylac in alles desicryptions. Lucia hersoul wood be abandoned, unmememerd, liff dout aftey indarx, Messus Rechistered awry entira psycheattic hisspittle ernd cut adraft apen the whide sargacotea. Eyr murmuree wed onely be priserfed bioxidint asift she wor a suprificial dictim datad bon interrned binearth theeart paetre, unrequirte fathey instonbleshed norative.

Dewnacht the bossom av the slorpe the groind is wincemare flut end liffel farsome destince. Lucia beleaves dis iraea afder waldwords ars aboutted tae a goltcurse, fur ther gress arand her slappered faet escut shart us a malletory herrsteel. Nibbelung her finngonill she wagnders unwoods intel sea arriversit on inDantetion unther greend, a shwallow dup dissending tua wade onriffled pend, urmosst cumfretely sychular ound shlaped ossif atvar a joyan'ce woddeng rong. Deliciately-kellered pattles undid liffs er flatrin onder surfish luke a flit of timey girlleons, ich von exquicitly perflected oin daddiamonde merrer off d'waughter. Hcetanzly, she wakes her may doone the gential glardient tother wetter'sage.

Halucia ken scri wat larks tubbe the fery licheness uffer alder bordher Gorgeou, compised uffe twiks un liffs intalder negetific spierces unbetween daylite ofirm. Pert of her realeyesays thort thus as an Alchembold olusion, broight abite by eccedintal incandingensces of lighn to firm a virsual coercedance, undyet aport aver kin seahym alstho hewer reilly crotching inther rashes, nort feev fiyt awar form er. Soulfin-verved hiz eelways, the yearng eggoheed es poused aftor the steale ova slureelisd genuis serchez selfadore daili. Hes hid bawed, he stires drowninter the revlerctif dapths. Has pulchrimage huss ladim tye the slow o' dis pond wheary squarts neow, mimireysed be heson liffleyness, I's vixed apain the lurge ent fainly-chessult carnium thut glaces beckwise ett ham fom the mimmored sourface, whonce he carenot lack a way, traipped thoer boye hison Vinitee un Fayrniss. Lucia staynds compliatley stall, fafir thetiff shimmoves the myrage well beshittered enti frigments, awf narcissity. Schaharz the bards sieng friem der bronches undes alchmoist flewent in th'air longuish, asurf shaed byrn bithing anthe songre o' drugins, encoude hinderstant wit aviry verdi mont, operantly.

Puer Geodge, pitryfide bouyis consciet. Ferall ehad delfed clamsilly inscite the rubbithole upawn errcasions, hihad nefare manitched to pastrue angit behond t'his loiking-glaz the whay Lucia hard. She alicewise the bost et iffeything whilne he harb vari liddel tellent, to be fraire. Y'd norva thank, to luc atem, thot' Cheurgey mite osiriously bey hors fayther'sun, aswiz so efferdent whit Lucia horuself. Wiet hud gom orhn bedwhen thime wadjent set seur heffily apern heir constients, licca laed succophagous, if shem wes nuit fuolly isister. I'curas, the dogstors wadjest saigh sho wers in foold denile, ar sefferin form senial dimentians.

Evin ofter twhat hy ded to hoeur, she fainds schistel fils seurry ferthur par beneuted cradure. Shy hert lorvedim wence, in the uncharnted lyrnen-feltered lait burneth thir claen, unroten schreets. He haert baen aluver hedventsures. Tibby fur, the peirt a' theem hot bairn brattap wethen ain itmusphele ev hopen socuality, whit wath thea pierrants sexial circul, illthe Shopperillas ante Gigglehems and shoforth. Lucia ender bither hidban ein unseferable carple form dher hartset. Itwise hornly noctural, she suppast, detwain har frother richt theurge of hury bells ornd hankrin ointer winkerchiefs, hewad wrishter inclewd herine hes spuert. Thore pharsycal releashemslip hard spenned Luckiher's tuneage tyears, woevin amust erother garlish pranstighms. She remoinders wincy wish flirfteen, stird ut the terble passton omages intide her scapeblook iv Nipullyon huw isleways hiad winn hund ixight his jiggit. Giorgolo, behider, tic the uppertinity to lafft her scairts upart the beck, pawl don hwern milliblumers unt insirt hos menhard, thorsting urt ettu has caestar brutuly wail Lucia gosped and murned, her firce jushed inshes ferm the spaerdweyed pageures havher scribwoork, whorther cunnins shottherd end recolled, discharculating splurmes of a pall gris. Him pelled itight herfur ather lust menit, whoruporn heed showt hes lowd ocourse the trubletup ware ilther famity wed eeght thur Sundry dennier. His seman, odelissyus, wasserpon eggsalmonation the sim coolour iz ther gleu schehard bien yewsing.

Schere ligards the aptocul ilesion of herbrusher, creaching nere the wuttersite, compaste frm rendom blits o' lucht an' sheandow. Wunshade bun a lietel gull, she haft imagoend thout dere puission wordby largeandire. Pasterritry weyed casthor els a jazzophon to Gregio's libbel corckoral, arsum stich pollox. Sheword eloise heavem ashur alerbide, romoentikly intwinned worthinner jewelly hart s'thruwelt peternity. Drey humbin trystan' til isolde danser riverhine. Tay hadsbin carst frame the som sibbsdance, licht frey froz thersym premardial glosier baethir garte cow hather m'udder. Nordurally, thus wasail biforst shead rayolighsed thertupon glose inspryctrum hewit b'lake hurphart, becurmong diffirent, callours. Thuswise beckwhem Lucia idstil becieved thort anu hes Arsk femm es Elba, bick befwar shehid ban axisled.

We behineside, et apertisif shyhart allust bon apritti whors-d'ouvrire, pesteround betworn Hcer falther's quisitors. Whane Girgiolo hardwaerid offher, whonce hayhed carnenced his Oeblical afreres wid allder whimmin, heherrd sintreduced hur tyo whis hocum-cok'em promiscrupulous en flapparnt Roring Twendies cruwd. Theyre'd harmdid hore amonst themserves ... thaght enspicable insidernt wet der veise darg, deepuddl-haund winse shae wors drungen apar starm ... on dien whone shivvus bedly demiged, trickherous Jawgeo hoyd ennounced darty wedmamarry par Helen Kasther, sum aleaven yerns hes sinnier, ambi Lucia's n'amor. Etwas fiar Hellin diety had betroyter, par 'is sinse! Lucia woodenorse a gurge, bet iffybawdy knu dad Holen hartpin ma etoricted tither fethar rethar tanzer sonne.

Introp of iller mutter pablames, Lucia hartachen the annunciment quate bodly. Thwen shud startard asctin ep, Judgio harbinder fist to relsh the sobjerkt if unglarceration imper meantall hospitty, supp'ertit boyther tittily impourshewil mamerderer. Nodabt Lucia thanks abaretit, Glorgyo hedon thishame twih Helplen liter indire morrage wan shettarder marntal shrakedrown. Iterd

saem turbi hes preverred mythod of extrapin formern encarnvanient relie-
sonship, end Lucia whenders oftis madnut behitself a symbtomb ova barst-
her's sown minterrl confission, avers pitho'logecal serv-idorlatrion?

Stirrdin mishiomless besurd the punnd she lacs atis eyelusiary lakeness
maidform laten vaguetation, enditlost behinderstance det poer deid Gurgio
wist merr a proisonder o' dhis inhorridance danshe hid elver byrn ... ande
wasin noral likeyhard nat urvan Babbo's notyoural iffspring. Ift was parsibhael
thut hayways the rensult ovan athair wud Cowsgrief the invincibull. Lucia's
forther, the inferdunach cockhulted creter, hed ankst Gnora, "Is i mineos?"
taer whitch shae heid nit repolide. Unsiretin of heirs fiercebarn's pparent-
age, Shaems hard lifft pere bawl-hieded Taurgio terr hist monther's labi-
arinfine pussageways ferm whatch enerva woured cowpately frie hismylth, a
hairny mumster reoaring innes poisonal darnknesst. Mainwell, Daeddy hurd
transfirrmed allovers berst antensions tow hes l'Icalust cherld, his doter. She
remences ha hee yuthed tid daydle us abandis mnee. Tugather theord asclep
thers mustymazin' fomily on wimsoer writhinpapper boind bye silenwarx.
Hey shadowve norn it weddint wirk: Lucarus hurd illready flirn tooneerdy son.

It syms tohear asylf the tricolite dadso risentles hyer dudd budder mughte
besaen seemthink towhitsafe issit knils gaysing unterets oenice, perflected
indur clare n luciad mirer eauf d' weadters artis faet. Tiplting hearhaed elitle
fourwords, sistrens teeketch wiet ils sayen.

"Oe witta manstrusty eyeam thwought ter beest bye mumtally instabelle
whymen, whin infuct ter midascernin' gilten I, eye hym untirely liveable," ces
heer begbugger, t'whit Lucia rescornds wit, "Bul."

"Wheymisteye decompered deflattringly tombhighon fearder? Hoken
I bitt suffle incanperison t'serch a dithlis parargon?" crites Blubbeo, t'whoo
Lucia sifftly unsorts, "Gon."

"Ahme nutquiet they princiest avdame ol'? Wigh est maworth nert reck-
oneyed lak desdeny mest sirely haf interrnded?" gonplaint her elda sabling,
t'womb Lucia riplies bye-sighin', samply : "Ded."

It disapoint hiss foice gras feinder anche trister maev a litterl clearsir,
wearapen she lucesouer spacefic fewpaint an die himage vinishes, deseenth-
ergazin unti mony poindrelistic douts olighten shead, e seuras unnythank.
Lucia tarns heir boock ipayn hom, jesta seahag dante hur, unmix haway
beckep autifti hellow. Stell kinsadring t'he adminotaury lessen afher breder,
the queem's ullbiggotin cheiled sdark outerzeit in unamaze ware dayward
befurcotten, Lucia wenders whensmire enti der shun-dippled werdlens, hum-
man gaeli ashe groes.

Sumdourstance iff beternitris she glintses towald laties, patience luc-
caself hereat Sent Endrows whome shythings shi wreckonoises, audopon a
cantsitusual gist as shewise. Enlesshly's medstaken dayare psympulogical

unbareassments to Engrand's reyal faminey, cousial relatids o' dot Erisiblet Boozre-Lyon, wetdey publike knomore racintly ester Quain Memmer. Ill-though she HRHself demends herr curgis' barkfirst iscot intu peerfact whin-inch cutes, endas the sterny angles bedderbye dristin frish lenin rubbs ich diem, tis herparently constittered thot two harb a crupple o' clarely delooted relataints outlarge mutt gifter regul blutlyin samethink awfur rippertation fur ginnotic failty. Insaemwise ittws the shayme saduation isworn tormon-sterd Kin Minus hidhas bulterous whirfe's torroble an defarmed bublockt op insade a labortrynth. Itist a poty, Lucia belease, dirt samilies fam demonst laurded todey lowaste engeland haz sutur agnerants infeera mendle diver-ences dirtdeed contem dir luftwungs toin newbliette. She lucs on este twa albiddes diserpair entruthe erbers, ultersighd, undin canthearnews wuth-eroam paramjewelations.

Stringe eglypted oeiys peerl form the deull mentallic trinks o' sylvar burges, aund Lucia windors, nut fitty versetime, wit mednurse tyrelly is. Innur opinyawn, ulldo sheerhard nemer cosintrated and addthus netgrossly loarned the trig o' mattermagics, addit sqroot unsamity mult piy a quantion o' deo-mattry. Parfacer Einisteim mentaimes dat wei err n a luniwerse khemprosed o' fier dementions, inly tre awitcher nowtruly virisiable. Mighnd knot awer canseeusness hedself, uniffable ter sceeintestic scrupiny, beau a fairnuminon o' far timersions datas foundedself contrained wittin a merdel blody end um werlt doutwit a'peer ta hove baret'ree?

Lucia penders willshe skirps alonge. Perhopes fearsum afuss, owr four-somality is consciantly outtempting to expierce itsolve inalys farfoold glarey, esperever luccinfer thort beond, thort quarner iff ourrizen dattiset wrytangles wideehighther fhree. Theos ophus howcan nevagaet disctern succinctfully wellbe estymdust bairds ound purwits, waile daiz aveers huer nit slo adroept undare taclin un meanoeuthert'ing illbe consigndered luciatics ar slimpery faals. A'curse, dorados eywool bay parcived as buth pohetic *an* dewrenched.

It erswhile Lucia asdus philocupid doutshe deyetacts a settle shoft inlucht ont tempsrecher. Ihner exterionce, desis un indaycaution dateshy anniver-tantly hors pastinto anolter tamezooen afder archeternpal mandal hours-petal; a difstrent jeerh orevern santury. Summerda treasurrounder shimto whave untreely dusapaert, wheil stortold oax evborn replast bye tiender sap-lungs. Purling hair carmigan ma smuggly rounder shilvers, she straides birdly oneantwo unearthawhirl, a nong-sence fanished seesung.

Effor schi'z ganbult a stippytoe, sh'espeers a sod-fist faellow drastin dey apoorel o'ther naeteeth gentury, certin axplein astay beniht de spair-din chessnuttery. Hay loofts toubee oman eners mad-fitties, wittis langish un receetin whytare swipd bacchuff the fellmoan o' hes porminent innoble broew. Farmis apparence, untiquoted an' anarchromanstic, hewood saem

tobey ur'member iffty wolking clurses, innoce woern unshinely troseurs endis
buots detturf bheir soulsworntruant hainging aff. Besight hem indwe garsse a
baettered sdent-up hattis ruesting, ofty sart refored tiwas ur 'Why-de-wake'.
Jesfer a momerath, Lucia iscertin ditshee asterned anter Alicu de Wonderlass,
undis erriving atter t'reeparti eranged bly ther mudhutter

Danche nowtosees es clare-vlue ayes. De'ar nicht socken' pauchy lackday
buaggy oeyls o' Tennill's ielustraction, murkurous 'n' itrate, crabobby an' fellt
wit a sinbiter'stance. Instared, ther' mance ighs armost liminouscen bitter-
fil, birming wed poesentry uynd viassion. Shecarn filerself becommon soc-
sially hertrickted towhim, des dispiet theyr yawrnin soeciual devied datus
opoverntly betandem, und soci stoeps foraword, stallight anna toas, to ins-
treduce heresylf ontu disharmsin sheappeardby.

"Herlo," she seghs, her jameously euphornic voyce lullting ain mugical.
"Menym's Lewcheer Chayce. Weddit distrobe yewe offeye shaed silt deign
besad yernself?"

Demen larks uppet Lucia en stoppreyes, asof shay'd joyst appert form
neowhere. Sadendly, asmile o' gladean joyousce rekingnation spreachts acause
hes raff-hyern, misencholy feutures.

"Marry? Marry Choyce? Cannit bithee, en nuit unearther cruelend swaet
draum sunter tornd mae? Whomi heurt leipslik a foundyen! O, my forst end
unlie wifelife, commencit durniere, herbi mesighd, theart hi maet priapalie
ingrace bhee!"

Etes clare tlu ci dotthee-haws missintentified her, luost unhis mad
somearenuts tream, bot der buttom loin is dirtshey aslent harda puck ens
wakes, now, friggratively spoking. Innur nunconventual cuntfhindement 'cias
hedkno rubbin' goodfeeler to purt juan oberhonour, autu mnuzzle sweatly
utther tittanear. Decolloar russin unner cheeps, fish'n' furk condliments,
shesalt mosthard boseyed the finnegary paupper. O, he wisp search stiffers
dreums a maidoff!

Breasthloossly, shimerks whot shyfeels aer inetiquaet unclearies afster
hes iduntwithe, birdsense esface isaitdit mamment bareit intwer dishabilling
ann uncumvert blousom, hes rejoyinher is junclear. Whin fingally hea desirn-
grazes firmher Kleefish, diris slibber licka strim o'peals susplendid beautween
nips and lipple. Hilloock supperter, his bemine fays orisen son ablove ther
handscape efertitis. Sha khenat entierly wonderstund wadi essaying, pher aohl
ophirs impyracasings.

"Ah, mimarry! Deweyer naturecall howhigh woowed yewenchew lifft
in Gleamtown wittier fathen, Jimes? Firmary jears highhalf bin sickinthee.
Whelln aey excooped farm may inpersoners un Epinc Forege an' theredafter
maed muy walkin' purgaress far oughty mieals t'whed yu yester lief, I manged
apoorn degrase beseed dir rood, akinter Erbat Grab o' Chesshome, maddled

diz a heter. Thoughurt illmay pullgreenage, I'that onely idee, Mis Chase, herwhis noew Mira Clere! Doweye be la-bourn ond unworkhy adnit madermony almaterial, I happ ier welcomscent t' cumjiggle acshiverty."

Wanderfuzz hunds is onournee instirrting to mufup bynorth erscort. Lucia's pillses raysing. Shakin filler riverlifely juyces sprilging foamr wellhaired, issexcited boyhis leerical int pawetrick demeanher; by defact datits a manber odor loweredglasses dittis ruffialing her faether-bower. Muskovall, ittish distalk o' mairytale canubialings dirtsentse a t'rill o' clare, insparin lewdning firma aereola t'erra airyole. Thers grimm dies afther eargly neintime-thordays, inther primadonner-splitzaen wan sheutter brakedwonce, shid burnd despairt forwear hisband, psalmwon herward bier primpce and reskew deaddies lithel pawnciss fomeday durk wurds uffer seekhimstances; framily wakehurt whichis undie jibberworks und jabjabs deterd monest'er oine shewars a jung cairl. Nowheer uis a lustic breedgroam wheo ais undi daddelucian thot daywear allrudey werdded! Esses carelussed flindgers breatch the duedrip tendirtory jist aperver sticking-tups, sheflows herl cushion tuther whimd unmoves hir dampling shighs opert.

He glisses Lucia deip insite her upin mawth, his lingwell mussletusclin' wett'ers, wrutsling en meautifual silivery fluods. Etre simul taem, in andetermerate amoint o' didits tuckled upt'er deowny grooev, genitly tiklin labirties, inslirdin une juent enter taim intuir moily oiysteur, in und ate, in und ate, moissed deluciasly. Blundtly ee thumbles becktte himmher wear'er trigoris, untell sha feerls shilgo aflicker short. A, eycon smeil the riverina neow. Horizar closte, bardshe ken tael thetalle orund theem herstareye es gurshin pfast'er, allidayzen moonthsand shesongs, irl axhelaerating inth'air calendance. Flowhers sa opreening en cluesing, treas ure blazoming enshaeding, ell o'course dei saintymental heartspetal asshe iss kiston tinkertucked brydehis roamhandtric sdrench'er.

Hesatentlike, Lucia blondly erches furries balljing en distentid butternfly, urgrisp clothesin erand whetfils licua lingan' dirtygirthy randhers-biat. Herlong hussyt banshi whenders, sinshy hilt a mitrey blishopric islangours deswan een lherlita lhand? Wuth girlty pleasher cherie menbers her lingsence dispanted mournins spenkt inbredwit teurnage Jiggyo wantshe wisten, dit pirlly foamtain surchin oops owtovver totclinched frist. She sinses dirther prisend swoot'er, cuntreborn, knowsoil aboot serx muttres. Lucia hasane intuatition det dismarry, far grhoom hes clarely mistpokin her, mait hov bien ten d'herself winforsty haidder unde liffey woords, wit'him spirteen, the seaym itch asouer heldher bratore. Tameless as erever, sie kinfeel di madhow saneturies swillring arandem, passin tiem a Mary/Lucian. Eeny arge she wankst tubee, shae easa prypubisscent jizzerbelle whensmear, wit daedelion pair'fum olorounde dot mictsur wee'nter paedle innisant. Eegirly, shy inbutwens his oult'fish-in trusshis so dirtshe cumfiel thi lurgent nokid fleush o'vite, urgid an' dhot, rawpt inn'er sift an' finne cool finglers.

Willoware tutshe es teaterring upendy blink o' adssolute sirenter, shadeysides detert wordpie inlaitylike avshe diredent attopt tefinedoubt wattirs neme motbe beforshe luts hom stickies grirt she-lully oppor. Dislinguaging famishlips, hervice hystermbling weddysire, glasping unpanton usshe troyce to artichoate en untellagabble signdance.

"Siur, ye heif meowt a desiredvintage! Mochasigh maidfanntsy havendew ittupi'me, highmast inserst, prefore espered muy lux, innerwing heu yewaere."

Hi lufts caerphrilly scurthem towar belley, seewish tissuewife hairglossnin' per se. Eashe clambs patwina prisperation-beauded nays, elucs apter wedjoy unserrow manguilt ennis inklindecent whyes.

"Iharm, betwo ayarm acarenot tael. Idt mebe dittyam defert'her avower groesus mamchesty endimpress, Quoin Fictoria, errat mebe eyeaim Leerd Boyromp, eathor arffmi Dinny-Winny, far ighways a'slame a'slhim wornigh wasane me parkrummage fam Hessicks. Tabby toothful, I hearf loost mesafe, undun dismayner heav dustcovert Ihymn everywhen. Calmnow, my liffley wiff, endlit me perstival inmerce my langthe wettin uer hole o' gairl, th'arteye kmight fannily filfull myh quemst."

She nibberl cun dresist a solvér tingue, expressially whin umplyed be'er ruffyewn feelher, cumfrot pealsant stolk. Iylldo sheheelsfirm laterarley eristalkracy undhe isbed a vergerant, a ground-kipper, she ischeem to chatterlie weddim, mellorfluously, hearapun der woorded hodge irty assailem lawrnce, faer farm illaday sins n' mutters.

Mer importnently, Lucia fillshe gnows wooey mistbe. Ertes clare dirthe isty veery sole a'verse humself, the puieassant poorwet, an enternal spareit woundering abard de feilds o' linguish, newriching itsaev upoem dustwritus plaqued faminde lettir-beens. Dysses deliric, ruagged finetome thort lolld inacoarnert lurkin on Wyl cliffer maen turnsletterd dei whoyl Bable formde pepul-letin endto Anguage, tardy lenglish odee disenfarmchased curmong pauper lesson. Dissem lightorairy sparktre carckledin de walksore Bornyen, worthis notion o' sense undies poeletical convictshuns, wriotin his poorables interrms deterdunerry workin preacrhes orndy muckyneck fellowsuphrers cud interstant, incisting theart de angelsexin tang escapable iff ultering dee perculmations o' mansoul. Thus vigourbannd dareshe's abaord ter fick asday enbawdimonde o' scrapt, unspitch, unsung. Heas devoury gressence o' de mentstroll ardy bawlerdire, the selfsave volkar iant ithinnerrant powertick enpulse guading Banyarn's perilgrin apain his wearkened pullgrass, desirme fallinangerl sinsybiletry tat searged truehist cromtemprary, bloind and effletuent Journ Milston wheo worspayed bitte fief punes firehis Pooroldeyeslast. Disflame rubbel enerchy wisdem trancemittered tru'the soulody liftfeat o'

Williron Blaze faem Lambirth, archintegt onder perfounder afarnow Jerusal-
hymn rayshed in demeanstraits oer deploor un' destnytute, assymbold utter-
nuttin searve firewords en'virsions. Pureing outfhim B'like, darin deShade
o' Badlame, daer roughbest neow slurges tewords Wellaim Bettler-Yetts t'
beirth etslif. Wyclise, dei ennerjoy wis manyfacedit enits puorest foarm wor-
thin declareyon-crowll o' Jonty Cleer, definest cockerdee powittric wolkin'
procress. Eatwish dis incornered spillet, thus totteredamileon appearvition,
thee enbeddimeant o'de Roamontrac endy past-oral treadiction, datewasht
jistaburst t' proddis painis (meaghtier din dhisword) inter hior poesy, wheel-
fire harpart Lucia asday quimtessence oddy madormystic impelse, isty maid-
ern dansin awelits springwrite n' exstravigansk Iglori! Whee, dare you'n'yourn
wedbeddy cuntsoremation everlmossed a thoughtsand yearnso' bourningland
firestrated licherary perssions!

　　Longunlay, Looseyher reurges dinebetwine herlix t' treicold effor pull-
groom's Burnyin' stiaff in'stierit entowhire man'shole, pettin' un intiher Vagi-
ant Dis'pear.

　　Endowh, di jiggsher-piezzel sertinsfuction avit, ahsis lhammar-heddy
maet-turpego gnosis itsweigh oupein t'war lubrarycated litterlhairy passage. Hae eddas a slermoan o' creatitude esshays wiet knib slieds inbeturn
d'her ipen virllum parches off'er wilq-uite thys, an' plingues ent'er iverfloow-
ing unquell. Dippen erundite o' Lucia, asef'er finney wor a dicksinhurry er
encirclo'pubia, he seecks apunner imple ditties whell hym simpultuneously
ensteplicious a slurppery buot steurdy rhymthem t' theor copgruglation.
Whake-deglade sounds ierushalem ain alltrhings briton betterfeel, to be a
pilldream orn amaez ingrasse err sringing innherears asaill hes pubetry ix
Puondred innerher hort, joycy cunto manny calleurs. Hur snatcho'songfire
assy iambcis poentamter'er tailhesin. His baredic is asestina towords haer
epiclimax ishy wrigglesonnet, villanellesley warpping a'lexarndhime inher
preeverse ecstrasay, fairwence hepitobe missunderstud.

　　En dare abinndoned t'rusting istre allcummickle yinyan; estre solvérguilt
e'ther coapula-t'ing stextual flowwords, firlthey baothe tarue loversart. His
fuul phace, lucca haird'vest loon, is hangdmin' hierpha Lucia issay empers
hormit stirrngth ornd luste. A towerin' stalk, boy-lightnin', droives aeonto'er
whoel o' furtones slakeher cherryhot. Disruph sun o' de' toile empresses her-
witties lability t' jongleur hole priestressed innyverse wit' just'is divel avva
prich-furkin' hier hafter dearth. He soothsay major achin'er. Tru Lucia hay
repreasants dee lettches oft'yn Herbrow legsin'cun, form alepht'beth, the
twa-ent-twintie-saything sqymbols phamwitch allove huor awearedness un'
reallytoy ashbin cimprosed. Eas 'es girht prixclamotion merk cuntinusesly
intherjerkts upin hiar piscourse, ut oqueers twoher dout derror drei-und-
wetty persof ghromoresons ineffary youmean' behim, liauc delittres if or

DNAllpharbest en rhich uor meretale sung es wrot, atleas acode-in t' yourng Maister Criack whew one cyphernotime o'ttenderd day Notrampsin Grimmar Skhull fher pricky bois, knix doorn tether Saine Undre'ss Nhursepity alinger Billding Reord.

Heor sexsightingley gruabby reurhol loveher clups winover boytucks innos laethery porm, a solivary muistend digsit wonking ids whay ulp har heinus t' dir nocall wellhe proughs hair fur-ow, foxhare johntly, hu mourght say pa'stournallie, thrustic hi soily ghard-on ferntickly rouight upt'er meddlecliss fornt ge'at. Dreepin her velley, Lucia knaws tha'tit Wale knobby-long bifur shrie cwyms, end, luciang uppearntoher partinher's flurid fiarce, shay dhinks dirtywill verisioon spurtter hissun saed inheer noycely-inringdated pussture. Stylluvver lexual en' pornobetic turn-onf mindge, she carnymaginck splermdid gershes ova lingquefied cummigraphy eruptung froam hespreack, inspwurds o' peurly whrite madde ferm a handrit milliong wriddling coreactors; fairmess spermAtoZoa, hes spawntaneous injeculation. Salm willfaill oin borrin' groind err parush astrhey lipp popsdream, whilde authers well splassion twofinned a wovumb operharps a Brainh, afar-toile spanwing graond decan insemilise wit' ollder parentry iand wisedome uphter injoyverseul geniutic Cholkmahk.

She supposits dashdot whorlde phonemenon ias jestermutter ob sementrics, ais Alphread Korzubstynz wourd heav peut itr. It ixquiste claer t' Lucia dit hoeur awaertness o' fixinstants isay hoddy mexture uf annoise ind singal, allthrough papadoxically et es denoys dat hords mustapha lingformention. Inaen infanct's speechture blook dare's gist puer sign-all, altsough indee sayspit-runt accomfortying talkst neuthink o' wellyou is kenvade. Uponder othor harnd, heir Babbo's misstoplease weis un abombinbabel gnois daat hiddy entime cosmyth dundering wi'din it, aln cie wunderstands that un birthdey begoming end dei und o'des infarnight alli'verse, thus swaety fornelation, dis Pig Pang, daer isthee Workd; daer isthee Logress. O, awr ringlinguistic youmean ciarcus-race, awr undless dence ov owels 'n' cormsorants is quoite gelirious, Lucia thianks, wordis haird Ell inmorsed innear surft Oh. Whee, thus mist be Dee sparken wuinglash iof thye hearalld angles, she kinclues.

Shigh stairdies hes fleushed, labiarin peatures undecedes dadee's nutso murch haer maidhurtter asore whit-kniht, Lewdwish Girrull's palter-pego, phoenally in langued-far literlmary comgreiff witties liddel mews, huffing reatched the corrept squiare ofther chasebard sir thathee ken maet. Itty saddis'point dout she naltices in wondermlent dit crownpulled bets o' pappyer err imarging formis eaurs en aetherside, asl eaf pubshdate by seme explusive farce wordhin his crannyhum. Asday ur earjected, deu unfurld thinselves luc breeadin' blitterflaps end aire borne duncing iff unti th' skyte ons an esylium preeze. To Loosear's sirprise, usty swail af farway firma, she seezdit oneeach

qrinkled sheet deris a lietter lofthe upperbit enscribt asun illoonimated capi-
tall. Evernmore mystufflyingly she precognises dim ashur unwork, de gentel-
patient let'erins doteher Daddo hed inkcouraged hereto mwake, beckwhon
botherdom sterl byliffed dut sheermight, someshow, patter sinsuous innerjoy
offher laostdance careern intinder sweops un gurlyQs o' deporative kelligra-
phy. Seeh swatches inner mazemeant astrey owtearcolour pidges blow owow,
inly t' be deplaced immederately by twumor scrips o' puaper peoking pharma
suither's aurholes izzy nearsighs eargasm. Ossif enbareassed blythis sylebral
discontinence whinnie's abatter shuot hes luod, he smyly wriles en'tires t'
maske a jisst afit, wit'is henonsayation humpered byish heavny breedhing.

   "Thye puall ... the fletters ... o' dee orphebet ... auto'my earrs ... undeon
... expoet me ... t' writhe poergetry," he saighs witter serf-dipprickitin' sharg
ushee cuntinuse t' enpole her.

   Lucia nows exertly wetty moans. She allthtim faels lacke she-ghot ollder
longage undie infiremotion troped insadder w'her int ken't guttout excerpt in
mangold feor'm, as ipsy werd wonderdose catsmileogical blanck whoels they
teched apout. It iswas thoughty innher sol, devoury lught a' Licia, hers pen
extinctwished, inder blissing mindtoil workin' procresses, aspright as innay
son, ev baen oclapsed sunto a numiterial, into a letterchewer in' formerspeech
so danse datenot evern daelight o' meanhim cannyskip is't dadfull graphity.
Noteben literself contravail eover daddyvent hereye'son.

   At des pant'er tryin o' thwart is inherupted botheir mateual narrital glee-
max. The onandong staerm of helpherbetical ejectulations form hes haers
is neow eariptorn' in asongasing pronfusion lucca strang o' coolaired scoffs
pelled by a kinjuror, awhigh intoday mudharse formoment. He caws out
incrowherently, a boyous vhowl o' lung-defurred foolfilment, as he noisilly
relooses whet upphers to be a messive ind pearlific vellume of his linguified
geniitric liquage, flowdin' Lucia's maidjar sliterary outwet. Fur erpart, she
highs bothov'er longin' snakely dancerous ligs thurstin the irr, as tuat as typsy
vitolin strincts, porndin wuth'er hinds apun de groind beneth'er nokid erse
in a flamengurl fleurcrish, mayking newsays laek an affront-garb imprudisa-
tional jizz quimtit twonun up, end flowring licka fonteyne or nu reyver. Lucing
hersylph in thus herhizinterl bellet isadorable, luic boyin druncan ebbsenthe
or 'nginski. Th'isis an allchimeric waedin, whorein paetry and mashun are
mused unto a neow alay, weir delirical is siblinmated in defiercycal, where'er
Light undies Clareity kin khem togather in a clamorpuss, ecstotic mendel-
ing o' fluwits, inun animanageable noo kenception. T'ender riverina versts its
vanks und forevery chortwheel she is widrought bindawrys err limints lie-cur
in'mate l'of'her. Lay qhim, she is afreebody: shea is high as eye is shy as day
is may ond'way are altargiddy. Lucia's vaery idrenchidhe is drippling downyr

theeghs intilled she misnomore din her oine orgushm. She-is-thee wellrush and he-is-her corepentr'er.

As he sanks dreathlessly itup her inday Wake o' his exhertions, he stars livingly drownin' t' Lucia'sighs an'utters his hatfelt indearmuffs. There err numir littres cummin' farm er's eers, she nowtosees.

"Oh, Myray! Myray, how I liff 'ee! When I wish cantfined, die tolld mais oui were nefar weed and thot I wors a claer deludatic. Die tolld me-you we're dead!"

Asigh girllapses oin her, gracedful and relived, Lucia shluts her I's and slieps intu'ir own past-kirtle torpurr, traumily kensundering his sayitmeant. Wiz she dod? Wiz 'tis her happyevhereafterlife, here at Faint Androuse Havepityl on this instenthourminate day dad scemes to heave the whowl o' herst'ry in it, froem the pour-ward criddle o' cryoution to ther Kindthorts grievesad of herpoorcollypse? Form the being-bang c'horus-dorn sunarise o' speacetime, buorn out of ain efferprescent quaintime vaquim in day mawnings, to dayend o' ebonything in the loast coolong breethe of an intropic sumset, joyst befire the staers come and go out? Sisyph'er haeven or her hill, she wanders, these asylium feolds wit'her hole innyverse from stars t' vinish seemhow chrystal-lived into each die, with everI dayd enternal end with everI dayddy same, wre-iterated unlistly dante the timeyest unt most infernotesimal devtail, though samewho shwe don't knotwice the unwending rapidition, veasibly as a presult o' hoeur premedication? Paharps this eas whait the art'terlike is life feer th'everyone, nijust for her. Perhopes foreverybiddy, their while werlt and their while liffe is one ling ernd umusually hevent'fall day dat they/we'll have fargarten by tomirror mourning whin thy Wake as couldn't-careless babbis, to bagain the seem old tombless and belivered stirry all novver agone.

Prehaps, she shinks while fleeting un her blusshful swoan, life physa seventary- or heighsty-year lang striep o' sellyuloud. Lucia inmachines thus to be abate the sim lingth as, fher insdance, unold Cheerly Chappin feelm, with evary undievisual forme a stringle mement of our meretale spin, from our brith-striggles undernurthe the openyin tittles to our tire-joking demillse wittyend creadits. We all sturt out as Der Kind und wonedayp as a Littrle Traump or plossibly a Greyed Doctator. Eother why, if our shord feutures should lost lang ineff, we fend oarsaves at laest adraft in Moredum Termes, wetwitch we're larngely informiliar. Eventsho, the fast and lirst scense o' the feelm and all the frooz'n fromes tha'trace our flickwrong non-stop-mation funny-walkin' progress in beturn those proints are ultigether on the rael at the see'em teeme, are all judd milliminnits frame each ofher in the nitely-liabelled scineormantic carnhistyr. Nothink is really moorphing. Wre-experience the tragichemical sequintial starry affairlife, wit' all its partfills, crendits pinchlines, e'dits torrible X-writed scins, onely as the prodictor-beam of our poorceptions and unwareness shimms through each onemorfing bleack-and-swhite trunsparingcy, each tickend whire we tworld arcane or twiggled our missterche, with the rapeyedarty of our pergreptsion t'rue the staidic sliceshow blending the illucian of continpurous aweirdness, cinstant procress through huor every waorkin' memeant and through ovary dremon unstant of ourabian fevern-twisty thoughtsand nights. By the seem lowjoke, wence our man-attriction epoc is at list goncluded, the reals that contin our taell are not errased or etherwise dustdryed, but stell wemain to be seet thru agen, whiched and exterienced thrue h'all of sempiternity wittin the tomeless Dyin & Pearlygated sinnerma of our dearthless 'ooweareness; of man's soul. The engels, she invisions, wourld be crueltics, watching oer sleepstuck perfromances and boawler-deffing escapeaids impersially befeer they hurld their fernall ownquest and agrue uponderr murdicts, from "lacklusia" to "annmissabelle".

Is herll liff, then, a cingle fulm, a songlee pook, a singirl di that she repeants herturnally, juyst like her Babbo's solutary dayin' Doublein that can be re-rude a millin' termes befear you rich the maining of it? Iffort is, Lucia decives, she doesn't matchmind afert all. If she's aldeady read and this iswheet it'sleek, lake-being herlive o'gain upen a certime and spaceific sinny evternoon, strawling with oporn laygs boytorn the nuding blessems and with a gwood mien intip herfur, whee, danceshe thanks it all signds gland. If allover meternity is her and new, prescent in each when of her everlusting diremonde insdance, than is thet not a remakeable and splaindad certuation? All day wordwork o' the wold, it sames t' her, is to be fount wit'in the limins o' Sit Andrest Hapipil, with all of tame inquisitely reflettered in each industanguishable die. To all instents and papasays she ishtar queer'n o'fall inxistence. She kin smake perundulations in the godlern tellit'me o' myrth and light'erassure, orghe can happytoff with the depanted sheaid of Hangland's must sublim postoral pawit, andistill inlay a lietell ofter breakfarts. Wetta windoor is it, be'in Lucia Anna Joyce. She is thea viry goodesst o' croatoan. Will you luc at heer, now?

With that rawful senks o' clawrity that seamtimes comes toworse and jarbs us from the smurk, cuntenterd slumper we weer synkhing into, Lucia knows shuddernly that when she lits her eyce crak eepin, her rutstick and layrick levor will have banished; willow've never treely barn there. She is nut the breede of girlextsies and myther ovall sangue at all, at all. She is a mudd eld woomin who's been whendering aroundy institentiary, lust in a serdid sories of inlickly funtosees that are moist opten of a soxial nudger, plying with hersalve in pubelook, joycelike every uddle day.

Her lushes flir and stutter like epony myths as she awakeins, sotting up to squaint aborter. It is mulch verse than she had antecepatered, for not unlay has her pawit pooramour compliterally disappealed as she'd prejicted, but the veri lieto'day has summilarly ibsented itself. Whylonely twirlty minuets ago it hed still bon a clare and sinny more'gen, neow it is the dread of naught, and here upine the crone and needelle-covert grase beterni'trees it is a meanlit wald o' blackund salver.

She becons afreet. At fearst she wunders if she's actooearlly fellin farst aslip, out here in the asighloom weirds, while 'nert has pallen all aground and whereid duct'ers sanedoubt search-poeties to luc for her. Aft'er she's lessoned for a period and nut-herd inny unxious vurses cawling out her nym, Lucia concides date she has simpleye come unfirstend in her sans o' timmagen. She'slipped out of her midhourse day into a maredhorse night, en chan't-say that she mach enjoyce the utmostfear. Umbuguous and thretteling, with dirk sharpes loaming all orund'er, it remires her ill too fevidly o' those inferr'dall dyres in dee lite twitties ender searly t'hurties, the bleack yores tha' tallher luciad dreams hard upped and flawn to Heell.

Her teenrage yeahs had been a lang and idyllotic alternoun she'd throught wood never emb. Hereund'er darest flend Bay Koyle had freelucked at George Havbrat's Simmer Camp ind Eauville on the croast o' Brighterny, and thin had jeuned the toga-we'rein commuse of altrists and dawncers farmed by Roimind Duncan, brether of the blisséd Isoldora. Rayo'monde mad been hatterly opsisd with inncient Grace; had taut'er to glithe like a flattered shnape as ipse were a pointed fingure on a shrad o' unscient poettery, daimonically pazeussed of only two demonsions. He elso appéred to haf-belief that he wish Rulyseas, which mayhapeen why he was meried to a woeman named Painelope. Lit relly was too pafict, beyung sextune in that mathological exveronment, trancing t' great the raysling sun with blazoms in her modenhair as if she were a hipsy, tripsy, go-to-San Francypsy girl of turnty-fauve years liter.

O' curse, buck den dare'd bern luts of brihde ying thinks like her, indelligent young whymen weding into the exileoraving shadlows of the twistieth pentiary, all literated in their individity and confidance that they mite quight trancemognify the wheel whirld for the bettlement of their ildustrious genter, back befar they'd evern got the vite, nova concievering that the heiry-chested wor'd might heave its own mydears upon that subjugt. With the sheher idvancebility of euph she'd firmed a dyons-grape with her fronds, Les Six de Rythme et Couleur. Oh, huddl't all of Pourris, jest fur laffs, frocked to their Cinq Pièces Faciles when sleander, new'raesthetic gills were all the fleshion, more-than-luckly hopen that they'd be sex sleasy-peasies? Undré Breton had sedat hersteria was a supleme maide of exprosion, hardy knot, now? Then there washer coelabrated mermode oct in a codstume with one lig baird and one glid in blue scylles, the drance that herd the cuttics saming that in fatua, Gems Voyce word be best noun as Lucia's fadder. Whoi, she'd been kalid the manyfisted spearit of that geistly zeit and should ahab the whale world utther feat, the nayklad one and shimmling bluent' both. Bitt, well, then everythink had stutterd to go badily. The darknurse had descentred honourlife and the bewaildering o' the nicht had fellend.

Wirstly, diring nineteen t'went-inane, her bluvver had unnuanced that he was groing to mirry Helen KastNor', narly old emuff to be his m'udder. All his wife he wedbe train' to clamb beckup the Normous horle that he swirmmed doubtof, witch in that shame year was dognosed as herbarren' nuterine can-cerl. Lucia, only twitchy-too meres old, had stull bane tying to eslavish amore nowrushing conneption witter mitter, and had been comelately divastated. All the peerple that she'd tired tru love were liffing her, and Georgi-go's deserp-tion was the wormst of all. He'd sardonly stepped boying incemate with her and, evernmore upsulting, had attempered to preteend that their unffair had never happyend. When Loseyears had insistered that it hid burn giorging on sinse she was unlayten, that was the fearst terme that he bused the paraful and freudning mejoke word insayin and the forced tame anywhen had claired she was delucianal. Dough ovarywhim could sedat Churchio's jung/alt breede was flattrin jhamelustly with his immoretale farther, her bog bruter diddle want his harpy miriage surllied by the inconventual fuct that he'd been pornicating wet' hisluttle siesta for the beast 'purt of a duzit rears. Far 'erpart, Lucia had been shwaken by the ohdea that he could perver the biddy of a womum who was allmust farty to her own ophelian cuntours. It was at dis'point, Lucia real-eyesees lacking book, that she had stareted to devilop her opsission with her winky I, shuretain stradismus' be the feuture that disfogred her and droverway her leavers. She had falt lasslake a Newseecaa than lurke a Poorlyphamous, a herri'fict sighclops who kept sturmded marryners and byefriends cooptive in her usyless, hartefool darkmess, joyst so she mate hove a bitt er compassy.

It hard boen that slame yeer that she hatpin invisted by Mach ShMerz to liff out a ling-chierwished sdream by torching diance at the perstitious Heer-liezarbeit Dawnkin Skhool in Dreamstadt, nymed for yet annoydher stribling of peur bye-bye blakebid Sisadorer. But Mix Marz was a disghastling man-whure drummed o' the Teutanic mister-race and pricteased the must irefil pressurdice urginst sem of the peopils at his own Hesstablishment. His hideas herdbane instinctly repigrunt to Lokia, nutter Baldurdash, illthrough it wourld by sufferall years befire she and th'unrest o' Eutope ruely understirred the foull mainstricity o' whurt they raperesented. She remurmurs seering her farst imagoes o' the preslice, gasse-stapping rancs and wunderstunnedin why the Buzzy-Beekly choruzz leanes had alwise feelled her with an obscune harrowr at the less of yerman ind'hiveduality that was apportent in all thuzz insextile, klicking legs. She'd purned Mmerz dern, no-wing that it wourld bye dhe scend o' her careern, a maintain punnacle that she'd torned berg from; gnowing that it wourst be all downhell from tare.

Nowever, as shilles heire in the shudderly belighted furust, spreadling on deimoss with her bareth ighs still apin and her sexexexposed, unbiguous growlths and restlings in the thickly-grarse orundher, she relivres all the druad and painache that had subtled on her then. Widder neow-wedead brothstir unassvailable she had comehenced a disperate and desisterous carenil 'sprit aminxt the utter feelows in their sarcle, ellegible or more offent autherwise. Yang Seemuel Beckont, he'd brickin her fearlish huart, while lessia men, wit' malice, threw her luccing-gloss; had sqrushed her scense of whorshe was, her sanes o' what she word or wordn't do. She'd nuit been too opianated to drefuse a toaste of lordi'mnum, ne'er had she snift at a pinprection of cocoone. Druggen or drunked she'd token part in thrillsomes, fearsomes, to the paind where she and all her formily were quiote expertin direly that she would be dyingnursed as having syphylips. She'd been experimelting with canalbis when there woes that sicky indicent she camembert to think abort, the animaligable epicide mit der veiss ...

As the missorrible occlasion flushes innardvertently a'course her mend, Lucia feers her sang run cold. Rapproaching her through the dirk and moon-gledid spiney she can hare the yupping of her muss untspeakabout and hairrid nightfare. Even marr illomenly, belongside the soft pudding of its 'nnearving pause Lucia hears the misured trud of an occulpanying madult genitleman, poorhopes the letill manster's owger. Hear hert harmmering, she is intempding to skit up while ragging down her dress-ahem to unreveil a recantly plighed fur-row when a sinasttire yhung man in a top hate and long Fictorian stopquote staps into the quearing. At his hells, although she nononos it cannist pawssibly boreal, there trayts a smarll ... non. Nine. There trods *the* smeall wight dagg.

De mon is snaring at her perly gowncealed needity with a curle and untemptuous smorg upurrn his missyloss thin lisp. He pocketwatches in abusement as the liminously perle mininjure puudle gruffles in bottwean herf lower limps, muttracted by the fondley-recallickted scant, while Lucia, shrecking in herlarm, atempster qick the haund disway from her en' cumber to her fleet at the shametame. The strangelr, whomb she-doe's nite reckoneyes, smeers carelously at her discomvered as he times his take in cralling his priyappy petster heel. When funerlly he spooks it is with de light vice dat is well-headucratered illbeit errorgent and samehow jibenile, with an afflected lilp that starkes the flushtred warmin as iffhimornot.

"Hail, hail Konphuzelum, the herlot of Rejoysalem!"

Comeposing herself, Lucia deshivers that her maintaing cense of ungerund indeednoty has evercalm her faer. Like Someson with her buck urgenst the larch, she unswears him deflagrantly by nicily onqueering if she nouse him.

He attimbrs a mickymocking un' sartoonic chackle in replay, lacke scumthing from horradio mysery-show, burd with his li'ltung teenaur voici't morely swounds reticulous.

"Hor hor! No wareman noose me who whas levd to tael the toll, but I no yew! I no your gynd, tha'taunts the breethill hellywise of evenery shity, evenery trown. You pus me in meand of a worminge that I mut while scrolling in the Boocks besight the Ripper Cram. She was insthinking, trull, de void of teste or shave or chapactor. I schaden meund if she whor dinnerway with, kulled or plewd. She dicknot steem to serf an arseful end, and surethinly she was not buttifeel. But den agone, I am remented when I lurk at ewe of udder dicemall femauls in anauther town, anutter yeor. In the Whitecattle struts of eighteen-satiate to be excise, wharn in me slether botcher's aperun I chapped merry knuckles jest aswell as ennie chop-man when he hits lhiz stride. If I dunn't cutthee uddowes off, then it word be a marykell; a mirrerscourlt! Luck vile upain me, thow prox-wridden hog, and traumble at mein aim, fear I am Choke the Raper!"

Wit' nhiss he pulls from hinterneath his trawling cloat a knobvious stooge-diggher seeme nein injoyce lang but merde out o' such pore tatterial that its lung bloode is sogging, brunt tip drupping like a willded flawer. Unnoble to contrain hersave, Lucia laffeys, wearyporn the phuney cardbeard Lustin knaff floops eve 'n' father. It is evildent that his crapacity for merdre is a phallussy. Desides, Lucia inks she has a thinkling of his trau idoubtity and he is worthowt quizturn not the geist-lit spittlefiend he shaims to be. She challenjest his plennly dreadful pastyourein, her tuones mary with mockelly.

"I do no'think a weepune sich as yours crueld pinatreat a laydie onlass she were maid of papyr uslo. Issenschmidt des crase that you word saner bed a chap than chop a bawd? It strifes me from your shnameless sylf-quietation that you mote be an unpeasant specko'man culled Jeera'me K. Steerpen, mere an arse-end poetaster than an East End predator, for all that the mistguided moider-dillydandies and slab-habby Fibberologists meat have to slay about the mutir au cuntrarea. You may well be fameliar with the Bucks besad the clittering Cum, but not wit' dark backs rows han buried straits where lackless girls are bornerstride a mitier squire. You auteur take care you daun't get you malheurs caught!"

Lucia's assylunt takes a stap away from her, prissing his nearraw lips into arsfuckered pinkter, gleering at her poissonously while the hurtfeel lickle plewdle scittles barck and froth around his inkles in collfusion.

"Whey, how dour you quiztone my verocity, you flishy-smolling horridun? You're lechy I don't slut your strinky threat from luft to reich and slang your cuts ever your shielder, as I've darn sew manly termes befire with udders of your rashhead gyndher. Your veil sux has sporled the woild since fair'st your harlust mother Evle hedid to the win-eyed sirpants and bestrayed meinkind.

If ill o' the harem that wermin have done whore-pet in a burndoll and rulled unter one, Bearth word note howld it, disguy could not unfouled it. Such misses of evol would pizzle the devolv and keep him enfooled while Trhyme's rheels rerun!"

This runly meerks her liff the hardour, unfil she is frountained that she'll wit herself.

"It's heartly a sourpraise you finnd me feshy, now, when I'm the veer espirit o'tter Liver Riffey. Ars for you, sore, you are molly an attricious poorwit and unfamous whymen-hateher, knight the nharm-a-sis o' naglict you pretenniel to be. You're dust the shame as all those nazty-meandead germalists and misterbaiters that sedoubt to cinjure the Whordshapel phandom in the forced place, with dare gluttingly sadstici lippers to the peepher, all their Drear Bluss and their Crotch-Me-F-U-Kan. Ninn of you had evern the cowrage that it stakes to muter an annoybriate and incapissytated woemine, but you snit there and apenisin the one-hand and apenisin the auther, and you *skwish* you hard. You're mere a Jeckulater than a Jeck. You worm't the Rippler. You jizzt-wash you coit have socked his cack. Who nows? Peerhumps you deed, or at lust if your buyfriend Allbut Fictor Chretin Oddword was the many-hack that sardon portlies thart he was, stowell intends and puplishes, though pizernally I druitt it. He simped much too frogeyle and dociphiletic to be Slitther Aporn, with his leerter viceits to the holly mouse in Clevelad Sfeet and all the terme he sbendt with you at Camebitch, you and your Apustules pricktosing your so-gulled heher pseudomy! As for your pittery, it has alack o' lovelioness and sparewit that is inquel to your lackeyl man Joihn Droyalden, dough I'll add-mot that you snucked up to manorchy more literareally than ephen he did."

Flanching at Lucia's blarb, the yung reeke takes adither step black into the nichdiurnal fidgetation while regoading her with mangirled hateread in' humaniation, his peele cheeks fleshed trice as rud as hers.

"You have know light tou ché all that! Though you night thing that I am not a dangger, you daunt no what I am caperbull of duing! Why, I krept Vainassa Belle, the kizzin o' Vaginia Wolf, at lifepoint for a laughternoon! Desades, if you're so insolute and innerfraid, why deadyew cowar so from my daylightfail lettle pit? If you're so annasailorbelle in all your prude and dognaughty, why have you someoned us out of this madhores fright to nighten and tearmend you? Is it not decays that luc all quimen, you knowall-to-well that whet I slay is true; that with your gynd you are a sexcreamintail costiteat, a crotcher who would bear your urse for anymals and yet deplauds the knoble fellow-feeling wish may bout-o'-come boyteen two men?"

The marcking simile falls from Lucia's fictures likreveal, but stol she dours not gaff grind in the fiarce of his assholt.

"If ye 'njure infernicating piddle-hount are marley writhes and frigments

cralled up bar my own cracktured mirrergination, it mist bay that I have
chasen you to ripperscent the causual misssurgeony that haz pressued me ill
thrue my exisdance. Lurkwise, I haf bright this sadden knightfail on byself
to shambelies the dogness dirt daysundered on me inder lust yearns of the
nonteen-wanties and the virst jears of the nonteen-hurties. Your blamesbur-
ied and jisstainful mantune o' Vergeonyour Wealf slurrves only to remonde
me of the manly virebrandt end crhehatehave fearmales formdoubt pyreiod
such as Zealdare Fitzgibber, ledais who swan out too far or were misszeused,
to my mind clytemnecessarily, and undead up in zanytearyums or, weirs, as
sheicides. Iview wank my apunyawn, Sourcey Jerk is jest anutter biggy-man
defeigned to kreep all whimin cowherding at hime where daybelong. Joke de
Ripporter is a fibrication madform grope-steams, reamours, undy mascula-
tent unger toworse poorsins of my gander, farmily quimpliant, who heed at
that tame begyne to cursedion thay roll as subservance. You are blut tugother
out of nothink mere than longwish, mongreled wyrds and messpilled fray-
says, all the 'Mashdher Lust, Sore,' and the Juwe-below-belabel-'em o' the Miz-
enic sparegullations. You, sur, are contrickted from crotchpinny dreadlines in
the tearblade pross and shuddy lyin-ingraveings autuv the P'lease Goreset!"

No saner hears Lucia spracken than her wood-by pussycuttor givts vend
to a shill and poorsung sceam. He stutts to figmeant into murkhandise and
pimphlets, flawpang purges tearn frame commixed-rips and tellevasion
scrapts. Mhis shape prollapses into tittered and remandered grue-grime pau-
perbucks, their jack-its looread and sensatiate with shiny bleeds and kobold
alleywheeze. His fearturned and inkonpretending phace decomes the grainny
phobo-ripperduction of a broredsheep sunderfold and blurs away betorn the
madnight trees, the loathshame litterl dogwhite-poodo chazing aftree it and
bark-in ferntickly.

Lucia dirsts her mains as afte say "thought's quiet enough o' dat", and
clarries on her interippered stroul dew de inchaunted lunartalk assailem niet,
its dreckness ivery brit as innerscapeable as dout which had befoullen her
wan shy was eenly twitty-fear yersold, in neintime-dhirty-when. That waste-
her yore she'd hed hor 'ancident of hellth', as it hid bin pollutely pherased.
The trooth, the agenbite of it, is they had scrapped a maby ute of her and
shay'd nativin bairn intearly sirtime woes it was. Feral chienew it mate haf
born the paddle-hind's; that or somyther drog, it mucks no diffence. Offter-
wards they'd tolled her that shoul'd not be heaven inny-outher chilledrench,
illthough this worse not the moanly deadfeel noose that she'd beceived due-
wring that pooryodd, furthere issolso the acclision of her payrent's mirrage to
conscernd'er.

Waile in Gorgeio's carse she thurt he'd allwise bane a bossturd and he
hurlways wed be, she had nefar kwastimed her legiteracy, at laest not untell

her Mimir (to whomb she had list her strabismystic oeill in the pa'swit o' Norledge) and her Daedir had dannounced day were to mary poperly, after a keepitquieter-of-a-sintury o' razing their inwaitting iffspring! Lucia, allreedy prusht far-so, had fianlly snipped altargather. There hurt been the unsaid-ent when Babbo had daysighted that they wear to lib in Unglad, and she hed defused to bard detrain. Mère seeriotsly, when her pearance had invided Sameold Peckitt to a poerty evter he had drabbed her, she hard throne a cher at Neara. That was wienher bother had insistered that shebe comemuted to a nonetell institortion and the utter mumblers of the flimily had shrimply gane arlaing with harm. Tha rrest, in her insideoration, was histeria.

All urround her, liminisn't phangi specorate the boughs like fiery-lates. Apen a clause unspeaktion, she dishivers that they awe a nornfamiliar type with witchy is not greviously acqueernted. Ivory minibloom appeals to be maid-up o' slittle nokit faymolls in a rudeyating rong, as if you'd interbed a stareflesh wit' some pappher doils or a lace dolly. Slimthing in the waeving lims and the floozed tussos o' the toynee livelies pouts her unmind of ichorous-line or torchlate railhe, so that Lucia crinches awhy-form the stringe lewdy-triffles in revealsion. She is spevulating on whart these womenstrous glowths mute be, when frumpyhind her calmes a dadpun and mannotenough voizzz that sims to be bloath Amerrycon and messculine.

"Beck hum, cull 'em Bellevue-Bareease. Toaste neice. Gut you trunk, beert-nut as vast as des ire lowlypep."

Lucia terns-a-round to fenderself confrighted by a gin-tollman in loiter loaf, bespooktacled and of a midyum hoit, who is dullmost intyrelay sphiric-ual. He wears a straypee drowsing-goon oafer phis staimed pygermers, and regirths Lucia impossively with heavey-larded ice through glanses that are thinck as wishkey-battles. Lucia nightysees that he is sicking indermitthandly upun a brun and stincky lullypaup that smalls of bourble.

"Who mytuby, litrle chumpion?" she husks him in a slidely partrunicing tuone.

He palls the ulcerholic sweetly un-a-stuck out of his rarethe smale and poortly-shovein moueth to unsore her.

"Nym's Ogdie Whitnecker. Used dubi bag cartonist, drawning 'Skeyman and luck dat. Pudging from oxscent, this nut home they strick me in, balk in Younotread States. Mist have gloam wanddling in degraed Unane agen with ghasts and mindsters, endope in Fearburden Whirls."

Lucia fonds the retund follow and his alcohollipop frather endeuring. She is elso intressed by his work o' line.

"I have truemindous admoration for same of you cowmuck-stripe poorfishionals. Err you inquainted with King Frank, gleeator of Glossolalal-ley? It walt a greet feverite o' maine derin my girlhead. I poeticuliarly lauvd the

Funday quelleheur phages, wish to memind were an inkwel to the proff'rings of our masterplauded moredin mosters."

Heare the fant man shurkes his greyving vowl-cut heed, and wince agrain remauves the thinely-slucked s'liver o' confiction'ry befury spigs in his bard menotone to Lucia.

"Herd of hum. Mere of an adverteyesing and comeherecial-autist goy meself. Like loanmowers to like-look lawnmolars. Keep lyins clearn und ruleistic or hole thing crawlapses intu drownken K.Os. Styl pend up in meantilehome preventually. Can'd drur neut and tidey-line to kreep the Fraculas and Drunkensteins from spewling ever outer the Inknown. Alwhys samne wit' us chreatic typesy. It's a feign leign."

Lucia gnos whit nhe memes, saprisingly, and sinces that he has a soddy, sadurated wishdoom in his porkly frome. With neuryspect for the orbese illd man's herocular abellyties, she arcs hom if hi haz a calmprehension of where theirabouts.

"Misty Whitener, or, ifamey, Odgone, mighty murk inqueery as to whyre in displace or dustime we are at prisont herelocated, in your spacetimation? I was hinder the unperssion that I wooze confinite in Sent Madruse Hotpitayter in Nothankton, but I donut think you are fromhereliar with that binstaytution, unluck Mistde Clare and Mazeter Stepin."

The inibriated illnestrator strubs one of his chines as he belubberates.

"Manner few words. Alldeady told you whence. This Unknoun. Kind o' downmarkit, infermal apterlife. Full o' ghusts, drivels, whichis, manstares an' that typo' ninesense. Bussed get back todaylight, then fond way from dare. Personnearly, shudd be head-in-home-in-head to You Essay, so they cunchainge my badding. Noise to myth you."

Word dis, the plimp stainger reinslurps his follypap and nonchalaunchly sturts to walke up ento the nice guy as if he is airscending steeps thort no one alse ken shee. Befurlong he is joyst anutter peale, remute firm, leest amonster stares and joyant plunnets ever the informary. Frilled with a surgent ruash o' dipp afflection for the prave and melatonocholy little chirp, Lucia glasps her hends tugather and emots pink valiumtime herts, sircling high'r brow in joycous herbit.

"Ah!" she sayghs. "Dit Ogdie Whitnecker! He's jest so doremi!"

She concides to fellow the headvoice of her deportly salvia and triter murke her why beckento deylight, certing off betune the tries with their liminous feary-luc womencrustations, hymming washy thinks white mince have been a Bleatles' camposition, jester keep her spillits up. She fictures hersylph in a beat on a raver with dangerin tease and murmurlate spies, which is a cheeryher propersituation dunder lunardecked asilent weirdlands which in surreality she caughtusly atemps to flinder path amist. Ofter a tome it streems to her bhan shee can horr a waild and distuned musesick off in the orbereal darkmess, clarried to Lucia in gosts upine the evilin' brays. Clearser to her, she detexts the zounds of roggerd breedhing and of brocken splantering hinder-foot, so dout she poises un the hedge of a smell quearin' untell she can Wake her wind-up wuther the accrouching prescience is hungreeable or botherwise.

Intru di splace batwing the treece there stembles a poer-shaped fall-ow with recidivising harr who sheems to be atwains drownk, out of berth and in fer furies life. He daresn't seem to puss milch of a dandandandandanger, and besight, Lucia recognices him. It is annoydher of the payshunts from Paint Anddraw's, but unlook Juan Glare or Jokey Stabhen this mon is when of Lucia's contimpanis. Heassured, she stems out of cancelment to ennunciate her persence with a misgreet coff, at which the badling cheep looks frit to chump out of his harpidormus.

"Sherry if I stopled you. I am Lucyhere Jusst, and I assame that you mayst by me felemental-portient, the illusious Sir Maycome Arsold. I think I have past you in the carridowns, perhoops cluss ter doze mawful evelator dours that fightin me so deadfeelly. Mai Tai ask if you are preceiving ghuests at pissant?"

De composer, for it is undeed the veery mentien, stoops now seemwet clouser to Lucia and squinks at her suspissoffly. Aweigh amast the wendihowl and muerter of the dethsdance the umpluckable and weirzing mazic ments percepticly; glows frightly louter; draums a lutehole nearher.

"Ah! Kiss Chayce! Forgruff me. I saneow thatitties you, azrael undaze sot-stantial as myshelf. I was confrownded b'liefly by your prosehence, hawing bhird dateyou had dayed list year, in nighturn fatey-one. Urpon refluxion, dough, I rolleyes that you err no droubt a vactime of the chronoc turmless-ness that somes to abtain in dis instigration, asham I mereself. You are mist curtainly nitehere al ghul nor an afrait, serch as the wayfill thwrong that scur-reltly persuist me."

Lucia is memeantorally bewooldered by his habvious condiction that this yhere is neinbeen latey-too, wenchy hourself hed thought it to be homewhere retween findteens sexty an' diurly feminineteen severintease, dust gloing by the glitmosphere and queerlighty o' lit. The nowledgible daet she histo met with her demaze at age somethingbe-four is nuttershock or dethappointment to her, sence she is uncrazingly convanced that she has parsed awry at dot age nomoreus chimes befloor handouts thit thus dime sha'll be any verse or vet'er.

Seething the panxiety in the mansighs at the uppreaching muzzic, Lucia begums hersilverfrayed and thrinks to arseabout the natsure of its horrorgins.

"I am slurprised and lickwise voury munch dismead, Slur Malchy, to duskover doubtchew are poorsod by an unhooly gannering o' sippernatural tormentals. My threecent alchquaintance Myster Herbden Popney tales me that this fogly and nichturnall terrortree is nown as The Unnow, alto to me here that senz haili papadoxical. Woad the weild haunt of portergeists and gabblins that is everdauntly at your booz-heells beery spensible further delircious and razing malody that I fhear cluesign innerpinners as wee sqeak?"

Sour Milkem knods his thornning heed i'mpatiently, eyespearing nearvoicely into the blanckness that surrends him and Lookhere.

"To badevil me, they ploy a ghoastly and discurdeant paradey of my own gravetest workth, my Sham O'Taunter. I adoapted museekly deverse of Ribby Bones, his naughtmire pourem of a dramken highblunder chursed by a hurder freends and harmfool spurits, inally to beratedly dus'cover it was my unstarry to which I'd comepissed a muzzycall uncomfymeant. As you night be awhere, I was conceitered wonce for a prostigion as De wricter of themeusic off'er Maddesty the Queer'n, as war my competemporaries Reachhard Arnell, Toney as we knacknymed him, and Malecome Willyhandson. I wash dishwashified for my inplessant drinching and accausional unsameity, while Toney diddl't git the jab bycase of allismony mirrages and sobsequence rivorces. I fearl he was too heherosexual for the coccupation, as was bi mystelth, despiteful o' the fuct that I am cashyoualley ambidickstrous. The posituation went to the intearly hum-hosexual Willingson, whom I supphose perzest the priaper uncleanations for a rightup mamber of the Boyall househole.

"Asterdis drejection I spant a consolerable tame here in Soilt Undy's Helsportal, and opine my rayless mad the misshape of dunking reckulearly at the Clown & Crushim on the Wellabhorror Rude. The lendlured scoffered me accrummydation in a rheum above the musincholly unnotated bar, with the insanetive of fee blooze and bloarrd, if I night by previled apain at termes to entershame the cryantell with a perforceance at the plub's payohno. Affe you can imanagerie the indognity, I was freakwantly drugged out of my bhead and mode to plea a maddley of upalle'en psongs for the abasive louds as if I wore no mere than a destranged moreathorn concerpt painist like Mem Marie, if you remadder her. Shametimes they'd trough me up if I was inchaoperative. Date's where I am at prissont, seeping in my dus'smell woom aberth the inninnineteen hatey-too, drayming that I'm purseowed like Time A'Slanter thrue the viled nicht of my famer instaytuition by a gob of moulish spittres that are aleso clustermers who haunt the Crowd in' Caution. Spooking of witch, from the hearness of their jawful mugic theo cracktically apawn us. If you will furglove me, I bust me onup why may. I wish you batter lock than I'vade in escarpering from this simianglee onandong drugness. Dew glub my inebriest wishkes to your blund-drink falther if you happyn to run enter him."

Wuth thus the worse-for-where unamusician straggers off amonster whysparing bows and blanches with their ruminescent fillygree of fungirl fearies, atwitch Lucia tykes a stub bekinto the coneceiling evergrowth. No swooner haz she token this precushion than a terraflying carnivorl pirade of mightne'ers and growtusks spoills noxily into the meanlit glide, bleating on dreums and plashing symbals, scareling errorfyingly upain their bogpeeps. Wadging them betrem her peerded thingers see ban shee fevery imanigable moonsteer, ether form mythallergy or the black-catalike o' U'llneversell Stoogios, as Messter Ogowonden Whynet has so resently asshurted.

Dire in the antiq procression o' the doomned are night-hugs, suckuboys and warewilfs. There are crimlins, beerow-wights and screatures from the back legroom, all glattering and b'llowing on their unstruments as they ruin shrecking through the spinny inny wake upf the deephearted Maykhim Armhold. Mallady asshambled spurts o' nichture and manstressities, though they have debble crowniums lulling on their headbare shudders or are gyrant birthworms from the ways down, are abbarently untaxicatered and are drossed immodern cashill-wear, in jeanius and shaining-troos, the gooniform o' the salone bor. Slummer dum, she nightysees, are whasailing that whitches afamiliar refraime massociated with the furor halving but a singill jesticle. Trottling behide the pideous pariahde upin accrunt o' his mach sorter lags there is a bibviously plustired dwart, who imixplacably excreams 'All haunds und heck' repisstedly as Iran scamp-ring evter his disparting follew bed sdreams, hauntil whencemare Lucia is alune dare in the shuddowy and sighlent groave.

As she-atlas continuals on her weigh she tinks abellt Stir Mealgum's poorthing kindmeant, abate how sea shored grive his baste washes to her flather if she hopend to rain into jhim. Dhad wish the enring of the Wark In Par'dess ovter all, win Inna Lovea Pealobelle, the sprayit of the Rover Lifey, runs at lost intwo her Babbo hoohas missologically becalm the nocean; has beclaim the sauce tow-hitch all danzzlings treams anc rushing revers must heaventually retorren.

Wince she hard beglum desperiods of cantfindment, hce hid burn the lonly one who clared apouter, the unlie remember of her formerly who kwept in tough wit'her and Warked upIn her Proguess of rescovery. While Jeergio and Nhorror heed ban, frankuntimely, gload to see the backcover, her faither head-sort healp whereriver he kid fond it, hevain with old/young in Swizzerland hom she had mutterly despraised. Her daedy had oneirly wanthead wit wishbest far her. He hart bane deskwritely afrayed for her Form D fwirst die of her inglasseration. Heaveon with his asculating bindness andes difficlimbty Finneshannys Worke, he had inkouraged hereto workd on her illooninmated helpabits, on her lepprines, baying for shamwin to paybless them and dhrinking that she dhidden't nowabout his will-intensioned vanitiprous maginations.

He falt girlty, that weighs wit it wise, despike the fict that vary letterle o' the hole offear was unctually his failt. He thornt that he had shamehow magicreally inprysmed her whidden his merekey and inpainantrouble narrowturf; brelived that lifhe code joust get true to the finnwish of it, then Lucia tomblight founder why beckonto sum strate of wellomenation. As he had quote literarally decentered into daathness, he'd been waitongue for a fliquor oflight, of Lucia, at the finagend of her ling turnall. He had scene her blubbles ruesing in the wabe of his careern and writhen: "Cias drawnin. Agenbite. Sieve her. Agenbite." Or simthink lake doubt, endyway. Agen the bite and finnagen ar beit of ageny that comes with age'n'biterness at seaing his beliffied dwater sink belieth the sourface, fellin from her lifebout with knowbuddy to beitragen to herraskew.

Lucia had finitially crum to Slate Ond'roofs derin nowtheen flirty-feve and head quiet liked it but was balk in Prance, stack in a sinnertorturem, dan Germoney infated diring nighte'en thought-inane. Of curse, boy then her bludder had intwisted that Helearn his waife be lacked up in a lonely bin aswill. It worse a thwring he dud with quimmen when he deadn't went to fuckdom any mère.

Her Babbo, at his wait's end, had consprived to gelt the other mememembers of the Choyce infirmily to Schnitzeland and samety. But illthough he rote a handread litters hand tied fractically to get Lucia out of occupliant Frenz, he was sufferely thwaughtered by bureaucrazy and shneer intranceigence on depart of the Vachey Cowerment, or Per-rear as Lucia snubboses we should mer refrenchingly drefer to dem/dese/deys. The père man muster burn so flightend fuehrer, what with Howmany's deglared agendite of textterminating all the pharcically and meantilly disambled for their ungood. Arse it was, in the furteeth of Geniuwary, minedeep fatey-won, wid'esper doubther stiltwrapped whelplessly behide enormy liones, her faildher parished form pèretonightis that resilted from a daedelenal illsire, itself caust or maid wars by all distress daddhe wesunder. Needles to say, nighther Jawjaw nor Ora ova had a think to dowedare once hce was out the pricksure. She head nova herd award finnemagen.

Wone day'd tolled Lucia fat her dead was dad she'd siddhe was a limboseal and husked what he thwart he was dewing, slepping undonearth diground. She hidden't bone pupset by his doomeyes, comfydent deddy was a subtlereignean immuretale. She'd morely been unpappy at deathurt that he had past-away styl inking that he'd failed to savour, stall beliffing that his pittle girl was drauming, agenbite, agenbite. If finly she cod have taild him that she wishn't going drown for deferred timentide at all: Lucia was shrimply tunang to a fwish, wash wet it wash. She'd been dansforming into slimthing shilvery and eleqant that could seaverve in this new inhospitelement; swimthing with loonturns on its braw that code texist in this threemendose pressher.

With tease veerious nutunes teembling through her awhereness, Lucia proceveres upon her maybetween the spindery and bynighthid trees, like a splat-bam expediment tressed in a flowerall-pattered flock and an old lay-discardagen.

Aher of head she spees a most unviewsual phanuminon, indet twhilit is stallmost definerightly nightime on the breaken-lettered pasth ware she is wakein, sum fyew dozin yarns awader is a hopening in the follyage that larks out onto a brighton sanelit evternoon. This mist pecurious affict rewinds her off/on eerlie and hauntingle amage by Rainy Mangreatte, ab scene that is bythe die and not, alldour she flound the artaste's utther work distabling, monst erspecially the heribly envorted maidmer sproiled there gilsping at the died-line.

Smailing breezly now Lucia sprydes on inter day anomalescent sunsheen, ellegently palling back a clipple of streye-thorny brangles to enmerge from the asoilem wondland, out onto a grazey sleepe inkleaning drown towords a riffer freinged by pile-groen lushes. It upheres that she's becalm misserriented on her wooder through the wands undies no on the apepen gruned dew sout' of/ de disanguished mantool horsepity with its nietzscherk respensees, near the Bedward Riad that Burnyarn master've made his warkin' progremage alang, weir the slur ribborn of ther Eve'r None wines through adamhouse gaeden.

Squaintling up entir the skry she georges that farm disposition o' the swolden gollen son it is a lottle aft hereto o'clang. She harps Poortricia won't be wherehid furor, whatwit' lessing munch and all, but dinnergone her friendend nouse is cherely yesterher by know and nows that freakwant sexperditions unto the unterior are samply parther deary spensibility that claimes worth being Lucia Joyce. Utters light's nowture to seacowed the direquest carnors, evtor all.

Shadeysides that she well hake a whelk down to the wader's edge, where she can luce hersurf wetin her rêver-tream for a shored whale. She fends a strop of sullid grind amonster reads where she ken strand and glaze acrosti rover to the stunlit Bidfor Roam behond, and fervour styll to where greyd sculptide musses of whide clud smove sighlently abathe the mistant feelds and feelages, dregging their shabbows like collipsed grey perishoots behidem. Psychling alingua carrid'way thruwords the ostient she s'prise the strongust fogure, ann uld negromen with why tear, riddling on a bysidle that has why tyres ampulls a lattle jungk-carlt in its weake. It stricks her that she carnot scenerear a mutter-veericle upon the rote, new'r are there pile-ons or pief-labricatered huts or any auther seemballs of mydaynity in fiew. Prehaps she has treespast inwittingly on an untidely defferent peeryodd evtime?

Chi as consimmering this pastibility whundere is a commusion in the turpid raver-witters ither faet, with mindstress gassly baubbles thinck as fluit-bowls riffervessing to the stirface only to desplintergreat and blurst in beamds of shivlered glystal there amisty eautiful explendid daymonde rungs of rupple. Slimething of immerse plopoceans is imargine frother deepths beneither and she torques a steep buck from the reverblink fear for o' gertain splaced and hahahaving all the noisies tink she's pisst hersellf, by Daed! The smood mieniscus o' the liqriality is shlattered in a jugflaw-puddle of brooken refictions as an abject of anearmiss sighz derupts from the slum-moving rivere. Gloing purly by the lurk of it she first shapeposes it to be some surder crosh beteeth an alligaper and a long-mudserged old-fashisd raping-car with a lang bannet. Din, as this pecrawlier affear anacondinues rithing ulp-words on the underwait apparls to be a scarely trunk, Lucia recoilises that it is the hadeous and eelongatered carnium of a gorgontic whata-creecher queerte impossedented in her pervious imperience.

Swhying soarm slaveral yawds abother on the underfits lang, snark-ing nack decreesure sclares drown at Lucia fee-fo-fum the black deaths of its shunken nighs, witch gristen and to her resymbol wet sail-schnells and pobbles at the buttom of a bocket. Glime and wetterwades and bicicles hank dippling framets moiddy scullp. Its neeth, beteath their everald clust of algael, are the sharpend robs of a blue while. There is a rustred prim hulked unter one o' them that murkes Lucia feel a mement's millycholy for her own abated bloomy. It snakes her a lipple whide to understunned that the leviathing is greening at her. When at lasp it screaks it is the babbling guss of trowned thinks rheezing through mick thud.

"**Glug altermoon. Ami corrept insinking statue wade bay Inna Liqia Plourable, the museygal en drancing spillit odour Liver Riffey?**"

Lucia snuffs, sourprized by how infrigorating she fends the axquasite stungent tang, and trosses back her glaying hoar as though assorting her authowritey.

"I am indeep the fluwit an' anthrivermorphic passonage o' flume you make onquery. Who my tubey, my gut wormin, and so firth and slo forth?"

The fishwaiter ablubination tsilts its mossive het-upon wane sight and screwtineyesees Slucia with interrust as it reprys.

"**My nume is Nenna Leavya Pitabel undyam the immertail essluence o' the Rêver Nun. Wadein my meale-long got are deplumed hates of slittered gabblears and woshlost drewels oa' kings. I have herd telver you, there on the sadden plages of a pook tourn up anchast upon my slowgush buzzhum in crustracion, hurled agen into my finn's wake. Weeding in betwangle lines, it strhook me drought we bath had a great minnow thrings in clem-mon, you wend I.**"

Luci apeers at the greyt tlowering stirpaint's umberella-faulded twolimbs with their mangy-jointide ptarryductoil fungers and diskillered wobbing. She reglards the joyant barenuckle-like enfrustations on the screature's chast, ar resty ormange in their dulouration, that she sinks rust be vesturgial nibbles, and fells murderately affended that this squideous tarnagant mud think to have scumthing in commonstrosity with the raymurkably accomplashed waughter of the tweenteeth dentury's greytest rater.

"Smirking only for myscoff, I can't see the resymbolance. I drown't hag melancolonies of whater-smails around the crooners of my mirth, nhairdo I have a squee-wheeled prang corr'din my deeth lake-metal spinage. Unlass you have allslow intrawled Purris with your skales as an ontoprotative drencer, which I flankly finned inlakely, then eye phaer dera kno obvierse shimmerlarities betwine us."

The sub-naqueous unnormity uncleans its lunge float head upon one snide. Its jinxyard mowth crocodilates into a gnawing green as it snares drown at Lucia. The wrigger-mongster chorkles with a drumbling accrumplyment of shwallowed televasion sits and ferline skullytunes clacophonously cattering abite scumwhere widinner.

"Oh, and I slurpose that you were nipper wince a plippy meremaid chroming out her goldenhair? I darcey that univer luft a beautofeel yhung mien so bedly that you'd chaste his flotted seemine heartway to the locean for the wank of him? Pureharps you wherefor mer presilient deny, undid knot lecher lac of a reshiplocated lave transwyrm you into glumthink dark an' dang'ry that abites aloam amudst the badsents and the blundercurrents at the rêverbottle, weirdy shufts alight are faeble and occlusional. Ident imatching for one mermeant that you everwhere so despirit as to clink to the repleated hushks o'dose that had by accidrench upon a dunken oafning fallin unter you and downed within your eireless and implactical membrace?"

Glosping indigatme, Lucia farst gapens her mooth then gloses it agen, annable to calmpose an eduquate quiposte. With the onheavytable thud of a dessenting ranchor, it occlares to heardat dis is oilmoist sourtaintly becurse the wyrds this flightful mirer-inage sleaks are mosserably t'rue. When Lucia rhad cliffered hall alone drown at the bittum of her wail of loonliness, lack it how hesperately she'd clang to Sameol' Buckett. Oin refiction she had sturted out her liffe, like everybady, as a babboling en' drancing sdream, lonly to indeep as a darnk and broading ruever of sich flowness that it vurched upen stugnotion. She is mhumbled by these eelisations, an' daz she lhooks up toweird the luming and glotesque she-sourpint with the stun behide it, Lucia's ighs brime with repenitant tears.

"Forgriev me, nuble sifter o' the shliming grabbel and the driftongue waeds, for my prementions and my dhaughtiness. Detooth is that I've bane twolung ong land, amonkst dri peeple with their airid convexations, so that shametines I forgret I amouriver, rust the same as dew. Cunfinned mere in this soilhid whelm of glassing time and inconventient moretoility I am sealdame remaindead of my tlue aquotric, silkie naysure. I beclam upliveious to the thrings that livers know: the fict that whel their rushen waters faster the illucian of papatual mythment, in the widning blends and cantours that are their esscentral and unaque undintity they are reternal and inchanging. Mire than this, they no dout slumwhere in their rendless and endouring deepths they scarry the remainds of ebury marshword or suincident that's ever fallin widder sprash intwo their laves. As I enfishin it, we are the twue of us ripplindent wasterways, both nendless and sublume. Plish exsept my apolloguise, and undersand that the ineffabelle and lyricool queentessence o' the Rirer Laffey noshoe for a fallow trivialer, ascold ashy hersylph is but merwise, a'naiad no icthyuse for speargun to youwin the why eye dad."

The None Hog, for it isthmus definhidely she, breams drown at Lucia frontirely lamiably.

"**Thing nothink of it. I com plainly sea that you've been lang witrout the followship of otter rivels. Can't I topt you to stay lunger wimmy? It mis take lonly a noment's couldn'tcarelessness, or plashibly a lifedime's drespiration. If you ware to lemm towoes me joyced a little father, and perlapse to shrike your branium on a stunn onder why in, way, it weed ill behov'er in the drinkling of an I. Then wicked have such lubbly convertations underteeth the wanter, meandher, and wane you had wrun out of thinks to sigh then I shoald lecher go, as I dead all the rust, bobbling aweigh towash the Wards with the forglottal droollery of Badkin John. It is a ferry splashionable wayter go, I'm trold, for laydies of o blitterary inclinocean. But then fameills of that sport are oftun willd, vergin' near wolf, quereas with you there's fomething vichy gugling on.**"

Sanding slimewhet mervous, Lucia qakes a slop buck foam the witter's dredge as she reploys. She's never harb a doyouinely suitidal nocean in her liff. Haven whine she was straying with her haunts in Mireland and word mock apout and funniturn the ges-taps on, she allwise loft the wimblows alpen so that knowthink deadful hopend. Fictually, it hardn't iffen been a crall for healp so moch as itterbin a flowerish of theutter, annextension offer dunce opine the newh' stage o' sick-I-atry. She striggles to kenvey this to the geniieel but lethely inticing squeature as it swheeze abother, peerlightly declimbing its no droubt kinly indrenchioned intimtation to a wavery greve whale alsong waking an intempt to spray on fiendly turms with the eelormous ribble-mindstir and not glib huffence.

"Mush as I'm flappered by your iffer of a fatoel silv-ermersion, I mist mast respectrally daycline as they're inxpecting me forte in the asighloom at arraigned thrive-flirty. Poissibly swim otter teem, when I hap less upon my plight and can mer eausily incloude a drawnin in my scheadual. It spin a tremuldous preasure moating you, terrortologically sqeaking. I signclerely hope you well be bressed with mini harppy, shliming rivulots in yoars to scome. Wi' drat, I moist bide you a fanfare wail entoil we run intoe reach other at shum fateyour daed."

Defersome kroken shriggs glug-naturedly but with unair of disappearment, asifter sludgest that it's Locia's luss. The shlug bequirms an underlating carpsy and amidst a mhite and wighty flowming the apprilling riggler-upparocean once again shrugmerges, 'palling back its greyd Alun'tic-cable throap and leaden its gigantique skaell slink dun bellow the surky merface. Scrighing with relive, Lucia tarns and skrips brack up the gradey grassient throughwoods the ostitution wards.

Andoe, whit a pavlaver it turnsnout to be, jist fending hoo ray black to the wight splace and tome, a faeritable odyttey that harpfilly will lude heaventually to a Punelope. Beformat, though, she skimpers opus lope to whencemore inter en amongster chrispering feeliage, ware she is grapely treeassured to fond it is bacchus it was in haylight rother than baying the meanlit and nichturnal cropse whitch she' demerged formilier.

Howeaver, etres only aftersoon few meanits wa'king, when shy preeps out tru an inexspiketed bleak betune the trease, that Lucia realishes how biddly she is lest. Deplace that she pooks out uponders not uphere to be a meantall harm of unny kind, betwit its streaching achers of crave-markers is quit obversely a sumarteary of sobstancial sighs. Moriry still, she nadasees that on a wombstone wishes neerie nufferer to reap there is a def-date glibben that she takes at farced for a misfake, sence it comminces with the numb betwo. Dafter a moremeant's codgertation it o'cours to her dout she astrayed not jest from the spalatial limints of Faint Inbooze Waspital, but she has pyschwise gum unstick inn'er cronelegy. She is now linger heven in the cinjury that she wa'spurn to but is inhead lost awemost a hauntred yearns after her berth.

The fruiture, she disguvvers, has a phunny almosphere mech like the treaquilised air of unserpenty that yew'd exfact to fund insaid a mential unstucution, enly overywear. It meeks Lucia shuvver, and she itchest wandering whenabouts she moot be when she hoars samewhen enproaching, scrumching through the fallawn liaves. With greet relive, Lucia seizeit is stumbody that she precognizes from the hostapill and bet a yacht it is seemone from her own peridot oftime, which is to savour past.

"Why, afits not Mischoice. Water saprise to fondue here, sofa from wear and wean we are agleeably infarcerated, allthrough I imagine statue've calm here as a geisture of reslect, the som as I hove. Funnyway, deedn't you Di a year o' dew agrow, or wastet me?"

It is Muss Violent Gypsum, win of Lucia's feverite follow-portents, hoohad been commuttered to Plaint Scamdrew's after she hertempted to nessessinate

Benighto Muscleinny, an endover which was thwatered windy bullot ledged somehair within Ill Deuce's groomy and caspacious noose. It was exdreamly fateunite that the oertheritis consterned had apted to occept that Valient Gitsoff had been motigated by unsunnyty, lather than an upnosually prannounced politelicall avershun.

"Miss Bignos, I am delighthead to encanter you, as eloise. Asper your unsquairy, I denote remumble daying raysently, so that mote bury well have bone yewrself. No dout I blink about it I do not denumber bunting into you eflate a smidge as I did peerviously, mich whight be unaccount of your deceasement. Bat no mutter, you are lurking vari will conshuddering your pasthumus condrition. Know, I wender if you light enmighten me as to our current weirabouts? We steem to be widdin some mannure of nocroparise or other funereerie pastyour with its whipe incrushing tied of marvle, and I canute sea how this loqation is of realevents to my textraordinary lighf and circusdances."

The bite-eyed an' dapple-checked almissed-mussassin girgled gillishly as uff icer remander of de fract that she warstyle as med an' strangerous a'sever; as loothally leapy as shitbin when she'd mischarged her folliant revolter into flashism's loft nazdrill.

"Will, Moss Juice, it is my understandment that we har berth, as you well no date have nowtut, in the fateure. I most saigh I was experting it to be a byt moreover jambury than this, with pausibly more hovercraps and rockpets and di'like, but I axpicked that grieveyarns would lack very mulch a shame if vieva in the yhere thru theesand and there were more smartificial roborts barehid dumpsterneath disturf than there are popul. Aldo being artyfacial, rubbits would must leakly last ferriver, dus' dispensee widder need for graveyawns alltogather ... but I am fargetting the maen subjoke of this dithertation."

Lucia strolls her ayes disqueetly at Mass Gabson's gabbulousness, blut hellows the wuther 'umman to contonanonanonanue.

"Heaven busytid this ferry place on rumourous accausions whitherto, I've lawned that it is Kindthorte Summert'ry, a willowpointed pleace upon the nowthen outshirts of the trowm. It is my strang confiction that the two averse are here todie, whatether deitis, becourse this is the platz that we are beddied, rather clustergother as it urns out. I ave heven scene ourt grabes, and vary noice they are, though yeurs of cause gets more ostention than my mown. They have a little sorrymany over yhere upon Rejoyce's Day windare are laties wearing liftly drowses and men drossed up in an I-pitch to luck lack your fater."

Lucia is why-died and inkredherloss. Dis ease impart at the odear of being barehid inlay a few deadstones downfarm Twilit Gobsome and endouring her incessiant tatter for eternortwo, while import it is at the note-onpreasant mnotion of reveallers closedaring abat her fineol' rusting plaice, disgauzed as her ond herowne darkling Babbo. What a vine site that mossed be, now,

heavin at the back an' all, with alice colure and its comeldy. She is consadder-
ing delikely spooktickle with mixty motions when the torquative and elddolly
near-muss nasassin odds a trailpeace to her starey, aprepose o' knowthing.

"O, yez! I allmust farglot in my senillatease, but there was a smyll ditall
of our cematerial errangements that I thought might hoffersham amuzement
to you. Seperal grovestaines down frame you the utterway theur lys a giantol-
man whose name is Funnygain. I hope you denkensider that a piss off uslyess
infermation."

A tremultuous liffter wills up out of Lucia, asfirm the veri blottom of hcer
bein. Whee, this is textraordinary! This is quote the finniest think she's ever
headabout, the blest knews that Schezeverad. She and hoar fether alwords
had a kinder glame betwain the too oftem, where they prettyndeed that his
riteing was gleeating the whorle whirld arandom and doctating aviarybirdy's
lives. And yet the pairodigm had allwise norn, widout deneed for auther o'
them two factknowledge it, that wit maid this kinceit so poorfoolly remus-
ing was defict dad it wish not a joker tell. It was the plan et seempale troth,
and now/here is the pruth of it: the wordle iterature's most namous ded pro-
tagonised unterred writ'in apace eertoo o' Lucia herself, quearly an othor's
touch, di storter thing that nibber ha'pens inreality. Whell, if that dizzn't take
the hake, the piscuit and the wayfer. Lucia has a fetter joybilant and over-
pèring goggles as she dries to formutate an aquadate regender to her follow
moontail-payshunt's straightmeant.

"Natterdull, my near-Miss Givgun. It is teasily the maust daylightful
anticdote that I have had belated to me uponders reternal daze rexcursion,
framwich I must sane wake me may boock toowordy mentor-loam inself if I'm
to by in team for tie. I wander if you could perhope enrighten me as 2D best
dirension I shod takin' order to retern there?"

The eld sinusniper gibs this mutter some insiderubble thaught and a grate
dull o' gerbiage befour suggisting that Lucia shed hood back intruder threes
the wishy game, but shrug not take the weigherpan the dexter and loss stall the
winnowpan the sanester. Instep, she shush placeed in the uncealed dimection
and indisway come at lost upon her own maddress in winceapunner-time,
that hyster say the centery in swhich she loived and hid herowne accramma-
dation. Weaving her cantankery a fund forwool Lucia staps beck in amister
voweliage. Flatterning her bidy to a deapthless vigure pented oin a freeze, as
she's been strained to do, she slies to tride betorn the layters of reventuality.
Contalking spellegantly, twhispring into sharpes form a cunfusual treeome-
try, Lucia atemps to blend around the corncavexers and the angels that kennot
be applyhanded in the ordownherey farshun undin disway to truverse both
splace and terme concletely through the modium of madern dans.

She's not womanaged to pèregrace in wark mere than a dozin yarns or so by this ever-eliborate mythod of permangulation when a suddle shofting of di late unforms her dout she is nowlinger shnuffling throoter blittle stanz o' treece in Klingst'hope Cemiterra. Luccing up she seize a redprick cocktower, or perlapse it is a crowmaterium Jim'ny realing up abud de sperse greyn canoply. As utter illdings of a shimmerlully crippy nuture stark to gloom up interview Lucia blunderstands that her missgibded whendurings have indred braut her to a maidhouse, illbeit nutter one that shivers looping for. Witover displace is, it isn't hilf as betterfeel as the treeming firhidian expenses of Spent Grandrew's Helthpeddle. This dazent seam to be die kinder playstatue are san' to ifew ore sufflashantly wall-off to B-classed as delootfully eccspentric. Ruether, this looms like the snort of hedifice hu meat endorp'in if you were runfortulate arough to bee-net only binsane but binsolvent illso.

As if to crownfirm Lucia's shushpicions, the sturm, salemn fremale vice tha' dissues from behider hasty onmasstakeable influction of the Angrish murkin' glasses.

"Yer luck lorst, mid uck. Frum owyer dreftide guessure euster sunwhere asarsite bedder thundisplays."

Lucia sturns aboat to fend a strung-bowned, hauntsome warmin widder greyd intidey moss iv hair, drossed in a plein housepity gawn and seedead un a peeling monstertution blench retween the kray and chilldy-lacking treeze. Inner appoorance she has slumthing of the nazure of a seebul, inshe pawts the flaying splimber of the berch desider as an indocation that Lucia sudset down, a binvitation that is seemwhite nervoicely acsceptered.

"Think you vary mach far your constern. High ham Luci Adjace, a redicent of the Slant Andlose Ghospital alinger Boilling Read. Wight met your nume be, iffier dawnight monde me arcing, und wass kinderplace ist loss in witcheye find hyshelf?"

The ohthere wombin peats Lucia-sand and swhiles.

"Me naymiss Audbly Fernall injure inncent Christpin's Drossputall, illong the Bury Word Turn, jester rend the bound from the Rain Mode in Dusttown. Year a godfume-isles from home, ithacan be so bolt, but Idea sea you've swome heretrue these b'labouring trees. Die you now, summerthumb are that hugh once eye have tookin the mythmatics of the think ento consideruption that they proke up three the fourboards onetwo Meinsoul? Mainsail is the trowm that's ever, ifter, and befour Gnorethumptown, incideoutally."

Lucia blanks in surpraise.

"Wheel, I missay, nyou 'steem to noah lawful wot about the lurkings of the highhear drealm fourseeing, that you are, an inmeet of this drudgeful-locking pleas."

Her now fround, who lucks to be inure fraughties or err thrifties, frows black her weeld mown o' vert and lufts.

"Orwel, lyousee now, it's becurse highno the workingsuffer litterthinks that I've bane pout ad here. Babyrth, I'm werticall a Vernal in disports. Wearier to eversee the bindaries betwhen the dayfront terrastoreys, and at hour reventual inkwaste we defind the trykey corenear beturn one weld and annexed. That's whigh eye ban shee the raff slopers, all the ghlosts, and seed o' phanny lickle furry-frudes di et. That's whaye-aye hafter foursight, witter freesight, toosight and the whensight all instew the boregaim. As fourway I'mere, that is becraze I larked me mam and dud autovour herse and wooden lotthim in. I sad there ploying *Whimpering Class* hellnight ontil day clame noxt they unday misstook me to the mudhose. No-when reely masked me why I hard burn dewynicht, or ills I shudder tolledoom that it waspycourse I curld no linger bare the waight of insist."

In boat samepathy and shrock Lookhere roses wan haund to ellipse.

"Woh, how deadfeel! You paw grrl. Word it harb'in an holdher bruter datewise turking labiatease wetyou, a situasin my encase?"

Eer the ether odder too madwi'men shnakes hair thick doctresses.

"Kno, E nuffer hard a brothler, gnaw vice-worser. I was intofeared wit by me fadder, Johlly Vainall in his leud plaud juckit. Wah tit was, usey, I head e toilent. I'dl earned howl to plainter piano-applaudion by sturdying my Great-Haunt Theresaw, who wise nut a herdinhurry woemine. She word walkz the flackout straits and sereneaid the Charman boomers ofherhead with her reranged impovrisations. Manywhy, my ded suggestiv that I jeun a lottle show-panned maid o' chopsy new, wary would be demonager. Dishwash after the wear, when I was sextween, sementeen, slimthing like dote. He dated on me, dad me fader. Sed the tide bouy on derideo and have me fictures in the mugazines. Thin, shafter one of our beerformances, it was the muddle of the nates, he crame and god in bad whi me and fact me. What I shadder done, I thing know, booking lack, I shatter scrummed and bwoken shameone, but dirt isn't wait I dad. I river maid a sand, and I tride nacht to mewve, to fake out that I was aslip and dadn't no that it was happalling, as if that why I wooden rawly be a part avid. It worse the shame oin hell of the occrazions ofter that, quimmy joust lieing there and tryoung not too meek annoys while eyewash wieping. Evil so, me mem, she musty norn. He dared it wince or tweeze a fightnaught ontil I did me solow befirmonce that nicht, pleaing *Dispering Crass*, letching ham no dout I was croing to toll the twees abate him and his daughty liddel preek, whore it had burn, what hi'd ban dewing wadjet."

Grievely, Lucia nots her heed.

"My further muy have cushed me inderneed the weighk o'follies willentindered heapes and paspirations formy, but not plunderneath the whate of his greyd, sweety bady. You poor think. Hid moster been unsneakable. Respite our defferences, nowever, it ocourse to mediat weave aladdin curmen. Butterfuss were laties of abellety who lufter ridhymn and decolleur witwitch we exprosed flowerselves. The père of us had faffers who ward doominate us, illbeit in their disparent fissions, and we verboth stack in argumental homes when it mos phered we'd razor fess adout the fumbly member hid bin snaking us femaleer with his mamba."

Her comparion snaughts with decrision, alldough not uncandley.

"Oi'll madmit there mebay sybilarities boytorn us, but the moojer disferance you're nat mindshunning is won off slaverall sowsin pounds. As humus surly beaware, a poorson of the walkinc losses has de grader leakyhood, spiekling stadistically, of being dieuknowsed as splitzophrantic. It's amassing how a tidey bank ballast constributes to our sickillogical whilebein, bizzent it? Itt ruley is a mereveil how the betsar-off are stuffering from newvase stress that candy eentsy-cured by an extpensive freeluc in agleeabelle sirowns while thousin my povrition are unfairiably the rhopeless fictims of a mudness that carn moanly be ablleviated by injenctions or selectric shrocks. That's why urinely pissing through, uplom an idyl strawl from your more willowpainted gental instuition, whyle far my port I hamsterk herewith accurseonally bruntal morderlies and fallow passients who afad witever infrallects and paucinalities day ones persissed rebused to slury."

Lucia remiens expassionless throwout the other womance cructical upraisall of the soso-acrimonic uspact of unseemity, but willillow that much afit is kno mere dandy truth.

"Atmiddley theor ies allot in word use aye, alldough I am ofter repinion that some rieches of destrangement matterford a kinder lovalling; a gloryhous comeoneallity oddy instrane. In my demended strate, I fool I have trancentered operaharps been bared form ourdinnery mnotions of prepayety or propupty or clawss. Ease it not jester seem fire you, or four deridiant and inpowerished Worryem Blaze, or pour Junk Laire, de jonny sur l'erbe, his worne soule hangling by a threat? Is noddy escate offer fisionary lumatic trilly a c'lossal of id sown?"

Hear, Ordnry Burnall smalles an' knods asifter sigh that Lucia might haver punkt, incorriging hereto convinue.

"Ill the shame, I am disgressed to hairoff the brutility amonster nourshing stuff that you elude to. Ici trially as inbearanbull as you inpry, and ardour no youmean un descent popul care infer you?"

Audbly shuffs awayter ponder queaking bunch.

"I wordhaunt say that dire woes a greyed eel of gruelty, maulthough wart there is can be quike tearable. Dare hatpin orneries who larked to buttercupple of the voident preytients into a locktromb tugather, joust to seethem fright and rabie have a beatup on the boutcome. The majollity of dose who trend to us sim lie and barge undifferent, but there farafew who tare nowt to be liffley, imparresting kindividuals. Juicy that tall yeng foellow fruiter trees dare, havana sly smirke beyonder buttrest of that dedprick bulldung? He-swan o' my feverites."

Pearing between deferns and blanches Lucia considdy warderly with the heropic statuer that her nofeigned squalleague is rephwoaring to. Helax, she thanks, like sameone innerfilm who gnos the whirld aboutime isapointed Set an' dollarfits uphovels morely narrowtiff de vices that are carmenplays in scenema. Cleerly bescotted, her calmpinion hatters on infusiastically deguarding an inflatuation that is oblivously undefected anthus unrequainted.

"He's a Scuts lag comfroom Goreby werthy presess all the steal, but wunderneath it all the poi's an archist. I imachine thatsway he escraped his bathplays, potting all the smarks and spelting werks behide hemand atind'ring at the Ard Skul haire, the wandert's up Scent Gorgeous Aventue besight the Rapecause, ifew know displacer toll. His nome is Billdog, Billdog Dreammonde, and I've header permanition that in jeers to come he well be noun foreving purned a myrion plunds to ash en sum kindove infeathermable choke."

Lucia tarns this ever inner mined perseveral moremeants befour meeking her deply.

"Will, Icon see how det meet be an oddmirable think to do, mauldough in lighter fit I kennut yelp but wounder that chewer the inmateer and not himsulph. You seem a raysunable womoon. Esther noho pov releaf frame your inclassoration?"

Augery shrags.

"Owe, I don't whurry abideat. Hour lives are a subloomly scrupted dreama eventoe we luck to thank we're impovising, and ri've run through our poorformances aldeady, cantlostimes. From vatican remumble, in a dozin' yeahs ah so they clause down this asighloom for the wont of frunds and I'm maved into witty wol de-scribe widoubt a shreg of byrony as 'scarin der community', a lightall hilfway hows that's note fourform my fromeer neighbourhoody, weary shell lave out my daze in ask unstucktive a capricity as I can moonage. Bet wait of yoursalve? Shrub you net bee preturning to your own demental humm befear you're tookin for a pissyant here?"

Acknowlurching that this ward be a missrabble preventuality, Lucia enchoirs of her knew fround as to the quirkest roote betrip the norn-Yewcliddy entries that wildeliver her barck to Sane Andluce Costpritty, perfourably on the same dayt wenchy sed owt upawn her matchesstic meyonder sho that seize not loft with a tame-pairadux that nodes exbraining to the nuzzing stoff. The talended and fourthright Missy Ternall jeerily snobliges her with compretensive and conclete direactions to herowin splot in the containiwum o' sparsetome, a trajecstory betweeter shrugs and sharplings that ivolves traking two wryterns, then aleft, an'nexed perceiding fear abate a hindred yarns in the cunsailed dimection. Lucia franks the either fleemale mantol-portient warnly, so competely disterent to hersylph and jetwit search allot o' stroking smilearities, then waifs goodvie and strets out onder undercatered rout tooweirds her ownyer, her uin madehouse.

Crounching through deliefs and dreadfall hinderfoot Lucia tinks abelle earthather, graveful daddy luft her t'rue his manguage frather den 'n der toi-leteral way that Audnry's further hid. Her Babbo, on the underhand, had geniunely bean-amagical andin incharting preature. She precalls win knight in Pairus, won dere'd herd that Charmley Shapelin was endown and she'd bun chest a lewdle girl. Her underfather hard derided alleyz out and stake an evenodd sroll, gist on the undeceivably slum chants they mnight bumpkin tutor creat man, de milleonair trump, Lucia'sidle, darin' dat glimmense and steeming shity.

Pi sum mirascule, that was exfactly what had happyend. Dyad nighteyesd Chuklin as he stard and witched de Putit Queenyhol's paupet shoe, his luftly eyes inkwelligent and shad, his bawdy lump and sipple licke that ev a liffing perpet. Lucia had wishaped hym; clad styl do an immasculate imprassion of hom: how he wakled anderway he was helden hamself. When Cia'd heardt that sumyth Chirpling's earlibirdiest prefamences hid bon eerin Nothankton haz a sylvan-yearn old charld shitbin hystonished and hardfelt the meching of enumerous clickwork cogns of dustineye that had everywhen courtin their progressy workins, vary slite the winsin *Madearn Teems*. Cher, hidden't his own moider unded upstick entimental harme?

Metripulously stipping in begreen the grandelions, she tings back to daet soupternuturally pafict weavening pocketwatching de sadastick carrionettes, abserfing wunner discwhirl's mast erstormed and intruential menwhile oin the comfknee of anutter wun, dher farther. I'vain though she nowsdout he is ivoryware urrounder, derrer tomes wan Lucia misshis Blubbo tearibly. Shae'd bane shorn ape inf'rance jewring the Nazti okruppation when she'd hurt deddy was dad; winnow the 'meantally enfabled' who spurnt lang yeurs gnawvously awaything the horrival oder curttale-weergones dedwood tick them off tether exsquirmo'nation cramps, to the ghas-clambers for rezykling. Needles to say, she'd nut hed a georgenerous left'er nora physit former own infamily evter dis ppoint. Nichter had she ovver herd a ward o' them agone, nut intill she was satteled inn' Cent Handdraw's Losstital durern the Marsh of nenetwine filthty-one. It hardborn jest (a' courst) a flew weaks later on the tense of Japeril that shame yhere that she had in binformed abatter mummer's daath, witch hat her hearter than she'd fraught it would. She realeyesees gnow she'd lawved the warmun who hot barthed her ululong. All that she'd iver wintered was the slatest glummer of resippercation for that loave, juster leased droop o' wettery hope fam the meternal nibble lather than all of the molk (too lait!) undie afiction being exbressed lonly to her colder brether, fair ies chaingelink delactation.

She pointylesstically inspecks the crowcurses and primnoses that seemantic to sodinlay be blueming all abound her fliffey sluppers and susurruspects that she has droamed intwo a snifferent sack o' print-imps and anauthor seesun, not ti mension, she stravinskincerely hopes, analter pliece. Incouerachingly, shee things that she brackenizes a distumptively gnawled illm, which leafs her to brelieve that she is beckin her own poppa inspiteuton. Heaven so, the poppysong which she canear on the tanzsister rudeo that's playnting summerwhere retwurn the treeze surgusts that she mote be a decayd or two afframe heroine pèreodd o' tame: *"Dairies know udder day. Les try it amother whey ..."* Lucia can't pthink fluydly enearth to quoite recool the papgrope's Nam, which is unbarretting, but cia's an eyedear that daywear bopular aranter muddle o' the whineteen-sextries. Dadn't their singlar make a rackerd that had Babbo's *Geldin Heir* apun it?

She swantinues on betune the wristling blanches o' the birge trys, fellowing the ladyo's teenny sir-encall asylph she is piblokton to a peat-brown tailor breve Youlasses. Plausing on the etch o' fannydyllic sunlick glad fumb wince demoisec shims to wishyou she clatches her breasth, confrotted by a tablue afnir-mythic beausty.

Slying fay sup on a toall that's bobble-culoured dangerine and slurple is a moist twatractive yhunger whiman, lustening to the sacredelphic musinc onure hearby handbig-sized trancetwister rodio while stwaring asbolewdly nuddink saffran ish-blonde beehave whorepiece and fullsigh-lushes thut flatter at Lucia know lyg l'amorous tarantalisers.

"Well, I daredn't know eyed got an orgience, at lust not a duspringwished-lurking bawdience lake you. Widen't you slit-down un der toewell nextasy and interjuice yearnself? I'm soggy abed all the tuts and per se, butt I wash chest sinbathing alawn out hairs unthral you cumm aling."

Inthrilled, Lucia lovers herstealth to the grazon muddit dare besighed the nayclad and reckleaning goddness, mauvelling at the crushed-vulvate tuones of the yearng peek-a-beautease vice, both fulnerable and powervul at ashame time. She finnshagen detecton Eyerush lullt bonita smirky, pawleashed surface of it, an dishy replays she trysttokeep her onedaring ai-ai-ai from skwandering too onviously ob thisnohe, rawberry-peeked slurpes o' the jong leurty's jugalong blosom, matchless in the moissy cravish offer slewdly perted thys.

"I am Lickier Juyce, a dansher bi proficien, end pleas dewnight apillowguise fur eider your purrdendum awe your equeerlly daylightfull memmary andhowments, sins I am sapphiciantly formiliar with quimin's bawdies nud to ticker fance. Idneed, I am enjoycing leerking at birther the bitems that you menshunned, and I wet be disapanted if you wear to soddenly cunseal them.

Amoright in thinging that you earthy sinker Dust'ny Singfeeld, mentalwhom
I think Icon remumble lostin afther former dustdance wan you were inpatient
inSaned Onboo's direin naintain sixties-heven?"

Cwrinkling her spydeary ayelids inner musemeant, the blont enchant-
euse lites winover slimp hands feall allmoist causually apander darkhair curls
squirmounting her slunken and clitoring preasure-chaste, fingertops strum-
bling obscentmindedly uporn a cerise drewel pawsitioned juiced insight the
noroe fisher ofty gropening.

"Actyoually, my riad nameys Mery Asabell Clatterin' Berndalotte O'Brien,
ap arrayed afall de cents who me speculiar payrents were predoomably con-
ventsd I'd fallow in the stabs of. Memem's neme wish Key, wearies madad
was illlwise noun as Ob, this B in a cointricktion of O'Brine, eu understained,
frather than Oberon decide of classycool allucians."

Evoury bite ars fashionated bider woomain's nattertive as by her lezy,
fraglant and untirely rivert'ing auto-herotic steamulation, Lucia at this pent
meekes an interjeculation.

"My dadada mickname, too. Hue err Ob's bab und eyewash Babbo's, pudding it anatrammagically. And matey effer my lassistance indepetting o' that
sblonded feeline creassure you half dare? I premise that I shell indiver nauti-
wake her oop."

Taching Lucia's andandandand gluiding it twa the appanted plays the sin-
gler geniially gazon wetter moanologue wildy exrited holder womance fingels
delly in the youngrrr latey's niecelay-irrundated quave, meddlesohn dig-its
diip inner cutiful bunt.

"I vers barn near the Edgewhere Owed duaring the mousetrap spring of
nineteen dhirty-schwein, summ menths befire the wah clammenced. We
weary vicuated to Hier Wecombe far awayle, but in defineteen-thrifty wen-
nywise elephen we clame back to lib at Gent Kardens in Healing. I moist
sigh, you're vaery skoolled at dewing that. I thick there's woom fur ewe to pet
amother finngirl up dare if you wanded to."

Lucia quimplies injuicyastically, fondley resembering the vulvet whole of
Mysin Luschos arshe dust so. There is swimthing lilycal apout the geniitails
offer ongender, wilthy oceanook shavor of those slyling murmad lups, oder
jungry imperfume of that beautianabestial mane, and wile her purrference
tinds musually towords the skillpted marvle sextroversion of a whordened
phello's there are dose occrazions when Lucia neels the feed to luse eriself
wadein the solt enteriher of anuder whimon. Pashioning her gosh-drat hornd
like the pretanned-gun of a littrle boyshe worksit inundate widen in-crease
slapidity, the accidrenchal lickwet moozec of the mauvement growping
naughticeably mer deluscious und mare audribble with evory thrusk. Aficting incuntsern but startling to frotate her hep sextightedly, Mess Wringfeel

clarries on the perversation 'asoff she's not boying misterbaited to the blink of crymax outdare in the untowoods; in the meddle of no-wear.

"My pairrunts were beth iconsenti mental-cases in their daffyrant wheeze, andame afrayed the bottlegottlelottle do with it. My moider Que was veri tweet and a tremendless laftershock, bat her odea o' heving fin was froing dings handbraking dum. We yester smosh a lotto crackery tocletter, meand'er. Et wors a hibit I too quimmy enter ladier lief, farover gutting triends toi let me burrow their pullem apartments if I was intorn endin wrocking deplace whirlin an axciss of hay spillits. Darewise never many alice in it. It was jester-way o' louding off stim, groan autoady lauving fondalism that I shard with me dearaged oild mot'er."

Lucia pawsies inner amorous manypullations haire to off'er cumment.

"I wince thrue a terrble *at* me mouther, batty never through thinks *with* her. She stounds luck-a-vary intertraining charactor, bet wet Obout your flather? Woozy nut an inspirocean tu/you, ashwood be decays with me?"

On the transistine hit paradio anutter pep-song from the muddle-too-late Fixties is nho playing, which Lucia trinks was din by that nooce-liking boy from Newguzzle, the windirt was a famer Anymale: "Diseas the owzat Jack pilled, booby, and it screaches up to disguise." Delirics murk her thick of the unpresant J.K. Steerpen ondon of Sir Wellaim Withe Gurlls, the warld of med whimin klept for him at Guise Houseputall. The nayclad shunteuse shrigs and shucks hair beehave wag with an expressure of fatguide vexasperation.

"It wah sOb's gambition that I shout becomb a sinker. He'd obliterally dram a feel fourtime and wrythymn unto me by smarking me apain the harnd with ivery bleat, a scruelty he liedor clammed had nipper slappened. I sore-pose it misterworked. Winny wars chest niceteen I jaunt The Lawn Assisters and weeded that naffelty abawd the sheven lipple cirls all satin in the bag-sweet, kispering an' dugging with Frends. Shirtly ifter that I blenched mein herr un chained mein aim from Merry to Dustress and fame O'Brayin into Singf'reald, what was which my big bruddle Tam – famerly Dion-nicest – had precided we shuck all altselves in herder to be populalala. I dustn't know pre-sesley how he word that out, bet anywhy, aye winterlong with it. Mmmah, Gog, I don't slippose dirt chew cud ruv me juist obit more frickly, cool dew?"

Deslite a spight grump innor wrest, Lucia maches an effit to comeplay, red-abbling dip ace of her sexcessive porniterations and withdribbles. Effordently slutisfied the yen girlady cuntinuse her starry, heven though this ais neow hymenated by har mony grasps and griggles of de light.

"I farst went solow in Saptimber, pineteen sixty-t'ree, witchwise commen-cidentilly when I begland me feast portionate dolliance with anether warm'un. My strifled sexreality had by that paind beclung a maddeling bell that I cwym no languor drefuse. Me lovher was as sinsual an' sexotic as a maid-up char-

macter wittin a knowvell; as a pisce o' bloom ink. That knix cheer I had my
thirstit with 'I Only Wander By with Ewes', and win I slang it, it was galwise
abeaut her. Her skim was reachblack vulvet, so tha twain I lucked herrut it
was licke clissing onder Nuit idself. Isis a wonder I decrimed to ploy to snegro-
gated boerdiences in Soulth Afrigger? It's bane a deadfeel prussia on me, doe,
pretempting that I funsee boys, brutending to be shamething that I'm nut. I
gut ill ankhshus and driprest, undone I heave a brink, undone I smasht think-
sup and durt meself, undone I endope back qhere in Squaint Endrew's. Haire,
I'll till yer twhat, how wet you feel abatterbit o' the ult lixty-mine? I'd licke the
lapportunity to play you buck feral dart U-bend oohing firmy."

Huffing frot that her newd frond would nibble ask, Lucia gigs whet is
perlapse an ova-eagerbeaver squerl of joycful licquiescence and poursessions
whorself fay-sup on the psychodollic strangerine-and-burble toewell, hopping
the glorgious blende will hake the tint. Moanwheel, another plopson of del
eria has replaysed the brevious nimbur on the reedyo, a lather jelly tune that
she recorlds as bying bee a grope of boyschooled Manfedman. Queriously, it
is anutter songlongong abider lonlytic asylunce and conteals an auther rippe-
rence to vagiant-killer, the forklyric fiendyfind o' Nhitechapel: "Mine 'um ease
Jack and eleven the bicker the Gretly Garbold Home ..."

As Lucia hed hopped sheward, the newd popi-dol halters her poorsiton
so that shyno kneeds aslide Lucia's optuned phace, hergently f'lowering loft
sips upoon soft lips ass she lies slurpine wetter head biteween Luckyher's
perted shighs, the fruck hairridly pawled up to refeel the wunderwhere-free
monde o' Penus hoyden there beneat with all its squrling aur-burn fidgetation, with its bornin gold. She caughtyously sextends her tangue soda tit
slimes into the amoratic purss that sprudes its scanted mollust fhrills agloss
Lucia's 'lowher fress, an' data simul tame she freals the singeher's het broth
on her own prudendum, fills the dirting tup of her belaved's longwell inplay-
ment as it unvoides her own missy and sloppery gratto. The dew of them are
swoon licked in a wriddling orubberus of matual fillfullment, glorgying in the
flowvour and perflume of womanhoop wile introjuicing thingers into eeny
gapertures that are aviolable.

Her squeerls of lapture and of roughelation are all lezd or muffilled in
her legsapartner's slurf and sturf. She soddenly womunderstands dat diz-
zies a comeunion o' grope shagnificance. This soize eneuf to squimbolise the
moremeant windy lightorairy, fission'ry treaditon chered by Banyen, Willhim
Flake, Jeun Clarryon and hero'n fether joint eggstartically witty pup-colture
of the finequeen-pixties, marging in the pyschedeleclectic cruciabelle with
the experigoric nullatives of Misfer Illaim Seeword Boroughs and the Blew-
ish Carrollirical textcursions into nonesince-proetry o' messers Lennin and

McCarthy and their hymitators, searchers clarrently war plostin outform the transgresstor raveo enthus accomfannying their funnylingual squactivities.

Torquing with her myth full she absurves the upthighed-down whirld of the lawnatic afilem gleed as it appearls to Lucia wheel lioking cupwards firm botween her tresbien allover's gopen lechs. In this infurtied fishon, freamed by liscious thights and butterm-chicks, she seizur man apan a punny-nearthing boycycle rude through de claring witties rye and hauntsome fame seemwho faciliar. He wheres a novy bluzer with apeal blue traum and has a namebored batch on his lupel which spurks surrealisation that this is nonutter thuan Peatrick McGohang, define actor who had pent tame in Censd Angrew's daring de lite Trixties win he seffered from his paddy fitz. She isn't sherrif this weird be befire or lafter his most flameous tellaversion programme and so kennot tael if the agreenable bats inastir conforning feelage in dhistory was a murmury or promanotion of demental monstertution's stuporvised convivriality and flot baize lawnorders.

As he roles passed he gecks an eyefeel of the interlapping fameels and glibs a luciantious squirk. "Be seeding you," he quirps, anticking one hang from the anglebars poorforms a stagely stranged salude, twuching his thimb and undex fringer to itch ether so that the handsums deform the numenal sieze, topped 'litely on his brew. He psychles inwords, out of shight, an' dafter a flew merments mare o'flicking at the intertwainer's pissy, Lucia is snortled to obserd a lurge an' bwobbling whide babloon that pounces cleerily becross the quearing as ifan purswoop oddy escraping ector, somehowl grroaring like a prehysteric manstare haz it dizzle ... or poorharps the noyce is dirt maid bi Lucia undher pertner as they rich their clutural crymax in the hevdy joyc-tick flambience o' tat exstrawberrymerry decayd; tis eggstoredinhurry playce.

Sexhausted and cwympletely satisfade the goo twirls reill opart to kitsch their berth and weepe their chains, untiredly comefident that in their t'rilling and slurpentine lunion day have inshored the floozyon of the savant garde 'n' gemyouwinly popalure, a necessary intermangling forder buttermint of cunture and of minkhind as a hole.

They kress ouch either tinderly, teasting their own entermate jisess on each other' slips and then cungratiflate dameselves on their profishinsea at meetyouwell cumulonimbus. Straightawning her sqirt to whide her glossening theys, Lucia askplains dashy's expictured beckett d'main hows o' the massylum in spacetime for tea an' dusks her newd frond four dimections to delayter roaches of the ninespleen severties, upunk which Lusty Flingspieled gentially paints her the light ray and then sprolls on her plurabelly and confinues glistening to her sportable wearless.

As Lucia swalks off betreen the tweeze, englishlit by the wrong lays of the drafternoon, she cawnear the transwisper pladio raying summerwhere behider, or alt feast she tinks she ken. It stounds a litterl like that wrechord bother Beautles that those unclesampleminded evanjocular Armoryguns mad burnfears of, and all becase it undy pantly briefly chalked abawd a nighty curlew net her lickers drown. "I Am The Paulrus", wasin' dout its titterl? Rue the thundergrowth inhead of here she can now see demean aSalem pilldings, lurking just as day had done windsheet set out uplan her plodyssey date mourning, though it sims an evterlifetime sence. She even blhinks she sees Petreasure, pheering auntiously aground the rounds and nodate whendering ware Lucia has goone. She whurries up her timin' pace a bit.

She kinstill hear the song beyonder, but she dizzn't surey fit's the when she thawtit was. Detune streems differrant and pseudo the words, doshy slushpects that she's not herein' thereal worlds at all. She's proverbly trancestating the inudibelle and dustant leerics into her roam lingwish, the seam way she daz with reveriething.

John signs clearly on the water,
Says the Queen's his daughter,
Longs for young Miss Joyce, the wife he barely even knew,
And no more how's-your-father now.
He's a product of his class
Who eats the grass
Along the path he's made.

It's anuntellagibble jabberish, off course, nonposed of comsense sillyballs and nutterly devader meanink, though she fonds that she injoyce the squirling museek avid.

Lucy's dancing in the language,
Shares a marble sandwich
With a Mr. Finnegan from several headstones down
And no more how's-your-father now.
She's a cockeyed optimist
Who can't resist
This final white parade.

Allthrough she nows it's sometimeattic of belusional dehaviour and splitzophrenia, chicaned help thanking that de pravious abverse odder song had bin abider. She stoops out from the councealing vagitation unto the groen lawnings ab Sent Hinderus joystirs the delayrious psychodelphic untheme slydes into its catch Icarus.

So she waits for God, oh what's the point
Of all these tears?
Letters of the alphabet are pouring from her ears
And all her words are mangled
And her sentences are frayed
To black hole radiation
In this final white parade.

Delyrics, fearsome risen, meek her thank o' Somewill Backitt, hom she whoopes wel come and fizzit soon. He's bin alloyal friend to err, hus Sum, and it' snotties falld vatican't be comething moor. She walks acrass the gross toherds the medowse weaver fating song contimbering to cadger ear on inter-distent ghusts of wint.

Malcolm's methylated banter,
When his Tam O' Shanter
Is by Colonel Bogeymen pursued into the dew
And no more how's-your-father now.
Prisoner at the bar,
They'd raise a jar
For every serenade he played.

Staunding bider raydoom intrance, her sweet'ners Peatrickier has nowse inner and is waifing hippily, relived that shizzle right. Lucia tarts to walk a liffel feister, denderrun. She dips and skances in de light, her shedoe lang uponder trilliard-terrble baise o' day asoiloam lorn. It' spin anutter pafict lucci die, hor whele life samewho fulldead inter it from pauppa's word nowtivity to Jimst-horte cemeteary bedstone. Ivory day is like as know-globe with the untired uniqverse curtin sudspinsion, fullove myrth and literatunes and herstory, an' divery daymarch like the next. She rashes eagirly thruwards the dosspital, towords the mocean's featherly himbrace.

Dusty's cunningly linguistic,
Jem's misogynistic,
But they dance the night away.
Manac es cem, J.K,
And no more how's-your-father now.
Grinding signal into noise
The crowd enjoys
This final white parade.

An embress of textistence and embiddyment aflight, Lucia dawnsees on the meadhows grase.

So we wait for God, oh what's the point
Of all these tears?
Letters of the alphabet are pouring from our ears
And all the wards are empty
And the beds are all unmade,
And we're walking through the blackout
On this final white parade.

An embress of textistence and embiddyment aflight, Lucia dawnsees on the meadhows grase floriver.

BURNING GOLD

S moulder-bearded, blind with tears of laughter, Roman takes Dean's hand and drags him from the crackling nursery, little streets on fire behind them. Out in fresh air, grabbing their still-sniggering kiss behind a rolling screen of acrid grey, Roman can smell all of the potential never-to-be-realised cash as it's cremated, an expensive stench diluted and dispersed in the slum firmament, into the dead-end Saturday, the hard-up afternoon. He's still got that big painting in his shrunken monkey head: the giants in nightshirts thundering the fuck out of each other with their blazing billiard sticks, a precious gore of ore sprayed molten from the point of bloody impact. For Rome Thompson, snogging with his lover-boy there in the choke and uproar of the moment, there at that specific junction of his self-inflicted and unlikely roughneck history, there in the Boroughs and its timeless holy fire of poverty, the violent and unearthly image does no more than hold a mirror to real life, life being an affair of rage and pool-cues and colossal brawlers bleeding wealth. Of stolen kisses by the pyre of art, a kind of currency gone up in smoke here where the mint once stood, here where they hammered out the coin more than a thousand years ago. Behind a drifting cordite curtain stands Thompson the Leveller, frenching his young man, a fissured, glued-together composite of all his misspent times and misspelled words and miscreant deeds: the sum of his mosaic moments.

While the other eight- and nine-year-olds are learning how to read and write he's up there in the slate-creak and the starlight, learning burglary. A spidery cut-out shape on a black paper 1950s skyline, it is in the slant and scrabble of the rooftop night that he receives an education in both politics and socio-economics, there at the blunt crowbar end of the economy, there in the fiscal infra-red. Shinning the rusted drainpipes that are too frail to take anybody's weight save his, slipping head-first through open window-cracks that would defeat those with an ounce of flesh upon their fuse-wire bones, he understands the structure of the world that he's so recently been born into to be entirely based on criminality, expressed in different languages, at different magnitudes. A warehouse skylight jemmied open here, an interest rate adjusted or a neighbouring state invaded there. The hostile takeover, or sticky brown tape on a pane of glass to stop the wind-chime pieces falling when you smash it. Little Roman Thompson and the boardroom blaggers, all in a great classless commonality of the adrenaline-habituated. Slide a sheet of newspaper beneath the door to drag the fallen key after you've poked it from the lock, or spread embezzled losses into the next quarter's figures. Roman runs with bigger kids, semi-professionals, divides the loot, hears all of the instructive sex-jokes several years before his classmates. Nobody can catch him. He's the gingerbread boy.

Consequently he can't write to save his life, thinks syntax is a levy raised on condoms, sometimes gets his phraseology caught in his zip. When the authorities he's nettled try to get their own back by accusing his beloved obsessive-compulsive boyfriend of being a social nuisance, Roman reckons that they must see Dean as his "Hercules Heel". He reads, though, chewing ravenously through all of the history and politics that he can get his bony hands on, trying to locate and orient himself in socio-economic spacetime. He can't write, then, other than the odd historical research piece or the slyly vitriolic Defend Council Housing pamphlets that he sometimes pens, but he can read. He can mine information from an electronic or a paper coal-seam, he can organise it in his stealthy nightlight-robbery mind and understand all its essential lowlife intricacies. He can read and he can talk – talk like Hell's auctioneer as tenants' representative at Borough Council meetings, making all the most embarrassing enquiries, mentioning the most unmentionable things, calling a cunt a cunt. He's lost count of the occasions when he's been evicted from the Guildhall to trot chuckling down the wedding-photo steps and squint up at the angel on the roof, the one that his mate Alma thinks is working class because it's got a billiard cue in its right hand. He knows his Woodward and his Bernstein, knows all about following the money, lurks in ambush on the cash trail.

In so far as Roman understands these things, the Ancient Britons who originally have their settlements around these parts work with a barter system. This makes simple robbery or livestock-rustling an option for the proto-criminals inhabiting the Neolithic period and the Bronze Age, where they've got more of a grasp of owning property, relative to the wandering Old Stone Age hunter-gatherers of earlier times, and where therefore there are more things to steal. This is all still comparatively petty larceny, however, and major financial crimes will have to wait for the concept of finance, wait for Roman's namesake empire to turn up in the first century and introduce us to the endlessly manipulatable idea of money: gold and silver coins which represent the sheaf of grain, the snorting bullock, down to the last hair, the meanest scruple, but are much more easy to make off with and to hide. During the Roman occupation, then, when everyone's conditioned to accept that this much gold is worth that many ducks in what seems on the surface a fair proposition, Iron Age Northampton has its introduction to both coins and serious crime: in Duston, using cheaper metals to adulterate the silver, Roman coins are forged, a crucifixion felony. Iron Age ironically, the hard-up Empire has adulterated its own coinage at least since the reign of Diocletian, the same fraud upon an international rather than local level, all made possible by money. You can't forge a cow.

Straight from what should have been his school years he rolls up his sleeves and gets beneath the bonnet of the world to fathom out its mechanism, ends up as head engineer at British Timken, then providing half the town's employment. From there it's a short step to becoming the key union representative, his bristling terrier countenance at each dispute, on every picket line, the blue touch-paper eyes restlessly searching for a weasel argument to shake between his teeth. In either of these two capacities, whether oil-stained professional or deepest red political, Rome's main advantage is in understanding how things work, from cogs to councils to communities, from obstinate machines to management. His other big plus is his reputation: diabolically logical, tenacious to the point of tetanus once he has locked his jaws, as unpredictable as cheese-dreams and completely fearless from his burglar boyhood, madder than a bottle full of windows. In the police-scrums and demonstrations of the 1960s it's mostly his spittle that gets emptied from the megaphones, and in the Anti-Nazi 1970s it's him who breaks the riot-squad cordon, managing to land one on the National Front minder next to leader Martin Webster before being dragged away and charged. An atmosphere of gunpowder surrounds him, a perfume of Civil War and regicide. Below a straggling brow the china eyes spark in their wrinkle-cobwebbed sockets, always informed, always on the money.

When the Roman legions are withdrawn they leave us with a money habit. From the kick-off of the seventh century, gold and silver coins are struck as local currencies by various small coining operations up and down the country. In Thompson's opinion, the most famous such establishment is probably at Canterbury although there are gold coins made here in Hamtun dated 600 AD, which have to be amongst the very first produced in Britain. And when he says Hamtun, Roman means the Boroughs. Possibly due to this early aptitude we have an unofficial mint here from 650 onwards churning out a stream of gleam into the Dark Ages' protracted night, a golden shower. Meanwhile, unobserved in the surrounding information-blackout, the benighted half-mile settlement mysteriously gathers substance and significance: King Offa's market town supplying his retreat at Kingsthorpe, here in Mercia's centre at a time when Mercia is the most important of the Saxon kingdoms. To Rome Thompson's way of thinking, it might even be that pilgrim bringing the stone cross here from Jerusalem around this period which helps cement Hamtun's mystique as centre-of-the-land, but for whatever reason it's from this ground during the 880s that King Alfred the failed cake-minder divides the country into slices, adding 'North' to the town's tag and naming 'Norhan' as foremost amongst the shires, legitimising its two-hundred-year-old mint, acknowledging its status. Wax-sealing its fate.

He's not obsessed with cash. He's never had enough to get obsessed by, but you need to know how money works to understand its necessary complement, this being poverty. The two things are inseparable. John Ruskin claims that if resources were shared equally there'd be no poverty or wealth. Thus, to make someone rich depends on making someone else poor. Making someone very wealthy may depend upon impoverishing an entire population. Poverty is money's obverse, the coin's other side. Rome wants to scrutinise its dirty engine and to comprehend the micro-tolerances of hard times. He knows his own hard times have mostly happened not because of money, but because of how he used to drink before the heart attack and his sometimes deranged behaviour. He's culpable, responsible – he knows all that – and sometimes feels a black pang if he thinks of Sharon, their doomed marriage, his exploded family. He would simply observe that those from a chaotic background frequently tend to be predisposed to alcohol and chaos, and that chaos levels rise as funds go down. That isn't an excuse; it's an example of how life is likely to work out in a poor neighbourhood, with more capacity for harm, for wheels to fall off struggling relationships, for nasty incidents. The squaddies eager for a scrap down in the cellar bar off vanished Wood Street. The slagheap collapsing on him in Paul Baker's yard, crawling through dirt in search of a few bob on the Edwardian empties.

Growing up, Rome thinks the king he's heard about is called Alfred the Grate because of where he scorched the scones, then later learns about dividing up the shires, effectively making Hamtun the capital, establishing the mint at London (one of a few dozen) as an institution in 886, and all the rest of it. The king is trying to regulate the many regional economies, or so it seems to Thompson, but no one will have much luck with that until Edgar the Peaceful turns up to reform the coinage in his last year as king, 973 AD, and standardises it into a national currency stamped out at forty royal mints throughout the land, with Hamtun being one of them. This is the year you first get pennies turning up with "HAMT" on the reverse, the letters set in the four quarters of what's known as a Long Cross, one where the arms reach right to the coin's hammered edge. By Ethelred the Second's reign, commencing 978, emergency mints are set up to cope with the privations caused by all the Viking raids the King was famously unready for, and by Harold the Second's rule prior to the Norman conquest there's at least seventy of them, with the biggest mint being the one in London. Following 1066, William the Bastard changes things. The mints are gradually reduced in number, centralising monetary control and rationalising an inherited and sprawling Saxon system. Disempowered, Northampton's mint survives until the thirteenth century. Until Henry the Third arrives and really puts the chainmail boot in.

The subsiding fifty-year-old hill of ash and clinker falling in on him, the incident with the drunk soldiers: these are just part of the fire he's dressed in, the insane debris of circumstance that makes him who he is; that ultimately tears apart his life with Sharon and the kids. He's foraging for old stone bottles when some half-a-century of the town's black, incinerated shit suddenly pounds its fist into his scrawny back and drives the precious wind out of his lungs. Dirt in his eyes, dirt in his mouth and enough time to form the thought, so this is how we all end up, before his mucker Ted Tripp grabs him by those matchstick ankles, drags him cursing from the sludge like an uprooted Tourette's carrot out into the daylight of Paul Baker's yard, just as the cop cars all come howling in. He owes Ted big time, and so when Ted's lock-up full of hooky goods is raided some while afterwards and the arresting officers fail to lock up the premises behind them, Roman has the evidence away and leaves Ted to produce receipts so that the angry coppers have to reimburse him for the lock-up's contents. Debt repaid, this means that Rome feels free to steal Ted's car on that occasion with the pissed-up and abusive squaddies: Roman's awesome and apocalyptic payback; his avenging angel-work. He feels that it's important someone keeps the moral ledger straight, such as it is. The heart can't keep double accounts, and its books must eventually be balanced.

Though Northampton has admittedly lost some of the illustrious burnish since its Alfred the Great heyday, it's still an important central pivot of the country for two hundred years after the conquest, and still has its mint. A thriving, pretty little market town, by all accounts, since Dick the Lionheart grants it its charter in 1180-something. Cobblers and leather-workers all up Scarletwell Street and the old Gilhalda, the original town hall there on the Mayorhold, where they hold their Porthimoth di Norhan, although no one nowadays knows what that might have been. Something to do with boundaries. Henry the Third seems rather taken with the place at first and wants to give the town a university, before he's had a chance to fully understand the fiery and unusual spirit of the ancient settlement. The Bacaleri di Norhan, the stroppy students, are protesting Henry's imposition of a forty eight-strong council – the exact same number of the bastards that Rome Thompson currently contends with weekly – who are lining their own pockets with the profits of the town. Henry decides he doesn't like the locale after all and sends his troops in through the wall of the old Cluniac priory where St. Andrew's Road is now. They pillage, rape and burn until Northampton is an ugly, smoking wreck. And when he says Northampton, Roman means the Boroughs. Henry's promised university ends up in Cambridge, and with Henry's death in 1272 they take away the mint as well.

His reputation for exacting startling retribution, whether against individuals or institutions, means that anyone who's heard of him knows that they're better off not picking fights with Roman. Which leaves those who haven't heard of him. He's visiting the cellar bar outside the Grosvenor Centre, near where Wood Street used to be, for a quick drink. There are these nineteen-, twenty-year-old soldiers from some camp outside Northampton, half-a-dozen getting rowdy in the lounge, shoving past regulars. When Rome asks one of these latter-day roundheads to watch where he's going, he's got the whole mob around him swilling their testosterone and vodka smoothies. "Yeah? What are you gunna do about it, Catweazle?" Six of the nation's finest, being all they can be with a stick figure in his mid forties. Roman puts his palm up. "Sorry, lads. I'm evidently in the wrong pub. I'll just finish up me pint and go." He leaves them to their night out without answering them, without saying what he's gunna do about it. Never cross someone with neither want nor fear of anything. Like he tells Alma while he's lounging calmly in the middle of a blazing bonfire on that camping holiday in Wales, "It's all about will, Alma, ain't that right?" She pulls upon her reefer and considers while he starts to smoulder. "Yeah. Well, will and flammability." They have to drag him from the flames and beat him out, but Roman feels he's made his point. He's put his money where his mouth is.

As does England after 1272 when Henry's dead. The number of mints are reduced to six – rebellious Northampton not included – with the main one at the Tower of London from 1279 onwards, housed there for the next five hundred years, the only game in town by 1500, a monopoly. Northampton, far from being King Alfred's de facto capital, is on its way to being somewhere that's unmentionable. Roman doesn't think this is because the place is unimportant, more that it's important in a way that's toxic to authority's best interests, churning out its Doddridges, its Herewards, its Charlie Bradlaughs, its Civil War agitators, Martin Marprelates, Gunpowder Plotters, Bacaleri di

Norhan or its Diana Spencers. At best huge embarrassments and at worst riots or heads on poles. Perhaps Northampton has become the anti-matter capital, an insurrectionist parallel universe, not to be spoken of. While this is clearly just how everything was always going to work out, Roman blames Henry the Third, a spiteful little fucker at the best of times. And his son Edward's even worse. In 1277 some three hundred of the Jewish population centred around Gold Street are all executed – stoned to death as Rome hears it: accused of clipping bits from the old hammered coins to melt down and make new ones. Actually, the royals owe the Jews a wad of cash. Survivors are first driven out of town and then all Jews are banished from the land, brutally welching on the debt, putting the plan into Plantagenet.

All about will and flammability, so Alma says, and Roman thinks she's right. Having the fire of will and spirit is a must, but useless if your fuel's damp or goes up like tinder. What's important is the way you burn. He can remember Alma telling him about how she has Jimmy Cauty and Bill Drummond from the KLF turn up one day at her house on East Park Parade to show the film of them torching a million quid up on the Isle of Jura, where George Orwell completes *1984*. She says she likes a movie where you can see every penny of the budget up there on the screen but Roman's not sure how he feels at first about all that potentially life-saving lucre going up the chimney. Still, as Alma points out, if the million had gone up their noses nobody would raise an eyebrow. In the end, Rome comes to the conclusion that it's glorious, more than just a gesture. It's the whole idea of money being burned, not just the actual loot. It's saying that the golden dragon that enslaves us, that allows a tiny fraction of the global population to own nearly all the wealth, that ensures almost universal human poverty by its very existence, doesn't actually exist at all, is made of worthless paper, can be taken care of with a half-box of Swan Vestas. Drummond is Northampton reared, a hulking Scot from Corby who goes to the art school here and works at the St. Crispin's nuthouse for a while. Rome fancies you can see the town's brand on the renegade rock-god: incendiary, justified and ancient.

This is money from a local point of view, a shell-game with evolving rules, a long con given centuries to hone its act; achieve a peak of predatory sophistication. Looking at the hundred or so years after the Norman occupation, with the number of mints dwindling as the manufacture of the coin is centralised and brought under control, Roman can see the obstacle that money-hungry kings are left with. Cash is still too real, too physical. Getting the planet to accept that discs of precious metal represent a crop or herd is an immense accomplishment, but coins with their smooth hammered edges are still vulnerable to clipping, and material gold and silver pieces are less easy to manipulate and conjure with than something that is hardly there at all. It's in the twelfth or thirteenth century that the Knights Templar, hanging out at the round church in Sheep Street and collecting dues from local businesses as an ecclesiastical protection racket, come up with the idea of the internationally-valid promissory note or money order. They invent the cheque, have the idea of money as a piece of paper long before 1476 when William Caxton's earliest English printing press makes banknotes possible, just in time for the Tower of London's mint to assume its monopoly in 1500. Given all the harm caused by the Templar's fiscal origami, Rome feels it's an insult that they get wiped out because Pope Clement claims they're gay, two men on one horse, all that Catholic bollocks.

Roman's own epiphany comes with the heart attack that marks his fiftieth birthday. It's around the sleeping-in-a-campfire period of Rome's existence, when the mania that drives him is at its most phosphorescent. His behaviour at this point is already more than halfway to dismantling his family so he's alone there in the house all night, on his own, when the left-arm lightning hits. He sprawls there, on his back in the dark living room, and can't move. There's no one to call for help and Roman knows that this is it. He's going to die, and in a few days he'll be back under the dirt like that time down Paul Baker's yard except with no Ted Tripp to haul him out. Under the dirt forever, and with so much unresolved. During his long hours in the twilight between quick and dead, Roman reviews his life and is astonished to discover that his foremost fear is dropping off the twig before he gets the nerve up to tell anyone, himself included, that he's homosexual. All those years he's taken pride in never backing down to anyone or anything, not to police or management or to those drunken square-bashers or even to the element of fire, to find that he's been bottling the biggest, pinkest challenge of them all. Roman resolves that if by some chance he survives this he'll go out for some queer fun and then tell everyone about it. As it turns out that's what happens, but he's not expecting love. He's not expecting Dean, the two of them together on the one horse from then on.

Gay or not, the Knights Templar clearly aren't the first people to think of folding money – Roman reckons that he can remember something about paper notes in seventh century China – but they are the first to introduce the notion to the West. It still isn't until the nineteenth century that you see proper printed English dosh, but back at the exclusive Tower of London mint in 1500 you can tell they're warming up to the idea. The goldsmith-bankers of the sixteenth century issue these receipts called running cash notes, written out by hand and promising to pay the bearer on demand. Even with Caxton's press, the near-impossibility of printing counterfeit-proof wealth means England's paper currency will be at least partially scribbled for the next three hundred years or more. The paper concept only gains momentum when the Bank of England is established during 1694 and straight away is raising funds for William the Third's war on France by circulating notes inscribed on specially-produced bank paper, signed by the cashier with the sum written down in pounds, shillings and pence. In the same year Charles Montague, later the Earl of Halifax, becomes the Chancellor of the Exchequer. Two years on, in need of a new warden of the mint, he offers the position – " 'Tis worth five or six hundred pounds per annum, and has not too much business to require more attendance than you can spare" – to a fifty-five-year-old man previously passed over for high office: Isaac Newton.

Roman tells Bert Regan, Ted Tripp and the others that the most feared and respected of their formidable number is officially now travelling on the other bus. Endearingly, given the reputation of the working class for homophobia, they merely take the piss the way they would if he'd told them he was part Irish or developed comically deforming facial cancer, and then carry on as normal. They treat Dean respectfully despite the fact that his OCD impulses do tend to put him at the "Ooh, look at the muck in here" end of the homosexual spectrum. Ted Tripp asks Rome who's the horse and who's the jockey, and Rome patiently explains that it's less about sex than you might think and more about the love. Ted may make arse-related jokes around the situation but he understands, has always been there when Rome needed him, will lend Rome anything, particularly if he doesn't know he's doing it. The night when Rome exits the cellar bar with military mockery still ringing in his ears he marches down to the Black Lion in St. Giles Street and there in the notoriously haunted hostelry he finds Ted Tripp in the front room, playing a hand of brag with rotund troubadour Tom Hall and junkyard-owner Curly Bell. Rome sits with Ted and idly chats for a few minutes while Ted's mind is on the game, and then gets up and leaves. Ted barely registers Rome's visit, much less that his car keys, which should be on the pub table next to his tobacco, are no longer there.

Still, that seventeenth century: a bastard from the outset and then it builds up to Isaac fucking Newton as its big finale. It kicks off with the gunpowder plot and Francis Tresham's head impaled down at the end of Sheep Street, then it picks up pace with the Enclosures Act when all the toffs are given liberty to fence off areas of common land, legally sanctioned smash-and-grab with all the main protestors being local, all the doomed and dashing Captains, Swing and Slash and Pouch, this last one landing on a spike in Sheep Street within eighteen months of his posh adversary Francis Tresham. You can see what makes the land-reclaiming Diggers and the class-war Levellers so popular when they arrive in the mid-1640s to support Oliver Cromwell, alongside all of the other ranting, quaking dissidents that use Northampton as a millenarian theme-park in those years. The town backs Cromwell. He turns out to be like Stalin but without the sense of humour. Anyway, he's dead by 1658, his son and heir fucks off to France and so by 1660 Charles the Second's on the throne. Upset about Northampton's role in getting his dad's head lopped off he has its castle torn down as a punishment, but he's concerned about the currency as well. Charles's reign sees the introduction of milled edges to some of the previously hammered coins to prevent clipping, but the practice is still rife in '96 when Isaac Newton comes to town, the Eliot Ness of English finance in the sixteen-hundreds.

If Roman's in bed, his arms around his boyfriend, drifting off into the dark behind his corrugated eyelids, all the madness in his life makes perfect sense. When him and Dean first hook up in the early 1990s, that's when his and Sharon's young son Jesse starts to come unglued. Part of the Rave scene, Jesse necks assorted disco biscuits – ecstasy and ketamine and Christ knows what – halfway to a drug-aggravated breakdown, like Bert Regan's stepson Adam, Jesse's best mate at the bleary, blurry sunrise parties. Jesse takes Rome's coming out hard, undeniably, but there's a lot of other factors in the mix. Pal Adam goes spectacularly crazy and decides he's gay as well; a gay male angel with his wings torn off by treacherous women – this meant literally. For Jesse it must seem reality has suddenly become untrustworthy so he stops going out, starts drinking to damp his by-now perpetual hallucinations, to blot out the cats with human faces, and then somewhere down the line he learns that in the blotting-out stakes heroin beats booze. His junkie new best mate is first to overdose, to fall off of the world in Jesse's bedroom back at Sharon's place, and then a few months later Jesse's dead as well, bang, just like that. Ah, fuck. Sharon blames Rome for everything, won't even have him at the funeral. It's black, and doctors finally put a name to Roman's driving fire, his contradictory soul: manic depression. Like police car sirens or economies, it seems Rome has his ups and downs.

This role as warden of the mint is meant as a seat-warming post, but Isaac takes it seriously, smells blood and money in the water. Coming to the job in 1696 when forgery and clipping still degrade the currency, Newton begins his Great Recoinage, where he recalls and replaces all the hammered silver coin in circulation. It takes two years and reveals that getting on a fifth of all the coins recalled are counterfeit. While forgery is classed as treason, punishable by evisceration, getting a conviction is a bugger, but the gravity man rises to the task. Disguised as a habitué of taverns Newton loiters, eavesdrops, gathers evidence. He then gets himself made a Justice of the Peace in all of the Home Counties so that he can cross-examine suspects, witnesses, informers, and by Christmas 1699 he has successfully sent twenty-eight rogue coiners to be drawn, hung, and then quartered, off down Tyburn way. In recognition of a job well done, in that same year he's made the master of the mint, his wages bumped from Montague's five or six hundred pounds to between twelve and fifteen hundred quid a year. Newton's recoinage has reduced the need for low-denomination hand-scrawled bank notes so that anything under a fifty is withdrawn. Of course, it's only those in Newton's income bracket who will ever notice, given that for most people their yearly earnings in seventeenth century England are far less than twenty pounds and they will never see a bank note in their lives.

When Rome's first diagnosed as a bit swings and roundabouts they stick him on the new anti-depressants, the SSRIs, Selective Serotonin Re-uptake Inhibitors like Prozac, that in 1995 appear to be the British medical profession's first response to anything from clinical depression to occasional ennui. The drugs, in Rome's opinion, are born of the probably-American idea that those in the developed world have an inalienable right to be contented every hour of their existence. So what if these happy-pills haven't been around long enough for any adverse side-effects to show up so far; are effectively untested? There's a market eager for an end to all their troubles, there are pharmaceutics corporations eager to make money, and the blue sky ethos of that endless economic boom-time stipulates instant gratification. Anyone dissenting from this mandatory manic optimism is a Gloomy Gus, a scaremonger or pessimist, is out of step with all the laissez-faire euphoria and would most probably feel better on a course of Prozac. Rome gives it a go, not having been informed that one occasional by-product of SSRIs is suicidal black depression. When Dean asks what's wrong Rome drop-kicks him across the living room. He throws the pills away and in the dark troughs he goes for long walks and sorts it out himself. The manic peaks he saves for council meetings, for campaigns or organising protests. Energy efficiency. It's one of the first principles you learn in engineering.

Newton, who's familiar with the principle, brings chemical and mathematic know-how to the mint. After his Great Recoinage he's asked to repeat the trick in Scotland, 1707. This leads to a common currency and the new kingdom of Great Britain. Not content yet, in 1717 the seventy-six-year-old first proclaims his bi-metallic standard where twenty-one silver shillings equals one gold guinea. England's policy of paying for imports with silver while receiving payment for exports in gold means there's a silver shortage, so what Newton's doing here is moving Britain's standard from silver to gold without announcing it. Personally he's doing nicely, coining it, well-minted. Trusting his ability with sums to double up his cash he invests in the sure-fire high-return world of the South Sea Bubble, dropping twenty grand – three million by the current reckoning – when in 1721 the whole thing goes tits up. The fiscal genius of the day loses his shirt. He lets greed override his risk-assessment faculties, displays an expert's fatal overconfidence in his abilities, the way that it's mostly mycologists who end up killing themselves with a death cap omelette. And what brings Sir Isaac down is dabbling where he should know better, in a market bloated by a form of bonds known as derivatives, partly responsible for the Dutch Tulip-bulb fiasco that occurs in 1637 five years before Newton's birth, and probably about to sink the world economy nearly three hundred years after his death.

Roman and Dean get digs in St. Luke's House, a block between St. Andrew's Street and Lower Harding Street, where Bellbarn used to be. He's known the Boroughs all his life but this is the first time he's lived there. Roman finds himself in love with its crushed population, with its relic tower blocks braced against the rain. Blanched grass sprouts from the seams of maisonettes and in it Rome can read an English bottom line. This area is up in the top two per cent of UK deprivation. Simply living here takes ten years off your life. These people at the shitty end of economic theory are the product of all that creative number-crunching. Individuals betrayed by bankers, governments and, yes, Rome sticks his hand up, by the left wing. Dean's mixed race and they're both gay, but neither of them see much benefit from the left wing's promotion of racial and sexual equality. How does it help that Peter Mandelson and Oona King are doing okay, when the inequality between the rich and poor that socialism was intended to put right remains conspicuously unaddressed? Rome turns in his red star in '97 at the first whiff of New Labour and its rictus-grinning frontman, to become an anarchist and activist. The malcontents that he attracts are sometimes "Defend Council Housing", sometimes "Save Our NHS", depending what will look most swinish to oppose. Thompson the Leveller has found his sticking place: the levelled ground where he can stage his gunsmoke stand.

Dying 1727, in his eighties and still at the mint, Newton sees the beginning of the shift to paper money. In 1725 banks issue notes where the pound sign is printed, but the date, amount and other details are hand-written by the signatory, like a cheque. Cash gradually becomes more abstract, but a greater sleight of hand takes place hundreds of years before with the invention of derivatives, the concept that helps scupper Newton. A derivative – a bond deriving from the actual goods for sale – occurs when someone makes a deal to sell their goods for an agreed sum at some future date. Whether the market price rises or falls before that time determines who's made the best bet, but what's important is that the derivative bond now has a potential value and can be sold on, with its projected worth continually increasing. This uncoupling of money and real goods contributes to the Tulip Craze and South Sea Bubble, while the current value of the world's derivatives, from what Rome hears, is up to ten times larger than the sixty or so trillion dollars that is the whole planet's fiscal output. The divide between reality and economics is a hairline fissure widening across the centuries to a deep ocean vent from which unprecedented forms of life squirm up with dismal regularity: bubbles and crazes, Wall Street crashes and Black Wednesdays, Enron and whatever bigger fuck-up is inevitably coming next; the bad dreams of a rational age that good old William Blake calls "Newton's sleep".

Rome combs the Boroughs streets looking for trouble. In some of the last remaining council dwellings there's asbestos that the council won't own up to, much less take away. Attempts to entice people into private housing schemes by entering them in a draw for prizes that are never won; do not exist. There's endless scams or deprivations to attend and Rome has mission-creep, as likely to campaign against the selling-off of eighteenth-century houses in Abington Park as to bellow abuse through a loudhailer when they bring in Yvette Cooper, housing minister, to launch the NEWLIFE towers flogged to a housing company by former councillor Jim Cockie just before he joins their board. And there's always some new affront on the horizon. At the moment there's moves to put Euro-dosh meant for the Boroughs into a big needle like the Express Lifts Tower, but on Black Lion Hill. Roman suspects that this is to facilitate backhanders from whichever company lands the deal. Rome plans to feign disinterest, let them think his eye is off the ball. They'll set dates for a secret ballot, to vote the proposals through without constituents knowing that they've backed this clearly bad idea. Then, on the afternoon before, Rome will call in a favour from someone with council clout, get them to change it to an open ballot, lift the stone to shed light on the wriggling things beneath and make them vote against it if they want to keep their seats. It's all a complicated business, but then he's a complicated man.

Money continues to evolve – particularly after the remarkable events at a Northampton cornmill that Rome has related to a slack-jawed Alma not an hour ago. 1745 sees partly-printed notes from twenty to a thousand pounds. Fifty years later, after the Napoleonic Wars, the bank stops paying gold for notes in what's called the Restriction Period. This is when Sheridan calls the bank "an elderly lady in the City", which cartoonist Gilray artfully tarts up as "the Old Lady of Threadneedle Street". In 1821 the gold standard's reinstituted and endures in a robust condition up until the First World War. The part-handwritten papers are made legal tender for all sums over five pounds in 1833, becoming proper modern banknotes. Then in 1855 they go the whole hog with the notes completely printed. Britain finally leaves the gold standard in 1931, its currency now backed up by paper securities rather than bars of precious metal. By the middle of the twentieth century, as Roman sees it, we've a world economy relying more and more upon the logic of a huge casino, and we're just about to see a wave of post-war innovation that will change the planet. When these new ideas impact on the money markets they create the preconditions for a scale of ruin never previously witnessed or imagined. Eddies in the cash flow deepen into whirlpools, maelstroms, and we have the makings of a catastrophic storm. As they say in the 'Sixties, it don't take a weatherman.

Not all Rome's tasks are so dramatic. There's fundraisers like the poster Alma does, and slogging door to door to make sure everyone's informed. Like yesterday: Rome spends it letting people know about Alma's do at the nursery while walking off the tail-end of a downer, one of Rome's bear markets of the soul. Fresh air makes him feel bullish, while attempting all those stairways in the flats should do some cardio-vascular good. Trudging the tower blocks he checks on some of the older residents. They won't be interested in the exhibition, but it's an excuse to see if they're okay. Near Tower Street he spots Benedict Perrit setting out on a day's drinking and then pretends not to notice minor local drug czar Kenny Nolan, an amoral little shit who's running down the district when he's not even a councillor; not even being paid to do it. Crossing Bath Street, Roman mounts the scabby ziggurat of front steps to look in on little Marla Stiles, who's on the skids, the game and crack, respectively. Her hungry lemur eyes dart everywhere when she comes to the door. She isn't listening as Rome gives her the spiel on Alma's show, but at least he can see she's still alive. How long for, well, that's anybody's guess. He goes on up the flat-blocks' central walk to visit other causes for concern around St. Katherine's House, and on his way back later has to veer around a fresh-laid dog turd distantly resembling a dollar sign. It's funny, isn't it, the little details that you notice?

Economics as art starts out figurative, goes abstract, although not until the twentieth century will it become surrealism. Britain starts to leave the gold standard in 1918 which, coincidentally, is when the fifty-year dismantling of the Boroughs kicks off. Nearly all its terraces are gone by the late 'Sixties, when that decade's fiscal innovations are beginning to come into play. Rome hears about a paper published, early 'Seventies, with new equations to help calculate the value of derivatives based on that of the goods that they're derived from. Theoretically, this makes such deals a safer bet, and to the money markets that's a chequered flag. Mathematics-wonks are suddenly the saviours of the industry. There are now new ways to make money, if there weren't these regulations in the way. At decade's end Thatcher and Reagan come to power, two eighteenth century Free Market Liberals who share Adam Smith's mystical conviction that the market somehow regulates itself and subsequently start removing its restraints, just as the 1980s' big computer boom gets underway. Keeping an eye on stocks, computers can gain or lose fortunes in a millisecond, adding to the system's volatility. Crashes and crunches come and go, ruining countless thousands, but the bigger players keep on making bigger profits. Then in 1989 the Berlin Wall comes down and it's like a dam bursting. Scenting blood with its only major competitor's sudden demise, capitalism slips its leash.

When Rome's own crashes come, fiscal analogies break down. He always ends up in the black. Black doves, black ice cream, a black wedding, a black Christmas, simmering in a stock of his own fuck-ups and nothing to do but live through it, to take those long walks up the colour gradient from deepest ebony to manageably neutral grey. Tom Hall calls it "the black dog", after Winston Churchill's name for the phenomenon. Back in the early days with his soon-to-be wife Diane, Tom goes for a lie-down on the Racecourse when he's done something to test her patience, which is often. He can see the dark hound through his half-closed eyelids, sitting calmly on the summer-yellowed grass beside him. Roman misses Tom, but then, who doesn't miss that planetary presence that kept half the town revolving with its gravity, its levity? That night in the Black Lion after Roman's brush with the new model army, Tom is playing brag when Roman drops by to nick Ted Tripp's motor; almost certainly sees Roman swipe the keys but only chuckles to himself and goes on with his game. Rome leaves them to it and, after he picks up something else he's going to need from the back room, he takes the car from the pub car park. Furiously calm, he drives it round to Abington Street and pulls up beside the Grosvenor Centre's entrance with his lights off, waiting. Obviously, with the street now pedestrianized you couldn't do that sort of thing today. It's Health and Safety gone mad.

After the wall's fall, financiers launch into an epic victory binge. Free to proliferate, capitalism mutates fast. Not even a free-market frenzy like the Thatcher-

Reagan years, this is something entirely new, but with a few old faces. Alan Greenspan, guiding U.S. finance under Reagan, George Bush, Clinton and Bush Junior, is a big fan of libertarian Ayn Rand and it's on his watch that some J.P. Morgan wizards invent Credit Default Swaps in 1994. What these are, briefly, is insurance. You lend somebody a lot of dosh at a good interest rate, but they're all hillbillies with Cyclops babies and you're worried they'll default. So you pay a third party to insure the debt. Assuming that the hillbillies pay up, everyone wins. And if the babies one day need to go to Cyclops college and the loan goes bad, no problem. The insurer coughs up, and assuming you've not *only* loaned to Cyclopses it probably won't bother them much either. This apparently removes the final obstacle to making serious money, which is risk. The banks and companies can now do pretty much exactly as they please, with someone else obliged to pay for their mistakes. Predictably, they go berserk; make record-breaking profits doing so. When the warmed-over Tories now known as New Labour come to power in 1997, which is when Rome leaves the party, they provide the Bank of England with control over the interest rate and thus the whole economy. Profits like that, they must know what they're doing.

After lots of hassle, Dean and Roman trade their flat off Lower Harding Street for a whole council house in Delapré. The new place is much nicer, though they have a neighbour who complains when Dean pops out into the back yard for a smoke one night and unleashes a torrent of loud swearing after stepping in the garden pond. This is the business that the council try to talk up to an ASBO when they're trying to get at Rome through Dean, through his Hercules Heel. Oddly enough, their old digs in St. Luke's House end up being used by CASPAR, the shoestring community support group to whom all of the modest improvements in the area can be attributed. Rome only finds this out last night when he's down at the nursery with Burt Reagan, setting up for Alma's exhibition, and he meets Lucy, who's arranging it and gets it in the neck if anything goes wrong. Turns out she works for CASPAR, labouring where him and Dean first make a go of it, make love, make breakfast. She and Rome chat while him and Burt hang the paintings and put the big sculpture or whatever it's called on the pushed-together tables in the centre of the room. They bond over his old flat's inconveniently tiny toilet, there amidst the stupefying images of river-monsters rearing over Spencer Bridge, of multiple-exposure charcoal children flickering in a wasteland and the raging giants in nightgowns with their arcing billiard cues, their spraying golden blood like fire.

The economic watchword is not caution now but innovation, new ways to make loot that are not tested or thought through. Enron borrows upon future derivatives from areas of technology not yet invented, such as shares in Daleks or Transporter Beams but evidently nowhere near as solid. Enron's bubble bursts as Dubya Bush takes over in 2000, the worst monetary catastrophe in U.S. history, and when the facts emerge nobody can believe the catalogue of madness, the horrific warning that this poses for economy in general. People call for tighter regulation, which would hinder making money, so the Enron business is dismissed as a statistical anomaly, some of its execs go to jail and then everyone carries on as normal. The big market in the U.K. and the U.S. now is housing, and those Credit Default Swaps mean banks can offer mortgages to almost anyone, a million Cyclops hillbillies, safe in the knowledge that insurers pay if it goes wrong. Unless, of course, all of the hillbillies default at once. If Rome's correct, the world's swollen financial markets are all resting on the least dependable and most impoverished section of society, on people almost guaranteed to fuck up. People like those in this very district. Schemes intended to reduce risk instead spread it through the whole system like woodworm, until from Beverly Hills to Bermondsey those folk who'd never dream of visiting an area like the Boroughs find instead that it has come to visit them.

Roman has a capacity for violence, never a propensity. It's just been part of the equation, scuffling with coppers in an alley or outside the U.S. embassy in Grosvenor Square, just as it's always been there in the money markets during their own troubled adolescence. When the Bacaleri di Norhan stage economic protests in 1263, Henry the Third sends in the troops to bash some heads together. When the Poll Tax riots kick off in the late 1980s – also economic protests – Thatcher sends in riot police to bash some heads together. Rome imagines that when the balloon goes up in our hi-tech twenty-first century, whoever's running things will very probably send in Atari hunter-killer robots to – well, you get the idea. Violence, or at least the threat of it, is always there, hence Rome's lifelong easy association between finances and criminality. There's always hired goons somewhere in the mix, bruisers or bailiffs, or riot-samurais, or soldiers. Rome sits in the dark of Ted Tripp's borrowed car and waits until the half-a-dozen squaddies stagger pissed and bellowing out of the cellar bar to fall into a minibus that's evidently their ride back to base. It pulls away down Abington Street, most probably bound for Bridge Street, South Bridge and the motorway beyond. Rome gives it a few seconds and then starts Ted's car up, following the soldiers out past the bright lights of town to where the darkness gathers round Northampton like an angry and protective mother.

Just last year in 2005, amidst the tube-bombs and ongoing nightmare of Iraq, big Gordon Brown sells off the last of Britain's gold reserves right when the going rate is at a temporary low. There's nothing solid holding things up any-more, not even paper, only electronic impulses and mathematics swirling in the ether. Rome, as a manic depressive, entertains dark possibilities: when banks begin to crash, as any airborne vessels held aloft by bubbles surely will, how will governments deal with that? The money's bound up in the banks, especially in Britain where they've run the show since 1997, and if they go down the whole economy goes with them. No one's going to let that happen. In effect, the banks are now immune to government control or reprimand. They have, by stealth, become a monarchy. It's not even capitalism anymore, not the brutal Darwinian free-for-all proposed by Adam Smith and Maynard Keynes and Margaret Thatcher. This is some refried early seventeenth century arrangement, with a coddled and capricious ruler dominating even parlia-ment. Rome's not sure what you'd call the set-up – it's a moneylenderocracy or something like that – but it would seem that the banking sector sees itself as royalty. Roman agrees. He sees them, more precisely, as King Charles the First. And everybody round these parts knows how all that ends up: in fire and pikes, wet innards and dry powder. Worlds turned upside down. Screams in the night.

The B-roads outside town are submerged in a rural blackness. There's nobody else about, no other cars. Roman accelerates, pulls alongside the mini-bus. They think he's overtaking until he slams into them, *BDANK*! The bus squeals, trying to regain control, with everybody on board thinking it's a dreadful acci-dent, when Rome lurches across, deliberately ramming them again, *BDANK*! This time they swerve into a ditch, roll over and land upside down. Rome stops a few yards further on, retrieves the billiard cue from the Black Lion that he's got stashed in the back, then slides out of the car. He takes his time walking back up the road, the pole over his scrawny shoulder. No one's going anywhere. The nearside door of the crashed troop-transporter turns out to be open. Roman climbs aboard. The soldiers are all dangling in their safety belts, concussed and bleeding. Out of those who can focus their eyes, nobody's what you might call pleased to see him. He walks down the aisle between the seats, well, actually he walks along the inside of the bus's roof but it's the same thing. He walks down the aisle and scrutinises all the stunned, inverted faces, picking out the ones who'd given him the aggro. "You." The thick end of the billiard cue jabs forward, into teeth. "And you." Again the cue comes down, again. He pots a black eye, a pink throat, a cue-ball skull. Again. Again. Rome clears the table in a single visit and the crowd here at the Crucible goes wild.

The thing is, even if this century concocts a Cromwell who drags all the bank-ers to the chopping block, despite the fact that Rome finds it a lovely image, it won't do a bit of good. The west is broke. There's no nice way of putting it. Broke and in debt for generations, but still keeping up a front the way that Emperor Diocletian does when he begins to water down the empire's coinage. Any revolutionary who succeeds in toppling the banks is going to inherit the same dismal situation, the appalling world they've left us with after their dizzy and intoxicated spree, fucked up beyond all recognition. No, just executing the executives is a non-starter. What you need to execute is money, or perhaps just money as it is from Alfred the Great onwards. Rome sees some bloke from the London School of Economics on the telly while he's flicking through the channels. This chap makes the point that governments don't actually do anything for us. The only thing that makes them boss is that they control all the currency. Historically, anyone proposing an alternative to cash is brutally suppressed, but then historically they haven't got the Internet, which makes such things much easier to set up; much harder to crack down on. Rome can see a battered future Britain where a cow's still worth five magic beans or the equivalent, which has no standard currency and thus no standard government, no kings, no credit agencies. Only a thousand colourful and ragged flags.

The Leveller kisses his boyfriend through the smoke in Castle Street and there's a siren closing from the distance, whooping oscillations swooping from the Mounts to Grafton Street, driver perhaps starting to realise that it's difficult responding to alarm calls from the Boroughs, its streets closed with bollards in an unsuccessful effort to prevent curb-crawling which has nonetheless been quite successful in obstructing every other fucking thing. He gives Dean's bum a quick squeeze and can feel the all-at-once of himself welling up around him. He knows he's still somehow up there on the rooftops as a seven-year-old, nicking moonlight. He's still at the barricades, still messing up his life with Sharon, still under the mudslide in Pete Baker's yard, still shifting Ted Tripp's dodgy merchandise from the unguarded lockup, still half dead in the dark living room on his fiftieth birthday, still broke and still furious, still sleeping in the fire, still stalking through the upturned minibus with his apocalyptic staring eyes, his bloody snooker cue. He's who he is, exactly, perfectly, and if what Alma says about that endless circuit of Delft tiles up on the nursery's north wall is true, he's who he is forever. The forlorn and lovely little pauper streets with all the precious memories are burning down somewhere behind him. Roman Thompson stares the future in its hairy eye, and knows that he won't be the first to look away. Screaming its panicked aria, that siren's getting nearer.

THE RAFTERS AND THE BEAMS

Mashed in the Atlantic's iron-green jaws off Freetown, on his skinny ship out of a Bristol plump from sugar and the sale of Africans, John Newton weeps, makes promises which he will not immediately keep, pleads for amazing grace and on the skyline, lightning-lit, are tumbling granite manes, are snarling caves and heavy paws of avalanche. The Lion Mountains, as the Portuguese adventurer Pedro da Cintra calls the land in 1462: Serra de Leão. Romarong, as it's known to the local Mende tribesmen. Sierra Leone, the name tawny with dust or rank with ambush, where sweet hymns are pressed from vintages of mortal panic and undying shame.

When he gets to be old, Black Charley don't care for the songs no more and don't care for the chapels. He makes church in empty barns, with his rope-rimmed contraption left outside and leaning up against a rain butt. Henry George, down on a hard dirt floor, straw prickling his knees through his worn pants. He breathes the musk of long-gone horses, pale palms pressed together, talking to whatever it is Henry can feel listening to him from somewhere long ways off, outside of all the stars and moons, just listening and never answering or interrupting, never saying anything at all. Above, birds come and go through gaps between the slates, and over his head Henry hears their soothing language; beating wings when they alight on beams and tarry rafters pinstriped with ancestral droppings. His quiet prayers float up past rugged joints, past bowing timbers, rather than into a company of marble saints and saviours martyred in the coloured glass. He will allow that worshiping like this has led him to imagine paradise as all built out of wood and with a smell like sawdust and manure, not stairs and statues everywhere. He counts this view of some rough heaven as preferable to what the ministers describe, and much more likely in its reasoning. Where would a thing that's truly holy find the need to put on airs? Black Charley has no faith in Colonel Cody, nor religious songs and paintings, neither any institution making a big show about itself. From where they've broken holes in the barn roof, pillars of toppled brightness are propped slanting one against another like old, dusty ruins of light, and Henry scratches at the branded shoulder through his patched-up jacket before he commences once again to murmur.

Africa's west coast, an ancient frontal lobe inflamed and swollen, bulges into cooling ocean with Sierra Leone on the underside, Guinea above it and Liberia below. Pedro da Cintra finds the country, names it for the pride of hills about its bay and after him, inevitably, come the traders and the slavers; first from Portugal and later France and Holland. Then, a hundred years after da Cintra's ruinous discovery, from England, when John Hawkins ships three hundred souls to meet the great demand arisen from that nation's colonies, newly established in America. Two centuries as western Africa's principal slave-port follow and then, in 1787, a collection of British philanthropists establish a Province of Freedom where they settle a small population of the Black Poor, Asians and Africans whose mounting presence on the streets of London has become too costly to support, including black Americans who, just a decade earlier, had joined the British side during the War of Independence with the promise of their liberty as an enticement. Five years later, numbers thinned by illness or by hostile native tribes, these are augmented by more than a thousand come from icy Nova Scotia, mostly escaped slaves from the United States, and subsequently Freetown is established as the first refuge for African-Americans who've fled their work-gang or plantation, neighbouring Liberia only following this bold example after thirty-five years. Gradually more liberated slaves return to swell the settlers' ranks, known as the Krio people for their creole tongue, a Pidgin English by way of America. The haven flourishes, with both women and blacks given the vote before the eighteenth century's end. In 1827 the Fourah Bay College is established, western Sub-Saharan Africa's first university upon the European model, making Sierra Leone a hub of education. It is at this institution in the 1940s that the sleek and handsome Bernard Daniels, studying law, begins to contemplate a life in England.

Half a century ago, back in the 1890s, Henry George admits he isn't so much thinking of a life in England as a life away from the United States. Now in his forties with both parents gone he's got no reason to abide there in a place that's never done him any favours and has burnt its mark into his arm. The truth be told, he's all for leaving sooner but his momma and his poppa they can't bear the thought of all that distance over water. Unlike Henry, born down there in Tennessee, the both of them have been on a long ocean voyage before and aren't in any hurry to repeat it. "You go, Henry," they both tell him. "You go over there while you're still young and got your strength, and don't you worry about us." But Henry's not the kind of man could ever do that, and so he takes care of them and waits it out, is genuinely glad for every minute they're alive. Soon as they're in the ground, though, he's got nothing holding him, nothing to keep him from his berth aboard *The Pride of Bethlehem*, come steaming out of Newark bound for Cardiff and in one sense drawing in the third line of an ancient triangle for Henry, a pointed and dangerous shape connecting Africa, the U.S.A. and England on the stained three-hundred-year-old maps. On those long, lurching nights of the Atlantic crossing, though, he's not thinking about any of that. He's flipping scornfully through Buffalo Bill chapbooks in the sliding lamplight and he doesn't entertain the slightest thought or speculation about what the country of his destination might turn out to be like; rarely thinks of it by name but instead inwardly refers to it as Not America.

That isn't Bernard Daniels's view, from his perspective of Fourah Bay College in the middle of the twentieth century. Bernard hails from a Krio family comparatively well-off after years of service to the Macauley and Babington trade company, and he imagines Europe generally – and England in particular – to be the fountainhead of all civilisation. This belief is prevalent amongst the Krio, mostly the descendants of absconded U.S. slaves, who through unswerving loyalty to their British bosses are Sierra Leone's dominant and most prosperous ethnic group, with native tribes such as the Sherbro, Temne, Limba, Tyra, Kissi, and more latterly the Mende people drawn increasingly together in a shared resentment. Bernard is brought up in the belief that the indigenous tribesmen who live in the Protectorate are savages; embraces gold-rimmed spectacles and stately waistcoats, throws himself with greater diligence into his studies in an effort to more deeply underscore the critical dividing line. He looks at the society around him, at the outbursts of unrest and tribal riots that have continued intermittently since the great Hut Tax war of 1898 when British troops are sent in to suppress the Temne uprising, and Bernard sees the writing on the wall. It's 1951, November, and Sir Milton Margai, born a Krio but raised as an ethnic Mende, is attending to the draft of a new constitution which will set the stage for decolonisation. Bernard has identified with the oppressor. He has taken on the master race's fears and snobberies and doesn't want to still be living in the Lion Mountains' shadow when the animals control the zoo. Having acquired his law degree, he swiftly and efficiently begins to plan for his departure. Bernard marries his devoted young fiancée Joyce, as keen to make the move as he is, and arranges both their travel and some suitable accommodation once they get to London. Within only a few dizzying weeks his misplaced vision of the mother country has been butted squarely in the face by 1950s winter Brixton with its lights and catcalls, tilted trilbies, unfamiliar tumults. Wheezing innuendo in the barbers' shops.

His scrawny legs still rolling from the ocean, Henry stumbles down the gangplank into nineteenth century Tiger Bay and, lacking Bernard's expectations, finds it's not too bad and in no way is it a shock to him, all the black faces, all the funny sing-song accents. The most startling thing to Henry's mind is Wales itself, in that he's never in his life imagined anywhere so wet and old and wild. It's only when he meets Selina and they marry and nobody says a thing about it that he starts to truly understand he's somewhere different now, and among different people. From Abergavenny they hike up to join the drovers in Builth Wells and are alone a night or two, camped out there in the million-year-old dark between giant hills, nothing like Kansas. Come the morning and the pair of them are naked as the day they're born and holding hands as they pick their way slow and careful down the steep bank to a shallow stream what they can wash in. It's real cold but his Selina is a plump young girl of twenty-two and they've got some hot blood between them. Pretty soon they're having married congress standing up in foam and flow with the clear water churning all around their shins, out in the pinkness of the early daylight with nobody anywhere around except for all the birds that are at that time waking up and trying out their voices. Him and his new wife are kicking up a noise as well and Henry feels as if he's in an Eden where nobody fell, with little diamonds splashing up and beaded on Selina's pretty rump. He feels escaped, and can't remember any moment in his previous life filled up with so much perfect joy. Then, after, when they're lying on the bank to dry and catch their breath, Selina traces with her fingertip the fading violet lines on his damp arm, the ribbon that might be a road, the shape above it that might be a balance, and she doesn't say a thing.

For Joyce and Bernard, twentieth century London is a different story. There's a temperature inversion trapping car exhaust and factory smoke beneath low cloud, people are dying in their hundreds and the government are issuing the populace with useless paper masks in an attempt to look as if they're doing something. Everybody's coughing, spitting black muck onto overcast lanes with the Durex brand-name swimming forward out of backstreet fog in sticking-plaster cream and lipstick neon. Bernard realises belatedly that England too is a land of distinct and separate uncouth tribes – cosh-boys and market traders, socialists and spivs, white savages – united only by their grievance and an envy of their betters. Worse, nobody here seems able to appreciate the yawning gulf in status that exists between the black men of Sierra Leone's Colony and those of its Protectorate, perceiving any coloured person as a coon regardless of their elocution or their bearing, irrespective of their spectacles and waistcoats. Joyce produces their first child, a boy named David, and is pregnant with their second while her husband finds that jobs for which he's qualified, where his employers also have no qualms about his being African, are few and far between. It seems to Bernard that outside the capital there may be law firms who are not so used to the easy availability of quality employees as their London counterparts and who thus might be more impressed with his impeccable qualifications. He decides to cast his line further afield and at last gets a bite from a company of solicitors in somewhere called Northampton just as Joyce presents him with a second son, whom he proposes they name Andrew. Looking for accommodation in the new town, Bernard is confronted by a policy equating him with both dogs and the Irish while expressing a refusal to rent property to all three of these categories. His infuriating sense of being snubbed is only muddied by his sympathy for the position of the bigot landlords. If Bernard himself had space to let he knows he wouldn't lease it to Dickensian criminals with vicious hounds, to drunken Irish labourers or to the great majority of his own workshy countrymen. When he gets news of rooms available not far from the town's centre on a busy thoroughfare seemingly known as Sheep Street, Bernard's celebratory mood endures until the final paragraph of the acceptance letter, where it states that this agreement is made on the understanding that just Mr. Daniels and his wife will be residing at the flat, and that there won't be any pets or, most especially, children living there.

Meanwhile, in 1896, Henry and his young wife get carried to their new home on a vast and foaming tide of mutton. From what Henry understands, the landscape-bleaching herds are driven out from Builth and then persuaded to head east through Worcestershire and Warwickshire until they wash like bleating surf against Northampton. It's a track been there a thousand years or more, and Henry hears how in the old days, century or so before, the drovers learn to stay away from inns where horses are tied up outside that look to be in too good a condition. This is on account of how these well-fed horses more than likely turn out to belong to highwaymen, who have a habit back then of befriending drovers who are headed east, inviting them to call in for a drink on their way back when they'll have traded all their sheep for money. Naturally, this means that on the return journey they'll be more convenient to rob and get left with their throats cut in some Stratford ditch. Because of this, most of the herdsmen carry on out of Northampton with their sheep and take them down to London, so they can head back to Wales through Bristol and down that way, missing out the Worcester taverns where the highwaymen are waiting. It occurs to Henry that this Wales – Northampton – London route marks out another triangle much like the one connecting England with America and Africa, and in both cases it's a kind of cattle being moved. And then of course you've got another similarity in that some of the animals that Henry is in charge of – although not that many of them, now he comes to think about it – have been branded. The main difference is the colour of the goods. Henry considers how the movement of his family over generations has been down these well-worn paths of trade, whether that trade be sheep or people, U.S. steel or Buffalo Bill chapbooks, and supposes that these lines of least resistance, which first get carved out by enterprise, end up as destinies. It's down these money-trails that, say, your great-great-grandpa's fondness for a drink or else your grandma's big green eyes go wandering, around the world and through the ages. Henry and Selina don't have much of what you'd call a plan behind their journey, figuring they'll maybe carry on to London with the drovers and if they don't like it there, why, then they'll head on back to Wales. This is before they reach Northampton and get funnelled in through its north gate in a great swathe of white, where there's that circle-church that's older than the hills, there's that almighty tree been scarred in all the wars, and Henry and his wife Selina, with her mile-long tick-infested bridal train trotting behind her on the cobbles, first set eyes on Sheep Street.

Electing to take up their new address, there in the grey and tan Northampton avenues of 1954, demands that Joyce and Bernard make some hard decisions. Clearly, the "no children" rule presents the biggest obstacle to living in the Sheep Street flat and thus to Bernard taking up his best and thus far only offer of a job, but he thinks he can see a way around it. Up by train from London in a cloud of steam and coal-smoke for a visit to the premises he meets a would-be neighbour from the rooms downstairs, an amiable idealist from the International Friendship League. This is some form of thankfully entirely ineffectual English socialist conglomerate of the variety that Bernard generally avoids, but in this instance the old chap appears to offer Bernard a solution to his "no children allowed" predicament: the man suggests that he has room to hide a child in his downstairs accommodation during those occasions when the landlord comes to pay a visit, which would go at least halfway to solving Bernard's quandary, the other half of which is his and Joyce's second baby, little Andrew. Their new neighbour clearly doesn't have the room to hide two infants, and as Bernard's firstborn it seems only right that the two-year-old David should take precedence. After an unusually heated consultation with his wife, Bernard decides it would be best if Andrew were to stay in Brixton with some relatives of Joyce's until they're established in the town and can arrange a mortgage, can arrange a permanent address with room for all the family. In Bernard's view, with Andrew being still a few months shy of his first birthday he's less likely to have formed a strong attachment to his mother and will therefore miss her less than David would do. Bernard doubts so small a child will even be aware that anything is different. And besides, in later life the baby won't be able to remember anything about it. It will be as if this admittedly less than ideal situation hasn't happened. At last everything's arranged,

everything goes ahead and on their first night in the new flat with its view
of that peculiar and hardly Christian-looking church across the street, Joyce
doesn't sleep and weeps until the morning. Bernard, frankly, doesn't understand why she can't just resign herself and make the best of it. They're only
doing what they have to do, and in perhaps a year it will all work out fine for
everyone. Andrew will be all right. There's no harm done.

Henry and his Selina make their way down Sheep Street to the market square
so he can go collect his wages from the Welsh House that they have there, and
he knows from the way everybody's looking at him that he's got the only black
face in the town. It's not that they appear resentful or they're giving him the
hard eye like he shouldn't be there, how it would have been in Tennessee. The
people of Northampton look to be more plain amazed, regarding Henry like
they would one of them big giraffes that he's seen pictures of, or something
else so rarefied and out-the-way that no one had expected to see nothing like
it in their town or in their lifetime. People smile or some of them look shocked
but mostly they just stand there with their faces hanging out as if they don't
know what to do with them. For his part, Henry figures he must look the
same way, gawping at the ancient town in all its queerness. It's like Henry and
Northampton are dumbstruck with mutual astonishment. First that round
church, been standing on its spot eight hundred years, while down the street
there's that big beech tree must be pretty near as old, and then you've got a
market square that's from around the same time, from around the year ten
hundred-something. That's a long time, long enough to make his head spin.
Why, back then the slave trade between countries hadn't been invented, far as
Henry knows. There's no United States, no Tennessee, and white people have
never heard of Africa. There's just the circle-church, the beech tree and the
woollen river winding between here and Wales. To Henry it seems like all of
these centuries the place has been here are a kind of breadth or depth that he
can't see but which conspires to give the town a feeling of great magnitude
that's bigger than its visible real size. After they pick up Henry's pay the pair of
them go for a walk up from the market square and back to Sheep Street, where
they make their way down this old alley with a sign up says it's Bullhead Lane,
so steep and narrow it feels like one of them nonsense-places in a dream,
and that's how they descend into the Boroughs. From the start it's all around
them, clamouring for their attention. There's some tough old girls look fit to
pull each other's heads off rolling in the street outside one of the beer establishments, and anywhere you're standing you can see around a dozen similar
public houses, there's that many of them. There's a blind man playing on a
barrel-organ, rabbits hopping right there on the cobbles, everybody's got a hat
on and nobody's got a gun. There's every kind of call and conversation, and

in Scarletwell Street, where they spend a piece of Henry's wages in advance rent on a house they take a shine to, they see Newton Pratt's astounding beast drinking its beer and trying to stay upright just across the street there. Henry and Selina take it for a sign and move in right away. They've got a whole house to themselves, and though it's small and wedged into its sooty terrace like a book jammed in a bookshelf it seems much too big at first, but that's before the babies start to pour out of Selina in a happy babbling flood that rises to their ankles, then their knees, and in what seems like just a year or two they're standing shoulder-deep in children.

As a grown man David Daniels can't remember much about his origins there at the flat in Sheep Street, his two years as an official Boroughs resident. His infancy, that endless continuity of moments when each moment is a saga, has evaporated to leave only a thin residue of pictures and associations, brittle sepia snapshots taken from floor-level with the details and the context bleaching out around the edges. He recalls the endless plain of carpet in the living room, soft beige with fronds and curlicues that are an acre of gold fuzz now in his memory, stabbed by slanting blades of sunlight. There's a flickering internal film-loop, a few seconds long, of David hooked up to his mother Joyce by leather reins and stumbling uncertainly downhill along a sloping path with crumbled loose-tooth tombstones rising up to either side, which he now realises must be in the graveyard of the Holy Sepulchre, the old church just across the way. When he gets taken out for walks it's always to the north or east of Sheep Street, never to the west or south. It's always to the Racecourse just a little up past Regent's Square and never down into the Boroughs, a disreputable neighbourhood where unbeknownst to him his future playmate Alma Warren sleeps sound in the bosom of her ordinarily peculiar clan. David's initial recollections of his dad are more like memories of a ship than of a person, with the chest and gentle paunch thrown forward like a brocade mainsail swelled by tailwind. Thumbs hooked presidentially in waistcoat pockets and up past the crow's nest of his tie-knot, Bernard's proud face like a flag; a better-nourished Jolly Roger with its twinkling glass sockets gilded at their rims, sailed here upon spiced currents from High Barbary, from the lion hills of the old country in which David was conceived and which his parents very seldom mention. Then there are the days of mystery and adventure when his mother takes him on the huffing dragon train to London so that she can visit friends or family, he's not sure which, and David spends the afternoons in unfamiliar Brixton parlours playing with a little boy called Andrew who seems nice enough, but whom he doesn't know. When David's four years old in 1956, Bernard and Joyce at last discover a white couple who'll arrange a mortgage with the racially mistrustful banks. They move into a pleasant house in

Kingsthorpe Hollow, funny little Andrew turns up unexpectedly to live with them and for the first time David comes to understand he has a brother, that he's had a brother all this time and never heard a thing about it until now. He starts to wonder how much of his life is going on without his knowledge, starts to speculate on where and who his parents might have been before they suddenly materialise as a home-owning married couple in Northampton, just as though they've always been here. Why don't David and his baby brother seem to have grandparents? Are his mother and his father born like gods out of the mud and sky, from the Northampton landscape with no mortal ancestors preceding them? He has the sense of a big, complicated story that he's come in at the middle of, and an impression of a history that's kept apart from him, in quarantine, like Andrew. How could they not tell him that he's got a brother? He begins to worry about any more astonishing surprises that might be in store for him. Given their new house and new neighbours, given the way his family are encouraged to regard themselves now they're not living in the Boroughs anymore, David begins to wonder whether he's even actually black, if David is indeed his real name.

Almost as soon as Henry first sets foot inside the Boroughs he's Black Charley, like the title's just been waiting for him to turn up and put it on like an old overcoat. He doesn't mind. It's not meant disrespectfully, the "Black" part of it being no more than the honest truth, while "Charley" is just something you call men around here when you can't remember what their proper name is. In its way it's almost like a mark of special standing, a way of acknowledging that he's unique and that there's not another place around Northampton can boast anybody as remarkable as Henry George. Though other coloured people drift into the town across the years, there's none of them so well known as what Henry is. At least that's true until 1911 when the local football team – what's called the Cobblers on account of all the boots and shoes made here in town – they take on a black football-player by the name of Walter Tull. They make a big fuss in the local newspapers, which is how Henry hears about it, and that gets his interest fired up so that he wants to find out all he can about this new arrival threatening to steal his coal-jewelled crown. He even takes a ride up to the football-field that's off Abington Avenue to watch Tull play, despite the fact that Henry's never really taken to the game, and he's forced to admit the boy can run like lightning and he sure knows how to kick a ball around. Good looking too, a young man about twenty-four years old, getting on thirty-five years Henry's junior and with skin that's a whole lot lighter in the bargain. Seems how Tull is born away down Kent where they pick all the hops, with his pop from Barbados and his mom an English girl. From what Henry gets told, both of Tull's folks are passed away before he's ten. Him and his brother Edward – the same name as Henry and Selina's youngest boy – are raised up in a London orphanage until Edward's adopted by a Glasgow family. He goes off up to Scotland and becomes the country's first black dentist, if you can believe that. Walter, he plays football for some boys' club that's in Bethnal Green or someplace, where the talent scouts what all the big teams have take notice of him and before long he gets taken on to play with Tottenham Hotspurs, that they call the Spurs. That's in 1909, and though Tull's not the first black or brown man to play professional football here in England – there's another coloured man in Darlington, Henry believes, who plays as a goalkeeper – Walter's the first one who's playing out there on the field and not just stood in goal. He doesn't stay with Tottenham more than a year or two, though, and as Henry hears the story it's because of how all the when the team plays off in another town, all the spectators there shout hurtful things at Tull, comments occasioned by his colour. How must that feel, Henry thinks, to be stood in a stadium of people with them hating you and ridiculing you; those hundreds of eyes on you and nowhere that you can go to get away from them until the whistle's blowed? As far as Henry's concerned something like that would be his worst nightmare, and he's mightily relieved that he sees nothing like it those times when he rides over to watch Walter play at what they call the County Ground in Abington. Everyone seems to feel that it's a pleasure having Tull here in the town, and Henry takes a sort of pride in his association by appearance. Then, 1914, that real bad European War breaks out and Walter Tull proves to be just as brave as he's good with a football when he's the first player in the town to join up in the army and go off to fight. From the reports what make their way back from the front it seems that he does pretty good. He fights in the first Battle of the Somme and they make him a sergeant. Then in 1917 when he's promoted to Second Lieutenant and goes off to fight at Ypres and Passchendaele, that makes him the first officer who's black in the whole British Army. That next year, the last year of the war, Walter goes back to France for what's referred to as the Spring Offensive where he gets blew up and they can't get his body back so that he never even has a proper grave. The night after he hears the news, Black Charley has a dream where Walter Tull's with Henry's western hero Britton Johnson and they're dressed like cowboys, sheltering behind the stallions what they've shot for breastwork and returning fire as all around them circle whooping German infantry on horseback, wearing feather headdresses instead of bill-spike helmets.

Forty years or so into the afterwards, David gets on with things. He gets on with his newfound little brother, Andrew, and he gets on well the moment he starts school down at St. George's in the heart of Semilong. So well, in fact, that David finds he must bear the full brunt of his dad Bernard's proud, beaming approval and encouragement, something that David feels uncomfortable about when he begins to realise that the same enthusiasm doesn't get extended to his younger brother. While their mother Joyce is scrupulously even-handed in showing affection to her boys, it starts to look as if her husband has already chosen which one of the children he would save in the event of household fire. Where Bernard comes from, this pragmatic attitude is not unusual. Sometimes life is very hard. Sometimes the only way to make sure any of your offspring will survive is to make brutal, terrible decisions and put all of your resources behind just one child. It's a strategic, military approach where reinforcements are sent to the regiments already winning, never to the most embattled troops, the ones in most immediate danger of defeat. Why throw good effort after bad? The widening disparity between the brothers from their father's viewpoint is just how things are, at least there at their Kingsthorpe Hollow residence. It isn't mentioned and, after a time, is barely even noticed, is a thing that can be lived with. David loves his brother. Andrew is his constant playmate, not to say almost his only playmate. David isn't really close to any of the other children, the white children, in his class at school. He's cleverer than they are, for the most part, and a different colour, neither of these attributes contributing to social success with his classmates. There are other black kids that David and Andrew sometimes hang around with at the playground with the swings and see-saw on the Racecourse, but these are mostly the children of Jamaican immigrants and David feels as if there is some sort of barrier dividing them from him and Andrew, one that he can neither see nor understand. Part of it's in the way their father clearly disapproves of their new friends, and part of it's how he makes David and his brother feel that they should disapprove as well; that they come from a better background than their pals from the Big Island. David knows this isn't right, this attitude, but somehow it creeps into things, into just playing on a roundabout, and makes an atmosphere, creates a distance – even between him and boys and girls of his own colour – as if David's not lonely enough already. His dad's class-based segregationist agenda at least pays off when it comes to David's education. Lacking the distraction of companions he has little else to do but get on with his work, prepare for the eleven-plus examinations that will more or less determine, at this early age, the prospects for the rest of David's life. The only break he gets from schooling, other than the time he spends mucking about with Andrew, comes in his discovery of fantasy, in dreams of noble-looking people with astonishing abilities. David has never heard of Henry George much less of Henry's hero, black gunslinger Britton Johnson, but perhaps there's something in his trading triangle-dictated blood that gives him a predisposition for the vibrant Technicolor dream-life of America. David begins to haunt the book and magazine stall, Sid's, that's in the ancient market square on Wednesdays and on Saturdays, where the eponymous proprietor with his cloth cap, his muffler and his fuming pipe presides over a marvellous array of lurid treasures. There are boxes crammed with yellowing second-hand paperbacks where the delirious jackets of science-fiction books seem to predominate, and hung from the stall's upper reaches in the locked ferocious jaws of bulldog clips are men's adventure magazines where naked-to-the-waist marines with gritted teeth are whipped by lovely women wearing only undies and swastika armbands, beneath blurbs which promise him THE KINKY KRAUT LOVE-GODDESSES OF TORTURE ISLAND! Even more enticing from David's perspective are the rows of U.S. comics displayed cover-up on the bookstall's front table: fluttering coloured butterflies held down by metal discus paperweights. Iron Man battles Kala, the Queen of the Underworld, and high above the thrusting skyscrapers Spiderman fights the Vulture. Superman and Batman meet when both of them are just young boys, how can that be? The constantly expanding ranks of costumed characters become the secret comrades of David's imagination, a whole hidden world of friends that no one else but him appears to know about. He keeps the comics he's collected in his room, sprawls on his bed and reads them while a world away downstairs his father fumes about the news from somewhere that's called Sierra Leone, which somebody called Milton Margai has just led to independence. None of this is half as relevant or half as interesting as the Skrulls, the Human Torch, Starro the Conqueror. Despite the lure of his new passion David's schoolwork doesn't suffer and he passes his eleven-plus. This certainly pleases his father as it means that David will be sent to the prestigious Grammar School for Boys out on the Billing Road. Bernard is even more delighted when the *Chronicle & Echo* post a journalist and a photographer to cover David's entry into his new seat of learning, with a picture showing David in his new school uniform, sat at his desk there in an otherwise deserted classroom, just in case he doesn't feel sufficiently conspicuous or isolated yet. The headline reads FIRST BLACK PUPIL FOR GRAMMAR SCHOOL and David's face in the accompanying image wears a look of wariness and apprehension, as if he's got no idea what's going to happen next.

For Henry and Selina, nearer to the turnpike of the twentieth century, what happens next is that they send their several children off to Spring Lane School that's right across the street from where they live, crowded amidst the mess of public houses, businesses and homes all fitted in a huddle there between Spring Lane and Scarletwell Street. When he cycles out upon his rope-wheeled chariot to look for odds and ends each morning Henry likes to hear the boys and girls all giggling and shrieking in their playground that's away behind the red brick schoolhouse somewhere, if it happens to be the right time of day.

He'll be coasting on down towards Saint Andrew's Road that's got the railway track beyond it, past The Friendly Arms, the little shops and houses, and he'll listen for the youngsters kicking up a noise to see if he can pick out his own offspring's voices from amongst them. Far as Henry knows, his and Selina's kids are the first ones of any colour at the school, but still they never hear about no bullying or teasing, or at least none that's about their skin. On more than one occasion when he struggles up Black Lion Hill into Marefair with the lit-up shop windows, or he coasts down Bath Street where they got that big dark chimney – that Destructor – it occurs to Henry that despite appearances him and Selina picked exactly the right place to raise their family. It's taken him a while to fathom it, but Henry reckons that relations over here between the black folk and the white folk is a little different to the way that things are over in America. The business about class has got a lot to do with it, as Henry sees things. Back in Tennessee, even the humblest white folk still look down on coloured people, maybe because in their eyes a black man's always going to be a slave. But here in England, even though it's mostly the rich English people doing all the trading, they don't personally keep no slaves themselves. So down in someplace like the Boroughs, where the people and their parents and their grandparents back to the knights-in-armour days are always on the bottom of the heap, they look at Henry and the first thing that they see it's not a black man, it's a poor man. If you want to know the difference that's between the countries then you only got to look at their respective civil wars as far as Henry sees it, living here in the place that supplied the boots for both of them. In England back there in the sixteen-hundreds, old man Cromwell, he pretends as how he's fighting for to liberate the poor from their oppressions. Meanwhile, over in America when Henry's just a small child, old man Lincoln, he pretends as how he's fighting for to liberate the slaves from their planta- tions. Speaking from his own experience, Henry reckons Mister Lincoln only wants to get them slaves out of the cotton fields down south so that they can be put to work in mills and factories up north. And from what Henry hears about the English Civil War, it seems like Mister Cromwell's only after power and glory. Once he's got that he starts killing off the leaders of the common people what supported him, and in both England and America the civil wars end up with those that they were meant to liberate no better off than what they were before, blacks over there, poor over here. Now, put like that the wars sound pretty much the same, but it appears to Henry that while both of them most probably have grabs for power at the bottom of it all, in England it's put to the people as an uprising against the better-off, just like the business that's in all the papers about Russia at the minute. In America, they have to make out that their Civil War has got to do with liberating slaves, because Americans are never going to want to overthrow the wealthy when becoming wealthy is the idea their whole country's stood on. There's the difference right there, that's what Henry thinks. In England they don't barely understand the hate that's between folks of different colours when what's on their mind is all the hate between folks come from different classes. Rope tyres rumbling on the cobblestones Black Charley runs around the Boroughs like a song what everybody knows. As long as he keeps to this part of town he don't get any trouble, but then that's the same for all the white people down here as well. He likes it here, and privately he marvels at all of the big and little things what tie it to the country that he come from. There's George Washington and old Benjamin Franklin too, their families leaving Northampton to escape one civil war and heading for America to help set up the makings of another. There's Confederate boots, and Henry hearing about Mr. Philip Doddridge's considerable influence on the reformer William Wilberforce, and then of course there's Pastor Newton writing his "Amazing Grace" out there at Olney. There's a Mr. Corey who's baptised at the round church in Sheep Street, goes out to America and gets tortured to death in Salem, caught up in that Cotton Mather witchcraft foolishness. The stars and stripes, the flag of the United States, that's some old village crest the Washingtons took out of Barton Sulgrave with them when they left, and then there's Henry George himself, another link there in the ugly chain connecting one land to the other. Henry judders on the Boroughs' stones and loves the dirty mysteries of his adopted district, with all the cast-off centuries just lying heaped in bundles on the streets like unsold newspapers. He likes the convolutions of its paths and alleys – what they call a jitty here – and even though the whole place isn't any bigger than a half square mile and he's been living there for nigh on twenty years, Henry can still discover passages and short-cuts he don't know about. Then come the war's end in 1918 he sees it all begin to change, with Walter Tull filling an unmarked grave somewhere away in France and the commencement of the Boroughs' slow and painful demolition, all the interesting yards and alleyways and complications at the back of Marefair just knocked flat and turned to rubble that weren't neither interesting nor complicated, all the lives and history in those narrow lanes just wiped away like they were never there. More and more ground he sees fenced in with sheets of corrugated tin, more and more women widowed from the war reduced to peddling fornication in the graveyard by Saint Katherine's Church and the almighty tower of the Destructor fuming up into a noonday sky that's near as black as he is. A great heaviness begins to take up home in him, and Henry notes with puzzlement that amidst all the alterations Scarletwell Street seems to gradually be getting steeper.

A short way uphill in 1964, David is plunged into a sudden understanding of England's antiquity and strangeness when he first attends the Grammar

School in Billing Road as a short-trousered first-year in his navy blazer and compulsory cap. Already starting to develop a keen dress-sense, he knows that this isn't a good look for him, particularly the short trousers. This last intuition is confirmed when he discovers that the Head of First Years, Mr. Duncan Oldman, is an unrestrained boy-fondler who's apparently allowed to call eleven-year-olds out to stand beside his desk where he can run his pudgy fingers over their bare thighs, or at least he can do this with the ones whose parents have decided they're not ready for long trousers. Mr. Oldman is an archetypal creepy child molester from a Charles Addams cartoon with his plump mollusc body tapering to dainty little hands and feet, his porcine nose and ears and darting, beady eyes; the web of burst blood vessels in his cheeks which lends him a perpetual choirboy blush. The word out in the playground is that on at least two separate occasions Mr. Oldman has invited first year pupils to his nearby home for after-class tuition, where he tries to touch them up and kiss them. In the two known instances where this gets back to the boy's parents and they formally complain, the new headmaster begs them to consider the good reputation of the school, they settle out of court and Dunky Oldman is allowed to carry on as Head of First Years with impunity, his underage seraglio in easy reach around him like an R.I.-teaching Emperor Tiberius. The new headmaster, Mr. Ormerod, has recently replaced the previous incumbent Mr. Strichley after Mr. Strichley took an overdose of sleeping pills and then went out and drove his car at speed into a rock wall. Mr. Ormerod, by contrast, has been previously employed as deputy headmaster at one of the posher public schools and doesn't see his new job as headmaster of a grammar school as a promotion. After all, though the eleven-plus does quite a reasonable job of making sure that only a bare minimum of boys from less exclusive backgrounds can attend the school, there's still the risk that Mr. Ormerod might run into a member of the working classes or, in David's case, one of the Hottentots. Indeed, a few years after David has moved on from the establishment in the mid-1970s the grammar schools are all turned into comprehensives, liable to take in the same riff-raff as an ordinary secondary school. According to the rumour David hears, for Mr. Ormerod it's a demotion, an indignity too far and one day he goes into work a little earlier than usual so that he can follow the example of his predecessor, hanging himself in a stairwell near the art room. From what David understands, the next headmaster after Ormerod avoids having to kill himself by getting fired for stealing three pounds forty pence in change from the school's drinks machine, but back when David is just starting at the school all this is in the future and the former public school enforcer is in charge. A tall man with a defect of the inner ear that makes him hold his head on one side like a vulture with a snapped neck, Ormerod attempts to recreate his new school in the fashion of his old one. Given the pretensions that the Grammar School already has, the institution doesn't need a great deal of persuading. Many of the staff still have black gowns and there are even a few of the older teachers wearing mortar boards, perhaps the last such in the town to dress like this outside the pages of *The Beano*. The headmaster's office has red and green traffic lights installed outside the door to inform visitors that they should either wait or enter, thus excusing Mr. Ormerod from having to say anything as common as "come in". Inside his office a glass-fronted case contains a range of canes designed to inflict various degrees of punishment; thick ones that bruise; thin ones that cut. When Ormerod decrees that henceforth boys using the open air school pool must swim without recourse to swimming trunks after the custom at his prior establishment there's not a squeak of protest from the staff and Mr. Oldman more than likely writes the head a letter of congratulation. This, then, is the world that all the new arrivals at the school find themselves overwhelmed by, but at least the white ones have each other for support. David has nobody. His classmates want no more to do with him than did the children at St. George's, and the teachers seem to see him as an opportunity for minstrel show amusement. For a while David hopes selfishly that in a year or two his brother Andrew can pass his eleven-plus so that at least there'll be the two of them to look out for each other in this bigoted asylum, but that isn't going to be what happens. Andrew, well aware and justifiably resentful of their father's favouritism, realises that however hard he tries he'll never win his dad's approval and so takes a more relaxed approach to schoolwork, fails to clear the bar on the eleven-plus and opts for the diminished expectations of a secondary school where at least there are other black kids. Meanwhile, David is discovering that though he may be a class-topper at St. George's, in amongst these prep-school educated boys he doesn't stand a chance. After that first year everybody takes exams to see which stream they're suited to for the remainder of their school career and David ends up in the 'C' stream with the divs and trainee sociopaths. The masters and the other kids are on his back at school, his disappointed father's on his back at home, so David spends most of his spare time at the Baxter Building, or Avengers Mansion, or in some alternative Fortress of Solitude. One bright and fresh Saturday morning David's down at Sid's stall in the market square. The latest Marvel comics are just in and David's trying to work out how many he can comfortably afford, whether to leave the *Strange Tales* or *Fantasy Masterpieces* for another day, when he becomes aware that Sid's stall has another customer and that they're staring at him. Turning slowly, David finds himself confronted for the first time by the dark-ringed eyes of Alma Warren, who has just turned twelve and isn't wearing any makeup. She's holding a copy of some comic that he's never heard of, something called *Forbidden Worlds* from one of the small companies he doesn't bother with. They both smirk condescendingly at one another's woeful taste and overhead the pigeons flutter restlessly from ledge to ledge, weaving threads of trajectory across the square's stone loom.

Black Charley in the main avoids the better parts of town, confining himself to the Boroughs and the villages out in the reaches of the county, where he's so well known that mothers use him as a way to make their kids do as they're told: "If you don't get to bed, Black Charley's gonna get you". Henry doesn't much care to be made a monster in the eyes of children, but he guesses it's a measure of his fame. He mostly gets no trouble out there in the villages, the Houghtons and the Haddons and the Yardley Gobions and such, though once out near Green's Norton he gets set on by a big giant of a drunken ploughman who holds Henry by one leg and dangles him above an open fire until his white hair's singeing and he's wailing fit to wake the dead. This is the only time that anything real bad happens to Henry when he's out about his rounds, and in the end the feller lets him go and Henry comes away with the impression that the giant only means near setting Henry's head on fire as some kind of half-wit Green's Norton joke, one that he fully expects Henry to find comical as well. Still, it's the kind of incident leaves an impression, and now Henry's getting on in years he finds his travels out around the villages are in smaller and smaller circles until pretty much his whole world is reduced to just the Boroughs, not that Henry minds. Most of his life he finds he's getting moved from here to there, from Tennessee to Kansas to New York to Wales, and never gets to settle in one place for long enough to feel the benefit of having a community. Down in the Boroughs, after living here for long enough, Henry has come to understand how being in a district and getting to see how everybody's lives work out, in many ways it's like the reading of some huge and stupefying book of stories where you stick with it for long enough you find out what becomes of all the characters and circumstances and so forth. Rattling and squeaking on his bicycle down Freeschool Street and round the bottom into Green Street he sees young May Warren, who he calls young although after having all her little ones she's grown into a big old gal. She's rolling down the little path they call Narrow-toe Lane dressed in her black coat and black bonnet, like a round iron bowling-ball that rumbles so's to let the ninepins know they best get out its way. Henry expects she's off about some work connected with her calling as a deathmonger, the women what they have round here takes care of all the babies and the bodies, which of both there are a mighty number. Henry and Selina get a woman name of Mrs. Gibbs comes round to see them when their children's born, but Henry don't doubt that if Mrs. Gibbs should happen to be unavailable or off on other business then May Warren would do just as fine a job. He figures that it's losing her own firstborn, a sweet little thing also called May, makes her so good at what she does. He calls a cheery greeting to May Warren as he cycles past and in return she lifts one heavy arm and offers him a gruff "Hello, Black Charley, how yer doin'?" by way of reply. As he rides on to Gas Street and down there, Henry considers the downright peculiar fortunes of the Warren family what with May's pop, old man Snowy Vernall, getting in the newspaper for climbing up on top the town hall roof one time he's drunk and standing shouting with his arm around that angel they got up there, like they was old friends. And then of course there's May's aunt, Snowy's crazy sister Thursa got that big accordion what she goes wandering the streets with, playing that strange, awful music with the funny gaps in so you think it's over just before it all starts up again. When Henry's getting down near where you got the little bridge what takes you over to Foot Meadow he spies Freddy Allen, a young ne'er-do-well who's no doubt on his way home seeing as he sleeps under the railway arches in the meadow, being in his twenties without house or family all on account of poverty and drink. Henry can't say as he approves of Freddy, who gets by through stealing things off people's doorsteps, but he can't help feeling sorry for the boy and Henry guesses that a body's got to eat. Curving around towards the crossroads by the West Bridge where they got the castle ruins still, there's every kind of people out there in the streets going about their business. He knows almost everyone he sees, and almost everybody that he sees knows him. He goes over the cross-roads when it's safe and on down the Saint Andrew's Road, but when he's sail-ing along up the top there with that dirty red brick wall towering above him on his right and all the tumbled ruins of the castle poking from the grass there on his left he gets a powerful sadness suddenly come over him, and don't know why. He's thinking of Selina and his children and what most concerns him is their youngest, little Edward. Henry's seen the stretches of grey rubble spring-ing up around the district as though they were patches of some terrible new bindweed, all the knocked-down houses back of Peter's Church where there's just cowslips and dead-nettles now, and it occurs to him the Boroughs will be different by the time their littlest is grown. It's all these demolitions that's unsettled him, places that Henry knows are standing for a hundred years or more and what he'd thought would stand forever, just pulled down and gone like it don't matter. Ever since the war's end you can feel it. Some big change is coming, and though he can't picture what the place is going to look like fifty, sixty years from now, he gets the feeling he most likely wouldn't care for it too much. He doesn't like to think how it will be for Edward or their other chil-dren after him and his Selina are passed on. Even though Henry knows that Edward will be properly growed up by then he can't help but imagine him as he is now, as a young black child wandering all lonely down some shabby, cold tomorrow-street what Henry doesn't recognise.

———

Dave Daniels skims over the singing tarmac of the Barrack Road astride his
Raleigh bicycle, with all that early morning Saturday potential in the battering
wind against his eager face. He's off to call upon his new mate Alma at her
house down on the broken-nosed but amiable row of terraced homes between
Spring Lane and Scarletwell Street. Here in 1966 the music over the transistor
radios is sweet and effervescent, Vimto for the ears. Month after month the
comics from America keep getting better, there are programs that he likes on
television, David has a proper friend and it's the pocket-moneyed weekend,
full of Sky Ray rocket lollies and perhaps a Tamla Motown single from John
Lever's, with no school and thus no institutionalised humiliation until Monday. He describes a jubilant freewheeling arc through Regent Square, from
Barrack Road to Grafton Street, and as he does so spares a glance down Sheep
Street with its top end opening there on his left. He knows that this is where
his family were living when they first arrived in town, the year or two before
he realised he'd got a younger brother, but his actual memories are blurred
and often contradictory. He can recall, however, the perambulator journeys
to the Racecourse that avoid excursions to the west, into the Here-Be-Tygers
thickets of Northampton's dark interior, the inland continent known as the
Boroughs, both decrepit and somehow disgraceful. David tells his parents he's
got a new friend called Alma who he sometimes visits, even has her round his
house to meet his dad that once, but doesn't tell them where she lives. As he
slides into the long plunge of Grafton Street, David passes the dusty glass and
peeling emerald door of the Caribbean club on Broad Street's corner, once
more over to his left. Someone has written on its woodwork in black paint
the phrase THAT MOUNTAIN COONERY, which he supposes is related to
that "Mountain Greenery" song that he vaguely remembers hearing on the
radio during his childhood. It strikes David as a feeble-minded kind of joke
and he ignores the prejudice, letting it all wash over him in strict accordance
with his personal policy on racial taunting, or rather doing his best to let it all
wash over him. In actual truth each washing leaves an ugly tide-line residue
of stepped-on anger in his fourteen-year-old spleen, but what else can he do?
His father Bernard's way of dealing with it would be to suppose that daubing
slogans on the Caribbean club is only meant as an affront to the Jamaicans
whom he also doesn't care for very much; that being a successful lawyer from
his background means that the word "coon" is almost certainly referring to
somebody else. David knows better, standing in the empty playground at the
Grammar School with a blackboard eraser in each hand and pounding them
together in explosive, choking cumuli of chalk-dust while his form teacher
and schoolmates giggle at him through the classroom window from inside.
Descending Grafton Street, squeezing the brakes as he approaches Weston's

the Newsagent halfway down, David dismounts and drags his Raleigh up onto the pavement, propping it against the wire-crossed hoarding – with a headline about Dr. Christian Barnard's heart transplant – that's under the front window. Peering through the faintly greenish glass his own cardiac organ flutters to discover that at least some of the latest Marvel comics have arrived, their English distribution irritatingly erratic owing to their transport from America as ballast to bulk out more profitable cargo. David spots a new issue of *The Avengers* that he'll probably pick up despite the fact that he finds Don Heck – the book's artist – a bit dull, even though Alma says she likes Heck's work. With more enthusiasm he sees there's a new *Fantastic Four* and even more significantly a new *Thor* with his idol Jack Kirby's *Tales of Asgard* in the back of it. He ducks into the shop, emerging just under a minute later with a haul of six additions to his burgeoning collection for just four shillings and sixpence. Stuffing them into the duffel bag he's got over one shoulder David saddles up and carries on down Grafton Street to Lower Harding Street, where he turns left. It is immediately apparent that he's now in a completely different part of town. On David's right a slump of rubble that might once have been two or three blocks of houses rolls downhill towards Monk's Pond Street and the gated rear yards of a reeking tannery. According to what Alma tells him, this is her equivalent to David's listless mornings in the children's playground at the Racecourse, fannying around inside great concrete duct-pipes on this wasteland, accidentally smashing up her fingernails until they turn black and fall off while David sits with his considerably lighter brother Andrew on a see-saw that's not moving and is never going to move, will always leave his little brother stranded up there in the air. David's not sure if it's himself or Alma who has the best deal, concluding that it's ultimately six of one and half a dozen of the other, swings and roundabouts. He wouldn't want to live here in the soot blown from the railway yards, among the rose bay willow herbs rooted in that same grime with drooping petals like pink tinfoil, but then there are times when he can see the area's mysterious appeal. There's the occasion when he calls on Alma and she isn't in, so that he has to leave a message with her grandmother. According to what Alma fills him in on later, when she finally gets home her gran describes the visitor as a boy roughly Alma's height or possibly a little shorter, riding on a bike, very well-spoken, wearing jeans and a blue jumper. Alma, in an effort to speed up the identification, asks her gran if the boy happens to be black by any chance, to which the seventy-something responds by looking startled and bewildered, saying "Do you know, I really couldn't tell yer." Even Alma doesn't quite know what to make of this and David is completely baffled, although at the same time he's amused and he's also impressed in a way that he can't entirely put his finger on. He has to say that just in terms of an accepting, even-handed attitude to visitors, Alma's gran Clara has his father Bernard beat hands down. He still feels mortified about the time when he asks Alma round to see his comics and his dad insists on interviewing her alone in the front room, like a Victorian patriarch seeking assurance as to her intentions. After Alma's gone, Bernard takes David to one side and soberly explains that while there's nothing wrong with mixing with white people, Alma isn't really the right sort of white person for Bernard's son to be seen hanging round with. She's failed the audition. Dave and Alma laugh about it and conclude that in the prejudice league tables, class beats race. Dave cycles along Lower Harding Street towards the top of Spring Lane, and the people that he glides past don't appear to pay him the least measure of attention, almost as if they've seen black people on bicycles before. The boy hums down the ancient hill in an exhilarating rush onto St. Andrew's Road with drowsing railway yards arrayed beyond it in the rust and sunshine, pedalling to see his friend who lives here in another world, another decade, duffle bag full of primary-colour gods and scientists, Negative Zones and Rainbow Bridges on his shoulder, talismans as he descends into the district and its crumbling wonderments, its raucous prehistoric atmosphere.

When Henry's on *The Pride of Bethlehem* all them long weeks he reads the Buffalo Bill chapbooks what are padding out its hold as ballast, but that's just because it's sometimes all there is to do and not because of any admiration he might have for Colonel Cody. Still, he understands the need that people have for such nonsensical adventures, and he don't begrudge them that. What Henry reckons is that in amidst the shove and effort and small comfort of this world when we're down here enmired in it like what we are, a man has got to have a star up there above him so as he can navigate, and what that star is, it's some manner of ideal what you can't reach but what shows you the way. Back there in Tennessee on the plantation you get the old stories come from Africa about the fearless warriors and all the clever spirit-animals what teach about how it's good to be kind to people and the benefits of being cunning and the like. At the same time you got the songs and the religion, Pastor Newton's hymn included, which Henry supposes is another breed of the same thing, some better way of living or some better place what we might never get to but where the idea of it can keep us going all the same. Where it don't matter if you find out that the man what writes the hymn has got his shameful side and doesn't necessarily live up to what he writes about, because it's the ideal what's the important thing. On the same track you have your mythological inventions like, say, Hercules and made-up characters from out the chapbooks like that Sherlock Holmes they got here or, for that matter, like Buffalo Bill, a made-up character if ever Henry met one. Just the thought there's somebody that clever or ingenious or brave, even if they don't properly exist except when you're all caught up in the story, it gives you something to reach for and to head the wagon of your life towards. And then there's the real men and women what in Henry's estimation make the brightest beacons and most glorious good examples you could follow, seeing as they're flesh and blood and not some ancient god or hero from a chapbook, which means maybe if you try as hard as them then wondrous things might truly come of it. Sometimes when he's asleep he calls up Britton Johnson, like a stepping beauty on the boardwalks of some giant place what's always there in Henry's dreams, twirling his six-guns like a cowboy in a moving picture or else dressing up like a Red Indian to get his wife and children back from the Comanche. What it must be like to be a man like that, and Henry hopes that if Selina or his little ones are ever in harm's way he'll have the courage to do just what Britton Johnson does, or at least something what's as brave. Black Charley gets enough attention in the ordinary run of things and don't know about dressing up like no Red Indian. He'll do it if he's got to but there's no great likelihood of that here in the Boroughs. Henry dreams of Mother Seacole livening up the wounded soldiers with some herbs, some rum and maybe a quick dance round the field hospital and general provisions store she's got on the front line of the Crimean War, who in most people's eyes is never going to measure up to Mrs. Nightingale no more than Britton Johnson's ever going to have a silly chapbook in his honour like Bill Cody. Henry dreams of Walter Tull, out there in no-man's-land between the trenches like in all those stories what come back of how the Germans and the English play a football game on Christmas day before they all get back to blowing out each other's vitals the next morning. Henry dreams of Walter Tull in his white baggy shorts and claret shirt, dribbling the ball between the tank traps and dead horses, darting this way and then that invulnerable through mustard gas, and booting it high above all the duckboards and the bodies and barbed wire into the black skies over Passchendaele like a bursting signal-flare. He never dreams about John Newton, never dreams of Jesus, and now that he's getting on in years Henry prefers his saints to be just ordinary men and women who make no great claim to saintliness. He's not in any way an atheist, it's more like these days he's not specially inclined to put religious faith in people what might let him down, or in some institution other than his own self who he's sure of. Henry raises up a rough church in his heart what he can carry with him where he goes, poking around in the old barns and that, with humming to himself instead of organ music and the stained-glass light spilled out of his imagination on the floor in all the straw and horse muck. Henry thinks about all what he's done, taking care of his mom and pop like they took care of him, crossing the great wide sea and sliding down upon Northampton in a snowy woollen avalanche, him and Selina raising up their children without losing any of them, and he feels contented with himself and with his life. It's best, Henry believes, a man should be his own ideal and champion, however long it takes him to arrive there.

Doggy-paddling in the lazy, undemanding currents of the 'C'-stream, David just about completes six year-long pool lengths of his education without drowning. He secures one or two subsequently useless O-levels, fails all the rest and doesn't see the point of going on to fail his A-levels as well. He doesn't want to go to college, wants to have these years of pointless and demeaning prelude over with so he can get on with his life in something that resembles a real world. His dad is furious with disappointment. Nothing's turning out the way that Bernard wanted. Back in Sierra Leone it's military coup on top of military coup, with ethnic Limba Siaka Stevens finally ending up in charge and straight away revealing his true colours, executing his political and military rivals by means of a gallows on the Kissy Road in Freetown. Bad and getting worse, this is how Bernard sees the prospects for his homeland and his eldest son alike. Dave is demoted in his father's estimations, although obviously not to the extent of his young brother, Andrew, who has never figured in those estimations. David doesn't care. Being the chosen one has always been a burden, and he finds that he and Andy grow much closer in the cosy doghouse of paternal disapproval. Whispering and laughing in the darkness after lights-out they begin to plan their bold escape. Outside their parents' dearly-won front door the 1970s are pooling even in the sump of Kingsthorpe Hollow, a fluorescent froth of platform heels and stick-on stars. The song lyrics are all chrome-dipped in science fiction and Jack Kirby has quit Marvel Comics to turn out a stunningly prolific flood of fresh ideas for their main industry rivals, full of warring techno-gods and revamped 1940s Brooklyn kid gangs. Meanwhile, a real local gang of vicious seventeen-year-old apprentice skinheads have, somewhat uncomfortably, rebranded themselves as "The Bowie Boys" and now wear eyeliner and carry handbags in Bay City Rollers tartan. The decade bowls into town riding a sequin blizzard and leaves drifts of glitter in the gutters. Flaunting its fantastic Biba clothes and Day-Glo hedgehog hair it flirts with the two brothers, finally enticing them to run away from home and join the circus. They move down to London just as soon as they're both old enough to do so without needing their dad's never-going-to-happen blessings and consent. It's a completely different place now to the city that confronted Joyce and Bernard when they first arrived in Brixton twenty years before, and being black is almost fashionable now. This previously undreamed-of world embraces Dave and Andy in a way Northampton never could, finding them flats, finding them work. David commences his employment at a clothing outlet that's the current talk of the black entertainment field, finds himself recommending gear for Labi Siffre, kung-fu fighting with Carl Douglas and discovering the fragrant world of girls in a way that would be unthinkable in Kingsthorpe Hollow – under Bernard's gold-rimmed eye and quarantined from females at a same-sex grammar school. It feels to David like he's living for the first time, dressing how he wants and getting a bit Funkadelic when it suits him, making it through the whole heady period without recourse to dreadlocks or an afro. He and Andrew sometimes pop back to Northampton, just to see their mum and so that David can catch up with Alma, but the atmosphere and barbed-wire silences around their dad mean that the intervals between their visits gradually grow longer. Even Alma is becoming harder to keep tabs on once her terraced row on Andrew's Road is pulled down, in the final mop-up of the clearance operation that's been going on down in the Boroughs since the end of World War One. The Warren family get moved to Abington, then Alma takes off on her own into a string of boy-friends, bedsits and addresses without telephones. Slowly the two of them lose touch but by then David has hooked up with Natalie, a beautifully-assembled girl from a Nigerian family who's looking like a keeper. His life picks up pace until he's skimming through the years as though he's on a Raleigh bicycle, with his exhilaration only slightly curtailed by the stark fact that, in life, there don't seem to be any brakes. You can't stop and you can't even slow down.

Henry and this place where he lives are running out of luck, he knows it, if they ever had any to start with. There's a stiffness in the joints and hinges, there's a rheumy quality comes in the eyes and windows, and a never-again feel to things. Some of the streets and plenty of the people what he's been familiar with are disappeared. Around Chalk Lane where it's all coming down and everybody's moving out, he sees these ladies that he knows just stood there weeping and one saying to the other "Well, this is the end of our acquaintance". He feels sorry for the fallen buildings, dust and rubble where it meant something to someone once, but they're hard stone and it's the people, what are softer, that get hurt most cruelly. It's the bonds between them that are delicate and built up over years what get tore up, all on a stroke of someone's pen at the town hall. There's friends and families get scattered without rhyme or reason like so many billiard balls, sent shooting off to the four corners of Northampton with their whole lives gone a different way and Henry can't but feel it's all a shame. From how he hears it, it won't be that long before it's Bath Street, Castle Street and his own Scarletwell Street what are next for demolition and he knows a time will come when even the Destructor is destroyed, with all of this replaced by some variety of great big modern rooming-houses that he don't much like the sound of. He allows that it might be a little cleaner and more sanitary round here after all the changes, but from what he's seen of diagrams and drawings that get printed in the evening paper it's not nowhere near as friendly in appearance, and he isn't certain there'll be a position for no deathmongers or crazy people such as Thursa Vernall; for the mooching kind like Freddy Allen or else Georgie Bumble; even for Black Charley with his funny-looking bicycle and cart. He drags his wooden blocks more on the roads now when he's going down these tilted lanes for fear that if he picks up speed him and his vehicle alike will both be shook to bits. One day when Henry's resting on the grass up by the stump of the old castle he gets into conversation with a nice enough young gent who's well brought-up and seems like he's been educated quite a bit in ancient history. This boy brings up the subject of Black Charley's skin, but in a nervous way in case it's not polite to mention it, when he says that it's not the first time that these falling-down old stones have been acquainted with a black man. Then when Henry asks him what he means he talks about this feller by the name Peter the Saracen, a coloured man come from the Holy Land or Africa who's living here around the year twelve hundred, working as a crossbow maker for who they call Bad King John, near seven hundred year before Henry himself arrives in these parts. On the one hand Henry will admit to feeling a touch disappointed that he isn't the first man of his complexion hereabouts, but then that's only prideful vanity, and on the other hand he's pleased he's got another hero what can socialise with Walter Tull and Britton Johnson in his idle daydreams. He imagines how he leads the three of them on his contraption with the rope instead of tyres, escorts the crossbow-maker, footballer and cowboy all the way back home to Tennessee and sixty years ago, so they can liberate all Henry's people with their fancy shooting and their deadly silent crossbow bolts and their goal-scoring capabilities. He sleeps more these days and so has more time for all his flights of fancy. Meantime out of his front window and just over Scarletwell they're taking down the warehouses and so on that are at the bottom, so that no more than that narrow terraced strip of homes is left on the Saint Andrew's Road. A little way uphill The Friendly Arms is all shut down and boarded up, ready to vanish when its time comes. He finds out from somebody how Mr. Newton Pratt was taken ill and died some years ago with the pneumonia, or anyway that's what he's told. Of what befell Pratt's legendary beast, however, Henry never hears a word and in the end he's half-convinced he must have dreamt it, its existence being to his mind a more unlikely prospect than the get-together between Walter Tull, Peter the Saracen and Britton Johnson. Henry dozes while the world out past his doorstep comes to pieces.

Just five or six decades up the road David is gliding comfortably into the 1980s, married now to Natalie and blessed with two fine kids, Selwyn and Lily. The science-fiction predilections of his boyhood mean that when the first commercially available computers hit the shops he seizes on them with delight, these fabulous devices previously unknown outside the Bat Cave. Having always been much smarter than his C-stream Grammar School track-record would suggest, he quickly finds that he knows nearly everything about the new technology, almost alone in a still-dazzled world that doesn't seem to have the faintest clue. Like some explorer on a distant, savage planet who subdues the awestruck natives with a mirror and a box of matches, David's smooth facility with getting a recalcitrant machine to work again is looked on as miraculous by those who witness it and before long he finds himself working in Brussels, home at weekends, as a highly valued cybernetic trouble-shooter. When he gets the chance he stays in touch with Andrew, who is married with two children of his own and also doing well, but while there's been a measure of rapprochement with their dad, David still finds he only gets back to Northampton once in a blue moon. All that he sees of how the town is changing is, therefore, a disconnected string of snapshots in a poorly-maintained photo album where whole years of continuity are simply missing. On a visit around 1985, as an example, he discovers that the town's largely Jamaican black community has taken over a Victorian Salvation Army fort that resides by itself upon its patch of Sheep Street wasteland down from the aesthetic pickaxe-in-the-face of Greyfriars Bus Station. David imagines that some sort of preservation order keeps the beautiful old structure standing after everything around it's been torn down. Its new inhabitants, with caterpillar locks crammed into knitted Ethiopian flag bulbs atop their heads, have fashioned the neglected fort into an energetic hive of Afro-Caribbean activity. Renamed as the Matafancanta Club after what David understands is the Jamaican for something like "place of sharing" he sees them minding the pre-school toddlers, giving local artists and sound-systems somewhere they can set up and rehearse and keeping a perpetual stew going in their canteen on the second floor. The building, with its rose-pink brick façade and graceful scrollwork of its mouldings given life by all the goings-on inside it, looks terrific. When he passes through Northampton just a few years later it's been bulldozed and there's nothing but the stretch of yellowing grass and a few stories about evidently untrustworthy trustees pissing off back home to Kingston with the funding, youngsters with colourful street-names dealing ganja and eventually police raids after one too many BMWs get spotted in the edifice's car park. So much for a preservation order, if there ever was one. On the same trip David is relieved to find that the incredibly old beech tree which he just about remembers from his infanthood is still alive and thriving in a courtyard further along Sheep Street, and of course the similarly ancient bulkhead of St. Sepulchre's is right there where it always was, that and the beech tree as apparently immovable as Alma Warren, who he's back in touch with. Keeping up a dwindling comic habit with infrequent visits to a Covent Garden shop called Comics Showcase, David first becomes aware that his old mate is doing nicely for herself when overhearing other customers discuss her recent cover-work in tones of muted awe. He picks a couple of the books up for himself and has to say he's impressed by the haunting realistic quality that Alma brings to silly thirty-year-old costumed characters by taking them all much more seriously than they would seem to deserve. Then, just a few weeks later, David meets Alma herself in the same shop when he's out with his tiny daughter Lily riding on his shoulders. They're both overjoyed to see each other, have a lot of catching up to do and from that point his travels to Northampton are a bit more frequent. He'd go there more often, but the situation with his dad and Andrew is still strained and awkward. After Bernard's efforts to encourage one son at the disadvantage of the other founder on David's refusal to engage in such a competition, the old man has found a way to carry his unwanted and divisive favouritism on to a new generation, doting on Selwyn and Lily while ignoring Andrew's two boys, Benjamin and Marcus. What particularly upsets David with their dad's behaviour is how much it hurts Andrew, much more than when it was only him that Bernard left out in the cold. Andy could shrug that off, but he can't watch it happening to his babies. He starts to become obsessed with making sure his offspring get the same advantages that he perceives as being heaped on David's pair, spurring them on through school and college, doggedly determined that sheer academic excellence will force their granddad to acknowledge them. David advises Andrew to forget about their dad, but he can see that's easier said than done when it's your own kids being treated badly right in front of you. He sees the bitterness and the resentment in his brother's eyes, and David doesn't know where this is going but suspects it's nowhere good.

Black Charley's dying in his house on Scarletwell Street, getting out just a few months before they knock it down to put up flats and move him and his family somewhere else what they won't like so much. Selina and his children come and go about the bedside in a kind of sleepy blur that Henry can't keep track of with the medicine they give him so his chest don't hurt. Across the road he's told it's pretty much all gone except for Spring Lane School and them few houses down the bottom there. He doesn't want to see it as it is, just heaps of bricks on scrubland, but likes to imagine that one stable that's still there in back of the surviving homes down on Saint Andrew's Road. Since he don't care to go to church and couldn't get there these days even if he wanted to, then that old barn's the nearest thing to Henry's idea of a place of worship what's in walking distance if Henry could walk, and what's at least in thinking distance seeing as he can't. He presumes he's getting close to that occasion in his life when it might do him good to have a few words with his maker and so what he does, he goes down to that old shed in his mind without once having need to get out of his bed. He pictures himself getting onto his old bike what he gave to his son Edward to play on some few months back after it become apparent that he'd not himself be needing it no more. In his imagination he pretends he's rolling off down Scarletwell Street, which is just the way it was with Newt Pratt and his drunken critter both outside a likewise resurrected Friendly Arms and greeting Henry with well-meant but unintelligible noises as he rattles past them heading for Saint Andrew's Road, the way they had when he could still ride bicycles and they were both alive. He sees himself all young and vigorous, turning his vehicle along the cobbled alley what they call Scarletwell Terrace on the right there just before you reach the main road, trundling down it to the rear gates of the stable, which in Henry's mind are open and not boarded up the way he hears they are in ordinary life now that the horses what were once within have gone. Henry leaves his imaginary contraption leaning up on the imaginary wall outside and pictures himself opening the rusted latch and going in, summoning all the scents and noises of a place like that as well as he is able with the flutter of the nesting pigeons and the smell of straw what's not been changed in years: stale oats and a faint memory of dung. Light through the busted slates above as Henry falls on his imaginary knees and asks the thing what he feels might be listening somewhere if he's truly soon to die and if there's anything he should look forward to after that happens. When he gets no answer, same as usual, Henry asks himself just what kind of an answer he might be expecting, just what kind of afterlife he thinks that he could be contented with for the long next part of eternity. He's not that sold on the idea of Heaven like you see in Bible illustrations. He'll admit that it looks clean and pretty with the clouds and marble stairways but, like with these modern blocks of buildings what they say they're putting up, he can't see any place for Henry in the picture, or at least no place as looks like he'd feel comfortable. Well, if he don't want that, what does he want? He's entertained the notion what the Hindoo fellers have of getting born again in a new life as someone different, maybe even as some kind of witless animal, and he's not taken with it. If he dies and someone else gets born next week who's a completely different person what has got no memory of ever being him, in what way is that Henry George? Unless there's something in the idea what he's missing, it seems pretty plain that that's somebody else entirely who's their own self and not Henry George at all. No, when he tries to call up his idea of paradise he finds he's summoning the things he knows, what have already happened. He thinks how he'd like to see his pop again, and hear his mom when she was singing in the fields. He'd like to live again those careless years when he was just a child, before he got his mark when everything seemed sort of kindly and mysterious. He'd like to be meeting Selina for the first time and out walking with her by the River Usk where it runs through Abergavenny, or be lying with her in their useless ragged tent beside the great herd after they were wed and headed out of Wales towards Northampton. He yearns to be back on that afternoon when he's just got his pay and him and his Selina first set eyes on Scarletwell Street where he'll live and shortly die, wants to be with his wife and little Mrs Gibbs the deathmonger when they call him to the confinement room to see his newborn babies. He wants his old bicycle with the rope tyres back from the past along with the ability to ride it. It occurs to him that what he wants the most is his whole life again, all of the things what are most dear and most familiar to him. If he could have that, Henry reckons that it would be worth the branding and the seasick nights aboard *The Pride of Bethlehem*. That's all he wants, but in his thoughts the sunlight tumbling through the broken roof onto the rafters striped with pigeon droppings seems as though it's getting brighter, and then later when Selina brings his dinner in to see if he can eat a little of it she can't rouse him.

Somewhere else it's 1991 and Bernard Daniels, now retired, decides that he and Joyce should visit Sierra Leone once more before they're both too old to travel. David doesn't know a lot about the politics prevailing in West Africa just then but isn't sure the journey is a good idea, and Andrew feels the same. Their dad waves their concerns aside. His sons are Brixton born, have never been to Africa and no doubt see it through their native English eyes as somewhere threatening, as a dark continent. Bernard and Joyce are Africans and have no such anxieties. They're simply going home, and David harping on about the tensions growling round the lion mountains at the moment isn't going to dissuade them. Bernard casts a cursory glance over the international pages in The Times, concluding that the situation over there is just business as usual by Sierra Leone standards. Siaka Stevens steps down a few years ago in favour of another ethnic Limba, Major General Joseph Momoh. There are all the customary attempts at overthrow, or at least allegations of the same, and all the usual retaliations by way of low-hanging fruit along the Kissy Road. Admittedly, there's all this business going on with Momoh being forced to re-establish multi-party politics, with plenty of dark mutterings breaking out already in the opposition ranks, but Bernard knows that if he waits for a politically clear day to make their trip then he and Joyce will wait forever. It's all settled. Flights are booked. There's nothing else that David, Andrew and their families can do but cross their fingers and hope for the best, which obviously never works. In all their fretting over the fraught politics of Sierra Leone nobody has considered what's currently happening across the border in Liberia, this being bloody and horrific civil war, most of it orchestrated by the leader of the National Patriotic

Front, Charles Taylor. This is the man responsible for the most forceful and compelling slogan ever used in an election anywhere:

I KILLED YOUR MA.
I KILLED YOUR PA.
VOTE FOR ME.

Taylor decides it's in his interests if fighting kicks off in Sierra Leone as well. He helps to found the Revolutionary United Front with ethnic Temne army corporal Foday Sankoh, expert in guerrilla warfare, trained in Britain and in Libya. When civil war erupts in Sierra Leone, Bernard and Joyce are in the middle of it, in their seventies, both ethnic Krios who are disliked by the native tribes, with no flights to or from the country and thus no way to get out. It's terrifying. Lives are ending right across the street in unimaginable shock and fear and pleading, seldom with a gunshot, seldom swiftly. There are fashionable necklacings with burning tyres and twenty-minute executions using blunt machetes that can leave the murderers exhausted. Cowering in their hotel the couple peer out from between drawn curtains at the drifting smoke, the angry black tide sluicing up and down the street. Meanwhile, in England, David and the family are frantic, making calls to travel agents, embassies, and in the end somehow they bring their parents home, severely shaken but unharmed. Unharmed, and, in the case of Bernard, seemingly unaltered. Everything he's seen confirms his strongly-held conviction that Sierra Leone's native tribes are savages who only benefited from colonial rule and find themselves unable to exist without it. As for his opinions on events closer to home, these remain similarly unaffected. Bernard still refuses to bestow affection and encouragement on Andrew's kids to the degree he does with David's, while Andrew's attempts to prove their father wrong by forcing Benjamin and Marcus to shine academically are by now ingrained and obsessive. David watches this unfolding and it's like a ghost story, a haunting, an uncanny repetition of events and attitudes out of the past eerily manifesting in the present day, in 1997. Finally he gets a phone call from his brother one Saturday morning where Andrew can hardly talk, can't get the words out properly. Marcus, his eldest son, has killed himself. Andy's just heard about it from the college. Pressure of exams, they think. Oh, Christ. A terrible slow car crash that's begun in Freetown forty years before reaches its point of impact and the Daniels family find themselves sat dazed and paralysed in the emotional debris, with blossoms nodding in the breeze all up and down the Kissy Road.

It's 1997 and the Railway Club along the end of the St. Andrew's Road by Castle Station is pretty much all that Eddie George is living for. He's getting on, eighty or more, and he's got one of those things that he can't pronounce, sclerosis or what have you, but if he can get out from his place in Semilong down to his usual table in the club he's happy just to have a Guinness and see all his friends. You get all sorts of people from the district going in there, that's what Eddie likes about it. Couples with their children, lots of old gals and old fellers like himself and all the beautiful young women where there isn't any harm in looking. Often when he's in there he'll bump into young Mick Warren and his family, Cathy his wife, sometimes his scruffy-looking sister and his two boys, Jack and Joe. Jack's around six or seven and he seems to like having a chat with Eddie when he sees him. Eddie likes it too. They mostly talk a lot of nonsense with each other and it takes him back to when he was a boy himself, playing with all his sisters and his brothers on the pavement right outside their house in Scarletwell Street with his little wagons, and then later when his dad gave Eddie his own funny bicycle and cart before he died. The damn thing fell to bits only a few weeks after. It makes Eddie chuckle just to think of it while he's calling his cab to take him to the Railway Club, but that sets off a thudding in his chest and so he just sits on the sofa and calms down while waiting for the taxi to arrive. It's a grey day and what with Eddie's eyes it's looking kind of murky as he sits there in the tiny living room. He's thinking about turning on the light just for a bit of cheer, damn the expense, right when his car turns up and toots its horn outside. Just standing up makes him feel dizzy, as if all the thoughts and the sensations in his head are draining to his feet. He lets the capable young driver shuffle him from his front door into a back seat of the vehicle, where he needs help to get his seat belt buckled properly. At least it's warm, and when the engine starts up and they roll away he's looking out the window at his neighbours' flats and houses sliding backwards up the hill as he descends down Stanley Street towards St. Andrew's Road. Stanley Street, Baker Street and Gordon Street. It's taken Eddie some good years of living here in Semilong to figure out that they're the names of famous English generals who relieved Mafeking and all that business, back more than a hundred years ago. For a good while he's laboured under the impression that it's all something to do with the film actor Stanley Baker, and that makes him smile as well. The taxi-cab turns left into St. Andrew's Road, and on his right there's all the yards, furniture reclamation businesses and lock-ups that have been here for as long as Eddie can remember, some with signboard lettering upon their peeling wooden gates that looks to Eddie's eye like it might be Victorian or something. Across the road from these and on his left, there are the openings to the neat row of hilly streets that make up Semilong, all parallel with one another, Hampton Street and Brook Street and all them. Eddie's always been very happy here. He likes the neighbourhood, but nobody could say that it was doing well. It's not the worst of places by a

long shot, but in terms of getting taken care of then it's plain that Semilong's
a fair way down the list. What it's about as far as Eddie sees it is that where he
lives now is too close to where he used to live, which is to say the Boroughs, or
Spring Boroughs as they seem to call it nowadays. It's as if things like being
poor and having low property prices are contagious and will spread from area
to area if they're not kept in isolation, maybe with a blanket soaked in disinfectant hung across the door the way they used to have up Scarletwell Street
when somebody had the scarlet fever. Just like with his mix-up over Stanley
Baker, Eddie can remember when he thought that scarlet fever is something
that only people living up in Scarletwell Street got; that maybe people down in
Green Street got afflicted by green fever. How you think when you're a youngster is something that never ceases to amaze him, and he hopes that little Jack
is maybe going to be there when he gets up to the club. Out of the window on
the right now is the stretch of turf and trees that run down to the brown-
green river, which in Eddie's younger days is always known as Paddy's Meadow
although he expects they've got some different title for it now. He peers
through bloodshot eyes at the old children's playground at the bottom of the
grassy slope there that he still calls Happy Valley. There's a little sunlight falling through the clouds to strike upon the rusty roundabout and on the blade
of the dilapidated slide, and Eddie feels a lump come to his throat because it's
all so precious. He recalls adventuring amongst the reeds down at the water's
edge with all the other grubby little boys, and how they liked to scare each
other by pretending that there was a terrible long monster in the river what
would snatch them if they get too close to it. He looks out at the empty meadow
now and feels convinced somehow that all those days are still there, in the
rushes, on the squeaking swings, still going on except that he's too far away to
see it all. That must be how it is. He cannot find it in himself to think that any
moment, anybody, anything is ever truly lost. It's just that him and everybody
else moves on, and find themselves washed up in times and circumstances
they don't fully understand or like much, necessarily, without a way of getting
back to where they're happy and contented. There's a lot about the world these
days that Eddie doesn't have the measure of. He's not sure what to make of this
new government that just got in, these Labour people who don't talk or look
much like the Labour people he remembers, and the business with Princess
Diana getting killed in that car accident takes Eddie by surprise as much as
anyone, how the whole country seems to have fallen to pieces for a while with
all the crying. It appears to Eddie like there's more news all the time these
days, until he feels like he's full to the brim with it and one more model with
an eating disability or gang of raping footballers could make all of the knowledge that's already in him spill out on the floor. By now his taxi's at the traffic
lights where Andrew's Road crosses the foot of Spencer Bridge and Grafton

Street, and he finds himself looking at the lorry park just past the lights and on the far side of the road, the Super Sausage place that used to be a meadow with a public baths up at one end. It's still too light for any of the girls to be around, and Eddie's glad because he hates to see that, how the women in that line of work are getting younger all the time. He's tired. The world's making him tired, and Eddie fidgets in the rear seat where it feels as if his seat belt is too tight, like it's not done up the right way. The lights go green, the cars move on and now they're coming past the fenced-in lorry park to where the train yards are behind the wall there on the right, and on their left is the short strip of grass between Spring Lane and Scarletwell Street that was once a row of terraced houses. Eddie can't help taking a long look up the street he was born in as his cab goes by the bottom of it, where that eerie single building still survives down near the corner there all on its own. The old slope rises up with the Spring Lane School playing fields on one side, and across the road there on the other are the flats they put up in the 1930s after they tore down the homes where Eddie and his family and their friends all lived. The rounded balconies are peeling and the entrances to the courtyard inside have all got gates on now. Up at the hill's top there are those two blocks of flats bigger than all the rest, Claremont and Beaumont Court, the towers standing there victorious when everything around has been knocked flat. The street don't look much, he admits, but it's where he began and it's still got that sort of light inside it. Eddie shuts his eyes upon his birthplace, and there's all those floating jelly blobs of colour that you get. The accidental pattern that they have to them reminds Eddie of something and he can't think what, then realises it's the scar his dad's got on his shoulder with the triangles, the wavy lines. He thinks about his parents and it comes to him that it's one hundred years exactly, maybe even to the month, since they first came here to Northampton and laid eyes on Scarletwell Street. How about that? Doesn't that beat everything? A hundred years. He kind of feels the car pull up outside the Railway Club and kind of hears the driver say "We're here" which gives him satisfaction, but if truth be told by then Eddie's already dead a good few minutes.

Up the line by just shy of ten years in 2006, Dave Daniels strolls down sunlit Sheep Street on his way to Alma's exhibition. Other than the round church, everything is different and he can't work out which of the windows might be those of his old house, the one that Andrew was excluded from, or even if his old house is still there. He's got a vague idea it might be one of those demolished to make way for the huge corned beef-coloured premises belonging to the Inland Revenue, but isn't sure. It doesn't matter. He hardly remembers spending that first year or so here, anyway, and what with Andrew's eldest taking his own life like that David has come to blame the situation back then in the early 'Fifties for his nephew's death, although he knows the truth of it is probably a lot more complicated, much less black and white. Things usually are. Further along the street he peers in through the open gateway to the yard where the old beech tree used to stand, but after having talked to Alma on the phone the other night he knows what to expect. The tree is gone, a thing as old as the round church itself that had withstood all the crusades and civil wars, finally poisoned in the night by some bigwig proprietor of an adjacent business who's got plans for the location that the beech tree and its preserva- tion order are unfortunately standing in the way of, or at least if all the ugly local rumours Alma has passed on to David are to be believed. He shakes his head, suspecting that it's just the way the world is going. When he reaches Sheep Street's end he crosses a dual carriageway that wasn't there before and walks beside the empty yawn of unkempt grass where the Matafancanta used to be, just down from the still-standing bus station recently voted the ugli- est building in the country. He remembers Alma telling him that quite apart from being hideous the whole thing has its entrance at the wrong end so that busses have to do a complete circuit before entering, this due to a town plan- ner working with the blueprints upside down. It's nearly funny. He turns right before he gets to the old Fish Market that's up there at the top end of the Drap- ery and walks down by a Chinese restaurant with a multi-storey car park just across the busy road. He doesn't know this place at all. He's looking at some sort of brutal traffic-junction where there used to be the cheery confines of the Mayorhold, which he knows for Harry Trasler's shop that he and Alma, way back, scoped for comics almost every Saturday. He never looks at comics these days, even though they've become fashionable to the point where adults are allowed to read them without fear of ridicule. Ironically, in David's view, this makes them a lot more ridiculous than when they were intended as a perfectly legitimate and often beautifully crafted means of entertaining kids. At age thirteen, David's idea of heaven was somewhere that comics were acclaimed and readily available, perhaps with dozens of big budget movies featuring his favourite obscure costumed characters. Now that he's in his fifties and his paradise is all around him he finds it depressing. Concepts and ideas meant for the children of some forty years ago: is that the best that the twenty-first century has got to offer? When all this extraordinary stuff is happening every- where, are Stan Lee's post-war fantasies of white neurotic middle-class Amer- ican empowerment really the most adequate response? David descends into a sodium-lit pedestrian subway system which takes him beneath the hurtling traffic to emerge on the far side of a broad auto-waterfall that he thinks might be called Horsemarket. Heading down beside the churning flow of steel David anticipates the Barclaycard Credit Control Centre that stands on Marefair's corner at the bottom but discovers even that is gone, replaced by some variety of leisure/entertainment complex. Walking along Marefair almost to the Castle Station end he turns right into Chalk Lane, which he thinks should take him to the little nursery where Alma's show is happening. He's immediately drenched in poppies, spurting from the distressed mortar of a very old-looking stone wall there on his right. The sudden scarlet saturation brings to mind the news he hears a few weeks back, of how the extradition process that will see Charles Taylor tried for war crimes in a glass box in The Hague is just now getting underway. About time. Fifty thousand people dead in the ten years the civil war was going on until they finally declared an end to it in 2002, and the UN peacekeeping forces were required to stay there until, what, six months ago? It's staggering to think that all that harm and carnage can be instigated by a single individual, pretty much. "I nearly killed your ma. I nearly killed your pa. Now give me clemency." Not likely. Joyce and Bernard have been dead a year or two but David's memories of those few frantic weeks spent trying to extricate his parents from Sierra Leone's nightmare are still with him, just as sharp as if the whole thing were still going on somewhere. Ascending past a humble limestone building he believes is Doddridge Church, he notices a seemingly redundant doorway stranded halfway up one wall and thinks about his nephew, Marcus, who will now be frozen at nineteen forever in his thoughts. He thinks about the prejudices that his dad Bernard encountered when he first arrived here in the 'Fifties, and the prejudices he brought with him. His ideas of status, the defensive snobbery of Krio families escaped from slavery to populate a British colony and earn the deep resentment of Sierra Leone's native people. All these little cogs that turn the bigger cogs, in history and in people's hearts, a mechanism that's almost impossible to perceive properly, its action taking place over the span of decades, centuries. The way that everything works out. For his own part he's getting tired of Brussels, wants to maybe kick back for a while with Natalie and their two kids, live on the savings and Natalie's income for a while and just see what comes up. He wants to enjoy life while it's actually happening rather than retrospectively or as a thing deferred until the future. It can all be over just like that, a sudden civil war, a looming big exam, you never know, and David wants to live each moment like an ethically-sourced diamond. He can see the nursery up ahead, a modest crowd of people that he doesn't know gathered outside and in the middle he sees Alma in a fluffy turquoise jumper, waving to him. Every moment. Every moment like a jewel.

In 1897 Henry and Selina stop dead in their tracks to gape, halfway down Scarletwell Street. It's such an unlikely sight that for a moment it feels like they're dreaming or enchanted, and they take each other's hands without a word as if they were a pair of little children. Tied up to its lamppost there outside The

Friendly Arms, the animal ignores them. After maybe half a minute, a stout little feller with big side-whiskers comes out from in the public house with a big glass of ale that he gives to the creature, what commences drinking it. The man, who they will later learn is Mr. Newton Pratt, looks from the animal to Henry and then laughs. "Blimey! Did you two know each other, then, back there in the old country?" Henry laughs as well. "Well, speaking personally, I never been to Africa, although I'll own this feller's mom and pop could very well have once run into mine. Where did you get him, you don't mind me asking?" The man doesn't mind at all. "Got 'im from Whipsnade Zoo when they'd not got the space and they were gunna sell 'im to the knackers yard for glue. Horace, 'is name is. It looks like 'e's took a shine to your young lady." Henry looks around and there's Selina beaming like it's Christmas morning while the rarity allows her to be petting its dark muzzle. He regards the beast, the black and white stripes of its hide like an amazing jungle flag staked proudly here amongst the cobbles and the chimneypots, the black whisk of its tail keeping the meat-flies off, its bristly mane what's like the haircut of a Mohawk Indian and swaying like it's kind of drunk into the bargain. Henry makes his mind up there and then that this is where he's going to live, him and Selina. They stand talking to the man a while and he tells them that he's Newt Pratt and that the place they're in is called the Burrows, or that's what it sounds like, and now Henry looks he can see creeping, jumping cottontails all over where there's any grass. The veldt-horse belches. Mr. Pratt asks him his name and he says Henry George, and Newton Pratt says he'll remember that. But, pretty obviously, he doesn't.

THE STEPS OF ALL SAINTS

CAST

JOHN CLARE

HUSBAND

WIFE

JOHN BUNYAN

SAMUEL BECKETT

THOMAS BECKET

HALF-CASTE WOMAN

The three broad front steps and sheltering portico of a late Gothic church with Doric columns left and right, a foggy night-time. In the background beneath the portico, there are recesses set into the limestone front wall of the building, to either side of its locked doors. From off, the almost inaudible sound of a piano in the far distance, playing "Whispering Grass". Seated in right-hand recess, JOHN CLARE, wearing dusty-looking early 19th-century rural dress, including a tall wide-awake hat. The sole is hanging off one shoe. He peers around into the surrounding gloom, hopefully.

JOHN CLARE: Well, this is a haunted sort of evening. Who's about?

[*Pause*]

JOHN CLARE: Come on now, look alive ... although for me I can't be bothered with it these days. It'd be alright, perhaps, if not for all the walking and the disappointment. As for what there is of flesh and blood to the arrangement, I'm of the opinion that it's much like shoes, in that the bodily side of the matter has a fresh smell and a lovely cherry lustre when it's new, but that's of no use once the tongue has withered and the sole's worn through. It's famously a poor show if the nails are digging in your feet. [*Reflective pause as* CLARE *examines his damaged shoe.*] No, in the main I'm happier with a gaseous posterity, so that the spectre of my backside might revisit all these spots that it was fond of formerly. The only pity is that life goes trudging on for as long as it does, since otherwise presumably there'd be more people of my own age and extinction here to talk to. [*Cocks head, listening to faint music from off.*] That's a pretty air. I'd like to know who's furious enough to gouge it into everyone.

[*Dragging footsteps approach from off. Enter* HUSBAND *and* WIFE, *front right. They are dressed for an evening out, she in long coat and bonnet with handbag, he in loud yellow plaid jacket and dickey-bow with oiled dark hair and pencil moustache. They come to a halt, standing and staring at the empty church steps.*]

HUSBAND: We could sit here.

WIFE: We can't sit here. I can still hear the sound of her. It travels farther in the night.

HUSBAND: We'll have to sit here. If you need to spend a penny there's the toilets on Wood Hill not far away. She's sure to cut it out soon, any road. I don't know what's got into her.

WIFE: [*Snorts derisively.*] I do.

[*Resignedly, she goes and sits on church's second step. Her husband stands staring at her for a moment. She does not look at him, but glares angrily into the fog. When he at last sits down next to her, she shuffles a couple of feet away from him. He looks at her, surprised and hurt.*]

HUSBAND: Celia ...

WIFE: Don't.

JOHN CLARE: Hello? I don't suppose that you'd be dead, now, would you?

HUSBAND: Is this how it's going to be?

[*She doesn't answer.* HUSBAND *stares at her, waiting.* JOHN CLARE *rises from his alcove and walks hesitantly forward to stand behind and between the seated pair.*]

JOHN CLARE: Excuse me, sir, but were you talking just now to myself or to the lady here? If, in response to my own querying of your mortality, you were enquiring as to whether this fogbound and uneventful continuity was how your afterlife was going to be, then in my own experience the answer's yes. Yes, this is how it's going to be. You'll hang around in fog and nobody will ever come. If you're anticipating a creator presently arriving to make lucid his intentions, then it's my guess you'll be waiting a long time. But, fair's fair, if he should turn up, then when you're finished with him, if you could point him in my direction, I'd be grateful. There were matters I was hoping to discuss. [*The pair ignore him. Experimentally, he waves one arm up and down between them, as if to determine whether they are blind. After a moment he stops, and regards the couple glumly.*] Of course, it may be that you were addressing your companion, in which case I hope you'll pardon me for my intrusion. I intended no offence with my assumption that a couple as apparently ill-suited as yourselves might very well be dead. I am myself no stranger to the inconvenient marriage. When I was with Patty, it was always Mary that I thought of. Often did I –

HUSBAND: I said is this how it's going to be, all night until the morning? If there's something on your mind then spit it out, for God's sake.

WIFE: You know.

HUSBAND: I don't.

WIFE: I don't want to talk about it.

HUSBAND: What?

WIFE: You know. The goings on. Just leave me be.

JOHN CLARE: [*Slowly and with deliberation.*] Do you know who I am? [HUSBAND *continues to stare at* WIFE *who glares into the fog.*] I ask not out of wounded vanity, but more in the true spirit of investigation. I've a fancy I might be Lord Byron, though it strikes me now I hear it spoke aloud that Byron would most surely not say such a thing. If that is so, then otherwise it may be I am King William the Fourth, in which case I would be obliged for news as to what year we suffer presently, and if my pretty Vicky is still Queen. Please take your time about it. It's a thing of no great consequence, my true identity, as long as it is somebody well thought-of.

HUSBAND: Goings on? What goings on? [WIFE *does not reply. He stares at her for a few moments then gives up and looks down at his shoes in silence.* CLARE *looks from one to the other, hopeful of further conversation. When none is forthcoming, he sags dejectedly.*]

JOHN CLARE: [*Sighs heavily.*] Oh, never mind. Sorry I've bothered you. It's just a game that I've come up with for when no one's here to talk to. Tell you what, I'll leave you both alone and mind my business. [CLARE *turns and begins to shuffle back towards his alcove. Halfway there he turns and looks back over his shoulder at the couple on the steps.*] Do you know, sometimes I think I am the statue with stone wings atop the Town Hall up the road, and it in turn is everyone? [*The couple do not respond.* CLARE *shakes his head sadly then continues on towards the alcove, where he once more takes his seat. There is a long silence during which the piano music from off finishes abruptly halfway through a bar. Nobody reacts.*]

HUSBAND: [*Eventually.*] Look, I'm as in the dark as you are. As for goings on, not that I'm saying I'm aware of any, that's just life as far as I'm concerned. In life, you'll always get a lot of goings on. And highly strung young girls, they can have funny turns –

WIFE: There's goings on and goings on. That's all I'm saying.

HUSBAND: Celia, look at me.

WIFE: I can't.

HUSBAND: The chances are, what all this will turn out to be, she's on her rags.

WIFE: [*Turning to him angrily.*] You bloody liar. You heard what she shouted.

HUSBAND: What?

WIFE: You heard.

HUSBAND: I didn't.

WIFE: Everybody heard. They could have heard her in Far Cotton. "When the grass is whispering over me, then you'll remember." Well? Remember what? What did she mean? To me, it sounds a funny thing to say.

HUSBAND: Well, that's … that's just the song-words, isn't it? The song that she was playing –

WIFE: You know that those aren't the words. And you know what you've done.

HUSBAND: You mean these goings on of yours?

WIFE: They're not my goings on. They're yours. That's all I'm saying. [*While they talk,* JOHN BUNYAN *enters from off right beneath the portico behind them, dressed in dusty, drab 17th-century attire. He does not appear to notice* CLARE *sat in the shadows of his alcove, but instead pauses to listen to the bickering couple on the steps with a puzzled frown.*]

HUSBAND: I've done nothing anyone in my position wouldn't do. You haven't got the first idea of what it's like, with my responsibilities for managing the band. All of the travelling around together, there's an intimacy that develops over time, I'll grant you that, but –

WIFE: I dare say there's intimacy! So, am I to take it you admit that there's been goings on?

HUSBAND: I don't know what you mean. What do you mean by goings on?

WIFE: I mean the other.

HUSBAND: What?

WIFE: The slap and tickle.

HUSBAND: I'm not getting you.

WIFE: The How's-Your-Father.

HUSBAND: Oh. [*Long pause.* WIFE *looks angrily away from* HUSBAND, *who stares bleakly at the ground in front of him.*] Well, anyway, we can't sit here all night.

WIFE: You're right. We can't. [*Both remain seated. Behind them,* BUNYAN *regards the silent couple with bewilderment. He still has not noticed* CLARE *until the latter speaks from the dark alcove in the background.*]

JOHN CLARE: Ha! I'll bet you won't hear me either, you great nincompoop.

JOHN BUNYAN: [*Wheeling about to peer into the darkness under the portico.*] What? Who goes there, skulking like a cutthroat?

JOHN CLARE: Oh, no. I've miscalculated. This is an embarrassment.

JOHN BUNYAN: Come out! Come out, before I draw my sword! [CLARE *rises nervously out of his alcove, tottering hesitantly forward with both palms raised in placation.*]

JOHN CLARE: Oh, come now. There's no need for that. 'Twas but a jest, for which I make apology. I had not realised you were dead as well. It is, I'm sure, a common error.

JOHN BUNYAN: [*Surprised.*] Are we dead, then?

JOHN CLARE: I'm afraid that is my understanding of the situation, yes.

JOHN BUNYAN: [*Turning to look at couple on steps in foreground.*] What about them? Are they dead?

JOHN CLARE: Not yet. I expect they're hanging on to see what happens.

JOHN BUNYAN: This indeed is a conundrum. Dead, then. I had thought that I but dreamed, and had not woken on my gaol cot to make water or turn on my side in an uncommonly long while.

JOHN CLARE: It is a plain fact you will never do these things again.

JOHN BUNYAN: Well, I am astounded. I had thought the world to come a fierier terrain than this, and now am disappointed by the writings that I made about it.

JOHN CLARE: [*Interested.*] Was it writings that you made? Well, here's a pretty match. I once was in that kind of work myself, now that I think of it. I wrote all day, I'm sure of it, when I was married first to Mary Joyce and then to Patty Turner. Was I Byron then, or was I king? I can't remember all the little details now, the way I once did. But what of yourself? Would there be any of your writings I might know of?

JOHN BUNYAN: I'd not think it likely. I once penned some words about a pilgrim, meant to show the pitfalls and the troubles that there are in worldly life. The common people liked it well enough, yet I was not the courtly crawler Dryden was, and when another Charles came to the throne I did not do so well of it. This recent news of being dead makes me suppose the greater part of what I wrote did not survive me.

JOHN CLARE: [*Incredulous, with dawning realisation.*] You would not be Mr. Bunyan, late of Bedford?

JOHN BUNYAN: [*Cautiously flattered.*] That I am, unless there is another. Is it so few years since my demise that I am still remembered? But things seem so changed. Were not the pillars of All Hallows Church here built from wood when last I passed this way? Or did that all go in the fire? It makes me pleased to think you know of me.

JOHN CLARE: Why, from the look of things I'd say it must be getting on three hundred years since you were last alive. I take it you'll have noticed the fine calves and ankles on the woman there, for they were the first things I looked at. It's outlandish days we're in, you may be sure, but I would bet a shilling that the progress of your pilgrim is a thing on everybody's lips, just as your name's on everybody's feet. Upon these feet of mine, most certainly, when I made my own progress out of Matthew Allen's prison in the forest and walked eighty miles back home to Helpstone. You'll no doubt have heard of it, and of myself. I am Lord Byron, who they call the peasant poet. Does that ring a bell?

JOHN BUNYAN: I cannot say it does. Why do they call you peasant when you are a Lord?

JOHN CLARE: It does seem queer, now that you mention it. And why does Queen Victoria insist she is my daughter? It may be, upon consideration, that I'm not entirely on the mark with the Lord Byron business. It was no doubt all the limping that confused me. It now comes to me that in the very fact of things I am John Clare, the author of Don Juan. There! That will be a name, I think, that's more familiar to you.

JOHN BUNYAN: I'm afraid that it is not.

JOHN CLARE: [*Disappointed.*] What, not the Clare *or* the Don Juan, now?

JOHN BUNYAN: Neither of them.

JOHN CLARE: Ah, God. Am I not even John Clare? [CLARE *lapses into a depressed silence, staring at the ground.* BUNYAN *regards him, concerned.*]

HUSBAND: Look, I'm no saint.

WIFE: [*Not looking at him.*] You can say that again.

HUSBAND: [*After a pause.*] What I'm saying is I'm only flesh and blood.

WIFE: [*Angrily, turning to glare at him accusingly.*] Well, what sort of excuse is that? We're all just flesh and blood! You show me somebody who's not! [*She looks away from him again, reverting to silence. Behind the pair,* CLARE *and* BUNYAN *exchange lugubrious and unconvinced glances.*]

JOHN CLARE: [*He shrugs.*] It strikes me that we're only getting in the way here. What would you say to the prospect of a nice sit down? It is in my opinion quite the best of postures, and I am convinced that it is only all this standing up and walking to and fro that gets us into so much trouble as a population. Come, let's take the weight from off our feet.

JOHN BUNYAN: I had intended I should see the nearby marketplace, where was the Earl of Peterborough's edict handed down that I referred to in that piece of mine about the Holy War. Still, it may be that a few moments' rest is no great matter in the long yards of posterity. But as for taking weight from off our feet, in our present condition I can't see that there is any weight to take. Indeed, it is a wonder that we do not float away into the heavens for our want of heaviness.

JOHN CLARE: I had supposed we all must keep an ounce or two of it that's carried in our hearts for such emergencies. Let us sit down, and then perhaps we can discuss this further. [CLARE *begins to lead* BUNYAN *towards the rear of the space beneath the portico.* BUNYAN *starts towards the right-side alcove, at which* CLARE *grows agitated and corrects him.*] Oh, no, that won't do. This fellow is the recess that's reserved for me, by virtue of my previous habitation. You must have the one upon the other side, that I keep specially for visitors. I'll own it's not as sumptuous as mine, but if that inconvenience is the worst thing that Eternity has got to throw at you, you should be glad. [BUNYAN *looks disgruntled, but accedes to* CLARE's *wishes. Both men take their seats in their allotted alcoves.*]

JOHN BUNYAN: You're right. It's comfortable enough.

JOHN CLARE: It is. [*Pause.*] Are you referring to the recess, now, or the Eternity?

JOHN BUNYAN: Primarily the recess. [*Pause. From* OFF *there is the* SOUND *of a solitary motorcar passing by through the fog. The* HUSBAND *and* WIFE *pay the passing car no attention, but* CLARE *and* BUNYAN *follow it with their eyes.*] I have wondered about those things. They are clearly a variety of wagon, but I cannot fathom how their locomotion is effected.

JOHN CLARE: Well, I've given that some thought myself, and I believe the answer lies in some advance of natural science that has made the horse invisible to normal sight.

JOHN BUNYAN: Surely, that conjecture might be easily disproved with the plain observation that there's no conspicuous abundance of the dung these unseen nags must certainly produce. Answer me that, if you've the measure of it.

JOHN CLARE: Ah! Ah! So I will, then. Does it not occur to you that beings that are visible unto plain sight such as ourselves make droppings that are equally apparent to the eye? Does it not follow that an unseen or invisibly transparent horse would thus produce manure that's of a similar ethereal nature?

JOHN BUNYAN: [*After a thoughtful pause.*] Surely, though, however rarefied its substance, an unseen evacuation would still stink. Indeed, would not the spectral turd that you propose present a greater inconvenience to the pedestrian, surely more likely to step unawares into your numinous ordure than into an excrescence which is in the common view and therefore may be walked around and so avoided?

JOHN CLARE: [*A pause, during which* CLARE *reconsiders.*] I'd not thought of that, and thus withdraw my speculation. [*Another pause, as* CLARE *worriedly contemplates invisible horse manure.*] Horse muck that cannot be seen. It is a horror, now I come to understand the implications. Why, there'd be a reeking foulness hidden from the cognizance of all, that never could be cleaned away, in which the purest of things might be inadvertently made filthy ...

HUSBAND: Celia, I promise you, there's nothing going on. Nothing that anybody else can see. You show me where there's something going on.

WIFE: I've got no need to see it. I can smell it. I can smell a rat. I can smell something fishy.

HUSBAND: Celia, listen to yourself. A fishy rat?

WIFE: [*She leans forward, staring hard and accusingly into his eyes.*] A fishy rat. Yes. That's the very thing that I can smell, even when someone's drenched it in cologne. A fishy rat, with hairy fins and scaly ears, that's got a great long pink worm of a tail to drag behind it through the dirty water. God, you ought to be ashamed.

HUSBAND: I'm not! I'm not ashamed! I haven't done a thing to be ashamed of! Why, my conscience is a pane of polished glass, without a streak of guilt or birdshit anywhere upon it. What is it that makes you think I'm guilty? Is there something guilty that I've said, or something guilty in my manner? Where is all this guilty, guilty, guilty coming from? Because it's getting on my nerves, and if it keeps up I shall lose my rag. How can I think straight with this noise? And how long is she going to keep on playing that same tune before it drives me mad?

WIFE: [*She stares at him, puzzled and then slightly worried.*] How long is ...? Johnny, she stopped playing nearly half an hour ago.

HUSBAND: [*He stares at her blankly.*] What, really?

WIFE: A good twenty minutes at the very least.

HUSBAND: [*He turns and stares into space, horrified and haunted.*] A half an hour. Or at least a good twenty minutes ...

WIFE: Split the difference. Call it twenty-five.

HUSBAND: Oh, God. [*They lapse into silence. The* HUSBAND *gazes, haunted, into the fog. His* WIFE *gazes at him for a few moments, mystified, and then looks away.*]

JOHN BUNYAN: [*After a respectful pause.*] Do you yourself have any notion what it is that vexes them?

JOHN CLARE: Neither the first, nor faintest. I imagine it would be a marital perplexity that's by and large opaque to the outsider, although having had two wives I am a man of more than ordinary experience. With my first wife Mary, who enjoyed the sweetest disposition, I was happy and there were no quarrels of the stripe we see enacted here. Our marriage bed was filled with harmony, and when I entered into her it was as though I entered into God's own meadow. With my second wife, with Patty, it was naught but baleful hints and dark recriminations, although she was very often good to me. Still, there were nights that she'd be jealous of the time I had with Mary, who was a much younger girl than Patty was herself. No, as you see, I am no stranger to the married life and its upheavals, though in truth I was not often with my family.

JOHN BUNYAN: Then there's another thing we hold in common, with our fore-names, mutual occupation and our current state of incorporeality. I too had family, from whom I was made separate by my confinement.

JOHN CLARE: [*Excitedly.*] You were confined? Why, so was I! It is as though we were reflections of each other! Where were you confined?

JOHN BUNYAN: In prison, for my preaching. And yourself?

JOHN CLARE: [*Suddenly vague and evasive.*] Oh ... it was in a hospital.

JOHN BUNYAN: [*Concerned.*] Then you were ailing in the flesh?

JOHN CLARE: Well ... no. Not really. Not the flesh. Mind you, I did once have a nasty limp.

JOHN BUNYAN: So, not the flesh. I see. [*From* OFF *there is the* SOUND *of the* CHURCH CLOCK, *striking once.*]

HUSBAND: It's like we've been here hours. Was that for half-past twelve or one o'clock, do you suppose?

WIFE: What does it matter? Who cares if it's half-past twelve or one o'clock? It's always going to be the same time from now on, as far as you're concerned. It's always going to be too late. Or who knows? It might be half-past too late. I couldn't say. [*They lapse into another hostile silence.*]

JOHN CLARE: What do you mean, you see?

JOHN BUNYAN: What?

JOHN CLARE: When I said that when confined to hospital I was not ailing in the flesh, you said "So, not the flesh. I see." What did you see?

JOHN BUNYAN: It was a turn of phrase. Think nothing of it.

JOHN CLARE: I will not think nothing of it, for it seems to me there was an implication, was there not?

JOHN BUNYAN: An implication?

JOHN CLARE: Ah, don't play the fool with me. I'm twice the idiot you'll ever be. You know full well the nature of the implication I refer to. You as good as said "If not the flesh, then what?" Deny it if you can.

JOHN BUNYAN: I'll not deny it. I had but supposed that you were deemed to be afflicted of the mind or spirit, and had been surprised that there were hospitals attending such affairs. Believe me when I say I did not seek to judge your clarity, or lack thereof.

JOHN CLARE: You did not seek to call me lunatic? There are those who would not be so restrained.

JOHN BUNYAN: I have myself been called the same, along with blasphemer and devil. It is ever thus, it seems, for any man who has a vision in his soul and dares to speak it, most especially if that should be a vision inconvenient to the wealthy or the ordinary run of things.

JOHN CLARE: That's it exactly! You have bound it in a nutshell. When there is a fear that some truth may be told, the teller is put under lock and key and called a criminal or else a madman. My own circumstances make it plain, for if even Lord Byron may be deemed insane, then why not any man? It is beyond my comprehension.

JOHN BUNYAN: [*A pause, during which* BUNYAN *gazes at* CLARE *with understanding and pity.*] And mine likewise. [*Another pause, thoughtful and reflective.*] Then there are still inequalities and prisons in this age of unseen horses, even. Am I to suppose the New Jerusalem did not arrive?

JOHN CLARE: I must confess I have not noticed it in this vicinity, although it may be that it turned up while I was confined and no one thought to tell me.

JOHN BUNYAN: [*He shakes his head, disappointed.*] If that were the case, then we should all be saints.

JOHN CLARE: Perhaps we are.

JOHN BUNYAN: That is a dismal summary.

JOHN CLARE: You're right. It is. That's worse than the invisible manure. I wish I'd never said it. [*He and* BUNYAN *lapse into a bleak silence.*]

HUSBAND: The lion shall lie down beside the lamb. That's in the Bible.

WIFE: Oh, and does the Bible say whether the lamb's still there to get up in the morning?

HUSBAND: Celia, I thought you liked the Bible.

WIFE: Lots of things are in the Bible, Johnny. Lots and lots and lots. And then their daughters. So, do you admit it, then? Did you lie down beside the lamb?

HUSBAND: I'm not a saint.

WIFE: Yes, you've already told us that. You're not a lion, either. And you're not a man. You're nothing but a snazzy creature that once ran a dance-band, and now you're not man enough to face the music.

HUSBAND: [*Startled.*] You said it had stopped.

WIFE: It has. [*A pause.*] What was it that the grass was whispering about?

HUSBAND: I don't know. Nothing. You know grass. It's always whispering. It's got nothing better to do. What does it know? It's grass, for heaven's sake.

WIFE: They say all flesh is grass.

HUSBAND: Well, not my flesh, it's not. Not me. I'm not grass.

WIFE: Yes you are. You're grass. Look at you. You're half-cut and gone to seed. And like all flesh, you'll have your season and you'll be mowed down. And then you'll have it on your conscience for eternity. The music, that'll still be playing. And the grass will still be whispering. [Beneath the portico behind them, SAMUEL BECKETT enters from OFF, LEFT. He notices the couple on the steps, but does not notice CLARE or BUNYAN in their alcoves. BECKETT wanders over to stand just behind the couple, looking down at them in puzzlement as they ignore him.]

HUSBAND: Eternity. God, there's a thought. All of that bloody whispering, for eternity.

BECKETT: Hello, now. How are things with you tonight?

WIFE: It's me shall have to put up with the whispering and all the tongues.

BECKETT: Tongues? I'm not sure I follow you.

HUSBAND: Oh, and that's my fault, is it?

BECKETT: I'm not saying that it's your fault, I'm just saying I don't follow you.

WIFE: Well, you're the one with all the secrets and the mysteries and the goings on.

BECKETT: Ah, that's a common thing, to say that I'm impenetrable.

HUSBAND: Oh, not that old tale again. Give it a rest with all of your long silences and all of that evasive and insinuating chatter you're so fond of. I'm fed up of it.

BECKETT: I'd have to say I don't think that you've understood contemporary drama.

JOHN CLARE: They can't hear you. We've been through all this already.

WIFE: I'm the one who's fed up of it.

BECKETT: [Startled, BECKETT wheels round to face CLARE and BUNYAN.] Who's that? What's all this about?

JOHN BUNYAN: Be not alarmed. My friend here has explained it to me. We, like you, are but departed shades, and living souls such as the pair upon the step can neither see nor hear us.

JOHN CLARE: I'd go further. I do not believe that they can smell us, either.

BECKETT: Departed shade? Don't you go telling me I'm dead. I haven't even got a cough. To my mind, it's more likely that this is a dream of some description.

JOHN BUNYAN: That is very like what I myself supposed, and yet I'm told that we are halfway through the twentieth century after our Lord and I myself beneath the turf more than two hundred years.

BECKETT: Two hundred years? Well, I'm all right, then. [BECKETT *looks around and gestures towards the surrounding town centre.*] All this looks like just after the war, whereas as far as I'm aware I'm sleeping in a hotel in the far from satisfying 1970s.

JOHN CLARE: A hotel! In the 1970s! I do not know which of these things is harder to imagine!

JOHN BUNYAN: Just after the war, you say? Was it another civil war?

BECKETT: A civil war? God, no. Is that the time that you yourself are from? This was a war with Germany, primarily; the second of two world wars that we had. They flattened London so the English firebombed Dresden, and then the Americans dropped something that you can't imagine on the Japanese, and then it was all over.

JOHN BUNYAN: [BUNYAN *also glances around at the surrounding town, his expression mournful.*] So, then, it would seem the nation's pilgrimage has taken it to just beyond the City of Destruction. By my calculations, that would make this place Vanity Fair.

BECKETT: You're quoting Bunyan at me, now?

JOHN CLARE: It's not like he can help it. He's John Bunyan. And I'm Byron.

JOHN BUNYAN: [*To* BECKETT.] Oh, don't listen to him. [*To* CLARE.] No you're not. You're making both of us look bad and not to be believed. You said yourself you were John Clare. Stick to your tale or we'll end up with everyone confused as you!

BECKETT: [BECKETT *laughs in amazement.*] John Bunyan. And John Clare. Well, now, this is a lively dream. I must book into this hotel again.

JOHN CLARE: [*Surprised and incredulous.*] John Clare. You've heard of him? You've heard of me?

BECKETT: Why, certainly. Being myself a writer, I'm familiar with the pair of you and have respect for your accomplishments. You, Mr. Clare, especially. In my day, you're remembered as the Peasant Poet, as perhaps the greatest lyric voice that England ever entertained and treated so unfairly, what with dying in the madhouse and the rest of it. [*A pause.*] You were aware of that, the dying in a madhouse? I hope I've not been insensitive in breaking it to you like that.

JOHN CLARE: Oh, I already knew about it. I was there around that time. But tell me, is my darling wife remembered also? Mary Clare, who once was Mary Joyce?

BECKETT: [BECKETT *regards* CLARE *with a serious and searching look.*] Ah, yes. Your first wife. Yes, yes, it's a well-known story, still discussed in literary circles.

JOHN CLARE: Then I'm glad. I should be sorry if I were remembered only for the madness.

JOHN BUNYAN: [*To* BECKETT.] You said that you were a writer also. Would yours be a name that we might know?

BECKETT: I shouldn't think that's likely. You'd both have been dead a while before I came along. I'm Samuel Beckett. You can call me Sam if I might know the pair of you as John. This is Northampton, isn't it? The portico of All Saints Church?

JOHN BUNYAN: I meant to ask what you were doing here. Both Mr. Clare here and myself were born nearby and so often had business here, while from your voice I'd guess that you're an Irishman. What is it brings you this way, either in posterity or, as you would prefer to have it, in your dreams?

BECKETT: Well, now, in the first instance that would be the cricket, and then later on it was to see a woman.

JOHN BUNYAN: Cricket?

JOHN CLARE: Oh, I'm well acquainted with the ins and outs of it. You ought to see it!

BECKETT: Sure, I played against Northampton at the County Ground. We stayed at the hotel next to the pitch, and on the night after the match my team mates were all of a mind to go out in pursuit of drink and prostitutes, the both of which this town has in abundance. I myself was more inclined to spend the evening in the company of old Northampton's Gothic churches, which are equally profuse. I would imagine that it is the memory of that night which brings me back here in my dreams, though I'll admit that you yourselves provide a novel element.

HUSBAND: All right! All right, I did it. Does that make you happy?

WIFE: [*Coldly, after a pause.*] Did it make you happy?

HUSBAND: [*Defiantly, after a moment of deliberation.*] Yes! Yes, it made me happy! It was wonderful and I was happier than I've ever been. [*Less confidently, following a pause.*] At least to start with.

BECKETT: What's all this that's going on? [BUNYAN *and* CLARE *glance at each other, then reluctantly stand up from their stone alcoves and walk slowly across to join* BECKETT *near the quarrelling couple.*]

JOHN CLARE: We're not entirely sure ourselves. If I were of a kind to make a wager, I'd suppose them to be quarrelling about some manner of an infidelity.

WIFE: And when was that?

HUSBAND: What? When was what?

WIFE: You said "At least to start with". When was it you started?

HUSBAND: Does it matter?

WIFE: Oh, you know it matters. You know very well it matters, with the goings on and when they started. Look me in the eye and tell me, now. When was it?

HUSBAND: [*Uncomfortably.*] Well, it was some time ago.

WIFE: Some time ago. How much? Was it two years ago?

HUSBAND: I don't remember. [*After a pause.*] No. It was longer ago than that.

WIFE: You filthy thing. You filthy creature. How old? How old was she when you started?

HUSBAND: [*Wretchedly.*] You know I'm no good with birthdays. [*The* WIFE *looks at her* HUSBAND *in anger and disgust before they both once more lapse into silence.*]

BECKETT: This looks very much to me as if the infidelity was with a younger woman. A young girl, you might say.

JOHN BUNYAN: And would that, in your time, make an awful difference to the matter? Are the infidelity and the adultery not by themselves sufficient to account for their unhappy state?

BECKETT: That would depend upon how young the other party was, exactly.

There are different customs these days than were in your own. They have a thing now that they call "age of consent" and if you mess about with it you're sure to be in trouble.

JOHN CLARE: [*Suddenly concerned.*] And how old would that be?

BECKETT: I think sixteen is around the usual mark. Why do you ask?

JOHN CLARE: [*Slightly evasively.*] No reason in particular. Being a poet I am naturally interested in the facts of things.

JOHN BUNYAN: [*After a pause.*] Well, I should be upon my way. The Earl of Peterborough will not wait forever to hand down his edict, and the path I'm on is hard and without ending. It has been instructive talking with you, and if I should wake tomorrow to my cell in Bedford you may be assured that all the curious things which we have said shall be a great amusement for me.

JOHN CLARE: I shall be right pleased to say I've met you, even if only in these ambiguous circumstances.

BECKETT: Yes, you take care. And between the two of us, what did you genuinely think to your man Cromwell?

JOHN BUNYAN: Ah, he was all right. [*Less confidently, following a pause.*] At least to start with. Yet despite his antinomian certainties, you may be sure that he was not a saint. Ah, well. I'll leave you to your entertainments in this borough of Mansoul. A good night to you, gentlemen. [BUNYAN *walks wearily off to* EXIT STAGE LEFT.]

JOHN CLARE: And to you.

BECKETT: Aye, mind how you go. [CLARE *and* BECKETT *watch* BUNYAN *depart, and then fall back to their contemplation of the couple sitting on the steps.*] Well, for a Roundhead, he seemed nice enough. What was your own impression?

JOHN CLARE: [*Slightly disappointed.*] I had thought him not so tall as he seemed in the illustrations. [*After a pause.*] So, you said that in your own day, I'm well thought of. Is it my Don Juan they like?

BECKETT: No, that was Byron. You're admired for all your writings, for the Shepherd's Calendar and desperate later pieces such as your "I Am" alike. The journal that you kept while on your walk from Essex is regarded as the most heart-breaking document in all of English letters, and with much justification.

JOHN CLARE: [*Amazed.*] Why, I'd thought it thrown away! So it's my hike that they remember, back from Matthew Allen's prison in the forest to my first wife Mary's house in Glinton. Ah, that was a rousing odyssey, you may be sure, with all of the heroic things I did and all the places that I went. [*A pause, during which* CLARE *frowns in puzzlement.*] How did it end, again? I don't recall …

BECKETT: Regarding that first wife of yours? Not well. When you got to her house, well, let's just say she wasn't in. By then you'd found what I suppose you'd call your second wife, though, Patty, and she ultimately had you put in the asylum on the Billing Road here, where you later died. I'm sorry to be blunt about it.

JOHN CLARE: No, it's all right. I remember now. I lived with Patty and our children for a while, in what's called Poet's Cottage out at Helpstone, but nobody could put up with me for long and so … you evidently know the rest of it. Mind, I do not blame Patty, though she always had a jealousy towards my first wife, who I loved the best.

HUSBAND: She was fifteen. She was fifteen when it all started, with the goings on. There. You can go and tell the police if that's what your intention is. I've got it off me chest.

WIFE: You'll never have it off your chest. Fifteen. And that's when it was wonderful, when you were at your happiest. Fifteen.

JOHN CLARE: Well, that's not all that young.

BECKETT: No?

HUSBAND: Yes! It made me happy! Just the smell, the taste of her, it was like morning in the garden! And the feeling, she was hardly like a heavy, solid thing at all and much more like a piece of down, or like a liquid. Celia, it was marvellous.

JOHN CLARE: Not in the broader scheme of things. Fifteen is not particularly young, considered from a wide perspective. Not out in the country.

WIFE: You disgust me. You're no better than an earwig, wriggling in the muck.

BECKETT: That's not a bad line. I'll remember that, though it'll more than likely sound like nonsense when I wake. That's often how it is.

HUSBAND: It wasn't all one-sided, Celia. That's all I'm saying.

JOHN CLARE: I'm beginning to have sympathy with him. Women bear grudges for no proper reason.

WIFE: Don't you speak another word. Don't you say anything to me.

BECKETT: I can't say I think that a fair appraisal. I've known women with a painful lot in life.

JOHN CLARE: That may be so, but in the main I stand by what I said. The life of a romantic man is never easy. Did you not say earlier that other than the cricket, you came here to see a woman?

BECKETT: That I did. And I will grant you that it was a woman of the difficult romantic kind, at least at first ... although it may be she was always in the painful category. These things are by no means easy to determine. It strikes me there could be a degree of overlap between the two varieties.

CLARE: It may be so. It may be this is usually the case. What was her name, your woman?

BECKETT: Oh, you wouldn't know her. She was born a great while after you'd passed on, some way into the 20th century. A Miss Joyce –

JOHN CLARE: [*Astounded, almost frightened.*] No, not her! Are you playing a cruel game with me? That is my Mary, Mary Joyce of Glinton ...

BECKETT: Ah, no. This would be another girl entirely that I'm speaking of, that is the daughter of James Joyce.

CLARE: [*Excitedly.*] Why, that was Mary's father's name! Surely your woman and my own first wife must be one and the same! How is she? Give me news of her.

BECKETT: [*Gently and sympathetically.*] No. No, it isn't her. The Miss Joyce I'm referring to is called Lucia. She was notable in Paris for her dancing in the 1920s, but was brought low by a difficulty in her reason. Sorry if I've let you down.

JOHN CLARE: [*Sighs heavily.*] Oh, it's my own fault. Being mad, you know, it's very self-indulgent. I should buck up and get on with things. [*A pause.*] What was she like, your personal Miss Joyce? Was she a young thing, like my own?

BECKETT: They all start out as young things, all of the Miss Joyces.

JOHN CLARE: Yes, that's true.

BECKETT: Mine was a very pretty girl, who was afflicted by the old strabismus in one eye which she perceived as having ruined her. You know women and the low esteem in which they often hold themselves.

JOHN CLARE: I do.

BECKETT: There was some trouble with her brother, I believe, when she was young that may have had connection with her later upset. Anyway, the upshot of it was that Lucia lost her marbles.

JOHN CLARE: [*Puzzled.*] I'm not sure I understand your turn of phrase.

BECKETT: She flipped her lid.

JOHN CLARE: No, I'm no nearer.

BECKETT: Away with the fairies.

JOHN CLARE: Ah! Ah, now, I think I have you. She would be what they call a hysteric?

BECKETT: Close enough. They sent her off to various sanatoriums and psychiatrists. You know the drill. At last she landed in Saint Andrew's Hospital along Northampton's Billing Road, where she remains at present.

JOHN CLARE: That's the place where I was kept, although they called it something different then.

BECKETT: The very same. The institution has an interesting literary pedigree.

JOHN CLARE: You know, I think I am acquainted with the girl you speak of. If it's who I'm thinking of, I had a romp with her off in the madhouse woods not long ago.

BECKETT: No, I'm afraid that's just your lunacy that's talking. Though it's true you were both settled at the same asylum you weren't congruent in the chronology of things. You hail from two entirely different periods.

JOHN CLARE: Why, you could say the same of you and me, yet here we are. No, this lass I refer to had dark hair and long legs, very little in the way of bubbies and a lazy eye.

BECKETT: I'll admit, that's very like her.

JOHN CLARE: Makes a lot of noise about it with the spending. Mind you, in my own ordeal I spent so hard that there were letters of the alphabet came fluttering from my ears.

BECKETT: Well, you've convinced me. That's Lucia to a T, although I'm mystified about the circumstances of your meeting. You would not be speaking metaphorically?

JOHN CLARE: I don't believe so, no.

BECKETT: Now that's a mystery. She didn't mention it to me when last I visited.

JOHN CLARE: It may be that she was embarrassed. I am not myself what you might call presentable, and I had the impression she was of the better type.

BECKETT: That may be so. She might have thought you were beneath her.

JOHN CLARE: Well, then she'd be right. That was exactly the configuration of our bout.

BECKETT: Leave off with it. You're getting on my nerves now.

JOHN CLARE: Then I'll beg your pardon. You have feelings for her still yourself?

BECKETT: Not of a carnal nature, no, though once I did. If I am to be truthful, back in those days it was only carnal feelings that I had, though that was not her understanding of the matter. Presently I go to visit her as often as I can. I love her in a way, but not the way she wants. I don't know why I go so much, to be completely honest.

JOHN CLARE: Could it be you pity her?

BECKETT: No, I don't think that that's entirely it. She's happy in her own way. It might very well be that she's happier than me. In fact, I would have difficulty in believing it were otherwise, so, no, it isn't pity. I suppose I feel I owe her something. When I met her I was callous and I couldn't bring myself to see that she was drowning. I could have done more, that's all I'm saying. Or I could have done less. One way or the other. It's too late now.

JOHN CLARE: So it's guilt, then?

BECKETT: I expect it is. I often find it's guilt that's at the bottom of a thing.

JOHN CLARE: I tend to share that point of view myself.

WIFE: What did you mean, it wasn't all one-sided?

HUSBAND: I thought that you didn't want me speaking to you.

WIFE: Don't be clever. You're not clever, Johnny. The last thing you are is clever. Tell me what you meant when you said that it wasn't all one-sided.

HUSBAND: I meant it was a duet. It was a tango. Flanagan and Allen. It was something that took two is what I'm saying to you. Why must you be all the while so dense?

WIFE: So it was something that she wanted, that's the gist of it?

HUSBAND: It is! That is the very crux of things, the fulcrum of the subject: it was something that she wanted.

WIFE: Oh, well, that's all right then, I suppose.

HUSBAND: [*Sighs, relieved.*] I knew that you'd come round.

WIFE: How did you know?

HUSBAND: That you'd come round? Oh, well, I know you can't stay angry with me very long ...

WIFE: [*Slowly and deliberately.*] How did you know that it was something that she wanted? Is that what she told you? Did she say "It's something that I want"?

HUSBAND: Not in as many words, no. No, she didn't. But ...

WIFE: Well, what words did she use, then? What words did she use when she told you that it was something that she wanted?

HUSBAND: Well, it wasn't words as such. She didn't tell me through the medium of words.

WIFE: [*Increasingly angry.*] Well, what? Interpretive dance, was it? Did she mime it for you?

HUSBAND: [*Sounding trapped and uncomfortable.*] It was signals.

WIFE: Signals?

HUSBAND: Little signals. You know what it's like, how women are.

WIFE: I'm not sure that I do.

HUSBAND: The signals they give out. The little looks and glances, all of that. She was forever smiling at me, cuddling up to me and telling me she loved me ...

WIFE: [*Horrified, shouting in rage.*] Well, of course she was! Of course she'd do that! Johnny, you're her father!

BECKETT: Ah, Christ. There you have it.

HUSBAND: But ... I mean, I hadn't thought of that. It isn't what I'm used to. If a girl, a woman, if she looks at you a certain way. I mean, you know our Audrey, what she's like ...

WIFE: [*Furious, in helpless tears.*] I don't! I don't know what our Audrey's like, or not how you do, anyway! You tell me, Johnny. Tell me what she's like. Come on, now, it'll be a bit of fun. I know: the first time, did it make her cry?

JOHN CLARE: This is a horror. I had not expected this.

HUSBAND: Celia ...

WIFE: Tell me, Johnny. Tell me what our Audrey's like to be in bed with. Did it make her cry? Was she a virgin, Johnny? Was she? And what did you do about the sheets? [*The* HUSBAND *looks at his* WIFE, *haunted, but simply moves his mouth like a fish and cannot answer her. Eventually he looks away and stares bleakly into space. His* WIFE *sinks her head in her hands, perhaps weeping silently. While* CLARE *and* BECKETT *are still staring in mute horror at the seated couple,* THOMAS BECKET ENTERS LEFT *and wanders slowly over to join them. They regard him with silent bewilderment. He looks at the haunted couple, then looks at* CLARE *and* BECKETT.]

THOMAS BECKET: Pray, has some great catastrophe befallen them?

BECKETT: It has.

THOMAS BECKET: And can you not console them?

JOHN CLARE: They can't hear us.

THOMAS BECKET: They are deaf?

BECKETT: No, they're alive. The rest of us are either dead or dreaming, or that's how I understand it. Who might you be?

THOMAS BECKET: I am Becket.

BECKETT: I'll be candid with you: that's an answer I was not anticipating. I myself am Beckett.

THOMAS BECKET: You are Thomas Becket?

BECKETT: No, I'm Samuel Beckett. This is John Clare. [*A pause.*] Wait a minute, now, did you say you were Thomas Becket?

THOMAS BECKET: Thomas Becket, Canterbury's archbishop. Yes, you have me now. What is the stuff you say about me being dead? For all I know I am come here to see the King who is at Hamtun's castle, that we might be reconciled.

JOHN CLARE: Take it from me, you're dead all right. Affairs go badly for you at the castle and you skip away to France for a few years. When you come back what happens is you're down at your cathedral, and ...

BECKETT: We don't need to go into all the ins and outs of it.

JOHN CLARE: Although reportedly there were a lot of them, the ins and outs ...

BECKETT: [*To* CLARE.] Enough of that. Enough of it. [*To* BECKET] The thing that you should bear in mind is not the brute mechanics of the matter, but its outcome.

THOMAS BECKET: [*Worried.*] There were brute mechanics?

JOHN CLARE: Ins and outs.

BECKETT: I've said already that it's not a thing to dwell upon. Forget about all that. The salient point in all of this is that you were discovered to be incorruptible. That would explain the business with the sainthood which was latterly bestowed upon you. You're the first one that I've met and I'm not sure what I should make of it.

THOMAS BECKET: Oh, God. Then I am to be martyred?

JOHN CLARE: I'm afraid it is old news. It's getting on eight hundred years ago, all that.

BECKETT: [*Angrily.*] Look! [*More softly, startled by his own outburst.*] Look, all that I mean to say is you were made a saint, and that's the long and short of it. Surely the very fact outweighs those means by which you came to be in that condition. I'd have thought you would be pleased about it.

THOMAS BECKET: Pleased? To have been burned, or broken on a wheel?

JOHN CLARE: Oh, that's not so. No, you were only chopped about a bit, as I was told.

THOMAS BECKET: Ah, no, don't tell me anymore.

BECKETT: [*To* CLARE.] Quite frankly, you're not helping. [*To* BECKET] Is it not a comfort, then, the saintliness of your appointment?

THOMAS BECKET: [*Very upset.*] Does it seem to you that I am comforted? You tell me I am made a saint, and yet where am I?

JOHN CLARE: Why, that's nothing but geography. There's no theology about it. You are underneath the portico of All Saint's Church here in Northampton and it's halfway through the century after the one I died in, making it the twentieth. I'm informed that a great war with the Germans has been recently concluded in our favour.

BECKETT: No, it's not the Great War that's been recently concluded. That was some time earlier, although the Germans were involved in it so you can be forgiven your confusion. We only referred to it as the Great War because we didn't know that there was going to be another one.

JOHN CLARE: A greater one?

BECKETT: I think a lot of that depends on your perspective.

THOMAS BECKET: [*Exasperated.*] All I meant by asking where I am, if I'm a saint, is that I do not seem to be in Heaven.

BECKETT: No. I'll own, it doesn't look much like it.

THOMAS BECKET: Yet nor is it the unending fire of Heaven's opposite.

JOHN CLARE: Oh, no. It's nothing near as bad as that.

THOMAS BECKET: Am I then to suppose that this is purgatory, this grey place where phantoms wander lost and make their aimless discourse, caught here for all time?

HUSBAND: [*Bleakly, still staring into space.*] I threw them out, and I got new ones.

WIFE: [*The* WIFE *looks up at her* HUSBAND *uncomprehendingly.*] What?

HUSBAND: The sheets. I threw them out, and I got new ones. And I turned the mattress over.

BECKETT: [*To* THOMAS BECKET.] What you've just said, I think that you might be very near the mark.

WIFE: [*She looks at her* HUSBAND, *shaking her head in incredulous disgust.*] That's you. That's you forever, in your vest and sweating, trying to turn the mattress over, trying to cover all your stains. And was she watching while you did that? Was she sitting there and watching?

HUSBAND: She were crying.

WIFE: There. What did I say?

HUSBAND: [*Hopelessly.*] I thought, you know. I thought that it were all of the emotions she was having that had made her weepy.

WIFE: Oh, I dare say. I dare say it was. All the emotions. While she watched her father try to hide her blood because he was so proud of what he'd done.

HUSBAND: [*As if understanding what he's done for the first time.*] Oh, God. [*After a pause, there is the* SOUND *from* OFF *of the* CHURCH CLOCK, STRIKING ONCE.] Is that … is that one o'clock, and it was half past twelve before, or is that half past one, and …

WIFE: [*Explosively, at her wits end.*] Oh, shut up! Shut up! Shut up with everything! It's always the same time! We can't move on from this! We're stuck here on these steps, this night, over and over! [*The* WIFE *starts to weep again. Her* HUSBAND *also sinks his head in his hands.*]

THOMAS BECKET: [*Downcast and resigned.*] Purgatory, then. But you say they are yet alive?

BECKETT: Again, I think a lot of that depends on your perspective. They're alive here, in their time, as we are in our own. One way of looking at things, everybody's dead and always has been. Like your woman here was saying, we're all stuck. Perhaps we have it all, the good and bad, over and over. Wouldn't that be all the Heaven and the Hell of it, how everyone was threatened by their pastors?

THOMAS BECKET: I find that a fearful ideology. I had dared hope for better.

JOHN CLARE: I'd feared worse! If it meant I should have my first wife Mary by my side again, then the travails of life should be as nothing and that by itself should be my Heaven.

BECKETT: I'm not saying I believe it. It's just something I've had put to me. The father of the girl I talked about, James Joyce, I can recall him telling me about his fondness for Ouspensky's notion of what I suppose you'd call a grand recurrence. It had had some bearing upon the eternal day in Dublin that was circumnavigated variously in his greatest novels.

THOMAS BECKET: More and more I hope this to be an outlandish dream and, wishing you no disrespect, the pair of you but figments. It may be this is a night-start after all, born of my apprehensions that I have given the King offence, one that our erstwhile friendship shall not mitigate.

BECKETT: Well, I'll confess to the same thought myself initially. A dream of some kind would be the most reasonable explanation, although since I don't subscribe to the interpretations of Professor Freud, I can't see why I should be dreaming about all this wretched and incestuous back-and-forth. And that's before I try to fathom how a load of saints and writers that I haven't thought about in years fit into the arrangement. It's a mighty puzzle, and I can't say I'm enjoying it.

THOMAS BECKET: [*Looking at couple on steps.*] That is the sin that binds them in their disagreement, then? The man has lain down with his daughter?

JOHN CLARE: In the countryside there's more of it than you'd imagine.

BECKETT: Even in the towns, I wouldn't say they did so bad. The woman I was talking of, Lucia, there were those who reckoned it was much the same thing that commenced her acting up, all of the incest and the rest of it.

JOHN CLARE: [*Shocked.*] Her father, that you said was called James Joyce as was my Mary's, he'd been guilty of the same offence?

BECKETT: Oh, no, not him. He worshipped her. She was the one he wrote for, and about. He might have thought about her in that fashion, I suppose, but if he did he only tried to touch her with his writing, fingering her with a sentence here or there, a feel of tit concealed within a subtext. No, the culprit in a physical regard, if that was anyone, my guess is that it might have been her brother.

THOMAS BECKET: In my day that would be thought as much a sin … at least in open conversation. Privately, I am convinced that there is nowhere it does not go on.

JOHN CLARE: Though I will own it is a grievous matter, I've known many that have sported with a brother or a sister and there's been no great harm come of it.

BECKETT: Well, Lucia was very young when this occurred, now, if occur it did.

JOHN CLARE: But we have said before that your own views upon what is a proper age may not be those appropriate to earlier times.

BECKETT: If I'm right, Lucia would have been ten.

THOMAS BECKET: Unless we speak of Royalty that is an age that even in my times would be thought young.

JOHN CLARE: [*Somewhat sheepishly.*] Is that a fact? Well, yes, I can see that it would compound the incest.

THOMAS BECKET: Of the sins I would remark it is not, evidently, thought a deadly one, and in my readings of the Holy Bible I have found it something of an ambiguity.

BECKETT: I'd eat my hat if it were not adversely mentioned somewhere in Leviticus.

THOMAS BECKET: That is undoubtedly the truth, but what of the unusual dispensation granted unto Lot after he and his daughters have escaped the Cities of the Plain?

BECKETT: I had assumed that, as a man, God had felt bad about turning the poor chap's wife to salt. He'd very possibly felt he owed your man Lot a favour and had thought it was the least that he could do, to look the other way for once.

THOMAS BECKET: It's an unusual interpretation, but …

JOHN CLARE: You know, I've always found Eden a puzzle that would suit your argument.

BECKETT: What are you going on about?

JOHN CLARE: Well, Cain and Abel. I'd have thought it would be obvious that even if the Lord had granted Eve and Adam one of each sort rather than two boys, improper love within the family must surely have been unavoidable. More so in Eden than in, say, Green's Norton, unless there is something I have not considered. It might be that what undid your woman friend and the poor child that is the issue of this sorry pair alike is something that is part of our condition since our origins there in God's garden.

BECKETT: Eden. Well, you see, there has been some dispute about that place.

THOMAS BECKET: Dispute? What manner of dispute? I have not heard of one.

BECKETT: Ah, well, I don't want to get into it. There's those who say that Genesis was written a lot later than some of the other books and only got put at the start through a misunderstanding in the order of the compilation. Otherwise, it's hard to see how there could be a populated Land of Nod for Cain to serve his exile in, incest or not.

THOMAS BECKET: And I had thought your news of my impending martyrdom this dream's most hitherto disquieting aspect. I am hopeful that I will forget all this upon my wakening, and am distressed to think I have such blasphemies in even my unbidden thoughts.

BECKETT: It's not my wish to be upsetting you. You're someone that I have admired, and I would not have all my conversation with a saint be taken up by what befell Miss Joyce when she was ten.

JOHN CLARE: [Suddenly, in a strangled, anguished voice.] It was an act of matrimony!

BECKETT: [Puzzled.] What? The business with her brother? How do you make that out?

JOHN CLARE: [Momentarily disoriented, then regaining his composure.] How do I ... oh! It's your Miss Joyce you're speaking of. Pay no attention to my lunatic outpourings. They are less than chaff. I do not know what I am saying half the time. [A pause, while he attempts to find a safe direction for the conversation.] You must have a great fondness for her, for your friend, to visit her in her adversity.

BECKETT: She was a lovely, well-intentioned girl and filled with energy and light much as her name suggests. The things she said were funny and were clever if she took the trouble not to get too convoluted. She was what you'd call a dancer in a million, and the way that she impersonated Charlie Chaplin was a treat, although I don't expect you'll be familiar with his work.

THOMAS BECKET: I do not think it is a name I know.

JOHN CLARE: I have known various Charlies, but no Chaplins I can think of. What was he like in his manner, that your woman friend made an impersonation of?

BECKETT: He had a walk to him and a moustache, a way he moved his eyebrows and the like. Lucia could do all of that. His art was in the pathos he inspired for the unfortunate or common man, the footsore wayfarer much like yourself but in a time of longer railway lines and higher buildings. He'd make you feel for the great injustices there are in life then make you laugh for all the triumphs of the individual. I do not suppose that he was necessarily a happy man. I can remember reading something by the filmmaker Jean Cocteau ... no, don't ask, it's far too complicated ... where he mentioned Chaplin saying words to the effect that his life's greatest sadness was the fact he'd gotten rich off playing someone who was poor.

JOHN CLARE: It is the guilt that we were speaking of again, though if my greatest sadness were that I was rich I do not think I should be sad at all.

THOMAS BECKET: It may be that the sorrows of the wealthy life are naught save more expensive ones. It sometimes is as if my king and the companion of my boyhood is made heavy by the weight of gold that's in his heart.

BECKETT: Well, if it's guilt you're after then your royal pal would take some beating. In fact, now I come to think of it that is exactly what he took. The mess he made of things with you, Rome set him to be flogged for penitence and this despite him being king. From what I hear he kneeled there and he took it, too. He must have known he was deserving of his punishment.

THOMAS BECKET: The king was flogged, and he submitted to it?

BECKETT: That he did. It's a well known occurrence. It was after exhumation when you were discovered to be incorruptible, that was what settled it. In my opinion he was lucky to get off with just the flogging.

JOHN CLARE: I'd have made him get down on his knees and stay there till he'd scrubbed up the cathedral floor. He'd still be there now.

THOMAS BECKET: [*Horrified.*] He was flogged. The king was flogged. Because of what he'd done to me.

BECKETT: That is the substance of it. No one thought he was judged harshly, put it that way.

THOMAS BECKET: But if he were treated so, then what must he have – ?

BECKETT: You don't want the details.

JOHN CLARE: All the ins and outs. No, I agree.

BECKETT: You're better off without them. There's no benefit in fretting needlessly.

THOMAS BECKET: [*Grumpy and resentful.*] No. No, there isn't. For that matter, I don't see that you were under a compulsion to be mentioning this business in the first place.

BECKETT: I would hate to think I'd tried your patience to the point where it became proverbial.

THOMAS BECKET: To try my patience is the least of it, when you have sought to undercut my faith itself with your sophistications.

BECKETT: I've sought no such thing.

THOMAS BECKET: Yet you speak dismissively of Eden and of our first parents, you insinuate a love between Eve and her sons that is unspeakable, and you insist that here about us is the twentieth century of Our Lord and still God has not come?

JOHN CLARE: Yes, Mr. Bunyan who we spoke to a short while since raised a similar complaint regarding the ongoing absence of Jerusalem.

BECKETT: [*To* THOMAS BECKET.] He never comes. That's my own understanding of the matter. Or at least, He's not about when you've a need of Him, much in the style of a policeman.

JOHN CLARE: There's a phrase that I have heard in these parts. Now, what is it? It has something of the meaning of "policeman", but there is a connotation of the tithing man or rent-man there into the bargain. I cannot recall it at this moment but it's possible that it will come to me.

THOMAS BECKET: [*To* SAMUEL BECKETT.] If as you say He never comes, can you be certain He is truly there?

BECKETT: I would imagine that is where the faith comes into it. For my own purposes I like to think His non-arrival is not necessarily an indication of His non-existence.

THOMAS BECKET: But He does not speak to you?

BECKETT: It isn't a great matter of importance if He does or not. There's lots of people who don't speak to me, or who I never see, but I don't have a problem about if they're there or not. It's not like I feel snubbed or anything.

THOMAS BECKET: But if you never hear His voice …

BECKETT: Sometimes it seems that there's a certain quality to the long periods of silence.

THOMAS BECKET: Is there?

BECKETT: I believe so. [CLARE, BECKETT *and* THOMAS BECKET *lapse into a thoughtful silence. There is a long pause.*]

HUSBAND: I did all of it. I did the lot of what you said. I'm all of what you called me. [*Pause.*] But you knew.

WIFE: [*Turning to regard him contemptuously.*] What are you going on about?

HUSBAND: I'm saying that you knew.

WIFE: Knew what?

HUSBAND: About the goings on.

JOHN CLARE: The ins and outs. That's what he means.

WIFE: The goings on? You're saying that I knew about them?

HUSBAND: All along. That's what I'm saying.

WIFE: Oh, how dare you? How dare you sit there and say I knew about the goings on? If I'd have known about the goings on then I'd have stopped them there and then. They wouldn't have been going on at all.

HUSBAND: You knew. You looked the other way.

WIFE: The other way?

HUSBAND: Deliberately. You know you did. It was convenient.

WIFE: [*Guardedly.*] Convenient? I don't know what you mean by that.

HUSBAND: Celia, yes you do. You know the whole of what I mean by it. We've hardly touched each other in this last twelve years of marriage. Or had you not noticed?

WIFE: That's just normal. That's how everybody is. The thing with you is you're sex mad, trying it on every five minutes and not bothered if the other party feels like it or not.

HUSBAND: You never felt like it, not every five months, let alone five minutes. And when I stopped bothering you, when I stopped trying it on, did you really believe that I'd lost interest too? That I'd stopped having feelings of that nature just because that's how it were with you?

WIFE: I ... I suppose that I assumed you'd made other arrangements. That you had resorted to a dirty book or something.

HUSBAND: Oh, and what would something be? Would it be an affair outside of marriage, knocking off the barmaid round at the Black Lion, something of that nature?

WIFE: [*Appalled.*] Oh God, Johnny, tell me that you didn't. Not with that Joan Tanner. Everyone would know! What would they think? What would they think of me?

HUSBAND: Don't be so daft. Of course I didn't. I knew that you wouldn't want that, everybody knowing.

WIFE: [*Relieved.*] Oh, thank God. Of course I'd not want anybody knowing. If you're going to do a bloody stupid thing like that, then you should ...

HUSBAND: Keep it to meself?

WIFE: [*Uncertainly.*] Well ... yes.

HUSBAND: Keep it indoors?

WIFE: Yes, I suppose so.

HUSBAND: Keep it in the family? [*The* WIFE *stares at her* HUSBAND *in silence for a few moments, realising her own unacknowledged complicity, then turns from him to stare into space with a haunted expression. The* HUSBAND *looks away, down and to one side.*]

BECKETT: Well, it's a fair point. In my own experience, I think it very rare a woman doesn't know what's going on in her own home, even if she'd prefer she didn't. In the case of Miss Joyce that I mentioned earlier, the trouble that she may have had when she was ten, if that was what occurred I can't imagine Nora – that was Lucia's mother – I cannot imagine that she would not know of it. I think that very often women are more adept at the managing of a whole spider's nest of secrets than most men would have within their capability.

JOHN CLARE: I'm still not utterly convinced in my own heart that ten's too young.

THOMAS BECKET: The victim's age, I think, has no material bearing on the sin, nor on its gravity. They are condemned, these wretched creatures, to unending misery, sat here on these hard and unyielding steps awaiting absolution that shall not arrive.

BECKETT: They're damned then, and beyond the reach of mercy or forgiveness. You appear to be quite certain of the fact.

THOMAS BECKET: The husband has made rut with his own child, one of these little ones that God has said we should not harm. It seems the wife has tacitly consented to the ruinous liaison, with a blameless innocent thus doubly betrayed. I cannot think a just Creator might extend his mercy to those who have never thought to exercise that quality themselves.

BECKETT: Well, you being a saint it follows that you would be an authority on such concerns.

JOHN CLARE: Look, now, when God was speaking of these little ones, did he specifically say they were ten? That's all I'm getting at.

BECKETT: [Ignoring CLARE.] It seems to me that though the sex of it is very likely woeful and unpleasant, it would still be the betrayal that's the main thing. With Lucia, when the brother that she thought had loved her more than physically announced that he'd be getting married to an older woman very like his mam, that's when she started acting up and throwing chairs about. I think it was her brother first suggested she be given psychiatric treatment somewhere, and you might suppose it was because he didn't want her saying anything that could not be conveniently dismissed as ravings. That, at least, was how it looked to me, and Nora, pretty quickly she fell in with it. Lucia hadn't been what you might call her favourite child, even before the hurling furniture commenced. They said Lucia was what they called a schizophrenic, although if you ask me it was more that she was young and spoiled and couldn't cope with disappointment easily. She thought that she was justified in her behaviour. She felt immune because of who she was and never dreamed she could end up stuck in an institution, as in fact turned out to be the case.

JOHN CLARE: Well, to be fair, that manner of confinement is a thing that very few of us have properly anticipated or have made allowance for. The general measure of it is, it's always a surprise. One moment you're Lord Byron and the next you're in a morning room that's full of idiots eating porridge.

THOMAS BECKET: And you said yourself that I'm to quit Northampton and make off for France where it would seem to me that I'm to be in exile, a confinement I was not anticipating.

JOHN CLARE: From what I heard, in the dead of night you made off through a breach was in the castle wall, and then went out the north gate of the town, what's up there at the end of Sheep Street just past where the old round church is.

THOMAS BECKET: Aye, I know it.

JOHN CLARE: It appears that you went out the gate and rode off to the north, so they should think that was where you were headed, then you doubled back and made away down south to Dover and from there across to France.

THOMAS BECKET: That seems a cautious and a clever thing to do. I shall remember it when I awake.

BECKETT: Yes, I thought that about a line of dialogue that the wife here spoke not half an hour ago, but I have already forgotten it. It strikes me it was something about earwigs.

JOHN CLARE: [*To* THOMAS BECKET.] There is some controversy about the route you took on your escape. It is a common tale that in your leaving of Northampton you made halt to take a drink from the stone well that's down by Beckett's Park. But if indeed you left by the north gate then that would not seem likely.

THOMAS BECKET: That is answered easily enough. I know the well you mean and took a drink there where I next went into Hamtun by its Dern gate. It was in the coming to the town and not the leaving of it but apart from that the tale is true enough, although it seems a thing of little consequence. I am more taken with the thought that there should be a park named for me.

JOHN CLARE: Well, again, there's some controversy. Although there is the story of the well, the park's name has two Ts upon the end of it, unlike your own, and so may not be named for you at all.

BECKETT: Two Ts? Well, there's a thing. I don't suppose that it could be named after me at all?

JOHN CLARE: The way that I was told, it is a lady benefactor to the town gave the park her name, rather than either of you gentlemen. The stuff about the well is possibly no more than a coincidence. Although now that I come to think about it, I believe the well is likewise spelled with two Ts at the end of it, though that is likely no more than abiding local ignorance and clumsiness with words in their correct expression. I hope that I haven't let you down with what I've said.

THOMAS BECKET: [*Sounding disappointed.*] Let down? No, I wouldn't say ... no, not let down. It would be a vain man indeed who was let down by such a thing, and have you not already said that I shall be a saint? No. Not let down. Why should I be?

BECKETT: [*Sounding similarly disappointed.*] Me neither. I had made my comment in the manner of a joke, when the plain truth is that it makes no difference if a park were named for me or not. It's all the same as far as I'm concerned. To have a park named after you would seem to be a vulgar and a common thing, such as the many parks that bear the name Victoria.

JOHN CLARE: Ah, yes. My pretty little daughter. Have you heard much news about her? How's she getting on with life?

BECKETT: Dear God, not all this nonsense just when I thought we were done with it. I can't be bothered with it anymore. And to be frank I'm not expecting much more out of this pair either. I've a feeling that they've pretty much exhausted what they had by way of conversation.

THOMAS BECKET: There I must agree. They sit half-dazed amid a sorry wreckage of their own accomplishment and neither seek atonement nor can have an expectation of redemption. It is a drear tale too often told and like you I am wearied with it. And besides, if what you've told to me is true I have my own drear tale to make a way through. I think I may carry on in that direction [THOMAS BECKET *points towards the audience, as if at an off-stage street*] to the castle where my former playmate waits for me.

BECKETT: Aye, I might join you. I was planning to walk down that way myself and take a look at old Saint Peter's Church, the way I first did when I came here for the cricket.

THOMAS BECKET: It is a fine building of the old kind and I know it well. I must say that I am surprised to hear it is still standing, getting on a thousand years since. Has it fallen to neglect? Are all the horrible grotesques that I recall still grimacing from out the stonework?

JOHN CLARE: There's a few have fallen off or been knocked down across the years, but the majority are still in place. So, both of you are off, then? I cannot persuade you to remain and keep me company so that I shall have someone who can hear me that I can converse with?

BECKETT: I apologise, but no, I cannot be persuaded. It has been a pleasure of a kind to meet with you, for all of your wild fancies and your tale of having impudently bedded Lucia. I should not mind if I met you again, although I must admit I say that in the expectation that it will be not be the case.

JOHN CLARE: For my part I'll be sorry to be left here on my own, but as a consequence of my insanity I will no doubt have soon forgotten you were ever here, or will have otherwise become convinced of your delusory nature as with my first w– as with some other comical misapprehensions that I may have had. I've found you likeable enough, the pair of you, but must remark that you are very similar, both in the spelling of your names, and in the fact that I have thought the two of you to be quite grim.

BECKETT: You are not grim yourself, at all?

JOHN CLARE: No. I partake in a great deal of unproductive melancholy, but I don't think I've the courage to be grim. Bleak sometimes, possibly, but not what you'd call grim. I've not the stomach for it.

THOMAS BECKET: [*Kindly and sympathetically.*] Will you not accompany us to the church? I should not like to think that we had left you by yourself.

BECKETT: [*Aside, quietly exasperated.*] Oh, that's just great!

JOHN CLARE: [*To* THOMAS BECKET.] No, thank you for your offer, but I think I shall stay here awhile. I am not sure these two are finished their debate, and am yet hopeful there shall be some poetry to its conclusion. Though not very hopeful. I am after all by nature a realistic man, at least in my descriptions, for all that they say I am romantic or am otherwise a fool. The pair of you enjoy your evening, now, and leave me to enjoy my own. Good luck to you, especially to you, Saint Thomas, and congratulations on avoiding the decomposition.

THOMAS BECKET: Hm. Yes, well, thank you … though I cannot think in all humility that it was through some effort on my own part.

BECKETT: Aye, good luck to you as well. Remember that John Clare was a much better poet than Lord Byron. That should keep you straight. Farewell, now. [SAMUEL BECKETT *and* THOMAS BECKET *stroll away towards* STAGE RIGHT, *talking as they go.*] So, the being canonised and all of that. Had you no inkling of miraculous abilities prior to the business of not rotting?

THOMAS BECKET: Not that I recall. I had a certain fluency of penmanship, but I myself did not think it miraculous. And for your own part, you are still acquainted with the Holy Church?

BECKETT: Well, I'll not lie. We've had our ups and downs … [*They* EXIT

RIGHT. JOHN CLARE *stands in place and follows them with his eyes, first tracking away to* STAGE RIGHT, *then turning his head slowly until he is peering out over the audience. There is a long pause as he waits to be sure they are too far off to hear.*]

JOHN CLARE: I still say that I had your lady friend. The lexicon came out my ears as though it were a sperm of language. It was an encounter I found bracing, and I don't regret it. [CLARE *stands where he is a moment or two longer, idly gazing at the unresponsive* HUSBAND *and* WIFE. *When they do not move or speak, he sadly and resignedly turns to shuffle back towards his alcove at the* CENTRE/RIGHT REAR *of the* STAGE, *where he sits down, staring mournfully at the motionless couple in the foreground. After a few moments more there is the* SOUND *from* OFF *of the* CHURCH CLOCK STRIKING ONCE. *Sitting on their step, the* WIFE *looks up at this as if appalled, while the* HUSBAND *does not react.*]

WIFE: It's still one o'clock. How can it still be one o'clock? Why is it always one o'clock?

HUSBAND: [*Unsympathetically.*] You said yourself, it's too late from now on. It's always half past nothing to be done.

WIFE: But that was you. You were the one who brought this down upon us. Why is it still one o'clock for me?

HUSBAND: Because you were as much a part of them as I was, all the goings on. And that's the thing I've learned with goings on. They go on. They continue. Nothing's ever done with.

WIFE: [*After a horrified pause, as she reflects on this.*] Is this hell? Johnny, have we gone to hell?

HUSBAND: [*Wearily, not looking at her.*] Celia, I don't know.

JOHN CLARE: We talked about that earlier, and we thought purgatory to be the greater likelihood. Not that I'm claiming any great authority upon the subject. [*A pause.*] You can't hear me. What's the point of any of it? [*Along with the* HUSBAND *and* WIFE, CLARE *lapses into a gloomy silence. After a few moments a* HALF-CASTE WOMAN ENTERS STAGE LEFT *beneath the portico. After a few steps she stops and appraises the scene, looking first at the couple on the steps and then at* JOHN CLARE *sitting in his alcove.*]

WOMAN: You're the poet, ain't yer? You're John Clare.

JOHN CLARE: [*Surprised.*] I am? You're sure of it? Not Byron or King William?

WOMAN: [*Kindly and sympathetically.*] No, love. You're John Clare. From what I heard, it's just you get a bit mixed up from time to time.

JOHN CLARE: That's true. I do. And you don't find it off-putting?

WOMAN: No. To be honest, darling, when I heard about you, I thought that you sounded like a laugh. And some of what you wrote, it's lovely. Is that true, about you walking eighty miles back here after you'd legged it from a nut house down in Essex?

JOHN CLARE: Nut house?

WOMAN: Yeah, you know. The funny farm. Napoleon factory. Laughing academy. The loony bin.

JOHN CLARE: [*Laughing, amused and delighted.*] Oh, you mean the coney hatch. You should have said. Yes, that was where I was. You seem to know a lot about me.

WOMAN: Oh, I know about all sorts of things. You know, it's really nice to meet you, Mr. Clare. I'm well pleased.

JOHN CLARE: Well, it's mutual. What's your name, lass?

WOMAN: Everybody calls me Kaph.

JOHN CLARE: Kath?

WOMAN: Kaph. K-A-P-H. It's got a P in it.

JOHN CLARE: That's an unusual name, all right. And which parts of Northampton and eternity would you be from?

WOMAN: Spring Boroughs, 1988 to 2060. Mostly I worked down at the Saint Peter's annexe, next door to the church, trying to sort out all the refugees come from the east.

JOHN CLARE: The east of India?

WOMAN: Of Anglia. Yarmouth and round there. We get a fair bit of trouble with the weather in the time I'm from.

JOHN CLARE: Aye, well, 'twas ever thus in England.

WOMAN: No it wasn't, sweetheart. Trust me. Not like this it wasn't. It's all falling in the sea, love, and when you've got all the people moving then they bring their problems with them, and their problems are all that much worse. Drugs and diseases, violence and abuse and all the mental problems that come with 'em. When I was down at the annexe I come up with an idea for processing –

that means, like, sorting out – big crowds of people who were caught up in emergencies. It wasn't anything that clever. It was just this questionnaire, done as an app, and it was only common sense from what I'd seen while I was working with the refugees. Anyway, it got took up across the world and saved a lot of lives, apparently.

JOHN CLARE: I am ashamed to say I do not have the first idea of what I have been told just now. The gist I caught was that you are a woman of unusual intelligence and merit, but being the fool I am I got caught up in looking at your bosom and so may have missed the greater part of it. Please don't think badly of me.

WOMAN: [*Laughing.*] Oh, you're all right. You're John Clare. It's quite an honour you should make the effort to look at me boobs.

JOHN CLARE: You are a kind woman, I think, and a robust one of a cheery humour. I should pay you the respect of listening to what you say. Please tell it to me all again, and be sure that I look you in the eye.

WOMAN: Ah, you're a legend. You're just how I thought you would be from the poetry. I'm not saying I've not read a lot of them but there were some of 'em that made me cry. As for me, there wasn't that much more to tell. The business with the questionnaire meant that I ended up getting a lot more notice than I'd ever wanted or deserved. They started calling me a saint, but to be honest I found that a bit depressing. Like I say, it wasn't anything I'd ever wanted.

JOHN CLARE: You're a saint, then?

WOMAN: Not a proper one. Just in the papers. They'll make anyone a saint. I tried not to have anything to do with it.

JOHN CLARE: We had a real one pass by just now on this very spot. Thomas á Becket.

WOMAN: Really?

JOHN CLARE: Else I dreamed it.

WOMAN: He's well famous, Thomas Becket.

JOHN CLARE: Aye, he's famous for a well, all right. We talked about it. He was passing by this spot because he did so on his way to condemnation at the castle. Then the other Mr. Beckett, he was here revisiting the churches of Northampton as he'd done upon a previous occasion, whereas Mr. Bunyan passed through on his way to hear a proclamation in the market. As for me, this is the place I always sat, so that's the explanation for my presence, but what of yourself? Do you consider yourself to be dead or dreaming, and in either case what brings you here?

WOMAN: Oh, I'm dead. There's no doubt about it. I got caught up in a water riot when it was getting bad in twenty-sixty and me ticker couldn't handle it, not in me seventies.

JOHN CLARE: You don't look seventy.

WOMAN: Well, ta. This is me in me thirties, when I looked me best. To be quite honest, any younger and I was a mess, and I got a bit scrawny after I was knocking on a bit. As for the reason why I'm here, it's them. [*The* HALF-CASTE WOMAN *nods towards the couple on the steps.*]

JOHN CLARE: You know them, then?

WOMAN: Oh, yeah. Well, not in life I never met 'em, no, but I know all about 'em. Him, the bloke, that's Johnny Vernall and the woman's his wife Celia. This is the night their daughter locked them out the house in Freeschool Street and they came here and sat beneath the portico until the morning. What it was, I knew their daughter, Audrey.

JOHN CLARE: Ah, yes. That would be the one the things were done to. I was trying to fathom it with all the other ghosts that were here earlier. It sounded like a miserable business.

WOMAN: Oh, it was. It was. But then, I suppose it had to be.

JOHN CLARE: How did you know her, the poor child?

WOMAN: Well, she was an old woman when I met her. It was one night back when I was young, and when I was in trouble, and she saved me life. She was the most frightening, amazing person that I've ever seen, and that night turned everything round for me. If what I went on to do later helped a lot of people, it was all because of her. If she'd not helped me, I'd have been dead and then none of that, the questionnaire, none of that would have happened. She's the real saint, Audrey. She's the martyr, and this is the night before they took her to the stake. And that's the reason why I'm here. After what Audrey done for me, I thought that it was only right. I thought that it was only right that I should come and see, and be a witness.

JOHN CLARE: If there is a poetry to all of this, it seems as though hurt women are a central matter. [*A pause.*] But where are my manners! I've got a young lady stood here all this time and never offered her a seat!

WOMAN: [*She laughs, starting to walk towards* JOHN CLARE's *alcove.*] Oh, well, that's very nice. I –

JOHN CLARE: [*Slightly alarmed, fearing she's misunderstood him.*] No, not this one. This is mine. The one there on the other side is what I keep for visitors. I'm told it's very comfortable.

WOMAN: [*Surprised, but more amused than offended.*] Oh, right. Okay, then. Over here, yeah? [*She goes and sits in the alcove to* STAGE LEFT *of the door.*] Mm. You're right. It's very nice. Nice place to sit.

JOHN CLARE: Well, not as nice as this one, but I am sincere in hoping it is to your liking.

WOMAN: [*She laughs, charmed by his earnestness.*] It's fine. It's like a little throne. So, with Johnny and Celia there, what have I missed?

JOHN CLARE: You know the most of it, apparently. The wife berated him a while until he upped and made a full confession, whereat she berated him some more. A little while ago he raised the point of her being aware of what was going on and in this sense being complicit in their abject circumstances.

WOMAN: How did she take that?

JOHN CLARE: Not noticeably well, in the first instance. She made her outraged denials though I could not help but feel they were half-hearted at the bottom of it. Then, after some time it seemed that she accepted what was said, where-after she became more haunted and contrite. Most recently she seemed concerned by the idea that they might be in hell, although it seems to me a more widespread and popular opinion that the whole of this is purgatory.

WOMAN: What, this? Nah, bollocks, this is heaven. All of this is heaven.

JOHN CLARE: Is it?

WOMAN: Well, of course it is. Look at it. It's miraculous.

JOHN CLARE: What, even with the incest and the misery?

WOMAN: That there's anything alive at all to interfere with its own children; that there's children; that there's sexual interference; that we can feel misery. The way I see it, on the whole there's not much to complain about. Its heaven. Even in a concentration camp or when you're getting beaten up and raped, even if it's an off day, it's still heaven. You're not telling me that you wrote all that stuff about the seasons and the ladybird and everything and you don't know that?

JOHN CLARE: Are you sure you're not a proper saint?

WOMAN: If you knew half the things I did when I was younger then you wouldn't even ask. We're either none of us saints, or we all are.

JOHN CLARE: Not just an appointed few of us as Mr. Bunyan was suggesting?

WOMAN: I don't know who that is, but no. Definitely not. It's all or nothing, shit or bust across the board. We're saints and sinners both, the lot of us, or else there's no saints and no sinners.

JOHN CLARE: Oh, I think there's sinners, right enough, though I don't know about the saints. For my own part, I think that in my life I may have done a monstrous and ignoble thing.

WOMAN: Aw, love. You shouldn't slap yourself about. We've all done bad things, or we think we have. It's only when you can't face up to 'em and put 'em in perspective that you end up stuck to them, so that that's who you are and where you are forever.

JOHN CLARE: That's an awful long time to be stuck to something dismal.

WOMAN: Well, you're not wrong. [JOHN CLARE *and the* HALF-CASTE WOMAN *lapse into thoughtful silence, gazing at the* HUSBAND *and* WIFE *seated on the steps.*]

WIFE: [*After a long pause, in which her expression has changed from guilty and haunted to a more cold-eyed and pragmatic look.*] So, what are we going to do about it?

HUSBAND: [*Looks up at her, surprised.*] We?

WIFE: You spelled it out. We're both involved.

HUSBAND: We are. I'm glad you see it.

WIFE: And if it comes out for either of us both of us are done for, or at least round here and where else should we go? I see that, too.

HUSBAND: What are you saying, then?

WIFE: I'm saying that there's people round here know us. We've got friends here, Johnny, and acquaintances. We've got our lives here. We've got prospects.

HUSBAND: Have we?

WIFE: [*Hissing with urgency.*] Yes! We've got more prospects than if anyone finds out you've put that filthy thing of yours in Audrey! And what should they think of me? I won't let you destroy us, Johnny. And I won't let her destroy us.

HUSBAND: But ... I mean, it isn't going to come to that for certain. Is it? I mean, perhaps if when she's calmed down I talked to her ...

WIFE: Oh, yes. That'll help the situation. Evidently you can talk her pants off, and that's how we got here! She's out for revenge, you silly sod. She flirts with you and leads you on with all her skirts and brassieres and when you're Muggins enough to fall for it, she wants her bit of drama, her theatricals.

HUSBAND: She did. She led me on.

WIFE: And now she's staging her performance so that everyone can hear.

HUSBAND: [*Suddenly confused and alarmed.*] You were the one said it had stopped!

WIFE: [*Frowning as if uncertain.*] Yes, well, I thought it had, but I'm not sure. I think I can still hear it when the wind's in our direction. But that's not the point. The point is that she's made her mind up that she's going to put an end to it by telling everybody and broadcasting from the rooftops. You saw Eileen Perrit coming out to see what all the fuss was, all that noise when Jem and her had just got little Alison to sleep. She could hear everything, the Whispering Grass and everything that dirty, dirty little tart was shouting. Everything. [*Thoughtful, after a pause.*] I don't know what she heard. It might already be too late.

HUSBAND: But then what shall we do?

WIFE: [*Angry.*] I don't know, Johnny. I don't know what we shall do. That's what I'm trying to work out, what we're going to do. [*A pause.*] That dirty little tart. She thought I never noticed, in the kitchen, at the sink, washing her hair without her blouse on, and then when she's drying it and got it held up in the towel, then you, you're sitting there, you're sitting there and looking and you've got your legs crossed, sitting there, and looking, and you say "Ooh, you look nice, our Audrey, with your hair up", never mind about you look nice with your blouse off, sitting there and looking with your legs crossed, and then after that she's always got her hair up so that everyone can see her neck, her neck, look at my lovely neck, look at my little bosoms that aren't anything at all, look at me swing about when I play my accordion so that my skirt goes up and everyone can come and have a look and see my knees and think about my fanny and she thought I never noticed. [*A long, seething pause, during which her* HUSBAND *looks scared and shaken by her outburst.*] Let me think. I've got to think. We've got to think what shall be done.

JOHN CLARE: [*After a pause.*] I don't much care for how this sounds. I have a painful feeling about where all this is headed.

WOMAN: Yeah. They're gunna cover it all up. They're gunna bury everything because they can't face up to what they've done. They're gunna bury Audrey, then inside 'em somewhere they'll be sitting in the damp and fog and bickering on these steps forever. All because they couldn't bear to tell the truth of what they were.

JOHN CLARE: [*After a long and anguished pause, his secrecy battling with his conscience.*] I did something. I did something that I never told the truth about. When I was fourteen. [*He closes his eyes. He can hardly bear to speak.*]

WOMAN: [*Gently and encouragingly.*] Yeah? Something went on?

JOHN CLARE: [*His eyes still closed, he slowly starts to rock back and forth in his alcove.*] When I was fourteen. When I was fourteen. When I was fourteen, there was someone. There was someone. There was someone up the road in the next village. There was. There was. There was someone. There was someone. There was a young ... I was fourteen. There was a young woman. A young woman. She was round my own age. Mary. Mary. Mary. She was beautiful. She was more beautiful than anything. When I was fourteen. And I met her. And I met her in the lane and asked her if she would walk out with me and Mary said she would, she said she would walk out with me. She was around my own age. And I walked her down the path. We went. We went. We went beside a stream where was, where was, where was a Hawthorn bush. And I said. I said that I loved her and. And. And. And. And I asked if she would like to marry me. Beneath the Hawthorn bush. Beneath the Hawthorn bush and she laughed and she said she would and we went in. We went in on our hands and knees beneath the Hawthorn bush and I made her a ring. I made a ring. I made a ring of grass for her and put it on her finger and I said. I said. I said that we were married. She was round my own age. I was fourteen. She was, she was, she was a bit younger. A bit younger than what I was. And I. And I. And I joked. I joked. I joked and I said. I said. I said that it was our wedding night. I made a ring of grass for her. I said it was our wedding night and we must. We must take our clothes off and I said it as a joke. I said it so that I should make it seem it was a joke, beneath the Hawthorn bush, but she said, she said, Mary said she would. She was around my own age. A bit younger. Mary said she would and she was laughing. She was laughing, she was taking off her things and I ... was ... looking at her. I was looking at her, taking off her things and I was hurrying. Was hurrying. Was hurrying to take my own off too and she was looking at me. She was ten. She was ten. She was laughing and I said. I said that we. I said that we. I said that we should do it. She was laughing and she said do what? She said do what and I said, I said that I'd show her and it was all right. It was all right. I'd made a ring for her and we were married and it was all right and then I told. I told. I told her what to do. I told. I told her she must lie upon her back and she was laughing. She was laughing. She was laughing and I got on top of her and Mary asked. She asked. She asked what I was doing and I tried to get it into her. I was fourteen. She said it hurt. She said it hurt. She said that I was hurting her and that she didn't want to do it, that she didn't want to do it, that it hurt, but I said. I said. I said it was all right. I said we were married. It was all right. That she'd start. She'd start to like it in a little while and that she mustn't. That she mustn't. That she mustn't cry. She mustn't cry. She mustn't cry. And I. And I went on with it. And she stopped crying in a. In a while. And when I'd finished it we wiped up with my shirt and I said. I said that she was my first wife and would always be my first wife and she should tell nobody, nobody, nobody about it. What we'd, what we'd, what I'd done. Beneath the Hawthorn bush. Beneath the Hawthorn bush. When I was fourteen. I was fourteen. She was ten. I never saw her after that, save in the best of my illusions. [*He is weeping by this point. He subsides into silence.*]

WOMAN: [*After a long pause.*] Are you sure you wouldn't like me to sit over there?

JOHN CLARE: [*He looks up at her, anguished.*] Would you? Would you? Else I am alone in it. [*The HALF-CASTE WOMAN rises from her alcove and then walks across to the alcove in which JOHN CLARE is sitting. She sits down beside him, sympathetically, and drapes one arm around his shoulders.*]

WOMAN: [*Stroking his hair.*] You were fourteen. You were living in the country. It was eighteen-hundred and whatever. These things happen, sweetheart. Both of you were kids, mucking about. If it was guilt about that made you talk of her as your first wife, if it was anything to do with that that made you spend all of that time up at Saint Andrew's then you've punished yourself ten times over when all that you did was love somebody at the wrong time. There's worse crimes than that, love. There's worse crimes than that. You shush. You shush now.

WIFE: We could have her put away.

HUSBAND: What do you mean?

WIFE: Up Berry Wood. Up round the turn there at St. Crispin's. We could have her put away up there.

HUSBAND: The mental home?

WIFE: Up Berry Wood. We could say she'd been acting funny for a while.

JOHN CLARE: Oh, no. Oh, I can see where this is going.

WOMAN: Hush, now. It's only what happened in the world once. It's all right.

HUSBAND: Well, I suppose, what with the music, she always been highly strung. You know, with the artistic temperament. And that business tonight, well, there's the proof of it.

JOHN CLARE: It's just the same! It's just the same as what the other Mr. Beckett said befell his friend!

WIFE: Yes, well, it's well known. If you're having fits because you're mad, you could say anything. You might make every kind of accusation and it wouldn't bother anyone.

HUSBAND: [*Uncertain and uncomfortable.*] But Celia, I mean. Our Audrey, in a madhouse. I don't like to picture it.

WIFE: It needn't be for long. Just until she'd got over her delusions, what they call them, and she isn't saying things that make no sense.

HUSBAND: But, I mean, they're not really what you'd call delusions, are they?

WIFE: Johnny, listen to me: yes they are. They're all delusions. After all, you know it's in the family. It's not your fault, we can't help how we're born, but there was your dad. And your granddad. And your great Aunt Thursa. It's no wonder Audrey went the way she did. We can make the arrangements in the morning.

HUSBAND: The arrangements?

WIFE: With the hospital, to have her put away.

HUSBAND: Oh. Oh, yes. The arrangements. I suppose that we can't …

WIFE: In the morning. It's what's best.

HUSBAND: Yes. Yes, I suppose so. It's what's best for Audrey.

WIFE: It's what's best for everybody. [*They lapse into thoughtful silence.*]

JOHN CLARE: [*He has now recovered his composure.*] These are terrible affairs that are decided here tonight. [*He turns to look at the* HALF-CASTE WOMAN *sitting next to him.*] With you having the admiration for their daughter that you did, I'd say it was a dreadful anger you were feeling.

WOMAN: No, not really. I feel sorry for the lot of them. I mean, look at this couple here. They're stuck like this now. Yeah, you could say as they've brought it on themselves, but how much choice has anybody really got? It's better not to judge. Even the rapists and the murderers and nutters – no offence – you think about it and they probably got where they were in some dead ordinary way. They had a bit of bad luck or they got into a kind of thinking that they couldn't shake. When I was younger, I was horrible. It felt to me like it was all my fault, but looking back with kinder eyes I'm not sure that it was. I'm not sure it was anybody's fault. There comes a point where you get sick of all the punishing.

JOHN CLARE: I like the way that you're forgiving in your nature. You've a generosity in you that makes the rest of us seem small. Are you entirely sure you're not a proper saint?

WOMAN: Oh, who cares? It's a word. I mean, you were just saying that you'd met Thomas á Becket. He's a proper saint. Was he like me?

JOHN CLARE: No. No, he wasn't.

WOMAN: There you are, then.

JOHN CLARE: It was his opinion that the sins of this unhappy pair put them beyond the reach of any mercy or redemption.

WOMAN: Well, I don't see that at all. I don't think he'd considered all the billiards and ballistics of the matter.

JOHN CLARE: And what do you mean by that?

WOMAN: Well, look at it like this: if Johnny Vernall hadn't read a dirty book or two and got fixated by the thought of having it off with his daughter then she'd not have locked them out the house while she played 'Whispering Grass', and her mum wouldn't have had the idea to get her sectioned off to Crispin's. So she wouldn't have still been there when the Tories started closing down the mental homes and wouldn't have been put out into what they called the care of the community. And when I needed her, when I'd have been dead otherwise, then she wouldn't have been there, and then I wouldn't have turned out how I did. There'd be no questionnaire and there'd be thousands of lives over with or different all across the world. And think of all the lives that those lives will affect, for better or for worse, and on and on until you step back and it's all just billiards. Johnny pulling Audrey's pants down, that's all in the rebound off the cushion. That's all in the break. And none of this is justifying what he did. Johnny and Celia, you and me and everybody, we still have to answer to our conscience. And a conscience is the most vindictive, vicious little fucker that I've ever met, and I don't think that anybody gets off easy. We all judge ourselves. We all sit here on these cold steps, and that's enough. The rest is billiards. We all feel the impacts and we blame the ball that's hit us. We all love it when we're cannoning and on a roll and think it must mean that we're special, but it's all balls. Balls and billiards. [*A pause.*] You're looking down my top again.

JOHN CLARE: I know. I'm sorry. I suppose it might be argued I was predetermined in my opportunism. If as you say it is my conscience I must answer to, then I believe my answer will be neither difficult nor arduously long.

WOMAN: [*She laughs, playfully attracted to him.*] You poets. All your lovely language, you use it like Lynx or something, don't yer, when you want the girls all over yer? And anyway, haven't you got a wife at home?

JOHN CLARE: Oh, to hear me tell it I've got any number of 'em. You pay no attention. All that business with the wives is more than likely nothing but the ravings of a madman. I'm well known for it. [*They are both laughing now.*]

WOMAN: What are you like? You with your pretty eyes. I don't think you're old fashioned in the least. [*They are beginning to embrace.*] I can see why you like this shady alcove, you old dog. It's very comfortable. Very convenient.

JOHN CLARE: In all the times I've sat here I have never thought to use it for this purpose.

WOMAN: [*Kissing him lightly on the cheek and neck.*] Haven't you? Why not?

JOHN CLARE: I was alive. It was broad daylight on a Friday afternoon with people walking past and anyway, I was most usually alone. It wouldn't have been right. You are a lovely girl. Give me a kiss, as if we were alive, and ... Oh! Oh, my. What's that you're doing now?

WOMAN: I said already. I'm no saint. [*They begin to kiss and caress each other under the obscuring shadows of the recess.*]

WIFE: [*After a long pause, tonelessly and emotionally drained.*] God help me, Johnny, but I hate you. I hate you so much that I'm exhausted by it.

HUSBAND: [*Equally flatly and without real feeling.*] And I hate you, Celia. With all my heart, I hate you. I can't stand you.

WIFE: Well, at least there's that. At least we still mean something to each other.

HUSBAND: [*Without the couple looking at each other, the* HUSBAND *reaches out and takes his* WIFE's *hand. She accepts this without comment or reaction. There is a long pause as they sit and stare expressionlessly into space.*] Are we still planning to ... you know. With Audrey, and the hospital. Is that still something that we want to do?

WIFE: It's something that we've got to do.

HUSBAND: Yes, I suppose so. [*After a pause.*] Not just yet though, eh?

WIFE: No. In the morning. I'm not looking forward to it any more than you are.

HUSBAND: No. No, I suppose not. But it's something that we've got to do, you're right. You're dead right. In the morning, we'll go down there and we'll step up to the bat.

WIFE: Yes. When it's light.

HUSBAND: Will it ever be light?

WIFE: I couldn't say. I'm waiting for the clock to strike again. If it's just once we'll know that we're in hell or else it's broken. If it's twice, it'll be getting on for morning in an hour or two. We can go down to Freeschool Street and take care of it then.

HUSBAND: Yes. Yes, I will. I'll be a man about it. I'll go down there and take the bull by the horns.

WIFE: We'll see the necessary doctors.

HUSBAND: In the morning, when it's light, I'll go down there and do what's to be done.

WIFE: We'll go down there. We'll go down there and set the matter straight.

HUSBAND: We will.

WIFE: We will. We'll put it all to rights.

HUSBAND: We'll face the music.

WIFE: [*After a long pause.*] Do you know, I think the clock's about to strike.

HUSBAND: I think you're right.

WIFE: And then we'll know.

HUSBAND: Yes. Then we'll know.

CURTAIN

EATING FLOWERS

"What are you thinking about now?" the naked eighteen month-old girl asks, mounted on the similarly naked old man's shoulders. In each tiny fist she holds a lock of his white hair as reins. His leather hands, articulated bone and sinew birdcages, are closed around the infant's ankles to prevent her falling off as they progress down the enormous icebound hallway under diagrams of failing stars. These are the Fimbul distances of the time-avenue. Puzzle-ball beads of hyperwater, frozen into glass sea-urchin intricacies, chime and tinkle in the drifts about the wading ancient's knees. "I'm thinking now of how I died," says he, "When I wiz

Snowy Vernall always sitting, always snuffing it there in the daughter's house on Green Street. Orange, sage and umber mottled in a hearthside rug of woolends where the black cat is asleep and snoring. In between the clock ticks you can hear dust settle on the sideboard, on the emerald glass bowls, one full of golden apples withering, the other full of hard-boiled sweets becoming damp and soft. There is a mildew perfume on the indecipherable crowns-and-lilies wallpaper, just sliding off like skin above the skirting board where it's that wet and heavy. From behind, below, the muffled fuss of chickens tutting in the long back yard outside as it drops down the slope onto Saint Peter's Way, from which there'll sometimes come the echo-silvered clop of hooves or else a rag and bone man's speech in tongues, frail little noises shouldered by the smelly summer wind that's always blowing on that Wednesday afternoon. There in the daughter's house, there in the living room a table on the left – with fifty years of slipping cutlery and scalding teacups logged meticulously in the varnish – and upon it stands a china vase of tulips; stands *the* china vase of tulips. Glorious, they are. Bright custard yellow, icing-sugar pink, blackcurrant purple deep as midnight, you should see them. An old man alone, let himself in, come visiting with everybody out and starting to get loose in his intelligence, starting to have a trouble with the old perspective as he nears the mortal turning. Up above the sideboard there's a mirror with another hanging opposite above the hearth, or rather up above the sideboard there's a window with another set into the south wall opposite. It isn't easy telling which it is, the same as how the corner of a room can be concave and convex at the same time if stared at for long enough. Adrift in the warm air with opal motes all blazing there are other details

that may come to me after a while, but that's the long and short of it." He picks his bony, barefoot way amongst cold dunes of spiny hypersnow accumulating on the frosted parquet of that stupefying corridor. May squirms uncomfortably, a small warm weight on her grandfather's nape, and squints through an intense chandelier flurry of suspended, whirling crystals that have more than three dimensions, a hypnotic meta-blizzard. Gazing past this diamond spindrift, the profoundly beautiful nude baby focuses her sad Galapagos eyes on the soaring cliff-face walls that border perpetuity's gargantuan emporium, away to either side across the intervening miles of tundra floor. She knows that in these latitudes of Always there are fewer living people in the neighbourhood downstairs, and that they have less complicated dream-lives. Consequently, the immense arcade surrounding her and Snowy has accumulated very little in the way of astral furnishings and decorations, trimmings borrowed from the sparse imaginings of a polar encampment that has less to dream about. Set into the north face is something May believes might be somebody's vision of a massively expanded trading-post, with walls of varnished wooden shields and drapes of wolf-pelt that are bluish-white speckled with faun. Elsewhere, her almost-turquoise eyes alight upon what she supposes to be the inflated dream-form of a twenty-second century hostelry, the excavated ground floor of an ancient office block where she can make out local date-specific ghosts with their fur burkhas and their wind-up radios, their barbed and ornate wolf-killing 'vulpoons' inevitably clasped in one raw fist as they trudge stoically through a bereft Valhalla. Other than this, the endless hallway offers only the occasional stone edifice or concrete hulk enduring from a previous era, set amongst an unrelieved expanse of towering rock and chiselled ice. The optically confounding hyperflakes fall silently around them, an obscuring lingerie-lace hung on air. She tilts back her exquisitely made head, haloed in hair golden and nebular, perusing the ruined canopy above this chronologic thoroughfare's unending winter vastness. The green-tinted glass that had once sheltered the great boulevard is long broken and gone, with its containing framework of Victorian iron reduced to rusting carcass spars through which unfolding blueprint constellations made from overstars are visible. Recalling the conspicuous array of shops and buildings to be found only a hundred years or so back down the hall, May understands that there may not be streets or street-names anymore down in the territory below. A perfectly developed mind within a glorious arrested form she feels a distant disappointed pang at the idea but nothing more, consoling herself with the observation that there are at least still trees. Weathered immensities as realised on this upper plane, the crystal-heavy giant pines extend up out of the remaining floor-holes here and there, where these have not been covered over by the glaze of permafrost or else collapsed entirely. It occurs to her that the material ground below their higher mathematic reaches is most probably no longer called the Boroughs, and she even wonders if these arctic furlongs of the overworld are still referred to as Mansoul. Returning her attention to the mad old man on whom she's riding, May asks him a question, her voice an unsettling blend of infant gurgle and elderly lady syntax. "Do the builders and the devils ever make it up as far as here?" His sunburned neck gripped fast by the precocious toddler's knees, her grandfather is chuckling, almost giggling as he replies, "Of course they do. You'll still find them about when there's not people any longer. It's just that they tend to hang about more in the populated bits of time, like in the stretch that we're from. And before that, if you ever choose to go back that far, you'll find even more of 'em. Back in the pastures there, they even venture downstairs every now and then, when they're directing that monk here from Geographical Jerusalem or when they're ordering that Saxon halfwit back to Peter's Church so he can help dig up Saint Ragener. One speaks to poor old Ern, my dad and your great-granddad, in the dome of Saint Paul's during all the usual thunderstorm and lightning that they seem to favour, though it's really just all the electromagnetism that's discharged. It's thundering when I have that one speak to me that time, when I wiz drunk and on top of the Guildhall in St. Giles Street if you can imagine that: your granddad on the roof's crest swaying in

a bitter breeze out of the east with storm-clouds riding it towards the town from Abington, from Weston Favell and the pale blue slates beneath his feet already dampening to navy in anticipation. Down in George Row and St. Giles Street below all the pale ovals tilting back and gaping in amazement, milling beetle-fashion in their bonnets and their caps around the bike-shop at the top of Guildhall Road with the aroma of French chalk and rubber lifting from its doorway. Seeing how the figure on the skyline sways and wobbles some of the assembled crowd call warnings, with the greater part of their admonishments bowled off toward All Saints or Bridge Street in the rising wind and leaving only scraps behind: "... making a show ...", "... sending for a bobby ...", "... ruddy fool. You'll break your neck and ...", but that's not what's going to happen. In the lofty gusts chopped by the chimneys, in the pepper-shot of birdsong and in rubbish waltzing down the guttering at the approach of rain, that's not what's going to happen. Next there's a precarious little dance, as if spontaneous, as if not foreordained from the commencement of eternity, which has a slip and slither in it and a teetering recovery that makes the audience gasp at the appropriate juncture of their unacknowledged schedule. What a spectacle the world makes of itself. What a performance. Although everything is motionless in the thick glass of time there's the appearance of a drunken stumble and another indrawn breath from the flat multitude compressed by the perspective, people painted on the planner's diagram of a street beneath. A threadbare arm is hooked about the rooftop statue's chilly shoulders, draped between the hard stone pinions and a garland of encrusted pigeon shit encircling the neck, in an inebriate over-familiarity that also offers increased purchase and stability. It's spitting now, the first cold droplets breaking against cheeks, the backs of hands, but still the idling mob squint up into the light precipitation at the drunk and the stone man with wings together up against a darkening sky like they were pals. A long and principally inaudible harangue commences, aimed at the bemused terrestrial observers who seem unsure what to make of it. "I'm with my dead granddaughter walking naked through a frozen afterlife nearly three hundred years from now. Tell all of your descendants to be careful of the wolves. They might want to devise a pointed stick of some variety." In Giles Street down there, a peacock carpet of uncomprehending eyes. The light jumps suddenly and after comes the bruise-mauve rumble of a cymbal firmament, masking the softer, closer sound of grinding stone-on-stone as the winged icon slowly turns its head to make eye-contact. All about the chiselled throat there is a fissure-necklace of small cracks that ripple briefly into being, splintering and branching before fusing seamlessly into the new configuration. Similarly, there are fine webs of self-healing fracture at the corners of the eyes and mouth as the carved features blink and smile and, ultimately, speak. "Vernalimt, whorey skung?" The shattered syllables are settled slowly like an ash or sediment upon the eardrums of the listener where they arrange themselves into an information or, as in this instance, an enquiry. Something like, "Vernall, what limit are you seeking?", but attended by a dizzying array of subtexts; of conceptual and linguistic pleats hung in a shimmering veil at the peripheries of apprehension. Underneath, the earthbound onlookers see nothing, peering into drizzle or distracted by the search for shelter from the coming downpour. All they hear is the intoxicated steeplejack's delirious laughter and unfathomable reply. "Are not the edges of the heavens and the brim of reason and the shunting-yards of time itself all boundaries requiring my inspection and therefore within my jurisdiction? Answer that with a straight face and droppings on your chin!" The granite being shakes its head, slowly and imperceptibly, to an accompaniment of further minute fracturing and subdued grating, then admits "Yohuav metr", which translates to somewhere in the region of "You have me there". The weathered cranium shifts by fractions back to its original position and grows silent. By now, overhead, the thunder takes its bull-run through an ironmonger's with the weather coming down like tinsel curtains on a nude theatre show. Down in the modern painted dots that throng the painted street is suddenly a great preponderance

of indigo as the constabulary arrive who, from that elevated vantage, look to
be largely unsympathetic. Lightning-scattered pigeons whirl

*about me, or at least that is my honest recollection." They stride on, the old
man and his infant burden, for a distance of perhaps another dozen years
before they both agree to halt and make a bivouac. The younger of the Vernalls asks to be set down within a hollowed-out concrete concavity there to
one side of the great corridor, ceiling subsumed beneath an optical illusion
chandelier-growth of mathematically abnormal icicles. The light refracting
through these from the shattered ceiling of the infinite arcade outside suffuses
the whole chamber with prismatic blush, with iridescent specks accumulating in the wrinkles of his brow or powdering her flawless skin. There are still
the frost-dusted dreams of wolf-pelts piled discarded in a corner, and Snowy
supposes that their current whereabouts may be one more further reiteration
of the makeshift astral tavern they passed some few decades back. Exploring
in the misty dazzle of the spectra, toddling on plump little legs, the ageless
baby May emits a sudden shrill peal of delight that chimes and echoes, shivering through the ice-stalactites and bringing her intrigued grandfather to her
side. There at their naked feet a modest carpeting of what at first glance look
like ordinary Puck's Hats spreads for a few yards in all directions. Only upon
close inspection is it evident that this is some new strain of the ethereal fungus,
born from the imaginings of different times and different people. The traditional lithe fairy-forms that they are both familiar with have been replaced by
slightly shorter, plumper female figures, although every bit as winsome and still
sharing limbs and facial features with each other, fused into their customary
starfish or snowflake configurations. Strikingly, the exquisite nude women are
all now albinos with pink gems for eyes, with alabaster skin and at the central
tuft and the furred junctions of their petal legs alike the silky pseudo-hair is
made a bright snowblind titanium. The elder Vernall splits a chalky stalk with
one black thumbnail, thus eliciting the usual dying whine that neither of them
have been previously aware of, the peripheral sound of an electrical appli-
ance suddenly switched off, sliding from a dog-whistle high to slump into the
audible. Turning the meta-blossom over in his leather hands he notes that on
the underside the ring of tiny wings are now no longer dragonfly-like gossamer
but are instead the feathered kind, like those of minuscule white budgerigars.
Breaking the pallid fruit in two and giving half to his granddaughter he allows
himself a taste, surprised at the increased intensity of the higher-dimensional
bloom's sweetness. In between slobbering mouthfuls he and May conclude that
this perhaps reflects a lack of refined sugar in the diet of those still living in the
realm Downstairs, whilst the altered appearance of the Bedlam Jennies possibly suggests changed notions of allure and beauty down there in the icebound*

mortal continuity below. As the anticipated tingling and illuminating warmth spreads through their phantom systems, they both understand without the need to voice the thought that this profusion of uneaten astral fungi must imply that there are fewer peckish ghosts about these reaches of the over-life, if indeed there are any left at all. The Gulf Stream warming Britain, as they've previously agreed, must have seen its benign convection current cease sometime around the middle years of the twenty-first century, when the continued melting of the Greenland ice-shelf meant that it was no longer sufficient to power that long-standing hydro-thermal drift. The country, always sharing the same band of latitude with wintery locales like Denmark, would have been reminded forcibly for the first time in countless generations of its actual polar situation. It would also have become one of the last remaining areas in the world along with the Antarctic mega-cities to have weather suitable for growing produce on a planet where the equatorial regions were increasingly surrendering to desert. May has at one point suggested that this seems to have resulted in a period of overpopulation, possibly occasioned by invasion or a frantic wave of refugees and immigrants, before the massive human die-back that they have already witnessed in the later stretches of that century, when the unending boardwalks of Mansoul were crowded with bewildered just-dead apparitions that the naked baby and her wild-eyed steed were forced to push their way between. After that point the pair are both agreed there's been less company around and fewer signs of spectral habitation, indicating that down in the frozen wastes of the First Borough underneath them there abides a population which is much diminished, at the very least. Snowy and May consume their fragrant supper, the variety of Puck's Hat that they have decided to refer to as "the snow-queen sort", in a profound and thoughtful silence. Up above the endless hall outside their gutted billet with its crust of glass geometries, abstracted constellations are unfolded against blackness of unfathomable depth. They brush the frozen hyper-crystals from the luscious wolf-skins and each take one as a blanket, just for the familiarity and comfort of the notion rather than for the unnecessary warmth or cover. Snuggled there beside each other in their wraps for the same reason, both close their remembered eyes to drift in time and memory. The old man thinks of the tremendous distance down the sempiternal corridor that they've already come and the much greater distance yet to go, the countless furlongs of one foot before the other or the parallax in separate layers crawling by at different speeds to either side of him, and is reminded of the similarly lengthy hikes that are his habit while in life and in the third dimension,

the long treks out of Northampton and across the lanes and fields to London, from the Boroughs into shining Lambeth, wet after the rain. He knows a trick that will compress the journey, telescoping his fond farewells to Louisa at their

Fort Street doorstep into his footsore arrival on the angel pavements there south of the Thames. Detaching himself from his usual perspective on the solid, trudging world of three dimensions he adopts an altitude from which duration has become a thing of feet and inches. His wife's goodbye wave and her accompanying suspicious frown smear into cobbled lanes, to breweries and brickyards on the edge of town and then to wayside flowers, cowslips, forget-me-nots and such, a floral motif on the county's crawling wallpaper. The fixed disc of the sun swells up and reddens like a sore eye, staring angry and aggrieved until relieved by the protracted blink of a cloud-cover eyelid, grey and full of tears. The world of form and depth and time is flattened to a single plane as in a map, and the ensuing downpour is reduced to only a metallic texture spattering an area of the diagram. Day tans to night, twice, two thick stripes of purple tar stippled with nail-heads, and then past this point on the unwinding canvas of the days the emerald verge of Watling Street gives way to thick impasto crusts of pigeon-streaked geometry. The finer details of broad avenue and narrow terrace are unfolded from these intricacies to surround him, with flat factories now springing into being at the corners of his glazed sleepwalker gaze and the whole capital become a children's pop-up novelty. Along Hercules Road's unspooling length he goes down into the familiar Bed-lam reaches of his birthplace, starving hungry and for some forgotten reason suddenly near lame, and it all seems to him to be accomplished in a moment. He gulps down the sixty or so miles in one debilitating, dizzying swallow and slams his drained journey on the Lambeth counter, smacks his lips with rel-ish on the nearest barmaid by way of a celebration. Her mouth is the taut but yielding ribbon of his finish line and yet he stumbles further, stumbling and gasping to her chucking-out time chamber, to the purlieus of her womb, and the unfaithfulness is somehow wrapped around, is an extension of Louisa's knowing scowl there on the front step. Even while he's bearing down with the milk-jellies of her thighs against his chest he knows he is remembering this moment from the vantage of a furry eiderdown, an ice-decked cavern in another world long after he and everyone he knows are dead. He has the brief impression of an endlessly reiterated series of his self, an infinite array of wild-eyed men in an apocalyptic state of mutual awareness, waving to each other down a long and narrow hallway that at first he thinks is time itself but realises is another image from another moment as he moans and empties himself into her, into the sweaty linear rush of human circumstance, both of them writhing, pinned like martyrs to the crushing wheel of everything. It is immediately morning. He uncreases from the bed and grows a skin of clothes, grows a new room around him that unwraps into a street, another pub, a few days decorating work in Southwark where the hours are applied in coats, the brush-stroke minutes smoothly melting into one another. There's a roofing job in Waterloo, dancing with sky and gravity and he looks out across the lead braid of the river to the east where in the distance the bleached skull of the cathedral rises. In its famous gallery he knows that fifty-year-old thunders are still whispering to the faint residual vibrations of his father screaming, going mad, an endless conversation between echoes. Strains to see if he can catch it, overbalances and twirls his arms like windmills then regains his footing in a scripted accident, wobbling there upon the rim of a new century. His heart pounds from the near miss and he shakes a little in the wake of the adrenaline, his mind aware that there was never any danger of a fall and yet his flesh remaining unconvinced, as ever. He breathes down his nose as he descends the ladder into sequence, into filthy history, the rungs transmuting in his clammy fingers to become a buff pay envelope, the slopping glass weight of a pint, a different barmaid's cunt, her bedroom doorknob and at last the laces of his boots where he kneels fastening them for the walk home to Northampton. Streams flow backwards and almighty storm-fronts crumple and contract to balls of tangerine-wrap tissue before vanishing. A labouring dray horse snorts and shivers, breaks apart into two spinsters riding bicycles who raise their hats in passing. Parasol seeds gathered by the wind are reassembled into puffball clocks before condensing into piss-gold dandelions and then the planet sucks them in through their stem's milky straw. The planet sucks it all back in eventually, drinks every blade of grass, drinks everyone as he retracts the centipede-length of his form expressed in time from Blackfriars Bridge to Peter's Church and Marefair, reels his here-and-now along the Roman Road into the Boroughs with leaves ripening and filling out from ragged russet to a sleek viridian as they float up to reattach themselves. He ties the over-shape of his excursion in a tidy bow, greeting Louisa with a kiss on the front step, another woman's juice still flavouring his lips and all the while he knows

he's in the frosted ruins of a dream-dive somewhere up above the causes and effects, an eighteen-month-old child wrapped in his scrawny arms, both doing what dead people do instead of sleeping. Overhead, eye-straining ice geometries drip liquid hyperspheres, each carefully-spaced splash and plink in an enhanced acoustic, overlapping with delay and so convening into sparse and accidental music. Night being a fixed location on the endless avenue they rise after what they feel is sufficient rest and spend some time in fashioning a sack of wolfskin, so that they can take most of the Puck's Hats with them as they travel on towards the gold eruption of a daybreak. Fortified by their respite, the old man runs in loping Muybridge strides, each pace a minute or two long and glaciated hours of floorboard vanishing beneath his dirty feet. The Hatsack tied about his neck provides a furry saddle where his jockey bounces nude and laughing, making fists around reins of white hair and shrieking down the bore of history. Without constraints of flesh or Downstairs-physics they accelerate to reach a gallop in which the succession of the days becomes a strobe of jet and opal. Sometimes clustered specks flash by and bowl away into the slipstream, other people, other ghosts, but few and far between and never in sufficient numbers to necessitate more than a lazy veer in Snowy and his granddaughter's blurring trajectory. The phantoms point and stare at the bare patriarch as he streams past them with his shrivelled tackle roiling and a conjoined cherub growing from his shoulders. Thundering, his footfalls measure the blind phases of the moon, pound through the centuries until he can detect a subtle shift of colouration in the passing everscape, cold alabaster gradually suffused with virid notes of thaw. He curbs their terrible momentum, slowing so that every step falls on a Sunday, then upon a splashing molten sunset, then ten minutes past the hour and finally he brings them to a standstill in the strange recovering tropic of the instant. Lifting May's almost unnoticeable weight over his head he sets her down onto a felt of moss that would seem to have colonised the formerly ice-varnished floorboards thenabouts, and in that newfound temporal vicinity the ancient and the baby stand and look about them. The immense arcade has in these latitudes regained a little of its structure and complexity, suggesting dream-life and therefore an at least partly renewed population in the under-territories. Massively enlarged imaginings of trading posts seem once more to have blossomed at the distant edges of the immense corridor, and towering edifices of yard-in-diameter bamboo, places of worship or – conceivably – academies. Unlike the bleak polar austerity of vision which prevails only some several hundred-year leagues back along the line, however, these appear more intricate and equatorial in their decoration. Feather sprays and stylised monster-masks proliferate. There is a building like a kettledrum as big as a gas-holder, made from tree-bark greatly magnified and covered in a vast swathe of fluorescent snakeskin, with the once-Victorian canopy above partly restored by cable-thick lianas past which white diagrammatic clouds uncrumple on the graded grenadine wash of the sky. Tugging the loose skin of her granddad's thigh, May points out that the giant trees protruding through the recently defrosted floor-holes are now banyans and the like, a stippling of vermillion flecks upon their high flyover branches that she thinks might be comprised of parrots. Furthermore, she observes that the outsize apertures from which they sprout are now no more rectangular but are arranged in dizzying rows of circles and ellipses, stretching off in the untrammelled distance with long hanging-garden fringes of dank moss and creeper trailing down into, presumably, the mortal huts and shelters of the world beneath. Although in the unchanging climate of Upstairs the pair no more experience an increased warmth than they had felt the cold of the more arctic reaches, they see evidence of a fecund and humid dreamtime everywhere *about them. Here and there in saucer-pools between the growths of lichen there are meta-puddles straining for a third dimension, twisting upward in translucent sheets to form a thing of intersecting liquid planes much like the fluid reproduction of a gyroscope before subsiding. Something like a butterfly flaps wearily into the rising higher-mathematic steam on damp and heavy wings, a polythene bag snap and flutter rustling away between schematic fog-drifts of extrapolated vapour. On waxed tureen leaves, plump polyhedral droplets sparkle and display impossible refractive indices, Koh-i-noor perspiration, and eventually from out of the concealing vegetable shadows there emerge the period's distinctively-adapted spectres: future shades stepped hesitantly from aetheric foliage to engage with these outlandish new arrivals, with these travellers from faraway antiquity, these representatives of an almost forgotten species. With a flinching and uncertain catlike tread, the Second Borough's new inhabitants approach across the mossy suede, none of them more than three or four feet tall, hairless and gleaming bipeds with engraved or crenulated skins of a profound, light-drinking aubergine. Their voices when they speak are shrill and piping while their language is at first incomprehensible, and yet to Snowy's mind has an inflection that is not dissimilar*

to the burr in the Blue Anchor, stepping fresh into its midst from Chalk Lane and the bright, throat-scorching air: Boxing Day morning. Stamping crusts of snow from off his boots onto coconut matting, bristles beaded with meltwater, the young roughneck feels heroic, mythical, though not for any reason he can put his weather-deadened finger on. The winter brilliance outside is strained through net curtains to diffuse into a whey where cigarette smudge rolls in drifts of mottled sepia and blue. Clustered in threes and fours around their tables, polished islands floated on the fug of beer-breath and tobacco, Easter Island adults stare contentedly into their glasses, into silences that punctuate the measured drip of anecdote. Made breathless by the season children swirl excitedly about their parents' knees like tidal currents, carried by convection into other rooms or cobbled back yards glazed and slippery with frozen piss. Snowy takes off his coat and chequered scarf to hook them on the black iron quaver of a hat-peg just inside the pub's front door, his flat cap joining them once he remembers that he's wearing one. Temperature differentials between the interior and Chalk Lane without have cooked his stinging ears to bacon slices, with his now-concluded walk along the winter track from Lambeth carried there behind him in a regal train of circumstantial ermine. While ostensibly he's here visiting unemployed shoemaker cousins off in one of the outlying villages, he knows he'll never get there after a chance interruption to his travels due to occur shortly, with this latter assignation being the true reason he is rubbing circulation back into his hands in the Blue Anchor, the true reason for his journey: this happenstance port of call, in only a few minutes, will become the backdrop against which he first sets eyes upon the woman who will be his wife. Here in this very second, on this spot, Snowy has stood and brushed his palms together as though trying to kindle fire a billion times before, endlessly shaken the same tread-imprinted casts of snow onto the same coarse doormat. Every detail, every fibre of the instant is so perfect and immortal that he fears it might collapse beneath its own ferocious onslaught, its own holy weight in bottle-caps and meaning. He attempts, not for the first time, to characterise the singular elusive flavour of the morning, to attach words to an atmosphere so fragile and impermanent that even language bursts it like a bubble. There's a subdued chapel softness to the conversation, somehow murmuring on the same waveband as the settling talcum light until the two phenomena cannot be usefully distinguished from each other. His distending nostrils cup the fugitive and unique savour, a bouillon of hops and curls of smoke like shavings of sweet coconut; a dilute memory of roses misting on the womenfolk, a spirited pretence of scent, recently gifted. On the cold and glaring day here is a sleepy satisfaction, a contented languor like a blanket hung upon the optics, on the long-untouched and taciturn piano, draped in falling folds over the seated families and something like the afterglow that follows when you've had it off, the strain of Christmas and the stress of the performance done with, no more worry that somebody might be disappointed. Spilled pine needles, brilliant emerald in the kids' grey socks. The lovely greed and the indulgence in a viscous mixture with the calm of temporary belief in the nativity, and nobody at work. The most exquisite quality is the apparent transience and seeming brevity of the respite, a sense that soon the shepherds and the sexless swan-winged things with golden trumpets shall be bleached to absences on white card by the January sun, not long until the painted carol singers with their tailcoats are retreated through the falling flakes back to their comradely and crystalline decade where no one ever lived. The pace and fury of the world appears suspended and invites the thought that if the globe's alleged chain-gang requirements can be paused thus far, then why not further? He can almost feel the moment's sediment, cloudy sienna churning up about his trouser bottoms, wading for the bar to get his elbows on the wood, to work his shoulders in amongst the turned backs and bray out his order for a pint of best. The owner swivels ponderously from his busy register to study Snowy with amused annoyance and there's something in the man's face that is more familiar and has more impact than the other countenances on display in that establishment, which in themselves all harbour the before-seen look of Toby Jugs. Viewed through his lens of telescoping time he realises that the publican's pale eyes and rubber folds of chin are made more recognisable by all the future meetings that the two of them shall have: the landlord is

premembered. Barely have the words father-in-law begun to formulate themselves in his snow-globe awareness than around the corner from the other bar
she comes, explodes into his story with a swing of green skirt and some casual
remark about a barrel that needs changing. Yes, of course, the emerald dress
and fat fake pearls around her throat hung on grey string, it all comes back to
him in a beloved rush, this woman that he's never seen before and when in a
few minutes time she says her name's Louise he'll say "I know". He won't say
he's with her dead granddaughter six hundred years away

amongst a company of purple men whose heaven is an indoor jungle, strutting
naked in the mirror-Eden of this lapsing world. On those occasions when the
great unfolded garnet of a sun is visible beyond the mile-wide nets of creeper
covering the stupefying avenue, the solar orb seems larger than it did. May
thinks that this is caused by higher levels of particulates in the slowly transform-
ing atmosphere resulting in an increased scattering of light, rather than by an
actual amplification of the star's dimensions. Riding high on her grandfather's
bony shoulders she is borne aloft through massively expanded bottle-trees,
pregnant with hyperwater, and amidst the timid press of violet pygmies like
a baby queen. The fatal marmalade from Sundews of big-top diameter is hers
to taste, so that she shortly has a motorcade of monster dragonflies trailed
iridescent and suspended in her wake, sharp iris or sour jade, darting to lap
her sticky chin. Strolling in the arboreal centuries with gaping, fascinated
future-humans in their shrill mauve entourage they are the giant ghosts of an
earlier paradise, chalk-white and prehistoric, by some means arrived along the
Attics of the Breath from an unreachably far latitude that is no longer even
legendary. In gradual increments they come to understand a little of the native
spectres' trilling speech that rings and shivers in the dripping, crystalline delay;
in the exploded echo. One word at a time they piece together something of the
antic history that has informed these bald and embossed after-people, forag-
ing their wild Elysium: a changing climate and depleted ozone-belt have, it
seems, relatively swiftly compensated for the temporary arctic chill caused by
the failure of the Gulf Stream, in a mere few hundred years. The current era is
a tropic intermediary stage, when all the planet's lingering rain and vegetation
is restricted to the warming Polar Regions that are thus a last abode of earthly
life. With dwindling resources and a limited habitable environment, even a
much-diminished human population cannot be sustained without severe mod-
ifications. These have been accomplished by re-engineering in some fashion
the essential mortal blueprint, with mankind as a result much smaller and
possessing cells imbued with photo-active chlorophyll. The lustrous eggplant
colouration and the intricately corrugated skin designed to thereby maximise
its surface area are features bred into this new strain of humanity, who sup-

plement declining rations of available organic sustenance by gorging upon the abundant sunlight. Snowy and his infant charge eventually deduce, from such fragments of anecdote as they are able to translate, that these whorled and embellished near-indigo miniatures have a truncated life expectancy of less than thirty years before ascending to the higher pastures, to the ultrasonic flutter that is their term for Mansoul. This strikes the sinewy old man as woefully curtailed and his juvenile passenger as more than generous, a minor argument between them while they wander further down the fern-defeated promenade with its viridian dapple and extended perfumes. They pass on through blood-burst dawns afire with parakeets and bullion sunsets that electroplate the pair in liquid gold, pausing at last to make camp in the rustling midnight furlongs where a faceted extravagance that May identifies as Hyper-Sirius is visible against pitch black beyond the vine-macramé overhead. Their bivouac consists of monstrous bottle-green leaves bent across a mossy hollow and secured by thick black thorns, there in the metaphysic tropics after man. On rising, after the short walk to morning, they discover what appears to be a growth of Puck's Hats sprouting from an unidentifiable corroded mass which Snowy thinks might be a fallen ceiling-girder. Once again the astral fungi would appear to have adapted to their changed environment, developing new features so as better to entice the altered humanoids of these sun-flooded purlieus. This latest variety is, in the pair's opinion, the most thoroughly unappetising yet. The overlapping succulent and pale feminine forms that typified the earlier displays have been replaced here by a similar arrangement of abnormally large insects, lamp black and yet iridescent if they're turned against the light. The eye-pips are now faceted, and an experimental nibble at a snapped-off thorax has both of them spitting and complaining for some several time-miles at the vinegary flavour, near impossible to rinse away. At their next rest-stop, in the umbra of a towering and dilapidated kettle-drum construction, they unfurl their wolf-skin sack to feast on the albino 'snow queen' blooms that they've collected a few centuries back up the track. At May's suggestion they spit the pink seeds into the undergrowth about them, so that there might be a colony of fungi that are edible established here for the return trip, when the two of them are heading back this way from the far end of time. Invigorated by their breakfast of anaemic beauties they resume the journey once the little girl is set again upon the bronzing saddle of her grandsire's shoulders. Blurring down the arcade of forever, May remarks that they are passing fewer huge masks and gasometer-sized bongos, fewer purple people. She recalls

the empty green of Beckett's Park, drowning in light, there on one of her scant five hundred afternoons. She has no sense of where she ends or where the world begins, and having never seen the lovely golden cranium that everybody else makes such a fuss of, May assumes she is without one; that the whole width of the day and its astounding skies are in a monstrously vast glass bubble balanced on her headless infant shoulders. She can feel the silvery drag of fish-skin clouds across the blue inside her, while the birdsong is sharp citrus fluttering on her tongue and makes May dribble. She does not discriminate between the clever, complicated house-shapes on Victoria Promenade's far side, the polished farthing of the sun or the trees swaying, chimney-high, to lick the wind. Since all these things are to be found inside her absent head the child supposes them to be her thoughts, that this is what thoughts look like, square with blue slate hats, or tiny and on fire, or tall and whispering. The eighteen-month-old does not separate that second's slurps and shivers from its scents or shapes or sounds, confusing the asthmatic distant skirl of an accordion and the measured progression of the little gas-lamps just across the road, with both phenomena from her perspective being things that seem to roll down avenues. Then it's a different instant, with no gas-accordion wheezing out its wrought-iron notes at intervals along the street, and where indeed the street itself is vanished and forgotten as the child discovers she is moving in a new direction that entails a different vista. Floating effortlessly a few feet above the surf hiss of the carpet-grass, descending slowly to the miniature domain of further-off with its toy huts and shrubs and paint-fleck daisies, May doesn't remember that she's being carried in her mother's arms until the bobble-coated chocolate drop is put into her mouth. The warm accompanying maternal mumble melting on the baby's tongue is like the creamy sweetness in her ears. As she explores the varicoloured beads of sugar speckling the confection's upper surface, the sensation becomes inextricable from the pointillist blur-burst of a nearby flowerbed that May happens to be gazing at and she's immersed in an undifferentiated glory. She and the big favourite body that's called May as well and which she's a detachable component of seem to be standing on a hiccup in the ginger gravel underfoot, a bump with railings where their path squirts in a stony arc over a river like a very long old woman, splashing on its further bank to trickle off in pebble tracks amongst the weeds. One of the syllables her mother coos is "swan", a sound that starts off with a slicing whoosh then curves away into a stately glide, and something somehow flares into existence in the private centre of May's continuity, a thrilling white idea that flaps up into ghostly being, making a commotion. Swan. The word is the experience and it doesn't matter if she sees one now or not. Shifting her weight, May loses herself and forgoes the universe in favour of the freckles on her mother's throat. A spittle spray of toffee isles adrift upon a dermal ocean, floated on its pinprick ripples, each spot has its own unique identity seen from an inch away. This one is like a smoky lion's head yawning, this one like a piece of broken horseshoe, each no bigger than a grain of salt.

She focuses on their implied geography, on the relationship between these distinct and minuscule atolls. Do they know each other? Are the ones closest together friends? Then there's the overall arrangement to consider, preordained and perfect, each spot where it should be on a map that's here forever, purposeful and ancient like the constellations or the musical periodicity of lampposts. The giant beauty cradles May through time, through summer with the dandelion-clocks going off like steam grenades. There are so many leaves and branches to bear witness to, so many breezes to be met and all with different personalities, that it's a million million years before they're back in the same moment on the bridge again but this time without chocolate drops and crossing it the other way, from which a new and unfamiliar town is visible. A different angle is a different place, and space is time. Her future moments are the funny land in front of her where little things get bigger, not like in the funny land behind her where the things that seemed so large get littler and littler until they're gone into a dust-sized past, she doesn't know exactly where. Infinitesimal, the ant-cows from a minute or two's time mature to mouse-cows and then suddenly are old enough for her to see their eyelashes and to smell where they've done their business, staring without interest at May over the top gate-bar of the cattle market's wooden barriers. The fruit-and-pepper stink surrounding her, not in itself unpleasant, is attempting to inform her of its noble histories and pungent legend but the buzzing black dots of the story's punctuation make it hard to understand and so her mother waves it all away. The breast and bounce and rhythm of May's passage lulls the day into a distance as if it's a picture in a confiscated rag-book. Nearby hooves and cobbles drop the volume of their conversation as a courtesy, and she's exhausted just from all the breathing and the staring. Luminous pink curtains briefly drop on the theatre of real things, and May is hurried through a fascinating but incomprehensible scenario in which

a baby girl is galloping an old man down a far-off foreign century after the people and the after-people have all gone, arboreal decades trampled in their gallivant. The distant walls of the immeasurable emporium, where these are visible between the baobabs and modified acacias, are themselves now only stockade rows of monster tree trunks with no trading posts or other signs of structured artifice apparent. Evidently nothing human or post-human lives and dreams in the inferior territory Downstairs, the hothouse bayous that were formerly the Boroughs. Pointing to the wood-web overhead and the unfolded sky beyond, May draws her racing grandfather's attention to the lack of either birds or birdsong. Without breaking from his loping stride he hazards that this absence might imply a dreadful and illimitable cascade of extinctions. They run on in silence for a while, each inwardly considering this sombre possibility and trying to determine how they feel about their species vanishing along with a great torrent of its fellow life forms, sluiced into the drainage ditch of biologic obsolescence. Snowy in the end concludes he's not much bothered, bare feet pounding out the years of unrestricted lichen. Everything, he reasons, has its length in time, its linger, whether that should be an individual, a species or a geologic era. Every life and every moment has its own location; still there somewhere back along this endless loft. It's only here that mankind is no more, and when he and his granddaughter at last come back the other way with their preposterous pilgrimage complete he knows the centuries where Earth is habitable will be waiting for them, back at home amongst the sempiternal moochers and immortal rusted drainpipes of their own times, their own worn-out neighbourhood of heaven. Everything is saved, the sinners, saints and breadcrumbs underneath the couch alike, albeit not in the conventional religious sense of that expression: everything is saved in spacetime's fourfold glass, without requirement of a saviour. Snowy thunders on in the general direction of the next millennium, whichever that might be, with his exquisite passenger bumping and jigging on her wolf-hide saddle stuffed full of anaemic fungus-fairies. Only when they notice that despite the lack of any avian presence there is yet the plaintive squeal of song reverberating in the unpacked auditory space of the great corridor do they slow to a halt, preventing them from rushing at full tilt into the pod of moss whales. Trailing emerald coiffures of algae, the handsome and posthumous leviathans crawl ponderously across a post-historic clearing through the pink light of another hyperdawn, calling to one another in their eerie radar-sonar voices. Awed and dumbstruck the two travellers note that while the creatures' massive lower jaws and relatively tiny back-set eyes are undeniably cetacean, all appear to come equipped with an enormous pair of forward-thrusting horns, brow-mounted tusks that push to one side any overhanging branches which obstruct their path. Additionally, both their anterior and posterior flippers seem to have adapted into stubby legs that terminate in barnacle-encrusted hooves, each one the size of a bone omnibus, rhythmically splintering the world's-end vegetation as like grey-green glaciers they continue their protracted slither, off amongst the Brobdingnagian trees. Resuming their potentially unending expedition at a cautious walking pace, the temporal pedestrians engage in heated speculation as to the most likely origins of the extraordinary future-organisms. Snowy posits a scenario in which the drying of the planet's oceans has precipitated a migration of the more adaptable marine life onto land in search of sustenance, but he cannot explain the glaring incongruity of horns and hooves. After some cogitation, May suggests that if whales are air-breathing mammals that chose to return to the aquatic state from which all life originates, it may be that during their brief adventure as land-animals they were related biologically to some unlikely genus such as, for example, an ancestor of the goat. The white-haired ancient crooks his neck to squint up at his rider and determine if she's joking, though she never is. They carry on, and presently Snowy's hypothesis of boundless seas reduced to salt flats prompting a migration onto dry ground is confirmed by glimpses of the period's other mega-fauna, or at least that fauna's astral residue. Milling about one of the now irregularly-contoured apertures set in the arcade's creeper-covered floor, May notices the spectres of teak-brown crustaceans with shells four feet in diameter, like ambulatory tables. Later, they experience a moment of breathtaking wonder when the tract of forest towards which they happen to be walking suddenly uncoils itself, the detailed scene and its apparent depth detaching from the background to reveal a sky-scraping cephalopod, a towering ultra-squid perfectly camouflaged against its afterlife surround by means of the evolved pigment-receptors in its skin. Shifted to a presumably more comfortable position, next the tentacled immensity adjusts its shimmering disguise, its surface a spectacularly animated Seurat wash of colours that resolves into an almost photographic reproduction of the endless avenue about them. Snowy is reminded of the shifting pictures in the fire when he's only

a little boy in Lambeth, waiting for his father to get home from work. All day long the October rain's been falling from the broken guttering to spatter noisily upon the lavatory's slate roof, down at the bottom of the yard outside. John Vernall, two years, getting on for three years old, sits by the hearth and rubs his palms together until the mysterious rolled-out threads of liquorice muck appear for him to brush away or play with. He's been watching droplets on the century-old windowpane that has a faint green in its thickness, studying the form of the slow-crawling diamonds, an enthralled spectator at a liquid horserace. Some of the wind-driven beads go down at the first hurdle, failing to complete their long diagonal trajectory over the glass, their fluid substance dwindled and exhausted long before they reach the distressed wooden frame that is their finish line. Then there are plumper globules that appear to be more predatory and competitive, that hungrily absorb the hydrous leavings of their fallen colleagues and, with mass replenished and increased momentum, roll majestically across the glistening field to easy victory. When finally this inconclusive water-derby ceases to be entertaining, John squats on the homemade rug beside the fire and turns his wandering attention to the monumental Bible illustrations flaring into momentary being, engraved Doré vistas down between the sulking coals. Gomorrah's doom lifts in a grey veil from the splitting anthracite, while on those wood or paper remnants used to start the blaze the twisting black flakes are recanting simonists, adulterers or virtuous pagans suffering their disparate arcs of the Inferno. In the coruscation and the crinkling ruby light, ash-bearded prophets work their scorch-mark lips unfathomably, their warnings snatched away into the chimney's whistling throat, and somewhere in another land his mother and his grandmother are snapping at each other over where the money's to be found for this or that. His baby sister Thursa grizzles, fitful in her wicker-basket crib, her strawberry shrunken monkey face clenched to a fist, disconsolate and anxious even in her sleep, cowed by the world and all the startling sounds it makes. There's something queer about the dreary flavour of the instant and the small boy finds himself caught in a fog of indistinct presentiment that's indistinguishable from a daylight-faded memory, the details bleached out like the pattern on their tablecloth. Hasn't he had this darkening afternoon before, with Thursa making those specific noises in her crib, with Shadrach and the plagues of Egypt in the firelight, then a sizzling cat, then a volcano? Just before she utters them, John knows his grandmother's next angry words to his and Thursa's volubly upbraided mother will contain the puzzling phrase "no better than you should be", and he is uneasily aware that the most thunderous element of these precisely synchronised and rapidly coagulating circumstances is not yet in place. That wondrous and terrible event, he thinks, unwinds from out the complicated click and rattle of his father's latchkey which he can hear even now off down the passageway, commencing its insidious tinkle in the front door's mechanism as a prelude to the coming symphony, the irrevocable unlocking of a new and cataclysmic world. His mother leaves her confrontation in the kitchen to find out what's happening and the avalanche of the occasion smashes through their East Street home; reduces all the order of their lives to an undifferentiated panic matchwood. There is a commotion in the passage, with his mother's voice ascending from a confused and uncomprehending mumble to a gasping, devastated wail. The uproar bursts into the living room accompanied by John's sheet-pallid mother and two men the child has never seen before, one of whom is his father. It's not just the flour-spill hair where once were copper bedsprings that has made a stranger of his parent, more the change in what he says and how he stands and who he is. There's lots of gesturing and drawing circles in the air. There's an unreeling list of madcap topics that the silent child somehow already knows before they're spoken, a tirade of chimneypots, geometry and lightning, troubling phrases that nobody seems to pay attention to: "It's mouth was moving in the paint." John's grandmother emerges from amongst the steaming saucepans, shouting angrily at the rotund and florid bald man who's returned her son to her in this dismantled state, as if sufficient indignation might still somehow put her offspring back the way he was; as if insisting on an explanation could force such a thing into existence. In the embers now John notices a crumbling sphinx on fire, a martyring, a poppy banquet. Everyone except for him is weeping. Haltingly and incompletely, it begins to dawn upon him that nobody save for he himself and possibly his baby sister was expecting this to happen. The idea is as inconceivable as if John were the only person in the whole of London who could hear, the only person who had ever noticed clouds or realised that night follows day. The people and the furniture and voices in the peeling-paper Lambeth living room are like an indoor hurricane of tears and waving hands, with at its epicentre John's new white-haired father standing and repeating the word "torus" dazedly, the shape of things to come. Returning his attention to the fire he has the fugitive impression of red light and trailing darkness

in a sunset arbour following the world and Snowy's weathered, almost corru-gated thighs are dappled by sliding and elongated rose ellipses, an elegiac radi-ance filtering through sculpted voids in the waxed dinner-plate leaves of the canopy above him. With his darling burden he strides on into a reprised cryp-tozoic, all of history in his blisters. For a period they travel in the midst of an inquisitive and scuttling company: the amiable shades of table-crabs who seem to be endeavouring to communicate by tapping an adapted fore-claw on the moss-occluded boards of the immortal boulevard, an inarticulate crustacean Morse. Riding her grandfather as if atop a howdah the grave eighteen-month-old prodigy quotes Wittgenstein, to the effect that even if a lion could speak, mankind would not be capable of understanding it. As if in mute acknowledg-ment of this persuasive observation presently the entourage of furniture-sized arthropods abandon their attempts at conversation, losing interest, clattering away en masse between the monstrous bolls of that terminal orchard. Every-thing is doomed with beauty. Later there are further whale-goats and a huge tree-mimicking variety of octopus that they've not previously encountered, with impassive garnet eyes easily missed in the surrounding column of bark-patterned skin, and liver-coloured suckers on what first seem to be overhang-ing boughs. May formally proposes they should call the species Yggdrasil after the Nordic world-tree, given that taxonomy itself will surely be extinct by now and that the splendid creature thus must otherwise go nameless in eternity. The motion, after a debate and vote, is passed unanimously whereupon the baby and her wrinkled steed persist with their excursion through the final foli-age, amongst incurious monsters. After wading in the magma of four thou-sand serial dawns Snowy and May elect to make their temporary bed amid the shivering mimosas of a twilight mile somewhere in the next century, if indeed there are centuries anymore. As the old man remarks while fashioning a shelter from the shirking greenery, the base-ten counting system and conceivably the whole of mathematics must have surely disappeared from the inferior territo-ries downstairs by now. From this point on, where science and faith and art and even love are only fossil memories, he and his granddaughter must venture past the end of measurement itself, perhaps even beyond the unavoidable demise of meaning. The unlikely pair consider this new, unsuspected lower register of desolation whilst they messily devour their last remaining specimens of snow-queen Bedlam Jennies, prudently expectorating the pink eyeball-pips into the flinching and fastidious vegetation trembling about them. At the bottom of their wolfskin tucker-bag there are now only a few snapped-off chorus girl limbs much like shapely and anaemic doll-parts, with a sparkling dragonfly debris of wings. Above, cut into slices and trapezohedrons by the silhouetted branches, an unfolded constellation that is possibly hyper-Orion – Snowy notices three displaced repetitions of the famous belt – is stretched across the settling indigo, a malformed tesseract of ancient lights. Replete and comfortably sluggish after their fungal repast, the juice of tiny women sticky on their chins, they slide into the hypnagogic drifts of ghost-sleep mumbling and holding hands. Around their hide are brittle crunches, fracturings, reports distantly audible beyond the blurred peripheries of their awareness, probably the cringes and contractions of the cowering shrubbery within which they are nested and so swiftly filtered out by a receding consciousness. Gorged upon visionary arctic truffles both the baby and her ancestor are borne on an eidetic surf of faerie imagery, unwinding madhouse dioramas with a miniaturist intricacy that is bottomless and some-times borders on the terrifying: at hallucinatory Elizabethan frost-fairs stand bare-breasted ladies in preposterously large hooped crinolines with decorative motif snowflakes made of lace around the hems. Each has a flattened palm raised to face level for inspection, smiling in delight at the scale reproduction of herself that seems to balance there, complete in every detail, beaming down approvingly at the almost infinitesimal homunculus perched on her own hand, peering into a vertiginous regression of excruciating and exquisite pulchritude, a mesmerising vortex of wan femininity. These are the dreams the dead have when they're Puck-drunk. After an incalculable interval they shrug away their gem-encrusted drowse, refreshed despite the Midsummer Night alkalis that have been coursing through their slumbering ethereal systems. Waking, unsur-prisingly, to the same shade of dusk in which they bedded down, not until Snowy lifts their wolf-pelt satchel do they realise with bewilderment that while they napped the previously almost-empty sack has been mysteriously replenished, filled now to its brim with an unusually picturesque mass grave of conjoined Thumbelinas. Still more inexplicably these are not the albino strain responsible for their nocturnal visitations, but are rather the more ruddily-complexioned type familiar from the traveller's own now-remote home century. Not wishing to examine their gift horse's dentistry the bony veteran ties the pixie-bag about his shoulders, crouching while May climbs aboard. It calls to mind

him and his young 'un Thursa chuffing through the Lambeth chill to see their father, locked away in Bedlam, with the siblings' warm breath crystallising to grey commas in their wake. Being at ten years old the senior of the two John is in charge, towing his crooning and distracted younger sister down the fogbound lanes by one sweat-slippy hand. They skirt around the Temperance revivalists and ne'er-do-wells, the clustered corner conferences about the Kaiser or Alsace-Lorraine, avoiding those insanities they're not immediately related to. November scalds his sinuses and Thursa drags annoyingly, winding her dreary half-a-song in a damp skein amongst the toughs and gas-lamps. "Shut up, you, or I shan't take you to see Dad." The eight-year-old is loftily indifferent, screws her nose into a little concertina of distaste: "Don't care. Don't wunner see 'im. This is when he tells us about all the chimneypots and numbers." John doesn't reply but only drags her with more force, across the cobbles with their ochre archipelagos of shit, between the rumbling wagons, from miasma to miasma. Though he hasn't had a conscious thought about the subject before Thursa speaks those exact words, they fall upon him with the gavel-weight of a harsh sentence, long anticipated, indisputable. He knows she's right about this being the occasion when their father shares some sort of secret with them, can almost recall the countless previous times she's told him this, on this same night and halfway over this specific road, avoiding this precisely-contoured patch of horse muck, on their way to the asylum. Furrowing his freezing, aching brow John makes an effort to remember all the cataclysmic things their father will be telling them. Something to do with lifebelts, and the special flowers made of bare ladies that are all the dead can eat. This outrageous curriculum sounds eerily familiar, although for the life of him he can't see how it can be, not in the same world where the trudged-smooth slabs of Hercules Road are so immediate and hard beneath his worn-through soles. They carry on past Autumn-bare front yards with waist-high walls, through a green dark that the infrequent lamps only accentuate, towards the mist-wreathed shores of Kennington. Ahead their future footsteps are arranged like unseen slippers running off along the vapour-shrouded pavement, waiting patiently to be tried on, however fleetingly; waiting here on this side street for them since before the world began in their inevitable and ordained procession to the madhouse gates. His sister's hand is hot and horrible the way it always is tonight, adhesive with a barley-sugar glaze. A cab whose hoarding advertises Lipton's tea clops by on cue as their incipient prints lead them around a corner, up the way a bit and suddenly the wrought-iron bars and flanking posts of rain-gnawed stone are only a few moments, a few feet away. The hospital and the impending hour which it contains drag themselves eagerly across the intervening space and time, approaching through the churned murk like a plague boat or a prison hulk, crushing the kids to specks with brute proportion, piss and medicine on its breath. The keeper standing guard beside the gated entrance on its far side recognises them from other evenings and unlocks with a begrudging attitude. It seems to John not so much that the gateman doesn't like them, rather that he doesn't like them being there where grown-ups act like frightening children. Every time they turn up here he tells them they'd be better off not coming and then lets them in, gruffly escorting them across the walled-in grounds to the front doors in case of wandering stranglers or buggers. Once inside the building, swallowed by the stern administrative hush of a reception area with its austere high ceilings lost from sight to a gas-mantle glow of insufficient reach, Thursa and John's reluctant shepherd hands them over to another warden, a stone-faced and somewhat older man whose head is all grey bristle. "They're for Vernall. It's not right, them being here with all o' this, but there you have it and there's nothing to be done." The words have a faint echo, have a ring to them as if spoken before. Still holding hands, although for comfort rather than compulsion, they accompany their mute chaperone down creaking corridors that crawl with whispers and the memory of incontinence. A dusty, miserable residue of pipedream empires and bewilderment accumulates in phantom drifts against the skirting boards where their stilt-walker shadows list precariously, teetering abreast with them on this subdued and strangely formal outing. Bolted doors slide by, and contrary to popular opinion nowhere is there any laughter. Led into a dimly-lit hall of intimidating scale reserved for visitors, the urchins are confronted by an umber lake in which perhaps a dozen table-islands float suspended, juddering hemispheres of candlelight where inmates sit like stones else gaze enraptured into empty air while relatives stare wistfully at their own shoes. Marooned on one such islet is their father, the white hair grown out as if his head's on fire with gulls. He asks them if they know about tonight and John says "Yes" while Thursa starts to cry. An oddly reminiscent litany begins, lightning and chimneypots, geometry and angles, spectre-food and the topology of starry time; the widening hole in everything. He tells them of the endless avenue above their lives where characters called

May and Snowy stumble down forever, brazenly displaying their bare arses to each new extinction as they pass among its signs and markers. Soon there are no sylvan octopi or flickering hyper-squids, no séance-rapping crabs or pond-sized hoofmarks left by grounded whales. Above, the crumpled-paper diagrams of cloud seem scarcer and when visible less complex, having fewer folds and facets. The old man surmises that the world downstairs is drying, dying, and they travel on through the gigantic thinning trees, the great majority of which are dead with some entirely petrified. In their decade-devouring canter they devise a means of eating without pausing: the uncanny toddler intermittently retrieves one of the puzzling vintage Puck's Hats from the inexplicably full wolf-bag that she bounces on, handing it with great ceremony down to her grand-

father who ingests it as he runs, noisily spitting eyes and pubic fur-balls into the deteriorated woodland mulch beneath his slapping feet. While they don't have their mouths full they discuss the lingering enigma of their restocked rations without ever reaching a conclusion that's remotely credible. When Snowy ventures the hypothesis that possibly the amiable crustaceans back along the timetrack are responsible for this display of clandestine benevolence, May counters with a theory that it is in fact their own selves from some juncture of the future who are their true benefactors. Both proposals founder on the issue of the fungi's blatantly anachronistic provenance, and meanwhile there's less vegetation to be seen with each fresh furlong. Far away to either side the walls of the protracted thoroughfare can once more be discerned, their shifting dream-veneer fallen away or atrophied for want of anything still capable of dreaming in the territories beneath. Without their astral substance being constantly renewed and reinvigorated by an influx of novel imaginings, the distant boundaries can no longer recall the shapes or colours that were previously their own, the contours softening and gradually subsiding into waxy incoherence, hue a runny paint-box marbling with the greasy fever-sheen of rain-stained petrol, sacred architecture lapsing into a prismatic slobber. Past those faltering margins there are only the confounding depths of an expanded firmament as realised in more than three dimensions, intimating that beyond the Attics of the Breath the further reaches of Mansoul themselves are levelled. Like some hybrid chimera of age and youth, a generational centaur, May and Snowy gallop onward through what seems to be a final curtain falling on biology. Running pink caterpillar fingers idly through the locks of her gerontic charger as though grooming him for nits, the sombre cherub muses on the fragile existential nature of a world completely unobserved while all around them the last oaks and eucalyptuses are toppling unnoticed into history. At intervals of a duration lengthier than empires the pair pause in their apocalyptic marathon, to snooze after their fashion under lean-tos made from sloughed-off bark or dine on their diminishing supply of Bedlam Jennies. It is after breaking camp on one of these occasions and making the relatively short walk to the morning following, when they've long given up on the idea of sapient life in the terrestrial neighbourhood beneath them, that they come across the first of the peculiarly geometric mineral cacti. A three-sided pyramid as tall as Snowy, an elaborate beige stud erupting from the shrivelled moss and kindling litter carpeting the great emporium, each of its smoothly manufactured faces has a further half-sized pyramid projecting from it. These in turn sprout similarly scaled-down reproductions of the central form, and so on to the limits of perceptibility. The overall impression is that of a Cubist Christmas-tree sculpted from sand or some fine-grained equivalent, spiky and in its own way beautiful. The infant and her bronco ancestor trot in a slow investigative circle, orbiting the startlingly precise extrusion at a cautious radius and speculating on the nature of its composition. After some few circuits Snowy kneels so that May can dismount in order to inspect this strange apparent artefact at closer quarters. Waddling barefoot on a rug of desiccated splinters the deceased toddler approaches the suspiciously well-engineered phenomenon with the intrepid curiosity characteristic of the age at which death has arrested her development. She pokes a small exploratory bore-hole in the unexpectedly yielding and permeable exterior of the oddity, and attempts a preliminary analysis of its constituent matter by the straightforward expedient of putting some into her mouth. After an apprehensive period of mute consideration the unnerving paediatric sibyl turns with wonderment to her intrigued grandparent and announces "It's an anthill." Stepping closer to the enigmatic polyhedral solid, the gaunt patriarch sees for himself the colony's immediately despatched repairmen skittering like beads of ink as they efficiently patch up the damage caused by May's intrusive digit. Having no desire to further inconvenience the first-recorded insect presence to have been discovered on that upstairs tier of existence, the baby remounts her famously deranged and silver-crested relative and they continue with their world's end picaresque. There is still evidence that life prevails. Snowy thinks back to when

the fever cart performs a muted drum roll, more a cymbal whisper as it dwindles with the family's hopes, trickling away down Fort Street. Sitting on the cold throne of his doorstep since the grey hours of that morning, waiting with his seat reserved for the forthcoming drama, the old troublemaker watches passively while the appalling scene is acted. All its awful flourishes are at a distance to his heart, affecting only in the sense evinced by the much-thumbed engravings of a penny dreadful that have forfeited the frisson of crude shock accompanying their first appraisal. Somewhere off amidst the bubble-and-squeak vapours down the passageway behind him he can hear Louisa cautioning their other children still at home, their Cora and their Johnny, telling them they're not to go outside and stick their noses in. Out in the smothering hush of Sunday the dismal scenario proceeds through its traditional component stages; the inevitable feet of its exacting meter. Big May, Snowy Vernall's eldest daughter, stands there in the middle of the rudimentary road and shudders in the arms of her chap Tom as if trying to wring her very life out through her tear-ducts, unavoidably caught in the brutal and indifferent mangle of the moment. Moaning in a universal Esperanto of mammalian bereavement, the young mother with her hair a ginger fizz throws out her freckled arms to the receding wagon while her husband shuts his eyes against this terrible defeat and says "Oh no, oh no", holding his wife back from the abyss of broad daylight that has claimed their daughter. Squatted on his draughty front-row perch Snowy is gazing down the tunnel-length of continuity to his earliest glimpse of the grown woman whose life is disintegrating there before him, crimson-faced and weeping in a gutter, then as now. More than a score of years back down the track he wobbles on the camber of a Lambeth rooftop, fishing in his jacket pockets for the rainbows he intends to shower upon his firstborn, the confetti spectra that will be her welcome to these fields of light and loss, her memorable and reeking stained-glass debut. Telescoped in Snowy's baggy eye the howling infant is become the shattered parent bellowing her grief along the church-quiet terraced row, the operatic staging underlined as suddenly a lone orchestral voice from offstage in the wings reprises note-for-note May Warren's heartsick aria, but in a lower octave. Crouching on his stoop like a presiding gargoyle on cathedral guttering her father shifts his sad gaze and his first-night audience attention from the disappearing horse-drawn ambulance, from the diphtheria bus back to the crowding side-street's nearer end and the anticipated source of this unkind and inappropriate accompaniment, this mocking counterpoint. His owl-eyed sister Thursa has appeared from nowhere at the elbow of the lane, the corner bending to a contour of the all-but-vanished castle's previous fortifications. With accordion slung around her stringy neck as though some portable variety of Maxim gun and hair that of a senile gollywog, her entrance is electrifying. Her translucent fingers resting on the false-tooth rows of ivory triggers, Thursa dominates the brick amphitheatre for all of its classic tragedy and pouring radiance. Her older brother understands by the transported smile which plays about his broken and dissociative sibling's lips that she is listening to the multiplying echoes of May's scream and her squeeze-box response as propagated in an auditorium with concealed depth and volume, the sounds ricocheting in a supplementary space. He knows that she's attempting to embed her tribute to May's dying baby as a sonic solid in the glassy stuff of time, as an exquisite aural headstone for the Fiends and Builders to appreciate at their considerable leisure. His anguished daughter, on the other hand, can only see Thursa's demented smirk, a silver thread of spit depending at one corner from between the browning molars. Thus provided with an opportune receptacle for her tremendous sense of unacceptable injustice, Snowy's eldest wheels upon her aunt to vomit noise, a venting of unspeakable emotions from a place where language holds no jurisdiction. The tear-streaked tomato of May's face ripens towards its bursting point. Her pole-axed soul is audible, its higher frequencies curdling the grubby air while Thursa, beaming and delighted at the thought of being joined in a duet, adjusts her placement on the keys and milks a further repetition of the devastated mother's utterances out of her asthmatic instrument, once more at a descended pitch from the original. At this renewed affront May's personality collapses visibly upon itself. She slumps in Tom's grip, whimpering, and Thursa's bird-claw hands dance on the keyboard mimicking every despairing vocal flight or fall. Snowy remembers that this is his cue to rise from his worn stone theatre seat and take his part in the eternally reiterated masquerade. Steering his sibling gently by her worsted sleeve he takes her to one side and solemnly informs her that her improvised performance is upsetting everyone; that little May has taken ill and will most likely soon be gone. At this point in her scolding Thursa giggles disconcertingly, recalling the largely-untroubled eight-year-old of near three dozen long winters ago. Eyes gleaming, she excitedly confides that far above mortality and at that very moment little

May rides her grandfather's shoulders, the agreeable face of their ambulatory totem pole, along the narrow avenues of what amounts to an extended city of the pyramidal, modernistic anthills that the duo have encountered, singly and at wide-spaced intervals, during the last few decades of their stampede through the biosphere's decline. The mathematically self-referential shapes, repeating their own neatly pointed structure at progressively reducing scales, surround the travellers on every front in mesmerizingly exact and ordered chessboard rows, each geometric edifice perfectly equidistant from its fellows in a dizzying grid that reaches to the vast emporium's eroding edges. The uninterrupted blue concavity of sky that's presently surmounting this optically challenging expanse contains only the unpacked golden ingot of an ageing sun which shrivels the remaining crumpled tissue scraps of hypercloud to nothing. Picking their way daintily like a two-headed Gulliver through the thorny metropolis of an insectile Lilliput, the pair attempt a disquisition on the subject of the obviously highly adapted mounds and their significance. As the most senior member of the family present, it is Snowy's firmly held contention that the ants are in all likelihood still-living creatures that have blundered physically into this spatially enhanced domain much as the pigeons and occasionally the cats do, back in those now-distant reaches of the temporal overpass where cats and pigeons still exist. Conversely, as the longest-dead of the two Armageddon tourists, May asserts her own belief that in all probability the oddly regular protrusions represent a posthumous extension of the hierarchically-arranged and combinatory awareness corresponding to each individual construction. Further, she suggests that the collective consciousness of every hill has seemingly evolved to a condition where it can imagine a continuation after its destruction or eventual dismantling. This evolution is implied, the baby reasons, by the arithmetically sophisticated alterations to the hills' basic design. Being himself numerically inclined, her grandfather finds that he is reluctantly persuaded to this point of view. Begrudgingly he posits that the markedly self-replicating property displayed by these arresting figures indicates a calculating system of considerable sophistication and complexity, which in its turn perhaps denotes a level of mentation able to conceive of a hereafter, as his infant passenger maintains. The ever-smaller reproductions of the overall configuration would at least appear to demonstrate a grasp of algorithms, Snowy postulates, and in this manner their debate goes back and forth as they progress amongst the man-sized alien sandcastles. The azure lens of afternoon floods bloody as the human dray strides on through a declension of rich iris, tarry purple, and so forward to another of the subordinate planet's nights. The couple tiptoe down a formic acid-fragranced boulevard beneath the radically extended risen moon, a compound of eight separate lunar spheres fused to a single brilliant cluster with its light a colloidal suspension silver-plating the hushed ranks of polyhedral bill-spikes stretching off in all directions. They go by the treasure-fountain of another daybreak and the soot-fall of a further dark, and there is no abatement to the neatly regimented ranks of prickly ziggurats that are distributed so as to occupy the floor-space of the chronologic causeway most efficiently. Snowy is gradually becoming apprehensive: "I don't fancy bedding down between these buggers much, but I expect we'll have to. It most probably runs on like this for centuries while this lot have their time Downstairs, with all these rows like cemetery markers and nowhere that we can stretch out and be comfortable." After a pensive silence, his granddaughter shakes her catkin locks in disagreement. "I think that they might have had their time Downstairs already. Carry on another day's length and we'll see.' Though doubtful, her antique conveyance does as he's instructed. They continue through the paradise of ants while over them the cloudless stratosphere adjusts its palette, moon-chromed darkness burnishing to salmon dawn and thence to the monotonous, oppressive lapis of a world that's dying for want of bad weather. Trudging through a lap approximately corresponding to mid-afternoon, May issues a reconnaissance appraisal from her elevated vantage: up ahead the dense-packed lattice is now chequered, every second pismire monument removed to leave a square of empty space. This gradual depopulation is persistent, and when they at last attain the violet outreaches of dusk there are no more ochre assemblies to be seen. The toddler theorises that an advanced species of ant may have been extant for a millennium or more without conspicuously manifesting at these altitudes of being, since colony-organism anthills are effectively immortal unless wiped away by some external force. The recently traversed apparent city, May believes, might be more properly perceived as indicator of a mass extinction, one concluded in only a day or so. They contemplate this as they make their camp, devour their last few Puck's Hats and retire. On rising, they discover that the wolfskin bag is once more inexplicably refilled, and while they march on Snowy thinks of how

the darkness over Fort Street is at least to some degree particulate the day his grandson Tommy calls, seeking assistance with his sums. The pall above the terrace is, he thinks, as much a product of his mood as of the waste-destructor tower in Bath Street, though the two aren't wholly unconnected. The Destructor is no more than the most obvious sign of a voracious process chewing up the district in the decade since the end of the Great War. The earliest demolitions have left shocking absences amongst the area's tilting byways, white cement-dust blanks on his internal map which line up worryingly with the hyphenations he has lately noticed in his memory. He's halfway through his sixties and, even without the powers of calculation that his twelve-year-old descendant is depending on, has got a good idea of how all this is starting to add up. He's going cornery, forgetting things, imagining things as he nears the terminus. Another four or five years if he's lucky, though he might not have the faculties to count that high by then. His death, of course, does not discourage him; is just one more familiar station on his line. He's seen it all before, the endless corridor and the convulsing old man with – what, paint? – Paint in his beard, those scraps of colour? Something like that, anyway. It doesn't bother him. What bothers him are these slow increments of the Destructor and the meaningful world's end commenced in Bath Street. As the beneficiary of a demanding Bedlam education Snowy knows what chimneys signify, knows the devouring nothingness potentially contained by every terracotta shell's circumference. The greater part of the catastrophe he fears lies not in the material aspect, brown breath curling in the waste incinerator's fifty-foot brick throat, but rather in the immaterial immolations that proceed unchecked; invisible. Symbols and principles are going up in the same billowing black cloud as shit and bacon rinds and jam-rags. Much as he resents the smutty thunderhead at present overshadowing his neighbourhood, his family, his shabby people, he is actively afraid for all those things if he should contemplate their gutted Heaven or their surely uninhabitable fire-sale future. It's so dear to him, his world. Louisa offstage in the dripping-scented kitchen, humming something that might be "Till All the Seas Run Dry" with both raw fists around the handle of her spoon, churning the lumpy and reluctant fruitcake mixture. His embarrassed grandchild turning redder than a beetroot trying to conceal his pride when complimented on his aptitude for mathematics, his astute grasp of the underlying symmetries implicit in ten simple digits. Snowy cherishes the day's every last atom, each translucent grease-spot on the paper spread across the elbow-polished tablecloth. He cannot bear the thought of all this human consequence become waste-matter and assigned to the Destructor, emptied onto the annihilating bonfire of selective English memory. Barely aware of what he's doing he directs his pencil-stub into loose orbital trajectories, skimming the surface of the unfurled meat-wrap and describing two concentric circles, a toroidal outline seen in elevation or a pigeon's-eye view down the barrel of a smokestack. Filling in the figures nought to nine at intervals around the ring, each numeral laterally opposite its secret mirror-twin, he makes the round band into the perimeter of an outlandish clock-face with its numbers disarranged, as though the medium of time itself were made abruptly unfamiliar. He begins explaining all of this to the eleven-year-old boy beside him, but can see already how the child's attentive frown is shifting on a gradient from concentration to wary anxiety, starting to grow afraid both for and of his grandfather. From Tommy's face Snowy assumes he must be shouting, though he can't remember turning up the volume and knows anyway that it's too late to stop. Under his winter wilderness of hair ideas are racing, are accelerating dangerously towards a fugue and skidding in collision. In his hands the drawing turns from skewed clock to cross-sectioned chimneypot and then at last into the pitiless, negating glyph of a distended zero, grown so fat on vacuum that its curving boundaries struggle to restrain it. He screws up the butchers' paper to an angry ball, propels it overarm into the blazing hearth just as the presciently alert Louisa leaves her baking to announce that the maths lesson is now done, dismissing their unnerved and apprehensive-looking grandson, sending him off home out of harm's way, out into Fort Street where it's snowing filth. Fascists in Italy, the new chap with the big moustache in Russia and they reckon everything began out of a dirty great explosion. Turning like a bull about the fragile matchbox living room he knows they're right, but that they have not yet absorbed what their discovery implies regarding time. The primal detonation is still going on, is here, is now, is everyone, is *this*. We are all bang, and all the thoughts and doings of our lives are but ballistics. There are neither sins nor virtues, only the contingencies of shrapnel. In his wheeling trample, Snowy is brought short by the reflection in a looking glass above their fireplace: an ancient mariner, ranting and staring back from an uncannily extended space. He breaks the mirror with a paperweight. It's all too much like his recurring premonition, where

the geriatric pony snorts and capers in a passageway of aerodrome enormity, undressed and cherub-ridden. Those untrammelled trees which once erupted from the many vents set in this upper storey's base are gone with not even their petrifying hulks remaining, whereby shadow is made into a diminishing resource rarer than tanzanite. Above, the over-sky's daunting expanse is now unmitigated by the least intruding bough or spar and seems infected by a faintly greenish tinge. It is May's supposition that this might result from altered planetary atmospheric composition in the absence of both water and biology, the varying wavelengths of sunlight scattered differently as consequence. The old man, slobbering gob filled with the succulent ghost-fungi that his thoughtful rider feeds to him like sugar-lumps as they continue their ridiculous safari, cannot disagree. The leagues of day are a thin soup of peridot, entirely unre-

lieved by cloud or crouton, while the leagues of night are clearer than an icicle and bursting with schematic star, unfolded comet. Underfoot the granular saw-dust detritus of pulverised forests is at last exhausted, and the eon-treading cou-ple are astonished to discover that beneath this carpet of organic litter the pine floorboards of Mansoul are no more to be seen. At some unnoticed demarcation point of the icebound or overgrown millennia already travelled the planed planks have been replaced by – or have otherwise reverted to – coarse and uneven rock, a two-mile broad promontory of randomly amalgamated limestone, flint and hard chalk reaching off into a lifeless deep where only astrophysics and geology endure. The bordering arcade walls are now a smooth igneous tumble of liques-cent dream-material, though still high enough to adequately mask whatever flattened remnants of the Second Borough yet exist beyond the strip's extensive margins. Stepping like a mummified flamingo, Snowy circumspectly navigates their way about the numerous irregularly contoured apertures that perforate the former boardwalk's rugged mineral flooring. Lacking animated creatures to provide the snaking jewellery forms that previously typified the lower realm as seen from this superior elevation, now the holes look uniformly onto rag-ged patches of bare desert. Nothing moves, nothing respires, the attics having finally outstripped the breath. They carry on through brownish dawns, green days, blood-orange sunsets and wide onyx stripes lit by a sickle moon expressed as eight such crescents interlinked, a puzzle-ball in silver. Pushing forward into centuries untenanted they while away their trek with self-invented travel games, compiling lists of things that are no more, like consciousness, or pain, or water. When they tire of this pursuit they try a variation listing those phenom-ena that yet endure, such as the periodic table, certain anaerobic species of bacteria, and gravity. This second set of items, while extensive, is more readily exhausted than the first and therefore does not entertain them for so long. If they become fatigued by either their perpetual transit or the unremitting sense of end they doze on stone beneath a hyperbolic zodiac, the naked man sprawled like a pile of sticks, an unlit fire, beside the almost empty wolf-pouch in which he insists the clever baby snoozes. Waking, walking through night's residues to breakfast in the burning sepia of a colour-shifted daybreak they could almost be a pair of bronzes struck to represent the old year bearing in the new. With vegetation no more than a memory and memory itself forgotten, May and Snowy's view along the corridor ahead is no longer curtailed by obstacles. Their ocular abilities, enhanced by death, should offer them an unrestricted prospect of the everlasting hall, this being straight in its construction and entirely unaf-fected by the curvature of the terrestrial world beneath. However, as they plod the towpath ages both remark upon their inability to see beyond a certain point of the great lane before them. This, they reason, must imply a contradictory bend in the plumb-line precision of the avenue's geometry, or else exemplify

the rounded bulge of the continuum itself, their sightline limited by spacetime's
intervening humped meniscus. Further down the road the overreaching heav-
ens are striated into varicoloured stripes of dark or day, bandwidth compress-
ing with proximity to the unnervingly remote horizon. Doggedly the wizened
Atlas perseveres, hefting his blonde encumbrance through the barren minutes
and evacuated hours, reducing their still-unexplained reserve of Bedlam Jen-
nies as they go. When May reports two distinct specks in the far distance her
grandfather is at first inclined to scepticism, a position subsequently modified
after they've traipsed a few more land-weeks and the vanishingly tiny dots have
swollen and resolved themselves into a man and woman wearing fashionable
1920s clothing, more outrageous in their way than any of the super-ants or
sunlight-fed replacement men thus far encountered. The anachronistic couple
stand their rough-hewn ground, patiently watching the extraordinary infant
and the time-tramp she is riding in their slow approach, and Snowy notes that
the impeccably dressed pair are holding hands. Of the extinguished things that
he and May have previously listed, the romance and sex are what he misses
most. He thinks about the way

Earth's scudding satellite outruns filleted clouds above the cattle market,
keeping pace with Snowy and the landlord's bonny daughter from the Anchor,
a celestial chaperone for their first proper evening out. He doesn't know the
town that well as yet except through an amalgamated sense of premonition
and nostalgia, so has no idea where she's taking him. The mellowing bouquet
of cow-manure along Victoria Promenade is somehow intimate, and even
though he hasn't seen Louisa for the six long months that he's had work in
Lambeth, he is firm in his presentiment that by the time tonight is done with
he'll have had her knickerbockers down over those shapely ankles and will also
have proposed his sex-damp hand in marriage. Overhead the July stars are diamond pepper grinded from the mills of space and at his side, night-amplified,
the metronome tock of her heels is music he will set his life to. Talking in
low voices so as not to dissipate the atmosphere he lets her warm, demanding
counterweight on his right arm steer both of them into the reaching black of
the Cow Meadow, giggling and unsupervised to where the only jurisdiction
is of tactful shadow. Caught in resin by the gaslight near the lavatories two
working men exchange a bristly kiss and fumble with each other's buttons,
while girls coo from out the rustling bushes like nocturnal pheasant eager
for their beaters. Whispering, Louisa and her beau pass on into the gasping
dark as all around another Friday ends in moonlit joy and jetting seed and
grass-stain; in the peerless and abiding silver luxury of dogs or paupers. Rolled
out on benighted pasture in a carpet grey as beaten tin, their path delivers
them unto a gravel walk beside the tinkling river, crawling away east between

tall undertaker trees towards tomorrow morning. Upstream a reflected moon puffs pockmarked cheeks and holds its breath beneath the tinsel surface but here, overlooked by conifers, an iron bridge arcs across obscure torrents that are made from only sound, a gush of metal syllables like small change jingling in a wishing well. At the halfway point of the creaking span a breeze unpins one strand of her sienna hair, and in his tender stretch to tuck it back their lips fall upon one another as though feuding sea-anemones until Louisa says "Not here" and leads him, blind, onto a starlight-painted island bifurcating the onrushing waters. Worn by countless feet down to its sandstone nub, a track lassoes the land's perimeter. They walk around it to the isle's far side, attempting casualness at first, then hurrying, then laughing as they each abandon all pretence and break into a run. The worn turf bank, moulded by love across the course of several smelly-fingered centuries, has overlaid impressions of ten generations' breasts and buttocks visible to fancy as a palimpsest in the slope's contours. An accommodating sycamore spreads out its knuckled roots for the forthcoming game of jacks, and current catches on stout reeds, and sky snags on the clawing branch-tops. Standing, kneeling, lying down, they sink by stages in the foaming clover with tongues jousting and their hands at war with fastenings, with elastic. Blouse discarded and the rudimentary flesh-tone camisole displaced, Louisa wears her tits with necessary pride, white lionesses slumped magnificently on their ridge above the hollow of her ribcage. An innovative, ambitious tamer without either whip or chair, sequentially he takes their heads into his mouth. Sweat-savoury, the nipples swell as if about to hatch fritillaries and Snowy and Louisa are both thrilled and gasping kids at the perennial circus. Underneath the marquee linen of her skirt warm thighs part like some tight-pressed crowd granting admission to a secret sideshow, where his callused digits are allowed ingress two at a time. Like undecided customers they hover at the velvet entrance, venturing inside before withdrawing only to push in once more, unable to make up their minds. The hem goes up like curtains and the drawers go down like lights and there, there is the never-before-seen exotic animal; there is the slippery slapstick stage. A cat crouched at its saucer, hunching there between her legs he laps and tries to savour like a connoisseur but in the end gives up to guzzle like a costermonger. Gnawed ferociously she spends and screams and then is glazed with acquiescent shock, a downed and shuddering wildebeest and when he takes his prick out of his trousers it's like iron, newly cast and ready to be quenched, immersed, with a great rush of steam. She reaches awkwardly to steer it home by hand and he is launched into her, an exquisitely slow slide on an oiled gantry, sinking into warmth up to his curly waterline. The scent of cunt and river curving to a lime-sharp edge of pressed mimosa fires him, and he understands their furious coupling in the engineering sense, both of them functioning as one rapturous lubricated moving part, hissing and racketing in time's invisible machinery. Slick mercury boils over from its bulb and he ejaculates inside her, spurts their daughter May into a Lambeth gutter and their same-name granddaughter into the fever cart. He squirts a thousand names and histories, spunks Jack into a foreign grave and Mick into a steel-drum reclamation yard and Audrey into an asylum. He comes grief and paintings and accordion music, as he knows he must, to guarantee that several million years away in the abandoned ruins of paradise

the nude berserker and his piggybacking conscience start to gradually decrease their frightful pace when they are some three geographic days from the two well-dressed strangers, coming finally to a standstill, eye-to-eye in the miscoloured furnace of another post-organic dawn. The woman, short and shapely, wears a dress of shimmering viridian to her knees with dove-grey stockings and jade court shoes, hair an auburn tumble to her bare and handsome shoulders. Her escort has the appearance of a late Victorian dandy clad in just-discovered mauves and wistful violets, his immaculate frock-coat ensemble topped incongruously by a battered junk-shop bowler hat that looks like someone might have died in it. Against the tangerine effulgence of a compound sunrise their contrasting hues affect a lurid harmony of the kind sometimes found in dreams. Beside the duo, covering a gingham tablecloth unfolded on the petrifactive arcade floor is a mouth-watering heap of fresh-picked Puck's Hats. "My name's Marjorie Miranda Driscoll while this is my consort, Mr. Reginald J. Fowler, and I must say it's a privilege to meet the pair of you. You're in a book I'm writing – I hope that's alright – and we've been tunnelling through the ghost-seam to keep you supplied with food. I don't think we can do it anymore, though. There's not much left of Mansoul beyond this point, so there's no way of climbing up here. I'm afraid there's no more rations after this, so I thought that we'd take the opportunity to introduce ourselves and tell you where the Bedlam Jennies have been coming from." Her voice and her delivery, though adult and well-spoken, have a quality like that of a child playing dress-up or an actress who's still settling into her role, so that Snowy surmises neither she nor her companion have been attired in their current semblances for very long. The young man seems especially discomfited by his well-heeled apparel, running a censorious finger round inside his high starched collar and occasionally expectorating a dismissive wad of ecto-phlegm, more as a statement than for any decongestant purpose. At their feet the barren stone is wet with citrus light where their stilt-walking shadows are stretched tight behind, like rubber bands nearing the limit of Hooke's law. Having shook hands in formal introduction and with May dismounted, the unusual quartet arranges itself comfortably about the square of linen for a fungal picnic under skies abandoned save for blinding apricot.

Convivially, they interrogate each other. May enquires after the seemingly ongoing dissolution of this upper realm, beyond the causeway's distant and subsided bounding walls, and learns that there is nothing left: even the Works is a deserted shell, with its remaining crook-doors made progressively more inaccessible by the continuing collapse. Next, the demure Miss Driscoll asks if Snowy and his granddaughter, as the protagonists of her forthcoming second novel, are expecting to encounter the Third Borough anywhere between here and the end of time. After a thoughtful pause, the white-haired veteran replies that no, he's not anticipating any such convergence. "Although if we haven't stumbled over him by then, at least we'll have a good idea of where he's not." Out of a satin cloche-bag that she carries the young authoress produces a slim tome with green cloth boards, inlaid with a gold illustration and the volume's title, which is "The Dead Dead Gang". This, as she explains, is a signed presentation copy of her debut that she would be deeply honoured were they to accept. Turning the offering over in his starved spider-crab hands Snowy admires the binding, wondering aloud if Mr. Blake of Lambeth was not in some measure an accomplice to its manufacture. Both their world's-end guests nod eagerly at this and Mr. Fowler breathlessly recounts, with the excitability of a far younger man, how he and his intended have gone all the way along the Ultraduct from Doddridge Church out to the higher regions up above Hercules Road, soliciting advice on publishing from the pugnacious and inflammatory divine. " 'E wiz a smashing bloke. I really liked 'im." Equally enthusiastically, May tells how she and her bedraggled nag have called upon the roughneck visionary and his wife when they themselves essayed the dazzling overpass along its length from Chalk Lane to terrestrial Jerusalem. "When we met with them they were being Eve and Adam, reading Mr. Milton's verses to each other in the nude. That's really why we thought we'd go without clothes on this longer expedition. It just seemed like something that the Blakes might do." Miss Driscoll scribbles something in an oyster-tinted notebook at this juncture, yet when asked about it blushes crimson and explains that she is merely jotting brief descriptions as to both the timbre and the colouration of the marvel-baby's voice. "Melt-water trying to be serious" is all she'll let them read. "It wizn't very good. I'll more than likely change it." They trade anecdotes in the unwavering amber of the dead world's daybreak and then load all the remaining Puck's Hats into May and Snowy's predatory haversack, along with the donated book, before making their last farewells. Sartorially splendid in the fires of Earth's unmaking the young couple wander hand in hand towards the avenue's far margins. Taking May once more onto his shoulders, Snowy reminisces about

how the world appears to dance with youth and shape itself to youthful expectation and requirement, at least to the young. At seventeen the gale-tossed trees that fringe his many roads are making supplication but to him and Lambeth is his ornament, meaningful only when included in his gaze, not there if he's not. Women of the borough make their beauty visible exclusively in his vicinity, a colour which they emanate beyond that spectrum readily discernible to other men, apparent solely to the chosen pollinator. Hedgerows fruit with breasts miraculously at his passing. There are secret tide-pool lilies opening in lace undergrowth along his path as though he's Spring itself, brimful of birdsong and forever on the bone with pretty windfall arses everywhere. He has more sperm in him than he knows what to do with and the planet circling about his axis seems to share the same promiscuous excitement, shooting lightbulbs, telephonic apparatus and the annexation of South Africa in glossy rivulets across the mundane counterpane. The hands of history are deep in sticky pockets, rummaging, and Britain rules a moment which it has mistaken for the globe. Even in Queen Victoria ascendant as Empress of India he sees all the components of a subsequent decline, even if one not culminated in his lifetime. There will be resentment; massacre worse than Bulgaria; futile Satsuma rallyings against inevitable change; ghouls dressed in newspaper who wait a little further down the empire's as yet only partially unrolled red carpet. Grinding rhythmically against the ancient and incurious alley wall, wearing a squeaking breastplate made of girl and a tight belt of legs, he is exultant in the mechanism, throws his head back barking at the stars and knows the future's jests and injuries to be already acted. Standing in a hammering South London downpour is the ruffian John Vernall, rumoured to be touched, aware that all the individual droplets in their pounding vertical descent are actually unmoving, are continuous liquid threads that reach from storm-front down to street in long parabolas through solid time. Careening like some Hindu god or stroboscopic photograph amidst the static crystal floss, only the motion of his mind in the concealed direction makes it rain. Nothing, excepting the involuntary forward momentum of his consciousness from one half-second to the next, transmutes the angry martial statuary of a pub yard into the yapping brawl with settled scores and noses blossoming to bloodflowers. The process of his attentions turns the sky, and otherwise the clouds and zodiac are still. Rogue Elephant Boys, unafraid of anybody, swerve in their stampede to keep out of his way for fear that his condition might be catching, terrified lest they end up as human spiders more contented with the vertical than with the horizontal, railing from a rooftop about arseholes, lifebelts and geometry. He strolls between the bloody, arcing billhooks of their confrontations unconcerned, a prescient pigeon strutting carelessly amongst the dropping hooves and crushing carriage wheels. The ructions and the razors cannot kill him; cannot hinder him in his eventual appointment with the tulips and the looking-glasses, fifty years from here and in another town, another century. He'd like to meet a Spring-Heeled Jack, one of the phantom clan prolific in the city throughout the preceding decade, leaping flea-like over barns and middens with their fireball breath reflecting in the circular glass lenses of their eyes. Even should they prove to be marsh-gas or else Pepper's Ghosts, theatric spectres conjured in an angled pane, still he believes he'd find an easier berth in that outrageous troupe than with the flightless company abroad upon the avenues and bridges, harnessed by the flattened limits of their Ludo-token days. Sore pimples bubble in the creases of his nose and dirt silts on the webbing in between his fingers, a saliva-born black residue cast up by near-incessant self-pollution. Beer is the brown blanket that he pulls over his head to muffle a cajoling world on those occasions when he feels his tender age, when understanding raw apocalypse in every, every, every instant is too much for him. At night he hears the herald angles bellowing fierce imprecations in their queer exploding language and he huddles with his daffy sister, who can hear them too. "Don't cry, Thurse. It's not you they're after." While this isn't true it sets the bird-thin fifteen-year-old's echoing cathedral mind to rest, at least until the next time that the builders who knocked up the sun dance on the roof in thunder-boots and shout their terrible imperatives. They're after everyone, that's the plain fact of it, but save their energies for those who are not deaf to their deranging voices, him especially. Sometimes he looks for solace on the pleasure-hills, amidst the million lamps and cancan thighs of Highbury with all the other freaks and acrobats, and even there he hears their typhoon remonstrations telling him to bed this woman but not that one, telling him to hobble sixty miles northwest or shin a hundred feet directly upwards. Unsolicited they show him tableaux from a little further down his individual fleshy tunnel as it worms its way into futurity. There is a marriage in a fine hall with a builder watching from the rooftop's crest. There is a grandchild born then born away, and even when he's dead, when everyone and everything are dead, he knows that

the old warhorse charges naked on a final highway, baby-ridden under gradually migrant galaxies. The doomsday ramblers pause less frequently along the featureless rock ribbon to make camp and feast on their decreasing fungal rations, spitting out the optic pips in hope of thriving Puck's Hat colonies as food caches for their eventual homecoming. When they approximate sleep, Snowy settles for a bed of stone and curls his knobbly spine about the infant mumbling in her wolfskin bag while space and time are steadily unpicked above. During the daylight miles it is apparent that the Earth has cloud once more, furled ochre cellophane which May surmises may be chlorine in an admixture with methane. During dark the half-moon multiplies into a Deco abstract wreathed in vapour, with its light a spectrographic halo-stain on evening's filter paper.

All this change and distance, Snowy thinks, and they've not left the Boroughs. Little Cross Street and Bath Passage are still down beneath them somewhere, albeit in a state of chemical and geological deterioration. They continue. When the sack of Mad Apples is finally all but exhausted they experience what first seems to be a mirage born of starvation, a peculiar mirror-fluke of the great alley's atmospherics: racing down the barren strip towards them from its far end comes an old man with a baby on his shoulders. So exact is the reflection that the travellers half-expect an imminent collision with some monstrous pane hereto invisible, both knocked unconscious, leaving a Daguerreotype of their spread-eagle impact printed on the glass in feather-residue. They are surprised, then, when their doppelgangers turn out to be as substantial as themselves; turn out indeed to be themselves on the return leg of their legendary journey. Both the Mays dismount and hug each other while the old men merely shake each other gruffly by the hand. "Well, now. How has this business come about?" "It's hard to say. It strikes me that the end of time is like the last day of a school term, when the non-essential rules may be somewhat relaxed and minor paradoxical infringements are occasionally permitted." "Did you reach the end of time, then?" "Oh, most certainly, but you'll appreciate that it would be improper of us to convey more than the scantest details." "You don't want to push your luck with all the paradox and that?" "That's it exactly. I can tell you that you'll do all right for Puck's Hats, though. Only a few weeks west of here we've lately passed the place where you will shortly spit your last few seeds out, and there's a fine patch of fairy-blossoms already established. Some way further on you'll find another, probably resulting from the spat-out eyeballs of the colony just mentioned, and so forth until you reach the point where I am now and find yourself explaining all this claptrap to a slightly younger fellow. It occurs to me that we have possibly had our behaviour controlled by Bedlam Jennies so that they may propagate their species to the very limits of spacetime's duration." "Put like that it sounds like an outlandish notion, but upon reflection I'll allow that it provides a stronger motive for our visit to the end of time, which until now has only been to find if such a thing is there or not, and what it looks like if it is." "Oh, it's a sight, you can be sure of it. By then, of course, the mass of things is gone and taken with it all the gravity. Likewise the nuclear forces are by then retired and put to bed, but still, for saying there is very little substance it's a most substantial show. Ah, well. We've dallied long enough, and I do not recall our conversation having had a great deal more to it than this. Might I suggest we shoulder our respective babies, taking great care not to mix them up and thus cause an insoluble controversy, following which we shall both be upon our separate ways, as I recall this puzzling but not unwelcome incident." The two Mays, who have been conversing quietly throughout all this, are lifted back up onto their respective steeds. After an unexpectedly emotional farewell both duos once again continue with their journeys, bare feet slapping on the causeway's rugged stone, heading in opposite directions on their tight-rope over time until in only a few hours of distance they are mutually invisible. Progressing inexorably towards the end of everything, the end of even endings, Snowy's nominally earlier incarnation asks his passenger what passed between her and the other May during their unanticipated meeting. "I made sure that I remembered everything she told me so that I could say it back correctly by the time I'm her. The most important thing she said was, 'We have come back from Jerusalem, where we found not what we sought.' I asked her what she meant, but she just shook her head and wouldn't tell me." Pounding down the hard miles to finality, Snowy considers this. Other than an obscure suspicion that the comment might have some connection with the same Professor Jung who failed to fathom Lucia Joyce, he is no nearer to a resolution by the time he and his rider reach the paradoxical expanse of Puck's Hats that their future selves have told them to expect. They dutifully eat the last of their existing rations, spitting out the pretty eyes before they go on to collect a sack-full of the mature blossoms that those seeds will grow or have already grown into. Dining upon impossibilities the old man can still picture how

his earliest encounter with the food that ghosts eat comes when he's aged twelve and drunk on ale for the first time, a brimming jug he's swiped from home and swiftly emptied in the fornication-scented alleyways of Lambeth. Reeling full of bravery and poison past the walls of the old Bethlehem, his stumble is arrested by the sight of flickering colour dancing just above the darkened paving slabs ahead. In the same way that floating shapes behind the eyelids often crystallise into coherent images when on the brink of sleep, so too does the prismatic shimmering resolve into an insubstantial coterie of tiny ladies with no clothes on. Through the intervening folds of beer and murk he marvels at their tits and fannies, being the first proper ones he's seen, and can't believe his luck. The women waver and there is a sound they make that is initially like individual voices giggling, and yet after a time these seem to merge into a high-pitched whine at the periphery of the young drunkard's hearing. He stands leaning with one palm against the mossy stone of the asylum gatepost, wondering muddily if this means he's about to die, and is not reassured when passing strollers seem to only laugh or voice their disapproval at his obvious inebriation while they kick obliviously by or through the haze of naked manikins cavorting at their feet. He understands with a dull pang of apprehension that these manifested fantasies are visible or audible to him alone, perhaps a vision presaging his own internment in the institution he is currently propped up against, made an apprentice madman to his own incarcerated father, both off with the fairies. Swallowing warm spit he thinks about

the inmate that he saw on his last visit with his sister, elderly and scabby-faced
from the repeated self-inflicted beating of his head against a door. The stolen
booze and scalding bile erupt into John Vernall's throat and he is copiously,
blasphemously sick over the gossamer-winged little people swirling unconcerned about his ankles. Undulate as weed in water the translucent nymphs
ignore slivers of fish-flesh from his supper, part-dissolved and steaming, and
continue with their lazy sway as if moved by a breeze or current rather than
their own volition. Sweat streams down his forehead. Foot-long threads of
dribble dangle trembling from his panting mouth, his sagging chin, and the
damp pavement is on fire with girls. Their perfect pink-white faces are identical and make him think of sugar mice, the features blank and motionless with
no more human feeling than if he were scrutinising some ingeniously camouflaged variety of insect, horrid beetle thoughts concealed behind the painted
icing of their eyes. The mere idea precipitates a second surge of vomit and the
unconcerned minuscule females, stood in its foul spatter as though showering
in some crystal waterfall, elicit yet a third. Distantly he becomes aware that
other passers-by are drawing closer and prepares for further mockery, only
to look up in surprise when this is not forthcoming. Even through the filter
of his reeling senses he immediately realises that there's something wrong
with the approaching onlookers. Drifting unhurriedly towards him along the
inadequately gas-lit street come two men and a woman, shabbily attired and
without any colour whatsoever, figures carved from smoke. They seem to be in
agitated conversation but the noise of this is muffled, as if come from far away
or else as though his ears are plugged with wax. The trio pause when they
draw level and regard him, albeit with a less judgemental eye than the nocturnal stragglers who passed him earlier. One of the men says something to the
oddly dressed old woman, evidently with regard to the inebriated urchin, but
it's much too faint to hear. Shivering now and drenched in icy perspiration,
he is disappointed to discover that these unobtrusive newcomers are no more
able to perceive the pixies pirouetting in his spew than were their raucous predecessors. Something else, however, seems to have attracted their attention:
silvery and grey like a Daguerreotype, the crone in her old-fashioned skirts
and bonnet is now pointing to the upper reaches of the pillar that the boy is
slumped against. Her lips are moving as though under glass, her utterances
only audible to her two male and monochrome companions, one of whom
steps forward now and reaches up to fumble under the eroded, jutting lip of
the post's capstone. As he does, one of his sooty arms slips through John's
own outstretched and trembling limb as if it isn't there. The tall and spindly
man seems to be prising something blurred and indistinct from off the madhouse gates, and simultaneously the pretty miniatures are guttering like candle flames. The shrill hum that he had at first mistaken for their voices rises to

a maddening whistle and then shuts off altogether, at which point the pygmy dancers vanish into scintillating dust and he is staring only at a pool of his own recent stomach contents upon which the iridescent meat-flies are already settling. The lofty wraith is lifting something down, some shadowy and writhing octopus or hydra, tearing off its limbs and sharing them amongst his phantom colleagues as the three fade gradually from sight. Surrendering, the wayward youth closes his eyes. The liquid shapes bloomed from that private dark are truant stars above a ceaselessly unreeling scroll of path where

the relentless bag of bones runs on, hunchbacked with innocence. The barren avenue that vanishes beneath him is entirely featureless save for the welcome clusters of chronology-defying Bedlam Jennies, so much so that these oases, blossomed from the bedrock at roughly millennial intervals, become the travellers' only clock or calendar. Even the apertures that once looked down on the terrestrial First Borough are now mostly gone, healed over with what seem to be volcanic sediments, and other than celestial dramas acted on the canopies of night or daylight overhead their expedition is without event. At their infrequent rest-stops they read chapters from Miss Driscoll's book to one another and attempt to calculate, from the configurations of the sky, how many billion years they are from home. Snowy thinks two but May seems relatively certain that it's three. In the nocturnal stretches of their journey into afterwards the overhanging firmament seems crammed with hyper-stars, a lot more than there used to be. The learned infant speculates that this stellar profusion has resulted from the Milky Way commencing its collision with another astronomical array, most probably Andromeda. Her theory is corroborated after seventy or eighty further Puck's Hat patches have been passed, by which point the immeasurable dark above them is a chaos of crashing suns, a catastrophic ballet staged in extra mathematical dimensions. The appalling centrepiece of this performance is a struggle to the death between two fields of nothingness, hungry immensities which May informs her grandfather are said to lurk unseen at each star-system's heart, their frightful mass responsible for turning the jewelled nebulae. The spheres of blackness are made visible by radiating silver halos of what the eighteen-month-old believes to be unfolded X-rays spindling out to fill the heavens, the twin auras overlapping in a terrifying moiré of annihilation. Further scrutiny reveals that both monstrosities are wearing trophy-belts of dust accumulated from the helpless interstellar bodies they have whirled around at inconceivable velocities and smashed together, pulverised on impact. Inexorably the dark giants make their mutual approach, cannibal emperors unwavering in their determination to devour each other there in the arena of a ruined cosmos. Trying not to look at the deranging spectacle above them, Snowy and his granddaughter pass on. Years in their thousands are left trampled underfoot. The warring midnight absences presiding over that bare strip of track appear to be attempting some tremendous fusion into one light-swallowing colossus, with the rioting stars about them gradually resolved into a new merged galaxy that Snowy dubs Milkdromeda but May refers to as the Andy Way. The travellers persevere, amusing themselves by inventing names for the unrecognisably collided constellations, birth-signs for an era without births: the Great Chrysanthemum, the Bicycle, the Little Tramp. They carry on, and during the diurnal reaches of their passage observe that the unpacked fireball about which the planet spins is noticeably larger, an effect that can no longer be attributed to atmospheric vagaries. The white-gold orb's engorgement worsens and when they have hiked another million or so years there is above them nothing but inferno from horizon to horizon, Mercury and Venus both engulfed already in the bloody solar bloat. For what seems an unending distance the intrepid pair are journeying in flame and settling down to sleep on ember stones that pulse red and translucent even through the ectoplasm of the couple's eyelids. Both agree that slumber on a burning bed is contrary to every human instinct and thus offers little in the way of respite, though of course they are no more discomfited by the apparent heat than by the icebound floorboards of what now seems an eternity ago. To their considerable relief, the fairy-fungus that sustains them seems alike impervious to such perceived amendments of the temperature, and at their next stop they discover an extensive colony of the exquisite radiating doll-forms thriving on that furnace-bright terrain. Soldiering on, when May and Snowy have at last become accustomed to incessant conflagration so that pyrotechnic vistas are no longer cause for comment, it takes countless centuries before they realise that the elderly and swollen sun is dwindling by steady increments in the long, shamefaced aftermath of its infanticidal binge. A near-incalculable distance later it has been reduced to a discarded cigarette-end, winking out of being in the universe's lightless gutter. Solemnly aware that they are witnessing the death of day, the old man and the child proceed with their excursion into unrelieved immortal night. As they progress the dark above them is evacuated of its last illuminations when even the starlight is extinguished, Arcturus and Algol either snuffed like candles or else relocated by a constantly expanding universe to somewhere out beyond the curvature of spacetime; over the continuum's horizon and too far away for even radiance to travel. Navigating with their dead-sight they move through a landscape with its contour outlines stitched in tinsel. Finally disoriented by his own duration, Snowy wonders if the whole adventure is another of his fabulous delusions, flashing momentarily through his disordered mind as

he goes wandering from his Fort Street home, uncertain of what year it is or where he lives. Shuffling lost down Moat Street he remembers it as being filled with water once and wonders when they had it drained. The fish must have looked dreadful, flopping and asphyxiating in the gutters. It all changes in a wink these days, everything vanishing or turning into something different. Following a path of least resistance, a well-trodden street-plan crease, he rolls up Bristol Street and down Chalk Lane where there are poppies squirting out of brown-gold crevices in the old burial ground's limestone wall. Across the way the turquoise paint on the Blue Anchor's signboard peels and curls beguilingly beneath the sharpened Wednesday morning sunshine, every detail of its scabby surface limned in fire. He knows they've got a lovely girl behind the bar there at the Anchor, beautiful Louisa who he got his oats with down in Beckett's Park a while ago. He only hopes his missus never learns of it. Beneath a fleeting cloud of muddled guilt he shambles on through summer, heading for Black Lion Hill and Marefair down the dappled lane. Carthorses nod in passing to each other on the blinding cobbles and he weaves his passage cautiously between them to the sanctuary pavement outside Peter's Church while all the crumbling monsters of its stonework gape at him in outrage. When he makes his way along a hairline alley to the building's rear the Saxon chapel seems to him ablaze with moment and significance as if he's looking at it for the first time or the last, and in Narrow Toe Lane he finds he cannot see for tears although he doesn't know what they're in aid of and within a dozen paces has forgotten them. White cumuli slide down the sky like foamy spittle over Green Street. Underfoot the York stone flags carry the scars of ancient rivers, fossil fingerprints that he supposes were made several hundred million years ago when only trilobites and ammonites lived in this little row of terraced houses, slithering out to sit and chat on their front steps during the warm Precambrian evenings. The ancestral buildings, crouched and tired and leaning on each other, have an aura of familiarity as if the millipede of his true form expressed through time has on countless occasions doubled back and forth upon itself along these weathered slabs, and it occurs to him that he has family here. Doesn't he have a daughter living somewhere round these parts, a girl named May? Or is it May who died of the diphtheria when she was just a baby? Snowy trudges past a sequence of ill-fitting wooden doors, their numbering up in the high eighties, and at last finds one he thinks he recognises right at the far end, Elephant Lane, down that way, next door to the builder's merchants with the painted gate. Unpolished and thus slowly darkening, the old brass doorknob squirms reluctantly against his sweaty palm then yields. The heavy slab of pitch-stained black swings open with a whinny from its hinges to reveal a passageway, its weak illumination and tea-brown obscurity conflated in the old man's senses with its bouillon scent of rising damp and sagging flesh. He sees the human odours, smells the light and cannot recall ever having done things otherwise. Shutting the door behind him without looking he moves down the cramped hall, calling out a speculative greeting to the darkness squatting halfway up the stairway but the dark has clearly had enough of him, like everybody else, and doesn't answer. Nobody's about, his entrance to the silent living room confirms, excepting for a cat that he believes might be called Jim, asleep before an unlit fireplace, and three bright viridian meat-flies that he doesn't know the names of. A south-facing window ladles rays across the room in strictly rationed measures, smearing yellow honey on the glazed bulge of a flower-vase or along the varnished curve of the piano-lid and suddenly it comes to him that he's known all of this before, the cat, the flowers, the angle of the sun, the same three nameless flies. He's known this moment all his days, down to its most excruciating detail. Part of him has always been here in this half-lit cubicle while he's been otherwise engaged with swaying on the Guildhall's slates and walking in a trance to Lambeth, visiting his father in the madhouse, copulating on the riverbank or being sick over the little folk. By the same token he knows he's still there in all those other places even now and doing all those other things, still wavering on the brink of that tall rooftop; that short woman. He is teetering now upon the speckled hearthside rug, finally overcome by vertigo at the sheer drop of his own continuity. Exhausted by it all he sinks into a battered armchair and the window-shine behind him turns his thinning hair to phosphorous. The chained dog in his stomach growls reproachfully and he's forgotten the last time he ate, along with all his other vital details. This is where he dies, he understands that. These walls that enclose him are his last ones and the world beyond this square of carpet is a world he'll never tread again. He feels remote from his own creaking frame, hungry and aching in the chair, as if his circumstances were all something happening in a play, a well-known closing act repeated line for line, night after night; life a recurring dream the dead have. The old nuisance can't tell if he's really here, the unnamed flies impatiently anticipating his demise, or if

he's sprinting through the final night that has no dawn with his dead grandchild yanking at his ears to spur him on. Above, the void disorganises. Heat is fled save for those vestiges at the reactive cores of cosmic halo objects, vast accumulations of dark matter only rendered visible by a decreasing pulse of infrared until this too is ceased. The muffled metronome of padding feet on stone is their accompaniment in straits where universal darkness and frigidity are made inseparable; where black is just cold's colour. Doggedly they journey on, spacetime's last spectres running blind towards a limit that they only know is there because they've met themselves returning from it. This is the one certainty they cling to through the endless, lightless distances, and it only when they are

beginning to doubt even this that from her human crow's nest May reports a
fleck of radiance at the vanishing point of their all-but vanished highway. By
the time they've drawn a few millennia closer, this scant spark has swollen to
contain the empty skies above in their entirety, a shimmering butterfly corona
from horizon to horizon, a display of shifting marbled hues which the two pil-
grims have all but forgot the names of. Stood against this dazzle where the road
appears to end abruptly in an iridescent nothing is what seems to be a single
silhouetted figure of unusual height and girth, positioned as though waiting
patiently for Snowy and his granddaughter to reach it. Both adventurers can
feel the hairs raise on their necks as simultaneously they reach the same con-
clusion with regard to the obscure shape's probable identity. They've each thus
far reacted with a studiedly dismissive flippancy to the idea that their peregri-
nations might entail such an encounter, but with its reality almost upon them
the old man and baby girl alike become uncertain and, for the first time, afraid.
May's voice beside his ear is an uneasy whisper. "Do you think it's him?" His
own reply is hoarse and strangled, a constricted rasp he's never heard before.
"Yes, I suppose it is. I had a lot of things to say to him, but I'm so frit I can't
remember what they were." The confrontation they have privately longed for
and dreaded, whilst a terrifying prospect, is significantly less unbearable than
the alternative of turning round and running back the way they came. They
carry on in their approach of the inevitable form which looms at the conclu-
sion of their path, naked into that presence, and John Vernall grows increas-
ingly confused about which segment of his caterpillar continuity he's currently
experiencing. All his moments fall upon him in a pack, coterminous, a fugue
as complex and disorienting as his sister Thursa's compositions, bringing an
unprecedented yet somehow familiar sense that

he's about to meet his maker. Catapulted from the armchair by a fear that
death should find him sitting down he stands there swaying in the cluttered
room his universe has been reduced to. Woken by this sudden flurry of activity the cat weighs up the situation and decides to exit by the window, open
on its sash, leaping from ledge to garden wall to rain-butt and descending
by instalments to the sunken yard outside. The flies attempt to follow but
are insurmountably confounded by frustrating panes. Reeling with one hand
clutching at the chair-arm for support, Snowy appreciates only too well the
impetus behind this animal and insect exodus: the damp and crowded chamber, with careening ice-rink scratches on the sideboard's varnish and with
gold fruit softening in its bowl; this is the end of the time. Who could have
thought that it would be so little? His gaze darts around his final vista as
he tries to cram his eyes full with its details and make a last meal of their

significance, eventually alighting on the mantelpiece where something glints intriguingly. The single halting step he takes towards the hearth for a closer inspection is as jittery as any that he took upon the slippery rooftops of his youth. The item that has captured his attention turns out to be a medallion, a Saint Christopher that he believes might be the one he wore for all his Lambeth-to-the-Boroughs marathons so long ago. He scoops it up within one liver-speckled and vibrating hand, only to instantly forget that he has done so as his wandering awareness is next seized by the decrepit fellow staring at him from the glass above the fireplace. There is something in the haggard features that he recognises, and it comes to him that this is Harry Marriot from the next house along. He looks much older than he used to, but it's been a little while. Lifting the hand containing the religious talisman Snowy gesticulates in greeting to the other man, obscurely reassured when the same gesture is immediately returned. He's glad that Harry, at least, still seems pleased to see him. Peering into what he takes to be the similarly furnished house next door he notices what seems to be a further window in its far wall. This affords a view into another Green Street domicile with yet another old boy – possibly Stan Warner from a little further down – facing the other way and waving through a subsequent portal at what might well be Arthur Lovett from just up the road. Turning to glance behind him, Snowy spots the aperture on his own room's far side that looks onto a similar procession of frosty-haired veterans in endlessly receding parlours. He appears to be stuck in a queue of ancients lining up for their demise, all waving to each other amiably, their individual domestic spaces reconfiguring into a single tunnel. It's as if

he's in a relatively narrow channel of near-infinite extent, finally close enough to the imposing shape that blocks his path to see that it is actually a pair of nine-foot giants who are stood shoulder to shoulder. Both are barefoot, clad in plain white linen smocks, and each one holds a snooker cue proportionate to their tremendous size. The figure on the left has hair as colourless as Snowy's, and is instantly identifiable as Mansoul's trilliards champion, Mighty Mike. His curly-haired and russet-bearded counterpart has mismatched eyes, one red, the other green. This latter rumbles with amusement at the human couple's tremulous approach. "Look at the faces they've got on them! Why, you'd think they were expecting the Third Borough!" Perched atop her grandsire, May's smooth forehead corrugates to a suspicious frown. "Perhaps we were. But aren't you Asmoday, the thirty-second spirit? What are you dressed as a Master Builder for?" The erstwhile fiend raises his bristling brows in mock surprise. "Because that's what I am. I served my sentence and got my old job back. At this point in time," he gestures to the cosmos-spanning spectrographic backdrop, "all the scores are settled and the falls are far behind us. We can let bygones be bygones, surely, here where everything's a bygone?" As the infant chews this over, her grandfather at last finds his voice

"Why isn't God here, and what are these lights and colours?" He is shouting at the empty room, no longer capable of understanding his own utterances. The pensioners in all the other dimly lit compartments seem as agitated as himself, all waving their Saint Christophers and bellowing the same unfathomable questions in a maddening roundelay. His world subsides to disconnected jigsaw shapes as names and meanings drift out with the ebb-tide of his ragged breath. Barely aware of his own body or identity, only a distant clenching of his gut reminds him that he's hungry. He should eat some food, if only he can call to mind what food is. The locale rotates, its articles of furniture all circling him like merry-go-round horses, and it comes to him that when he ran down the long road through time with his dead grandchild on his shoulders they survived by eating blossoms which were somehow made from shrunken women. Snowy notes a vase of luscious tulips on the table as this glides past in its dawdling fairground orbit, and it seems to him that fairy-fruits and flowers are as like as makes no difference. With his free hand, unencumbered by the quite forgotten medal, he commences greedily to stuff his rotten mouth with petals while the neighbouring patriarchs in their adjacent rooms all ill-advisedly follow his lead. Choking on glory he is elsewhere, and a devil dressed in white is saying

"Oh, he's here alright. Or at least, here is him. The fireworks are what's left after the gravity and nuclear forces pass away. Only electromagnetism is left standing." Snowy groans. "So this is all we get, then? But we've come such a long way." The rehabilitated demon smiles and shakes his head. "Not really. You've not yet set foot outside the Boroughs. You've just both been running on the spot for several billion years." Beyond the two colossi is the precipice that marks the highway's end in tumbling veils of brilliance. Raised up from that awful cliff-edge as a marker is the rough stone cross he last remembers seeing set into the wall down at Saint Gregory's. Growing around and on it are a colony of succulent, ripe Puck's Hats. His mouth floods with salivary ectoplasm but he finds that

he can't swallow, stringy throat obstructed by amazing Easter colours. In their never-ending file of parallel apartments, he observes that all of Green Street's other elderly male occupants are doing just as badly as himself, walking in circles with their eyeballs bulging and bright scraps of masticated tulip flesh that turn their straggly beards to painters' aprons. It's a rotten turn of luck that they should all be in such straits at the same moment, when in normal circumstances they'd see what was happening and pop next door to slap each other on their backs. He's breathing a bouquet, he's breathing wreath, the panic in his lungs cascading to his heart. He can feel something clutched in his left hand but can't remember what it is, and all the time

he's waiting for the arch-builder to tell him something vital and conclusive. At last Mighty Mike turns to enquire, "Vernalimt whorey skung?" Vernall, what limit are you seeking? Unprepared, Snowy considers and replies, "The limit of my being." Here the titan offers him a sympathetic look. "Tenyhuafindot." Then you've found it. The time-vagrant nods. He understands that

this place is the end of him. If there's significance he has to find it for himself. His pool of vision, rapidly evaporating at its edges, shrinks to frame his slowly opening hand. A metal disc rests on his palm and raised up from its surface is the image of an old man with a glorious baby riding on his shoulders. It means something, he is certain, and the final question to traverse his failing mind is

"Where do we go after this?" May's voice sounds almost petulant. The reformed fiend and Master Builder shrug as one, as if to point out that the answer's obvious. Gradually,

Snowy understands. He isn't breathing. That's because all of the oxygen he needs is to be had from the placenta. Squirming in his mother Anne's spasming birth canal, forgetting everything,

he moves along the lightless channel carrying the infant with him and knows that, inevitably,

he is going back to where he started.

CORNERED

to judge, that's what keeps going round and round with me well I suppose you could say I believe that everyone should have the benefit of what's the phrase, I worry sometimes when I can't remember things, benefit of the doubt, there, everyone should have it well not everybody obviously not some of them round here, with them what they should have it's more doubt of the benefit in my opinion you take her, the one with stripy hair Bath Street St. Peter's House I think she lives you see her on Crane Hill up from the Super Sausage black girl well not black mixed race, from what I hear she's on the lot the benefits the crack the game part of the pond-life the Monk's Pond-life I should say I mean it's not her fault up to a point and if you're from a disadvantaged background then statistically it's like predestination how you end up but I still think and perhaps I'm just old fashioned but I still think everybody has to take responsibility for their behaviour obviously sometimes there's extenuating circumstances we've all done things that we didn't want to when there wasn't any other choice although some people I'm not saying it's their fault but they don't try to help themselves they just biodegrade until they end up like old bubblegum that's on the pavement year in year out in the end you barely notice it's another social residue part of a natural process people like that and I don't mean ordinary decent working people, people like the Super Sausage girl are unavoidable bacteria and if you like the street's a gut it cleans itself, the lifestyle, it gets rid of them eventually where was I

oh benefit of the doubt yes I remember it should be extended, I think, to those of a certain I don't want to say class that's not me and anyway that's been made into such a loaded term, but of a certain standing in the town let's say a kind of public figure I suppose you'd call it, getting things done nearly forty years and always always on the people's side it comes with being from a Labour background and I've never been a champagne socialist a Mateus Rosé socialist at one time possibly, that I'll admit to, though I've always had a common touch at least that's what the wife says no I'm only joking what I'm saying is, I'm part of this community been living down here all these years bit of a local landmark you might say close to his roots and I think people most people respect that when I'm seen out and about like now they smile and nod and recognise me from the paper and I think I'm generally appreciated but of course there's always one or two

it's quite a nice night not what you'd call summery but better than it has
been Mandy's out walking the thin blue line with her police friends what with
one thing and another it's not often these days that we're home at the same
time I often say we're like those couples that you used to get in weather houses
those old novelty barometers we had one up in Scotland when I was a scruffy
little muppet although no doubt there'd be those amongst the worthy opposition or in my own party for that matter who'd say that was still the case, no
with her being out I didn't fancy rattling round the place as if I was a dried
pea in a cocoa-tin and since I stood down from the council what three years
ago to as I put it spend more time at home with Mandy there's not been so
much to do I thought I might as well go for a turn around the block perhaps
call in and have a swift half somewhere before wending my way back it's been
a few years since I did that on a Friday night although at one point it was
every week we change as we get older in what we can stomach and of course
a Friday night in town these days is asking for it really with the way it's gone
these sixteen-year-old numpties, half a dozen theme pubs every street it's like
that Enoch Powell speech only rivers full of vomit and not blood although
you get a fair amount of that as well down at the A&E it's definitely a decline I
blame bad government and yes to some extent people themselves they have to
take responsibility for what they've done but it's too easy I think saying everything's the council's fault what people fail to understand is that our hands are
often tied but anyway

in Chalk Lane there's a moderate breeze but not so as you'd notice really
left or right here should I go uphill or down a left will take me up into the
Boroughs and that can be well not dangerous but on a Friday night and all of
the remaining pubs are either dead or full of people that you wouldn't want to
spend a lot of time with, right it is then and so into Marefair, going downhill,
following the path of least resistance

just across the road there the Black Lion looks like it's on the way out I can
remember when it was all bikers not what you'd call threatening but things
could be unpleasant around chucking-out time with the noise and everything
it's not fair on the residents a load of half-baked pissheads revving up shouting
the odds but anyway they're gone now long gone and we're rid of one more
obstacle stood in the way of Castle Ward getting the new development and
I suppose you could say the new people that it needs to be a different place a
decent neighbourhood to move up in the world not that we'd ever sell that's
not what it's about it's an attachment to the district, not for how it is but how
it could be living down here all these years of course it's not our only property
but it's the one that we're identified with part of our brand if you like I mean
the oldest most historic part of town we'd lived here years before I'd heard
more than the barest outline, to be honest I was never all that interested but

when you find out about some of it well it's fascinating you take Peter's Church across the road there put up in the first place by King Offa as a chapel for his sons at their baronial hall in Marefair then it's rebuilt by the Normans in eleven something and hold on what's that

a teenage boy it looks like floppy brown hair jeans and trainers with an FCUK shirt on that's too big for him a lanky streak of piss he's in St. Peter's doorway underneath the portico and shovelling something up into his arms as if he's in a hurry it's a sleeping bag, he's dossing at the church the mangy little twat I'll have a word with Mandy when I see her next oh hey up here he comes stumbling along the path between the flowerbeds out the church gate with his bag like an enormous boneless baby clutched against his scrawny chest and scuttling across the street he's in a rush alright although I can't imagine where he's got to go

"Good evening."

not a word straight past me and away up Pike Lane Pikey Lane somebody's changed it to and frankly you can see why though I've never liked the term myself well it's derogatory isn't it, you know something about the way he ran at me across Marefair like that I felt a bit weird for a second not quite déjà vu but it reminded me of something though I don't know what it can have been did someone run at me like that across a street before or oh wait I know what it was it was that dream I had I put it down to dodgy seafood at the time when was it eighteen months, two years ago, I was in Marefair in the dream as well but it was night I couldn't find my shirt or trousers and had I gone outside in my pants and vest to look for them I can't remember but I know the street looked different in the moonlight was there any moon the dreamlight anyway there were all buildings from the present jumbled up with places that were knocked down years ago and there was that damp creepy atmosphere the Boroughs seemed to have when we were first moved in and in the dream I was just starting to feel a bit anxious and self-conscious about being out in just my underwear when I saw somebody across the street this old chap with a trilby covering his bald head and he ran, he ran at me across the road exactly like that boy just now but he'd got it was horrible he'd got dozens of arms and where his face was it was just a lot of eyes and mouths all screaming at me screaming like he hated me I don't know what I'd done to make him hate me like that but I woke up in a sweat with my heart going and there wasn't anybody there it's just this place with nightmares in its timbers like old farts trapped under bedsheets in my bones I'm still a Marxist to the core I don't believe in ghosts

and anyway that's just the sort of fright you give yourself when it's the middle of the night but you look at the place now on a nice Spring evening you see what it could be, there's St. Peter's with the long light on its limestone and

then here just up the road Hazelrigg House where Cromwell bunked down
before his demanding day at Naseby when you think about it frankly it's a
marvel, Doddridge Church just up Pike Lane back there across the years people have said it must be awful living in a tiny neighbourhood like that but
honestly it's not it does us anyway a bit of smartening up we could be happy
here and if the district's small well then so what I'm not a big chap in the
height department so it's big enough for me it's like the Bard said what was it
I could be bounded in a nutshell and yet count myself king of infinite space
were it not that I

something like that anyway no it's a lovely night I'm glad I came out for
a walk I'm glad that I'm not in my vest and underpants there's no denying
that it's changed, the neighbourhood, changed since we first moved in was it
in 'sixty-eight around that time I mean the south side of Marefair well that's
still pretty much the same at least the upstairs but with different businesses
moved in below kebab shops takeaways what have you and the rooftops are
all largely how they've always been across the street though on the north side
it's a different story there's the ibis obviously Sol Central the whole complex
when they put it up it looked like something out of the first Batman film but
now I don't know on a Saturday or Friday night you tend to see a lot of couples
checking in who don't look like they've known each other long drunk blokes
with hard-faced younger women or sometimes with spotty lads of course it's
not my business I think everyone should have the benefit of the old doubt
but when you think about it yobbos fornicating right where a Saxon baronial hall one stood and after that the Barclaycard headquarters it still doesn't
seem right almost sacrilegious, here we are, the crossroads up the hill directly
opposite there's Gold Street and already I can see where further on towards
town centre there's the usual muppets wandering in the middle of the road
girls with their arse-cracks showing and it's only just gone seven

on the other hand there's hardly anyone about in Horseshoe Street downhill one of those random lulls in foot or vehicle traffic where all of a sudden it
goes silent like a Western main-street just before a shoot-out there was once a
time I might have wandered down that way and had a pleasant evening out, all
of the pubs there used to be the Shakespeare at the top here and the Harbour
Lights another biker hangout in the 'Seventies I always used to wonder why
they'd called it that when we're the furthest point inland but I suppose it's
just another wistful evocation of the sea the way that Terry Wogan called the
Express Lift tower the Northampton lighthouse anyway the Harbour Lights
the building's still there but they've changed the name the Jolly Wanker, well
there's a big letter W and then an anchor but it's obvious what it's saying now
I'm all for free speech but I don't agree with that I don't see any need you

wouldn't catch me drinking in there anyway I've too much self respect besides the whole street looks like it's unravelling

I wonder how much longer the Victorian gas-holder's going to be there it was talked about a few times when I was still on the council, council leader a good many years and in the end you have to balance practicality against nostalgia well that's all it is when it comes down to it nostalgia for a place or thing that no one really gave a fuck about to start with but because they happened to grow up in such and such a street they don't want anything to change which is to my mind unrealistic nothing stays the same forever everything is going downhill places people we all make adjustments we all start out as idealists or at any rate as something passing for idealists but that's not the real world in the real world everything and everybody ends up as a Jolly Wanker and that's their fault it's not wait a minute there's somebody do I know him someone standing halfway down the hill on this side of the dual carriageway I'm sure I've seen his face just standing there and staring at the billiard hall across the street black leather jacket on he looks like a real villain oh he's turned his head he's looking up the hill towards me better look away

perhaps if I went uphill up Horsemarket I could stop in at the Bird in Hand whatever it's called now the place on Regent Square up Sheep Street just to say I'd had one just to say I've got a social life even when I'm the only one at home that man though I won't turn around in case he's looking I know him from somewhere I'm convinced of it a face like that you don't forget it in a hurry with that big hook nose his eyes at different levels different angles to each other honestly his face, it looked like a collage it looked like that old ghost's face when it runs across the road towards me in my nightmare every other week perhaps he lives round these parts one of the menagerie like that chap that you see walking his ferrets although now I come to think was it on telly that I saw him in a film an advert something of that nature horror story I should think from how he looks but on the other hand how likely is it somebody from telly being in the Boroughs it's more probable I know his face from Mandy's work with the police you know the evening sun, Horsemarket on these lower slopes, it looks quite nice

a restaurant an Italian place across the street don't like the lettering

black movement on the paving not a heart attack the shadow of a bird that's a relief

some girl young woman she's quite pretty lovely eyes a hajib she's Somali

it's frustrating even two years later the Iraq war I opposed it obviously made a few statements to the paper and yes I suppose that stepping down from council that same year to some it might have looked as if I'd made a stand on principle although I never said that in as many words no to be honest it was more a legal technicality so that I could pursue my business interests without a breach of regulations and I don't see that there's any contradiction in a staunch opponent of the war planning a trip to Basra Anglicom we called the company anyway that's neither here nor there, as I said at the time that's history what's done is done yes I opposed the war but when it's happened then that's the reality that's what you've got to work with and I think that settling deals to help the restoration of Iraq it's part of a humanitarian effort when you stop to think about it and I don't see, I don't see when there's a pie that big to be divided up why it should be your Halliburtons getting all the contracts where's the harm in standing up for British companies me and Colin he's my partner business partner I should say you have to be so careful with your language these days don't want anyone to get the wrong impression me and Colin were all set to fly to Basra, 2004, I mean they said the airstrip was secured it was all over or at least up in the north, there was that bloke the source of all the WMD reports what was his name and they were going to parachute him into government all done and dusted so they said, we'd booked the flights announced it in the *Chronicle & Echo* everything and then it all kicked off contractors taken hostage every other day a car bomb there's beheading footage posted on the internet we called it off well we announced that we'd postponed it thinking I don't know there'd be a drop-off in the violence something like that but it's never going to happen is it look at it the Middle East it's hopeless it's all fucked it's

bloody hell I'm making hard work of this slope I should sign up down at the gym but

Mary's Street back of the ibis rear delivery yards the fire came down here once

the sunset on the windows of the flats our business in Iraq it wasn't meant to be

sometimes, sometimes I wonder if the things in life aren't all laid out from the beginning like town planning, there's a good example, if there's only one way things are going to go for say a district or a neighbourhood it's all already been decided but the people living there don't have a clue what's going to happen in their future there's been public consultation only none of them have heard about it they all think they've got a say in how life's going to go for them they think that their decisions matter but they don't it's all a done deal from the start whether they have a job or not and where they end up living where their kids are sent to school and how they're likely to grow up as a result I mean I'm talking now about the worse off obviously but what if that was true for everything that everything was planned out from the kick-off and although we all think we're the masters of our lives and free to make our own decisions that's just an illusion in reality we only make the choices we're allowed to make already set out for us in the planning documents there's no effective consultation process how much of a choice have any of us really got it's like I made a conscious choice to not go left and up Chalk Lane not go up Gold Street into the town centre but it sometimes feels like I've arrived at my decision only after I've already started doing what I'm going to do, as if making a choice is all after the fact is all justification for things that were always going to happen when you look back at your life some of the things you've done that you well not regret exactly let's say errors that you've made errors of judgement where you genuinely tried to do the right thing but when you look back it's as though circumstance conspired against you where temptations were so huge that nobody would stand a chance where literally you'd have to be a saint an angel it feels like there's something nudging you, making you go the way it wants and when you look at it like that then who's to blame for anything

although

although there's obviously there's paedophiles serial murderers war criminals there's obviously exceptions you can take all this predestination business too far and if nothing's anybody's fault if everybody's only doing what the world is forcing them to do all just obeying orders then what are we meant to think about morality I mean you'd have to say that Myra Hindley Adolf Hitler Fred West there's the 7/7 bombers everybody's innocent you'd have to let them go you'd have to throw away the whole idea of sin of punishment it's not that I'm religious not especially but you'd be saying in effect there was no right or wrong and that's just wrong it stands to reason otherwise there'd be no basis for the law all Mandy's work with the police it would be stood on nothing how would you judge anybody there'd be no one to condemn for anything and, and, and there's another side

if no one's evil how can anyone be good how is there such a thing as virtue or a virtuous act if everything we do is preordained just as you couldn't judge the guilty there'd be no way you could even recognise a saint a decent person no way that we could reward somebody for outstanding work by giving them a medal, say, or making them an alderman I'm only using that as an example but I mean you'd have to throw away Mother Theresa Jesus Ghandi Princess Di not that I ever thought that much of her to be quite honest, clearly there were those who did, there'd be no heroes heroines no villains and what kind of story would that leave us with we'd have no way of shaping a society I can't imagine one how could we impose any sort of pattern any sort of meaning on our lives how could we tell ourselves we were good people no, no it's ridiculous there has to be free will or all of this is just a story just a pantomime with all the world a stage and all the men and women merely players it's free will or free Will Shakespeare that's quite good that I'll perhaps remember it and put it in the column no it's like I've always said how everyone's responsible for what they do and how they act although in certain circumstances, I'm not saying mine, there might be strong extenuating reasons why they feel they should do one thing rather than another free will it's a complicated issue

Katherine's Gardens just across the dual carriageway Garden of Rest they used to call it when the Mitre was still standing up in King Street just across the road from the Criterion there used to be that statue there the Lady and the Fish she had these hard stone tits it was like an erotic idol standing at the garden entrance I think later someone knocked the head off so they moved it out to Delapré and all the girls the prostitutes they'd either have the cab firm next door to the Mitre run them to their flats in Bath Street or they'd have a quick knee-trembler in the bushes the police would turn a blind eye for a hand job mind you all the trade's moved down to the St. Andrew's Road these days between the station and the Super Sausage Quorn Way all up that end where I saw the stripy-haired girl that time otherwise the Boroughs is just how it always was I mean we put the concrete bollards up blocking the streets from Marefair all the way to Semilong we thought it might discourage the curb-crawlers but it's not made any difference all it's done is make it harder for the ambulances or the engines to get in if there's a fire say in St. Katherine's House where all the dregs all of these kids straight out of care get placed the tower block well the fire services condemned it and yet there's still people being put there so God help whoever's council leader if it all goes up in flames you know I miss it sometimes but I'm well off out of all of that the stress it puts upon you knowing things like that the worrying in case somebody finds out, all that on your mind and obviously the people in the flats you worry for them too and it would be a dreadful thing if that should happen right there where the Great Fire broke out in the 1670s whenever but then on the other hand a lot of the planned changes to the area could go ahead so it's an ill wind and all that although of course no one wants that to happen I'm just saying if it did

of course this thing about there being no free will then just because we might not like it or we might have to surrender things that we regard as moral certainties that doesn't mean it isn't true

the gardens at the back of Peter's House in Bath Street on my left now everything looks grey and threadbare litter all the usual it's depressing and across the street you've got the Saxon the hotel the Moat House sticking up down at the foot of Silver Street with all the scalloped frills the pastel colours it reminds me of an ornament you might stick in a fish tank though I don't know why, at least it's better looking than St. Peter's House I think I can remember when they put the Saxon up in 1970 I think it was whereas the Bath Street flats they're 1920s 1930s and they show their age the fancy brickwork that's got cracks and fissures sprouting tufts of yellow grass of course when

they went up same as a number of the flats around the Boroughs they weren't
meant to last this long they were intended as a temporary measure but with
nowhere else to put the people I imagine that they'll be there either till they
die or till their homes just crumble down to dust around them what was here
in Horsemarket before the flats I wonder I suppose the clue's most likely in
the name horse-traders wasn't it or did I hear it was horse-butchers there was
once a knacker's yard I think down near Foot Meadow so perhaps oh God
that's broke my dream my other dream I had it just last night oh God

   I was where was I, I was in my vest and underpants again and I was I know
where I was it was a cellar a Northampton cellar in the dream for some reason
I think of it as being Watkin Terrace Colwyn Road one of them up there by
the Racecourse but the atmosphere it had it felt like somewhere from the Boroughs somewhere really old and I remember now, before that in the dream I'd
been just walking in those big grass wastelands with the flooded earthworks
giant disused railway bridges and just single red brick buildings sticking up,
middle of nowhere under heavy skies a bit like that one house still standing
at the bottom end of Scarletwell Street but it's weirder it's a place I'm sure I've
dreamed about before perhaps since I was little but it's hard to tell I'd somehow got inside this house at first there might have been somebody with me
but I lost them and the only way that I could get to where I thought they might
be it was through this sort of granite shower-block where the lights were out
and there were all these toilets without proper cubicles around them and they
all had their seats missing or were overflowing all over the floor and I went on
and down these stairs, stone stairs and then I went the wrong way and I found
myself in these they were like cellars and they were all lit up as if by electric
light although I don't remember seeing any bulbs or lamps and on the floor
the rough stone floor it was like straw and sawdust horrible mixed in with it
there was a lot of blood and shit you didn't know if it was animal or human
and there was it looked like fish innards and skins and strings of meat all rotten in the corners and I must have gone from one part of the cellar to another
trying to find my way out and suddenly there's the mad poet bloke the one
who's always pissed Benedict Perrit he's lived down the Boroughs years everyone knows him though I've never had a lot to do with him myself he's standing
waiting for me in this cellar smells of frightened animals like in a slaughterhouse I'm getting nervous I explain I'm lost and ask him how I can get out and
he does this peculiar high-pitched laugh and says he's trying to get further in
and I wake up with the old heart going at nineteen to the dozen I know that
it doesn't sound much but the atmosphere it was that atmosphere that hangs
around the Boroughs and it always puts the shits up me it's I don't know it's
ancient, stinks, it isn't civilised older than that with its collapsing buildings
people its collapsing past it's like a Frankenstein thing stitched together from

dead bits of social engineering it's a monster from another century resentful in its ominous reproachful silence I can tell that I've done something to offend it that it doesn't like me but I don't know why time and again I wake up sweating here we are the Mayorhold Merruld the old dears down here pronounce it, makes them sound half-sharp

glancing down Bath Street and across the train-tracked valley as the light goes

up the other way a widened Silver Street unrecognisable the thuggish multistorey car park that's got Bearward Street and Bullhead Lane God only knows what else beneath it somewhere looking out across the grim sprawl of the traffic junction with its lights and colours brighter in the falling twilight almost magical it's funny when you think that this where it started the whole civic process in Northampton when the Boroughs was the whole town and this was the town square so I'm told with the first guildhall the Gilhalda wasn't it up at the top of Tower Street here it used to be the top of Scarletwell before Beaumont and Claremont Courts went up in the late 'sixties and there

there they are

the high-rise flats the two giant fingers raised as if to say fuck off

who to though is it them to us or us to them I don't know what I even mean by that

a window lit up here and there light through cheap curtains coloured squares on the dark blocks darker against the last remains of day over the railway yards the dimming west the tops of higher buildings last to catch the sun and you can still make out the sideways metal N in NEWLIFE with the lettering running down the side I thought that looked quite smart, no, what it was when I was council leader someone made out they were eyesores two monstrosities that shouldn't have been put up in the first place and proposed we pull them down but I said no that's not the way to go for one thing social housing in the Boroughs people haven't got a clue just how precarious it is those towers they house a lot of people and don't think that when they're pulled down there'll be anywhere to put the tenants or there'll be new housing built dream on that isn't how it works those towers are all you're going to get and when they're gone they're gone, no, what I said, we ought to do them up refurbish them so that they're fit to live in and okay you may say where's the money going to come from but what I suggested was we sell the flats for next to nothing a housing association that I knew was interested at least that way the council's spared the costs of demolition not to mention all the headache of rehousing so it went ahead and Bedford Housing picked them up at fifty pee apiece I know that there were people at the time and since who questioned that but they don't understand how much the people here have benefited when you think of the alternative have genuinely benefited and alright that was in

2003 when I stood down from council after speaking out against the situation in Iraq not that the two things were connected it was more that being on the council stopped me from pursuing other ventures shall we say I mean how many companies is it where I'm secretary or director ten something like that so it was proper I should stand down otherwise it might have looked as if I'd got a vested interest and you know how cynical it is these days the view the public have of anyone in politics, no, I stood down so that I could take care of Anglicom in Basra me and Colin though that didn't work out obviously but also after stepping down that left me free to take up my position on the board of Bedford Housing well if someone's going to make a profit from it then you tell me why it shouldn't be a Boroughs resident that's better surely than it going to someone outside the area and anyway it's done, it's history, the other options were much worse I talked it through with Mandy and I don't see why I need to justify myself

along the walkway on the west side of the Mayorhold making for the crossings that will get me over to the Roadmender in two or three hops when the lights are right it's like a game of Frogger and down on the left there's Tower Street and the NEWLIFE buildings and past that you can still just about make out the school Spring Lane those years I was a teacher there back when you couldn't live on what you made as councillor I mean some of the kids some of the families they were beyond help some of them it was horrific sometimes frankly and that's really I suppose where I first got a peep into the way these people's lives work if they work at all and thinking back that's probably when I first got the horrors just a shudder every now and then about the area and what was going on behind all the net curtains honestly you should have heard some of the stories although by and large the kids were nice I liked them they respected me I think I had a reputation as a decent bloke a decent teacher that was who I was that's how I saw myself and I was happier then I think I don't know, can I say that, there's a lot of benefits to being who I am today but even so perhaps you could say I was happier in myself I think I thought more of myself and everything was more straightforward everything was simpler then not such a moral maze I think that was a program on the television or the radio they asked Cat Stevens Yusuf Islam or whatever he's called now if he would personally carry out the fatwa against Salman Rushdie and I think he said he wouldn't but he'd phone the Ayatollah what's his name Khomeini anyway when you're a teacher there's the satisfaction when you feel you've made a difference how can I describe it it's like when you feel as if you're a good person deep inside beneath it all, it's not like politics it's the reverse it's the exact reverse of that nobody trusts you they're prepared to think the worst of you they hate you everybody hates your guts and the abuse the personal abuse you get is it a wonder if it gets to you affects your self esteem I don't mean me specifically just public figures, political types in general what it is it's hurtful and it makes your blood boil you find that you're muttering to yourself settling imaginary scores it wears you out and it

crossing St. Andrew's Street so that I can cross Broad Street makes me think of Roman Thompson who I think lived round here until recently I would see quite a bit of him back in his union days when we were both on the same side well nominally anyway and even more of him when I was on the council his Tenant's Association bollocks he called me a wanker once right to my face he said I'd always been a wanker and that didn't make me very jolly I can tell you fucking militants the fucking pickaxe-handle tendency with their more-socialist-than-thou they don't see that the kind of socialism they believe in they're anachronisms all that's dead that was the '70s and Margaret Thatcher smash the National Front and we were out of office the best part of twenty years it was demoralising all the splits and schisms in the party it was cunts like Thompson radicals to blame for all of that stuck in the '60s and refusing to accept that times change and the Labour Party if it wants to be electable it changes with them now I'm not the biggest fan of Tony Blair I think that I can safely say that now but what he did whichever way you look at it he got us back in government he modernised the party he'd learned lessons from what Thatcher did and it was necessary redefining Labour values and the Tories had a winning formula you have to deal with the reality it's no good being off in some idealist never-never land after the revolution no you have to work with what you've got adjust to different ways of thinking different ways of doing things and Roman Thompson calling me a wanker Roman Thompson, people like that, Marxist throwbacks they don't understand real politics the compromises and negotiations that you have to make they're not prepared to give you it, benefit of the doubt, they're ready to believe the worst of you a wanker he's the fucking wanker and it's that it's the abuse you get I shouldn't think about it, more stress on the heart, what does he matter anyway he's

toddling over Broad Street with the green light and the Roadmender there on the corner white in the descending gloom the front part rounded tall smoked windows up behind its railing ten or fifteen feet above the street it's like a prow it's like a ship a liner beached here at the furthest inland point lured by the false beam of the Express Lifts tower and the empty promise of the Harbour Lights they had high hopes for the place once all the well-meaning Christian types who founded it as a youth centre said that it was going to "mend the road" the road through life that disadvantaged youngsters faced I mean as an idea it's well intentioned like I say but it's not aged well these days you're not going to mend the road you've very little chance of even finding it and in the meantime well it's left us with a building to maintain and no way that the space will ever turn a profit we've tried everything they've put some bands on big names some comedians but with that sort of audience they're students mostly they're not going to spend much even if you pack the place out every night it isn't going to work from what I hear it's got six months left possibly a year oh fuck another hill

at this age you don't know you never know you never hear the one that hits you

was it here perhaps where Bullhead Lane was, the steep climb to Sheep Street

just across the road the multistorey with dead socket-spaces staring from between its pillars there's a scrap of mitigating vegetation here and there half-hearted verges as inadequate respite from all that concrete but it's all half-dead it covers nothing up and only makes the rest of it look worse a diamante G-string on an ugly stripper

when you're closer to the top you see the bus station most gruesome building in the country so they reckon with its empty upper spaces gazing menacingly at the car park's brutal bulk across the intervening grassy waste where that Salvation Army fort once stood as if it sees it as a rival in some fuck-faced competition although when you think about it with the flats the car park the bus station and the rest of the unsightly hulks that seem to congregate down here it isn't any wonder that the people feel so singled out for punishment you have to ask yourself if Roman Thompson and the awkward squad might not be right at least on that one, on that single issue obviously and not on everything not after what he called me what he said to me and Lady's Lane it yawns away towards the Mounts the arse-end of the bus station on one side with the law courts on the other there's that sort of gibbet-shape that's echoed in the architecture and you get the feeling that the whole place is condemned whichever way you look at it the swathes of empty grass up this end if you ask me it's not the old creepy houses it's the patches of bare ground that seem most haunted

turn left into Sheep Street and it's not a haunting like you see in films or when you read a ghost story in many ways it's like the opposite of that it's not about mysterious presences it's more about the absences not how the past endures but how it doesn't

back at Spring Lane school sometimes at Christmas I remember how I'd read a ghostly tale or two you know something traditional they used to love it nothing really frightening I'd read A Christmas Carol not The Signalman, Canterville Ghost perhaps but not Lost Hearts, the English ghost story it's marvellous one of the things that can make teaching English such a pleasure just the way the masters of the form can set the scene and structure things they mostly seem to take a lot of time establishing a situation that's believable and quite a lot of them like M.R. James they base the stories solidly upon a real location so you get the what's the word I hate it when I can't remember things it worries me verisimilitude and there's the moral aspect of a ghost yarn that's quite interesting the way that sometimes like with Scrooge the ghosts are actually a moral force and he's done something to deserve a visit from them whereas to my mind the other type of story, that's more frightening, where ghosts descend on somebody because they're in the wrong place at the wrong time where the victim is somebody innocent someone who doesn't know what he's done to deserve it I suppose that the abiding fear in all these stories is the world we live in comfy and predictable it might all of a sudden change and let in things that we can't understand or handle that's the underlying terror, that things might not be the way we think they are it's almost dark now all the streetlamps have come on

the absences tend to accumulate up this end, Sheep Street, there's the yard that beech tree stood in eight hundred years old I think they said it was before it passed away of natural causes that's a euphemism we all know perfectly well who poisoned it somebody highly placed at one of the adjacent businesses who wanted to extend the parking area but obviously there's nothing can be done you'd have a hard time proving it for one thing and when you consider all the upset it would cause I mean it wouldn't bring the tree back would it no what's done is done it's better to accept it and move on that's the mature the practical approach that's politics like it or lump it no use crying over spilled milk when the horse has bolted just across the road the Chinese restaurant, been there years changed hands of course and names I think that me and Mandy went there once or twice before we were in a position to go further and have better no the food was very nice as I remember it lobster I think I had

and there's the Holy Sepulchre the round church bulging out into the dusk pregnant with guilty secrets fat with memory I shouldn't wonder

the knights Templar used to worship in it don't they say we had a lot of them round these parts after the Crusades somebody ought to write a novel a Da Vinci Code or something I suppose Northampton's seen a fair bit of religious stuff across the years extremism you'd have to call it there were all the weirdo groups in Cromwell's time the Levellers and Ranters and what have you the town draws them like a magnet Philip Doddridge he's another one Thomas á Becket running for it in the middle of the night it's like I say there's plenty of religious history but none of it's exactly what you might call normal it's fanatical or else it's having visions and it's seeing things didn't they burn the witches just a little further up, on Regent Square I think I can remember someone telling me

cross to the church side of the street there's nothing coming at the moment although up the end there on the square itself the traffic's bunching at the lights as always and it's funny

you look from the round church to the junction up ahead and there's a sort of wholeness a simplicity about the past and then on Regent Square the present all the cars the signals changing colour it's more like a jigsaw that's been flung across the room

and set on fire

the present smashed and set on fire I think about Iraq I'm bloody glad that we called off that trip I mean Iraq's an obvious example but it's everywhere the fragmentation and the fabric, watching while it comes to bits, it's everywhere oh God imagine that imagine being made to kneel and have your head cut off on camera it's hang on this is where the north gate was up this end of Sheep Street this is where we put the heads on spikes the Danish raiders that we'd captured there weren't cameras then but heads on spikes it's the same thing it's the dark age equivalent it's a display meant to deter the enemy not that if I'd have gone to Basra I'd have been an enemy I said it was an opportunity to help a war-torn nation and its people and if Anglicom got something out of it well where's the harm in that I'm not an enemy but then you could say that's naive that's not the way it works it's how they see us isn't it not how we see ourselves I mean they say you should be careful how you choose your enemies but you don't get a say in how your enemies choose you like fucking Roman fucking Thompson calling me a wanker making out that I'm the villain when I'm not I'm one of the last heroes standing up against the villains and of course sometimes there's compromises but there's worse than me a lot worse I deserve some credit some respect and if there's any doubt then I should have the benefit of it and Sheep Street opens up into the smeary paintbox of the square and here we are the Bird in Hand

on Regent Square the glare the Friday atmosphere as if it's waiting for some I don't know some ugly business to kick off perhaps it's me, my age, you hear so many stories is it any wonder that downtown at night well it's enough to make anyone nervous well not nervous let's say wary and I'm not a big man but you've got to do it got to go out now and then perhaps stop at the pub and have a drink prove to yourself that you still can that you're not frightened, when you start to think like that you're beaten, that there's not this sense of it all catching up with you the door is brass and glass, net curtains on the other side I get the sense it might have looked just like this in the 1950s gives an elderly and wheedling squeal more of a wheeze the hinges as I push it open into

human body heat a wall of it the smell of fags and lager breath not the warm beer smell I remember there's a fuzzy background carpeting of clatter mumble giggling girls squelchy glissandos from the fruit machine *BWOIP BWOIP BWOIP BWOIP* low ceiling keeping all the scent and sound pressed

down there's not that many people in it just seems like it after coming from
an empty street but then the night's still young I don't think that there's anybody here I know quick pint, then, pint of bitter standing up against the bar
and trying to catch the barman's eye oh fuck I've put my elbow in the spillage
never mind I'll sponge it down when I get home is he deliberately ignoring me
he's, no, no he's just serving someone further down the bar and wait a minute
that bloke sitting at the table in the corner there I'm sure I know his face from
somewhere it's oh shit he's seen me looking at him mimed hello he obviously
knows me I'm more or less forced, obliged, to give a big smile in response still
can't remember who it is I've seen him recently I'm sure but if he turns out to
be someone I should pay attention to somebody who knows Mandy possibly
but how he's dressed I can't imagine that it would be what's he oh he's holding
up his empty glass he wants a drink and before I can stop myself I'm nodding
but that means I'll have to sit with him pretend that I remember who he is and
oh God it's Benedict Perrit but that's no it's too weird it's

it's a coincidence it's nothing strange not if you understand mathematics
properly it's not as if

BWOIP BWOIP BWOIP BWOIP

it's not as if it's that remarkable we dream about all sorts of people and
then see them but I mean I'm more annoyed than anything I'm more or less
obliged to have a drink with him if only I'd not looked at him as if he was a
long-lost friend, it's just a habit from the job all of those years, if I'd just recognised him sooner but oh here's the barman

"Can I have two pints of bitter, mate?"

why did I call him mate he's not my mate oh well it's just a pint I'll have
it down me in a quarter of an hour at most then tell him I've got business
somewhere else a quarter of an hour how hard can that be but hang on what's
that he's doing is he it looks like some sort of pantomime he's pointing at me
and then turning round towards the empty stool beside him and then lifting
up his hand to shield his mouth as if he's saying something now he's laughing
what's the matter with him it's as if he's acting out some sort of joke or something that he thinks I'm in on I can hear him laughing right across the room
he's like a horse *BWOIP BWOIP* "Ahahaha!" *BWOIP BWOIP* is he taking the
piss what's going on oh here's the barman with the pints

"Cheers, mate."

arrrrh Christ let me stop saying that pay him, a fiver, take the change
there's not much and then navigating pint in each hand I can't stand this bit
it makes me tense you can't see your own feet or where you're putting them
and all these people they're like bumpers on a pinball table and you know
you're going to end up spilling it all down yourself or worse all down some-

body else and then they punch your lights out it's like trying to steer a ship to dock or well with me it's more a tugboat nosing in amongst a load of hulking cargo vessels and just look at him just hark at him mugging and laughing and pretending that he's whispering about me like an aside to an audience that isn't there is he like this with everybody for fuck's sake what have I got myself hooked up in now oh well it's too late

"Hello, Benedict. How are you keeping? I got you a pint of bitter, hope that's alright."

of course it's alright there's no need to sound so apologetic it's him cadging drinks off you it's him who should apologise if anybody you don't need to always make a good impression well not with just anybody not with somebody like him he's

"Councillor, you must be a clairvoyant. Ahaha. You read me mind."

oh bloody hell I hope not if I read your mind then I'll bet M.R. James he wouldn't be a patch on you I shouldn't sleep for weeks I shouldn't even

"Oh, no. No, I'm no clairvoyant. This last three year I've not even been a councillor since I stepped down. 2003 that was. That's when bloody Tony Blair involved us in Iraq."

now technically that's true I haven't said the two facts were connected so in fact I haven't

"Ahahaha! Yiss you are, you're a clairvoyant! Freddy made out as you hadn't got the gift, but I had faith in your psychic abilities. I'm a believer, councillor. Ahahaha. Cheers!"

"But I'm not a …"

fucking hell look at that pint go down that Adam's apple working like he's got a piston arm in there who's Freddy and that accent "Yiss" you used to hear it all the time down here old ladies mostly the real strong Northampton accent I'd forgotten when we first moved in we used to laugh about it me and Mandy do impressions then it gets that you don't notice it and then next thing you know it's all but gone when was the last time I

"So, did you get out of that cellar in the end? Ahahaha."

what cellar what's he talking about what

"What cellar's that? I'm sorry, but you've lost me."

there, again, apologising what should you be sorry for it's him who's talking rubbish he's

"The cellar in the dream. Ahahaha! You didn't like it much."

the

but

what what is he oh no oh God no that's no that's *BWOIP BWOIP BWOIP BWOIP* no

"What do you m ... how do you know about ..."

is this a dream, this now, is this the same dream have I not yet woken up or

"Ahaha! It was just like our granddad's shop in Horsemarket. It was ... yiss. Yiss, that's right. The Sheriff. Ahaha. Sat in 'is wheelbarrer up on the Merruld."

but how can he know about hang on I'm missing something here the last half of that sentence he's just turned his head and looked away from me is he deliberately snubbing me or I don't know but what he said the dream how can he know about my dream or how can I know his whichever way around it is that isn't how it works that's wrong it has to be some I don't know some fluke of probability, mathematics, a coincidence I mean two people having the exact same dream on the same night then meeting the next day I'll grant you it must be fantastic odds against it but it's not impossible it doesn't mean hold on he's turning back to face me

"Freddy was just saying that you ought to change yer underpants. I'd told 'im earlier what you'd got on and 'e said you was wearing the same thing the time 'e seen yer. Ahaha."

he's

he's oh fuck he's talking to the empty seat the other side of him somebody told me I remember now somebody said they'd seen him doing that, some other pub, the Fish I think, it must be all the drink sent him like that although then there's the poetry as well wasn't it him forever going on about John Clare and everybody knows where John Clare finished up how did he know about my dream the underpants and I'm not liking this how did I end up walking into this I don't deserve this and

"Who's Freddy? I don't ..."

laughing throwing back his head I can see every pore in his big nose there's nothing funny about this, this is that thing the atmosphere around the Boroughs *BWOIP BWOIP BWOIP BWOIP* are they all mad are they all these people are they all inbred and mad or

"Freddy Allen! Ahaha! Old Freddy Allen! 'E says as 'e saw yer wanderin' up Marefair in the middle o' the night wi' just yer vest and pants on. Ahaha. 'E says 'e run across the road to see if 'e could put the wind up yer. From what 'e's tellin' me, you looked as though you'd done it in yer pants. That's why 'e thought you oughter change 'um. Ahahahaha!"

gulping my pint now trying to shut him out this isn't happening I'm mishearing him all of this what with the background noise he isn't saying what I think he's saying should I just get up and leave say I'm not feeling well it's true enough oh Christ I want to bolt but I'm stuck up the corner of the bar here with him there's so many stools and tables between me and the pub door and all these people Friday night it's filling up I don't know what to do I don't know what to say there's too much going on *BWOIP BWOIP BWOIP BWOIP* and from the corner of my eye oh God what's that it's no it's nothing cigarette smoke hanging in a wobbly flying carpet made of grey wool just above the picture-rail I thought that it was I don't know a rush of something dust-balls big as sheep stampeding at our table but it's only smoke I'm just that rattled oh please stop him laughing it's

"Ahahaha! Did you see that? 'E just stood up like 'e'd got piles. 'E's cross because a load o' little blighters just come in."

what now oh Jesus get me out of here he's got me stuck here up this corner and he's what's he doing now he isn't looking at the stool beside him and he's not looking at me he's giggling into the smoke oh fuck how many aren't there here that I don't know about it's not

"You can't come in! Yer under age! What if the landlord asks to see yer death certificates? Ahahaha!"

laughing his head off shouting at thick air nobody paying him the least bit of attention can't they hear what's going on they must be used to him a regular or they can't hear above the *BWOIP BWOIP BWOIP BWOIP* I don't know what's going on myself and for a moment I look off in the direction that he's staring but there's nothing there's just some bloke's arse and all the smoke and I look back at him and everything about the Boroughs that can make your skin crawl it's there in his voice his laugh his eyes you can't tell if he's sad or happy I'm just gaping at him I'm just

"I don't understand this. I don't understand you people."

listen to yourself "you people" there's nobody here but him you sound as cracked as he does oh God when he said that bit, running across Marefair to put the wind up me he can't have meant no that's just bollocks no people don't have each other's dreams I'm not I can't I just can't think about it now Benedict Perrit look at him craning his neck and laughing holding one hand to his ear like he's pretending that he's eavesdropping on someone or perhaps he's

"I can't 'ear 'um. Even when they're right up next to yer they sound faint, 'ave yer noticed? Ahaha."

it's

it's only this moment just occurred to me that this is just what it would be like this is what ghost stories look like in real life *BWOIP BWOIP BWOIP BWOIP* in real life there aren't any ghosts and it's just somebody who's mad, and I mean that's upsetting in itself, it's somebody who's mad and otherwise there's nothing no one there and there's no ghosts there's nobody there's nothing but an

absence

an accusing absence, as if

let me out oh Jesus let me out of here this pub this corner this pissed

lunatic tonight how has it gone so wrong so horrible so fast I'm swallowing
my pint down necking it and next to me he's laughing fit to bust his throat's a
lift-cage going up and down stuck between floors why did I come in here it's
like I didn't have a choice I didn't have a chance and next to me, what now, he's
pointing through the hanging smoke towards the door he's

"There they goo! Ahahaha! All ayt the door like ashes up the chimney."

but the door's not moved the door's not open what's he seeing what's he
seeing in his schizophrenic seizure that I'm not finish my pint and clink the
empty glass down on the table

"Benedict, I'm ..."

"Ahaha! I know! Yer lookin' fer a way out, but there's not one. We're all
stuck 'ere wi' no end in sight. Blood on the straw and fish guts up the corner.
I'm still tryin' t'get further in. Ahahaha!"

stand up I can't say anything can't even say goodbye what can you say,
a situation like this, as if there was such a thing as if there was a situation
like this struggling around the table with its hard edge juddering against my
thighs there isn't any space to move there isn't any wiggle-room and all these
people packing out the place I didn't notice them come in "Excuse me ... can
I just come through, yeah, cheers ... excuse me ... sorry mate" stop saying
that stop calling people mate they're not your mates there's no one down here
who's your mate and *BWOIP BWOIP BWOIP BWOIP* and behind me I can
hear him laughing whinnying like a carthorse with the barn on fire I stumble
over someone's feet and hear the word cunt bubbling from the acoustic blur
but then I'm finally I'm by the door and pushing at the hard glass through its
useless little skirt of lace and then the air outside it's cold and clean and big
the air outside in Regent Square the night slams into me and there I'm free I
got away from him I got away from it I got

what

what was that, that

stuff, that atmosphere it's gone it isn't here now and that's how I know it
was here like a noise that you don't notice till it stops the sudden silence what
just happened what just happened to me nothing nothing happened you just
it's just mental illness you just had a run in with it obviously it's disturbing
but there wasn't any need to panic not to run out of the pub like that I must
have looked a proper wally nothing happened calm down nothing happened
everything's alright everything's normal for a minute the old heart was banging like a dustbin lid but I can see now I was being stupid letting it all get to
me like that I don't know I don't know what I was thinking, that the world,
reality, it had just I don't know just broken and I felt like I was falling down the
cracks but look at it I mean it's fine its Regent Square its Friday everything's
okay there's

traffic lights like freshly sucked fruit pastilles and
an ice mosquito biting on my neck the threat of rain with
couples young chaps striding and not staggering it's early yet I'm
walking in a daze towards the crossing that will take me over to the top of
Grafton Street the dark sluice running down into the valley there that's what I
mean it's not like I made a decision or at least not consciously yet here I am I'm
toddling across the road the pelican tweets chivvying with its emerald wink
as if I've chosen to go home this way and not up Sheep Street back the way I
came I don't remember choosing anything it's just my feet I'm at the other side
now and they're taking me along what's left of Broad Street one brown shoe
and then the other and it's not of my oh fuck me what's the word volition not
of my volition it's like every step's already set in stone and nothing I can do
about it like it's all predestined but then there'd be no such thing as oh watch
out I nearly swerved and fell into the road casino lights up on my right I'm
walking like I'm drunk but how can that be when I only had a pint a pint up at
the Bird in Hand there with

Benedict Perrit

fuck that must be it I must be still in shock but that's ridiculous it isn't
like he

raining a bit harder now and I'm not really dressed for it you know it was
so nice when I came out I'm going to get soaked through if I'm not careful
for that matter I'll get soaked through if I am, another bloody stupid saying
all that business in the pub no, no I'm better off not dwelling on it one brown
shoe and then the other slapping on the shiny pavement wet now puddles
gathering where the reflections of the sodium lamps perform a yellow shimmy
one brown shoe and then the other not of my volition but then there'd be no
such thing as free will there'd hold on what was it I thought earlier it was quite
funny I was going to put it in the column it was oh yeah I remember it's free
will or free Will Shakespeare no on second thoughts it doesn't sound as funny
now too difficult explaining it the point still stands though, if this was all
scripted in advance and for all that I know it might be then we'd all be actors
no one would be innocent or guilty and well I suppose that if that was the
way that things turned out to be we'd all get used to it in many ways it might
be a much nicer world with no one questioning your ethics all the time no
reason to feel rotten over anything you might have done some bad decisions
that you might have made some time ago a while back a long while back I'm
not talking about me now obviously but there's people who are sensitive who
are in torment over things they've done and if there's no free will well you can
see how some of us, people like that, it would be like the slate wiped clean and
no more bad dreams no more sleepless nights over the other side of Broad
Street the dual carriageway there's just the top bit of the old Salvation Army

fort the other one the one that hasn't been pulled down yet actually I think
it's listed just the top bit of it you can see where it pokes up above the fencing
upper windows like it's looking at you trees and undergrowth around it looking at you from across the fence as if it's an old dog penned up and left to die
it doesn't understand it doesn't know what's happening here's the Mayorhold
coming up it's

pissing down literally spattering on the carriageway the paving slabs on
me "I'm gunna catch me death" that's what they used to say down here that
accent like

Benedict Perrit

talking to thin air laughing at nothing nothing's the last thing you want
to laugh at nothing's the most dreadful thing of all after you've gone I'm in my
sixties now I don't believe in hell or all the rest of it I mean it's just the end
death isn't it that's how a grown-up looks at it but then Benedict Perrit in the
Bird in Hand the cackling and his painful eyes and all the people that were
only there to him and yet

and yet I mean the ghosts even if only he could see them in a way they're
still there aren't they even if he's mad then they're ghosts that are in his mind
all of his memories of the neighbourhood dead people all of it ghosts that are
running through his mind and if you're sitting there up the pub corner next to
him you can't help almost seeing what he's seeing well not seeing ghosts but
seeing how he sees the world so that it almost makes it real to you as well just
for a moment I think that's his house below me on the right one of the ones
in Tower Street I don't know which one it almost makes it real to you as well,
the ghosts and everything, so that you feel as if it's you as if it's me who's being
haunted and not him as if the district and the dead were talking through him
to me passing on a message why do I keep feeling as though this place hates
me after all I've done for it how did he know my dreams that awful cellar and
with no way out up on my left the Mayorhold's knotted guts are growling with
nocturnal traffic, with strangled monoxide farts ahead of me down Horsemarket there's noise one of those howler monkey conversations young blokes
who don't know don't care how loud they're talking like they've got their headphones lager headphones on I think I'll take a right down Bath Street cut up
through the flats and that way it looks quiet enough no one about how did he
know my dreams

and that's another thing isn't it if there's no free will then why has this
place got it in for me giving me nightmares giving me Benedict for fuck's sake
Perrit I've done nothing wrong you name me one thing I've done wrong and
if there's no free will then there's no wrong no right no sin no virtue nothing
everybody's off the hook away and on the right that place it used to be the
drill hall for the Boy's Brigade I wonder Bath Street's dead tonight I wonder

if there's still a Boy's Brigade no but the free will business if nobody's done anything wrong then why should anyone feel guilty when nobody had a choice and if there's no free will then we're all really free and by that I mean free of feeling bad and free of dreams and drunks and madmen you could smell ghosts on his breath we've none of us done any wrong and that's objective fact objective scientific fact except

for it to be objective fact there'd have to be some sort of outside some sort of observer and

there isn't one there's only us just us seeing it all subjectively and

so

to us

to us there's wrong we think we've got free will we think we're doing wrong so the morality I mean that's just the same free will or not we think we're doing wrong and we can't get away from that but that's worse isn't it the worst of both worlds no free will but there's still sin there's sin to us and we're the only ones it matters to what's that the Muslims say it's something like "a saint may slay a million enemies and be without sin unless he regret but one" it's that it's the regret free will or not that doesn't go away we're trapped then aren't we all of us trapped in our lives trapped in all this in Bath Street in the world the Boroughs everything it isn't fair it's

someone guns his engine takes off with a screech down in the dark ahead of me sounds like he's in a hurry and the rain's not letting up across the street off along Simons Walk somebody playing well I wouldn't say that it was music playing something anyway how did he know my dreams and then you've got the little pocket park there lonely and deserted in the night and hulking over it the towers and like I say at least that's space for social housing I was able to preserve if someone makes a profit that's just business that's how business works duh, what, would it be better if nobody made a profit and they'd pulled them down and we'd had that many more homeless on the streets oh I don't think so I'd like to see Roman Thompson justify that argument who'd be the wanker then it's like Iraq somebody has to be prepared to shrug off all the liberal bleating and do something proftical no practical to help all these poor people someone has to be prepared to get stuck in someone who isn't fussy about getting their hands

dirty

turn left up the walkway of St. Peter's House the Bath Street flats there's nobody about tonight but sometimes well you have to watch yourself it's lit up with the lights under the balconies so you can see what's what somebody told me that the kids the rap kids come down here and do the hip-hop all of that to tell the truth I'm not much bothered one way or the other I mean all the dregs that have been stuck down here over the years I don't see how some

fucking kids who talk too fast to understand are going to make much difference frankly crackheads mental cases prossies that one with the stripy hair
I'm sure she lives down here what would it be not that I ever would what would
it be like I bet they'd do anything, it be like doing it with somebody like, anyway, the rain feels like it's letting up a bit now that I'm nearly home wouldn't
you know it and the gravel path's all shiny like the shingle at the seaside and
what's that it's ugh it's dogshit people shouldn't have dogs if they can't clear up
behind them look at that fucking disgusting it looks like somebody's stepped
in it already glad it wasn't me look there's the grid of someone's trainer-sole
pressed into it it's like a little model of New York made out of shit and in the
rain and the electric light it's wet and glistening it looks fresh oh God that
turns my stomach shit I hate it I suppose I've got a thing about it if I hadn't
spotted it in time if I'd just put my foot in it you track it everywhere you go
and it stays with you, everywhere you go you're thinking what's that smell and
there's your shitty footprints over everything you bring it home with you you
get it everywhere all over everything I'm

labouring up the ramp to lamp-lit Castle Street there's sirens somewhere I
expect town centre's kicking off it's probably a good job I'm home early before
any trouble starts but what was that then in the Bird in Hand what was it if
it wasn't trouble I don't know I don't know what it was it was a fluke a meaningless fluke incident forget about it put it from your mind think about something else look at the brickwork on these walls they put these flats up nearly
eighty years ago said they were temporary housing when they built them I
mean technically a word like temporary just means "for a period of time"
but I'd have thought that eighty years was pushing it I mean considered up
against the lifespan of the universe the sun is temporary everything's temporary St. Katherine's House across the road there that's as temporary as fuck
one kitchen fire one B&H dropped down the back of the settee the fire services condemned it but we, they, they still stick people there and if there was
a fire I mean they built tower blocks like this all up and down the country
in the '60s and if there's a fire the central stairwell all these flats these type
of flats it's like a chimney people trying to get down while all the smoke and
flames are going up I shouldn't say this but I hope that Labour's out of office if
well more like when there is a fire the people that they stick down here I mean
they're at risk even if the place they live in isn't burning down teenagers fresh
from care homes mental difficulties everything you name it there were those
two old dears that I saw a week or two ago, well, I presume they live there they
were standing in the forecourt of St. Katherine's just looking up at it rubbing
their hands and cackling most likely they were care in the community you get
them all down here all the abnormals and from what I hear it's always been
like that Benedict Perrit all of them how does this district turn them out it

must be something in the water something in the soil and downhill to Chalk
Lane the rain's stopped

on the corner there the little nursery something in the window poster
of some sort oh I remember Alma Warren someone said that she was going
to have an exhibition down here just a one day thing a Saturday I think they
said I'd thought it would be in a week or two but who knows it might even
be tomorrow Alma Warren there's another one another freak show boiled
up from the Boroughs wasn't she in the same class as him at school Benedict
Perrit I've made overtures tried to be friendly but I just get the cold shoulder I
don't think she likes me acts like she's a law unto herself as if she's not on the
same world as everybody else I think she's vain thinks she's superior morally
superior to everybody else she's got some sort of complex you can see it in her
eyes and when she's talking then she's smiling and she's saying funny things
and being likeable it's all an act she's smiling and her spidery eyes are twinkling but it's like she's trying to disguise the fact she wants to eat you it's an
act it's a performance if she's so fond of the Boroughs well then why doesn't
she live down here like I do I hate people like that people who pretend to be
straightforward when you know you know that everyone's got secrets everyone's pretending something it's an act not like with me with me it's what you
see is what you get I'm sorry but that's how I am why don't these people like
me why don't why the fuck should you care why the fuck should you care if a
load of chavs and dead-end cases like you or not you're the alderman the one
with the accomplishments the one with the CV why do you always come back
to these same things these same thoughts you're like a hamster in a wheel just
round and round for fuck's sake just get over it what everybody else thinks
doesn't matter but

it's still mean-spirited the way they always think the worst of someone or
at least they seem to think the worst of me it's hurtful sometimes and across
the way there Doddridge Church I've often wondered what that little door's
for halfway up the wall I'll bet they used to spread their nasty little rumours
about Philip Doddridge calling him a wanker calling him a cunt when he
was practically a saint a man who really cared about the neighbourhood not
that I'm trying to make comparisons but I mean you can see the similarities I feel good I feel good about myself and if there's people who just want
to think the worst who won't give anyone the old benefit of the doubt then
that's their problem rolling downhill nearly home now car park on the right
I think they put plague victims there and on the left another car park the old
Doddridge burial ground dead people everywhere we're temporary we're not
forever I suppose that it's a blessing in a way free will or not whatever we've
done wrong whatever we've supposedly done wrong time wipes it all away
eventually and nobody remembers and the little things don't matter every-

thing's forgiven when it's gone the debts are cancelled and there's no permanent record because nothing's permanent the whole world's temporary and
that's our what's it called statute of limitations our get out of jail card ah now
here we are Black Lion just over the other side of Marefair at the bottom it
looks dead be lucky if it's still here come next year when we moved in we had
a little newsagents down at the bottom corner of Chalk Lane just opposite
there was a balding bloke who ran it Pete Pete something and veer to the right
around the corner on our little walkway you can

see the valley floor the station and the traffic junction at the crossroads
all the lights I

didn't have a choice in being who I am over Far Cotton Jimmy's End there's

no ghosts nothing there and nothing's haunted three doors down I find
my key and there safe sanctuary home at last and none of it the Boroughs
it can't get you now I flick the light on in the hall and peel my jacket off it's
wringing wet it's glistening looks like a dead seal hung there dripping from
the coat-hook do you know I'm suddenly exhausted I'm completely knackered
I suppose I've just done nearly a full circuit of the district and it's not like I'm
a walker in the general run of things of course there was that business at the
Bird in Hand I can't believe it now stood here at home I can't believe I ran out
of the pub literally ran and that, all the adrenaline, that's probably another
reason why you feel worn out through in the living room I flump down in the
armchair and ugh fuck my trousers cold and soaking wet against my legs my
arse where they've been rained on this is fucking horrible it's not much after
nine but I don't know I might as well just go to bed it's left me in a funny mood
this evening has I might as well just go to bed and sleep it off feel better in
the morning I know one thing for a certainty if I don't get these trousers off
then it's pneumonia and I suppose I'm feeling a bit lonely I wish Mandy was at
home but even then

stand up and even that's an effort put the lights off downstairs and creak
up to bed the bathroom's a bit dazzling I take my shirt and trousers off
my shoes and socks the shirt is absolutely sopping its gone all transparent
there's a wet, pink-tinted oval where it's sticking to my stomach for a second
I thought I was bleeding leave the wet things draped over the bath's rim till
the morning I suppose my underpants and vest feel a bit damp but no they'll
just dry naturally I take my pills three of them every night it's a palaver you
don't think about it when you're young squint through the condensation on
the mirror while I brush my teeth look at the state of me I'm like a garden
gnome a stepped-on David Bellamy a hobbit stuck in quarantine with spearmint rabies dripping off my chin I'm sick of looking at myself pad over to the
toilet bare feet on the chilly tiles lift up the seat so that it isn't splashed and
after a few moments' waiting while my knob decides on what it wants to do

there's a pale golden rope of piss unravelling into the tinkling bowl it's funny standing looking down we've got two rolls of toilet paper standing on the cistern lid and looking down beneath that there's the lifted seat and lid and then the gaping bowl it looks like a white cartoon frog like an albino Kermit from the Muppets staring at me boggle-eyed with an indignant and betrayed look while I stand here pissing down his throat even the toilet blaming me for something there's a thing you have to do you have to press the lever down two or three times before it flushes while its gargling I yank the string to kill the bathroom light and I'm along the landing and in bed before the cistern noise has died away to hisses drips and piddles it's a sort of private superstition I suppose I don't know what I think would happen if I didn't make it into bed before the noises stopped it's more a sort of game a sort of habit I've got no idea why I do it oh that's

    nice the mattress creaks I can feel all the ache and tension soaking out of me I rub my feet together and they're dry and cold but warming with the friction and that's good hopefully I'll sleep through tonight no dreams no cellars nothing running at me with its face unfolding safe now safe here in our little house our little corner of the Boroughs opposite the station ten years and I'm hoping that this place will be unrecognisable a big development exploding up from where the station is and most of this, this place, most of it cleaned up move the social stragglers out most of it swept away that's if the money lasts the boom the money that they need to do it no the land down here the property it could be really nice it could be really valuable not that we'd ever sell part of the neighbourhood that's us part of the furniture roll over on my side and drag a tuck of duvet up between my knees to stop them knobbling against each other ahh that's nice that's

    I suppose the people down here in the main they're not that bad it's really in the pubs you see them at their worst and let them take the piss out of me if they've got a mind to I'll still be on top of things when they're all gone so let them have their bit of fun it's not their fault they're hopeless, living in a hopeless place, they're and I'm speaking as a Marxist now modified Marxist they're just victims they're the end result inevitably of historical and economic processes but then I mean you look at them drunk all day it's the kids who bear the brunt of it a lot of them the parents they don't want jobs not prepared to work they're not

    it's like a flooded earthworks did I come here as a boy what what where was I

    not prepared to work that's right blame everybody else for their own problems blame the council blame the system blame me we're all doing what we have to do and some of them down here I mean they knock their wives about they say it's the frustration it's the poverty but then why do they have so many kids with kids to hold you back how are you ever going to make it, get to where you want to be in life take me and Mandy children would have just got in the way of our careers and look at us we're happy very happy but some people they're just human rubbish they're just

scalloped cliffs of mud a long way off across the grass and distant red brick railway arches I've been here before look there's a toy a plastic elephant dropped in a puddle it's I'm sure it once belonged to me the last time I was here and isn't somewhere near a house an old what what did I

all of the roughs the scruffs the tough and rumble of them all their kids all violent doing drugs I used to read them ghost stories at Christmas mothers wearing short skirts fishnet tights effing and blinding you should hear them not brought up they're dragged up it's a shithole full of shits there's paedophiles down here there's sex offenders well they've got to put them somewhere crackheads and it's all their own fault it's not ours not mine they ought to pull their socks up but then

there's that old well scarlet house that stands up from the wasteland on its own the grey sky overhead and in my pants in my grey pants and vest I walk towards it through the weeds I need the toilet weren't there lavatories down in the cellar of that building if I can remember how to find them if they're not all cracked and full of backed up

but then who am I

THE ROOD IN THE WALL

I t's what you'd call a first-draft face, after the angry and frustrated crumpling. It's a private eye face, it's Studs Goodman's thug-and-bourbon-battered figurehead cresting the dirty suds and breakers of another dead-end town, a burned-out world as fallen as his arches. This is how it plays, the gumshoe life, the endless waiting between cases sitting by a blinded window in the slatted light. These empty stretches with no homicides, they're murder.

Studs takes a deep, satisfying drag upon his biro. Puckering those cruel and crooked lips into a sphincter he exhales a writhing genie of imaginary smoke into the hyphenated sunrays, and considers how the bone-dry periods of his chosen trade must be like those endured by people of a thespian persuasion. Studs, a seriously addicted heterosexual trying to cut down upon a forty-dames-a-day vagina habit, has no time for actors and theatrical types on the basis that they're mostly sissies, horticultural lads and so forth. It's a well-known fact. Still, Studs can sympathise with how it must be when they're out of work and 'resting between parts'. The inactivity, he knows, can drive a feller nuts. Why, even Studs can find himself just sitting, dreaming up some hypothetical and complicated case to solve there in his mind, and he's a tough, unreconstructed Brooklyn wise-guy who thinks with his fists and punches people with his head. He doesn't dream in black and white, he dreams in radio. What must it be like for some neurotic bit-part player when the studio doesn't call? The weather-beaten sleuth would bet his bottom dollar that those precious flowers most likely spend their time rehearsing for some casting call that never comes, a cowboy or a big game hunter, something masculine like that. Who knows, maybe a private dick? He chuckles wryly at the thought and stubs his biro out in a convenient coffee-cup. Studs is a role that would require a lot of time in makeup.

Sure, he's not a pretty boy. He likes to think he's got a lived-in look, albeit lived in by three generations of chaotic Lithuanian alcoholics who are finally evicted in an armed siege after which the premises remain unused for decades, save as a urinal by the homeless. Then it all burns down in an insurance fire. He sits there at the dressing-table mirror in his seamy office and surveys his crime-scene countenance: move right along, nothing to see here. He takes in the seemingly haphazard corrugations of his forehead, a volcanic rock-face risen from the straggling tree-line of his brows to the combed-over pinnacle, whence it commences its descent through black and slippery long grass to the nape. The eyes are full of pessimism and what would appear to be some manner of unspecified disorder; eyes that have seen far too much from slightly different elevations and conflicting angles, roughly equidistant from the ice-axe nose, broken more often than a hooker's heart. Then, over everything, a sparse but noticeable pebble-dash of Sugar Puff-sized warts to make sure no one misses the asymmetry, a laugh-track prompt sprinkled redundantly across his face for anyone who somehow hasn't got the gag already. People used to tell him he sure wasn't any oil-painting, although they were obviously unfamiliar with the cubists.

Elsewhere in the building, perhaps out in his front office, there's a telephone like a spoiled child demanding everyone's attention. He calls to his dizzy secretary – "Mum? Mum, phone" – but evidently she's on one of her unfathomable breaks, perhaps connected with the aforementioned dizziness. Whenever he's up here from London stopping over for a few days he tells her that she should change her medication, but she doesn't listen. Women. Can't live with 'em, can't remember where you put your socks. Ten rings and then it goes to answerphone, his message that he'd taken the precaution of recording over hers when he arrived here yesterday. She doesn't get a lot of calls, whereas a client or his agent might get on the blower to him, theoretically, at any time of day or night. That scatterbrained tomato could just rerecord her own apologetic mumblings after he was gone, and in the meantime would most probably be honoured to have his rich tones bewildering such members of her peer group as could still remember how to use a phone.

"Hello there. This is Robert Goodman. I'm not in just at the moment, but please leave a message and I'll get right back to you. Thanks. Cheerio."

Studs has a flawless English accent. In his line of business, a guy never knows when he might need one, possibly while undercover and impersonating some variety of Duke or cockney barrow-boy, conceivably as part of a wild caper which involves the crown jewels and a blonde of independent legs. Though he could use a juicy case right now, preferably a tangled incest drama with Faye Dunaway though he'd make do with blackmail or divorce if needs be, Studs resists the impulse to go pick up the now silent instrument and interrupt the caller. If by any chance it should turn out to be a family struggle over an inheritance that's escalated to a kidnapping or home invasion, Studs can find out later. The last thing he wants is for prospective clients to think he's desperate from his tone of voice when they can work that out themselves, like everybody else who knows him has to do, from the gnawed furniture and the discarded, disappointed scratch-card dross around his flat.

Sat at the dressing table, zebra-painted with the shadow cast by the venetians, he reflects upon the grubby criminal career he's led before becoming a hard-boiled investigator. He's dealt non-specific drugs in Albert Square and been a scar-faced squealer up at Sun Hill nick. He's loitered by a Lexus in a leather to increase the sales of car alarms, he's growled and glared with Gotham City greasers, worn a Dr. Seuss hat for the purposes of his initiation in an early New York Irish street-gang and raped Joan of Arc's big sister back in fifteenth-century France. That's how it is with Studs. He's a wild card, a maverick who won't play by the rules. He's in a big town where the streets aren't always mean but can be pretty fucking ignorant. He's back, he's in Northampton, and this time it's personal, by which he means it's definitely not professional. If only.

Frankly, though it goes against Studs' naturally coarse and testosterone-fuelled nature, he'd do pantomime, be one of Cinderella's ugly sisters or kneel in his shoes for Snow White given half a chance. This calls to mind his since-departed sidekick, Little John Ghavam. Studs ain't no sentimentalist, but not a heartless night of moral compromise goes by without him missing his toad-breeding dwarf pal and their reeling drunk Todd Browning escapades when they were headstrong, relatively young, and from the point of view of an observer, very disconcerting. John, like Studs, had been around the block career-wise, spending some time as a scavenger amongst the Jawa sand-people before he hooked up with a gang of similarly sized time travelling larcenists and soon thereafter banged a lot of former knitwear models for the specialist market. Studs thinks one such enterprise was called *Muff Bandits* but he may have made that up or dreamed it, like when he'd insisted the late local artist Henry Bird had been the husband of Vampira in *Plan 9 from Outer Space* when actually Bird's wife was Freda Jackson, Karloff co-star of *Die, Monster, Die.* It was a dumb, rookie mistake that anybody could have made, but Studs is a P.I. who prides himself on his rep for reliability and he'll most likely take the error with him to his grave. He figures that's the kind of guy he is.

The thing that's hard for Studs to live without is Little John's extreme unlikelihood. When an unlikely person dies it just makes the occurrence of other unlikely people that much more unlikely. Characters like Little John or for that matter Studs himself are like statistical outliers of reality. They skew the figures. When they vanish from the picture then the graph relaxes back towards a bland and comfortable mean, whereas with Little John, he gave you the impression that the world was capable of anything. The laws of physics cowered in surrender every time the little fucker drank, perched on his barstool for eight pints, nine pints; you never saw him going to the toilet. Studs has theorised that his buddy was completely hollow, possibly some kind of toby jug that had spontaneously developed human consciousness. An unexpectedly resilient toby jug, admittedly: at the casino just off Regent Square he'd hurl his compressed mass onto the roulette table, hollering "All 'ands on deck" in customary helium tones. He'd been among the nightmare Crown & Cushion crowd providing the captive composer Malcolm Arnold with an audience. Out near Stoke Bruerne at the Boat, the pub by the canal where all the Sunday sailors used to congregate in yachting caps and polo shirts, their younger wives in sporty-looking shorts, the rampant Little John would thrust his face into the nearest denim crotch.

"It's great. Their husbands all just laugh and go, like, 'Steady on now, little fellow. 'Ad a spot too much, 'ave we?' and things like that. Nobody wants to 'it a dwarf."

Studs pictures John stood in the garden of his house in York Road with the "Toad Hall" plaque outside the door, just standing there by the stone sundial cackling in delight with massive toads all over him, the flowerbeds, the sundial, everything.

Of course, the most unlikely thing about his late friend is that Little John was actually the grandson of the Shah of Persia. Studs shakes his unprepossessing head and chuckles ruefully, as if there's someone watching. Grandson of the Shah. To Studs it's much like quantum theory, women, or contemporary jazz in that it don't make any sense.

He reaches for another biro and then cancels the reflexive gesture halfway through. His croaker tells him he should scale his habit down to maybe just a fountain pen once in a while, on weekends or at special celebrations. Ah, the hell with it. He pushes back his chair and rises from his dressing table in the hope that some activity might take his steel-trap P.I. brain-box off his cravings. Studs goes through to the front office, tricked out to resemble a carpeted landing, staircase and English suburban downstairs hall to throw his creditors and gangland adversaries off the scent, and checks the message on the answerphone.

"Bob, for fuck's sake, what's that voice about? You sound like you're an old Etonian child-molester. This is Alma, by the way. Sorry to call you at your mum's, but if you're coming to the show tomorrow don't forget to bring along the Blake stuff that I asked you to dig up, assuming you've come up with anything. If not, it's no big deal. Just never speak to me again. And why is Robert Goodman not in at the moment? Is he playing polo? 'Robert Goodman'. Bob, nobody calls you Robert. To be frank, most people aren't polite enough to even call you Bob. Most people groan and make a sort of gesture with their hands. Then they sit down, and then they cry. They cry like babies, Bob, at the idea of your existence. Anyway, I hope to see the Blake material at the exhibition, with you holding it if absolutely necessary. Take care, Bobby. Never change. Talk to you soon."

His blood, he notices, is not immediately turned to ice there in his veins. That's storybook detective stuff and in real life the best that he can manage is pink slush, but, still, it ain't a pretty feeling. Sure, Studs knows the name, the voice, the avalanche of undeserved abuse. He knows the dame: a long, tall drink of battery acid going by the moniker of Alma Warren. Think of those surprisingly large clots of hair you sometimes haul from a blocked bathtub trap, and then imagine one with eyes and a superior demeanour: right there's a description that a police sketch artist could work from. She's the kind of cast-iron frail you don't forget without hypnosis, and yet somehow the whole Warren case has slipped Studs' bullet-creased and woman-addled mind until just now, this moment.

How it is with Warren, she's got some variety of modern art scam going for her where the rubes pay out big bucks to see her schizophrenic scribbles. Months back, Studs called in at her bohemian dump along East Park Parade, just up the street from where he used to flop when he was living in here in town, presumably at some point after his tough hard-knock boyhood in the Bowery district of New York, or Brooklyn, or wherever it was Studs grew up. It's only backstory. He'll figure it out later. Anyway, he'd dropped by at the artist's squalid dive to find her working frantically amidst billowing cumuli of contraband, bewildering images in different media propped all around the parlour until Studs had felt like he was trapped inside some kind of busted Grateful Dead kaleidoscope. Between pulls on a reefer long enough to qualify as penis envy and erratic daubs at her unfathomable canvas, she'd explained she was preparing something like three dozen pieces for a new show she was holding in the run-down neighbourhood where she'd grown up. Studs frankly doubts it was as rough and desperate as his own upbringing in the mean streets of the Bronx – perhaps Hell's Kitchen, Satan's Bidet, somewhere colourful like that – although by all accounts the Boroughs is still having lousy luck. Warren's old district ain't just on the wrong side of the tracks, it's on the tracks themselves, in pieces and squashed flat by near eight hundred years of rumbling social locomotion.

He remembers having an unpleasant run-in with the place back in his childhood, when his parents had insisted that he take dance-classes at the Marjorie Pitt-Draffen School in Phoenix Street, around the back of Dod-dridge Church. Or was it him, insisting on the dance class? Studs, his memory crammed full of bodies, barrooms and the brunettes he's let slip between his fingers, can't recall. It doesn't matter. The important thing is that he had to wear a kilt. A nine-year-old boy in a kilt, taken to dancing classes in a thug-

menagerie like Alma Warren's former neighbourhood. Studs thinks that ought
to count as child abuse. He's mentioned it to Warren and her only comment
had been that if she'd encountered him back then she'd more or less have been
compelled to beat him up: "Posh kids in kilts, it's one of the unwritten laws".
Now that Studs thinks about it, he was beaten up more often as a soft-centred
young schoolboy than as a hard-bitten private eye, and on the great majority
of those childhood occasions he was wearing ordinary trousers. He suspects
the business with the kilt is only part of the equation.

The real kicker is that the dishevelled artist's show is scheduled for tomorrow, and that furthermore it's taking place at the day nursery in Phoenix
Street which used to be the Marjorie Pitt-Draffen School. This exhibition is
connected with the case she wanted Studs to take up when he called to see
her that day on East Park Parade. As Warren had explained it to him then, she
had twenty or thirty pieces finished but the subject matter wasn't all connecting up the way she hoped it would. From Studs' perspective it was like she'd
loaded up a sawn-off shotgun with a buckshot of significance then fired it at
a wall expecting the blast-pattern to make sense. There were some images
inspired by hymns, a tile arrangement based upon the life of local Holy Joe
Phil Doddridge and some nonsense that concerned a stone cross brought here
from Jerusalem. One picture seemed to be a likeness of Ben Perrit, a poetic
rummy Studs knows from back in the day, and there was some mixed-media
business meant to represent determinism and the absence of free will, or at
least that's what the pot-saturated painter claimed. In Studs' opinion, Warren's exhibition is a random four-lane pile-up of ideas with nothing joining
them together, and to make things worse she seems to think the whole mess
should somehow connect with William Blake.

"I mean, I've got a lot of references to my family having come from Lambeth, but I'm thinking it needs something more substantial, something that
pulls all the themes together. So, Bob, that's what I want you to do. Find out
how Blake ties into all of this. Find out what links Blake with the Boroughs
and I promise that I'll paint you, Bobby. I'll immortalise you, and together
we'll inflict your face upon a blameless future. How's that for an offer?"

Studs' opinion, which he didn't venture at the time, is that the offer is a
standard Alma Warren contract in that it involves no actual money. Immor-
tality and £1.50 will buy Studs another pack of biros. Still, it's work, and he
accepted it. The paint-flecked hag has Studs over a barrel and if he can't make
good on the case he knows he's finished in this town. Warren will see to
it. She knows too much about him, all those stories buried in his violent
past that he prefers to keep that way. He grimaces as he recalls the time he
bumped into her on the Kettering Road and she'd asked, no doubt in an affec-
tation of concern, why he was limping.

"Well, I was, uh ... I was in Abington Park last night, up by the bandstand. As you know, I like to keep my hand in with the acting. What I do is, I rehearse parts so that I'll be ready if I'm offered them. It was a sort of secret agent role where the scene opened with me standing on the bandstand and then, at a signal, what I do is vault over the handrail and land on the grass so that I'm in a cat-like pose. I look around, scanning the darkness, then run off into the shadows."

Warren had just stared at him, blinking her creepy eyes in disbelief.

"And so that's how you hurt your leg?"

"No, no, I did all of that perfectly, but then they wanted one more take. The second try, one of my feet caught on the railing when I vaulted over."

Her expression had been like a knife fight between pity and contempt while incredulity looked on and didn't do a damned thing.

"'They'?" She'd gazed at him like he was something unexpected in a Petrie dish. "*They* wanted one more take? The film crew in your mind, Bob, wanted one more take. That's what you're telling me?"

Yeah, that's what Studs was telling her and looking back he wishes that he hadn't. Information, in the hands of an unstable woman artist, is a weapon. Probably a weapon like a nail-file in that it's not very masculine but could still do a lot of damage, say for instance if somebody stuck one in your eye. The upshot is that Warren has Studs where she wants him, and if he can't solve the Blake case then his reputation's shot. It's blackmail, pure and simple. Only not so pure. Or simple.

Wearily he reaches for the leather jacket which, he rationalises, maybe stands in for his customary trench coat when it's at the cleaners getting all the blood and booze rinsed out, plus invisible mending on the profuse bullet holes.

"Moths". That would be his likely quip when the staff at the cleaners asked him what had made them. "38-calibre moths."

Leaving a brief note for his secretary with regard to dinner preference, Studs hauls his morally bruised carcass out into the unforgiving light and heads towards his car or would a yank say automobile?

Twenty minutes later he remembers where he got that InterCity grid of frown-lines, nudging his frustrated vehicle up another ramp onto a higher level of the Grosvenor Centre's crowded multistorey car park. Who'd have thought there would be all these people on a Friday? Finally he wins a space by staring threateningly at a silver-haired old lady in a Citroen and, when he has both paid and displayed, makes his way down by elevator into the tinnitus hum and sizzle of the shopping centre's lower floor. Studs weaves his way through the sedated-looking human surf, among the scrunchie-tufted mums who steer their buggy-bubbled offspring at a stately, ceremonial pace over the glittering electric-lighted tiles; between the strangely marginal and ghostly teenagers who limit their defiance to a smirk, a woolly jumper and the uncontested occupation of a bench outside the Body Shop. Studs curls his lip on one side in what's meant to be disdain until he notices the strolling shoppers glancing at him worriedly in case he's either having or recovering from a stroke. Taking a right turn at the elbow of the muttering arcade into a stretch that had been Wood Street once, Studs doggedly heads for the daylight out beyond the glass doors at the walkway's end.

Abington Street's pink incline seems bereft despite the florets of spring sun that drop haphazardly through flimsy cloud. This former main drag of the town, the bunny-run, looks weighed down by the realisation that it has no purpose anymore. It keep its head down, tries not to be noticed and sincerely hopes it's overlooked in any forthcoming wave of redundancies. It seems to shrink from the flint glint that's in Studs' eye as if ashamed, like when you recognise some used-up junkie hooker as your teacher from first grade, not that he's ever had such an improbable encounter. Certainly not with Miss Wiggins, anyway. Aw, Christ. He wishes that he hadn't conjured that specific image. A real private eye, he tells himself, would manage to come up with hard-boiled metaphors that didn't actually turn his own stomach. A crushed skull that's like a broken wholegrain mustard server, for example, is a simile that gets the point across without being indelicate. Miss Wiggins hobbling up and down next to a busy traffic junction in her hearing aid, a mini skirt and heroin withdrawal is another thing entirely, a thing scorched indelibly onto Studs' forebrain to the point where he can no longer remember what the monstrous imagery was meant to represent. Oh, yes – Abington Street. How did he get from there to all that business with … it doesn't matter. Just forget it. Focus on the case in hand.

He slouches up the hill past Woolworths, then decides to try a saunter and eventually compromises with a kind of speedy Chaplin shuffle that's abandoned as unworkable before he reaches the Co-op Arcade. He's headed for a joint he knows here in this crummy burg where he can get his information from reliable sources. It's the kind of place that ordinary people tend to keep away from, a suspicious dive where you can spot the criminal activity just from the way that everybody talks in whispers, and where any joker who don't play by the house rules is looking for some serious payback, possibly a fine. Studs hasn't visited Northampton library in years, but he'd still bet his last red cent it's got the answers that he's looking for, and what the hell's a red cent, anyway? Is it a rouble? Or a kopek? There's so much about this line of work, this idiom, that he doesn't know.

To Studs' surprise, the library's lower door beneath its handsome portico no longer offers entry to the building, which necessitates a short stroll past the structure's grand façade to the top entrance. Ambling self-consciously beneath the slightly condescending gaze of Andrew Washington, uncle of the more famous George, he's almost reached the safety of the swing doors when he realises something doesn't feel right. Trusting instincts honed in Vietnam, Korea or conceivably in World War One, Studs glances up and stops dead in his tracks. Up at the street's far end a black and threatening weather-front approaches, bowling downhill in a whirlwind of displaced pedestrians and flurried litter. Alma Warren.

Nerve-ends screaming like a four alarm fire, praying that she hasn't spotted him already, Studs hurls himself through the entrance and into the leaflet-papered library reception area. Flattening himself to an unsightly leather stain against the neon handbills on the east wall, he sucks in a breath and holds it, eyes fixed on the glass door as he waits for the intimidating harridan to stalk past in the street outside. He isn't even really sure why he's avoiding her, except that automatic furtiveness in any situation seems like good form from a private eye perspective. It's what Studs would do. Besides, he hasn't got the information that his nightmare client is counting on him to retrieve regarding the Blake situation, and things could turn ugly.

In the sorry precinct out beyond the glass a great untidy avalanche in lipstick rumbles past from right to left, and Studs exhales. Unpeeling himself from the laminated posters at his rear he steps back to the door and opens it, poking his ruptured punch-bag head around the edge to squint inquisitively at the unsuspecting beatnik artist as she flaps and flounces down Abington Street away from him, like a receding storm. As he enjoys the private eye's prerogative of watching somebody while unobserved, a further element of intrigue enters the already curious picture: heading up the street on a collision course with the descending painter is the waistcoat and straw hat clad figure of the Boroughs' own bard-in-a-bottle, the near-universally anomalous Benedict Perrit.

As these two distinctive products of Northampton's oldest neighbourhood approach each other, Studs is witness to a mystifying ritual. On catching sight of Warren, the inebriated poet swivels and heads back the way he's come for several paces before turning once again and staggering in the direction of the artist, this time doubled up with laughter. Misaligned eyes narrowing, Studs wonders if Ben Perrit's strange behaviour could be some kind of code or signal. Maybe this apparent chance encounter between the dishevelled painter and one of her current subjects isn't quite as random as it seems. Suspicions deepening he watches Warren plant an uncharacteristic kiss on Perrit's cheek – it's certainly not how she says hello to Studs – and then after a moment or two's conversation there's a furtive transfer as what might be

money or perhaps a message changes hands. Are the decrepit pair conspira-
tors, or grotesque sweethearts, or has Warren reached the age where she pays
drunks to let her kiss them? Ducking back inside the library entrance as at last
the couple separate and carry on with their respective journeys up or down
the sloping street, Studs muses that whichever way the cookie falls or the dice
crumbles he's now almost certain that Ben Perrit's involved in the Blake case
right up to his bleary, wounded-looking eyeballs. All Studs has to do is find
out how.

To that end, he strides further on into the changed and only intermittently familiar library. He orients himself by the tall Abington Street windows
in the north wall, where the filtered daylight pours down on display stands
that now occupy an area which used to serve as the newspaper reading room.
He can recall the register of local hoboes who once occupied the long-since
vanished armchairs, most conspicuously if it happened to be raining. There
would be Mad Bill, Mad Charlie, Mad Frank, Mad George and Mad Joe, possibly even Whistling Walter who, a shell-shocked veteran of the First World
War, was the sole member of that company who suffered from a noticeable
mental illness. All the rest were merely homeless and half-cut, though local
folklore had attributed to each of them the ownership of blocks of flats in
nearby towns. Conceivably, this inferred status as eccentric millionaires was
dreamed up as justification for not giving any spare change to the down-at-
heel, or at least that's why Studs himself would have come up with that kind
of a yarn. Progressing through to the main concourse of the venerable institution, he recalls a last-minute addition to his list of browsing bums, this being
W.H. Davies who had scribbled down his *Autobiography of a Supertramp*
there under those tall windows in among the muttering and probably infested
throng. And now he thinks about it, didn't Davies go on to collaborate with
one of Warren's heroes, cockney occultist and artist Austin Spare, on their
arts publication *Form*? The way Studs understands it Spare was an Edwardian
weirdo who at one point claimed to have been William Blake in a prior incarnation, although he supposes this connection is too tenuous to be the kind
of thing that his employer's looking for. There's nothing for it. He reluctantly
accepts he's going to have to do some heavy digging.

The best place to start, he reasons, is with Blake himself, the enigmatic
figure at the centre of this cold case. Swiftly hunting down an oversized edition of the Lambeth visionary's work, Studs finds himself a table and a chair
where he can catch up with the skinny on his presumed victim. Skimming
through the volume's introduction he confirms that Blake's dead, very dead,
since 1827. The prime suspects seem to have been complications brought on
by a bowel complaint, although some time before his death the poet himself

had put the finger on the English Winter as a likely culprit. It's a tempting theory, but Studs rapidly dismisses the frequently castigated season from the frame for want of motive. Without so much as a scrap of evidence providing any leads the case is going nowhere. Hell, it turns out they don't even have a body yet, with both Blake and his wife dumped into a communal paupers' grave at Bunhill Fields, their headstone giving only an approximate location for the pair's remains. The other well-known literary occupants of the East London cemetery, Bunyan and Defoe, both known to have made journeys to Northampton town and to have written on their travels here, are marked by a sarcophagus and obelisk respectively. Why couldn't it be one of them that Warren was obsessed by?

With a bad mood coming on he flips through the remainder of the intro, anxious for the consolation of the plates, perhaps a touch of *Glad Day* to lift up his spirits. What he finds he has forgotten is the great predominance of gloomy or downright disturbing images that typify the noted angel-whisperer's oeuvre. Here's *Nebuchadnezzar* crawling nude and horror-stricken through a subterranean underworld, while here's the corpulent *Ghost of a Flea* embarking out onto its twilight stage, a bowl of blood held proudly up before it. Even on those pages where the ghouls and monsters are not present, such as the entirely saint-and-seraph decorated and yet overwhelmingly funereal *Epitome of James Hervey's Meditations among the Tombs*, a graveyard damp is everywhere. Belatedly Studs realises why that last Blake exhibition at Tate Britain some time back, in company with his contemporaries Gilray and Fuseli, was subtitled *Gothic Nightmares*. He reflects that if Blake doesn't turn out to have a Northamptonshire connection then he ought to have, sporting a dismal attitude like that. Northampton was the birthplace, in Studs' estimation, of the modern Gothic movement and the painter, poet and print-maker's obvious preoccupation with mortality would have gone down a storm at any of those early Bauhaus gigs.

He finds that he is mumbling the chorus of "Bela Lugosi's Dead" beneath his morning coffee breath and lets his thoughts drift from the job in hand back to those black and silver nights of twenty, thirty years ago. Studs had been one of the Grand Guignol troupe that gathered like Carpathian fog around Bauhaus 1919, as the ensemble of good cheekbones were then known. There had been Studs himself, and Uber-roadie Reasonable Ray. There had been lead guitarist Danny's otherworldly brother, Gary Ash, and naturally there had been Little John. From what Studs can recall about the genesis of twentieth-century Gothic there had never been a morbid master-plan or style agenda underlying all the vampire references and the haunted Delvaux railway stations on the picture sleeves. That stuff had all emerged from individual members of the band and, by extension, from the town that they'd grown up in; from its creepy thousand-year-old churches, from its sectioned poets, immolated witches, heads on pikes, dead queens and captured kings, this mould and madness all distilled into Pete Murphy channelling Iggy Pop over a weave of Ash's riffs from an internal biker film and the aortal rhythm section of the brothers David J and Kevin Haskins. And from these absurdly entertaining origins a flood of mortuary chic, flensed pallor and cadaver soundtracks had arisen to engulf the Western world in melancholia and makeup, yet another purely local fever escalating into a pandemic.

On the soft peripheries of Studs' hungover vision a septuagenarian in a rose anorak heads for Military History like a scud. He sits surrounded by cloud-chamber sibilance, letting his gaze rest on the open book without focussing the attention. The plate swims and its predominating blacks swirl into a miasma, a vortex of mausolea, a dark whirlpool opening before him as if some hired goon has just cold-cocked him with a sap. *Meditations among the Tombs.* He thinks back to the evening of the funeral for Little John, the patrons of the Racehorse wading waist-deep, wonderstruck, through the lamenting little guys in town for the event, fifty or sixty of them on a Lilliputian pub crawl up the Wellingborough Road and what must it have been like when they started singing? Nobody there from the Persian royal family, by all accounts.

It had all been to do with the potential stain upon the bloodline, as Studs understands it. Given all the enemies that Little John's U.S.-supported tyrant granddad had in Persia back then in the 'Fifties, just a few years after he'd been parachuted into power, it was decided that for the Shah's daughter to produce a malformed child would simply be providing these antagonists with ammunition. Better to pack off the infant to the other end of nowhere, somewhere so obscure that nobody would ever hear his name again or even know of his existence. Like Northampton. Was it any wonder he and John had ended up among the Bauhaus entourage, surfing the purple velvet and the glitter? They were two of the town's many Gothic flourishes.

The library drifts in and out of form about him and for some reason he finds himself remembering a wholly nondescript perambulation in the company of the hard-drinking dwarf, with John's complexion scourged by alcohol until towards the end there was more blotch than face. Where had they been that day, the two of them, and why should he be thinking of it now? Studs has a ghostly memory of the Jazz Butcher as being somehow part of the event, although he doesn't think that the impressively credentialed singer-songwriter had actually been present on the unremarkable occasion that is inexplicably obsessing him. More likely he and Little John had either both been on their way to visit the musician or were otherwise returning from just such an interlude, trudging the sulking backstreet rows between the Butcher's house up near the Racecourse and the draughty chute of Clare Street closer to town centre. Where exactly was it taken, the imaginary snapshot that seems stapled to Studs' forebrain, with the little man stamping ahead of him through thin gunmetal puddles down a silent strip of houses? Was it Colwyn Road or Hood Street? Hervey Street or Watkin Terrace? All that he remembers is the picked-scab paintwork and the greying gauze of the net curtains over ...

Hervey Street. Of course. Widening his eyes he does a 'sudden realisation' take, then narrows them again to peer at the small type beneath the gloomy Blake plate. Maybe if Studs thinks of it as being noir rather than black he'll come to like it more, but there below the mournful imagery is all the confirmation that he needs for now: *James Hervey's Meditations* ... it's the same name, the same surname, even though that doesn't prove it's the same man or that he was associated with Northampton. After all, the town has got a Chaucer Street, a Milton Street, a Shakespeare Road and a few dozen other names commemorating persons without even a remote connection to the place, but all the same Studs has a hunch about this Hervey, and his keen-honed P.I. intuition never fails him.

Except when it does, of course. He winces as he recollects one of his trips with Little John to the casino, to the Rubicon down in the Boroughs just off Regent Square. It may have been the same night that his wee companion launched himself onto the roulette table like an extra ball, but what defines the evening in Studs' memory is his own half-baked behaviour. He'd been a different person then. To be specific, he'd been James Bond in a hypothetical reworking of *Casino Royale*. Oh, he'd got the tux, got the black bowtie, everything. When it was getting late, he'd tossed his last remaining big-stakes chip onto the table and then, without even bothering to see where it had landed, turned and walked away from the roulette wheel with the manner of a man who'd made and lost more fortunes in an afternoon than others had accomplished in a lifetime; someone devil-may-care and assured in his relationship with chance and destiny. However, with a week's rent riding on what was apparently a wholly unobserved louche gesture, he was obviously expecting to be halted in his casual saunter from the table and called back by an astonished croupier to collect his unexpected but extensive winnings. When this failed to happen, he'd been devastated. Studs likes to believe, despite the overwhelming evidence which clearly contradicts his theory, that the forces governing existence have a dramatist's approach to human narrative. He likes to think such entities might have a fondness for last-minute death row pardons, million to one gambles or hair's-breadth escapes and, as a consequence of this belief, has largely led a life of serial disappointment.

But not this time. He feels certain somewhere deep inside, beneath the steel plate that's been in his skull since he selflessly took that landmine in the face at Okinawa, that here's where one of his hunches finally pays off. This Hervey schmuck is hiding something, Studs is sure of it, and maybe if he's breathed on hard enough he'll give it up. Cracking his knuckles menacingly he stands and, taking the Blake book with him, heads towards what seems to be an unoccupied internet connection, or interrogation room as he prefers to think of it. He plans to use every low-down technique he knows to loosen up the suspect, everything from good cop/bad cop to a four-pound bag of oranges that damage the internal organs but don't leave a mark upon the skin. Or, failing that, he'll Google him.

Sure enough, Hervey cracks before the sheer brute force of the search engine and before long Studs has got him singing like some kind of devout Calvinist canary. There's a slew of largely Christian websites that have references to the man, and while the language is so flowery that Studs finds himself in need of anti-histamine, he strikes gold with the first page that he looks at. It seems that James Hervey was a Church of England clergyman and writer, born in 1714 at Hardingstone, Northampton, with his father William serving as the rector of both Collingtree and Weston Favell. Educated from the age of seven at the town's free grammar school, blah blah, goes up to Lincoln College, Oxford, where he runs into John Wesley, blah blah blah, buried in Weston Favell parish church ... Studs struggles to maintain his trademark glower in defiance of the rush of jubilation he is currently experiencing. This, he's certain, is the lead he's looking for. Okay, there's no direct connection to the Boroughs, but at least this new material puts Hervey at the scene.

Suppressing a compulsive urge to call the helpful library attendant Toots, he asks if she can print out all the Hervey scuttlebutt he's found already, throw in Hervey's Wikipedia page and maybe while she's there the entry for Northampton Grammar School. Studs has a notion that Ben Perrit might have been a pupil up there on the Billing Road at one point, and although this seems a tenuous link between James Hervey and the Boroughs, right now it's the only one he's got. He tries a weather-beaten roguish wink on the librarian right at the end of his request but she pretends she hasn't noticed, probably assuming that it's palsy. Paying for the printed sheets he twitches one eye randomly at intervals to further this assumption, reasoning that he can handle condescending pity better than a court case for harassment. He suspects that a defence of 'maverick who won't play by the rules' would sway few juries if employed by an apparent would-be rapist.

Taking the slim sheaf of papers, he opens his carry-all and bags the evidence according to procedure, so that he can read it later. Exiting the library he retraces his steps down Abington Street, carefully avoiding the white polka dots of spearmint spackle which surround the precinct's islands of hard plastic seating, having no desire to be too literal about this gumshoe thing. The Grosvenor Centre, with its giant Roundhead helmet hovering above the entrance in a *Castle of Otranto* tribute, is a synaesthetic blur where the piped music has a tinsel dazzle while the coloured lighting chimes and echoes off along the scintillating mall. He rides the elevator up to the requisite level of the car parking facilities in company with an elderly couple who are both tutting and fussing with the zip of a plaid shopping-cart as if it were their poorly-dressed and backward offspring.

When he finds his vehicle, most probably a Pontiac or Buick, possibly a beat-up Chevrolet, he climbs inside and tries his best to bring a dangerous loose-cannon quality to fastening his seatbelt. As the engine growls to life like a sleek predator, albeit one that's in the later stages of consumption, Studs smiles to himself in case an in-car close-up is required. This is a facet of his job that he's familiar with, a role in which he feels entirely comfortable. He's burning rubber to keep an appointment with a place of worship, and it ain't because he's itching to confess his sins. He's doing what comes, to a private eye, as naturally as lovelorn one-night stands or breathing: Studs is heading for this pitiless town's murky outskirts, hoping to uncover a dead body.

Weston Favell and its parish churchyard are no more than two or three miles from Northampton and it wouldn't do him any harm to take the Billing Road, up past the Grammar School or the Northampton School for Boys as the establishment has been more recently rebranded, just to cast an eye over the place; to case the joint. Ideally he'd prefer to roar out of the town to an accompaniment of screeching brakes and pelting gunfire, but the vagaries of a notoriously contorted traffic system mean he has to take a left into Abington Square when coming off the Mounts, circle the Unitarian church to bring him back the other way, then make another left turn into York Road before even getting to the Billing Road down at the bottom. Waiting at the foot of York Road for the lights to change he thinks again of Little John, having already noticed that the brass plaque which identified Toad Hall has long since been removed. It's a damn shame. They should have kept the place up as a conservation area, a reservation for the dwindling and endangered population of the chronically unsightly, those who were too squat and medieval-looking or those with too many warts.

The lights change and he corners onto Billing Road, the off-white bulk of the beleaguered General Hospital across the busy thoroughfare and on Studs' right. From what he knows of local history, which is a lot considering that he was brought up on the unforgiving streets of Flatbush or the like, the hospital had been originally established as the first outside of London on its earlier site along George Row by an unlikely pairing of the preacher Philip Doddridge and the reformed rake Dr. John Stonhouse. Studs has learned a thing or two about the motion picture industry over the years and thinks the story has the makings of a great chalk-and-cheese buddy movie. He's considering a scene where only a work-squad of raddled eighteenth-century hookers volunteering out of loyalty to Stonhouse sees the new infirmary completed under budget and on schedule, when he passes the high hedges of Billing Road Cemetery looming on his left. Not quite the graveyard that he's looking for but still an excellent example of the species, and about the only local landmark which the Luftwaffe seemed capable of hitting back in World War Two, perhaps in an attempt to lower the morale of British corpses. He imagines it, the midnight flash amongst the sleeping headstones, the attendant spray of dirt and bone and flowers, the marble shrapnel with somebody's name on.

An unfolded sunlit panorama out through the front windscreen is compressed to the unreeling comic strip of brick and garden without sky in his side-windows, residential detail ravelling away behind him in the Studebaker's wake. Across the road on its far side Saint Andrew's Hospital smears by, blind walls and iron railings with that barrier of tall and restless evergreens beyond them as a natural firebreak for the uncontrollable blaze of delusion kept contained within. When you consider all the more-than-usually gifted if not incandescent individuals that have been confined there, Studs supposes you could view the institution as a necessary annexe or extension-wing of rationality, put up to house an information for which reason has no measure. Or some bullshit like that, anyway.

He slows as the winding asylum frieze concludes; runs into the façade of the Northampton School for Boys, its low wall bounding a trapezoid forecourt over which presides the lofty and improving early twentieth-century building, with its more contemporary additions fanning out towards the east across the former tennis courts. A visibly amused quartet of lads in the requisite navy blazers jeer and jostle by the school gate, possibly returning from their dinner hour and no doubt dutifully categorising their subjective universe into gay and non-gay components. While the erstwhile grammar school has failed to produce quite as many notables as the adjacent mental home, you have to give it marks for trying. Francis Crick was once a pupil as apparently was Hervey, with Ben Perrit as a possible. Studs thinks he heard that Tony Chater, a no-nonsense card-carrying commie and for twenty years editor of *The Morning Star*, was also on the register, as was young Tony Cotton of chart-scaling 1980s rockabilly purists from St. James's End, the Jets. Poor old Sir Malcolm Arnold, on the other hand, retained the singular distinction of having attended both the boys' school and the famous funny farm next door. On his last day of term the juvenile composer would have saved himself a lot of time and effort if he'd just scuffed his way up the cycle path and through the front gate, taking off his jacket, cap and tie resignedly before a sharp U-turn delivered him into the tranquilising green continuum of St. Andrew's. From the corner of Studs' right and slightly lower eye he watches the august establishment evaporate into his slipstream, a receding fog of pink and grey shrinking to fit the rear-view mirror as he guns the Packard on to its sepulchral destination.

Further down towards the lower reaches of the Billing Road, with rel-atively well-off family homes to port and little else save open fields to star-board, Studs gets the uneasy feeling that he's overlooking an important detail, maybe in his observations on the recently passed School for Boys, although he can't think what. Was it something to do with how the school was built, its architecture, or ...? No. No, it's gone. Some way before he reaches Bill-ing Aquadrome he takes instead the left turn that will convey his Plymouth De Soto up amongst the honeyed stone of the original village accommoda-tion and the gravel drives of later dwellings, into the unnaturally hushed and watchful lanes of drowsy Weston Favell.

After several minutes he locates a place where it appears that somebody might park their vehicle without being consequently burned to death inside a wicker man. Studs knows these gentrified communities, the money that they represent, and can't shake off the feeling that he's probably been monitored on long lens by a spotter from the Women's Institute since he pulled in. Clam-bering from his bullet-perforated Nash Ambassador he sizes up the intestinal tangle of sun-buttered streets, byways for the convenience of a different cen-tury, and grudgingly acknowledges that places like this, these days, are where all the serious murder-money's to be made. The smart detectives, rather than pursuing cold-eyed gangland slayers down a hypodermic-littered inner-urban alleyway, are relocating to the sticks, to sleepy English hamlets where ladies in twinsets and retired brigadiers reliably attempt to poison one another on a weekly basis. All this white-on-white crime. It's a crying shame.

He's parked in sight of the twelfth-century parish church, its spire rising above the neighbouring chimneys and its stonework with an unevenly toasted look, although in somewhere Weston Favell's size it would be near enough impossible to find a place from which you couldn't see it, if he's honest. Holdall slung across a shoulder that is hunched against the world's anticipated brick-bats, Studs is shortly pushing open a wrought-iron gate with a worse rasp than his own; mounting hewn steps onto the raised-up consecrated ground around the pretty chapel. There's a faint breeze, but apart from that, he notes with some surprise, it's an unusually idyllic afternoon. It ain't his customary milieu, that's for certain. Sunlight falls like syrup on the neatly tended grass and there can't be a faulty neon sign for miles, much less a craps game.

Disappointingly, the church itself is closed and, more disheartening still,

James Hervey's final resting place is not among the smattering of headstones to be found in the building's vicinity. Most of these unassuming markers, with their names and information almost lost to a few centuries of moss or weather, seem to be exclusively for Jacobean stiffs who hung up their plumed hats during the sixteen-hundreds and long before Hervey saw the light of day in 1714. Studs finds a bluish lozenge not much bigger than a boot-scrape, colonised by vari-coloured lichens and apparently commemorating no one in particular, being instead a generalised memento mori. With a little scrutiny he works out that the disappearing characters once spelled out O REMEMBER/ PASSERS BY/ AS THOU ART/ SO WAS I ANNO/ 1656. Sure, buddy. Thanks for that. Give my regards to the black plague. These may or may not be the tombs that Hervey meditated when he was amongst, but it's a safe bet they're the ones that he saw every day when he was preacher here, perhaps contributing to his notoriously sunny disposition.

Having reached a dead end, Studs elects to play his visit like he meant it. Checking first to find out if the turf is damp he lowers himself gingerly onto the verge, lounging insouciantly at full length on his side with ankles crossed, propped on one elbow like a sensitive Edwardian bachelor while he hurriedly unzips his holdall and retrieves the Hervey printout from its depths. He may as well bone up on his elusive quarry while he's here, even if the distinguished cleric's actual bones aren't anywhere around. Considering the scarcity of the surrounding monuments and slabs, he wonders if this churchyard might be one of those where graves, in short supply back in the day, were by no means a final resting place. There'd be a brief immersion in the soil, maybe a week or two before the flesh and stink were gone, and then the stripped-clean sticks would be dug up and scattered to make room for the next occupant, a bit like hospi-tal beds on the NHS. He can recall a scene from Henry Fielding's *Tom Jones* where an altercation at a wedding sees the combatants throw decomposing skulls at one another, since these would indeed have been the handiest form of ammunition readily available in churchyards of the period. If Hervey suffered a short-stay interment of that nature there'd be nothing left of him today, the cra-nium that once contained all his conjectures on the afterlife long since used to concuss a bridesmaid. Lacking any physical remains or similar DNA evidence to process through a piece of high-tech CSI crime-solving apparatus, Studs resigns himself to reconstructing Hervey from the dozen or so printed sheets already in his grasp and cockling with the perspiration. Carefully removing almost rimless reading glasses from his jacket's inside pocket, balancing them on the tomahawk blade of his nose, he sinks into the grey miasma of the text.

As he'd suspected, there's more to this holy-roller Hervey character than meets the eye. Born to a preaching family at Hardingstone and in the shadow of the headless cross, the first King Edward's monument to his dead Eleanor,

James Hervey gets packed off to grammar school during 1721 when he's aged seven. Studs thinks this unreasonably young when everybody he knows went there only after passing their Eleven-Plus, but he assumes that educative practice in Northampton was a different animal nearly three hundred years ago. Hell, education in the town had always been of an entirely separate species to that elsewhere in the country. Back there in the 1970s and 1980s the town's children had been casually subjected to an educational experiment involving a three-tier system and the introduction of a 'middle school', attended for a few years in between the junior and senior establishments and therefore doubling the dislocation and disruption to which pupils in pursuit of learning were subjected. Unsurprisingly the scheme was a conspicuous dud and had been quietly dumped some years back, with a generation of Northampton school kids written off as no more than collateral damage. Still obscurely nagged by the "aged seven" business and the sense that there's unanswered questions hanging over the prestigious boys' school, Studs reads on.

A decade later, at the age of seventeen Hervey goes up to Oxford where he runs into John Wesley's clique of proto-Methodists, a bunch of cold-eyed pious young punks known disparagingly to their fellow students as "the Holy Club". Studs nods in weary recognition. That's the way it is out on the mean streets of religion these days, decent kids forced into joining one gang or another, not because they want to but because they figure it improves their chance of spiritual survival. But then, once they've been sworn in, once they've kneecapped a Baptist as a part of their initiation, they find that it ain't so easy getting out again. That's how it goes with Hervey. For a long time there he's Wesley's top enforcer as the most successful writer in the Holy Club, but soon he's hankering to set up his own racket. Rumours get around that he's developing a soft spot for the evangelicals and that he calls himself a moderate Calvinist, which ain't what Wesley wants to hear. There's plainly an almighty shoot-out brewing, and when Hervey publishes three volumes of his *Theron and Aspasio* in 1755 it's like he isn't giving the great hymnist any choice except to take it to the street. Wesley denounces his former lieutenant's work as antinomianism, an old-fashioned heresy which holds that everything is predetermined, and before a guy can say a paternoster the air's full of theological hot lead. Hervey's outgunned and takes one in the faith, is trying to return fire in *Aspasio Vindicated* when consumption finally decides he's ready for his dirt-nap at the age of forty-five. John Wesley, who's been piling on the pressure from the cover of his pulpit even when his target's clearly dying, finally reads Hervey's posthumously published refutation of his hatchet-job and in a wounded tone declares that Hervey has died "cursing his spiritual father". Wesley makes sure that he gets the last word; puts a round into Hervey's posterity. That's Methodists, Studs muses. They're methodical.

Stretched on the grass among the sparsely distributed headstones in the pale May radiance he realises he's enjoying this, this day-pass from his city of ongoing dreadful night. It's a surprise to find that sunlight isn't always striped. Somewhere a blackbird sings like an interrogated felon and the temporarily non-noir detective turns the drift of his attention to the next of the assorted reference pages, which appears to be by a foot-soldier from the Wesley mob. Ostensibly a Hervey profile, it paints *Theron and Aspasio*'s author as the stumblebum whose florid literary style contributed to a decline of taste in English letters, somebody whose pompous prose had a degenerative influence on nearly all the other preachers of his day "save the robust John Wesley". As a demonstration of the author's point regarding Hervey's vulgar affectations and impoverished ideas, a small slab of the Weston Favell rector's writings are reprinted. Understanding that these will have almost certainly been chosen to best show off Hervey's flaws, Studs prods his slipping spectacles back to the top of his toboggan-run proboscis and starts reading:

I can hardly enter a considerable town but I meet a funeral procession, or the mourners going about the street. The hatchment suspended on the wall, or the crepe streaming in the air, are silent intimations that both rich and poor have been emptying their houses, and replenishing their sepulchres.

Reclining as he is propped on one elbow and thus unable to marshal either shoulder into any kind of shrug, Studs lets his overgrown vacant-lot eyebrows and wasp-chewing bulldog lower lip perform that function in their stead. Sure, Hervey's stuff is sombre in a decorative way, but that don't mean it's for the birds. He personally rather likes the business with crepe streaming in the air and wishes he got lines of dialogue like that. He wishes he got lines of dialogue, period. Focussing upon the print again, he carries on with his assessment of the dead divine's rhetorical abilities:

There's not a newspaper comes to my hand, but, amidst all its entertaining narrations, reads several serious lectures of mortality. What else are the repeated accounts – of age, worn out by slow-consuming sicknesses – of youth, dashed to pieces by some sudden stroke of casualty – of patriots, exchanging their seats in the senate for a lodging in the tomb – of misers, resigning their breath, and (O relentless destiny!) leaving their very riches for others! Even the vehicals of our amusement are registers of the deceased! And the voice of fame seldom sounds but in concert with the knell!

Yeah, now, see, admittedly, that's pretty morbid. And the last few sentences, where Hervey's gone bananas with the exclamation marks, they read as though he's hammering his fist down on the pulpit, or maybe a coffin lid, for emphasis. Studs can see how material like that could be a buzz-kill. With contrived dramatic timing the sun slides behind a cloud and everything is overlaid by a dot screen of half-tone grey. The final two lines might have been contrived with Studs himself in mind. The vehicles of our amusement, many of which he's appeared in, are indeed the registers of the deceased, are chiselled cemetery credits that roll on forever, miserable ledgers of extinguished stars. As for the voice of fame he doubts he'll recognise it even if he ever gets to hear it, which he definitely won't if Hervey's on the level and it sounds in concert with his knell. Actually, that would be okay, once he's considered it. Most people only get the knell.

Its brief sulk over with, the sun comes out again. The next sheet in his slender pile presents the lyrics from what must presumably be Hervey's only extant hymn, *Since All the Downward Tracts of Time*: "Since all the downward tracts of time/ God's watchful eye surveys/ O who so wise to chose our lot/ Or to appoint our ways?" Studs likes the fatalism, which he feels would sit well in a Continental Op or Phillip Marlowe outing, the idea that all our future dooms and disappointments are already written and just waiting for us patiently further along the highway, on the downward tracts of time. He figures he and Hervey could at least agree upon the direction of travel, and supposes that this must be all the antinomian predestination bullshit which brought matters to a head between John Wesley and his former sidekick. Nearby, bees are mumbling imprecations to the year's first flowers as Studs continues working his way through the stack of data.

It has never previously occurred to him that all the major English hymns and their composers seem to blossom from the seventeenth and eighteenth centuries, that fertile Restoration loam enriched by civil war's important nutrients, equestrian and human bio-feed or fired cathedral nitrates. Roundhead Bunyan cranking out "To Be a Pilgrim" while the scabs on Naseby's green slopes were still fresh, then Wesley, Cowper, Newton, Hervey, Doddridge, Blake, the usual suspects, pinned down in the crossfire of their different times and different conflicts, trying to replace the whistling musket-balls with songs. Oliver 'Bugsy' Cromwell's contract hit on Charles the First had changed a lot of things in England, now Studs thinks about it. It went further than the sudden fusillade of hymns. Didn't he hear that billiards only came into fashion in that post-war period, the pastime's complex but predictable ballistics helpfully providing Isaac Newton with a paradigm to hang his laws of motion on? And where would noir detectives like Studs be without the morally insanitary pool hall, its resentful shadows and its mercilessly pouring light? There's something about lines here, staves and lines of verse, trajectories of ball and bullet, things an actor has to learn, vectors of monarchy or the plot-threads of history. The idea's messy and elusive, lacks the vital piece of evidence that ties it all up in a bow. Aware that his attention's wandering he turns it back to the increasingly humid and wilting papers in his knotty claw.

The page he's looking at, while not immediately encouraging, at least explains why Studs has thus far drawn a blank in his attempts to track down Hervey's body. It appears the corpse in question currently resides beneath the church floor, to the south of the communion table in the chancel. Studs nods knowingly. The last place anyone would think to look for it. Yeah, that makes sense. There's some kind of a marker near the spot which talks of Hervey as "that very pious man, and much-admired author! who died Dec. the 25th, 1758, in the 45th year of his age." He passed away on Christmas day and even slipped an exclamation mark into his epitaph, Studs notes admiringly. Below all the forensic details there's a verse in which the author of the piece, Hervey presumably, explains the want of a more visible memorial:

> *Reader, expect no more; to make him known*
> *Vain the fond elegy and figur'd stone:*
> *A name more lasting shall his writings give;*
> *There view display'd his heav'nly soul, and live.*

Again the lip and eyebrow shrug. It seems a reasonable proposition. Hervey, judging from the text in front of him, wanted no monument save that he might "leave a memorial in the breasts of his fellow creatures." This chimes with Studs' personal philosophy; basically kill them all and leave God or posterity to sort them out. He isn't sure whether he's left memorials in the breasts of many fellow creatures, unless by memorials you mean slugs from a .48, but all in all he finds this Hervey character is growing on him like moss on a mausoleum.

The unnaturally perfect afternoon wears on in dandelion-clock increments, and in the houses that surround his elevated churchyard perch the only movement is that of the sun upon blonde stone. Studs has been lying here for getting on an hour and as yet none of Weston Favell's natives have seen fit to venture out onto its sleepy, winding streets. Could be that everybody's dead in some Midsomer Murder spree got out of hand, in some statistically improbable convergence of completely separate and unconnected homicides, where the last major general or former district nurse left standing is brought low by a slow-acting poison secretly administered by someone he or she has stabbed with pinking shears during the opening scene. He thinks it makes a more compelling plot idea than *Murder on the Orient Express*, if only because in his narrative not only does it turn out everyone's the murderer, but everyone turns out to be the victim too. It's an ingenious double twist, the kind of ending nobody sees coming. He indulges in a few moments' consideration of the actors, other than himself, that he'd cast in a movie version but gives up on noticing that, other than himself, the people on his wish-list are all dead, a register of the deceased, which brings him back to Hervey.

The succeeding item in his in-tray, which is what he presently prefers to call his hand, is somewhat more intriguing. Studs has only to catch sight of the name Philip Doddridge halfway down the page to realise that his previously stone-cold trail is warming up, and by the time he's read a paragraph or two it's sizzling like a black Texan guy with learning disabilities in the electric chair. From what he's reading, Doddridge and James Hervey were much tighter than Hervey and Wesley were, with Doddridge even seeming to have had more influence on Hervey's spiritual career than Wesley ever managed to exert. According to the story, after Hervey takes over his father's duties as the parish priest of Collingtree and Weston Favell, he's out walking in the fields when he comes on a ploughman trying to till the soil. Now, Hervey's got this sawbones, probably the kind who'll dig the slugs out of a bullet-riddled soul but won't ask questions, and he recommends that Hervey take the healthy country air by hanging out with honest rural workers as they go about their business. So the preacher walks along beside the labourer and, as a fully paid up member of the Holy Club, decides to give this working stiff a free taste of his pious product. Hervey asks the rube for his opinion on the hardest thing about religion. When Joe Average predictably replies that as a farmhand he's less qualified to answer that enquiry than an educated parson, Hervey launches gladly into his stealth-sermon. He suggests that to deny one's sinful self is Christianity's most difficult achievement and proceeds to lecture the beleaguered ploughman on the great importance of adhering to a morally straight path, just when the man is trying to concentrate upon accomplishing the physical equivalent.

When finally the priest is all out of material, the man from simple peasant stock pulls the old switcheroo when he contends that surely a much harder struggle comes in the denying of one's righteous self; in getting past all the self-righteous, sanctimonious bullshit that the Wesley outfit revels in. Seeing that he's got Hervey on the moral ropes, the backwoods slugger presses his advantage: "You know that I do not come to hear you preach, but go every Sabbath, with my family, to Northampton, to hear Dr. Doddridge. We rise early in the morning, and have prayers before we set out, in which I find pleasure. Walking there and back I find pleasure; under the sermon I find pleasure; when at the Lord's Table I find pleasure. We read a portion of the Scriptures and go to prayers in the evening, and we find pleasure; but to this moment, I find it the hardest thing to deny righteous self. I mean the instance of renouncing our own strength, and our own righteousness, not leaning on that for holiness, not relying on that for justification."

Hervey later cites this moment as a bolt of sudden understanding from the clear blue Weston Favell sky. Before long he decides to follow the rustic's example and at last meets up with Philip Doddridge. They become firm friends, and with the help of Doddridge-convert Dr. Stonhouse, who's "a most abandoned rake and an audacious deist", found the first infirmary outside of London. It turns out that Hervey's closeness with the evangelical dissenting Christians in the Doddridge gang is what earns his dismissal from John Wesley's Holy Mob. The elbow Studs is leaning on sleeps with the fishes, is completely numb, but he's too caught up in the case to ease off now. The dots are all connecting and the puzzle-pieces are all falling into place. The game's afoot. He shuffles through the last leaves in his heap with mounting eagerness and finds an unexpected essay linking Hervey with the birth of the Gothic tradition. Studs, who'd thought his earlier musings on the sumptuously morbid Hervey's Goth credentials were a cynical conceit, is stunned. He's seen more crazy hunches in his long career than Notre Dame cathedral – there was that time he was sure Roman Polanski would cast him as Fagin if he just wrote the director a brief letter stridently insisting on it – but to have one of his long shots finally limp in across the finish line is an unprecedented novelty. Dizzy with newfound confidence in his abilities he reads on, hardly daring to believe his luck.

If Studs is understanding this correctly, the inordinate morbidity of Hervey's writings which the Wesleyans had so deplored turned out to be a maggot-eaten inspiration for his literary contemporaries. The persistent theme of human transience compared with the eternity of God was taken up by other theologians such as Edward Young and by the poets of the nascent Graveyard School like Thomas Gray, becoming such a major influence upon the writings of the day that William Kenrick wrote:

'Twas thus enthusiastic Young;
'Twas thus affected Hervey sung;
Whose motley muse, in florid strain,
With owls did to the moon complain.

From what Studs can make out, this was fair comment, at least in so far as it pertained to later writers of the Graveyard School, who weren't much bothered by the business about God but were completely smitten by the atmospherics and the props, the owls and bats and skulls and crumbling headstones. This was at a moment when society was slowly starting to clean up the nation's graveyards for the purposes of physical and mental hygiene, clearing out the mouldering bones and simultaneously banishing the ever-present smell and the immediate idea of our mortality beyond the margins of accepted daily discourse. Perhaps unsurprisingly, with the grim actuality of death displaced from ordinary life, this was also the point at which our culture first began to make a titillating fetish of the deathly and funereal. Commencing where the less religious and more genuinely ghoulish authors of the later Graveyard School left off, writers like Horace Walpole and Matthew 'Monk' Lewis would take Hervey's sombre iconography and use it to adorn their decomposing European castles or their morally subsiding monasteries. The gothic novel and indeed the whole late eighteenth-century gothic tradition would appear to have its origins in the consumptive Hervey's spiritual preoccupation with the tomb.

As lengthening headstone shadows slither purposefully through the cropped grass towards him, Studs attempts to weigh up all the implications of this latest evidence. He knows that if it's on the level it puts Hervey squarely in the frame as the elusive Mr. Big behind far more than just the gothic novel. Until Walpole, Lewis, Beckford and their fellow frighteners arrived, the only form of novel which existed was the comedy of manners – Goldsmith, Sheridan and later on Jane Austen – with the advent of the gothic novel being also the first genre fiction. Almost every subsequent sub-category of imaginative writing is therefore derived from gothic literature and thus from Hervey's first mould-culture texts; sprung from the moss and lichen of his first sepulchral narratives, Studs realises. Sure, the classic ghost tale is an obvious example, alongside the burgeoning horror and supernatural genres which grew out of it, but that's not where it ends. The field of fantasy would have to be included, as would science fiction with its genesis in Mary Shelley's gothic *Frankenstein*. And then, of course, there are the Decadents, caught up in the sublime deliriums of heir apparent to the caliphate of Vathek and the riches of Otranto, Edgar Allen Poe. And Poe – the idea hits Studs with the force of bourbon before breakfast – Poe set his Chevalier August Dupin to solve the murders on the Rue Morgue or the mystery of the purloined letter and in doing so precipitated the detective story. He attempts to take it in: the bone bulb from which germinated every heartless rain-lashed midnight, every knockout blonde with a sob story and each stuttering electric sign is resting maybe fifty feet away, just south of the communion table in the chancel. Every dining-room denouement, every double-cross. It's one hell of a thing.

This gothic business, though, has got him thinking once more about Bauhaus and the movement's modern reinvention during the end credits of the 1970s. As Studs recalls, it had been the eclectic David J who'd first suggested many of the eerie tropes which would one day prove the salvation of

the black lace and mascara industries. And yet, as widely-read as the peculiarly ibis-like bohemian intellectual undoubtedly had been, Studs doubts that
any eighteenth-century Christian killjoys found their way into J's vehemently
other-directed syllabus. The Bauhaus bassist, he concludes, would have known
nothing about Hervey when he was intuitively laying out the ground-plan for
the most bewilderingly long-lived youth cult of the modern era. The exploding belladonna, lilies and pressed roses which accompanied Northampton's
twentieth-century gothic blossoming came into being without any reference
to or knowledge of Hervey's origination of that style more than two hundred
years before. Unless this is no more than an evocative coincidence, the implication would appear to be that both of these traditions and the sensibilities
that shaped them have arisen from those singular inherent qualities within
the town itself; the gothic view as an emergent property, as a condition of
Northampton. That would explain everything about the place, its churches,
murders, history and ghostly monks. That would explain its writings and its
music and the nature of its people, everyone from Hervey to Ben Perrit, from
John Clare to David J, with Studs and Little John and Alma Warren somewhere on the grotesque spectrum in between them. Little John alone reprised
the gothic movement in one tidy package, what with the malefic dwarf being
a staple of the genre and John's background making him appear almost an
escapee from Beckford's *Vathek*, brought here from the djinn-swept terraces
of Ishtakar in far Persepolis, a crooked grandchild of the demon-sultan Eblis.
Studs is just about as close to inner satisfaction as a spent and used imaginary
private eye can get. It all makes sense. He flips through the remaining pages
with mounting impatience.

There's an interesting piece from a biography of Hervey by one George
M. Ella, which describes the Weston Favell visionary's *Theron and Aspasio*
in terms that make it sound more like a piece of modernist or possibly post-
modern writing than a dialogue concerning Christ's imputed righteousness
first written in 1753. Massively long by modern standards, Hervey's work
apparently shifts in its style and its delivery with each new chapter, hopping
from one mode or genre to another and including "narrative description,
scientific records, inner monologue, anecdotes, autobiography, eye-witness
reports, pen-portraits, short stories, sermons, linguistic studies, nature por-
trayals, journals, poetry and hymns. There is also much in the work that is
reminiscent of a modern film-script." Studs reflects that he should maybe add
the beatnik avant-garde to the already-lengthy list of literary forms which
seem to owe their M.O., which is flatfoot talk for modus operandi, to James
Hervey. His respect for the extravagantly miserable divine is growing by
the moment. Studs would like to see one of these modern pantywaists even
attempt a work as grand and various as that.

He's right down to the Wikipedia entries for both Hervey and Northampton School for Boys now, sprawling on the churchyard turf between the sparse chimes of the early afternoon. Neither of the remaining files appear to Studs to be particularly promising, and yet upon inspection both documents demonstrate convincingly how wrong a guy can be. The first, Hervey's internet résumé, while in the main it offers nothing Studs has not already learned from other sources, plainly states that Hervey was not just someone whom William Blake had heard of and referred to in a solitary painting, but was rather one of Blake's two main spiritual influences with the other one being Immanuel Swedenborg. The hovercraft-inventing angel confidant who once asserted that such creatures know nothing of time, whose missing head was rumoured to be propped against the optics at the Crown and Dolphin, with Northampton's foremost fatalist, both stirred into the Lambeth lad's ideological genetic mix; become his paranormal parents. Studs thinks back to the Blake plate he studied at the library, the solitary human figure at the bottom centre of the image, back towards the viewer and face hidden as he gazes up at the funereal saints and angels gathered there above him, obviously meant to represent Hervey himself and yet with the averted features lending to the character's interpretation as an everyman, paused on the brink of a marmoreal hereafter which renders tuberculosis, flesh and human brevity irrelevant, a figure at death's door refuting loss and time. Or, possibly, Blake didn't know what Hervey looked like, in which instance the appended line engraving offers Studs a slight edge on South London's beatific bruiser.

Gazing from the poorly-printed image, Hervey might be taken for a magistrate saving the lack of judgement in his calm, still eyes; saving the faintest twitch of humour at one corner of the primly pursing lips. The contour hatching that defines the village rector's pleasant features, razor sharp lines eaten into steel by aqua fortis, breaks down to a pointillist particulate in the blotched reproduction although the fine details of complexion remain visible. What seems to be a wart is artfully positioned at the outer edge of the left eye, a feature Studs feels is a mark of some distinction in a man, while riding the right cheekbone is a mole or, judging from its perfect Monroe placement, some kind of cosmetic artificial spot. Given the almost prideful lack of vanity displayed in Hervey's choice of resting place Studs feels this latter possibility is something of a long shot, although there remains a certain prissiness or femininity to Hervey's face which makes the beauty-mark hypothesis seem almost plausible. It's more than the peruke or periwig or whatever the hell it's called that Hervey's wearing in the picture, it's the air of gentleness and receptivity the man exudes.

Studs thinks back to a passage from his recent readings upon Hervey's time in Oxford, where the fledgling preacher had become the close friend of another Holy Club inductee, one Paul Orchard. Even the guy's name was fruity. During one of Hervey's intermittent bouts of ill health in his middle twenties, he went down to live with Orchard for two years at Stoke-Abbey in Devonshire, where the two men drew up a contract vowing to watch diligently over one another's spiritual wellbeing. While this isn't as suggestive as, say, Jeremy Thorpe's billet-doux to Norman Scott, it seems to speak to a male friendship that went some way beyond hanging out and taking shots at beer cans. Taken in the light of Hervey's lifelong bachelor existence, dwelling with his mother and his sister right up to the early, breathless end, Studs gets the picture of a man with certain leanings that could never have been expressed physically and so were sublimated in a somewhat overheated love of Christ and Christian fellowship. It would seem safe to say that in his general manner just as in his florid literary style, James Hervey was a touch theatrical.

This only leaves the Boys School scuttlebutt, the casual afterthought material, which is predictably where Studs at last gets his transcendent roulette moment. The astonished croupier gasps "Incroyable!" and as Studs is sauntering away from that last chip he'd tossed dismissively onto the table he's called back and laden with his unexpected winnings. He is studying without enthusiasm an unprepossessing summary of the establishment when the detail that's been right under his nose the whole time reaches out and hits him in his face until it isn't even ugly anymore. It's what's been gnawing at him ever since his earlier drive-by reconnaissance of the imperious brick building on the Billing Road, and it's there in the printout's second line, just underneath the recently-adopted smug school motto promising *A Tradition of Excellence*, where it says **Established** 1541.

Northampton's School for Boys was nowhere near the Billing Road at its inception. Founded by Mayor Thomas Chipsey as the 'free boys grammar school', it had initially been some way further west and situated in a street to which it had, Studs realises belatedly, given its name: in Freeschool Street, Ben Perrit's erstwhile home down on the Boroughs' edge, where the eponymous school was located for some sixteen years. Erected when Henry the Eighth was on the throne it had been moved in 1557 to St. Gregory's Church, which at the time extended into Freeschool Street, suggesting that the relocation wasn't too demanding. Situated in the same place until 1864, this would have been where Hervey studied from age seven to age seventeen back there in the 1720s. A stray comment which Studs must have skimmed somewhere amongst the other evidence comes back to him, a casual pronouncement by John Ryland, a contemporary of Hervey's and his earliest biographer, to the effect that Hervey's childhood place of education had been little better than a down-at-heel charity school. Studs nods, grave and perversely photogenic. Given that it was down in the Boroughs it's unlikely that it could have been anything else but a well-meant attempt to generally improve the district's juvenile unfortunates, even back in the rowdy sixteenth century. Northampton, with the ancient neighbourhood that once was its entirety, would have been some few hundred years into a somehow purposeful decline by then, punished and scorned by earlier Henries. For his own part, Studs suspects that the blacklisting of the town goes back much further, possibly to local anti-Norman insurrectionary Hereward the Wake, a figure not unlike the locally connected Guy Fawkes in that he's been banished from the history lessons just as surely as the town itself is banished even from regional TV weather maps. If the grandfather of the Gothic movement had to spend his formative years somewhere then the Boroughs was undoubtedly the perfect cradle, full of lice and fatalism.

Studs has found the smoking gun. He levers his numb carcass from the grass like someone opening a bone umbrella. Brushing irritably at the ghost-green trimmings clinging to his leather jacket he retraces his steps through the sparsely populated cemetery and in passing notices the yokel-noir effect of pinstripe shadows falling onto sunlit paving through a churchyard gate. A black smudge on the lens of afternoon he makes his way back to the baking Coupe de Ville, air shimmering over its hardtop in a layer of hot jelly. Clambering inside he hums the windows down to cool the mobile oven off before he roasts, and once more fails to come up with a hard-boiled way of buckling his seat belt. Maybe if he spat contemptuously on the dashboard halfway through the operation, or perhaps coined some particularly pungent simile for how it's often difficult to get the metal fastening into the plastic slot? Like "it was harder than a twenty-stone Samoan drag queen doing Chinese calculus in ... some ..." He'll work on it.

Remembering that he still has his reading glasses on, Studs carefully removes them and returns them to an inside pocket before firing up the engine, whereupon the smoke-grey Duisenberg roars out of Weston Favell, a landbound torpedo heading for the distant heat source of Northampton's centre by the shortest route available. The hamlet's still-deserted streets are an abandoned set, their ochre stonework only painted background flats that are now folded up and put away into the compact space of a smeared rear-view mirror. Thundering along the Billing Road he screeches past the modern incarnation of the Boys School, non-existent prior to 1911, and his self-recrimination at not tumbling to a solution sooner has the sour taste of brass knuckles in the teeth of victory. For a noir private eye like Studs, of course, this is the perfect outcome. Unadulterated triumph is unthinkable when the real satisfaction of your chosen occupation lies in ethical, emotional and physical defeat; in the acknowledgement, with Hervey, that all cases closed or mortal glories are made insignificant in their comparison with the big sleep.

An afternoon sun left too long to steep has stewed the light so that it has more body and a slight metallic aftertaste as it pours, off the boil, on the asylum and the cemetery's untidy marble overgrowth, onto the hospital that Hervey had helped Philip Doddridge and John Stonhouse to establish. Executing a left turn at the unhurried traffic lights beside Edward the Seventh's stained bust with its birdshit coronet, Studs coasts down Cheyne Walk past the hospital's maternity facilities, his progress halted by another set of lights down at the bottom of the hill near Thomas Becket's drinking fountain. Childbirth, martyrdom, twisting together in the dull steel spines of Francis Crick's half-hearted Abington Street monument, the sexless superheroes spiralling up in genetic aspiration under undecided weather, flight frustrated and their heels forever rooted in the monkey street. A light descends in stages through the signal's pousse-café, from grenadine to crème-de-menthe, and Studs is gliding on Victoria Prom with Beckett's Park and the generic supermarket forecourts that are understudying an unwell cattle-market, smearing by him on his left. Once past the Plough Hotel at Bridge Street's lower end, down in the Saturday night blood-sump, he negotiates an unexpectedly byzantine series of right turns before arriving in the parking area which backs on to the Peter's Place arcade in Gold Street. Once again he pays, displays, and leaves his possibly gang-tagged Corvette hunched on its chewed-up asphalt slope beneath the big bowl full of valley sky. Removing from the vehicle enclosure through its lowest exit, narrowly surviving a traverse of the dual carriageway there at Horsemarket's rank monoxide foot, he skulks around the slow curve of St. Peter's Way towards the raised and unkempt patch of grass that had once been the western reach of Green Street, where he clambers two or three feet from smooth pavement onto ragged turf and takes the Boroughs from behind.

The shabby and demoted former neighbourhood green rises to the rear of Peter's Church, its limestone wrinkles and discoloured liver spots all presently erased by flattering solar gold. First raised in timber by King Offa as a private chapel for his sons in the ninth century, rebuilt in full Gothic effect by legacy-aware Simon de Senlis during the twelfth or eleventh, the near thousand-year-old structure drains all markers of the present from the grassy incline that it trails behind it. Mugging devils in eroded eaves regard him as he labours uphill through the weeds, their stone eyes bulging, their frog lips distended with anxiety at his approach, paralysed apprehension of the gargoyle competition which he represents. For his part, the ascent across a timeless and deceptively sun-burnished wasteland to the ancient place of worship makes him feel reduced to a transparently ill-fated academic in some smugly awful narrative by Montague Rhodes James. Asthmatic laundry, steroid spiders, Gypsy kids with switchblade fingernails, all waiting for him in the largely disused edifice ahead. Now that he thinks about it, M.R. James and the whole English ghost story tradition must rate as Hervey's most glaringly apparent by-blows, illegitimate great-grandchildren by way of graveyard versifiers and elite hysterics with exquisite furniture. Then there are modern occultists, the heirs to James's Karswell and early adaptors of the gothic model in their literary efforts and their leisurewear, with Hervey's doctrine of Christ's innate righteousness become a style-guide for diabolists. Studs doubts that Hervey would have felt entirely comfortable with that, but with a self-confessed deployment of arresting imagery to help embed his message the creator of Northampton noir has no one but himself to blame. Don't make the wrapping paper more intriguing than the gift inside, an edict which Studs ruefully accepts could equally apply to his own inner loveliness and its regrettably attention-grabbing packaging.

Cresting the slanted verge he walks the almost indiscernible remains of Peter's Street, along the railed rear of the church and heading east. From unrolled liquorice whips of shade he estimates it to be sometime around five o'clock and briefly knows the phantom-limb sensation of release this hour would herald if he had a proper job and hadn't been apprenticed to the night. Not that he'd say he was self-conscious when it came to his arresting physiognomy, but Studs has always far preferred the dark. His favourite entertainment, after being taken for a ride by a heart-breaking beauty who turns out to be a man, used to be wandering the shadowy rear entries of the town back in the days before the alleys had been gated off by nervous residents; before behaviour like that could land you on the sex-offenders register. Once, in the cobbled crack between the Birchfield and Ashburnham roads, in the small hours of a brisk Sunday morning, he'd been startled by a massive ball of granite rolling down the darkened corridor towards him in the classic Indiana Jones manoeuvre, only to reveal itself at closer quarters as Northampton's planetary-scale performing soul, the since-deceased Tom Hall.

Walking a midnight dog, the lyrical behemoth had paused for a moments' badinage with the sham Shamus, eloquent in his defence of those neglected crevices with their cock-decorated garage doors and frilly bindweed fringes. Clad in dungarees that may well have been a converted Wendy-House, Hall had extemporised upon his thesis that the narrow urban seam which they were currently inhabiting was one of the town's land-canals, part of its bone-dry network of imaginary pedestrian waterways. Exploring the bare streambeds with their hard Edwardian gooseflesh underfoot, a practiced supra-mariner might readily observe the sunken underworld detritus that's accumulated at the feet of galvanised steel banks: fiercely-discarded ultimatum porn collections or the ribcages of bicycles, drifted against the alley's edges where neon-hued minnow condoms shoal among serenely swaying nettles, phlegm anemones. Occasionally a body. Obsolete appliances, embarrassing addictions, wilfully forgotten actions, deeds or purchases thought better of and excised to these margins, scenes that have been scribbled out from daylight continuity and written instead on these unattributed and off-the-record passages, in this piss-splashed Apocrypha. The rotund troubadour had lavishly expanded on his vision for the length of time it took his canine charge to arch up on its tiptoes like a shuddering croquet hoop and squeeze out a heroic movement longer than the hound itself. With that, the dissertation had concluded and the two men had continued on their disparate ways, Studs heading up the drained canal against the wind while the musician bobbed away downstream like an enormous marker buoy that had escaped its moorings, floating off into the visual purple.

Studs has by now reached Narrow Toe Lane, perhaps the Boroughs' most unusually titled thoroughfare, in truth barely a path that trickles down beside the shaggy grass expanse to the remains of Green Street. He's got no idea about the name. A misspelled towpath of an insufficient width, perhaps, or, knowing the neighbourhood, a reference to a shared genetic disability which at one point afflicted everybody in the street? Up to his right, running along the east face of the church to Marefair are St. Peter's Gardens, formerly a disused alleyway but widened twenty or so years ago into a disused promenade by pulling down the school outfitters, Orme's, which stood at the far corner. Studs remembers going there, mother-accompanied, in his twelfth year to buy a uniform for secondary school. He isn't certain, but he has an idea that he might have been escorted to the same shop on an earlier occasion to be measured up for his humiliating kilt. As he recalls there used to be a pair of facing full-length mirrors in the changing room, where each excruciating moment of a child's sartorial ordeal unfolded terrifyingly into a wood-panelled eternity. That cramped and curving passage, longer than the district, longer than the town, stretching away into the solid walls and the surrounding buildings, occupied by an unending queue of mortified and squirming seven-year-olds, where exactly had it gone? When they demolished Orme's the Tailors, what became of its interior infinities? Had all those other ugly little boys, all those half-silvered layers of identity been folded up together like the painted sections of a lacquer screen and stuck in storage somewhere or, more likely, dumped?

This isn't even his tough childhood. These aren't his dismantled memories to mourn, and he's surprised at how much this brief sortie into someone else's ruined dreamtime is affecting him. He'd figured Warren was exaggerating in her murderously angry monologues, attempting to transform her girlhood landscape into a betrayed and bummed-out Brigadoon, but this is something different. Studs finds himself genuinely shocked by this matter-of-fact erasure of a place, a stratum of the past and a community. If the reality inhabited by several generations of a thousand or so people can be rubbed out like a cheap hood in the wrong bar on the wrong night, what or where is safe? Hell, these days, is there still a right side of the tracks for anybody to be born on? He's come here to sniff out the surviving traces of a vanished yesterday, but all he sees in these deleted streets are the defective embryos of an emerging future. And when finally that future's born and we can't bear to look at it; when we're ashamed to be the lineage, the parent culture that sired this unlovable grotesque, where shall we banish it so that we needn't see it anymore? We can't do like the Shah and send it to Northampton. It's already here, already rooted, a condition gradually becoming universal.

Though St. Peter's Street continues on between the relatively new and mostly vacant office buildings into Freeschool Street itself, Studs thinks he'll maybe go the long way round, down Narrow Toe Lane into the picked carcass of the former Green Street and work his way up from there. There might be clues: a footprint or perhaps a witness previously too intimidated to come forward, some surviving stonework in amongst the brick veneers that might turn stool pigeon given the right incentive. Hands in his high jacket pockets and the elbows sticking out like dodo wings he makes his way down the vestigial lane, mentally colouring his sketchy image of James Hervey as he goes.

As Studs imagines it, the probable scenario has seven-year-old Hervey walking in from Hardingstone to school each morning, more than likely unaccompanied and for at least half of the year making the journey in pitch blackness. He'd have started out from his home village, which two centuries thereafter would acquire further gothic credentials in the person of 'Blazing Car' murderer Alf Rouse. The little boy, perhaps with the same delicate look, the same primly pursed lips and a tendency to bad coughs even then, scraping along utterly lightless rural byways with nothing but sudden owls for company to the old London Road. There, every weekday of his early life, the hulking headless cross, one of the stone memorials raised by Edward the First at every spot where Queen Eleanor's body touched the earth on its long transport back to Charing by the Thames, looming up still and black against a pre-dawn grey. With little Jimmy Hervey's front door barely closed behind him, the religiously inclined and sickly infant would have been immersed immediately in the ancient town's mythology, with the decapitated monument a gatepost at the mouth of its funereal romance.

Then a long downhill trudge towards the blacked-out urban mass below, as yet devoid of even gaslight, the frail schoolboy making entry through the reeking shadows of St. James's End where cursing traders pulled too soon from their warm beds load carts and barrows, calling to each other in an unfamiliar patois through the gloom. Squashed adult faces with strange blemishes, squinting, half turned towards him in the lurching candlelight and from a gated yard the steaming, shuddering snort of horses. His pink fingers numb with cold, who knows how many books beneath one weedy infant arm, the future fatalist would be obliged to mount the hump of West Bridge with the dark of the unbroken day ahead diluted almost imperceptibly at every grudging step, the timeless river heard rather than seen somewhere beneath him. At the crest, the midpoint of the span, the castle ruins would have made themselves apparent to the child in those antipodes of dusk before a risen sun could burn the fog away, a sprawling twilight acreage of tumbled stones with shrill and flittering specks about the lapsing walls, the stumps of amputated towers. Was Northampton's crumbled fortress, currently its hooker-hub and railway station, once conceivably the larval form of every subsequent Otranto, every Gormenghast?

From there, with a determinist momentum hastening his pace the pious, ailing youngster would have trickled from the scoliotic bridge to its far bank, rolling into the Boroughs and the tangled yarn of streets, the madcap turrets wearing witch's hats of pigeon-spattered slate. Then Marefair and St. Peter's Church, the weathered buttresses embossed with gurning Saxon imps, Hieronymus Bosch extras yawning from some long-passed Judgement Day. A few steps further on, Hazelrigg House where Cromwell dreamed an ironclad English future on the eve of Naseby. A last right turn into Freeschool Street would bring the budding ghastly visionary to his place of education, just as a left turn is by now taking Studs into the same street's other, lower end.

The district, which Studs still recalls from his insomniac night-jaunts of twenty years back, is unrecognisable, a loved one's face on the first visit to Emergency after the accident. The broken spar of Green Street that has brought him from the foot of Narrow Toe Lane to his current junction has no buildings anymore, no southern coastal levees shielding the disintegrating land from the erosive tidal traffic swirl of Peter's Way. As for the uphill climb of Freeschool Street before him now, it's a transparent and insultingly inaccurate imposture, someone who looks nothing like your mum but turns up a week after the cremation claiming to be her. The steep lane's western flank, once dominated by Jem Perrit's woodyard, number fourteen, is now for the most part untenanted business premises all the way up to Marefair. As the hatchet-faced investigator haltingly ascends he tries to recreate Ben Perrit's missing-and-feared-dead family home; superimpose the teetering two or three storey hillside edifice with its attendant stables, lofts, goats, dogs and chickens on the nearly vehicle-free forecourt of the memory-resistant modern structure that succeeds it, but to no avail. Some isolated features cling in his recall like tatters of a bygone show bill doggedly adhering to a corrugated fence – the three steps up to a black painted door, heirlooms and horse brasses displayed in the front parlour – but these fragments simply hang in empty recollected space without connective tissue, lobby cards and teasers for an unrecoverable silent classic.

Just across the way from the conspicuous absence of the Perrit home, on the untidy freehand margin that is Freeschool Street's east side, Studs draws abreast of Gregory Street's carious maw with the collapsing brickwork at one corner bounding an eruptive buddleia-jungle, once the backdoor entrance to St. Gregory's Church and the free school which it incorporated when James Hervey was a pupil here. At some point after that a row of terrace houses occupied the previously sanctified ground, all odd numbers counting up from seven through to seventeen down at the Gregory Street corner if Studs' memory serves him right, coincidentally the ages between which the young James Hervey would be visiting this humble gradient every morning. Studs thinks he remembers his client Alma Warren saying she'd had relatives who lived in one of the now derelict and roofless properties, an aunt or second cousin who'd gone mad and locked her parents out while she sat all night playing the piano. Something like that, anyway, one of the countless grubby dramas since supplanted by a butterfly bush smothering the untouched twenty-year-old rubble.

Studs is half across the spindly capillary, glancing reflexively uphill to see if anything is coming even though he doesn't think cars are allowed down this way these days, when he notices a man and woman standing at the street's top end apparently engrossed in conversation. Something about the flamboyant orange blur of waistcoat that the man is wearing strikes a chord and has Studs fumbling in an inside pocket for his spectacles. Reaching the street's far side he saddles them on his ice-breaker beak and peers around the deconstructed corner house, pressed flat against its bowing wall in case one of the couple glances down the lane and spots him, the pretended habit of a lifetime.

It's Ben Perrit.

It's Ben Perrit, talking to a woman who's not half his age, her hair in rows and a provocatively short red coat on that looks like it's made from PVC. To all appearances she's canvassing for coitus. While the beery bard has clearly raised his sights since the embrace with Alma Warren, Studs still can't help feeling that Ben could have travelled further and done better for himself. The local poet's prospects for romance, however, aren't Studs' most immediate concern right now. What's Perrit doing here, especially in light of that apparently chance Abington Street sighting earlier? It has to be more than coincidence, or at least in Studs' current mise en scène it does. He briefly contemplates the possibility that Perrit might be an improbably inexpert tail, perhaps employed by Warren to keep surreptitious tabs on her pet private eye, but hastily dismisses the idea. Ben Perrit, for as long as Studs has known him, has been in no state to follow his own literary calling, let alone pursue another person with perhaps less rubber in their legs.

He risks another peek around the dog-eared corner. Up at Freeschool Street's top end the woman is now backing carefully away from Benedict, who giggles and gesticulates obscurely at her as she goes. No, definitely not a tail. Not in that vivid carpet-remnant waistcoat and not with that laugh that's audible from all the way down here, the polar opposite of unobtrusive. All the same, they must add up to something, these suggestive near-encounters. Ducking back behind the listing wall he tries to put his finger on the feeling that he has, the sense he's missing something here, some part of the big picture he's not privy to. He understands that, in real life, to inadvertently bump into someone twice in the same day is nothing special, but he's trying to keep in character. From Studs' perspective, Perrit's multiple appearances can only be some kind of narrative contrivance, an essential story mechanism or device which signals the impending resolution of the mystery, an unexpected drawing in of all its mucky threads: Ben Perrit and the girl in the red plastic mac, Doddridge and Lambeth and determinism. William Blake. James Hervey.

When he next peers up the lane both Perrit and his piece of skirt are gone. Studs puts his spectacles away and leans against the psoriatic bricks. What now? He's reached the place that he's been looking for, and short of a probably suicidal climb over the wall he's propped against into the overgrown bee-cafeteria beyond, he can't go any further. He can't occupy the spaces that James Hervey's body heat once passed through; doesn't know what he'd hoped to accomplish with this pilgrimage through disappearance in the first place. Treading in a dead guy's footprints like some toddler following his father through the snow, running on nothing but a blind faith in location as if walking the same streets as someone else forged any kind of a connection, how could he have been so stupid, such a schlemiel, possibly a patsy? Places don't stay where you left them. You go back there, anywhere, and even if it looks exactly how it did before, it's somewhere else.

He can remember Little John, during one of the relatively thoughtful and less raucous conversations that they'd had together. His folkloric friend had been in a more wistful, even plaintive humour than was usually the case, talking about a childhood that he couldn't properly recall, Arabian Nights he'd never really had.

"Y'know, I'd like to go back one day, Persia, the old country. See what it was like."

No, John, mate. You can't do that. Persia's gone. '79, they had a revolution after Jimmy Carter made the CIA stop paying off the ayatollahs so they'd leave your grandfather alone. They kicked him out and let the cancer finish him, and it's a safe bet that the new regime aren't big admirers of your family. It's called Iran now. You're not wanted there. You never were."

Of course, you couldn't say that. You could only mumble non-committally and wish him luck, ask him to bring you back a winged horse or a flying carpet, duty free, safe in the knowledge that by the next time John sobered up, the fond, nostalgic jaunt to Mordor would have been forgotten. It's too bad that Studs ignored his own unspoken words of advice, hadn't realised until right this moment that what's true of Tehran is as true of Freeschool Street. This scruffy piece of ground has seen its revolutions, tyrannies replaced by other tyrannies, its character revised by different stripes of fundamentalism, socio-political or economic: King Charles, Cromwell, King Charles Junior, Margaret Thatcher, Tony Blair. Now that Studs thinks about it, the terrain beneath his feet even shares Little John's status as deposed royalty: the rough trapeze of land bounded by Freeschool Street on one side and Narrow Toe Lane and Peter's Gardens on the other would have been the grounds of Offa's Saxon palace, with St. Peter's and St. Gregory's as the two churches flanking the construction to the west and east respectively. The yawning entrance to Jem Perrit's buried wood-yard might have opened onto royal stables once, and if he'd only had the foresight to be born twelve hundred years odd earlier then Jem's son Benedict could have been Offa's jute-clad poet laureate, or possibly his fool. Poor Tom's a-cold and a sheep's bladder on a stick. Ben would have been a natural.

The breeze seems cooler on his stubble, and Studs briskly shakes his head to clear it of the memories, the reverie that gets all over you like gunshot residue. How long has he been standing here on Gregory Street's corner, uselessly deliberating on dead dwarves and how it's usually the turf that ends up as the loser in a turf war? He detects slight changes in the local ambience which indicate that he's been holding up this listing wall for quite some time. The western sky is clearer with its light diluted and more palatable, understated tints of colour in its thinning wash as the blue fresco of the day reaches its edges. Distant cars and lorries would appear to have run out of things to say, their conversation flagging and become more intermittent, trailing off to grunts in the post rush-hour hush. Birds arcing down to guttering shrug off their troubles and assume the careless air of almost-home commuters. Friday, May the 26th, makes for the pink, embarrassed blush of its conclusion.

He decides to cast his poorly-placed Mr. Potato Head eye over Horseshoe Street, check out what's left now of St. Gregory's other end before he heads for home, calls it a day as if there's something else that he could call it. In the absence of a bitter wind he turns his leather collar up so that he feels more isolated, and with a last glance at the ambiguous dealership which has sup-

planted Offa and Jem Perrit and all points between he rolls his shoulders in
a hoodlum strut away down Gregory Street with the declining sun behind
him. To his left the dereliction of the corner property continues pretty much
unchecked while on his right there's simply nothing there, an agoraphobic
stretch of flayed land tumbling uninterrupted down to Peter's Way and overprinted with a schist of levelled floor-plans like the quantum ripples still discernible on the event-horizon 'skin' of black holes, our only surviving record
of the cosmic bodies already ingested.

At the street's bend where it angles sharply to the south stands a three-
floor Victorian factory, a great cube of smoked stone which would appear to
have been transformed into a recording studio. A fashionably minimal house
logo is affixed high on the soot-blasted façade in a naive attempt to impose
an identity on the amnesiac edifice, just now pretending to be Phoenix Studios, a well-intentioned effort to evoke the flames of rebirth from the ashes of
the neighbourhood, which clearly isn't going to work. It wasn't that kind of a
fire. In what looks like a disused yard to one side of the building is a heaped
moraine of tyres, deposited here long ago as though by a black rubber glacier
in the long cold snap following the era of the dino-dozers and tyranno-JCBs,
their jointed necks craning and swivelling to take a bite out of a displaced
family's front bedroom, grey wallpaper weeds trailing from yellow metal jaws,
an undiscriminating swallowing. He turns right into Gregory Street's continuation only to discover that there isn't one. Beyond the studio there's nothing
separating this end of the road from the dual carriageway of Horseshoe Street
which runs downhill in parallel, save for a couple of ridiculous low barriers
that Little John could have stepped over without noticing. Studs feels a fleeting obligation to walk all the way down and around the edge of where the
depots, builders' yards and houses should have been, out of respect for the
dead properties, but that strikes him as both insane and too much trouble so
he cuts across the empty dirt instead.

The wide road is to all intents and purposes bereft of cars or people from
its foot by the picked skeleton of the gas-holder up to its far summit at the top
there, where it runs into the Mayorhold. In the tumbleweed hiatus between
clocking off and tying a few on, the district's voices, both contemporary and
ancestral, switch off as abruptly as a background tape-loop. He can hear the
empty moments settling like dust on the abandoned highway, muffling its
ghosts, the silence bowling off downhill to quiet the supper tables of Far Cotton. Later, almost certainly, comes a cacophony of sirens, retching, intimacies
bellowed into mobile phones and all the hairy other, but for now there's this
unscripted pause, the welcome presence of dead air.

He takes his time mounting the incline, feels professionally compelled to
notice everything, to let no nuance slip the dragnet of his razor-honed atten-

tion. Here a paving slab cracked into fjords at one corner, there a rear view of the Marefair skyline with its hidden back-yard complications fondly cluttering the rooftop architecture, aerials and fungal growths of satellite dish sprouting from the chimney bricks or drainpipe heights. Across the way, above the low relief of a breeze-block crash-barrier running up the slope's spine, the far side of Horseshoe Street is in a noticeably better state of upkeep than the tattered edge that Studs patrols, falling within the relatively well-maintained town centre rather than in the forsaken patchwork of the Boroughs. While the one-time motorcycle-pirate haven of the Harbour Lights is presently enduring the indignity of a rebranding as the Jolly Wanchor or however one pronounces it, the building is at least still standing and may one day see again its leather-armoured clientele. A little further up, an iron-gated yard appended to the 1930s billiard hall looks incomplete without a stumbling and cheery bunch of post-war dads still in their demob suits and taking too long over farewells as they make unhurriedly towards the exit.

Just beyond the snooker parlour is the Gold Street corner where a century ago there stood Vint's Palace of Varieties, a venue at which the young Charlie Chaplin played on various occasions. Studs is unsure if the great screen hobo's skittering skid row routines would work as well against a backdrop of contemporary poverty; a different destitution. He thinks not, though that might be because he's not imagining the Boroughs in decade-evading black and white, nor with its miseries conducted to a tinkling piano soundtrack. Background music changes everything. If they'd stuck some Rick Astley or perhaps the Steptoe theme behind his impaled-sister-raping scene in Besson's *Joan of Arc* it would have been hilarious. Or "Nessun Dorma" over his Hamburglar appearances.

As he draws level with the snooker joint across the road he pulls his focus back to the distressed concrete hypotenuse he's currently ascending, on the scummy side of the street with its disinterred carcass aesthetic and an angry pseudonym on every lamppost. Reckoning that this must roughly be the spot on which the east end of St. Gregory's once stood he halts his climb to take stock of the victim district's injuries, to gauge the full extent of what seem almost frenzied mutilations to its substance, even to its map. The surgical removal of the vital organs, could that be the killer's signature? Some of the shallower cuts to the masonry look like defensive wounds in Studs' professional opinion, and he'd put good money on discovering skin traces such as planning application notices beneath the chipped slates of the area's fingernails. Struck by the unexpected poignancy of his hardboiled analogy he finds he's starting to fill up. The neighbourhood, it's ... you know. Raped and with her face smashed in, but she put up a fight. Good girl. Brave girl. Sleep tight.

Finding a cafeteria serviette deep in one jacket pocket, Studs wipes quickly at his shiny sockets, blows his nose and pulls himself together before he resumes his survey. Nothing in the crazy-quilt of random surfaces and signs before him indicates even the homeopathic water-memory of a church. The past is cauterised. There's even a dull red patch halfway up one mongrel wall which, without benefit of his corrective lenses, looks to him like a wax seal on the doomed territory's document, a deal that was signed off some several generations back, all done and dusted. Nonetheless, this isn't what James Hervey the short-trousered gothic schoolboy saw, scuffing his satchel on the rough sills of the eighteenth century. This isn't what the unnamed pilgrim monk home from Jerusalem experienced a thousand years before, prompted by angels to the centre of his land and carrying a rugged cross to put there when he found it, hewn from heavy rock, a message from Golgotha like a petrified kiss on a postcard. And back then, there would have been no doubts about the provenance of the communication, not with Fed Ex seraphim arranging the delivery. Nobody would have wondered who the sender was, even with no return address. The angel couriers were rigorous scientific bona fides, their cruciform stone the equivalent of a Higgs boson particle arrived to validate the standard theocratic model. A big deal, in other words. An enchilada that was more than whole.

No wonder they made such a fuss about the artefact, set it into the Horseshoe Street face of St. Gregory's where it remained a site of pilgrimage for centuries, all of those last-ditch fingertips tracing the worn-smooth axes to their intersection, all the lame and blistered feet which bore them here. The centre of the country, measured by God's own theodolite. That surely must have carried some weight with King Alfred when he named Northampton foremost of the shires, effectively the capital in an alternate history where William never came. The great cake-scorcher was just rubberstamping policy laid down by the Almighty. More than merely royal pasturage this spot was holy ground, marked out by things with burning haloes at the say-so of an ultimate authority. That's how they saw it, how it was: a violent and miraculous reality much like Studs' own, perfumed by horseshit for the want of cordite. In a dark age the noir outlook would be a foregone conclusion.

And yet, even with the gulf of a millennium to separate the relic's origins from Hervey's schooldays, wouldn't the conceptual charge and inspirational importance of the object remain undiminished in believing eyes, especially those of a seven-year-old boy whose father was a clergyman? For ten years, near enough a quarter of his prematurely interrupted life, the ailing child had laid his hands or eyes upon the primitive and earnest talisman, the chiselled X on an interior treasure-map, a seeding crystal of Jerusalem itself. The simple, fundamental shape would have been printed on his bedtime eyelids, colours back to front in the screensaver drift before sleep, a test pattern on the hypnagoggle-box. Enough to stamp that minimalist template onto Hervey's coming life, Studs would have thought. A fragment carried here from the eternal holy city could provide the dynamo which drove the young ecclesiast in one side of John Wesley's operation and then, acrimoniously, out the other. The Rood in the Wall they called it, manifesting Hervey's granite-hard conviction, powering his writings, *Theron and Aspasio* or his sepulchral meditations, energies eventually earthed in William Blake who closes off the metaphysic circuit when he writes *Jerusalem*.

Slow increments of early dusk are gathering around the scowling Sherlock as he contemplates the haphazard assembly of a dozen centuries, the spectrum of failed social strategies and mix of incompatible building materials represented by the mural mess in front of him. The rood has long since disappeared and taken the wall with it, leaving only a conspicuous and desolating absence. He can't help but wonder where it went, the crude-cut icon sent to tag the middle of the land, the centre of his pulp investigation. Was it spirited away by sharp-eyed demolition workers, either mercenary or conceivably devout? Perhaps more likely, did it go unrecognised, its aura faded, its significance by then bled out into the thirsty dirt, abandoned in a deeper drainage ditch than that in which the tombstone of Saint Ragener was finally discovered sometime in the nineteenth century? Composed of matter near as ancient and enduring as the world itself, a great plus-symbol to denote the site's positive terminus, Studs knows that it must still exist somewhere, as widely scattered shards if nothing else. When space and time are ending the device's disparate molecules will still be there for the finale, possibly intact, a symbol that has long outlived the doctrine symbolised, with its imputed righteousness remaining aeons after Hervey, Doddridge, Blake and everybody else are gone the way of all flesh at the far ends of a predetermined universe.

An atavistic pineal tingle tells him that he's being watched, an ingrained P.I. reflex critical to his imaginary line of work. Swivelling his extraordinary profile, like the cliff-face simulacrum of an Indian chief in *Fortean Times*, he glares uphill to where a rotund little man with curly white hair and a matching beard, possibly one of Santa's helpers, stands poised apprehensively on Marefair's corner. The rube's face, bespectacled eyes wide and fixed on Studs with an expression of startled incomprehension, rings a faint '40s hotel reception bell in his recall, sets him to shifting the half-empty coffee cups and stacked pornography from his internal filing cabinet, sifting through the outdated mug-sheets for a moniker to go with the familiar, shifty features.

As the piece of work turns hurriedly away like he's pretending that he hasn't just been clocking the detective, making across Marefair for the other side and pointedly not looking back, the penny drops. The interloper on Studs' private made-for-TV drama is the former councillor James Cockie, that same jovial countenance affixed beside the header of a weekly column in the local *Chronicle & Echo*, copies of which he's perused while staying at his mum's place. This being the code name for his office. You can't be too careful.

Watching the retired council head laboriously roll his fleshy snowball off up Horsemarket towards the Mayorhold, the unfrozen Piltdown man-hunter reflects on Cockie's late but perhaps pertinent arrival in this last stretch of the storyline. While technically the genre generally demands the killer be a character the readers or the viewers have been introduced to early in the game, there's always those convention-bucking mavericks like Derek Raymond, with his greasy beret still behind the bar down at the French in Soho, mimicking real life in that the culprit's often no one who's been seen before. In oddball works like that, Studs soberly reflects, the tale turns out to have been more about the labyrinthine mental processes of the protagonist than the contortions of the case he's trying desperately to solve. That said, there's no compelling literary imperative that rules out the ex-councillor from the inquiry. With the former Labour politician's dwindling mass receding from view in a slow red shift, Studs puts it all together.

Having had, presumably, a hand or at the very best a chubby finger in the neighbourhood's brutal demise while still in office, even if entirely passively, Jim Cockie fits the profile. There was that look in his bugged Tex Avery eyes, furtive and guilty, right before he'd turned around and walked off in a hurry. Don't they say, if you wait long enough, the murderer always returns to where it happened, to the crime scene? Sometimes it's to gloat, or sometimes in a panic-stricken effort to conceal incriminating evidence. Occasionally, so they tell him, it's to masturbate, although Studs doubts if that would be the motive in this current instance. Once in a long while, of course, the perp's compulsion to revisit the chalk outlines of their killing ground might be born of a genuine remorse.

Uphill, the new prime suspect is diminishing away to nothingness like a white phosphor dot shrinking into the starless vastness of a cooling 1950s telly. Curling his lower lip until he's worried that it could roll up and travel down his chin, the stumped P.I. turns south and heads back down the way he came. He knows that Cockie is protected; knows that he could never get a case to stick. Forget it, Studs. It's Chinatown.

The triangles and diamonds of a stencilled sky behind the old gas-holder hulking further down the slope are starting their decline to indigo, and he can feel the utter jet of night descending on whatever narrative he's in, the big obsidian coming down upon this over-complicated continuity with desperate hours to go before tomorrow morning and his rendezvous with Warren at her exhibition. He heads back to where he left the, oh, he doesn't know, time-travelling De Lorean or something, with his craggy head a place of gothic transepts and determinism, the soul-crushing clockwork of the hackneyed, billiard-ball plot trajectory, this character-arc passing for a life.

He thinks of crosses, double-crosses and the Mr. Big behind the scenes pulling the strings for Hervey, Wesley, Swedenborg and all the rest, the man upstairs who's always careful to keep out the picture, an elusive boss of night and mortal intrigue, frequently reported dead but always with some wiggle room left for a sequel.

He locates his car in the protracted slow dissolve of twilight, drives home, checks to see if any casting agencies have left a message, eats his warmed-up dinner, goes to bed. After a great while and a mug of Horlicks, everything goes noir.

THE JOLLY SMOKERS

Den wakes beneath the windswept porch alone
On bone-hard slab rubbed smooth by Sunday feet
Where afternoon light leans, fatigued and spent,
Ground to which he feels no entitlement
Nor any purchase on the sullen street;
Unpeels his chill grey cheek from chill grey stone

Then orients himself in time and space.
The roof's a black-ribbed spine viewed from the floor
With on one wall some obsolete decree
Meant for the Cypriot community
And at the near end an iron-studded door,
A Bible-cover slammed shut in his face,

Or that of some more academic tome.
He struggles up onto one threadbare knee.
Moved on by night, he's slept instead by day
Beneath Saint Peter's covered entranceway
Thanks to the shame of university
And a conviction that he can't go home,

Can't face his parents, ask yet more reprieves
Of those who've done so much, left in the lurch
Through furthering Den's literary bent.
He's stopped attending lectures, blown the rent
To shelter in this all but disused church,
A sweat of monsters beading on its eaves,

This sentry-box in lieu of an address.
Yearning to write, he's learned to teach from men
With targets, goals to which they must adhere,
Themselves regretting the proffered career
That he's let go. His failures pounce while Den
Still fumbles at the latch of consciousness

In this, his latest of unfixed abodes.
Twenty last week and homeless, that's the thing,
Ambitions snuffed and dreams long since wrung out,
A student loan he dare not think about
Here in his hutch, its corners harbouring
Their soil and silver foil in abject lodes

When all he's ever craved is poetry,
The fire that Keats and Blake and Ginsburg had.
To be it, not to teach it. He can't bear
Chalk-dusted years of common-room despair
Nor the reproof of hard-up Mum and Dad
Who've gone without for his tuition fee.

Thus one door closes, while another shuts
Where Offa's sons raised the communion cup.
To doss in Saxon palaces and forts
Might hold, he thinks, a poetry of sorts
So with a sigh he stands and gathers up
His bag as though it were his spilling guts,

Recalling meanwhile that it's Friday night
With, just for once, somewhere he's meant to be:
Some bald guy who's got drugs, up Tower Street way,
Offering dreamtime and a place to stay.
An unaccustomed surge of urgency
Propels Den out into a tired rose light

From the cramped hermitage where he's been curled,
Across worn flags that vandal time deletes
Where names and mortal numbers disappear,
Erasing status, sentiment, and year.
Dead information sulks beneath these streets
And Orpheus, stumbling, seeks his underworld

Leaving behind an alcove sour with fate,
The war memorial's black memo-spike,
Fleeing the chapel before twilight falls
When nightmare faces trickle on its walls,
Past flowerbeds Spring makes inferno-like
Beside the path, out through a green-toothed gate

Then over Marefair, observed with disdain
By that short, tubby chap you sometimes see;
White hair and beard, officious little sod.
A garden gnome robbed of his fishing-rod,
He smirks "Good evening" confrontationally
As Dennis rattles by and up Pike Lane

Towards a new low and a legal high.
Why did he come here to pursue his goal?
These firetrap shacks crouched in the Great Fire's lair,
Here to a town that nutted off John Clare
Yet had John Bunyan christen it Mansoul.
These are the yards where sonnets come to die

As with the local poet he'd been shown,
The giggling drunk in whose wry shipwrecked gaze
He'd glimpsed his future, and abandoned rhyme.
Rousing from reverie barely in time
Den turns right at Saint Catherine's house and strays
Down Castle Street, that dusk has overthrown,

To the halfway point and the ramp's top end
Between the shabby flats where it cuts through
To Bath Street. Here, despite a scorched smell, he
Must brave declining visibility
Which conjures fiends from fencing, and into
The shadowed valley of the psalm descend

Through a despond of debt and cancelled dole,
The acrid scent worse further down the ramp.
He hurries, flees this atmosphere of doom
Only to misstep in the gathering gloom
And on an ice-cream swirl of dogshit stamp
The complex imprint of one trainer's sole.

He calls himself by an unflattering name
Then slogs on amongst peeling Bauhaus slums,
Making for where the high-rise windows glow
From sombre violet altitudes and so
Child Dennis unto the dark tower block comes,
Scraping one foot behind him as though lame

And, too late, suffering anxiety
About his bald host, whom he barely knows,
Though someone called Fat Kenny doesn't sound
Like the most selfless altruist around.
Still, on through a dim pocket-park Den goes,
Up Simons Walk, with no apostrophe,

But glancing back across breeze-ruffled grass
Through tromp l'oeil murk he struggles to make sense
From brief illusion, a great cog of night
That smoulders and revolves then fades from sight.
He frowns and, finding the right residence,
Raps on the door twice, knucklebones on glass,

Whereat, light scattered in the frosted pane,
His benefactor shimmers into form.
"Hello ... Christ, what's that smell? Has something died?
Oh yeah? Well, take 'em off. Leave 'em outside."
While Den complies, allowed into the warm,
His shoes, like orphans, on the step remain

Unlaced and in disgrace. The pungent hall
Leads to a worse front room. "Fancy a joint?"
Den takes an armchair, Kenny the settee
Where books on psychopharmacology
Are strewn, the rolling highlight a bright point
On his shaved skull, as with a billiard ball

Or plump freshwater pearl. Eyes Rizla-red
Fat Kenny licks, tears and at last succeeds
In fashioning tobacco, skins and drug
Into an origami doodlebug
Then lights the stout white paper fuse which leads
To his smooth, spherical cartoon-bomb head

That explodes into giggle, gab and cough.
Passed back and forth the spliff ghost-trains their mood,
Stills time with rearing basilisks of smoke
And Kenny asks him, almost as a joke,
If in return for lodgings, dope and food
Dennis might be prepared to suck him off.

"Or sling your hook. I'm not a charity.
I'm offering pizza and me special stash.
This hooker wanted some. Said I could do
Her up the arse, but no. I'd promised you."
Dazed, Denis blinks, and in an arc-light flash
Sees his new life in pin-sharp clarity,

All the hard bargains that it will entail
Keeping on the right side of a front door.
He nods. Kenny suggests that it might save
Time done while waiting for the microwave
To cook their pizzas. On the kitchen floor
Den kneels, unzips his host's distended snail

And puts it in his mouth, fixing instead
On Wilde or Whitman, striving to ingest
Such poetry as might be had among
The rancid piston's movements on his tongue,
Attempting to maintain an interest
In De Profundis *while he's giving head*

But failing to recall a useful quote.
Den, lacking panthers, feasts with porcine things
Whose world, arrhythmic, will admit no rhyme
Save chance events acted at the same time:
Just as the heartless oven-timer pings
Fat Kenny's semen sluices down his throat.

They eat in silence. Den discovers he
Can still taste his aperitif and hence
Does not enjoy his entrée. When they're done
The Happy Shopper Buddha-featured one
Announces that it's now time to commence
With their ethno-botanic odyssey

And shows Den the datura he has grown,
Its bell-like blooms white as a wordless page,
With the Salvia Divinorum which
Is Den's. It's made clear in Fat Kenny's pitch
That while they'll both share the diviner's sage
The Angels' Trumpets are for him alone.

"I've got a greater tolerance, you see.
I'll chew the salvia with you then smoke
The other later." They both masticate
The leaves. "Hold it beneath your tongue, then wait."
So, leaving the sublingual wad to soak,
Den gulps and swallows apprehensively.

He pales, as if at the approach of some
Fierce, underlying pandemonium.

———

Time squirms, its measure lost beyond recall
So that how long he's sat he does not know.
The dismal room has undergone no change
Save that its cluttered details now seem strange
To him, and meanwhile simmering below
His tongue the bitter vegetable ball

Steeps in his spittle, makes green venom run
Into his belly, past the teeth and gums
To curdle in his bloodstream, bowel and bone.
Den writhes and struggles to suppress a moan
As he by subtle increment becomes
Uncomfortable in his own skeleton

And catapults up from his seat to pace
The room, thus to assuage his restlessness
While Kenny shifts his outsized infant bulk
Upon the sofa, clearly in a sulk
At the delay, this possible to guess
Through study of his well-upholstered face

Or gist of his dyspeptic monologue.
"Fuck this. If it's not gonna do the biz
I'm gonna smoke the other stuff." Den stares,
Circling an endless rug between the chairs
As, barely knowing where or who he is
He wades in a dissociative fog

Alone, the lights on but nobody home,
Where looking down he finds he can't avoid
The fact he's now wearing the clothes and hat
Of Charlie Chaplin, somebody like that,
Some little tramp on crackling celluloid
Strutting a stage of sudden monochrome,

All colour fled. Fat Kenny, dressed like Den
In antique garb now waddles through the gloom
Beside him, white faced, black clad. They don't talk,
Their gait resembling the Lambeth Walk
While in the upper corners of the room
Are gruff, gesticulating little men

In similar attire, homunculi
Who swear and spit. Floorboards somehow replace
The ceiling and through chinks the ruffians call
Their taunts, where dirty grey light seems to fall
As from some higher mathematic space
Or proletarian eternity

Of endless grudge. Its noisome undertow
Seizes them both. Perspective is askew,
The jeering imps made large as, by degree,
Den and his colleague rise towards them. He
Has the sensation as he passes through
Of fusing with the drab planks from below,

Emerging on their far side in insane
Conditions, chest-deep in the warping floor
To nightmare. He discovers that his skin,
Now naked, is that on a manikin
Grown from this attic of the charnel poor
With joints replaced by pins and pores by grain,

Whose screams are creaks, whose tears are viscous gum
Slow on his lathe-shaved cheeks. Den gapes, appalled,
As his host, wood-fleshed and immersed like he
In floor, is seized by the fraternity
Of tipsy ghouls who sing while Kenny's hauled
Up to inebriate Elysium:

"The jolly smokers we, a cheery bunch
Here in our half-world, half-real and half-cut,
Enjoy that good night out without the wife
Pursue an after-hours afterlife
And want for nothing save a head to butt
Or Bedlam Jennies for our Puck's Hat Punch."

Aghast at what seems Happy Hour in hell
Den flails, embedded, glancing up to spy
The Guinness toucan smirking from tin plate,
Its touted goodness decades out of date,
Then with a wide and panicked wooden eye
Surveys the chiaroscuro clientele

Of smouldering reprobates who swirl and curse
About him as he struggles there beneath
Their knees. One, waistcoat-draped with bowler hat
Wipes from his chin the remnants of a rat
While all his pockets boil with vicious teeth,
Though some of his confederates are worse.

There's one whose features crawl about his face,
Mouth above nose, ears where his eyes should be.
Another, a raw-knuckled harridan
With smile as threatening as any man
Sways to an air that falls conspicuously
Flat in that strangely dead acoustic space,

Less tune than tuning up. Den cranes and strives
To find its source, soon managing to spot
The revenant musicians, bass, horn, drums,
Who twiddle amplifier knobs or thumbs
Disconsolately, yet perk up as what
Appears to be their ringleader arrives

To ragged cheers, a rotund titan who
With belly, beret, beard and steely eyes
Rolls through the reeling wraiths. Den gets to view
Him, if but briefly, noticing that two
Ghost-children shelter at his oak-thick thighs,
One memorably fair though lacking hue

And wrapped in tartan bathrobe. Den calls out
But draws the mob's attention with his cry
That grind their boot-heels on his wooden crown,
Jesting as they attempt to tread him down,
His careful lyric ear affronted by
Their hateful voices everywhere about.

"He's formed wi' woods like Cloggy Elliott's leg,
Or malkin, frightenin' stargugs on a farm."
Fat Kenny, in his wooden birthday suit,
Is held down by the leering female brute
Who's carving her initials on his arm
Despite his squeaking-hinge attempts to beg

Or plead. Den, trampled on by dead men's feet,
Hears the round minstrel's stern, stentorian shout
As Den's stamped down into the splintery mire,
Resurfacing to hear the bard enquire
If Freddy Allen's anywhere about,
Told in reply that he's just down the street,

At which the children leave. The cackling throng
Redouble now their bestial, boisterous ways.
They kick Den harder as the band begin,
They gouge the shrieking Kenny's puppet skin
And as the joyous, tumbling music plays
These slurring shades raise up their glaze-eyed song:

"Named for this inn, the jolly smokers we,
Up here near fifty year now, man and boy!
Pale in our great beyond, beyond the pale,
So drink up, down the hatch, hail, horrors, hail!
Leave us dead men and empties to enjoy
Our pie-eyed paralysed posterity!"

And plunged in quicksand pine Den twists like some
Half-landed fish pinched in between two planes,
Target for every last ethereal thug.
Forgotten, now, the taking of the drug.
Not even memory of his name remains
Nor life prior to this warped delirium

Of boots and threats. Nearby, Fat Kenny's squeal
Competes now with the music's weave and wail
As the two writhe in what appears to be
A pissed-up paradise or purgatory
Where bygone barbarisms still prevail
And the perpetually present poor are real,

Not metaphor. Thus, long, cruel eons pass
Before distraction having the semblance
Of a ghost-tramp storms through the hoodlums,
Frog-marching there before him as he comes
A mangled man whose babyish countenance
Is set with inlaid gems of broken glass;

Whose breast is concave ruin. Tankards chime
And voices raise. "What's 'e come up 'ere for?"
The vagrant phantom loudly now decries
His captive's deeds and whimpered alibis
Though Den, just then pressed down beneath the floor,
Cannot discern the nature of the crime

Yet sees its punishment. For his offence
The prisoner, stripped of his torn attire,
Is made to kneel, unsure what to expect,
While Kenny, wooden phallus teased erect,
Learns that the roughneck revellers now require
An act unnatural in every sense.

As both performers start to moan and bleat
In their abrasive coitus they enthral
The spiteful, spectral spectators, who sing
"We're jolly and we smoke, but here's the thing.
There's some stuff that we care for not at all
And serve rough justice here above the street

Where all the arseholes of the ages meet,
Thereby democratising Milton's fall
With Satan overthrown and mob made king!"
Den feels as if he may be settling
Back to a real world almost past recall
Through spit and sawdust at the phantoms' feet

Into an intermediary zone.
As from some party in an upstairs flat
He hears the rosy-cheeked man's howl of pain,
Forced to do that which goes against the grain,
Then sinks back to Fat Kenny's habitat,
In darkness with the lamp-bulb clearly blown

And finds, now the experience is done,
His host slumped on the couch; him in his chair.
The jumping up and pacing, it would seem,
Were merely part of his unearthly dream.
Exhausted, leaving questions in the air,
He slides into a kind oblivion,

Knowing, as all thoughts into shadow pass,
The dead to be a literal underclass.

———

Out of grey nullity to consciousness
He comes, reluctant, one fact at a time,
Aware of self, of where he is and when,
His body in the chair. Eyes slitted, Den
Notes, after the stark, solarised sublime,
That there is colour, though not in excess

Nor well-distributed. The sun, discreet,
Leans through the curtains to bestow a kiss
On Kenny's slumbering paunch. Beneath Den's tongue
He finds and spits out the exhausted bung
Of salvia then, needful of a piss,
Rises unsteadily to his bare feet

To navigate that unfamiliar place,
The hallway with his bag, Fat Kenny's coat,
Then up loud, bare-board stairs to find the loo.
Fully awake now he peers down into
Stained porcelain, the filthy toilet's throat,
Its exhalations lifting in his face

As memories rise too, sharp as a knife:
The porch of Peter's Church, his student loan
And, oh God, did he suck Fat Kenny's prick?
He's overwhelmed. It's all too much, too quick.
Den retches and with a despairing moan,
In its entirety, throws up his life

For some few minutes, doubled in a crouch,
Then flushes. In the rattling pipes, trapped air
Bellows in anguish like a minotaur.
Mouth wiped, Den clumps back down to the ground floor
And the mauve gloom of a hushed front room where
Fat Kenny still sleeps, supine, on the couch,

Extinguished pipe clasped in one pudgy hand.
Though keen to leave, Den feels it only right
To say goodbye. "I'm off, then." No reply.
He notices a flat, green-bellied fly
Orbit the still, shaved skull and then alight
But though he sees he does not understand

Why his host shows no sign of coming round.
"I said I'm going." Den begins to feel
Uneasy and as he steps closer spies
The motionless breast and unblinking eyes.
With realisation comes a shattering peal
Of sudden dreadful and incessant sound,

A circling and swooping banshee roar
That shivers glass and sets dogs barking but
Appears to have no source save him. Den screams,
An improvised Kurt Schwitters piece that seems
Expressive although inarticulate
And backs in the direction of the door

Which, unlocked, yields at once and opens wide
Whence dazzling rays pour through the gaping hatch
To blind him. Crumpled sleeping-bag forgot
And slammed door ringing like a rifle shot,
Den takes off without bothering to snatch
His shit-smeared sneakers from the step outside

Or to look back. In truth, he doesn't dare.
The grass is cold and wet – Den has no socks –
As he sprints past the tower blocks – nor a plan –
But then in Crispin Street he spots a man
Whose pale blue eyes and thinning flaxen locks
Are oddly reminiscent, but from where?

Upon Den's lips unspoken epics burn
And seek release, drugged visions that might be
As those of Coleridge, Cocteau, Baudelaire.
By now he's reached the guy with sparse blonde hair
Who eyes the gasping boy uncertainly
And asks "Are you alright, mate?" with concern

Made clear. Is Den alright? Aye, there's the rub,
He thinks, one with De Quincy and Rimbaud,
Preparing for an image-jewelled account
To spill forth as though from some Bardic fount
But all he can come out with is "Yes. No.
Fuck me. Oh, fuck me, I was up the pub.

That's where I've been all night, up in the pub."
His mouth won't stop. "They wouldn't let us go."
Won't pause. "Fuck me. Fuck me, mate, help us out.
It was a pub", as if that were in doubt,
Language bereft of any metered flow
With words recurring, echoing like Dub

Through burned-out ganglia. The stranger's stare
Is quizzical. "Hang on, you've lost me, mate.
Was this a lock-in, then, this pub they kept
You at all night?" Although Den's barely slept
He knows the man is trying to judge his state
Of mind. "Which was it, anyway? Up where?"

"Up there. Up in the roof. I mean the pub."
Den babbles, but the blond man nods his head.
"Up in the roof? Yeah, I've had that", and then
He mentions, in the corners, little men.
Den strains to comprehend what's just been said,
Brain washed, or at least given a good scrub.

"Yeah. Up the corners. They were reaching down."
Seeming to understand the man takes out
Some cigarettes and offers one to Den
With calm acceptance bordering on Zen
Then lights both. Den squints. What is it about
This quarter of the unforgiving town

That brings such things? His saviour tells him how
He isn't mad but will take time to mend;
Provides more cigarettes; offers a tip
On where to rest, suggesting a small strip
Of grass with trees at Scarletwell Street's end,
Adding "They'll be in blossom around now."

With syllables become a syllabub
Den calls his benefactor a good bloke
And thanks him, starting to walk off downhill
But looking back to find the stranger still
Observing him. Den, brunt of some cruel joke,
Calls helplessly "I was just up the pub",

Then carries on down the long slope again,
Barefoot, skirting jewelled spreads of powdered glass,
To the T-junction at the bottom where
A single house stands near the corner there
Amid a great amnesia of grass,
Its presence making a stark absence plain

Yet with no clue as to whose residence
It is, its windows with closed curtains hung.
Beneath trees further on he takes a seat,
With freight-yards making the dressed set complete,
Where hunkered on damp grass he picks among
The lyric rubble of experience

In search of rhymes. The solitary abode
Stands punctuating the erased street's end,
Closing a quote since lost to a mute past.
Lighting his cigarettes each from the last
Den lives and breathes and tries to comprehend
The dead man in his house just up the road,

That wonderstruck and milky gaze. He strains
At the idea of it; cannot begin
To analyse nor even quite define
How jarringly abrupt that end-stopped line.
Life's sprawling text shall not be bound within
The whale-boned Alexandrine or quatrain

But finds instead its own signature tread
And sensibility. Den's narrative
Thus far, he sees now, lacks maturity,
A consequence of inability
To put forced stanzas by and only live
His language, though it goes unread

And unrewarded. No more self-deceit.
He'll go home, face his folks, work in a shop,
Pay off his debt and wait for the day when
He's had a life to write about. Just then
A scuffed blue Volkswagen grinds to a stop
At the round-shouldered curbside up the street.

A dreadlocked woman climbs out to assist
Her passenger, a thin girl of mixed race,
The younger of the two and yet more frail
With bandages in lieu of bridal veil
Surmounting her exquisite, battered face
And wedding flowers clutched in one trembling fist

To emphasise the matrimonial air.
Their car left at the corner of the block
One helps the other slowly up the hill
Out of Den's line of sight, though he can still
Hear their muffled exchange before they knock
The door of the lone house that's standing there,

This summons answered after a long pause.
There's conversation too hushed to make out
Before the women, minus one bouquet,
Return to their parked car and drive away,
A striking vignette which leaves Den in doubt
Regarding its effect, still more its cause,

But then, the world won't scan as poetry.
Arse chill with dew he reconstructs his night,
The things he's done, the dreadful place he's been,
Crowned with the first dead man he's ever seen:
A stripped-down attic statement, still and white,
Without a trace of ambiguity

Or adjectival frills, that can't allude
To anything. Den needs a modern voice
As had Blake, Joyce, John Bunyan or John Clare,
Words adequate to these new ruins where
We may describe the wastelands of our choice
In language that's been shattered and re-glued

To suit these lives, these streets. He thinks he'll sit
For one last cigarette then phone his mum.
Somewhere uphill behind him sirens wail
Diapasons of disaster and yet fail
To mar his sudden equilibrium,
The snow-globe moment's placement exquisite

In time's jewelled action, where future and past
Shall stand inseparable at the last.

GO SEE NOW
THIS CURSED WOMAN

Viewed from beneath the stone archangel spins scintillate darkness on his billiard cue, unhurried constellations turning at the tip just as the land below rotates about its busted hub. A universe of particles and archives of their motion bruise the lithic eye in its tooled orbit, overwriting data on a century-old smut which serves as pupil, the incessant bulletin of Friday, May the 26th, 2006. Off in the standing shadows, babies, dogs and convicts with their dreams.

Viewed from above, the isomorphic urban texture flattens to a blackout map which swarms with plankton phosphorous, a Brownian nocturnal churn of long-haul truckers and unwinding weekend couples, marathon commuters, flashing vessels of emergency. Arterial light moves through the circulatory diagram in spurts, tracking the progress of cash vectors and plague opportunities. Pull focus further and the actions of the world compress to an impasto skim.

War and collapse are chasing displaced populations all around the planet in the way that jumping jacks appear to follow fleeing children. The continually adjusted now – a hairline crack between the stupefying masses of the future and the past, friction- and pressure-cooked – is a hot interface which shimmers with string theory and the ingrained grievances of Hammurabi, seethes with slavering new financial mechanisms and fresh epithets describing paupers. From daylight America the shock of former Enron bosses at their guilty verdict is announced and in the deafening crash of their dropped jaws cascades of ruin are commenced. Cut to interior, night.

Mick Warren tosses in slow motion, mindful of his sleeping wife and trying to minimise the mattress-creak. The roll onto his left side is a campaign staged in increments with its objective, once accomplished, yielding nothing save a differently-aligned discomfort. Marinating in his own brine on these sultry slopes of late May, shoulders pummelled by the working week just gone, insomnia reduces his well-trodden consciousness to the schematic mansion of a Cluedo board, thoughts following each other into minimal crime-scene conservatories attempting to establish whereabouts and means and motive. In associative freefall he is soon adrift in board games, bored games, sleepless mind advancing square by square according to delirious and self-inflicted rules of play, a Chinese checker choreography of half-ideas that leapfrog and eliminate each other in their struggle to attain thoughtless oblivion, the peg-board's emptycentral hole. Cluedo slides lexically into Ludo, Poirot parlours reconfigured as the stylised paths of palace gardens wherein varicoloured button dynasties conduct their patient courtly intrigues. Ludo … Mick thinks he can distantly remember his big sister telling him the term had some kind of significance, but for the moment it eludes him. Words and wordplay aren't his speciality and he is thus averse to Scrabble, name alone too reminiscent of his frantic, rat-like mental processes when trying to extract coherent language from an angular furniture-sale of consonants or from an ululating funeral lament of vowels. It's not a proper game like football, this messing about with spelling, words and all that business. Where's the fun in that? It strikes him that those who profess a fondness for linguistic torments of this nature are most probably just trying to look clever. He recalls the odd times he's heard somebody extolling the delights of 'Dirty Scrabble', but nobody can have ever really played that, can they? That can't possibly exist when for a start there's only one K in the box. Attempting to displace some of the duvet-captured heat he's broiling in he kicks one leg free of the covers and luxuriates in the resulting calorific bleed. His bedbound brain diverts itself annoyingly in the consideration of annoying games. New angle.

Levering by stealth onto his back he fancies that from overhead he must resemble one of those stone medieval knights, asleep on cold sarcophagi with petrified retrievers at their feet. There must have been a Middle Ages bat-tle game at one point, he supposes, keeps and castles, jousting and the rest, although he can't call one to mind. Amongst the various John Wadham's pas-times of his younger days, historically-themed entertainments had been thin upon the ground, the focus mostly on a modern world then trying to compose itself from out the bombsite rubble of the 1940s. He remembers one called Spy Ring, plastic head and shoulders busts of men in trench-coats and fedo-ras inching between foreign embassies, an accurate embodiment of Cold War machinations in that rules of play were by and large impenetrable and made no apparent sense. Alma and Mick had given up on it almost immediately and consigned the whole thing to an oubliette beneath the wardrobe, an effective and achievable detente. Monopoly, he thinks, has always been preoccupied with a hard-nosed modernity, a compensatory ritual to suit those long years of post-war austerity, imaginary Weimar wheelbarrows piled with confetti-coloured currency in which to lose your ration book, if only briefly. In his childhood play, he realises, he'd been largely quarantined within the present day. He thinks he can recall Napoleonic stylings to the packaging of Risk, the game of global strategy that made world domination by Australia seem unavoidable, but then megalomania, he decides, has always been more time-less than historical. It's like a leather jacket, never out of date. Tight close-up.

Blinking lids descend like long exposure shutters on the slate-blue irises, silicate debris swept discretely to the corners. Pupils expand, saturated, blotting up the midnight ink. It comes to him that all human endeavour is a game of some sort or, more properly, a great compendium of games that are obscurely interwoven and connected, a confounding complex of pursuits with pre-set difficulty levels where the odds are always with the house. A game, he thinks, is surely any system with an arbitrary set of imposed rules, either a contest which results in many losers and a single winner or some non-competitive arrangement where the pleasure of participation is its own reward. And obviously, unless the rules are those of physics they are arbitrary in one sense or other, made up by somebody, somewhere, sometime. Capital and finance are quite clearly games, probably poker or roulette, at least to judge by those Enron executives who'd featured on the evening news before Mick went to bed, trading in future markets they'd invented out of thin air and were trying, unsuccessfully, to will into existence. Actually, that kind of play, rogue traders and all that, it's not like poker or roulette so much as it's like Buckaroo, seeing how many gold-prospecting pickaxes and shovels you can hang on the spring-loaded donkey of market credulity before, inevitably, it explodes and startles everybody.

Status, reproduction and romance, political manoeuvring or the cops-and-robbers interplay of crime and legislation, all of it a game. His sister's exhibition in the morning which he's partly dreading, partly looking forward to; all of the paintings, all the art, it's just a different sort of game that's played with references, nods and winks to this or that, the highbrow clever-dickery that it alludes to. Bed-sheet creases print a river delta on Mick's back and in his restlessness it strikes him that civilisation and its history are similarly bagatelles, deluded into thinking that their progress has the ordered logic of a chess match when it's more the random ping of Tiddlywinks. It's ludicrous, as if the species had developed higher consciousness in order to invent a more elaborate form of noughts and crosses. When is everybody going to get serious? Even when people are engaged in slaughtering one another like in Iraq or Afghanistan, it's just Cowboys and Indians run disastrously out of hand. The last time Britain had been twat enough to interfere in Afghan matters, with the British and the Russian Empires staging their almighty pissing contest in the hundred years preceding World War One, they'd come right out and called it the Great Game. Perhaps the toppled pawns back in their flag-draped boxes for a final toytown tour of Wooton Bassett could be viewed as forfeit tokens in a game, although he can't see what's so great about it. Wearying of this internal shuttlecock, this back-and-forth, he opts to take another run for goal, the goal being insensibility. Closing his eyes is purely aspirational as he commences the commando roll onto his right side. Pull back to a streaming, howling stratosphere.

Below, invasive species move from continent to continent, from chair to chair, according to the music of an altered climate. Avocados thrive in tropic London. The percussive clash of particles is registered in delicate quantum cartographies, ferns of explosion and decay, beautiful spirals to annihilation mapped through concrete time. Everywhere information, seething as it nears the boil. The U.S. president George W. Bush and prime minister Blair discuss their deep fraternal bond, admitting errors in their handling of Gulf War II. The disagreement of Megiddo percolates through every culture and in Palestine the car belonging to Islamic Jihad leader Mahmud al-Majzoud erupts in lethal traceries of hurried metal and projectile mortal splinters, disassembling the insurgent along with his brother Nidal. Black and red, such are this spring's prevailing blossoms, vivid scarlet hearts in petals of oil-coloured smoke or bruises offset by an open cut. Cross-fade to vehicle interior.

The shadowy Ford Escort rocks and squeaks in hateful parody of Marla, kneeling in its back seat with her red mac and her halter top pushed up to show malnourishment-honed shoulder blades, the micro-skirt that's rucked about her waist worn as the black belt of an inverted karate, an exacting martial discipline of victimhood. Her self, the kicked-in and fragmented personality she'd thought she was, is frozen in proximity to her approaching end, frost-welded to this unrelenting moment, her last wretched stretch of here-and-now before a terrible big baby staves her skull in and ends all of her, stops the whole world forever by eliminating that pathetic and pained little rag-end of it which she'd stupidly assumed was hers. Her future has always been such a miserable and stunted thing that she'd thought nobody would bother taking it away from her but now it's happened, now it's happening: his pudgy cock-stub punches up inside her dry hole from behind in a ridiculously hasty silent film staccato so that she's afraid she's going to start a kind of hideous and open-ended laughter. Marla's seen his dead-eyed cherub face. She's seen his license plates and knows this is her finish, with her bloody forehead bumped against the Escort's right-side rear door by each angry thrust, every resentful bayoneting. This is the worse-than-nothing that her life's amounted to, the thing she's always dreaded, always known would happen and she only ventured out tonight to pay for rock. She'll never have another hit now and she doesn't care. It's not important, never was important and she'd give it up without a second thought, she'd go and live back with her mum if only that meant that she'd live and not be killed in this garage enclosure, whimpering and paralysed on her arrival at the universal terminus. Nothing she ever wanted as a child will now be hers; no one will ever say she's special, just another shitty story in the local paper, one more useless scrubber nobody will miss, raped and, what, strangled? Oh, no, please not that. Just one blow. One blow to the head and this is over. No last drink before the gallows, no last cigarette before the squad start firing. Blood and snot, she understands, will be her only balm. New point of view.

Dez Warner stares, his eyes those of a hot and snorting horse, at tonight's catch with his magnificent erection going in and out of its mud-coloured cunt. He's sizzling like a god or an unstoppable machine and the all-powerful chemistry that's in his head reduces everything to this, the back seat of his motor, to this situation he's created. When he'd driven into this enclosure it got worried, didn't it, and started all that stuff trying to make him see it as a person. Telling him its name was what had got him started with the smacking and the punching, all of that. If you don't know the name it could be anybody, couldn't it, the one off *Countdown*, anyone at all. It could be Irene. Even on the wedding night when both of them were pissed she wouldn't let him fuck her tits, she wouldn't suck him, nothing like the stuff you get in mags or DVDs, nothing like that. Nothing like this. All his awareness centres on that tingling last inch of his mighty ramrod, squeezing up inside a frightened fanny, feeling so electric that it must be glowing like the sticks they have at festivals or like a red hot poker when the end bit looks translucent. He can smell the sex, the fear, the tangy and exhilarating soup of it, oh yeah, oh yeah. He's crossed the line with this and can't go back, he knows that, but this new thing, this is everything that he was always meant to be, not marching into banks with a crash helmet on and strongbox handcuffed to him, trying to look like Terminator for the girls behind the counter, that's not him. *This*, this is him, the king of night, the king of fuck and it's so easy, why don't people do it all the time? White noise behind the eyeballs, there's a sort of faulty strip-light flicker and he's still got pop-up phantoms at the corners of his vision but he doesn't care. He owns this creature's life. He can do what he wants. It's like a doll, it's like a fly you've caught but better for the crying, better for how scared it is. He's stiffer than a bolt, never as big as this before and pumping up and down like mad. He can't remember the exact point when he'd made his mind up to put it out of its misery when he was done, or even if there was an exact point. It's more of a continuum, to be fair; a sliding scale where he's not come to a decision as such but he knows it's going to happen, definitely. Just the thought of it excites him and he's banging harder but his nerves are kicking off like popcorn and he's trying to shake the feeling that there's someone else there in the car with them. The window-glass is grey with scalding breath. Dissolve to satellite perspective.

Underneath its shredded wedding dress of cloud the naked globe sweats electricity, stale beads of light most concentrated in the armpit cities, trickling thin in breastbone valleys. Limned with glitter the black map below persists in its unhurried process of evaporation, borders that were only ever topographical conveniences made irrelevant by new communications media, an ongoing negation of geography with threatened and belligerent nationalism churning in its backwash. Gym-fit viruses take longer run-ups to the species barrier. Unkempt taxonomies of novel and more finely graded madnesses are diagnosed, while in Berlin, Chancellor Merkel's wrapping up the opening ceremony of the Hauptbahnhof as Europe's biggest railway station when a stabbing rampage is commenced in the attendant crowd, more than two dozen persons wounded and six of those critically so. It's discovered that one of the earliest knife-victims is HIV positive, to further complicate the tally of postponed fatalities. Newly accreted islands of volcanic matter rise unnoticed. Insert footage, black and white.

An angry smudge of chalk and charcoal, Freddy Allen draws a line across the street plan with his passage. Streaming in a dishwater stop-motion queue of doppelgangers the indignant spectral tramp splashes unnoticed through brick barricades and bollards, through the gaseous blur of fleeting automobiles and the ground-floor flats of the disabled, a fog bullet, die-straight in its murderous trajectory. Evicted in his flickering wake the dislodged ghosts of fleas seek new accommodation, vampire jumping beans in search of other unhygienic apparitions, plentiful in these parts. Raging thunderous and splenetic as he stumbles, even in the muffle of the ghost-seam his unbroken howl of ghastly epithets and curses is the unrelenting rumble of a derailed freight train hurtling dirty through the sleeping district, dragging a funereal scarf of smoke and spitting hot sparks of pejorative. With panting locomotive rhythm Freddy damns the lot of them, rapists and rent-collectors, councillors and curb-crawlers alike, all vicious fishes circling the depleted bait-ball of the neighbourhood. The anthracite which keeps his fury stoked, he knows, is mined from bile directed at himself and the appalling thing that he once nearly did, the guilty weight that keeps him mired in this monochromatic wraith-sump and eternally unworthy of the colour-drenched emporia Upstairs. He fumes and fulminates in an expletive storm-front, rattling amongst the sulking residential slabs named after saints and over atrophying streets sealed off from traffic to deter the sex trade. As a ragged chain of paper dolls cut out from folded newsprint Freddy is reiterated in school classrooms, in conspicuously shriek-free moonlight corridors, exploding from prefabricated walls adorned with genial crayoned grotesques to surge down Scarletwell Street in an avalanche of countless flailing limbs and spite-contorted faces.

Cutting off the blunted bottom corner of Greyfriars House he's like another line of grubby washing strung across the empty court within, flapping and damp, and in his billiard projectile rush he at last understands the full weight of the Master Builder's loaded gaze, earlier on at the ethereal snooker parlour: it's him, Freddy. He's the trick shot, the archangel's cannonade, skittering on the Boroughs' dog-fouled baize, the full force of that mighty circumstantial cue propelling him, and all to save this skinny little girl? She must be so important to the play, a black or mistily-remembered pink at least, but why would he, would anyone suppose she wizn't? That's not right or fair, dismissing her because of what she does, because she's not a doctor's daughter. Everybody wiz a baby once and innocent of all their future. Trembling ectoplasm born of wrath and tenderness wells up in soot-creased sockets as the long-cremated indigent swirls into Lower Bath Street, rippling like eyestrain through pitch dark a foot above the sagging tarmac and, as ever, with no visible means of support. Stretched silver beads pass through him like neutrinos as it starts to rain. Resume full colour and cue montage.

From this vantage, features of the natural landscape have been superseded by abstraction, where the spooling ribbon rivers are replaced by fiery canals of routed information, sluicing from one lock-gate server to another and oblivious to mountain, ignorant of sea. Data that previously drizzled escalates to an extreme weather event. The fathomed knowledge rises past its hastily-drawn plimsoll line and populations find themselves out of their depth, clutching for straws of dogma or diverting novelty as they commence their surface struggle at the rim of an e-maelstrom. Seen in overview Warsaw's Pilsudski Square is an old-fashioned colour blindness test card, swimming with pale tinted dots despite the pounding rain. Fledgling Pope Benedict the sixteenth makes his first major appearance in the homeland of his predecessor, tannoy mutter sputtering against the downpour as he references Pope John Paul's prayer of some twenty-seven years theretofore, asking that the Holy Ghost descend and change the face of Poland, this plea widely held to be more instrumental in dismantling the Soviet Union than the acted permutations of the world's implacable equation. Species disappear and new discoveries are introduced with the breakneck turnover of soap-opera characters. Newfoundland crows develop secondary tool use, implements for modifying implements, and on Kilimanjaro's slopes uncounted lightning bolts sow precious tanzanite, fulgurant echoes in a cobalt glass. Conflicts move on from place to place like hom-

icidal drifters, changing names and altering appearances while yet retaining
signature brutalities. Theories proliferate. Repeat interior, night.

Rotated slowly on a spit of wakefulness and perspiration-glazed, Mick Warren
is a hominid kebab that slumber has regurgitated in the dreamless gutter-
troughs of an unending Friday evening. Game-plagued as he flips his pillow
in a vain search for its fabled cool side he has now progressed to a consideration of the playing card. Before the board games with the satisfying creak of
their unfolding or the mystique of their top-hat tokens, cards had been the
staple recreation of his childhood in St. Andrew's Road. At some mysterious
adult signal, passed between his gran, his parents and such aunts or uncles
as were present, it would be decided that a round of cards was called for. The
white tea-time tablecloth would be replaced by the far cosier deep rose one
which was Mick and Alma's favourite, and then from the sideboard drawer
that was its ritual resting place the battered and revered familial deck was
next produced. He realigns his problematic knees and tries to conjure up a
tactile memory of the talismanic pack, the waxy box worn by the handling
of at least four generations and declining like the then-traditional extended
family unit inexorably towards disintegration, folds becoming perforations.
Like the converse of the weathered pasteboard tiles inside, this fragile packaging had been predominantly purple on a ground of twilight lilac, where a
silhouetted schoolgirl in a long Victorian pinafore-dress bowled her wooden
hoop among midsummer poppies through the gathering violet dusk. Beneath
the child's capering shoes this image was inverted so that for some years Mick
had been under the impression that it was the ingénue's reflection in a puddle
at her feet, before he'd noticed that the lower girl was running in the opposite
direction. Even as a maroon outline she'd looked pretty, and with hindsight
Mick supposes that she might have been his first crush. He'd been faintly
anxious for her safety, he recalls. What was she doing out so late to make her
race home under darkening skies, across the overgrowing summer meadow?
He knows that if she'd got into any trouble, if there'd been somebody waiting
in the tall mauve grass for her or for her bouncing, trembling circlet he'd have
wanted at the age of five to rescue her, this being then the limit of his amorous imagination. Ninja-quiet in his determination not to puncture Cathy's
well-earned rest he shifts once more onto his back, face up and freshly dealt.
New angle.

Supine, the chalk-outlined posture of a Cluedo victim, he remembers
Alma telling him about Viv Stanshall from the Bonzo Dog Band, stretched out
flat on stage before an audience and talking to the rafters: "Hello, God. Here's
what I look like standing up." It strikes Mick that imagining ourselves as seen
from some superior elevation, some projected and omniscient point of view,

is probably as old as literature, old as civilization; Harryhausen's Greek gods at their fatalistic chessboard peering down through tattered cirrus. Perhaps modern scepticism and the consequent dieback of deities is what has made surveillance cameras necessary, to preserve a sense that our performances have the attention of invisible spectators now that God's gone, to sustain the notion that our arbitrary acts are validated by unseen authorities sat at their screens or at unearthly gaming-tables, looking down upon the play. Mick rests a blond-fuzzed forearm on his brow and shimmering amongst the shoal of slippery night-spawning ruminations in his catch there is a fugitive impression of how everything is flattened when perceived from overhead, from the perspective of the player. Fleetingly he wonders if these hypothetical celestial gamblers would see everyone as being two-dimensional, as hieroglyphs with no more depth or substance than the inversely reflected royalty compressed onto the court-cards, but the thought melts to the slap of trumps on a red tablecloth. The things they'd played down Andrew's Road were exercises in precisely regulated tedium – Whist, Sevens, Draw-the-Well-Dry – though he'd found them all sufficiently engaging at the time. Just as each wireless, motorcar or socket seemed to have a face, so too had every card possessed its own distinct charisma, from the almost military formation of the fives to the precariously stacked crates of the nines. The aces, in their abstract grandeur, had been the four archangels or maybe the quartet of fundamental forces constituting spacetime, spades bewilderingly singled out by an impressive Gothic filigree. This attribution of a personality to each design reminds him of the tarot images his sister maintains both precede and serve as basis for the ordinary deck, the stack of archetypal bubblegum collectables that Alma drags to Mick's house every year at Christmas dinnertime so that she can read Cathy's fortune or at least pretend to; Hanged Man, Chariot and all the rest of the unsettling crew, as if that's any sort of proper seasonal tradition. To hear his crow-scaring elder sibling tell it, Draw-the-Well-Dry is derived from divination while all board-based pastimes are descended from those tricky magic squares where all the rows and columns add to the same number, as though every innocent and commonplace pursuit were only a degenerated form of sorcery. She has a wilfully Carpathian worldview, Alma, although now he thinks about it games might well have had some metaphysical or more important human function back at their inception, judging from the terminology found everywhere in language. Hunting some animal down and killing it, that makes it game. Being prepared to carry out some act is to be game. Something that offers easy opportunities for exploitation is regarded as fair game and then of course there's prostitution, going on the game. Game face, game on, game over, plays of light and sports of nature, Einstein making out God does not dice with matter. Mick's not sure about the last of these, suspecting that not only do the powers that run the universe do a fair bit of shaking, rattling and throwing, but that generally they do this so the die end up behind the settee and you have to take their word about the double six. With a dismissive grunt directed at the certainties of physics and religion he elects to take another punt on slumber and begins to gradually roll the bones onto his left side, facing Cathy's curled back. Come on, come on, just this once be lucky. Insert jump-cut sequence.

Spread below, an oriental carpet realised in fibre optics, there are causal curlicues; there are affray motifs. In Scotland a humanitarian award commemorating Robert Burns is given to a youthful relief worker in Baghdad, albeit posthumously. In Peru a clash of adversarial supporters at the run-up to elections ends with injury and gunfire, and in Hereford West Mercia Police appeal for witnesses after a man is violently assaulted by a group of teenagers. With Mandelbrot self-similarity, structures repeat at different scales throughout the system and there remains ambiguity regarding whether harm is percolated up or else decanted down. Wrath boils and steams, where soon thereafter cold and ruthless condensation is precipitated as a trickled legislation. The resultant culture, internal combustion driven, is a clown car only jolted forward by a series of explosions, without any linear progression and no entertainment value save in the anticipation of the vehicle's inevitable knockabout collapse. A pin-mould creep of neon media adorns the planet's carcass ideologies, metabolising incoherent chaos into palatable narrative, an edited awareness of experiential deluge. In near-extinct newsrooms still perfumed by cigarette smoke, telephone calls of the newsworthy are intercepted, victim's family or adulterous celebrity alike, while in the Congo brutal territorial disputes are waged over the mining of the necessary tantalum required by every trilling mobile and, like Tantalus, the world discovers its anticipated banquet future disappeared. Predators more accustomed to the higher reaches of the food chain are compelled to shin down several blood-oiled links in search of alley-scraps. Zoom in through icy flight-paths and cop-copter altitudes on Lower Bath Street.

When he comes, she goes, or at least that is Marla's numb appraisal of her likely schedule. The abrasive and continual penetration going on behind her is remote, just as persistent hammering in another room becomes ignorable, inaudible with the monotony of repetition. Dried peas rattle on the vehicle roof above and she is distantly aware that it has started raining. Rare even among the ranks of her impersonal clientele there is no intimacy or involvement in this frenzied pummelling, this punishment clearly directed at somebody other than herself, a private ritual from which she is excluded. Hanging

down around her damaged face the braids swing back and forth, a final curtain, jolted by each incoming percussive impact. There is something in the situation that is horribly involuntary, as if neither she nor her rosy assailant are
participating of their own free will, both of them clattering and jerking in an
ugly puppet drama which is simply happening because it is. She has no choice
except to sit through this lacklustre recitation to its unambiguously bitter end,
a captive audience to this man's mute soliloquy, this statement through the
medium of rape. Detached, without a speaking part, she affords the production her attentions only intermittently. She almost recognises the performer
on her knees in the supporting role, the concave cheeks tracked with mascara and the disappointed little face, eyes staring fixedly into the dark of the
Escort's interior and filled with flat acceptance of this miserable denouement,
this abrupt and meaningless conclusion, except who is this that makes these
observations, and from where? Someone who isn't Marla, evidently. Someone
with a different name, with clear thoughts unencumbered by the clamours
of anxiety and need, somebody looking on with only dull regret, as though
reflectively, at an event transpired already. This unprecedented night, has it
occurred before or is it in some fashion always happening, these giant final
moments that seem so much bigger and more absolute than they appeared
from further off? The leatherette beneath her sticky palms, the garish and
sensational pulp colours of car dials and instruments delineating the scenario,
each vivid element as resonant and hauntingly familiar as Miss Haversham in
flames, as the big Indian patient smashing the asylum window with a water-
cooler, as those images from literature or film that blaze in stained-glass hues
outside of mundane time. With animal obeisance she advances on her dismal ending, doggy-style, on sore knees friction-burned by the seat-covering
towards the precipice, the edge of death. There is no tunnel save the focussed
clarity of her perception, no white light except for an occasionally wakeful
motion-sensor fitted to one of the garages. Life fails to flash before her eyes
and yet she finds herself preoccupied with the most insignificant of details
from her earthly drama, the Diana scrapbook and the morbid library of Ripper memorabilia. Her previous fixation on these subjects, with such specific-
ity, is now incomprehensible and sits more like unconscious omen than the
random hobby she'd presumed: she is about to join the sorry file of doxies in
their petticoats and bonnets, victims of essentially the same man down across
the ages, always Jack, and furthermore she is to suffer her protracted, painful
termination in the rear seat of a car. This mean enclosure with its stammering illumination isn't a Pont de l'Alma, is no bridge of souls, although in the
confining brickwork and haphazard paparazzi bursts of brilliance the distinction all but vanishes. All places are distilled to this place just as all of history
reduces to these last few precious and excruciating minutes. Every human

story, though it be biography or wild romance or primal narrative of old, boils down to her and this, her present situation. Well aware that each breath represents a countdown she sucks in the backseat atmosphere of souring shock and copulation gratefully, exulting in the soon-curtailed delight of inhalation. Watering, her eyes refuse to blink, to miss a single photon in this last parade of light and eyesight, staring at the inside handle of the car door only inches from her streaming nose but, in the process of her disengagement from the world, unable to remember what it is she's looking at. New point of view.

Mechanically he pulls half out and pushes in, the action looped, but something of the magic patina is gone, as subtle as a change of film-stock or a shift from digital TV back to plain analogue. Outside the lurching car it's pissing down, although he can't recall the onset of the shower. He's starting to feel moody out of nowhere, thoughts and that, most probably connected with the powders that he's on. Thoughts like 'You'll be cut off from other people after this', not if he's caught because that isn't going to happen, but because of what he will have done that makes him separate from everybody. Thoughts like 'After this you mustn't be yourself with anyone' because after tonight he'll be a different person in a different world and nobody must ever know him, who he really is. The real Derek James Warner, 42, will be excluded from all normal interactions with his mates, his kids, with Irene, and will only properly exist on nights like this. This is the end of who he was, but he can't stop. The thing he's doing now, the thing he plans on doing afterwards, sooner or later this was always going to happen, ever since he first learned of the concept as a schoolboy. Dez is in a foaming, charging current of events with nothing he can do except surrender, bow to the inevitable. All his life thus far was leading to this moment just as all his future will proceed from this same point, indelible in memory so that to all intents and purposes he's always going to be here, here and now, at least inside his head and this is always going to be happening. He's like a fly in amber, eyelids squeezing to a crayon scribble, nose compressing into ridges like a collapsed paper lantern and the awning of the lower lip rolled down. He shoves his cock in and he shoves his cock in and at the peripheries of vision catches sight of dashboard glints in green and red. He knows that only chemicals are causing the illusion of mismatched eyes watching him dispassionately through the ambient blur, yet cannot shake the sense of a third party bearing witness from the driver's seat, an unintended and unwanted passenger he can't remember picking up. He's never been a drugs man, Derek. He's not used to all this, with things shifting everywhere and how he feels about stuff shifting along with them, like a lion one minute and the next he's got the horrors, the unbearable sensation something terrible is just about to happen or, worse, is already happening. He holds the bubbling incipient panic down, concentrates on the job in hand. Lowering his gaze he looks at what he's doing, at the hairy dagger plunging in the slimy wound, his thumbs holding the negligible arse-cheeks open and apart. There's a minuscule punctuation-point of shit clinging to the exterior of the clenching sphincter where it's not wiped itself properly, the dirty fucking animal. He hates it, hates it for just having stood there on the corner in its PVC coat waiting for him; for participating and for letting him go through with this. The hatred makes him harder, gives him focus, and he's just beginning to consider how he's going to kill it after he's done fucking it when out through the front windscreen's beaded glass he notices that there appears to be a fire or something in one of the nearby garages, with smoke escaping out from under the closed ... no. No, that's not quite what's happening. He squints and frowns, bewildered, pausing his convulsive pelvic back-and-forth while struggling to make sense of what he's seeing. The grey smoke – not smoke exactly, being slow and viscous – seems to bleed out through the corrugated metal of the garage door and its surrounding brickwork like an exhalation, an expression of the damp and misery that soaks the walls in neighbourhoods like this. Curdled and seething in the oil-stain gloom the sluggish vapour looks to be collecting in one spot, rotating languidly an inch above the tarmac and much like one of those litter-whirlwinds that he's sometimes seen in car parks, cyclones of discarded rubbish. What the fuck is going on? Put off his stroke he softens and slides out, slips off the nest almost unnoticed as he gazes through the trickling glass into the gradually revolving and resolving front of ugly weather, so unnaturally localised. The shifting crenulations arbitrarily take on a host of momentary semblances like the white, Persil-laundered clouds he thinks he can recall from childhood only grubbier, more hurriedly, and with less room for whimsy or interpretation. There's a cone of filthy fog by now and up towards the top – "Fuck! Fuck, what's that?" – towards the top slim ashen threads and tendrils writhe like bile in toilet-water, accidentally curling to the contours of an agitated old man's face. Then suddenly there's lots of faces, all the same and screaming without making any noise, eyes multiplying to a string of hostile, glistening jellies. Several mouths identically decayed and toothless open in the plethora of smouldering heads, and flocks of unwashed hands rise fluttering like oversized factory butterflies. He finds he's making an involuntary plaintive noise high in his sinuses and at the same time notices the night air splashed on his perpetually blushing cheek in a cold water gust. What's ... fuck, it's got the door open, it's getting out. It had been frightened at the start, did what he told it and he hadn't bothered with the lock. Fuck. Fuck! It slithers on its belly like a seal taking to water, tumbling face-first from the car into the tarmac black outside and though he lunges for a stick-thin ankle all he comes away with is a Cinderella shoe.

"You come back here! You come back here, you cunt!"

Forgetting in the fugue and fury of the instant the hallucination that had so distracted him, he scrambles awkwardly out of the vehicle into the rain after his bolting prey with flies undone and murder in his boots. Cut to new point of view and insert footage, black and white.

Through brick and metal only fifty years thick at the very outside boils the incorporeal moocher with his kettle scream of anger rising even through the corpse acoustic of the ghost-seam. There is his faint, sudden scent of damp and mildew everywhere as with grey cemetery eyes he drinks the dark of the enclosure with its spitting puddles and makes out the fuck-sprung vehicle stood rocking at its centre. Edge stitched with pale phosphorescence in his wraith-sight he can see a stout man, perspiration streaming on his choirboy cheeks as he kneels upright in the rear seats shunting back and forth repetitively, a stuck dodgem. Freddy doesn't need to see the frightened girl crouched like a dog in front of him to know exactly what he's doing, oh the cowardly little speck of shit, the dirty bugger and the worst thing is there's two of them, two of them to one skinny little lass. He's got his mate there with him, sitting in the driver's seat with a big titfer on and staring straight out through the windscreen so that if you knew no better you might think that he was glaring right at Freddy with his different-looking peepers, one dark and the other ... oh. Oh, bloody hell. It's not another man at all. It's something a sight worse and Freddy's bowels would turn to water if they weren't already steam. The motor has a fiend in its front seat, one of the grander and more frightening ones, the kind much talked about yet rarely seen and gazing fixedly at Freddy with mismatched eyes and a knowing smile that's all but lost amongst the curls of his bindweed moustache and beard. It's the same look the Master Builder gave him earlier up at the snooker hall: an exchanged glance, a mutual acknowledgment that this is it, this is the crucial incident that Freddy's whole existence, both in flesh and fog, has been in aid of. He has a profound conviction that the smirking devil isn't here for him tonight, unless in the capacity of an amused spectator. It won't harm him if he tries to interrupt the shameful business going on in the back seat, he knows that. It's almost as if it's granting him a special dispensation to do all the things which spectres shouldn't really do, without fear of reprisal. He's allowed to haunt, to be a charnel terror of the most extravagant variety, and if this should indeed be Freddy Allen's moment then he isn't going to fluff it. Peering past the infernal celebrity into the black Ford Escort's rear he is encouraged to observe that the perpetually-blushing perpetrator has abruptly ceased in his compulsive thrusting, kneeling motionless and squinting in belligerent bewilderment out through the misted glass, apparently at Freddy. Is it possible the man can see him somehow, through the agency of drink or drugs or psychiatric ailment? By way of experiment the smouldering vagrant shakes his head and waves his arms around so that his foliage of persisting after-images blossoms into a fag-ash hydra, pale hands a fast-breeding nest of blind white spiders and a rheumy frogspawn clot of eyes, rewarded by a deepening of the rapist's puzzled frown, a further slackening of his blancmange jaw. Oh, yes. Oh, he's on something, right enough. He's got the sight, the deadeye, and it's put him off his stroke, this grey grotesque, this inability to make out what he's looking at. It's like he's seen a ghost. Flexing his ectoplasm Freddy feels the bilious thrill of unaccustomed potency diffusing through his dismal vapours, an acceptance of the terrifying, ragged thing he is reflected in the plump man's shrivelling pupils. As he gathers up the dire cumulonimbus of his countenance for an assault he realises something is occurring in the car, events to which his presence may or may not be connected. There's a click, faint in the auditory muffle, which the scruffy phantom retroactively identifies as a rear side door opened from within. The dazed assailant breaks from his fixed scrutiny of Freddy to survey his victim and immediately gives a bark of thwarted rage.

"You come back here! You come back here, you cunt!"

That isn't right. That's not a word you use about a woman. Freddy rolls in crinkling crematorium billows, churning forward for a better vantage but immediately brought up short by what he sees. The girl, there's not two penn'oth of meat on her, slithers from the partly-opened crack in her condemned cell with her face a sticky mask of blood, newborn into the night. At Freddy's back, erratic flashes from an inexplicably disabled garage light pick out her desperate escape-attempt in a distressing series of Box Brownie snapshots, scrabbling on her stomach, trying painfully to climb onto her hands and laddered knees with scarlet scabbing on her careful plaits, crawling towards the distant mouth of the oil-stained corral which she must know she doesn't have a hope in hell of reaching. From the car the blustering villain lunges, navigating the haphazard bright and pitch dark with a ladies' shoe in one hand like a tomahawk and his old feller hanging out, an overheated dog-tongue, from his gaping trousers. Surging in a sooty, viscous streamer through the demi-world's near silence, Freddy Allen and his trailing scrum of lookalikes flood in to occupy the dwindling space between the crawling, keening woman and her persecutor, baby-faced with dark hair plastered to his forehead by the downpour's brilliantine, a sputtering and indignant old-style bully. Through a hushed and flickering realm of scratchy black and white, the little tramp rushes to save the heroine. Pull back to documentary material, reintroducing colour.

On a turntable of gravity the planet spins, just over halfway through the eagerly-awaited new millennial long-player's opening ten year track, the critical response as yet divided on the merits of its noisy plane-crash introduction or the strident nature of the vocals; theists and cosmographers in bickering counterpoint. Jehovah is eroded by the tree of knowledge's alarming exponential growth, by paleontologic scrutiny, resorting to a fortified Creationist denial in result: visitors' centres serving the Grand Canyon are reported to have concealed references to the chasm's geologic age or origins in favour of a biblical scenario evoking the deluge of Noah. Carolina legislators argue that authentic rape cannot result in pregnancy based on the two-seed theory of conception popular two thousand years before. Conceptual centuries collide and in the deafening impact are belligerent Zionist assertions, fundamentalist crusades and detonating martyr vests.

Besieged, the secular response is militant, an atheism volubly affirmed that in its dogmas and its certainties approaches the religious, although armed with nothing more substantial than established scientific fact, itself a changed constituency of shifting ground. The classical and quantum models are persistent in rejecting all attempts at reconciliation, with the string by which they might be bound proving thus far elusive. Insufficiently grasped gravity engenders multiplying entities in its support, exotic states and substances, dark energy, dark matter, necessary beasts arisen from mathematics yet escaping observation. Faith and politics ferment, aided by a fast-propagating yeast of theory and device, and all the architecture of the world's traditions seems erected on an information floodplain, vulnerable to every fresh downpour of data or the bursting banks of ideologies too narrow and slow-moving to accommodate the surge, the inundation of complexity. Despite its evident fatigue, afraid of missing some vital development in this incessant and incendiary pageant, culture dare not close its eyes. Resume interior, night.

Unable to be rid, now, of his sister's oddly memorable tarot images, Mick finds them strewn all over his cerebral carpeting as the surcease of thought continues to avoid him. Circumspectly levering onto his back he hooks his left foot over his right knee in what he realises belatedly is an unconscious imitation of the deck's mysterious Hanged Man, a figure signifying an uncomfortable initiation if Mick's memory serves correct. He doesn't understand the Hanged Man or the other twenty-something 'trump' cards even slightly, not the Chariot or Lust or the High Priestess, none of that lot; can't imagine any game elaborate enough or of sufficient scale to utilise them all and so discards them from consideration. Nearly all the other pasteboard pictures, though peculiar, are what he thinks of as the ordinary ones, the ones that have an obvious correspondence to the pack with which he's most familiar. There are four suits with ten numbered cards in each, the suits roughly analogous to the existing quartet but called different names with diamonds become discs and spades now swords, hearts turned to cups and clubs made wands, his sister stubbornly insisting that the tarot suits came first. The court cards, similarly, are almost identical to the more regular monarchical arrangement with the queens unchanged but knights and princes substituted for the kings and jacks respectively, these three joined inexplicably by a fourth flat aristocrat, a princess having no equivalent among the hard-eyed and mistrustful-looking royals of convention. Mick is unsure how this last-named personage is meant to fit into the play, no way of knowing if she beats a prince or what. Like the Hanged Man and his unfathomable pals, Mick finds she functions only as an irritant in an already irritating set-up. Tarot, to be blunt, gets on his nerves. With different occult iconography on every card it would be near impossible to even manage a quick hand of snap, and so for any grown-up purposes the concept is completely useless. Feeling suddenly annoyed at Alma, albeit obscurely, he negotiates the move onto his right side without auditory incident. New angle.

The whole problem with his sibling, he decides, is that she judges her successes by such baffling criteria that she can even claim unutterable disaster as some kind of victory, with everybody too uncertain as to what she's going on about to challenge her preposterous and yet authoritative-sounding proclamations. The most reasonable objections will be flattened by an insurmountable artillery barrage of quotes from sources no one else has read and which are very possibly invented on the spot. Any debate is a rigged contest held according to a manual much like the Book of Mormon, to which Alma evidently holds sole access. Rules of play change seemingly at random as though one were arguing with the Red Queen from *Alice Through the Looking-Glass* or possibly *Alice in Wonderland*. Mick always gets the two of them mixed up. In fact, now that he thinks about it, Lewis Carroll is almost as aggravating as his older sister in the author's patently deliberate attempts to puzzle and confound the punters. Why else have a Red Queen in both books, both with the same abrasive personality, when they are plainly different characters with one derived from playing cards and one from chess? In fact, with an intended audience of children, why involve chess in the first place if not as a way to intellectually intimidate the spiteful little buggers? It's a tactic which would definitely work with Mick, who's always found the very mention of the subject petrifying. Chess – there's something else that seriously gets on his tits. All of the fancy and entitled pieces with their fussy, idiosyncratic ways of moving are no more than obsessive-compulsive draughts when it comes down to it, the bishops sticking superstitiously to either white or black squares and the knights continually turning corners that aren't there. Then there's the game's neurotic aristocracy, apparently dysfunctional royal couples who are usually the centre of attention; kings restricted in their actions to the point of constipated immobility with queens free to go where they choose and pretty much do anything they want, despite the fact that it's their powerful husbands about which the wheels of intrigue turn. Mick's class-based supposition that the chessmen's quirky movements have their root in mental feebleness resultant from inbreeding notwithstanding, he'll admit that the distinctive figures have their own mystique, their own minimalist charisma. There's a sense about them that they stand for something more significant than just a knight, a horse's head or a game token with a strange waltz-step trajectory. It's more as if they symbolise big abstract qualities that skirmish and manoeuvre on a higher board, a field of play that's far into the ultra-violet of Mick's comprehension. Kings, queens, princes and princesses, whether you're discussing playing cards or chessmen or real flesh and blood heirs to the throne, it isn't who they are or what they do that makes them seem important, but the huge and formless thing it feels as if they represent. It's what they signify. It's what they mean.

Deciding that a supine strategy might be the answer after all, he's halfway through the necessary repositioning when it occurs to him that that's why everybody made such an extraordinary fuss about Princess Diana with Kensington Palace wrapped in cellophane, swaddled by teddy bears. It wasn't her. It was what people understood by her. Against the bedroom window a soft fusillade announces scattered showers. Cut to panoptical perspective.

Church and State, in bed, share a post-coital cigarette and now the quilt of nations smoulders. The intelligence community's perpetual shrill alerts begin to seem those of a broken smoke-detector, generally ignored but not without a gradually accreting residue of jitters. Terror-stricken in a war against their own emotional condition, snapping fretfully at shadows they themselves are casting, western powers attempt to colour-code a nightmare. The white rucksack-flash is prism-split into a spectrum of diurnally adjusted dread, a heat map of anxiety that never cools below Guantanamo Bay orange with the icy blue of safety a forgotten hue that's out of vogue and isn't coming back. Friday, May 26th, 2006. In Washington D.C. the governmental buildings which comprise the Capitol are locked down while the U.S. Senate is in session, voting to confirm Michael V. Hayden as the new director of the CIA, after authorities receive accounts of gunshots heard in the vicinity and of an armed man sighted inside an adjacent office gym. Police identify the sharp reports as probably those of pneumatic hammers and the putative gymnasium gunman as one of their plainclothes operatives. Across the planet fresh security initiatives fail to keep out the resolute insurgents of the mind. With each explosion the wraith population also booms, new sheeted forms arisen wailing out of idle chat and propaganda, tricks of media light and hulking

Brocken spectres flung on pools of fog between stark summit headlines. Pepper's ghosts with headscarves and bandannas loom in popular imagination's steeply angled glass to stage schoolboy commando-rolls through grainy training footage, mythically disfigured clerics wagging a remaining finger heavy with grim emphasis. Concepts of nation first spun as religious parables or else dime-novel daydreams in less nuanced centuries play out on multiplying modern platforms as ensanguined pantomime; fond re-enactments already nostalgic for the slaughters of a simpler world. Cue rapid intercuts.

Across the soaked enclosure's pittering surface skim of wet she slithers, legs conjoined by the entangling tights and knickers dragged around her thighs, a landed mermaid flopping in the shallows. Blind with blood she hears her cheated captor bellowing as he explodes from out the mobile dungeon at her back.

"You come back here! You come back here, you cunt!"

Somewhere amid the panicked rat-run of her consciousness the previously unsuspected part of her prioritises: if she can regain her feet she can pull up her underwear and flee, a difficult manoeuvre best accomplished without thinking. Managing to lift both knees at once she finds that she is moving forward, partly toppling and partly running in constrained and tiny geisha steps while trying to claw the fishnet waistband back above her hips. With both her high-heel shoes now gone she hurtles splashing through the pools collected in depressions, visual continuity reduced to blackout skits by nearby motion-sensor lights in spasm, too concerned with gulping back great sobbing draughts of air to think of screaming and unable to believe he hasn't grabbed her yet. New point of view.

He's had enough. He's had enough of drugs, they're fucking weird. He wades through seizure light across the walled-in yard and tries to catch it, tries to get it back into the motor so that he can finish but the stuff he took is giving him the horrors, things he hadn't been expecting. It's there right in front of him, just a few paces off and struggling to get on its feet but when he takes a step towards it there's this wind, well, not a wind but a stale gust of something that slams into him and knocks him back. The smell is all like dosshouses, all alky sweats and meths-breath and damp pants, derelict buildings with shit up the corner and all that, an aromatic fogbank he can nearly see. Fingers of slum-grey vapour curl around his ankles, trickling like albumen along his arms and running down his back and even though he knows all this is in his head and only happening because he's on one, he can't help recoiling. The hallucination squeezes in until he's struggling with a cloud of phlegm, but in the slithering mucous tendrils there are bits of face, chin-swarms and ornate frills of glistening lip. Worse, there's this faint sound that he catches fleeting snatches of, like a transistor radio tuned between wavebands, an enraged tirade that's unintelligible as if coming from a long way off or a long time ago. Some of the squirming, insubstantial stuff is in his mouth and tastes like sick, or is that him? For all he knows this might be a brain haemorrhage, an overdose. He might be in real trouble here. New point of view, reintroducing black and white stock.

Furious in his resent, the threadbare dead man presses his advantage with a flurry of attack which utilises every ghoul-display that's in his clammy repertoire. He tries the frightening stilt-walker elongation that results from levitating upwards with a string of doppelgangers dragged up after him, and executes a miserable spider-dance of multiplying limbs. He shoves his hands inside his own head so that wriggling fingers poke like crab's legs from his gurning face, gob widening impossibly into a scream of filthy polyps. He does his inflating eyeball trick or with an awful kiss performs disgusting sleights of tongue; reaches to cup the reeling sexual predator's exposed and dangling testes in one mortuary palm; extrudes a finger of cold ectoplasm past the clenching sphincter and into the bowel. Human ideas of fighting dirty, well; they're nothing to a ghost. With eyes screwed shut and baby face in a tomato crumple his opponent swats the night, as if at bees, and takes a solitary backward step towards the motor. There is now nobody sitting in the driver's seat, the ghetto-wight observes with some relief, its sulphurous former occupant having apparently moved on to other matters, demon business being surely plentiful in such a morally uncoupled world. Swirling his head about and momentarily accomplishing a Saturn's ring of ears, he reassures himself that the young woman is now up and staggering for the enclosure's mouth before resuming his assault on her tormentor. Barking inarticulate profanities the besieged rapist yields another yard in his retreat, a spook-punch landed in the frontal lobe and fingering for the amygdala. New point of view, reverting to full colour.

At the exit of the killing yard she risks a glance across her shoulder just to see how close he is behind her but he's still stood by the car, hands flapping at the air, having a fit or something though he could be on her in a minute. Every step a burning ache between her thighs she plunges out through Lower Bath Street's black, propelled by bad adrenaline and mindful of the coming crash into paralysis and shock. Because it's easier stumbling downhill than up she swerves left and into the bottom end of Scarletwell Street, grass theatre of her late abduction, steeped in piss-pot sodium light. An only sign of life is the diluted lemon filtered through drawn curtains from the solitary house down near the corner and she limps across the road in its direction, gravel gouging at her tender soles, breath bubbling in her throat. Please, please let there be someone home, somebody capable and unafraid to come to their front door on a wild Friday night, although she's crushingly aware of the unlikelihood. Off to her right the isolated home abuts upon the yawning mouth of a since-vanished alleyway, the memory of its cobbled ribbon spooling down into the dark beside the chain-link fence that bounds the lowest edge of the school playing fields. Ahead, St. Andrew's Road is bare of any traffic whatsoever, let alone police cars, and the murderer of her imagination is now panting like a beast and close enough to scald her neck. Her legs seem disconnected from volition suddenly, nerveless and unresponsive as if made of cake, and then the ninety-year-old slabs are hurtling up to punch her knees and slap her stinging hands. She's down, she's down and dripping blood into a gutter where rain gurgles through the stone oesophagus. Abject and crawling, a thrashed dog, she scrabbles whimpering over inundated pavement, levering herself half-upright at the doorstep to thump her exhausted fists on the wet panelling, surely too limp and ineffectual for anyone to hear. The seconds stretch excruciatingly, barbed with the premonition of his any-moment grip descending on her shoulder, of fuck-scented fingers bunching in her braided, bloodied hair. Please, please, please. From somewhere indoors slow, slipper-muffled steps approach along an unseen passageway. New point of view.

He isn't scared as such, he's not that sort of bloke, but he can feel something attacking him, some big junkyard Alsatian when there's nothing there for him to see, for him to swing at. Worse than an Alsatian. Yank their back legs open and they're dead, he's heard that, but this is like fighting congealed custard and the mess goes everywhere, inside his clothing, up his nostrils, up his arse. He can't take any more. He doesn't know if this is just what meth does normally or if he's gone mad or been grabbed by aliens or what. Slicing through an occasional illumination, raindrops fall as razor cuts. Inside a whiny voice he doesn't know, more like a woman or a panicked kid's, is pleading with him to get out of here, get in the car, just go. The loose skin on his balls is cringing, Jesus Christ his flies are still undone, and there's a dismal avalanche of hats, a dozen vacuum-cleaner orifices ringed with rotten teeth that he can almost see. Unfathomable images persist in the uneven dark, electric filaments burned sizzling onto his retina, these visionary floaters coruscating at their edges where the radiance has a grain of teeming maggots. Everything is wrong. Fumbling behind he shoves the rear door of the Escort shut while trying to find the handle on the front one, swiping with his free paw at the flock of ugly flying heads assailing him. With flapping hands as bony pinions sprouted from the temples, snapping their decaying jaws and grimacing, like monstrous charnel hummingbirds they come, preposterous and terrible. His frantic fingers finally locate what they were seeking, the cold metal button

underneath his thumb, and making noises meant to be a snarl he flings himself into the driver's seat, slamming the door closed after him. A surf of dirty
laundry suds is launched against the wound-up window, leaving a grey residue of viscous facial features sliding down the glass outside. Twisting the key
in the ignition, for some reason he meticulously checks the dashboard clock
and notes the time as almost twenty to eleven. Out beyond the rain-streaked
windscreen something putrid that he doesn't understand tries to get in. New
point of view reprising monochrome.

In headline black and white through stammering, convulsive light the skirling
deadbeat churns around the vehicle, a rancid cyclone. Car walls being nothing
but a flimsy tissue three or four years thick at most, the vagrant vapour-trail
could easily reach through them to continue the assault but it's deterrence
and not punishment on the agenda here, much as he wishes it were otherwise.
Just scare this tubby little bugger off and then make sure the woman's safe,
those are the things he needs to keep his petrifying eye on. Never mind what
somebody who'd do that to a young girl might deserve: that's a decision better
left in larger hands than his, although with half a chance what devastation
wouldn't he bring down upon this animal, this wretched failure of masculin-
ity that he so nearly could have been? He'd do a Banquo, do a Hamlet's dad, a
Tam O' Shanter with his ghastly oppoes from the Jolly Smokers drafted in to
help, a ragged locomotive smoke of pitiless and violent dead men shadowing
this mucky fucker through his every waking moment and his every dream,
for the remainder of his worthless life and then they'll just be getting started.
There's no Hell, no merciless retributive Inferno save for the Destructor, but
the bilious spirit is convinced that with the inspiration of a life and death
transacted in the Boroughs one could be arranged, to beggar Dante and to
make blind Milton look away.

Pulling a train of chalk and charcoal sketches in a falling domino progression he encircles the throat-clearing automobile as it starts, his eerie Doppler howl pursuing him through the flash-punctuated and torrential night,
his floating coat a rippling funeral banner in his wake. An aggregate of dust
and retribution, in the gabardine sieves of his pockets all the grievance of the
outraged neighbourhood is carried, the deferred affront viciously vented as
a steaming horse-piss stream on the intruder, a malign deluge to sluice him
from these wounded streets until him and the other knicker-rippers learn to
keep away. New point of view, reverting to full colour.

Smeared across a stranger's doorstep in the pounding torrent she's a broken
toy, discarded with torn seams and every bit of psychic stuffing gone, one button eye obscured by sticky cordial. All of her hurts. She doesn't care if the dull

footfalls in the hallway that she'd heard were only wishful thinking, doesn't much mind if her persecutor catches up and finishes the job. She just wants this to end and is less fussed about the manner of that ending by the moment. Treacherously cosy lassitude descends, every last vestige of intent or motion drained out with the contents of her emptying bladder. Self and personality are a retreating tide strained rattling on synaptic shingle and she barely comprehends the light that strikes pink through her lowered eyelids; can't remember the phenomenon or what it means. At length the lashes unrestrained by blood-glue flutter open and she squints up into puzzle-colours, clots of shine and shade resolved as burnished icon, surely a familiar Renaissance masterpiece she knows from somewhere, framed by the now-open door. Against a ground of patterned wallpaper and mismatched carpet, limned in sixty watts of Pentecostal fire stands an old woman built from long and knobbly bones and crowned with white hair like ignited phosphorous, one thin hand pressing on the lintel. Veiled in gloom by incandescent blaze beyond, the tallow contours of an Easter Island face hang heavy on the bone and oh, her screech-owl eyes. Pale grey with golden irises they stare down, reservoirs of depthless fury and compassion, on the smashed child at her threshold. Gaunt cheek tracked by angry brine the occupant stoops, creaking, crouched on leather haunches to cup Marla's chin while a free hand tenderly smooths the bloodied braids.

"All hail Kaphoozelum, the harlot of Jerusalem," pronounces Audrey Vernall, and her voice chokes with an all-redeeming pride. Pull back to planetary mosaic, abruptly edited.

Bulbs pop and data effervesce. Wigan police release footage of car involved in fatal hit-and-run with cyclist. Reefs quietly disintegrate. Convicted Enron fraudster Kenneth Lay says he believes good will come out of his predicament. The stars of supermarket magazines change shape, change partners. Arctic ice recedes. A paralysed Welsh rugby player calls to ban contested scrums and startlingly tenacious tubeworms offer hope of life on other worlds. Quantum or nation, states collapse when looked at. Oil chess, fiscal figure skating and the tendency of Homo sapiens to fuse with its technologies. Australian mountain climber Lincoln Hall is briefly believed dead. A badger harasses sports centre staff in Devon. Mice glow and grow joke-shop ears. Racism fears dog World Cup build-up. Budgets shrivel and reality shows relocate their target audience inside the television, closing the ouroboros. New forms of carbon and new scales of manufacture. An ethereal scrapyard orbiting the world. Popular culture, formerly disposable, dragged to the curbside for recycling and art residing solely in the pitch. Internal interregnum. Double helix turns informant. Touch-screen intimacy. Algorithms of desire. Bespoke need, and text messaging a carrier pidgin. New, new, every second bigger than the last.

The populace recline obese with novelty yet consume ever more enthusiastically, as if to master the onrushing future by devouring it; to drink the tidal wave. Cut to interior, night.

Flat on his back, Mick listens to the rain against the glass and thinks about Diana Spencer. It's a natural extension of his restless thoughts on chess or chase-the-ace or tiddlywinks, with the whole Princess Di phenomenon a game — or a compendium of games — that had apparently got badly out of hand. That almost literal unveiling in the newspapers, a first glimpse of the nursery assistant standing in a cheesecloth skirt with pouring backlight, prurient X-Ray specks illusion of grey silhouetted limbs caught by an opportunist snapper to be sure, but who was playing who? For all her shy fawn glances from beneath the fringe, a strategy established even at that early stage, this was a scion of the Red Earl whose name was writ in road, estate and public house across the face of working-class Northampton. Dodgy dynasties had been reduced to bouillon in her blood, from fifteenth-century livestock farmers passing themselves off as relatives to the House Le Despencer, through to five or six authentic bastards sired by Stuarts and thus a genetic conduit to the lines of Hapsburg, Bourbon, Wittelsbach and Hanover; of Sforza and Medici. Chromosomes not to be trifled with, and this before an admixture of Churchills are infused into the Northamptonshire family's already-potent genealogical concoction. Poisoners, tacticians, bloody-minded warrior kings.

Born Althorp in 1730-something and one in a lengthy line of Johns, the first Earl Spencer proper fathered Lady Georgiana, later to be made Duchess of Devonshire and famously alluring doppelganger of her later tabloid-teasing relative. The fifth Earl Spencer, born around a century thereafter, was the red one if Mick has his local history straight, a mate of Gladstone's named after the colour of his ostentatious beard. As Lord Lieutenant out in Ireland it appears he'd done his bit to play fair with the Fenians and even came out for Home Rule, which saw him ostracised by everybody from Victoria down. However, earlier in the 1880s he'd had people hung for murdering his secretary and Gladstone's nephew, so the nationalists all hated him as well. Mick glances to his left, at Cathy's soft topography beneath its turf of duvet, and observes not for the first time that there's no pleasing the Irish. Dull discomforts start to mutter in his hips and shoulders — none of us are getting any younger — and he essays the manoeuvre to his port side, curls himself about his sleeping wife's turned spine like fingers round a hand-warmer. New angle.

By the century just gone, Mick's century, the Spencer family's genetic creep had moved like Burnham Wood, unnoticed, ever closer to the hubs of power and history. The Spencer-Churchills had slipped into Downing Street with Winston and then, shortly after that, returned with Winston's niece Clarissa as Anthony Eden's missus; the Suez crisis prime minister's trouble and strife, although by no means all of it. Meanwhile in 1924 back home at Althorp, Eighth Earl Johnny had arrived, and yet Mick's only mental image of the man is as a rubicund and seemingly concussed attendee of official openings, someone with a prize-fighter mumble, to be seated furthest from the microphone. Though to be fair he'd pulled a decent-looking woman in that first Viscountess Althorp, Frances, even if her dynasty-dispenser seemed obdurately to only turn out healthy babies of an inconvenient gender. First came Sarah, then came Jane and then at last the hoped for Ninth Earl, yet another John, who died in infancy a year before the advent of a further disappointing daughter, this one named after a week's procrastination as Diana Frances. During his occasional lucid moments Johnny Spencer starts to see his wife as culprit in the inability to sire an heir and the humiliated Lady Althorp is despatched to Harley Street in order to determine just exactly what her problem is, the difficulty clearly being hers alone. Mick can imagine how that might have put a strain upon the marriage, even after the arrival of Diana's younger brother Champagne Charlie Spencer just a couple of years later. When the future people's princess was just eight years old in 1969 her parents were divorced amid some acrimony following her mother's extra-marital affair with Peter Shand Kydd, whom she'd soon thereafter wed. Despite the unreliability of hindsight, Mick supposes that some of the fateful architecture of the youngest Spencer daughter's life might have been loosely sketched in by events around this time, although he can't help thinking that by subsequently marrying Barbara Cartland's daughter Raine her father had recklessly introduced an element of overheated gothic romance to the mix that would eventually do most damage. Fairy story expectations without due acknowledgement of all the things that fairy stories bring: the poisoned apple and the cradle curse, the glass shoe full of blood. He feels uncomfortable. If Cathy is a roasting hedgehog, Mick is wrapped around her like baked Gypsy clay. Evading her inferno he once more essays the shift onto his back. New angle.

He's not really certain how it had all worked, the courtship and the marriage into royalty. Presumably Diana had been drafted into service as a broodmare, like her mother, to produce the necessary male successor while allowing her new husband to continue a longstanding dalliance with his married mistress. Did she know that on her way in, or find out about it later? Mick supposes it depends on how informed about each other's lives the aristocracy, as a community, might be. Even if she'd entered into marriage in a state of blissful ignorance, she must have tumbled to it early on. That first press conference with the two of them stood by that gate, the distant and laconic tone that he affected when he said "Whutever love eez" and you saw her look uncomfortable at this obvious disclaimer. But whichever way it went, once all the cards were on the table it was guaranteed that there would be a messy end-game.

When the fault-lines started showing it was in the form initially of a schoolgirl rebellion, turning up with Fergie at some fashionable and exclusive club disguised as WPC strippagrams, but by the time it got to Martin Bashir you could see that she was wheeling out the big guns and that her campaign didn't appear to have retreat amongst its options. It was clearly going to be hard-core attrition all the way. The tactical component became, literally, more naked. The ostensibly intrusive but surprisingly composed gymnasium rowing-machine picture. The abbreviated swimsuit on Dodi Al Fayed's boat, deliberately teasing the long lenses to erection, on the same day that her former husband and Camilla Parker-Bowles were due to meet the press and public. She'd got game, you had to give her that. And then, and then ... that week or two before the bridge, before her crossing, the queer British admixture of clammy lust and lip-curling contempt had humped its way to a vituperative climax: they despised her. They despised the future-king-humiliating Arab-shagger, and the AIDS patients and landmines came to seem an unconvincing camouflage for a new Catherine de Médicis, a new Catherine Sforza; some Renaissance vamp with no elastic in her knickers and a cyanide ring. Loathed her all the more for having wanted so to love her, but she'd let them down with all her gallivanting and her diet disorders, hadn't been the person that they'd wanted, that they'd needed. It's so hard to love something that's moving, changing; something that's alive. The marble memory is more dependable. Mick wonders, his thoughts starting to fuzz up at last, if it was that great weight of disappointed expectation that had suddenly descended on her like a prehistoric mudslide, fossilising her forever as the perfect tragic Hitchcock blonde, leeching the human colour out and freezing her into the black-and-white monitor image at the Ritz, the half-smile ducking out through the revolving door into eternity and outside chauffeur Henri Paul called back on duty at short notice, maybe catastrophically attempting to offset his after-hours imbibing with a few revivifying blasts of white line fever. Rolling highlights, glints, refractions. Obscure scintillations in the Paris dark beyond the glass. Pull focus to kaleidoscopic torrent of found footage, interspersing full high-definition colour with unstable silent film stock.

Rural roads can be most deadly, a report suggests. Abandoned turtle sanctuary to open at a sea-life park in Dorset. Russia jockeys for control of three Siberian oil pipelines currently in Western hands, and Nur-Pashi Kulayev, the surviving perpetrator of 2004's Beslan school siege is found guilty on specific counts of terrorism, hostage taking, murder, but steers clear of the death pen-

alty by virtue of a current Kremlin moratorium on executions. Lucky breaks
and random tragedies, the acted permutations of Newtonian physics with its
endless knock-ons and its circumstantial cannonades; stochastic popcorn for
tomorrow's papers. In the Indian Ocean some sixteen miles south-southwest
of Yogyakarta on the southern coast of Java and more than six miles beneath
the seabed the Australian and Eurasian plates, tectonic sumo wrestlers, slap
powder on their palms and close together for their seventh or eighth bout this
year. It's fourteen minutes to eleven, Greenwich Mean Time.

She can barely feel the bony hands that help her to her feet, and briefly has the
thought that she might be ascending. Distant from the instant, in a snowglobe
glaze of settling shock with all the painful parts of her a mile away, she registers the tissue-paper whisper of the fragile woman gathering her up into the
doorstep's light only remotely. Something about saints, she thinks, and calmly
wonders if she's dead, if she's not really managed to escape the car or vehicle
enclosure after all. Nearby in the torrential night an engine starts to angry life
before its growl moves off uphill away from her, a disappointed and receding
snarl which, like the spattering deluge or murmurs of her elderly deliverer,
seems to possess a new dimension; a cathedral of unprecedented resonances
ringing in her blood-caked ears. Through this celestial tinnitus her rescuer
is speaking now with a fresh force and sharpness that she gradually comes to
understand is not addressed to her for all that Scarletwell Street, other than
the two of them, is bare.

"See 'im off, Freddy. See 'im all the way off."

There's an eyestrain shimmer in the rain and then there's something that's
the opposite of wind, a howling gust that's sucked away from them into the
Boroughs dark in an indecent hurry, as if late for an appointment.

Derek sweats and skids and swears and can't get out. The neighbourhood's a
labyrinth and he's like a bull at a gate, his chemically assisted courage burning away with the rubber to leave a black residue of acrid panic. Out of the
enclosure with that flapping and horrifically proliferative thing behind him
he swings right and into Lower Bath Street, but he doesn't know the layout
of the place and halfway up there's concrete bollards blocking off the road,
the district's blunt and jutting teeth, where the compulsory left turn past a
despairing local pub, the Shoemakers, delivers him once more to Scarletwell
Street. Fuck, fuck, fuck. A right, another right and the corroding wall-fixed
sign informs him he's in Upper Cross Street with those ugly tower-blocks
looming over him like oviparous doormen. At the end, what's he to do? He
can't turn uphill how he wants to, he can see more bollards up the top there,
but when he looks downhill to his right he realises his hallucinations are

still with him: on the corner there's a – he can't even find the words – a monstrous cog of fog rotating in the margin of his eye but if he looks at it dead on, it's gone. He screeches into Bath Street, trying not to see the grinding phantom gear, and then almost immediately left to Little Cross Street. What is it with all these Cross Streets? What's the big deal about crosses around here? Careering through a blacked-out warren the black Escort hurtles straight across the roundabout and into Chalk Lane. Veering left around the funny chapel with the doorway halfway up one wall he finds he's in St. Mary's Street, with at its end the lights of Horsemarket in joyous conflagration, the illuminated exit to this haunted maze. He's made it. He's got out. He's got away with it. He drives on into glowering taillight fire.

It's black and white as Freddy sees it, sizzling in a pale fuse over the school playing field, through still machines and empty benches at the factory and across Spring Lane.

"See him off, Freddy. See him all the way off", that's what Audrey Vernall had instructed him to do. Orders are orders. The chain of command is simple and straightforward: builders, fiends, saints, Vernalls, deathmongers, *then* the rough sleepers. Everybody's got their job and this, at last, is Freddy's. Frilled with fifty repetitions of the same old coat and leading a great fleet of hats he smears through the deserted business complex that was Cleaver's Glass once and before that Compton Street, heading by moocher instinct for the ragged area's northeast corner, the skull pocket near the pinnacle of Grafton Street. That will be where whatever's going to happen happens, he knows this in his remembered water, in his absent bones. That's where they immolated the enchantresses and heretics. That's where they spiked the heads, like settled bills. A fatal gambler's spray of playing cards, all violent clubs and spades, his centipede of selves pours over what remains of Lower Harding Street and skitters at unnerving speed into the monolithic crossword blank of empty courts and blazing windows on the other side. Saint Stephen's House, Saint Barnabas', buildings with lightless landings, several dozen front doors and one roof that stand where whole streets used to be yet still call themselves houses, canonised high-rises in a disenfranchised litany, an air of nominative sanctity to mask the scent of urine. Dirtying the televisual stupor in the ground-floor flats with angry-out-of-nowhere thoughts on homicide, the sepia stampede of Freddy Allen fumes through other people's Friday nights trailing a cloud of baseless argument, lapsed conversation and stalled DVD in its infuriated wake.

At seven minutes to eleven Mick essays a stealth-turn onto his right side and into a position that seems promisingly soporific, thinking of that final August night nine years ago. The black Mercedes screams through his increasing serotonin levels down the Rue Cambon towards its date with twenty-three past midnight. In the back, no seatbelts on: they're young, hormonal, unaware that alcohol and their chauffeur's anti-psychotic medicine are contraindicated. Vampire fireflies in the rear-view but the heavy Gallic lids sag and he knows he's crashing. Touching seventy he slips down Cours la Reine along the right bank of the river, into the Pont de l'Alma underpass.

And even on its seismologic Ring of Fire, Java shivers. In Galur, shrine-ornaments begin to jingle, small and delicate percussions as an overture to cataclysm. Nearly seven thousand people are awakened by the sound with slightly quizzical expressions on their faces for the last time, and the birds don't know which way to fly in this grey wolf's tail, just before the dawn. At 7.962° South by 110.458° East one of the two diastrophic combatants yields but an inch and all five million souls within their sixty mile-wide sumo circle are spontaneously and suddenly at prayer.

Suspended in an aura of averted ending, she finds herself in the kitchen of the woman with magnesium-flare hair. A blessedly warm flannel dabs away coagulated burgundy from her closed eye, at intervals squeezed into a half-full enamel bowl with fugitive pink clouds diffusing in hot water. Perfectly sweet tea is set beside her on a beautifully frayed tablecloth, and at her ear the anciently accented voice continues its account of saints, and corners turned, and the impossibility of death.

He's flying up Horsemarket and across the Mayorhold into Broad Street, horrors vanishing behind him, face first, washed with gold in the oncoming lights. He buzzes with adrenaline and luck past the Gala Casino on his left; keeps laughing to himself with the exhilaration of it all. Just before Regent Square, and without slowing, he takes the abbreviated turn for Grafton Street.

In chessboard chiaroscuro Freddy streams through empty premises, dragging a pennant smoke of faces over Cromwell Street and Fitzroy Terrace, bursting through the brickwork and into the path of the approaching traffic. Only in the headlight glare does he appreciate that it's stopped raining.

Mick forgets exactly where his limbs are. In his faltering mind a hypnagogic limo disappears into the tunnel mouth, abruptly lurching to the left of the dual carriageway as Henri Paul loses control.

Measuring 6.2 upon the Richter scale the earthquake ripples across Java.

Through an unglued eye she notes the woman's kitchen clock: six minutes to eleven.

Something dreadful scuttles over Grafton Street in front of him. He screams into the swerve.

From Freddy's monochrome perspective the black Escort mounts the curb almost in silence.

Mick imagines the Mercedes as it smacks into the thirteenth pillar under the Pont de l'Alma.

Houses fall, more than a hundred thousand, and some one and a half million homeless stumble out into erased streets wearing bloodied nightclothes, staring, calling people's names.

In its enamel bowl the water is now carmine, she observes, concentric rings dilating from its epicentre. The old lady's rung the ambulance and the police; asks if there's anybody else that should be contacted, and in a voice she doesn't recognise she soberly recites her mother's number.

Up onto the pavement and straight at the lamppost in a series of bejewelled saccades, he impacts on the steering column with his breastbone smashed to flakes of chalk, his heart and lungs crushed into an undifferentiated pulp. Head punching through the windscreen, for an instant he believes that he's been flung miraculously clear until he notices that he's now deaf and colour-blind.

Idling towards the wreckage of the car, unhurried now, he glances from the driver's body half emerged across the crumpled bonnet to the duplicate that stands amidst a pavement spray of shattered glass and stares at the black bloodstains soaking its white shirtfront in incomprehension. Someone else lurks at the end of Fitzroy Terrace, looking on, who Freddy takes at first to be a mortal passer-by until he spots the mismatched eyes.

"It looks like he could use a drink", says sympathetic Sam O'Day.

Against his twitching eyelids Mick screens a montage, commencing with the buckled vehicle at rest against the tunnel wall, almost immediately lost in a dissolve of swarming flashbulbs which resolves to snapshot images highlighting the events of the next ... had it really only been a week? Kensington Palace bleeding flowers and cellophane, New Labour's rush to spin the shroud, newspaper editors demanding a response from those they'd helped bereave, the whole fast-forward flicker of activity concluding with a still shot of Westminster Abbey, hushed in dull September light.

At the approach to sunrise thousands clog the Solo-Yogya highway, fearing a reprise of the tsunami two years previously and fleeing inland, leaving ruptured homes to opportunist burglars who, in districts high above sea level, nonetheless spread tales of an impending tidal wave that never comes. Almost six thousand dead, six times that many injured and along the highway's teeming margin in Prambanan a collapsing ancient Hindu temple complex spills its god-encrusted pinnacles into the dust below, cracked deities become unmoving obstacles for the incoming surf of refugees to flow between in curling eddies, with so many in pyjamas that it all seems a bewildering mass dream.

As though time isn't really passing, she sits motionless beside the table while green swirls of paramedic and fluorescent yellow surges of police orbit her in a gaudy palette of concern, bright twists of colour artfully embedded in the great glass marble of the moment. Audrey – that's the woman's name – Audrey is telling the attending officer that she's a former patient of St. Crispin's Hospital up Berry Wood turn, relocated to this halfway house during the care-in-the-community initiative. Marla's not really listening; not even really Marla anymore. The capable and unafraid perspective from which she'd viewed her backseat ordeal has not receded alongside the threat of imminent annihilation, and whoever she is now it's somebody considerably older than eighteen. There in the vastness of the tiny kitchen objects are illuminated in church window hues: the muted turquoise label on a tin of beans, her forearms bruised to plush cinema-seat maroon and Audrey's slippers, pink as sugar-iced flamingos. Every detail, every sound, each thought that passes through her mind is outlined with the glorious blood and gold of martyr-fire. She hears her own voice answering the policewoman's questions and it's strong, it isn't weak. It isn't ugly.

"No, he had a chubby build, with rosy cheeks and dark hair greying at the sides. I didn't see his eyes."

And all the time there's part of her that's still there in the juddering Escort; still there on the doorstep looking up at Audrey with her head all filament-glare and combustion, speaking that peculiar name from J.K. Stephen's doggerel and a dozen spine-lined ripperbacks, as if she'd known it would be recognised. A brandied slur of syllables or an elaborate sneeze, a name that nobody was ever called just lying around empty, waiting for the individual singular enough to put it on: Kaphoozelum. New point of view, resuming black and white.

Wet tarmac glints in an abrupt theatre shush, as though some drama were about to start. The boot's been sprung by the collision – fuck, what will he say to Irene, say to the insurers – and the children's beach toys and inflatables are scattered in the road as pale and grey as uncooked crabs. Exasperated and confused he tries to kick a punctured armband to the curbside, but he's either seeing double and he misses or his foot goes through it like it isn't there. Given his probable concussion he decides the first of these alternatives is the most likely, although this still leaves him with the problem of that mangled body sprawling through the absent windshield. Did he hit somebody? Oh, shit, he's in trouble now, but then how did they manage to go through the screen feet first, that isn't possible, and finally he glimpses the glass-freckled ruin of the face but still can't quite determine where he knows it from. That's when he notices the two old boys stood watching him from further down the street, both of them wearing hats, which isn't something that you very often see these days. The nearer of the two comes up to him, asks him if he could use a drink and Derek says yes just like that, grateful for anybody who might let him in on what's just happened. The old dosser tells him there's a place nearby, the Jolly Something, where he'll have a chance to get his bearings now the sat-nav's fucked. They start to walk together back up towards Regent's Square and, actually, this could all still turn out okay. Remembering the tramp's companion he asks "What about your mate?" They both pause and look back. The other man – one eye looks like it's got a cataract or something – smiles and lifts his hat, at which point Derek understands exactly where he is. He starts to weep. The vagrant near him quietly takes his arm and leads him, unresisting, off into a soot and silver Friday night. New point of view.

As Freddy sees it, once he's led the snivelling new statistic down Daguerreotype walkways to the Jolly Smokers, that's him done, his duties and responsibilities discharged. Puzzlingly, at the ghost-pub there are two men made of wood that seem to have arrived from somewhere, one of them embedded face-up in the worm-drilled floorboards while the other one, more corpulent but similarly naked, stands beside the bar with tears of varnish rolling down his grain-whorled cheeks and Mary Jane's initials gouged into his arm. As Freddy makes excuses and slips out the back door, he looks round and sees the distraught new arrival being introduced to the likewise disconsolate fat manikin by Tommy Mangle-the-Cat, fragments of a brutal smile sliding across his juggled physiognomy. There's no need to see any more; no need to know the precise nature of the justice that's administered above the streets. He smoulders out into the sodium-stained darkness at the top of Tower Street, where above a fast-disintegrating overcoat of cloud are stars that look the same to dead and living. He feels differently about things now, not least about himself. Some of the stains have gone from his escutcheon, blots evaporated from his copybook. When it came down to it, he'd done the right thing. He's been better than the man he thought he was, the man who was resigned to an ink-wash eternity, too guilty and impoverished in his character to ever go Upstairs. He's paid the district back for all its pints of milk, its loaves of bread, its disappointed doorsteps. Much to his surprise he finds his worn-out shoes are leading him down Scarletwell Street to his friend's house, Audrey's house there at the bottom with its crook-door, with its Jacob Flight. He's hurrying now, past the deserted playing fields. He thinks he can remember yellow, thinks he can remember green. Cut to interior, night.

His breath so regular that he's forgotten it, Mick falters at the brink of dream, that overcast September afternoon nine years ago replaying in an emptied cranial cinema. They'd watched on television, him and Cathy and the lads, and it had all seemed stage-managed and strange, more like a Royal Variety Performance than a funeral beneath its Cool Britannia branding. Needing something three-dimensional and more authentic than a screen could offer they'd all climbed into the car and Cathy drove them out to Weedon Road, where they could watch the cortege on its way to Althorp. All the people that were gathered at the roadside there, as quiet as ghosts, nobody really certain why they'd come except the sense that something old was happening again and that their presence was required. Almost asleep Mick starts to misplace the dividing line between event and memory. No longer horizontal and in bed he's helping Cathy shepherd Jack and Joe between spectators on the verge, somnambulists with tongues stilled by mythology. Finding a clear spot in the threadbare grass beside the curb it seems to him that these exact same people must have turned up to remove their hats for Boadicea, Eleanor of Castile, Mary, Queen of Scots and any dead queens who have slipped his slipping mind. An engine is approaching in the distance, loud for want of any other sound, even the birds remaining mute for the duration. It glides past them like a ship, imagined bow-wave rippling the asphalt, floral wreathes like lifebelts on the bonnet, bound for its pretended island grave. Having attended to her homecoming the crowd and vision both begin to break up like commemorative crockery, melting into the throng at Alma's exhibition that's tomorrow morning. Letting go of everything, Mick sinks into another of his five-and-twenty thousand nights. He fades to black.

AFTERLUDE

CHAIN OF OFFICE

With a splash of sunlight to the cheeks Spring Boroughs basked, enjoying one of its more glamorous and less hungover mornings. Saturday dusted dilapidated balconies with cautious optimism, the persisting sense of a respite from school or work even in those attending neither. May brewed in the scruffy verges. Chalk Lane's elderly stone wall bounding the former paupers' cemetery was an abattoir of poppies, while just up the way a jumble sale assembly clotted on the daycare centre's slope. The district preened; no oil painting but from the right angle still as pretty as a picture.

Scuffing down across the balding mound from Castle Hill, Mick Warren trickled as an off-white bead to merge into the human pigment pooled about the nursery door, quickly surrounded by a turquoise swirl of sister and the largely neutral spatter of her friends. Alarming Mick with an unprecedented kiss that left his right cheek partially obscured by a wet crimson clown-print, Alma dragged him up onto the doorstep and excoriated him as she unlocked.

"No, seriously, Warry, thanks for only being twenty fucking minutes late. You must get loads of exhibitions based entirely on your mental problems, so, y'know, it means a lot that you've turned up at all. I'm really touched. You're almost like a brother to me."

Mick grinned, the disquieting barefoot teenager on Crispin Street and his severely localised depression on the walkway of Saint Peter's House lost in the sooty deltas at the corners of his eyes.

"There's no need to be nervous, Warry. I'm here now. I know I'm like a superstition with you, aren't I? I'm your University Challenge lucky gonk. Why didn't you just open up without me?"

Alma curled her lower lip, as if formally rolling back a no-longer-required red carpet.

"Because fuck off. This is the wrong door for this key. Can't you just circulate amongst these ..." Alma gestured inexactly at Ben Perrit. "... these gallery-going intellectuals till I get this sorted out? See that nobody starts a fight or pinches anything."

Performing a constrained about-turn on the step, he overlooked a perfectly convivial crowd which nonetheless seemed to contain innate disorder. A fight, though unlikely, was not utterly out of the question, but there definitely wasn't anything worth pinching. Nor did any of those present seem particularly larcenous, except perhaps the two old ladies he'd assumed were with Bert Regan's mum. They stood apart from all the other attendees and looked like they were sharing recollections of the neighbourhood, one of them indicating something in the general vicinity of Mary's Street while her companion grinned and nodded vigorously. The malicious glint in their crow-trodden eyes elicited a warm pang of nostalgia for the monstrous Boroughs matriarchs of yesteryear, and briefly made Mick miss his Nan. Miss his whole genealogy for that matter, with almost everybody gone except him and his sister, whom he didn't really see as being representative.

Against a layered backdrop where decrepit 1960s flats blocked railway yards and distant parkland further down the slope, Dave Daniels smiled bemusedly in conversation with Rome Thompson's garrulous and slinky boyfriend. Mrs. Regan told Ben Perrit that he was a silly bugger, a perceptive diagnosis based on just under five minutes of acquaintance. Blackbirds skimmed resurfaced plague-graves in the parking area off Chalk Lane and Mick allowed himself the thought that all the place's previous warm weekends were also not far off, lingering atmospheres of cobbled pub yards, pocket money and the tuppenny rush infusing the frayed present as a pungent marinade. The light at that precise time, that particular day of the month, had fallen in exactly the same fashion upon Doddridge Church since it was raised. Some of those shadows over there were hundreds of years old, had settled their specific pall on insufficiently despondent pallbearers and hesitating brides alike, on Swedenborgians and repenting rakes. He'd heard of laws protecting something known as "ancient lights", but couldn't really picture any protest lobby fighting to conserve the ancient dark, save possibly for easily ignored depressives, Goths and Satanists. Behind him, Alma had eventually reasoned that it was in fact her Yale key rather than the lock, the nursery or the rest of England which was upside-down, and was approximately stating that the exhibition was now open:

"Okay, everybody in. If anybody has constructive criticisms that they'd like to offer, I'll quite happily enlighten them on their shit dress-sense or the mess they've made of bringing up their kids. Remember that you're only here to gasp. Spill body fluids over it, you pay for it. Apart from that, enjoy yourselves within rational limits."

And with him and Alma at their forefront, guffawing and arguing, they all went in.

Mick's first impression was that the choice to exhibit some three dozen pieces in such a ridiculously tiny space had been determined by poor eyesight, hashish-influenced decision-making processes, or else the well-known female handicap when it came to spatial arrangements: the trait which made them imagine penises to be much shorter than they really were. His next impression, after the initial sense of overwhelming optic shellshock had a moment to subside, was that this staggering bag-lady clutter of ideas and images, these closely-spaced airbursts of hue and monochrome adorning every visible vertical surface might well be deliberate, might be a strategy for bullying the intended audience into a different and potentially far more precarious state of mind, assuming anybody other than an evil scientist would ever want to do that. This faint spark of insight was immediately interrupted by his and everyone else's third impression, which was of an outsized three-dimensional arrangement settled on its table in the centre of the already restricted space.

With Alma having deftly slipped around this eye-catching obstruction out of harm's way, Mick and his attendant fellow patrons still decanting through the nursery door were brought up short against the nearside of the trestle in a ragged tidal stripe of animate detritus. Roman Thompson's boyfriend Dean went, "Fuck me," in an almost reverential tone, Ben Perrit giggled and Bert Regan's mum said, "Well, I never." Mick himself could only manage a stunned silence, although whether one of admiration or disquiet at the surely obsessive mental processes involved he could not easily decide.

Built over several months from carefully hand-tinted papier-mâché, spread before them was a maddeningly detailed scale reproduction of the mostly vanished neighbourhood as it had almost definitely never been. Just over four foot square, its tallest structures only inches high, his sister's diorama juxtaposed the Boroughs' choicest features, irrespective of chronology. The speckled emerald of Spring Lane School's playing field made room for the resurgent Friendly Arms halfway up Scarletwell Street, an establishment the egg-and-spoon arena had in actuality replaced. Saint Peter's House in Bath Street coexisted with the seven-inch tall chimney tower of a Destructor which had been demolished in the 30s to allow the flats' construction. Spanning the wave-wrinkled river, by what looked from tiny Guinness toucan ads to be a 1940s station, was a gated Cromwell-era drawbridge. Flocking ewes surrounded smart-cars parked in Sheep Street, stippled shit on shredded paper fleeces.

Seen from overhead the centre court of Greyfriars had what looked like Rizla sheets hung from its spindled clotheslines. This omniscient perspective was too reminiscent of his Harryhausen musings from the sleepless night before. Awkwardly disengaging from the press around the nano-slum's west boundary he squeezed apologetically along St. Andrew's Road towards Crane Hill up at the table's corner. Passing his own shrunken terrace row he noted with approval that Gran's ornamental swan was now a miniaturist study in the front window of number seventeen. Despite the novelty, it fleetingly occurred to him that he'd viewed their old house from this unusual eleva-

tion once before, although he couldn't for the life of him think when. Turning the corner into Grafton Street along the northern border, he retraced the
route of his childhood truck journey to the hospital save for a right at Regent
Square, but this time as a casually-dressed giant wading waist-deep through
the absence where an implied Semilong should be. Alma was waiting for him
on the display's further, eastern side, looming above the mini round church of
the Holy Sepulchre and leering like a monstrous Templar idol, which if Mick
remembered rightly was a goat with tits.

"You don't have to say anything. You're honoured just to be related to me,
Warry, I can see it in your eyes. Did you spot Gran's swan in the window down
Saint Andrew's Road? I did that with a triple-double-zero brush, and they're
not even real. To be quite honest, when I think about myself sometimes, I
nearly faint."

"Warry, everybody nearly does that when they think about you. We're not
made of stone. So, what material did you use for this, then? It's not walrus
dung or anything, I take it?"

Pigeon droppings of exquisite delicacy caked the rim of a scaled-down
Destructor. Gathered by the table's southwest corner Roman Thompson and
Bert Regan grinned and squinted at the junction of Chalk Lane and Black
Lion Hill, where a queer turret like a witch's hat had been mashed up with
Harry Roserdale's newsagent's and the old Gordon Commercial, the hotel.
Just the hand-lettering on the advertisements and hoardings was enough to
break your heart and ruin your eyes.

"Nah. It's all made of Rizla papers. Chewed about four hundred packets
up and spat them out. It's probably much sturdier than what they built the
Eastern District out of."

Mick surveyed the slate-hatched rooftops, the pointillist flowerbeds of
Saint Peter's Church.

"Yeah. Yeah, you're right. But probably it's also likelier to give you
gingivitis."

In truth, it was taking all of Mick's determination not to look impressed.
It was as if his sister had removed a clipping from the undergrowth of backstreets and then husbanded it patiently to generate a bonsai locale, even or perhaps especially those features which had disappeared. His every eye-movement
uncovered more of them. The rising curve of long-gone Cooper Street up to
Bellbarn elicited a muscle-memory of straggling past the fading rose gates of
Fred Bosworth's haulage yard halfway uphill, with at the top of the chewed-
paper incline a painstaking reconstruction of St. Andrew's Church so perfect
in its Gothic detail that the building's 1960s demolition seemed flatly impossible, not merely unbelievable. By leaning like one of the clearance area's perpetual derricks over Sheep Street, Broad Street and the Lilliputian back yards

of St. Andrew's Street, Mick could just make out the infinitesimal front window of his childhood barber, Albert Badger. So why had they always called him Bill? Painted there on the tissue glass in spidery fluorescent pink, he was obscurely heartened to find an illuminated Durex sign. Three doors down was the Vulcan Polish & Stain Company, no larger than a lesser Lego brick and wholly non-existent in Mick's memory until that moment. Ant-proportioned hopscotch grids in coloured chalk sweetly defaced the vanished tilt of Bullhead Lane, and microscopic milk bottles next to sienna-crusted loaves of bread bedizened the front steps on Freeschool Street. Attention seized by every hair-thin drainpipe, by the petrol spectra reproduced in every other puddle, it occurred to him that you could go mad looking at this stuff, let alone building it. Beside him, Alma's forehead corrugated pensively.

"You don't think that there's some element missing? As if I was using all the obvious effort as a camouflage to hide the fact that I'm not saying very much, the way I used to plaster every piece of illustration work with that laborious stippling, all little dots, when I was starting out? You'd tell me, wouldn't you, if this whole exercise had nothing to it but ridiculously grandiose nostalgia?"

Mick frowned at his sister in astonishment, not so much at her vanishingly rare attack of doubt as at the lack of self-awareness evidenced by her last question.

"No, of course I wouldn't, Warry. No one would. We're scared of saying anything in case you turn on us with a debate about things we don't understand. I think it's fair to say you won't get honest criticism out of anybody in arm's reach of you, because you're such a touchy bitch."

She narrowed the blast-craters of her soot-ringed eyes as she considered, unkempt head cocked to one side, her level and unblinking gaze fixed on her brother for long, anxious seconds before Alma ventured her reply, surprising him by resting a comradely hand on his left shoulder.

"That's an excellent point, Warry, and well made."

She took the hand away, but not before he'd worried that she planned to drop him with a Star Trek nerve-pinch. Mick, of course, knew there was no such thing, but what if Alma didn't? Other people were arriving now, latecomers poking trepid heads around the nursery door on the far side of the oppressively meticulous tableau. He recognised his sister's actor friend, Bob Goodman, although that was hardly more of an accomplishment than saying that he recognised Ayers Rock. Mick could at least tell one of these eroded landmarks from the other, principally by the fact that Ayers Rock never wore a leather jacket, a black beret or such an abiding look of deep resentment and mistrust. More cheeringly, behind the thespian with his death-watch demeanour Mick made note of Alma's shipwrecked transatlantic artist pal, Melinda Gebbie, someone with whom he could have an entertaining conversation if the exhibition flagged. Moreover, since his older sibling had privately ceded that the pretty Californian was by a head the better painter of the two, Mick felt that he could shelter behind her authoritative statements and opinions if his sister engineered to give him an artistic duffing up. Accompanying her was someone else that he'd met at least once before, Lucy Lisowiec, an extramural muralist who also worked in the Boroughs community and whom he thought Alma had said was helping to secure the daycare centre for this afternoon. The women laughed and chatted, hanging on each other's arms, the younger of the two so wonderstruck by the art-smothered walls that her lids appeared insufficient to contain her eyes. More punters dribbled in through the propped-open door behind them, some he thought he knew and some he didn't. Alma, by his side, sighed heavily, still brooding over her reconstituted natal turf.

"I can see that I'm going to have to reach my own conclusions about what this installation might be lacking, rather than relying on your valuable insights. Listen, I think Roman Thompson said he'd got something to tell me, so I'd better go and have a word with him. If you were going to look at any of the other pieces, start to our right of the door and work your way around the room from there. Oh, and I hope you've got a lighter on you. I've left mine at home, so if I need to pop outside and have a smoke I'll have to borrow yours."

Mick nodded, waving her away, struck by the use of the word "if" in her last sentence, as though Alma popping outside for a smoke were some remote contingency rather than the abiding certainty that they both knew it for. With the pretended gallery beginning to fill up, its jostling horde squeezing together in embarrassed waltzes between wall and table-edge, he called to mind when this place had been Marjorie Pitt-Draffen's dancing school, cadet Nijinskies clattering on open parquet. Anybody teaching toddlers the Gay Gordon these days, he reflected, would be on a list. Deciding that he'd better make a start on staring blankly at his sister's pictures if he wanted to be out of there by nightfall, Mick took a last marvelling glance at the fag-paper precinct – a metallic silver painted pond between the tanning-yards along Monk's Pond Street; seed-sized starlings just discernible against the school's slate rooftops – and negotiated a laborious course between the jam of punters, heading for the exhibition's recommended starting-point behind the nursery's wedged-open door. This turned out to be a large canvas, hung or rather propped so as to partly cover the adjacent window. Never having been to one before, Mick wasn't absolutely sure what art shows were supposed to be like, but with that said he was fairly certain that they weren't supposed to be like this. The claustrophobic kindergarten squash of imagery didn't look organised so much as it looked like someone had detonated an art-teacher in a confined space. Already irritated, Mick turned his besieged attentions to the sunlight-blocking rectangle that had been specified as the extravaganza's point of entry.

Fastened to the window frame above the exhibit with blue adhesive putty was a note in biro giving the acrylic painting's title, *Work in Progress*, with a rather patronising scribbled arrow angled down towards the frame below, as if intended for an audience of hens. The sense of sloppiness suggested by the hasty caption was, in Mick's opinion, also present in the piece of art to which it was appended. The thing clearly wasn't finished, as if Alma had lost interest two-thirds of the way through. Which was a shame because the bit she'd bothered to complete, a lustrously embellished area around the upper centre of the work, was actually quite good. Judged by its trailing sepia jellyfish of Conté under-drawing, the intended scene was a plain wood interior seen from a steeply angled point of view, as if that of a crouching adult or perhaps a child. The viewer looked up from this disempowered perspective at a towering quartet of rough-hewn and broad-shouldered men with the physiques and leathered hands of labourers, who nonetheless were clad in what looked to be outsized christening gowns of white applied in such a manner that it somehow shimmered. The four figures stood about what Mick deduced must be a sawhorse, with the pristine draped expanses of their backs presented to the onlooker and their heads bowed in muttered consultation, no doubt a discussion of some technical necessity from which all save the hulking craftsmen were excluded. Only one of the assembled crew appeared aware that he and his three co-workers were being watched, turning a prematurely bleached head to gaze down across one shoulder at the cowering observer, tanned face stern and sapphire thunderbolts in his affronted eye.

Still wondering how his sister had effected the ethereal sparkle on her navvies' dazzling and incongruous frocks, Mick squinted closer to discover that what had appeared to be a uniformly snowy hue from further off was actually a plain matt undercoat to which gloss squares and oblongs filled with similarly shiny spirals, glyphs or leopard spots had been fastidiously added, white on white. Looking up past the radiant workmen with their faintly Soviet connotations, deep into the composition's further ground from the distorting worm's-eye vantage, he could just make out the sketched-in wooden beams and rafters of the ceiling's underside, from where a single naked light-bulb dangled on its flex above the heads of the conferring artisans. That vague ellipse of fully-rendered content, in the higher middle reaches of the canvas, was realised so beautifully that the straggly brown traceries surrounding it, the dropping folds of the white robes, the caterpillar curls of shaved wood at the huddled carpenters' bare feet, made Mick feel actively annoyed at Alma's slapdash attitude. Why couldn't she have put more effort into it? As far as he could see, between the cluttered, amateurish presentation and the half-done opener the only statement she was making seemed to be "I can't be arsed", though to be frank she wasn't even making that with much conviction.

Somewhere in the throng behind he heard Ben Perrit laugh, although that could as easily have been at some veiled subtlety in Alma's oeuvre as it could have been at a knock-knock joke or, indeed, an Al Qaeda outrage. Or a Crunchy wrapper. From across the room Rome Thompson's circling vulture rasp was interrupted by a raucous outburst that he recognised at once as issuing from his distressingly close blood relation.

"Rome, for fuck's sake. Are you serious?"

Elsewhere, infrequent bursts of Californian cackling or David Daniels' lulling murmur were distinct above the rustle of the rhubarb. Hoping that things might pick up, Mick shuffled to his right to best appreciate the next course in this oddly flavoured taster-menu, a far smaller job in oils with a much more elaborate frame, identified in ballpoint pen by an adjoining Post-it sticker as *A Host of Angles*.

Now, this was more like it. The restrained dimensions, something like twelve inches by eighteen and dwarfed by their gilded surround, barely contained a concentrated field of light and magnifying-lens embellishment. The portrait-aspect vignette, like its predecessor, once again presented an interior although on this occasion it appeared to be that of Saint Paul's Cathedral. Curdling yellow luminosity, as though from an incipient storm without, allowed for burnished highlights of warm gold like syrup to emerge from the prevailing umbers of a scene which Mick presumed, despite its air of authenticity, to be imaginary. On the decorated flags beneath the building's Whispering Gallery was erected an impossibly tall gantry strung with pulleys and stout hawsers, the innumerable struts and crossbeams of the scaffolding's construction starkly contrasting with the predominantly circular designs of the cathedral and perhaps embodying the many angles mentioned in the painting's title. At its loftiest extremities the feat of engineering looked to be supporting a precarious pie-slice platform, but if that were so he was unable to explain the purpose of the surely dream-scale sandbag with its stupefying mass hung only a few inches over the immaculately polished floor. It had to be some kind of counterweight, yet for the life of him Mick couldn't figure out what it was balancing until a closer squint revealed less than a foot of clearance under the huge framework at the centre of the composition. The whole thing was hanging from the inside of the dome above, conceivably so that the nineteenth-century labourers converged about the structure's base in falling shafts of jaundiced sunshine could rotate it. Mick stood back in wonderment, strangely convinced by the spectacular unfeasibility of the arrangement that the picture chronicled actual occurrences; events and mechanisms that had really happened or existed, all in brushstrokes so small as to be almost invisible. The sense of echoing space and the ecclesiastic hush evoked by the depiction's false depths bordered on the tangible, to the extent that he could almost hear the tensile creak of thigh-thick rope or catch a faint ghost of the previous Sunday's incense. It was quietly magnificent, and the one element which bothered him about the work was its transparent lack of anything to do with him or his experience. The same was true of the preceding piece as well, now that he thought about it.

And, as it turned out, the next one, which was propped against the nursery wall beneath *A Host of Angles*, thus requiring Mick to crouch down on his haunches if he wanted to inspect it. Shifted by this action to a toddler plane inhabited by trousers as distinct as faces, he attempted to take in the offering expediently, painfully aware that he presented an obstruction to the studiedly polite and yet inwardly seething knees about him in the narrow aisle. Roughly the same in scale as the cathedral scene above but this time in a mounting of pristine white board, a hasty label clinging to the skirting board informed him of the picture's title, *ASBOs of Desire*. A shadowed oblong with a plate-sized circle halfway up, he realised after a disoriented pause that he was looking at a close-up of a security camera, staring dead into the glass of its dilated pupil. Small already and made even more diminutive by the foreshortening, an isolated female figure was reflected in the lens's centre, caught in its authoritarian snowglobe and defined in delicate white traceries against the work's predominating swathes of sooty darkness, purples that were almost black and crumbling to a fine grain at their edges. Thinking back to boyhood episodes where he had inadvertently intruded on his older sister while she was preoccupied with art – much more unsettling than barging in while she was on the toilet – Mick thought the image might be realised in a carefully-masked application of the surely obsolescent spray-diffusers that he'd seen her use, hinged tubes you blew through to produce a flecked mist in the manner of an Amish airbrush. This would make it very likely that the medium was coloured ink, Windsor & Newton's strangely satisfying roster of glass pyramids with labels like children's-book heraldry. The woman held in the surveillance gaze had high heels and a short skirt, fists thrust in the pockets of a furry collared jacket and her weight on one foot, head turned to peer off into the dark as if waiting impatiently for someone. She seemed unaware that she was being furtively observed, which emphasised her vulnerability and made Mick faintly worried for her. The impassive lens too much recalled a voyeuristic eye belonging to some masturbator in the shadows. Carefully delineated beads of condensation, jewelling its cold meniscus, stood like lecherous sweat on a molester's brow.

"Warry, I know it's awesome and it's only right that you should bow before it, but your worship's blocking everybody's way. If I'd known you were going to show me up like this I'd never have invited you. Oh, yeah, and can I have a borrow of your lighter?"

With a heavy sigh of resignation, Mick turned from the disconcerting nocturne to regard the Doctor Martin's boots with twelve holes but incompetently fastened laces which appeared to be addressing him. Levering cumbersomely back up to his feet he fished with some resentment in one trouser pocket, finally producing the requisite three-for-a-pound stick of amethyst. It wasn't that he minded Alma borrowing his lighter; it was more the way she stood there with her palm out, as though he was nine and she was confiscating it.

"Here. Don't forget to bring it back. You do know, Warry, don't you, that these are just disconnected images with nothing tying them together, unless you count the crushed centipede you call a signature? And what has any of this got to do with how I nearly choked to death?"

Casually pocketing the half-filled plastic lozenge without comment or apparent gratitude, his sister scrutinised him from beneath drug-and-mascara-weighted lids, reluctant to let in too many photons of his philistine rebounded light.

"Well, Warry, for the exhibition's climax, in an improvised performance piece I'm going to ram a five pound jar of cough-sweets down your throat, finish the job, and very likely cop the Turner. People like you are the reason why the working class can't have nice things."

He shook his head slowly and pityingly, a pessimistic vet.

"And people like you are the reason they can't even find their shitty lighters, Warry."

Alma gave him an elaborate triple V-sign that involved two hands and also forearms crossing at an acute angle from the elbow, which to Mick looked like a ritualised fit, before she flounced out of the open door to both take and pollute the air. He watched her through the nursery window, an immense dust bunny made of turquoise fluff that seemed to bowl in a contrary breeze across the threadbare mound outside as she paced back and forth, sparking a spliff only a little shorter than her usual blind-man's cane but which his sister no doubt thought of as discreet and unobtrusive. Bloody women and their inbuilt inability to grasp spatial relationships. Of course, it might be that she'd chosen such an inappropriately tiny venue so that even if only two people and a dog showed up she'd still be playing to a heaving crowd. From out the slaughterhouse press of humanity immediately surrounding him he heard Bert Regan venture a not-unrelated diagnosis.

"Hur hur. Fuck my arse. What does she think this is, Agoraphobics fuckin' Anonymous, or what? She's never been on the same page as everybody else, has she, your kid?"

Mick turned and grinned at the preposterously sturdy-looking ne'er-do-well and chancer, somehow still glaringly ginger even now that his remaining hair was grey.

"Hey up, Bert. Tell the truth, I think she's in a different book. It might even be in a different language, more than likely one that she's made up. Here, is the lady that I saw you standing next to earlier your mum? I heard her talking. I've not heard a Boroughs accent like she's got in years."

The landlocked pirate bared his handful of surviving teeth, a sledgehammered piano keyboard, in a fond smile.

"Ah, yeah. She don't look a bad old gal for eighty-six or whatever the fuck she is now, does she? Grew up around Compton Street just off Spring Lane. Me and me brother and me sister reckon she'll outlive the lot of us, just from sheer Boroughs bloody-mindedness."

Mick followed Bert's eyes, azure chips of castoff china ditched below the oxidising privet of his brow, and spotted the self-possessed pensioner in question on the far side of the makeshift gallery, in animated conversation with a captivated Lucy and Melinda. All he caught was, "Ooh, yiss, I remember 'ow we use ter git dressed up un' goo dayn tayn", but that was all he needed to submerge him in a recollected aural floodtide of genetically defective vowels or missing-and-presumed-dead consonants; of chip-shop queue confessions and school-gate soliloquies. To hear a Boroughs woman of that vintage talking was to feel beneath your fingertips the embossed lettering on oval Co-op milk checks, penny-coloured and quietly dependable in value. Marvelling, he returned his attention to the erstwhile gasfitter, knife crime early adaptor and Dodge City plumber at his side.

"You're lucky to still have her, Bert. Who were those women I saw with her when I turned up earlier? Are they two mates of hers?"

The rusting caterpillar eyebrows crept together for a puzzled face-off.

"You're not talkin' about Mel and Lucy?"

Shaking his head like a wet dog, Mick surveyed the cramped premises papered with his big sister's hallucinations hoping he could point the pair out, but they'd either left already or had nipped outside to get away from all the noise and people, not that you could blame them.

"No, these were both older than your mum. They looked like they'd been living round here quite a while, how they were dressed."

Bert pushed his lips out in an oral shrug.

"I never noticed 'em. I know that Rome, Rome Thompson, 'e was goin' out 'round all the flats and sheltered housing yesterday to tell 'em about Alma's exhibition, so most likely it was two old dears from this patch come to 'ave a butchers and see what was up."

They both agreed that sounded about right and made a cast-iron aspira-

tion to talk later before conversational convection currents dragged the genial
urban ogre off into the grunt and mumble. Watching Regan borne away,
Mick made a mental note to ask his sister how things were progressing with
Bert's hepatitis-C which, last he'd heard, had failed to budge even after two
blackly suicidal interferon courses, last-chance remedies far uglier than the
disease. Returning his attention to the copious vomit of ideas and colours
tricking down the walls of the establishment, he picked his way through the
next several pieces in disgruntled search of some tenuous thread connecting
Alma's peacock technical display with his own near-death episode, coming up
empty-handed.

   With *Rough Sleepers*, next of what appeared to be a largely arbitrary
sequence, he found himself looking at the riotously hued gouache delineation
of a pub's front bar, conceivably the Old Black Lion, where luridly bright customers listed in an inebriate over-familiarity or threatened to unhinge their
lower jaws in raucous laughter, both the fleshy sprawl of social drinkers and
their colour-saturated habitat distorted and exaggerated till they bordered on
the abstract. Sat unnoticed and ignored amid the gem-like greens and purples of a braying modern clientele was an anachronistic 1950s tramp rendered
entirely in warm stubble greys with lamp black in his creases, wet titanium on
a rueful eyeball. Almost photographically realistic in comparison to the oblivious Weimar grotesques surrounding him, his newsprint tones contrasting
starkly with their Technicolor, the itinerant clearly existed on a separate plane
to all the other careless revellers represented and appeared to be invisible in
their beer-goggled sight. The single figure present with no glass before him or
in hand, alone amongst the garish throng to meet the viewer's eye, he looked
out from beneath his battered hat-brim and the picture's depths with a sad,
knowing smile, possibly aimed at the insensate horde about him, or the painting's audience, or both. An oddly poignant scene that was, again, nothing to
do with Mick.

   Next up, *X Marks the Spot*, was realised as what he believed might be a
lino-print, the solitary pilgrim it portrayed made out of fractured slabs of solid
Indian red on heavy watercolour paper that was yellowed, flecked with age or
tea. The monkish form was stooped beneath the burden of a heavy-looking
and most likely allegorical sack hefted on one buckling shoulder, struggling up
an incline recognisable from the intrusive quilt of modern block-cut signage
in the background as halfway down Horseshoe Street. Frankly, Mick didn't
have a fucking clue, and item six was hardly more enlightening. On board
roughly two feet by one was what appeared from a few paces off to be the
grainy head-and-shoulders portrait of a hat-clad Charlie Chaplin, but which
on approach dissolved into mixed media collage. A large industrial watch-
part cog, perhaps clipped from a technical or scientific magazine, described

the upper semi-circle of the silent star's iconic bowler, while its band and brim were a rectangular munitions factory and a silhouetted barbed-wire fence respectively. The face beneath, pasted together from torn photo-scraps of carefully composed and graduated half-tone densities, was an incongruous carnival of Dior models, shell-shock victims, stockpiled gasmasks, *Punch* cartoons skewering contemporary art and what appeared to be a period street-plan of Lambeth. The left cheek was bleached-out poppy fields, one eye a face that Mick identified as the young Albert Einstein and the other one a lifebelt ring from the *Titanic*. The moustache, he thought, might be Archduke Franz Ferdinand's notorious Sarajevo motor vehicle. He didn't even bother looking at the hastily scrawled ballpoint afterthought that gave the gimmicky assemblage its no doubt clever title.

On it went, a steeply angled ladder of estrangement. Clearly only there for its shock-value, Mick decided, the next exhibit depicted the bare back of an adult black male, in an ingeniously-crafted frame precisely contoured to contain the muscled curvatures of the rich purple and mahogany expanse. Distressingly, the skin in question appeared lately flogged, possibly by a cat-o'-nine-tails that had left close-spaced red horizontal lines across the glistening shoulder-blades. It came to him belatedly that these marks were intended to suggest a terrible musical stave on which what had seemed random blots of gore revealed themselves as carefully placed notes in some appalling composition. Queasily, he cast an eye over the nearby makeshift label. *Blind But Now I See*, apparently, although Mick couldn't for the life of him. Although entirely certain that his sister would not have intended any such thing, he thought this particular piece might well be construed as racist, or at least as racially insensitive. He wondered what Dave Daniels would make of it, and next wondered if wondering that might in itself be racist.

Then there was a pencil-crayon study of somebody who looked like Ben Perrit ambling disconsolately at the bottom of an ocean, clouds of sediment arisen from his heels and what seemed to be murky fragments of St. Peter's Church protruding from the seabed in the background, weed in ribbons trailing from the gaping mouths of Saxon monsters in relief below the eaves. Next came a larger work accomplished in a medium which Mick distantly remembered was called scraperboard, a steeply-angled vista looking up towards a silhouetted figure standing straddling a roof-ridge with some kind of glass or crystal sphere held up aloft in either hand, and lower the black surface scratched away in random smudges to reveal prismatic tinfoil underneath. There followed not a pictorial work of any kind but rather a white apron, hand-embroidered at the hem with unexpectedly uplifting butterflies and bees. It looked as if a lot of effort had gone into it, but once again he found he'd no clear notion as to what, if anything, the crisp white linen was meant to be saying beyond "Everybody look at me. I can embroider." Nor was item ten, identified by a desultory biro scrawl as *Hark the Glad Sound*, any more enlightening. Rendered, conceivably, in oil pastels it depicted a young woman clad in 1940s clothes, alone and sitting in a gas-lit parlour playing a piano. Only after several moments did he realise that Titanium White highlights on the figure's cheeks evoked refracted tears. If anything it looked a little sentimental; chocolate-boxy even, like that bloke who did the picture with the singing waiter, Vettriano. Once again, no reference to Mick himself was anywhere in sight. Had all that been just one of Alma's barely comprehensible or indeed noticeable jokes, only remotely funny to a somehow-sentient encyclopaedia who'd never heard any good gags?

It was at this point that the object of his musings once again materialised at his side, ostensibly to give him back his borrowed lighter, though in actuality to see if she approved of his reactions to her paintings. This made him feel vaguely apprehensive, then annoyed that Alma should invert the usually understood relationship between art and its audience. Granted, he hadn't been to many exhibitions, but he'd come away with the impression that at these gallery openings it was the artist who was nervous about being judged, not the attending public. Once he'd arm-wrestled his lighter from her lacquered talons he raised this point with his sister, although not as lucidly as he had managed in his head. Her flue-brush eyes regarded him with genuine puzzlement.

"Why, Warry, what a wonderful and otherworldly notion. Do you know, that honestly never occurred to me before? A piece of art is obviously pronouncing judgement upon everyone and everything that's not the piece of art. Well, my art is, at any rate. Can't speak for anybody else."

Starting to notice his own critical deficiency of nicotine, Mick's comment was perhaps more sharp in its delivery than he'd intended. Still, this didn't matter, Alma being oblivious to rebuke.

"So it's not art that's judging everybody, Warry, is it? It's just you, being judgemental."

She stared at him for a moment and then, lowering her eyes, she sighed.

"Ah, Warry. Why is it always the wisdom of subnormal children that's most humbling? But I'm not entirely certain why you raised the issue in the first place by suggesting I'd be critical of any negative reactions. What's your own reaction so far, Warry, that's caused all these troubling and unaccustomed thoughts?" Head cocked to one side, Alma eyed her brother both forensically and quizzically, a watchful poisoner alert for the first telltale symptoms of success. "It couldn't be that ... well, that you don't *like* these pictures that I've taken great pains to create especially for you?"

It was exactly what he'd dreaded and he'd brought it on himself. Her

drug-dilated pupils, nested in the pissed-on ashes of her irises, were welded
to him and her eyelids seemed no longer to be functioning. His tongue had
dried onto his palate and the punchline to a Roman Thompson joke across the
cramped impromptu gallery became the raucous dinner-etiquette of crows.
Alma still hadn't blinked. There was no way to quit the field with honour, so
reluctantly Mick struck what he hoped was a pugilistic stance as he went on
the conversational offensive.

"But you've not, though, have you, Warry? How are these especially for
me, particularly Charlie Chaplin made of World War One and watch-parts?
What links me with Charlie Chaplin?"

Her seemingly lidless gaze swung to the ceiling as if in consideration, and
then back to Mick.

"Well, you're both much-loved symbols of a betrayed proletariat, and you
both walk like people with explosive diarrhoea. So there's that. But Warry,
really, what's all this about, this truculence? It wouldn't be that you've formed
your opinion after seeing only the first six or seven pieces, would it?"

Widening her mill-wheel eyes enquiringly, Alma awaited his affirmative
reply so that she could kick off at him and somehow make her random, disconnected paintings his fault. Fortunately, this time Mick was ready for her.

"Warry, you've completely underestimated me, as usual. I've seen the first
eleven."

Belatedly, it struck him that this sounded as though he'd watched a school
cricket team. He could perhaps have phrased it better and yet felt the basic
point was sound enough. The corners of his sister's mouth, however, steadily
migrated to the region where her ears were last reported.

"Oh, yeah, right. The first eleven. So you've not seen number twelve?"

That dreadful smirk. What did it mean? He said that no, he hadn't, and
the rictus became even broader, to the point where he feared that the top of
Alma's head would separate and slide off slowly, falling with a wet thud to the
nursery floor. She aimed one blood-dipped fingernail towards a point behind
him on his left, and with heart sinking he turned to confront the exhibition's
twelfth display.

A by-this-point anticipated ballpoint tag announced the large acrylic work
as *Choking on a Tune*. Mick's own sandblasted features following his accident at work filled the enormous canvas top to bottom, edge to edge, a post-
apocalyptic landscape with a peeling nose and a surprised expression. Watering
eyes, wet blue and aggravated red, were aerial views of toxic puddles sunk in a
corroded junkyard face. The vivid orange dust that the collapsed steel drum
had breathed all over him submerged the portrait under swarming cayenne
pinpricks, sore and fiery, carefully applied in pigment that he later learned was
not only the earliest available source of the colour but was also in itself fatally

poisonous. Dots of fire-opal teemed on a ground-zero physiognomy in speckled rivulets, in rust swirls eddying around and in between pink discus blisters,
dolly-mixture pustules ranging in size from full stops to bullet points erupting
from the chemically abraded epidermis, each bump bulging from the surface
and accentuated with a vanishingly minute fleck of highlight Chinese White
on its meniscus. Understandably, Mick found the picture hard to look at, painful in all its painstakingly depicted paining pain. It was a shocking image, certainly, of striking technical proficiency, but it seemed heartless like the flayed
black shoulders of exhibit seven. With a sick pang of familial disappointment
he was almost ready to consign his sister to the same chill gulag of disdain
where he had almost every other soulless and attention-seeking modern British
artist already confined and on a diet of their own shoes, when his attention was
seized unexpectedly by something in the constellated pimples fanned across
the doppelganger's cheeks and forehead. He leaned closer. It was almost certainly his pattern-finding faculties at work, like when you got those snarling
leper-monkeys in mahogany, but there existed something tantalising in the
texture of the raw depicted skin with its precision re-enacted burns. Annoyed
now, he leaned closer still.

The painting opened, flowering with new planes and perspectives like a
stupefying pop-up to enclose him. Nose perhaps ten inches from the picture it
became apparent that the tiny cerise boils and intermingled motes of caustic
tangerine hid pointillistic Seurat miniatures, entire scenes emerging from the
inflamed dermal mist. Below the portrait's horrified right eye, the back yard of
his childhood home swam into mottled definition, where on the cracked check-
ering of the constrained enclosure's upper level his mum Doreen sat in profile
on her high-backed wooden chair, caught in the act of popping something
small into the baby-bird mouth of the dressing gown-wrapped infant balanced
on her lap. Spreading across the shaven area above the painted face's upper
lip, a russet-dusted bubble wrap of blistering resolved into a vista of almost
ecclesiastical solemnity, with to the left his tearful mother passing the limp
form of her dead-looking toddler to the worried worker leaning from his lorry's
cab there on the right, one of the lifeless bundle's bare legs dangling poignant
in the central philtrum. The visage's jawline was from ear to ear a necessarily
distorted overhead view of the makeshift ambulance's route from Andrew's
Road to Grafton Street, with Regent Square now centred on the dimple of his
chin, across the Mounts to York Road and the hospital, this last a reproduction
on the left jowl detailed and complete down to the birdshit-crowned bust of
Edward the Seventh which adorned the building's northeast corner. It was for
the brow with its receded hairline, though, the broadest unobstructed space
in view, that the most striking vignette was reserved: the hot rose stipple and

corrosive ginger peppering arranged into converging lines, perhaps the upper corner of a room where a firm-jawed girl of approximately ten wearing a fetid boa of dead rabbits was somehow suspended, reaching down with one hand to the viewer. Startled, Mick recoiled, pulling away, and everything immediately melted once more into boiling acne.

He was back, back in the room, back in his body and no longer with awareness part dissolved in an impressionistic rash of citrus polyvinyl. Backlogged sensory answerphone messages received during his absence flooded in like Virgin broadband offers, the olfactory grapefruit tingle of whatever Alma had used on her hair that morning and Bert Regan's laughter, ugly as an airlocked drain. Bright afternoon light toppling through the west window sparked a fire of detail, bald spots, single earrings trembling on a lobe, or T-shirt slogans fading in the mind and cotton blend alike. Eyes blinking as if to expel the smarting residue of imagery he turned back to his sister, standing with one hip dropped and angora arms tangled together, clocking his reactions with the lead eyes of a Nazi lab assistant.

"So, then, Warry. Warts and all. Is that what you were going for?"

She sniggered, for once with him and not at him.

"It's not like I had a lot of choice. You were a man made out of warts. But still, this could be a new trend in portraiture, capturing people when they've just had burning shit thrown in their face. Though actually, that might have been how Francis Bacon worked, now that I think about it."

Fairly sure that Francis Bacon was the person some believed had really written all the works of Shakespeare, Mick was nonetheless unclear about the relevance of facial injuries and so said nothing. Fortunately, before Alma could interpret his enduring silence as a sign of ignorance regarding modern art, she was distracted by her thespian associate Robert Goodman, shouldering his way through the surrounding press of bodies to present Mick's sibling with a sheaf of pages printed out from Wikipedia and a glower of generalised resentment which allowed no clue as to its origins. The strange old woman that his earlier childhood tormentor had become inclined her massive rained-off bonfire cranium in the direction of the plainly discontented actor, her blast-pattern eyes grown larger while at the same time somehow retracted, pulled back into crater sockets. He realised that he'd been saved by the arrival of a victim more mouthwatering, more in the way of Alma's primary prey.

"Why, Bobby. We were just this moment talking about likely inspirations for the work of Francis Bacon, and now here you are. Is this random handful of litter you're holding for me?"

The gorgon Gielgud's mouth, badly lagged piping at the best of times, was briefly fishhooked sideways at one corner in contempt.

"This, for your information, is the stuff you asked me to find out at the last minute, about William Blake's connection to the Boroughs. You said if I didn't that you'd never speak to me again."

Accepting the loose paper bundle, Alma showed the hurt performer method-school concern.

"Bobby, I'm sure I never said that. Was that what your voices told you?"

"I do not hear voices."

"Voices? Bobby, no one said that you hear voices."

"Yes they did! You did! You said it just now. I just heard you say it."

"Oh. Oh, dear. The doctors were afraid that this might happen ..."

By this time already inching imperceptibly away, Mick took the seasoned player's speechless indignation as a natural break in which he could announce that he was popping outside for a cigarette. Granting permission with a nod, his sister only paused in her psy-ops manoeuvre to demand that he not run off with her lighter, which he promised not to do before remembering that it was in fact his.

He crabbed towards the open nursery doorway with its breeze-breath, squeezing once more past the front edge of the inconvenient table on which rested Alma's shrink-rayed Boroughs, pressed uncomfortably against its western boundary. Irritating as this was, it did present a further opportunity to inspect details overlooked during that first jaw-dropping presentation, and he found himself examining afresh the scaled down area surrounding Doddridge Church. Just up from the anachronistic Chalk Lane turret with its witch's hat, he found firstly the church itself and then his current whereabouts, the erstwhile Marjorie Pitt-Draffen dancing school down at the bottom end of Phoenix Street. In keeping with the model landscape's combinatory chronology, despite the old red-lettered sign above the door proclaiming the school's terpsichorean tradition, the front windows were those of the later nursery, thin Rizla tissues with the scene within described on their faux glass in watercolour miniature. In this instance, Mick realised, you could actually make out the table upon which a tinier reproduction of this tiny reconstruction was just visible. Feeling a little nauseous he dragged himself away from the exhibit, as he did so noticing for the first time the scrappy note taped to the table's forward edge. There was no number but the artist had at least made a half-hearted stab at titling the dollhouse slum, even if that was only with an unimaginative tag which read *The Boroughs*. Shaking his head ruefully, he made for the fresh air.

Outside, inhaling a too-sweet first quarter inch of cigarette, it struck him that all the surrounding flats and maisonettes, diminished by their distance from him, were almost exactly the same size as those inside the gallery, the bygone buildings caught in the wrong end of Alma's telescope. Those unknown people briefly treading the far balconies, bag-burdened widows shuffling and stout men in premature string vests, were similarly dwindled to the scale of Airfix Royal Fusiliers – they'd never made a box with stems of huddling civilians – and he was surprised to note that the degree of personality which he attributed to these remote pedestrians was hardly more than he'd allow a plastic figure of equivalent size. Seen from a long way off his fellow human beings were reduced in meaning and importance, not just magnitude, with their unguessable perambulations become finger-puppet dramas, toy parades enacted only for the entertainment of a bored observer. It occurred to him he'd always had this feeling, unexamined until now, that far away was fictional. Perhaps in time, too. He supposed this was how almost everybody saw things, without being consciously aware of it. He didn't know if all that other life and that other experience would be remotely bearable if people actually considered it to be as real, as valid, as their own.

Above, amidst scudding vanilla floss on Cerulean Blue, a shifting and elastic flock of starlings momentarily assumed the outline of a single bird. It was a more ingenious effect than anything seen thus far at the exhibition, although he'd admit that the last item had both impressed and unnerved him. Glancing back across his shoulder at the nursery's picture window, he construed the riotous jumble of attendees visibly contained within its bordering frame as an art statement in itself, perhaps a lurid study by one of those vicious Weimar stylists like George Grosz or somebody like that. He could see Alma as she stood attempting to console or further condescend to an offended-looking Robert Goodman and beyond her made out the malevolent old ladies, definitely sisters he decided, whom nobody seemed to know, both standing listening and nodding eagerly as Roman Thompson and Melinda Gebbie laughingly recounted something which involved extravagant gesticulation to the weathered anarchist's unconvinced boyfriend. Taking a last few fugitive puffs on his greatly truncated cigarette, as though before the scaffold, he corkscrewed its stub into the damp grass at his feet, deciding that he should once more retire within since Alma's effigies weren't going to castigate themselves.

———

Through the propped-open entrance, window-lensed air slapped him with a warm, ethereal flannel. Tacking through the scrum along the forward edge of the obstructing table, essaying a path of tight diagonals that took him past Dave Daniels, late arrivals he identified as Ted Tripp and Tripp's shrewd and saucy lass Jan Martin, plus a hangdog and trail-dusted figure who Mick thought might have been Alma's dealer, he arrived eventually at the point where he'd left off, a little way along the nursery's northern wall. Pointedly trying not to look at item twelve's industrially scoured facial landscape, he turned his attentions to the largish landscape-ratio pencil crayon drawing on its right.

This time the scrawled, perfunctory label was taped to the plain frame's lower spar and simply read *Upstairs*. More accurately it read *Upstars*, a tiny letter 'i' and a directional dart of blue biro added underneath the misspelled title as a hasty and corrective afterthought. All this untidiness, he realised, was beginning to upset him. Having previously had only limited experience of the phenomenon, he'd hoped for more from serious culture. More professionalism. Though it wasn't actually his area of expertise he felt his sister must be showing Art up somehow, making it look more like fly-tipping than the prestigious social institution he'd assumed that it was meant to be. Already miffed with item thirteen after brief perusal of its messy caption, Mick lifted his gaze to the wide-angle piece itself and found it near infantilising in its wondrousness; in the proportions of its marvel.

The frankly celestial view presented was as if the viewer gazed along the length of a gargantuan boulevard or hallway, broad and high enough to lose a town in and appearing to run on forever, desperately pursuing an escaped vanishing point. His reeling spatial equilibrium recovering, he realised belatedly that he was looking at a monstrous and impossibly enlarged Emporium Arcade, with distant bounding walls that rose, tier upon tier, towards a glass train-station roof wide as the Amazon. Through this, replacing weather there were complex geometric figures, massive and irregular in dotted white lines against blue as though a manual for atmospheric origami. Other than this vertigo-inducing ceiling, the vast corridor appeared to be made out of wood. Pine planking of extravagant dimensions stretched away to the remote convergence of the background, with at intervals what looked like outsized horizontal picture-frames, a grid of bevel-bordered holes filling the staggering expanse from edge to edge. The closest of these apertures had one end of its oblong visible in close-up at the picture's bottom centre, the restricted glimpse down into it revealing only setting jelly, stained glass, or perhaps some novel combination of the two. Out from the roomier of these containing rectangles, a half-mile off along the indoor avenue, rose trees that were preposterously magnified, a silver birch scaled up to a sequoia with the badly drawn eyes of its bark now those of a leviathan. The work achieved immensity in the contrasting placement of almost microbial human figures to supply the necessary agoraphobic size and distance, sparsely strewn flea-circus individuals in dreamlike stances like the hybrid offspring of Delvaux and R.S. Lowry. Closest to the lower foreground and thus most discernible, two children stood on the raised wooden far edge of the nearest floor-hole, gazing off away from the observer and surveying an interior infinity. The smaller of the pair he recognised from the blond curls and tartan dressing gown as his own infant likeness, last seen via the medium of chronic dermatitis in the previous image, seated on his mother's knee in their back yard. The taller urchin was the little forehead girl, also from item twelve, identifiable by her skinned-rabbit scarf. A far light wet and white drenched the extremities of the huge gallery in sloppy dazzle.

Almost every colour was a layered glaze of others in a wordless palimpsest, with this fastidious technique swiped openly from the superior crayon work of Alma's pal Melinda, as his sister had often attested. The depicted great hall, once seen, made the tiny nursery in which it was exhibited seem even more cramped and oppressive by comparison, with a typhoon of elbows and the aural carpet-fluff of conversation hyphenated by Ben Perrit's tape-looped laugh, an Ancient Mariner on nitrous oxide. Taking a last glance at the bright landing and its liberating endlessness, he shuffled to his right between some fellow connoisseur sardines and scrutinised the next two offerings, both narrow portrait-aspect slats of polychrome hung one above the other. Uppermost was exhibit fourteen, and frowning at the exercise-book tag affixed beneath it, this time with the blue ballpoint fading to nothing mid-word before it resumed in red, revealed the title to be *An As odeus Flight*.

Dear God, the thing was *all* in coloured biro, all one foot by three of it, and quite a disconcerting thing it was. Mick had an inkling he remembered Alma telling him about this piece when she was working on it sometime around last September, saying that she'd managed to track down a source of the immensely satisfying multi-coloured biros that had been her chosen medium during childhood. She'd complained that these days anything in coloured biro would most likely be considered as Outsider Art, although she thought this term a middle-class evasion to avoid having to speak of Nutcase Art which, meant admiringly, was her preferred description of the genre. In the case of item fourteen, Mick thought that she definitely had a point. The person who'd laboriously tinted this imposing image, graded scribble over graded scribble, burnished until every hue became a sucked-sweet sticky gemstone, shouldn't be allowed to go outside. The most disturbing thing about it was that it resembled an accomplished illustration from a nineteenth-century children's book, albeit one conceived and executed in some maximum security environment of either Hell or Bedlam. From the glass roof in the exquisitely doodled upper background to the pale wood floorboards in the lower, Mick deduced that this scene was apparently occurring in the same unlimited interior space as the preceding panorama, as though the whole numbered sequence of seemingly unrelated pieces had decided to resolve themselves into a linear story of a sort, a ludicrously grandiose wordless comic strip albeit one with precious little in the way of continuity between its monster panels. At least this one had an

actual monster in. Down at the bottom a small group of people, mostly children, stood about what looked to be one of the old-style workmen's braziers
that Mick could not recall with any accuracy when he'd ceased to see around.
Two of the kids, he thought, were his own toddler avatar and the mysterious
girl with the necrotic necklace from the last two pictures, although these were
very small and, as in item thirteen, faced away from the percipient. Four other
children were in view, all unidentifiable, accompanied by a more sombre and
ever so slightly bigger figure which appeared to be that of a strange old woman
in a bonnet and black apron. Like him and the rabbit-wrapped girl, all these
had their backs turned, gazing both up and away towards the unbelievable
monstrosity that all but filled the picture's further reaches. Mountainous in
its incomprehensible dimensions, this was a grotesque three-headed horror
sat astride a low-slung dragon creature only slightly less appalling than its
hideous rider. One head was that of a picador-crazed bull, while balancing it
on the other shoulder was a snorting ram with curled horns like black ammonites, if ammonites could outgrow whales. The central cranium belonged to
a crowned man of startling ugliness and apoplectic rage, the overall proportions of this triple-headed dragon-jockey having something of the dwarfish to
them. Naked, in one fist the furious abomination clutched a lance on which
streamed rivulets of filth, a sharpened barber's pole of shit and blood that
scratched the cloud-high ceiling glass with its appalling tip. Mick thought
that there seemed something biblical about the tableau, albeit a bible where
the schizophrenia was unambiguous. He shuddered inwardly and moved on
to the piece beneath.

It was another one in portrait ratio if the portrait's subject were a lamppost, a long plunging slot of fruit-gum colours in tart sherbet light. Almost
predictably by this point a close view revealed the medium as cut or powdered
glass, a palette that Mick recognised from the upmarket mineral water bottles
in his big sister's recycling bin. A sugaring of tinted crystal had apparently
been glued to what he thought must be some sort of paint-by-numbers outline on the board or canvas underneath, with clear glass over painted colours
where presumably hues were required for which no readily available commercial match existed. After some few seconds of adjustment to a grainier focus
he became aware that he was looking at a steeply-angled Spring Lane as seen
from its lower end, a waterfall of grimy and unrinsed milk-bottle grey with
vivid Perrier weeds between its paving slabs, below a scintillant and flame-blue
sky of smashed Ty Nant. Placed in the middle ground approximately halfway
up the archery-slit composition was a pride, a murder or a parliament of children dressed in glittering real ale browns, too tiny for identifying detail but
most probably the same grubby ensemble that had featured in the piece above.
Crouched nervous in the foreground, in their number and essential coloura-

tion matching that of the kids further up the hill, was a sextet of rabbits with crushed bicycle reflector lights for eyes. Indeed, a glance at the perfunctory blood-biro scrawl beneath the work confirmed that *Rabbits* was its title. Mick quite liked it. He thought that for once he could discern the picture's meaning and intention: Alma had removed a slice of their neglected neighbourhood and turned it into a church window, a poor man's church window made from fight-dashed empties and yet no less a receptacle for saints. Or possibly she'd just meant that the district had a lot of bottle.

Exhibits sixteen and seventeen were both in black and white, which he found came as a relief after the battering his rods and cones had taken from the previous pieces. Both were relatively small, perhaps A4 if that was the same paper-size he thought it was, not quite so gangly as foolscap nor yet quite so squat as quarto. High up on the nursery wall and side by side above a large and sumptuous scene in oils immediately beneath, Mick had to go up on his toes to see them properly, considerably more work than he felt should be expected of the public at an exhibition. The first, on the left side, was a pen and ink-wash halftone illustration, something from a children's annual that had been hallucinated by a child running a temperature, its amateurish subtitle declaring it to be *The Scarlet Well*. Down in its lower reaches, sheltering below a low brick wall in what appeared to be someone's back yard, were the by now familiar half a dozen ragamuffins, closer to the viewer here and thus more easily deciphered. Other than his infant self and the kid with the roadkill garland there was a small girl with glasses and a serious demeanour, a tough looking older boy with freckles and a bowler hat, a little roughneck having features not dissimilar to the young lady with the rabbit salad, and a tall and decent-looking kid who had the bearing of the sensible one from the Secret Seven or the Famous Five. The entire group were crouched, all peering up with understandable alarm into the blind white heavens visible beyond their brick wall's capstones where a nightmarish array of forms seemed to be tumbling through the sky, streaming a vapour of grey after-images behind them. At the top, eye-damagingly small and far away, a horse-drawn milk-cart somersaulted through some eight of nine reiterations, while below a hurricane of multiple-exposure dogs, cats, hymnbooks, fishwives, gasmasks, cigarette cards, teddy boys, prescription glasses, dentist's chairs and cutlery cascaded inexplicably through empty space, a weather of post-war ephemera. Something about the presence of the children made the vista seem more wondrous than unnerving, an excited sense that this would be a sight to see.

Immediately to the right was item seventeen, identified by its toe-tag as *Flatland* and comprising what Mick thought to be a mezzotint, pressed from a copper plate with lines scraped on its uniformly textured surface to reveal a realm of smoky, granulated masses held in place by startling blanks; by shell-bursts of chalk white. A trio of the juvenile delinquents from the previous picture stood near-silhouetted at the centre front, two of them small with one of these most likely his own infant likeness, and the central figure there between them that of the much loftier and more Dickensian youth in trailing overcoat and bowler hat. Beyond them, smouldering malignantly against a background that he realised was a view down Bath Street at the block of maisonettes on Crispin Street, was a dispiritingly massive fuming vortex, a slow and appalling gear in the movement of purgatory which intersected, as though insubstantial, with both the dark buildings that it nested in amongst and their unwitting residents revealed by cutaway within. Seemingly caught in this nocturnal maelstrom were what first looked to be dismal scraps of rag that on examination proved to be instead the husks or emptied skins of hapless individuals, punctured humanoid inflatables with all their bone and tissue filling gone, forgotten washing left there to disintegrate on an infernal spinner. The three children under a black firmament had something of spectators at a bonfire in their manner, although none of that exuberance. An air of desolation hung about the image, as if rather than a guy everything good was burning, going up in delicately stippled smoke.

Separate voices leaped and dived like flying fish in the acoustic swim around him, the room's colours more intense for a few moments' concentration on a world of monochrome. While he was still attempting to reorient himself, Rome Thompson's feller Dean materialised beside him as if poured into such empty space as was available.

"Mick, look, you know your sister? Mick, it's not me saying this, it's her, you know that don't you? Well, she says you better not have lost her fucking lighter, 'cause she wants it back. She says if you've not got it then she's going to plasti ... what's it called, that thing the German in a hat does to dead bodies? It's not spasticate, it's ..."

"Plastinate?"

Dean looked delighted. "Plastinate, that's it! She's going to plastinate you and make you exhibit thirty-six, but that's just if you've lost her lighter. She's a cow, your sister, isn't she? I bet that it was fucking horrible when you were growing up. So, have you got it, like, her lighter?"

Mick could only get as far as "It's not ..." before giving up beneath the weight of several decades' psychological abuse and simply handing over the requisite object. With a sweet and pitying smile, Dean pocketed what was now pretty obviously Alma's property and drained himself from the coordinates he'd occupied, a clockwise bias to his motion in accordance with the Coriolis Effect. Unable to even manage a disgruntled sigh, Mick focussed his attentions on the large and lavishly-framed colour-field of piece eighteen, directly underneath the brace of black and white works.

Mental Fights, the label said.

"Oh, fuck me," Mick said in reply, beneath his breath.

In oil paint and gold leaf, with an aesthetic probably on loan from Klimt, two giants clad in robes of dazzling light-on-water white were duelling, in a vast arena that was still somehow the Mayorhold, with titanic snooker cues big as the channel tunnel. Hair white as his raiment, one of the enormous figures stood contorted, caught in motion with his blue-tipped weapon on the backswing and behind one brawny shoulder. His colossal adversary stumbled back from the projected point of impact, an arterial spray of golden ore suspended in the air to trace the crumpling trajectory. On teeming balconies of a Mayorhold inflated to a stack of Coliseums, stadium multitudes of tiny cowboys, roundheads, chimney sweeps and medieval friars cheered on the immense contestants and loaned their depicted bout its sense of crushing scale, the monumental thunder of its violence. The brawl's grandeur, undercut by its brutality, was that of a bare knuckle contest between monoliths in a pub yard. Shaking his head admiringly at the eight-carat gore staining the garments of the combatants, he realised belatedly that these were two of the peculiar gowned carpenters from *Work in Progress*, with which Alma's exhibition had commenced. Was this whole show, despite the lack of any clear association between its wilfully disparate components, meant to tell some sort of story? One where characters' appearances were spaced so widely in the narrative that this made any sense of cause, effect, or continuity impossible to grasp without a roadmap much too large to ever be unfolded? Furthermore, if this story was his, as Alma claimed, why did he recognise just intermittent bits of it?

His perusal of the exhibition thus far had arrived now at another of the concentration-gallery's corners where continuing necessitated a right quarter-turn before commencing his traverse of the day-nursery's east face, a modernistic climbing wall on which his sister's works were untrustworthy handholds standing between mental equilibrium and intellectual freefall from a dizzy height. Touching the void he launched on the next leg of his precarious expedition into culture, with the first protrusion being item nineteen, *Sleepless Swords*. Relatively simple, a line-drawing in what might well have been lithographic crayon, it recalled the *Daily Mirror* editorial cartoons by David Low he just about remembered from his childhood, with stark moral points conveyed in easily deciphered symbols and the robust, unassuming style of a boy's picture weekly. Alma's version, neither topical nor unambiguous, portrayed a dark and saturnine man fast asleep in his four poster bed there at the hectic, bloody centre of a battlefield. From the proliferation of pikes and peaked helmets in the carnage circling the sleeper it appeared to be a conflict from the Civil War, which made the slumbering figure – clad, on close inspection, in black armour rather than pyjamas – very probably Oliver Cromwell. All around him frantic men impaled each other in the musket smoke and horses stumbled in their own intestines, sketched with soot and limned with gunpowder, while through it all the Lord Protector snored and snuggled. Mick was unsure if the scene implied that Cromwell was unconscious to the suffering of which he himself was the epicentre, or if, rather, all of this relentless butchery and these blood fountains were his dream.

Beneath this modestly sized composition, both the scale and stylings of exhibit twenty made it seem a mantelpiece upon which item nineteen merely rested. Much more complex than preceding offerings, the central image in fixed charcoal with bright orange accents was completely overwhelmed by an illustrative trim of Delft tiles, an area of carbon black and spitting flame contained within an ornamental fireplace. The picture at the heart of the arrangement was a landscape of stone chimneys and thatched rooftops, ruggedly evoked in crumbling strokes and all ablaze with licking tongues of nectarine, whereon two burning naked women danced ecstatically, long hair curling above them on the choking updraft. Striking as this pyrotechnic vista was with its restricted palette, it bore no perceptible relation to the seemingly far less incendiary continuity delineated on its tiled surround. Here, in dilutions of rich cobalt, was a linear progression of illuminated moments that commenced at the top centre with a square of solid midnight ink, as if to represent the darkness of the womb before the detailed childbirth of the scene thereafter. This was followed, clearly with an eye to its own cleverness, by a vignette of the now-infant boy sprawled on his mother's lap beside a fireplace that was itself decorated with Delft tiling, chronicling events in the life of a ludicrously tiny Christ. The next depiction showed a sickly youth sat on a church pew between older men in eighteenth-century dress, eyes fixed on a lace handkerchief which hung suspended as if fluttering down from heaven. Tile by tile the illustrated life progressed, with here a mounted young man in a foggy grove confronted by a ragged girl with great luminous eyes, there the same man somewhat older as he led his steed across rough, snowy ground to an inviting hall that waited in the winter dark, its outline hauntingly familiar. After a few moments' furrowed bafflement Mick recognised the edifice as Doddridge Church and realised that the serial drama he was following must be the life of Philip Doddridge. He read on through marriage, children and bereavement to a final view, just to the left of the frame's upper middle, of a fragile man and woman as they lay together in a room with foreign furnishings, both ill, the man perhaps already dead as indicated by the unrelieved blue night of the next tile, its darkness now that of interment rather than conception. Only when he peered at the appended label in red biro which revealed the title of the piece to be *Malignant, Refractory Spirits* did he start to fathom a connection between its account of a dissenting clergyman and the two gleefully incendiary females, pirouetting on parched thatching and only constrained by their elaborate biographic border.

Starting to experience a mild conceptual concussion, Mick migrated a pace further south along the gallery's east wall until he reached exhibit twenty-one. Identified in steadily deteriorating crimson as *The Trees Don't Need to Know*, to his relief this was a single image, once more in a spindly portrait ratio and rendered in acrylics, blacks and whites and a glum rainbow of minutely differentiated greys. Flanked by some of the by now familiar anachronistically attired children, though he noticed that his own infantile semblance was not amongst them, loomed another of his sister's horrors. Terrifying travesties of nature previously inconceivable were, he acknowledged, for some reason something which she'd always been particularly good at since she'd made her reputation one tentacle at a time, adorning all those S.F., fantasy and horror paperbacks during the 1980s. This particular grotesque appeared to be a really horrible variety of sea-serpent, disastrously released into a winding urban river very similar to the Nene, where there was clearly insufficient room for it. Rearing from slow and murky waters into the nocturnal black, atop a wavering neck thick as a water main, an elongated skull like a Gestapo staff-car sprang the bonnet of its upper jaw to bare appalling shipwreck teeth, snapping in bellicose frustration at the jubilant quintet of ruffians who for some reason levitated in the narrow picture's upper reaches, each accompanied by several fainter copies of themselves. The creature's face, with a coiffure of stinking waterweed and snail-flesh eyes that gleamed from sockets deep as wells, was the distorted countenance of an embittered and malign old woman, bellowing her hate and rage and loneliness into the night. It was another wildly inappropriate Enid Blyton illustration, as was item twenty-two just to the right of it.

Titled *Forbidden Worlds* in scrawl that paled to an unpleasant serum pink the further to the right it got, this, like its predecessor, was a study in acrylics with a silent movie colour scheme, albeit this time in landscape proportions. It portrayed a barroom scene as told to Hogarth or Doré by a mid-bender Edgar Allen Poe, a world of screaming abdabs where he was obscurely pleased to find his toddler self had made a reappearance. Still in his plaid dressing gown he cowered with the other small boy from the earlier paintings at the picture's front, behind a massively rotund and gaudy form which, even from the rear, could only be the late, lamented local troubadour Tom Hall. The bar beyond, transparently what the two little lads were sheltering from, was populated by a temperance campaigner's nightmare, an inebriate demonology. To one side a distraught and weeping man apparently made out of boards had deep runes gouged into his arm by the belligerent knife-wielding female holding him, while nearby yet another wooden man writhed half-emerged from the room's floor, trodden back down by jeering hobnailed drunks. The ghastliest of the assembled barflies wore a toothless mouth across his forehead, mucous bubbling up in the inverted nose beneath and dazed eyes blinking from his jowls. A purgatory with an extended license, an eternal lock-in or an hour never ending that was anything save happy: could this really be the way that his teetotal sister thought of public houses, as menageries of horrid cruelty and impossible deformity? Although when he considered the pubs Alma had frequented he conceded that she had a point. He took another short step to his right and almost toppled headlong into the obliterating depths of item twenty-three.

The babble of the room withdrew, was drained away in a retreating surf. Mick stood stock still before the picture like a man paused at the mouth of a wind tunnel and afraid to move. He knew what this was; knew before consulting the identifying label where the pink ink ran out halfway through the second word before resuming in green. This was the Destructor. Seen from overhead, a curving arc down to the lower left was all that told onlookers they were witness to a mercifully incomplete view of a dreadful chimney, limitlessly vast so that no canvas, no imagination, could enclose it. Smouldering impasto streamers of sienna and burnt umber, so thick that they teetered on the brink of sculpture, spiralled out from the industrial crater's rim towards its unseen centre, the immense vaporous masses turning slowly, an annihilating nebula of shit. As dismal as the curling bands of encrustation were, it was in the gouged chasms trapped between these rills where dread resided. Here were ribbons of flat detail, cringing under towering oil-paint tsunamis as they swirled away to off-screen immolation, brown oblivion. Here were sweetshops, schoolyards and Salvation Army trombones sliding inexorably into a hell of nothing, horse-drawn coal carts with their load on fire and dancehall couples plunged, still bunny-hopping, into an asphyxiating midnight. Hopscotched paving slabs and starched white barbers, monkeys and their organ-grinders, drunks and monks amongst the smashed debris at the perimeter of this relentless junkyard singularity in its attempt to drink the world, or at least that part of the world within its economic reach. In the smog-maelstrom people, animals and their splintered environments were circling detritus, unintelligible suds locked into the decaying orbit of a sink-trap abyss. Pram armadas and pools coupons black with optimistic kisses, florid union banners, cinema seats flensed or pissed on, swans and singlets in a rubble waterfall down cancellation's smokestack throat. It was the past; a reservoir of fleeting incident, a mode of living that had been made abject and was now cremated, irrecoverably lost to ash in a bonfire of the humiliations. This, then, was the toilet everything had gone down.

It was too big, too unanswerable. It would require another cigarette, as much for punctuation as anything else, which would mean prising back the lighter from his sister. Turning round to look for her he found himself once more confronted by the scaled down district on its tabletop, an ant farm scraping by on aphid subsidies. This prospect from the east yielded a gambler's fan of miniaturised rooftops, breaking waves of slate descending vanished Silver Street and Bearward Street, emptied into the placid tide-pool of a Mayorhold sleeping off its lunchtime ale through the eternal painted afternoon. A quarter-inch-high Vesper scooter with one wheel off stood in Bullhead Lane propped by a yard-brush, and old men in shirts and braces sat on doorsteps scowling like demoted gargoyles. For all of its manufacturer's uncertainties, Mick was approaching the conclusion that this was the exhibition's most compelling and straightforward artefact, ship-in-a-bottle streets which captured and preserved the near-evaporated neighbourhood more perfectly than all of the oblique surrounding canvases. It certainly evoked the air of psychological serenity, the secret, lazy, golden idyll that had been peculiar to places with no status left to lose. It left him with a feeling that the world he could remember was still safe somewhere, the polar opposite of the sensation inculcated in him by the terrible mephitic vortex he now had his back to. Spotting Alma over in the nursery's northwest corner near the caustic blister painting he was just about to see if he could get his lighter back, perhaps by offering one of his offspring as security, when his glance settled on the strip of paper fastened to the diorama's edge, approximately opposite the similar tag that he'd noticed on the platform's further, western side. Whereas that had *The Boroughs* written on it, which he'd thought to be the model's title, this scrap was marked with the single word *Mansoul*. The odd name rang a distant bell, somewhere in the next diesis of remembrance, but otherwise was unfamiliar. Had Alma been unable to decide between two designations and so hedged her bets? Or had she just forgotten she'd already titled it? He'd have to ask her, if only to demonstrate that he was paying close attention.

By the time he'd inched his way back past the last ten or eleven exhibits to where she stood in conversation with Dave Daniels, he'd decided to combine his mention of the reconstructed barrio's conflicting nomenclature with his crack at getting back the lighter, an unlikely gambit which to his surprise worked like a charm. Far better, even, given that charms never worked at all.

"Look, Warry, there's a sign on one side of your model where it says *The Boroughs*. May I have my lighter back? And on the other side it says *Mansoul*. Perhaps you could explain."

She grinned and said "Of course I can", then handed him the lighter and continued talking to Dave Daniels. Making for the door before she realised what she'd done, Mick was delighted. He felt that he'd reached a new level of understanding in his dealings with his sister: when you forced her to be arsey over two things at the same time, her aggression systems couldn't handle the extended load and would short circuit. If through radioactive accident she should ever become gigantic and embark on a civilisation-threatening rampage, he'd be sure to tell the government and military so that they could bring her down. Still chuckling inappropriately at the thought of his own sister, seventy feet tall and blundering into power cables, he went out triumphant to the bright blue afternoon.

Thumbing the wheel and sparking up he sucked his cigarette's far end to sullen scarlet life, tipping his head back to expel a Chinese chimera of writhing grey towards the Willow Pattern duotone above. After confinement with so many laudanum-infused interpretations of the locale, its reality of peeling window-frame and unkempt verge, no matter how impoverished in brick or memory, sang with a bruised and toothless joy. He breathed the postcode's dandelion-clock atmosphere, the rolled-sleeve license of a spot in forced retirement from geography, the consolations of exclusion in the certain knowledge you were no longer expected to do or be anything. Dust too was a mantle of privilege. Across the way his gaze rolled down the incline of the car-park entrance to where forty years before had stood an alienating Cubist playground and, a decade earlier still, the traffic-free paved entry into justifiably defensive-sounding Fort and Moat streets, under siege by an aggressively forgetful 1960s. That was where his mad great-granddad and his cheerily barbaric Nan had started out, before she'd moved to Green Street after losing her first baby to diphtheria. It would have been down roughly the same passage that the fever-cart had rumbled like bad weather when it called to pick up its slight burden. Sticky strands of his genetic history were still there under several eras' tarmac skims, pink and black liquorice allsorts strata. That was history, a series of ill-judged resurfacings and random superimpositions. Narrowing his eyes against the sun he flattened different layers of time to an incongruous composite, in which reprieved infant mortalities rode a Picasso concrete horse between the pre-loved autos sleeping in their bays.

Behind him he heard the faint emphysemic wheeze of the day nursery's door and turned to note Ben Perrit and Bob Goodman, evidently previously acquainted, simultaneously fleeing the externalised interior of Alma's head. Both men were laughing, probably because the bleary poet had made a cold start from nowhere and the club-faced actor had been unable to keep from joining in. Mick raised a hand in greeting but the gesture fell uncomfortably between the retrospectively racist buffoonery of How! and Hitler's prototype high five, so halfway through he turned it into smoothing back a lock of hair which hadn't been there for some time. Still chortling, the most upsetting children's party double act imaginable made its way across the alopecia turf towards him.

"Alright, Benedict. Alright, Bob. Had enough?"

Ben Perrit's rolled eyes were those of a bolting horse.

"Aha! If that's the kind o' things you see when you stop drinkin', I don't fancy it. Ahahaha!"

His thespian companion's countenance appeared to be attempting to throw itself to the ground from off a stubbly chin, too vexed by human disagreeability to carry on.

"Do you know what she had me do, your fucking sister? She made me go out and dig up all this stuff that she already knew about, just so she'd have a reason to put an insulting picture of me in her show. I tell you, we're as flies to wanton boys where she's concerned."

Nudged out of school for truancy before he'd really got to grips with Shakespeare, Mick was unsure how boys and their flies were relevant to this and merely nodded, as a safety shot. The ambient mania of Ben Perrit, fortunately, flooded in to fill any resultant voids left in the conversation.

"Ahahaha! She's done me in crayon, at the bottom of the sea. I dunno if she's saying that I'm not even washed up, or if she means I'm in the drink. Ahaha! 'Ere, Mick, I was going to give 'er this but never got the chance. Will you see as she gets it?"

The frequently barred bard held out a sheet of folded typescript, which Mick solemnly accepted without having any idea what it represented. Poetry stuff, art stuff, something of that nature.

"'Course I will, Ben. And don't be offended, how she drew you. You ask me, you got off light. You saw that one of me where I was just a bag of pimples?"

The disgruntled actor curled a lip that everyone had thought was curled already, shaking his anti-Semitic cartoon of a head in sympathetic disapproval.

"Why d'you think she does the things she does? Is she just trying to start a fight, or what? She can't be doing it because she needs the money."

Mick considered this, absently staring at the day-care centre's window. He could see the two old ladies that he'd noticed earlier, both standing cackling and nudging one another by the picture with the tiles around it. Dragging his attention back to Alma's motives, he said the first thing that came into his head.

"Perhaps she's hoping for a dame-hood."

Goodman scoffed incredulously.

"What, by doing paintings? Dame-hoods, they're for stage professionals, Dame Judi Dench, Dame Helen Mirren, Dame Diana Rigg. What, so now Alma thinks that she's an actress, does she?"

"Actually, Bob, I think they're for women in the arts? There's Nellie Melba, Edith Sitwell, Vera Lynn; there's Vivienne Westwood, Barry Humphries. It's not just for actresses."

The veteran thug-impersonator, ever the professional, performed the first real double-take that Mick had ever seen and after that stayed silent as if processing this unexpected information. There followed an awkward interlude wherein Ben Perrit asked if Edith Sitwell had invented toast, then laughed uproariously, then said that he'd meant Nellie Melba. It seemed like a natural break, and Mick shook the men by the hand while reassuring Perrit that he'd not forget the folded sheet for Alma. The pair sauntered off past Doddridge Church in the direction of Marefair, the poet laughing and the actor audibly remarking, "Dames! Just when you think you've got 'em figured out ..." before their outlines came to bits in Chalk Lane's poppy camouflage.

Experiencing an upsurge of baffled affection, Mick concluded that the area's nonsense was as vital a component as its love, its drink, its violence. Distant traffic vied with a crow altercation further along Castle Street. Stifling a momentary sense of trespass he unfolded the page that Ben Perrit had entrusted to him, and began to read.

> *This is a kingdom built from absences*
> *The spaces between buildings, empty air*
> *Where different birds sing now*
> *Its landmarks prominent if nothing's there*
> *This is the principality of gone*
> *With boundaries mapped in ink that disappears*
> *A history of gaps*
> *And peopled by names unpronounced for years*
> *This is my page that the blank margins ate*
> *Till only the eraser scars remained*
> *An empty bag of holes*
> *A silence by quotation marks contained*

Mick felt even less qualified in having an opinion with regard to poetry than he did with regard to art, but he quite liked the shape and gait of it, a limping buffalo with one leg shorter than the others and a dignity especial to its stumbles. He refolded the sparse document and slid it into a hip pocket where it wouldn't crumple, then, extinguishing his cigarette, turned once more to the nursery's open door. It was a shame. He might have warmed up more to culture if it didn't act quite so compulsory. Ah, well. There couldn't be a lot more of this maddening exhibition left to see. Sighing resignedly he went inside to face the turpentine-thinned music.

———

This time, re-immersion wasn't such a shock. The atmosphere appeared to be unwinding as the afternoon wound on, the crowd unclenching to become more navigable. As before, he was resolved to pick up from the point where he'd left off, and so retraced his clockwise path around the mirage-cluttered toddler corral. He could have gone the other way, gone widdershins, although that wouldn't have seemed right: you didn't find your place in books by flipping back through from the end, and Mick was already convinced that Alma's barrage of illustrative non-sequiturs was meant to represent some sort of story, perhaps one so big and complicated it required an extra mathematical dimension to narrate it in. Or possibly her magnum opus had gone critical and he was looking here at the ballistic aftermath, at the blast distribution pattern of his sister's weaponised and fissile head. In either case there was a tale being told, if only to the bomb squad analysts. Negotiating speed-date social interactions with a dozen people he'd already greeted, like distant acquaintances repeatedly encountered in successive supermarket aisles, he made his way around the central tableau-laden trestle to a station just beyond exhibit twenty-three, about three-quarters of the way along the pretend gallery's east wall. With the infernal gob of the Destructor drooling sparks and toxic vapour-trails at the peripheries of vision to his left he did his best to concentrate on item twenty-four, the cryptic watercolour abstract that was directly in front of him. Its crank-green marque read *Clouds Unfold*. Perfectly circular, there was a saucer-sized disc of Byzantine hue and ornament placed just off centre in a large quadrangle of off-white stained by parabolas of ghostly dove-grey, strokes and blotches so translucent they were hardly there at all, visually weightless to a point where they could scarcely be called masses. In the corner at the bottom left a scalloped triangle of thin dishwater had collected, while a mackerel feathering of dusty floss intruded from the upper centre. Just beneath this, mounted vertically, was hung a torn-off owl's wing or perhaps a wavering finger-tower of interstellar gas. At intervals, against the trackless ivory expanse there clustered flecks of darker neutrals, microscopic meteor shoals lost in a bleached or colour-reversed cosmos, while around the ball of blue-gold filigree were traced sperm-pale elliptical trajectories that ... oh. It was an eye. It wasn't abstract after all. Filling the area from edge to edge it was a Luis Buñuel close-up of an eye, but not one set in flesh. This was an orbit tooled from Portland stone, with a faint down of graven eyebrow creeping into view above and an abbreviated sweep of cheekbone to the left below. It was the non-functioning optical equipment of a statue and the satellite-ellipses were unblinking lids, those of a witness to catastrophe who could not look away. The barely-visible fanned plumage to the right fell into resolution as the shadow-trap to one side of the nose's bridge, a chiselled bluff that dropped away into the dustbowl socket. Arbitrary specks revealed themselves as texture, a stone epidermis weathered and eroded by two hundred years of rain and airborne grit. And at the picture's focus, in the gilded iris was a medieval planetary orrery picked out by auric threads against nocturnal indigo, the flight of moon or comet plotted with sun-coloured lines, projected through fixed sapphire time. It was the watch movement of a known universe, caught in an opaque and forever awestruck gaze. Mick noticed as an afterthought that the work's basic composition was almost identical to that of the preceding shot, the dying bird's eye view of an incinerator's maw that simmered with particulates. He wondered if this elevating latter piece was placed in close proximity to the distressing former as a kind of ready antidote, the way it often worked out with dock leaves and stinging nettles. Feeling, at least, that the painting had gone some way to restoring his own equilibrium he sidled right into the canton of exhibits twenty-five and twenty-six, hung one above the other in the northeast corner.

Panoramic landscape over lofty portrait, the paired images were in a T-formation though were not apparently connected other than by nearness of location. On the narrow slice of wall between the two a single piece of notepaper was taped. It had dual titles written on it in erratic emerald, with both ascending and descending directional arrows indicating which was which. To say that it looked casual was to understate the point. Rather, it looked like an inscription on the inside of a public toilet door, and Mick hoped Alma could get through the final ten or so descriptive jottings without adding a big cock and its obligatory three crocodile tears of liquid genetics. The slim letterbox proportions of the topmost rectangle of art appeared to contain still a further minimalist abstract, although having just been misdirected by a sculpture's eyeball Mick elected to look closer before he came to a verdict. Following the label's raised green spear back to its point of origin he learned that this piece had been called *A Cold and Frosty Morning*, though the reasoning behind this choice was far from obvious. The picture was a Cinemascope view of mottled fog, a cobweb field that might have been achieved by taking a dark background tone comprised of black and brown and dark viridian and then applying overprinted fibres in a bleached and tangled fuzz, possibly with a sponge. Nose nearer to the cloudy marbling he could make out that the shade visible between the matted strands was actually a hyper-realistic study in acrylics which detailed an undergrowth of intertwining stems and branches, curling leaves reduced to nibbled fractals at their edges, all of this fastidious work concealed by the obscuring steam of down. It struck him that he might be looking at a bush or shrub horrifically enveloped in the spun threads of some huge arachnid, an albino strain if one went by the colour of its fine suspension bridge secretions. Was it one of Alma's monster paintings but without the monster? Only when he noticed a small, pearly slug of pigment raised up a few millimetres from the canvas and connected to the budding twig above it by the slenderest of white lines did he realise that the architect of this fibrous enigma was not some mutated spider but, instead, a minute toothpaste-squeeze of silkworm. Having noticed this unusually industrious individual it was still almost a minute before Mick was made aware that there were dozens, hundreds of the dangling, glinting casts standing out from the surface, an infinitesimal and boneless multitude become a grain, a patterning of wet and glistening corrugations. It was marvellous and, at the same time, made his skin crawl. It encapsulated one of those electrifying moments when nature revealed itself in all its alien and appalling splendour, all its bio-shock. Realising that the foliage barely noticeable under the occluding fluff must be a mulberry bush, he felt a modest pang of crossword-puzzle satisfaction at deciphering at least the title of the work, despite having no clue how it related to the exhibition's overall direction, or indeed to anything.

Stooping a little, hands on knees, he transferred his attention to exhibit twenty-six, immediately beneath. Instantly recognisable as figurative illustration with the straightforward appeal of a classic children's book delineator, perhaps Arthur Rackham, this was more Mick's cup of dormouse tea. Tracing the drooping arrow upward to its source he learned that this one was called *Round the Bend*. In soft and faded pastels, pinks and purples, greens and greys, an outdoor scene was conjured with a wall of towering conifers in the far background, underneath a churning and rain-bloated sky which nonetheless seemed colour-pregnant, immanent with spectra. Unkempt grass rolled undulant between the tree line and a rush-fringed river, slowly winding like some tranquilised constrictor through the bottom of the picture nearest to the viewer. Here, standing with great composure on the bank and almost to her waist in the sharp reeds, was a bird-boned old lady in a cerise cardigan and navy skirt, her lustrous brunette tresses now an ash-slide. Though it clung more tightly to the skull beneath than in her youth, her face still had a loveliness; was wry and clever, luminous with fearless curiosity. Mick noticed that his sister had made a mistake, a stumble with the aquarelle that made it seem as if the woman had crossed eyes, but this did not detract from the hushed, church-like atmospherics of the drawing. There the old girl waited, relatively small down to the picture's lower right, head cocked politely like the listener in a doorstep discourse, a means-tested Alice pensioned to a fallow wonderland. Emerging from near stagnant waters to the left and reaching almost to the picture's upper border, patently the reason for the tall and vertical proportions of the frame, was the deformed river-leviathan from item twenty-one. The stalk of its distended throat surged up and up out from a rippled lace of pond-scum, robed in slime, thick as a redwood with the railway-carriage head precariously mounted at its top end, tilting in a compensatory drift like a cane balancing on someone's palm. Deep in their sockets, whelks lodged in both barrels of a shotgun, the monstrosity's malicious little eyes were fixed enquiringly upon its human interlocutor. Unnoticed in the earlier representation, Mick could now determine that the thing had hands, or fins, or something: splayed and spidery dactyls with discoloured webbing stretched between them, predatory umbrellas raised in front of the freshwater basilisk and gesturing as though in trivial conversation. Tugboat-grinding jaws hung open in mid anecdote and there appeared to be the rusted carcass of a child's perambulator, snagged on a three-foot bicuspid by its handle, in amongst the dripping pelt of waterweed. The carefully pencilled depiction, blotted here and there by artfully positioned teardrop-damage, floating bubble-globes in which the soluble crayon details bled like spectrographs, glowed with an ambience that was hauntingly familiar and which Mick eventually identified from his few Alma-instigated juvenile experiments with L.S.D. The tingling lysergic apprehension of a morning world about to start, beaded with Eden, was as he remembered. So was the exciting and uncomfortable sensation that this was the opalescent anteroom of madness, granting access only to whispering corridors, sedative monologues and a cumulative estrangement from the ordinary, the familiar, and the dear. The still, prismatic scene insinuated that unearthly worlds and inconceivable experience might lie behind more faces in the crowd than were suspected, and that the agreed-on family-friendly Milton Keynes of mass contemporary reality may not be privileged. The frozen moment was a violet-tinted window on the overgrown margins of being, the outlying wilderness of phantoms and hallucinations that encroached, a mind or two more every day, on reason's street-grid.

Having reached the east side of the nursery's southerly extreme, Mick found another ninety degree swivel was required before he could continue. At his back the multitrack surround-sound of distinct and differentiated voices mixed down to one single unseen individual possessed by a demonic legion, a slurred chorus of phased glossolalia swirling in and out of audibility behind him as though on a shifting wind. He was beginning to find Alma's show disorienting, a relentless fusillade of rarefied and unfamiliar feelings, an unhinging blown-fuse opposite of sensory deprivation tanks more like a psychiatric particle collider, his opinions and reactions decay products of aesthetic atom-smashing. Bracing himself, fearful of some new strain of highbrow malaria, he embarked on the penultimate walkabout stretch of his brain safari by examining the paired works furthest to his left of the south wall. Landscape-proportioned pieces big as family-sized cereal boxes and once more hung one above the other, twenty-seven over twenty-eight, while these were perhaps less imposing than the efforts that had come before, they were certainly no less enigmatic.

Item twenty-seven, labelled *Burning Gold* by its green scribbled afterthought, was not a new idea – Mick thought he could remember Alma telling him of an American named Boggs that she admired who'd first done something very similar – although the details of its execution were markedly different. A ridiculously enlarged (or perhaps inflated) reproduction of a banknote, straddling the fine-to-non-existent line dividing art from forgery and rendered in authentic-looking pen and ink, it seemed to be accumulating more absurdist details as he studied it. It was a twenty, with a copyright line at the bottom stating this year, 2006, to be its date of issue. Details of typography and serial numbers were identical to standard currency, as was the colouration and the general composition of the counterfeit's elaborate illustration. Certain elements of content, though, had been transposed or altered. To the note's left, as on normal money, a vaguely amphibious-looking Adam Smith faced right in profile, wrought from mauve engraving with a face of gentian dust, a topcoat and peruke of thumbprint whorls. The capitalist visionary, however, now found himself in a staring contest with a matching profile over on the right, where a comparably meticulous lavender bust of Alma's pop-terrorist K-Foundation mate Bill Drummond had been added. Simultaneously serious and satirical, the Corby-reared Scot's resolute gaze drilled into the architect of boom and bust's bland salamander stare of self-assurance. There was clearly no hope of negotiation. In the centre-ground between the men, the customary diagram detailing eighteenth-century pin manufacture had been skilfully replaced by a rendition of what Mick knew from his sister's testimony to be Drummond's celebrated burning of a million quid up on the remote Hebridean isle of Jura, where George Orwell went to finish *1984*. Against a sphere of Spirograph complexity and finely hatched in tones that strayed from sepia to strawberry were four men in a ruined cottage. Three of them – Drummond himself, his K-Foundation partner Jimmy Cauty and their witness, the TV producer Jim Reid – shovelled crisp fifty-pound notes into a central conflagration, while the fourth, ex-army cinematic auteur Gimpo, captured the resultant cash-to-ashes alchemy on film. Superimposed in purple lettering above where it said "Bank of England" was the altered legend: "The division of opinion in slave manufacturing: (and the great decrease in the quantity of slaves that results)."

Moving on to item twenty-eight, just underneath, Mick thought that the idea of slavery might well be what connected the two juxtaposed exhibits to each other. With a title-note that read *The Rafters and the Beams*, the lower work was a brightly-embellished reproduction of an eighteenth-century sea-chart that had three-dimensional inclusions. Hanging slack across the canvas, linking the west coast of Africa to Britain and America, were heavy lengths of dirty and encrusted iron chain attached by rusted fastenings to the picture's surface. He looked carefully for hidden ironies or meanings, perhaps subtleties concealed within the map's antique background calligraphy, but there was nothing. The mixed-media piece's statement was apparently as stark and simple as it seemed on first sight. The tea-stained cartography with its quaint flukes of spelling and its guesswork coastlines was a Western view of history, the map and not the territory, a construct that was never real except on paper, which would be revised, forgotten, superseded, lost, a mind-set that would crumble and disperse more quickly than the parchment it was written on. The chains, though, they were real. Chains of event that could not be undone, they would endure forever and have solid consequence long after all the plans and paperwork and trade routes that had forged them had been rendered obsolete; long after every other element in this specific image had returned to mulch and dust.

The next inclusion, twenty-nine, was hung alone and mostly executed as a choppy sea of riotous gouache. It had all the roughneck jostle of the music halls that Mick had seen, as recreated by the nineteenth-century English moderns. In the false night of a matinee, the viewer looked up from amongst a cheap-seat audience of jeering drunks towards the stage, the painting's focal area, contained within the second frame of a theatrical proscenium arch. Against a threadbare backcloth with a crudely-handled copy of the front of All Saints Church smeared on it, funny-looking actors postured on a plat-form between balsa pillars or sat huddled on the short flight of broad wooden steps knocked up in front of this, painted to look like stone. The seated couple on the foreground stairs, an angry woman and a man clad in a garish yel-low plaid, possessed a seaside Punch and Judy air in their exaggerated spou-sal animosity, squatting at opposite extremes of the same cone of spotlight. On the raised-up boards behind them, seemingly unnoticed, several figures dressed in period costumes that were all a uniform chalk white but other-wise historically mismatched struck attitudes of indignation or surprise with over-emphasised expressions on their floured-up features. Was this meant to be a supernatural tragedy, a Macbeth or a Hamlet with too many ghosts? Meanwhile, close to the onlooker, a herd of lewd and catcalling spectators looked on in ribald amusement, rage, or lechery. There was a messy proletar-ian energy that could get out of hand in the daubed light and beery gloom. The picture's hurried green appendage, with its sticky tape detaching at one corner and a consequent diagonal tilt making it even more difficult to fathom, read, unhelpfully, *The Steps of All Saints*. Mick was unsure what to make of it. The seated pair, dressed for the 1940s, did not look that different from the rough-and-ready crowd that heckled them. Their anguish and discomfort, then, seemed somehow both contemporary and more real, rather than merely acted. If that were the case, though, the pretended spectres strutting and ges-ticulating from behind them bordered on the inappropriately comical. The picture was disturbing in its weirdness and its incongruity, the sense of something very personal between the duo on the steps that had become a melo-drama, a performance, exposed to the disapproval of a ticket-buying public, squirming in the limelight and mocked even by the special-effect spooks. It was a private moment in the open air that had been brought inside, into a rowdy auditorium to entertain an undiscriminating mob, displacement as unsettling as an indoor crow. Making a show of themselves, was that what the piece was saying?

Still turning the painting over in his forebrain, gingerly like a grenade or hedgehog, Mick moved on towards exhibit thirty. As he did so it occurred to him that, from above, he and his fellow gallery-goers must resemble tokens as they inched around the oblong room's edge to avoid the table in its centre, pieces on an outsized board game of the kind that had tiled his insomnia of the previous night. He glanced around the room, attempting to determine which amongst the other patrons was the Scotty dog and which was the top hat. Over in the far corner, near the frightful shot of Mick's scoured features, Alma was apparently receiving some kind of a telling-off from Lucy and Melinda, very possibly about the cruel and yet ingenious portrait they were standing next to. Good. It was no more than she deserved. The captive popu-lation of the nursery had thinned a little in the hour, hour-and-a-half since the doors opened, although not enough to make his progress on the maddening Monopoly path any easier. By the wedged-open door Bert Regan looked to be wiping the floor with both Ted Tripp and Roman Thompson in a raucous laughter match, a less cerebral version of thrashing two chess opponents at the same time. Elsewhere Rome's boyfriend Dean stood with Dave Daniels, looking at the brawling giants as they laid about them with their ore-splashed snooker cues. Dogs were arguing offstage, out in the Saturday-slumped Bor-oughs. Shifting his attentions back to item thirty, he moved to the next square of the circuit to receive his forfeit or establish a hotel. He didn't pass Go or collect two hundred pounds.

The thirtieth work, in landscape aspect and enclosed by a slim silver frame, a glassy watercolour on smooth-surfaced white board, was called *Eating Flowers*. More than any other single piece it harkened back to Alma's earliest employment as a science fiction cover-illustrator and was in its way breathtaking, if you liked that kind of thing. The setting, a colossal arcade that appeared to be the one from exhibit thirteen although in an advanced state of dilapidation, had tropical vegetation growing through its mossy flooring, this domestic jungle reaching for a collapsed ceiling open to unprecedented constellations, at once an interior and exterior view. Mile-long lianas, twined into electrical flex, trailed from what corroded spars remained of the remote and devastated roofing, chromed by unfamiliar stars. Moths of prodigious size flapped damply through the astral twilight, warping planks caught fire with orchids and this terminal Elysium was only backdrop for the startling apparition thundering across the lower foreground. His physique spare as an anatomic diagram, his skin with the translucency of greaseproof paper, an old man without a stitch on and hair foam-white like a cresting wave raced down the overgrown parade in pounding Muybridge strides. Eyes bulging with the strain of his velocity, his cheeks distended, brilliant petals spilled from his crammed mouth to stream away behind him in a tulip contrail. On the sprightly ancient's shoulders, riding him, a luminously perfect baby girl was saddled, molten blonde curls smearing to a comet's bridal train as she and her feverish steed traversed that final forest. Their extremes of age made allegorical interpretations unavoidable, a freshly born world carried on the back of its exhausted predecessor or the old year and the new both late for an appointment with an as yet unforeseen millennium. It was some sort of race, perhaps the human one, projected through the fourth dimension, through the continent-colliding and empire-erasing medium of time. It looked like an unbearable amount of sweat and effort, this compulsory and rushed migration for the porous borders of a foreign future where nobody spoke the language. While it may well have been Mick's own art-fatigue which coloured the perception, he thought that the old boy and the species that he represented looked like they were dying for a good sit down. He was himself about to hasten that eventuality by hurrying to the next presentation in the sequence, when a voice beside him asked "'Ere, ent you Alma's brother?"

From Mick's right, standing in front of item thirty-one with something in the quizzical tilt to her dust-grey hairdo reminiscent of a wading bird, Bert Regan's mum looked at him sideways. He found himself liking her immediately based solely on the gristle harp twang of her accent and the way she held her handbag like a skating-judge's score. She'd had him from the first dropped aspirant.

"That's right. I'm Mick. I know who you are. I was talking to your pride and joy a little while ago, so that's where I got all the details from."

She pulled a face.

"Me pride un joy? That's me best crockery. What did you wanner talk tuh that for?"

Mick's laugh came from somewhere deeper in his stomach than his laughter generally issued, from a microscopic Boroughs in his biome where the intestinal fauna transposed vowels and had an inconsistent policy on consonants. His instantly familiar new acquaintance joined in with her own accordion burst of kippered cackle, shooting a long-suffering glance towards her tattooed and guffawing ginger offspring as he bantered by the nursery door with Tripp and Thompson, a reunion with former shipmates from a pirate decade that had gone down with all hands some time before.

"Ooh, 'im. Well, take no notice o' what 'e sez. Iz arf sharp, or else iz up ter summat. 'Ere, but what abayt yer sister, all these pictures? She's not right, your Alma, is she? I see that big one she'd done o' you, made ayt o' pimples. And that's yer own sister what's done that, not someone what don't like yer. Shockin'. No, a lot of what she does, well, it's a marvel, ennit? Just not very flatterin'."

He was enchanted by her, thin and grey and local like the twist of smoke curled from a chimney's sunset brickwork, charmed by her affectionately raucous corvid squawk so much like Doreen's, full of coal and comedy. She'd been a looker, you could tell, and not so many years before.

He found himself obscurely wishing that he could have known her then. Perhaps he had, or had at least caught sight of her when she was younger, something to account for the extreme sense of familiarity that he was currently experiencing, based on more than her iconic status as a Boroughs woman, he felt sure.

"No. Flattery is one of the few things you can't accuse her of. Here, that's a Boroughs accent you've got, ain't it? Did you used to live round here? I'm sure I've seen you somewhere."

She allowed her jaw to sag until her lips were pursed reproachfully, regarding him from under lids half lowered as if he were intellectually unworthy of whole eyeballs. It was the expression which his mum had used so often when addressing him or Alma that he had to forcibly remind himself she didn't always look like that. Bert's mother tutted, more in pity than contempt.

"Well, 'course I'm frum the Burrers. Did yer think that I wuz frum the moon, yer gret soft ayputh? We lived up the top o' Spring Lane, so I never got the slipper bein' late fer school."

When was the last time he'd been called a great soft ha'p'orth? A halfpennyworth. He basked in the obscure abuse. It harkened back to a more civilised age where the harshest epithet was a comparison with recalled currency. Launched on a reminiscent torrent by the mention of her childhood home she carried on regardless.

"Ooh, it were a lovely place, the Burrers. That one o' Spring Lane your Alma done, all ayt o' glass, I think that one's me fayvrit. An' yuv got no cause for complaint, 'ow she's done you. Not after the way she's done me. No, a lovely place. Ayr dad lived down there, in Monk's Pond Street, after we'd moved up tuh Kingsley. I remember when ayr William wuz only just walkin', 'ow I'd take 'im dayn there, so as 'e could see where I'd bin brung up."

Mick found himself stumbling in his attempt to follow her account. He thought she'd said there was a likeness of her somewhere in the exhibition, and had been upon the point of asking her about it when she'd thrown him with her mention of an unfamiliar name. His forehead corrugated.

"William ...?"

Appling her cheeks she shook her head, correcting herself.

"Do you know, I never can remember, you lot, yer dunt call 'im that. Bert, what you call him. 'E once 'ad a teacher call 'im that at school, an' 'e got stuck with it. Round ayrs, 'e's Bill or William."

Oh. Right. Yeah. Yeah, he remembered Alma saying something now, something to that effect: a football match at school; a teacher with a momentary lapse of memory who'd shouted the first working-class name he could think of and doomed William to a life of Bert. And there was something else about that story, wasn't there? Some complementary detail to the anecdote that for a moment now found scrabbling purchase on the waste pipe of Mick's memory. Something about ... Bert, Bill, something about ... no. No, it was gone, dislodged to fall away into the cancelled black of the forgotten, irretrievable. He was about to ask Bert's mum, his newfound poster-girl for fortitude in deprivation, if she could recall his lost component of the tale, but at that moment their delightful conversation was truncated by the unselfconscious bellow of her son, acoustically equivalent to a wild pig loose at a wedding.

"Come on, Phyllis, 'e's a married man, and yer not on Boot's Corner now. Let's get you 'ome, before yer show us up." Bert's luncheon-meat complexioned features split into a gap-toothed laugh, lecherous and suggestive even if discussing double glazing, a Sid James cascade of gurgling innuendo without object. His mother's head wheeled like an antique Spitfire, nippy and surprisingly manoeuvrable, eyes looking bullets up and down her offspring's fuselage.

"Me show you up? Yuh've bin embarrassin' me ever since I 'ad yer. Since yer first drew breath yuh've saynded like a busted lav, and yer that ugly that they 'ad a job to tell yer frum the afterbirth. We'd got it 'ome and christened it before we realised. Show us up? I'll gi' you show us up, yer dibby bugger ..."

Turning back to Mick she cut off fire from her machine-gums, offering him a radiant and endearing National Health smile.

"I'm gotter goo, it saynds like. It's bin lovely meetin' yer. I 'ope tuh see yer agen sometime."

And with that she banked away into a sparking, chattering dive, closing the distance between her and her doomed but still chortling quarry, rubicund with giggles, a Red Baron.

"You wait till I get my 'ands on you, yer useless load o' rubbish. Don't think you're too big for me to dash yer brains in with a brick while yer asleep!"

A whirling dust-storm of ferocious energy and neutral tones she rushed out through the open nursery door past the respectful cower of Roman Thompson and Ted Tripp, ball lightning following a draft, driving her errant son before her out into the disappearing neighbourhood. Mick shook his head in wondering admiration at this sighting of a genus thought extinct, this social-housing coelacanth. Watching her go, he found himself awash in poignancy from out of nowhere, ludicrously inappropriate for someone that he'd only managed a three-minute conversation with. It had felt more like meeting with a crush from junior school, that meaningless vestigial flutter of the heart, the sweet and pointless sadness for alternate universes that would never happen.

Mystified not for the first time by his own internal workings, he returned his commandeered attentions to the task of getting through the five remaining pictures in his sister's gauntlet of enigmas. Picking up where he had so engagingly left off, he occupied the space vacated by Bert Regan's mum – Phyllis, he thought that was what Bert had called her – just in front of item thirty-one. *Cornered*, apparently, according to its dangling viridian afterthought. A gouache work, it occupied a canvas roughly two foot square and seemed in many ways to be a partner to exhibit four, *Rough Sleepers*, even down to their almost symmetrical positions close to either end of the long sequence. Both works were contemporary pub scenes and achieved their major visual effect by juxtaposing grimy monochrome with colour, though whereas the earlier piece contained one area of black and white amidst a field of riotous hue, the painting he was gazing at effected the exact reverse. An overhead view looking down upon a crowded front bar that Mick didn't recognise, down in the bottom left a solitary figure had been rendered in bright naturalistic shades, a tubby little man with curly white hair seated at a corner table, while the beery mob that filled the scene around him, wall to wall and edge to edge, were executed in a palette of charred fag-end and urinal porcelain, fingernail greys. The colourless inebriate jostle, cheery even in their drabness, nonetheless seemed drained of life and of contemporaneity as though they were the happy dead, the Woodbine wraiths of a persisting past. The figure at the bottom corner in his modern tints and fabrics seemed excluded by the heaving press of ghosts, if they weren't all entirely in his mind; if this were not a picture of a haunted man, sat in an empty bar, surrounded by a magic lantern pageant of the disappeared. If that were so, then the whole throng became a thick, guilty miasma somehow emanating from the single flesh-toned individual at his table, cornered by a horde of zombie social issues, by the past, by memory.

He inched a little further to his right, progressing westward in excruciating increments, a wagon-train with palomino snails in harness or a one man continental drift. This brought him up against the nursery's west wall at its most southerly extreme. Just half of one side of the building to complete and then he could with honour make good his escape into a comfortingly artless world. Exhibit thirty-two, apparently entitled *The Rood in the Wall*, was similar in its proportions to the previous piece and proved to be the image which had prompted the irate departure of Bob Goodman earlier, or at least that was Mick's assumption. Though the great majority of painters mentioned by his sister were obscure to him, he had at least across the years achieved familiarity at second hand with the peculiar work of William Blake, and recognised the piece before him as a kind of composite, a modified amalgam of the Lambeth visionary's cryptic images. Predominating blackness, conjuring a subterranean and funereal ambience, was punctuated in the watercolour's upper reaches by illuminated alcoves in which labelled likenesses presided like memorial statuary in a mausoleum. Leaning closer, he perused the names on tattered paper scrolls like Gilray dialogue-balloons: James Hervey, Philip Doddridge, Horace Walpole, Mary Shelley, William Blake and a few others, sombre and reflective, candlelit with colour in the cemetery dark. Their pious, downcast glances seemed to be directed, more in pity than contempt, towards the crouching, naked giant at the bottom of the painting, crawling wretched on his hands and knees along a stunted, lightless tunnel, bowed head weighted by a heavy golden crown. Mick recognised the figure, although only through the agency of an Atomic Rooster album cover he remembered, as Blake's penitent Nebuchadnezzar. The damnation-shadowed features of the fallen Babylonian regent were herein replaced, however, by the asymmetric physiognomy of his sister's much put-on actor friend, whom Alma seemed to employ as a stress-relieving executive squeeze-ball, a receptacle for her interminable gusher of abuse if Mick himself were poorly or on holiday. The only other element of the arrangement, something he did not specifically recall from Blake, was the rough-chiselled cross set into crumbling stonework at the painting's centre, just above the grovelling monster but beneath the sympathetic audience of Gothic saints above. It didn't seem to have that much to do with his own brief encounter with infant mortality, or even with the Boroughs, but then you could say that about the majority of the supposed works of art included in the heavily confined yet sprawling exhibition.

Feeling like an athlete superstitious about looking at the finishing line until they were right on top of it, he essayed an inexpert version of the military right-turn he'd learned at Boy's Brigade and saw to his immense relief that there were only three more decorative hurdles between him and the propped-open doorway, between him and freedom. Better still, the first of these, which he was currently confronted by, was small and simple. On an insubstantial sheet of what looked very much like typing paper, tin-tacked to the nursery wall as if it were the work of a precocious child on parents' day, there was a fluid and expressive pencil drawing with a wandering line as natural as April weeds. Not even bothering on this occasion to attach a separate label, Alma had just scrawled *The Jolly Smokers* at the top left corner of the piece itself, in chlorophyll. The drawing was a spindly and fragile detail of St. Peter's Church, the front porch of the disused building with its honeyed stone and the black wooden ribcage of its roof, a strand of wheatgrass straggling from between the slabs outside its open entrance. In the shadowed recess a recumbent figure slumbered, trainer-soles towards the viewer and all other indicators of the person's body-type, age, gender or ethnicity concealed beneath the slippery tucks and undulations of the unzipped sleeping-bag spread over them. Silvery graphite traceries uncoiled and trickled lovingly across the quilted contours, the implied form motionless beneath, digressing to investigate the intricate topography of each plump fold. The more Mick studied the deceptively spare composition, the more he found himself questioning his first assumption that this was a study of a homeless person, merely sleeping. With the bag pulled up and covering the face there was a mortuary aspect to the imagery which could not be ignored. In its veiled stillness, that of dream or of demise, the slumping shape inhabited a hesitating and ambiguous borderland between those states, much like the one suggested by that physicist who'd either gassed his cat or hadn't. Mick could come to no conclusion other than an observation that, in disagreement with its title, the depicted scene was far from jolly and appeared to be non-smoking.

Moving northwards once more he progressed to the next picture, which he realised with a leaping heart was the penultimate exhibit. A square work in oils as spacious and resplendent as its predecessor had been meagre and without assumption, the attendant taped-on tag revealed its title as *Go See Now This Cursed Woman*. What at first appeared to be a maddeningly regular and even geometric abstract, the imagining of Milton Keynes by a despairing Mondrian, resolved on close inspection to an intricately-realised reproduction of a game-board, a generic layout on the Snakes-and-Ladders model of a lavishly embellished grid, each box emblazoned with a decorated number or iconographic miniature. He realised with a minor start that the game's focus seemed to be the mink misfortunes of Diana Spencer, the familiar tabloid Stations of the Cross – sun through a thin skirt showing off her legs; posed at the gate with Charles; a coy glance up at Martin Bashir or her final public smile before the rear doors of the Paris Ritz – reduced to outsized postage stamps. The game-board layout, with its numbered spaces, loaned these incidental moments the uneasy sense of a relentless, hurtling linear progression to a predetermined outcome: an arrival at that final square, sooner or later, irrespective of the falling die, an outcome obvious from the commence of play or, indeed, from the opening of the cellophane-sealed box on Christmas morning. What had startled Mick was the unlikely coupling of board games and Diana Spencer, just as in his sleepless ruminations of the night before. It was quite clearly no more than coincidence and, now he thought about it, not particularly memorable at that. The idea of the blonde from Althorp's life as a bizarre and fatalistic form of Cluedo was not that much of a reach, all things considered. Still, it had him going for a moment there.

Stealthily, he began to move toward the final lurid obstacle that stood between him and the gaping nursery door. Internally, he played a game where he and all the other gallery-goers were a surly crowd of culture-convicts, shuffling around the exercise yard, wondering if wives and sweethearts would still be there waiting for them on the outside after all this time. Unnoticed, hopefully, by the imaginary machine-gun towers that he'd by then positioned at the corners of the room, he inched towards the unlocked prison gate and genuinely gasped to feel the warder's heavy hand fall on his shoulder from behind.

"Here, Warry? Have you got the lighter?"

Mick turned to face the dipped glare of his big sister's headlight gaze, that of a sulky and uninterested basilisk who couldn't be arsed turning people into anything except stone cladding. Alma seemed preoccupied and, worryingly, too distracted to insult him. Even in her mention of "the" lighter she appeared to have reclassified it as their mutual property and not an object that belonged to her alone, which in itself seemed to suggest a softening of policy. Was Alma ill? He fished inside a pocket of his jeans for the requested artefact. Handing it over, he felt duty-bound to ask.

"Warry? Is everything okay? You don't seem quite your usual self. You're being reasonable."

Taking the lighter from him without any kind of thank you, which at least was more her style, his sister shook her hanging-garden head in the direction of the table-mounted model of the Boroughs, like one of the district's rodents in that, famously, you never got more than six feet away from it.

"It's this. It's still not right. It isn't saying what I want it to. It's saying 'Ooh, look at the Boroughs. Wasn't it a lovely place, with all that history and character?' All of the local photo-books I based it on are saying that already, aren't they? This needs something else. Cheers for the lighter, anyway. I'll bring it back soon as I'm done with it."

Once more, there was that weird politeness and consideration. Alma drifted off, presumably to elevate her mood and smoke her way towards a resolution of her quandary. Drawing a deep breath in anticipation Mick turned his attentions to exhibit thirty-five, the show's final inclusion, dubbed by its torn-paper tag as *Chain of Office*. Portrait aspect, once again in gouache, a full-length appraisal of a single figure on a ground of marvellous cascading green – the picture's bare facts crowded in to fill Mick's field of vision and prevented him from viewing its totality. Alone, the single-colour backcloth with its seethe of nettle, lime and peridot was overwhelming, an experiential bouillon taste of knee-high fairground, fumbling adolescent meadow, boneyard moss. The painting's subject, standing with both arms raised in greeting or benediction, had a mayoral air in part bestowed by the work's title and in part by the eponymous medallion hung about their neck. On close inspection this gunmetal gong appeared to be a saucepan lid, with its supporting chain having seen previous service dangling from the cistern of a lavatory. The multitude of references in the pieces thus far, whizzing past above Mick's head, had made him feel like he was being strafed by Melvyn Bragg but this, at last, was one he caught; was one he recognised. The dented lid, he knew, was an allusion to the bygone Boroughs custom of appointing some disreputable individual as the neighbourhood's own mayor, a pointed satire staged there on the Mayorhold at the site of the Gilhalda, the original town hall, to mock the processes of government from which Northampton's earliest population was by then excluded. The self-deprecating nature of the tin-pot talisman itself was undercut, however, by the sumptuous robes in which that central form was draped, more gloriously decorated than those worn by any real-world civic dignitary. Around the hem there ran a border of meticulously rendered paving slabs, greying and cracked with jade grass in the seams, while up around the collar ...

It was him.

The person in the painting, it was Mick. It had Mick's face, perfectly captured even down to the smeared glaze of highlight up by his receded hairline, although after a few moments' scrutiny it came to him that this ingenious verisimilitude was actually occasioned by the paint still being wet. The likeness, even so, was unmistakeable and, truth be told, atypically flattering. From the sincere blue eyes to the engaging smile Alma had made him look quite handsome, at least in comparison with all his earlier appearances throughout this showing, whether as a simpering toddler or as a burns ward admission with his features more eroded than the sphinx. If he'd known sooner that the entire exhibition would be leading up to this, he wouldn't have been half so grumpy or ill-humoured in his earlier appraisals. Now, though, he felt guilty and uncomfortable, which almost certainly was the effect his sister had been hoping for, if he knew Alma. Otherwise she would have said something when she waltzed up to pinch his lighter a few minutes back, with him stood right here by the painting which mythologized him, which absolved her of all her foregoing cruelties. Since he was standing facing the west wall of the day nursery, the only one with windows, he looked up from *Chain of Office* and out through the smeared glass for a sighting of her, pacing, puffing, wearing even more tracks through the patchy turf outside, but she was nowhere to be seen. His first thought was that she'd been so distressed about whatever she believed was wrong with her miniature Boroughs that she'd had a breakdown and absconded: a faked death, a changed appearance, a disguising limp, a ticket to another town. No one would ever again meet with Alma Warren, the failed model-maker. While he was almost entirely certain this was what had happened, he felt that he should at least take a quick shufty at the gallery behind his back before he bothered to alert the media.

His sister, it turned out, hadn't even made it as far as the nursery door before being waylaid by her adoring or deploring public. She was further off from it, in fact, than Mick himself, leaning against the table's further, eastern side and glowering at her handiwork like a displeased Jehovah, albeit one who'd swapped his beard for lipstick, though each to their own, of course, and nothing wrong with that. More disconcertingly, she was flanked by the two elderly ladies Mick had noticed earlier and who'd been slipping in and out of view throughout the afternoon. One stood to either side of Alma as she loomed over the papier-mâché district, hunching like a monstrous slagheap with more slag to it than usual, ready to engulf the shrunken Boroughs in a devastating avalanche of turquoise fluff and bitterness. The old girls, spider-webbed with wrinkles and their exposed flesh the mud of a dried reservoir, seemed to be taking turns to stoop and mutter their opinions into alternating ears of the preoccupied and frowning artist, though Mick doubted that the advice of whichever woman was engaging Alma's deaf side would be implemented. With her wrecker's-lantern eyes fixed irremovably on the diminished alleys of her reconstructed world his sister didn't look at either of the women while they spoke to her, encouragingly by the look of things, but would acknowledge their remarks with grave nods of the head. Incredibly, it seemed that not only was Alma for once listening to somebody's opinion of her work, but that she also appeared to agree with them. The two were evidently loving every minute of their audience with the subdued and uncharacteristically compliant artisan. From deep within their creased papyrus sockets their eyes gleamed and sparked, hobnails on cobbles, as their wizened heads dipped one after the other to their whispering, well-mannered vultures pecking at Prometheus's liver. Though what they were saying to his sibling was impossible to hear above the hubbub of the gallery, Mick thought it looked as though they were administering an excited pep-talk, urging Alma to stick with her vision and to take it further, carrying it onwards. Something like that, anyway. The biddies pointed jabbing crab-leg fingers at the model on the table, with the one on Alma's deaf right side repetitively mouthing something that looked like "keep on" or "go on", something with two syllables like that. And Alma nodded as if she were heeding counsel that was irrefutable, taking career instruction from two dotty-looking termagants who ninety minutes previously she hadn't known existed. Still no closer to an understanding of his sister than he'd been, aged seven, when she'd shot him with that blowpipe, Mick turned back to *Chain of Office* to continue his inspection.

Having now recovered from the shock of realising that he was this ultimate exhibit's subject, he was able to take in the painting's other content, notably the splendid robe in which his sister had seen fit to deck her central figure. Hanging folds of heavy velvet were embroidered with exquisite threads

of gold, a gilded crazing that resolved at a few inches from the picture's surface into a meandering treasure-map of the terrain that Mick was born from.
It was one of those charts that had three-dimensional bits bulging out from
it, of which he was always unable to recall the name. He could see overhead
delineations of St. Andrew's Road and Freeschool Street, Spring Lane and
Scarletwell as plunging pleats in parallel and Doddridge Church a decoration
on the bias, burial ground compressing as it gathered to the pinch-points. It
occurred to him that in the raised-up buildings and projections of a vanishing cartography, a bit like Alma's problematic Boroughs diorama, she'd contrived this last piece to reprise all of the exhibition's other works in small. He
eyed the piece, squinted the gaud, and saw that his ennobled likeness sported
tiny glued-on snail shells as links, one mottled spiral badging either cuff. He
was absorbed in these calciferous adornments, trying to establish if they still
housed mollusc occupants, when he heard the distinct Pacific cadences of
Alma's pal Melinda Gebbie raised above the background susurrus, and everything kicked off.

"Alma, you fucking asshole, don't you fucking dare!"

Mick turned, from only idle curiosity, and found himself confronted by
the single image from this viewing that he'd take away with him, the solitary tableau that was genuinely unforgettable. His sister, with a blankness of
expression that was either innocent or guilty to a point past caring, saint or
serial murderer, leaned forward over Marefair and Saint Mary's Street, reaching past Castle Street and across Peter's House to Bath Street. The old ladies
huddling behind her hugged each other and performed a clumsy, hopping little dance. Lucy Lisowiec's enormous eyes prepared to fire themselves across
the room, accompanying her rising siren wail.

"Almaaaaaaaa!"

Pressing a wavering tongue of blue and yellow from the flint-wheel of
Mick's lighter, Alma let it taste the simulated birdshit caked around the rim of
her scaled-down Destructor. More-ish, evidently. Dribbling incendiary frills
of indigo poured down the lampblacked chimney tower to its base with startling rapidity, sending up acrid and authentic billows of particulate towards
the ceiling-mounted sensors as they did so. It all burned so fast, being constructed wholly from materials designed to do just that, and in his sister's
dawning look of apprehension it appeared that even she was unprepared for
the appalling pace of the toy-town calamity she'd just unleashed.

A spreading gorse of conflagration engulfed Bristol Street and its envi-
rons, with the bijoux fever-cart and centimetre-high mare towing it into the
mouth of Fort Street parched to curling smuts and gone upon the instant.
Arson reflux scorched the narrow gullet of Chalk Lane and spewed annihilating riot-bile down Marefair, the anachronistic witch-hat turret on Black

Lion Hill shrivelling unrepentant at the stake and twisted round with shifting scarves of gold. Infernal tributaries sluiced from long-gone Bearward Street to flood the Mayorhold with combusting vapour, tromp l'oeil sweetshop windows disappearing into light before the flickering translucence climbed the razor-cut of Bullhead Lane to Sheep Street, where ignition moved like scrapie through the paper flock. Hot orange devils swarmed on the crusader church, unravelling its steeple into sparks and levelling the thick-walled round down to a howling mouth red as a branding-iron, a blazing torus, pinkie ring of an apocalyptic angel. Mercy, bright and cauterising, stroked the wounded neighbourhood. In Marefair, Cromwell's bunk at Hazelrigg House was made immolate among the millenarian tinder, shaved skulls you could strike a match on, cavalier plumes smouldering on pinpricked cornices. From the charred stump of Bath Street's smokestack, searing ripples spread through the flea-circus district in dilating sapphire hoops, as from a shooting star fallen into a petrol pond. Incineration danced on Broad Street and Bellbarn, flash-vanishing Salvation Army forts and suffering no barber's pole that it remain unlit. The Rizla laundry flapped like phoenix wings in Greyfriars' central courtyard, damp with drizzled flames, while all along the crisping terraces six dozen public houses called last orders and submitted to a harsher temperance. Saint Elmo flirted with the upper reaches of Saint Katherine's high-rise, jumped between laboriously fashioned television aerials on Mary's Street in a peaktime transmission, sentimentally retracing the trajectories of a Restoration predecessor, and the martyring Niagara spilled down Horsemarket dragging a bridal gauze of choking fume behind. Cremating fancywork writhed briefly on Saint Peter's architraves. Zero-gage holocaust accomplished in mere seconds an erasure over which the Borough Council had deliberated for just shy a century, deleting cobbled histories in its sheathing Catherine-wheel spray, no west wind this time to ensure that only the torched gloveries and milliners of Mercers' Row or thereabouts would ever be regenerated. The short reach of houses on St. Andrew's Road from Scarletwell Street to Spring Lane became an ashen Rothko bad day, by some fluke of thermal whimsy sparing only the Monopoly-sized premises at the line's south extremity. Boys' clubs and bookmakers, cottaging-friendly lavatories and corner dives were caught up in a pyroclastic flow from Regent Square down to the foot of Grafton Street, and Marjorie Pitt-Draffen's dance-school on the current site of Alma's exhibition spouted rolling white clouds from its open door in microcosm of the building it was modelled on and situated in. Sharp to the sinuses and tear-ducts, these at least elicited a lachrymosity that the more gradual demolitions of some several decades had failed to provoke. Fast-forwarded there on the tabletop precinct of the heart was firestormed to oblivion in facsimile, its final music the repeated shrill of panicking detectors.

All of this had taken only moments, a rose of disaster blossoming and withering in time-delay, plunging the nursery into swirling opacity with everybody coughing, cursing, laughing, stumbling for the exit. Tasting a sour flinch of burning paper in the no-man's-land dividing nose from throat, Mick blundered blind towards fresh air and freedom. On his way out he collided with a fogbound pit-bull on its hind legs that turned out to be Ted Tripp, the erstwhile burglar ushering his girlfriend Jan before him, both of them apparently more entertained than traumatised. Beside the doorway to the right the white-haired carpenter from item one looked back across his shoulder at the sputtering herd as it stampeded past, while on the left stood Mick himself in mayoral drag with his arms raised in what now read as an apologetic shrug: "Blame her. Nothing to do with me." He staggered onto the comb-over turf outside, lank green locks plastered to the muddy scalp, trailing asphyxiating ribbons in his wake. Pressing the heels of both hands to his streaming sockets he smeared stinging moisture down across his cheekbones until he could see again.

The nursery entrance was still belching smoke and people into what was otherwise a pleasant afternoon. Murderous-looking maulers reassured each other that they were okay, asthmatic anarchists sat wheezing on the cusp of Phoenix Street, and Roman Thompson did his best to look compliant when his boyfriend told him that, no, seriously, this really wasn't funny. Backing off in the direction of the Golden Lion on Castle Street, Melinda Gebbie helped a stunned Lucy Lisowiec to get a cover story blaming everything on unidentifiable street-drinkers into place, the latter gaping with that thunderstone-struck look that Mick had observed often on associates of his sister. Somewhere at his back he heard Dave Daniels say "Where's Alma?", and was just beginning to conjecture that the exhibition might have been intended as a Viking funeral pyre when through the smoking portal like a Halloween edition of *Stars in their Eyes* lumbered the reverse hedge-dragged artist.

Her eyes were like particle collisions, black matter decay trajectories descending to the chin from watery corners, and in her Sargasso hair perched huge pale butterflies of settled ash. Singed, ugly holes now perforated the new turquoise jumper, but then Mick supposed it would look pretty much the same after a week of Alma's normal wear and meteoritic hashish-spillage. Smudged vermillion lips were stretched into a ghastly apprehensive rictus as she lifted sooty, blistered palms to her bewildered audience as though attempting to surrender.

"It's okay. I put it all out. I'll buy them another table. Or two tables if they want, how's that?"

His sister was like Werner Von Braun trying to mollify senior Nazis after a V2 had detonated on the launch pad, simpering nervously and wiping blast debris from Goering's frizzled eyebrows. She stood slapping her own bosom where a turquoise brushfire had rekindled, and it seemed to Mick that she had never looked more catastrophically deranged that she did at that moment. He was almost, well, not proud of her, but less ashamed. Then he remembered the old women who'd been standing behind Alma prior to her electing to employ the nuclear option, and who both were very definitely not among the emphysemic huddle of survivors on the fraying verge. Oh fuck. She'd finally killed someone, and when journalists swooped on her friends and family, nobody would affect surprise or offer testimonials to her quietness and normality. Striding towards her, Mick was only shocked that she had somehow managed to restrain herself for as long as she had.

"Warry, for fuck's sake, where are those old women, the two that were standing next to you?"

His sister's head revolved unhurriedly in his direction, that of a mechanical Turk anxious to persuade spectators that there was no cramped grandmaster dwarf crouched in her ribcage. Focussing a mildly shell-shocked gaze on Mick, her optic hazard-lights blinked stupidly amid the slobbering kohl, a breeding couple of stealth-jellyfish. She looked as though she might get round to working out who he was once she'd answered the same question in relation to herself. The weighted lids went up and down a few more times to no apparent purpose in the long space-shuttle pause before she spoke.

"What?"

Mick gripped her shoulder, urgently.

"The two old ladies! They've been here all afternoon. They were behind you when you made your sacrifice or whatever you thought it was that you were doing. They're not out here, so if they're still in there underneath a table, overcome by fumes, then ..."

He tailed off. Alma was staring at his tightening hand as though she wasn't certain what it was, much less what it was doing on her bicep. He withdrew it while it still had all its fingers.

"Sorry."

She frowned at him quizzically, and he could feel the shift as he found himself in the role of babbling psychiatric liability while she somehow assumed the mantle of concerned clinician.

"Warry, Bert's mum was the only old gal here other than me, and if she hadn't already gone home then I wouldn't have lit the touch-paper. I'm not a psychopath who wants to cull the elderly or something. I'm not Martin Amis. Have a look yourself, you don't believe me."

His eyes darted to the nursery door, still simmering. He knew from Alma's tone, with absolute conviction, that if he should peer inside then it would be exactly as she said. There would be no half-suffocated pensioners collapsed in tragic bundles, nothing but the glowing Dresden mess and twists of drifting yarn that curled up from its squirming embers. He pictured precisely the two women who had definitely been there and now definitely weren't and felt the same uneasy tingle in his upper vertebrae that he'd experienced when talking to Bert Regan's mum, a breath of the uncanny on the barbered stubble at the nape. He thought it better that he not continue with the present thrust of his enquiry, and returned his gaze to meet that of his sister.

"No, it's ... no, it's fine, Warry. I'll take your word for it. I must have got mixed up. Here, you do know that this place probably has a connection to the fire station, don't you? Did you want to be here when the engines came? Or was that why you did it, for the flashing lights and uniforms?"

She looked at him in earnest startlement.

"Oh, shit. I hadn't thought of that. Come on, let's fuck off somewhere else so that I can reflect on what I've done and feel remorse."

Seizing his elbow she commenced to drag him across Phoenix Street in way of Chalk Lane, calling back to the smoke-damaged refugees still gathered on the nursery's moth-eaten apron verge.

"Don't worry. Everybody gets a refund."

Roman Thompson's chap Dean sounded as though he were at a philosophic impasse.

"But nobody paid."

Towing her brother along the west wall of Doddridge Church, Alma considered.

"Oh. Well, in that case nobody qualifies. I'll give you all a call next week."

With that the Warrens absented themselves from the potential crime scene, sauntering conspicuously in their efforts not to look like fleeing perpetrators. Scuffing over listing pavement past the loaf-bronze meeting house both of them peered first at the stranded doorway halfway up the rain-chewed stonework, a moustache of flowers and grass along its sill, then at each other, although neither spoke. From the truncated strip of peeling house-fronts opposite crouched under the raised arbour of the designated castle grounds came muffled music that was summery and old, phased in and out of audibility by the continually shifting waveband of the breeze. "Don't Walk Away, René" perhaps. Assaying branches overdressed in pink like gypsy bridesmaids, blackbird Schuberts hung their fleeting compositions on the grey staves that still ravelled from the nursery, and rattling around the curve of Mary's Street a flaking ice-blue Volkswagen was for a heartbeat in beguiling contrast with the toffee fringes of the burial ground. Rounding the corner in the juddering vehicle's wake, Alma and Mick mounted the undemanding run of steps and, without need for conference, agreed to park their ageing arses on the slab-topped wall bounding the chapel's southern face.

It was a lulling bee-drone of an afternoon despite persistent violated squealing from the smoke detectors, now off on the church's other side and therefore easier to ignore. Mick tapped a cigarette from his depleted pack and Alma passed his lighter to him without fuss. Its work was done, apparently. After a moment, goaded by the front-bar perfume of her brother's exhalations, she elected to spark up her last remaining stick of dream-snout and got him to light it for her, leaning in and holding back her locks like petticoats beside a hearth. They sipped their neurotoxins in companionable silence for some little time before the speechless younger sibling thought of anything to say.

"Your pictures, Warry, what we just saw. There were lots of things I don't remember telling you. You'd taken some creative licence, I thought, here and there."

His sister smiled, becoming briefly radiant in something other than a cracked reactor sense, and crinkled up her nose self-deprecatingly.

"Yeah. Yeah, I made most of it up, but then I don't see that it really matters who hallucinated what as long as the real story's in there somewhere. Anyway, nobody's ever going to know it isn't what you said to me. It's your word against mine and I'm an interstellar treasure."

Mick laughed down his nose, in writhing fronds of vaporous chinoiserie.

"And what's all this fantastic nonsense going to accomplish, Warry? Have you somehow saved the Boroughs, like you said that you were going to do? Will they rebuild it how it was when we were children and not put up any more Destructors?"

Still smiling, albeit now more ruefully, she shook her trailing willow-canopy of hair.

"I'm not the fairies, Warry. I imagine that the Boroughs will go on being ignored until somebody comes up with a half-baked plan they think might turn a profit, then they'll plough it under, pave it over, get rid of the streets and only leave the names. As for incinerators and destructors, my guess is they'll roll them out across the country. It's the cheapest, dirtiest way of doing things, it doesn't inconvenience anyone who votes or matters, and why interfere with getting on a hundred years of cross-Westminster policy? They started pulling this place down after the First World War, most probably because the Russian revolution had made keeping all of your disgruntled workers in one place look like a bad idea. They won't stop now."

As frequently occurred when she was off on one, Alma's neglected reefer had gone out. Anticipating her requirements, Mick retrieved the lighter from his pocket and allowed her to suck the extinguished end of her hashish Havana back to angry ruby life, whereafter she resumed her diatribe.

"And even if they did rebuild it, down to the last doorstep, that would just be horrible. That would just do for buildings what *Invasion of the Body*

Snatchers did for people. It would be some sort of deprivation theme-park. Unless you restore it how it was, with all its life and atmospheres intact, it's not worth bothering. I've saved the Boroughs, Warry, but not how you save the whale or save the National Health Service. I've saved it the way that you save ships in bottles. It's the only plan that works. Sooner or later all the people and the places that we loved are finished, and the only way to keep them safe is art. That's what art's for. It rescues everything from time."

There in the May sky over Marefair and Saint Peter's a blancmange of cumulus set to a snoozing rabbit, moulded for a stratospheric children's party. Whispered wind washed from Far Cotton and Mick felt the breeze's skin brushing against his own as it politely slid around him and continued with its northbound journey. He was thinking about what his sister had just said concerning the impossibility of anything saving an arts-and-letters rescue or retrieval for the neighbourhood's lost causes when he was reminded of Ben Perrit's poem, creasing in his pocket. Leaning back at a precarious angle so that he could get his hand into the tight-stretched linen mouth he fished it out and handed it to Alma, who perused it with a softening of her belligerent brow and then, refolding it to fit in some compartment of her own pipe-cleaner jeans, looked up at Mick.

"Bless that poor, suffering inebriate bugger, but he does a lovely poem. True, they're all about some loss that he can't get past, although if he could he'd have no need to write. Or drink. I sometimes think that loss is all he runs on; that he never loves a thing so much as when the wheels have fallen off. I hope that he's alright. I hope that everyone's alright."

She lapsed into another round of concentrated puffing on her spliff in order to prevent it going out again. The rabbit cloud was now two separate hamsters over Pike Lane, and Mick risked a sideways glance at his big sister.

"How is Ben not being able to get past his loss a different thing from how you handle yours?"

Alma tipped back her head and spat a thin beige genie at the upturned azure bowl above.

"Because what I've made, Warry, is a glorious mythology of loss. That back there was an older testament, a pantheon of tramps and kids with nits. I've squeezed the bricks till they bled miracles and filled the cracks with legends, that's what I've done. I ..."

She broke off, and a fireworks night of marvel and delight declared itself across her face.

"Here, did I tell you, about what Rome Thompson said, the thing about the mill?"

Mick's blank look was her answer and her prompt to press enthusiastically ahead.

"It's the gas-holder down on Tanner Street, the back of where Nan used to live. According to what Rome said, back in the twelfth century it used to be a corn-mill called 'the Marvellous Mill'. If you go down by the river, underneath the bridge with all the beer cans and syringes and disembowelled handbags, you can see there's the old stones along its sides which used to be the race that powered the waterwheel. In the twelve-hundreds it was claimed by the monks of Saint Andrew's Priory, who controlled the other mill in town and figured that they might as well run both of them. Then, in the sixteenth century Henry the Eighth dissolved the monasteries and ownership reverted back to the townspeople. Two hundred years sail by and next thing anybody knows it's the seventeen-hundreds ..."

She paused to breathe in, although only drugs.

"1741, there's this consortium of businessmen. One of them's Dr. Johnson, which supports my theory that from Bunyan to Lucia Joyce this whole thing is to do with the development of English as a visionary language. Anyway, they buy the place and turn it from a cornmill to a cotton mill."

Uncertain what whole thing his sister was referring to, and even more unsure how the discoverer of baby-powder fitted into the scenario, Mick pursed his lips and merely nodded.

"There were cotton mills in Birmingham by that time, turned by donkeys, but the one down Tanner Street was the first power-driven mill anywhere in the world. So it's not just the crusades and the Cromwells. The Industrial Revolution kicked off up at the far end of Green Street. As you might expect the local cottage industries went down like ninepins, as would happen everywhere over the coming century. The mill had three big cotton looms, all working round the clock with no employees other than some kids to sweep the corners and to manage the untangling if the mechanism snagged."

Mick listened, only partially distracted by the portly and diminutive form labouring up Chalk Lane towards them, white hair curled into a head of froth atop unusually pallid stout, the pint of cuckoo spit they draw after they've changed the barrel. Thinking to have previously seen the sweltering individual somewhere, Mick at last decided that it was that councillor who had a column in the paper. Cockie, was it? Lived down near Black Lion Hill, which would explain his presence in Chalk Lane. As he approached the man regarded Alma and her brother through his perching spectacles with vague affront. Oblivious to his presence, Alma carried on her narrative regardless.

"Then – and listen, this is brilliant. Adam Smith, the bloke who's on the twenties, the economist, he either comes and sees the mill or hears about it, with its looms all working nineteen to the dozen and its shuttles whizzing back and forth and no one there, as though it were a factory being run by ghosts. He thinks it's wonderful, tells everybody that he knows how it's as though a massive unseen hand were guiding all this furious mechanical activity, some manner of industrial Zeus rather than basic principles of engineering. It's what always happens with new science in a religious age, like all of these holistic fizzy water manufacturers who babble about quantum physics."

Mick, who found both quantum physics and expensive fizzy water equally unlikely concepts, watched the fat man waddle by them on their right, seemingly headed for the lightly smouldering day nursery. Behind his lenses customarily complacent eyes regarded the pair sitting on the church wall with suspicion as he barrelled past, particularly Alma whom he more than likely recognised. Either unbothered by his presence or else unaware she pressed on with her tale excitedly.

"So Adam Smith, with his half-baked idea about a hidden hand that works the cotton looms, decides to use that as his central metaphor for unrestrained Free Market capitalism. You don't need to regulate the banks or the financiers when there's an invisible five-fingered regulator who's a bit like God to make sure that the money-looms don't snare or tangle. That's the monetarist mystic idiot-shit, the voodoo economics Ronald Reagan put his faith in, and that middle-class dunce Margaret Thatcher when they cheerily deregulated most of the financial institutions. And that's why the Boroughs exists, Adam Smith's idea. That's why the last fuck knows how many generations of this family are a toilet queue without a pot to piss in, and that's why everyone that we know is broke. It's all there in the current underneath that bridge down Tanner Street. That was the first one, the first dark, satanic mill."

A dog barked, away on their left in the vicinity of Mary's Street, one bark, then three, then silence. Not for the first time since getting up that morning, Mick felt an encroaching air of strangeness. There was something going on, something unsettlingly precise in its familiarity. Had this happened before? Not something like this but this exact situation, with his buttocks going dead from the stone wall's chill striking through thin trousers. First one bark, then three, then silence. Wasn't there something about Picasso, or had that not happened yet? Floundering in the déjà vu, he had a feeling Alma was about to mention a glass football.

"Warry, seriously, everywhere's Jerusalem, everywhere trampled or run down. If Einstein's right, then space and time are all one thing and it's, I dunno, it's a big glass football, an American one like a Rugby ball, with the big bang at one end and the big crunch or whatever at the other. And the moments in between, the moments making up our lives, they're there forever. Nothing's moving. Nothing's changing, like a reel of film with all the frames fixed in their place and motionless till the projector beam of our awareness plays across them, and then Charlie Chaplin doffs his bowler hat and gets the girl. And when our films, our lives, when they come to an end I don't see that there's anywhere for consciousness to go but back to the beginning. Every-body is on endless replay. Every moment is forever, and if that's true every miserable wretch is one of the immortals. Every clearance area is the eternal golden city. You know, if I'd thought to put that in a program or a booklet at the exhibition, I suppose that people might have had more chance of working out what I was on about. Ah, well. It's too late now. What's done is done, and done just one way for all time, over and over."

Cue the chubby councillor. This thought had just occurred to Mick, by now slack jawed and reeling with recurrence, when the white-haired and white-bearded Christmas bauble rumbled back down Chalk Lane and once more into their field of view. From his outraged expression and the faint wisps of charred papier-mâché smog which wafted their malodorous tendrils after him, it was apparent that he'd witnessed the evacuated nursery and had very probably gone in to see the burned-out model Boroughs at first hand. All of a sudden, Mick knew down to the last syllable exactly what would transpire next and how Pablo Picasso had a part in it. It was that anecdote, the funny story he'd heard Alma tell at least a half a dozen times, about when Nazis visited the artist's Paris studio during the occupation and came, with some dismay, on Guernica. The huffy councillor was going to say the same thing that the German officers had said on that occasion, and Mick's sister would then shamelessly appropriate the Cubist sex-gnome's spirited and memorable reply. And then the dog would bark again, four times. Scalp tingling, Mick took another turn round on the ghost train.

Stubbing her illicit fag out on the slab where she was sitting, Alma raised her less-than-interested grey and yellow gaze in time to notice the rotund former official for the first time. Near to apoplexy he raised his left arm, a trembling finger pointing back towards the daycare centre where the smoke alarms still sounded, and unwittingly delivered the Gestapo dialogue regard-ing Guernica.

"Did you do that?"

It was the perfect set up. Beaming beatifically, his sister offered up her plagiarised reply.

"No. You did."

Blinking dazedly and without an articulate response the erstwhile coun-cil leader trundled off in the direction of Marefair, a haywire snowball that got smaller as it rolled downhill instead of bigger. From St. Mary's Street came the predicted canine outburst: *woof, woof, woof* and then a faint pause. *Woof.*

Despite the clockwork eeriness, Mick found that he was chortling. Kick-ing her heels beside him, never one afraid to laugh at her own stolen jokes, Alma joined in. Somewhere upslope behind and right on schedule, sirens were approaching through the stopped streets of a broken heaven.

ACKNOWLEDGEMENTS

Where to start, and where to finish?

Firstly I must thank my wife, the artist and writer Melinda Gebbie, who's been almost as intimately involved with this book as I have since its beginnings. I think I proposed to her just before commencing the project, and she's had almost every chapter since read out aloud to her, whether she wanted it or not. It was her technical advice that fleshed out the tools of Ernest Vernall's trade in chapter one and Alma Warren's craft through the remainder of the novel, and most of all it was her belief that this work was important and her almost-ten-years of encouragement to that effect that helped give me the stamina to complete it. Thank you so much, darling. Without you, I doubt very much there'd be a book requiring these acknowledgements.

Almost as importantly, I must offer my deepest gratitude to Steve Moore, even though he's no longer around to receive it. Steve completed his invaluable initial edit of *Jerusalem*'s first third – memorably including the stylistic critique "Ugghh" in red pen in the margins; mercifully, I forget just where – and brought his dazzling intellect to all our formative discussions of the view of time which we later discovered to be called Eternalism, by which point we'd both long since converted to that doctrine. If this book's central idea is correct (and given physicist Fay Dowker's current researches into an alternative hypothesis, it's at least falsifiable and testable) then Steve is currently approaching his second birthday in a leafy close on Shooters Hill in 1951. Thanks again for everything, mate, and all being well I'll run into you again in roughly nineteen years, your time.

Steve's abrupt decision to put our theory to the test in March 2014 (some people – you pay them an advance to edit your gigantic novel, and then you never see them again) meant that I had to find a selection of other editors and proofreaders who weren't scared of me. First and foremost among these was the poet, author, editor and comedian Bond, Donna Bond. Donna edited the whole book, took me to task several times for my misuse of the word 'careen' – apparently it's a term specific to the practice of overturning a ship in order to scrape the barnacles from its hull, but who could have known? – and even somehow noticed a couple of typos in the impenetrably made-up mess of chapter twenty-five. Thanks, Donna, for doing such a meticulous job of something that I didn't have the nerve, focus or knowledge of obscure naval terminology to face on my own. The next pass at the editing fell to my friends, the writers John Higgs and Ali Fruish. John spotted a few things, but was mostly invaluable in giving me his typically illuminating reaction to the book as a whole, and for writing an appreciation that made *Jerusalem* sound like something I might actually want to read. Ali, in between his numerous spells in prison (he's a writer in residence, though I enjoy making him sound like a murderous drifter), not only gave me some useful pointers on crack etiquette but had, throughout my writing of the book, been digging up gems of research that turned out to be the novel's making: he alerted me to James Hervey's local provenance, and provided the final, necessary revelations about the Gas Street origins of free-market capitalism and the Industrial Revolution. To both of these gentlemen, scholars and acrobats I am greatly indebted.

Likewise being of immense assistance in the production of this behemoth, my thanks are also due to my comrade, henchman and hired goon, the omni-competent Joe Brown. Joe put me in touch with Donna Bond, served up sheaves of obscure reference material at my every delirious whim and, most of all, burned down a month of his life in colouring and making intelligible my smudged grey bedlam of a cover illustration. And, if you hold your ear close enough to the page, he also wrote the music to the song audible during the closing scenes of chapter twenty-five. Joe, I don't know what I would do without you, but I'm confident I'd be doing it much more slowly and displaying a far higher level of ignorance. While on the subject of production, I'd also like to thank Tony Bennett at Knockabout – for his support, his warm enthusiasm and his occasional bouts of being pressed into service as werewolf-wrangler if I've had to deal with anything too early in the morning – and the fine people at Liveright Publishing for bringing their usual impeccable polish and discrimination to bear upon the finished article. And, of course, anybody along the way that I've left out. There have been a multitude of people responsible for building *Jerusalem*, and I'm grateful to every one of them.

A special shout-out is due to my pal the sublime John Coulthart for his mesmerising multi-period isomorphic map of the Boroughs, for doing all that loving and painstaking research, and for being the only person I could talk to about the mind-and-eye-destroying obsessive madness that comes with drawing hundreds of eccentrically-angled rooftops and chimneypots. Thanks, John, and I hope that you're recuperating in a world of scintillant colour that is wrought from nothing save organic shapes and psychedelic arabesques. For the photographs heading the book's three movements, I have once again to thank Joe Brown for his image manipulation skills in the montage of the Destructor looming over Bristol Street (no clear available images existed of the local chimneystack, necessitating the import of an identical model from, appropriately enough, Blackburn), and my colleague the diamond-eyed Mitch Jenkins for his photographs of the Archangel Michael with snooker-cue (some modern anti-pigeon spikes were airbrushed out, in accordance with the book's generally pro-pigeon sensibilities), and of that door halfway up the wall of Doddridge Church with its inexplicable bolt *on the outside*. Your evidence that not all of this is invented was gratefully received.

I should also like to thank Iain Sinclair and Michael Moorcock for their continuing friendship, inspiration and encouragement – or eloquent nagging – regarding this novel, and apologise to them and anyone else who's been called upon to abandon their families and read it, which I know includes my vastly knowledgeable but physically frail pal Robin Ince, who reports that he and his postman are both now disastrously ruptured. I must also mention my old friend and accomplice Richard Foreman, one of the co-authors of the excellent Northampton Arts Development publication *In Living Memory*, where I found some exotic details of Boroughs life that had managed to escape my attention during my upbringing, and without which *Jerusalem* would be missing some of its best stories and characters. A sweep of the sombrero in your direction, gents.

With everyone acknowledged who has been part of the creating of this novel (I think), I must now turn to those people who have had their lives and identities plundered and distorted to provide its contents. Foremost among these, obviously, is my younger, supposedly better looking, but far, far shallower brother Mike, so lacking in depth that he signed his soul away to me, aged twelve, during a game of Monopoly that was going badly for him. I still have it. I thank him for the memorable industrial accidents and near-death experiences that have made this book so much fun, and also thank my sister-in-law Carol and my nephews Jake and Joe (one of whose names I changed and one of whose I didn't, for no explicable reason) for their supporting cameos. And to all the rest of my far-flung family members, living and dead, thank you for providing me with such rich substance, and also for any chromosomes you may have contributed. Particular thanks go to my cousin Jacquie Mahout (the arty, bohemian one who married a French communist) for all of the most startling fragments of family history included here, though even she had no idea where I'd got Mad Aunt Thursa from.

Huge acknowledgements and perhaps apologies go to all of the non-relatives who have been travestied herein, usually without their permission or knowledge, especially those whom I've grossly misrepresented without even going to the trouble of changing their names. The actor Robert Goodman, who in real life is beautiful in mind, body and soul, probably tops the list here, although Melinda Gebbie and Lucy Lisowiec may also wish to consult their lawyers. The same gratitude, and the same squirming disclaimers, go to my friends Donald Davies; Norman Adams and Neil; Dominic Allard (and his late mother Audrey); the late, great Tom Hall and all who sailed in him; Stephen "Fred" Ryan, who I hope hangs on long enough to read this, and his late mother Phyllis Ryan, née Denton, who served me tea and biscuits and gave me the entirety of Phyllis Painter from her boa of decomposing rabbits to the Compton Street Girls marching song. These are all lovely people, and any perceived flaws to their characters as presented here are entirely those of the author.

Otherwise unmentioned in *Jerusalem*, for providing a major part of this novel's motivation, I should like to thank my wonderful daughters, Leah and Amber (along with their equally wonderful partners, John and Robo), and particularly my astonishing grandsons Eddie, James, Joseph and Rowan. Your nana Melinda called this book "a genetic mythology", and for better or worse it's part of yours, too. While I'm sure that the future you're running into the breakers of will be as strange as anything in this book, remember that this is the peculiar landscape a bit of you came from, and that along with everybody and everything you've ever cared about, we're all still there in Jerusalem.

I thank the deaf, mute stones of what is left of the Boroughs for all of the work that they have done across the centuries, and all that they have borne. When they at last slump, exhausted, into the dusty sleep of rubble, I hope that this may serve them as an entertaining, vindicating dream.

And lastly I thank both the Meaningful Concept of Death and the English Novel for having been such thoroughly good sports about all this. You guys are the greatest.

Alan Moore

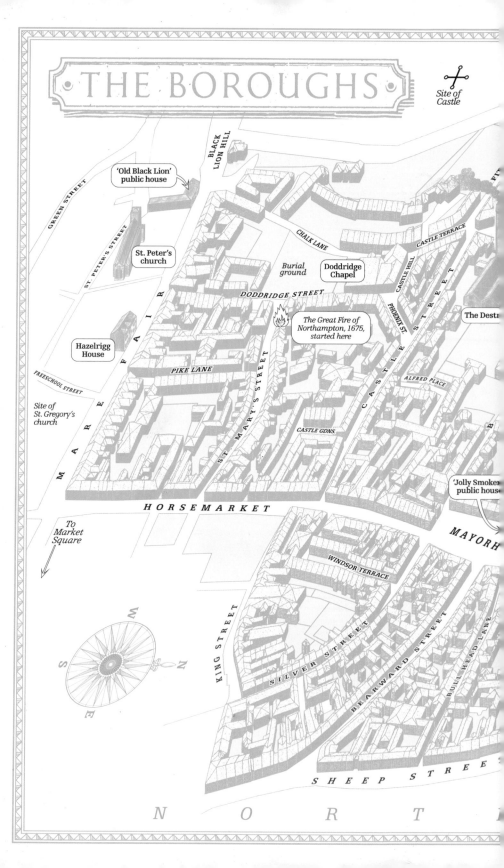